W9-CQH-616

The Norton Book of Science Fiction

The Norton Book of Science Fiction

North American Science Fiction, 1960–1990

Edited by Ursula K. Le Guin

and Brian Attebery

Karen Joy Fowler, *Consultant*

W · W · Norton & Company · New York · London

Printed in the United States of America

First Edition

The text of this book is composed in Avanta (Electra),
with the display set in Bernhard Modern.
Composition and manufacturing by the Haddon Craftsmen, Inc.
Book design by Antonina Krass adapted by Jack Meserole.

Library of Congress Cataloging-in-Publication Data

The Norton book of science fiction / edited by Ursula K. Le Guin and Brian Attebery.
p. cm.
1. Science fiction, American. I. Le Guin, Ursula K., 1929–
II. Attebery, Brian, 1951–
PS648.S3N66 1993
813'.0876208—dc20 93-16130

ISBN 0-393-03546-8

W. W. Norton & Company, Inc., 500 Fifth Avenue, New York, N.Y. 10110
W. W. Norton & Company Ltd., 10 Coptic Street, London WC1A 1PU

1 2 3 4 5 6 7 8 9 0

CONTENTS

1966

1967

1968

1969

1971

1978

1980

1981

1982

1983

1984

1985

1986

1987

1988

1989

1990

SPECIAL THANKS

Many friends gave us invaluable suggestions and counsel. Several people took the time to make out lists for us of works and writers we might otherwise have missed; some gave us immense help locating elusive stories or evasive authors. People we contacted in Canada, particularly at the Merril Collection of Science Fiction, Speculation, and Fantasy at the Toronto Public Library, were most generous, helping us make this a genuinely North American anthology.

The three of us, individually or jointly, particularly and personally, wish to thank Douglas Barbour, Richard Curtis, Ellen Datlow, Bud Foote, Joan Gordon, Donald M. Hassler, Veronica Hollinger, Elizabeth Anne Hull, Kathryn Hume, John Kessel, David Ketterer, Virginia Kidd, Damon Knight, Rob Latham, Colin Manlove, Vonda McIntyre, Scott Meredith, Judith Merrill, Pat Murphy, Frederik Pohl, Delores Rooney, Brian Stableford, Lorna Toolis, and Ralph Vicinanza.

This is also the place to honor editors of anthologies, who take stories from the all too ephemeral issue of a magazine and put them between the covers of books, thus giving them a shelflife of more than a few weeks. Science fiction has had a very distinguished series of anthologists, and we were fortunate to have their work to draw on. Among the editors whose anthologies we found reliable sources of excellent stories in our period, we'd like particularly to mention Frederik Pohl for the *Galaxy* anthologies of the sixties, Damon Knight for the inimitable *Orbit* series of original stories, Robert Silverberg for outstanding reprint and original collections, James Gunn for his notable historical series, Judith Merrill for founding the brilliant *Tesseracts,* Pamela Sargent for the invaluable *Women of Wonder* collections, Gardner Dozois for the big, generous *Bests* throughout the eighties, and most particularly Terry Carr, probably the finest editor the field has yet had, who left a marvelous legacy of reprint and original anthologies.

INTRODUCTION BY URSULA K. LE GUIN

Facilmente aceptamos la realidad, acaso porque intuimos que nada es real.
(We accept reality easily, perhaps because we sense that nothing is real.)

—*Jorge Luis Borges,* El Inmortal

Storytelling reveals meaning without committing the error of defining it.

—*Hannah Arendt,* Men in Dark Times

Process

When the publisher invited me to edit this book, I knew I wanted to do it, but I wanted not to do it alone. I needed advice on what to read, help with the great task of reading and selection, and colleagues to work out ideas and argue about stories with. I asked for Brian Attebery and Karen Fowler as my partners, and got them, though only one could be included in the full partnership I hoped for. I know how seriously they took our job. I know and rejoice in their carefulness, their imagination, their resourcefulness, their generosity as fellow workers.

We worked as a team, finding and reading stories, researching, recommending, sending copies to the others, hunting out half-remembered pieces in obscure places, discussing, wordcounting, and finally going through the awful task of fitting the thousands of pages of stories we wanted into the 750 pages we had. We allowed ourselves a limited veto power: basically, each of us could nix *one* story without explanation or argument, which we did. Both the Fowler and the Le Guin stories were selected with the author's consent but without her advice. Late in the selection process, when it got down to making some tough choices, we voted. The vote led us to omit some stories that one or another of us wanted very much to include, but no stories were included that any of us dislike. Altogether, the general procedure turned out to be less a settling of arguments by compromise than an arrival at consensus by finding out we already agreed.

Fully as Karen Fowler shared it with us, Brian Attebery and I feel that the responsibility is ours. Criticism for choosing this story and not that one, putting So-and-So in and leaving So-and-So out, and all other matters of judgment, should be addressed to the Editors; we will accept it. The only criticism we won't accept is that which ignores our clearly stated and firmly maintained criteria.

Criteria (Clearly, Firmly, etc.)

This is a book of science fiction stories written in English by North American writers and published in North America between 1960 and 1990.

I established that description of the book at the start, and we held to it. It was intended mainly to narrow our task to a possible size, and to give the contents some unity in (as you might say) the spacetime continuum.

It was hard to leave out all Britain, all Europe. It was hard to leave out authors whose work we admire immensely but whose best writing was done before 1960—and some whose bright light began to shine just post-1990. Some excellent authors are not in this book because we found their best work to be inarguably fantasy rather than science fiction (attempts at making that distinction will follow later in this introduction). We very much regret the absence of several powerful and imaginative novelists who write little or not at all in the short-story form. Again, the long story, classified as novelette or novella, is one of the prime forms of science fiction, and a number of writers do their best work in it; but if we had included more than a few pieces over thirty pages long, we would have had to leave out half our short stories. And we regret the absence of the one author who refused us the story we wanted, offering us instead a recipe for pudding, which we found did not meet our criteria.

On the other hand, we enjoyed our freedom to include any writer of our period/area who used the techniques and imagery of science fiction, an option available to all artists willing to learn how to use it, whether or not they define themselves by genre. We tried not to let an author's reputation—high, low, or nonexistent, in the field or out of it—influence our judgment of the stories themselves. Three decades and two nations of a large continent offered a wide enough spectrum of styles and approaches to provide, I think, a good picture of what science fiction can do and has been doing.

I wish science fiction were not as white as it is. I wish I understood why it is still so white. I am glad of and proud of the African American and Native American presences in this book, but sorry there are not more, nor any Asian or Latin voices. After another three decades I hope there will be very many more.

I wish science fiction were not as male as it is, but it isn't as male as it was, not by a long shot. The strong and brilliant female presences in this book give me joy, and that so many of them are young gives me confidence. We have regendered a field that was, to begin with, practically solid testosterone. (I was going to remark here that one of the longest and most powerful stories in the book is by a woman using a male pen name; but then I remember how, when that story first came out, women read it and were amazed, delighted, jubilant, that a man could write such a story. . . . And then when the author revealed her real name, the revisions of thought, the revelations of prejudice, we all had to go through, to realize that a woman had written such a story. . . . I think I should leave it to you who don't know which author I'm talking about to discover her, and so to experience those amazements.)

Certain ethical considerations influenced our judgment and should be mentioned. We were not receptive to stories promulgating racism or homophobia, of which in any case there are very few in current science fiction (though it seems to be nearly as straight as it is white), or to misogynistic stories, which are somewhat commoner. Misogyny usually occurs in the socially approved form of fictions of violence against women, presenting women as objects of degradation, rape, torture, murder; the pattern is often so brainlessly repetitive as to debase stories otherwise inventive and imaginative. The use of prolonged description of violence (against anybody) to provide the emotional whammy of a story is a technique that fits better in horror, porn, or survivalist propaganda than in science fiction. I cannot myself untangle ethical from aesthetic standards in these matters.

Decades and Fashions

Our chronological ordering of the book may lend it a spurious air of historical intent. Excellent, scholarly, historical collections of science fiction exist; we intend no competition with them. We gave ourselves the freedom *not* to include any story because it was "important," or "seminal" (or ovular, as the case may be), or typical of its period, or for any reason other than its inherent excellence as science fiction and as story. The stories are arranged chronologically because there had to be an order, and when we tried that one, it worked. Arranging the stories in order of the year of their publication presented a fortuitous but fortunate balance of themes, tone, and length.

And, even if we were not trying for it, the chronological order gives some glimpse of the story of science fiction itself during the first thirty years of its maturity. It is hard not to think in decades, and our three decades do each have a certain character, or plot function, in the story.

Without in the least dismissing or belittling earlier writers and work, I think it is fair to say that science fiction changed around 1960, and that the change tended towards an increase in the number of writers and readers, the breadth of subject, the depth of treatment, the sophistication of language and technique, and the political and literary consciousness of the writing. The sixties in science fiction were an exciting period for both established and new writers and readers. All the doors seemed to be opening. Yet the sixties were also a period of intense anxiety; the genocidal posturings of the cold war, the escalation of the Viet Nam war, the realization that prophecies of overpopulation and ecological disaster were being fulfilled, and the strains of dissidence from the left, from blacks, from women—all were reflected in the dark mirror of science fiction. Optimism, the often rather blustering faith in American Know-how and the technofix, became rarer; science fiction increasingly explored failures, limits, ends, final things. But even as "The Future" grew cloudier, more threatening, more complex, the fiction that uses the future as its metaphor gained in complexity and human relevance. Authors of the sixties, abetted by several brilliant editors, abandoned the market-bound, limited-audience pulp mentality, and used the Matter of Science Fiction not only as a set of dazzling intellectual ploys and gimmicks, but as source material for a serious and responsible literature.

This seriousness and responsibility—which, since we're talking about art, is mostly manifested as playfulness and daring—consolidated and strengthened in the seventies. The seventies have been dismissed as a feeble and aberrant era in science fiction, by people suffering from nostalgia for an illusionary "Golden Age" of "hard" science fiction. The phrase "hard science fiction" is both descriptive and evaluative. It denotes a fiction using hi-tech iconology with strong scientific content, solidly thought out, well researched, tough-minded; it also often connotes a fiction whose values are male-centered, usually essentialist, often politically rightist or militaristic, placing positive ethical value upon violence. Its implied counterpart is a "soft" fiction of the left, without gender bias, which does not posit violence either as an ethical standard or a necessity of plot. This, indeed, describes a good deal of the excellent writing of the seventies. I would suggest that the useful difference is not on a hard-soft scale, but on a scale of maturity. "Hard" science fiction becomes interesting to the adult reader pretty much as it departs from simplistic moralism and explores the implications of techno/scientific change with a rigorous, but not rigid, intelligence. There are brilliant stories by "hard" science-fiction writers in this book, some of them from the seventies. It is a strong and permanent element of the field, and needs no disinformational propaganda. What is needed is recognition of the strengths of seventies writing—its generosity, courage, and innovation.

When I began reading stories from the eighties for this anthology, I had not been keeping up with the magazines or collections, and had vague notions that much of science fiction had become artsy, druggy, and repetitive—that instead of going on from Philip Dick, the writers had settled for imitating the film that travestied one of his novels. Indeed I found some pretentious murk and a lot of weird chemicals in eighties science fiction; but my prejudices were, like all such judgments, based on ignorance, and I happily abandoned them. Half the stories (33, a yang number) in this book are from the years 1960 through 1980, and half (34, a yin number) from the decade of the eighties. This preponderance of the recent is common to anthologies not historically structured. We swore to avoid it, before we began reading for the book; but the recent work, the new stuff, was too seductive, too exciting.

What had discouraged me from reading science fiction was the publishers' huge output of formula fiction, a flood of flashily dreary imitations in which it was hard to see the islands of durable excellence. Fad had also discouraged me: the hullabaloo about cyberpunk, for example. One writer and a gaggle of low-quality clones? Looking closer, we found some very savvy writers using the cyberpunk iconology for their own purposes. Another eighties trend was pastiche, some effective, but much of it bloodless. The fad for pastiche is of course not limited to science fiction; it is a (frequently dead-end) form of metafiction.

Metafiction, self-reflexive narrative that openly draws not only on "reality" and "imagination" but also on the body of existing fiction, is a major element in contemporary literature, including magical realism and all postmodernist narrative. Science fiction during the three decades of our collection has increasingly shared in that reflexive movement, using the mature body of science fiction as poets use the tradition of all poetry, to explore and test the possibilities and potentialities of form, emotion, and significance.

Clearly and Firmly into the Tar Pit

"North American English-language science-fiction stories from 1960 to 1990"—No problem with *English-language North America.* No problem with *1960–1990.* Not much problem with *stories.* But what do we mean by *science fiction?*

An anthology, by what it contains and omits, is an implicit definition. As editors, we remained in the implicit zone, avoiding definitional discussions, until we felt the question forced on us, Is this story science fiction or not?

We answered that question editorially; and the editor owes the reader some attempt to be explicit.

What is science fiction?

Why are all the answers to that question either brisk evasions or labored partialities?

I think of the statues at the Tar Pits in Los Angeles: a mammoth, sinking in the dreadful ooze, lifts her trunk in a vain and perpetual bellow, while all around her lie vast sunken corpses of the unwary, preserved for paleontologists. I would prefer not to step into this pit. I would prefer to be not a mammoth, but a small primate, skipping briskly away.

Science fiction is "a genre," we are told, briskly. But the validity of the concept of genre (not to mention the problem of how to pronounce it in English) is problematical.

The definition of a genre is often an act of offense, or of retaliation. The professors and critics who for most of the century have controlled the modernist literary canon define and dismiss science fiction—frequently in absolute ignorance of its texts—as "genre fiction," that is, not "literature," in order to restrict "literature" to the privileged mode, realism. In defiant and often ignorant resentment of "the highbrow establishment," some practitioners of science fiction define it defensively as "popular entertainment," not "literature." Some chic critics go slumming trendily with them. None of this posturing advances understanding.

Genre is a useful concept only when used not evaluatively but descriptively. Authors and readers of any genre form a community, with certain shared interests and expectations. Modern poetry is a good example of genre as community. So is science fiction.

Professor Thomas Roberts, author of *The Aesthetics of Junk Fiction,* * makes this parallel, pointing out that people who read poetry "follow

*(Athens, GA: University of Georgia Press, 1968). These quotations are from an interview by Marcia Biederman: "Genre Writing" in *Poets and Writers* (January–February 1992).

poetry rather than poems"—that is, they read the genre, not only certain authors, because the *body of work* is at least as important as the individual writers. Excellence within a genre is seen not as a miraculous anomaly of "genius," but as a high point in a tradition. The artist is not expected to reinvent the wheel—only to use it well.

Genre writers and readers share a common stock of concepts, icons, images, manners, patterns, precisely as the musicians and audiences of Haydn's and Mozart's time shared a *materia musica* which the composer was expected, not to shatter or transcend, but to use and make variations on. "The pattern," says Roberts, "has to be fixed, partly because that's enjoyable in itself, partly because that makes it possible to be surprised and delighted by a diversion from the pattern." Transcendence, as in the case of Mozart, may of course occur; it's wonderful, but it really isn't the point. We have let the modern fixation on the Hero-Genius, that phallological fellow who towers in tremendously visible solitude from Byron on, obscure our view of how literature actually works. It works through accreting a tradition. A genre is a formal tradition.

All right. I say that science fiction is a literary tradition, a genre of fiction, like realism.

But we have not yet defined it. The Tar Pit waits.

And the brisk evasions continue, as do the boasts and the dismissals. One well-known writer in the field recently informed readers of *The Atlantic* that science fiction "is for children," thus exhibiting his superiority both to science fiction and to children. Others earnestly proclaim it to be "the mythology of the modern world," which sounds fine, but generally begs the question of what myth is and does. Damon Knight says science fiction is what he's pointing at when he points at it, and I agree; but it isn't very useful unless you can see where he's pointing.

I will not try to summarize the efforts of scholars to define science fiction; serious, complicated, and various, they are outside the scope both of my expertise and of this introduction. Those interested should obtain Brian Attebery's Teaching Guide to this volume. They will find there an excellent summary of critical opinion. They will not find a nice, neat, final definition of "what science fiction is."

Indeed I wonder: is the non-definability of science fiction perhaps an essential quality of it?

Items and Icons

Perhaps any close, fixed definition of a genre tends not towards a broader critical understanding, but towards a mere limitation to formula. (Thus, while "the genres" are defined in order to reduce them to formula, "literature" is defined by its exemption from the requirement that it be defined: Le Guin's Conspiracy Theory of the Canon.)

Formula fiction is not a literary tradition but a commercial commodity. Formula fiction is inherently definable, self-limited, not to a shared treasury of living *patterns,* but to a set of stock figures, motifs, props, locutions—a list of *items.* In cases of extreme formulization, such as some series romances, the list is actually furnished to the writer by the publisher.

When you ask the Common Reader what science fiction is, the answer is likely to include ideas or images from a list of items or elements (often derived from film rather than fiction) such as:

the future
"futuristic" science, technology, weaponry, cities, etc.
spaceships, space voyages
time machines, time travel
other worlds
alien beings
monsters
robots
mutants
parapsychology
mad scientists

The Common Reader who has actually read science fiction might add complex non-formulaic patterns, such as:

alternative history, alternate or parallel worlds
thought experiments in physiology, psychology, physics, etc.
experimental models of society

Elements of the first list may occur both in formula/commodity science fiction and genre/literary science fiction. They may serve as dead items to be manipulated as in a game, or living patterns to be used in the work of art. They are infinitely reusable until (probably) finally exhausted or outmoded. Professor Gary K. Wolfe calls them "icons," a useful word.* Looking at the tremendous vitality of some of them, such as the Robot, the Spaceship, the Alien, which long ago escaped from fiction to become common elements of our entire culture, I would incline to call them archetypes, in much the sense in which Jung used the word: mind-forms, iconic modes of thought. William Gibson deals with something

**The Known and the Unknown* (Kent, OH: Kent State University Press, 1979).

very similar in his story, "The Gernsback Continuum": "They're semiotic phantoms, bits of deep cultural imagery that have split off and taken on a life of their own."

The Common Denominator

Even from a capsulized notion of "sci fi" as formula, one may work towards an open conception of science fiction as field, by noting the common element of most icons/items on the list. They generally derive from or employ assumptions basic to science, scientific technology, and scientism.

Materialistic cause and effect; the universe conceived as comprehensible object of exploration and exploitation; multiculturalism; multispeciesism; evolutionism; entropy; technology conceived as intensive industrial development, permanently developing in the direction of complexity, novelty, and importance; the idea of gender, race, behavior, belief as culturally constructed; the consideration of mind, person, personality, and body as objects of investigation and manipulation: such fundamental assumptions of various sciences or of the engineering mind underlie and inform the imagery and the discourse of science fiction.

The content may be not scientific but scientistic, when science and technology are presented as deity (or negatively as demon).

Science is all-powerful: it can create anything (destroy everything). Science will save us (destroy us). It can solve any problem (it is the problem). It is the essence of the human (it creates monsters). The scientist is superhuman (subhuman). Science is a purely rational process (the scientist is mad). It is objective, excluding all emotional consideration; hence its judgment is unappealable. Science is gendered (male). It is inherently virtuous (immoral). Science is the sum of knowledge: hence it predicts or prescribes the future. Science progresses inevitably "forward" or "upward": hence technological advance and civilization are synonymous. Science disproves and replaces religion.

That is the mythos of scientism, positive or negative. All its elements can and do enter into science fiction, along with the actual content of science.

Science fiction, then, commonly uses techniques both from the realistic and the fantastic traditions of narrative to tell a story of which a referent, implicit or explicit, is the mind-set, the content, or the mythos of science and technology.

In his *Strategies of Fantasy,* Brian Attebery shows how science fiction uses science as its "megatext." The nourishing medium, the origin of the imagery, the motive of the narrative, is to be found in the contents, assumptions, and world view of modern science and technology. "Science surrounds, supports, and judges SF in much the same way the Bible grounds Christian devotional poetry."*

Such reciprocity is of course not limited to one kind of fiction. The Western partly reflected actual frontier/ranch life, partly invented the ethos and mythos of western America. The realistic novel both grew from and helped create the middle class, and has defined and defied it for two hundred years. All living art is connected to the central concerns of its society and has a social and intellectual function. It seems strange that one has to say so. But the idea of "pure" art, "high" art as socially functionless, above use, apolitical, is still so diligently cherished by many critics that it must be directly addressed.

The social function of narrative is not limited to "primitive" people sitting around the fire telling each other where Fire came from and why they're sitting around it. Intellectual content and moral function are equally essential elements of "civilized" fiction. In his book *Retelling and Rereading,* Karl Kroeber discusses the Modernist attempt to relegate narrative to the nursery or the savages. "More attention to narrative as narrative," he says, "might assist in developing a responsiveness that does not flinch from art that is more than 'aesthetically' interesting. Throughout human history, stories have been the preferred form for expression of moral commitments. . . . Narrative is a primary means for testing with concrete particularizations the benefits and disadvantages of specific ethical decisions. Narrative retellability and rereadability ensure that such examinations will not too easily crystallize into mere dogma."†

Science fiction, in reflecting and reflecting upon both the passing dogmas and the tragic ethical questions of the Age of Science, has carried a narrative load which realistic fiction was encouraged to abandon in favor of concentration on the individual psyche and personal relationships. In the postmodern era, thanks largely to feminist criticism and the extraordinary contemporary flourishing of fiction by non-white, feminist, and other marginalized writers, the literary canon based on "pure" aesthetic value is in question. The hidden social agenda of "pure" art may be discussed. And narrative may again be valued as much for its intellectual, political, and ethical content as for its psychological depth and its beauty.

This revaluation has already enhanced the critical study of science fiction. But there are dangers here. When science fiction was considered as without aesthetic merit, as "not literature," it was overvalued for its

***Strategies of Fantasy* (Bloomington, IN: Indiana University Press, 1992), p. 107.
†*Retelling and Rereading* (New Brunswick, NJ: Rutgers University Press, 1992), p. 189.

intellectual content, studied as if it were a matter of ideas only. And this habit of mind continues. An acute contemporary writer in the field says:

> . . . Science fiction is art—conscious or unconscious, but art, and whatever artistic can be found in it is freely assimilable into the growing body of study of science fiction as an art. Curiously enough, although this school of thought lends weight to the product of intellect, it contains at its core the statement that art is independent of intellect. That is a true statement, in my experience, but few scholars who have elaborated the "literary" view of science fiction appear at all willing to work with or discuss it, and most "literary" critics write as if authors always build their fabulations in every detail on some sort of scrupulous intellectual model.*

I cannot agree that "art is independent of intellect," but I do absolutely agree that art does not originate in the intellect, and that it cannot be judged adequately as a product or expression of intellect. Science fiction may be, as its lovers love to call it, "a literature of ideas," but it is no less a literature. It has no mandate to produce or explain ideas, nor is it reducible to intellectual schemata. It behooves our critics to study its literary techniques and devices as well as its intellectual content. Critics of landscape paintings don't analyze and judge the actual hills and rivers painted by the artist; they discuss the paintings. "An idea," to a writer, is a very different thing from a scientist's "idea," and the writer's pursuit of it is not an intellectual but an aesthetic one.

Real and Fake Science

Therefore, though science is the megatext, science-fiction stories cannot be judged according to their actual scientific content. Serious writers in the field take pride in careful research and fact-checking, in, as S. R. Delany says, "not denying what is known to be known," and in making plausible extrapolations from current knowledge. Many of them are real experts in one science or another (some are practicing scientists), and their fictions can be used as trustworthy introductions to various fields or theories. But there are serious and beautiful science-fiction stories in which the science is completely imaginary and the technology not only implausible but impossible.

A perfect example, which our geographical limitation forbade us to include in this book, is Robert Shaw's "Light of Other Days." Shaw imagines a kind of glass which slows the velocity of light. Light takes

*Algirdas Jonas Budrys, "SF in the Marketplace," in *Nebula Winners 12,* ed. Gordon R. Dickson (New York: Harper & Row, 1978), p. 114.

days or even years to pass through a slow-glass window pane, which thus becomes a literal window on the past. This is a lovely idea. It is not a scientific idea, in that there is absolutely no theory or technique that could explain or accomplish it. Yet the story does call upon the scientific megatext: the author knows what is known of the behavior of light, and he presents slow glass, not as a miraculous substance, but as a natural development of scientific technology, a product, an amenity. The beauty of "Light of Other Days" is not in the scientific probability of the concept, but in its coherent development, its convincingness, its imaginative resonance—all aesthetic qualities—and its aesthetic function as "the idea" of a moving and elegant story.

Thus time machines, parapsychology, and faster-than-light spaceships, though scientifically disreputable and technologically inexplicable, are elements of the discourse of science fiction, not of fantasy. They are efforts to conceive or comprehend or control imagined phenomena *within the context of materialist cause and effect,* not as interventions from a realm of the supernatural. A time machine may be impossible, but it is a genuinely rational conception. It is conceived as functioning according to (as yet undiscovered) natural laws, not as a subversion or transcendence of natural order. Its medium is not the fantastic but the scientific imagination.

Wish-fulfillment, of course, may influence the scientific imagination, and not only in fiction. The great boondoggle, popularly and accurately known as "Star Wars," is an instance of governmental sci fi—a rationally conceived but technologically absurd program based on wish-fulfillment. Much cold war thinking, the rationales and scenarios of "parity," "overkill," and so forth, was science fiction of this type. The kind that stays inside book covers, testing assumptions and decisions with thought experiments instead of money and lives, costs us a great deal less.

Certain commonplaces of science fiction lacking scientific explanation or validity are widely used and accepted because they are powerful icons and/or because they facilitate narrative. A good example is faster-than-light travel for spaceships (FTL, warp drive, etc.). If people are to get around the galaxy exploring and meeting one another to make war or love, they need to move a great deal faster than light. If they went as fast as our space probes go—even if, obeying the laws of physics as we currently understand them, they went as fast as but no faster than light—it would take them eons to get anywhere and meet anybody. So science fiction has for decades used FTL, sometimes explained with variously plausible and beautiful motive forces such as ion drives, lightsails, wormholes, and sometimes not explained at all. But also, writers may accept the scientists' hypothesis of lightspeed as the speed limit, and use it to structure their stories: then we have tales of time dilatation, and stories of generation ships, tiny self-contained worlds where a hundred generations may live out their lives before the ship comes to any destination. Nobel Prize winner Harry Martinson's *Aniara* is such a tale.

Science fiction is sometimes harshly critical of science; it abounds with cautionary parables of the misuse of technology, the dangers of social or genetic engineering, and so forth. Whether the attitude is positive or negative makes no real difference. The megatext is the same. Whether a pastor preaches about Heaven or Hell, he's talking Christianity; whether a story dwells on the wonders of exploring the universe or on the horrors of tampering with the universe, it's science fiction.

What Is, What Might Be, What Can't Be

Our finest in-house critic, S. R. Delany, has defined the area of science fiction as "subjunctive reality."* Reporting and history, in Delany's schema, deal with what happened; realistic fiction, with what could have happened; fantastic fiction, with what could not have happened. And science fiction deals with what has not happened.

He refines this useful distinction further to apply to three major types of science-fiction stories: the extrapolative, the cautionary, and the alternate-world. The predictive or extrapolative story deals with what has not happened, but might happen. The cautionary tale deals with what hasn't happened—yet. And the tale of parallel or alternate worlds deals with what might have happened, but didn't.

But this last overlaps, quite evidently, with the area of realism. Realistic and naturalistic fiction tells about events that could have occurred, people who might have existed, although factually/historically they didn't. And therefore, says Delany: "Naturalistic fictions are parallel-world stories in which the divergence from the real is too slight for historical verification."

I would suggest that the issue is not so much one of verification—it would be possible to verify that Prince Andrey and Natasha were not historical figures of the Napoleonic era in Russia—as one of value. In a realistic novel such as *War and Peace,* the divergence of the fiction from historical actuality is not valued; rather it is minimized, disguised, played down, so skillfully that Tolstoy can include historical figures such as Napoleon among his fictional characters without any shock to our credence. In the alternate-world novel, such as Philip K. Dick's *The Man in the High Castle,* the divergence of the fiction from history/actuality is

*"About 5750 Words," in *The Jewel-Hinged Jaw: Notes on the Language of Science Fiction* (New York: Berkley, 1977).

the very center and value of the book; it is deliberate, it is major, setting up what Delany calls a "tension between reality and fantasy." We know that Germany and Japan lost the Second World War: that knowledge plays against our absorption in an absolutely convincing story set in an America that lost the war: and this tension between what "really" happened and what happens in the story, with all its emotional, intellectual, and ethical resonances, is one of the effects particular to science fiction.

A good deal of science fiction, however, plays down its aberration from actuality, just as realistic fiction does. This is why many stories are set in a deliberately indeterminate near future, very much resembling the present day. Plausibility is given by the mundane, familiar setting, while the readers aren't forced to believe in events—nuclear holocaust, alien invasion, or the invention of a cure for the common cold—which they know haven't, as of now, occurred. Reality, however, ineluctably catches up with every fictional near future. Some stories are hopelessly dated, once their future has become our past; they must be strong and self-contained fictions to survive. Has *1984* survived 1984?

Delany's point, that the difference between realistic fiction and science fiction may be one of degree and not of kind, deserves very careful thought. He points out that any sentence from realistic fiction could appear in a science-fiction story, but that the reverse is not true. The sun rose. Both suns rose. The first sentence could slip into any story in any genre; the second makes that story into science fiction. If science fiction can absorb any amount of reality, but realism cannot absorb any noticeable variation on reality, "which then," Delany asks, "is the major and which the subcategory?" A question nicely designed to irritate the proponents of literature-as-realism.

Grandmother and the Kids

Realism is a quite recent fictional mode, a few hundred years old. Science fiction is an even more recent development of the same movement. The difference between these young genres, realistic and science fiction, is less than the difference of both of them from fantasy.

A rough but serviceable distinction of fantasy from non-fantasy is that fantasy includes or invokes the supernatural, and non-fantasy (including realistic and science fiction) avoids it. The admitted presence of magic in a story makes that story fantasy. By magic, I mean causes and effects presented as inherently inexplicable in terms of natural law, not answerable to scientific question, miraculous. Writer and reader of fantasy agree to accept as narratively real what they know to be factually impossible.

Fantasy is, I suppose, the oldest kind of fiction, and the most universal.

Why is the fiction of the impossible the primary form? Perhaps because human thinking is predicated on our capacity (related to our capacity for language?) to conceive of what is *not true*—and because this faculty (for lying, for imagining) gives us, like all our faculties well used, intense delight and the knowledge of power. Or perhaps because the imagination, by short-circuiting a laborious imitation of the actual, gives us direct access to truths that everyday actuality only masks from us. Or perhaps because we think in symbol and metaphor, and the metaphors of the dreaming, fantasizing, imagining mind are infinitely flexible and complex methods for comprehending the actual. Or because we need to think about what is not in order to know what is. *Acaso porque intuimos que nada es real* . . . I don't know; but I think fiction begins in dream and myth, and all its oldest forms are fantasies.

At the moment, most literary critics carefully use terms such as "magical realism" for fantasies they approve of, and take no notice whatever of the popular and commercial forms of fantasy. Mindless fantasy novels that manipulate trite symbols in formulaic "battles of Good and Evil" are certainly negligible; but the existence of muzak does not disprove the existence of music. Fantasy is the grandmother of all fictions. Grandmother may be a bit sleepy from time to time, but she wakes. One of the central books of twentieth-century English literature, which will not go away no matter how the Guardians of the Canon shudder and cry anathema, *The Lord of the Rings,* was written during one of her waking hours.

The existence and permanence of a narrative mode which does not even pretend to imitate "real life" demands critical attention. That most children are creators and insatiable hearer/readers of fantasy, and that most oral literatures are describable as fantastic, in no way justifies a reductionism that dismisses fantasy as childish or "primitive." The contemporary acceptance of fantasy by intensely sophisticated authors and readers is neither regression nor aberration. The realistic mode is insufficient to what such writers as Italo Calvino, Gabriel García Márquez, Toni Morrison, Gloria Naylor, Leslie Silko, and many others have to say. To know why they use fantasy, how they use fantasy, that they use fantasy, is essential to any comprehension of postmodern fiction.

Having carefully distinguished fantasy from science fiction, now I must add that they constantly overlap. Science fiction, while remaining in the realistic mode, behaves like fantasy in making up things which we know don't exist, even things which we know can't exist, though the latter are disguised by occurring in the megatext of science and realism. Fantasy in return often borrows images from science fiction, and plays with its rationalistic language. The two kinds of writing miscegenate promiscuously, like all healthy artforms. But this is an anthology of science fiction not of fantasy, and in selecting stories we had to interrogate both the story and ourselves: Is this fantasy rather than science fiction? Does it invoke or rely upon the supernatural? Does it use magic, miracle? Does it occur in addictspace, a drug-induced reality where the connection of cause and effect is denied? In rejecting stories we thought to be essentially fantasy, as I said above, we sadly excluded some very fine authors.

And there may be question about some we included—for instance, Orson Scott Card's "America." The story tells of a series of prophetic or true dreams, leading to the re-enactment of a myth. But the telling is realistic and rationalistic; the actors of the myth know they will be seen as superhuman, but know themselves as human. The beauty of the story and, I think, its science-fictionality, lie in the subtle, strong, unresolved tension between a possible supernatural and a vivid materialism.

Another story that might be seen as fantasy is Fritz Leiber's "The Winter Flies." This tale certainly occurs in addictspace (alcohol), and no rational explanation of the rescue of Heinie's non-existent spaceship is possible. To my sternly questioning colleagues I insisted that the story really is science fiction at its most intensely metaphorical and metafictional, innerspace fiction, the story of a desperate and triumphant effort to wrest the universe *out* of the realm of the supernatural and re-establish a shared, rationally confirmable reality. I may be wrong. But one of the reasons I wanted to edit this book was to include "The Winter Flies." The story has haunted and delighted me since I first read it; and I am glad that I could tell Fritz Leiber that, before he died, in September 1992.

"I'm Just Not Human till I've Had My Coffee"

Literalization of metaphor is a characteristic of science fiction. In teaching the craft to people new to it, I use Delany's phrase "subjunctive tension" to alert them to a challenge not present in realistic fiction: the way in which the open context of science fiction brings the language alive.

In a story where only what ordinarily occurs is going to occur, one can safely use such a sentence as, "He was absorbed in the landscape." In a story where *only the story* tells you what is likely to happen, you had best be careful about using sentences like that.

Her eyes dropped to the floor. . . . He was walking on air. . . . The chairman kept putting out feelers. . . .

Realistic fictional context keeps such imagery safely dead; science-fictional context revives it, re-embodies it.

Literality of metaphor is in fact an essential maneuver of science fiction, serving to put reality into question, making us aware of our assumptions concerning what is real, as well as our perceptions or convictions of continuity and identity. The reader can't take much for granted in a fiction where the scenery can eat the characters. And this is one reason why science fiction, marginal during the Modernist period with its exclusive focus on realism, has moved during the past thirty years towards the center: because it provides some of the things contemporary and postmodern writers and readers want from narrative—among them, an open context allowing a fluid, unfixed, often multiple, indeterminate apprehension of experience. No authority. Nothing taken for granted.

Literality of imagination is a related asset of science fiction. Not only language but perception itself can be renewed by the same maneuver of taking nothing for granted. Gravity, for instance. We all know what gravity is. But a girl in John Varley's "Lollipop and the Tar Baby," having lived all her life in freefall, doesn't. What's gravity? she asks, and is told: "People on planets have to worry about that all the time. They have to put something strong between themselves and the center of the planet, or they'll go down." It had never occurred to me that a floor is something strong that I have to keep between myself and the center of the planet. The factual precision of the observation, like the startling exactness of poetry, causes me wonder and pleasure. Maybe this, indeed, is the "sense of wonder": the revival of intense, exact perception, by short-circuiting habits of mind that insulate us from the world. T. S. Eliot's bird was of the opinion that humankind cannot bear very much reality, but I think the bird was wrong. We crave reality, hunger for it; that's why we read poetry and fiction.

In comparing a certain effect of science fiction to that of poetry, I don't mean to imply that science fiction uses the language or devices of poetry. The language of science fiction and the structure of its narrative was, for a long time, strictly prosaic. Even as prose it was conservative—straightforward, direct, plain, non-experimental, its main virtues being clarity and a vigorous pace. Such language and structure is not of great interest to most critics, who find simplicity very hard to discuss, and this helped keep science fiction in low critical esteem. In *Romantic Fantasy and Science Fiction,* Karl Kroeber points out that early science fiction adapted "from its technological model an assumption of uncomplicated relations between language and what it represents."* Often a good deal better than scientists at explicating scientific ideas, science-fiction writ-

*(New Haven, CN: Yale University Press, 1988), p. 22.

ers shared the scientistic assumption that reality is completely describable and that rational language is capable of describing it.

Very few scientists any longer take that assumption for granted; and science-fiction writers since the sixties increasingly use a language whose relationship with what it represents is deliberately complex, and structures that imitate or create an irrational or unreliable or multivalent reality. As such, their work is more attractive to the scholars, as well as having genuinely heightened aesthetic interest. But Philip K. Dick could question reality, and the connection of language with reality, in a language apparently plain, direct, straightforward to a fault. I'd like to see a good critic explain how he did it.

Looking Back

It might be entertaining to look briefly at some well-known older tales of science fiction in the light of my discussion of what science fiction does, to sketch their relation to science and scientism, how they used the icons, or what their influence may have been.

Science as creator of monsters is the myth on which Mary Shelley founded science fiction early in the nineteenth century, and a continuing theme. In the middle of this century, our Frankenstein was usually atomic war and its spawn of hideous and/or supernally gifted mutants.

Jules Verne was a hugely successful visionary in the extrapolative mode; his dazzling mixture of technological goshwowery and male-bonded adventurism still dominates some science-fiction writing and most sci-fi films.

H. G. Wells's Scientific Romances and a number of his short stories set an intellectual, ethical, and aesthetic standard that serious science fiction still honors. His themes are far too complex to go into here, but it is worth noting that practically everybody's idea of what a time machine is comes from *The Time Machine,* and that the themes and imagery of that tale and of *The War of the Worlds* and *The Invisible Man* have been reworked right through the twentieth century without wearing out at all. Freud invented the unconscious; Wells put the Morlocks into it; even the Marxists couldn't get them out.

E. M. Forster similarly struck a vein that would be mined for decades in his dystopian vision "The Machine Stops." Rudyard Kipling's adventure stories of the tanks and air warfare of the future set a style that served well up to the sixties; but his uncanny gift for presenting ships and trains (as well as pythons, engineers, and Buddhists) as passionate and intelligent beings came out in stories the influence of which is probably far deeper, though harder to trace.

Ray Bradbury's work often yearns toward a nostalgic rural simplicity, but the imagery of his stunning early stories is brilliantly technological, and the title of his most famous cautionary tale is an elegant scientific reference: 451 degrees Fahrenheit is the combustion point of paper.

The literal imagination of science fiction is evident in one of the purest and neatest uses of the myth of science as omnipotent: Arthur Clarke's "The Nine Billion Names of God," in which a computer, by printing out the divine names heretofore laboriously written down by monks, closes down the universe.

Isaac Asimov's "Nightfall," mythlike in its evocation of a world that has never known darkness, also draws upon the mythology of scientism: without scientific, rational knowledge of why the darkness falls, human beings are shown as mindless prey to panic fear, madly setting their cities afire to make light.

In the sixties, science fiction began drawing on ecology for both imagery and ethic. Frank Herbert exemplified the mode in such stories as "Greenslaves" (regrettably too long for this book) in which the consequences of the industrial abuse of the planet are drawn in brilliant and frightening imagery. What has been called ecofiction, using scientific observation of the effects of mismanaged technology to criticize scientific/technologic endeavor, offers rational caution against uncritical trust in human undertakings and intentions. Its opposite is the technofiction in which only "man" exists, other species and planets being considered only as inimical or exploitable, without consideration of the interdependence of organic processes or the psychological effect of species-isolation on human beings. Though considerably more sophisticated than during its so-called Golden Age, this expansionist, androcentric mode still exists, still drawing on a basically uncritical belief in technology as saviour-god.

Isaac Asimov's "Laws of Robotics" were brilliant ethical abstractions made in an experiential void: there were no robots, and there are still no androids, on whom these behavioral laws might be tested. But this thought experiment may yet find practical application, with the development of AI (artificial intelligence). The record of science fiction in actually "predicting the future" is about as good as that of most fortune tellers. The prettiest case of accurate prediction I know is Robert Heinlein's invention, in a story called "Waldo," of the manipulative devices now called, in deserved recognition, waldoes.

Until Stanley Weinbaum's "A Martian Odyssey" came out, the only good aliens were dead ones. That vivid and charming story (first published in 1934) opened the door to a great domain of science fiction, replacing tentacled horrors with fully imagined non-human physiologies and societies. By the fifties the theme of "first contact" was a reliable source of invention and ethical dilemma. I don't know when the first story was written with only alien characters, no human; but this anthropological Copernification has proceeded, and by now the universe, which used to be shown as waiting for Earth to tell it what to do, is generally not perceived as having us at its center.

Stories drawing on anthropological experience and ethic were the precedent for the *Star Trek* series' "Prime Directive," a rather Taoist taboo on human interference in alien societies, which has proved an inexhaustible source of plots, mostly based on the relationship of industrial and pre-industrial societies on Earth. At least this degree of sophistication now underlies most stories of human/alien contact, no matter which group is considered "superior" or how superiority is defined.

The curiously nineteenth-century Empires of formula science fiction, the endless wars between good worlds and bad worlds, the conception of power as the natural privilege of a tiny elite ruling innumerable faceless nobodies—such scenarios may reflect not only a naive social Darwinism, but also the exemption of scientific and technological research from social responsibility. Science still sets up a claim that its "objectivity" sets it "above" politics, and fiction may imitate it in cutting itself off from the very chain of cause and effect which science posits as reality, and thus from social and ethical answerability. But "objectivity" was also a literary totem, for a while, and literature was also supposed to be exempt from the taint of politics. It's funny to find the lean, bronzed Captains of the Galactic Empire in the same boat with T. S. Eliot and his bird.

Our Stories: Topics, Times, and Lawki

Where and when—with all the Galaxy and all Time to choose from—do our sixty-seven stories take place?

Fifty of them are set on Earth. Four take place on spaceships, and thirteen on other planets (of this or a distant solar system). Most of the "off Earth" stories are from the decade of the sixties, only four from the eighties.

Six stories involve the past. Two of these, Robinson's "The Lucky Strike" and Waldrop's ". . . the World, as we Know't," are set in a deliberately altered past, and thus are parallel-world stories; different as they are, each is exemplary of the mode. Kessel's "Invaders," moving between the present day, an imagined near future, and the historical past, alters history only at the very end. Others visit the historical past through memory or time shift from a conventional present-day or near-future setting. Bryant's "Precession" traps its protagonist in an unnerving back-slip and echo-effect of time. Only one story, Simak's "Over the River and Through the Woods," involves time travel as a technology, and the story's concern is people, not technology.

The presentness or futurity of many of the stories is not really determinable. As I remarked above, science-fiction writers often set their story just a bit in advance of "now," in order to keep it in a world familiar to the reader while freeing it from the plausibility-damaging question, "If that happened, why haven't I heard of it?" To divide "now or pretty soon" from "the future," I used any notable change in technology, such as passenger spaceships or robot popes, or any evidence of radical social discontinuity, such as an alien invasion. Omitting the two alternate-history stories, I made out that thirty-two stories are set mostly in the present or near future, and thirty-three take place in a future that is either remote in time, or radically different from Lawki—Life As We Know It.

Of the thirty-three stories from the sixties and seventies, twenty-two are set in the far future; of the thirty-four stories from the eighties, only half as many. Eighties writers were writing more about here and now.

It appears, in fact, that many of the icons and images that are used to characterize science fiction have been gradually dropping out of the fiction, being relegated to film and other media. The writers of our three decades don't often go far afield either in space or time. The spaceship doesn't figure largely in our collection, the time machine not at all. This may have something to do with the editors' taste; but I can say that none of us is aware of any prejudice against far-future or far-planet or deep-space or time-travel stories—quite the contrary. There simply seemed to be fewer of them, or fewer good ones, being written as our three decades went on.

To some extent the short-story form itself favors the contemporary mundane setting, which can be instantly presented and taken for granted. An alien world or an altered future must be described, with explicit or implicit explanations, in order to ground the reader. It can take a while to make a world. Novella and novel offer more room for it. But there are stories in this volume that create a vivid, total, and totally unfamiliar reality in a very few pages; it is indeed a test of the science-fiction writer's craft to be able to do so. And the form can't explain a change in content. I think that in fact this drift away from the depths of Space and Time, this withdrawal towards Earth and Now, has been going on in science fiction since at least the fifties, and must reflect a large slow movement of what I wish I knew another word for than *Weltgeist.* It may well reverse itself, as the *Weltgeist* has a habit of doing.

What about the "Space Aliens" beloved of the trash tabloids? Aliens are definitely still with us. My figures may, however, be disputed. Are long-dead aliens discovered by archeologists *in* the story or *not* in the story? Are animals aliens? Under what circumstances or from what point of view are humans aliens? I solved these problems with about as much finesse as Alexander showed with his big hard knot. My very rough count is that there are twenty-one stories with aliens in them, and forty-six alien-free stories containing only humans, though some of the humans in some of the stories are pretty weird.

McIntyre's "The Mountains of Sunset, the Mountains of Dawn" is the only story with no humans in it at all to clutter the pure dream of love and death and flight. In Delany's "High Weir," though the aliens (our only Martians) are not present, the story is profoundly one of alienation. In Wolfe's "Feather Tigers," visitors from elsewhere study an Earth on which humans are extinct (although when discussing Wolfe's stories, the verb "to be" must be used with extreme caution). And Atwood's "Homelanding" deftly and tenderly turns the concept of alienness inside out and empties it.

For the most part, the non-humans are seen through human eyes; but frequently they look back, in one way or another, and in Ellison's "Strange Wine" they look both ways. "Social science fiction," one of my own favorite varieties, which presents a complete picture of an alien culture, is best developed in long works; alien mores in the short story are often satirical or polemical comments on our own. But Lafferty's "Nine Hundred Grandmothers" transcends irony, achieving the true mystical hilarity; as, in an absolutely different way and direction, does Gotlieb's "Tauf Aleph." Indeed, three of the funniest stories in this book, these two and Silverberg's "Good News from the Vatican," have to do with religion, a fact I have no intention of trying to explain.

Woman and Other

It is notable that many of the stories about aliens are by women, and/or have to do in one way or another with a relationship between woman/women and alien/aliens. The story may involve love between a woman and an alien being, as in Anderson's "Kyrie." Or the connection may be sexual, exploitive, or something else entirely, as in Blish's "How Beautiful with Banners." In Hess's "When I Was Miss Dow" the alien is literally identified with a human woman. The frequency of this woman/alien theme is striking; it is the subject of very different, very powerful stories. Among them are Emshwiller's "The Start of the End of the World," Cadigan's "After the Days of Dead-Eye 'Dee," Wilhelm's "And the Angels Sing," and Murphy's "His Vegetable Wife."

Obviously, "the alien" may be a metaphor of alienation. Its frequent use as a means of examining the nature of gender may imply that in fact the assignment to gender roles is a central cause or nexus of alienation, especially but not solely among women. The exemplary story of this kind is Tiptree's "The Women Men Don't See," which permanently redefined the scope of the genre by its delicate exploration of the social construction of gender, its literalization of woman as Other. In Kress's "Out of All Them Bright Stars," gender is one element in the painful question of human responsibility. Goldstein's "Midnight News" has another take on the identification of woman and alien, the dehumanization of the old, the plain, the women men don't see.

Russ's "A Few Things I Know About Whileaway" (which has no aliens in it, unless women who get along without men are considered to be non-human) deconstructs the myth of What Women Want with good-natured polemical directness. In quite a different mode, Gloss's "Interlocking Pieces" posits a dilemma of both gender and identity, and leaves us poised, most poignantly, upon the horns of it.

Hunting the Icons

There are characters who find the social construction not only of gender but of humanity to be intolerable, and come up with a truly original way to get around it, such as Coney's "Byrds." Equally ingenious is Gunn's entomological solution to the problems of office management. Grimmer forms of alienation are found in Bunch's cybermen of "2064, or Thereabouts," in Dorsey's harshly brilliant reversal of the cyberpunk wet-dream in "(Learning About) Machine Sex," or in Haldeman's unflinching "Private War of Private Jacob," a perfect example of the literalization of metaphor. Glancy's "Aunt Parnetta's Electric Blisters" deals with two kinds of alienation—racial (again, who are the aliens?) and technological, the alien and inimical technology being represented, absolutely convincingly, by a refrigerator (which, as Parnetta sadly remarks, is white).

I find no monsters in this book. Monsters have mostly gone back to fantasy (where, if they are supernatural, they belong) and horror stories. The nearest we come, perhaps, is Varley's chatty black hole in "Lollipop and the Tar Baby." The beasts in Swanwick's "Midwinter's Tale" are in no way monstrous, though terrifying and marvelous. Probably the truest monsters in the book are in Davidson's "The House the Blakeneys Built," and the Blakeney family is perfectly and horribly human.

We're low on robots, too. Silverberg gives us the only straightforward tin man; the arrangement in Knight's "The Handler" is rather more ambiguous. There is a good deal of highly intelligent machinery, however. Certainly the ship in Dick's "Frozen Journey" is a well-meaning Artificial Intelligence, and in Malzberg's "Making It All the Way," part of the problem people have is telling themselves from androids. "Alpha Ralpha Boulevard" is typical of Cordwainer Smith's work, in that the line between machine and human and the line between human and animal has become so complicated that it partakes (like a coastline in Chaos theory) of the infinite.

A parenthesis for praise: "Alpha Ralpha Boulevard," when it was first published in 1961, revised, once for all, my ideas of what science fiction was and what it could do. Cordwainer Smith (Paul Linebarger; like the other employee of the U.S. intelligence services in this book, he used a pen name) wrote a series of stories set in a far, strange future. It is an extraordinary body of work, not yet adequately appreciated by critics, and only erratically reprinted. Many of the stories have a deeper political interest than this one, and a more controlled subject matter; but I honor this one for its romantic flamboyance, its hallucinatory imagery, its emotional intensity, and its beauty. I hope readers may discover in it what I did: the opening of a door into a new poetry.

While in parenthesis, I want to pay homage also to Philip K. Dick, a writer of very quiet, very great originality and strength. His short stories have recently been reprinted, and it is an impressive series of volumes, but I think he needed the scope of the novel to do his best work. "Frozen Journey" is typical Dick in its terrifying reality-slippage—reading him can be like losing your footing on a scree slope. He was an obsessional and visionary writer. His science-fiction novels, highly praised by French critics and receiving intelligent notice from postmodernist critics here, are just beginning to get their due.

To return to the items and icons that are supposed to characterize science fiction: we have no mutants; nobody glows. And not a single mad scientist, unless the narrator of Blumlein's "The Brains of Rats" qualifies, and there's method in his madness. What about "psi," paranormal powers or altered states of consciousness which affect reality? Our stories using this matter are rather bleak. Mental powers in the tabloids express wish-fulfillment, but these stories emphasize the price. Zelazny's "Comes Now the Power" presents telepathy in images of loss and pain, though finally of solace; Sargent's "Blue Roses" has no solace. My "New Atlantis" seems to suggest that the connection between a dying world and one rising towards birth is one of consciousness. But the force that draws MacLean's protagonist through the mean streets of "Night-Rise" is not supernatural or paranormal, though one might wish it were.

Science appears as god/demon in two stories from 1982, Waldrop's "The World" and Bear's "Schrödinger's Plague." In both, science is responsible for catastrophe. But they are also linked with other stories throughout the book by a different theme: the scientist as moral individual, the scientist's responsibility to knowledge, to society, to family. "Exposures" by Benford, a practicing physicist, plays this tune most artfully. Both Willis's "Schwarzchild Radius" and Preuss's "Half-Life" explore with delicacy and passionate ethical feeling the experience of scientists who were historical figures, founders of modern physics. Here, as we shall see again and again, enters the question of responsibility. Who is responsible, answerable? For what?

Finding the Patterns

What I'll talk about from here on are not formulaic items or icons but commonalties, shared literary themes of these particular science-fiction texts, which I noticed as I read and reread the stories. They are not topics prescribed in a definition of the genre; they are subjects or motifs that I see writers in the genre mutually and severally pursuing. My indication of them is anything but methodical or exhaustive. Study of the stories will turn up many more themes and connections than my brief and partial survey.

Identity is a major theme of twentieth-century fiction, and throughout this book. Bradley's "Elbow Room" literalizes the question "Who am I?" to make a classic spaceship story. Many other stories, such as those by Gloss and Leiber, and several of the woman/alien stories, ask the question more or less directly. Some carry it into metafiction, like Arnason's "The Warlord of Saturn's Moons," an unusually honest account of the peculiar relationship of actual and fictional selves.

I was struck by how many children there are in the book, and how often a familial or parental responsibility is important in the story. These are not subjects one thinks of as counting for much in science fiction. Zenna Henderson's stories were nearly all about schoolchildren; some were sentimental, others vivid and original. "As Simple as That" is a by no means simple tale about reality as a social construct and the urgency of the need to work together on the construction. Theodore Sturgeon, most of whose major, highly original work was written before the period of this book, sentimentalized kids sometimes, but he knew them. "Tandy's Story"—named for one of his own—uses what may be ultimately a Christian motif, innocence as a vehicle of true communication. The child can hear/speak to the Other as the adult cannot. James H. Schmitz's nice kids at home on an alien world enact a similar drama, with a more unsettling implication, at least if one considers our autonomy essential to our humanity; for in "Balanced Ecology," a fable of the necessity of interdependence in organic systems, the humans aren't in control.

Children figure also in the two stories which are directly concerned with language, though in Elgin's "For the Sake of Grace" the girl who is the center of the tale never appears in it; we see only the exotic and rigid society which her genius will probably remodel. And at the end of Butler's fearful parable, "Speech Sounds"—the first story I know that has asked, What if we couldn't talk *at all?*—the narrator takes parental responsibility for two children, in whom lies hope.

The Los Angeles of Butler's story is a familiar locus of science fiction: the city in which community has broken down and violence is the only order. The cities of dreadful night favored by cyberpunk are a variant, in which street smarts provide the ethic in a world modeled on the contemporary inner city, the rock scene, the drug scene, and hackers' dreams of glory. Kelly's "Rat" uses this stage set to extraordinary effect, and is the only story about international drug smugglers that I would ever think of comparing favorably with *The Wind in the Willows.*

The father of cyberpunk is here represented by a gentler nightmare, "The Gernsback Continuum," a metafiction in which the future of the past begins to complicate the present. Things in science fiction are always getting out of hand; Pandora's box is part of the deep-structure grammar of the genre.

Not surprisingly, things are terribly out of hand in the two stories concerning the Viet Nam war—Fowler's achingly restrained "The Lake Was Full of Artificial Things," and Shiner's "The War at Home," which, by taking a slogan literally, vastly enlarges its significance. In fact, things are out of hand in all the war stories but Robinson's World War II one, where the past gets changed for the better. In Willis's World War I story, the image is the information sink, the black hole, where everything gets out of hand forever.

Black holes turn up in several other stories; they seem to be a deep-space phenomenon/hypothesis that particularly resonates with these writers.

It is possible that the actual "conquest" of the Moon and implementation of the space program, however limited, had something to do with turning science fiction away from space exploration. It was only a dream till we did it.

But some of the dreams of early science fiction are now part of our lives, and still part of science fiction. Television is one. Along with related (sometimes not yet invented) electronic media, TV plays a part in a good many of these stories. Weiner's "Distant Signals" brings together the Oater and the Alien to ask (im)pertinent questions concerning Art. Pohl's "Day Million" provides a new meaning to the phrase "Live on

TV," along with a truly dazzling array of special effects. Sheckley's "Life of Anybody" gives us a video-vérité which validates the common confusion of existence with soap opera (TV tends to induce questions of ontology). And in Crowley's "Snow," imagery of the video bug and the home video provides subtle, complex metaphors of memory, time, and loss.

The computer is of course another piece of science fiction which became real and ate the world. There are fewer computer stories than I expected in this book. Bishop's "Bob Dylan Tambourine Software" is a superb conflation of computer programming with market hype, capitalism, and the Messiah; and Dorsey's "Machine Sex" is genuinely knowledgeable about who programmers are and how they work. But we found that a lot of computer stories have more jargon than content. Their noise to information ratio is poor. The technology and theory has probably been moving too fast for fiction to keep up with. However boldly imaginative it may seem, and even when you can write it very, very fast on a word processor, fiction grows from experience and knowledge taken into the mind and body and composted till it produces something new, whether familiar or unfamiliar. And you can't hurry compost.

For example: "Virtual Reality" is a lovely notion that is being played with in actuality (those who play with it like to claim it will replace fiction, a silly notion, since VR has little or nothing to do with words and fiction is nothing but words). It has long been present in science fiction in foreshadowings and approximations, such as the dream technology in Fowler's story, or the idea of cyberspace; but we found no good stories using actual VR technology. It hasn't been composted yet.

Finally, one of the major historical themes of the modern world, the destruction and assimilation by Western industrialism of every culture it comes in contact with, has been represented in science fiction for a long time. In the pulps it mostly appeared in march tempo with tubas: the Triumph of Science over Stupid Superstition, Man's Conquest of the Universe, Anglo Hero vs. Alien Slime, Dick White and his Ray-Gun against the Mongloobian Hordes. Leukocentrism was no worse in science fiction than anywhere else, but no better, either. I remember, not too clearly, a story about some aliens who came to look humanity over to see if we would make good slaves; the smart-American-white-male-hero presented some Eskimos to the aliens as typical humans. The Eskimos did nothing but grunt illiterately and smell fishy and chew blubber—we all know Eskimos are incapable of anything else—and so the aliens went away to wait a few millennia till humans got civilized enough to be worth enslaving. I believe that story was published in the sixties. We've come a long way, Baby. Some of us.

One story simply reverses the whole myth of Western superiority, stands it on its head: Sterling's "We See Things Differently." Resnick's "Kirinyaga" subverts it by setting two ethical systems, two moralities, on a head-on collision course, without overtly favoring either. In "Aunt Parnetta," Glancy, not a member of the conquistador culture, writes with an authority that needs no emphasis. Card's "America" dreams forward to a future where the whole tragedy of the Conquest, having played itself out, reaches a politico-mythical resolution—or reversal. Finally, I am glad that Kessel's "Invaders" closes our book, not only because it handles this urgent, difficult theme with wit and passion, but because its last words are the last words of all the words of all the stories in the book, and they are: "and everyone lived happily ever after."

The Norton Book of Science Fiction

DAMON KNIGHT

THE HANDLER

When the big man came in, there was a movement in the room like bird dogs pointing. The piano player quit pounding, the two singing drunks shut up, all the beautiful people with cocktails in their hands stopped talking and laughing.

"Pete!" the nearest woman shrilled, and he walked straight into the room, arms around two girls, hugging them tight. "How's my sweetheart? Susy, you look good enough to eat, but I had it for lunch. George, you pirate—" he let go both girls, grabbed a bald blushing little man and thumped him on the arm—"you were great, sweetheart, I mean it, really great. Now HEAR THIS!" he shouted, over all the voices that were clamoring Pete this, Pete that.

Somebody put a martini in his hand, and he stood holding it, bronzed and tall in his dinner jacket, teeth gleaming white as his shirt cuffs. "We had a show!" he told them.

A shriek of agreement went up, a babble of did we have a *show* my God Pete listen a *show*—

He held up his hand. "It was a good show!"

Another shriek and babble.

"The sponsor kinda liked it—he just signed for another one in the fall!"

A shriek, a roar, people clapping, jumping up and down. The big man tried to say something else, but gave up, grinning, while men and women crowded up to him. They were all trying to shake his hand, talk in his ear, put their arms around him.

"I love ya *all*!" he shouted. "Now what do you say, let's live a little!"

The murmuring started again as people sorted themselves out. There was a clinking from the bar. "Jesus, Pete," a skinny pop-eyed little guy was saying, crouching in adoration, "when you dropped that fishbowl I though I'd pee myself, honest to God—"

The big man let out a bark of happy laughter. "Yeah, I can still see the look on your face. And the fish, flopping all over the stage. So what can I do, I get down there on my knees—" the big man did so, bending over and staring at imaginary fish on the floor. "And I say, 'Well, fellows, back to the drawing board!' "

Screams of laughter as the big man stood up. The party was arranging itself around him in arcs of concentric circles, with people in the back standing on sofas and the piano bench so they could see. Somebody yelled, "Sing the goldfish song, Pete!"

Shouts of approval, please-do-Pete, the goldfish song.

"Okay, okay." Grinning, the big man sat on the arm of a chair and raised his glass. "And a vun, and a doo—vere's de moosic?" A scuffle at the piano bench. Somebody banged out a few chords. The big man made a comic face and sang, "Ohhh—how I wish . . . I was a little fish . . . and when I want some quail . . . I'd flap my little tail."

Laughter, the girls laughing louder than anybody and their red mouths farther open. One flushed blonde had her hand on the big man's knee, and another was sitting close behind him.

"But seriously—" the big man shouted. More laughter.

"No seriously," he said in a vibrant voice as the room quieted. "I want to tell you in all seriousness I couldn't have done it alone. And incidentally I see we have some foreigners, litvaks and other members of the press here tonight, so I want to introduce all the important people. First of all, George here, the three-fingered band leader—there isn't a guy in the world could have done what he did this afternoon—George, I love ya." He hugged the blushing little bald man.

"Next my real sweetheart, Ruthie, where are ya? Honey, you were the greatest, really perfect—I mean it, baby—" He kissed a dark girl in a red dress who cried a little and hid her face on his broad shoulder. "And Frank—" he reached down and grabbed the skinny pop-eyed guy by the sleeve. "What can I tell you? A sweetheart?" The skinny guy was blinking, all choked up; the big man thumped him on the back. "Sol and Ernie and Mack, my writers, Shakespeare should have been so lucky—" One by one, they came up to shake the big man's hand as he called their names; the women kissed him and cried. "My stand-in," the big man was calling out, and "my caddy," and "Now," he said, as the room quieted a little, people flushed and sore-throated with enthusiasm, "I want you to meet my handler."

The room fell silent. The big man looked thoughtful and startled, as if he had had a sudden pain. Then he stopped moving. He sat without breathing or blinking his eyes. After a moment there was a jerky motion behind him. The girl who was sitting on the arm of the chair got up and moved away. The big man's dinner jacket split open in the back, and a little man climbed out. He had a perspiring brown face under a shock of black hair. He was a very small man, almost a dwarf, stoop-shouldered and round-backed in a sweaty brown singlet and shorts. He climbed out of the cavity in the big man's body, and closed the dinner jacket carefully. The big man sat motionless and his face was doughy.

The little man got down, wetting his lips nervously. Hello, Harry, a few people said. "Hello," Harry called, waving his hand. He was about forty, with a big nose and big soft brown eyes. His voice was cracked and uncertain. "Well, we sure put on a show, didn't we?"

Sure did, Harry, they said politely. He wiped his brow with the back of his hand. "Hot in there," he explained, with an apologetic grin. Yes I guess it must be, Harry, they said. People around the outskirts of the crowd were beginning to turn away, form conversational groups; the hum of talk rose higher. "Say, Tim, I wonder if I could have something to drink," the little man said. "I don't like to leave him—you know—" He gestured toward the silent big man.

"Sure, Harry, what'll it be?"

"Oh—you know—a glass of beer?"

Tim brought him a beer in a pilsener glass and he drank it thirstily, his brown eyes darting nervously from side to side. A lot of people were sitting down now; one or two were at the door leaving.

"Well," the little man said to a passing girl, "Ruthie, that was quite a moment there, when the fishbowl busted, wasn't it?"

"Huh? Excuse me, honey, I didn't hear you." She bent nearer.

"Oh—well, it don't matter. Nothing."

She patted him on the shoulder once, and took her hand away. "Well excuse me, sweetie, I have to catch Robbins before he leaves." She went on toward the door.

The little man put his beer glass down and sat, twisting his knobby hands together. The bald man and the pop-eyed man were the only ones still sitting near him. An anxious smile flickered on his lips; he glanced at one face, then another. "Well," he began, "that's one show under our belts, huh, fellows, but I guess we got to start, you know, thinking about—"

"Listen, Harry," said the bald man seriously, leaning forward to touch him on the wrist, "why don't you get back inside?"

The little man looked at him for a moment with sad hound-dog eyes, then ducked his head, embarrassed. He stood up uncertainly, swallowed and said, "Well—" He climbed up on the chair behind the big man, opened the back of the dinner jacket and put his legs in one at a time. A few people were watching him, unsmiling. "Thought I'd take it easy a while," he said weakly, "but I guess—" He reached in and gripped something with both hands, then swung himself inside. His brown, uncertain face disappeared.

The big man blinked suddenly and stood up. "Well *hey* there," he called, "what's a matter with this party anyway? Let's see some life, some action—" Faces were lighting up around him. People began to move in closer. "What I mean, let me hear that beat!"

The big man began clapping his hands rhythmically. The piano took it up. Other people began to clap. "What I mean, are we alive here or just waiting for the wagon to pick us up? How's that again, can't hear you!" A roar of pleasure as he cupped his hand to his ear. "Well come on, let me hear it!" A louder roar. Pete, Pete; a gabble of voices. "I got nothing against Harry," said the bald man earnestly in the middle of the noise, "I mean for a square he's a nice guy." "Know what you mean," said the pop-eyed man, "I mean like he doesn't *mean* it." "Sure," said the bald man, "but Jesus that sweaty undershirt and all . . . " The pop-eyed man shrugged. "What are you gonna do?" Then they both burst out laughing as the big man made a comic face, tongue lolling, eyes crossed. Pete, Pete, Pete; the room was really jumping; it was a great party, and everything was all right, far into the night.

(1960)

CORDWAINER SMITH

Alpha Ralpha Boulevard

We were drunk with happiness in those early years. Everybody was, especially the young people. These were the first years of the Rediscovery of Man, when the Instrumentality dug deep in the treasury, reconstructing the old cultures, the old languages, and even the old troubles. The nightmare of perfection had taken our forefathers to the edge of suicide. Now under the leadership of the Lord Jestocost and the Lady Alice More, the ancient civilizations were rising like great land masses out of the sea of the past.

I myself was the first man to put a postage stamp on a letter, after fourteen thousand years. I took Virginia to hear the first piano recital. We watched at the eye-machine when cholera was released in Tasmania, and we saw the Tasmanians dancing in the streets, now that they did not have to be protected any more. Everywhere, things became exciting. Everywhere, men and women worked with a wild will to build a more imperfect world.

I myself went into a hospital and came out French. Of course I remembered my early life; I remembered it, but it did not matter. Virginia was French, too, and we had the years of our future lying ahead of us like ripe fruit hanging in an orchard of perpetual summers. We had no idea when we would die. Formerly, I would be able to go to bed and think, "The government has given me four hundred years. Three-hundred-and-seventy-four years from now, they will stop the stroon injections and I will then die." Now I knew anything could happen. The safety devices had been turned off. The diseases ran free. With luck, and hope, and love, I might live a thousand years. Or I might die tomorrow. I was free.

We revelled in every moment of the day.

Virginia and I brought the first French newspaper to appear since the Most Ancient World fell. We found delight in the news, even in the advertisements. Some parts of the culture were hard to reconstruct. It was difficult to talk about foods of which only the names survived, but the homunculi and the machines, working tirelessly in Downdeep-downdeep, kept the surface of the world filled with enough novelties to fill anyone's heart with hope. We knew that all of this was make-believe, and yet it was not. We knew that when the diseases had killed the statistically correct number of people, they would be turned off; when the accident rate rose too high, it would stop without our knowing why. We knew that over us all, the Instrumentality watched. We had confidence that the Lord Jestocost and the Lady Alice More would play with us as friends and not use us as victims of a game.

Take, for example, Virginia. She had been called Menerima, which represented the coded sounds of her birth number. She was small, verging on chubby; she was compact; her head was covered with tight brown curls; her eyes were a brown so deep and so rich that it took sunlight, with her squinting against it, to bring forth the treasures of her irises. I had known her well, but never known her. I had seen her often, but never seen her with my heart, until we met just outside the hospital, after becoming French.

I was pleased to see an old friend and started to speak in the Old Common Tongue, but the words jammed, and as I tried to speak it was not Menerima any longer, but someone of ancient beauty, rare and strange—someone who had wandered into these latter days from the treasure worlds of time past. All I could do was to stammer:

"What do you call yourself now?" And I said it in ancient French.

She answered in the same language, "Je m'appelle Virginie."

Looking at her and falling in love was a single process. There was something strong, something wild in her, wrapped and hidden by the tenderness and youth of her girlish body. It was as though destiny spoke to me out of the certain brown eyes, eyes which questioned me surely and wonderingly, just as we both questioned the fresh new world which lay about us.

"May I?" said I, offering her my arm, as I had learned in the hours of hypnopedia. She took my arm and we walked away from the hospital.

I hummed a tune which had come into my mind, along with the ancient French language.

She tugged gently on my arm, and smiled up at me.

"What is it," she asked, "or don't you know?"

The words came soft and unbidden to my lips and I sang it very quietly, muting my voice in her curly hair, half-singing half-whispering the popular song which had poured into my mind with all the other things which the Rediscovery of Man had given me:

> "She wasn't the woman I went to seek.
> I met her by the merest chance.

> She did not speak the French of France,
> But the surded French of Martinique.
>
> "She wasn't rich. She wasn't chic.
> She had a most entrancing glance,
> And that was all . . . "

Suddenly I ran out of words, "I seem to have forgotten the rest of it. It's called 'Macouba' and it has something to do with a wonderful island which the ancient French called Martinique."

"I know where that is," she cried. She had been given the same memories that I had. "You can see it from Earthport!"

This was a sudden return to the world we had known. Earthport stood on its single pedestal, twelve miles high, at the eastern edge of the small continent. At the top of it, the Lords worked amid machines which had no meaning any more. There the ships whispered their way in from the stars. I had seen pictures of it, but I had never been there. As a matter of fact, I had never known anyone who had actually been up Earthport. Why should we have gone? We might not have been welcome, and we could always see it just as well through the pictures on the eye-machine. For Menerima—familiar, dully pleasant, dear little Menerima—to have gone there was uncanny. It made me think that in the Old Perfect World things had not been as plain or forthright as they seemed.

Virginia, the new Menerima, tried to speak in the Old Common Tongue, but she gave up and used French instead:

"My aunt," she said, meaning a kindred lady, since no one had had aunts for thousands of years, "was a Believer. She took me to the Abba-dingo. To get holiness and luck."

The old me was a little shocked; the French me was disquieted by the fact that this girl had done something unusual even before mankind itself turned to the unusual. The Abba-dingo was a long-obsolete computer set part way up the column of Earthport. The homunculi treated it as a god, and occasionally people went to it. To do so was tedious and vulgar.

Or had been. Till all things became new again.

Keeping the annoyance out of my voice, I asked her:

"What was it like?"

She laughed lightly, yet there was a trill to her laughter which gave me a shiver. If the old Menerima had had secrets, what might the new Virginia do? I almost hated the fate which made me love her, which made me feel that the touch of her hand on my arm was a link between me and time-forever.

She smiled at me instead of answering my question. The surfaceway was under repair; we followed a ramp down to the level of the top underground, where it was legal for true persons and hominids and homunculi to walk.

I did not like the feeling; I had never gone more than twenty minutes' trip from my birthplace. This ramp looked safe enough. There were few hominids around these days, men from the stars who (though of true human stock) had been changed to fit the conditions of a thousand worlds. The homunculi were morally repulsive, though many of them looked like very handsome people; bred from animals into the shape of men, they took over the tedious chores of working with machines where no real man would wish to go. It was whispered that some of them had even bred with actual people, and I would not want my Virginia to be exposed to the presence of such a creature.

She had been holding my arm. When we walked down the ramp to the busy passage, I slipped my arm free and put it over her shoulders, drawing her closer to me. It was light enough, bright enough to be clearer than the daylight which we had left behind, but it was strange and full of danger. In the old days, I would have turned around and gone home rather than to expose myself to the presence of such dreadful beings. At this time, in this moment, I could not bear to part from my new-found love, and I was afraid that if I went back to my own apartment in the tower, she might go to hers. Anyhow, being French gave a spice to danger.

Actually, the people in the traffic looked commonplace enough. There were many busy machines, some in human form and some not. I did not see a single hominid. Other people, whom I knew to be homunculi because they yielded the right of way to us, looked no different from the real human beings on the surface. A brilliantly beautiful girl gave me a look which I did not like—saucy, intelligent, provocative beyond all limits of flirtation. I suspected her of being a dog by origin. Among the hominids, d'persons are the ones most apt to take liberties. They even have a dog-man philosopher who once produced a tape arguing that since dogs are the most ancient of men's allies, they have the right to be closer to man than any other form of life. When I saw the tape, I thought it amusing that a dog should be bred into the form of a Socrates; here, in the top underground, I was not so sure at all. What would I do if one of them became insolent? Kill him? That meant a brush with the law and a talk with the Subcommissioners of the Instrumentality.

Virginia noticed none of this.

She had not answered my question, but was asking me questions about the top underground instead. I had been there only once before, when I was small, but it was flattering to have her wondering, husky voice murmuring in my ear.

Then it happened.

At first I thought he was a man, foreshortened by some trick of the underground light. When he came closer, I saw that it was not. He must have been five feet across the shoulders. Ugly red scars on his forehead showed where the horns had been dug out of his skull. He was a homunculus, obviously derived from cattle stock. Frankly, I had never known that they left them that ill-formed.

And he was drunk.

As he came closer I could pick up the buzz of his mind: . . . *they're not people, they're not hominids, and they're not Us—what are they doing here? The words they think confuse me.* He had never telepathed French before.

This was bad. For him to talk was common enough, but only a few of the homunculi were telepathic—those with special jobs, such as in the Downdeep-downdeep, where only telepathy could relay instructions.

Virginia clung to me.

Thought I, in clear Common Tongue: *True men are we. You must let us pass.*

There was no answer but a roar. I do not know where he got drunk, or on what, but he did not get my message.

I could see his thoughts forming up into panic, helplessness, hate. Then he charged, almost dancing toward us, as though he could crush our bodies.

My mind focussed and I threw the stop order at him.

It did not work.

Horror-stricken, I realized that I had thought French at him.

Virginia screamed.

The bull-man was upon us.

At the last moment he swerved, passed us blindly, and let out a roar which filled the enormous passage. He had raced beyond us.

Still holding Virginia, I turned around to see what had made him pass us.

What I beheld was odd in the extreme.

Our figures ran down the corridor away from us—my black-purple cloak flying in the still air as my image ran, Virginia's golden dress swimming out behind her as she ran with me. The images were perfect and the bull-man pursued them.

I stared around in bewilderment. We had been told that the safeguards no longer protected us.

A girl stood quietly next to the wall. I had almost mistaken her for a statue. Then she spoke,

"Come no closer. I am a cat. It was easy enough to fool him. You had better get back to the surface."

"Thank you," I said, "thank you. What is your name?"

"Does it matter?" said the girl. "I'm not a person."

A little offended, I insisted, "I just wanted to thank you." As I spoke to her I saw that she was as beautiful and as bright as a flame. Her skin was clear, the color of cream, and her hair—finer than any human hair could possibly be—was the wild golden orange of a Persian cat.

"I'm C'mell," said the girl, "and I work at Earthport."

That stopped both Virginia and me. Cat-people were below us, and should be shunned, but Earthport was above us, and had to be respected. Which was C'mell?

She smiled, and her smile was better suited for my eyes than for Virginia's. It spoke a whole world of voluptuous knowledge. I knew she wasn't trying to do anything to me; the rest of her manner showed that. Perhaps it was the only smile she knew.

"Don't worry," she said, "about the formalities. You'd better take these steps here. I hear him coming back."

I spun around, looking for the drunken bull-man. He was not to be seen.

"Go up here," urged C'mell, "They are emergency steps and you will be back on the surface. I can keep him from following. Was that French you were speaking?"

"Yes," said I. "How did you—?"

"Get along," she said. "Sorry I asked. Hurry!"

I entered the small door. A spiral staircase went to the surface. It was below our dignity as true people to use steps, but with C'mell urging me, there was nothing else I could do. I nodded goodbye to C'mell and drew Virginia after me up the stairs.

At the surface we stopped.

Virginia gasped, "Wasn't it horrible?"

"We're safe now," said I.

"It's not safety," she said. "It's the dirtiness of it. Imagine having to talk to her!"

Virginia meant that C'mell was worse than the drunken bull-man. She sensed my reserve because she said,

"The sad thing is, you'll see her again . . . "

"What! How do you know that?"

"I don't know it," said Virginia. "I guess it. But I guess good, very good. After all, I went to the Abba-dingo."

"I asked you, darling, to tell me what happened there."

She shook her head mutely and began walking down the streetway. I had no choice but to follow her. It made me a little irritable.

I asked again, more crossly, "What was it like?"

With hurt girlish dignity she said, "Nothing, nothing. It was a long climb. The old woman made me go with her. It turned out that the machine was not talking that day, anyhow, so we got permission to drop down a shaft and to come back on the rolling road. It was just a wasted day."

She had been talking straight ahead, not to me, as though the memory were a little ugly.

Then she turned her face to me. The brown eyes looked into my eyes as though she were searching for my soul. (Soul. There's a word we have in French, and there is nothing quite like it in the Old Common Tongue.) She brightened and pleaded with me:

"Let's not be dull on the new day. Let's be good to the new us, Paul. Let's do something really French, if that's what we are to be."

"A café," I cried. "We need a café. And I know where one is."

"Where?"

"Two undergrounds over. Where the machines come out and where they permit the homunculi to peer in the window." The thought of homunculi peering at us struck the new-me as amusing, though the old-me had taken them as much for granted as windows or tables. The old-me never met any, but knew that they weren't exactly people, since they were bred from animals, but they looked just about like people, and they could talk. It took a Frenchman like the new-me to realize that they could be ugly, or beautiful, or picturesque. More than picturesque: romantic.

Evidently Virginia now thought the same, for she said, "But they're *nette,* just adorable. What is the café called?"

"The Greasy Cat," said I.

The Greasy Cat. How was I to know that this led to a nightmare between high waters, and to the winds which cried? How was I to suppose that this had anything to do with Alpha Ralpha Boulevard?

No force in the world could have taken me there, if I had known.

Other new-French people had gotten to the café before us.

A waiter with a big brown moustache took our order. I looked closely at him to see if he might be a licensed homunculus, allowed to work among people because his services were indispensable; but he was not. He was pure machine, though his voice rang out with old-Parisian heartiness, and the designers had even built into him the nervous habit of mopping the back of his hand against his big moustache, and had fixed him so that little beads of sweat showed high up on his brow, just below the hairline.

"Mamselle? M'sieu? Beer? Coffee? Red wine next month. The sun will shine in the quarter after the hour and after the half-hour. At twenty minutes to the hour it will rain for five minutes so that you can enjoy these umbrellas. I am a native of Alsace. You may speak French or German to me."

"Anything," said Virginia. "You decide, Paul."

"Beer, please," said I. "Blonde beer for both of us."

"But certainly, m'sieu," said the waiter.

He left, waving his cloth wildly over his arm.

Virginia puckered up her eyes against the sun and said, "I wish it would rain now. I've never seen real rain."

"Be patient, honey."

She turned earnestly to me. "What is 'German,' Paul?"

"Another language, another culture. I read they will bring it to life next year. But don't you like being French?"

"I like it fine," she said. "Much better than being a number. But Paul—" And then she stopped, her eyes blurred with perplexity.

"Yes, darling?"

"Paul," she said, and the statement of my name was a cry of hope from some depth of her mind beyond new-me, beyond old-me, beyond even the contrivances of the Lords who moulded us. I reached for her hand.

Said I, "You can tell me, darling."

"Paul," she said, and it was almost weeping, "Paul, why does it all happen so fast? This is our first day, and we both feel that we may spend the rest of our lives together. There's something about marriage, whatever that is, and we're supposed to find a priest, and I don't understand that, either. Paul, Paul, Paul, why does it happen so fast? I want to love you. I do love you. But I don't want to be *made* to love you. I want it to be the real me," and as she spoke, tears poured from her eyes though her voice remained steady enough.

Then it was that I said the wrong thing.

"You don't have to worry, honey. I'm sure that the Lords of the Instrumentality have programmed everything well."

At that, she burst into tears, loudly and uncontrollably. I had never seen an adult weep before. It was strange and frightening.

A man from the next table came over and stood beside me, but I did not so much as glance at him.

"Darling," said I, reasonably, "darling, we can work it out—"

"Paul, let me leave you, so that I may be yours. Let me go away for a few days or a few weeks or a few years. Then, if—if—if I *do* come back, you'll know it's me and not some program ordered by a machine. For God's sake, Paul—for God's sake!" In a different voice she said, "What is God, Paul? They gave us the words to speak, but I do not know what they mean."

The man beside me spoke. "I can take you to God," he said.

"Who are you?" said I. "And who asked you to interfere?" This was not the kind of language that we had ever used when speaking the Old Common Tongue—when they had given us a new language they had built in temperament as well.

The stranger kept his politeness—he was as French as we but he kept his temper well.

"My name," he said, "is Maximilien Macht, and I used to be a Believer."

Virginia's eyes lit up. She wiped her face absent-mindedly while staring at the man. He was tall, lean, sunburned. (How could he have gotten sunburned so soon?) He had reddish hair and a moustache almost like that of the robot waiter.

"You asked about God, Mamselle," said the stranger. "God is where he has always been—around us, near us, in us."

This was strange talk from a man who looked worldly. I rose to my feet to bid him goodbye. Virginia guessed what I was doing and she said:

"That's nice of you, Paul. Give him a chair."

There was warmth in her voice.

The machine waiter came back with two conical beakers made of glass. They had a golden fluid in them with a cap of foam on top. I had never seen or heard of beer before, but I knew exactly how it would taste. I put imaginary money on the tray, received imaginary change, paid the waiter an imaginary tip. The Instrumentality had not yet figured out how to have separate kinds of money for all the new cultures, and of course you could not use real money to pay for food or drink. Food and drink are free.

The machine wiped his moustache, used his serviette (checked red and white) to dab the sweat off his brow, and then looked inquiringly at Monsieur Macht.

"M'sieu, you will sit here?"

"Indeed," said Macht.

"Shall I serve you here?"

"But why not?" said Macht. "If these good people permit."

"Very well," said the machine, wiping his moustache with the back of his hand. He fled to the dark recesses of the bar.

All this time Virginia had not taken her eyes off Macht.

"You are a Believer?" she asked. "You are still a Believer, when you have been made French like us? How do you know you're you? Why do I love Paul? Are the Lords and their machines controlling everything in us? I want to be *me.* Do you know how to be *me?*"

"Not you, Mamselle," said Macht, "that would be too great an honor. But I am learning how to be myself. You see," he added, turning to me, "I have been French for two weeks now, and I know how much of me is myself, and how much has been added by this new process of giving us language and danger again."

The waiter came back with a small beaker. It stood on a stem, so that it looked like an evil little miniature of Earthport. The fluid it contained was milky white.

Macht lifted his glass to us. "Your health!"

Virginia stared at him as if she were going to cry again. When he and I sipped, she blew her nose and put her handkerchief away. It was the first time I had ever seen a person perform that act of blowing the nose, but it seemed to go well with our new culture.

Macht smiled at both of us, as if he were going to begin a speech. The sun came out, right on time. It gave him a halo, and made him look like a devil or a saint.

But it was Virginia who spoke first.

"You have been there?"

Macht raised his eyebrows a little, frowned, and said, "Yes," very quietly.

"Did you get a word?" she persisted.

"Yes." He looked glum, and a little troubled.

"What did it say?"

For answer, he shook his head at her, as if there were things which should never be mentioned in public.

I wanted to break in, to find out what this was all about.

Virginia went on, heeding me not at all: "But it did say something!"

"Yes," said Macht.

"Was it important?"

"Mamselle, let us not talk about it."

"We must," she cried. "It's life or death." Her hands were clenched so tightly together that her knuckles showed white. Her beer stood in front of her, untouched, growing warm in the sunlight.

"Very well," said Macht, "you may ask . . . I cannot guarantee to answer."

I controlled myself no longer. "What's all this about?"

Virginia looked at me with scorn, but even her scorn was the scorn of a lover, not the cold remoteness of the past. "Please, Paul, you wouldn't know. Wait a while. What did it say to you, M'sieu Macht?"

"That I, Maximilien Macht, would live or die with a brown-haired girl who was already betrothed." He smiled wrily, "And I do not even quite know what 'betrothed' means."

"We'll find out," said Virginia. "When did it say this?"

"Who is 'it'?" I shouted at them. "For God's sake, what is this all about?"

Macht looked at me and dropped his voice when he spoke: "The Abba-dingo." To her he said, "Last week."

Virginia turned white. "So it does work, it does, it does. Paul darling, it said nothing to me. But it said to my aunt something which I can't ever forget!"

I held her arm firmly and tenderly and tried to look into her eyes, but she looked away. Said I, "What did it say?"

"Paul and Virginia."

"So what?" said I.

I scarcely knew her. Her lips were tense and compressed. She was not angry. It was something different, worse. She was in the grip of tension. I suppose we had not seen that for thousands of years, either. "Paul, seize this simple fact, if you can grasp it. The machine gave that woman our names—but it gave them to her twelve years ago."

Macht stood up so suddenly that his chair fell over, and the waiter began running toward us.

"That settles it," he said. "We're all going back."

"Going where?" I said.

"To the Abba-dingo."

"But why now?" said I; and, "Will it work?" said Virginia, both at the same time.

"It always works," said Macht, "if you go on the northern side."

"How do you get there?" said Virginia.

Macht frowned sadly, "There's only one way. By Alpha Ralpha Boulevard." Virginia stood up. And so did I.

Then, as I rose, I remembered. Alpha Ralpha Boulevard. It was a ruined street hanging in the sky, faint as a vapor trail. It had been a processional highway once, where conquerors came down and tribute went up. But it was ruined, lost in the clouds, closed to mankind for a hundred centuries.

"I know it," said I. "It's ruined."

Macht said nothing, but he stared at me as if I were an outsider . . .

Virginia, very quiet and white of countenance, said, "Come along."

"But why?" said I. "Why?"

"You fool," she said, "if we don't have a God, at least we have a machine. This is the only thing left on or off the world which the Instrumentality doesn't understand. Maybe it tells the future. Maybe it's an un-machine. It certainly comes from a different time. Can't you use it, darling? If it says we're us, we're *us.*"

"And if it doesn't?"

"Then we're not." Her face was sullen with grief.

"What do you mean?"

"If we're not us," she said, "we're just toys, dolls, puppets that the Lords have written on. You're not you and I'm not me. But if the Abba-dingo, which knew the names Paul and Virginia twelve years before it happened—if the Abba-dingo says that we are us, I don't care if it's a predicting machine or a god or a devil or a what. I don't care, but I'll have the truth."

What could I have answered to that? Macht led, she followed, and I walked third in single file. We left the sunlight of The Greasy Cat; just as we left, a light rain began to fall. The waiter, looking momentarily like the machine that he was, stared straight ahead. We crossed the lip of the underground and went down to the fast expressway.

When we came out, we were in a region of fine homes. All were in ruins. The trees had thrust their way into the buildings. Flowers rioted across the lawn, through the open doors, and blazed in the roofless rooms. Who needed a house in the open, when the population of Earth had dropped so that the cities were commodious and empty?

Once I thought I saw a family of homunculi, including little ones, peering at me as we trudged along the soft gravel road. Maybe the faces I had seen at the edge of the house were fantasies.

Macht said nothing.

Virginia and I held hands as we walked beside him. I could have been happy at this odd excursion, but her hand was tightly clenched in mine. She bit her lower lip from time to time. I knew it mattered to her—she was on a pilgrimage. (A pilgrimage was an ancient walk to some powerful place, very good for body and soul.) I didn't mind going along. In fact, they could not have kept me from coming, once she and Macht decided to leave the café. But I didn't have to take it seriously. Did I?

What did Macht want?

Who was Macht? What thoughts had that mind learned in two short weeks? How had he preceded us into a new world of danger and adventure? I did not trust him. For the first time in my life I felt alone. Always, always, up to now, I had only to think about the Instrumentality and some protector leaped fully-armed into my mind. Telepathy guarded against all dangers, healed all hurts, carried each of us forward to the one-hundred-and-forty-six-thousand-and-ninety-seven days which had been allotted us. Now it was different. I did not know this man, and it was on him that I relied, not on the powers which had shielded and protected us.

We turned from the ruined road into an immense boulevard. The pavement was so smooth and unbroken that nothing grew on it, save where the wind and dust had deposited random little pockets of earth.

Macht stopped.

"This is it," he said. "Alpha Ralpha Boulevard."

We fell silent and looked at the causeway of forgotten empires.

To our left the boulevard disappeared in a gentle curve. It led far north of the city in which I had been reared. I knew that there was another city to the north, but I had forgotten its name. Why should I have remembered it? It was sure to be just like my own.

But to the right—

To the right the boulevard rose sharply, like a ramp. It disappeared into the clouds. Just at the edge of the cloudline there was a hint of disaster. I could not see for sure, but it looked to me as though the whole boulevard had been sheared off by unimaginable forces. Somewhere beyond the clouds there stood the Abba-dingo, the place where all questions were answered . . .

Or so they thought.

Virginia cuddled close to me.

"Let's turn back," said I. "We are city people. We don't know anything about ruins."

"You can if you want to," said Macht. "I was just trying to do you a favor."

We both looked at Virginia.

She looked up at me with those brown eyes. From the eyes there came a plea older than woman or man, older than the human race. I knew what she was going to say before she said it. She was going to say that she *had* to know.

Macht was idly crushing some soft rocks near his foot.

At last Virginia spoke up: "Paul, I don't want danger for its own sake. But I meant what I said back there. Isn't there a chance that we were *told* to love each other? What sort of a life would it be if our happiness, our own selves, depended on a thread in a machine or on a mechanical voice which spoke to us when we were asleep and learning French? It may be fun to go back to the old world. I guess it is. I know that you give me a kind of happiness which I never even suspected before this day. If it's really us, we have something wonderful, and we ought to know it. But if it isn't—" She burst into sobs.

I wanted to say, "If it isn't, it will seem just the same," but the ominous sulky face of Macht looked at me over Virginia's shoulder as I drew her to me. There was nothing to say.

I held her close.

From beneath Macht's foot there flowed a trickle of blood. The dust drank it up.

"Macht," said I, "are you hurt?"

Virginia turned around, too.

Macht raised his eyebrows at me and said with unconcern, "No. Why?"

"The blood. At your feet."

He glanced down. "Oh, those," he said, "they're nothing. Just the eggs of some kind of an un-bird which does not even fly."

"Stop it!" I shouted telepathically, using the Old Common Tongue. I did not even try to think in our new-learned French.

He stepped back a pace in surprise.

Out of nothing there came to me a message: *thankyou thankyou goodgreat gohomeplease thankyou goodgreat goaway manbad manbad manbad* . . . Somewhere an animal or bird was warning me against Macht. I thought a casual *thanks* to it and turned my attention to Macht.

He and I stared at each other. Was this what *culture* was? Were we now men? Did freedom always include the freedom to mistrust, to fear, to hate?

I liked him not at all. The words of forgotten crimes came into my mind: *assassination, murder, abduction, insanity, rape, robbery* . . .

We had known none of these things and yet I felt them all.

He spoke evenly to me. We had both been careful to guard our minds against being read telepathically, so that our only means of communication were empathy and French. "It's your idea," he said, most untruthfully, "or at least your lady's . . . "

"Has lying already come into the world," said I, "so that we walk into the clouds for no reason at all?"

"There is a reason," said Macht.

I pushed Virginia gently aside and capped my mind so tightly that the anti-telepathy felt like a headache.

"Macht," said I, and I myself could hear the snarl of an animal in my own voice, "tell me why you have brought us here or I will kill you."

He did not retreat. He faced me, ready for a fight. He said, "Kill? You mean, to make me dead?" but his words did not carry conviction. Neither one of us knew how to fight, but he readied for defense and I for attack.

Underneath my thought shield an animal thought crept in: *goodman goodman take him by the neck no-air he-aaah no-air he-aaah like broken egg* . . .

I took the advice without worrying where it came from. It was simple. I walked over to Macht, reached my hands around his throat and squeezed. He tried to push my hands away. Then he tried to kick me. All I did was hang on to his throat. If I had been a Lord or a Go-Captain, I might have known about fighting. But I did not, and neither did he.

It ended when a sudden weight dragged at my hands.

Out of surprise, I let go.

Macht had become unconscious. Was that *dead?*

It could not have been, because he sat up. Virginia ran to him. He rubbed his throat and said with a rough voice:

"You should not have done that."

This gave me courage. "Tell me," I spat at him, "tell me why you wanted us to come, or I will do it again."

Macht grinned weakly. He leaned his head against Virginia's arm. "It's fear," he said. "Fear."

"Fear?" I knew the word—*peur*—but not the meaning. Was it some kind of disquiet or animal alarm?

I had been thinking with my mind open; he thought back *yes.*

"But why do you like it?" I asked.

It is delicious, he thought. *It makes me sick and thrilly and alive. It is like strong medicine, almost as good as stroon. I went there before. High up, I had much fear. It was wonderful and bad and good, all at the same time. I lived a thousand years in a single hour. I wanted more of it, but I thought it would be even more exciting with other people.*

"Now I will kill you," said I in French. "You are very—very . . ." I had to look for the word. "You are very evil."

"No," said Virginia, "let him talk."

He thought at me, not bothering with words. *This is what the Lords of the Instrumentality never let us have. Fear. Reality. We were born in a stupor and we died in a dream. Even the underpeople, the animals, had more life than we did. The machines did not have fear. That's what we were. Machines who thought they were men. And now we are free.*

He saw the edge of raw, red anger in my mind, and he changed the subject. *I did not lie to you. This is the way to the Abba-dingo. I have been there. It works. On this side, it always works.*

"It works," cried Virginia. "You see he says so. It works! He is telling the truth. Oh, Paul, do let's go on!"

"All right," said I, "we'll go."

I helped him rise. He looked embarrassed, like a man who has shown something of which he is ashamed.

We walked onto the surface of the indestructible boulevard. It was comfortable to the feet.

At the bottom of my mind the little unseen bird or animal babbled its thoughts at me: *goodman goodman make him dead take water take water . . .*

I paid no attention as I walked forward with her and him, Virginia between us. I paid no attention.

I wish I had.

We walked for a long time.

The process was new to us. There was something exhilarating in knowing that no one guarded us, that the air was free air, moving without benefit of weather machines. We saw many birds, and when I thought at them I found their minds startled and opaque; they were natural birds, the like of which I had never seen before. Virginia asked me their names, and I outrageously applied all the bird-names which we had learned in French without knowing whether they were historically right or not.

Maximilien Macht cheered up, too, and he even sang us a song, rather off key, to the effect that we would take the high road and he the low one, but that he would be in Scotland before us. It did not make sense, but the lilt was pleasant. Whenever he got a certain distance ahead of Virginia and me, I made up variations on "Macouba" and sang-whispered the phrases into her pretty ear:

"She wasn't the woman I went to seek.
I met her by the merest chance.
She did not speak the French of France,
But the surded French of Martinique."

We were happy in adventure and freedom, until we became hungry. Then our troubles began.

Virginia stepped up to a lamp-post, struck it lightly with her fist and said, "Feed me." The post should either have opened, serving us a dinner, or else told us where, within the next few hundred yards, food was to be had. It did neither. It did nothing. It must have been broken.

With that, we began to make a game of hitting every single post.

Alpha Ralpha Boulevard had risen about half a kilometer above the surrounding countryside. The wild birds wheeled below us. There was less dust on the pavement, and fewer patches of weeds. The immense road, with no pylons below it, curved like an unsupported ribbon into the clouds.

We wearied of beating posts and there was neither food nor water.

Virginia became fretful: "It won't do any good to go back now. Food is even farther the other way. I do wish you'd brought something."

How should I have thought to carry food? Who ever carries food? Why would they carry it, when it is everywhere? My darling was unreasonable, but she was my darling and I loved her all the more for the sweet imperfections of her temper.

Macht kept tapping pillars, partly to keep out of our fight, and obtained an unexpected result.

At one moment I saw him leaning over to give the pillar of a large lamp the usual hearty but guarded *whop*—in the next instant he yelped like a dog and was sliding uphill at a high rate of speed. I heard him shout something, but could not make out the words, before he disappeared into the clouds ahead.

Virginia looked at me. "Do you want to go back now? Macht is gone. We can say that I got tired."

"Are you serious?"

"Of course, darling."

I laughed, a little angrily. She had insisted that we come, and now she was ready to turn around and give it up, just to please me.

"Never mind," said I. "It can't be far now. Let's go on."

"Paul . . . " She stood close to me. Her brown eyes were troubled, as though she were trying to see all the way into my mind through my eyes. I thought to her, *Do you want to talk this way?*

"No," said she, in French. "I want to say things one at a time. Paul, I do want to go to the Abba-dingo. I need to go. It's the biggest need in my life. But at the same time, I don't want to go. There is something wrong up there. I would rather have you on the wrong terms than not have you at all. Something could happen."

Edgily, I demanded, "Are you getting this 'fear' that Macht was talking about?"

"Oh, no, Paul, not at all. This feeling isn't exciting. It feels like something broken in a machine—"

"Listen!" I interrupted her.

From far ahead, from within the clouds, there came a sound like an animal wailing. There were words in it. It must have been Macht. I thought I heard "take care." When I sought him with my mind, the distance made circles and I got dizzy.

"Let's follow, darling," said I.

"Yes, Paul," said she, and in her voice there was an unfathomable mixture of happiness, resignation, and despair . . .

Before we moved on, I looked carefully at her. She *was* my girl. The sky had turned yellow and the lights were not yet on. In the yellow rich sky her brown curls were tinted with gold, her brown eyes approached the black in their irises, her young and fate-haunted face seemed more meaningful than any other human face I had ever seen.

"You *are* mine," I said.

"Yes, Paul," she answered me and then smiled brightly. "*You* said it! That is doubly nice."

A bird on the railing looked sharply at us and then left. Perhaps he did not approve of human nonsense, so flung himself downward into dark air. I saw him catch himself, far below, and ride lazily on his wings.

"We're not as free as birds, darling," I told Virginia, "but we are freer than people have been for a hundred centuries."

For answer she hugged my arm and smiled at me.

"And now," I added, "to follow Macht. Put your arms around me and hold me tight. I'll try hitting that post. If we don't get dinner we may get a ride."

I felt her take hold tightly and then I struck the post.

Which post? An instant later the posts were sailing by us in a blur. The ground beneath our feet seemed steady, but we were moving at a fast rate. Even in the service underground I had never seen a roadway as fast as this. Virginia's dress was blowing so hard that it made snapping sounds like the snap of fingers. In no time at all we were in the cloud and out of it again.

A new world surrounded us. The clouds lay below and above. Here and there blue sky shone through. We were steady. The ancient engineers must have devised the walkway cleverly. We rode up, up, up without getting dizzy.

Another cloud.

Then things happened so fast that the telling of them takes longer than the event.

Something dark rushed at me from up ahead. A violent blow hit me in the chest. Only much later did I realize that this was Macht's arm trying to grab me before we went over the edge. Then we went into another cloud. Before I could even speak to Virginia a second blow struck me. The pain was terrible. I had never felt anything like that in all my life. For some reason, Virginia had fallen over me and beyond me. She was pulling at my hands.

I tried to tell her to stop pulling me, because it hurt, but I had no breath. Rather than argue, I tried to do what she wanted. I struggled toward her. Only then did I realize that there was nothing below my feet—no bridge, no jetway, nothing.

I was on the edge of the boulevard, the broken edge of the upper side. There was nothing below me except for some looped cables, and, far underneath them, a tiny ribbon which was either a river or a road.

We had jumped blindly across the great gap and I had fallen just far enough to catch the upper edge of the roadway on my chest.

It did not matter, the pain.

In a moment the doctor-robot would be there to repair me.

A look at Virginia's face reminded me there was no doctor-robot, no world, no Instrumentality, nothing but wind and pain. She was crying. It took a moment for me to hear what she was saying,

"I did it, I did it, darling, are you dead?"

Neither one of us was sure what "dead" meant, because people always went away at their appointed time, but we knew that it meant a cessation of life. I tried to tell her that I was living, but she fluttered over me and kept dragging me farther from the edge of the drop.

I used my hands to push myself into a sitting position.

She knelt beside me and covered my face with kisses.

At last I was able to gasp, "Where's Macht?"

She looked back. "I don't see him."

I tried to look too. Rather than have me struggle, she said, "You stay quiet. I'll look again."

Bravely she walked to the edge of the sheared-off boulevard. She looked over toward the lower side of the gap, peering through the clouds which drifted past us as rapidly as smoke sucked by a ventilator. Then she cried out:

"I see him. He looks so funny. Like an insect in the museum. He is crawling across on the cables."

Struggling to my hands and knees, I neared her and looked too. There he was, a dot moving along a thread, with the birds soaring by beneath him. It looked very unsafe. Perhaps he was getting all the "fear" that he needed to keep himself happy. I did not want that "fear," whatever it was. I wanted food, water, and a doctor-robot.

None of these were here.

I struggled to my feet. Virginia tried to help me but I was standing before she could do more than touch my sleeve.

"Let's go on."

"On?" she said.

"On to the Abba-dingo. There may be friendly machines up there. Here there is nothing but cold and wind, and the lights have not yet gone on."

She frowned. "But Macht . . . ?"

"It will be hours before he gets here. We can come back."

She obeyed.

Once again we went to the left of the boulevard. I told her to squeeze my waist while I struck the pillars, one by one. Surely there must have been a reactivating device for the passengers on the road.

The fourth time, it worked.

Once again the wind whipped our clothing as we raced upward on Alpha Ralpha Boulevard.

We almost fell as the road veered to the left. I caught my balance, only to have it veer the other way.

And then we stopped.

This was the Abba-dingo.

A walkway littered with white objects—knobs and rods and imperfectly formed balls about the size of my head.

Virginia stood beside me, silent.

About the size of my head? I kicked one of the objects aside and then knew, knew for sure, what it was. It was people. The inside parts. I had never seen such things before. And that, that on the ground, must once have been a hand. There were hundreds of such things along the wall.

"Come, Virginia," said I, keeping my voice even, and my thoughts hidden.

She followed without saying a word. She was curious about the things on the ground, but she did not seem to recognize them.

For my part, I was watching the wall.

At last I found them—the little doors of Abba-dingo.

One said METEOROLOGICAL. It was not Old Common Tongue, nor was it French, but it was so close that I knew it had something to do with the behavior of air. I put my hand against the panel of the door. The panel became translucent and ancient writing showed through. There were numbers which meant nothing, words which meant nothing, and then:

Typhoon coming.

My French had not taught me what a "coming" was, but "typhoon" was plainly *typhon,* a major air disturbance. Thought I, *let the weather machines take care of the matter.* It had nothing to do with us.

"That's no help," said I.

"What does it mean?" she said.

"The air will be disturbed."

"Oh," said she. "That couldn't matter to us, could it?"

"Of course not."

I tried the next panel, which said FOOD. When my hand touched the little door, there was an aching creak inside the wall, as though the whole tower retched. The door opened a little bit and a horrible odor came out of it. Then the door closed again.

The third door said HELP and when I touched it nothing happened. Perhaps it was some kind of tax-collecting device from the ancient days. It yielded nothing to my touch. The fourth door was larger and already partly open at the bottom. At the top, the name of the door was PREDICTIONS. Plain enough, that one was, to anyone who knew Old French. The name at the bottom was more mysterious: PUT PAPER HERE it said, and I could not guess what it meant.

I tried telepathy. Nothing happened. The wind whistled past us. Some of the calcium balls and knobs rolled on the pavement. I tried again, trying my utmost for the imprint of long-departed thoughts. A scream entered my mind, a thin long scream which did not sound much like people. That was all.

Perhaps it did upset me. I did not feel "fear," but I was worried about Virginia.

She was staring at the ground.

"Paul," she said, "isn't that a man's coat on the ground among those funny things?"

Once I had seen an ancient X-ray in the museum, so I knew that the coat still surrounded the material which had provided the inner structure of the man. There was no ball there, so that I was quite sure he was *dead*. How could that have happened in the old days? Why did the Instrumentality let it happen? But then, the Instrumentality had always forbidden this side of the tower. Perhaps the violators had met their own punishment in some way I could not fathom.

"Look, Paul," said Virginia. "I can put my hand in."

Before I could stop her, she had thrust her hand into the flat open slot which said PUT PAPER HERE.

She screamed.

Her hand was caught.

I tried to pull at her arm, but it did not move. She began gasping with pain. Suddenly her hand came free.

Clear words were cut into the living skin. I tore my cloak off and wrapped her hand.

As she sobbed beside me I unbandaged her hand. As I did so she saw the words on her skin.

The words said, in clear French: *You will love Paul all your life.*

Virginia let me bandage her hand with my cloak and then she lifted her face to be kissed. "It was worth it," she said; "it was worth all the trouble, Paul. Let's see if we can get down. Now I know."

I kissed her again and said, reassuringly, "You do know, don't you?"

"Of course," she smiled through her tears. "The Instrumentality could not have contrived this. What a clever old machine! Is it a god or a devil, Paul?"

I had not studied those words at that time, so I patted her instead of answering. We turned to leave.

At the last minute I realized that I had not tried PREDICTIONS myself.

"Just a moment, darling. Let me tear a little piece off the bandage."

She waited patiently. I tore a piece the size of my hand, and then I picked up one of the ex-person units on the ground. It may have been the front of an arm. I returned to push the cloth into the slot, but when I turned to the door, an enormous bird was sitting there.

I used my hand to push the bird aside, and he cawed at me. He even seemed to threaten me with his cries and his sharp beak. I could not dislodge him.

Then I tried telepathy. *I am a true man. Go away!*

The bird's dim mind flashed back at me nothing but *no-no-no-no-no!*

With that I struck him so hard with my fist that he fluttered to the ground. He righted himself amid the white litter on the pavement and then, opening his wings, he let the wind carry him away.

I pushed in the scrap of cloth, counted to twenty in my mind, and pulled the scrap out.

The words were plain, but they meant nothing: *You will love Virginia twenty-one more minutes.*

Her happy voice, reassured by the prediction but still unsteady from the pain in her written-on hand, came to me as though it were far away. "What does it say, darling?"

Accidentally on purpose, I let the wind take the scrap. It fluttered away like a bird. Virginia saw it go.

"Oh," she cried disappointedly. "We've lost it! What did it say?"

"Just what yours did."

"But what words, Paul? How did it say it?"

With love and heartbreak and perhaps a little "fear," I lied to her and whispered gently,

"It said, 'Paul will always love Virginia.' "

She smiled at me radiantly. Her stocky, full figure stood firmly and happily against the wind. Once again she was the chubby, pretty Menerima whom I had noticed in our block when we both were children. And she was more than that. She was my new-found love in our new-found world. She was my mademoiselle from Martinique. The message was foolish. We had seen from the food-slot that the machine was broken.

"There's no food or water here," said I. Actually, there was a puddle of water near the railing, but it had been blown over the human structural elements on the ground, and I had no heart to drink it.

Virginia was so happy that, despite her wounded hand, her lack-of-water and her lack-of-food, she walked vigorously and cheerfully.

Thought I to myself, *Twenty-one minutes. About six hours have passed. If we stay here we face unknown dangers.*

Vigorously we walked downward, down Alpha Ralpha Boulevard. We had met the Abba-dingo and were still "alive." I did not think that I was "dead," but the words had been meaningless so long that it was hard to think them.

The ramp was so steep going down that we pranced like horses. The wind blew into our faces with incredible force. That's what it was, wind, but I looked up the word *vent* only after it was all over.

We never did see the whole tower—just the wall at which the ancient jetway had deposited us. The rest of the tower was hidden by clouds which fluttered like torn rags as they raced past the heavy material.

The sky was red on one side and a dirty yellow on the other.

Big drops of water began to strike at us.

"The weather machines are broken," I shouted to Virginia.

She tried to shout back to me but the wind carried her words away. I repeated what I had said about the weather machines. She nodded happily and warmly, though the wind was by now whipping her hair past her face and the pieces of water which fell from up above were spotting her flame-golden gown. It did not matter. She clung to my arm. Her happy face smiled at me as we stamped downward, bracing ourselves against the decline in the ramp. Her brown eyes were full of confidence and life. She saw me looking at her and she kissed me on the upper arm without losing step. She was my own girl forever, and she knew it.

The water-from-above, which I later knew was actual "rain," came in increasing volume. Suddenly it included birds. A large bird flapped his way vigorously against the whistling air and managed to stand still in front of my face, though his air speed was many leagues per hour. He cawed in my face and then was carried away by the wind. No sooner had that one gone than another bird struck me in the body. I looked down at it but it too was carried away by the racing current of air. All I got was a telepathic echo from its bright blank mind: *no-no-no-no!*

Now what? thought I. A bird's advice is not much to go upon.

Virginia grabbed my arm and stopped.

I too stopped.

The broken edge of Alpha Ralpha Boulevard was just ahead. Ugly yellow clouds swam through the break like poisonous fish hastening on an inexplicable errand.

Virginia was shouting.

I could not hear her, so I leaned down. That way her mouth could almost touch my ear.

"Where is Macht?" she shouted.

Carefully I took her to the left side of the road, where the railing gave us some protection against the heavy racing air, and against the water commingled with it. By now neither of us could see very far. I made her drop to her knees. I got down beside her. The falling water pelted our backs. The light around us had turned to a dark dirty yellow.

We could still see, but we could not see much.

I was willing to sit in the shelter of the railing, but she nudged me. She wanted us to do something about Macht. What anyone could do, that was beyond me. If he had found shelter, he was safe, but if he was out on those cables, the wild pushing air would soon carry him off and then there would be no more Maximilien Macht. He would be "dead" and his interior parts would bleach somewhere on the open ground.

Virginia insisted.

We crept to the edge.

A bird swept in, true as a bullet, aiming for my face. I flinched. A wing touched me. It stung against my cheek like fire. I did not know that feathers were so tough. The birds must all have damaged mental mechanisms, though I, if they hit people on Alpha Ralpha. That is not the right way to behave toward true people.

At last we reached the edge, crawling on our bellies. I tried to dig the fingernails of my left hand into the stonelike material of the railing, but it was flat, and there was nothing much to hold to, save for the ornamental fluting. My right arm was around Virginia. It hurt me badly to crawl forward that way, because my body was still damaged from the blow against the edge of the road, on the way coming up. When I hesitated, Virginia thrust herself forward.

We saw nothing.

The gloom was around us.

The wind and the water beat at us like fists.

Her gown pulled at her like a dog worrying its master. I wanted to get her back into the shelter of the railing, where we could wait for the air-disturbance to end.

Abruptly, the light shone all around us. It was wild electricity, which the ancients called *lightning.* Later I found that it occurs quite frequently in the areas beyond the reach of the weather machines.

The bright quick light showed us a white face staring at us. He hung on the cables below us. His mouth was open, so he must have been shouting. I shall never know whether the expression on his face showed "fear" or great happiness. It was full of excitement. The bright light went out and I thought that I heard the echo of a call. I reached for his mind telepathically and there was nothing there. Just some dim, obstinate bird thinking at me, *no-no-no-no-no!*

Virginia tightened in my arms. She squirmed around. I shouted at her in French. She could not hear.

Then I called with my mind.

Someone else was there.

Virginia's mind blazed at me, full of revulsion, *The cat girl. She is going to touch me!*

She twisted. My right arm was suddenly empty. I saw the gleam of a golden gown flash over the edge, even in the dim light. I reached with my mind, and I caught her cry:

"Paul, Paul, I love you. Paul . . . help me!"

The thoughts faded as her body dropped.

The someone else was C'mell, whom we had first met in the corridor.

I came to get you both, she thought at me; *not that the birds cared about her.*

What have the birds got to do with it?

You saved them. You saved their young, when the red-topped man was killing them all. All of us have been worried about what you true people would do to us when you were free. We found out. Some of you are bad and kill other kinds of life. Others of you are good and protect life.

Thought I, is that all there is to *good* and *bad?*

Perhaps I should not have left myself off guard. People did not have to understand fighting, but the homunculi did. They were bred amidst battle and they served through troubles. C'mell, cat-girl that she was, caught me on the chin with a pistonlike fist. She had no anesthesia, and the only way—cat or no cat—that she could carry me across the cables in the "typhoon" was to have me unconscious and relaxed.

I awakened in my own room. I felt very well indeed. The robot-doctor was there. Said he:

"You've had a shock. I've already reached the Subcommissioner of the Instrumentality, and I can erase the memories of the last full day, if you want me to."

His expression was pleasant.

Where was the racing wind? The air falling like stone around us? The water driving where no weather machines controlled it? Where was the golden gown and the wild fear-hungry face of Maximilien Macht?

I thought these things, but the robot-doctor, not being telepathic, caught none of it. I stared hard at him.

"Where," I cried, "is my own true love?"

Robots cannot sneer, but this one attempted to do so. "The naked cat-girl with the blazing hair? She left to get some clothing."

I stared at him.

His fuddy-duddy little machine mind cooked up its own nasty little thoughts, "I must say, sir, you 'free people' change very fast indeed . . . "

Who argues with a machine? It wasn't worth answering him.

But that other machine? Twenty-one minutes. How could that work out? How could it have known? I did not want to argue with that other machine either. It must have been a very powerful left-over machine—perhaps something used in ancient wars. I had no intention of finding out. Some people might call it a god. I call it nothing. I do not need "fear" and I do not propose to go back to Alpha Ralpha Boulevard again.

But hear, oh heart of mine!—how can you ever visit the café again?

C'mell came in and the robot-doctor left.

(1961)

THEODORE STURGEON

Tandy's Story

This is Tandy's story. But first, take a recipe: the Canaveral sneeze; the crinkled getter; the Condition adrift; the analogy of the Sahara smash; Hawaii and the missing moon; and the analogy of the profit-sharing plan. There is no discontinuity here, nor is the chain more remarkable than any other. They are all remarkable.

If this were your story, it might compound from the recipe of a letter that never got mailed, a broken galosh clip, a wistful memory of violet eyes, the Malthusian theory and a cheese strudel. However, it is Tandy's.

We begin then with the Canaveral sneeze, delivered by a white-gowned, sterile-gloved man in a germ-free lab, as gently he lifted a gold-plated twenty-three-inch sphere into its ultimate package. Not having a third hand at the time, he was unable to cover his mouth in time. *Gesundheit.*

And now to Tandy's story.

Tandy's brother Robin was an only child for the first two years of his life and he would never get over it. Noël, her sister, was born when Tandy was crossing that high step into consciousness called Three Years Old. (Timothy, the other brother, wasn't until later. Anyway, this isn't his story. This is Tandy's story.)

When Tandy was five, then, it was clear to her that while the older Robin was bigger, stronger, more knowledgeable and smarter (he wasn't, but she hadn't been around long enough to learn that yet) and could push her around at will until she yelled for help—while, to put it another way, she was attacked from above—the sister below was excavating the ground under her feet. Noël unaccountably delighted everyone else, even Robin, for she was a blithe little bundle. But her advent necessarily drained off a good deal of parental attention from Tandy, who lost the household position of The Baby without gaining Robin's altitude as The Firstborn. It didn't seem fair. So she did what she could about it. She yelled for help.

It wasn't any ordinary yell, if an ordinary yell is a kind of punctuation or explosion or communicative change-of-pace. There were times when it wasn't, except for its purpose and figuratively, a yell at all. It was at times a whine—a highly specialized one, not very loud but strident, that could creep in and out of her voice twice in a sentence. Or it might be merely a way of asking for something, and asking and *asking,* so that she couldn't even hear a "yes" and was not aware of the point at which it furiously turned to a "no." Or perhaps an instantaneous approach to tears, complete with filling eyes and twisting mouth, where anyone else might use the mildest emphasis: "It *was* Tuesday I wore the blue dress, not Monday," and the equally instantaneous disappearance of the tears (which, somehow, was the annoying part). Or utter, total, complete, unmoving non-response to an order through the third, the fourth, the fifth repetition, and then a sudden shattering screech "I *heard* you!"

Tandy had, in short, a talent approaching genius for getting under one's skin and prickling.

This established, it is mere justice to all concerned to report also that Tandy was loved and lovable as well. Her parents took the matter of child-rearing seriously. The reasons (over and above innate talent) for Tandy's more irritating proclivities were quite known to them. And Tandy, long-lashed, supple, with hair the color of buckwheat honey and golden freckles spattered across her straight perfect nose, was an affectionate child, and her parents loved her and showed it very often.

And this did not alter one whit her position as No. Two Child, her distaste for the rôle, her yelling for help and therefore, for all the love, the concurrent war of abrasion.

There were times when she and Robin got along as contemporaries and splendidly. And of course almost anyone could get along with the biddable Noël. But these times were more wished-for than often. When they occurred, they were so welcome that one is reminded of the lady with the perennially battling children who called out into an unwonted silence one mid-morning: "What are you kids doing?" From under the porch a young voice replied, "Burning the wrappers off these razorblades with matches, Mommy." "That's nice," she replied, "Don't fight . . . "

At such times, in short, they could get away with practically anything, and Tandy's usual occupations were staged alone and away from people.

Yet never completely away.

Perhaps as a result of her crowded loneliness, she liked to be on the outside looking in or on the inside looking on, but not *of* the group. When the neighborhood gathered on the lawn for hide-and-seek or kickball, and the game was well started, Tandy would be seen forty paces off, squatting by the driveway, making a cake-sized cake of earth, perhaps, and decorating it with pebbles and twigs; or acting out some elaborate dialogue with her doll Luby (whether or not Luby was with her), bowing and mugging and murmuring the while in a number of voices. Tandy spoke beautifully. She had since the beginning, and her command of idiom and tone was too expert to be cute. There were times when it was downright embarrassing, as when the father overheard her demanding of a peonybush, with precisely his own emphasis, "*What the hell are you, hypnotized?*" There were times when these performances at the edge of the activity of others attracted considerable attention. She was surprisingly deft for a five-year-old, being one of these kids who from birth, apparently, can with a single movement draw a closed figure so that you are unable to see where the ends of the line join, and whose structures with blocks never seem jumbled, but quite functional (as indeed, to the fantasy of the moment, they are). Once in a while she drew quite a gallery of the curious with, say, six careful rows of red Japanese maple leaves and deep pink trumpetvine blossoms alternating on the lawn, before which she would posture severely, murmuring under her breath and pointing to one and another with a stick. At such times she seemed quite oblivious to six or eight children magnetically drawn round her, who watched mystified. Sometimes she would answer and sometimes she would not. Sometimes it would take drastic measures, as for example Robin's shuffling through the careful arrangement of leaves and petals, before it could be learned (the hard way, in this case) that she was teaching school, that the leaves were boys and the trumpets girls, and that she was now going to tell Mama to throw Robin's Erector set into the garbage, and a good deal more—precisely what more, no one knew, for by then the screech would have destroyed intelligibility.

The crinkled getter was placed near the base and inside the metal envelope of an RF amplifier tube in the telemetry circuit of the big rocket's second stage. The getter's function was to absorb the residual gases in the tube and harden the vacuum therein. Its crinkle was an impurity, but so slight as to cause no trouble until the twelfth hour of countdown. Then rarefied gas began to ionize and *foop!* discharge and ionize and *foop!* discharge again.

To replace the tube required that they go back to twenty-four hours and start the countdown again. The extra twelve hours delay enabled sneeze-mist to dry on the sphere, and certain bacilli to die, and others to encyst, and a smear of virus, sub-microscopically, to turn to a leathery, almost crystalline jelly.

Tandy lived in a house in the woods which in turn were in, or nearly in, the very middle of the upstate village, a pleasant accident derived from the land-grabbing, landholding traditions of three neighbors' fathers, and grandfathers, and great-grandfathers. The three acres on which Tandy's house stood were surrounded by perhaps twenty acres of other people's woods and a small swamp; yet the house was barely ten minutes on foot away from the village green.

Somewhere, then, in house or garden, lawn, swamp or wood, the brownie came to Tandy.

It had that stuffed-toy, left-out-in-the-rain aspect possible only to stuffed toys which have been left out in the rain. It was about nine inches high. Its clothing, or skin (properly, the outside layer was both), was variously khaki-colored and mottled green. The appellation "brownie" derived from what appeared to be a tapered hat, though once the father was heard to remark that it was the damn thing's head that was pointed. The arms and legs were taut and jointless, and looked like sausages on which lived lichens. For hands there were limp yellow-pink leaves of felt, and for feet, what might have been the model for a radical cartoonist's rendering of the knotted moneybags of Old Moneybags. As for a face—well, it was a face. That's all. Black disks for eyes, so faded you couldn't tell whether they were supposed to be open or closed, a ditto-mark for a nose and a streak below which may have been some clumsy whimsy—a smile up on the right scowling downward to the left—or a streak of dirt.

In the light of all that happened, one would think there would be a day of discovery, an hour of revelation, an open-the-package kind of Event. But there wasn't.

The brownie was kicking around the place for weeks, months maybe; they had all seen it, kicked it aside, used it as a peg for that parental sigh, "Got to clean out all this junk sometime . . . " Robin dug a grave for a dead cat once and then couldn't find the cat, so buried the brownie instead. Noël had taken it to bed with her once, and the mother had thrown it out the window during the night. It was one of those things, along with the bent but not quite broken doll carriage, the toy electric motor with the broken brush and Noël's wind-up giraffe, which needed new ears. So the brownie wove its indistinct thread into the tapestry of days, in and out of the margin between toys and trash.

The exact beginnings of Tandy's preoccupation with the brownie were also vague, and even when first her interest was total, it made little impression, because Tandy was . . . well, for example, the caterpillar. Once when she was four she caught a tent caterpillar and kept him in a coffee can for two days and named him Freddy and fed and watered him and even covered him at night with a doll blanket. During the second night she awoke crying, agonizing after Freddy, inconsolable until the can was found and brought and shown to her. Her grandmother, who was around at the time, said sagely, "*That* child needs a pet!" and everybody nodded and conversed about pets. The next morning Tandy put Freddy on the flagstones out front "so he could go for a walk." He went for a walk. Altogether.

For half a day people tiptoed around Tandy as if she were full of fulminate and had dined on dynamite.

But not only did she not ask about Freddy, she never even mentioned him. She stumbled over the can and almost fell and kicked it away and did not even glance at it. Thereafter Tandy's preoccupations were beyond judgment or prediction; they might be blood-sistership, like the affair with her doll Luby Cindy, or they might be passing passions like Freddy. The brownie . . . well, people became aware not that Tandy had a new one, but that for some indeterminate time she had been orbiting around this artifact. And when Tandy orbited, so did the cosmos or it—all of it—would be accountable to Tandy.

Mention of orbit brings up the Condition adrift. No other name for it will do, and even that is inaccurate. It was . . . well, matter; but matter in such a curlicue, so self-involved in stress, that Condition is a better word than Thing. It had been made where it was useful to its makers, and one might say it had a life of its own though it had not used it in some millions of megayears. By a concidence as unlikely as the existence of the reader of this history or a world to read it on, but as true, the Condition adrift found itself matching course and speed with the golden ball in space. It contacted, interpenetrated, an area of the golden surface four by eight microns, and happily found itself a part of organic material—a dried and frozen virus and two encysted bacteria. The latter it dissected and used. The former it activated, but in a wild reorganizing way so radical its mammy amino wouldn't have recognized it. The Condition became then a Thing (without losing its conditional character) and it scored itself across and divided. And divided again. And that was the end of that, for it had used up its store of a certain substance too technical to mention, but as necessary as number. Such was the nature of this organism that once alive it must grow, but if it could not grow it must cease dividing, and if it ceased dividing it must undergo an elaborate, eons-long cycle before it could come round to being again a mere Condition adrift. But unless it could begin that cycle it must die.

By means known to it, it flowed through the lattices of the sputtered gold, quartered the sphere, searched and probed, and at last stopped.

It turned its attention to the great globe underneath.

Some time or other—it was in the early spring, though Tandy herself could never remember just when—she got the brownie a house. Actually it was an old basketwork fishing creel she had found behind the garage, but the one thing one learned most quickly about Tandy was that things were what she said they were. Anything else was only your opinion, to which you were not entitled. And there was a certain justice in her attitude, for it did not take long for such an object to lose its creelship and become what she said it was.

She set it against the back wall of the garage, in the tangled ground between the wall and the old stone fence, under the shelter of the adjoining carport—for a wall-less shelter had been hung to the side of the garage to accommodate the second car they hoped for some day. It was a nice sort of outdoors-indoors place. She drove a row of stakes in front of the creel and on it placed a rectangle of discarded plywood—a miniature of the carport—but as time went on she added walls. First they were cardboard. The creel was the bedroom and the rest of it was the living room.

At Easter she saved her basket and it was a bed. She got the brownie up every morning and put him to bed every night, and on weekends he took his nap too.

She fed him.

She had a small table—not a cream cheese box, a table!—for him, and on the table were clamshell plates and an acorn cup, and a pill-bottle—strike that; a flower vase—which, from the time spring first started to show her colors, she kept supplied. But before that she was feeding him snow ice cream, sawdust cereal, mushroom steaks, and wooden bread. She talked to him constantly, sometimes severely. And in that unannounced way of hers, she spent all her free time with him.

No one noticed it especially, in March and almost through April, except perhaps to be grateful for the quiet. A minute spent with the brownie was a minute without Tandy's moaning, whining, sobbing, screeching or otherwise yelling for help. Of course, there had to be minutes spent away from the brownie. Most of them were at school.

School was kindergarten, of course, and it may have been that there was just too much of it for Tandy. Due to factors of distance and necessities of school buses, the kindergarten was not, as is usual for such establishments, a nine-to-noon affair, but instead lasted for the whole school day, ending at three. In spite of a long rest period after lunch, it was the opinion of many that this was asking too much of five-year-olds. It may have been the teacher's opinion as well. It was certainly Tandy's opinion. Her first report card was not resoundingly good, and her second one was somewhat worse. Neither was bad enough to cause concern, but the parents were jolted by the specific items on which she scored worst. Beside the item *Speak clearly and distinctly* the teacher had marked the symbols which meant "Hardly ever," and beside *Knows right from left* was the mark for "Seldom." The parents looked at one another in amazement, and then the father said, "That can't be right!" and the mother said, "That can't even be Tandy. She's given her the wrong report card!"

But she had not, as the mother found out by visiting the teacher at school one afternoon.

The mother, going in like a lion, came out numb with awe for the teacher's forbearance, and for the second time (Robin had done this to her once, on another matter) suffering that partly amused but nonetheless painful experience of learning how little one knows of one's own. Or as the bemused father put it, "It's a wise father who knows his own child." For, fully documented and with inescapable accuracy, the teacher had described a Tandy they never saw around the house—a Tandy recalcitrant, stubborn, inactive, disobedient and, most incredible of all, talking incessant baby talk. The teacher's ability to see below the surface, to know that the child wasn't *really* as bad as all that, helped the overall picture not at all, because it became manifest that Tandy did not know right from left on purpose; that she spoke baby-talk by choice; that she fell from grace in matters of handkerchiefs and handwashing not because she forgot, but because she remembered.

Above and beyond everything else was that the degree of this behavior was by no means excessive. She had never once been subjected to the routine punishment of being made to stand out in the hall. She could always stop just short of outright delinquency. She was the foot that drags, the pressure which is not quite toothache, the discomfort which is not yet heartburn.

The parents conferred unhappily with each other and then with Tandy, who answered every "*Why?*" with "I just—" and an infuriating shrug, rolling upward of the eyes, flinging the hands out and down to flap helplessly against the thighs. It was the mother's exact gesture, which of course is precisely why it was infuriating.

So the father, his anger at last arriving, drew a bead on Tandy with his long forefinger and declared, "This is a *rule.* No more brownie."

The analogy of the Sahara smash is the anecdote of one of the desert crashes of a B-17 in Africa. Unlike tragic others, this one had a happy ending, and this is why: the crew made no attempt to trek out of there in a body, but instead assigned one man to march out and get help. The significant thing is that he carried with him not only a compass, but almost their entire water supply. The rest of the crew rationed themselves down to three tablespoons a day and lay as still as possible buried in the sand under the broken fuselage. So it was that the organism on the golden satellite told one of itself to ooze patiently out to the tip of one of the whip antennae; then, by means known to it—for as related, it contained unheard-of stresses, neatly curled up and intertwined—it bent the whip double and released it, and out into the emptiness, in the opposite direction from orbital motion, was snapped this infinitesimal fleck of substance. It tracked along with the satellite for a long time, but separating always, until it was lost in the glittering emptiness. But with it it carried all but a fraction of the organic substance available to the whole. Three parts were left quiescent, waiting moveless to die or be saved. The fourth fell toward Earth, which took—as long as it took . . .

Now there is a school of control-by-giving (hits in the head or ice cream) and a school of taking away, and the father, when aroused, tended to the latter. In extreme cases a child can learn never to express preference or fondness for anything lest he qualify it for the disciplinary list. This was not that extreme. It would not be because of the mother, who despised this kind of thing and whose reactions were very fast. One glimpse of Tandy's stricken face at this "No more brownie!" dictum and she added, " . . . if you go on making people unhappy." And, ignoring the father's stifled cry of rage, she went on, "Now you run on out and talk it over with the brownie."

Tandy did as she was told, leaving her parents to instruct one another about child-rearing, and communed with the brownie: and perhaps this was the real beginning of it all.

For she had done a great deal for this brownie. Now, for the first time, she had made it clear that there were things that needed doing for her.

If things changed at school, it was naturally not immediately apparent at home. Things at home did not change. That is, the busy-ness with the brownie continued to use up the whining time, the screeching time, the opportunities for chance medley and battle royal with Noël and Robin.

One weekday morning the mother had hung out a lineful of clothes and, being face to face with the garage, was moved to go round and see how Tandy was coming along with Project Brownie. She hadn't seen it for some weeks. She recalled vaguely that the cardboard sides had been replaced, and she knew that the tiny flower-vase had borne violets, and baby's breath, and alyssum. And she recalled the time she had turned out her sewing basket and the kitchen gadget drawer and rearranged them, all in one morning, and had given the detritus to Tandy for her brownie. Time was when Tandy would have gathered up such a treasure-trove with a shrill shriek of joy, would have fought selfishly and jealously with the other children over the ownership of every ribbon-end, every old cork and worn-out baby-bottle nipple, only to leave bits and pieces exasperatingly all over the house and yard within the next couple of hours. But this time she had spread the whole clutter out on the living room table, darted her deft small hands in and out of the pile, and in a few seconds had selected the blunt end of a broken nutpick, the china handle of a Wedgwood pitcher, a small tangle of pale blue nylon-and-wool yarn, and a brass wing-nut. "He wants these," she said positively. "That's all?" the mother had asked, astonished. And Tandy had replied, precisely mimicking the father, "Now what would a brownie want with all that junk?" It wasn't so much the modesty of Tandy's wants that had surprised the mother. It was the absolute and unhesitating certainty with which she chose.

Thinking of this, the mother rounded the garage and saw the brownie's house.

The old creel was still the bedroom, but the rest of the structure had vastly altered. The cardboard walls had been replaced with wood—some ends of shiplap that used to lie under the sleeping porch—and since the mother had heard nothing of any carpentry by or for Tandy, she could see that the stony ground had been carefully and laboriously dug to various depths so that the little boards, buried upright, could present an even eaveline. On one side were two small square window-openings, glazed with cellophane; on the other was a longer opening like a picture-window. The roof, still the castoff piece of plywood, had been covered with a layer of earth, and smoothly, brilliantly, it was thatched with living star-moss.

The mother knelt to look inside. The floor of the house was covered with a blinding-white powder of some kind. She took a pinch of it and felt it and smelt it and even tasted it a little without recognizing it; she'd ask Tandy later. The table was covered with a cloth which had once been part of a dust-rag which had once been one of the mother's dresses; it was spotlessly clean—it seemed to have been ironed—and was so folded and placed that the torn edges were out of sight. On the table was the pill-bottle flower-vase, just half full of clean water, in which stood a single stem and blossom of bleeding-heart. The effect was simple, tasteful, sort of Japanese-y. And further inside was the creel bedroom, with an oval dresser (despite the neat cloth cover and skirt, she recognized the lines of an inverted sardine tin) over which was the mirror which had been in Tandy's birthday pocketbook, and before which was a handsome little round chair, made of a bit of cardboard glued to a large wooden thread-spool, also covered and skirted with a scrap of material matching the dresser. And in bed was the brownie.

The mother had to go down almost flat on her stomach to see what it was which covered his pillow so whitely, so clean and thick-textured. A luxury material indeed—dogwood petals. He was covered with a quilt (she couldn't bring herself to call it one of her old pot-holders) and he was sleeping.

She chuckled at herself. How were those round black painted eyes to look open or closed? . . . and she looked again and thought they were open. She almost said "Excuse me!" and she actually did blush at disturbing his nap. Wagging her head, she backed away and stood up.

Between her and the old stone fence was usually a carpet of weeds. There was no pretense of making lawn or garden out of the stony soil here. Actually, the front lawn had been grown on trucked-in topsoil. Yet—

Yet this area was not planted. A row of early marigolds between the brownie's house and the onetime weed-bed. And, from there to the fence, a dark-green plant, low, spidery, in rows. She did not recognize the plant except perhaps as just another weed.

Speechless, she returned to the house.

Trouble on the school bus that day; Robin came home bloody and triumphant.

Mother had meant to talk about brownie, but it was some time before events sort themselves out. It appeared that a "big kid" had started chanting the well-known chant about "I seen Tandy's underwear," and Robin had punched him and gotten clobbered for it. The bus monitor broke it up, and in spite of Robin's having gotten the worst of it, he came home bursting with pride and Tandy awash with admiration.

The mother felt both. It was the first time Robin had ever brought arms to bear in defense of his sister, and after the question and cross-question and verbal jigsaw-puzzling which is always necessary to get an anecdote out of a child, and the awkward telephone conversation with the parent of the party of the other part, she found herself alone not with Tandy, but with Robin, Tandy having escaped to her preoccupation behind the garage.

"Robin, I don't like fighting but I must say, I like the way you took up for Tandy."

"Aw, she's okay," said Robin, not noticing how the mother of what he usually called that little tattletale, that squeaky wheel, that pushfaced squint-eyed bow-legged stoop . . . how the mother of this repulsive sibling let drop her jaw, and slumped into a chair.

She was still sitting there, trying to recover her strength, while Robin pedalled away on his bicycle and while, a moment later, Tandy came in. She came totteringly, mounded down with clean laundry. The mother leapt up to help her get the screen door open and then had to sit down again. "Tandy!" she cried.

"Well, they was all dry, Mommy, so I brought them in."

"They *were*," said the mother weakly.

"Sure they were. Mommy . . ."

She was going to ask for something. If it was a diamond tiara, the mother thought, she'd get her one if she had to murder for it. "Yes, honey."

"Mommy, would you teach me how to set the table? I could do it every day while you get dinner."

So for the time being the mother utterly forgot to ask any questions about the brownie.

The mother thought about the brownie a good deal, although—perhaps it was a remnant of her comical embarrassment at having caught him in bed—she seldom went back there to look at the house. But one afternoon, thinking about the neatness of the little table, the dresser and chair and mirror, the shining white floor (what *was* that stuff, anyway?) it occurred to her that the three-year-old Noël would find that arrangement back there irresistible, and she shuddered at the mental picture of Noël bellying delightedly into the careful structure, churning up the white floor, leaning too hard on the cheese-box table, tumbling the mossy roof. "Noël . . . "

"?"

"Noël, we've all got to be specially careful of Tandy's brownie house. You wouldn't ever play with it unless she asked you to, would you?"

Noël gravely shook her helmet of tight curls. "I not allowed."

The mother tipped her head to one side and regarded the child. There were a number of things Noël was not allowed to do which she . . . "But all the same, you won't go back there by yourself."

"I not *allowed,*" said Noël with great emphasis, and simultaneously the mother thought (a) that she'd like Tandy's formula for not allowing if it worked like this and (b) let's keep an eye on Noël all the same.

It was demonstrated, about ten days later, just how unnecessary it was to stand guard over the brownie's house. It was a Saturday. The father was home, Robin was off somewhere on his bicycle, and Tandy was slaving happily away behind the garage. The father, from the front of the house, called out, "Do you know what happened to the hand cultivator?"

The mother's photographic memory saw it lying beside a row of green. Oh, of course. "Noël, darling, run out behind the garage and get the cultivator. Tandy'll show you."

Pleadingly, "No, Mommy!"

"Noël!"

"I not *allowed* to!" said Noël, and incredibly, for she was a cheerful child, she began to cry.

The first impulse was to lay on some muscle and authority, the next a deep sympathy for the little one. "Oh . . . Noël . . . "

"I gon' *hide*!" shrieked Noël in something very like Tandy's special rasping shriek; and go she did, hide she did, ineffectively (the mother knew she was in the baby's blue chiffonier) but with great purpose. Apparently her "not allowed" was big enough to make it worth while defying the giants. Sighing, the mother went to the back door. "Tandy!"

"Yes, Mommy . . . "

"Bring Daddy's cultivator to him, he needs it!"

"The handle-fingers?"

"That's right, dear.'

She watched Tandy, in a yellow dress, bounding from behind the garage and heading for the front lawn. She waited until she saw the flash of yellow again and called her to the back steps.

"Tandy, you must have been terribly rough to Noël about not playing with your brownie. She's afraid to go back there because you said she's not allowed."

"No, I didn't, Mommy."

"Tandy!" (The explosion of the name alone was the mother's favorite curb.)

For the first time in many weeks Tandy began to pucker up, the eyes grew bright, the mouth trembled. "I reely, reely, reely . . . "

Moving on impulse, the mother stepped forward and took Tandy's wrist. "Shh, honey. Take me out and show me what you're doing."

Tandy immediately shut it all off and they went back of the garage, Tandy skipping. The mother was prepared to be complimentary as one normally is, multiplied by the wonder of what she had seen before; but she was not prepared for what she found.

One wall had been removed from the little house, the shiplap scraps unearthed and tossed aside. The roof was still supported by the other side and the top of the creel. A heap of flat stones lay near, and a small sack of ready-mixed concrete. A seed-flat was doing service as a miniature mortar-board, and a discarded pancake-turner as a trowel.

Tandy was composedly replacing the wooden wall with one of fieldstone.

"Tandy! Why, I never . . . who taught you to do this?"

"I asked Mr. Holmes-the-gym-teacher." (Tandy's teachers' names were all compounded like this.)

"But—but . . . where did you get the concrete?"

"I boughted it. I saved my 'lowance money and all my ice-cream money. That's all right, isn't it? I didn't go into town, Robin did on his bicycle." She slopped water from a toy sand-bucket and began to mix the concrete.

"Robin never told me," said the mother faintly.

"I guess you never asked him, Mommy."

"I guess I never." The mother wet her lips. "Tandy, how did you ever think of all this?"

"I didn't think of it. I just did it, that's all." She picked up a slather of cement and ladled it on to the top course of her new wall. "You wouldn't expect a brownie to go on living in a ol' wood house, now, would you?" she demanded in grandmotherly tones.

"No, I—I suppose not . . . Tandy, I saw the dresser and the little chair and the tablecloth. They're lovely. Tandy, did someone iron the tablecloth for you?"

"Oh, it irons itself," said Tandy. "You wash it an' rinse it and stick it on a window an' when it's dry it's ironed."

"What's that lovely white floor?"

Tandy selected and hefted a stone, then carefully laid it on the course. "Borax," she said.

"And you bought that with your ice-cream money too?"

"Sure. Brownies like borax and the little lumps off roots and that stuff there." She pointed to the rows of dark green weed.

"What is that?"

"The brownie's farm."

"I mean, the plant."

"I don't know what the real name is. I found it through the woods there, there's a whole patch. I call it brownie spinach. Look, over there's the lumps. It's like candy to a brownie." She pointed to a heap of roots, from some legume or other—the mother couldn't tell, for the leaves were gone; but the root-hairs had clusters of the typical nitrogenous nodules. "Tandy, how on earth do you know so much about brownies?"

Tandy gave her an impish glance. "I guess the same way you know about little girls."

The mother laughed. "Oh, but I had little girls of my own!"

Tandy just nodded: "Mm-hm."

The mother laughed again. When she left Tandy was fitting a whiskey-bottle—the three-sided "pinch" bottle—full of water, into the wall she was building, taking infinite pains to have it slant just so.

The mother wasn't laughing, though, later when she told her husband about it. As such things occasionally do, these developments had come about invisibly to him, having shown themselves mostly when he was away during the day. He listened, frowning thoughtfully, and when the children were glued to the television set the parents went out to look at the brownie house. All he said—all he could find to say, over and over, was: "Well, how about that."

When they left he snapped off a sprig of the dark green weed and put it in his pocket.

"And she sets the table every night," breathed the mother.

After she finished the fieldstone house (even the roof was stone, laid over the plywood from which the mossy earth had been swept away) Tandy seemed to abandon the brownie and his house altogether. She went back to one of her earlier passions, modelling clay, and spent her time studiously working it. But not ducks, not elephants. She would make thick rectangular slabs of it, and draw, or score, deeply into it. Some of the channels she cut were deeper than others, some curved, some straight but cut with her stylus at an acute angle, so that portions were undercut. "Looks like a three-dimensional Mondrian," said the father one night when the kids were asleep. He worked in a museum and knew a great many things, and had access to a great many more. That plant, for example. "It's *astralagus vetch,*" he told his wife. "And I knew I'd read something about it somewhere, so I looked it up again. It's a pretty ordinary sort of vegetable except for some reason it has a fantastic appetite for selenium. So much so that proposals have been made to mine selenium—and you know, that's that light-sensitive element they use in TV tubes and photocells and the like—by planting the vetch where selenium is known to be in the soil, harvesting the whole plant, burning it and recovering selenium from the ash. All of which is beside the point—what on earth made the little fuzzhead pick the stuff up and plant it?"

"Brownies like it," the mother said, and smiled.

It was the very next morning that Tandy was missing from the breakfast table.

There was only a small flurry about it; the mother knew just where to look. The child was busily packing armloads of vetch and tangles of knobby roots into a hole in the solid front of the brownie house. The brownie himself sat against the garage, its face turned toward her, its not-closed, not-open eyes seeming to watch. "I'm sorry, Mommy," Tandy said brightly, "but I'm not late for school, am I?"

"No, dear, but your breakfast is ready. What on earth are you doing to the brownie's house?"

"It isn't a house any more," said Tandy, in the tones of one explaining the self-evident to one who should know better without asking, "it's a factory." She put both hands in the hole and pushed hard. Apparently the house was baled full of weeds and roots. She daubed mortar around the opening quickly.

"Come, dear."

"Just finished, Mommy." She took a flat stone and set it into the opening, which must have been prepared for it, for it seemed a perfect fit. Another slap of mortar and she was up smiling. "I'm sorry, Mommy, but this is the day I had to do that."

"For the brownie."

"For the brownie." They went back to the house.

In Hawaii, a specialist, who should have been but was not more than a sergeant at the missile tracking station, grunted and straightened away from the high definition screen. "Lost it." He pulled a tablet toward him, glanced at the clock, and started filling in the log.

Nobody saw the faint swift streak as the satellite died. But if there had been a witness to that death—placed not to see faint swift streaks, but right on the scene, with a high-speed stroboscopic viewing device, he would have had some remarkable pictures.

As the golden sphere surrendered to the ravening attack of fractional heat, in that all but immeasurable fragment of time wherein parts became malleable, plastic, useful—they were used. Selenium from the solar cells, nitrogen from the pressurized interior, borosilicates ripped from refractory parts, were gleaned and garnered and formed and conformed. For a brief time (but quite long enough) there existed a device of molten alloy bars and threads surrounding a throat, or gate, which was composed of a pulsing, brilliant blue non-substance.

Anything placed within this blue area would cease to exist—not destroyed in any ordinary sense, but utterly eliminated. And the laws of the universe being what they are, such eliminated matter must reappear elsewhere. Exactly where, depends of course on circumstances.

That morning the mother was hanging clothes when a flash of light caught her eye. She put down her clothes-basket and went to the back of the garage.

The brownie sat with his back to the garage, staring glumly at the torn-up remnants of his "farm." The mid-morning sunlight, warm and bright in this clear dry day, struck down through a gap in the trees and poured itself on and over the pinch bottle, half in and half out of the near wall of the little house. The colors were, she found by screening her vision through her eyelashes, lovely and very bright—flame-orange and white—why, the bottle itself seemed to be alight.

Or was it the inside of the little house?

There was a violent, sudden hiss as the bottle, full of water, popped its cork and sent a gout of water inside the little stone structure. Steam rolled up and then disappeared, and she took a pace back from the sudden wave of heat. Terrified, she began to think of hose, or extinguisher . . . the garage, all these trees, the house . . . and then she saw that the side of the brownie's house which adjoined the wooden garage was fieldstone too. The heat, whatever it was, was contained.

It seemed to diminish a little. Then the glass bottle wavered, softened, slumped and fell inside. Heat blasted out again and again diminished.

She stepped closer and peered down through the hole left by the bottle. She could clearly see, lying on the floor of the stone chamber, the clay slab Tandy had made, with its odd, geometrical system of ditches and scorings. But they seemed filled with some quivering liquid, which even as she watched turned from yellow to silver and then dulled to what could only be called a chalky pewter. The lines and ditches, filled with this almost-metal, made a sort of screen, but not exactly. It was too tangled for that. Say an irregular frame about an irregular opening in the center of the slab. And this center area began to turn blue and then purple, and then throb in some way she would never be able to describe. She had to turn her eyes away.

Looking away seemed to snap the thread of fascination with which she had leashed fear. She fled to the house, dialed the telephone, got her husband. "Quick," she said, and stopped to pant, alarming him mightily. "Come home."

It was all she could manage. She hung up and sank into a couch. She was therefore unaware of Noël, who came trotting across the back of the house and straight and fearlessly behind the garage. She stood for a while with a red lollipop in her mouth and pink hands behind her, watching the heat-flickers over the stones, then circled them carefully to windward and squatted down where she could peer inside. Carefully then, and much more steadily than even a deft three-year-old might be expected to move, she reached down with her delicate lollipop and probed the molten slag.

"Oh, don't, don't!" the mother said later back of the garage, as the father stabbed angrily at the hot stones with a crowbar. "Tandy might . . . she might . . . oh, it's meant so much to her . . . "

"I don't care, I don't care," he growled, stabbing and slashing and ruining. "I don't like it. Just say it's about fire, like playing with matches. We won't punish her or anything."

"No?" she said woefully, looking at the ruins.

"And this," he said, "damn devilish thing." He scooped up the brownie and thrust it among the scorching rocks. It flamed up easily. The last thing to go was the pair of dull eyes. The mother was at last sure they had been open the whole time. "Just tell her we almost had a fire," growled the father.

. . . which was the selfsame day Tandy brought back her report card, the absolutely perfect report card, and the note:

> . . . truly the first absolutely perfect report card I have ever made out in my twenty-eight years of teaching school. The change in Tandy is quite beyond anything I have ever seen. She is an absolute delight, and I think it is safe to say that probably she always was; her previous behavior was, perhaps, a protest against something which she had now accepted. I shall never be able to express my gratitude to you for coming in for that talk, nor my admiration of you for your handling of the child (whatever that was!). It might be gracious of you to say that perhaps I had something to do with this; I would like to forestall that compliment. I did nothing special, nothing extra. It is you who have wrought the most pleasant kind of miracle.

It was signed by her teacher, and it left them numb. Then the mother kissed Tandy and exclaimed, "Oh darling, whoever in the world magicked you?"

Exclamation or no, Tandy took it as a question and answered it directly: "The brownie."

There was a heavy silence, and then the mother took Tandy's hand. "You have to know about something," she said, and urgently to the father, "You come too."

They went out behind the garage, the woman touching Tandy's shoulders with ready mother hands. "There was a fire, honey. It all burned up. The brownie burned too."

The father, watching Tandy's face, which had not changed at the sight of the ruin (was this that un-seeing you read about, when people in shock deny to themselves what they see?) said suddenly and hoarsely, "It was an accident."

"No, it wasn't," Tandy said. She looked at her father and her mother but they were both looking at their feet. "And anyway *he* isn't burned up, he wasn't in that fire."

"He was," said the father, but she ignored him. "Anyway," the mother said, "I'm terribly sorry about your pretty little house, Tandy."

Tandy poked out her lips briefly. "It wasn't a house, it was a factory, I told you," she said. "And anyway it's all finished with anyway."

"You better understand," said the father doggedly, "that brownie did burn."

"You remember. You left him sitting right there," said the mother.

"Oh," said Tandy, "*that* wasn't a brownie! You can't see a brownie, silly. I've got the brownie. Don't you know that? Didn't you see the 'port card?"

"How did the . . . " She couldn't say it.

"It was easy. Any time I got to do something, I think about should I or not, and if I should, how I should do it; when I think of the right way, something inside here goes *bwoop-eee!*" (she made a startlingly electronic sound, the first syllable glissading upward and the second flat and unmusical, like a "pure" tone) "and I know that's what I should do. It's easy. And that's the brownie."

"Inside you."

"Mm-hm. That dirty old doll, that was just a way to get some fun out of all that hard work. I couldn't've done it without having some sort of fun. So I made it easy for brownies to live in this whole world and they make it easy for me."

The mother thought about a metallic twisted thing with a purple mystery atremble in it. It was like looking through a window into a—another place. Or a door.

"Tandy," she said, moved as she sometimes was by sheer impulse, "how many brownies came through the door?"

"Four," said Tandy blithely, and began to skip. "One for me, one for Robin, one for Noël and one for the baby. Could I have some juice?"

They walked back to the house. Robin was home. He was giving Noël back her lollipop and saying "Thank you" the way they always wished he would. Noël always was a generous child. She had already given the baby a lick.

The analogy of the profit-sharing plan appears as we imagine a self-satisfied tycoon at his desk and a bright-eyed junior exec sprinting in bearing mimeographed sheets. "Gosh, J.G., this is that first look I had at the new plan. You're doing a lot for your people here, J.G., a whole lot." And homiletically the great man inclines his head, accepting the tribute, and says "A happy worker is a loyal worker, my boy." And while bobbing his head, the junior executive is thinking, "Yeah, and what's good for the happy workers is good for management, how about that?"

Yet enlightened and cooperative self-interest is not always to be sneered at. Ask any symbiote. Whatever it was that bubbled up out of that blue orifice had been designed simply and solely to adapt a host fully to its environment, in order to induce that cardinal harmony called—joy.

Not satisfaction, not contentment, not pleasure. These can be had in other ways, and by using less than all of the environment. A surge of joy within the host created that special substance on which the symbiote fed, and it was as simple as that. Oh happy worker. Oh happy management . . .

"Well, thank God anyway she's back to normal," said the father. He came in from the porch where he and the mother had stood watching the neighborhood kids and Robin and Tandy playing on the lawn. The mother did not point out to him that Tandy, in and of the whole group now, may have been playing normally, but she wasn't back to it; she'd come to it. The mother stood watching, silent, happy, and frightened.

Inside, the father picked up his newspaper and threw it down again when he heard one of those special in-group code sounds which come to families like secret ciphers. This one was the click of heavy glass against hardwood, and meant that the baby, who had been put down in the crib in the master bedroom, had lashed out with a strong left hook in his random way and belted his bottle out of his mouth and up against the crib bars.

The father stopped just inside the bedroom. His jaw dropped, and all he could do was slowly to raise a hand to his chin and close it and hold it closed. For the baby, the six-months-old Timothy, who only yesterday could hopelessly lose a bottle five-eighths of an inch away from his hungry face, pulled himself to a sitting position by the bars, half-turned to the left and pulled the pillow on which the bottle had been perched away from the side of the crib and up to a formal position across the end of the mattress; half-turned to the right to grasp the bottle, then lay back.

He not only took the bottle firmly in his two hands; he not only got his mouth on it; he also elevated it so it would flow freely.

And for a long moment there was no sound but his suckings, his rhythmic murmurs of sheer joy, and the faint susurrus of tiny bubbles valving back into the bottle; for the father was holding his breath. At last the father inhaled and opened his mouth to call his wife witness to this miracle. He then thought better of it, closed his mouth, wagged his head and quietly left the room.

As he entered by one door, Robin, the firstborn, bounded in at the front. The screen door went to the stretch, and uncorked a curve that promised to tear out the moldings when it hit. The father squinched up his face and eyes in preparation for the crash, but Robin, for the first time in his life—a boy has to be at least eleven before he stops slamming screen-doors, and Robin was only eight—Robin reached behind him without looking and buffered the door with his fingertips, so it closed with a whisper and a click. He galloped past the unthunderstruck father and went into the kitchen; a moment later he was seen, all unbidden, lugging the garbage out.

The father fell weakly back into the big wicker chair.

"Daddy . . . "

He put down his paper. Noël came to him with a long cardboard box stretching her three-year-old arms out almost straight. She pleaded, "You wanna play chest with me?"

He looked at her for a long moment. Many times they had sat on the carpet and made soldier-parades with the chessmen. But now he—he . . .

He shuddered. He tried to control it but he couldn't "No, Noël," he said. "I don't want to play chest with you . . . " But oh, that's Noël's story, not Tandy's.

(1961)

DAVID R. BUNCH

2064, OR THEREABOUTS

He was just a tall spot moving slow out of the Down Provinces when first I picked him up on the Warn. But he came on dogged and inexorable until he stood dour and spent-seeming, frowning at my armored gates, the noon sun of a sun-flashing day glinting upon his sheathed face.

I allowed him through my gates one by one, when the weapons report and all the decontaminators signaled he was clean, and I saw that his heart was exposed as well as some of the gears activating the breath bags. There were tatters of flesh, and torn metal, over half of his upper shell. It was as though some giant claw, I thought, had ripped him across the chest in some accidental quick encounter. Or more it was, I thought, like a madman might work and rip at himself after some long time of frustration.

"You're hurt!" I impulsively said, a strange compassion working through me as I stared into his rusted sorrowing eyes.

"NO!" he said, putting down the small easel he carried, "not the way that you think I am hurt. The heart works well still, and the covering being off the gears of the chest does not slow them one whit. But I am hurt, deep-wounded, daily killed by the long unrewarded years of looking, not finding." He dropped his head forward then and his shoulders were bent, and I knew enough about burdens to know that he had one. "Each of us seeks for his own view of the Dream," he went on, "each in his limited way, each to his own degree of time-spent-in-searching looks for his Ultimate. Mine has been almost a total involvement, and the years seem growing late now, mine and the world's. That's why when you saw me, though perhaps I did not seem to be, I was speeding. I was up almost to total maximum with my hinges and braces working, oh, I was on the trail of the Dream again, hotly. Coming down here."

"But why" I stammered, "why have you, an artist, come to this place of an obvious involvement in strength, a citadel of real firmness? I suppose you are en route?"

"NO!" He snapped his head up, the old shoulders straightened and the white metal strings in his beard trembled. His head shook on the spring-strips in his neck. "No, I am not en route, except in that larger sense that we are always en route as we wander here and look here. But I hope I am Here now, arrived. I hope I have found—after this to wander no more the Long Search."

"I—I don't understand." In my general uncertainty and surprise I trembled more than I meant to. Instinctively I looked to the better positioning of weapons men and edged a little nearer a steel sentry who stood nearby. "This is no artist's colony," I blurted, "nor an old painter's rest home. This is a working Stronghold, and we hold no dances for maimed Dream Seekers here. I would hope not to have to be unkind."

He ignored my words almost entirely. "Through the Down Provinces," he continued, "word spread of a most wonderful armed place by the plastic land of the steel dogs near the Valley of Witch. A man was in a citadel there, according to rumors passed round, a New Processes man of New Processes Land, replaced, metal-shored, flesh-stripped to the very minimum of flesh allowable for mortal man. That man sat serenely living, month in month out, years long, decades long, never influenced by family or friend or enemy, completing his great self through the days of his living, really living a Life. Surrounded by so many security devices and Walls and all the Wonderful Appliances of the Sciences that serve and nourish mankind in this year of Our Discoveries, 2064, he lounged like a superb nut, a giant seed in a great shell, ripening day by day to new Meanings. After wandering life-long, frantically, the fear-tossed world and not finding—well, to see such beauteous calm—and Life-Meaning—I must before I die!

"Yes, I have been of the wanderers," he talked on, "the lost and searching wanderers, who sometimes never find because we pick, to look for, a Dream too shining to ever be." He plucked a small raveling piece of metal loose from his malleable nose. "Yes, they replaced me, metal-alloyed me, gave me there at the last mostly a mechanical metallic heart, one perhaps as faultless and smooth-working as yours or your great master's. But I was never content to go behind some weapons and a Wall to live with the Wonderful Appliances. In short, I could never quite find my place in the stability of the New Processes society. Something writhed unfed, always.

"Frantically it seems I was always chasing the wind to the edges of frightening bottomless caverns of Despair, while such as your great master, with what must have been a surer grasp of The Values, slipped with effortless beauteous calm into the chair of The Dream. I have longed to make some enduring monument; I have hungered after the Great Painting; ever haunted by questions I have tried throughout a long failure to express the Life-Meaning, the essence of YOU and ME. And now, changing my course a little, I have come to do it as a single portrait, one of your great firm master calmly in his chair! Right here in this Stronghold!"

More than a trifle alarmed now I looked at the gauntness of him where he stood trembling, his rusted metal flexing, sending up small squeaks and screams. And I noted how his flesh-strips with the years had gone all wrinkled and sere. There was a stench about him of old grease in the hinge joints, and certainly he needed an oil bath to brighten his metal shell. What poor specimens profess to our greatest dreams and questions, I reflected. This smelly vagrant, I thought with the greatest contempt, peasant-robot-thing, probably doesn't have a single Wall or weapons man to his name, and yet he staggers addle-waddle over the countryside, with his easel and paintbrushes, talking about his Ultimate, talking about Meaning. As though such as he had any right to question and conjecture! But when his rusting eyes with all their piercing sorrow looked into mine again, I felt a queer watery feeling, that was not fear, flood through my flesh-strips. "Perhaps you have not had your introven," I said. "Perhaps you have food-hunger." I went for a needle and a cup of the special fluid that serves to nourish our flesh-strips, that small part of mortality the Rebuilders have had to leave between metal and metal, even here in Moderan.

When I came back he was lying along the floor, looking like the small beginnings of an interesting stack of scrap steel. His hands were over his face, the fingers spread, and except his eyes gleamed through his fingers like two brown fires, I would have thought him entirely "done with it all." With the snap of a rusty spring he came to a sitting position. "I do not wish to dine," he said. "I am quite well and strong, really. It's just that so near to Dream's find, to trail's end, to final realization one grows a little fluttery in the dream bag, a little tight in the think box, oh God! oh God! A kind of tightening around the mind cups it is; a kind of great hammering of the heart that has waited so long comes on. And a throbbing beats just under the gears of the eyes to make one see phantom wings. One feels suddenly tired and close to death on the brink of the Great Jubilation. That's why I lay down."

He stood erect, just unfolded up from the floor with a snap of all his joints. In some ways it reminded me of an automatic tree coming out of the plastic earth-shell, the way they do when spring comes round to Big Calendar and someone thumbs the switch to Green Things in Season Control. "Take me to him," he cried, "for it grows late, late in my years as well as old in the years of the world. Let us waste no more time. Take me to your great master, that man who sits living like a great firm nut, a splendid seed, the earth's finest fruit, ripening in the hull of his Walls, guards and guns. His Meaning I would record; such an adaptation, such a fearless calm in the face of the ever-lurking Disaster is surely the Beauty I have sought."

Unfortunately, at that juncture I had one of my panic times. Certain wheels had spun round, the slots had been spread, and in my mind now it was time for my cowardice. While he stood there waiting to be conducted to the Great Calm Face, I passed totally into the Trembly Country of Fear, my own personal Nation of Dread. While he stood watching, wondering, I went completely into my Cycle of Anguish, and I could not help how it was. I trembled violently; metal parts clanked and zinged; my face steel became so gaunt and distorted that metal-complaint started up a high shriek-and-whine. I started wildly to think of all the happenstance things that might befall me and my fort. Though the sound-buzz was constant now, meaning that all was well in the Wonderful Appliances that often served me so well, how long would it be so? Let a wheel falter a thousand miles away, let a shaft break where a billion phantom buckets dropped uncountable billions of power droplets upon a blade, upon a thousand blades, and lights would blink, the wonderful buzz would go scratchy, and my fort would cough and catch its breath and flounder like a bent-down sick old man. And the sun! what of the sun? the giver of all. The sun burns up! The sun falls out of the sky! A bigger sun comes flying flaming out of the Great Yon and burps and my sun is wafted away, or even it eats my sun! opens up like some great boa mouth and gulps a small flaming egg. Fears, Fears, FEARS! In my personal cycle, far in the Kingdom of Dread, I think of all the fears, fears founded, fears unfounded, fears old, fears new, fears not before dreamed up perhaps by any man.—An attack! a space launch from far-off dangerous old Mars! Some strange metal-rot works all unknown, unsuspected, in my hinge joints for years! I fall into chaos and parts. Suddenly.—What else is there but fears ever for any reasonable man? What? WHAT?

When I came back to a calmer place and found somehow the small firm Fortress of Hold in my groping mind, I saw how he waited and stared. A pounding as of hammers on huge steel tubes filled my metal ears then; wave on wave of shame washed up from my mortal strips. I clung to two steel men and braced my feet hard on a pillar of iron fitted around marble slabs. Fighting hard I managed to meet the intensity of his gaze. "There's no one here but me—I swear," I finally said, "I'm master here.—I'm the one you would paint! Shall we move to my calmness chair?"

For a moment too intense to measure in the long hurling on of Time the brown balls of his eyes seemed awash in his battered head. His face steel wrinkled and screamed, the white threads of his beard trembled as if a sharp wind passed through. I watched the Dream finally die in the iron face of a man, and being what I was, there was no thing I could do. "I'm sorry," I heard him say as from some immeasurably great distance, and I felt something of how sorry he really was for us all.

After awhile he left, clutching his empty unused easel in a kind of greater desperation, it seemed—out through all the launchers and the Walls, the weapons tracking him, and seeing him go I felt I was watching a Dream at the very end of its road. He reeled toward the plastic valley of the steel dogs, and I went deeper into my complex to take me a calmness bath, and later I aimed to try with new nerve-strip rays to stay that trembling that had started up again all through my flesh-and-steel shell. Later I heard how he was met at the edge of the Valley by a little masquerade new-metal dog carrying the barest of plastic bones marked THIS FOR THE MEANING SEEKER. Of course it was a wide joke sent up from the Palace of the Witch, and that was why the air over the White Valley was suddenly alive with big clown-faced balloons and the long guns of laugh salvoing out a full Ho-ho salute. The masquerade dog, the gears and the punched cards in his head working perfectly, backed carefully away while the artist examined his bone. Handling it in other than the one prescribed way, of course, the artist caused the mined bone to explode, and his heart and colors and empty easel, as well as his metal shell and the few flesh-strips he owned, for a moment joined the Ho-ho salute and the big-balloon clown carnival high over White Witch Valley.

Considering his high seriousness, as well as the intensity of his try, it did seem, even to me, a most unsatisfactory way for him to go.

(1964)

JAMES H. SCHMITZ

Balanced Ecology

The diamondwood tree farm was restless this morning. Ilf Cholm had been aware of it for about an hour but had said nothing to Auris, thinking he might be getting a summer fever or a stomach upset and imagining things and that Auris would decide they should go back to the house so Ilf's grandmother could dose him. But the feeling continued to grow, and by now Ilf knew it was the farm.

Outwardly, everyone in the forest appeared to be going about their usual business. There had been a rainfall earlier in the day; and the tumbleweeds had uprooted themselves and were moving about in the bushes, lapping water off the leaves. Ilf had noticed a small one rolling straight towards a waiting slurp and stopped for a moment to watch the slurp catch it. The slurp was of average size, which gave it a tongue-reach of between twelve and fourteen feet, and the tumbleweed was already within range.

The tongue shot out suddenly, a thin, yellow flash. Its tip flicked twice around the tumbleweed, jerked it off the ground and back to the feed opening in the imitation tree stump within which the rest of the slurp was concealed. The tumbleweed said "Oof!" in the surprised way they always did when something caught them, and went in through the opening. After a moment, the slurp's tongue tip appeared in the opening again and waved gently around, ready for somebody else of the right size to come within reach.

Ilf, just turned eleven and rather small for his age, was the right size for this slurp, though barely. But, being a human boy, he was in no danger. The slurps of the diamondwood farms on Wrake didn't attack humans. For a moment, he was tempted to tease the creature into a brief fencing match. If he picked up a stick and banged on the stump with it a few times, the slurp would become annoyed and dart its tongue out and try to knock the stick from his hand.

But it wasn't the day for entertainment of that kind. Ilf couldn't shake off his crawly, uncomfortable feeling, and while he had been standing there, Auris and Sam had moved a couple of hundred feet farther uphill, in the direction of the Queen Grove, and home. He turned and sprinted after them, caught up with them as they came out into one of the stretches of grassland which lay between the individual groves of diamondwood trees.

Auris, who was two years, two months, and two days older than Ilf, stood on top of Sam's semiglobular shell, looking off to the right towards the valley where the diamondwood factory was. Most of the world of Wrake was on the hot side, either rather dry or rather steamy; but this was cool mountain country. Far to the south, below the valley and the foothills behind it, lay the continental plain, shimmering like a flat, green-brown sea. To the north and east were higher plateaus, above the level where the diamondwood liked to grow. Ilf ran past Sam's steadily moving bulk to the point where the forward rim of the shell made a flat upward curve, close enough to the ground so he could reach it.

Sam rolled a somber brown eye back for an instant as Ilf caught the shell and swung up on it, but his huge beaked head didn't turn. He was a mossback, Wrake's version of the turtle pattern, and except for the full-grown trees and perhaps some members of the clean-up squad, the biggest thing on the farm. His corrugated shell was overgrown with a plant which had the appearance of long green fur; and occasionally when Sam fed, he would extend and use a pair of heavy arms with three-fingered hands, normally held folded up against the lower rim of the shell.

Auris had paid no attention to Ilf's arrival. She still seemed to be watching the factory in the valley. She and Ilf were cousins but didn't resemble each other. Ilf was small and wiry, with tight-curled red hair. Auris was slim and blond, and stood a good head taller than he did. He thought she looked as if she owned everything she could see from the top of Sam's shell; and she did, as a matter of fact, own a good deal of it—nine tenths of the diamondwood farm and nine tenths of the factory. Ilf owned the remaining tenth of both.

He scrambled up the shell, grabbing the moss-fur to haul himself along, until he stood beside her. Sam, awkward as he looked when walking, was moving at a good ten miles an hour, clearly headed for the Queen Grove. Ilf didn't know whether it was Sam or Auris who had decided to go back to the house. Whichever it had been, he could feel the purpose of going there.

"They're nervous about something," he told Auris, meaning the whole farm. "Think there's a big storm coming?"

"Doesn't look like a storm," Auris said.

Ilf glanced about the sky, agreed silently. "Earthquake, maybe?"

Auris shook her head. "It doesn't feel like earthquake."

She hadn't turned her gaze from the factory. Ilf asked, "Something going on down there?"

Auris shrugged. "They're cutting a lot today," she said. "They got in a limit order."

Sam swayed on into the next grove while Ilf considered the information. Limit orders were fairly unusual; but it hardly explained the general uneasiness. He sighed, sat down, crossed his legs, and looked about. This was a grove of young trees, fifteen years and less. There was plenty of open space left between them. Ahead, a huge tumbleweed was dying, making happy, chuckling sounds as it pitched its scarlet seed pellets far out from its slowly unfolding leaves. The pellets rolled hurriedly farther away from the old weed as soon as they touched the ground. In a twelve-foot circle about their parent, the earth was being disturbed, churned, shifted steadily about. The clean-up squad had arrived to dispose of the dying tumbleweed; as Ilf looked, it suddenly settled six or seven inches deeper into the softened dirt. The pellets were hurrying to get beyond the reach of the clean-up squad so they wouldn't get hauled down, too. But half-grown tumbleweeds, speckled yellow-green and ready to start their rooted period, were rolling through the grove towards the disturbed area. They would wait around the edge of the circle until the clean-up squad finished, then move in and put down their roots. The ground where the squad had worked recently was always richer than any other spot in the forest.

Ilf wondered, as he had many times before, what the clean-up squad looked like. Nobody ever caught so much as a glimpse of them. Riquol Cholm, his grandfather, had told him of attempts made by scientists to catch a member of the squad with digging machines. Even the smallest ones could dig much faster than the machines could dig after them, so the scientists always gave up finally and went away.

"Ilf, come in for lunch!" called Ilf's grandmother's voice.

Ilf filled his lungs, shouted, "Coming, Grand—"

He broke off, looked up at Auris. She was smirking.

"Caught me again," Ilf admitted. "Dumb humbugs!" He yelled, "Come out, Lying Lou! I know who it was."

Meldy Cholm laughed her low, sweet laugh, a silverbell called, the giant greenweb of the Queen Grove sounded its deep harp note, more or less all together. Then Lying Lou and Gabby darted into sight, leaped up on the mossback's hump. The humbugs were small, brown, bobtailed animals, built with spider leanness and very quick. They had round skulls, monkey faces, and the pointed teeth of animals who lived by catching and killing other animals. Gabby sat down beside Ilf, inflating and deflating his voice pouch, while Lou burst into a series of rattling, clicking, spitting sounds.

"They've been down at the factory?" Ilf asked.

"Yes," Auris said. "Hush now. I'm listening."

Lou was jabbering along at the rate at which the humbugs chattered among themselves, but this sounded like, and was, a recording of human voices played back at high speed. When Auris wanted to know what people somewhere were talking about, she sent the humbugs off to listen. They remembered everything they heard, came back and repeated it to her at their own speed, which saved time. Ilf, if he tried hard, could understand scraps of it. Auris understood it all. She was hearing now what the people at the factory had been saying during the morning.

Gabby inflated his voice pouch part way, remarked in Grandfather Riquol's strong, rich voice, "My, my! We're not being quite on our best behavior today, are we, Ilf?"

"Shut up," said Ilf.

"Hush now," Gabby said in Auris's voice. "I'm listening." He added in Ilf's voice, sounding crestfallen, "Caught me again!" then chuckled nastily.

Ilf made a fist of his left hand and swung fast. Gabby became a momentary brown blur, and was sitting again on Ilf's other side. He looked at Ilf with round, innocent eyes, said in a solemn tone. "We must pay more attention to details, men. Mistakes can be expensive!"

He'd probably picked that up at the factory. Ilf ignored him. Trying to hit a humbug was a waste of effort. So was talking back to them. He shifted his attention to catching what Lou was saying; but Lou had finished up at that moment. She and Gabby took off instantly in a leap from Sam's back and were gone in the bushes. Ilf thought they were a little jittery and erratic in their motions today, as if they, too, were keyed up even more than usual. Auris walked down to the front lip of the shell and sat on it, dangling her legs. Ilf joined her there.

"What were they talking about at the factory?" he asked.

"They did get in a limit order yesterday," Auris said. "And another one this morning. They're not taking any more orders until they've filled those two."

"That's good, isn't it?" Ilf asked.

"I guess so."

After a moment, Ilf asked, "Is that what *they're* worrying about?"

"I don't know," Auris said. But she frowned.

Sam came lumbering up to another stretch of open ground, stopped while he was still well back among the trees. Auris slipped down from the shell, said, "Come on but don't let them see you," and moved ahead through the trees until she could look into the open. Ilf followed her as quietly as he could.

"What's the matter?" he inquired. A hundred and fifty yards away, on the other side of the open area, towered the Queen Grove, its tops dancing gently like armies of slender green spears against the blue sky. The house wasn't visible from here; it was a big one-story bungalow built around the trunks of a number of trees deep within the grove. Ahead of them lay the road which came up from the valley and wound on through the mountains to the west.

Auris said, "An aircar came down here a while ago . . . There it is!"

They looked at the aircar parked at the side of the road on their left, a little distance away. Opposite the car was an opening in the Queen Grove where a path led to the house. Ilf couldn't see anything very interesting about the car. It was neither new nor old, looked like any ordinary aircar. The man sitting inside it was nobody they knew.

"Somebody's here on a visit," Ilf said.

"Yes," Auris said. "Uncle Kugus has come back."

Ilf had to reflect an instant to remember who Uncle Kugus was. Then it came to his mind in a flash. It had been some while ago, a year or so. Uncle Kugus was a big, handsome man with thick, black eyebrows, who always smiled. He wasn't Ilf's uncle but Auris's; but he'd had presents for both of them when he arrived. He had told Ilf a great many jokes. He and Grandfather Riquol had argued on one occasion for almost two hours about something or other; Ilf couldn't remember now what it had been. Uncle Kugus had come and gone in a tiny, beautiful, bright yellow aircar, had taken Ilf for a couple of rides in it, and told him about winning races with it. Ilf hadn't had too bad an impression of him.

"That isn't him," he said, "and that isn't his car."

"I know. He's in the house," Auris said. "He's got a couple of people with him. They're talking with Riquol and Meldy."

A sound rose slowly from the Queen Grove as she spoke, deep and resonant, like the stroke of a big, old clock or the hum of a harp. The man in the aircar turned his head towards the grove to listen. The sound was repeated twice. It came from the giant greenweb at the far end of the grove and could be heard all over the farm, even, faintly, down in the valley when the wind was favorable. Ilf said, "Lying Lou and Gabby were up here?"

"Yes. They went down to the factory first, then up to the house."

"What are they talking about in the house?" Ilf inquired.

"Oh, a lot of things." Auris frowned again. "We'll go and find out, but we won't let them see us right away."

Something stirred beside Ilf. He looked down and saw Lying Lou and

Gabby had joined them again. The humbugs peered for a moment at the man in the aircar, then flicked out into the open, on across the road, and into the Queen Grove, like small, flying shadows, almost impossible to keep in sight. The man in the aircar looked about in a puzzled way, apparently uncertain whether he'd seen something move or not.

"Come on," Auris said.

Ilf followed her back to Sam. Sam lifted his head and extended his neck. Auris swung herself upon the edge of the undershell beside the neck, crept on hands and knees into the hollow between the upper and lower shells. Ilf climbed in after her. The shell-cave was a familiar place. He'd scuttled in there many times when they'd been caught outdoors in one of the violent electric storms which came down through the mountains from the north or when the ground began to shudder in an earthquake's first rumbling. With the massive curved shell about him and the equally massive flat shell below, the angle formed by the cool, leathery wall which was the side of Sam's neck and the front of his shoulder seemed like the safest place in the world to be on such occasions.

The undershell tilted and swayed beneath Ilf now as the mossback started forward. He squirmed around and looked out through the opening between the shells. They moved out of the grove, headed towards the road at Sam's steady walking pace. Ilf couldn't see the aircar and wondered why Auris didn't want the man in the car to see them. He wriggled uncomfortably. It was a strange, uneasy-making morning in every way.

They crossed the road, went swishing through high grass with Sam's ponderous side-to-side sway like a big ship sailing over dry land, and came to the Queen Grove. Sam moved on into the green-tinted shade under the Queen Trees. The air grew cooler. Presently he turned to the right, and Ilf saw a flash of blue ahead. That was the great thicket of flower bushes, in the center of which was Sam's sleeping pit.

Sam pushed through the thicket, stopped when he reached the open space in the center to let Ilf and Auris climb out of the shell-cave. Sam then lowered his forelegs, one after the other, into the pit, which was lined so solidly with tree roots that almost no earth showed between them, shaped like a mold to fit the lower half of his body; he tilted forward, drawing neck and head back under his shell, slid slowly into the pit, straightened out and settled down. The edge of his upper shell was now level with the edge of the pit, and what still could be seen of him looked simply like a big, moss-grown boulder. If nobody came to disturb him, he might stay there unmoving the rest of the year. There were mossbacks in other groves of the farm which had never come out of their sleeping pits or given any indication of being awake since Ilf could remember. They lived an enormous length of time and a nap of half a dozen years apparently meant nothing to them.

Ilf looked questioningly at Auris. She said, "We'll go up to the house and listen to what Uncle Kugus is talking about."

They turned into a path which led from Sam's place to the house. It had been made by six generations of human children, all of whom had used Sam for transportation about the diamondwood farm. He was half again as big as any other mossback around and the only one whose sleeping pit was in the Queen Grove. Everything about the Queen Grove was special, from the trees themselves, which were never cut and twice as thick and almost twice as tall as the trees of other groves, to Sam and his blue flower thicket, the huge stump of the Grandfather Slurp not far away, and the giant greenweb at the other end of the grove. It was quieter here; there were fewer of the other animals. The Queen Grove, from what Riquol Cholm had told Ilf, was the point from which the whole diamondwood forest had started a long time ago.

Auris said, "We'll go around and come in from the back. They don't have to know right away that we're here . . . "

"Mr. Terokaw," said Riquol Cholm, "I'm sorry Kugus Ovin persuaded you and Mr. Bliman to accompany him to Wrake on this business. You've simply wasted your time. Kugus should have known better. I've discussed the situation quite thoroughly with him on other occasions."

"I'm afraid I don't follow you, Mr. Cholm," Mr. Terokaw said stiffly. "I'm making you a businesslike proposition in regard to this farm of diamondwood trees—a proposition which will be very much to your advantage as well as to that of the children whose property the Diamondwood is. Certainly you should at least be willing to listen to my terms!"

Riquol shook his head. It was clear that he was angry with Kugus but attempting to control his anger.

"Your terms, whatever they may be, are not a factor in this," he said. "The maintenance of a diamondwood forest is not entirely a business proposition. Let me explain that to you—as Kugus should have done.

"No doubt you're aware that there are less than forty such forests on the world of Wrake and that attempts to grow the trees elsewhere have been uniformly unsuccessful. That and the unique beauty of diamondwood products, which has never been duplicated by artificial means, is, of course, the reason that such products command a price which compares with that of precious stones and similar items."

Mr. Terokaw regarded Riquol with a bleak blue eye, nodded briefly. "Please continue, Mr. Cholm."

"A diamondwood forest," said Riquol, "is a great deal more than an assemblage of trees. The trees are a basic factor, but still only a factor, of a closely integrated, balanced natural ecology. The manner of interdependence of the plants and animals that make up a diamondwood forest is not clear in all details, but the interdependence is a very pronounced one. None of the involved species seem able to survive in any other environment. On the other hand, plants and animals not naturally a part of this ecology will not thrive if brought into it. They move out or vanish quickly. Human beings appear to be the only exception to that rule."

"Very interesting," Mr. Terokaw said dryly.

"It is," said Riquol. "It is a very interesting natural situation and many people, including Mrs. Cholm and myself, feel it should be preserved. The studied, limited cutting practiced on the diamondwood farms at present acts towards its preservation. That degree of harvesting actually is beneficial to the forests, keeps them moving through an optimum cycle of growth and maturity. They are flourishing under the hand of man to an extent which was not usually attained in their natural, untouched state. The people who are at present responsible for them—the farm owners and their associates—have been working for some time to have all diamondwood forests turned into Federation preserves, with the right to harvest them retained by the present owners and their heirs under the same carefully supervised conditions. When Auris and Ilf come of age and can sign an agreement to that effect, the farms will in fact become Federation preserves. All other steps to that end have been taken by now.

"That, Mr. Terokaw, is why we're not interested in your business proposition. You'll discover, if you wish to sound them out on it, that the other diamondwood farmers are not interested in it either. We are all of one mind in that matter. If we weren't, we would long since have accepted propositions essentially similar to yours."

There was silence for a moment. Then Kugus Ovin said pleasantly, "I know you're annoyed with me, Riquol, but I'm thinking of Auris and Ilf in this. Perhaps in your concern for the preservation of a natural phenomenon, you aren't sufficiently considering their interests."

Riquol looked at him, said, "When Auris reaches maturity, she'll be an extremely wealthy young woman, even if this farm never sells another cubic foot of diamondwood from this day on. Ilf would be sufficiently well-to-do to make it unnecessary for him ever to work a stroke in his life—though I doubt very much he would make such a choice."

Kugus smiled. "There are degrees even to the state of being extremely wealthy," he remarked. "What my niece can expect to gain in her lifetime from this careful harvesting you talk about can't begin to compare with what she would get at one stroke through Mr. Terokaw's offer. The same, of course, holds true of Ilf."

"Quite right," Mr. Terokaw said heavily. "I'm generous in my business dealings, Mr. Cholm. I have a reputation for it. And I can afford to be generous because I profit well from my investments. Let me bring another point to your attention. Interest in diamondwood products throughout the Federation waxes and wanes, as you must be aware. It rises and falls. There are fashions and fads. At present, we are approaching the crest of a new wave of interest in these products. This interest can be properly stimulated and exploited, but in any event we must expect it will have passed its peak in another few months. The next interest peak might develop six years from now, or twelve years from now. Or it might never develop since there are very few natural products which cannot eventually be duplicated and usually surpassed by artificial methods, and there is no good reason to assume that diamondwood will remain an exception indefinitely.

"We should be prepared, therefore, to make the fullest use of this bonanza while it lasts. I am prepared to do just that, Mr. Cholm. A cargo ship full of cutting equipment is at present stationed a few hours' flight from Wrake. This machinery can be landed and in operation here within a day after the contract I am offering you is signed. Within a week, the forest can be leveled. We shall make no use of your factory here, which would be entirely inadequate for my purpose. The diamondwood will be shipped at express speeds to another world where I have adequate processing facilities set up. And we can hit the Federation's main markets with the finished products the following month."

Riquol Cholm said, icily polite now, "And what would be the reason for all that haste, Mr. Terokaw?"

Mr. Terokaw looked surprised. "To insure that we have no competition, Mr. Cholm. What else? When the other diamondwood farmers here discover what has happened, they may be tempted to follow our example. But we'll be so far ahead of them that the diamondwood boom will be almost entirely to our exclusive advantage. We have taken every precaution to see that. Mr. Bliman, Mr. Ovin and I arrived here in the utmost secrecy today. No one so much as suspects that we are on Wrake, much less what our purpose is. I make no mistakes in such matters, Mr. Cholm!"

He broke off and looked around as Meldy Cholm said in a troubled voice, "Come in, children. Sit down over there. We're discussing a matter which concerns you."

"Hello, Auris!" Kugus said heartily. "Hello, Ilf! Remember old Uncle Kugus?"

"Yes," Ilf said. He sat down on the bench by the wall beside Auris, feeling scared.

"Auris," Riquol Cholm said, "did you happen to overhear anything of what was being said before you came into the room?"

Auris nodded. "Yes." She glanced at Mr. Terokaw, looked at Riquol again. "He wants to cut down the forest."

"It's your forest and Ilf's, you know. Do you want him to do it?"

"Mr. Cholm, please!" Mr. Terokaw protested. "We must approach this properly. Kugus, show Mr. Cholm what I'm offering."

Riquol took the document Kugus held out to him, looked over it. After a moment, he gave it back to Kugus. "Auris," he said, "Mr. Terokaw, as he's indicated, is offering you more money than you would ever be able to spend in your life for the right to cut down your share of the forest. Now . . . do you want him to do it?"

"No." Auris said.

Riquol glanced at Ilf, who shook his head. Riquol turned back to Mr. Terokaw.

"Well, Mr. Terokaw," he said, "there's your answer. My wife and I don't want you to do it, and Auris and Ilf don't want you to do it. Now . . . "

"Oh, come now, Riquol!" Kugus said, smiling. "No one can expect either Auris or Ilf to really understand what's involved here. When they come of age—"

"When they come of age," Riquol said, "they'll again have the opportunity to decide what they wish to do." He made a gesture of distaste. "Gentlemen, let's conclude this discussion. Mr. Terokaw, we thank you for your offer, but it's been rejected."

Mr. Terokaw frowned, pursed his lips.

"Well, not so fast, Mr. Cholm," he said. "As I told you, I make no mistakes in business matters. You suggested a few minutes ago that I might contact the other diamondwood farmers on the planet on the subject but predicted that I would have no better luck with them."

"So I did," Riquol agreed. He looked puzzled.

"As a matter of fact," Mr. Terokaw went on, "I already have contacted a number of these people. Not in person, you understand, since I did not want to tip off certain possible competitors that I was interested in diamondwood at present. The offer was rejected, as you indicated it would be. In fact, I learned that the owners of the Wrake diamondwood farms are so involved in legally binding agreements with one another that it would be very difficult for them to accept such an offer even if they wished to do it."

Riquol nodded, smiled briefly. "We realized that the temptation to sell out to commercial interests who would not be willing to act in accordance with our accepted policies could be made very strong," he said. "So we've made it as nearly impossible as we could for any of us to yield to temptation."

"Well," Mr. Terokaw continued, "I am not a man who is easily put off. I ascertained that you and Mrs. Cholm are also bound by such an agreement to the other diamondwood owners of Wrake not to be the first to sell either the farm or its cutting rights to outside interests, or to exceed the established limits of cutting. But you are not the owners of this farm. These two children own it between them."

Riquol frowned. "What difference does that make?" he demanded. "Ilf is our grandson. Auris is related to us and our adopted daughter."

Mr. Terokaw rubbed his chin.

"Mr. Bliman," he said, "please explain to these people what the legal situation is."

Mr. Bliman cleared his throat. He was a tall, thin man with fierce dark eyes, like a bird of prey. "Mr. and Mrs. Cholm," he began, "I work for the Federation Government and am a specialist in adoptive procedures. I will make this short. Some months ago, Mr. Kugus Ovin filed the necessary papers to adopt his niece, Auris Luteel, citizen of Wrake. I conducted the investigation which is standard in such cases and can assure you that no official record exists that you have at any time gone through the steps of adopting Auris."

"*What?*" Riquol came half to his feet. Then he froze in position for a moment, settled slowly back in his chair. "What is this? Just what kind of trick are you trying to play?" he said. His face had gone white.

Ilf had lost sight of Mr. Terokaw for a few seconds, because Uncle Kugus had suddenly moved over in front of the bench on which he and Auris were sitting. But now he saw him again and he had a jolt of fright. There was a large blue and silver gun in Mr. Terokaw's hand, and the muzzle of it was pointed very steadily at Riquol Cholm.

"Mr. Cholm," Mr. Terokaw said, "before Mr. Bliman concludes his explanation, allow me to caution you! I do not wish to kill you. This gun, in fact, is not designed to kill. But if I pull the trigger, you will be in excruciating pain for some minutes. You are an elderly man and it is possible that you would not survive the experience. This would not inconvenience us very seriously. Therefore, stay seated and give up any thoughts of summoning help . . . Kugus, watch the children. Mr. Bliman, let me speak to Mr. Het before you resume."

He put his left hand up to his face, and Ilf saw he was wearing a wrist-talker. "Het," Mr. Terokaw said to the talker without taking his eyes off Riquol Cholm, "you are aware, I believe, that the children are with us in the house?"

The wrist-talker made murmuring sounds for a few seconds, then stopped.

"Yes," Mr. Terokaw said. "There should be no problem about it. But let me know if you see somebody approaching the area . . . " He put his hand back down on the table. "Mr. Bliman, please continue."

Mr. Bliman cleared his throat again.

"Mr. Kugus Ovin," he said, "is now officially recorded as the parent by adoption of his niece, Auris Luteel. Since Auris has not yet reached the age where her formal consent to this action would be required, the matter is settled."

"Meaning," Mr. Terokaw added, "that Kugus can act for Auris in such affairs as selling the cutting rights on this tree farm. Mr. Cholm, if you are thinking of taking legal action against us, forget it. You may have had certain papers purporting to show that the girl was your adopted child filed away in the deposit vault of a bank. If so, those papers have been destroyed. With enough money, many things become possible. Neither you nor Mrs. Cholm nor the two children will do or say anything that might cause trouble to me. Since you have made no rash moves, Mr. Bliman will now use an instrument to put you and Mrs. Cholm painlessly to sleep for the few hours required to get you off this planet. Later, if you should be questioned in connection with this situation, you will say about it only what certain psychological experts will have impressed on you to say, and within a few months, nobody will be taking any further interest whatever in what is happening here today.

"Please do not think that I am a cruel man. I am not. I merely take what steps are required to carry out my purpose. Mr. Bliman, please proceed!"

Ilf felt a quiver of terror. Uncle Kugus was holding his wrist with one hand and Auris's wrist with the other, smiling reassuringly down at them. Ilf darted a glance over to Auris's face. She looked as white as his grandparents but she was making no attempt to squrim away from Kugus, so Ilf stayed quiet, too. Mr. Bliman stood up, looking more like a fierce bird of prey than ever, and stalked over to Riquol Cholm, holding something in his hand that looked unpleasantly like another gun. Ilf shut his eyes. There was a moment of silence, then Mr. Terokaw said, "Catch him before he falls out of the chair. Mrs. Cholm, if you will just settle back comfortably . . . "

There was another moment of silence. Then, from beside him, Ilf heard Auris speak.

It wasn't regular speech but a quick burst of thin, rattling gabble, like human speech speeded up twenty times or so. It ended almost immediately.

"What's that? What's that?" Mr. Terokaw said, surprised.

Ilf's eyes flew open as something came in through the window with a whistling shriek. The two humbugs were in the room, brown blurs flicking here and there, screeching like demons. Mr. Terokaw exclaimed something in a loud voice and jumped up from the chair, his gun swinging this way and that. Something scuttled up Mr. Bliman's back like a big spider, and he yelled and spun away from Meldy Cholm lying slumped back in her chair. Something ran up Uncle Kugus's back. He yelled, letting go of Ilf and Auris, and pulled out a gun of his own. "Wide aperture!" roared Mr. Terokaw, whose gun was making loud, thumping noises. A brown shadow swirled suddenly about his knees. Uncle Kugus cursed, took aim at the shadow and fired.

"Come," whispered Auris, grabbing Ilf's arm. They sprang up from the bench and darted out the door behind Uncle Kugus's broad back.

"Het!" Mr. Terokaw's voice came bellowing down the hall behind them. "Up in the air and look out for those children! They're trying to get away. If you see them start to cross the road, knock 'em out. Kugus—after them! They may try to hide in the house."

Then he yowled angrily, and his gun began making the thumping noises again. The humbugs were too small to harm people, but their sharp little teeth could hurt and they seemed to be using them now.

"In here," Auris whispered, opening a door. Ilf ducked into the room with her, and she closed the door softly behind them. Ilf looked at her, his heart pounding wildly.

Auris nodded at the barred window. "Through there! Run and hide in the grove. I'll be right behind you . . . "

"Auris! Ilf!" Uncle Kugus called in the hall. "Wait—don't be afraid. Where are you?" His voice still seemed to be smiling. Ilf heard his footsteps hurrying along the hall as he squirmed quickly sideways between two of the thick wooden bars over the window, dropped to the ground. He turned, darted off towards the nearest bushes. He heard Auris gabble something to the humbugs again, high and shrill, looked back as he reached the bushes and saw her already outside, running towards the shrubbery on his right. There was a shout from the window. Uncle Kugus was peering out from behind the bars, pointing a gun at Auris. He fired. Auris swerved to the side, was gone among the shrubs. Ilf didn't think she had been hit.

"They're outside!" Uncle Kugus yelled. He was too big to get through the bars himself.

Mr. Terokaw and Mr. Bliman were also shouting within the house. Uncle Kugus turned around, disappeared from the window.

"Auris!" Ilf called, his voice shaking with fright.

"Run and hide, Ilf!" Auris seemed to be on the far side of the shrubbery, deeper in the Queen Grove.

Ilf hesitated, started running along the path that led to Sam's sleeping pit, glancing up at the open patches of sky among the treetops. He didn't see the aircar with the man Het in it. Het would be circling around the Queen Grove now, waiting for the other men to chase them into sight so he could knock them out with something. But they could hide inside Sam's shell and Sam would get them across the road. "Auris, where are you?" Ilf cried.

Her voice came low and clear from behind him. "Run and hide, Ilf!"

Ilf looked back. Auris wasn't there but the two humbugs were loping up the path a dozen feet away. They darted past Ilf without stopping, disappeared around the turn ahead. He could hear the three men yelling for him and Auris to come back. They were outside, looking around for them now, and they seemed to be coming closer.

Ilf ran on, reached Sam's sleeping place. Sam lay there unmoving, like a great mossy boulder filling the pit. Ilf picked up a stone and pounded on the front part of the shell.

"Wake up!" he said desperately. "Sam, wake up!"

Sam didn't stir. And the men were getting closer. Ilf looked this way and that, trying to decide what to do.

"Don't let them see you," Auris called suddenly.

"That was the girl over there," Mr. Terokaw's voice shouted. "Go after her, Bliman!"

"Auris, watch out!" Ilf screamed, terrified.

"Aha! And here's the boy, Kugus. This way! Het," Mr. Terokaw yelled triumphantly, "come down and help us catch them! We've got them spotted . . ."

Ilf dropped to hands and knees, crawled away quickly under the branches of the blue flower thicket and waited, crouched low. He heard Mr. Terokaw crashing through the bushes towards him and Mr. Bliman braying, "Hurry up, Het! Hurry up!" Then he heard something else. It was the sound the giant greenweb sometimes made to trick a flock of silver-bells into fluttering straight towards it, a deep drone which suddenly seemed to be pouring down from the trees and rising up from the ground.

Ilf shook his head dizzily. The drone faded, grew up again. For a moment, he thought he heard his own voice call "Auris, where are you?" from the other side of the blue flower thicket. Mr. Terokaw veered off in that direction, yelling something to Mr. Bliman and Kugus. Ilf backed farther away through the thicket, came out on the other side, climbed to his feet and turned.

He stopped. For a stretch of twenty feet ahead of him, the forest floor was moving, shifting and churning with a slow, circular motion, turning lumps of deep brown mold over and over.

Mr. Terokaw came panting into Sam's sleeping place, red-faced, glaring about, the blue and silver gun in his hand. He shook his head to clear the resonance of the humming air from his brain. He saw a huge, moss-covered boulder tilted at a slant away from him but no sign of Ilf.

Then something shook the branches of the thicket behind the boulder. "Auris!" Ilf's frightened voice called.

Mr. Terokaw ran around the boulder, leveling the gun. The droning in the air suddenly swelled to a roar. Two big gray, three-fingered hands came out from the boulder on either side of Mr. Terokaw and picked him up.

"Awk!" he gasped, then dropped the gun as the hands folded him, once, twice, and lifted him towards Sam's descending head. Sam opened his large mouth, closed it, swallowed. His neck and head drew back under his shell and he settled slowly into the sleeping pit again.

The greenweb's roar ebbed and rose continuously now, like a thousand harps being struck together in a bewildering, quickening beat. Human voices danced and swirled through the din, crying, wailing, screeching. Ilf stood at the edge of the twenty-foot circle of churning earth outside the blue flower thicket, half stunned by it all. He heard Mr. Terokaw bellow to Mr. Bliman to go after Auris, and Mr. Bliman squalling to Het to hurry. He heard his own voice nearby call Auris frantically and then Mr. Terokaw's triumphant yell: "This way! Here's the boy, Kugus!"

Uncle Kugus bounded out of some bushes thirty feet away, eyes staring, mouth stretched in a wide grin. He saw Ilf, shouted excitedly and ran towards him. Ilf watched, suddenly unable to move. Uncle Kugus took four long steps out over the shifting loam between them, sank ankle-deep, knee-deep. Then the brown earth leaped in cascades about him, and he went sliding straight down into it as if it were water, still grinning, and disappeared. In the distance, Mr. Terokaw roared, "This way!" and Mr. Bliman yelled to Het to hurry up. A loud, slapping sound came from the direction of the stump of the Grandfather Slurp. It was followed by a great commotion in the bushes around there; but that only lasted a moment. Then, a few seconds later, the greenweb's drone rose and thinned to the wild shriek it made when it had caught something big and faded slowly away . . .

Ilf came walking shakily through the opening in the thickets to Sam's sleeping place. His head still seemed to hum inside with the greenweb's drone but the Queen Grove was quiet again; no voices called anywhere. Sam was settled into his pit. Ilf saw something gleam on the ground near the front end of the pit. He went over and looked at it, then at the big, moss-grown dome of Sam's shell.

"Oh, Sam," he whispered, "I'm not sure we should have done it . . . "

Sam didn't stir. Ilf picked up Mr. Terokaw's blue and silver gun gingerly by the barrel and went off with it to look for Auris. He found her at the edge of the grove, watching Het's aircar on the other side of the road. The aircar was turned on its side and about a third of it was sunk in the ground. At work around and below it was the biggest member of the clean-up squad Ilf had ever seen in action.

They went up to the side of the road together and looked on while the aircar continued to shudder and turn and sink deeper into the earth. Ilf suddenly remembered the gun he was holding and threw it over on the ground next to the aircar. It was swallowed up instantly there. Tumbleweeds came rolling up to join them and clustered around the edge of the circle, waiting. With a final jerk, the aircar disappeared. The disturbed section of earth began to smooth over. The tumbleweeds moved out into it.

There was a soft whistling in the air, and from a Queen Tree at the edge of the grove a hundred and fifty feet away, a diamondwood seedling came lancing down, struck at a slant into the center of the circle where the aircar had vanished, stood trembling a moment, then straightened up. The tumbleweeds nearest it moved respectfully aside to give it room. The seedling shuddered and unfolded its first five-fingered cluster of silver-green leaves. Then it stood still.

Ilf looked over at Auris. "Auris," he said, "should we have done it?"

Auris was silent a moment.

"Nobody did anything," she said then. "They've just gone away again." She took Ilf's hand. "Let's go back to the house and wait for Riquol and Meldy to wake up."

The organism that was the diamondwood forest grew quiet again. The quiet spread back to its central mind unit in the Queen Grove, and the unit began to relax towards somnolence. A crisis had been passed—perhaps the last of the many it had foreseen when human beings first arrived on the world of Wrake.

The only defense against Man was Man. Understanding that, it had laid its plans. On a world now owned by Man, it adopted Man, brought him into its ecology, and its ecology into a new and again successful balance.

This had been a final flurry. A dangerous attack by dangerous humans.

But the period of danger was nearly over, would soon be for good a thing of the past.

It had planned well, the central mind unit told itself drowsily. But now, since there was no further need to think today, it would stop thinking . . .

Sam the mossback fell gratefully asleep.

(1965)

AVRAM DAVIDSON

The House the Blakeneys Built

"Four people coming down the Forest Road, a hey," Old Big Mary said.

Young Red Tom understood her at once. "Not ours."

Things grew very quiet in the long kitchenroom. Old Whitey Bill shifted in his chairseat. "Those have's to be Runaway Little Bob's and that Thin Jinnie's," he said. "Help me up, some."

"No," Old Big Mary said. "They're not."

"Has to be." Old Whitey Bill shuffled up, leaning on his canestick. "Has to be. Whose elses could they be. Always said, me, she ran after him."

Young Whitey Bill put another chunk of burnwood on the burning. "Rowwer, rowwer," he muttered. Then everyone was talking at once, crowding up to the windowlooks. Then everybody stopped the talking. The big foodpots bubbled. Young Big Mary mumbletalked excitedly. Then her words came out clearsound.

"Look to here—look to here—I say, me, they aren't Blakeneys."

Old Little Mary, coming down from the spindleroom, called out, "People! People! Three and four of them down the Forest Road and I don't know them and, oh, they funnywalk!"

"Four strange people!"

"Not Blakeneys!"

"Stop sillytalking! Has to be! Who elses?"

"But not Blakeneys!"

"Not from The House, look to, look to! People—not from The House!"

"Runaway Bob and that Thin Jinnie?"

"No, can't be. No old ones."

"Children? Childrenchildren?"

All who hadn't been lookseeing before came now, all who were at The House, that is—running from the cowroom and the horseroom and dairyroom, ironroom, schoolroom, even from the sickroom.

"Four people! Not Blakeneys, some say!"

"Blakeneys or not Blakeneys, not from The House!"

Robert Hayakawa and his wife Shulamith came out of the forest, Ezra and Mikicho with them. "Well, as I said," Robert observed, in his slow careful way, "a road may end nowhere, going in one direction, but it's not likely it will end nowhere, going in the other."

Shulamith sighed. She was heavy with child. "Tilled fields. I'm glad of that. There was no sign of them anywhere else on the planet. This must be a new settlement. But we've been all over that—" She stopped abruptly, so did they all.

Ezra pointed. "A house—"

"It's more like a, well, what would you say?" Mikicho moved her mouth, groping for a word. "A . . . a *castle*? Robert?"

Very softly, Robert said, "It's not new, whatever it is. It is very much not new, don't you see, Shulamith. *What—?*"

She had given a little cry of alarm, or perhaps just surprise. All four turned to see what had surprised her. A man was running over the field towards them. He stopped, stumbling, as they all turned to him. Then he started again, a curious shambling walk. They could see his mouth moving after a while. He pointed to the four, waved his hand, waggled his head.

"Hey," they could hear him saying. "A hey, a hey. Hey. Look to. Mum. Mum mum mum. Oh, hey . . . "

He had a florid face, a round face that bulged over the eyes, and they were prominent and blue eyes. His nose was an eagle's nose, sharp and hooked, and his mouth was loose and trembling. "Oh, hey, you must be, mum, his name, what? And she run off to follow him? Longlong. Jinnie! Thin Jinnie! Childrenchildren, a hey?" Behind him in the field two animals paused before a plow, switching their tails.

"Michiko, look," said Ezra. "Those must be cows."

The man had stopped about ten feet away. He was dressed in loose, coarse cloth. Again he waggled his head. "Cows, no. Oh, no, mum mum, freemartins, elses. Not cows." Something occurred to him, almost staggering in its astonishment. "A hey, you won't know me! Won't know me!" He laughed. "Oh. What a thing. Strange Blakeneys. Old Red Tom, I say, me."

Gravely, they introduced themselves. He frowned, his slack mouth moving. "Don't know them name," he said, after a moment. "No, a mum. Make them up, like children, in the woods. Longlong. Oh, I, now! Runaway Little Bob. Yes, that name! Your fatherfather. Dead, a hey?"

Very politely, very wearily, feeling—now that he had stopped—the fatigue of the long, long walk, Robert Hayakawa said, "I'm afraid I don't know him. We are not, I think, who you seem to think we are . . . might we go on to the house, do you know?" His wife murmured her agreement, and leaned against him.

Old Red Tom, who had been gaping, seemed suddenly to catch at a word. "The House! A hey, yes. Go on to The House. Good now. Mum."

They started off, more slowly than before, and Old Red Tom, having unhitched his freemartins, followed behind, from time to time calling something unintelligible. "A funny fellow," said Ezra.

"He talks so *oddly,*" Mikicho said. And Shulamith said that all she wanted was to sit down. Then—

"Oh, look," she said. *"Look!"*

"They have all come to greet us," her husband observed.

And so they had.

Nothing like this event had ever occurred in the history of the Blakeneys. But they were not found wanting. They brought the strangers into The House, gave them the softest chairseats, nearest to the burning; gave them cookingmilk and cheesemeats and tatoplants. Fatigue descended on the newcomers in a rush; they ate and drank somewhat, then they sank back, silent.

But the people of the house were not silent, far from it. Most of them who had been away had now come back, they milled around, some gulping eats, others craning and staring, most talking and talking and talking—few of them mumbletalking, now that the initial excitement had ebbed a bit. To the newcomers, eyes now opening with effort, now closing, despite, the people of the house seemed like figures from one of those halls of mirrors they had read about in social histories: the same faces, clothes . . . but, ah, indeed, not the same dimensions. Everywhere—florid complexions, bulging blue eyes, protruding bones at the forehead, hooked thin noses, flabby mouths.

Blakeneys.

Thin Blakeneys, big Blakeneys, little Blakeneys, old ones, young ones, male and female. There seemed to be one standard model from which the others had been stretched or compressed, but it was difficult to conjecture what this exact standard was.

"Starside, then," Young Big Mary said—and said again and again, clearsound. "No elses live to Blakeneyworld. Starside, Starside, a hey, Starside. Same as Captains."

Young Whitey Bill pointed with a stick of burnwood at Shulamith. "Baby grows," he said. "Rower, rower. Baby soon."

With a great effort, Robert roused himself. "Yes. She's going to have a baby very soon. We will be glad of your help."

Old Whitey Bill came for another look to, hobbling on his canestick. "We descend," he said, putting his face very close to Robert's, "we descend from the Captains. Hasn't heard of them, you? Elses not heard? Funny. Funnyfunny. We descend, look to. From the Captains. Captain Tom Blakeney. And his wives. Captain Bill Blakeney. And his wives. Brothers, they. Jinnie, Mary, Captain Tom's wives. Other Mary, Captain Bob's wife. Had another wife, but we don't remember it, us, her name. They lived, look to. Starside. You, too? Mum, you? A hey, Starside?"

Robert nodded. "When?" he asked. "When did they come from Starside? The brothers."

Night had fallen, but no lights were lit. Only the dancing flames, steadily fed, of the burning, with chunks and chunks of fat and greasy burnwood, flickered and illuminated the great room. "Ah, when," said Old Red Tom, thrusting up to the chairseat. "When we children, old Blakeneys say, a hey, five hundredyear. Longlong."

Old Little Mary said, suddenly, "They funnywalk. They funnytalk. But, oh, they funnylook, too!"

"A baby. A baby. Grows a baby, soon."

And two or three little baby Blakeneys, like shrunken versions of their elders, gobbled and giggled and asked to see the Starside baby. The big ones laughed, told them, soon.

"Five hundred . . . " Hayakawa drowsed. He snapped awake. "The four of us," he said, "were heading in our boat for the Moons of Lor. Have you—no, I see, you never have. It's a short trip, really. But something happened to us, I don't know . . . how to explain it . . . we ran into something . . . something that wasn't there. A warp? A hole? That's silly, I know, but—it was as though we felt the boat *drop*, somehow. And then, after that, our instruments didn't work and we saw we had no celestial references . . . not a star we knew. What's that phrase, 'A new Heaven and a new Earth?' We were just able to reach her. Blakeneyworld, as you call it."

Sparks snapped and flew. Someone said, "Sleepytime." And then all the Blakeneys went away and then Hayakawa slept.

It was washtime when the four woke up, and all the Blakeneys around The House, big and little, were off scrubbing themselves and their clothes. "I guess that food on the table is for us," Ezra said. "I will assume it is for us. Say grace, Robert. I'm hungry."

Afterwards they got up and looked around. The room was big and the far end so dark, even with sunshine pouring in through the open shutters, that they could hardly make out the painting on the wall. The paint was peeling, anyway, and a crack like a flash of lightning ran through it; plaster or something of the sort had been slapped onto it, but this had mostly fallen out, its only lasting effect being to deface the painting further.

"Do you suppose that the two big figures could be the Captains?" Mikicho asked, for Robert had told them what Old Whitey Bill had said.

"I would guess so. They look grim and purposeful . . . When was the persecution of the polygamists, anybody know?"

Current social histories had little to say about that period, but the four finally agreed it had been during the Refinishing Era, and that this had been about six hundred years ago. "Could this house be that old?" Shulamith asked. "Parts of it, I suppose, could be. I'll tell you what I think, *I* think that those two Captains set out like ancient patriarchs with their wives and their families and their flocks and so on, heading for somewhere where they wouldn't be persecuted. And then they hit—well, whatever it was that *we* hit. And wound up here. Like us."

Mikicho said, in a small, small voice, "And perhaps it will be another six hundred years before anyone else comes here. Oh, we're here for good and forever. That's sure."

They walked on, silent and unsure, through endless corridors and endless rooms. Some were clean enough, others were clogged with dust and rubbish, some had fallen into ruin, some were being used for barns and stables, and in one was a warm forge.

"Well," Robert said at last, "we must make the best of it. We cannot change the configurations of the universe."

Following the sounds they presently heard brought them to the washroom, slippery, warm, steamy, noisy. Once again they were surrounded by the antic Blakeney face and form in its many permutations. "Washtime, washtime!" their hosts shouted, showing them where to put their clothes, fingering the garments curiously, helping them to soap, explaining which of the pools were fed by hot springs, which by warm and cold, giving them towels, assisting Shulamith carefully.

"Your world house, you, a hey," began a be-soaped Blakeney to Ezra; "bigger than this? No."

Ezra agreed, "No."

"Your—Blakeneys? No. Mum, mum. Hey. Family? Smaller, a hey?"

"Oh, much smaller."

The Blakeney nodded. Then he offered to scrub Ezra's back if Ezra would scrub his.

The hours passed, and the days. There seemed no government, no rules, only ways and habits and practices. Those who felt so inclined, worked. Those who didn't . . . didn't. No one suggested the newcomers do anything, no one prevented from doing anything. It was perhaps a week later that Robert and Ezra invited themselves on a trip along the shore of the bay. Two healthy horses pulled a rickety wagon.

The driver's name was Young Little Bob. "Gots to fix a floorwalk," he said. "In the, a hey, in the sickroom. Needs boards. Lots at the river-water."

The sun was warm. The House now and again vanished behind trees or hills, now and again, as the road curved with the bay, came into view, looming over everything.

"We've got to find something for ourselves to *do,*" Ezra said. "These people may be all one big happy family, they better be, the only family on the whole planet all this time. But if I spend any much more time with them I think I'll become as dippy as they are."

Robert said, deprecatingly, that the Blakeneys weren't *very* dippy. "Besides," he pointed out, "sooner or later our children are going to have to intermarry with them, and—"

"Our children can intermarry with each other—"

"Our grandchildren, then. I'm afraid we haven't the ancient skills necessary to be pioneers, otherwise we might go . . . just anywhere. There is, after all, lots of room. But in a few hundred years, perhaps less, our descendents would be just as inbred and, well, odd. This way, at least, there's a chance. Hybrid vigor, and all that."

They forded the river at a point just directly opposite The House. A thin plume of smoke rose from one of its great, gaunt chimneys. The wagon turned up an overgrown path which followed up the river. "Lots of boards," said Young Little Bob. "Mum mum mum."

There were lot of boards, just as he said, weathered a silver gray. They were piled under the roof of a great open shed. At the edge of it a huge wheel turned and turned in the water. It, like the roof, was made of some dull and unrusted metal. But only the wheel turned. The other machinery was dusty.

"Millstones," Ezra said. "And saws. Lathes. And . . . all sorts of things. Why do they—Bob? Young Little Bob, I mean—why do you grind your grain by hand?"

The driver shrugged. "Have's to make flour, a hey. Bread."

Obviously, none of the machinery was in running order. It was soon obvious that no living Blakeney knew how to mend this, although (said Young Little Bob) there were those who could remember when things were otherwise: Old Big Mary, Old Little Mary, Old Whitey Bill—

Hayakawa, with a polite gesture, turned away from the recitation. "Ezra . . . I think we might be able to fix all this. Get it in running order. *That* would be something to do, wouldn't it? Something well worth doing. It would make a big difference."

Ezra said that it would make all the difference.

Shulamith's child, a girl, was born on the edge of a summer evening when the sun streaked the sky with rose, crimson, magenta, lime, and purple. "We'll name her *Hope,*" she said.

"Tongs to make tongs," Mikicho called the work of repair. She saw the restoration of the water-power as the beginning of a process which must eventually result in their being spaceborne again. Robert and Ezra did not encourage her in this. It was a long labor of work. They pored and sifted through The House from its crumbling top to its vast, vast colonnaded cellar, finding much that was of use to them, much which—though of no use—was interesting and intriguing—and much which was not only long past use but whose very usage could now be no more than a matter of conjecture. They found tools, metal which could be forged into tools, they found a whole library of books and they found the Blakeney-made press on which the books had been printed; the most recent was a treatise on the diseases of cattle, its date little more than a hundred years earlier. Decay had come quickly.

None of the Blakeneys were of much use in the matter of repairs. They were willing enough to lift and move—until the novelty wore off; then they were only in the way. The nearest to an exception was Big Fat Red Bob, the blacksmith; and, as his usual work was limited to sharpening plowshares, even he was not of much use. Robert and Ezra worked from sunrise to late afternoon. They would have worked longer, but as soon as the first chill hit the air, whatever Blakeneys were on hand began to get restless.

"Have's to get back, now, a hey. Have's to start back."

"Why?" Ezra had asked, at first. "There are no harmful animals on Blakeneyworld, are there?"

It was nothing that any of them could put into words, either clearsound or mumbletalk. They had no tradition of things that go bump in the night, but nothing could persuade them to spend a minute of the night outside the thick walls of The House. Robert and Ezra found it easier to yield, return with them. There were so many false starts, the machinery beginning to function and then breaking down, that no celebration took place to mark any particular day as the successful one. The nearest thing to it was the batch of cakes that Old Big Mary baked from the first millground flour.

"Like longlong times," she said, contentedly, licking crumbs from her toothless chops. She looked at the newcomers, made a face for their baby. A thought occurred to her, and, after a moment or two, she expressed it. "Not ours," she said. "Not ours, you. Elses. But I rather have's you here than that Runaway Little Bob back, or that Thin Jinnie . . . Yes, I rathers."

There was only one serviceable axe, so no timber was cut. But Ezra found a cove where driftwood limbs, and entire trees, was continually piling up; and the sawmill didn't lack for wood to feed it. "Makes a lot of boards, a hey," Young Little Bob said one day.

"We're building a house," Robert explained.

The wagoner looked across the bay at the mighty towers and turrets, the great gables and long walls. From the distance no breach was noticeable, although two of the chimneys could be seen to slant slightly. "Lots to build," he said. "A hey, whole roof on north end wing, mum mum, bad, it's bad, hey."

"No, we're building our own house."

He looked at them, surprised. "Wants to build another room? Easier, I say, me, clean up a no-one's room. Oh, a hey, lots of them!"

Robert let the matter drop, then, but it could not be dropped forever, so one night after eats he began to explain. "We are very grateful for your help to us," he said, "strangers as we are to you and to your ways. Perhaps it is because we *are* strange that we feel we want to have our own house to live in."

The Blakeneys were, for Blakeneys, quiet. They were also uncomprehending.

"It's the way we've been used to living. On many of the other worlds people do live, many families—and the families are all smaller than this, than yours, than the Blakeneys, I mean—many in one big house. But not on the world we lived in. There, every family has its own house, you see. We've been used to that. Now, at first, all five of us will live in the new house we're going to build near the mill. But as soon as we can we'll build a second new one. Then each family will have its own . . . "

He stopped, looked helplessly at his wife and friends. He began again, in the face of blank nonunderstanding, "We hope you'll help us. We'll trade our services for your supplies. You give us food and cloth, we'll grind your flour and saw your wood. We can help you fix your furniture, your looms, your broken floors and walls and roofs. And eventually—"

But he never got to explain about eventually. It was more than he could do to explain about the new house. No Blakeneys came to the house-raising. Robert and Ezra fixed up a capstan and hoist, block-and-tackle, managed—with the help of the two women—to get their small house built. But nobody of the Blakeneys ever came any more with grain to be ground, and when Robert and Ezra went to see them they saw that the newly-sawn planks and the lathe-turned wood still lay where it had been left.

"The food we took with us is gone," Robert said. "We have to have more. I'm sorry you feel this way. Please understand, it is not that we don't like you. It's just that we have to live our own way. In our own houses."

The silence was broken by a baby Blakeney. "What's 'houses'?," he asked.

He was shushed. "No such word, hey," he was told, too.

Robert went on, "We're going to ask you to lend us things. We want enough grain and tatoplants and such to last till we can get our own crops in, and enough milk-cattle and draft-animals until we can breed some of our own. Will you do that for us?"

Except for Young Whitey Bill, crouched by the burning, who mumbletalked with "Rower, rower, rower," they still kept silence. Popping blue eyes stared, faces were perhaps more florid than usual, large, slack mouths trembled beneath long hook-noses.

"We're wasting time," Ezra said.

Robert sighed. "Well, we have no other choice, friends . . . Blakeneys . . . We're going to have to take what we need, then. But we'll pay you back, as soon as we can, two for one. And anytime you want our help or service, you can have it. We'll be friends again. We *must* be friends. There are so many, many ways we can help one another to live better—and we are all there are, really, of humanity, on all this planet. We—"

Ezra nudged him, half-pulled him away. They took a wagon and a team of horses, a dray and a yoke of freemartins, loaded up with food. They took cows and ewes, a yearling bull and a shearling ram, a few bolts of cloth, and seed. No one prevented them, or tried to interfere, as they drove away. Robert turned and looked behind at the silent people. But then, head sunk, he watched only the bay road ahead of him, looking aside neither to the water or the woods.

"It's good that they can see us here," he said, later on that day. "It's bound to make them think, and, sooner or later, they'll come around."

They came sooner than he thought.

"I'm so glad to see you, friends!" Robert came running out to greet them. They seized and bound him with unaccustomed hands. Then, paying no attention to his anguished cries of "Why? Why?" they rushed into the new house and dragged out Shulamith and Mikicho and the baby. They drove the animals from their stalls, but took nothing else. The stove was now the major object of interest. First they knocked it over, then they scattered the burning coals all about, then they lit brands of burnwood and scrambled around with them. In a short while the building was all afire.

The Blakeneys seemed possessed. Faces red, eyes almost popping from their heads, they mumble-shouted and raved. When Ezra who had been working in the shed came running, fighting, they bore him to the ground and beat him with pieces of wood. He did not get up when they were through; it seemed apparent that he never would. Mikicho began a long and endless scream.

Robert stopped struggling for a moment. Caught offguard, his captors loosened their hold—he broke away from their hands and his bonds, and, crying, "The tools! The tools!", dashed into the burning fire. The blazing roof fell in upon him with a great crash. No sound came from him, nor from Shulamith, who fainted. The baby began a thin, reedy wail.

Working as quickly as they could, in their frenzy, the Blakeneys added to the lumber and waste and scraps around the machinery in the shed, soon had it all ablaze.

The fire could be seen all the way back.

"Wasn't right, wasn't right," Young Red Bob said, over and over again.

"A bad thing," Old Little Mary agreed.

Young Big Mary carried the baby. Shulamith and Mikicho were led, dragging, along. "Little baby, a hey, a hey," she crooned.

Old Whitey Bill was dubious. "Be bad blood," he said. "The elses women grow more babies. A mum mum," he mused. "Teach them better. Not to funnywalk, such." He nodded and mumbled, peered out of the window-look, his loose mouth widening with satisfaction. "Wasn't right," he said. "Wasn't *right.* Another house. Can't be another *house,* a second, a third. Hey, a hey! Never was elses but The House. Never be again. No."

He looked around, his gaze encompassing the cracked walls, sinking floors, sagging roof. A faint smell of smoke was in the air. "The House," he said, contentedly. "The House."

(1965)

CLIFFORD D. SIMAK

Over the River and Through the Woods

I

The two children came trudging down the lane in apple-canning time, when the first goldenrods were blooming and the wild asters large in bud. They looked, when she first saw them, out the kitchen window, like children who were coming home from school, for each of them was carrying a bag in which might have been their books. Like Charles and James, she thought, like Alice and Maggie—but the time when those four had trudged the lane on their daily trips to school was in the distant past. Now they had children of their own who made their way to school.

She turned back to the stove to stir the cooking apples, for which the wide-mouthed jars stood waiting on the table, then once more looked out the kitchen window. The two of them were closer now and she could see that the boy was the older of the two—ten, perhaps, and the girl no more than eight.

They might be going past, she thought, although that did not seem too likely, for the lane led to this farm and to nowhere else.

They turned off the lane before they reached the barn and came sturdily trudging up the path that led to the house. There was no hesitation in them; they knew where they were going.

She stepped to the screen door of the kitchen as they came onto the porch and they stopped before the door and stood looking up at her.

The boy said, "You are our grandma. Papa said we were to say at once that you were our grandma."

"But that's not . . . " she said, and stopped. She had been about to say it was impossible, that she was not their grandma. And, looking down into the sober, childish faces, she was glad that she had not said the words.

"I am Ellen," said the girl in a piping voice.

"Why, that is strange," the woman said. "That is my name, too."

The boy said, "My name is Paul."

She pushed open the door for them and they came in, standing silently in the kitchen, looking all about them as if they'd never seen a kitchen.

"It's just like Papa said," said Ellen. "There's the stove and the churn and . . . "

The boy interrupted her. "Our name is Forbes," he said.

This time the woman couldn't stop herself. "Why, that's impossible," she said. "That is our name, too."

The boy nodded solemnly. "Yes, we knew it was."

"Perhaps," the woman said, "you'd like some milk and cookies."

"Cookies!" Ellen squealed, delighted.

"We don't want to be any trouble," said the boy. "Papa said we were to be no trouble."

"He said we should be good," piped Ellen.

"I am sure you will be," said the woman, "and you are no trouble."

In a little while, she thought, she'd get it straightened out.

She went to the stove and set the kettle with the cooking apples to one side, where they would simmer slowly.

"Sit down at the table," she said. "I'll get the milk and cookies."

She glanced at the clock, ticking on the shelf. Four o'clock, almost. In just a little while the men would come in from the fields. Jackson Forbes would know what to do about this; he had always known.

They climbed up on two chairs and sat there solemnly, staring all about them, at the ticking clock, at the wood stove with the fire glow showing through its draft, at the wood piled in the wood box, at the butter churn standing in the corner.

They set their bags on the floor beside them, and they were strange bags, she noticed. They were made of heavy cloth or canvas, but there were no drawstrings or no straps to fasten them. But they were closed, she saw, despite no straps or strings.

"Do you have some stamps?" asked Ellen.

"Stamps?" asked Mrs. Forbes.

"You must pay no attention to her," said Paul. "She should not have asked you. She asks everyone and Mama told her not to."

"But stamps?"

"She collects them. She goes around snitching letters that other people have. For the stamps on them, you know."

"Well, now," said Mrs. Forbes, "there may be some old letters. We'll look for them later on."

She went into the pantry and got the earthen jug of milk and filled a plate with cookies from the jar. When she came back they were sitting there sedately, waiting for the cookies.

"We are here just for a little while," said Paul. "Just a short vacation. Then our folks will come and get us and take us back again."

Ellen nodded her head vigorously. "That's what they told us when we went. When I was afraid to go."

"You were afraid to go?"

"Yes. It was all so strange."

"There was so little time," said Paul. "Almost none at all. We had to leave so fast."

"And where are you from?" asked Mrs. Forbes.

"Why," said the boy, "just a little ways from here. We walked just a little ways and of course we had the map. Papa gave it to us and he went over it carefully with us. . . . "

"You're sure your name is Forbes?"

Ellen bobbed her head. "Of course it is," she said.

"Strange," said Mrs. Forbes. And it was more than strange, for there were no other Forbeses in the neighborhood except her children and her grandchildren and these two, no matter what they said, were strangers.

They were busy with the milk and cookies and she went back to the stove and set the kettle with the apples back on the front again, stirring the cooking fruit with a wooden spoon.

"Where is Grandpa?" Ellen asked.

"Grandpa's in the field. He'll be coming in soon. Are you finished with your cookies?"

"All finished," said the girl.

"Then we'll have to set the table and get the supper cooking. Perhaps you'd like to help me."

Ellen hopped down off the chair. "I'll help," she said.

"And I," said Paul, "will carry in some wood. Papa said I should be helpful. He said I could carry in the wood and feed the chickens and hunt the eggs and . . . "

"Paul," said Mrs. Forbes, "it might help if you'd tell me what your father does."

"Papa," said the boy, "is a temporal engineer."

II

The two hired men sat at the kitchen table with the checker board between them. The two older people were in the living room.

"You never saw the likes of it," said Mrs. Forbes. "There was this piece of metal and you pulled it and it ran along another metal strip and the bag came open. And you pulled it the other way and the bag was closed."

"Something new," said Jackson Forbes. "There may be many new things we haven't heard about, back here in the sticks. There are inventors turning out all sorts of things."

"And the boy," she said, "has the same thing on his trousers. I picked them up from where he threw them on the floor when he went to bed and I folded them and put them on the chair. And I saw this strip of metal, the edges jagged-like. And the clothes they wear. That boy's trousers are cut off above his knees and the dress that the girl was wearing was so short. . . ."

"They talked of plains," mused Jaclson Forbes, "but not the plains we know. Something that is used, apparently for folks to travel in. And rockets—as if there were rockets every day and not just on the Fourth."

"We couldn't question them, of course," said Mrs. Forbes. "There was something about them, something that I sensed."

Her husband nodded. "They were frightened, too."

"You are frightened, Jackson?"

"I don't know," he said, "but there are no other Forbeses. Not close, that is. Charlie is the closest, and he's five miles away. And they said they walked just a little piece."

"What are you going to do?" she asked. "What can we do?"

"I don't rightly know," he said. "Drive in to the county seat and talk with the sheriff, maybe. These children must be lost. There must be someone looking for them."

"But they don't act as if they're lost," she told him. "They knew they were coming here. They knew we would be here. They told me I was their grandma and they asked after you and they called you Grandpa. And they are so sure. They don't act as if we're strangers. They've been told about us. They said they'd stay just a little while and that's the way they act. As if they'd just come for a visit."

"I think," said Jackson Forbes, "that I'll hitch up Nellie after breakfast and drive around the neighborhood and ask some questions. Maybe there'll be someone who can tell me something."

"The boy said his father was a temporal engineer. That just don't make sense. Temporal means the worldly power and authority and . . ."

"It might be some joke," her husband said. "Something that the father said in jest and the son picked up as truth."

"I think," said Mrs. Forbes, "I'll go upstairs and see if they're asleep. I left their lamps turned low. They are so little and the house is strange to them. If they are asleep, I'll blow out the lamps."

Jackson Forbes grunted his approval. "Dangerous," he said, "to keep lights burning of the night. Too much chance of fire."

III

The boy was asleep, flat upon his back—the deep and healthy sleep of youngsters. He had thrown his clothes upon the floor when he had undressed to go to bed, but now they were folded neatly on the chair, where she had placed them when she had gone into the room to say good night.

The bag stood beside the chair and it was open, the two rows of jagged metal gleaming dully in the dim glow of the lamp. Within its shadowed interior lay the dark forms of jumbled possessions, disorderly and helter-skelter, no way for a bag to be.

She stooped and picked up the bag and set it on the chair and reached for the little metal tab to close it. At least, she told herself, it should be closed and not left standing open. She grasped the tab and slid it smoothly along the metal tracks and then stopped, its course obstructed by an object that stuck out.

She saw it was a book and reached down to rearrange it so she could close the bag. And as she did so, she saw the title in its faint gold lettering across the leather backstrap—Holy Bible.

With her fingers grasping the book, she hesitated for a moment, then slowly drew it out. It was bound in an expensive black leather that was dulled with age. The edges were cracked and split and the leather worn from long usage. The gold edging of the leaves was faded.

Hesitantly, she opened it, and there, upon the fly leaf, in old and faded ink, was the inscription:

To Sister Ellen from Amelia
Oct. 30, 1896
Many Happy Returns of the Day

She felt her knees grow weak and she let herself carefully to the floor and there, crouched beside the chair, read the fly leaf once again.

Oct. 30, 1896—that was her birthday, certainly, but it had not come, as yet, for this was only the beginning of September, 1896.

And the Bible—how old was this Bible she held within her hands? A hundred years, perhaps more than a hundred years.

A Bible, she thought—exactly the kind of gift Amelia would give her. But a gift that had not been given yet, one that could not be given, for that day upon the fly leaf was a month into the future.

It couldn't be, of course. It was some kind of stupid joke. Or some mistake. Or a coincidence, perhaps. Somewhere else someone else was named Ellen and also had a sister who was named Amelia and the date was a mistake—someone had written the wrong year. It would be an easy thing to do.

But she was not convinced. They had said the name was Forbes and they had come straight here and Paul had spoken of a map so they could find the way.

Perhaps there were other things inside the bag. She looked at it and shook her head. She shouldn't pry. It had been wrong to take the Bible out.

On Oct. 30 she would be fifty-nine—an old farm-wife with married sons and daughters and grandchildren who came to visit her on weekends and on holidays. And a sister Amelia who, in this year of 1896, would give her a Bible as a birthday gift.

Her hands shook as she lifted the Bible and put it back into the bag. She'd talk to Jackson when she went downstairs. He might have some thought upon the matter and he'd know what to do.

She tucked the book back into the bag and pulled the tab and the bag was closed. She set it on the floor again and looked at the boy upon the bed. He still was fast asleep, so she blew out the light.

In the adjoining room little Ellen slept, baby-like, upon her stomach. The low flame of the turned-down lamp flickered gustily in the breeze that came through an open window.

Ellen's bag was closed and stood squared against the chair with a sense of neatness. The woman looked at it and hesitated for a moment, then moved on around the bed to where the lamp stood on a bedside table.

The children were asleep and everything was well and she'd blow out the light and go downstairs and talk with Jackson, and perhaps there'd be no need for him to hitch up Nellie in the morning and drive around to ask questions of the neighbors.

As she leaned to blow out the lamp, she saw the envelope upon the table, with the two large stamps of many colors affixed to the upper right-hand corner.

Such pretty stamps, she thought—I never saw so pretty. She leaned closer to take a look at them and saw the country name upon them. Israel. But there was no such actual place as Israel. It was a Bible name, but there was no country. And if there were no country, how could there be stamps?

She picked up the envelope and studied the stamp, making sure that she had seen right. Such a pretty stamp!

She collects them, Paul had said. She's always snitching letters that belong to other people.

The envelope bore a postmark, and presumably a date, but it was blurred and distorted by a hasty, sloppy cancellation and she could not make it out.

The edge of a letter sheet stuck a quarter-inch out of the ragged edges where the envelope had been torn open, and she pulled it out, gasping in her haste to see it while an icy fist of fear was clutching at her heart.

It was, she saw, only the end of a letter, the last page of a letter, and it was in type rather than in longhand—type like one saw in a newspaper or a book.

Maybe one of those new-fangled things they had in big city offices, she thought, the ones she'd read about. Typewriters—was that what they were called?

> do not believe, *the one page read,* your plan is feasible. There is no time. The aliens are closing in and they will not give us time.
>
> And there is the further consideration of the ethics of it, even if it could be done. We can not, in all consciousness, scurry back into the past and visit our problems upon the people of a century ago. Think of the problems it would create for them, the economic confusion and the psychological effect.
>
> If you feel that you must, at least, send the children back, think a moment of the wrench it will give those two good souls when they realize the truth. Theirs is a smug and solid world—sure and safe and sound. The concepts of this mad century would destroy all they have, all that they believe in.
>
> But I suppose I cannot presume to counsel you. I have done what you asked. I have written you all I know of our old ancestors back on that Wisconsin farm. As historian of the family, I am sure my facts are right. Use them as you see fit and God have mercy on us all.
>
> Your loving brother,
>
> Jackson
>
> P.S. A suggestion. If you do send the children back, you might send along with them a generous supply of the new cancer-inhibitor drug. Great-great-grandmother Forbes died in 1904 of a condition that I suspect was cancer. Given those pills, she might survive another ten or twenty years. And what, I ask you, brother, would that mean to this tangled future? I don't pretend to know. It might save us. It might kill us quicker. It might have no effect at all. I leave the puzzle to you.
>
> If I can finish up work here and get away, I'll be with you at the end.

Mechanically she slid the letter back into the envelope and laid it upon the table beside the flaring lamp.

Slowly she moved to the window that looked out on the empty lane.

They will come and get us, Paul had said. But would they ever come? Could they ever come?

She found herself wishing they would come. Those poor people, those poor frightened children caught so far in time.

Blood of my blood, she thought, flesh of my flesh, so many years away.

But still her flesh and blood, no matter how removed. Not only these two beneath this roof tonight, but all those others who had not come to her.

The letter had said 1904 and cancer and that was eight years away—she'd be an old, old woman then. And the signature had been Jackson—an old family name, she wondered, carried on and on, a long chain of people who bore the name of Jackson Forbes?

She was stiff and numb, she knew. Later she'd be frightened. Later she would wish she had not read the letter, did not know.

But now she must go back downstairs and tell Jackson the best way that she could.

She moved across the room and blew out the light and went out into the hallway.

A voice came from the open door beyond.

"Grandma, is that you?"

"Yes, Paul," she answered. "What can I do for you?"

In the doorway she saw him crouched beside the chair, in the shaft of moonlight pouring through the window, fumbling at the bag.

"I forgot," he said. "There was something papa said I was to give you right away."

(1965)

JAMES BLISH

How Beautiful with Banners

1

Feeling as naked as a peppermint soldier in her transparent film wrap, Dr. Ulla Hillstrøm watched a flying cloak swirl away toward the black horizon with a certain consequent irony. Although nearly transparent itself in the distant dim arc-light flame that was Titan's sun, the fluttering creature looked warmer than what she was wearing, for all that reason said it was at the same minus 316° F. as the thin methane it flew in. Despite the virus space-bubble's warranted and eerie efficiency, she found its vigilance—itself probably as nearly alive as the flying cloak was—rather difficult to believe in, let alone to trust.

The machine—as Ulla much preferred to think of it—was inarguably an improvement on the old-fashioned pressure suit. Made (or more accurately, cultured) of a single colossal protein molecule, the vanishingly thin sheet of life-stuff processed gases, maintained pressure, monitored radiation through almost the whole of the electromagnetic spectrum, and above all did not get in the way. Also, it could not be cut, punctured or indeed sustain any damage short of total destruction; macroscopically it was a single, primary unit, with all the physical integrity of a crystal of salt or steel.

If it did not actually think, Ulla was grateful; often it almost seemed to, which was sufficient. Its primary drawback for her was that much of the time it did not really seem to be there.

Still, it seemed to be functioning; otherwise Ulla would in fact have been as solid as a stick of candy, toppled forever across the confectionery whiteness that frosted the knife-edged stones of this cruel moon, layer upon layer. Outside—only a perilous few inches from the lightly clothed warmth of her skin—the brief gust the cloak had been soaring on died, leaving behind a silence so cataleptic that she could hear the snow creaking in a mockery of motion. Impossible though it was to comprehend, it was getting still colder out there. Titan was swinging out across Saturn's orbit toward eclipse, and the apparently fixed sun was secretly going down, its descent sensed by the snows no matter what her Earthly sight, accustomed to the nervousness of living skies, tried to tell her. In another two Earth days it would be gone, for an eternal week.

At the thought, Ulla turned to look back the way she had come that morning. The virus bubble flowed smoothly with the motion and the stars became brighter as it compensated for the fact that the sun was now at her back. She still could not see the base camp, of course. She had strayed too far for that, and in any event, except for a few wiry palps, it was wholly underground.

Now there was no sound but the creaking of the methane snow, and nothing to see but a blunt, faint spearhead of hazy light, deceptively like an Earthly aurora or the corona of the sun, pushing its way from below the edge of the cold into the indifferent company of the stars. Saturn's rings were rising, very slightly aware in the dark blue air, like the banners of a spectral army. The idiot face of the gas giant planet itself, faintly striped with meaningless storms, would be glaring down at her before she could get home if she did not get herself in motion soon. Obscurely disturbed, Dr. Hillstrøm faced front and began to unload her sled.

The touch and clink of the sampling gear cheered her, a little, even in this ultimate loneliness. She was efficient—many years, and a good many suppressed impulses, had seen to that; it was too late for temblors, especially so far out from the sun that had warmed her Stockholm streets and her silly friendships. All those null adventures were gone now like a sickness. The phantom embrace of the virus suit was perhaps less satisfying—only perhaps—but it was much more reliable. Much more reliable; she could depend on that.

Then, as she bent to thrust the spike of a thermocouple into the wedding-cake soil, the second flying cloak (or was it the same one?) hit her in the small of the back and tumbled her into nightmare.

2

With the sudden darkness there came a profound, ambiguous emotional blow—ambiguous, yet with something shockingly familiar about it. Instantly exhausted, she felt herself go flaccid and unstrung, and her mind, adrift in nowhere, blurred and spun downward too into trance.

The long fall slowed just short of unconsciousness, lodged precariously upon a shelf of dream, a mental buttress founded four years in the past—a long distance, when one recalls that in a four-dimensional plenum every second of time is 186,000 miles of space. The memory was curiously inconsequential to have arrested her, let alone supported her: not of her home, of her few triumphs or even of her aborted marriage, but of a sordid little encounter with a reporter that she had talked herself into at the Madrid genetics conference, when she herself was already an associate professor, a Swedish government delegate, a 25-year-old divorcée, and altogether a woman who should have known better.

But better than what? The life of science even in those days had been almost by definition the life of the eternal campus exile. There was so much to learn—or, at least, to show competence in—that people who wanted to be involved in the ordinary, vivid concerns of human beings could not stay with it long, indeed often could not even be recruited. They turned aside from the prospect with a shudder or even a snort of scorn. To prepare for the sciences had become a career in indefinitely protracted adolescence, from which one awakened fitfully to find one's adult self in the body of a stranger. It had given her no pride, no self-love, no defenses of any sort; only a queer kind of virgin numbness, highly dependent upon familiar surroundings and unvalued habits, and easily breached by any normally confident siege in print, in person, anywhere—and remaining just as numb as before when the spasm of fashion, politics or romanticism had swept by and left her stranded, too easy a recruit to have been allowed into the center of things or even considered for it.

Curious, most curious that in her present remote terror she should find even a moment's rest upon so wobbly a pivot. The Madrid incident had not been important; she had been through with it almost at once. Of course, as she had often told herself, she had never been promiscuous, and had often described the affair, defiantly, as that single (or at worst, second) test of the joys of impulse which any woman is entitled to have in her history. Nor had it really been that joyous. She could not now recall the boy's face, and remembered how he had felt primarily because he had been in so casual and contemptuous a hurry.

But now that she came to dream of it, she saw with a bloodless, lightless eye that all her life, in this way and in that, she had been repeatedly seduced by the inconsequential. She had nothing else to remember even in this hour of her presumptive death. Acts have consequences, a thought told her, but not ours; we have done, but never felt. We are no more alone on Titan, you and I, than we have ever been. *Basta, per carita!*—so much for Ulla.

Awakening in the same darkness as before, Ulla felt the virus bubble snuggling closer to her blind skin, and recognized the shock that had so regressed her—a shock of recognition, but recognition of something she had never felt herself. Alone in a Titanic snowfield, she had eavesdropped on an . . .

No. Not possible. Sniffling, and still blind, she pushed the cozy bubble away from her breasts and tried to stand up. Light flushed briefly around her, as though the bubble had cleared just above her forehead and then clouded again. She was still alive, but everything else was utterly problematical. What had happened to her? She simply did not know.

Therefore, she thought, begin with ignorance. No one begins anywhere else . . . but I did not know even that, once upon a time.

Hence:

3

Though the virus bubble ordinarily regulated itself, there was a control box on her hip—actually an ultra-short-range microwave transmitter—by which it could be modulated against more special environments than the bubble itself could cope with alone. She had never had to use it before, but she tried it now.

The fogged bubble cleared patchily, but it would not stay cleared. Crazy moirés and herringbone patterns swept over it, changing direction repeatedly, and, outside, the snowy landscape kept changing color like a delirium. She found, however, that by continuously working the frequency knob on her box—at random, for the responses seemed to bear no relation to the Braille calibrations on the dial—she could maintain outside vision of a sort in pulses of two or three seconds each.

This was enough to show her, finally, what had happened. There was a flying cloak around her. This in itself was unprecedented; the cloaks had never attacked a man before, or indeed paid any of them the least attention during their brief previous forays. On the other hand, this was the first time anyone had ventured more than five or ten minutes outdoors in a virus suit.

It occurred to her suddenly that insofar as anything was known about the nature of the cloaks, they were in some respect much like the bubbles. It was almost as though the one were a wild species of the other.

It was an alarming notion and possibly only a metaphor, containing as little truth as most poetry. Annoyingly, she found herself wondering if, once she got out of this mess, the men at the base camp would take to referring to it as "the cloak and suit business."

The snowfield began to turn brighter; Saturn was rising. For a moment the drifts were a pale straw color, the normal hue of Saturn light through an atmosphere; then it turned a raving Kelly green. Muttering, Ulla twisted the potentiometer dial, and was rewarded with a brief flash of normal illumination which was promptly overridden by a torrent of crimson lake, as though she were seeing everything through a series of photographic color separations.

Since she could not help this, she clenched her teeth and ignored it. It was much more important to find out what the flying cloak had done to her bubble, if she were to have any hope of shucking the thing.

There was no clear separation between the bubble and the Titanian creature. They seemed to have blended into a melange which was neither one nor the other, but a sort of coarse burlesque of both. Yet the total surface area of the integument about her did not seem to be any greater—only more ill-fitting, less responsive to her own needs. Not much less; after all, she was still alive, and any really gross insensitivity to the demands and cues of her body would have been instantly fatal. But there was no way to guess how long the bubble would stay even that obedient. At the moment the wild thing that had enslaved it was perhaps dangerous to the wearer only if she panicked, but the change might well be progressive, pointed ultimately toward some saturnine equivalent of the shirt of Nessus.

And that might be happening very rapidly. She might not be allowed the time to think her way out of this fix by herself. Little though she wanted any help from the men at the base camp, and useless though she was sure they would prove, she had damn well better ask for it now, just in case.

But the bubble was not allowing any radio transmission through its roiling unicell wall today. The earphone was dead; not even the hiss of the stars came through it—only an occasional pop of noise that was born of entropy loss in the circuits themselves.

She was cut off. *Nun denn, allein!*

With the thought, the bubble cloak shifted again around her. A sudden pressure at her lower abdomen made her stumble forward over the crisp snow, four or five steps. Then it was motionless once more, except within itself.

That it should be able to do this was not surprising, for the cloaks had to be able to flex voluntarily at least a little to catch the thermals they rode, and the bubble had to be able to vary its dimensions and surface tension over a wide range to withstand pressure changes, outside and in, and do it automatically. No, of course the combination would be able to move by itself. What was disquieting was that it should want to.

Another stir of movement in the middle distance caught her eye: a free cloak, seemingly riding an updraft over a fixed point. For a moment she wondered what on that ground could be warm enough to produce so localized a thermal. Then, abruptly, she realized that she was shaking with hatred, and fought furiously to drive the spasm down, her fingernails slicing into her naked palms.

A raster of jagged black lines, like a television interference pattern, broke across her view and brought her attention fully back to the minutely solipsistic confines of her dilemma. The wave of emotion, nevertheless, would not quite go away, and she had a vague but persistent impression that it was being imposed from outside, at least in part—a cold passion she was interpreting as fury because its real nature, whatever it was, had no necessary relevance to her own imprisoned soul. For all that it was her own life and no other that was in peril, she felt guilty, as though she were eavesdropping, and as angry with herself as with what she was overhearing, yet burning as helplessly as the forbidden lamp in the bedchamber of Psyche and Eros.

Another metaphor—but was it after all so far-fetched? She was a mortal present at the mating of inhuman essences; mountainously far from home; borne here like invisible lovers upon the arms of the wind; empalaced by a whole virgin-white world, over which flew the banners of a high god and a father of gods and, equally appropriately, Venus was very far away from whatever love was being celebrated here.

What ancient and coincidental nonsense! Next she would be thinking herself degraded at the foot of some cross.

Yet the impression, of an eerie tempest going on just slightly outside any possibility of understanding what it was, would not pass away. Still worse, it seemed to mean something, to be important, to mock her with subtle clues to matters of great moment, of which her own present trap was only the first and not necessarily the most significant.

And suppose that all these impressions were in fact not extraneous or irrelevant, but did have some import—not just as an abstract puzzle, but to that morsel of displaced life that was Ulla Hillstrøm? No matter how frozen her present world, she could not escape the fact that from the moment the cloak had captured her she had been simultaneously gripped by a Sabbat of specifically erotic memories, images, notions, analogies, myths, symbols and frank physical sensations, all the more obtrusive because they were both inappropriate and disconnected. It might well have to be faced that a season of love can fall due in the heaviest weather—and never mind what terrors flow in with it or what deep damnations. At the very least, it was possible that somewhere in all this was the clue that would help her to divorce herself at last even from this violent embrace.

But the concept was preposterous enough to defer consideration of it if there were any other avenues open, and at least one seemed to be: the source of the thermal. The virus bubble, like many of the Terrestrial microorganisms to which it was analogous, could survive temperatures well above boiling, but it seemed reasonable to assume that the flying cloaks, evolved on a world where even words congealed, might be sensitive to a relatively slight amount of heat.

Now, could she move of her own volition inside this shroud? She tried a step. The sensation was tacky, as though she were plowing in thin honey, but it did not impede her except for a slight imposed clumsiness which experience ought to obviate. She was able to mount the sled with no trouble.

The cogs bit into the snow with a dry, almost inaudible squeaking and the sled inched forward. Ulla held it to as slow a crawl as possible, because of her interrupted vision.

The free cloak was still in sight, approximately where it had been before, insofar as she could judge against this featureless snowscape; which was fortunate, since it might well be her only flag for the source of the thermal, whatever it was.

A peculiar fluttering in her surroundings—a whisper of sound, of motion, of flickering in the light—distracted her. It was as though her compound sheath were trembling slightly. The impression grew slowly more pronounced as the sled continued to lurch forward. As usual there seemed to be nothing she could do about it, except, possibly, to retreat; but she could not do that either, now; she was committed. Outside, she began to hear the soft soughing of a steady wind.

The cause of the thermal, when she finally reached it, was almost bathetic—a pool of liquid. Placid and deep blue, it lay inside a fissure in a low, heart-shaped hummock, rimmed with feathery snow. It looked like nothing more or less than a spring, though she did not for a moment suppose that the liquid could be water. She could not see the bottom of it; evidently it was welling up from a fair depth. The spring analogy was probably completely false; the existence of anything in a liquid state on this world had to be thought of as a form of vulcanism. Certainly the column of heat rising from it was considerable; despite the thinness of the air, the wind here nearly howled. The free cloak floated up and down, about a hundred feet above her, like the last leaf of a long, cruel autumn. Nearer home, the bubble cloak shook with something comically like subdued fury.

Now, what to do? Should she push boldly into that cleft, hoping that the alien part of the bubble cloak would be unable to bear the heat? Close up, that course now seemed foolish, as long as she was ignorant of the real nature of the magma down there. And besides, any effective immersion would probably have to surround at least half of the total surface area of the bubble, which was not practicable—the well was not big enough to accommodate it, even supposing that the compromised virus suit did not fight back, as in the pure state it had been obligated to do. On the whole she was reluctantly glad that the experiment was impossible, for the mere notion of risking a new immolation in that problematical well horrified her.

Yet the time left for decision was obviously now very short, even supposing—as she had no right to do—that the environment-maintaining functions of the suit were still in perfect order. The quivering of the bubble was close to being explosive, and even were it to remain intact, it might shut her off from the outside world at any second.

The free cloak dipped lower, as if in curiosity. That only made the trembling worse. She wondered why.

Was it possible—was it possible that the thing embracing her companion was jealous?

4

There was no time left to examine the notion, no time even to sneer at it. Act—act! Forcing her way off the sled, she stumbled to the well and looked frantically for some way of stopping it up. If she could shut off the thermal, bring the free cloak still closer—but how?

Throw rocks. But were there any? Yes, there, there were two, not very big, but at least she could move them. She bent stiffly and tumbled them into the crater.

The liquid froze around them with soundless speed. In seconds, the snow rimming the pool had drawn completely over it, like lips closing, leaving behind only a faint dimpled streak of shadow on a white ground.

The wind moaned and died, and the free cloak, its hems outspread to the uttermost, sank down as if to wrap her in still another deadly swath. Shadow spread around her; the falling cloak, its color deepening, blotted Saturn from the sky, and then was sprawling over the beautiful banners of the rings—

The virus bubble convulsed and turned black, throwing her to the frozen ground beside the hummock like a bead doll. A blast of wind squalled over her.

Terrified, she tried to curl into a ball. The suit puffed up around her.

Then at last, with a searing invisible wrench at its contained kernel of space-time which burned out the control box instantly, the single creature that was the bubble cloak tore itself free of Ulla and rose to join its incomplete fellow.

In the single second before she froze forever into the livid backdrop of Titan, she failed even to find time to regret what she had never felt, for she had never known it, and only died as she had lived, an artifact of successful calculation. She never saw the cloaks go flapping away downwind—nor could it ever have occurred to her that she had brought anything new to Titan, thus beginning that long evolution the end of which, sixty millions of years away, no human being would see.

No, her last thought was for the virus bubble, and it was only two words long:

You philanderer—

Almost on the horizon, the two cloaks, the two Titanians, flailed and tore at each other, becoming smaller and smaller with distance. Bits and pieces of them flaked off and fell down the sky like ragged tears. Ungainly though the cloaks normally were, they courted even more clumsily.

Beside Ulla, the well was gone; it might never have existed. Overhead, the banners of the rings flew changelessly, as though they too had seen nothing—or perhaps, as though in the last six billion years they had seen everything, siftings upon siftings in oblivion, until nothing remained but the banners of their own mirrored beauty.

(1966)

R. A. LAFFERTY

Nine Hundred Grandmothers

Ceran Swicegood was a promising young Special Aspects Man. But, like all Special Aspects, he had one irritating habit. He was forever asking the question: How Did It All Begin?

They all had tough names except Ceran. Manbreaker Crag, Heave Huckle, Blast Berg, George Blood, Move Manion (when Move says "Move," you move), Trouble Trent. They were supposed to be tough, and they had taken tough names at the naming. Only Ceran kept his own—to the disgust of his commander, Manbreaker.

"Nobody can be a hero with a name like Ceran Swicegood!" Manbreaker would thunder. "Why don't you take Storm Shannon? That's good. Or Gutboy Barrelhouse or Slash Slagle or Nevel Knife? You barely glanced at the suggested list."

"I'll keep my own," Ceran always said, and that is where he made his mistake. A new name will sometimes bring out a new personality. It had done so for George Blood. Though the hair on George's chest was a graft job, yet that and his new name had turned him from a boy into a man. Had Ceran assumed the heroic name of Gutboy Barrelhouse he might have been capable of rousing endeavors and man-sized angers rather than his tittering indecisions and flouncy furies.

They were down on the big asteroid Proavitus—a sphere that almost tinkled with the potential profit that might be shaken out of it. And the tough men of the Expedition knew their business. They signed big contracts on the native velvet-like bark scrolls and on their own parallel tapes. They impressed, inveigled and somewhat cowed the slight people of Proavitus. Here was a solid two-way market, enough to make them slaver. And there was a whole world of oddities that could lend themselves to the luxury trade.

"Everybody's hit it big but you," Manbreaker crackled in kindly thunder to Ceran after three days there. "But even Special Aspects is supposed to pay its way. Our charter compels us to carry one of your sort to give a cultural twist to the thing, but it needn't be restricted to that.

What we go out for every time, Ceran, is to cut a big fat hog in the rump—we make no secret of that. But if the hog's tail can be shown to have a cultural twist to it, that will solve a requirement. And if that twist in the tail can turn us a profit, then we become mighty happy about the whole thing. Have you been able to find out anything about the living dolls, for instance? They might have both a cultural aspect and a market value."

"The living dolls seem a part of something much deeper," Ceran said. "There's a whole complex of things to be unraveled. The key may be the statement of the Proavitoi that they do not die."

"I think they die pretty young, Ceran. All those out and about are young, and those I have met who do not leave their houses are only middling old."

"Then where are their cemeteries?"

"Likely they cremate the old folks when they die."

"Where are the crematories?"

"They might just toss the ashes out or vaporize the entire remains. Probably they have no reverence for ancestors."

"Other evidence shows their entire culture to be based on an exaggerated reverence for ancestors."

"You find out, Ceran. You're Special Aspects Man."

Ceran talked to Nokoma, his Proavitoi counterpart as translator. Both were expert, and they could meet each other halfway in talk. Nokoma was likely feminine. There was a certain softness about both the sexes of the Proavitoi, but the men of the Expedition believed that they had them straight now.

"Do you mind if I ask some straight questions?" Ceran greeted her today.

"Sure is not. How else I learn the talk well but by talking?"

"Some of the Proavitoi say that they do not die, Nokoma. Is this true?"

"How is not be true? If they die, they not be here to say they do not die. Oh, I joke, I joke. No, we do not die. It is a foolish alien custom which we see no reason to imitate. On Proavitus, only the low creatures die."

"None of you does?"

"Why, no. Why should one want to be an exception in this?"

"But what do you do when you get very old?"

"We do less and less then. We come to a deficiency of energy. Is it not the same with you?"

"Of course. But where do you go when you become exceedingly old?"

"Nowhere. We stay at home then. Travel is for the young and those of the active years."

"Let's try it from the other end," Ceran said. "Where are your father and mother, Nokoma?"

"Out and about. They aren't really old."

"And your grandfathers and grandmothers?"

"A few of them still get out. The older ones stay home."

"Let's try it this way. How many grandmothers do you have, Nokoma?"

"I think I have nine hundred grandmothers in my house. Oh, I know that isn't many, but we are the young branch of a family. some of our clan have very great numbers of ancestors in their houses."

"And all these ancestors are alive?"

"What else? Who would keep things not alive? How would such be ancestors?"

Ceran began to hop around in his excitement.

"Could I see them?" he twittered.

"It might not be wise for you to see the older of them," Nokoma cautioned. "It could be an unsettling thing for strangers, and we guard it. A few tens of them you can see, of course."

Then it came to Ceran that he might be onto what he had looked for all his life. He went into a panic of expectation.

"Nokoma, it would be finding the key!" he fluted. "If none of you has ever died, then your entire race would still be alive!"

"Sure. Is like you count fruit. You take none away, you still have them all."

"But if the first of them are still alive, then they might know their origin! They would know how it began! Do they? Do you?"

"Oh, not I. I am too young for the Ritual."

"But who knows? Doesn't someone know?"

"Oh, yes, All the old ones know how it began."

"How old? How many generations back from you till they know?"

"Ten, no more. When I have ten generations of children, then I will also go to the Ritual."

"The Ritual, what is it?"

"Once a year, the old people go to the very old people. They wake them up and ask them how it all began. The very old people tell them the beginning. It is a high time. Oh, how they hottle and laugh! Then the very old people go back to sleep for another year. So it is passed down to the generations. That is the Ritual."

The Proavitoi were not humanoid. Still less were they "monkey-faces," though that name was now set in the explorers' lingo. They were upright and robed and swathed, and were assumed to be two-legged under their garments. Though, as Manbreaker said, "They might go on wheels, for all we know."

They had remarkable flowing hands that might be called everywhere-digited. They could handle tools, or employ their hands as if they were the most intricate tools.

George Blood was of the opinion that the Proavitoi were always masked, and that the men of the Expedition had never seen their faces. He said that those apparent faces were ritual masks, and that no part of the Proavitoi had ever been seen by the men except for those remarkable hands, which perhaps were their real faces.

The men reacted with cruel hilarity when Ceran tried to explain to them just what a great discovery he was verging on.

"Little Ceran is still on the how-did-it-begin jag," Manbreaker jeered. "Ceran, will you never give off asking which came first, the chicken or the egg?"

"I will have that answer very soon," Ceran sang. "I have the unique opportunity. When I find how the Proavitoi began, I may have the clue to how everything began. All of the Proavitoi are still alive, the very first generation of them."

"It passes belief that you can be so simpleminded," Manbreaker moaned. "They say that one has finally mellowed when he can suffer fools gracefully. By God, I hope I never come to that."

But two days later, it was Manbreaker who sought out Ceran Swicegood on nearly the same subject. Manbreaker had been doing a little thinking and discovering of his own.

"You are Special Aspects Man, Ceran," he said, "and you have been running off after the wrong aspect."

"What is that?"

"It don't make a damn how it began. What is important is that it may not have to end."

"It is the beginning that I intend to discover," said Ceran.

"You fool, can't you understand anything? What do the Proavitoi possess so uniquely that we don't know whether they have it by science or by their nature or by fool luck?"

"Ah, their chemistry, I suppose."

"Sure. Organic chemistry has come of age here. The Proavitoi have every kind of nexus and inhibitor and stimulant. They can grow and shrink and telescope and prolong what they will. These creatures seem stupid to me; it is as if they had these things by instinct. But they have them, that is what is important. With these things, we can become the patent medicine kings of the universes, for the Proavitoi do not travel or make many outside contacts. These things can do anything or undo anything. I suspect that the Proavitoi can shrink cells, and I suspect that they can do something else."

"No, they couldn't shrink cells. It is you who talk nonsense now, Manbreaker."

"Never mind. Their things already make nonsense of conventional chemistry. With the pharmacopoeia that one could pick up here, a man need never die. That's the stick horse you've been riding, isn't it? But you've been riding it backward with your head to the tail. The Proavitoi say that they never die."

"They seem pretty sure that they don't. If they did, they would be the first to know it, as Nokoma says."

"What? Have these creatures humor?"

"Some."

"But, Ceran, you don't understand how big this is."

"I'm the only one who understands it so far. It means that if the Proavitoi have always been immortal, as they maintain, then the oldest of them are still alive. From them I may be able to learn how their species—and perhaps every species—began."

Manbreaker went into his dying buffalo act then. He tore his hair and nearly pulled out his ears by the roots. He stomped and pawed and went off bull-bellowing: "It don't make a damn how it began, you fool! It might not have to end!" so loud that the hills echoed back:

"It don't make a damn—you fool."

Ceran Swicegood went to the house of Nokoma, but not with her on her invitation. He went without her when he knew that she was away from home. It was a sneaky thing to do, but the men of the Expedition were trained in sneakery.

He would find out better without a mentor about the nine hundred grandmothers, about the rumored living dolls. He would find out what the old people did do if they didn't die, and find if they knew how they were first born. For his intrusion, he counted on the innate politeness of the Proavitoi.

The house of Nokoma, of all the people, was in the cluster on top of the large flat hill, the Acropolis of Proavitus. They were earthen houses, though finely done, and they had the appearance of growing out of and being a part of the hill itself.

Ceran went up the winding, ascending flagstone paths, and entered the house which Nokoma had once pointed out to him. He entered furtively, and encountered one of the nine hundred grandmothers—one with whom nobody need be furtive.

The grandmother was seated and small and smiling at him. They talked without real difficulty, though it was not as easy as with Nokoma, who could meet Ceran halfway in his own language. At her call, there came a grandfather who likewise smiled at Ceran. These two ancients were somewhat smaller than the Proavitoi of active years. They were kind and serene. There was an atmosphere about the scene that barely missed being an odor—not unpleasant, sleepy, reminiscent of something, almost sad.

"Are there those here older than you?" Ceran asked earnestly.

"So many, so many, who could know how many?" said the grandmother. She called in other grandmothers and grandfathers older and smaller than herself, these no more than half the size of the active Proavitoi—small, sleepy, smiling.

Ceran knew now that the Proavitoi were not masked. The older they were, the more character and interest there was in their faces. It was only of the immature active Proavitoi that there could have been a doubt. No masks could show such calm and smiling old age as this. The queer textured stuff was their real faces.

So old and friendly, so weak and sleepy, there must have been a dozen generations of them there back to the oldest and smallest.

"How old are the oldest?" Ceran asked the first grandmother.

"We say that all are the same age since all are perpetual," the grandmother told him. "It is not true that all are the same age, but it is indelicate to ask how old."

"You do not know what a lobster is," Ceran said to them, trembling, "but it is a creature that will boil happily if the water on him is heated slowly. He takes no alarm, for he does not know at what point the heat is dangerous. It is that gradual here with me. I slide from one degree to another with you and my credulity is not alarmed. I am in danger of believing anything about you if it comes in small doses, and it will. I believe that you are here and as you are for no other reason than that I see and touch you. Well, I'll be boiled for a lobster, then, before I turn back from it. Are there those here even older than the ones present?"

The first grandmother motioned Ceran to follow her. They went down a ramp through the floor into the older part of the house, which must have been under ground.

Living dolls! They were here in rows on the shelves, and sitting in small chairs in their niches. Doll-sized indeed, and several hundred of them.

Many had wakened at the intrusion. Others came awake when spoken to or touched. They were incredibly ancient, but they were cognizant in their glances and recognition. They smiled and stretched sleepily, not as humans would, but as very old puppies might. Ceran spoke to them, and they understood each other surprisingly.

Lobster, lobster, said Ceran to himself, *the water has passed the danger point! And it hardly feels different. If you believe your senses in this, then you will be boiled alive in your credulity.*

He knew now that the living dolls were real and that they were the living ancestors of the Proavitoi.

Many of the little creatures began to fall asleep again. Their waking moments were short, but their sleeps seemed to be likewise. Several of the living mummies woke a second time while Ceran was still in the room, woke refreshed from very short sleeps and were anxious to talk again.

"You are incredible!" Ceran cried out, and all the small and smaller and still smaller creatures smiled and laughed their assent. Of course they were. All good creatures everywhere are incredible, and were there ever so many assembled in one place? But Ceran was greedy. A roomful of miracles wasn't enough.

"I have to take this back as far as it will go!" he cried avidly. "Where are the even older ones?"

"There are older ones and yet older and again older," said the first grandmother, "and thrice-over older ones, but perhaps it would be wise not to seek to be too wise. You have seen enough. The old people are sleepy. Let us go up again."

Go up again, out of this? Ceran would not. He saw passages and descending ramps, down into the heart of the great hill itself. There were whole worlds of rooms about him and under his feet. Ceran went on and down, and who was to stop him? Not dolls and creatures much smaller than dolls.

Manbreaker had once called himself an old pirate who reveled in the stream of his riches. But Ceran was the Young Alchemist who was about to find the Stone itself.

He walked down the ramps through centuries and millennia. The atmosphere he had noticed on the upper levels was a clear odor now—sleepy, half-remembered, smiling, sad and quite strong. That is the way Time smells.

"Are there those here even older than you?" Ceran asked a small grandmother whom he held in the palm of his hand.

"So old and so small that I could hold in my hand," said the grandmother in what Ceran knew from Nokoma to be the older uncompounded form of the Proavitus language.

Smaller and older the creatures had been getting as Ceran went through the rooms. He was boiled lobster now for sure. He had to believe it all: he saw and felt it. The wren-sized grandmother talked and laughed and nodded that there were those far older than herself, and in doing so she nodded herself back to sleep. Ceran returned her to her niche in the hive-like wall where there were thousands of others, miniaturized generations.

Of course he was not in the house of Nokoma now. He was in the heart of the hill that underlay all the houses of Proavitus, and these were the ancestors of everybody on the asteroid.

"Are there those here even older than you?" Ceran asked a small grandmother whom he held on the tip of his finger.

"Older and smaller," she said, "but you come near the end."

She was asleep, and he put her back in her place. The older they were, the more they slept.

He was down to solid rock under the roots of the hill. He was into the passages that were cut out of that solid rock, but they could not be many or deep. He had a sudden fear that the creatures would become so small that he could not see them or talk to them, and so he would miss the secret of the beginning.

But had not Nokoma said that all the old people knew the secret? Of course. But he wanted to hear it from the oldest of them. He would have it now, one way or the other.

"Who is the oldest? Is this the end of it? Is this the beginning? Wake up! Wake up!" he called when he was sure he was in the lowest and oldest room.

"Is it Ritual?" asked some who woke up. Smaller than mice they were, no bigger than bees, maybe older than both.

"It is a special Ritual," Ceran told them. "Relate to me how it was in the beginning."

What was that sound—too slight, too scattered to be a noise? It was like a billion microbes laughing. It was the hilarity of little things waking up to a high time.

"Who is the oldest of all?" Ceran demanded, for their laughter bothered him. "Who is the oldest and first?"

"I am the oldest, the ultimate grandmother," one said gaily. "All the others are my children. Are you also of my children?"

"Of course," said Ceran, and the small laughter of unbelief flittered out from the whole multitude of them.

"Then you must be the ultimate child, for you are like no other. If you be, then it is as funny at the end as it was in the beginning."

"How was it in the beginning?" Ceran bleated. "You are the first. Do you know how you came to be?"

"Oh, yes, yes," laughed the ultimate grandmother, and the hilarity of the small things became a real noise now.

"How did it begin?" demanded Ceran, and he was hopping and skipping about in his excitement.

"Oh, it was so funny a joke the way things began that you would not believe it," chittered the grandmother. "A joke, a joke!"

"Tell me the joke, then. If a joke generated your species, then tell me that cosmic joke."

"Tell yourself," tinkled the grandmother. "You are a part of the joke if you are of my children. Oh, it is too funny to believe. How good to wake up and laugh and go to sleep again."

Blazing green frustration! To be so close and to be balked by a giggling bee!

"Don't go to sleep again! Tell me at once how it began!" Ceran shrilled, and he had the ultimate grandmother between thumb and finger.

"This is not Ritual," the grandmother protested. "Ritual is that you guess what it was for three days, and we laugh and say, 'No, no, no, it was something nine times as wild as that. Guess some more.' "

"I will *not* guess for three days! Tell me at once or I will crush you," Ceran threatened in a quivering voice.

"I look at you, you look at me, I wonder if you will do it," the ultimate grandmother said calmly.

Any of the tough men of the Expedition would have done it—would have crushed her, and then another and another and another of the creatures till the secret was told. If Ceran had taken on a tough personality and a tough name he'd have done it. If he'd been Gutboy Barrelhouse he'd have done it without a qualm. But Ceran Swicegood couldn't do it.

"Tell me," he pleaded in agony. "All my life I've tried to find out how it began, how anything began. And you know!"

"We know. Oh, it was so funny how it began. So joke! So fool, so clown, so grotesque thing! Nobody could guess, nobody could believe."

"Tell me! Tell me!" Ceran was ashen and hysterical.

"No, no, you are no child of mine," chortled the ultimate grandmother. "Is too joke a joke to tell a stranger. We could not insult a stranger to tell so funny, so unbelieve. Strangers can die. Shall I have it on conscience that a stranger died laughing?"

"Tell me! Insult me! Let me die laughing!" But Ceran nearly died crying from the frustration that ate him up as a million bee-sized things laughed and hooted and giggled:

"Oh, it was so funny the way it began!"

And they laughed. And laughed. And went on laughing . . . until Ceran Swicegood wept and laughed together, and crept away, and returned to the ship still laughing. On his next voyage he changed his name to Blaze Bolt and ruled for ninety-seven days as king of a sweet sea island in M-81, but that is another and much more unpleasant story.

(1966)

SONYA DORMAN HESS

When I Was Miss Dow

These hungry, mother-haunted people come and find us living in what they like to call crystal palaces, though really we live in glass places, some of them highly ornamented and others plain as paper. They come first as explorers, and perhaps realize we are a race of one sex only, rather amorphous beings of proteide; and we, even baby I, are Protean also, being able to take various shapes at will. One sex, one brain lobe, we live in more or less glass bridges over the humanoid chasm, eating, recreating, attending races and playing other games like most living creatures.

Eventually, we're all dumped into the cell banks and reproduced once more.

After the explorers comes the colony of miners and scientists; the Warden and some of the other elders put on faces to greet them, agreeing to help with the mining of some ores, even giving them a koota or two as they become interested in our racing dogs. They set up their places of life, pop up their machines, bang-bang, chug-chug; we put on our faces, forms, smiles and costumes. I am old enough to learn to change my shape too.

The Warden says to me, "It's about time you made a change, yourself. Some of your friends are already working for these people, bringing home credits and sulfas."

My Uncle (by the Warden's fourth conjunction) made himself over at the start, being one of the first to realize how it could profit us.

I protest to the Warden, "I'm educated and trained as a scholar. You always say I must remain deep in my mathematics and other studies."

My Uncle says, "You have to do it. There's only one way for us to get along with them," and he runs his fingers through his long blond hair. My Uncle's not an educated person, but highly placed politically, and while Captain Dow is around, my Uncle retains this particular shape. The captain is shipping out soon, then Uncle will find some other features, because he's already warned it's unseemly for him to be chasing around in the face of a girl after the half-bearded boys from the spaceships. I don't want to do this myself, wasting so much time, when the fourteen decimals even now are clicking on my mirrors.

The Warden says, "We have a pattern from a female botanist, she ought to do for you. But before we put you into the pattern tank, you'll have to approximate another brain lobe. They have two."

"I know," I say sulkily. A botanist. A she.

"Into the tank," the Warden says to me without mercy, and I am his to use as he believes proper.

I spend four days in the tank absorbing the female Terran pattern. When I'm released, the Warden tells me, "Your job is waiting for you. We went to a lot of trouble to arrange it." He sounds brusque, but perhaps this is because he hasn't conjoined for a long time. The responsibilities of being Warden of Mines and Seeds come first, long before any social engagement.

I run my fingers through my brunette curls and notice my Uncle is looking critically at me. "Haven't you made yourself rather old?" he asks.

"Oh, he's all right," the Warden says. "Thirty-three isn't badly matched to the Doctor, as I understand it."

Dr. Arnold Proctor, the colony's head biologist, is busy making radiograph pictures (with his primitive X-rays) of skeletal structures: murger birds, rodents, and our pets and racers, the kootas. Dogs, to the Terrans, who are fascinated by them. We breed them primarily for speed and stamina, but some of them carry a gene for an inherited structural defect which cripples them, and they have to be destroyed before they are full grown. The Doctor is making a special study of kootas.

He gets up from his chair when I enter the office. "I'm Miss Dow, your new assistant," I say, hoping my long fingernails will stand up to the pressure of punchkeys on the computer, since I haven't had much practice in retaining foreign shapes. I'm still in uncertain balance between myself and Martha Dow, who is also myself. But one does not have two lobes for nothing, I discover.

"Good morning. I'm glad you're here," the Doctor says.

He is a nice, pink man with silver hair, soft-spoken, intelligent. I'm pleased, as we work along, to find he doesn't joke and wisecrack like so many of the Terrans, though I am sometimes whimsical, I like music and banquets as well as my studies.

Though absorbed in his work, Dr. Proctor isn't rude to interrupters. A man of unusual balance, coming as he does from a culture which sends out scientific parties that are 90 percent of one sex, when their species provides them with two. At first meeting he is dedicated but agreeable, and I'm charmed.

"Dr. Proctor," I ask him one morning, "is it possible for you to radiograph my koota? She's very fine, from the fastest stock available, and I'd like to breed her."

"Yes, yes, of course," he promises with his quick, often absent smile. "By all means. You wish to breed only the best." It's typical of him to assume we're all as dedicated as he.

My Uncle's not pleased. "There's nothing wrong with your koota," he says. "What do you want to X-ray her for? Suppose he finds something is wrong? You'll be afraid to race or breed her, and she won't be replaced. Besides, your interest in her may make him suspicious."

"Suspicious of what?" I ask, but my Uncle won't say, so I ask him, "Suppose she's bred and her pups are cripples?"

The Warden says, "You're supposed to have your mind on your work, not on racing. The koota was just to amuse you when you were younger."

I lean down and stroke her head, which is beautiful, and she breathes a deep and gentle breath in response.

"Oh, let him go," my Uncle says wearily. He's getting disgusted because they didn't intend for me to bury myself in a laboratory or a computer room without making more important contacts. But a scholar is born with a certain temperament and has an introspective nature, and as I'm destined eventually to replace the Warden, naturally I prefer the life of the mind.

"I must say," my Uncle remarks, "you look the image of a Terran female. Is the work interesting?"

"Oh, yes, fascinating," I reply, and he snorts at my lie, since we both know it's dull and routine, and most of my time is spent working out the connections between my two brain lobes, which still present me with some difficulty.

My koota bitch is subjected to a pelvic radiograph. Afterward, I stand on my heels in the small, darkened cubicle, looking at the film on the viewing screen. There he stands too, with his cheekbones emerald in the peculiar light, and his hair, which is silver in daylight, looks phosphorescent. I resist this. I am resisting this Doctor with the X-ray eyes who can examine my marrow with ease. He sees Martha's marrow, every perfect corpuscle of it.

You can't imagine how comforting it is to be so transparent. There's no need to pretend, adjust, advance, retreat or discuss the oddities of my planet. We are looking at the X-ray film of my prized racer and companion to determine the soundness of her hip joints, yet I suspect the doctor, platinum-green and tall as a tower, is piercing my reality with his educated gaze. He can see the blood flushing my surfaces. I don't need to do a thing but stand up straight so the crease of fat at my waist won't distort my belly button, the center of it all.

"You see?" he says. I do see, looking at the film in this darkness where perfection or disaster may be viewed, and I'm twined in the paradox which confronts me here. The darker the room, the brighter the screen and the clearer the picture. Less light! and the truth becomes more evident. Either the koota is properly jointed and may be bred without danger of passing the gene on to her young, or she is not properly jointed, and cannot be used. Less light, more truth! And the Doctor is green sculpture—a little darker and he would be a bronze—but his natural color is pink alabaster.

"You see," the Doctor says, and I do try to see. He points his wax pencil at one hip joint on the film, and says, "A certain amount of osteoarthritic build-up is already evident. The cranial rim is wearing down, she may go lame. She'll certainly pass the defect on to some of her pups, if she's bred."

This koota has been my playmate and friend for a long time. She retains a single form, that of koota, full of love and beautiful speed; she has been a source of pleasure and pride.

Dr. Proctor, of the pewter hair, will discuss the anatomical defects of the koota in a gentle and cultivated voice. I am disturbed. There shouldn't be any need to explain the truth, which is evident. Yet it seems that to comprehend the exposures, I require a special education. It's said that the more you have seen, the quicker you are to sort the eternal verities into one pile and the dismal illusions into another. How is it that sometimes the Doctor wears a head which resembles that of a koota, with a splendid muzzle and noble brow?

Suddenly, he gives a little laugh and points the end of the wax pencil at my navel, announcing, "There. There, it is essential that the belly button onto the pelvis, or you'll bear no children." Thoughts of offspring had occurred to me. But weren't we discussing my racer? The radiograph film is still clipped to the view screen, and upon it, spread-eagled, appears the bony Rorschach of my koota bitch, her hip joints expressing doom.

I wish the Doctor would put on the daylight. I come to the conclusion that there's a limit to how much truth I can examine, and the more I submit to the conditions necessary for examining it, the more unhappy I become.

Dr. Proctor is a man of such perfect integrity that he continues to talk about bones and muscles until I'm ready to scream for mercy. He has done something unusual and probably prohibited, but he's not aware of it. I mean it must be prohibited in his culture, where it seems they play on each other, but not with each other. I'm uneasy, fluctuating.

He snaps two switches. Out goes the film and on goes the sun, making my eyes stream with grateful tears, although he's so adjusted to these contrasts he doesn't so much as blink. Floating in the sunshine, I've become opaque; he can't see anything but my surface tensions, and I wonder what he does in his spare time. A part of me seems to tilt, or slide.

"There, there, oh dear, Miss Dow," he says, patting my back, rubbing my shoulder blades. His forearms and fingers extend gingerly. "You do want to breed only the best, don't you?" he asks. I begin within me a compulsive ritual of counting the elements; it's all I can do to keep communications open between my brain lobes. I'm suffering from eclipses; one goes dark, the other lights up like a new saloon, that one goes dark, the other goes nova.

"There, there," the Doctor says, distressed because I'm quivering and trying to keep the connections open; I have never felt clogged before. They may have to put me back into the pattern tank.

Profoundly disturbed, I lift my face, and he gives me a kiss. Then I'm all right, balanced again, one lobe composing a concerto for virtix flute, the other one projecting, "Oh Arnie, oh Arnie." Yes, I'm okay for the shape I'm in. He's marking off my joints with his wax pencil (the marks of which can be easily erased from the film surface) and he's mumbling, "It's essential, oh yes, it's essential."

Finally, he says, "I guess all of us colonists are lonely here," and I say, "Oh yes, aren't we," before I realize the enormity of the Warden's manipulations, and what a lot I have to learn. Evidently the Warden triple-carded me through the Colony Punch Center as a Terran. I lie and say, "Oh yes, yes. Oh Arnie, put out the light," for we may find some more truth.

"Not here," Arnie says, and of course he's right, this is a room for study, for cataloging obvious facts, not a place for carnival. There are not many places for it, I discover with surprise. Having lived in glass all my life, I expect everyone else to be as comfortable there as I am. But this isn't so.

Just the same we find his quarters, after dark, to be comfortable and free of embarrassment. You wouldn't think a dedicated man of his age would be so vigorous, but I find out he spends his weekends at the recreation center hitting a ball with his hand. The ball bounces back off a wall and he hits it and hits it. Though he's given that up now because we're together on weekends.

"You're more than an old bachelor like me deserves," he tells me.

"Why are you an old bachelor?" I ask him. I do wonder why, if it's something not to be.

He tries to explain it to me. "I'm not a young man. I wouldn't make a good husband, I'm afraid. I like to work late, to be undisturbed. In my leisure time, I like to make wood carvings. Sometimes I go to bed with the sun and sometimes I'm up working all night. And then children. No. I'm lucky to be an old bachelor," he says.

Arnie carves kaku wood, which has a brilliant grain and is soft enough to permit easy carving. He's working on a figure of a murger bird, whittling lengthwise down the wood so the grain, wavy, full of flowing, wedge-shaped lines, will represent the feathers. The lamplight shines on his hair and the crinkle of his eyelids as he looks down, and carves, whittles, turns. He's absorbed in what he doesn't see there, but he's projecting what he wants to see. It's the reverse of what he must do in the viewing room. I begin to suffer a peculiar pain, located in the nerve cluster between my lungs. He's not talking to me. He's not caressing me. He's forgotten I'm here, and like a false projection, I'm beginning to fade. In another hour perhaps the film will become blank. If he doesn't see me, then am I here?

He's doing just what I do when busy with one of my own projects, and I admire the intensity with which he works: it's magnificent. Yes, I'm jealous of it, I burn with rage and jealousy, he has abandoned me to be Martha and I wish I were myself again, free in shape and single in mind. Not this sack of mud clinging to another. Yet he's teaching me that it's good to cling to another. I'm exhausted from strange disciplines. Perhaps he's tired too; I see that sometimes he kneads the muscles of his stomach with his hands, and closes his eyes.

The Warden sits me down on one of my rare evenings home, and talks angrily. "You're making a mistake," he says. "If the Doctor finds out what you are, you'll lose your job with the Colony. Besides, we never supposed you'd have a liaison with only one man. You were supposed to start with the Doctor, and go on from there. We need every credit you can bring in. And by the way, you haven't done well on that score lately. Is he stingy?"

"Of course he isn't."

"But all you bring home in credits is your pay."

I can think of no reply. It's true the Warden has a right to use me in whatever capacity will serve us all best, as I will use others when I'm a Warden, but he and my Uncle spend half the credits from my job on sulfadiazole, to which they've become addicted.

"You've no sense of responsibility," the Warden says. Perhaps he's coming close to time for conjunction again, and this makes him more concerned about my stability.

My Uncle says, "Oh, he's young, leave him alone. As long as he turns over most of those pay credits to us. Though what he uses the remainder for, I'll never know."

I use it for clothes at the Colony Exchange. Sometimes Arnie takes me out for an evening, usually to the Laugh Tree Bar, where the space crews, too, like to relax. The bar is the place to find joy babies; young, pretty, planet-born girls who work at the Colony Punch Center during the day and spend their evenings here competing for the attention of the officers. Sitting here with Arnie, I can't distinguish a colonist's daughter from one of my friends or relatives. They wouldn't know me, either.

Once, at home, I try to talk with a few of these friends about my feelings. But I discover that whatever female patterns they've borrowed are superficial ones; none of them bother to grow an extra lobe, but merely tuck the Terran pattern into a corner of their own for handy reference. They are most of them on sulfas. Hard and shiny toys, they skip like pebbles over the surface of the colonists' lives.

Then they go home, revert to their own free forms, and enjoy their mathematics, colors, compositions and seedings.

"Why me?" I demand of the Warden. "Why two lobes? Why me?"

"We felt you'd be more efficient," he answers. "And while you're here, which you seldom are these days, you'd better revert to other shapes. Your particles may be damaged if you hold that female form too long."

Oh, but you don't know, I want to tell him. You don't know I'll hold it forever. If I'm damaged or dead, you'll put me into the cell banks, and you'll be amazed, astonished, terrified, to discover that I come out complete, all Martha. I can't be changed.

"You little lump of protagon," my Uncle mumbles bitterly. "You'll never amount to anything, you'll never be a Warden. Have you done any of your own work recently?"

I say, "Yes, I've done some crystal divisions, and regrown them in nonestablished patterns." My Uncle's in a bad mood, as he's kicking sulfa and his nerve tissue is addled. I'm wise to speak quietly to him, but he still grumbles.

"I can't understand why you like being a two-lobed pack of giggles. I couldn't wait to get out of it. And you were so dead against it to begin with."

"Well, I have learned," I start to say, but can't explain what it is I'm still learning, and close my eyes. Part of it is that on the line between the darkness and the brightness it's easiest to float. I've never wanted to practice only easy things. My balance is damaged. I never had to balance. It's not a term or concept I understand even now, at home, in free form. Some impress of Martha's pattern lies on my own brain cells. I suspect it's permanent damage, which gives me joy. That's what I mean about not understanding it; I am taught to strive for perfection, how can I be pleased with this, which may be a catastrophe?

Arnie carves on a breadth of kaku wood, bringing out to the surface a seascape. Knots become clots of spray, a flaw becomes wind-blown spume. I want to be Martha. I'd like to go to the Laugh Tree with Arnie, for a good time, I'd like to learn to play cards with him.

You see what happens: Arnie is, in his way, like my original self, and I hate that part of him, since I've given it up to be Martha. Martha makes him happy, she is chocolate to his appetite, pillow for his weariness.

I turn for company to my koota. She's the color of morning, her chest juts out like an axe blade, her ribs spring up and back like wings, her eyes are large and clear as she returns my gaze. Yet she's beyond hope; in a little time, she'll be lame; she can't race any more, she must not mother a litter. I turn to her and she gazes back into my eyes, dreaming of speed and wind on the sandy beaches where she has run.

"Why don't you read some tapes?" Arnie suggests to me, because I'm restless and I disturb him. The koota lies at my feet. I read tapes. Every evening in his quarters Arnie carves, I read tapes, the broken racer lies at my feet. I pass through Terran history this way. When the clown tumbles into the tub, I laugh. Terran history is full of clowns and tubs; at first it seems that's all there is, but you learn to see beneath the comic costumes.

While I float on that taut line, the horizon between light and dark, where it's so easy, I begin to sense what is under the costumes: staggering down the street dead drunk on a sunny afternoon with everyone laughing at you; hiding under the veranda because you made blood come out of Pa's face; kicking a man when he's in the gutter because you've been kicked and have to pass it on. Terrans have something called tragedy. It's what one of them called being a poet in the body of a cockroach.

"Have you heard the rumor?" Arnie asks, putting down the whittling tool. "Have you heard that some of the personnel in Punch Center aren't really humans?"

"Not really?" I ask, putting away the tape. We have no tragedy. In my species, family relationships are based only on related gene patterns; they are finally dumped into the family bank and a new relative is created from the old. It's one form of ancient history multiplying itself, but it isn't tragic. The koota, her utility destroyed by a recessive gene, lies sleeping at my feet. Is this tragedy? But she is a single form, she can't regenerate a lost limb, or exfoliate brain tissue. She can only return my gaze with her steadfast and affectionate one.

"What are they, then?" I ask Arnie. "If they're not human?"

"The story is that the local life forms aren't as we really see them. They've put on faces, like ours, to deal with us. And some of them have filtered into personnel."

Filtered! As if I were a virus.

I say, "But they must be harmless. No harm has come to anyone."

"We don't know that for a fact," Arnie replies.

"You look tired," I say, and he comes to me to be soothed, to be loved in his flesh, his single form, his search for the truth in the darkness of the viewing cubicle. At present he's doing studies of murger birds. Their spinal cavities are large, air-filled ovals, and their bone is extremely porous, which permits them to soar to great heights.

The koota no longer races on the windblown beaches; she lies at our feet, looking into the distance. The wall must be transparent to her eyes, I feel that beyond it she sees clearly how the racers go, down the long, bright curve of sand in the morning sun. She sighs, and lays her head down on her narrow, delicate paws.

Arnie says, "I seem to be tired all the time," and kneads the muscles of his chest. He puts his head down on my breasts. "I don't think the food's agreeing with me lately."

"Do you suffer pains?" I ask curiously.

"Suffer," he says, "what kind of nonsense is that, with analgesics. No. I don't suffer. I just don't feel well."

He's absorbed in murger birds, kaku wood, he descends into the darks and rises up like a rocket across the horizon into the thin clarity above. While I float, I no longer dare to breathe. I'm afraid of disturbing everything. I do not want anything. His head lies gently on my breast and I will not disturb him.

"Oh. My God," Arnie says and I know what it's come to, even before he begins to choke, and his muscles leap although I hold him in my arms. I know his heart is choking on massive doses of blood; the brilliance fades from his eyes and they begin to go dark while I tightly hold him. If he doesn't see me as he dies, will I be here?

I can feel, under my fingers, how rapidly his skin cools. I must put him down, here with his carvings and his papers, and I must go home. But I lift Arnie in my arms, and call the koota, who gets up rather stiffly. It's long after dark, and I carry him slowly, carefully, home to what he called a crystal palace, where the Warden and my Uncle are teaching each other to play chess with a set some space captain gave them in exchange for seed crystals. They sit in a bloom of light, sparkling, their old brains bent over the chessmen, as I breathe open the door and carry Arnie in.

First, my Uncle gives me just a glance, but then another glance, and a hard stare. "Is that the Doctor?" he asks.

I put Arnie down and hold one of his cold hands. "Warden," I say, on my knees, on eye level with the chessboard and its carved men. "Warden, can you put him in one of the banks?"

The Warden turns to look at me, as hard as my Uncle. "You've become deranged, trying to maintain two lobes," he says. "You cannot reconstitute or recreate a Terran by our methods, and you must know it."

"Over the edge, over the edge," my Uncle says, now a blonde, six-foot, hearty male Terran, often at the Laugh Tree with one of the joy babies. He enjoys life, his own or someone else's. I have, too, I suppose. Am I fading? I am, really, just one of Arnie's projections, a form on a screen in his mind. I am not, really, Martha. Though I tried.

"We can't have him here," the Warden says. "You better get him out of here. You couldn't explain a corpse like that to the colonists, if they come looking for him. They'll think we did something to him. It's nearly time for my next conjunction, do you want your nephew to arrive in disgrace? The Uncles will drain his bank."

The Warden gets up and comes over to me. He takes hold of my dark curls and pulls me to my feet. It hurts my physical me, which is Martha. God knows Arnie, I'm Martha, it seems to me. "Take him back to his quarters," the Warden says to me. "And come back here immediately. I'll try to see you back to your own pattern, but it may be too late. In part, I blame myself. If you must know. So I will try."

Yes, yes, I want to say to him; as I was, dedicated, free; turn me back into myself, I never wanted to be anyone else, and now I don't know if I am anyone at all. The light's gone from his eyes and he doesn't see me, or see anything, does he?

I pick him up and breathe the door out, and go back through the night to his quarters, where the lamp still burns. I'm going to leave him here, where he belongs. Before I go, I pick up the small carving of the murger bird, and take it with me, home to my glass bridge where at the edge of the mirrors the decimals are still clicking perfectly, clicking out known facts; an octagon can be reduced, the planet turns at such a degree on its axis, to see the truth you must have light of some sort, but to see the light you must have darkness of some sort. I can no longer float on the horizon between the two because that horizon has disappeared. I've learned to descend, and to rise, and descend again.

I'm able to revert without help to my own free form, to re-absorb the extra brain tissue. The sun comes up and it's bright. The night comes down and it's dark. I'm becoming somber, and a brilliant student. Even my Uncle says I'll be a good Warden when the time comes.

The Warden goes to conjunction; from the cell banks a nephew is lifted out. The koota lies dreaming of races she has run in the wind. It is our life, and it goes on, like the life of other creatures.

(1966)

ROGER ZELAZNY

Comes Now the Power

It was into the second year now, and it was maddening.

Everything which had worked before failed this time.

Each day he tried to break it, and it resisted his every effort.

He snarled at his students, drove recklessly, blooded his knuckles against many walls. Nights, he lay awake cursing.

But there was no one to whom he could turn for help. His problem would have been non-existent to a psychiatrist, who doubtless would have attempted to treat him for something else.

So he went away that summer, spent a month at a resort: nothing. He experimented with several hallucinogenic drugs; again, nothing. He tried free-associating into a tape recorder, but all he got when he played it back was a headache.

To whom does the holder of a blocked power turn, within a society of normal people?

. . . To another of his own kind, if he can locate one.

Milt Rand had known four other persons like himself: his cousin Gary, now deceased; Walker Jackson, a Negro preacher who had retired to somewhere down South; Tatya Stefanovich, a dancer, currently somewhere behind the Iron Curtain; and Curtis Legge, who, unfortunately, was suffering a schizoid reaction, paranoid type, in a state institution for the criminally insane. Others he had brushed against in the night, but had never met and could not locate now.

There had been blockages before, but Milt had always worked his way through them inside of a month. This time was different and special, though. Upsets, discomforts, disturbances, can dam up a talent, block a power. An event which seals it off completely for over a year, however, is more than a mere disturbance, discomfort or upset.

The divorce had beaten hell out of him.

It is bad enough to know that somewhere someone is hating you; but to have known the very form of that hatred and to have proven ineffectual against it, to have known it as the hater held it for you, to have lived with it growing around you, this is more than distasteful circumstance. Whether you are offender or offended, when you are hated and you live within the circle of that hate, it takes a thing from you: it tears a piece of spirit from your soul, or, if you prefer, a way of thinking from your mind; it cuts and does not cauterize.

Milt Rand dragged his bleeding psyche around the country and returned home.

He would sit and watch the woods from his glassed-in back porch, drink beer, watch the fireflies in the shadows, the rabbits, the dark birds, an occasional fox, sometimes a bat.

He had been fireflies once, and rabbits, birds, occasionally a fox, sometimes a bat.

The wildness was one of the reasons he had moved beyond suburbia, adding an extra half-hour to his commuting time.

Now there was a glassed-in back porch between him and these things he had once been part of. Now he was alone.

Walking the streets, addressing his classes at the institute, sitting in a restaurant, a theater, a bar, he was vacant where once he had been filled.

There are no books which tell a man how to bring back the power he has lost.

He tries everything he can think of, while he is waiting. Walking the hot pavements of a summer noon, crossing against the lights because traffic is slow, watching kids in swimsuits play around a gurgling hydrant, filthy water sluicing the gutter about their feet, as mothers and older sisters in halters, wrinkled shirts, bermudas and sunburnt skins watch them, occasionally, while talking to one another in entranceways to buildings or the shade of a storefront awning. Milt moves across town, heading nowhere in particular, growing claustrophobic if he stops for long, his eyebrows full of perspiration, sunglasses streaked with it, shirt sticking to his sides and coming loose, sticking and coming loose as he walks.

Amid the afternoon, there comes a time when he has to rest the two fresh-baked bricks at the ends of his legs. He finds a tree-lawn bench flanked by high maples, eases himself down into it and sits there thinking of nothing in particular for perhaps twenty-five minutes.

Hello.

Something within him laughs or weeps.

Yes, hello, I am here! Don't go away! Stay! Please!

You are—like me. . . .

Yes, I am. You can see it in me because you are what you are. But you must read here and send here, too. I'm frozen. I—Hello? Where are you?

Once more, he is alone.

He tries to broadcast. He fills his mind with the thoughts and tries to push them outside his skull.

Please come back! I need you. You can help me. I am desperate. I hurt. Where are you?

Again, nothing.

He wants to scream. He wants to search every room in every building on the block.

Instead, he sits there.

At 9:30 that evening they meet again, inside his mind.

Hello?

Stay! Stay, for God's sake! Don't go away this time! Please don't! Listen, I need you! You can help me.

How? What is the matter?

I'm like you. Or was, once. I could reach out with my mind and be other places, other things, other people. I can't do it now, though. I have a blockage. The power will not come. I know it is there. I can feel it. But I can't use . . . Hello?

Yes, I am still here. I can feel myself going away, though. I will be back. I . . .

Milt waits until midnight. She does not come back. It is a feminine mind which has touched his own. Vague, weak, but definitely feminine, and wearing the power. She does not come back that night, though. He paces up and down the block, wondering which window, which door . . .

He eats at an all-night café, returns to his bench, waits, paces again, goes back to the café for cigarettes, begins chain-smoking, goes back to the bench.

Dawn occurs, day arrives, night is gone. He is alone, as birds explore the silence, traffic begins to swell, dogs wander the lawns.

Then, weakly, the contact:

I am here. I can stay longer this time, I think. How can I help you? Tell me.

All right. Do this thing: Think of the feeling, the feeling of the out-go, out-reach, out-know that you have now. Fill your mind with that feeling and send it to me as hard as you can.

It comes upon him then as once it was: the knowledge of the power. It is earth and water, fire and air to him. He stands upon it, he swims in it, he warms himself by it, he moves through it.

It is returning! Don't stop now!

I'm sorry. I must. I'm getting dizzy. . . .

Where are you?

Hospital . . .

He looks up the street to the hospital on the corner, at the far end, to his left.

What ward? He frames the thought but knows she is already gone, even as he does it.

Doped-up or feverish, he decides, and probably out for a while now.

He takes a taxi back to where he had parked, drives home, showers and shaves, makes breakfast, cannot eat.

He drinks orange juice and coffee and stretches out on the bed.

Five hours later he awakens, looks at his watch, curses.

All the way back into town, he tries to recall the power. It is there like a tree, rooted in his being, branching behind his eyes, all bud, blossom, sap and color, but no leaves, no fruit. He can feel it swaying within him, pulsing, breathing; from the tips of his toes to the roots of his hair he feels it. But it does not bend to his will, it does not branch within his consciousness, furl there its leaves, spread the aromas of life.

He parks in the hospital lot, enters the lobby, avoids the front desk, finds a chair beside a table filled with magazines.

Two hours later he meets her.

He is hiding behind a copy of *Holiday* and looking for her.

I am here.

Again, then! Quickly! The power! Help me to rouse it!

She does this thing.

Within his mind, she conjures the power. There is a movement, a pause, a movement, a pause. Reflectively, as though suddenly remembering an intricate dance step, it stirs within him, the power.

As in a surfacing bathyscaphe, there is a rush of distortions, then a clear, moist view without.

She is a child who has helped him.

A mind-twisted, fevered child, dying . . .

He reads it all when he turns the power upon her.

Her name is Dorothy and she is delirious. The power came upon her at the height of her illness, perhaps because of it.

Has she helped a man come alive again, or dreamed that she helped him? she wonders.

She is thirteen years old and her parents sit beside her bed. In the mind of her mother a word rolls over and over, senselessly, blocking all other thoughts, though it cannot keep away the feelings:

Methotrexate, methotrexate, methotrexate, meth . . .

In Dorothy's thirteen-year-old breastbone there are needles of pain. The fevers swirl within her, and she is all but gone to him.

She is dying of leukemia. The final stages are already arrived. He can taste the blood in her mouth.

Helpless within his power, he projects:

You have given me the end of your life and your final strength. I did not know this. I would not have asked it of you if I had.

Thank you, she says, *for the pictures inside you.*

Pictures?

Places, things I saw . . .

There is not much inside me worth showing. You could have been elsewhere, seeing better.

I am going again . . .

Wait!

He calls upon the power that lives within him now, fused with his will and his sense, his thoughts, memories, feelings. In one great blaze of life, he shows her Milt Rand.

Here is everything I have, all I have ever been that might please. Here is swarming through a foggy night, blinking on and off. Here is lying beneath a bush as the rains of summer fall about you, drip from the leaves upon your fox-soft fur. Here is the moon-dance of the deer, the dream drift of the trout beneath the dark swell, blood cold as the waters about you.

Here is Tatya dancing and Walker preaching; here is my cousin Gary, as he whittles, contriving a ball within a box, all out of one piece of wood. This is my New York and my Paris. This, my favorite meal, drink, cigar, restaurant, park, road to drive on late at night; this is where I dug tunnels, built a lean-to, went swimming; this, my first kiss; these are the tears of loss; this is exile and alone, and recovery, awe, joy; these, my grandmother's daffodils; this her coffin, daffodils about it; these are the colors of the music I love, and this is my dog who lived long and was good. See all the things that heat the spirit, cool within the mind, are encased in memory and one's self. I give them to you, who have no time to know them.

He sees himself standing on the far hills of her mind. She laughs aloud then, and in her room somewhere high away a hand is laid upon her and her wrist is taken between fingers and thumb as she rushes toward him suddenly grown large. His great black wings sweep forward to fold her wordless spasm of life, then are empty.

Milt Rand stiffens within his power, puts aside a copy of *Holiday* and stands, to leave the hospital, full and empty, empty, full, like himself, now, behind.

Such is the power of the power.

(1966)

FREDERIK POHL

Day Million

On this day I want to tell you about, which will be about a thousand years from now, there were a boy, a girl and a love story.

Now although I haven't said much so far, none of it is true. The boy was not what you and I would normally think of as a boy, because he was a hundred and eighty-seven years old. Nor was the girl a girl, for other reasons; and the love story did not entail that sublimation of the urge to rape and concurrent postponement of the instinct to submit which we at present understand in such matters. You won't care much for this story if you don't grasp these facts at once. If, however, you will make the effort, you'll likely enough find it jampacked, chockfull and tiptop-crammed with laughter, tears and poignant sentiment which may, or may not, be worth while. The reason the girl was not a girl was that she was a boy.

How angrily you recoil from the page! You say, who the hell wants to read about a pair of queers? Calm yourself. Here are no hot-breathing secrets of perversion for the coterie trade. In fact, if you were to see this girl, you would not guess that she was in any sense a boy. Breasts, two; vagina, one. Hips, Callipygean; face, hairless; supraorbital lobes, non-existent. You would term her female at once, although it is true that you might wonder just what species she was a female of, being confused by the tail, the silky pelt or the gill slits behind each ear.

Now you recoil again. Cripes, man, take my word for it. This is a sweet kid, and if you, as a normal male, spent as much as an hour in a room with her, you would bend heaven and earth to get her in the sack. Dora (we will call her that; her "name" was omicron-Di-base seven-group-totter-oot S Doradus 5314, the last part of which is a color specification corresponding to a shade of green)—Dora, I say, was feminine, charming and cute. I admit she doesn't sound that way. She was, as you might put it, a dancer. Her art involved qualities of intellection and expertise of a very high order, requiring both tremendous natural capacities and endless practice; it was performed in null-gravity and I can best describe it by saying that it was something like the performance of a contortionist and something like classical ballet, maybe resembling Danilova's dying swan. It was also pretty damned sexy. In a symbolic way, to be sure; but face it, most of the things we call "sexy" are symbolic, you know, except perhaps an exhibitionist's open fly. On Day Million when Dora danced, the people who saw her panted; and you would too.

About this business of her being a boy. It didn't matter to her audiences that genetically she was male. It wouldn't matter to you, if you were among them, because you wouldn't know it—not unless you took a biopsy cutting of her flesh and put it under an electron microscope to find the XY chromosome—and it didn't matter to them because they didn't care. Through techniques which are not only complex but haven't yet been discovered, these people were able to determine a great deal about the aptitudes and easements of babies quite a long time before they were born—at about the second horizon of cell-division, to be exact, when the segmenting egg is becoming a free blastocyst—and then they naturally helped those aptitudes along. Wouldn't we? If we find a child with an aptitude for music we give him a scholarship to Juilliard. If they found a child whose aptitudes were for being a woman, they made him one. As sex had long been dissociated from reproduction this was relatively easy to do and caused no trouble and no, or at least very little, comment.

How much is "very little"? Oh, about as much as would be caused by our own tampering with Divine Will by filling a tooth. Less than would be caused by wearing a hearing aid. Does it still sound awful? Then look closely at the next busty babe you meet and reflect that she may be a Dora, for adults who are genetically male but somatically female are far from unknown even in our own time. An accident of environment in the womb overwhelms the blueprints of heredity. The difference is that with us it happens only by accident and we don't know about it except rarely, after close study; whereas the people of Day Million did it often, on purpose, because they wanted to.

Well, that's enough to tell you about Dora. It would only confuse you to add that she was seven feet tall and smelled of peanut butter. Let us begin our story.

On Day Million Dora swam out of her house, entered a transportation tube, was sucked briskly to the surface in its flow of water and ejected in its plume of spray to an elastic platform in front of her—ah—call it her rehearsal hall. "Oh, shit!" she cried in pretty confusion, reaching out to catch her balance and find herself tumbled against a total stranger, whom we will call Don.

They met cute. Don was on his way to have his legs renewed. Love was the farthest thing from his mind; but when, absent-mindedly taking a short cut across the landing platform for submarinites and finding himself drenched, he discovered his arms full of the loveliest girl he had ever seen, he knew at once they were meant for each other. "Will you marry me?" he asked. She said softly, "Wednesday," and the promise was like a caress.

Don was tall, muscular, bronze and exciting. His name was no more Don than Dora's was Dora, but the personal part of it was Adonis in tribute to his vibrant maleness, and so we will call him Don for short. His personality color-code, in Angstrom units, was 5290, or only a few degrees bluer than Dora's 5314, a measure of what they had intuitively discovered at first sight, that they possessed many affinities of taste and interest.

I despair of telling you exactly what it was that Don did for a living—I don't mean for the sake of making money, I mean for the sake of giving purpose and meaning to his life, to keep him from going off his nut with boredom—except to say that it involved a lot of traveling. He traveled in interstellar spaceships. In order to make a spaceship go really fast about thirty-one male and seven genetically female human beings had to do certain things, and Don was one of the thirty-one. Actually he contemplated options. This involved a lot of exposure to radiation flux—not so much from his own station in the propulsive system as in the spillover from the next stage, where a genetic female preferred selections and the subnuclear particles making the selections she preferred demolished themselves in a shower of quanta. Well, you don't give a rat's ass for that, but it meant that Don had to be clad at all times in a skin of light, resilient, extremely strong copper-colored metal. I have already mentioned this, but you probably thought I meant he was sunburned.

More than that, he was a cybernetic man. Most of his ruder parts had been long since replaced with mechanisms of vastly more permanence and use. A cadmium centrifuge, not a heart, pumped his blood. His lungs moved only when he wanted to speak out loud, for a cascade of osmotic filters rebreathed oxygen out of his own wastes. In a way, he probably would have looked peculiar to a man from the 20th century, with his glowing eyes and seven-fingered hands; but to himself, and of course to Dora, he looked mighty manly and grand. In the course of his voyages Don had circled Proxima Centauri, Procyon and the puzzling worlds of Mira Ceti; he had carried agricultural templates to the planets of Canopus and brought back warm, witty pets from the pale companion of Aldebaran. Blue-hot or red-cool, he had seen a thousand stars and their ten thousand planets. He had, in fact, been traveling the starlanes with only brief leaves on Earth for pushing two centuries. But you don't care about that, either. It is people that make stories, not the circumstances they find themselves in, and you want to hear about these two people. Well, they made it. The great thing they had for each other grew and flowered and burst into fruition on Wednesday, just as Dora had promised. They met at the encoding room, with a couple of well-wishing friends apiece to cheer them on, and while their identities were being taped and stored they smiled and whispered to each other and bore the jokes of their friends with blushing repartee. Then they exchanged their mathematical analogues and went away. Dora to her dwelling beneath the surface of the sea and Don to his ship.

It was an idyll, really. They lived happily ever after—or anyway, until they decided not to bother any more and died.

Of course, they never set eyes on each other again.

Oh, I can see you now, you eaters of charcoal-broiled steak, scratching an incipient bunion with one hand and holding this story with the other, while the stereo plays d'Indy or Monk. You don't believe a word of it, do you? Not for one minute. People wouldn't live like that, you say with an irritated and not amused grunt as you get up to put fresh ice in a stale drink.

And yet there's Dora, hurrying back through the flushing commuter pipes toward her underwater home (she prefers it there; has had herself somatically altered to breathe the stuff). If I tell you with what sweet fulfillment she fits the recorded analogue of Don into the symbol manipulator, hooks herself in and turns herself on . . . if I try to tell you any of that you will simply stare. Or glare; and grumble, what the hell kind of love-making is this? And yet I assure you, friend, I really do assure you that Dora's ecstasies are as creamy and passionate as any of James Bond's lady spies, and one hell of a lot more so than anything you are going to find in "real life." Go ahead, glare and grumble. Dora doesn't care. If she thinks of you at all, her thirty-times-great-great-grandfather, she thinks you're a pretty primordial sort of brute. You are. Why, Dora is farther removed from you than you are from the australopithecines of five thousand centuries ago. You could not swim a second in the strong currents of her life. You don't think progress goes in a straight line, do you? Do you recognize that it is an ascending, accelerating, maybe even exponential curve? It takes hell's own time to get started, but when it goes it goes like a bomb. And you, you Scotch-drinking steak-eater in your Relaxacizer chair, you've just barely lighted the primacord of the fuse. What is it now, the six or seven hundred thousandth day after Christ? Dora lives in Day Million. A thousand years from now. Her body fats are polyunsaturated, like Crisco. Her wastes are hemodialyzed out of her bloodstream while she sleeps—that means she doesn't have to go to the bathroom. On whim, to pass a slow half-hour, she can command more energy than the entire nation of Portugal can spend today, and use it to launch a weekend satellite or remold a crater on the Moon. She loves Don very much. She keeps his every gesture, mannerism, nuance, touch of hand, thrill of intercourse, passion of kiss stored in symbolic-mathematical form. And when she wants him, all she has to do is turn the machine on and she has him.

And Don, of course, has Dora. Adrift on a sponson city a few hundred yards over her head or orbiting Arcturus, fifty light-years away, Don has only to command his own symbol-manipulator to rescue Dora from the ferrite files and bring her to life for him, and there she is; and rapturously, tirelessly they ball all night. Not in the flesh, of course; but then his flesh has been extensively altered and it wouldn't really be much fun. He doesn't need the flesh for pleasure. Genital organs feel nothing. Neither do hands, nor breasts, nor lips; they are only receptors, accepting and transmitting impulses. It is the brain that feels, it is the interpretation of those impulses that makes agony or orgasm; and Don's symbol-manipulator gives him the analogue of cuddling, the analogue of kissing, the analogue of wildest, most ardent hours with the eternal, exquisite and incorruptible analogue of Dora. Or Diane. Or sweet Rose, or laughing Alicia; for to be sure, they have each of them exchanged analogues before, and will again.

Balls, you say, it looks crazy to me. And you—with your after-shave lotion and your little red car, pushing papers across a desk all day and chasing tail all night—tell me, just how the hell do you think you would look to Tiglath-Pileser, say, or Attila the Hun?

(1966)

FRITZ LEIBER

The Winter Flies

After the supper dishes were done there was a general movement from the Adler kitchen to the Adler living room.

It was led by Gottfried Helmuth Adler, commonly known as Gott. He was thinking how they should be coming from a dining room, yes, with colored maids, not from a kitchen. In a large brandy snifter he was carrying what had been left in the shaker from the martinis, a colorless elixir weakened by melted ice yet somewhat stronger than his wife was supposed to know. This monster drink was a regular part of Gott's carefully thought-out program for getting safely through the end of the day.

"After the seventeenth hour of creation God got sneaky," Gott Adler once put it to himself.

He sat down in his leather-upholstered easy chair, flipped open Plutarch's *Lives* left-handed, glanced down through the lower halves of his executive bifocals at the paragraph in the biography of Caesar he'd been reading before dinner, then, without moving his head, looked through the upper halves back toward the kitchen.

After Gott came Jane Adler, his wife. She sat down at her drawing table, where pad, pencils, knife, art gum, distemper paints, water, brushes, and rags were laid out neatly.

Then came little Heinie Adler, wearing a spaceman's transparent helmet with a large hole in the top for ventilation. He went and stood beside this arrangement of objects: first a long wooden box about knee-high with a smaller box on top and propped against the latter a toy control panel of blue and silver plastic, on which only one lever moved at all; next, facing the panel, a child's wooden chair; then back of the chair another long wooden box lined up with the first.

"Good-by Mama, good-by Papa," Heinie called. "I'm going to take a trip in my spaceship."

"Be back in time for bed," his mother said.

"Hot jets!" murmured his father.

Heinie got in, touched the control panel twice, and then sat motionless in the little wooden chair, looking straight ahead.

A fourth person came into the living room from the kitchen—the Man in the Black Flannel Suit. He moved with the sick jerkiness and had the slack putty-gray features of a figure of the imagination that hasn't been fully developed. (There was a fifth person in the house, but even Gott didn't know about him yet.)

The Man in the Black Flannel Suit made a stiff gesture at Gott and gaped his mouth to talk to him, but the latter silently writhed his lips in a "Not yet, you fool!" and nodded curtly toward the sofa opposite his easy chair.

"Gott," Jane said, hovering a pencil over the pad, "you've lately taken to acting as if you were talking to someone who isn't there."

"I have, my dear?" her husband replied with a smile as he turned a page, but not lifting his face from his book. "Well, talking to oneself is the sovereign guard against madness."

"I thought it worked the other way," Jane said.

"No," Gott informed her.

Jane wondered what she should draw and saw she had very faintly sketched on a small scale the outlines of a child, done in sticks-and-blobs like Paul Klee or kindergarten art. She could do another "Children's Clubhouse," she supposed, but where should she put it this time?

The old electric clock with brass fittings that stood on the mantel began to wheeze shrilly, "Mystery, mystery, mystery, mystery." It struck Jane as a good omen for her picture. She smiled.

Gott took a slow pull from his goblet and felt the scentless vodka bite just enough and his skin shiver and the room waver pleasantly for a moment with shadows chasing across it. Then he swung the pupils of his eyes upward and looked across at the Man in the Black Flannel Suit, noting with approval that he was sitting rigidly on the sofa. Gott conducted his side of the following conversation without making a sound or parting his lips more than a quarter of an inch, just flaring his nostrils from time to time.

BLACK FLANNEL: Now if I may have your attention for a space, Mr. Adler—

GOTT: Speak when you're spoken to! Remember, I created you.

BLACK FLANNEL: I respect your belief. Have you been getting any messages?

GOTT: The number 6669 turned up three times today in orders and estimates. I received an airmail advertisement beginning "Are you ready for big success?" though the rest of the ad didn't signify. As I opened the envelope the minute hand of my desk clock was pointing at the faceless statue of Mercury on the Commerce Building.

When I was leaving the office my secretary droned at me, "A representative of the Inner Circle will call on you tonight," though when I questioned her, she claimed that she'd said, "Was the letter to Innes-Burkel and Company all right?" Because she is aware of my deafness, I could hardly challenge her. In any case she sounded sincere. If those were messages from the Inner Circle, I received them. But seriously I doubt the existence of that clandestine organization. Other explanations seem to me more likely—for instance, that I am developing a psychosis. I do not believe in the Inner Circle.

BLACK FLANNEL (*smiling shrewdly—his features have grown tightly handsome though his complexion is still putty gray*): Psychosis is for weak minds. Look, Mr. Adler, you believe in the Mafia, the FBI, and the Communist Underground. You believe in upper-echelon control groups in unions and business and fraternal organizations. You know the workings of big companies. You are familiar with industrial and political espionage. You are not wholly unacquainted with the secret fellowships of munitions manufacturers, financiers, dope addicts and procurers and pornography connoisseurs and the brotherhoods and sisterhoods of sexual deviates and enthusiasts. Why do you boggle at the Inner Circle?

GOTT (*coolly*): I do not wholly believe in all of those other organizations. And the Inner Circle still seems to me more of a wish-dream than the rest. Besides, you may want me to believe in the Inner Circle in order at a later date to convict me of insanity.

BLACK FLANNEL (*drawing a black briefcase from behind his legs and unzipping it on his knees*): Then you do not wish to hear about the Inner Circle?

GOTT (*inscrutably*): I will listen for the present. Hush!

Heinie was calling out excitedly, "I'm in the stars, Papa! They're so close they burn!" He said nothing more and continued to stare straight ahead.

"Don't touch them," Jane warned without looking around. Her pencil made a few faint five-pointed stars. The Children's Clubhouse would be on a boundary of space, she decided—put it in a tree on the edge of the Old Ravine. She said, "Gott, what do you suppose Heinie sees out there besides stars?"

"Bug-eyed angels, probably," her husband answered, smiling again but still not taking his head out of his book.

BLACK FLANNEL (*consulting a sheet of crackling black paper he has slipped from his briefcase, though as far as* GOTT *can see there is no printing, typing, writing, or symbols of any sort in any color ink on the black bond*): The Inner Circle is the world's secret elite, operating behind and above all figureheads, workhorses, wealthy dolts, and those talented exhibitionists we name genius. The Inner Circle has existed *sub rose niger* for thousands of years. It controls human life. It is the repository of all great abilities, and the key to all ultimate delights.

GOTT (*tolerantly*): You make it sound plausible enough. Everyone half believes in such a cryptic power gang, going back to Sumeria.

BLACK FLANNEL: The membership is small and very select. As you are aware, I am a kind of talent scout for the group. Qualifications for admission (*he slips a second sheet of black bond from his briefcase*) include a proven great skill in achieving and wielding power over men and women, an amoral zest for all of life, a seasoned blend of ruthlessness and reliability, plus wide knowledge and lightning wit.

GOTT (*contemptuously*): Is that all?

BLACK FLANNEL (*flatly*): Yes. Initiation is binding for life—and for the afterlife: one of our mottos is Ferdinand's dying cry in *The Duchess of Malfi.* "I will vault credit and affect high pleasures after death." The penalty for revealing organizational secrets is not death alone but extinction—all memory of the person is erased from public and private history; his name is removed from records; all knowledge of and feeling for him is deleted from the minds of his wives, mistresses, and children: it is as if he had never existed. That, by the by, is a good example of the powers of the Inner Circle. It may interest you to know, Mr. Adler, that as a result of the retaliatory activities of the Inner Circle, the names of three British kings have been expunged from history. Those who have suffered a like fate include two popes, seven movie stars, a brilliant Flemish artist superior to Rembrandt . . . *(As he spins out an apparently interminable listing, the Fifth Person creeps in on hands and knees from the kitchen. GOTT cannot see him at first, as the sofa is between GOTT's chair and the kitchen door. The Fifth Person is THE BLACK JESTER,* who looks rather like a caricature of *GOTT but has the same putty complexion as the MAN IN THE BLACK FLANNEL SUIT. THE BLACK JESTER wears skin-tight clothing of that color, silver-embroidered boots and gloves, and a black hood edged with silver bells that do not tinkle. He carries a scepter topped with a small death's-head that wears a black hood like his own edged with tinier silver bells, soundless as the larger ones.)*

THE BLACK JESTER (*suddenly rearing up like a cobra from behind the sofa and speaking to the MAN IN THE BLACK FLANNEL SUIT over the latter's shoulder):* Ho! So you're still teasing his rickety hopes with that shit about the Inner Circle? Good sport, brother!—you play your fish skillfully.

GOTT (*immensely startled, but controlling himself with some courage*): Who are you? How dare you bring your brabblement into my court?

THE BLACK JESTER: Listen to the old cock crow innocent! As if he didn't know he'd himself created both of us, time and again, to stave off boredom, madness, or suicide.

GOTT (*firmly*): I never created *you.*

THE BLACK JESTER: Oh, yes, you did, old cock. Truly your mind has never birthed anything but twins—for every good, a bad; for every breath, a fart; and for every white, a black.

GOTT (*flares his nostrils and glares a death-spell which hums toward the newcomer like a lazy invisible bee*).

THE BLACK JESTER (*pales and staggers backward as the death-spell strikes, but shakes it off with an effort and glares back murderously at* GOTT): Old cock-father, I'm beginning to hate you at last.

Just then the refrigerator motor went on in the kitchen, and its loud rapid rocking sound seemed to Jane to be a voice saying, "Watch your children, they're in danger. Watch your children, they're in danger."

"I'm no ladybug," Jane retorted tartly in her thoughts, irked at the worrisome interruption now that her pencil was rapidly developing the outlines of the Clubhouse in the Tree with the moon risen across the ravine between clouds in the late afternoon sky. Nevertheless she looked at Heinie. He hadn't moved. She could see how the plastic helmet was open at neck and top, but it made her think of suffocation just the same.

"Heinie, are you still in the stars?" she asked.

"No, now I'm landing on a moon," he called back. "Don't talk to me, Mama, I've got to watch the road."

Jane at once wanted to imagine what roads in space might look like, but the refrigerator motor had said "children," not "child," and she knew that the language of machinery is studded with tropes. She looked at Gott. He was curled comfortably over his book, and as she watched, he turned a page and touched his lips to the martini water. Nevertheless, she decided to test him.

"Gott, do you think this family is getting too ingrown?" she said. "We used to have more people around."

"Oh, I think we have quite a few as it is," he replied, looking up innocently at the sofa, beyond it, and around at her expectantly, as if ready to join in any conversation she cared to start. But she simply smiled at him and returned relieved to her thoughts and her picture. He smiled back and bowed his head again to his book.

BLACK FLANNEL (*ignoring THE BLACK JESTER*): My chief purpose in coming here tonight, Mr. Adler, is to inform you that the Inner Circle has begun a serious study of your qualifications for membership.

THE BLACK JESTER: At *his* age? After *his* failures? Now we curtsy forward toward the Big Lie!

BLACK FLANNEL (*in a pained voice*): Really! (*Then once more to GOTT.*) Point One: you have gained for yourself the reputation of a man of strong patriotism, deep company loyalty, and realistic self-interest, sternly contemptuous of all youthful idealism and rebelliousness. Point Two: you have cultivated constructive hatreds in your business life, deliberately knifing colleagues when you could, but allying yourself to those on the rise. Point Three and most important: you have gone some distance toward creating the master illusion of a man who has secret sources of information, secret new techniques for thinking more swiftly and acting more decisively than others, secret superior connections and contacts—in short, a dark new strength which all others envy even as they cringe from it.

THE BLACK JESTER (*in a kind of counterpoint as he advances around the sofa*): But he's come down in the world since he lost his big job. National Motors was at least a step in the right direction, but Hagbolt-Vincent has no company planes, no company apartments, no company shooting lodges, no company call girls! Besides, he drinks too much. The Inner Circle is not for drunks on the downgrade.

BLACK FLANNEL: Please! You're spoiling things.

THE BLACK JESTER: *He's* spoiled. (*Closing in on GOTT.*) Just look at him now. Eyes that need crutches for near and far. Ears that mis-hear the simplest remark.

GOTT: Keep off me, I tell you.

THE BLACK JESTER (*ignoring the warning*): Fat belly, flaccid sex, swollen ankles. And a mouthful of stinking cavities!—did you know he hasn't dared visit his dentist for five years? Here, open up and show them! (*Thrusts black-gloved hand toward GOTT's face.*)

Gott, provoked beyond endurance, snarled aloud, "Keep off, damn you!" and shot out the heavy book in his left hand and snapped it shut on the Black Jester's nose. Both black figures collapsed instantly.

Jane lifted her pencil a foot from the pad, turned quickly, and demanded, "My God, Gott, what was that?"

"Only a winter fly, my dear," he told her soothingly. "One of the fat ones that hide in December and breed all the black clouds of spring." He found his place in Plutarch and dipped his face close to study both pages and the trough between them. He looked around slyly at Jane and said, "I didn't squush her."

The chair in the spaceship rutched. Jane asked, "What is it, Heinie?"

"A meteor exploded, Mama. I'm all right. I'm out in space again, in the middle of the road."

Jane was impressed by the time it had taken the sound of Gott's book clapping shut to reach the spaceship. She began lightly to sketch blob-children in swings hanging from high limbs in the Tree, swinging far out over the ravine into the stars.

Gott took a pull of martini water, but he felt lonely and impotent. He peeped over the edge of his Plutarch at the darkness below the sofa and grinned with new hope as he saw the huge flat blob of black putty the Jester and Flannel had collapsed into. *I'm on a black kick,* he thought, *why black?*—choosing to forget that he had first started to sculpt figures of the imagination from the star-specked blackness that pulsed under his eyelids while he lay in the dark abed: tiny black heads like wrinkled peas on which any three points of light made two eyes and a mouth. He'd come a long way since then. Now with strong rays from his eyes he rolled all the black putty he could see into a woman-long bolster and hoisted it onto the sofa. The bolster helped with blind sensuous hitching movements, especially where it bent at the middle. When it was lying full length on the sofa he began with cruel strength to sculpt it into the figure of a high-breasted exaggeratedly sexual girl.

Jane found she'd sketched some flies into the picture, buzzing around the swingers. She rubbed them out and put in more stars instead. But there would be flies in the ravine, she told herself, because people dumped garbage down the other side; so she drew one large fly in the lower left-hand corner of the picture. He could be the observer. She said to herself firmly, *No black clouds of spring in this picture* and changed them to hints of Roads in Space.

Gott finished the Black Girl with two twisting tweaks to point her nipples. Her waist was barely thick enough not to suggest an actual wasp or a giant amazon ant. Then he gulped martini water and leaned forward just a little and silently but very strongly blew the breath of life into her across the eight feet of living-room air between them.

The phrase "black clouds of spring" made Jane think of dead hopes and drowned talents. She said out loud, "I wish you'd start writing in the evenings again, Gott. Then I wouldn't feel so guilty."

"These days, my dear, I'm just a dull businessman, happy to relax in the heart of his family. There's not an atom of art in me," Gott informed her with quiet conviction, watching the Black Girl quiver and writhe as the creativity-wind from his lips hit her. With a sharp twinge of fear it occurred to him that the edges of the wind might leak over to Jane and Heinie, distorting them like heat shimmers, changing them nastily. Heinie especially was sitting so still in his little chair light-years away. Gott wanted to call to him, but he couldn't think of the right bit of spaceman's lingo.

THE BLACK GIRL (*sitting up and dropping her hand coquettishly to her crotch*): He-he! Now ain't this something, Mr. Adler! First time you've ever had me in your home.

GOTT (*eyeing her savagely over Plutarch*): Shut up!

THE BLACK GIRL (*unperturbed*): Before this it was only when you were away on trips or, once or twice lately, at the office.

GOTT (*flaring his nostrils*): Shut up, I say! You're less than dirt.

THE BLACK GIRL (*smirking*): But I'm interesting dirt, ain't I? You want we should do it in front of her? I could come over and flow inside your clothes and—

GOTT: One more word and I uncreate you! I'll tear you apart like a boiled crow. I'll squunch you back to putty.

THE BLACK GIRL (*still serene, preening her nakedness*): Yes, and you'll enjoy every red-hot second of it, won't you?

Affronted beyond bearing, Gott sent chopping rays at her over the Plutarch parapet, but at that instant a black figure, thin as a spider, shot up behind the sofa and reaching over the Black Girl's shoulder brushed aside the chopping rays with one flick of a whiplike arm. Grown from the black putty Gott had overlooked under the sofa, the figure was that of an old conjure woman, stick-thin with limbs like wires and breasts like dangling ropes, face that was a pack of spearheads with black ostrich plumes a-quiver above it.

THE BLACK CRONE (*in a whistling voice like a hungry wind*): Injure one of the girls, Mister Adler, and I'll castrate you, I'll shrivel you with spells. You'll never be able to call them up again, no matter how far a trip you go on, or even pleasure your wife.

GOTT (*frightened, but not showing it*): Keep your arms and legs on, Mother. Flossie and I were only teasing each other. Vicious play is a specialty of your house, isn't it?

With a deep groaning cry the furnace fan switched on in the basement and began to say over and over again in a low rapid rumble, "Oh, my God, my God, my God. Demons, demons, demons, demons." Jane heard the warning very clearly, but she didn't want to lose the glow of her feelings. She asked, "Are you all right out there in space, Heinie?" and thought he nodded "Yes." She began to color the Clubhouse in the Tree—blue roof, red walls, a little like Chagall.

THE BLACK CRONE (*continuing a tirade*): Understand this, Mr. Adler, you don't own us, we own you. Because you gotta have the girls to live, you're the girls' slave.

THE BLACK GIRL: He-he! Shall I call Susie and Belle? They've never been here either, and they'd enjoy this.

THE BLACK CRONE: Later, if he's humble. You understand me, Slave? If I tell you have your wife cook dinner for the girls or wash their feet or watch you snuggle with them, then you gotta do it. And your boy gotta run our errands. Come over here now and sit by Flossie while I brand you with dry ice.

Gott quaked, for the Crone's arms were lengthening toward him like snakes, and he began to sweat, and he murmured, "God in Heaven," and the smell of fear went out of him to the walls—millions of stinking molecules.

A cold wind blew over the fence of Heinie's space road and the stars wavered and then fled before it like diamond leaves.

Jane caught the murmur and the fear-whiff too, but she was coloring the Clubhouse windows a warm rich yellow; so what she said in a rather loud, rapt, happy voice was: "I think Heaven is like a children's clubhouse. The only people there are the ones you remember from childhood—either because you were in childhood with them or they told you about their childhood honestly. The *real* people."

At the word *real* the Black Crone and the Black Girl strangled and began to bend and melt like a thin candle and a thicker one over a roaring fire.

Heinie turned his spaceship around and began to drive it bravely homeward through the unspeckled dark, following the ghostly white line that marked the center of the road. He thought of himself as the cat they'd had. Papa had told him stories of the cat coming back—from downtown, from Pittsburgh, from Los Angeles, from the moon. Cats could do that. He was the cat coming back.

Jane put down her brush and took up her pencil once more. She'd noticed that the two children swinging out farthest weren't attached yet to their swings. She started to hook them up, then hesitated. Wasn't it all right for some of the children to go sailing out to the stars? Wouldn't it be nice for some evening world—maybe the late-afternoon moon—to have a shower of babies? She wished a plane would crawl over the roof of the house and drone out an answer to her question. She didn't like to have to do all the wondering by herself. It made her feel guilty.

"Gott," she said, "why don't you at least finish the last story you were writing? The one about the Elephants' Graveyard." Then she wished she hadn't mentioned it, because it was an idea that had scared Heinie.

"Some day," her husband murmured, Jane thought.

Gott felt weak with relief, though he was forgetting why. Balancing his head carefully over his book, he drained the next to the last of the martini water. It always got stronger toward the bottom. He looked at the page through the lower halves of his executive bifocals and for a moment the word "Caesar" came up in letters an inch high, each jet serif showing its tatters and the white paper its ridgy fibers. Then, still never moving his head, he looked through the upper halves and saw the long thick blob of dull black putty on the wavering blue couch and automatically gathered the putty together and with thumb-and-palm rays swiftly shaped the Old Philosopher in the Black Toga, always an easy figure to sculpt since he was never finished, but rough-hewn in the style of Rodin or Daumier. It was always good to finish up an evening with the Old Philosopher.

The white line in space tried to fade. Heinie steered his ship closer to it. He remembered that in spite of Papa's stories, the cat had never come back.

Jane held her pencil poised over the detached children swinging out from the Clubhouse. One of them had a leg kicked over the moon.

THE PHILOSOPHER (*adjusting his craggy toga and yawning*): The topic for tonight's symposium is that vast container of all, the Void.

GOTT (*condescendingly*): The void? That's interesting. Lately I've wished to merge with it. Life wearies me.

A smiling dull black skull, as crudely shaped as the Philosopher, looked over the latter's shoulder and then rose higher on a rickety black bone framework.

DEATH (*quietly, to* GOTT): Really?

GOTT (*greatly shaken, but keeping up a front*): I *am* on a black kick tonight. Can't even do a white skeleton. disintegrate, you two. You bore me almost as much as life.

DEATH: Really? If you did not cling to life like a limpet, you would have crashed your car, to give your wife and son the insurance, when National Motors fired you. You planned to do that. Remember?

GOTT (*with hysterical coolness*): Maybe I should have cast you in brass or aluminum. Then you'd at least have brightened things up. But it's too late now. Disintegrate quickly and don't leave any scraps around.

DEATH: Much too late. Yes, you planned to crash your car and doubly indemnify your dear ones. You had the spot picked, but your courage failed you.

GOTT (*blustering*): I'll have you know I am not only Gottfried but also Helmuth—Hell's Courage Adler!

THE PHILOSOPHER (*confused but trying to keep in the conversation*): A most swashbuckling sobriquet.

DEATH: Hell's courage failed you on the edge of the ravine. (*Pointing at* GOTT *a three-fingered thumbless hand like a black winter branch.*) Do you wish to die now?

GOTT (*blacking out visually*): Cowards die many times. (*Draining the last of the martini water in absolute darkness.*) The valiant taste death once. Caesar.

DEATH (*a voice in darkness*): Coward. Yet you summoned me—and even though you fashioned me poorly, I am indeed Death—and there are others besides yourself who take long trips. Even longer ones. Trips in the Void.

THE PHILOSOPHER (*another voice*): Ah, yes, the Void. Imprimis—

DEATH: Silence.

In the great obedient silence Gott heard the unhurried click of Death's feet as he stepped from behind the sofa across the bare floor toward Heinie's spaceship. Gott reached up in the dark and clung to his mind.

Jane heard the slow clicks too. They were the kitchen clock ticking out, "Now. Now. Now. Now. Now."

Suddenly Heinie called out, "The line's gone. Papa, Mama, I'm lost."

Jane said sharply, "No, you're not, Heinie. Come out of space at once."

"I'm not in space now. I'm in the Cats' Graveyard."

Jane told herself it was insane to feel suddenly so frightened. "Come back from wherever you are, Heinie," she said calmly. "It's time for bed."

"I'm lost, Papa," Heinie cried. "I can't hear Mama any more."

"Listen to your mother, Son," Gott said thickly, groping in the blackness for other words.

"All the Mamas and Papas in the world are dying," Heinie wailed.

Then the words came to Gott, and when he spoke his voice flowed. "Are your atomic generators turning over, Heinie? Is your space-warp lever free?"

"Yes, Papa, but the line's gone."

"Forget it. I've got a fix on you through subspace and I'll coach you home. Swing her two units to the right and three up. Fire when I give the signal. Are you ready?"

"Yes, Papa."

"Roger. Three, two, one, fire and away! Dodge that comet! Swing left around that planet! Never mind the big dust cloud! Home on the third beacon. Now! Now! Now!"

Gott had dropped his Plutarch and come lurching blindly across the room, and as he uttered the last *Now!* the darkness cleared, and he caught Heinie up from his spacechair and staggered with him against Jane and steadied himself there without upsetting her paints, and she accused him laughingly "You beefed up the martini water again," and Heinie pulled off his helmet and crowed, "Make a big hug," and they clung to each other and looked down at the half-colored picture where a children's clubhouse sat in a tree over a deep ravine and blob children swung out from it against the cool pearly moon and the winding roads in space and the next to the last child hooked onto his swing with one hand and with the other caught the last child of all, while from the picture's lower left-hand corner a fat, black fly looked on enviously.

Searching with his eyes as the room swung toward equilibrium, Gottfried Helmuth Adler saw Death peering at him through the crack between the hinges of the open kitchen door.

Laboriously, half passing out again, Gott sneered his face at him.

(1967)

SAMUEL R. DELANY

HIGH WEIR

I

"What do you know!" Smith, from the top of the ladder.

"What is it?" Jones, at the bottom.

And Rimkin thought desperately: Boiled potatoes! My God, boiled potatoes! If I took toothpicks and stuck them in boiled potatoes, then stuck one on top of the other, made heads, arms, legs—like little snowmen—they would look just like these men in spacesuits on Mars.

"Concaved!" Smith called down. "You know those religious pictures they used to have back home, in the little store windows, where the eyes followed you down the street? The faces were carved in reverse relief like this."

"Those faces aren't carved in reverse relief!" Mak, right next to Rimkin, shouted up. "I can see that from here."

"Not the whole face," Smith said. "Just the eyes. That's why they had that funny effect when we were coming across the sand."

Mak, Rimkin thought. Mak. Mak. What distinguishes that man besides the *k* in his name?

"They are handsome up there." That from Hodges. "A whole year of speculation over whether those little bits of purple stone were carved or natural—and suddenly here it all is, right on High Weir. The answer. Look at it: it means intelligence. It means culture. It means an advanced culture at least on the level of the ancient Greeks, too. Do you realize the spaces between these temple columns lead to a whole new branch of anthropology?"

"We don't know that this thing's a temple," Mak grunted.

"A whole new complex of studies!" Hodges reiterated. "We're all of us Sir Arthur Evans unearthing the great staircase at Knossos. We're Schliemanns digging up the treasures of Atreus."

I don't know where any of them are, Rimkin thought. Their voices come through the rubber-ringed grills inside my helmet. All these boiled-potato figures against the grainy rust; that one there who I think is Hodges; the sun blinds out the faceplate. And, for all I know, behind the plastic is a grotesquerie as deformed as those domed heads along the archetrave above us. . . .

"Hey, Rimkin, you're the linguist. Why aren't you poking around for something that looks like writing?"

"Huh . . . ?" And as he said it, without hearing their laughter, he knew that inside their onion helmets they were smiling and shaking their heads. Jones said:

"Here we are on Mars, and Rimky is *still* in another world. Is there any writing or hen-scratching up there where you are, Smith?"

"Nothing up here. But look at the surface of this eye, the way it's carved out!"

"What about it?"

And then Jimmi—Rimkin could always tell Jimmi because her suit was a head and a half shorter than any of the others—climbed up the rough stone foundation blocks and, with a beautiful "Martian lope" and a wake of russet dust, crossed the flooring, then turned back. "Look!" He could always tell her voice, no matter the static and distortion of the radios (short range; no fidelity). "Here's one that fell!"

"Here!" Rimkin said. "Let me see." They mustn't think he wasn't interested.

Her soft voice said in his ear: "I can't very well move it. You'll have to come up here, Rimky."

But he was already climbing. "Yes, yes. Of course. I'm coming." And there was the sound of somebody trying not to snicker, position concealed by lack of stereo.

The carving had fallen. And it had cracked on the stone flags.

He walked up to Jimmi. The top of her helmet came to the middle of his upper arm.

"It's so funny," she said with that oddness to her laughter the radio couldn't mask. "It looks just like a Martian."

"What?"

She looked up at him, small brown face behind the white frame. The movements of her laughter were displaced from the sound in his ear. "Just look." She turned back. "The great, high forehead, the big beady eyes, and hardly any chin. Wouldn't you have guessed? Martians would turn out to look just like a nineteen-fifties s-f film."

"Maybe . . . " A third of the face had fallen away. The crack went through the left eye. What remained of the mouth leered with prune-puckered lips. "Maybe it's all a joke. Perhaps some of the military people from Bellona came here and set this whole thing up like an elaborate stage-set. Just to play a joke on us. They *would,* you know! This is absurd, just the five of us taking the skimmer on a routine scouting trip across High Weir plateau, not sixty-five miles from the base, and coming across—"

"—across a structure as big as the Parthenon! Hell, bigger than the Temple of Zeus!" Hodges exploded. "Come off it, Rimky! You can't just sneak off in the morning and erect an entire stone ruin. Not one like this."

"Yes, but it's so—"

"Hey! You people!" Again, the voice came from Smith. "Somebody come up here and take a look at the eyes. Are they the same stone as the rest of the building, just very highly polished? Or are they some different material set in? I can't tell from here."

Jimmi bent awkwardly and ran her glove over the broken surface. She who is dark and slender and the definition of all grace, Rimkin thought, muffled against the blazing ruin beneath deep turquoise skies.

"It's an inset, Dr. Smith." She made a blunted gesture, and Rimkin bent to see.

The eyes were cylinders of translucent material perhaps nine inches in diameter and a foot long. They were set flush into the face, the front surfaces ground to shimmering concavities.

"Lots of them are different colors," Mak noted.

Rimkin himself had noticed that the great row of eyes gave off an almost day-glow quality, from across the dunes; up close, they were mottled.

"What are they made of?" Hodges asked.

"The building's that Marsite stuff," Jones said. The light, purplish rock "marsite" had been found as soon as the military base at Bellona had grown larger than a single bubble-hut. Rimkin, there with the Inter-Nal University group, had spent much time looking at the worn fragments, playing after-dinner games with the military men (who barely tolerated the contingent of scholars) speculating as to whether they were carved or natural. The purple shards could have been Martian third cousins to the Venus of Wellendorf, or they could have simply been eroded fragments tossed for millennia by the waterless waves.

"What are the eyes made of?" Hodges demanded. "Semi-precious stone? Is it something smelted, or synthetic? That opens up a whole world of possibilities about the culture."

"I can chip some off this broken one to take back—"

"Rimkin! No!" Hodges shouted, and in a moment the bumpy air suit had scrambled over the foundation. Hodges swayed on bloated feet. "Rimkin . . . look, wake up! We've just had the first incontrovertible proof that there is—or at any rate at one time there was—intelligent life beside us in the universe. In the solar system! And you want to start chipping. Sometimes you come on like one of those brass-decked thick skulls back at the base!"

"Oh, Hodges, cut it out!" Jimmi snapped. "Leave him alone. It's bad enough trying to put up with those thick-skulls you're talking about. If we start this sort of bickering—"

"Stop trying to protect him, Jimmi," Hodges countered. "All right, perhaps he's a brilliant linguist in a library cubicle. But he's absolute dead weight on this expedition. He spends all his time either completely uninterested in what's going on, or worse, making absurd suggestions like breaking up the most important archaeological discovery in human history with a sledgehammer!"

"I wasn't going to break up—"

Then: "Oh my—God. . . . No! This is—"

And Rimkin thought: Which one is it? Jesus, with all this distortion, I can't tell what direction the voices are coming from. I can place any accent on Earth, but I can't even recognize their individual voices any more! Which one?

Hodges turned around. "What is it?"

Jones, still down on the sand, called up, "What is it, Dr. Smith? What's happening up there?"

"This is just . . . no . . . this is amazing!"

They were all going to the base of the column against which the ladder was leaning. So Rimkin went too.

The white-suited figure on the top rung was peering into one of the eyes with a flashlight.

"Dr. Smith, are you all right?"

"Yes, yes. I'm fine. Please, just wait! But this . . . "

"That's a low-power laser beam he's looking in there with," someone began.

"He said be quiet," from someone else.

I can hear five people breathing in my ears, Rimkin thought. What could he be looking at? "Dr. Smith," Rimkin called.

"Shhhh!"

Rimkin went on doggedly. "Can you describe what you're looking at."

"Yes, I . . . think so. It's—Mars. Only, the way it must have been. A city, the city around this building. Roads. Machines that move, and a horizon full of man-made—buildings? Perhaps they're buildings. The picture moves—and the streets are full of creatures, like the statues. No, they're different. Some hurry . . . some go slowly . . . this whole plateau, all of High Weir must have been some incredible acropolis for a mammoth, cosmopolitan community. Wait! They're unveiling some sort of statue. Now, they're presenting one of them to the people. Maybe a priest. Or a sacrifice—"

After moments of silence, Mak said, "What pictures are you talking about?"

"It's like looking through a window onto what must have been here . . . on this plateau perhaps hundreds of thousands of years ago. As soon as I shine my lazer-light into the concaved surface, I'm suddenly looking out on three-dimensional moving scenes, just as real . . . just as strange . . . "

Mak turned to Hodges. "Is it some sort of animated diorama?"

"It's got to be some kind of hologram. A moving hologram!" At the top of the ladder, Dr. Smith finally looked down. "You've got to come up here and see this! I just wanted to look at the inside of the eye on this carving closely. I thought with the laser-light I might detect crystalline structures, perhaps get a clue to what the eyes were made from. But I saw pictures!" He started down the ladder. "You've all just got to go up there and take a look!" Smith's indrawn breath roared in Rimkin's ear. "It's the most amazing thing I've ever seen."

"Still think somebody came by and built this today just to get us off on a wild-goose chase, eh, Rimkin?" Hodges chided. "Let me go up and look. I've got my own beam, Dr. Smith." Hodges started up the rungs as Smith reached the bottom.

Frowning behind his faceplate, Rimkin took out his own flash. For a moment he fondled the tube; then he went back over the rusty sand tongues and purple stone to where the head had fallen. He looked at the whole eye. He looked at the broken one. He did not know what perversity made him crouch before the latter. He flicked on his laser-beam.

It took half an hour for Mak, Hodges, Jimmi, and Jones to climb the ladder, watch for two or three minutes, then climb down. They were gathering to go back to the skimmer when Jimmi saw Rimkin. She loped over to him.

She laughed when she saw what he was doing. "Now aren't we a bunch of dopes! Some of us could have looked at this one down here. Come on, we're going back now."

Rimkin switched off his beam, but still crouched before the tilted visage.

"Oh, come on, Rimky. They're starting back already."

Rimkin drew breath, then stood slowly. "All right." They started across the dressed stone flooring. The sand, fine as dust, spewed about their white boots like powdered blood.

II

The commons room of the skimmer was a traveling fragment of classical academia. The celitex walls looked depressingly like walnut paneling. Above the brass-fixtured folding desk surfaces, the microfilms were stacked behind Naugahyde spines lettered in gold leaf. There was a mantelpiece above the heating nook. Glowing plates shot pale flickerings across the fur throws. The whole construct, with its balcony library cubicles (and a bust of Richard Nielson, president of Inter-Nal University, on his pedestal at the turn of the stairwell) was a half-serious joke of Dr. Edward Jones. But the university people, by and large, were terribly appreciative of the extravagant facade, after a couple of weeks in the unsympathetic straits of the military back at Bellona Base.

Mak sat on the hassock, rolling the sleeves of his wool shirt over his truckdriver forearms. He had headed the Yugoslavian expedition that had unearthed Gevgeli Man. Mak's boulderlike build (and what forehead he had was hidden by a falling thatch of Sahara-colored hair) had brought the jokes in the anthropology department to new nadirs: "This is Dr. Mak Hargus, the Gevgeli Man . . . eh, man . . . "

Mak raised the periscope of his briar from his shirt pocket. "Tell me about holograms. I've seen them, of course, the three-dimensional images and all. But how do they work? And how did the ancient Martians store all those pictures that just pop up under laser-light?"

Ling Wong Smith dropped his fists into the baggy pocket of his corduroy jacket. He and Mak gazed over the ferns in the windowbox. Outside the tri-plex pane, across the dusty bruise of High Weir, the dark columns—twelve whole, seven broken—sketched the incredible culture they had viewed in the polished eyes along the carved lintel.

Jimmi pushed her dark braid back from her shoulder and leaned on the banister to look.

Ling Wong Smith turned away. "It's basically a matter of information storage, Mak." He lowered himself to the arm of the easy chair, meshed his long fingers and bent forward so that his straight black hair slipped forward.

"The Martians certainly stored one hell of a lot of information in those eyes," Hodges commented, coming jerkily down the stairs on her crutches. She was large, almost as large (and soft) as Mak was large (and hard). She had a spectacular record in cultural anthropology, and combined a sort of braying energy, enthusiastic idealism, and a quite real sensitivity (she had been a cripple since birth), with which she had managed to stagger through all sorts of bizarre cultures in East Africa,

Anatolia, and Southern Cambodia to emerge with thorough and cohesive accounts of religions, mores, and manners. Her spacesuit was a prosthetic miracle that enabled her to move as easily as anyone while she wore it. But outside it, she still used aluminum crutches.

From his go game with Jones in the corner, Rimkin watched her lurch down the stairs. She must think they're a psychological advantage, he decided.

"Go on, Ling. Now tell us all about holograms." She picked up one crutch and waved it at the Chinese psychologist, only just avoiding the venerable Nielson.

"Information storage," Smith repeated. "Basically it's a photograph, taken without a lens, but with perfectly parallel beams of light—the sort you get in laser light. The only scattering is that which comes from the irregularities of the surface of the object being recorded. The final plate looks like a blotchy configuration of grays—or mud if it's in color. But when you shine the parallel beams of a laser light on this plate, you get a three-dimensional, full-color image hanging over the plate—"

"—that you can walk around," Mak finished.

"You can walk around up to a hundred and eighty degrees," Smith amended. "It's just a completely different way of storing information than the regular photographic method. And it is far more efficient."

Jones said softly, from across the gaming board, "It's your move, Rimky."

"Oh." Rimkin picked up another black oval from his pot between his first two fingers and hesitated above the grid, dotted with white and black. Bits of information. He tried to encompass the areas of territory mapped below him, but they kept breaking up into small corner battles. "There." He clicked his stone to the board.

Jones frowned. "Sure you don't want to take that move back?"

"No. No, I don't."

"You can, you know," Jones went on, affable. "This isn't chess. The rules are that you can take a move back if you—"

"I know that," Rimkin said loudly. "Don't you think I know that? I want to go—" he looked around and saw the other watching— "there!" The click of his stone had been very loud.

"All right." Jones's stone ticked the board. "Double attari." But Rimkin was looking past Jones's small, heart-shaped, Nigerian face, to the others in the room, thinking, How can I tell them apart? They all just blend with one another. The room is round, their faces are round, stuck on little round bodies. Suddenly he closed his eyes. If they started talking, I know I wouldn't be able to tell any of them apart. How is one supposed to know? How?

And if I opened my eyes?

"Your move, Rimkin," Jones said. "I've got two of your stones in attari."

Rimkin opened his eyes on the grid of black and white. "Oh," he said, and tried to strangle up a laugh. "Yes. That was a pretty silly move after all, wasn't it?"

III

Such an absurd move; he lay in his bunk with his eyes closed and his lips open over his teeth in a leer, trying to think of a better one. He hadn't slept in two nights. An hour like this . . . maybe it was only a few minutes, but it seemed like an hour . . . and he sat up.

He swung the reading machine over his bed and rolled it to the closing of the *Tractatus.* He'd been rereading it the afternoon the skimmer had left Bellona; *Wovon man nicht sprechen kann.* . . . He pushed the machine aside and ran his hand under his undershirt. The skimmer would not leave till the morning. They should return to Bellona that night and report their discovery to Those Who Were in Charge of Such Things. But the university people (especially the anthropology department) treasured their brief freedom. One more examination of the site tomorrow, a few cursory readings and measurements . . .

Rimkin walked barefoot into the hall. It must have only been a few minutes, because strips of light from reading machines underlined three doors. Which room belonged to whom? He knew, and yet somehow there seemed no way to know. . . .

Down in the locks, he put his air suit on over his underwear. The plastic form-rings felt odd against his thighs and arms without the usual padding. He stepped into the lock.

Outside, sharp stars dropped frostlights. The sand was filled with great, slopping puddles of ink. Cold, cold outside. The little motor humming in the vicinity of his chin kept the silicone circulating between the double thickness of his faceplate to avoid frosting. He stepped. And stepped. The desert sucked his boots.

The others? It was not even that he disliked them. He was infinitely confused by them. Dune and shadow received him. As he walked, he looked up. One bright star was . . . moving. If he stood still, he could follow the movement distinctly. Phobos? Demos? He knew it was one of the two tiny Martian moons. But for the life of him, Rimkin could not remember whether it was Fear or Terror that coursed the frozen jewelry of the Martian night.

He saw the ruin.

He tried to blank the struggling anxieties that squirmed into the edges of his consciousness. Seven hundred and fifty-odd vitally important enzyme reactions are occurring constantly in the human body. Were any one of them to break down for even two/three minutes, the body would die. So, just to fix the free fear that ranged his mind, he worried about one of these seven hundred and fifty-odd complex reactions suddenly coming to a halt; until he lost the subject of his worry in the coils of sand. And fear moved free above him, tangible as the slender columns, the sculpted architrave.

He looked up at the faces, obscured by darkness. The eyes caught and grayed the starlight, and regarded him. Rimkin began to paw under the flap of his pack for his flash. He found it after much too much time—he had forgotten what he was looking for twice—and rotated the dispersal grid to break up the laser-beam into ordinary light.

He played the beam over the stones. They were gray, now. He wondered if the purple were actually only a reflection from the desert. No, it was just the weakness of his beam. He walked along the sand to the place where the foundation could be mounted. He started to climb, once more aware of the inside of his suit against bare skin. The heating was working adequately, but the plastic and metal textures were so odd. He wanted to take the suit off and place his hand on the stone, then grew terrified that he might; because the Martian night was almost a hundred degrees below freezing.

Rimkin stood on the edge of the foundation and fanned his light toward the fallen head. He approached across the sandy blocks. The smaller fragment of face lay like a saucer. Its half-eye had cracks all through. Rimkin squatted before the major portion of the face, leaned toward the fractured orb. He raised his flash, twisted back the dispersal-grid so that the bright, singular beam fell on the broken circle; flicker, and flicker, image and image. The fragmented orb began to weep the sights of ages.

Dawn comes quickly on worlds with thin atmosphere. It climbed the dunes behind Rimkin and laid its blazing hands on his shoulders. And the mechanism of his suit began to hum and twitter about him to prepare for the two-hundred-degree rise that would occur in the next twenty minutes.

"Rimkin . . . ?"

Who was breathing in his ear?

"Rimkin, are you up there?"

The voices had been calling for some time. But with just a sound coming out of a machine by your ear, how was he supposed to know what they were?

"Rimky, there you are! What are you doing? Have you been here all morning?"

He turned around—and fell over.

"Rimkin!"

He had been in one position for almost nine hours, and every muscle, once moved, was in agony. In the pain fogging his vision like heat, he watched the boiled potato, jogging toward him in a cloud of fiery dust.

Through his gasps he kept on trying to get out: "Why . . . who are . . . which . . . who are—"

"It's me, Evelyn."

Evelyn, he thought. Who was Evelyn? "Who . . . "

She reached him. "Evelyn Hodges, who did you think it was? Are you hurt? Has something gone wrong with your suit? Oh I *knew* I should have brought Mak out here with me. The outside temperature is about ten degrees Fahrenheit right now. But in fifteen minutes it'll be a ninety or more. I can't get you back to the ship by myself."

"No—No." Rimkin shook his head. "All right. My suit. I'm just—"

"What is it, then?"

The pain was incredible, but for a moment he was in control enough to get out: "I'm just stiff. . . . I was in one position for so long. I just . . . just forgot."

"How long is a long time?" Hodges demanded.

"Almost all night, I guess." His arms weren't so bad. He pushed himself up and propped himself against the stone.

Hodges bent down, picked up the flash (a feat she could only do with her specially constructed suit) and turned it around. "You've been looking at the pretty pictures?"

Rimkin nodded. "Eh . . . yes."

She made a sound that had something of confusion, something of frustration. "You just be glad I came looking for you!" she squatted beside him, and after much maneuvering, got herself seated. "I can never sleep past five thirty in the morning anyway, and I got to thinking that perhaps I'd let myself get carried away a couple of times with you. You know, back at the base, with all those ribbons and brass flapping around, saying all those stupid things, we've all been under a bit of pressure. Early this morning I was in the hall, saw the light from your reading machine, and thought you might be up. I peeped in, because the door was open, but you weren't in bed. I figured you must be in the library; but the doors down to the port were open and your suit was gone—well, this is the only thing around worth going out to look at. You've been here since last night?"

"Yes. I have."

"Rimky," Hodges said after a few moments, "we're all oddballs in our way. You're really not all that strange when you start looking at the rest of us. Maybe you're just a little less used to fitting your angles into other people's spaces. But I have been doing some thinking. And I have a feeling I've put my finger on the reason you were so . . . well, preoccupied all last evening. Give me a listen and tell me if I'm right."

She rocked a couple of times beside him to settle inside her blimp. "Yesterday I said something about the Martians having at least reached the level of the Greeks. But that was before we discovered the moving hologram records. That at least brings their technology—or one facet of it, at any rate—to a level comparable to the middle of the twentieth century. Or even well beyond. We still can't embed a moving hologramic image into a crystal that just starts to play back automatically under laser light. Now if they were all that advanced, then there should be scads of written evidence around here. If not things like books, then at least carved in the stone. But there isn't a scratch, not a dated cornerstone, no mayor's name carved over the doorway. Hell, there're at least mason's marks on the blocks in the Khufu Pyramid. Now you're our semanticist, Rimky, and it must be pretty important to you that there be some evidence of a Martian language. But the fact that there isn't any immediately visible about a structure this imposing, coupled with the fact that they obviously stored so much *visually* . . . " Her voice hung on the word as a card player's fingers might linger on a daring discard. "Well, there's a good possibility, Rimky, that they just weren't a verbal race, and they somehow managed to achieve this level of technology without ever employing written communication, sort of the same way the Incas and Mayas reached their cultural level and still managed totally to bypass the invention of the wheel. If that *is* the case, Rimky, that makes you sort of useless on this expedition. I could see that getting to you, upsetting you."

He could tell she was waiting for some great reaction of relief, now that a truth had outed. How did she expect to detect it? Perhaps the change in breathing would come through the suit phones. He tried to remember who she was. But there were all seven hundred and fifty-odd enzyme reactions to think about, to make sure that one of them didn't suddenly stop. . . .

"You know," she was going on (Hodges? Yes it *was* the Hodges woman), "I'm really the useless one on the expedition. You know what my talent is? I'm the one who can make friends with all sorts of Eskimos and jungle bunnies. And then there were the mountain cannibals in the Caucasus who wanted to make me their queen." She laughed metallically. "They certainly did. I don't care if I never see another piece of decayed yak butter again as long as I live. Rimky, I'm here just in case we run into a tribe of *live* Martians," She looked out across the barren copper. After a few more moments she said, "I think you'd pretty well agree there's a good deal more chance you'll find Martian writing than I'll find the models for those carvings up there, wandering around in nomadic tribes. And what's more, it *does* get under my skin. I guess, being on edge like that, I've occasionally said some things, some of them to you, I'd have best held in. If you've got a skill or a discipline, you want to use it. You don't want to drag it halfway across the solar system because there's a one-in-a-thousand chance somebody might just want a minute of your time." She patted his forearm. "Am I anywhere near it?"

Rimkin thought: Live Martians? If I were a live Martian, then I wouldn't have to worry about the seven hundred and fifty enzyme reactions that keep the human body alive. But then, there'd be others, different ones, even more complicated, even more dangerous, because they have to function over a much wider temperature range. Am I a Martian? Am I one of those strange creatures I watched in the beam of my flash, walking the strange alleys with the garnet-colored walls, driving their beasts, and greeting one another with incomprehensible gestures? But this woman, which one is she? "Where's Jimmi . . . ?" Rimkin asked.

He heard Hodges start to say something; then she decided not to, and began the complicated maneuver of her prostheses to stand. "Can you walk, Rimkin? I think I'd better get you back to the skimmer."

"The skimmer . . . ? Oh, yes. Of course. It's time to go back to the skimmer, isn't it?"

He ached. All over his body, he ached. But he managed to stand, thinking. Why does it hurt so? Perhaps it's one of the seven hundred reactions, starting to fail, and I'm going to . . .

"Let's hurry up," Hodges urged. "If you've been out here all night, you're probably on the third time through your air. I bet it's stale as an old laundry bag in there."

Rimkin started slowly across the stones. But Hodges paused. Suddenly she bent down before the cracked visage and shone Rimkin's laser on the broken iris. She looked for the whole minute it took Rimkin to reach the edge. She made puzzled "mmmmm" sounds twice.

When she joined him to climb down to the sand, she was frowning behind the white frame of her helmet. And a couple of times she made strange faces.

IV

The process of getting Rimkin to bed pretty well finished getting everybody else up. When Dr. Jones wanted to give him a sedative, Rimkin went into a long and fairly coherent discussion about the drug's causing possible upset in his enzymal chemistry, which the others listened to seriously until suddenly he started to cry. At last he let Jimmi give him the injection. And while the pretty Micronesian qualitative analyst stroked his forehead, he fell asleep.

Mak, in his weight allowance for Equipment Vital to the facilitation of Your Specialized Functions, had secreted a Westphalian ham and a gallon of the good Slivowitz, contending that breakfast was pointless without a hefty slice of the one and at least a pony of the other. But he was willing to share; the ritual of breakfast was left to his episcopacy. Anyway, he had the best luck among them beating dehydrated eggs back into shape. Now, in the small area under the steps where such things were done, he was clanking and fuming like a rum-and-maple dragon.

Smith came down the stairs.

A skillet cover rang on the pan rim. Mak grunted. "I didn't realize he was that bad, Ling."

Jones folded the gaming board; the pattern of white and black fell apart. He slid the pebbles into the pot, and pushed the stud on the pot base. "I guess none of us did." The pot began to vibrate. The white stones were substantially less dense than the black ones, so, after a good shaking, ended up on top. "Do you think Mars is just too much for him?" Dr. Jones had already noticed that the separation process took longer on this lightweight planet than at home.

"Naw." Mak ducked from under the stairs with his platter of ham and eggs. The steam rose and mixed with the pipe smoke. "This must have been building for months, maybe all his life, if Freud's progeny are to be trusted."

He leaned over hefty Miss Hodges and set the platter down. Then he frowned at her. "You look oddly pensive, ma'am."

Hodges, using her aluminum stalks, pushed herself around from the table so she could see Smith, who was at the bottom of the stairs. "What happens if you cut—or break—a hologram plate in half, Ling?"

"I guess you get half the image," Jimmi said. She was sitting on an upper step. Richard Neilson was staring directly at the top of her head.

"If I sit down at the table before the rest of you," Mak said, ducking under the steps for the coffeepot, "you're only going to get half your breakfast."

Smith, Jones, and Jimmi took their chairs. Mak set the steaming enameled pot (it too was from Yugoslavia, and had come with Equipment Vital) on the coffee tile, sat down and took four pieces of toast.

"Actually you don't." Ling passed the egg platter to Hodges. "If you think of it as a method of information storage, you'll understand. You take the ordinary hologram plate, cut it in half, and then shine a laser beam on it, and you get the complete, three-dimensional image hanging there, full size. Only it's slightly out of focus, blurry, a little less distinct." He folded a sliver of ham with blackened edges and skewered it to some toast. "And if you cut it again, the image just goes a bit more out of focus. Try and imagine a photograph and a hologram of the same object side by side. Every dot of light-sensitive emulsion on each is a bit of information about the object. But the information dots on the photographic plate only relate to one point of a two-dimensional reduction. The information dots on the hologram plate relate to the entire, solid, three-dimensional object. So you see, it's vastly more efficient and far more complete. Theoretically, even a square millimeter cut from a hologram will have something to tell you about the whole object."

"Does that 'theoretical' *mean* something," Mak asked, between burblings of his briar, "or is it just rhetoric?"

"Well," Ling said, "there is a point of diminishing returns. From what I've said, it would seem that most information storage is essentially photographic; writing, tape, punchcards—"

"But those are all linear," Dr. Jones objected.

"Photographic in that there's a one-to-one relation between each datum and each un-integrated fact—"

"Think of a photograph as composed of the lines of a television picture," Jimmi said, hastily swallowing eggs and toast. "A photograph can be reduced to linear terms too."

"That's right," Ling said.

"Diminishing returns. . . . " Hodges prompted.

"Oh yes. It's simply this: if you only have a relatively small number of addresses—cybernetics term for the places your data are going to go—" he explained to Jimmi's puzzled look, "then you're often better off with photographic or linear storage. That's because you need so many bits of holographic information before the image starts to clear enough to be—"

"—anything but a menacing shadow, a ghost, a specter of itself, a vague outline filled with the unknown and too insubstantial to contain it."

Everyone looked at Hodges.

"What *are* you talking about, Evelyn?"

"Rimkin." She gestured with her brandy glass to keep Mak from filling it to the brim. "Poor, crazy Rimky."

"Oh, he isn't crazy," Jones insisted. "He may be having a nervous breakdown on us, which is too bad. But he's a brilliant, brilliant man. He *did* end up beating me at go last night. Sometimes I'm just afraid these sorts of situations are merely occupational hazards."

"True, Jonesy." She smiled ruefully and sipped. "And that's all I meant by crazy."

"You brought this whole business up in the first place, about the broken holograms," Ling said. "Why, Evelyn?"

The inflamed light of the morning desert jeweled the glass in her puffy fingers. "Do you remember the head that had fallen from the frieze? It was cracked so that one of the eyes had broken in half. When I found him this morning, he'd been out all night with his laser beam looking at the images in the broken eye." She put her glass on the table.

After a while, Dr. Smith asked, "Did you take a look?"

Evelyn Hodges nodded.

"Well?" Mak asked.

"Just what you said, Ling. The images were whole. But they were slightly blurred, out of focus. I think there was something off with the timing too. That's all."

Mak leaned forward, made disgusted sounds, and began to batter his ashes over the detritus of crusts and butter on his plate. "Let's go out and finish up those measurements." He poked the stem in his pocket. The periscope dropped. "If he was up all night, that shot should keep him asleep till this evening."

V

It didn't.

Rimkin woke fighting the drug after they had been gone twenty minutes.

And he still didn't know where he was. Not where he should be, certainly. Because his head hurt; it felt as though the side had been broken away. His whole body was sore. He lurched from the bed and tried to focus on the dishes, on the table—but they all had haloes like the superimpositions from special-effect sequences in old color films.

Jimmi was sitting on the bottom step, reading. She had chosen (a little unwillingly) to stay with the patient.

Crash!

She looked up.

Richard Nelson was trundling down the steps toward her. And at the top, stood naked Rimkin. Jimmi leapt away as the bust struck the reader she had dropped on the steps.

"Rimky, are you . . . ?"

He came down the steps, three of them slowly, seven of them fast, the last two slowly. Then, while she was debating whether to try and restrain him physically, he was gone through the double doors to the lockers. She ran toward them—the two brass handles swung up and clicked. She crashed against them. But behind the veneer that looked like walnut was ribbed steel.

Inside the locker Rimkin fumbled the catches of his air suit and thought: Hot. Hot outside. Twice he dropped the contraption on the grilled floor. Boiled . . . boiled *something.* An Earthman would boil out there on the desert without a suit. But why was he worrying? He wasn't sure who or what he might be. But the streets with their shaggy pennants, and their elegant citizens walking their shambling beasts with blood-colored eyes; they were waiting for him there in the hot city, the dusty city, with high, Marsite facades from which the carven heads gazed down on dry gutters.

He didn't need a suit, of course. But the lock-release switch was inside the suit, and it wouldn't work unless the suit was sealed. He picked up the white, slippery material again. Sealing the suit was almost habit; and the habits must have been working, because the skimmer door was opening now. Through his faceplate he could almost see the great city of High Weir stretching away to the temple. But slightly out of focus, indistinct. . . . How was he supposed to know which were shapes of time-cast dust and which were the intelligent creations of the amazing culture of his people, his planet? He brushed his arm around his faceplate—but that didn't do any good.

He walked down the blazing, alien street.

And the street sucked his boots.

He was going to take off his air suit soon. Yes. Because there was no need for it in such a brilliant city. But wait just a few minutes, because things were still too unfocused, too amorphous. And sand, from when he'd brushed his arm across his faceplate, kept trickling down the plastic. Nor were the figures in front of him Martians. He didn't think they were Martians. They were white and bulbous and were busy about the shards of purple stone, doing things to the slim columns that rose to prick the Martian noon.

"Who are you?" he said.

Two of them turned around.

"Rimkin . . . !"

"I don't know who you are," he told them.

"Hey, what's he doing out here?"

"I'm a Martian," Rimkin told them. "You're nothing but . . . that's right, potatoes!" He tried to laugh, but it came out crying because his head hurt very badly, and he was dopey from whatever they had given him that morning.

"We've got to get him back to the skimmer! Come on, Rimky."

"I'm going to take off my air suit," he said. "Because I'm a Martian and you—"

But then they were all around him. And they kept holding his hands down, which was easy because he was weak from the drug. And the carved heads, the gleaming eyes, melted behind his tears.

"Rimkin! Rimkin! Are you out there? Evelyn, Mak, Rimkin's out there some place!"

"We've got him, Jimmi! It's all right. We're bringing him back to the skimmer."

"Who are you? I can't tell who you are!"

"Oh, Rimky, are you all right?"

"I'm a Martian. I can take off my spacesuit—"

"No, you don't, fellow. Keep your hands down."

"I think you're all crazy, you know? I'm a Martian, but you're all talking to somebody who isn't even here!"

"Rimkin, go on back with them and don't give them any trouble. For me, for Jimmi. They just want to help."

"I don't even know you. Why do I have to come back? This is my city. These are my buildings, my house. It's just not clear any more. And it hurts."

"Keep your hands down. Come on—"

"Jimmi, are you all right? How did he get out? He didn't hurt you, did he?"

"I guess the sedative wasn't strong enough. He surprised me, and managed to lock me in the study. I just found Evelyn's emergency keys in her room a minute ago so I could get down to the controls and radio you. What are we going to do with him?"

"I'm going to go to Mars. I can take off my spacesuit. I'm a Martian. I'm a Martian—"

"He doesn't seem to be dangerous. They'll get him back to Earth, fill him full of calming drugs, and in six months he'll probably be good as new. I wouldn't be surprised to find out he goes into this sort of thing periodically. I spent a couple of weeks in a hospital drying out once."

"Why can't I take off my suit? I'm a Martian—"

"Rimky, remember all those enzyme reactions you were going on at us about this morning when you didn't want to take your shot? You open your suit, and the temperature out here will work so much havoc with them you won't have time to blink. You'll also fry."

"But which ones? How can I tell which ones will . . . "

"Evelyn, I can't hit him over the head. I'll crack his helmet."

"I know, I know, Mak. We'll get him back. Oh, this is so terrible!

What causes something like this to happen to a perfectly fine—more than fine mind, Ling?"

"Don't hit me over the head. Don't . . . I'm a Martian. And it hurts."

"We won't hurt you, Rimky."

"Evelyn, we're out here exploring the ruins of new civilizations on other planets and we still don't know. We know much of it's chemical, and we can do something about a lot of it, but we still don't . . . Holograms, Evelyn . . . "

"What, Ling?"

"Nobody's ever been able to figure out how the brain stores information. We know the mind remembers everything it sees, hears, feels, smells, as well as all sorts of cross-referencing. People have just always assumed that it must be basically a photographic process, all the separate bits of data stored on the juncture of each individual synapse. But suppose, Evelyn, the brain stores hologramically. Then madness would be some emotional or chemical situation that blocked off access to large parts of the cerebral hologram."

"Then large parts of the world would just lose their sharpness, their focus . . . "

"Like Rimkin here?"

"Now *keep* your hands *away* from your suit catch!"

"Come on, Rimkin. Once we get you home, you'll be all right."

"It won't hurt any more?"

"That's right. Try to relax."

As they reached the lock, Rimkin turned to one of the white, inflated figures and his voice grew tearful. "Aren't I . . . aren't I really a Martian?"

Two white hands patted the shoulders of his air suit. "You're George Arthur Rimkin, Associate Professor of Semantics at Inter-Nal University, a very brilliant man who has been under a lot of pressure recently."

Rimkin looked out over beautiful rifts and dells, shapes that could have been sand dunes, that could have been the amazing structures of the great Martian city of High Weir, that could have been . . . He was crying again. "It hurts so much," he said quietly, "how am I supposed to tell?"

(1968)

POUL ANDERSON

KYRIE

On a high peak in the Lunar Carpathians stands a convent of St. Martha of Bethany. The walls are native rock; they lift dark and cragged as the mountainside itself, into a sky that is always black. As you approach from Northpole, flitting low to keep the force screens along Route Plato between you and the meteoroidal rain, you see the cross which surmounts the tower, stark athwart Earth's blue disc. No bells resound from there—not in airlessness.

You may hear them inside at the canonical hours, and throughout the crypts below where machines toil to maintain a semblance of terrestrial environment. If you linger a while you will also hear them calling to requiem mass. For it has become a tradition that prayers be offered at St. Martha's for those who have perished in space; and they are more with every passing year.

This is not the work of the sisters. They minister to the sick, the needy, the crippled, the insane, all whom space has broken and cast back. Luna is full of such, exiles because they can no longer endure Earth's pull or because it is feared they may be incubating a plague from some unknown planet or because men are so busy with their frontiers that they have no time to spare for the failures. The sisters wear space suits as often as habits, are as likely to hold a medikit as a rosary.

But they are granted some time for contemplation. At night, when for half a month the sun's glare has departed, the chapel is unshuttered and stars look down through the glaze-dome to the candles. They do not wink and their light is winter cold. One of the nuns in particular is there as often as may be, praying for her own dead. And the abbess sees to it that she can be present when the yearly mass, that she endowed before she took her vows, is sung.

> Requiem aeternam dona eis, Domine, et lux
>   perpetua luceat eis.
> Kyrie eleison, Christie eleison, Kyrie eleison.

The Supernova Sagittarii expedition comprised fifty human beings and a flame. It went the long way around from Earth orbit, stopping at Epsilon Lyrae to pick up its last member. Thence it approached its destination by stages.

This is the paradox: time and space are aspects of each other. The explosion was more than a hundred years past when noted by men on Lasthope. They were part of a generations-long effort to fathom the civilization of creatures altogether unlike us; but one night they looked up and saw a light so brilliant it cast shadows.

That wave front would reach Earth several centuries hence. By then it would be so tenuous that nothing but another bright point would appear in the sky. Meanwhile, though, a ship overleaping the space through which light must creep could track the great star's death across time.

Suitably far off, instruments recorded what had been before the outburst, incandescence collapsing upon itself after the last nuclear fuel was burned out. A jump, and they saw what happened a century ago, convulsion, storm of quanta and neutrinos, radiation equal to the massed hundred billion suns of this galaxy.

It faded, leaving an emptiness in heaven, and the *Raven* moved closer. Fifty light-years—fifty years—inward, she studied a shrinking fieriness in the midst of a fog which shone like lightning.

Twenty-five years later the central globe had dwindled more, the nebula had expanded and dimmed. But because the distance was now so much less, everything seemed larger and brighter. The naked eye saw a dazzle too fierce to look straight at, making the constellations pale by contrast. Telescopes showed a blue-white spark in the heart of an opalescent cloud delicately filamented at the edges.

The *Raven* made ready for her final jump, to the immediate neighborhood of the supernova.

Captain Teodor Szili went on a last-minute inspection tour. The ship murmured around him, running at one gravity of acceleration to reach the desired intrinsic velocity. Power droned, regulators whickered, ventilation systems rustled. He felt the energies quiver in his bones. But metal surrounded him, blank and comfortless. Viewports gave on a dragon's hoard of stars, the ghostly arch of the Milky Way: on vacuum, cosmic rays, cold not far above absolute zero, distance beyond imagination to the nearest human hearthfire. He was about to take his people where none had ever been before, into conditions none was sure about, and that was a heavy burden on him.

He found Eloise Waggoner at her post, a cubbyhole with intercom connections directly to the command bridge. Music drew him, a triumphant serenity he did not recognize. Stopping in the doorway, he saw her seated with a small tape machine on the desk.

"What's this?" he demanded.

"Oh!" The woman (he could not think of her as a girl, though she was barely out of her teens) started. "I . . . I was waiting for the jump."

"You were to wait at the alert."

"What have I to do?" she answered less timidly than was her wont. "I mean, I'm not a crewman or a scientist."

"You are in the crew. Special communications technician."

"With Lucifer. And he likes the music. He says we come closer to oneness with it than in anything else he knows about us."

Szili arched his brows. "Oneness?"

A blush went up Eloise's thin cheeks. She stared at the deck and her hands twisted together. "Maybe that isn't the right word. Peace, harmony, unity . . . God? . . . I sense what he means, but we haven't any word that fits."

"Hm. Well, you are supposed to keep him happy." The skipper regarded her with a return of the distaste he had tried to suppress. She was a decent enough sort, he supposed, in her gauche and inhibited way; but her looks! Scrawny, big-footed, big-nosed, pop eyes, and stringy dust-colored hair—and, to be sure, telepaths always made him uncomfortable. She said she could only read Lucifer's mind, but was that true?

No. Don't think such things. Loneliness and otherness can come near breaking you out here, without adding suspicion of your fellows.

If Eloise Waggoner was really human. She must be some kind of mutant at the very least. Whoever could communicate thought to thought with a living vortex had to be.

"What are you playing, anyhow?" Szili asked.

"Bach. The Third Brandenburg Concerto. He, Lucifer, he doesn't care for the modern stuff. I don't either."

You wouldn't, Szili decided. Aloud: "Listen, we jump in half an hour. No telling what we'll emerge in. This is the first time anyone's been close to a recent supernova. We can only be certain of so much hard radiation that we'll be dead if the screenfields give way. Otherwise we've nothing to go on except theory. And a collapsing stellar core is so unlike anything anywhere else in the universe that I'm skeptical about how good the theory is. We can't sit daydreaming. We have to prepare."

"Yes, sir." Whispering, her voice lost its usual harshness.

He stared past her, past the ophidian eyes of meters and controls, as if he could penetrate the steel beyond and look straight into space. There, he knew, floated Lucifer.

The image grew in him: a fireball twenty meters across, shimmering white, red, gold, royal blue, flames dancing like Medusa locks, cometary tail burning for a hundred meters behind, a shiningness, a glory, a piece of hell. Not the least of what troubled him was the thought of that which paced his ship.

He hugged scientific explanations to his breast, though they were little better than guesses. In the multiple star system of Epsilon Aurigae, in the gas and energy pervading the space around, things took place which no laboratory could imitate. Ball lightning on a planet was perhaps analogous, as the formation of simple organic compounds in a primordial ocean is analogous to the life which finally evolves. In Epsilon Aurigae, magnetohydrodynamics had done what chemistry did on Earth. Stable plasma vortices had appeared, had grown, had added complexity, until after millions of years they became something you must needs call an organism. It was a form of ions, nuclei, and force-fields. It metabolized electrons, nucleons, X rays; it maintained its configuration for a long lifetime; it reproduced; it thought.

But what did it think? The few telepaths who could communicate with the Aurigeans, who had first made humankind aware that the Aurigeans existed, never explained clearly. They were a queer lot themselves.

Wherefore Captain Szili said, "I want you to pass this on to him."

"Yes, sir." Eloise turned down the volume on her taper. Her eyes unfocused. Through her ears went words, and her brain (how efficient a transducer was it?) passed the meanings on out to him who loped alongside *Raven* on his own reaction drive.

"Listen, Lucifer. You have heard this often before, I know, but I want to be positive you understand in full. Your psychology must be very foreign to ours. Why did you agree to come with us? I don't know. Technician Waggoner said you were curious and adventurous. Is that the whole truth?

"No matter. In half an hour we jump. We'll come within five hundred million kilometers of the supernova. That's where your work begins. You can go where we dare not, observe what we can't, tell us more than our instruments would ever hint at. But first we have to verify we can stay in orbit around the star. This concerns you too. Dead men can't transport you home again.

"So. In order to enclose you within the jumpfield, without disrupting your body, we have to switch off the shield screens. We'll emerge in a lethal radiation zone. You must promptly retreat from the ship, because we'll start the screen generator up sixty seconds after transit. Then you must investigate the vicinity. The hazards to look for—" Szili listed them. "Those are only what we can foresee. Perhaps we'll hit other garbage we haven't predicted. If anything seems like a menace, return at once, warn us, and prepare for a jump back to here. Do you have that? Repeat."

Words jerked from Eloise. They were a correct recital; but how much was she leaving out?

"Very good." Szili hesitated. "Proceed with your concert if you like. But break it off at zero minus ten minutes and stand by."

"Yes, sir." She didn't look at him. She didn't appear to be looking anywhere in particular.

His footsteps clacked down the corridor and were lost.

—Why did he say the same things over? asked Lucifer.

"He is afraid," Eloise said.

—?—.

"I guess you don't know about fear," she said.

—Can you show me? . . . No, do not. I sense it is hurtful. You must not be hurt.

"I can't be afraid anyway, when your mind is holding mine."

(Warmth filled her. Merriment was there, playing like little flames over the surface of Father-leading-her-by-the-hand-when-she-was-just-a-child-and-they-went-out-one-summer's-day-to-pick-wildflowers; over strength and gentleness and Bach and God.) Lucifer swept around the hull in an exuberant curve. Sparks danced in his wake.

—Think flowers again. Please.

She tried.

—They are like (image, as nearly as a human brain could grasp, of fountains blossoming with gamma-ray colors in the middle of light, everywhere light). But so tiny. So brief a sweetness.

"I don't understand how you can understand," she whispered.

—You understand for me. I did not have that kind of thing to love, before you came.

"But you have so much else. I try to share it, but I'm not made to realize what a star is."

—Nor I for planets. Yet ourselves may touch.

Her cheeks burned anew. The thought rolled on, interweaving its counterpoint to the marching music. —That is why I came, do you know? For you. I am fire and air. I had not tasted the coolness of water, the patience of earth, until you showed me. You are moonlight on an ocean.

"No, don't," she said. "Please."

Puzzlement: —Why not? Does joy hurt? Are you not used to it?

"I, I guess that's right." She flung her head back. "No! Be damned if I'll feel sorry for myself!"

—Why should you? Have we not all reality to be in, and is it not full of suns and songs?

"Yes. To you. Teach me."

—If you in turn will teach me— The thought broke off. A contact remained, unspeaking, such as she imagined must often prevail among lovers.

She glowered at Motilal Mazundar's chocolate face, where the physicist stood in the doorway. "What do you want?"

He was surprised. "Only to see if everything is well with you, Miss Waggoner."

She bit her lip. He had tried harder than most aboard to be kind to her. "I'm sorry," she said. "I didn't mean to bark at you. Nerves."

"We are everyone on edge." He smiled. "Exciting though this venture is, it will be good to come home, correct?"

Home, she thought: four walls of an apartment above a banging city street. Books and television. She might present a paper at the next scientific meeting, but no one would invite her to the parties afterward.

Am I that horrible? she wondered. I know I'm not anything to look at, but I try to be nice and interesting. Maybe I try too hard.

—You do not with me, Lucifer said.

"You're different," she told him.

Mazundar blinked. "Beg pardon?"

"Nothing," she said in haste.

"I have wondered about an item," Mazundar said in an effort at conversation. "Presumably Lucifer will go quite near the supernova. Can you still maintain contact with him? The time dilation effect, will that not change the frequency of his thoughts too much?"

"What time dilation?" She forced a chuckle. "I'm no physicist. Only a little librarian who turned out to have a wild talent."

"You were not told? Why, I assumed everybody was. An intense gravitational field affects time just as a high velocity does. Roughly speaking, processes take place more slowly than they do in clear space. That is why light from a massive star is somewhat reddened. And our supernova core retains almost three solar masses. Furthermore, it has acquired such a density that its attraction at the surface is, ah, incredibly high. Thus by our clocks it will take infinite time to shrink to the Schwarzschild radius; but an observer on the star itself would experience this whole shrinkage in a fairly short period."

"Schwarzschild radius? Be so good as to explain." Eloise realized that Lucifer had spoken through her.

"If I can without mathematics. You see, this mass we are to study is so great and so concentrated that no force exceeds the gravitational. Nothing can counterbalance. Therefore the process will continue until no energy can escape. The star will have vanished out of the universe. In fact, theoretically the contraction will proceed to zero volume. Of course, as I said, that will take forever as far as we are concerned. And the theory neglects quantum-mechanical considerations which come into play toward the end. Those are still not very well understood. I hope, from this expedition, to acquire more knowledge." Mazundar shrugged. "At any rate, Miss Waggoner, I was wondering if the frequency shift involved would not prevent our friend from communicating with us when he is near the star."

"I doubt that." Still Lucifer spoke, she was his instrument and never had she known how good it was to be used by one who cared. "Telepathy is not a wave phenomenon. Since it transmits instantaneously, it cannot be. Nor does it appear limited by distance. Rather, it is a resonance. Being attuned, we two may well be able to continue thus across the entire breadth of the cosmos; and I am not aware of any material phenomenon which could interfere."

"I see." Mazundar gave her a long look. "Thank you," he said uncomfortably. "Ah . . . I must get to my own station. Good luck." He bustled off without stopping for an answer.

Eloise didn't notice. Her mind was become a torch and a song. "Lucifer!" she cried aloud. "Is that true?"

—I believe so. My entire people are telepaths, hence we have more knowledge of such matters than yours do. Our experience leads us to think there is no limit.

"You can always be with me? You always will?"

—If you so wish, I am gladdened.

The comet body curvetted and danced, the brain of fire laughed low. —Yes, Eloise, I would like very much to remain with you. No one else has ever—Joy. Joy. Joy.

They named you better than they knew, Lucifer, she wanted to say, and perhaps she did. They thought it was a joke; they thought by calling you after the devil they could make you safely small like themselves. But Lucifer isn't the devil's real name. It means only Light Bearer. One Latin prayer even addresses Christ as Lucifer. Forgive me, God, I can't help remembering that. Do You mind? He isn't Christian, but I think he doesn't need to be, I think he must never have felt sin, Lucifer, Lucifer.

She sent the music soaring for as long as she was permitted.

The ship jumped. In one shift of world line parameters she crossed twenty-five light-years to destruction.

Each knew it in his own way, save for Eloise who also lived it with Lucifer.

She felt the shock and heard the outraged metal scream, she smelled the ozone and scorch and tumbled through the infinite falling that is weightlessness. Dazed, she fumbled at the intercom. Words crackled through: " . . . unit blown . . . back EMF surge . . . how should I know how long to fix the blasted thing? . . . stand by, stand by . . . " Over all hooted the emergency siren.

Terror rose in her, until she gripped the crucifix around her neck and the mind of Lucifer. Then she laughed in the pride of his might.

He had whipped clear of the ship immediately on arrival. Now he floated in the same orbit. Everywhere around, the nebula filled space with unrestful rainbows. To him, *Raven* was not the metal cylinder which human eyes would have seen, but a lambence, the shield screen reflecting a whole spectrum. Ahead lay the supernova core, tiny at this remove but alight, alight.

—Have no fears (he caressed her). I comprehend. Turbulence is extensive, so soon after the detonation. We emerged in a region where the plasma is especially dense. Unprotected for the moment before the guardian field was reestablished, your main generator outside the hull was short-circuited. But you are safe. You can make repairs. And I, I am in an ocean of energy. Never was I so alive. Come, swim these tides with me.

Captain Szili's voice yanked her back. "Waggoner! Tell that Aurigean to get busy. We've spotted a radiation source on an intercept orbit, and it may be too much for our screen." He specified coordinates. "What *is* it?"

For the first time, Eloise felt alarm in Lucifer. He curved about and streaked from the ship.

Presently his thought came to her, no less vivid. She lacked words for the terrible splendor she viewed with him: a million-kilometer ball of ionized gas where luminance blazed and electric discharges leaped, booming through the haze around the star's exposed heart. The thing could not have made any sound, for space here was still almost a vacuum by Earth's parochial standards; but she heard it thunder, and felt the fury that spat from it.

She said for him: "A mass of expelled material. It must have lost radial velocity to friction and static gradients, been drawn into a cometary orbit, held together for a while by internal potentials. As if this sun were trying yet to bring planets to birth—"

"It'll strike us before we're in shape to accelerate," Szili said, "and overload our shield. If you know any prayers, use them."

"Lucifer!" she called; for she did not want to die, when he must remain.

—I think I can deflect it enough, he told her with a grimness she had not hitherto met in him. —My own fields, to mesh with its; and free energy to drink; and an unstable configuration; yes, perhaps I can help you. But help me, Eloise. Fight by my side.

His brightness moved toward the juggernaut shape.

She felt how its chaotic electromagnetism clawed at his. She felt him tossed and torn. The pain was hers. He battled to keep his own cohesion, and the combat was hers. They locked together, Aurigean and gas cloud. The forces that shaped him grappled as arms might; he poured power from his core, hauling that vast tenuous mass with him down the magnetic torrent which streamed from the sun; he gulped atoms and thrust them backward until the jet splashed across heaven.

She sat in her cubicle, lending him what will to live and prevail she could, and beat her fists bloody on the desk.

The hours brawled past.

In the end, she could scarcely catch the message that flickered out of his exhaustion:—Victory.

"Yours," she wept.

—Ours.

Through instruments, men saw the luminous death pass them by. A cheer lifted.

"Come back," Eloise begged.

—I cannot. I am too spent. We are merged, the cloud and I, and are tumbling in toward the star. (Like a hurt hand reaching forth to comfort her:) Do not be afraid for me. As we get closer, I will draw fresh strength from its glow, fresh substance from the nebula. I will need a while to spiral out against that pull. But how can I fail to come back to you, Eloise? Wait for me. Rest. Sleep.

Her shipmates led her to sickbay. Lucifer sent her dreams of fire flowers and mirth and the suns that were his home.

But she woke at last, screaming. The medic had to put her under heavy sedation.

He had not really understood what it would mean to confront something so violent that space and time themselves were twisted thereby.

His speed increased appallingly. That was in his own measure; from *Raven* they saw him fall through several days. The properties of matter were changed. He could not push hard enough or fast enough to escape.

Radiation, stripped nuclei, particles born and destroyed and born again, sleeted and shouted through him. His substance was peeled away, layer by layer. The supernova core was a white delirium before him. It shrank as he approached, ever smaller, denser, so brilliant that brilliance ceased to have meaning. Finally the gravitational forces laid their full grip upon him.

—Eloise! he shrieked in the agony of his disintegration.—Oh, Eloise, help me!

The star swallowed him up. He was stretched infinitely long, compressed infinitely thin, and vanished with it from existence.

The ship prowled the farther reaches. Much might yet be learned.

Captain Szili visited Eloise in sickbay. Physically she was recovering.

"I'd call him a man," he declared through the machine mumble, "except that's not praise enough. We weren't even his kin, and he died to save us."

She regarded him from eyes more dry than seemed natural. He could just make out her answer. "He is a man. Doesn't he have an immortal soul too?"

"Well, uh, yes, if you believe in souls, yes, I'd agree."

She shook her head. "But why can't he go to his rest?"

He glanced about for the medic and found they were alone in the narrow metal room. "What do you mean?" He made himself pat her hand. "I know, he was a good friend of yours. Still, his must have been a merciful death. Quick, clean; I wouldn't mind going out like that."

"For him . . . yes, I suppose so. It has to be. But—" She could not continue. Suddenly she covered her ears. "Stop! Please!"

Szili made soothing noises and left. In the corridor he encountered Mazundar. "How is she?" the physicist asked.

The captain scowled. "Not good. I hope she doesn't crack entirely before we can get her to a psychiatrist."

"Why, what is wrong?"

"She thinks she can hear him."

Mazundar smote fist into palm. "I hoped otherwise," he breathed.

Szili braced himself and waited.

"She does," Mazundar said. "Obviously she does."

"But that's impossible! He's dead!"

"Remember the time dilation," Mazundar replied. "He fell from the sky and perished swiftly, yes. But in supernova time. Not the same as ours. To us, the final stellar collapse takes an infinite number of years. And telepathy has no distance limits." The physicist started walking fast, away from that cabin. "He will always be with her."

(1968)

SUZETTE HADEN ELGIN

For the Sake of Grace

The Khadilh ban-harihn frowned at the disk he held in his hand, annoyed and apprehensive. There was always, of course, the chance of malfunction in the com-system. He reached forward and punched the transmit button again with one thumb, and the machine clicked to itself fitfully and delivered another disk in the message tray. He picked it up, looked at it and swore a round assortment of colorful oaths, since no women were present.

There on the left was the matrix-mark that identified his family, the ban-harihn symbol quite clear; no possibility of error there. And from it curled the suitable number of small lines, yellow for the females, green for the males, one for each member of his household, all decorously in order. Except for one.

The yellow line that represented at all times the state of being of his wife, the Khadilha Althea, was definitely not as it should have been. It was interrupted at quarter-inch intervals by a small black dot, indicating that all was not well with the Khadilha. And the symbol at the end of the line was not the blue cross that would have classified the difficulty as purely physical; it was the indeterminate red star indicating only that the problem, whatever it was, could be looked upon as serious or about to become serious.

The Khadilh sighed. That would mean anything, from his wife's misuse of their credit cards through a security leak by one of her servants to an unsuitable love affair—although his own knowledge of the Khadilha's chilly nature made him consider the last highly unlikely. The only possible course for him was to ask for an immediate full report.

And just what, he wondered, would he do, if the report were to make it clear that he was needed at home at once? One did not simply pick up one's gear and tootle off home from the outposts of the Federation. It would take him at the very least nine months to arrive in his home city-cluster, even if he were able to command a priority flight with suspended-animation berths and warp facilities. Damn the woman anyway, what could she be up to?

He punched the button for voice transmittal, and the com-system began to hum at him, indicating readiness for dialing. He dialed, carefully selecting the planet code, since his last attempt to contact his home, on his wife's birthday, had resulted in a most embarrassing conversation with a squirmy-tentacled creature that he had gotten out of its (presumed) bed in the middle of its (presumed) sleep. And he'd had to pay in full for the call, too, all intergalactic communication being on a buyer-risk basis.

" . . . three-three-two-three-two . . . " he finished, very cautiously, and waited. The tiny screen lit up, and the words "STAND BY" appeared, to be replaced in a few seconds by "SCRIBE (FEMALE) OF THE HOUSEHOLD BAN-HARIHN, which meant he had at least dialed correctly. The screen cleared and the words were replaced by the face of his household Scribe, so distorted by distance as to be only by courtesy a face, but with the ban-harihn matrix-mark superimposed in green and yellow across the screen as security.

He spoke quickly, mindful of the com-rates at this distance.

"Scribe ban-harihn, this morning the state-of-being disk indicated some difficulty in the condition of the Khadilha Althea. Please advise if this condition could be described as an emergency."

After the usual brief lag for conversion to symbols, the reply was superimposed over the matrix-mark, and the Khadilh thought as usual that these tiny intergalactic screens became so cluttered before a conversation was terminated that one could hardly make out the messages involved.

The message in this case was "Negative," and the Khadilh smiled; the Scribe was even more mindful than he of the cost of this transmittal.

He pushed the ERASE button and finished with, "Thank you, Scribe ban-harihn. You will then prepare at once a written report, in detail, and forward it to me by the fastest available means. Should the problem intensify to emergency point, I now authorize a com-system transmittal to that effect, to be initiated by any one of my sons. Terminate."

The screen went blank and the Khadilh, just for curiosity, punched one more time the state-of-being control. The machine delivered another disk, and sure enough, there it was again, black dots, red star and all. He threw it into the disposal, shrugged his shoulders helplessly and ordered coffee. There was nothing whatever that he could do until he received the Scribe's report.

However, if it should turn out that he had wasted the cost of an intergalactic transmittal on some petty household dispute, there was going to be hell to pay, he promised himself, and a suitable punishment administered to the Khadilha by the nearest official of the Women's Discipline Unit. There certainly ought to be some way to make the state-of-being codes a bit more detailed so that everything from war to an argument with a servingwoman didn't come across on the same symbol.

The report arrived by Tele-Bounce in four days. Very wise choice, he thought approvingly, since the bounce machinery was totally automatic and impersonal. It was somewhat difficult to read, since the Scribe had specified that it was to be delivered to him without transcription other than into verbal symbols, and it was therefore necessary for him to scan a roll of yellow paper with a message eight symbols wide and seemingly miles long. He read only enough to convince him that no problem of discretion could possibly be involved, and then he ran the thing through the transcribe slot, receiving a standard letter on white paper in return.

"To the Khadilh ban-harihn," it read, "as requested, the following report from the Scribe of his household:

> Three days ago, as the Khadilh is no doubt aware, the festival of the Spring Rains was celebrated here. The entire household, with the exception of the Khadilh himself, was present at a very large and elaborate procession held to mark the opening of the Alaharibahn-khalida Trance Hours. A suitable spot for watching the procession, entirely in accordance with decorum, had been chosen by the Khadilha Althea, and the women of the household were standing in the second row along the edge of the street set aside for the women.
>
> There had been a number of dancers, bands, and so on, followed by thirteen of the Poets of this city-cluster. The Poets had almost passed, along with the usual complement of exotic animals and mobile flowers and the like, and no untoward incident of any kind had occurred, when quite suddenly the Khadilh's daughter Jacinth was approached by (pardon my liberty of speech) the Poet Anna-Mary, who is, as the Khadilh knows, a female. The Poet leaned from her mount, indicating with her staff of bells that it was her wish to speak to the Khadilh's daughter, and halting the procession to do so. It was at this point that the incident occurred which has no doubt given rise to the variant marking in the state-of-being disk line for the Khadilha Althea. Quite unaccountably, the Khadilha, rather than sending the child forward to speak with the Poet (as would have been proper), grabbed the child Jacinth by the shoulders, whirling her around and covering her completely with her heavy robes so that she could neither speak nor see.
>
> The Poet Anna-Mary merely bowed from her horse and signaled for the procession to continue, but she was quite white and obviously offended. The family made a show of participating in the rest of the day's observ-

ances, but the Khadilh's sons took the entire household home by mid-afternoon, thereby preventing the Khadilha from participating in the Trance Hours. This was no doubt a wise course.

What sequel there may have been to this, the Scribe does not know, as no announcement has been made to the household. The Scribe here indicates her respect and subservience to the Khadilh.

Terminate with thanks.

"Well!" said the Khadilh. He laid the letter down on the top of his desk, thinking hard, rubbing his beard with one hand.

What could reasonably be expected in the way of repercussions from a public insult to an elderly—and touchy—Poet? It was hard to say.

As the only female Poet on the planet, the Poet Anna-Mary was much alone; as her duties were not arduous, she had much time to brood. And though she was a Poet, she remained only a female, with the female's inferior reasoning powers. She was accustomed to reverent homage, to women holding up their children to touch the hem of her robe. She could hardly be expected to react with pleasure to an insult in public, and from a female.

It was at his sons that she would be most likely to strike, through the University, he decided, and he could not chance that. He had worked too hard, and they had worked too hard, to allow a vindictive female, no matter how lofty her status, to destroy what they had built up. He had better go home and leave the orchards to take care of themselves; important as the lush peaches of Earth were to the economy of his home planet, his sons were of even greater importance.

It was not every family that could boast of five sons in the University, all five selected by competitive examinations for the Major in Poetry. Sometimes a family might have two sons chosen, but the rest would be refused, as the Khadilh himself had been refused, and would then have to be satisfied with the selection of Law or Medicine or Government or some other of the Majors. He smiled proudly, remembering the respectful glances of his friends when each of his sons in turn had placed high in the examinations and had been awarded the Poet Major, his oldest son entering at the Fourth Level. And when the youngest had been chosen, thus releasing the oldest from the customary vow of celibacy—since to impose it would have meant the end of the family line, an impossible situation—the Khadilh had had difficulty in maintaining even a pretense of modesty. The meaning, of course, was that he would have as grandson the direct offspring of a Poet, something that had not happened within his memory or his father's memory. He had been given to understand, in fact, that it had been more than three hundred years since all sons of any one family had entered the Poetry courses. (A family having only one son was prohibited by law from entering the Poetry Examinations, they told him.)

Yes, he must go home, and to hell with the peaches of Earth. Let them rot, if the garden-robots could not manage them.

He went to the com-system and punched through a curt transmittal of his intention, and then set to pulling the necessary strings to obtain a priority flight.

When the Khadilh arrived at his home, his sons were lined up in his study, waiting for him, each in the coarse brown student's tunic that was compulsory, but with the scarlet Poet's stripe around the hem to delight his eyes. He smiled at them, saying, "It is a pleasure to see you once more, my sons; you give rest to my eyes and joy to my heart."

Michael, the oldest, answered in kind.

"It is our pleasure to see you, Father."

"Let us all sit down," said the Khadilh, motioning them to their places about the study table that stood in the center of the room. When they were seated, he struck the table with his knuckles, in the old ritual, three times slowly.

"No doubt you know why I have chosen to abandon my orchards to the attention of the garden-robots and return home so suddenly," he said. "Unfortunately, it has taken me almost ten months to reach you. There was no more rapid way to get home to you, much as I wished for one."

"We understand, Father," said his oldest son.

"Then, Michael," went on Khadilh, "would you please bring me up to date on the developments here since the incident at the procession of the Spring Rains."

His son seemed hesitant to speak, his black brows drawn together over his eyes, and the Khadilh smiled at him encouragingly.

"Come, Michael," he said, "surely it is not courteous to make your father wait in this fashion!"

"You will realize, Father," said the young man slowly, "that it has not been possible to communicate with you since the time of your last transmittal. You will also realize that this matter has not been one about which advice could easily be requested. I have had no choice but to make decisions as best I could."

"I realize that. Of course."

"Very well, then. I hope you will not be angry, Father."

"I shall indeed be angry if I am not told at once exactly what has occurred this past ten months. You make me uneasy, my son."

Michael took a deep breath and nodded. "All right, Father," he said. "I will be brief."

"And quick."

"Yes, Father. I took our household away from the festival as soon as I decently could without creating talk; and when we arrived at home, I sent the Khadilha at once to her quarters, with orders to stay there until you should advise me to the contrary."

"Quite right," said the Khadilh. "Then what?"

"The Khadilha disobeyed me, Father."

"Disobeyed you? In what way?"

"The Khadilha Althea disregarded my orders entirely, and she took our sister into the Small Corridor, and there she allowed her to look into the cell where our aunt is kept, Father."

"My God!" shouted the Khadilh. "And you made no move to stop her?"

"Father," said Michael ban-harihn, "you must realize that no one could have anticipated the actions of the Khadilha Althea. We would certainly have stopped her had we known, but who would have thought that the Khadilha would disobey the order of an adult male? It was assumed that she would go to her quarters and remain there."

"I see."

"I did not contact the Women's Discipline Unit," Michael continued. "I preferred that such an order should come from you, Father. However, orders were given that the Khadilha should be restricted to her quarters, and no one has been allowed to see her except the serving-women. The wires to her com-system were disconnected, and provision was made for suitable medication to be added to her diet. You will find her very docile, Father."

The Khadilh was trembling with indignation.

"Discipline will be provided at once, my son," he said. "I apologize for the disgusting behavior of the Khadilha. But please go on—what of my daughter?"

"That is perhaps the most distressing thing of all."

"In what way?"

Michael looked thoroughly miserable.

"Answer me at once," snapped the Khadilh, "and in full."

"Our sister Jacinth," said his second son, Nicolas, "was already twelve years of age at the time of the festival. When she returned from the Small Corridor, without notice to any one of us, she announced her intention by letter to the Poet Anna-Mary—her intention to compete in the examinations for the Major of Poetry."

"And the Poet Anna-Mary—"

"Turned the announcement immediately over to the authorities at the Poetry Unit," finished Michael. "Certainly she made no attempt to dissuade our sister."

"She is amply revenged then for the insult of the Khadilha," said the Khadilh bitterly. "Were there any other acts on the part of the Poet Anna-Mary?"

"None, Father. Our sister has been cloistered by government order since that time, of course, to prevent contamination of the other females."

"Oh, dear God," breathed the Khadilh, "how could such a thing have touched my household—for the second time?"

He thought a moment. "When are the examinations, then? I've lost all track of time."

"It has been ten months, Father."

"In about a month, then?"

"In three weeks."

"Will they let me see Jacinth?"

"No, Father," said Michael. "And, Father—"

"Yes, Michael?"

"It is my shame and my sorrow that this should have been the result of your leaving your household in my care."

The Khadilh reached over and grasped his hand firmly.

"You are very young, my son," he said, "and you have nothing to be ashamed of. When the females of a household take it upon themselves to upset the natural order of things and to violate the rules of decency, there is very little anyone can do."

"Thank you, Father."

"Now," said the Khadilh, turning to face them all, "I suggest that the next thing to do would be to initiate action by the Women's Discipline Unit. Do you wish me to have the Khadilha placed on Permanent Medication, my sons?"

He hoped they would not insist upon it, and was pleased to see that they did not.

"Let us wait, Father," said Michael, "until we know the outcome of the examinations."

"Surely the outcome is something about which there can be no question!"

"Could we wait, Father, all the same?"

It was the youngest of the boys. As was natural, he was still overly squeamish, still a bit tender. The Khadilh would not have had him be otherwise.

"A wise decision," he said. "In that case, once I have bathed and had my dinner, I will send for the Lawyer an-ahda. And you may go, my sons."

The boys filed out, led by the solemn Michael, leaving him with no company but the slow dance of a mobile flower from one of the tropical stars. It whirled gently in the middle of the corner hearth, humming to itself and giving off showers of silver sparks from time to time. He watched it suspiciously for a moment, and then pushed the com-system buttons for his Housekeeper. When the face appeared on the screen he snapped at it.

"Housekeeper, are you familiar with the nature of the mobile plant that someone has put in my study?"

The Housekeeper's voice, frightened, came back at once. "The Khadilh may have the plant removed—should I call the Gardener?"

"All I wanted to know is the sex of the blasted thing," he bellowed at her. "Is it male or female?"

"Male, Khadilh, of the genus—"

He cut off the message while she was still telling him of the plant's pedigree. It was male; therefore it could stay. He would talk to it, while he ate his dinner, about the incredible behavior of his Khadilha.

The Lawyer an-ahda leaned back in the chair provided for him and smiled at his client.

"Yes, ban-harihn," he said amiably, having known the Khadilh since they were young men at the University, "what can I do to help the sun shine more brightly through your window?"

"This is a serious matter," said the Khadilh.

"Ah."

"You heard—never mind being polite and denying it—of my wife's behavior at the procession of the Spring Rains. I see that you did."

"Very impulsive," observed the Lawyer. "Most unwise. Undisciplined."

"Indeed it was. However, worse followed."

"Oh? The Poet Anna-Mary has tried for revenge, then?"

"Not in the sense that you mean, no. But worse has happened, my old friend, far worse."

"Tell me." The Lawyer leaned forward attentively, listening, and when the Khadilh had finished, he cleared his throat.

"There isn't anything to be done, you know," he said. "You might as well know it at once."

"Nothing at all?"

"Nothing. The law provides that any woman may challenge and claim her right to compete in the Poetry Examinations, provided she is twelve years of age and a citizen of this planet. If she is not accepted, however, the penalty for having challenged and failed is solitary confinement for life, in the household of her family. And once she has announced to the Faculty by signed communication that she intends to compete, she is cloistered until the day of the examinations, and she may not change her mind. The law is very clear on this point."

"She is very young."

"She is twelve. That is all the law requires."

"It's a cruel law."

"Not at all! Can you imagine, ban-harihn, the chaos that would result if every emotional young female, bored with awaiting marriage in the women's quarters, should decide that she had a vocation and claim her right to challenge? The purpose of the law is to discourage foolish young girls from creating difficulties for their households, and for the state. Can you just imagine, if there were only a token penalty, and chaperons had to be provided by the Faculty, and separate quarters provided, and—"

"Yes, I suppose I see! But why should women be allowed to compete at all? No such idiocy is allowed in the other Professions."

"The law provides that since the Profession of Poetry is a religious office, there must be a channel provided for the rare occasion when the Creator might see fit to call a female to His service."

"What nonsense!"

"There is the Poet Anna-Mary, ban-harihn."

"And how many others?"

"She is the third."

"In nearly ten thousand years! Only three in so many centuries, and yet no exception can be made for one little twelve-year-old girl?"

"I am truly sorry, my friend," said the Lawyer. "You could try a petition to the Council, of course, but I am quite sure—*quite* sure—that it would be of no use. There is too much public reaction to a female's even attempting the examinations, because it seems blasphemous even to many very broad-minded people. The Council would not dare to make an exception."

"I could make a galactic appeal."

"You could."

"There would be quite a scandal, you know, among the peoples of the galaxy, if they knew of this penalty being enforced on a child."

"My friend, my dear ban-harihn—think of what you are saying. You would create an international incident, an intergalactic international incident, with all that implies, bring down criticism upon our heads, most surely incur an investigation of our religious customs by the intergalactic police, which would in turn call for a protest from our government, which in its turn—"

"You know I would not do it."

"I hope not. It would parallel the Trojan War for folly, my friend—all that for the sake of one female child!"

"We are a barbaric people."

The Lawyer nodded. "After ten thousand years, you know, if barbarism remains it becomes very firmly entrenched."

The Lawyer rose to go, throwing his heavy blue cloak around him. "After all," he said, "it is only one female child."

It was all very well, thought the Khadilh when his friend was gone, all very well to say that. The Lawyer no doubt never had had the opportunity to see the result of a lifetime of solitary confinement in total silence, or he would have been less willing to see a child condemned to such a fate.

The Khadilh's sister had been nearly thirty, and yet unmarried, when she had chosen to compete, and she was forty-six now. It had been an impulse of folly, born of thirty years of boredom, and the Khadilh blamed his parents. Enough dowry should have been provided to make even Grace, ugly as she was, an acceptable bride for someone, somewhere.

The room in the Small Corridor, where she had been confined since her failure, had no window, no com-system, nothing. Her food was passed through a slot in one wall, as were the few books and papers which she was allowed—all these things being very rigidly regulated by the Women's Discipline Unit.

It was the duty of the Khadilha Althea to go each morning to the narrow grate that enclosed a one-way window into the cell and to observe the prisoner inside. On the two occasions when that observation had disclosed physical illness, a dart containing an anesthetic had been fired through the food slot, and Grace had been rendered unconscious for the amount of time necessary to let a Doctor enter the cell and attend to her. She had had sixteen years of this, and it was the Khadilha who had had to watch her, through the first years when she alternately lay stuporous for days and then screamed and begged for release for days . . . now she was quite mad. The Khadilh had observed her on two occasions when his wife had been too ill to go, and he had found it difficult to believe that the creature who crawled on all fours from one end of the room to the other, its matted hair thick with filth in spite of the servomechanisms that hurried from the walls to retrieve all waste and dirt, was his sister. It gibbered and whined and clawed at its flesh—it was hard to believe that it was human. And it had been only sixteen years. Jacinth was twelve!

The Khadilh called his wife's quarters and announced to her serving-women that they were all to leave her. He went rapidly through the corridors of his house, over the delicate arched bridge that spanned the tea gardens around the women's quarters, and into the rooms where she stayed. He found her sitting in a small chair before her fireplace, watching the mobile plants that danced there to be near the warmth of the fire. As his sons had said, she was quite docile, and in very poor contact with reality.

He took a capsule from the pocket of his tunic and gave it to her to swallow, and when her eyes were clear of the mist of her drugged dreams, he spoke to her.

"You see that I have returned, Althea," he said. "I wish to know why my daughter has brought this ill fortune upon our household."

"It is her own idea," said the Khadilha in a bitter voice. "Since the last of her brothers was chosen, she has been thus determined, saying that it would be a great honor for our house should all of the children of banharihn be accepted for the faith."

It was as if a light had been turned on.

"This was not an impulse, then!" exclaimed the Khadilh.

"No. Since she was nine years old she has had this intention."

"But why was I not told? Why was I given no opportunity—" He stopped abruptly, knowing that he was being absurd. No women would bother her husband with the problems of rearing a female child. But now he began to understand.

"She did not even know," his wife was saying, "that there was a living female Poet, although she had heard from someone that such a possibility existed. It was, she insisted, a matter of knowledge of the heart. When the Poet Anna-Mary singled her out at the procession . . . why, then, she was sure. Then she knew, she said, that she had been chosen."

Of course. That in itself, being marked out for notice before the crowd, would have convinced the child that her selection was ordained by Divine choice. He could see it all now. And the Khadilha had taken the child to see her aunt in her cell in a last desperate attempt to dissuade her.

"The child is strong-willed for a female," he mused, "if the sight of poor Grace did not shake her."

His wife did not answer, and he sat there, almost too tired to move. He was trying to place the child Jacinth in his mind's eye, but it was useless. It had been at least four years since he had seen her, dressed in a brief white shift that all little girls wore: he remembered a slender child, he remembered dark hair—but then all little girls among his people were slender and dark-haired.

"You don't even remember her," said his wife, and he jumped, irritated at her shrewdness.

"You are quite right," he said. "I don't. Is she pretty?"

"She is beautiful. Not that it matters now."

The Khadilh thought for a moment, watching his wife's stoic face, and then, choosing his words with care, he said, "It had been my intention to register a complaint with the Women's Discipline Unit for your behavior, Khadilha Althea."

"I expected you to do so."

"You have a good deal of experience with the agents of the WDU—the prospect does not upset you?"

"I am indifferent to it."

He believed her. He remembered very well the behavior of his wife at her last impregnation, for it had required four agents from the Unit to subdue her and fasten her to their marriage bed. And yet he knew that many women went willingly, even eagerly, to their appointments with their husbands. It was at times difficult for him to understand why he had not had Althea put on Permanent Medication from the very beginning; certainly, it would not have been difficult to secure permission to take a second, more womanly wife. Unfortunately he was soft-hearted, and she had been the mother of his eldest son, and so he had put up with her, relying upon his concubines for feminine softness and ardor. Certainly Althea had hardened with the years, not softened.

"I have decided," he finished abruptly, "that your behavior is not so scandalous as I had thought. I am not sure I would not have reacted just as you did under the circumstances, if I had known the girl's plans. I will make no complaint, therefore."

"You are indulgent."

He scanned her face, still lovely for all her years, for signs of impertinence, but there were none, and he went on: "However, you understand our eldest son must decide for himself if he wishes to forego his own complaint. Your disobedience to him wasn't your first, you know. I have become accustomed to it."

He turned on his heel and left her, amused at his own weakness, but he canceled the medication order when he went past the entrance to her quarters. She was a woman, she had meant to keep her daughter from becoming what Grace had become; it was not so hard to understand, after all.

The family did not go to the University on the day of the examinations. They waited at home, prepared for the inevitable as well as they could prepare.

Another room, near the room where Grace was kept, had been made ready by the weeping servingwomen, and it stood open now, waiting.

The Khadilh had had his wife released from her quarters for the day, since she would have only the brief moment with her daughter, and thereafter would have only the duty of observing her each morning as she did her sister-in-law. She sat at his feet now in their common room, making no sound, her face bleached white, wondering, he supposed, what she would do now. She had no other daughter; there were no other sisters. She would be alone in the household except for her serving-woman, until such a time as Michael should, perhaps, provide her with a granddaughter. His heart ached for her, alone in a household of men, and five of them, before very long, to be allowed to speak only in the rhymed couplets of the Poets.

"Father?"

The Khadilh looked up, surprised. It was his youngest son, the boy James.

"Father," said the boy, "could she pass? I mean, is it possible that she could pass?"

Michael answered for him. "James, she is only twelve, and a female. She has had no education; she can only just barely read. Don't ask foolish questions. Don't you remember the examinations?"

"I remember," said James firmly. "Still, I wondered. There is the Poet Anna-Mary."

"The third in who knows how many hundreds of years, James," Michael said. "I shouldn't count on it if I were you."

"But is it possible?" the boy insisted. "Is it possible, Father?"

"I don't think so, son," said the Khadilh gently. "It would be a very curious thing if an untrained twelve-year-old female could pass the examinations that I could not pass myself, when I was sixteen, don't you think?"

"And then," said the boy, "she may never see anyone again, as long as she lives, never speak to anyone, never look out a window, never leave that little room?"

"Never."

"That is a cruel law!" said the boy. "Why has it not been changed?"

"My son," said the Khadilh, "it is not something that happens often, and the Council has many, many other things to do. It is an ancient law, and the knowledge that it exists offers to bored young females something exciting to think about. It is intended to frighten them, my son."

"One day, when I have power enough, I shall have it changed."

The Khadilh raised his hand to hush the laughter of the older boys. "Let him alone," he snapped. "He is young, and she is his sister. Let us have a spirit of compassion in this house, if we must have tragedy."

A thought occurred to him, then. "James," he said, "you take a great deal of interest in this matter. Is it possible that you were somehow involved in this idiocy of your sister's?"

At once he knew he had struck a sensitive spot; tears sprang to the boy's eyes and he bit his lip fiercely.

"James—in what way were you involved? What do you know of this affair?"

"You will be angry, my father," said James, "but that is not the worst. What is worse is that I will have condemned my sister to—"

"James," said the Khadilh, "I have no interest in your self-accusations. Explain at once, simply and without dramatics."

"Well, we used to practice, she and I," said the boy hastily, his eyes on the floor. "I did not think I would pass, you know. I could see it—all the others would pass, and I would not, and there I would be, the only one. People would say, there he goes, the only one of the sons of the banharihn who could not pass the Poetry exam."

"And?"

"And so we practiced together, she and I," he said. "I would set the subject and the form and do the first stanza, and then she would write the reply."

"When did you do this? Where?"

"In the gardens, Father, ever since she was little. She's very good at it, she really is, Father."

"She can rhyme? She knows the forms?"

"Yes, Father! And she *is* good, she has a gift for it—Father, she's much better than I am. I am ashamed to say that, of a female, but it would be a lie to say anything else."

The things that went on in one's household! The Khadilh was amazed and dismayed, and he was annoyed besides. Not that it was unusual for brothers and sisters, while still young, to spend time together, but surely one of the servants, or one of the family, ought to have noticed that the two little ones were playing at Poetry?

"What else goes on in my house beneath the blind eyes and deaf ears of those I entrust with its welfare?" he demanded furiously, and no one hazarded an answer. He made a sound of disgust and went to the window to look out over the gardens that stretched down to the narrow river behind the house. It had begun to rain, a soft green rain not much more than a mist, and the river was blurred velvet through the veil of water. Another time he would have enjoyed the view; indeed, he might well have sent for his pencils and his sketching pad to record its beauty. But this was not a day for pleasure.

Unless, of course, Jacinth did pass.

It was, on the face of it, an absurdity, The examinations for Poetry were far different than those for the other Professions. In the others it was a straightforward matter: one went to the examining room, an examination was distributed, one spent perhaps six hours in such exams, and they were then scored by computer. Then, in a few days, there would come the little notice by com-system, stating that one had or had not passed the fitness exams for Law or Business or whatever.

Poetry was a different matter. There were many degrees of fitness, all the way from the First Level, which fitted a man for the lower offices of the faith, through five more subordinate levels, to the Seventh Level. Very rarely did anyone enter the Seventh Level. Since there was no question of being promoted from one level to another, a man being placed at his appropriate rank by the examinations at the very beginning, there were times when the Seventh Level remained vacant for as long as a year. Michael had been placed at the Fourth Level instead of the First, like the others of his sons, and the Khadilh had been awed at the implications.

For Poetry there was first an examination of the usual kind, marked by hand and scored by machine, just as in the other Professions. But then, if that exam was passed, there was something unique to do. The Khadilh had not passed the exam and he had no knowledge of what came next, except that it involved the computers.

"Michael," he said, musing, "how does it go exactly, the Poetry exam by the computer?"

Michael came over to stand beside him. "You mean, should Jacinth pass the written examination, even if just by chance, then what happens?"

"Yes. Tell me."

"It's simple enough. You go into the booths where the computer panels are and push a READY button. Then the computer gives you your instructions."

"For example?"

"Let's see. For example, it might say—SUBJECT: LOVE OF COUNTRY . . . FORM: SONNET. UNRESTRICTED BUT RHYMED . . . STYLE: FORMAL, SUITABLE FOR AN OFFICIAL BANQUET. And then you would begin."

"Are you allowed to use paper and pen, my son?"

"Oh, no, Father." Michael was smiling, no doubt, thought the Khadilh, at his father's innocence. "No paper or pencil. And you begin at once."

"No time to think?"

"No, Father, none."

"Then what?"

"Then, sometimes, you are sent to another computer, one that gives more difficult subjects. I suppose it must be the same all the way to the Seventh Level, except that the subject would grow more difficult."

The Khadilh thought it over. For his own office of Khadilh, which meant little more than "Administrator of Large Estates and Households," he had had to take one oral examination, and that had been in ordinary, straightforward prose, and the examiner had been a man, not a computer, and he still remembered the incredible stupidity of his answers. He had sat flabbergasted at the things that issued from his mouth, and he had been convinced that he could not possibly have passed the examination. And Jacinth was only twelve years old, with none of the training that boys received in prosody, none of the summer workshops in the different forms, scarcely even an acquaintance with the history of the classics. Surely she would be too terrified to speak? Why, the simple modesty of her femaleness ought to be enough to keep her mute, and then she would fail, even if she should somehow be lucky enough to pass the written exam. Damn the girl!

"Michael," he asked, "what is the level of the Poet Anna-Mary?"

"Second Level, Father."

"Thank you, my son. You have been very helpful—you may sit down now, if you like."

He stood a moment more, watching the rain, and then went back and sat down again by his wife. Her hands flew, busy with the little needles used to make the complicated hoods the Poets wore. She was determined that her sons should, in accordance with the ancient tradition, have every stitch of their installation garments made by her hands, although no one would have criticized her if she had had the work done by others, since she had so many sons needing the garments. He was pleased with her, for once, and he made a mental note to have a gift sent to her later.

The bells rang in the city, signaling the four o'clock Hour of Meditation, and the Khadilh's sons looked at one another, hesitating. By the rules of their Major that hour was to be spent in their rooms, but their father had specifically asked that they stay with him.

The Khadilh sighed, making another mental note, that he must sigh less. It was an unattractive habit.

"My sons," he said "you must conform to the rules of your Major. Please consider that my first wish."

They thanked him and left the room, and there he sat, watching first the darting fingers of the Khadilha and then the dancing of the mobile flowers, until shadows began to streak across the tiled floor of the room. Six o'clock came, and then seven, and still no word. When his sons returned, he sent them away crossly, seeing no reason why they should share in his misery.

By the time the double suns had set over the river he had lost the compassion he had counseled for the others and become furious with Jacinth as well as the system. That one insignificant female child could create such havoc for him and for his household amazed him. He began to understand the significance of the rule; the law began to seem less harsh. He had missed his dinner and he had spent his day in unutterable tedium. His orchards were doubtless covered with insects and dying of thirst and neglect, his bank account was depleted by the expense of the trip home, the cost of extra garden-robots on Earth, the cost of the useless visit from the Lawyer. And his nervous system was shattered, and the peace of his household destroyed. All this from the antics of one twelve-year-old female child! And when she had to be shut up, there would be the necessity of living with her mother as she watched the child deteriorate into a crawling mass of filth and madness as Grace had done. Was his family cursed, that its females should bring down the wrath of the universe at large in this manner?

He struck his fists together in rage and frustration, and the Khadilha jumped, startled.

"Shall I send for music, my husband?" she asked. "Or perhaps you would like to have your dinner served here? Perhaps you would like a good wine?"

"Perhaps a dozen dancing girls!" he shouted. "Perhaps a Venusian flame-tiger! Perhaps a parade of Earth elephants and a tentacle bird from the Extreme Moons! May all the suffering gods take pity upon me!"

"I beg your pardon," said the Khadilha. "I have angered you."

"It is not you who have angered me," he retorted; "it is that miserable female of a daughter that you bore me, who has caused me untold sorrow and expense, that has angered me!"

"Very soon now," pointed out the Khadilha softly, "she will be out of your sight and hearing forever; perhaps then she will anger you less."

The Khadilha's wit, sometimes put to uncomfortable uses, had been one of the reasons he had kept her all these years. At this moment, however, he wished her stupider and timider and a thousand light-years away.

"Must you be right, at a time like this?" he demanded. "It is unbecoming in a woman."

"Yes, my husband."

"It grows late."

"Yes, indeed."

"What could they be doing over there?"

He reached over to the com-system and instructed the Housekeeper to send someone with a videocolor console. It was just possible that somewhere in the galaxy something was happening that would distract him from his misery.

He skimmed the videobands rapidly, muttering. There was a new drama by some unknown avant-garde playwright, depicting a liaison between the daughter of a Council member and a servomechanism. There was a game of jidra, both teams apparently from the Extreme Moons, if their size could be taken as any indication. There were half a dozen variety programs, each worse than the last. Finally he found a newsband and leaned forward, his ear caught by the words of the improbably sleek young man reading the announcements.

Had he said—yes! He had. He was announcing the results of the examinations in Poetry. "—ended at four o'clock this afternoon, with only eighty-three candidates accepted out of almost three thousand who—"

"Of course!" he shouted. How stupid he had been not to have realized, sooner, that since all members of Poetry were bound by oath to observe the four o'clock Hour of Meditation, the examinations would have had to end by four o'clock! But why, then, had no one come to notify them or to return their daughter? It was very near nine o'clock.

The smallest whisper of hope touched him. It was possible, just possible, that the delay was because even the callous members of the Poetry Unit were finding it difficult to condemn a little girl to a life of solitary confinement. Perhaps they were meeting to discuss it, perhaps something was being arranged, some loophole in the law being found that could be used to prevent such a travesty of justice.

He switched off the video and punched the call numbers of the Poetry Unit on the com-system. At once the screen was filled by the embroidered hood and bearded face of a Poet, First Level, smiling helpfully through the superimposed matrix-mark of his household.

The Khadilh explained his problem, and the Poet smiled and nodded.

"Messengers are on their way to your household at this moment, Khadilh ban-harihn," he said. "We regret the delay, but it takes time, you know. All these things take time."

"What things?" demanded the Khadilh. "And why are you speaking to me in prose? Are you not a Poet?"

"The Khadilh seems upset," said the Poet in a soothing voice. "He should know that those Poets who serve the Poetry Unit as communicators are excused from the laws of verse-speaking while on duty."

"Someone is coming now?"

"Messengers are on their way."

"On foot? By Earth-style robot-mule? Why not a message by com-system?"

The Poet shook his head. "We are a very old profession, Khadilh ban-harihn. There are many traditions to be observed. Speed, I fear, is not among those traditions."

"What message are they bringing?"

"I am not at liberty to tell you that," said the Poet patiently.

Such control! thought the Khadilh. Such unending saintlike tolerance! It was maddening.

"Terminate with thanks," said the Khadilh, and turned off the bland face of the Poet. At his feet the Khadilha had set aside her work and sat trembling. He reached over and patted her hand, wishing there were some comfort he could offer.

Had they better go ahead and call for dinner? He wondered if either of them would be able to eat.

"Althea," he began, and at that moment the servingwoman showed in the messengers of the Poetry Unit, and the Khadilh rose to his feet.

"Well?" he demanded abruptly. He would be damned if he was going to engage in the usual interminable preliminaries. "Where is my daughter?"

"We have brought your daughter with us, Khadilh ban-harihn."

"Well, where is she?"

"If the Khadilh will only calm himself."

"I am calm! Now where is my daughter?"

The senior messenger raised one hand, formally, for silence, and in an irritating singsong he began to speak.

"The daughter of the Khadilh ban-harihn will be permitted to approach and to speak to her parents for one minute only, by the clock which I hold, giving to her parents whatever message of farewell she should choose. Once she has given her message, the daughter of the Khadilh will be taken away and it will not be possible for the Khadilh or his household to communicate with her again except by special petition from the Council."

The Khadilh was dumbfounded. He could feel his wife shaking uncontrollably beside him—was she about to cause a second scandal?

"Leave the room if you cannot control your emotion, Khadilha," he ordered her softly, and she responded with an immediate and icy calm of bearing. Much better.

"What do you mean," he asked the messenger, "by stating that you are about to take my daughter away again? Surely it is not the desire of the Council that she be punished outside the confines of my house!"

"Punished?" asked the messenger. "There is no punishment in question, Khadilh. It is merely that the course of study which she must follow henceforth cannot be provided for her except at the Temple of the University."

It was the Khadilh's turn to tremble now. She had passed!

"Please," he said hoarsely, "would you make yourself clear? Am I to understand that my daughter has passed the examination?"

"Certainly," said the messenger. "This is indeed a day of great honor for the household of the ban-harihn. You can be most proud, Khadilh, for your daughter has only just completed the final examination and has been placed in Seventh Level. A festival will be declared, and an official announcement will be made. A day of holiday will be ordered for all citizens of the planet Abba, in all city-clusters and throughout the countryside. It is a time of great rejoicing!"

The man went on and on, his curiously contrived-sounding remarks unwinding amid punctuating sighs and nods from the other messengers, but the Khadilh did not hear any more. He sank back in his chair, deaf to the list of the multitude of honors and happenings that would come to pass as a result of this extraordinary thing. Seventh Level! How could such a thing be?

Dimly he was aware that the Khadilha was weeping quite openly, and he used one numb hand to draw her veils across her face.

"Only one minute, by the clock," the messenger was saying. "You do understand? You are not to touch the Poet-Candidate, nor are you to interfere with her in any way. She is allowed one message of farewell, nothing more."

And then they let his daughter, this stranger who had performed a miracle, whom he would not even have recognized in a crowd, come forward into the room and approach him. She looked very young and tired, and he held his breath to hear what she would say to him.

However, it was no message of farewell that she had to give them. Said the Poet-Candidate, Seventh Level, Jacinth ban-harihn: "You will send someone at once to inform my Aunt Grace that I have been appointed to the Seventh Level of the Profession of Poetry; permission has been granted by the Council for the breaking of her solitary confinement for so long as it may take to make my aunt understand just what has happened."

And then she was gone, followed by the messengers, leaving only the muted, tinkling showers of sparks from the dancing flowers and the soft drumming of the rain on the roof to punctuate the silence.

(1969)

ZENNA HENDERSON

As Simple As That

"I won't read it." Ken sat staring down at his open first grade book.

I took a deep, wavery breath and, with an effort, brought myself back to the classroom and the interruption in the automatic smooth flow of the reading group.

"It's your turn, Ken," I said. "Don't you know the place?"

"Yes," said Ken, his thin, unhappy face angling sharply at the cheekbones as he looked at me. "But I won't read it."

"Why not?" I asked gently. Anger had not yet returned. "You know all the words. Why don't you want to read it?"

"It isn't true," said Ken. He dropped his eyes to his book as tears flooded in. "It isn't true."

"It never was true," I told him. "We play like it's true, just for fun." I flipped the four pages that made up the current reading lesson. "Maybe this city isn't true, but it's like a real one, with stores and—" My voice trailed off as the eyes of the whole class centered on me—seven pairs of eyes and the sightless, creamy oval of Maria's face—all seeing our city.

"The cities," I began again. "The cities—" By now the children were used to grown-ups stopping in mid-sentence. And to the stunned look on adult faces.

"It isn't true," said Ken. "I won't read it."

"Close your books," I said, "And go to your seats." The three slid quietly into their desks—Ken and Victor and Gloryanne. I sat at my desk, my elbows on the green blotter, my chin in the palms of my hands, and looked at nothing. I didn't want anything true. The fantasy that kept school as usual is painful enough. How much more comfortable to live unthinking from stunned silence to stunned silence. Finally I roused myself.

"If you don't want to read your book, let's write a story that *is* true, and we'll have that for reading."

I took the staff liner and drew three lines at a time across the chalk board, with just a small jog where I had to lift the chalk over the jagged crack that marred the board diagonally from top to bottom.

"What shall we name our story?" I asked. "Ken, what do you want it to be about?"

"About Biff's house," said Ken promptly.

"Biff's house," I repeated, my stomach tightening sickly as I wrote the words, forming the letters carefully in manuscript printing, automatically saying, "Remember now, all titles begin with—"

And the class automatically supplying, "—capital letters."

"Yes," I said. "Ken, what shall we say first?"

"Biff's house went up like an elevator," said Ken.

"Right up into the air?" I prompted.

"The ground went up with it," supplied Gloryanne.

I wrote the two sentences. "Victor? Do you want to tell what came next?" The chalk was darkening in my wet, clenched hand.

"The groun'—it comed down, more fast nor Biff's house," supplied Victor hoarsely. I saw his lifted face and the deep color of his heavily fringed eyes for the first time in a week.

"With noise!" shouted Maria, her face animated. "With lots of noise!"

"You're not in our group!" cried Ken. "This is our story!"

"It's everyone's story," I said and wrote carefully. "And every sentence ends with a—"

"Period," supplied the class.

"And then?" I paused, leaning my forehead against the coolness of the chalk board, blinking my eyes until the rich green alfalfa that was growing through the corner of the room came back into focus. I lifted my head.

Celia had waited. "Biff fell out of his house," she suggested.

I wrote. "And then?" I paused, chalk raised.

"Biff's house fell on him," said Ken with a rush. "And he got dead."

"I saw him!" Bobby surged up out of his seat, speaking his first words of the day. "There was blood, but his face was only asleep."

"He was dead!" said Ken fiercely. "And the house broke all to pieces!"

"And the pieces all went down in that deep, deep hole with Biff!" cried Bobby.

"And the hole went shut!" Celia triumphantly capped the recital.

"Dint either!" Victor whirled on her. "Ohney part! See! See!" He jabbed his finger toward the window. We all crowded around as though this was something new. And I suppose it was—new to our tongues, new to our ears, though long scabbed over unhealthily inside us.

There at the edge of the playground, just beyond the twisted tangle of the jungle gym and the sharp jut of the slide, snapped off above the fifth rung of the ladder, was the hole containing Biff's house. We solemnly contemplated all that was visible—the small jumble of shingles and the wadded TV antenna. We turned back silently to our classroom.

"How did you happen to see Biff when his house fell on him, Bobby?" I asked.

"I was trying to go to his house to play until my brother got out of fourth grade," said Bobby. "He was waiting for me on the porch. But all at once the ground started going up and down and it knocked me over. When I got up, Biff's house was just coming down and it fell on Biff. All but his head. And he looked asleep. He did! He did! And then everything went down and it shut. But not all!" he hastened to add before Victor gave tongue again.

"Now," I said—we had buried Biff—"Do we have it the way we want so it can be a story for reading? Get your pencils—"

"Teacher! Teacher!" Maria was standing, her sightless eyes wide, one hand up as high as she could reach. "Teacher! Malina!"

"Bobby! Quickly—help me!" I scrambled around my desk, knocking the section of four-by-four out from under the broken front leg. I was able to catch Malina because she had stopped to fumble for the door knob that used to be there. Bobby stumbled up with the beach towel and, blessedly, I had time to wind it securely around Malina before the first scream of her convulsions began. Bobby and I held her lightly, shoulder and knees, as her body rolled and writhed. We had learned bitterly how best to protect her against herself and the dangerous place she made for herself of the classroom. I leaned my cheek against my shoulder as I pressed my palms against Malina. I let my tears wash down my face untouched. Malina's shaking echoed through me as though I were sobbing.

The other children were righting my fallen desk and replacing the chunk of four-by-four, not paying any attention to Malina's gurgling screams that rasped my ears almost past enduring. So quickly do children adjust. So quickly. I blinked to clear my eyes. Malina was quieting. Oh, how blessedly different from the first terrified hour we had had to struggle with her! I quickly unwrapped her and cradled her against me as her face smoothed and her ragged breath quieted. She opened her eyes.

"Daddy said next time he had a vacation he'd take us to Disneyland again. Last time we didn't get to go in the rocket. We didn't get to go in anything in that land." She smiled her normal, front-tooth-missing smile at me and fell asleep. We went back to work, Bobby and I.

"Her daddy's dead," said Bobby matter-of-factly as he waited his turn at the pencil sharpener. "She knows her daddy's dead and her mother's dead and her baby brother's—"

"Yes, Bobby, we all know," I said. "Let's go back to our story. We just about have time to go over it again and write it before lunchtime."

So I stood looking out of the gap in the wall above the Find Out Table—currently, *What Did This Come From?* while the children wrote their first true story after the Torn Time.

Biff's House

Biff's house went up like an elevator.
The ground went up with it.
The ground came down before Biff's house did.
Biff fell out of his house.
The house fell on him and he was dead.
He looked asleep.
The house broke all to pieces with a lot of noise.
It went down into the deep, deep hole.
Biff went, too.
The hole went shut, but not all the way.
We can see the place by our playground.

It was only a few days later that the children asked to write another story. The rain was coming down again—a little less muddy, a little less torrential, so that the shards of glass in our windows weren't quite so smeary and there was an area unleaked upon in the room large enough to contain us all closely—minus Malina.

"I think she'll come tomorrow," said Celia. "This morning she forgot Disneyland 'cause she remembered all her family got mashed by the water tower when it fell down and she was crying when we left the sleeping place and she wasn't screaming and kicking and this time she was crying and—"

"Heavens above!" I cried, "You'll run out of breath completely!"

"Aw naw I won't!" Celia grinned up at me and squirmed in pleased embarrassment. "I breathe in between!"

"I didn't hear any in-betweens," I smiled back. "Don't use so many 'ands'!"

"Can we write another real story?" asked Willsey. ("Not Willie!" His mother's voice came back to me, tiny and piercing and never to be heard aloud again. "His name is Willsey. W-i-l-l-s-e-y. Please teach him to write it in full!")

"If you like," I said. "Only do we say, 'Can we?' "

"May we?" chorused the class.

"That's right," I said. "Did you have something special in mind, Willsey?"

"No," he said. "Only, this morning we had bread for breakfast. Mine was dry. Bobby's daddy said that was lucky 'relse it would have rotted away a long time ago." Bread. My mouth watered. There must not have been enough to pass around to our table—only for the children.

"Mine was dry, too," said Ken. "And it had blue on the edge of it."

"Radioactive," nodded Victor wisely.

"Huh-uh!" contradicted Bobby quickly. "Nothing's radioactive around here! My daddy says—"

"You' daddy! You' daddy!" retorted Victor. "Once I gots daddy, too!"

"Everybody had a daddy," said Maria calmly. " 'Relsn you couldn't get born. But some daddies die."

"All daddies die," said Bobby. "Only mine isn't dead yet. I'm *glad* he isn't dead!"

"We all are," I said, "Bobby's daddy helps us all—"

"Yeah," said Willsey, "he found the bread for us."

"Anyway, the blue was mould," Bobby broke in. "And it's good for you. It grows peni—pencil—"

"Penicillin?" I suggested. He nodded and subsided, satisfied. "Okay, Willsey, what shall we name our story?"

He looked at me blankly. "What's it about?" I asked.

"Eating," he said.

"Fine. That'll do for a title," I said. "Who can spell it for me? It's an ing ending."

I wrote it carefully with a black marking pencil on the chart paper as Gloryanne spelled it for me, swishing her long black hair back triumphantly as she did so. Our chalk board was a green cascade of water under the rain pouring down through the ragged, sagging ceiling. The bottom half of the board was sloughing slowly away from its diagonal fracture.

"Now, Willsey—" I waited, marker poised.

"We had bread for breakfast," he composed. "It was hard, but it was good."

"Mine wasn't," objected Ken. "It was awful."

"Bread isn't awful," said Maria. "Bread's good."

"Mine wasn't!" Ken was stubborn.

"Even if we don't ever get any more?" asked Maria.

"Aw! Who ever heard of not no more bread?" scoffed Ken.

"What is bread made of?" I asked.

"Flour," volunteered Bobby.

"Cornbread's with cornmeal," said Victor quickly.

"Yes, and flour's made from—" I prompted.

"From wheat," said Ken.

"And wheat—"

"Grows in fields," said Ken.

"Thee, Thmarty!" said Gloryanne. "And whereth any more fieldth?"

"Use your teeth, Gloryanne," I reminded. "Teeth and no tongue. Say, 'see.' "

Gloryanne clenched her teeth and curled her lips back. "S-s-s-thee!" she said, confidently. Bobby and I exchanged aware looks and our eyes smiled above our sober lips.

"Let's go on with the story," I suggested.

Eating

We had bread for breakfast.
It was hard but it was good.
Bobby's daddy found it under some boards.
We had some good milk to put it in.
It was goat's milk.
It made the bread soft.
Once we had a cow.
She was a nice cow but a man killed her
because he wanted to eat her.
We all got mad at him.
We chased him away.
No one got to eat our cow
because it rained red mud
all over her and spoiled the meat.
We had to push her into a big hole.

I looked over the tight huddle of studious heads before me as they all bent to the task of writing the story. The rain was sweeping past the windows like long curtains billowing in the wind. The raindrops were so fine but so numerous that it seemed I could reach out and stroke the swelling folds. I moved closer to the window, trying several places before I found one where no rain dripped on me from above and none sprayed me from outside. But it was an uncomfortable spot. I could see the nothing across the patio where the rest of the school used to be. Our room was the only classroom in the office wing. The office wing was the only one not gulped down in its entirety, lock, stock and student body. Half of the office wing was gone. We had the restrooms—non-operational—the supply room—half roofed—and our room. We were the school. We were the whole of the sub-teen generation—and the total faculty.

The total faculty wondered—was it possible that someone—some *one*—had caused all this to happen? Some one who said, "Now!" Or said, "Fire!" Or said, "If I can't have my way, then—" Or maybe some stress inside the world casually adjusted itself, all unknowing of the skim of life clinging to its outsides. Or maybe some One said, "I repent Me—"

"Teacher, Teacher!" Maria's voice called me back to the classroom. "The roof! The roof!" Her blind face was urgent. I glanced up, my arm lifting protectively.

"Down!" I shouted. "Get down flat!" and flung myself across the room, mowing my open-mouthed children down as I plunged. We made it to the floor below the level of my desk before what was left of the ceiling peeled off and slammed soggily over us, humped up just enough by the desk and chairs to save our quivering selves.

Someone under me was sobbing, "My paper's all tore! My paper's all tore!" And I heard Bobby say with tight, controlled anguish, "Everything breaks! Any more, everything breaks!"

We wrote another story—later. Quite a bit later. The sun, halo-ed broadly about by its perpetual haze, shone milkily down into our classroom. The remnants of the roof and ceiling had been removed and a canvas tarp draped diagonally over the highest corner of the remaining walls to give us shade in the afternoon. On the other side of the new, smaller playground our new school was shaping from adobe and reclaimed brick. Above the humming stillness of the classroom, I could hear the sound of blackbirds calling as they waded in the water that seeped from the foot of the knee-deep stand of wheat that covered the old playground. Maybe by Fall there would be bread again. Maybe. Everything was still maybe. But 'maybe' is a step—a big one—beyond 'never.'

Our chalk board was put back together and, except for a few spots that refused to accept any kind of impression, it functioned well with our smudgy charcoal sticks from the Art Supplies shelf.

"Has anyone the answer yet?" I asked.

"I gots it," said Victor, tentatively. "It's two more days."

"Huh-uh!" said Celia. "Four more days!"

"Well, we seem to have a difference of opinion," I said. "Let's work it out together.

"Now, first, how many people, Victor?"

"Firs' they's ten people," he said, checking the chalk board.

"That's right," I said, "And how many cans of beans? Malina?"

"Five," she said. "And each can is for two people for one day."

"Right," I said. "And so that'll be lunch for how many days for ten people?"

"For one day," said Malina.

"That's right. Then what happened?"

"All but two people fell in the West Crack," said Bobby. "Right—straight—down—farther than you can hear a rock fall." He spoke with authority. He had composed that part of our math problem.

"So?" I said.

"There were five cans of beans and that's ten meals and only two people," said Willsey.

"So?" I prompted.

"So two people can have five meals each."

"So?"

"So they gots dinners for five days and that's *four* days more than one day! So there!" cried Victor.

"Hey!" Celia was outraged. "That's what *I* said! You said *two* more days!"

"Aw!" said Victor. "Dumb problem! Nobody's gunna fa' down West Crack eenyway!"

"A lot of people fell in there," said Gloryanne soberly. "My gramma did and my Aunt Glory—"

In the remembering silence, the sweet creaking calls of the blackbirds could be heard again. A flash of brilliance from the sky aroused us. A pie-shaped wedge had suddenly cleared in the sun's halo, and there was bright blue and glitter, briefly, before the milky came back.

"A whole bright day," said Maria dreamily. "And the water in Briney Lake so shiny I can't look at it."

"You can't look anyway," said Ken. "How come you always talk about seeing when you can't even?"

" 'Cause I can. Ever since the Torn Time," said Maria. "I got blind almost as soon as I got born. All blind. No anything to see. But now I can watch and I can see—inside me, somewhere. But I don't see now. I see sometime—after while. But what I see comes! It isn't, when I see it, but it bees pretty quick!" Her chin tilted a 'so there!'

The children all looked at her silently and I wondered. We had lost so much—so much! And Maria had lost, too—her blindness. Maybe more of our losses were gains—

Then Bobby cried out, "What happened, teacher? What happened? And why do we stay here? I can remember on the other side of West Crack. There was a town that wasn't busted. And bubble gum and hamburgers and a—a escalator thing to go upstairs to buy color TV. Why don't we go there? Why do we stay here where everything's busted?"

"Broken," I murmured automatically.

The children were waiting for an answer. These child faces were turned to me, waiting for me to fill a gap they suddenly felt now, in spite of the endless discussions that were forever going on around them.

"What do *you* think?" I asked. "What do you think happened? Why *do* we stay here? Think about it for a while, then let's write another story."

I watched the wind flow across the wheat field and thought, too. Why do we stay? The West Crack is one reason. It's still unbridged, partly because to live has been more important than to go, partly because no one wants to leave anyone yet. The fear of separation is still too strong. We *know* people are here. The unknown is still too lonely to face.

South are the Rocks—jagged slivers of basalt or something older than that—that rocketed up out of the valley floor during the Torn Time and splintered into points and pinnacles. As far as we can see, they rise, rigidly vertical, above the solid base that runs out of sight east and west. And the base is higher than our tallest tree.

And north. My memory quivered away from north—

East. Town used to be east. The edge of it is Salvage now. Someday when the stench is gone, the whole of it will be salvage. Most of the stench is only a lingering of memory now, but we still stay away except when need drives us.

North. North. Now it is Briney Lake. During the Torn Time, it came from out of nowhere, all that wetness, filling a dusty, desert cup to brimming and more. It boiled and fumed and swallowed the land and spat out parts of it again.

Rafe and I had gone up to watch the magical influx of water. In this part of the country, any water, free of irrigation or conservation restrictions, was a wonder to be watched with fascinated delight. We stood, hand in hand, on the Point where we used to go at nights to watch the moonlight on the unusually heavy stand of cholla cactus on the hillsides—moonlight turning all those murderous, puncturing thorns to silvery fur and snowy velvet. The earth around us had firmed again from its shakenness and the half of the Point that was left was again a solid Gibraltar.

We watched the water rise and rise until our delight turned to apprehension. I had started to back away when Rafe pulled me to him to see a sudden silvery slick that was welling up from under the bubbling swells of water. As he leaned to point, the ground under our feet gave a huge hiccough, jerked him off balance and snatched his hand from my wrist. He hit the water just as the silvery slick arrived.

And the slick swallowed Rafe before my eyes. Only briefly did it let go of one of his arms—a hopelessly reaching arm that hadn't yet realized that its flesh was already melted off and only bones were reaching.

I crouched on the Point and watched half my boulder dissolve into the silver and follow Rafe down into the dark, convulsed depths. The slick was gone and Rafe was gone. I knelt, nursing my wrist with my other hand. My wrist still burned where Rafe's fingernails had scratched as he fell. My wrist carries the scars still, but Rafe is gone.

My breath shuddered as I turned back to the children.

"Well," I said, "what *did* happen? Shall we write our story now?"

What Happened?

Bobby's daddy thinks maybe the magnetic poles changed and north is west now or maybe east.
Gloryanne's mother says it must have been an atom bomb.
Malina's Uncle Don says the San Andreas fault did it.
That means a big earthquake all over everywhere.
Celia's grandfather says the Hand of God smote a wicked world.
Victor thinks maybe it was a flying saucer.
Ken thinks maybe the world just turned over and we are Australia now.
Willsey doesn't want to know what happened.
Maria doesn't know.
She couldn't see when it was happening.

"So you see," I summed up. "Nobody knows for sure what happened. Maybe we'll never know. Now, why do we stay here?"

"Because"—Bobby hesitated—"because maybe if here is like this, maybe everywhere is like this. Or maybe there isn't even anywhere else anymore."

"Maybe there isn't," I said, "But whether there is or not and whatever really happened, it doesn't matter to us now. We can't change it. We have to make do with what we have until we can make it better.

"Now, paper monitor," I was briskly routine. "Pass the paper. All of you write as carefully as you can so when you take your story home and let people read it, they'll say, 'Well! What an interesting story!' instead of 'Yekk! Does this say something?' Writing is no good unless it can be read. The eraser's here on my desk in case anyone goofs. You may begin."

I leaned against the window sill, waiting. If only we adults would admit that we'll probably never know what really happened—and that it really doesn't matter. Inexplicable things are always happening, but life won't wait for answers—it just keeps going. Do you suppose Adam's grandchildren knew what really happened to close Eden? Or that Noah's grandchildren sat around wondering why the earth was so empty? They contented themselves with very simple, home-grown explanations—or none at all—because what was, was. We don't want to accept what happened and we seem to feel that if we could find an explanation that it would undo what has been done. It won't. Maybe some day someone will come along who will be able to put a finger on one of the points in the children's story and say, "There! That's the explanation." Until then, though, explanation or not, we have our new world to work with.

No matter what caused the Torn Time, we go on from here—building or not-building, becoming or slipping back. It's as simple as that.

(1971)

ROBERT SILVERBERG

Good News from the Vatican

This is the morning everyone has waited for, when at last the robot cardinal is to be elected pope. There can no longer be any doubt of the outcome. The conclave has been deadlocked for many days between the obstinate advocates of Cardinal Asciuga of Milan and Cardinal Carciofo of Genoa, and word has gone out that a compromise is in the making. All factions now are agreed on the selection of the robot. This morning I read in *Osservatore Romano* that the Vatican computer itself has taken a hand in the deliberations. The computer has been strongly urging the candidacy of the robot. I suppose we should not be surprised by this loyalty among machines. Nor should we let it distress us. We *absolutely must not* let it distress us.

"Every era gets the pope it deserves," Bishop FitzPatrick observed somewhat gloomily today at breakfast. "The proper pope for our times is a robot, certainly. At some future date it may be desirable for the pope to be a whale, an automobile, a cat, a mountain." Bishop FitzPatrick stands well over two meters in height and his normal facial expression is a morbid, mournful one. Thus it is impossible for us to determine whether any particular pronouncement of his reflects existential despair or placid acceptance. Many years ago he was a star player for the Holy Cross championship basketball team. He has come to Rome to do research for a biography of St. Marcellus the Righteous.

We have been watching the unfolding drama of the papal election from an outdoor café several blocks from the Square of St. Peter's. For all of us, this has been an unexpected dividend of our holiday in Rome; the previous pope was reputed to be in good health and there was no reason to suspect that a successor would have to be chosen for him this summer.

Each morning we drive across by taxi from our hotel near the Via Veneto and take up our regular positions around "our" table. From where we sit, we all have a clear view of the Vatican chimney through which the smoke of the burning ballots rises: black smoke if no pope has been elected, white if the conclave has been successful. Luigi, the owner and headwaiter, automatically brings us our preferred beverages: Fernet-Branca for Bishop FitzPatrick, Campari and soda for Rabbi Mueller, Turkish coffee for Miss Harshaw, lemon squash for Kenneth and Beverly, and Pernod on the rocks for me. We take turns paying the check, although Kenneth has not paid it even once since our vigil began. Yesterday, when Miss Harshaw paid, she emptied her purse and found herself 350 lire short; she had nothing else except hundred-dollar travelers' checks. The rest of us looked pointedly at Kenneth but he went on calmly sipping his lemon squash. After a brief period of tension Rabbi Mueller produced a 500-lire coin and rather irascibly slapped the heavy silver piece against the table. The rabbi is known for his short temper and vehement style. He is twenty-eight years old, customarily dresses in a fashionable plaid cassock and silvered sunglasses, and frequently boasts that he has never performed a bar mitzvah ceremony for his congregation, which is in Wicomico County, Maryland. He believes that the rite is vulgar and obsolete, and invariably farms out all his bar mitzvahs to a franchised organization of itinerant clergymen who handle such affairs on a commission basis. Rabbi Mueller is an authority on angels.

Our group is divided over the merits of electing a robot as the new pope. Bishop FitzPatrick, Rabbi Mueller and I are in favor of the idea. Miss Harshaw, Kenneth and Beverly are opposed. It is interesting to note that both of our gentlemen of the cloth, one quite elderly and one fairly young, support this remarkable departure from tradition. Yet the three "swingers" among us do not.

I am not sure why I align myself with the progressives. I am a man of mature years and fairly sedate ways. Nor have I ever concerned myself with the doings of the Church of Rome. I am unfamiliar with Catholic dogma and unaware of recent currents of thought within the Church. Still, I have been hoping for the election of the robot since the start of the conclave.

Why? I wonder. Is it because the image of a metal creature upon the Throne of St. Peter's stimulates my imagination and tickles my sense of the incongruous? That is, is my support of the robot purely an aesthetic matter? Or is it, rather, a function of my moral cowardice? Do I secretly think that this gesture will buy the robots off? Am I privately saying, Give them the papacy and maybe they won't want other things for a while? No. I can't believe anything so unworthy of myself. Possibly I am for the robot because I am a person of unusual sensitivity to the needs of others.

"If he's elected," says Rabbi Mueller, "he plans an immediate time-sharing agreement with the Dalai Lama and a reciprocal plug-in with the head programmer of the Greek Orthodox Church, just for starters. I'm told he'll make ecumenical overtures to the rabbinate as well, which is certainly something for all of us to look forward to."

"I don't doubt that there'll be many corrections in the customs and practices of the hierarchy," Bishop FitzPatrick declares. "For example, we can look forward to superior information-gathering techniques as the Vatican computer is given a greater role in the operations of the Curia. Let me illustrate by—"

"What an utterly ghastly notion," Kenneth says. He is a gaudy young man with white hair and pink eyes. Beverly is either his wife or his sister. She rarely speaks. Kenneth makes the sign of the Cross with offensive brusqueness and murmurs, "In the name of the Father, the Son and the Holy Automaton." Miss Harshaw giggles but chokes the giggle off when she sees my disapproving face.

Dejectedly, but not responding at all to the interruption, Bishop FitzPatrick continues, "Let me illustrate by giving you some figures I obtained yesterday afternoon. I read in the newspaper *Oggi* that during the last five years, according to a spokesman for the *Missiones Catholicae,* the Church has increased its membership in Yugoslavia from 19,381,403 to 23,501,062. But the government census taken last year gives the total population of Yugoslavia at 23,575,194. That leaves only 74,132 for the other religious and irreligious bodies. Aware of the large Moslem population of Yugoslavia, I suspected an inaccuracy in the published statistics and consulted the computer in St. Peter's, which informed me"—the bishop, pausing, produces a lengthy printout and unfolds it across much of the table—"that the last count of the Faithful in Yugoslavia, made a year and a half ago, places our numbers at 14,206,198. Therefore an overstatement of 9,294,864 has been made. Which is absurd. And perpetuated. Which is damnable."

"What does he look like?" Miss Harshaw asks. "Does anyone have any idea?"

"He's like all the rest," says Kenneth. "A shiny metal box with wheels below and eyes on top."

"You haven't seen him," Bishop FitzPatrick interjects. "I don't think it's proper for you to assume that—"

"They're all alike," Kenneth says. "Once you've seen one, you've seen all of them. Shiny boxes. Wheels. Eyes. And voices coming out of their bellies like mechanized belches. Inside, they're all cogs and gears." Kenneth shudders delicately. "It's too much for me to accept. Let's have another round of drinks, shall we?"

Rabbi Mueller says, "It so happens that I've seen him with my own eyes."

"You *have*?" Beverly exclaims.

Kenneth scowls at her. Luigi, approaching, brings a tray of new drinks for everyone. I hand him a 5000-lire note. Rabbi Mueller removes his sunglasses and breathes on their brilliantly reflective surfaces. He has small, watery gray eyes and a bad squint. He says, "The cardinal was the keynote speaker at the Congress of World Jewry that was held last fall in Beirut. His theme was 'Cybernetic Ecumenicism for Contemporary Man.' I was there. I can tell you that His Eminence is tall and distinguished, with a fine voice and a gentle smile. There's something inherently melancholy about his manner that reminds me greatly of our friend the bishop, here. His movements are graceful and his wit is keen."

"But he's mounted on wheels, isn't he?" Kenneth persists.

"On treads," replies the rabbi, giving Kenneth a fiery, devastating look and resuming his sunglasses. "Treads, like a tractor has. But I don't think that treads are spiritually inferior to feet, or, for that matter, to wheels. If I were a Catholic I'd be proud to have a man like that as my pope."

"Not a man," Miss Harshaw puts in. A giddy edge enters her voice whenever she addresses Rabbi Mueller. "A robot," she says. "He's not a man, remember?"

"A *robot* like that as my pope, then," Rabbi Mueller says, shrugging at the correction. He raises his glass. "To the new pope!"

"To the new pope!" cries Bishop FitzPatrick.

Luigi comes rushing from his café. Kenneth waves him away. "Wait a second," Kenneth says. "The election isn't over yet. How can you be so sure?"

"The *Osservatore Romano,*" I say, "indicates in this morning's edition that everything will be decided today. Cardinal Carciofo has agreed to withdraw in his favor, in return for a larger real-time allotment when the new computer hours are decreed at next year's consistory."

"In other words, the fix is in," Kenneth says.

Bishop FitzPatrick sadly shakes his head. "You state things much too harshly, my son. For three weeks now we have been without a Holy Father. It is God's Will that we shall have a pope; the conclave, unable to choose between the candidacies of Cardinal Carciofo and Cardinal Asciuga, thwarts that Will; if necessary, therefore, we must make certain accommodations with the realities of the times so that His Will shall not be further frustrated. Prolonged politicking within the conclave now becomes sinful. Cardinal Carciofo's sacrifice of his personal ambitions is not as self-seeking an act as you would claim."

Kenneth continues to attack poor Carciofo's motives for withdrawing. Beverly occasionally applauds his cruel sallies. Miss Harshaw several times declares her unwillingness to remain a communicant of a church whose leader is a machine. I find this dispute distasteful and swing my chair away from the table to have a better view of the Vatican. At this moment the cardinals are meeting in the Sistine Chapel. How I wish I were there! What splendid mysteries are being enacted in that gloomy, magnificent room! Each prince of the Church now sits on a small throne surmounted by a violet-hued canopy. Fat wax tapers glimmer on the desk before each throne. Masters of ceremonies move solemnly through the vast chamber, carrying the silver basins in which the blank ballots repose. These basins are placed on the table before the altar. One by one the cardinals advance to the table, take ballots, return to their desks. Now, lifting their quill pens, they begin to write. "I, Cardinal ——, elect to the Supreme Pontificate the Most Reverend Lord my Lord Cardinal ——." What name do they fill in? Is it Carciofo? Is it Asciuga? Is it the name of some obscure and shriveled prelate from Madrid or Heidelberg, some last-minute choice of the anti-robot faction in its desperation? Or are they writing *his* name? The sound of scratching pens is loud in the chapel. The cardinals are completing their ballots, sealing them at the ends, folding them, folding them again and again, carrying them to the altar, dropping them into the great gold chalice. So have they done every morning and every afternoon for days, as the deadlock has prevailed.

"I read in the *Herald Tribune* a couple of days ago," says Miss Harshaw, "that a delegation of two hundred and fifty young Catholic robots from Iowa is waiting at the Des Moines airport for news of the election. If their man gets in, they've got a chartered flight ready to leave, and they intend to request that they be granted the Holy Father's first public audience."

"There can be no doubt," Bishop FitzPatrick agrees, "that his election will bring a great many people of synthetic origin into the fold of the Church."

"While driving out plenty of flesh-and-blood people!" Miss Harshaw says shrilly.

"I doubt that," says the bishop. "Certainly there will be some feelings of shock, of dismay, of injury, of loss, for some of us at first. But these will pass. The inherent goodness of the new pope, to which Rabbi Mueller alluded, will prevail. Also I believe that technologically-minded young folk everywhere will be encouraged to join the Church. Irresistible religious impulses will be awakened throughout the world."

"Can you imagine two hundred and fifty robots clanking into St. Peter's?" Miss Harshaw demands.

I contemplate the distant Vatican. The morning sunlight is brilliant and dazzling, but the assembled cardinals, walled away from the world, cannot enjoy its gay sparkle. They all have voted, now. The three cardinals who were chosen by lot as this morning's scrutators of the vote have risen. One of them lifts the chalice and shakes it, mixing the ballots. Then he places it on the table before the altar; a second scrutator removes the ballots and counts them. He ascertains that the number of ballots is identical to the number of cardinals present. The ballots now have been transferred to a ciborium, which is a goblet ordinarily used to hold the consecrated bread of the Mass. The first scrutator withdraws a ballot, unfolds it, reads its inscription; passes it to the second scrutator, who reads it also; then it is given to the third scrutator, who reads the name aloud. Asciuga? Carciofo? Some other? *His?*

Rabbi Mueller is discussing angels. "Then we have the Angels of the Throne, known in Hebrew as *arelim* or *ophanim.* There are seventy of them, noted primarily for their steadfastness. Among them are the angels Orifiel, Ophaniel, Zabkiel, Jophiel, Ambriel, Tychagar, Barael, Quelamia, Paschar, Boel and Raum. Some of these are no longer found in Heaven and are numbered among the fallen angels in Hell."

"So much for their steadfastness," says Kenneth.

"Then, too," the rabbi goes on, "there are the Angels of the Presence, who apparently were circumcised at the moment of their creation. These are Michael, Metatron, Suriel, Sandalphon, Uriel, Saraqael, Astanphaeus, Phanuel, Jehoel, Zagzagael, Yefefiah and Akatriel. But I think my favorite of the whole group is the Angel of Lust, who is mentioned in Talmud *Bereshith Rabba* Eighty-five as follows, that when Judah was about to pass by—"

They have finished counting the votes by this time, surely. An immense throng has assembled in the Square of St. Peter's. The sunlight gleams off hundreds if not thousands of steel-jacketed crania. This must be a wonderful day for the robot population of Rome. But most of those in the piazza are creatures of flesh and blood: old women in black, gaunt young pickpockets, boys with puppies, plump vendors of sausages, and an assortment of poets, philosophers, generals, legislators, tourists and fishermen. How has the tally gone? We will have our answer shortly. If no candidate has had a majority, they will mix the ballots with wet straws before casting them into the chapel stove, and black smoke will billow from the chimney. But if a pope has been elected, the straw will be dry, the smoke will be white.

The system has agreeable resonances. I like it. It gives me the satisfaction one normally derives from a flawless work of art: the *Tristan* chord, let us say, or the teeth of the frog in Bosch's *Temptation of St. Anthony.* I await the outcome with fierce concentration. I am certain of the result; I can already feel the irresistible religious impulses awakening in me. Although I feel, also, an odd nostalgia for the days of flesh-and-blood popes. Tomorrow's newspapers will have no interviews with the Holy Father's aged mother in Sicily, nor with his proud younger brother in

San Francisco. And will this grand ceremony of election ever be held again? Will we need another pope, when this one whom we will soon have can be repaired so easily?

Ah. The white smoke! The moment of revelation comes!

A figure emerges on the central balcony of the facade of St. Peter's spreads a web of cloth of gold and disappears. The blaze of light against that fabric stuns the eye. It reminds me perhaps of moonlight coldly kissing the sea at Castellammare or, perhaps even more, of the noonday glare rebounding from the breast of the Caribbean off the coast of St. John. A second figure, clad in ermine and vermilion, has appeared on the balcony. "The cardinal archdeacon," Bishop Fitzpatrick whispers. People have started to faint. Luigi stands beside me, listening to the proceedings on a tiny radio. Kenneth says, "It's all been fixed." Rabbi Mueller hisses at him to be still. Miss Harshaw begins to sob. Beverly softly recites the Pledge of Allegiance, crossing herself throughout. This is a wonderful moment for me. I think it is the most truly contemporary moment I have ever experienced.

The amplified voice of the cardinal archdeacon cries, "I announce to you great joy. We have a pope."

Cheering commences, and grows in intensity as the cardinal archdeacon tells the world that the newly chosen pontiff is indeed *that* cardinal, that noble and distinguished person, that melancholy and austere individual, whose elevation to the Holy See we have all awaited so intensely for so long. "He has imposed upon himself," says the cardinal archdeacon, "the name of—"

Lost in the cheering. I turn to Luigi. "Who? What name?"

"Sisto Settimo," Luigi tells me.

Yes, and there he is, Pope Sixtus the Seventh, as we now must call him. A tiny figure clad in the silver and gold papal robes, arms outstretched to the multitude, and, yes! the sunlight glints on his cheeks, his lofty forehead, there is the brightness of polished steel. Luigi is already on his knees. I kneel beside him. Miss Harshaw, Beverly, Kenneth, even the rabbi all kneel, for beyond doubt this is a miraculous event. The pope comes forward on his balcony. Now he will deliver the traditional apostolic benediction to the city and to the world. "Our help is in the Name of the Lord," he declares gravely. He activates the levitator jets beneath his arms; even at this distance I can see the two small puffs of smoke. White smoke, again. He begins to rise into the air. "Who hath made heaven and earth," he says. "May Almighty God, Father, Son and Holy Ghost, bless you." His voice rolls majestically toward us. His shadow extends across the whole piazza. Higher and higher he goes, until he is lost to sight. Kenneth taps Luigi. "Another round of drinks," he says, and presses a bill of high denomination into the innkeeper's fleshy palm. Bishop FitzPatrick weeps. Rabbi Mueller embraces Miss Harshaw. The new pontiff, I think, has begun his reign in an auspicious way.

(1971)

PAMELA SARGENT

Gather Blue Roses

I cannot remember ever having asked my mother outright about the tattooed numbers. We must have known very early that we should not ask; perhaps my brother Simon or I had said something inadvertently as very small children and had seen the look of sorrow on her face at the statement; perhaps my father had told us never to ask.

Of course, we were always aware of the numbers. There were those times when the weather was particularly warm, and my mother would not button her blouse at the top, and she would lean over us to hug us or pick us up, and we would see them written across her, an inch above her breasts.

(By the time I reached my adolescence, I had heard all the horror stories about the death camps and the ovens; about those who had to remove gold teeth from the bodies; the women used, despite the Reich's edicts, by the soldiers and guards. I then regarded my mother with ambivalence, saying to myself, I would have died first, I would have found some way rather than suffering such dishonor, wondering what had happened to her and what secret sins she had on her conscience, and what she had done to survive. An old man, a doctor, had said to me once, "The best ones of us died, the most honorable, the most sensitive." And I would thank God I had been born in 1949; there was no chance that I was the daughter of a Nazi rape.)

By the time I was four, we had moved to an old frame house in the country, and my father had taken a job teaching at a small junior college near by, turning down his offers from Columbia and Chicago, knowing how impossible that would be for mother. We had a lot of elms and oaks and a huge weeping willow that hovered sadly over the house. Our pond would be invaded in the early spring and late fall by a few geese, which would usually keep their distance before flying on. ("You can tell those birds are Jewish," my father would say, "they go to Miami in the winter," and Simon and I would imagine them lying on a beach, coating their feathers with Coppertone and ordering lemonades from the waitresses; we hadn't heard of Collinses yet.)

Even out in the country, there were often those times when we would see my mother packing her clothes in a small suitcase, and she would tell us that she was going away for a while, just a week, just to get away, to find solitude. One time it was to an old camp in the Adirondacks that one of my aunts owned, another time to a cabin that a friend of my father's loaned her, always alone, always to an isolated place. Father would say that it was "nerves," although we wondered, since we were so isolated as it was. Simon and I thought she didn't love us, that mother was somehow using this means to tell us that we were being rejected. I would try very hard to behave; when mother was resting, I would tiptoe and whisper. Simon reacted more violently. He could contain himself for a while; but then, in a desperate attempt at drawing attention to himself, would run through the house, screaming horribly, and hurl himself, head first, at one of the radiators. On one occasion, he threw himself through one of the large living room windows, smashing the glass. Fortunately, he was uninjured, except for cuts and bruises, but after that incident, my father put chicken wire over the windows on the inside of the house. Mother was very shaken by that incident, walking around for a couple of days, her body aching all over, then going away to my aunt's place for three weeks this time. Simon's head must have been strong; he never sustained any damage from the radiators worse than a few bumps and a headache, but the headaches would often keep mother in bed for days.

(I pick up my binoculars to check the forest again from my tower, seeing the small lakes like puddles below, using my glasses to focus on a couple in a small boat near one of the islands, and then turn away from them, not wanting to invade their privacy, envying the girl and boy who can so freely, without fear of consequences, exchange and share their feelings, and yet not share them, not at least in the way that would destroy a person such as myself. I do not think anyone will risk climbing my mountain today, as the sky is overcast, cirro-cumulus clouds slowly chasing each other, a large storm cloud in the west. I hope no one will come; the family who picnicked beneath my observation tower yesterday bothered me; one child had a headache and another indigestion, and I lay in my cabin taking aspirins all afternoon and nursing the heaviness in my stomach. I hope no one will come today.)

Mother and father did not send us to school until we were as old as the law would allow. We went to the small public school in town. An old yellow bus would pick us up in front of the house. I was scared the first day and was glad Simon and I were twins so that we could go together. The town had built a new school; it was a small, square brick building, and there were fifteen of us in the first grade. The high school students went to classes in the same building. I was afraid of them and was glad to discover that their classes were all on the second floor; so we rarely saw them during the day except when they had gym classes outside. Sitting at my desk inside, I would watch them, wincing every time someone got hit with a ball, or got bruised. (Only three months in school, thank God, before my father got permission to tutor me at home, three months were too much of the constant pains, the turmoil of emotions; I am sweating now and my hands shake, when I remember it all.)

The first day was boring to me for the most part; Simon and I had been reading and doing arithmetic at home for as long as I could remember. I played dumb and did as I was told; Simon was aggressive, showing off, knowing it all. The other kids giggled, pointing at me, pointing at Simon, whispering. I felt some of it, but not enough to bother me too much; I was not then as I am now, not that first day.

Recess: kids yelling, running, climbing the jungle gym, swinging and chinning themselves on bars, chasing a basketball. I was with two girls and a piece of chalk on the blacktop; they taught me hopscotch, and I did my best to ignore the bruises and bumps of the other students.

(I need the peace, the retreat from easily communicated pain. How strange, I think objectively, that our lives are such that discomfort, pain, sadness and hatred are so easily conveyed and so frequently felt. Love and contentment are only soft veils which do not protect me from bludgeons; and with the strongest loves, one can still sense the more violent undercurrents of fear, hate and jealousy.)

It was at the end of the second week that the incident occurred during recess. I was, again, playing hopscotch, and Simon had come over to look at what we were doing before joining some other boys. Five older kids came over. I guess they were in third or fourth grade, and they began their taunts.

"Greeeenbaum," at Simon and me. We both turned toward them, I balancing on one foot on the hopscotch squares we had drawn, Simon clenching his fists.

"Greeeeenbaum, Esther Greeeeenbaum, Simon Greeeeenbaum," whinnying the green, thundering the baum.

"My father says you're Yids."

"He says you're the Yid's kids." One boy hooted and yelled. "Hey, they're Yid kids." Some giggled, and then they chanted, "Yid kid, Yid kid," as one of them pushed me off my square.

"You leave my sister alone," Simon yelled and went for the boy, fists flying, and knocked him over. The boy sat down suddenly, and I felt pain in my lower back. Another boy ran over and punched Simon. Simon whacked him back, and the boy hit him in the nose, hard. It hurt and I started crying from the pain, holding my nose, pulled away my hand and saw blood. Simon's nose was bleeding, and then the other kids started in, trying to pummel my brother, one guy holding him, another guy punching. "Stop it," I screamed, "stop it," as I curled on the ground, hurting, seeing the teachers run over to pull them apart. Then I fainted, mercifully, and came to in the nurse's office. They kept me there until it was time to go home that day.

Simon was proud of himself, boasting, offering self-congratulations. "Don't tell mother," I said when we got off the bus, "don't, Simon, she'll get upset and go away again, please. Don't make her sad."

(When I was fourteen, during one of the times mother was away, my father got drunk downstairs in the kitchen with Mr. Arnstead, and I could hear them talking, as I hid in my room with my books and records, father speaking softly, Mr. Arnstead bellowing.

"No one, no one, should ever have to go through what Anna did. We're beasts anyway, all of us, Germans, Americans, what's the difference."

Slamming of a glass on the table and a bellow: "God damn it, Sam, you Jews seem to think you have a monopoly on suffering. What about the guy in Harlem? What about some starving guy in Mexico? You think things are any better for them?"

"It was worse for Anna."

"No, not worse, no worse than the guy in some street in Calcutta. Anna could at least hope she would be liberated, but who's gonna free that guy?"

"No one," softly, "no one is ever freed from Anna's kind of suffering."

I listened, hiding in my room, but Mr. Arnstead left after that; and when I came downstairs, father was just sitting there, staring at his glass; and I felt his sadness softly drape itself around me as I stood there, and then the soft veil of love over the sadness, making it bearable.)

I began to miss school at least twice a week, hurting, unable to speak to mother, wanting to say something to father but not having the words. Mother was away a lot then, and this made me more depressed (I'm doing it, I'm sending her away), the depression endurable only because of the blanket of comfort that I felt resting over the house.

They had been worried, of course, but did not have their worst fears confirmed until Thanksgiving was over and December arrived (snow drifting down from a gray sky, father bringing in wood for the fireplace, mother polishing the menorah, Simon and me counting up our saved allowances, plotting what to buy for them when father drove us to town). I had been absent from school for a week by then, vomiting every morning at the thought that I might have to return. Father was reading and Simon was outside trying to climb one of our trees. I was in the kitchen, cutting cookies and decorating them while mother rolled the dough, humming, white flour on her apron, looking away and smiling when I sneaked small pieces of dough and put them in my mouth.

And then I fell off my chair onto the floor, holding my leg, moaning, "Mother, it hurts," blood running from my nose. She picked me up, clutching me to her, and put me on the chair, blotted my nose with a tissue. Then we heard Simon yelling outside, and then his banging on the back door. Mother went and pulled him inside, his nose bleeding. "I fell outa the tree," and, as she picked him up, she looked back at me; and I knew that she understood, and felt her fear and her sorrow as she realized that she and I were the same, that I would always feel the knife thrusts of other people's pain, draw their agonies into myself, and, perhaps, be shattered by them.

(Remembering: Father and mother outside, after a summer storm, standing under the willow, father putting his arm around her, brushing her black hair back and kissing her gently on the forehead. Not for me, too much shared anguish with love for me. I am always alone, with my mountain, my forest, my lakes like puddles. The young couple's boat is moored at the island.)

I hear them downstairs.

"Anna, the poor child, what can we do?"

"It is worse for her, Samuel," sighing, the sadness reaching me and becoming a shroud, "it will be worse with her, I think, than it was for me."

(1972)

JAMES TIPTREE, JR.

The Women Men Don't See

I see her first while the Mexicana 727 is barrelling down to Cozumel Island. I come out of the can and lurch into her seat, saying, "Sorry," at a double female blur. The near blur nods quietly. The younger one in the window seat goes on looking out. I continue down the aisle, registering nothing. Zero. I never would have looked at them or thought of them again.

Cozumel airport is the usual mix of panicky Yanks dressed for the sand pile and calm Mexicans dressed for lunch at the Presidente. I am a used-up Yank dressed for serious fishing; I extract my rods and duffel from the riot and hike across the field to find my charter pilot. One Captain Estéban has contracted to deliver me to the bonefish flats of Bélise three hundred kilometers down the coast.

Captain Estéban turns out to be four feet nine of mahogany Maya *puro.* He is also in a somber Mayan snit. He tells me my Cessna is grounded somewhere and his Bonanza is booked to take a party to Chetumal.

Well, Chetumal is south; can he take me along and go on to Bélise after he drops them? Gloomily he concedes the possibility—*if* the other party permits, and *if* there are not too many *equipajes.*

The Chetumal party approaches. It's the woman and her young companion—daughter?—neatly picking their way across the gravel and yucca apron. Their Ventura two-suiters, like themselves, are small, plain and neutral-colored. No problem. When the captain asks if I may ride along, the mother says mildly, "Of course," without looking at me.

I think that's when my inner tilt-detector sends up its first faint click. How come this woman has already looked me over carefully enough to accept on her plane? I disregard it. Paranoia hasn't been useful in my business for years, but the habit is hard to break.

As we clamber into the Bonanza, I see the girl has what could be an attractive body if there was any spark at all. There isn't. Captain Estéban folds a serape to sit on so he can see over the cowling and runs a meticulous check-down. And then we're up and trundling over the turquoise Jello of the Caribbean into a stiff south wind.

The coast on our right is the territory of Quintana Roo. If you haven't seen Yucatán, imagine the world's biggest absolutely flat green-grey rug. An empty-looking land. We pass the white ruin of Tulum and the gash of the road to Chichén Itzá, a half-dozen coconut plantations, and then nothing but reef and low scrub jungle all the way to the horizon, just about the way the conquistadores saw it four centuries back.

Long strings of cumulus are racing at us, shadowing the coast. I have gathered that part of our pilot's gloom concerns the weather. A cold front is dying on the henequen fields of Mérida to the west, and the south wind has piled up a string of coastal storms: what they call *llovisnos.* Estéban detours methodically around a couple of small thunderheads. The Bonanza jinks, and I look back with a vague notion of reassuring the women. They are calmly intent on what can be seen of Yucatán. Well, they were offered the co-pilot's view, but they turned it down. Too shy?

Another *llovisno* puffs up ahead. Estéban takes the Bonanza upstairs, rising in his seat to sight his course. I relax for the first time in too long, savoring the latitudes between me and my desk, the week of fishing ahead. Our captain's classic Maya profile attracts my gaze: forehead sloping back from his predatory nose, lips and jaw stepping back below it. If his slant eyes had been any more crossed, he couldn't have made his license. That's a handsome combination, believe it or not. On the little Maya chicks in their minishifts with iridescent gloop on those cockeyes, it's also highly erotic. Nothing like the oriental doll thing; these people have stone bones. Captain Estéban's old grandmother could probably tow the Bonanza . . .

I'm snapped awake by the cabin hitting my ear. Estéban is barking into his headset over a drumming racket of hail; the windows are dark grey.

One important noise is missing—the motor. I realize Estéban is fighting a dead plane. Thirty-six hundred; we've lost two thousand feet.

He slaps tank switches as the storm throws us around; I catch something about *gasolina* in a snarl that shows his big teeth. The Bonanza reels down. As he reaches for an overhead toggle, I see the fuel gauges are high. Maybe a clogged gravity feed line, I've heard of dirty gas down here. He drops the set; it's a million to one nobody can read us through the storm at this range anyway. Twenty-five hundred—going down.

His electric feed pump seems to have cut in: the motor explodes—quits—explodes—and quits again for good. We are suddenly out of the bottom of the clouds. Below us is a long white line almost hidden by rain: The reef. But there isn't any beach behind it, only a big meandering bay with a few mangrove flats—and it's coming up at us fast.

This is going to be bad, I tell myself with great unoriginality. The women behind me haven't made a sound. I look back and see they're braced down with their coats by their heads. With a stalling speed around eighty, all this isn't much use, but I wedge myself in.

Estéban yells some more into his set, flying a falling plane. He is doing one jesus job, too—as the water rushes up at us he dives into a hair-raising turn and hangs us into the wind—with a long pale ridge of sandbar in front of our nose.

Where in hell he found it I never know. The Bonanza mushes down, and we belly-hit with a tremendous tearing crash—bounce—hit again—and everything slews wildly as we flat-spin into the mangroves at the end of the bar. Crash! Clang! The plane is wrapping itself into a mound of strangler fig with one wing up. The crashing quits with us all in one piece. And no fire. Fantastic.

Captain Estéban prys open his door, which is now in the roof. Behind me a woman is repeating quietly, "Mother. Mother." I climb up the floor and find the girl trying to free herself from her mother's embrace. The woman's eyes are closed. Then she opens them and suddenly lets go, sane as soap. Estéban starts hauling them out. I grab the Bonanza's aid kit and scramble out after them into brilliant sun and wind. The storm that hit us is already vanishing up the coast.

"Great landing, Captain."

"Oh, *yes!* It was beautiful." The women are shaky, but no hysteria. Estéban is surveying the scenery with the expression his ancestors used on the Spaniards.

If you've been in one of these things, you know the slow-motion inanity that goes on. Euphoria, first. We straggle down the fig tree and out onto the sandbar in the roaring hot wind, noting without alarm that there's nothing but miles of crystalline water on all sides. It's only a foot or so deep, and the bottom is the olive color of silt. The distant shore around us is all flat mangrove swamp, totally uninhabitable.

"Bahía Espíritu Santo." Estéban confirms my guess that we're down in that huge water wilderness. I always wanted to fish it.

"What's all that smoke?" The girl is pointing at plumes blowing around the horizon.

"Alligator hunters," says Estéban. Maya poachers have left burn-offs in the swamps. It occurs to me that any signal fires we make aren't going to be too conspicuous. And I now note that our plane is well-buried in the mound of fig. Hard to see it from the air.

Just as the question of how the hell we get out of here surfaces in my mind, the older woman asks composedly, "If they didn't hear you, Captain, when will they start looking for us? Tomorrow?"

"Correct," Estéban agrees dourly. I recall that air-sea rescue is fairly informal here. Like, keep an eye open for Mario, his mother says he hasn't been home all week.

It dawns on me we may be here quite some while.

Furthermore, the diesel-truck noise on our left is the Caribbean piling back into the mouth of the bay. The wind is pushing it at us, and the bare bottoms on the mangroves show that our bar is covered at high tide. I recall seeing a full moon this morning in—believe it, St. Louis—which means maximal tides. Well, we can climb up in the plane. But what about drinking water?

There's a small splat! behind me. The older woman has sampled the bay. She shakes her head, smiling ruefully. It's the first real expression on either of them; I take it as the signal for introductions. When I say I'm Don Fenton from St. Louis, she tells me their name is Parsons, from Bethesda, Maryland. She says it so nicely I don't at first notice we aren't being given first names. We all compliment Captain Estéban again.

His left eye is swelled shut, an inconvenience beneath his attention as a Maya, but Mrs. Parsons spots the way he's bracing his elbow in his ribs.

"You're hurt, Captain."

"*Roto*—I think is broken." He's embarrassed at being in pain. We get him to peel off his Jaime shirt, revealing a nasty bruise on his superb dark-bay torso.

"Is there tape in that kit, Mr. Fenton? I've had a little first-aid training."

She begins to deal competently and very impersonally with the tape. Miss Parsons and I wander to the end of the bar and have a conversation which I am later to recall acutely.

"Roseate spoonbills," I tell her as three pink birds flap away.

"They're beautiful," she says in her tiny voice. They both have tiny voices. "He's a Mayan Indian, isn't he? The pilot, I mean."

"Right. The real thing, straight out of the Bonampak murals. Have you seen Chichén and Uxmal?"

"Yes. We were in Mérida. We're going to Tikal in Guatemala . . . I mean, we were."

"You'll get there." It occurs to me the girl needs cheering up. "Have they told you that Maya mothers used to tie a board on the infant's forehead to get that slant? They also hung a ball of tallow over its nose to make the eyes cross. It was considered aristocratic."

She smiles and takes another peek at Estéban. "People seem different in Yucatán," she says thoughtfully. "Not like the Indians around Mexico City. More, I don't know, independent."

"Comes from never having been conquered. Mayas got massacred and chased a lot, but nobody ever really flattened them. I bet you didn't know that the last Mexican-Maya war ended with a negotiated truce in 1935?"

"No!" Then she says seriously, "I like that."

"So do I."

"The water is really rising very fast," says Mrs. Parsons gently from behind us.

It is, and so is another *llovisno.* We climb back into the Bonanza. I try to rig my parka for a rain catcher, which blows loose as the storm hits fast and furious. We sort a couple of malt bars and my bottle of Jack Daniel's out of the jumble in the cabin and make ourselves reasonably comfortable. The Parsons take a sip of whiskey each, Estéban and I considerably more. The Bonanza begins to bump soggily. Estéban makes an ancient one-eyed Mayan face at the water seeping into his cabin and goes to sleep. We all nap.

When the water goes down, the euphoria has gone with it, and we're very, very thirsty. It's also damn near sunset. I get to work with a bait-casting rod and some treble hooks and manage to foul-hook four small mullets. Estéban and the women tie the Bonanza's midget life raft out in the mangroves to catch rain. The wind is parching hot. No planes go by.

Finally another shower comes over and yields us six ounces of water apiece. When the sunset envelopes the world in golden smoke, we squat on the sandbar to eat wet raw mullet and Instant Breakfast crumbs. The women are now in shorts, neat but definitely not sexy.

"I never realized how refreshing raw fish is," Mrs. Parsons says pleasantly. Her daughter chuckles, also pleasantly. She's on Mamma's far side away from Estéban and me. I have Mrs. Parsons figured now: Mother Hen protecting only chick from male predators. That's all right with me. I came here to fish.

But something is irritating me. The damn women haven't complained once, you understand. Not a peep, not a quaver, no personal manifestations whatever. They're like something out of a manual.

"You really seem at home in the wilderness, Mrs. Parsons. You do much camping?"

"Oh goodness no." Diffident laugh. "Not since my Girl Scout days. Oh, look—are those man-of-war birds?"

Answer a question with a question. I wait while the frigate birds sail nobly into the sunset.

"Bethesda . . . Would I be wrong in guessing you work for Uncle Sam?"

"Why, yes. You must be very familiar with Washington, Mr. Fenton. Does your work bring you there often?"

Anywhere but on our sandbar the little ploy would have worked. My hunter's gene twitches.

"Which agency are you with?"

She gives up gracefully. "Oh, just GSA records. I'm a librarian."

Of course. I know her now, all the Mrs. Parsonses in records divisions, accounting sections, research branches, personnel and administration offices. Tell Mrs. Parsons we need a recap on the external service contracts for fiscal '73. So Yucatán is on the tours now? Pity . . . I offer her the tired little joke. "You know where the bodies are buried."

She smiles deprecatingly and stands up. "It does get dark quickly, doesn't it?"

Time to get back into the plane.

A flock of ibis are circling us, evidently accustomed to roosting in our fig tree. Estéban produces a machete and a Maya string hammock. He proceeds to sling it between tree and plane, refusing help. His machete stroke is noticeably tentative.

The Parsons are taking a pee behind the tail vane. I hear one of them slip and squeal faintly. When they come back over the hull, Mrs. Parsons asks, "Might we sleep in the hammock, Captain?"

Estéban splits an unbelieving grin. I protest about rain and mosquitoes.

"Oh, we have insect repellent and we do enjoy fresh air."

The air is rushing by about force five and colder by the minute.

"We have our raincoats," the girl adds cheerfully.

Well, okay, ladies. We dangerous males retire inside the damp cabin. Through the wind I hear the women laugh softly now and then, apparently cosy in their chilly ibis roost. A private insanity, I decide. I know myself for the least threatening of men; my non-charisma has been in fact an asset jobwise, over the years. Are they having fantasies about Estéban? Or maybe they really are fresh-air nuts . . . Sleep comes for me in invisible diesels roaring by on the reef outside.

We emerge dry-mouthed into a vast windy salmon sunrise. A diamond chip of sun breaks out of the sea and promptly submerges in cloud. I go to work with the rod and some mullet bait while two showers detour around us. Breakfast is a strip of wet barracuda apiece.

The Parsons continue stoic and helpful. Under Estéban's direction they set up a section of cowling for a gasoline flare in case we hear a plane, but nothing goes over except one unseen jet droning toward Panama. The wind howls, hot and dry and full of coral dust. So are we.

"They look first in the sea," Estéban remarks. His aristocratic frontal slope is beaded with sweat; Mrs. Parsons watches him concernedly. I watch the cloud blanket tearing by above, getting higher and dryer and thicker. While that lasts nobody is going to find us, and the water business is now unfunny.

Finally I borrow Estéban's machete and hack a long light pole.

"There's a stream coming in back there, I saw it from the plane. Can't be more than two, three miles."

"I'm afraid the raft's torn." Mrs. Parsons shows me the cracks in the orange plastic; irritatingly, it's a Delaware label.

"All right," I hear myself announce. "The tide's going down. If we cut the good end off that air tube, I can haul water back in it. I've waded flats before."

Even to me it sounds crazy.

"Stay by plane," Estéban says. He's right, of course. He's also clearly running a fever. I look at the overcast and taste grit and old barracuda. The hell with the manual.

When I start cutting up the raft, Estéban tells me to take the serape. "You stay one night." He's right about that, too; I'll have to wait out the tide.

"I'll come with you," says Mrs. Parsons calmly.

I simply stare at her. What new madness has got into Mother Hen? Does she imagine Estéban is too battered to be functional? While I'm being astounded, my eyes take in the fact that Mrs. Parsons is now quite rosy around the knees, with her hair loose and a sunburn starting on her nose. A trim, in fact a very neat shading-forty.

"Look, that stuff is horrible going. Mud up to your ears and water over your head."

"I'm really quite fit and I swim a great deal. I'll try to keep up. Two would be much safer, Mr. Fenton, and we can bring more water."

She's serious. Well, I'm about as fit as a marshmallow at this time of winter, and I can't pretend I'm depressed by the idea of company. So be it.

"Let me show Miss Parsons how to work this rod."

Miss Parsons is even rosier and more windblown, and she's not clumsy with my tackle. A good girl, Miss Parsons, in her nothing way. We cut another staff and get some gear together. At the last minute Estéban shows how sick he feels: he offers me the machete. I thank him, but, no; I'm used to my Wirkkala knife. We tie some air into the plastic tube for a float and set out along the sandiest looking line.

Estéban raises one dark palm. *"Buen viaje."* Miss Parsons has hugged her mother and gone to cast from the mangrove. She waves. We wave.

An hour later we're barely out of waving distance. The going is purely god-awful. The sand keeps dissolving into silt you can't walk on or swim through, and the bottom is spiked with dead mangrove spears. We flounder from one pothole to the next, scaring up rays and turtles and hoping to god we don't kick a moray eel. Where we're not soaked in slime, we're desiccated, and we smell like the Old Cretaceous.

Mrs. Parsons keeps up doggedly. I only have to pull her out once.

When I do so, I notice the sandbar is now out of sight.

Finally we reach the gap in the mangrove line I thought was the creek. It turns out to open into another arm of the bay, with more mangroves ahead. And the tide is coming in.

"I've had the world's lousiest idea."

Mrs. Parsons only says mildly, "It's so different from the view from the plane."

I revise my opinion of the Girl Scouts, and we plow on past the mangroves toward the smoky haze that has to be shore. The sun is setting in our faces, making it hard to see. Ibises and herons fly up around us, and once a big permit spooks ahead, his fin cutting a rooster tail. We fall into more potholes. The flashlights get soaked. I am having fantasies of the mangrove as universal obstacle; it's hard to recall I ever walked down a street, for instance, without stumbling over or under or through mangrove roots. And the sun is dropping, down, down.

Suddenly we hit a ledge and fall over it into a cold flow.

"The stream! It's fresh water!"

We guzzle and gargle and douse our heads; it's the best drink I remember. "Oh my, oh my—!" Mrs. Parsons is laughing right out loud.

"That dark place over to the right looks like real land."

We flounder across the flow and follow a hard shelf, which turns into solid bank and rises over our heads. Shortly there's a break beside a clump of spiny bromels, and we scramble up and flop down at the top, dripping and stinking. Out of sheer reflex my arm goes around my companion's shoulder—but Mrs. Parsons isn't there; she's up on her knees peering at the burnt-over plain around us.

"It's so good to see land one can walk on!" The tone is too innocent. *Noli me tangere.*

"Don't try it." I'm exasperated; the muddy little woman, what does she think? "That ground out there is a crust of ashes over muck, and it's full of stubs. You can go in over your knees."

"It seems firm here."

"We're in an alligator nursery. That was the slide we came up. Don't worry, by now the old lady's doubtless on her way to be made into handbags."

"What a shame."

"I better set a line down in the stream while I can still see."

I slide back down and rig a string of hooks that may get us breakfast. When I get back Mrs. Parsons is wringing muck out of the serape.

"I'm glad you warned me, Mr. Fenton. It *is* treacherous."

"Yeah." I'm over my irritation; god knows I don't want to *tangere* Mrs. Parsons, even if I weren't beat down to mush. "In its quiet way,

Yucatán is a tough place to get around in. You can see why the Mayas built roads. Speaking of which—look!"

The last of the sunset is silhouetting a small square shape a couple of kilometers inland: a Maya *ruina* with a fig tree growing out of it.

"Lot of those around. People think they were guard towers."

"What a deserted-feeling land."

"Let's hope it's deserted by mosquitoes."

We slump down in the 'gator nursery and share the last malt bar, watching the stars slide in and out of the blowing clouds. The bugs aren't too bad; maybe the burn did them in. And it isn't hot any more, either—in fact, it's not even warm, wet as we are. Mrs. Parsons continues tranquilly interested in Yucatán and unmistakably uninterested in togetherness.

Just as I'm beginning to get aggressive notions about how we're going to spend the night if she expects me to give her the serape, she stands up, scuffs at a couple of hummocks and says, "I expect this is as good a place as any, isn't it, Mr. Fenton?"

With which she spreads out the raft bag for a pillow and lies down on her side in the dirt with exactly half the serape over her and the other corner folded neatly open. Her small back is toward me.

The demonstration is so convincing that I'm halfway under my share of serape before the preposterousness of it stops me.

"By the way. My name is Don."

"Oh, of course." Her voice is graciousness itself. "I'm Ruth."

I get in not quite touching her, and we lie there like two fish on a plate, exposed to the stars and smelling the smoke in the wind and feeling things underneath us. It is absolutely the most intimately awkward moment I've had in years.

The woman doesn't mean one thing to me, but the obtrusive recessiveness of her, the defiance of her little rump eight inches from my fly—for two pesos I'd have those shorts down and introduce myself. If I were twenty years younger, if I wasn't so bushed . . . But the twenty years and the exhaustion are there, and it comes to me wryly that Mrs. Ruth Parsons has judged things to a nicety. If I *were* twenty years younger, she wouldn't be here. Like the butterfish that float around a sated barracuda, only to vanish away the instant his intent changes, Mrs. Parsons knows her little shorts are safe. Those firmly filled little shorts, so close . . .

A warm nerve stirs in my groin—and just as it does I become aware of a silent emptiness beside me. Mrs. Parsons is imperceptibly inching away. Did my breathing change? Whatever, I'm perfectly sure that if my hand reached, she'd be elsewhere—probably announcing her intention to take a dip. The twenty years bring a chuckle to my throat, and I relax.

"Good night, Ruth."

"Good night, Don."

And believe it or not, we sleep, while the armadas of the wind roar overhead.

Light wakes me—a cold white glare.

My first thought is 'gator hunters. Best to manifest ourselves as *turistas* as fast as possible. I scramble up, noting that Ruth has dived under the bromel clump.

"Quién estás? A socorro! Help, *señores!"*

No answer except the light goes out, leaving me blind.

I yell some more in a couple of languages. It stays dark. There's a vague scrabbling, whistling sound somewhere in the burn-off. Liking everything less by the minute, I try a speech about our plane having crashed and we need help.

A very narrow pencil of light flicks over us and snaps off.

"Eh-ep," says a blurry voice and something metallic twitters. They for sure aren't locals. I'm getting unpleasant ideas.

"Yes, help!"

Something goes crackle-crackle whish-whish, and all sounds fade away.

"What the holy hell!" I stumble toward where they were.

"Look." Ruth whispers behind me. "Over by the ruin."

I look and catch a multiple flicker which winks out fast.

"A camp?"

And I take two more blind strides. My leg goes down through the crust and a spike spears me just where you stick the knife in to unjoint a drumstick. By the pain that goes through my bladder I recognize that my trick kneecap has caught it.

For instant basket case you can't beat kneecaps. First you discover your knee doesn't bend any more, so you try putting some weight on it and a bayonet goes up your spine and unhinges your jaw. Little grains of gristle have got into the sensitive bearing surface. The knee tries to buckle and can't, and mercifully you fall down.

Ruth helps me back to the serape.

"What a fool, what a godforgotten imbecile—"

"Not at all, Don. It was perfectly natural." We strike matches; her fingers push mine aside, exploring. "I think it's in place, but it's swelling fast. I'll lay a wet handkerchief on it. We'll have to wait for morning to check the cut. Were they poachers, do you think?"

"Probably," I lie. What I think they were is smugglers.

She comes back with a soaked bandanna and drapes it on. "We must have frightened them. That light . . . it seemed so bright."

"Some hunting party. People do crazy things around here."

"Perhaps they'll come back in the morning."

"Could be."

Ruth pulls up the wet serape, and we say good-night again. Neither of us are mentioning how we're going to get back to the plane without help.

I lie staring south where Alpha Centauri is blinking in and out of the overcast and cursing myself for the sweet mess I've made. My first idea is giving way to an even less pleasing one.

Smuggling, around here, is a couple of guys in an outboard meeting a shrimp boat by the reef. They don't light up the sky or have some kind of swamp buggy that goes whoosh. Plus a big camp . . . paramilitary-type equipment?

I've seen a report of Guévaristo infiltrators operating on the British Honduran border, which is about a hundred kilometers—sixty miles—south of here. Right under those clouds. If that's what looked us over, I'll be more than happy if they don't come back . . .

I wake up in pelting rain, alone. My first move confirms that my leg is as expected—a giant misplaced erection bulging out of my shorts. I raise up painfully to see Ruth standing by the bromels, looking over the bay. Solid wet nimbus is pouring out of the south.

"No planes today."

"Oh, good morning, Don. Should we look at that cut now?"

"It's minimal." In fact the skin is hardly broken, and no deep puncture. Totally out of proportion to the havoc inside.

"Well, they have water to drink," Ruth says tranquilly. "Maybe those hunters will come back. I'll go see if we have a fish—that is, can I help you in any way, Don?"

Very tactful. I emit an ungracious negative, and she goes off about her private concerns.

They certainly are private, too; when I recover from my own sanitary efforts, she's still away. Finally I hear splashing.

"It's a big fish!" More splashing. Then she climbs up the bank with a three-pound mangrove snapper—and something else.

It isn't until the messy work of filleting the fish that I begin to notice.

She's making a smudge of chaff and twigs to singe the fillets, small hands very quick, tension in that female upper lip. The rain has eased off for the moment; we're sluicing wet but warm enough. Ruth brings me my fish on a mangrove skewer and sits back on her heels with an odd breathy sigh.

"Aren't you joining me?"

"Oh, of course." She gets a strip and picks at it, saying quickly, "We either have too much salt or too little, don't we? I should fetch some brine." Her eyes are roving from nothing to noplace.

"Good thought." I hear another sigh and decide the Girl Scouts need an assist. "Your daughter mentioned you've come from Mérida. Have you seen much of Mexico?"

"Not really. Last year we went to Mazatlán and Cuernavaca . . . " She puts the fish down, frowning.

"And you're going to see Tikal. Going to Bonampak too?"

"No." Suddenly she jumps up brushing rain off her face. "I'll bring you some water, Don."

She ducks down the slide, and after a fair while comes back with a full bromel stalk.

"Thanks." She's standing above me, staring restlessly round the horizon.

"Ruth, I hate to say it, but those guys are not coming back and it's probably just as well. Whatever they were up to, we looked like trouble. The most they'll do is tell someone we're here. That'll take a day or two to get around, we'll be back at the plane by then."

"I'm sure you're right, Don." She wanders over to the smudge fire.

"And quit fretting about your daughter. She's a big girl."

"Oh, I'm sure Althea's all right . . . They have plenty of water now." Her fingers drum on her thigh. It's raining again.

"Come on, Ruth. Sit down. Tell me about Althea. Is she still in college?"

She gives that sighing little laugh and sits. "Althea got her degree last year. She's in computer programming."

"Good for her. And what about you, what do you do in GSA Records?"

"I'm in Foreign Procurement Archives." She smiles mechanically, but her breathing is shallow. "It's very interesting."

"I know a Jack Wittig in Contracts, maybe you know him?"

It sounds pretty absurd, there in the 'gator slide.

"Oh, I've met Mr. Wittig. I'm sure he wouldn't remember me."

"Why not?"

"I'm not very memorable."

Her voice is factual. She's perfectly right, of course. Who was that woman, Mrs. Jannings, Janny, who coped with my per diem for years? Competent, agreeable, impersonal. She had a sick father or something. But dammit, Ruth is a lot younger and better-looking. Comparatively speaking.

"Maybe Mrs. Parsons doesn't want to be memorable."

She makes a vague sound, and I suddenly realize Ruth isn't listening to me at all. Her hands are clenched around her knees, she's staring inland at the ruin.

"Ruth. I tell you our friends with the light are in the next county by now. Forget it, we don't need them."

Her eyes come back to me as if she'd forgotten I was there, and she nods slowly. It seems to be too much effort to speak. Suddenly she cocks her head and jumps up again.

"I'll go look at the line, Don. I thought I heard something—" She's gone like a rabbit.

While she's away I try getting up onto my good leg and the staff. The pain is sickening; knees seem to have some kind of hot line to the stomach. I take a couple of hops to test whether the Demerol I have in my belt would get me walking. As I do so, Ruth comes up the bank with a fish flapping in her hands.

"Oh, no, Don! *No!*" She actually clasps the snapper to her breast.

"The water will take some of my weight. I'd like to give it a try."

"You mustn't!" Ruth says quite violently and instantly modulates down. "Look at the bay, Don. One can't see a thing."

I teeter there, tasting bile and looking at the mingled curtains of sun and rain driving across the water. She's right, thank god. Even with two good legs we could get into trouble out there.

"I guess one more night won't kill us."

I let her collapse me back onto the gritty plastic, and she positively bustles around, finding me a chunk to lean on, stretching the serape on both staffs to keep rain off me, bringing another drink, grubbing for dry tinder.

"I'll make us a real bonfire as soon as it lets up, Don. They'll see our smoke, they'll know we're all right. We just have to wait." Cheery smile. "Is there any way we can make you more comfortable?"

Holy Saint Stercuilius: playing house in a mud puddle. For a fatuous moment I wonder if Mrs. Parsons has designs on me. And then she lets out another sigh and sinks back onto her heels with that listening look. Unconsciously her rump wiggles a little. My ear picks up the operative word: *wait.*

Ruth Parsons is waiting. In fact, she acts as if she's waiting so hard it's killing her. For what? For someone to get us out of here, what else? . . . But why was she so horrified when I got up to try to leave? Why all this tension?

My paranoia stirs. I grab it by the collar and start idly checking back. Up to when whoever it was showed up last night, Mrs. Parson was, I guess, normal. Calm and sensible, anyway. Now's she's humming like a high wire. And she seems to want to stay here and wait. Just as an intellectual pastime, why?

Could she have intended to come here? No way. Where she planned to be was Chetumal, which is on the border. Come to think, Chetumal is an odd way round to Tikal. Let's say the scenario was that she's meeting somebody in Chetumal. Somebody who's part of an organization. So now her contact in Chetumal knows she's overdue. And when those types appeared last night, something suggests to her that they're part of the same organization. And she hopes they'll put one and one together and come back for her?

"May I have the knife, Don? I'll clean the fish."

Rather slowly I pass the knife, kicking my subconscious. Such a decent ordinary little woman, a good Girl Scout. My trouble is that I've bumped into too many professional agilities under the careful stereotypes. *I'm not very memorable* . . .

What's in Foreign Procurement Archives? Wittig handles classified contracts. Lots of money stuff; foreign currency negotiations, commodity price schedules, some industrial technology. Or—just as a hypothesis—it could be as simple as a wad of bills back in that modest beige Ventura, to be exchanged for a packet from say, Costa Rica. If she were a courier, they'd want to get at the plane. And then what about me and maybe Estéban? Even hypothetically, not good.

I watch her hacking at the fish, forehead knotted with effort, teeth in her lip. Mrs. Ruth Parsons of Bethesda, this thrumming, private woman. How crazy can I get? *They'll see our smoke* . . .

"Here's your knife, Don. I washed it. Does the leg hurt very badly?"

I blink away the fantasies and see a scared little woman in a mangrove swamp.

"Sit down, rest. You've been going all out."

She sits obediently, like a kid in a dentist chair.

"You're stewing about Althea. And she's probably worried about you. We'll get back tomorrow under our own steam, Ruth."

"Honestly I'm not worried at all, Don." The smile fades; she nibbles her lip, frowning out at the bay.

"You know, Ruth, you surprised me when you offered to come along. Not that I don't appreciate it. But I rather thought you'd be concerned about leaving Althea alone with our good pilot. Or was it only me?"

This gets her attention at last.

"I believe Captain Estéban is a very fine type of man."

The words surprise me a little. Isn't the correct line more like "I trust Althea," or even, indignantly, "Althea is a good girl"?

"He's a man. Althea seemed to think he was interesting."

She goes on staring at the bay. And then I notice her tongue flick out and lick that prehensile upper lip. There's a flush that isn't sunburn around her ears and throat too, and one hand is gently rubbing her thigh. What's she seeing, out there in the flats?

Oho.

Captain Estéban's mahogany arms clasping Miss Althea Parsons' pearly body. Captain Estéban's archaic nostrils snuffling in Miss Parsons' tender neck. Captain Estéban's copper buttocks pumping into Althea's creamy upturned bottom . . . The hammock, very bouncy. Mayas know all about it.

Well, well. So Mother Hen has her little quirks.

I feel fairly silly and more than a little irritated. *Now* I find out. But even vicarious lust has much to recommend it, here in the mud and rain. I settle back, recalling that Miss Althea the computer programmer had waved good-bye very composedly. Was she sending her mother to flounder across the bay with me so she can get programmed in Maya? The memory of Honduran mahogany logs drifting in and out of the opalescent sand comes to me. Just as I am about to suggest that Mrs. Parsons might care to share my rain shelter, she remarks serenely, "The Mayas seem to be a very fine type of people. I believe you said so to Althea."

The implications fall on me with the rain. *Type.* As in breeding, bloodline, sire. Am I supposed to have certified Estéban not only as a stud but as a genetic donor?

"Ruth, are you telling me you're prepared to accept a half-Indian grandchild?"

"Why, Don, that's up to Althea, you know."

Looking at the mother, I guess it is. Oh, for mahogany gonads.

Ruth has gone back to listening to the wind, but I'm not about to let her off that easy. Not after all that *noli me tangere* jazz.

"What will Althea's father think?"

Her face snaps around at me, genuinely startled.

"Althea's father?" Complicated semismile. "He won't mind."

"He'll accept it too, eh?" I see her shake her head as if a fly were bothering her, and add with a cripple's malice: "Your husband must be a very fine type of a man."

Ruth looks at me, pushing her wet hair back abruptly. I have the impression that mousy Mrs. Parsons is roaring out of control, but her voice is quiet.

"There isn't any Mr. Parsons, Don. There never was. Althea's father was a Danish medical student . . . I believe he has gained considerable prominence."

"Oh." Something warns me not to say I'm sorry. "You mean he doesn't know about Althea?"

"No." She smiles, her eyes bright and cuckoo.

"Seems like rather a rough deal for her."

"I grew up quite happily under the same circumstances."

Bang, I'm dead. Well, well, well. A mad image blooms in my mind:

generations of solitary Parsons women selecting sires, making impregnation trips. Well, I hear the world is moving their way.

"I better look at the fish line."

She leaves. The glow fades. *No.* Just no, no contact. Good-bye, Captain Estéban. My leg is very uncomfortable. The hell with Mrs. Parsons' long-distance orgasm.

We don't talk much after that, which seems to suit Ruth. The odd day drags by. Squall after squall blows over us. Ruth singes up some more fillets, but the rain drowns her smudge; it seems to pour hardest just as the sun's about to show.

Finally she comes to sit under my sagging serape, but there's no warmth there. I doze, aware of her getting up now and then to look around. My subconscious notes that she's still twitchy. I tell my subconscious to knock it off.

Presently I wake up to find her penciling on the water-soaked pages of a little notepad.

"What's that, a shopping list for alligators?"

Automatic polite laugh. "Oh, just an address. In case we—I'm being silly, Don."

"Hey." I sit up, wincing. "Ruth, quit fretting. I mean it. We'll all be out of this soon. You'll have a great story to tell."

She doesn't look up. "Yes . . . I guess we will."

"Come on, we're doing fine. There isn't any real danger here, you know. Unless you're allergic to fish?"

Another good-little-girl laugh, but there's a shiver in it.

"Sometimes I think I'd like to go . . . really far away."

To keep her talking I say the first thing in my head.

"Tell me, Ruth. I'm curious why you would settle for that kind of lonely life, there in Washington? I mean, a woman like you—"

"—should get married?" She gives a shaky sigh, pushing the notebook back in her wet pocket.

"Why not? It's the normal source of companionship. Don't tell me you're trying to be some kind of professional man-hater."

"Lesbian, you mean?" Her laugh sounds better. "With my security rating? No, I'm not."

"Well, then. Whatever trauma you went through, these things don't last forever. You can't hate all men."

The smile is back. "Oh, there wasn't any trauma, Don, and I *don't* hate men. That would be as silly as—as hating the weather." She glances wryly at the blowing rain.

"I think you have a grudge. You're even spooky of me."

Smooth as a mouse bite she says, "I'd love to hear about your family, Don."

Touché. I give her the edited version of how I don't have one any more, and she says she's sorry, how sad. And we chat about what a good life a single person really has, and how she and her friends enjoy plays and concerts and travel, and one of them is head cashier for Ringling Brothers, how about that?

But it's coming out jerkier and jerkier like a bad tape, with her eyes going round the horizon in the pauses and her face listening for something that isn't my voice. What's wrong with her? Well, what's wrong with any furtively unconventional middle-aged woman with an empty bed. And a security clearance. An old habit of mind remarks unkindly that Mrs. Parsons represents what is known as the classic penetration target.

"—so much more opportunity now." Her voice trails off.

"Hurrah for women's lib, eh?"

"The lib?" Impatiently she leans forward and tugs the serape straight. "Oh, that's doomed."

The apocalyptic word jars my attention.

"What do you mean, doomed?"

She glances at me as if I weren't hanging straight either and says vaguely, "Oh . . . "

"Come on, why doomed? Didn't they get that equal rights bill?"

Long hesitation. When she speaks again her voice is different.

"Women have no rights, Don, except what men allow us. Men are more aggressive and powerful, and they run the world. When the next real crisis upsets them, our so-called rights will vanish like—like that smoke. We'll be back where we always were: property. And whatever has gone wrong will be blamed on our freedom, like the fall of Rome was. You'll see."

Now all this is delivered in a grey tone of total conviction. The last time I heard that tone, the speaker was explaining why he had to keep his file drawers full of dead pigeons.

"Oh, come on. You and your friends are the backbone of the system; if you quit, the country would come to a screeching halt before lunch."

No answering smile.

"That's fantasy." Her voice is still quiet. "Women don't work that way. We're a—a toothless world." She looks around as if she wanted to stop talking. "What women do is survive. We live by ones and twos in the chinks of your world-machine."

"Sounds like a guerrilla operation." I'm not really joking, here in the 'gator den. In fact, I'm wondering if I spent too much thought on mahogany logs.

"Guerrillas have something to hope for." Suddenly she switches on the jolly smile. "Think of us as opossums, Don. Did you know there are opossums living all over? Even in New York City."

I smile back with my neck prickling. I thought I was the paranoid one.

"Men and women aren't different species, Ruth. Women do everything men do."

"Do they?" Our eyes meet, but she seems to be seeing ghosts between us in the rain. She mutters something that could be "My Lai" and looks away. "All the endless wars . . . " Her voice is a whisper. "All the huge authoritarian organizations for doing unreal things. Men live to struggle against each other; we're just part of the battlefield. It'll never change unless you change the whole world. I dream sometimes of—of going away—" She checks and abruptly changes voice. "Forgive me, Don, it's so stupid saying all this."

"Men hate wars too, Ruth," I say as gently as I can.

"I know." She shrugs and climbs to her feet. "But that's your problem, isn't it?"

End of communication. Mrs. Ruth Parsons isn't even living in the same world with me.

I watch her move around restlessly, head turning toward the ruins. Alienation like that can add up to dead pigeons, which would be GSA's problem. It could also lead to believing some joker who's promising to change the whole world. Which could just probably be my problem if one of them was over in that camp last night, where she keeps looking. *Guerrillas have something to hope for . . . ?*

Nonsense. I try another position and see that the sky seems to be clearing as the sun sets. The wind is quieting down at last too. Insane to think this little woman is acting out some fantasy in this swamp. But that equipment last night was no fantasy; if those lads have some connection with her, I'll be in the way. You couldn't find a handier spot to dispose of the body. Maybe some Guévaristo is a fine type of man?

Absurd. Sure. The only thing more absurd would be to come through the wars and get myself terminated by a mad librarian's boyfriend on a fishing trip.

A fish flops in the stream below us. Ruth spins around so fast she hits the serape. "I better start the fire," she says, her eyes still on the plain and her head cocked, listening.

All right, let's test.

"Expecting company?"

It rocks her. She freezes, and her eyes come swiveling around at me like a film take captioned Fright. I can see her decide to smile.

"Oh, one never can tell!" She laughs weirdly, the eyes not changed. "I'll get the—the kindling." She fairly scuttles into the brush.

Nobody, paranoid or not, could call *that* a normal reaction.

Ruth Parsons is either psycho or she's expecting something to happen—and it has nothing to do with me; I scared her pissless.

Well, she could be nuts. And I could be wrong, but there are some mistakes you only make once.

Reluctantly I unzip my body-belt, telling myself that if I think what I think, my only course is to take something for my leg and get as far as possible from Mrs. Ruth Parsons before whoever she's waiting for arrives.

In my belt also is a .32-caliber asset Ruth doesn't know about—and it's going to stay there. My longevity program leaves the shoot-outs to TV and stresses being somewhere else when the roof falls in. I can spend a perfectly safe and also perfectly horrible night out in one of those mangrove flats . . . Am I insane?

At this moment Ruth stands up and stares blatantly inland with her hand shading her eyes. Then she tucks something into her pocket, buttons up and tightens her belt.

That does it.

I dry-swallow two 100-mg tabs, which should get me ambulatory and still leave me wits to hide. Give it a few minutes. I make sure my compass and some hooks are in my own pocket and sit waiting while Ruth fusses with her smudge fire, sneaking looks away when she thinks I'm not watching.

The flat world around us is turning into an unearthly amber and violet light-show as the first numbness seeps into my leg. Ruth has crawled under the bromels for more dry stuff; I can see her foot. Okay. I reach for my staff.

Suddenly the foot jerks, and Ruth yells—or rather, her throat makes that *Uh-uh-hhh* that means pure horror. The foot disappears in a rattle of bromel stalks.

I lunge upright on the crutch and look over the bank at a frozen scene.

Ruth is crouching sideways on the ledge, clutching her stomach. They are about a yard below, floating on the river in a skiff. While I was making up my stupid mind, her friends have glided right under my ass. There are three of them.

They are tall and white. I try to see them as men in some kind of white jumpsuits. The one nearest the bank is stretching out a long white arm toward Ruth. She jerks and scuttles farther away.

The arm stretches after her. It stretches and stretches. It stretches two yards and stays hanging in air. Small black things are wiggling from its tip.

I look where their faces should be and see black hollow dishes with vertical stripes. The stripes move slowly . . .

There is no more possibility of their being human—or anything else I've ever seen. What has Ruth conjured up?

The scene is totally silent. I blink, blink—this cannot be real. The two in the far end of the skiff are writhing those arms around an apparatus on a tripod. A weapon? Suddenly I hear the same blurry voice I heard in the night.

"Guh-give," it groans. "G-give . . ."

Dear God, it's real, whatever it is. I'm terrified. My mind is trying not to form a word.

And Ruth—Jesus, of course—Ruth is terrified too; she's edging along the bank away from them, gaping at the monsters in the skiff, who are obviously nobody's friends. She's hugging something to her body. Why doesn't she get over the bank and circle back behind me?

"G-g-give." That wheeze is coming from the tripod. "Pee-eeze give." The skiff is moving upstream below Ruth, following her. The arm undulates out at her again, its black digits looping. Ruth scrambles to the top of the bank.

"Ruth!" My voice cracks. "Ruth, get over here behind me!"

She doesn't look at me, only keeps sidling farther away. My terror detonates into anger.

"Come back here!" With my free hand I'm working the .32 out of my belt. The sun has gone down.

She doesn't turn but straightens up warily, still hugging the thing. I see her mouth working. Is she actually trying to *talk* to them?

"Please . . . " She swallows. "Please speak to me. I need your help."

"RUTH!!"

At this moment the nearest white monster whips into a great S-curve and sails right onto the bank at her, eight feet of snowy rippling horror.

And I shoot Ruth.

I don't know that for a minute—I've yanked the gun up so fast that my staff slips and dumps me as I fire. I stagger up, hearing Ruth scream, "No! No! No!"

The creature is back down by his boat, and Ruth is still farther away, clutching herself. Blood is running down her elbow.

"Stop it, Don! They aren't attacking you!"

"For god's sake! Don't be a fool, I can't help you if you won't get away from them!"

No reply. Nobody moves. No sound except the drone of a jet passing far above. In the darkening stream below me the three white figures shift uneasily; I get the impression of radar dishes focusing. The word spells itself in my head: *Aliens.*

Extraterrestrials.

What do I do, call the President? Capture them single-handed with my peashooter? . . . I'm alone in the arse end of nowhere with one leg and my brain cuddled in meperidine hydrochloride.

"Prrr-eese," their machine blurs again. "Wa-wat hep . . . "

"Our plane fell down," Ruth says in a very distinct, eerie voice. She points up at the jet, out towards the bay. "My—my child is there. Please take us *there* in your boat."

Dear god. While she's gesturing, I get a look at the thing she's hugging in her wounded arm. It's metallic, like a big glimmering distributor head. What—?

Wait a minute. This morning: when she was gone so long, she could have found that thing. Something they left behind. Or dropped. And she hid it, not telling me. That's why she kept going under that bromel clump—she was peeking at it. Waiting. And the owners came back and caught her. They want it. She's trying to bargain, by god.

"—Water," Ruth is pointing again. "Take us. Me. And him."

The black faces turn toward me, blind and horrible. Later on I may be grateful for that "us." Not now.

"Throw your gun away, Don. They'll take us back." Her voice is weak.

"Like hell I will. You—who are you? What are you doing here?"

"Oh god, does it matter? He's frightened," she cries to them. "Can you understand?"

She's as alien as they, there in the twilight. The beings in the skiff are twittering among themselves. Their box starts to moan.

"Ss-stu-dens," I make out. "S-stu-ding . . . not—huh-arm-ing . . . w-we . . . buh . . . " It fades into garble and then says "G-give . . . we . . . g-go . . . "

Peace-loving cultural-exchange students—on the interstellar level now. Oh, no.

"Bring that thing here, Ruth—right now!"

But she's starting down the bank toward them saying. "Take me."

"Wait! You need a tourniquet on that arm."

"I know. Please put the gun down, Don."

She's actually at the skiff, right by them. They aren't moving.

"Jesus Christ." Slowly, reluctantly, I drop the .32. When I start down the slide, I find I'm floating; adrenaline and Demerol are a bad mix.

The skiff comes gliding toward me, Ruth in the bow clutching the thing and her arm. The aliens stay in the stern behind their tripod, away from me. I note the skiff is camouflaged tan and green. The world around us is deep shadowy blue.

"Don, bring the water bag!"

As I'm dragging down the plastic bag, it occurs to me that Ruth really is cracking up, the water isn't needed now. But my own brain seems to have gone into overload. All I can focus on is a long white rubbery arm with black worms clutching the far end of the orange tube, helping me fill it. This isn't happening.

"Can you get in, Don?" As I hoist my numb legs up, two long white pipes reach for me. *No you don't.* I kick and tumble in beside Ruth. She moves away.

A creaky hum starts up, it's coming from a wedge in the center of the skiff. And we're in motion, sliding toward dark mangrove files.

I stare mindlessly at the wedge. Alien technological secrets? I can't see any, the power source is under that triangular cover, about two feet long. The gadgets on the tripod are equally cryptic, except that one has a big lens. Their light?

As we hit the open bay the hum rises, and we start planing faster and faster still. Thirty knots? Hard to judge in the dark. Their hull seems to be a modified trihedral much like ours, with a remarkable absence of slap. Say twenty-two feet. Schemes of capturing it swirl in my mind. I'll need Estéban.

Suddenly a huge flood of white light fans out over us from the tripod, blotting out the aliens in the stern. I see Ruth pulling at a belt around her arm, still hugging the gizmo.

"I'll tie that for you."

"It's all right."

The alien device is twinkling or phosphorescing slightly. I lean over to look, whispering, "Give that to me, I'll pass it to Estéban."

"No!" She scoots away, almost over the side. "It's theirs, they need it!"

"What? Are you crazy?" I'm so taken aback by this idiocy I literally stammer. "We have to, we—"

"They haven't hurt us. I'm sure they could." Her eyes are watching me with feral intensity; in the light her face has a lunatic look. Numb as I am, I realize that the wretched woman is poised to throw herself over the side if I move. With the alien thing.

"I think they're gentle," she mutters.

"For Christ's sake, Ruth, they're *aliens!*"

"I'm used to it," she says absently. "There's the island! Stop! Stop here!"

The skiff slows, turning. A mound of foliage is tiny in the light. Metal glints—the plane.

"Althea! Althea! Are you all right?"

Yells, movement on the plane. The water is high, we're floating over the bar. The aliens are keeping us in the lead with the light hiding them. I see one pale figure splashing toward us and a dark one behind, coming more slowly. Estéban must be puzled by that light.

"Mr. Fenton is hurt, Althea. These people brought us back with the water. Are you all right?"

"A-okay." Althea flounders up, peering excitedly. "You all right? Whew, that light!" Automatically I start handing her the idiotic water bag.

"Leave that for the captain," Ruth says sharply. "Althea, can you climb in the boat? Quickly, it's important."

"Coming."

"No, no!" I protest, but the skiff tilts as Althea swarms in. The aliens twitter, and their voice box starts groaning. "Gu-give . . . now . . . give . . ."

"Qué llega?" Estéban's face appears beside me, squinting fiercely into the light.

"Grab it, get it from her—that thing she has—" but Ruth's voice rides over mine. "Captain, lift Mr. Fenton out of the boat. He's hurt his leg. Hurry, please."

"Goddamn it, wait!" I shout, but an arm has grabbed my middle. When a Maya boosts you, you go. I hear Althea saying, "Mother, your arm!" and fall onto Estéban. We stagger around in water up to my waist; I can't feel my feet at all.

When I get steady, the boat is yards away. The two women are head-to-head, murmuring.

"Get them!" I tug loose from Estéban and flounder forward. Ruth stands up in the boat facing the invisible aliens.

"Take us with you. Please. We want to go with you, away from here."

"Ruth! Estéban, get that boat!" I lunge and lose my feet again. The aliens are chirruping madly behind their light.

"Please take us. We don't mind what your planet is like; we'll learn—we'll do anything! We won't cause any trouble. Please. Oh *please.*" The skiff is drifting farther away.

"Ruth! Althea! Are you crazy? Wait—" But I can only shuffle nightmarelike in the ooze, hearing that damn voice box wheeze, "N-not come . . . more . . . not come . . ." Althea's face turns to it, open-mouthed grin.

"Yes, we understand," Ruth cries. "We don't want to come back. Please take us with you!"

I shout and Estéban splashes past me shouting too, something about radio.

"Yes-s-s," groans the voice.

Ruth sits down suddenly, clutching Althea. At that moment Estéban grabs the edge of the skiff beside her.

"Hold them, Estéban! Don't let her go."

He gives me one slit-eyed glance over his shoulder, and I recognize his total uninvolvement. He's had a good look at that camouflage paint and the absence of fishing gear. I make a desperate rush and slip again.

When I come up Ruth is saying, "We're going with these people, Captain. Please take your money out of my purse, it's in the plane. And give this to Mr. Fenton."

She passes him something small; the notebook. He takes it slowly.

"Estéban! No!"

He has released the skiff.

"Thank you so much," Ruth says as they float apart. Her voice is shaky; she raises it. "There won't be any trouble, Don. Please send the cable. It's to a friend of mine, she'll take care of everything." Then she adds the craziest touch of the entire night. "She's a grand person, she's director of nursing training at N.I.H."

As the skiff drifts out I hear Althea add something that sounds like "Right on."

Sweet Jesus . . . Next minute the humming has started; the light is receding fast. The last I see of Mrs. Ruth Parsons and Miss Althea Parsons is two small shadows against that light, like two opossums. The light snaps off, the hum deepens—and they're going, going, gone away.

In the dark water beside me Estéban is instructing everybody in general to *chingarse* themselves.

"Friends, or something," I tell him lamely. "She seemed to want to go with them."

He is pointedly silent, hauling me back to the plane. He knows what could be around here better than I do, and Mayas have their own longevity program. His condition seems improved. As we get in I notice the hammock has been repositioned.

In the night—of which I remember little—the wind changes. And at seven thirty next morning a Cessna buzzes the sandbar under cloudless skies.

By noon we're back in Cozumel. Captain Estéban accepts his fees and departs laconically for his insurance wars. I leave the Parsons' bags with the Caribe agent, who couldn't care less. The cable goes to a Mrs. Priscilla Hayes Smith, also of Bethesda. I take myself to a medico and by three P.M. I'm sitting on the Cabañas terrace with a fat leg and a double Margarita, trying to believe the whole thing.

The cable said: ALTHEA AND I TAKING EXTRAORDINARY OPPORTUNITY FOR TRAVEL. GONE SEVERAL YEARS. PLEASE TAKE CHARGE OUR AFFAIRS. LOVE, RUTH.

She'd written it that afternoon, you understand.

I order another double, wishing to hell I'd gotten a good look at that gizmo. Did it have a label, Made by Betelgeusians? No matter how weird it was, *how* could a person be crazy enough to imagine—?

Not only that but to hope, to plan? *If I could only go away* . . . That's what she was doing, all day. Waiting, hoping, figuring how to get Althea. To go sight unseen to an alien world . . .

With the third Margarita I try a joke about alienated women, but my heart's not in it. And I'm certain there won't be any bother, any trouble at all. Two human women, one of them possibly pregnant, have departed for, I guess, the stars; and the fabric of society will never show a ripple. I brood: do all Mrs. Parsons' friends hold themselves in readiness for any eventuality, including leaving Earth? And will Mrs. Parsons somehow one day contrive to send for Mrs. Priscilla Hayes Smith, that grand person?

I can only send for another cold one, musing on Althea. What suns will Captain Estéban's sloe-eyed offspring, if any, look upon? "Get in, Althea, we're taking off for Orion." "A-okay, Mother." Is that some system of upbringing? *We survive by ones and twos in the chinks of your world-machine . . . I'm used to aliens . . .* She'd meant every word. Insane. How could a woman choose to live among unknown monsters, to say good-bye to her home, her world?

As the Margaritas take hold, the whole mad scenario melts down to the image of those two small shapes sitting side by side in the receding alien glare.

Two of our opossums are missing.

(1973)

GENE WOLFE

Feather Tigers

"That big river down there is the Mekong," the skyacht said. "It's a very famous river. My masters fought a war on it and around it that lasted . . . well, you wouldn't believe how long it lasted."

"That's right," said Quoquo the psychologist, who was soft and blue and looked something like a childsized rabbit, "I would not. And I have never—never in all the time I've been here—really understood why your masters, as you call them, were moved to create machines that lie."

"I thought," the skyacht replied very respectfully, "that it was your business to understand them, those late, honored masters of mine. Surely—"

"Please be quiet," said Quoquo, who was recording this conversation for possible future use in his lectures, but would have preferred talking to one of his own species on the ground below by means of his belt communicator.

"Of course. Would you like me to fly lower? That way I could point out more places of interest. If you like, I could even make a few passes over Angkor Thom."

"Just go where you're told."

The skyacht spread its wings (they had been folded back for supersonic flight, so that it had looked like a silver dart; but with them spread and their thousand articulated surfaces set for landing the skyacht would have looked surprisingly like a phoenix as the flame from its rockets washed backward over its own indestructible skin, had there been any eye watching to which the phoenix was known) and settled down toward Biological Experiment Station 73, Quoquo's destination. "This used to be part of Cambodia when my masters were still alive," it informed Quoquo amiably. "But I can't give you the name of a city because there weren't any nearby. These are the Dangrek Mountains."

Quoquo merely grunted.

Later, Dondiil, the biologist who operated the station, said admiringly, "You came in one of *their* machines?"

"Certainly," snapped Quoquo. "I hoped I might learn something. Besides, they're much faster than ours."

"And did you learn anything?"

Quoquo smoothed his fur, parting it horizontally across the belly, the conventional way of implying a negative mixed with self-contempt. "I have spent thousands of hours questioning those machines already," he said morosely, "and I should have known better than to think . . . but one always hopes."

Dondiil assented with a body-shake. "I have found their machines," he said diplomatically, "to possess only a low degree of knowledge. Biological knowledge, that is."

Quoquo appeared not to have heard him. "They know history," he said, "and geography. The geography consists of place names and the history of unmotivated moving and fighting. A colleague of mine has spent over a score-score wakeperiods in establishing beyond contradiction that, as far as any surviving machine knows, Paris, France and Paris, Texas had nothing whatsoever in common but their names. *France* means 'the country of the Franks,' that is, of those who speak unadorned truth; *Texas* signifies 'the land of friends,' which is to say, of those who do not fight among themselves. The 'friends' for whom the country was named were cannibals. Do you find this suggestive?"

"Not psychologically," admitted Dondiil. "As a biologist I would expect a coastal or island area providing a diet deficient in mammalian protein."

"My present approach," said Quoquo, who had perhaps been following his own train of thought while Dondiil spoke, "is to study the creatures in their most primitive state."

"And how may I assist you?"

"In pursuit of my goal I have catalogued over ten score primitive groups, and have rated them according to the information available. One of the most primitive was called 'The People of the Yellow Leaves.' Does it happen that you are familiar with this group?"

Dondiil parted the hair on his belly horizontally.

"They inhabited precisely this area. And they possessed a remarkable superstition, one that does not seem to have been found among the human beings on any other part of this planet. They believed in the existence of 'feather tigers.' "

Dondiil's ears snapped into the position of maximum alertness. "You're aware of my work," he said quickly. "I'm attempting to restore that extinct species—that is, the animals that were called 'tigers.' " After a moment he added, "But I am afraid I fail to see how this impinges on your own problem—the disappearance of the race of intelligent beings who once ruled this world."

Quoquo stood, fluffing out his small tail before he began to pace the room. "We are aware," he said, "from our studies of the records they left behind, as well as from questioning their machines, that before they vanished several species of wildlife disappeared."

Dondiil body-shook vigorously.

"For example," Quoquo continued, "a certain pygmy tribe of the Congo basin—the Batwas—seems to have ceased to exist at about the same time as the lowland gorilla. Similarly, the French-speaking people of the lower Mississippi are no longer mentioned in the records after the disappearance of the brown pelican."

"And these People of the Yellow Leaves . . . ?" queried Dondiil.

"Vanished at about the same time as your tigers," finished Quoquo.

"But surely you are not hoping that the biological restoration of the tigers—"

"Will restore the associated tribe?" Quoquo laughed. "Certainly not. But as a psychologist I am eager to probe the effect the presence of the animals may have had upon these creatures' minds. In the other cases I mentioned it is not possible to do this because the animals themselves no longer exist. But you have restored the tiger for us, and done it in precisely the area in which the associated human group lived. I want to achieve empathy with those vanished beings. If I can learn to think, Dondiil, as they did—even a little—we will know far more than we do at present."

"But tigers," Dondiil objected, "were unquestionably real animals—I possess several complete skeletons. You said the feather tigers were a superstition."

"They were. The People of the Yellow Leaves believed that tigers—the actual living animals of your own interest—could detach their souls from their bodies and send them forth to locate prey. The presence of these hunting tiger-spirits could be detected by their influence on dapples of light and shadow, the patterns of foliage and such things, which they caused to resemble tigers." Quoquo fell silent.

"Why were they called 'feather tigers'?" Dondiil asked.

"If a wind stirred the leaves," Quoquo said, "these patterns naturally disappeared. The People of the Yellow Leaves accounted for this by saying that the tigers' spirits were very light, like feathers, and were blown away by the wind." He sighed. "When human beings from more advanced groups visited these primitives they were shocked by the amount of fear and suffering this belief caused them. Yet when the tigers became extinct the People of the Yellow Leaves seem to have vanished as well; perhaps they were even more closely linked to nature than those who visited them believed. Indeed, that seems to have been the case with the entire indigenous intelligent species."

"Would I be overstraining your patience," inquired Dondiil, "if I asked why the People of the Yellow Leaves were so called?"

"They were very much afraid of the far larger and more advanced group called the Siamese," Quoquo explained, "who killed them and stole their females; and for that reason they hid themselves in the most remote parts of the mountains, coming down into the valleys and onto the less inhospitable slopes only when food was difficult to find. This was most often in time of drought, just before the winter monsoons."

"I see," said Dondiil. "When the leaves turn yellow for want of moisture—particularly the bamboo."

Quoquo indicated approval. "Yes," he said. "This was the only time during which they were seen by outsiders. But now, may I see your tigers?"

The cages in which Dondiil housed the results of his breeding experiments were out-of-doors; his assistants, with brush hooks and heavy, complicated vegetation-slicing machines, maintained a twenty-hop cleared space around them. But on the farther side of this shaven lawn the montane jungle of East Asia presented a solid wall of trees and creepers, laced with clumps of bamboo. Quoquo stood for a moment studying it, then turned toward Dondiil's exhibits.

"Quite impressive," he said, "but are those flashy orange and black stripes authentic?"

"Absolutely," said Dondiil.

"Then tell me, how is this done? Just how do you go about re-creating an extinct animal?" (As Quoquo said this he bent his right ear with his left hand, a gesture indicating that though he was already familiar with the matter about which he was inquiring he considered it a courtesy he owed his host to submit his present ideas for amplification, and, if need be, correction.)

"We have records, including color photographs, left behind by the intelligent race," Dondiil said modestly. "As well as the skeletons I spoke of. And though the tiger became extinct, a number of smaller, related felines survived. I have bred these, now, for two score orbits of the home world, altering their genetic structure with beam-scalpels, and selecting the resultant mutants for size, coloration, and other tigerlike characteristics."

"But," asked Quoquo, raising one hand in the gesture of pointed interruption (despite the fact that Dondiil had finished speaking), "can you—and have you—selected also for the behavioral characteristics of the original animal? I see before me five large, striped beasts who watch me calmly with singularly beautiful eyes, but are these the fierce predators who terrified the People of the Yellow Leaves? They are motionless except for the twitching of their tails, and I confess that I fail to find them very frightening."

"It may be that I have failed in that regard," Dondiil said humbly, "though they kill the wild cattle we bring them quite efficiently."

"Animal psychology is not my field," said Quoquo, "but if you like, I can give you the address of a sound colleague who might advise you." He turned away from the tigers, and as he did one of them coughed. It was a deep, rattling sound, and it was followed by a loud, prolonged noise like the consonant *R* repeated over and over. "One of your beasts is sick," he told Dondiil.

"Oh, no," Dondiil explained, "that sound is characteristic of them. It is almost time for them to eat; they always become restless about now."

Quoquo turned back to look at the animals. One was sitting up now, and, meeting Quoquo's eye, it yawned. "They have splendid teeth," Quoquo observed.

"Oh, he's one of the small ones," Dondiil said. "You ought to see the big fellow back in the corner."

"Well, this has been interesting." Quoquo rubbed his hands together in the gesture of satisfaction with another's hospitality. "And I have stored my mind with a number of valuable images, but now I must be about my own business."

"You intend to go out into the jungle?"

"Certainly. There is no other way by which I can observe and photograph the leaf patterns, shadows and so forth I described to you. I have my belt communicator; so if you'll be so good as to send out a homing signal from the station here I cannot possibly become lost, and I'll take care not to fall off any cliffs."

"Wouldn't you like to see my animals fed?" Dondiil asked a little wistfully. He did not get company often.

Quoquo declined firmly. "I should be back at my desk by tomorrow at the latest." He was already examining his camera to make certain it was in working order. "Is there a break in that jungle somewhere where I can walk in, or will I have to blast my way?"

"Blast," said Dondiil. "That's what we have to do. Go in a straight line and sooner or later you'll strike a game trail."

Quoquo inclined his head (the conventional gesture of acquiescence) and taking his blaster from his belt dialed a semidiffuse beam and depressed the firing stud. A smoking hole a hop wide a hop high and a hundred hops long appeared in the green wall.

In two hours he had penetrated a considerable distance into the jungle, and photographed any number of shadows, waving leaves and fallen trees, none of which, he admitted to himself, looked in the least like

Dondiil's animals. Into his recorder he said: "I have now observed, in person and on foot, the rugged, jungle-clad slopes of the Dangrek Mountains, the area which was, at one and the same time, the homeland of the obscure primitive tribe known as the People of the Yellow Leaves and one of the last strongholds of the large carnivorous animal called 'tiger.' The experience has given me a lively awareness of the isolation of the People of the Yellow Leaves and of the difficulty of their struggle for survival—a struggle which they, sooner than less beleaguered groups, eventually lost. But it has not furnished me with any additional evidence in support of the theory which couples their disappearance with that of the tiger. The bars of light falling to the jungle floor through the leaves overhead often assume shifting and fantastic shapes, and the stems of the bamboos, though seeming quite inflexible to the hand, sway in the slightest of breezes; but at no time do these phenomena, nor any of the many others I have observed, assume a form suggestive of beasts. In short, I have seen no 'feather tigers.' "

He touched the switch that deactivated his recorder, and listened for a moment to the steady pinging of the homing signal on his communicator, debating whether he should continue his investigation or return to the station. He had just decided on the latter when the pinging ceased, replaced by Dondiil's voice.

"Quoquo!" the biologist called excitedly. "Quoquo, can you hear me?"

Quoquo activated the sending circuit. "I hear you," he said. "Has a message come for me?"

"Quoquo, my animals have escaped. I need your help."

"Are you serious?"

"It was feeding time," Dondiil babbled, "and one of my assistants had opened the cage door to drive in a bullock. Quite unexpectedly the tigers rushed for the opening instead of waiting for the animal to be herded into the cage for them. Once outside they appeared to become frenzied; they ignored the bullock and made for the path you blasted out. One of them clawed poor Aniipan in passing, and he's in critical condition. But the important point, as I'm sure you'll realize, is that the animals must be recovered. Their loss would set my program back disasterously. If you see one can I count on you to report it at once, and keep him under observation until we can reach the spot with a capture party?"

"Certainly," Quoquo said, unholstering his blaster as he spoke and checking the state of the charge. "But I must warn you, Dondiil, that I was already returning when I received your call, and I intend to continue to do so; and if I feel it's necessary to injure one of your specimens in order to preserve my own safety, that is what I will do."

"I understand," Dondiil said, and signed off.

Quoquo had not walked more than a hundred hops more when he saw the first tiger. It was ready to spring, and there was no time to notify Dondiil—or indeed to do anything but jerk his blaster to waist height and fire. A corridor of jungle disappeared in a sheet of flame, and after a moment, when his nerves had quieted somewhat, he advanced to see if any part of the tiger had been outside the beam and thus remained intact for examination. There was nothing but ashes, heat-split stones and scorched soil.

He killed the second before he had taken another fifty hops, and a third at thirty. By the time he saw the fourth he knew that at least some of the first three had not been real. He hesitated, his finger on the firing stud, and saw, with unspeakable horror, the striped beast slink silently away. Too late he fired, then instead of examining the result of his shot he stood rooted to the spot, turning his head slowly to scan the underbrush around him, his stare lingering longest on the shadows of the huge tree trunks. Feather tigers. Feather tigers everywhere. He screamed wordlessly and ran, and as he did so dark eyes, timid but bright with an intelligence not found in any animal, followed him from the depths of a thicket of yellowing bamboo.

(1973)

VONDA N. MCINTYRE

The Mountains of Sunset, the Mountains of Dawn

The smell from the ship's animal room, at first tantalizing, grew to an overpowering strength. Years before, the odor of so many closely caged animals had sickened the old one, but now it urged on her slow hunger. When she was a youth, her hunger demanded satiation, but now even her interior responses were aging. The hunger merely ached.

Inside the animal room, three dimensions of cages stretched up the floor's curvature, enclosing fat and lethargic animals that slept, unafraid. She lifted a young one by the back of its neck. Blinking, it hung in her hand; it would not respond in fear even when she extended her silver claws into its flesh. Its ancestors had run shrieking across the desert when the old one's shadow passed over them, but fear and speed and the chemical reactions of terror had been bred out of these beasts. Their meat was tasteless.

"Good day."

Startled, the old one turned. The youth's habit of approaching silently from behind was annoying; it made her fancy that her hearing was failing as badly as her sight. Still, she felt a certain fondness for this child, who was not quite so weak as the others. The youth was beautiful: wide wings and delicate ears, large eyes and triangular face, soft body-covering of fur as short as fur can be, patterned in tan against the normal lustrous black. The abnormality occurred among the first ship-generation's children. On the home world, any infant so changed would have been exposed, but on the sailship infanticide was seldom practiced. This the old one disapproved of, fearing a deterioration in her people, but she had grown used to the streaked and swirling fur pattern.

"I greet thee," she said, "but I'm hungry. Go away before I make thee ill."

"I've become accustomed to it," the youth said.

The old one shrugged, leaned down, and slashed the animal's throat with her sharp teeth. Warm blood spurted over her lips. As she swallowed it, she wished she were soaring and eating bits of warm meat from the fingers of a mate or a lover, feeding him in turn. Thus she, when still a youth and not yet "she," had courted her eldermate; thus her youngermate had never been able to court her. Two generations of her kind had missed that experience, but she seemed to regret the loss more than they did. She dismembered and gutted the animal and crunched its bones for marrow and brains.

She glanced up. The youth watched, seeming fascinated yet revolted. She offered a shred of meat.

"No. Thank you."

"Then eat thy meat cold, like the rest of them."

"I'll try it. Sometime."

"Yes, of course," the old one said. "And all our people will live on the lowest level and grow strong, and fly every day."

"I fly. Almost every day."

The old one smiled, half cynically, half with pity. "I would show thee what it is to fly," she said. "Across deserts so hot the heat snatches thee, and over mountains so tall they outreach clouds, and into the air until the radiation explodes in thine eyes and steals thy direction and shatters thee against the earth, if thou art not strong enough to overcome it."

"I'd like that."

"It's too late." The old one wiped the clotting blood from her hands and lips. "It's much too late." She turned to leave; behind her, the youth spoke so softly that she almost did not hear. "It's my choice. Must you refuse me?"

She let the door close between them.

In the corridor, she passed others of her people, youths and adults made spindly by their existence on the inner levels of the ship, where the gravity was low. Many greeted her with apparent deference, but she believed she heard contempt. She ignored them. She had the right; she was the oldest of them all, the only one alive who could remember their home.

Her meal had not yet revived her; the slightly curved floor seemed to rise in fact rather than in appearance. The contempt she imagined in others grew in herself. It was past her time to die.

Ladders connected the levels of the ship, in wells not designed for flying. With difficulty, the old one let herself down to the habitation's rim. She felt happier, despite the pain, when the centrifugal force increased her weight.

The voyage had been exciting, before she grew old. She had not minded trading hunting grounds for sailship cubicles; the universe lay waiting. She entered the ship young and eager, newly eldermated, newly changed from youth to adult; loved, loving, sharing her people's dreams as they abandoned their small, dull world.

The old one's compartment was on the lowest level, where the gravity was greatest. Slowly, painfully, she sat cross-legged beside the window, unfolding her wings against the stiffness of her wing-fingers to wrap the soft membranes around her body. Outside, the stars raced by, to the old one's failing sight a multicolored, swirling blur, like mica flakes in sand.

The habitation spun, and the sails came into view. The huge reflective sheets billowed in the pressure of the stellar winds, decelerating the ship and holding it against gravity as it approached the first new world the old one's people would ever see.

She dreamed of her youth, of flying high enough to see the planet's curvature, of skimming through high-altitude winds, gambling that no capricious current could overcome her and break her hollow bones. Other youths fell in their games; they died, but few mourned: that was the way of things.

She dreamed of her dead eldermate, and reached for him, but his form was insubstantial and slipped through her fingers.

Claws skittered against the door, waking her. Her dreams dissolved.

"Enter."

The door opened; against the dimness of her room light shadowed the one who stood there. The old one's eyes adjusted slowly; she recognized the piebald youth. She felt that she should send the youth away, but the vision of her eldermate lingered in her sight, and the words would not come.

"What dost thou wish?"

"To speak with you. To listen to you."

"If that's all."

"Of course it isn't. But if it's all you will allow, I will accept it."

The old one unwrapped her wings and sat slowly up. "I outlived my youngermate," she said. "Wouldst thou have me disgust our people again?"

"They don't care. It isn't like that anymore. We've changed."

"I know . . . my children have forgotten our customs, and I have no right to criticize. Why should they listen to a crippled parent who refuses to die?"

The youth heel-sat before her, silent for a moment. "I wish . . . "

She stretched out her hand, extending the sharp claws. "Our people should never have left our home. I would long be dead, and thou wouldst not have met me."

The youth took her hand and grasped it tightly. "If you were dead—"

She drew back, opening long fingers so her wing spread across her body. "I will die," she said. "Soon. But I want to fly again. I will see one new world, and then I will have seen enough."

"I wish you wouldn't talk of dying."

"Why? Why have we become so frightened of death?"

The youth rose, shrugging, and let the tips of the striped wings touch the floor. The vestigial claws clicked against the metal. "Maybe we're not used to it anymore."

The old one perceived the remark's unconscious depth. She smiled, and began to laugh. The youth looked at her, as if thinking her mad. But she could not explain what was so funny, that they had reached for the perils of the stellar winds, and found only safety and trepidation.

"What's the matter? Are you all right? What is it?"

"Nothing," she said. "Thou wouldst not understand." She no longer felt like laughing, but exhausted and ill. "I will sleep," she said, having regained her dignity. She turned her gaze from the beautiful youth.

Waking, she felt warm, as if she were sleeping in the sun on a pinnacle of rock with the whole world spreading out around her. But her cheek rested against chill metal; she opened her eyes knowing once more where she was.

The youth lay beside her, asleep, wing outstretched across them both. She started to speak but remained silent. She felt she should be angry, but the closeness was too pleasurable. Guilt sprang up, at allowing this child to retain desire for the love of one about to die, but still the old one did not move. She lay beneath the caressing wing, seeking to recapture her dreams. But the youth shifted, and the old one found herself looking into dark, gold-flecked, startled eyes.

The youth pulled away. "I am sorry. I meant only to warm you, not to . . . "

"I . . . found it pleasant, after so long in this cold metal. I thank thee."

The youth gazed at her, realizing gradually what she had said, then lay down and gently enfolded her again.

"Thou art a fool. Thou dost seek pain."

The youth rested against her, head on her shoulder.

"I will only call thee 'thee,' " she said.

"All right."

The flying chamber enclosed half the levels of a segment two twelfths of the habitation wide. Its floor and its side walls were transparent to space.

The old one and the youth stood on a brilliant path of stars. On one side of them, the sails rippled as they changed position to hold the ship on course. They obscured a point of light only slightly brighter than the stars that formed its background: the sun of the home planet, the star this ship and a thousand like it had abandoned. On the other side, a second star flared bright, and even the old one could see the changing phases of the spheres that circled it.

The youth stared out at the illuminated edge of their destination. "Will you be happy there?"

"I'll be happy to see the sky and the land again."

"A blue sky, without stars . . . I think that will be very empty."

"We became used to this ship," the old one said. "We can go back again as easily." She turned, spread her wings, ran a few steps, and lifted herself into the air. The takeoff felt clumsy, but the flying was more graceful.

She glided, spiraling upward on the gravity gradient. To fly higher with less and less effort had been strange and exciting; now she only wished for a way to test her strength to the breaking point. Her distance perception had weakened with time, but she knew the dimensions of the chamber by kinesthetic sense and memory: long enough to let one glide, but not soar, wide enough to let one stroke slowly from one side to the next, but not tax one's muscles with speed, deep enough to let one swoop, but not dive.

At the top of the chamber, she slid through the narrow space between ceiling and walking bridge; she heard the youth, behind her, falter, then plunge through. The old one had laughed when they built the crossing, but there were those who could not cross the chamber without the bridge, and that she did not find amusing.

Sound guided her. Sometimes she wished to plug her ears and fly oblivious to the echoes that marked boundaries. She had considered dying that way, soaring with senses half crippled until she crashed against the thick tapestry of stars and blessed the sailship with her blood. But she wanted to touch the earth again; so she continued to live.

She grew tired; her bones would ache when she had rested. She dipped her wings and slipped toward the floor, stretching to combat the rising end of the gradient. She landed; her wings drooped around her. The youth touched down and approached her. "I am tired."

She appreciated the concession to her dignity. "I, too."

The days passed; the youth stayed with her. They flew together, and they sailed the long-deserted ion boats in the whirlpools of converging stellar winds. At first fearful, the youth gained confidence as the old one demonstrated the handling of the sails. The old one recalled other, half-forgotten voyages with other, long-dead youths. Her companion's growing pleasure made her briefly glad that her dream of dying properly, veiled and soaring, had kept her from taking one of the boats and sailing until the air ran out or some accident befell her.

When the features of the new world could be discerned, the old one made the long walk to the navigation room. Her eyes no longer let her feel the stars, and so she did not navigate, yet though the young people could guide the ship as well as her generation had, she felt uneasy leaving her fate in the hands of others. From the doorway, she pushed off gently and floated to the center of the chamber. A few young adults drifted inside the transparent hemisphere, talking, half dozing, watching the relationships between ship, planet, primary, and stars. The navigation room did not rotate; directions were by convention. Streaked with clouds, glinting with oceans, the crescent world loomed above them; below, the ship's main body spun, a reflective expanse spotted with dark ports and the transparent segment of the flying chamber.

"Hello, grandmother."

"Hello, grandchild." She should call him "grandson," she thought, but she was accustomed to the other, though this child of her first child, already youngermated, had long been adult. She felt once more that she should choose a graceful way to die.

Nearby, two people conferred about a few twelfths of a second of arc and altered the tension on the main sail lines. Like a concave sheet of water, the sail rippled and began to fold.

"It seems the engines will not be necessary." They had begun the turn already; the stars were shifting around them.

He shrugged, only his shoulders, not his wings. "Perhaps just a little." He gazed at her for a long time without speaking. "Grandmother, you know the planet is smaller than we thought."

She looked up at the white-misted, half-shadowed globe. "Not a great deal, surely."

"Considerably. It's much denser for its mass than our world was. The surface gravity will be higher."

"How much?"

"Enough that our people would be uncomfortable."

The conditional, by its implications, frightened her. "Our people are weak," she said. "Have the council suggest they move to the first level."

"No one would, grandmother." Though he never flew, he sounded sad.

"You are saying we will not land?"

"How can we? No one could live."

"No one?"

"You are old, grandmother."

"And tired of sailing. I want to fly again."

"No one could fly on that world."

"How can you say? You don't even fly in the chamber."

He stared down at the shimmering, half-folded sails. "I fly with them. Those are all the wings our people need."

The old one flexed her wing-fingers; the membranes opened, closed, opened. "Is that what everyone believes?"

"It's true. The sails have carried us for two generations. Why should we abandon them now?"

"How can we depend on them so heavily? Grandson, we came onto this ship to test ourselves, and you're saying we will avoid the test."

"The ambitions and needs of a people can change."

"And the instincts?"

She knew what his answer would be before he did. "Even those, I think."

The old one looked out over space. She could not navigate, but she could evaluate their trajectory. It was never meant to be converted into an orbit. The ship would swing around the planet, catapult past it, and sail on.

"We felt trapped by a whole world," the old one said. "How can our children be satisfied on this uninteresting construct?"

"Please try to understand. Try to accept the benefits of our security." He touched her hand, very gently, his claws retracted. "I'm sorry."

She turned away from him, forced by the lack of gravity to use clumsy swimming motions. She returned to the low regions of the habitation, feeling almost physically wounded by the decision not to land. The ship could sustain her life no longer.

The youth was in her room. "Shall we fly?"

She hunched in the corner near the window. "There is no reason to fly."

"What's happened?" The youth crouched beside her.

"Thou must leave me and forget me. I will be gone by morning."

"But I'm coming."

She took the youth's hand, extending her silver claws against the patterned black and tan fur. "No one else is landing. Thou wouldst be left alone."

The youth understood her plans. "Stay on the ship." The tone was beyond pleading.

"It doesn't matter what I do. If I stay, I will die, and thou wilt feel grief. If I leave, thou wilt feel the same grief. But if I allow thee to come, I will steal thy life."

"It's my life."

"Ah," she said sadly, "thou art so young."

The old one brought out a flask of warm red wine. As the sky spun and tumbled beside them, she and the youth shared the thick, salty liquid, forgetting their sorrows as the intoxicant went to their heads. The youth stroked the old one's cheek and throat and body. "Will you do one thing for me before you leave?"

"What dost thou wish?"

"Lie with me. Help me make the change."

With the wine, she found herself half amused by the youth's persistence and naiveté. "That is something thou shouldst do with thy mate."

"I have to change soon, and there's no one else I want to court."

"Thou dost seek loneliness."

"Will you help me?"

"I told thee my decision when thou asked to stay."

The youth seemed about to protest again, but remained silent. The old one considered the easy capitulation, but the strangeness slipped from her as she drank more wine. Stroking her silver claws against her companion's patterned temple, she allowed her vision to unfocus among the swirls of tan, but she did not sleep.

When she had set herself for her journey, she slipped away. She felt some regret when the youth did not stir, but she did not want another argument; she did not want to be cruel again. As she neared the craft bay, excitement overcame disappointment; this was her first adventure in many years.

She saw no one, for the bay was on the same level as her room. She entered a small power craft, sealed it, and gave orders to the bay. The machinery worked smoothly, despite lack of use or care. The old one could understand the young people's implicit trust in the ship; her generation had built seldom, but very well. The air gone, she opened the hatch. The craft fell out into space.

Her feeling for the workings of the power craft returned. Without numbers or formulae she set its course; her vision was not so bad that she could not navigate in harbors.

Following gravity, she soon could feel the difference between this world and the home planet; not, she thought, too much. She crossed the terminator into daylight, where swirls of cloud swept by beneath her. She anticipated rain, cool on her face and wings, pushed in rivulets down her body by the speed of her flight. Without the old one's conscious direction, her wing fingers opened slightly, closed, opened.

She watched the stars as her motion made them rise. Refraction gave her the approximate density of the air: not, she thought, too low.

The ship dipped into the outer atmosphere. Its stubby wings slowed it; decelerating, it approached the planet's surface, fighting the differences of this world, which yielded, finally, to the old one's determination. She looked for a place to land.

The world seemed very young; for a long while she saw only thick jungles and marshes. Finally, between mountain ranges that blocked the clouds, she found a desert. It was alien in color and form, but the sand glittered with mica like the sand of home. She landed the ship among high dunes.

The possibility had always existed that the air, the life, the very elements would be lethal. She broke the door's seal; air hissed sharply. She breathed fresh air for the first time in two generations. It was thin, but it had more oxygen than she was used to, and made her light-headed. The smells teased her to identify them. She climbed to the warm sand, and slowly, slowly, spread her wings to the gentle wind.

Though the land pulled at her, she felt she could overcome it. Extending her wings to their limits, she ran against the breeze. She lifted, but not enough; her feet brushed the ground, and she was forced to stop.

The wind blew brown sand and mica flakes against her feet and drooping wingtips. "Be patient to bury me," she said. "You owe me more than a grave."

She started up the steep face of a nearby dune. The sand tumbled grain over grain in tiny avalanches from her footsteps. She was used to feeling lighter as she rose; here, she only grew more tired. She approached the knife-edged crest, where sunlight sparkled from each sand crystal. The delicate construct collapsed past her, pouring sand into her face. She had to stop and blink until her eyes were clear of grit, but she had kept her footing. She stood at the broken summit of the dune, with the sail-like crests that remained stretched up and out to either side. Far above the desert floor, the wind blew stronger. She looked down, laughed, spread her wings, and leaped.

The thin air dropped her; she struggled; her feet brushed the sand, but her straining wings held her and she angled toward the sky, less steeply than of old, but upward. She caught an updraft and followed it, spiraling in a wide arc, soaring past the shadowed hills of sand. This flight was less secure than those of her memories; she felt intoxicated by more than the air. She tried a shallow dive and almost lost control, but pulled herself back into the sky. She was not quite ready to give life up. She no longer felt old, but ageless.

Motion below caught her attention. She banked and glided over the tiny figure. It scuttled away when her shadow touched it, but it seemed incapable of enough speed to make a chase exhilarating. Swooping with some caution, she skimmed the ground, snatched up the animal in her hand-fingers, and soared again. Thrashing, the scaly beast cried out gutturally. The old one inspected it. It had a sharp but not unpleasant odor, one of the mysterious scents of the air. She was not hungry, but she considered killing and eating the creature. It smelled like something built of familiar components of life, though along a completely alien pattern. She was curious to know if her system could tolerate it, and she wondered what color its blood was, but her people's tradition and instinct was to kill lower animals only for food. She released the cold beast where she had found it and she soared away.

The old one climbed into the air for one final flight. She felt deep sorrow that the young ones would not stop here.

At first, she thought she was imagining the soft, keening whine, but it grew louder, higher, until she recognized the shriek of a power craft. It came into view, flying very fast, too fast—but it struggled, slowed, leveled, and it was safe. It circled toward the old one's craft. She followed.

From the air, she watched the youth step out into the sand. She landed nearby.

"Why didst thou come? I will not go back."

The youth showed her ankle bands and multicolored funeral veils. "Let me attend your death. At least let me do that."

"That is a great deal."

"Will you allow it?"

"Thou hast exposed thyself to great danger. Canst thou get back?"

"If I want to."

"Thou must. There is nothing here for thee."

"Let me decide that!" The youth's outburst faltered. "Why . . . why do you pretend to care so much about me?"

"I—" she had no answer. Her concern was no pretense, but she realized that her actions and her words had been contradictory. She had changed, perhaps as much as the young ones, keeping the old disregard for death to herself, applying the new conservation of life to others. "I do care," she said. "I do care about you."

And the youth caught his breath at her use of the adult form of address. "I've hoped for so long you might say that," he said. "I've wanted your love for such a long time . . . "

"You will only have it for a little while."

"That is enough."

They embraced. The old one folded her wings over him, and they sank down into the warm sand. For the first time, they touched with love and passion. As the sun struck the sharp mountains and turned the desert maroon, the old one stroked the youth and caressed his face, holding him as he began the change. The exterior alterations would be slight. The old one felt her lover's temperature rising, as his metabolism accelerated to trigger the hormonal changes.

"I feel very weak," the youth whispered.

"That is usual. It passes."

He relaxed within her wings.

The sun set, the land grew dim; the moons, full, rose in tandem. The stars formed a thick veil above the fliers. They lay quietly together, the old one stroking her lover to ease the tension in his muscles, helping maintain his necessary fever with the insulation of her wings. The desert grew cool with the darkness; sounds moved and scents waxed and waned with the awakening of nocturnal creatures. The world seemed more alien at night.

"Are you there?" His eyes were wide open, but the pupils were narrow slits, and the tendons in his neck stood out, strained.

"Of course."

"I didn't know it would hurt . . . I'm glad you're here . . . "

"We all survive the passage," she said gently. But something about this world or the changing one himself made this transition difficult.

She held him all night while he muttered and thrashed, oblivious to her presence. As dawn approached, he fell into a deep sleep, and the old one felt equally exhausted. The sun dimmed the veil of stars and warmed the fliers; the creatures that had crept around them during darkness returned to their hiding places. The old one left her lover and began to climb a dune.

When she returned, the new adult was awakening. She landed behind him; he heard her and turned. His expression changed from grief to joy.

"How do you feel?"

He rubbed his hands down the back of his neck. "I don't know. I feel . . . new."

She sat on her heels beside him. "I was hungry afterward," she said. She held up a squirming pair of the reptiles. "But I didn't have to wonder if the food would kill me." She slashed one creature's throat. The blood was brilliant yellow, its taste as sharp as the smell. She sampled the flesh: it was succulent and strong after the mushy, flavorless meat on the ship. "It's good." She offered him a piece of the meat she held. "I feel you can eat it safely." He regarded it a moment, but took the second beast and bit through its scales and skin. It convulsed once and died.

"A clean kill," she said.

He smiled at her, and they feasted.

He stood and spread his wings, catching a soft hot breeze.

"We *can* fly here," the old one said.

He ran a few steps and launched himself into the air. She watched him climb, astonished and delighted that he needed no assistance. He seemed unsure of distances and angles, unsteady on turns and altitude changes, but that would have improved if he had had the time. She heard him laugh with joy; he called to her.

Wishing she were still strong, she climbed the dune again and joined him. All that day they flew together; she taught him to hunt, and they fed each other; they landed and lay together in the sand.

Twilight approached.

The old one ached in every bone. She had imagined, as the air supported her, that she might somehow escape her age, but the ground dragged at her, and she trembled.

"It's time," she said.

Her lover started as if she had struck him. He started to protest, but stopped, and slipped his wings around her. "I will attend you."

He walked with her up the dune, carrying the veils. At the top, he fastened the bands around her fingers and ankles. The old one spread her wings and fell into the air. She flew toward the mountains of sunrise until darkness engulfed her and the stars seemed so close that she might pull them across her shoulders. Her lover flew near.

"What will you do?"

"I'll go back to the ship."

"That's good."

"I may be able to persuade a few to return with me."

She thought of his loneliness, if he were refused and returned nonetheless, but she said nothing of that. "I respect your decision."

She climbed higher, until the air grew perceptibly thinner, but she could not fly high enough for cosmic rays to burst against her retinas. She took comfort in the clear sky and in flying, and plucked a veil from her companion. After that, he slipped them into the bands, staying near enough for danger. She felt the cold creeping in; the veils drifted about her like snow. "Goodbye, my love," she said. "Do not grieve for me."

Her senses were dimmed; she could barely hear him. "I have no regrets, but I will grieve."

The old one stretched out her stiffening wings and flew on.

He followed her until he knew she was dead, then dropped back. She would continue to some secret grave; he wished to remember her as she had been that day.

He glided alone over the desert and in the treacherous currents of mountains' flanks, impressing the world on his mind so he could describe its beauties. At dawn, he returned to his craft. A breeze scattered tiny crystals against his ankles.

He dropped to his knees and thrust his fingers into the bright, warming sand. Scooping up a handful, he wrapped it in the last silver funeral veil and carried it with him when he departed.

(1974)

JOE HALDEMAN

The Private War of Private Jacob

With each step your boot heel cracks through the sun-dried crust and your foot hesitates, drops through an inch of red talcum powder, and then you draw it back up with another crackle. Fifty men marching in a line through this desert and they sound like a big bowl of breakfast cereal.

Jacob held the laser projector in his left hand and rubbed his right in the dirt. Then he switched hands and rubbed his left in the dirt. The plastic handles got very slippery after you'd sweated on them all day long, and you didn't want the damn thing to squirt out of your grip when you were rolling and stumbling and crawling your way to the enemy, and you couldn't use the strap, noplace off the parade ground; goddamn slide-rule jockey figured out where to put it, too high, take the damn thing off if you could. Take the goddamn helmet off too, if you could. No matter you were safer with it on. They said. And they were pretty strict, especially about the helmets.

"Look happy, Jacob." Sergeant Melford was always all smile and bounce before a battle. During a battle, too. He smiled at the tanglewire and beamed at his men while they picked their way through it—if you go too fast you get tripped and if you go too slow you get burned—and he had a sad smile when one of his men got zeroed and a shriek a happy shriek when they first saw the enemy and glee when an enemy got zeroed and nothing but smiles smiles smiles through the whole sorry mess. "If he *didn't* smile, just once," young-old Addison told Jacob, a long time ago, "just once he cried or frowned, there would be fifty people waiting for the first chance to zero that son of a bitch." And Jacob asked why and he said, "You just take a good look inside yourself the next time you follow that crazy son of a bitch into hell and you come back and tell me how you felt about him."

Jacob wasn't stupid, that day or this one, and he did keep an inside eye on what was going on under his helmet. What old Sergeant Melford did for him was mainly to make him glad that he wasn't crazy too, and no matter how bad things got, at least Jacob wasn't enjoying it like that crazy laughing grinning old Sergeant Melford.

He wanted to tell Addison and ask him why sometimes you were really scared or sick and you would look up and see Melford laughing his crazy ass off, standing over some steaming roasted body, and you'd have to grin, too, was it just so insane horrible or? Addison might have been able to tell Jacob but Addison took a low one and got hurt bad in both legs and the groin and it was a long time before he came back and then he wasn't young-old any more but just old. And he didn't say much any more.

With both his hands good and dirty, for a good grip on the plastic handles, Jacob felt more secure and he smiled back at Sergeant Melford.

"Gonna be a good one, Sarge." It didn't do any good to say anything else, like it's been a long march and why don't we rest a while before we hit them, Sarge, or, I'm scared and sick and if I'm gonna die I want it at the very first, Sarge: no. Crazy old Melford would be down on his hunkers next to you and give you a couple of friendly punches and josh around and flash those white teeth until you were about to scream or run but instead you wound up saying, "Yeah, Sarge, gonna be a good one."

We most of us figured that what made him so crazy was just that he'd been in this crazy war so long, longer than anybody could remember anybody saying he remembered; and he never got hurt while platoon after platoon got zeroed out from under him by ones and twos and whole squads. He never got hurt and maybe that bothered him, not that any of us felt sorry for the crazy son of a bitch.

Wesley tried to explain it like this: "Sergeant Melford is an improbability locus." Then he tried to explain what a locus was and Jacob didn't really catch it, and he tried to explain what an improbability was, and that seemed pretty simple but Jacob couldn't see what it all had to do with math. Wesley was a good talker though, and he might have one day been able to clear it up but he tried to run through the tanglewire, you'd think not even a civilian would try to do that, and he fell down and the little metal bugs ate his face.

It was twenty or maybe twenty-five battles later, who keeps track, when Jacob realized that not only did old Sergeant Melford never get hurt, but he never killed any of the enemy either. He just ran around singing out orders and being happy and every now and then he'd shoot off his projector but he always shot high or low or the beam was too broad. Jacob wondered about it but by this time he was more afraid, in a way, of Sergeant Melford than he was of the enemy, so he kept his mouth shut and he waited for someone else to say something about it.

Finally Cromwell, who had come into the platoon only a couple of weeks after Jacob, noticed that Sergeant Melford never seemed to zero anybody and he had this theory that maybe the crazy old son of a bitch was a spy for the other side. They had fun talking about that for a while, and then Jacob told them about the old improbability locus theory, and one of the new guys said he sure is an imperturbable locust all right, and they all had a good laugh, which was good because Sergeant Melford came by and joined in after Jacob told him what was so funny, not about the improbability locus, but the old joke about how do you make a hormone? You don't pay her. Cromwell laughed like there was no tomorrow and for Cromwell there wasn't even any sunset, because he went across the perimeter to take a crap and got caught in a squeezer matrix.

The next battle was the first time the enemy used the drainer field, and of course the projectors didn't work and the last thing a lot of the men learned was that the light plastic stock made a damn poor weapon against a long knife, of which the enemy had plenty. Jacob lived because he got in a lucky kick, aimed for the groin but got the kneecap, and while the guy was hopping around trying to stay upright he dropped his knife and Jacob picked it up and gave the guy a new orifice, eight inches wide and just below the navel.

The platoon took a lot of zeros and had to fall back, which they did very fast because the tanglewire didn't work in a drainer field, either. They left Addison behind, sitting back against a crate with his hands in his lap and a big drooly red grin not on his face.

With Addison gone, no other private had as much combat time as Jacob. When they rallied back at the neutral zone, Sergeant Melford took Jacob aside and wasn't really smiling at all when he said: "Jacob, you know that now if anything happens to me, you've got to take over the platoon. Keep them spread out and keep them advancing, and most of all, keep them happy."

Jacob said, "Sarge, I can tell them to keep spread out and I think they will, and all of them know enough to keep pushing ahead, but how can I keep them happy when I'm never very happy myself, not when you're not around."

That smile broadened and turned itself into a laugh. You crazy old son of a bitch, Jacob thought and because he couldn't help himself, he laughed too. "Don't worry about that," Sergeant Melford said. "That's the kind of thing that takes care of itself when the time comes."

The platoon practiced more and more with knives and clubs and how to use your hands and feet but they still had to carry the projectors into combat because, of course, the enemy could turn off the drainer field whenever he wanted to. Jacob got a couple of scratches and a piece of his nose cut off, but the medic put some cream on it and it grew back. The enemy started using bows and arrows so the platoon had to carry shields, too, but that wasn't too bad after they designed one that fit right over the projector, held sideways. One squad learned how to use bows and arrows back at the enemy and things got as much back to normal as they had ever been.

Jacob never knew exactly how many battles he had fought as a private, but it was exactly forty-one. And actually, he wasn't a private at the end of the forty-first.

Since they got the archer squad, Sergeant Melford had taken to standing back with them, laughing and shouting orders at the platoon and every now and then loosing an arrow that always landed on a bare piece of ground. But this particular battle (Jacob's forty-first) had been going pretty poorly, with the initial advance stopped and then pushed back almost to the archers; and then a new enemy force breaking out on the other side of the archers.

Jacob's squad maneuvered between the archers and the new enemy soldiers and Jacob was fighting right next to Sergeant Melford, fighting pretty seriously while old Melford just laughed his fool head off, crazy son of a bitch. Jacob felt that split-second funny feeling and ducked and a heavy club whistled just over his head and bashed the side of Sergeant Melford's helmet and sheared the top of his helmet off just as neat as you snip the end off a soft-boiled egg. Jacob fell to his knees and watched the helmet full of stuff twirl end over end in back of the archers and he wondered why there were little glass marbles and cubes inside the grey-blue blood-streaked mushy stuff and then everything just went.

Inside a mountain of crystal under a mountain of rock, a tiny piezoelectric switch, sixty-four molecules in a cube, flipped over to the OFF *position and the following transaction took place at just less than the speed of light:*

UNIT 10011001011MELFORD ACCIDENTALLY DEACTIVATED.
SWITCH UNIT 1101011100JACOB TO CATALYST STATUS.
(SWITCHING COMPLETED)
ACTIVATE AND INSTRUCT UNIT 1101011100JACOB.

and came back again just like that. Jacob stood up and looked around. The same old sun-baked plain, but everybody but him seemed to be dead. Then he checked and the ones that weren't obviously zeroed were still breathing a bit. And, thinking about it, he knew why. He chuckled.

He stepped over the collapsed archers and picked up Melford's bleedy skull-cap. He inserted the blade of a knife between the helmet and the hair, shorting out the induction tractor that held the helmet on the head and served to pick up and transmit signals. Letting the helmet drop to the ground, he carefully bore the grisly balding bowl over to the enemy's crapper. Knowing exactly where to look, he fished out all the bits and pieces of crystal and tossed them down the smelly hole. Then he took the unaugmented brain back to the helmet and put it back the way he had found it. He returned to his position by Melford's body.

The stricken men began to stir and a few of the most hardy wobbled to their hands and knees.

Jacob threw back his head and laughed and laughed.

(1974)

ELEANOR ARNASON

The Warlord of Saturn's Moons

Here I am, a silver-haired maiden lady of thirty-five, a feeder of stray cats, a window-ledge gardener, well on my way to the African violet and antimacassar stage. I can see myself at fifty, fat and a little crazy, making cucumber sandwiches for tea, and I view my future with mixed feelings. Whatever became of my childhood ambitions: joining the space patrol; winning a gold medal at the Olympics; climbing Mount Everest alone in my bathing suit, sustained only by my indomitable will and strange psychic arts learned from Hindu mystics? The saddest words of tongue or pen are something-or-other what might have been, I think. I light up a cigar and settle down to write another chapter of *The Warlord of Saturn's Moons.* A filthy habit you say, though I'm not sure if you're referring to smoking cigars or writing science fiction. True, I reply, but both activities are pleasurable, and we maiden ladies lead lives that are notoriously short on pleasure.

So back I go to the domes of Titan and my red-headed heroine death-raying down the warlord's minions. Ah, the smell of burning flesh, the spectacle of blackened bodies collapsing. Even on paper it gets a lot of hostility out of you, so that your nights aren't troubled by dreams of murder. Terribly unrestful, those midnight slaughters and waking shaking in the darkness, your hands still feeling pressure from grabbing the victim or fighting off the murderer.

Another escape! In a power-sledge, my heroine races across Titan's methane snow, and I go and make myself tea. There's a paper on the kitchen table, waiting to tell me all about yesterday's arsons, rapes and bloody murders. Quickly I stuff it into the garbage pail. Outside, the sky is hazy. Another high-pollution day, I think. I can see incinerator smoke rising from the apartment building across the street, which means there's no air alert yet. Unless, of course, they're breaking the law over there. I fling open a cabinet and survey the array of teas. Earl Grey? I ponder, or Assam? Gunpowder? Jasmine? Gen Mai Cha? Or possibly an herb tea: sassafras, mint, Irish moss or mu. Deciding on Assam, I put water on, then go back to write an exciting chase through the icy Titanian mountains. A pursuer's sledge goes over a precipice and, as my heroine hears his long shriek on her radio, my tea kettle starts shrieking. I hurry into the kitchen. Now I go through the tea-making ceremony: pouring boiling water into the pot, sloshing the water around and pouring it out, measuring the tea in, pouring more boiling water on top of the tea. All the while my mind is with my heroine, smiling grimly as she pilots the power-sledge between bare cliffs. Above her in the dark sky is the huge crescent of Saturn, a shining white line slashing across it—the famous Rings. While the tea steeps, I wipe off a counter and wash a couple of mugs. I resist a sudden impulse to pull the newspaper out from among the used tea leaves and orange peelings. I already know what's in it. The Detroit murder count will exceed 1,000 again this year; the war in Thailand is going strong; most of Europe is out on strike. I'm far better off on Titan with my heroine, who is better able to deal with her problems than I am to deal with mine. A deadly shot, she has also learned strange psychic arts from Hindu mystics, which give her great strength, endurance, mental alertness and a naturally pleasant body odor. I wipe my hands and look at them, noticing the bitten fingernails, the torn cuticles. My heroine's long, slender, strong hands have two-inch nails filed to a point and covered with a plastic paint that makes them virtually unbreakable. When necessary, she uses them as claws. Her cuticles, of course, are in perfect condition.

I pour myself a cup of tea and return to the story. Now my heroine is heading for the mountain hideout where her partner waits: a tall, thin, dour fellow with one shining steel prosthetic hand. She doesn't know his name and she suspects he himself may have forgotten it. He insists on being called 409, his number on the prison asteroid from which he has escaped. She drives as quickly as she dares, thinking of his long face, burned almost black by years of strong radiation on Mars and in space, so the white webbing of scars on its right side shows up clearly. His eyes are grey, so pale they seem almost colorless. As I write about 409, I find myself stirred by the same passion that stirs my heroine. I begin to feel uneasy, so I stop and drink some tea. I can see I'm going to have trouble with 409. It's never wise to get too involved with one's characters. Besides, I'm not his type. I imagine the way he'd look at me, indifference evident on his dark, scarred face. I could, of course, kill him off. My heroine would then spend the rest of the story avenging him, though she'd never get to the real murderer—me. But this solution, while popular among writers, is unfair.

I go into the kitchen, extract a carrot from a bunch in the icebox, clean it and eat it. After that, I write the heroine's reunion with 409.

Neither of them is demonstrative. They greet each other with apparent indifference and retire to bed. I skip the next scene. How can I watch that red-headed hussy in bed with the man I'm beginning to love? I continue the story at the moment when their alarm bell rings, and they awake to find the warlord's rocket planes have landed all around their hideout. A desperate situation! 409 suggests that he make a run for it in their rocket plane. While the warlord's minions pursue him, my heroine can sneak away in the power-sledge. The plan has little chance of success, but they can think of none better. They bid farewell to one another, and my heroine goes to wait in the sledge for the signal telling her 409 has taken off. As she waits, smoking a cigar, she thinks of what little she knows about 409. He was a fighter pilot in the war against the Martian colony and was shot down and captured. While in prison something happened to him that he either can't remember or refuses to talk about, and, when the war ended and he was released, he became a criminal. As for herself, she had been an ordinary sharpshooter and student of Hindu mysticism, a follower of Swami Bluestone of the Brooklyn Vedic Temple and Rifle Range. Then she discovered by accident the warlord's plot to overthrow the government of Titan, the only one of Saturn's satellites not under his control. With her information about the plot, the government may still be saved. She has to get to Titan City with the microfilm dot!

The alarm bell rings, and she feels the ground shake as 409's plane takes off. Unfortunately I'm writing the story from my heroine's point of view. I want to describe 409 blasting off, the warlord's rocket planes taking off after him, chasing him as he flies through the narrow, twisting valleys, the planes' rockets flaring red in the valley shadows and missiles exploding into yellow fireballs. All through this, of course, 409's scarred face remains tranquil and his hands move quickly and surely over the plane's controls. His steel prosthetic hand gleams in the dim light from the dials. But I can't put this in the story, since my heroine sees none of it as she slides off in the opposite direction, down a narrow trail hidden by overhanging cliffs.

I am beginning to feel tense, I don't know why. Possibly 409's dilemma is disturbing me. He's certainly in danger. In any case, my tea is cold. I turn on the radio, hoping for some relaxing rock music and go to get more tea. But it's twenty to the hour, time for the news, and I get the weekend body count: two men found dead in suspected westside dope house, naked body of woman dragged out of Detroit River. I hurry back and switch to a country music station. On it, someone's singing about how he intends to leave the big city and go back down south. As I go back into the kitchen, I think:

Carry me back to Titan.
That's where I want to be.
I want to repose
On the methane snows
At the edge of a frozen sea.

I pour out the old tea and refill the cup with tea that's hot.

The radio begins to make that awful beepity-beep-beepity sound that warns you the news is coming up. I switch back to the rock station, where the news is now over. I'm safe for another fifty-five minutes, unless there's a special news flash to announce a five-car pile-up or an especially ghastly murder.

The plan works! For my heroine, at least. She doesn't know yet if 409 got away. She speeds off unpursued. The power-sledge's heating system doesn't quite keep her warm, and the landscape around her is forbidding: bare cliffs and narrow valleys full of methane snow, overhead the dark blue sky. Saturn has set, and the tiny sun is rising, though she can't see it yet. On the high mountains the ice fields begin to glitter with its light. On she races, remembering how she met 409 in the slums of The Cup on Ganymede, as she fled the warlord's assassins. She remembers being cornered with no hope of escape. Then behind the two assassins a tall figure appeared and the shining steel hand smashed down on the back of one assassin's head. As the other assassin turned, he got the hand across his face. A moment or two more, and both the assassins were on the ground, unconscious. Then she saw 409's twisted grin for the first time and his colorless eyes appraising her.

There I go, I think, getting all heated up over 409. The radio is beginning to bother me, so I shut it off and re-light my cigar. I find myself wishing that men like 409 really existed. Increasingly in recent years, I've found real men boring. Is it possible, as some scientists argue, that the Y chromosome produces an inferior human being? There certainly seem to be far fewer interesting men than interesting women. But theories arguing that one kind of human being is naturally inferior make me anxious. I feel my throat muscles tightening and the familiar tense, numb feeling spreading across my face and my upper back. Quickly I return to my story.

Now out on the snowy plain, my heroine can see the transparent domes of Titan City ahead of her, shining in the pale sunlight. Inside the domes the famous pastel towers rise, their windows reflecting the sun. Her power-sledge speeds down the road, through the drifts that half cover it. Snow sprays up on either side of the sledge, so my heroine has trouble seeing to the left and right. As a result, it's some time before she sees the power-sledges coming up behind her on the right. At the same moment that she looks over and sees them, their sleek silver bodies shining in the sunlight and snow-sprays shooting up around them, her radio begins to go beep-beep-beep. She flicks it on. The voice of Janos Black, the warlord's chief agent on Titan, harsh and slurred by a thick Martian accent, tells her the bad news: 409's plane has been shot down. He ejected before it crashed. Even now the warlord's men are going after the ejection capsule, which is high on a cliff, wedged between a rock spire and the cliff wall. Janos offers her a trade: 409 for the microdot. But Janos may well be lying; 409 may have gotten away or else been blown up. She feels a sudden constriction of her throat at the thought of 409 dead. She flicks off the radio and pushes the power-sledge up to top speed. She realizes as she does so that 409 is unlikely to fare well if Janos gets ahold of him. Janos' wife and children died of thirst after the great Martian network of pipelines was blown apart by Earther bombs, and Janos knows that 409 was a pilot in the Earther expeditionary force.

I write another exciting chase, this one across the snowy plain toward the pink, green, blue and yellow towers of Titan City. The warlord's power-sledges are gaining. Their rockets hit all around my heroine's sledge, and fire and black smoke erupt out of the snow. Swearing in a low monotone, she swings the sledge back and forth in a zig-zag evasive pattern.

I stop to puff on my cigar and discover it's gone out again. My tea is cold. But the story's beginning at last to interest me. I keep on writing.

As my heroine approaches the entrance to Titan City, she's still a short distance ahead of her pursuers. Her radio beeps. It's Janos Black again. He tells her his men have gotten to the ejection capsule and are lowering it down the cliff. Any minute now, they'll have it down where they can open it and get 409 out.

Ignoring Janos, she concentrates on slowing her sledge and bringing it through the city's outer gate into the airlock. A moment or two later, she's safe. But what about 409?

Frankly, I don't know. I stand and stretch, decide to take a bath, and go to turn the water on. The air pollution must be worse than I originally thought. I have the dopey feeling I get on the days when the pollution is really bad. I look out the window. Dark grey smoke is still coming out of the chimneys across the street. Maybe I should call the Air Control number (dial AIR-CARE) and complain. But it takes a peculiar kind of person to keep on being public-spirited after it becomes obvious it's futile. I decide to put off calling Air Control and water my plants instead. Every bit of oxygen helps, I think. I check the bathtub—it's not yet half-full—and go back to writing. After a couple of transitional paragraphs, my heroine finds herself in the antechamber to the Titan Council's meeting room. There is a man there, standing with his back to her.

He's tall and slender, and his long hair is a shade between blond and grey. He turns and she recognizes the pale, delicate-looking face. This is Michael Stelladoro, the warlord of Saturn's moons. His eyes, she notices, are as blue as cornflowers and he has a delightful smile. He congratulates her on escaping his power-sledges, then tells her that his men have gotten 409 out of the ejection capsule. He is still alive and as far as they can determine uninjured. They have given 409 a shot of Sophamine. At this my heroine gasps with horror. Sophamine, she knows, is an extremely powerful tranquilizer used to control schizophrenia. One dose is enough to make most people dependent on it, and withdrawal takes the form of a nightmarish psychotic fugue. The warlord smiles his delightful smile and turns on the radio he has clipped to his belt. A moment later my heroine hears 409's voice telling her that he has in fact been captured. He sounds calm and completely uninterested in his situation. That, she knows, is the Sophamine. It hasn't affected his perception of reality. He knows where he is and what is likely to happen to him, but he simply doesn't care. When the Sophamine wears off, all the suppressed emotions will well up, so intense that the only way he'll be able to deal with them will be to go insane, temporarily at least.

The warlord tells her he regrets having to use the Sophamine, but he was certain that 409 would refuse to talk unless he was either drugged or tortured, and there simply wasn't enough time to torture him.

"You fiend!" my heroine cries.

The warlord smiles again, as delightfully as before, and says if she gives the microdot to the Titan Council, he will turn 409 over to Janos Black, who will attempt to avenge on him all the atrocities committed by the Earthers on Mars.

What can she do? As she wonders, the door to the meeting room opens, and she is asked to come in. For a moment, she thinks of asking the Titanians to arrest the warlord. Almost as if he's read her mind, he tells her there's no point in asking the Titanians to arrest him. He has diplomatic immunity and a warfleet waiting for him to return.

She turns to go into the meeting room. "I'll tell Janos the good news," the warlord says softly and turns his radio on.

She hesitates, then thinks, a man this evil must be stopped, no matter what the cost. She goes into the meeting room.

I remember the bath water, leap up and run into the bathroom. The tub is brim-full and about to overflow. I turn off the tap, let out some of the water, and start to undress. After I climb into the tub, I wonder how I'm going to get 409 out of the mess he's in. Something will occur to me. I grab the bar of soap floating past my right knee.

After bathing, I put on a pink and silver muumuu and make a fresh pot of tea. Cleanliness is next to godliness, I think as I sit down to write.

My heroine tells her story to the Titan Council and produces the microdot. On it is the warlord's plan for taking over the government of Titan and a list of all the Titanian officials he has subverted. The president of the council thanks her kindly and tells her that they already have a copy of the microdot, obtained for them by an agent of theirs who has infiltrated the warlord's organization. "Oh no! Oh no!" my heroine cries. Startled, the president asks her what's wrong. She explains that she has sacrificed her partner, her love to bring them the information they already had. "Rest easy," the president says. "Our agent is none other than Janos Black. He won't harm 409."

Thinking of Janos' family dying of thirst in an isolated settlement, my heroine feels none too sure of this. But there's nothing left for her to do except hope.

After that, I describe her waiting in Titan City for news of 409, wandering restlessly through the famous gardens, barely noticing the beds of Martian sandflowers, the blossoming magnolia trees, the pools of enormous silver carp. Since the warlord now knows that the Titan Council knows about his schemes, the council moves quickly to arrest the officials he's subverted. The newscasts are full of scandalous revelations, and the warlord leaves Titan for his home base on Tethys, another one of Saturn's moons. My heroine pays no attention to the newscasts or to the excited conversations going on all around her. She thinks of the trip she and 409 made from Ganymede to Titan in a stolen moon-hopper, remembering 409's hands on the ship's controls, the way he moved in zero-G, his colorless eyes and his infrequent, twisted smile. Cornball, I think, but leave the passage in. I enjoy thinking about 409 as much as my heroine does.

After two days, Janos Black arrives in a police plane. 409 is with him. Janos comes to see my heroine to bring her the news of their arrival. He's a tall man with a broad chest and spindly arms and legs. His face is ruddy and Slavic, and his hair is prematurely white. He tells her that he kept 409 prisoner in the warlord's secret headquarters in the Titanian mountains till the Titanian police moved in and arrested everybody.

"Then he's all right," she cries joyfully.

Janos shakes his head.

"Why not?"

"The Sophamine," Janos explains. "When it wore off, he got hit with the full force of all his repressed feelings, especially, I think, the feelings he had about the war on Mrs. Think of all that anger and terror and horror and guilt flooding into his conscious mind. He tried to kill himself. We stopped him, and he almost killed a couple of us in the process. By we I mean myself and the warlord's men; this happened before the police moved in. We had to give him another shot of Sophamine. He's still full of the stuff. From what I've heard, the doctors want to keep giving it to him. They think the first shot of Sophamine he got destroyed his old system of dealing with his more dangerous emotions, which are now overwhelming him. The doctors say on Sophamine he can function more or less normally. Off it, they think he'll be permanently insane."

"You planned this!" she cries.

Janos shakes his head. "The warlord gave the order, miss. I only obeyed it. But I didn't mind this time. I didn't mind."

I stop to drink some tea. Then I write the final scene in the chapter: my heroine's meeting with 409. He's waiting for her in a room at the Titan City Hospital. The room is dark. He sits by the window looking out at the tall towers blazing with light and at the dome above them, which reflects the towers' light so it's impossible to look through it at the sky. She can see his dark shape and the red tip of the cigar he smokes.

"Do you mind if I turn on the lights?" she asks.

"No."

She finds the button and presses it. The ceiling begins to glow. She looks at 409. He lounges in his chair, his feet up on a table. She realizes it's the first time she's seen him look really relaxed. Before this, he's always seemed tense, even when asleep.

"How are you?" she asks.

"Fine." His voice sounds tranquil and indifferent.

She can't think of anything to say. He looks at her, his dark, scarred face expressionless. Finally he says, "Don't let it bother you. I feel fine." He pauses. She still can't think of anything to say. He continues. "The pigs don't want me for anything here on Titan. I think I'll be able to stay."

"What're you going to do here?"

"Work, I guess. The doctors say I can hold down a job if I keep taking Sophamine." He draws on the cigar, so the tip glows red, then blows out the smoke. He's looking away from her at the towers outside the window. She begins weeping. He looks back at her. "I'm all right. Believe me, I feel fine."

But she can't stop weeping.

Enough for today, I think and put down my pencil. Tomorrow, I'll figure out a way to get 409 off Sophamine. Where there's life there's hope and so forth, I tell myself.

(1974)

BARRY N. MALZBERG

Making It All the Way into the Future on Gaxton Falls of the Red Planet

July 14, 2115, and here we are in Gaxton Falls of the famous red planet. Why we are spending this bright Bastille Day in Gaxton Falls when we could be just six, make it seven kilometers away, celebrating more properly in Paris is beyond me but impulse must always be respected and so here we are. Down the midway we see fragments and artifacts of reconstructed Americana: lining our path are the little booths and display halls where facets of that vanished time may be more closely observed. Betsy holds my hand tightly as well she may. Truly, she has never seen anything like this and neither, for that matter, have I.

"Isn't this the most remarkable thing?" she says, referring, I suppose, to the fact that Gaxton Falls is in most ways a faithful reconstruction of a medium-sized American city of 1974, one hundred and forty-one years ago, a wonderful time in which to be alive. "It just looks so real, Jack," she says and so it does, so it does indeed but I will not betray to her my own astonishment, concentrating as I am upon walking down the midway undisturbed by the blandishments and cries of the barkers who would have us stop at this stand, that display, these pieces of goods. It is a disgraceful thing what has happened to Mars; the place is a tourist trap. Truly one must be aware of this at all times: it was a grand thing to have colonized the planet fifty years ago and we will always be in the pioneers' debt . . . but fashions change, emphases shift and the good people generally steer clear of this place. We had to stop over to make the Ganymede switch but once is enough. Mars is economically viable now only because of the tourist business, which in turn bears the result of the reconstruction committees of the hated nineties . . . but all of this is boring, abstruse history. Even the rather colorful villages of Mars, the ruins I mean, do not move me and I cannot wait to get away from here. To some degree I hold it against Betsy that she responds to the place.

Still: we are in Gaxton Falls and must make the best of a bad time.

"Come in, sir," a man with a moustache calls to us through the sparse crowd, "come in and meet the iconoclast, do," and before I can protest, Betsy is tugging me by the hand toward the barker's stand which fronts a rather drab set of burlap curtains. "Fascinating and educational," the barker says, "and not only do you have a chance to hear the iconoclast speak, you may also argue with him, take exception to his points, get into a fascinating discussion." Like all the barkers he has a precise command of the idiom of this period although his pronunciation is foul. Obviously this man like so many of the others was imported from Venus where the excessive labor pool produces thousands like him. "What do you say, sir?" he says when we near him. His eyes are faintly desperate, his skin has a greenish cast from lack of sunlight. Clearly a Venusian.

"Let's go in," Betsy says. Her ebullience is a cover for doubt and I feel a lurch of pity; better go along with her. I give the barker his asking price in scrip, two dollars and fifty cents for each of us, and still holding hands we duck within the curtains, feeling the threads of burlap coming out to caress us like fingernails and into the enclosure itself which, expectedly, is smaller and more odorous than the front would indicate. An enormous man sits behind a simple wooden table shaking his head. We are the only customers in the enclosure. As we enter he begins speaking in an empty, rehearsed drone.

"We must abandon the space program," he says in the old accent, much better than the barker, "because it is destroying our cities, abandoning our underprivileged, leading people toward the delusion that the conquest of space will solve their problems and it is in the hands of technicians and politicians who care not at all for the mystery, the wonder, the intricacies of the human soul. Better we should solve our problems on Earth before we go to the Moon." He rams the table. "We won't be ready for space until we've cleaned up our own planet, understood our own problem."

"But don't you think," Betsy asks, entering into the spirit of this: an engaging girl, "that exploration is an important human need? We'll never solve our problems on Earth after all so we might as well voyage outward where the solutions might be." She squeezes my hand, pleased with herself. Indeed, her own mastery of the idiom is impressive although only guidebook deep.

"Certainly not," the iconoclast says, "that's a ridiculous argument." He does not really look at her; I wonder if he is machinery. Some of the exhibits are and some are not; it is hard to tell; humans and the more sophisticated androids are interchangeable anyway. "The era of exploration and discovery has shifted to the arena of inner space. We must know ourselves or die. To continue the space program would be madness. Happily it is being abandoned."

It is brief but I am already bored with this exhibit, which is rather predictable and limited. "That's nonsense," I point out. "You can't equate exploration with ignorance any more than your enemies could with knowledge."

"But of course I can!" the iconoclast booms. His eyes belie the energy however, they are dull and withdrawn; he is deep, then, into a programmed series of replies, and we are not discussing the matter but merely exchanging positions. "The two are exactly the same when you consider that the space program has produced in its fifteen years not one single positive contribution to the common lives of most men. Or women."

"Not so!" says Betsy. "Think of lasers, life-support systems, advances in pacemaker technique, adaptation to weightlessness, psychological studies, rare alloys . . . "

"No," the iconoclast says loudly. He pushes himself back from the table, his body sagging. Enormous: the exhibit must weigh over four hundred pounds. "That is specious and entirely wrong."

"Enough," I say. Abruptly my boredom has turned into physical disgust and I want to leave. Gaxton Falls is highly overrated and the iconoclast is typical of almost all its exhibits: cheap, programmatic, superficial. "We're going to leave."

"Jack," Betsy says, her head wrenching one way, her body another. "We may hurt his feelings."

"Don't be foolish," I say, using a double-lock on her wrist, "he's merely an exhibit, possibly an android, certainly hypnoprogrammed. He doesn't even know we're here; they wake up in a vat later. Anyway," I add, turning toward the iconoclast who has sat rigid through all of this, his face as bleak and empty as the sands which lie just to the rear of the Falls, stretching then into Paris, "besides you're a fool and you did not prevail. We returned to the Moon in 1980. We were on Mars by 1990. By 2050 we had established a scientific colony on Mars, a viable, self-supporting unit, had landed several times on Venus, were investigating the rings of Saturn at close range and were preparing to drop the first ship on Ganymede. It was, in historical perspective, merely a sneeze, this midseventies interruption of the program. You did not prevail."

The iconoclast puts his palms flatly on the table, tries awkwardly to rise, falls back into his flesh, gasping. Respiration makes his arms billow, he seems excited. Have I broken the program? "*You* are the fool," he says. "The space program was abandoned for all time. The great riots of the 1980s destroyed all of the centers and equipment, leaving nothing. It will be thousands of years before men even think of going into space again."

I look at him and see that he is serious. Whether programmed or working out of the program the iconoclast really believes this and I am filled with pity but pity has nothing to do with it. The air is dense. I want desperately to leave the tent. I tug Betsy by the hand, she swings like a pendulum and comes against me. The shock of the impact unbalances and I scramble on my knees, Betsy awkwardly straddling me. We cannot seem to disentangle.

"You fools," the iconoclast says, "you poor fools, just look, *look,*" and it is as if the tent falls away, the burlap turning to glass, then mist: the burlap opening toward an endless perspective of the dead landscape of Mars; in that landscape I see the fires, the fires of the 1980s which destroyed the center forever. They sear and rip away; it is momentarily more than I can take, I claw to ground desperately, knowing that when I open them again this will have gone away and I will see Gaxton Falls and its midway again, all of this a seizure, but when I do open them, see again after a long time it is not the midway I see but the flap of the tent opening and as I stare, two people enter, one of them Betsy, and look at me. The other looks familiar although I cannot quite place him. He seems to be a reasonable man, however, and I will do what I can to bring him around.

"We must abandon the space program," I say.

(1974)

URSULA K. LE GUIN

THE NEW ATLANTIS

Coming back from my Wilderness Week I sat by an odd sort of man in the bus. For a long time we didn't talk; I was mending stockings and he was reading. Then the bus broke down a few miles outside Gresham. Boiler trouble, the way it generally is when the driver insists on trying to go over thirty. It was a Supersonic Superscenic Deluxe Longdistance coal-burner, with Home Comfort, that means a toilet, and the seats were pretty comfortable, at least those that hadn't yet worked loose from their bolts, so everybody waited inside the bus; besides, it was raining. We began talking, the way people do when there's a breakdown and a wait. He held up his pamphlet and tapped it—he was a dry-looking man with a schoolteacherish way of using his hands—and said, "This is interesting. I've been reading that a new continent is rising from the depths of the sea."

The blue stockings were hopeless. You have to have something besides holes to darn onto. "Which sea?"

"They're not sure yet. Most specialists think the Atlantic. But there's evidence it may be happening in the Pacific, too."

"Won't the oceans get a little crowded?" I said, not taking it seriously. I was a bit snappish, because of the breakdown and because those blue stockings had been good warm ones.

He tapped the pamphlet again and shook his head, quite serious. "No," he said. "The old continents are sinking, to make room for the new. You can see that that is happening."

You certainly can. Manhattan Island is now under eleven feet of water at low tide, and there are oyster beds in Ghirardelli Square.

"I thought that was because the oceans are rising from polar melt."

He shook his head again. "That is a factor. Due to the greenhouse effect of pollution, indeed Antarctica may become inhabitable. But climatic factors will not explain the emergence of the new—or, possibly, very old—continents in the Atlantic and Pacific." He went on explaining about continental drift, but I liked the idea of inhabiting Antarctica and daydreamed about it for a while. I thought of it as very empty, very quiet, all white and blue, with a faint golden glow northward from the unrising sun behind the long peak of Mount Erebus. There were a few people there; they were very quiet, too, and wore white tie and tails. Some of them carried oboes and violas. Southward the white land went up in a long silence toward the Pole.

Just the opposite, in fact, of the Mount Hood Wilderness Area. It had been a tiresome vacation. The other women in the dormitory were all right, but it was macaroni for breakfast, and there were so many organized sports. I had looked forward to the hike up to the National Forest Preserve, the largest forest left in the United States, but the trees didn't look at all the way they do in the postcards and brochures and Federal Beautification Bureau advertisements. They were spindly, and they all had little signs on saying which union they had been planted by. There were actually a lot more green picnic tables and cement Men's and Women's than there were trees. There was an electrified fence all around the forest to keep out unauthorized persons. The forest ranger talked about mountain jays, "bold little robbers," he said, "who will come and snatch the sandwich from your very hand," but I didn't see any. Perhaps because that was the weekly Watch Those Surplus Calories! Day for all the women, and so we didn't have any sandwiches. If I'd seen a mountain jay I might have snatched the sandwich from his very hand, who knows. Anyhow it was an exhausting week, and I wished I'd stayed home and practiced, even though I'd have lost a week's pay because staying home and practicing the viola doesn't count as planned implementation of recreational leisure as defined by the Federal Union of Unions.

When I came back from my Antarctican expedition, the man was reading again, and I got a look at his pamphlet; and that was the odd part of it. The pamphlet was called "Increasing Efficiency in Public Accountant Training Schools," and I could see from the one paragraph I got a glance at that there was nothing about new continents emerging from the ocean depths in it—nothing at all.

Then we had to get out and walk on into Gresham, because they had decided that the best thing for us all to do was get onto the Greater Portland Area Rapid Public Transit Lines, since there had been so many breakdowns that the charter bus company didn't have any more buses to send out to pick us up. The walk was wet, and rather dull, except when we passed the Cold Mountain Commune. They have a wall around it to keep out unauthorized persons, and a big neon sign out front saying COLD MOUNTAIN COMMUNE and there were some people in authentic jeans and ponchos by the highway selling macrame belts and sandcast candles and soybean bread to the tourists. In Gresham, I took the 4:40 GPARPTL Superjet Flyer train to Burnside and East 230th, and then walked to 217th and got the bus to the Goldschmidt Overpass, and transferred to the shuttlebus, but it had boiler trouble, so I didn't reach the downtown transfer point until ten after eight, and the buses go on a once-an-hour schedule at 8:00, so I got a meatless hamburger at the Longhorn Inch-Thick Steak House Dinerette and caught the nine o'clock bus and got home about ten. When I let myself into the apartment I flipped the switch to turn on the lights, but there still weren't any. There had been a power outage in West Portland for three weeks. So I went feeling about for the candles in the dark, and it was a minute or so before I noticed that somebody was lying on my bed.

I panicked, and tried again to turn the lights on.

It was a man, lying there in a long thin heap. I thought a burglar had got in somehow while I was away and died. I opened the door so I could get out quick or at least my yells could be heard, and then I managed not to shake long enough to strike a match, and lighted the candle, and came a little closer to the bed.

The light disturbed him. He made a sort of snorting in his throat and turned his head. I saw it was a stranger, but I knew his eyebrows, then the breadth of his closed eyelids, then I saw my husband.

He woke up while I was standing there over him with the candle in my hand. He laughed and said still half-asleep, "Ah, Psyche! From the regions which are holy land."

Neither of us made much fuss. It was unexpected, but it did seem so natural for him to be there, after all, much more natural than for him not to be there, and he was too tired to be very emotional. We lay there together in the dark, and he explained that they had released him from the Rehabilitation Camp early because he had injured his back in an accident in the gravel quarry, and they were afraid it might get worse. If he died there it wouldn't be good publicity abroad, since there have been some nasty rumors about deaths from illness in the Rehabilitation Camps and the Federal Medical Association Hospitals; and there are scientists abroad who have heard of Simon, since somebody published his proof of Goldbach's Hypothesis in Peking. So they let him out early, with eight dollars in his pocket, which is what he had in his pocket when they arrested him, which made it, of course, fair. He had walked and hitched home from Coeur D'Alene, Idaho, with a couple of days in jail in Walla Walla for being caught hitchhiking. He almost fell asleep telling me this, and when he had told me, he did fall asleep. He needed a change of clothes and a bath but I didn't want to wake him. Besides, I was tired, too. We lay side by side and his head was on my arm. I don't suppose that I have ever been so happy. No; was it happiness? Something wider and darker, more like knowledge, more like the night: joy.

It was dark for so long, so very long. We were all blind. And there was the cold, a vast, unmoving, heavy cold. We could not move at all. We did not move. We did not speak. Our mouths were closed, pressed shut by the cold and by the weight. Our eyes were pressed shut. Our limbs were held still. Our minds were held still. For how long? There was no length of time; how long is death? And is one dead only after living, or before life as well? Certainly we thought, if we thought anything, that we were dead; but if we had ever been alive, we had forgotten it.

There was a change. It must have been the pressure that changed first, although we did not know it. The eyelids are sensitive to touch. They must have been weary of being shut. When the pressure upon them weakened a little, they opened. But there was no way for us to know that. It was too cold for us to feel anything. There was nothing to be seen. There was black.

But then—"then," for the event created time, created before and after, near and far, now and then—"then" there was the light. One light. One small, strange light that passed slowly, at what distance we could not tell. A small, greenish white, slightly blurred point of radiance, passing.

Our eyes were certainly open, "then," for we saw it. We saw the moment. The moment is a point of light. Whether in darkness or in the field of all light, the moment is small, and moves, but not quickly. And "then" it is gone.

It did not occur to us that there might be another moment. There was no reason to assume that there might be more than one. One was marvel enough: that in all the field of the dark, in the cold, heavy, dense, moveless, timeless, placeless, boundless black, there should have occurred, once, a small slightly blurred, moving light! Time need be created only once, we thought.

But we were mistaken. The difference between one and more than one is all the difference in the world. Indeed, that difference is the world.

The light returned.

The same light, or another one? There was no telling.

But, "this time," we wondered about the light: Was it small and near to us, or large and far away? Again there was no telling; but there was something about the way it moved, a trace of hesitation, a tentative quality, that did not seem proper to anything large and remote. The stars, for instance. We began to remember the stars.

The stars had never hesitated.

Perhaps the noble certainty of their gait had been a mere effect of distance. Perhaps in fact they had hurtled wildly, enormous furnace-fragments of a primal bomb thrown through the cosmic dark; but time and distance soften all agony. If the universe, as seems likely, began with an act of destruction, the stars we had used to see told no tales of it. They had been implacably serene.

The planets, however . . . We began to remember the planets. They had suffered certain changes both of appearance and of course. At certain times of the year Mars would reverse its direction and go backward through the stars. Venus had been brighter and less bright as she went through her phases of crescent, full, and wane. Mercury had shuddered like a skidding drop of rain on the sky flushed with daybreak. The light we now watched had that erratic, trembling quality. We saw it, unmistakably, change direction and go backward. It then grew smaller and fainter; blinked—an eclipse?—and slowly disappeared.

Slowly, but not slowly enough for a planet.

Then—the third "then"!—arrived the indubitable and positive Wonder of the World, the Magic Trick, watch now, watch, you will not believe your eyes, mama, mama, look what I can do—

Seven lights in a row, proceeding fairly rapidly, with a darting movement, from left to right. Proceeding less rapidly from right to left, two dimmer, greenish lights. Two-lights halt, blink, reverse course, proceed hastily and in a wavering manner from left to right. Seven-lights increase speed, and catch up. Two-lights flash desperately, flicker, and are gone.

Seven-lights hang still for some while, then merge gradually into one streak, veering away, and little by little vanish into the immensity of the dark.

But in the dark now are growing other lights, many of them: lamps, dots, rows, scintillations—some near at hand, some far. Like the stars, yes, but not stars. It is not the great Existences we are seeing, but only the little lives.

In the morning Simon told me something about the Camp, but not until after he had had me check the apartment for bugs. I thought at first he had been given behavior mod and gone paranoid. We never had been infested. And I'd been living alone for a year and a half; surely they didn't want to hear me talking to myself? But he said, "They may have been expecting me to come here."

"But they let you go free!"

He just lay there and laughed at me. So I checked everywhere we could think of. I didn't find any bugs, but it did look as if somebody had gone through the bureau drawers while I was away in the Wilderness. Simon's papers were all at Max's, so that didn't matter. I made tea on the Primus, and washed and shaved Simon with the extra hot water in the kettle—he had a thick beard and wanted to get rid of it because of the lice he had brought from Camp—and while we were doing that he told me about the Camp. In fact he told me very little, but not much was necessary.

He had lost about 20 pounds. As he only weighed 140 to start with, this left little to go on with. His knees and wrist bones stuck out like rocks under the skin. His feet were all swollen and chewed-looking from the Camp boots; he hadn't dared take the boots off, the last three days of walking, because he was afraid he wouldn't be able to get them back on. When he had to move or sit up so I could wash him, he shut his eyes.

"Am I really here?" he asked. "Am I here?"

"Yes," I said. "You are here. What I don't understand is how you got here."

"Oh, it wasn't bad so long as I kept moving. All you need is to know where you're going—to have someplace to go. You know, some of the people in Camp, if they'd let them go, they wouldn't have had that. They couldn't have gone anywhere. Keeping moving was the main thing. See, my back's all seized up, now."

When he had to get up to go to the bathroom he moved like a ninety-year-old. He couldn't stand straight, but was all bent out of shape, and shuffled. I helped him put on clean clothes. When he lay down on the bed again, a sound of pain came out of him, like tearing thick paper. I went around the room putting things away. He asked me to come sit by him and said I was going to drown him if I went on crying. "You'll submerge the entire North American continent," he said. I can't remember what he said, but he made me laugh finally. It is hard to remember things Simon says, and hard not to laugh when he says them. This is not merely the partiality of affection: He makes everybody laugh. I doubt that he intends to. It is just that a mathematician's mind works differently from other people's. Then when they laugh, that pleases him.

It was strange, and it is strange, to be thinking about "him," the man I have known for ten years, the same man, while "he" lay there changed out of recognition, a different man. It is enough to make you understand why most languages have a word like "soul." There are various degrees of death, and time spares us none of them. Yet something endures, for which a word is needed.

I said what I had not been able to say for a year and a half: "I was afraid they'd brainwash you."

He said, "Behavior mod is expensive. Even just the drugs. They save it mostly for the VIPs. But I'm afraid they got a notion I might be important after all. I got questioned a lot the last couple of months. About my 'foreign contacts.' " He snorted. "The stuff that got published abroad, I suppose. So I want to be careful and make sure it's just a Camp again next time, and not a Federal Hospital."

"Simon, were they . . . are they cruel, or just righteous?"

He did not answer for a while. He did not want to answer. He knew what I was asking. He knew by what thread hangs hope, the sword, above our heads.

"Some of them . . . " he said at last, mumbling.

Some of them had been cruel. Some of them had enjoyed their work. You cannot blame everything on society.

"Prisoners, as well as guards," he said.

You cannot blame everything on the enemy.

"Some of them, Belle," he said with energy, touching my hand—"some of them, there were men like gold there—"

The thread is tough; you cannot cut it with one stroke.

"What have you been playing?" he asked.

"Forrest, Schubert."

"With the quartet?"

"Trio, now. Janet went to Oakland with a new lover."

"Ah, poor Max."

"It's just as well, really. She isn't a good pianist."

I make Simon laugh, too, though I don't intend to. We talked until it was past time for me to go to work. My shift since the Full Employment Act last year is ten to two. I am an inspector in a recycled paper bag factory. I have never rejected a bag yet; the electronic inspector catches all the defective ones first. It is a rather depressing job. But it's only four hours a day, and it takes more time than that to go through all the lines and physical and mental examinations, and fill out all the forms, and talk to all the welfare counselors and inspectors every week in order to qualify as Unemployed, and then line up every day for the ration stamps and the dole. Simon thought I ought to go to work as usual. I tried to, but I couldn't. He had felt very hot to the touch when I kissed him good-bye. I went instead and got a black-market doctor. A girl at the factory had recommended her, for an abortion, if I ever wanted one without going through the regulation two years of sex-depressant drugs the fed-meds make you take when they give you an abortion. She was a jeweler's assistant in a shop on Alder Street, and the girl said she was convenient because if you didn't have enough cash you could leave something in pawn at the jeweler's as payment. Nobody ever does have enough cash, and of course credit cards aren't worth much on the black market.

The doctor was willing to come at once, so we rode home on the bus together. She gathered very soon that Simon and I were married, and it was funny to see her look at us and smile like a cat. Some people love illegality for its own sake. Men, more often than women. It's men who make laws, and enforce them, and break them, and think the whole performance is wonderful. Most women would rather just ignore them. You could see that this woman, like a man, actually enjoyed breaking them. That may have been what put her into an illegal business in the first place, a preference for the shady side. But there was more to it than that. No doubt she'd wanted to be a doctor, too; and the Federal Medical Association doesn't admit women into the medical schools. She probably got her training as some other doctor's private pupil, under the counter. Very much as Simon learned mathematics, since the universities don't teach much but Business Administration and Advertising and Media Skills any more. However she learned it, she seemed to know her stuff. She fixed up a kind of homemade traction device for Simon very handily and informed him that if he did much more walking for two months he'd be crippled the rest of his life, but if he behaved himself he'd just be more or less lame. It isn't the kind of thing you'd expect to be grateful for being told, but we both were. Leaving, she gave me a bottle of about two hundred plain white pills, unlabeled. "Aspirin," she said. "He'll be in a good deal of pain off and on for weeks."

I looked at the bottle. I had never seen aspirin before, only the Super-Buffered Pane-Gon and the Triple-Power N-L-G-Zic and the Extra-Strength Apansprin with the miracle ingredient more doctors recommend, which the fed-meds always give you prescriptions for, to be filled at your FMA-approved private enterprise friendly drugstore at the low, low prices established by the Pure Food and Drug Administration in order to inspire competitive research.

"Aspirin," the doctor repeated. "The miracle ingredient more doctors recommend." She cat-grinned again. I think she liked us because we were living in sin. That bottle of black-market aspirin was probably worth more than the old Navajo bracelet I pawned for her fee.

I went out again to register Simon as temporarily domiciled at my address and to apply for Temporary Unemployment Compensation ration stamps for him. They only give them to you for two weeks and you have to come every day; but to register him as Temporarily Disabled meant getting the signatures of two fed-meds, and I thought I'd rather put that off for a while. It took three hours to go through the lines and get the forms he would have to fill out, and to answer the 'crats' questions about why he wasn't there in person. They smelled something fishy. Of course it's hard for them to prove that two people are married and aren't just adultering if you move now and then and your friends help out by sometimes registering one of you as living at their address; but they had all the back files on both of us and it was obvious that we had been around each other for a suspiciously long time. The State really does make things awfully hard for itself. It must have been simpler to enforce the laws back when marriage was legal and adultery was what got you into trouble. They only had to catch you once. But I'll bet people broke the law just as often then as they do now.

The lantern-creatures came close enough at last that we could see not only their light, but their bodies in the illumination of their light. They were not pretty. They were dark colored, most often a dark red, and they were all mouth. They ate one another whole. Light swallowed light all swallowed together in the vaster mouth of the darkness. They moved slowly, for nothing, however small and hungry, could move fast under that weight, in that cold. Their eyes, round with fear, were never closed. Their bodies were tiny and bony behind the gaping jaws. They wore queer, ugly decorations on their lips and skulls: fringes, serrated wattles, featherlike fronds, gauds, bangles, lures. Poor little sheep of the deep pastures! Poor ragged, hunch-jawed dwarfs squeezed to the bone by the weight of the darkness, chilled to the bone by the cold of the darkness, tiny monsters burning with bright hunger, who brought us back to life!

Occasionally, in the wan, sparse illumination of one of the lantern-creatures, we caught a momentary glimpse of other, large, unmoving shapes: the barest suggestion, off in the distance, not of a wall, nothing so solid and certain as a wall, but of a surface, an angle . . . Was it there?

Or something would glitter, faint, far off, far down. There was no use trying to make out what it might be. Probably it was only a fleck of sediment, mud or mica, disturbed by a struggle between the lantern-creatures, flickering like a bit of diamond dust as it rose and settled slowly. In any case, we could not move to go see what it was. We had not even the cold, narrow freedom of the lantern-creatures. We were immobilized, borne down, still shadows among the half-guessed shadow walls. Were we there?

The lantern-creatures showed no awareness of us. They passed before us, among us, perhaps even through us—it was impossible to be sure. They were not afraid, or curious.

Once something a little larger than a hand came crawling near, and for a moment we saw quite distinctly the clean angle where the foot of a wall rose from the pavement, in the glow cast by the crawling creature, which was covered with a foliage of plumes, each plume dotted with many tiny, bluish points of light. We saw the pavement beneath the creature and the wall beside it, heartbreaking in its exact, clear linearity, its opposition to all that was fluid, random, vast, and void. We saw the creature's claws, slowly reaching out and retracting like small stiff fingers, touch the wall. Its plumage of light quivering, it dragged itself along and vanished behind the corner of the wall.

So we knew that the wall was there; and that it was an outer wall, a housefront, perhaps, or the side of one of the towers of the city.

We remembered the towers. We remembered the city. We had forgotten it. We had forgotten who we were; but we remembered the city, now.

When I got home, the FBI had already been there. The computer at the police precinct where I registered Simon's address must have flashed it right over to the computer at the FBI building. They had questioned Simon for about an hour, mostly about what he had been doing during the twelve days it took him to get from the Camp to Portland. I suppose they thought he had flown to Peking or something. Having a police record in Walla Walla for hitchhiking helped him establish his story. He told me that one of them had gone to the bathroom. Sure enough I found a bug stuck on the top of the bathroom door frame. I left it, as we figured it's really better to leave it when you know you have one, than to take it off and then never be sure they haven't planted another one you don't know about. As Simon said, if we felt we had to say something unpatriotic we could always flush the toilet at the same time.

I have a battery radio—there are so many work stoppages because of power failures, and days the water has to be boiled, and so on, that you really have to have a radio to save wasting time and dying of typhoid—and he turned it on while I was making supper on the Primus. The six o'clock All-American Broadcasting Company news announcer announced that peace was at hand in Uruguay, the president's confidential aide having been seen to smile at a passing blonde as he left the 613th day of the secret negotiations in a villa outside Katmandu. The war in Liberia was going well; the enemy said they had shot down seventeen American planes but the Pentagon said we had shot down twenty-two enemy planes, and the capital city—I forget its name, but it hasn't been inhabitable for seven years anyway—was on the verge of being recaptured by the forces of freedom. The police action in Arizona was also successful. The Neo-Birch insurgents in Phoenix could not hold out much longer against the massed might of the American army and air force, since their underground supply of small tactical nukes from the Weathermen in Los Angeles had been cut off. Then there was an advertisement for Fed-Cred cards, and a commercial for the Supreme Court: "Take your legal troubles to the Nine Wise Men!" Then there was something about why tariffs had gone up, and a report from the stock market, which had just closed at over two thousand, and a commercial for U.S. Government canned water, with a catchy little tune: "Don't be sorry when you drink / It's not as healthy as you think / Don't you think you really ought to / Drink coo-ool, puu-uure U.S.G. water?"—with three sopranos in close harmony on the last line. Then, just as the battery began to give out and his voice was dying away into a faraway tiny whisper, the announcer seemed to be saying something about a new continent emerging.

"What was that?"

"I didn't hear," Simon said, lying with his eyes shut and his face pale and sweaty. I gave him two aspirins before we ate. He ate little, and fell asleep while I was washing the dishes in the bathroom. I had been going to practice, but a viola is fairly wakeful in a one-room apartment. I read for a while instead. It was a best seller Janet had given me when she left. She thought it was very good, but then she likes Franz Liszt too. I don't read much since the libraries were closed down, it's too hard to get books; all you can buy is best sellers. I don't remember the title of this one, the cover just said "Ninety Million Copies in Print!!!" It was about small-town sex life in the last century, the dear old 1970s when there weren't any problems and life was so simple and nostalgic. The author squeezed all the naughty thrills he could out of the fact that all the main characters were married. I looked at the end and saw that all the married couples shot each other after all their children became schizophrenic hookers, except for one brave pair that divorced and then leapt into bed together with a clear-eyed pair of government-employed lovers for eight pages of healthy group sex as a brighter future dawned. I went to bed then, too. Simon was hot, but sleeping quietly. His breathing was like the sound of soft waves far away, and I went out to the dark sea on the sound of them.

I used to go out to the dark sea, often, as a child, falling asleep. I had almost forgotten it with my waking mind. As a child all I had to do was stretch out and think, "the dark sea . . . the dark sea . . . " and soon enough I'd be there, in the great depths, rocking. But after I grew up it only happened rarely, as a great gift. To know the abyss of the darkness and not to fear it, to entrust oneself to it and whatever may arise from it—what greater gift?

We watched the tiny lights come and go around us, and doing so, we gained a sense of space and of direction—near and far, at least, and higher and lower. It was that sense of space that allowed us to become aware of the currents. Space was no longer entirely still around us, suppressed by the enormous pressure of its own weight. Very dimly we were aware that the cold darkness moved, slowly, softly, pressing against us a little for a long time, then ceasing, in a vast oscillation. The empty darkness flowed slowly along our unmoving unseen bodies; along them, past them; perhaps through them; we could not tell.

Where did they come from, those dim, slow, vast tides? What pressure or attraction stirred the deeps to these slow drifting movements? We could not understand that; we could only feel their touch against us, but in straining our sense to guess their origin or end, we became aware of something else: something out there in the darkness of the great currents: sounds. We listened. We heard.

So our sense of space sharpened and localized to a sense of place. For sound is local, as sight is not. Sound is delimited by silence; and it does not rise out of the silence unless it is fairly close, both in space and in time. Though we stand where once the singer stood we cannot hear the voice singing; the years have carried it off on their tides, submerged it. Sound is a fragile thing, a tremor, as delicate as life itself. We may see the stars, but we cannot hear them. Even were the hollowness of outer space an atmosphere, an ether that transmitted the waves of sound, we could not hear the stars;

they are too far away. At most if we listened we might hear our own sun, all the mighty, roiling, exploding storm of its burning, as a whisper at the edge of hearing.

A sea wave laps one's feet: It is the shock wave of a volcanic eruption on the far side of the world. But one hears nothing.

A red light flickers on the horizon: It is the reflection in smoke of a city on the distant mainland, burning. But one hears nothing.

Only on the slopes of the volcano, in the suburbs of the city, does one begin to hear the deep thunder, and the high voices crying.

Thus, when we became aware that we were hearing, we were sure that the sounds we heard were fairly close to us. And yet we may have been quite wrong. For we were in a strange place, a deep place. Sound travels fast and far in the deep places, and the silence there is perfect, letting the least noise be heard for hundreds of miles.

And these were not small noises. The lights were tiny, but the sounds were vast: not loud, but very large. Often they were below the range of hearing, long slow vibrations rather than sounds. The first we heard seemed to us to rise up through the currents from beneath us: immense groans, sighs felt along the bone, a rumbling, a deep uneasy whispering.

Later, certain sounds came down to us from above, or borne along the endless levels of the darkness, and these were stranger yet, for they were music. A huge, calling, yearning music from far away in the darkness, calling not to us. *Where are you? I am here.*

Not to us.

They were the voices of the great souls, the great lives, the lonely ones, the voyagers. Calling. Not often answered. *Where are you? Where have you gone?*

But the bones, the keels and girders of white bones on icy isles of the South, the shores of bones did not reply.

Nor could we reply. But we listened, and the tears rose in our eyes, salt, not so salt as the oceans, the world-girdling deep bereaved currents, the abandoned roadways of the great lives; not so salt, but warmer.

I am here. Where have you gone?

No answer.

Only the whispering thunder from below.

But we knew now, though we could not answer, we knew because we heard, because we felt, because we wept, we knew that we were; and we remembered other voices.

Max came the next night. I sat on the toilet lid to practice, with the bathroom door shut. The FBI men on the other end of the bug got a solid half hour of scales and doublestops, and then a quite good performance of the Hindemith unaccompanied viola sonata. The bathroom being very small and all hard surfaces, the noise I made was really tremendous. Not a good sound, far too much echo, but the sheer volume was contagious, and I played louder as I went on. The man up above knocked on his floor once; but if I have to listen to the weekly All-American Olympic Games at full blast every Sunday morning from his TV set, then he has to accept Paul Hindemith coming up out of his toilet now and then.

When I got tired I put a wad of cotton over the bug, and came out of the bathroom half-deaf. Simon and Max were on fire. Burning, unconsumed. Simon was scribbling formulae in traction, and Max was pumping his elbows up and down the way he does, like a boxer, and saying "The e-lec-tron emis-sion . . . " through his nose, with his eyes narrowed, and his mind evidently going light-years per second faster than his tongue, because he kept beginning over and saying "The e-lec-tron emission . . . " and pumping his elbows.

Intellectuals at work are very strange to look at. As strange as artists. I never could understand how an audience can sit there and *look* at a fiddler rolling his eyes and biting his tongue, or a horn player collecting spit, or a pianist like a black cat strapped to an electrified bench, as if what they *saw* had anything to do with the music.

I damped the fires with a quart of black-market beer—the legal kind is better, but I never have enough ration stamps for beer; I'm not thirsty enough to go without eating—and gradually Max and Simon cooled down. Max would have stayed talking all night, but I drove him out because Simon was looking tired.

I put a new battery in the radio and left it playing in the bathroom, and blew out the candle and lay and talked with Simon; he was too excited to sleep. He said that Max had solved the problems that were bothering them before Simon was sent to Camp, and had fitted Simon's equations to (as Simon put it) the bare facts, which means they have achieved "direct energy conversion." Ten or twelve people have worked on it at different times since Simon published the theoretical part of it when he was twenty-two. The physicist Ann Jones had pointed out right away that the simplest practical application of the theory would be to build a "sun tap," a device for collecting and storing solar energy, only much cheaper and better than the U.S.G. Sola-Heetas that some rich people have on their houses. And it would have been simple only they kept hitting the same snag. Now Max has got around the snag.

I said that Simon published the theory, but that is inaccurate. Of course he's never been able to publish any of his papers, in print; he's not a federal employee and doesn't have a government clearance. But it did get circulated in what the scientists and poets call Sammy's-dot, that is, just handwritten or hectographed. It's an old joke that the FBI arrests everybody with purple fingers, because they have either been hectographing Sammy's-dots, or they have impetigo.

Anyhow, Simon was on top of the mountain that night. His true joy is in the pure math; but he had been working with Clara and Max and the others in this effort to materialize the theory for ten years, and a taste of material victory is a good thing, once in a lifetime.

I asked him to explain what the sun tap would mean to the masses, with me as a representative mass. He explained that it means we can tap solar energy for power, using a device that's easier to build than a jar battery. The efficiency and storage capacity are such that about ten minutes of sunlight will power an apartment complex like ours, heat and lights and elevators and all, for twenty-four hours; and no pollution, particulate, thermal, or radioactive. "There isn't any danger of using up the sun?" I asked. He took it soberly—it was a stupid question, but after all not so long ago people thought there wasn't any danger of using up the earth—and said no, because we wouldn't be pulling out energy, as we did when we mined and lumbered and split atoms, but just using the energy that comes to us anyhow: as the plants, the trees and grass and rosebushes, always have done. "You could call it Flower Power," he said. He was high, high up on the mountain, ski-jumping in the sunlight.

"The State owns us," he said, "because the corporative State has a monopoly on power sources, and there's not enough power to go around. But now, anybody could build a generator on their roof that would furnish enough power to light a city."

I looked out the window at the dark city.

"We could completely decentralize industry and agriculture. Technology could serve life instead of serving capital. We could each run our own life. Power is power! . . . The State is a machine. We could unplug the machine, now. Power corrupts; absolute power corrupts absolutely. But that's true only when there's a price on power. When groups can keep the power to themselves; when they can use physical power-to in order to exert spiritual power-over; when might makes right. But if power is free? If everybody is equally mighty? Then everybody's got to find a better way of showing that he's right . . . "

"That's what Mr. Nobel thought when he invented dynamite," I said. "Peace on earth."

He slid down the sunlit slope a couple of thousand feet and stopped beside me in a spray of snow, smiling. "Skull at the banquet," he said, "finger writing on the wall. Be still! Look, don't you see the sun shining on the Pentagon, all the roofs are off, the sun shines at last into the corridors of power . . . And they shrivel up, they wither away. The green grass grows through the carpets of the Oval Room, the Hot Line is disconnected for nonpayment of the bill. The first thing we'll do is build an electrified fence outside the electrified fence around the White House. The inner one prevents unauthorized persons from getting in. The outer one will prevent authorized persons from getting out . . . "

Of course he was bitter. Not many people come out of prison sweet.

But it was cruel, to be shown this great hope, and to know that there was no hope for it. He did know that: He knew it right along. He knew that there was no mountain, that he was skiing on the wind.

The tiny lights of the lantern-creatures died out one by one, sank away. The distant lonely voices were silent. The cold, slow currents flowed, vacant, only shaken from time to time by a shifting in the abyss.

It was dark again, and no voice spoke. All dark, dumb, cold.

Then the sun rose.

It was not like the dawns we had begun to remember: the change, manifold and subtle, in the smell and touch of the air; the hush that, instead of sleeping, wakes, holds still, and waits; the appearance of objects, looking gray, vague, and new, as if just created—distant mountains against the eastern sky, one's own hands, the hoary grass full of dew and shadow, the fold in the edge of a curtain hanging by the window—and then, before one is quite sure that one is indeed seeing again, that the light has returned, that day is breaking, the first, abrupt, sweet stammer of a waking bird. And after that the chorus, voice by voice: This is my nest, this is my tree, this is my egg, this is my day, this is my life, here I am, here I am, hurray for me! I'm here!—No, it wasn't like that at all, this dawn. It was completely silent, and it was blue.

In the dawns that we had begun to remember, one did not become aware of the light itself, but of the separate objects touched by the light, the things, the world. They were there, visible again, as if visibility were their own property, not a gift from the rising sun.

In this dawn, there was nothing but the light itself. Indeed there was not even light, we would have said, but only color: blue.

There was no compass bearing to it. It was not brighter in the east. There was no east or west. There was only up and down, below and above. Below was dark. The blue light came from above. Brightness fell. Beneath, where the shaking thunder had stilled, the brightness died away through violet into blindness.

We, arising, watched light fall.

In a way it was more like an ethereal snowfall than like a sunrise. The light seemed to be in discrete particles, infinitesimal flecks, slowly descending, faint, fainter than flecks of fine snow on a dark night, and tinier; but blue. A soft, penetrating blue tending to the violet, the color of the shadows in an iceberg, the color of a streak of sky between gray clouds on a winter afternoon before snow: faint in intensity but vivid in hue: the color of the remote, the color of the cold, the color farthest from the sun.

On Saturday night they held a scientific congress in our room. Clara and Max came, of course, and the engineer Phil Drum and three others who had worked on the sun tap. Phil Drum was very pleased with himself because he had actually built one of the things, a solar cell, and brought it along. I don't think it had occurred to either Max or Simon to build one. Once they knew it could be done they were satisfied and wanted to get on with something else. But Phil unwrapped his baby with a lot of flourish, and people made remarks like, "Mr. Watson, will you come here a minute," and "Hey, Wilbur, you're off the ground!" and "I say, nasty mould you've got there, Alec, why don't you throw it out?" and "Ugh, ugh, burns, burns, wow, ow," the latter from Max, who does look a little pre-Mousterian. Phil explained that he had exposed the cell for one minute at four in the afternoon up in Washington Park during a light rain. The lights were back on on the West Side since Thursday, so we could test it without being conspicuous.

We turned off the lights, after Phil had wired the table-lamp cord to the cell. He turned on the lamp switch. The bulb came on, about twice as bright as before, at its full forty watts—city power of course was never full strength. We all looked at it. It was a dime-store table lamp with a metallized gold base and a white plasticloth shade.

"Brighter than a thousand suns," Simon murmured from the bed.

"Could it be," said Clara Edmonds, "that we physicists have known sin—and have come out the other side?"

"It really wouldn't be any good at all for making bombs with," Max said dreamily.

"Bombs," Phil Drum said with scorn. "Bombs are obsolete. Don't you realize that we could move a mountain with this kind of power? I mean pick up Mount Hood, move it, and set it down. We could thaw Antarctica, we could freeze the Congo. We could sink a continent. Give me a fulcrum and I'll move the world. Well, Archimedes, you've got your fulcrum. The sun."

"Christ," Simon said, "the radio, Belle!"

The bathroom door was shut and I had put cotton over the bug, but he was right; if they were going to go ahead at this rate there had better be some added static. And though I liked watching their faces in the clear light of the lamp—they all had good, interesting faces, well worn, like the handles of wooden tools or the rocks in a running stream—I did not much want to listen to them talk tonight. Not because I wasn't a scientist, that made no difference. And not because I disagreed or disapproved or disbelieved anything they said. Only because it grieved me terribly, their talking. Because they couldn't rejoice aloud over a job done and a discovery made, but had to hide there and whisper about it. Because they couldn't go out into the sun.

I went into the bathroom with my viola and sat on the toilet lid and did a long set of sautillé exercises. Then I tried to work at the Forrest trio, but it was too assertive. I played the solo part from *Harold in Italy,* which is beautiful, but it wasn't quite the right mood either. They were still going strong in the other room. I began to improvise.

After a few minutes in E-minor the light over the shaving mirror began to flicker and dim; then it died. Another outage. The table lamp in the other room did not go out, being connected with the sun, not with the twenty-three atomic fission plants that power the Greater Portland Area. Within two seconds somebody had switched it off, too, so that we shouldn't be the only window in the West Hills left alight; and I could hear them rooting for candles and rattling matches. I went on improvising in the dark. Without light, when you couldn't see all the hard shiny surfaces of things, the sound seemed softer and less muddled. I went on, and it began to shape up. All the laws of harmonics sang together when the bow came down. The strings of the viola were the cords of my own voice, tightened by sorrow, tuned to the pitch of joy. The melody created itself out of air and energy, it raised up the valleys, and the mountains and hills were made low, and the crooked straight, and the rough places plain. And the music went out to the dark sea and sang in the darkness, over the abyss.

When I came out they were all sitting there and none of them was talking. Max had been crying. I could see little candle flames in the tears around his eyes. Simon lay flat on the bed in the shadows, his eyes closed. Phil Drum sat hunched over, holding the solar cell in his hands.

I loosened the pegs, put the bow and the viola in the case, and cleared my throat. It was embarrassing. I finally said, "I'm sorry."

One of the women spoke: Rose Abramski, a private student of Simon's, a big shy woman who could hardly speak at all unless it was in mathematical symbols. "I saw it," she said. "I saw it. I saw the white towers, and the water streaming down their sides, and running back down to the sea. And the sunlight shining in the streets, after ten thousand years of darkness."

"I heard them," Simon said, very low, from the shadow. "I heard their voices."

"Oh, Christ! Stop it!" Max cried out, and got up and went blundering out into the unlit hall, without his coat. We heard him running down the stairs.

"Phil," said Simon, lying there, "could we raise up the white towers, with our lever and our fulcrum?"

After a long silence Phil Drum answered, "We have the power to do it."

"What else do we need?" Simon said. "What else do we need, besides power?"

Nobody answered him.

The blue changed. It became brighter, lighter, and at the same time thicker: impure. The ethereal luminosity of blue-violet turned to turquoise, intense and opaque. Still we could not have said that everything was now turquoise-colored, for there were still no things. There was nothing, except the color of turquoise.

The change continued. The opacity became veined and thinned. The dense, solid color began to appear translucent, transparent. Then it seemed as if we were in the heart of a sacred jade, or the brilliant crystal of a sapphire or an emerald.

As at the inner structure of a crystal, there was no motion. But there was something, now, to see. It was as if we saw the motionless, elegant inward structure of the molecules of a precious stone. Planes and angles appeared about us, shadowless and clear in that even, glowing, blue-green light.

These were the walls and towers of the city, the streets, the windows, the gates.

We knew them, but we did not recognize them. We did not dare to recognize them. It had been so long. And it was so strange. We had used to dream, when we lived in this city. We had lain down, nights, in the rooms behind the windows, and slept, and dreamed. We had all dreamed of the ocean, of the deep sea. Were we not dreaming now?

Sometimes the thunder and tremor deep below us rolled again, but it was faint now, far away; as far away as our memory of the thunder and the tremor and the fire and the towers falling, long ago. Neither the sound nor the memory frightened us. We knew them.

The sapphire light brightened overhead to green, almost green-gold. We looked up. The tops of the highest towers were hard to see, glowing in the radiance of light. The streets and doorways were darker, more clearly defined.

In one of those long, jewel-dark streets something was moving—something not composed of planes and angles, but of curves and arcs. We all turned to look at it, slowly, wondering as we did so at the slow ease of our own motion, our freedom. Sinuous, with a beautiful flowing, gathering, rolling movement, now rapid and now tentative, the thing drifted across the street from a blank garden wall to the recess of a door. There, in the dark blue shadow, it was hard to see for a while. We watched. A pale blue curve appeared at the top of the doorway. A second followed, and a third. The moving thing clung or hovered there, above the door, like a swaying knot of silvery cords or a boneless hand, one arched finger pointing carelessly to something above the lintel of the door, something like itself, but motionless—a carving. A carving in jade light. A carving in stone.

Delicately and easily the long curving tentacle followed the curves of the carved figure, the eight petal-limbs, the round eyes. Did it recognize its image?

The living one swung suddenly, gathered its curves in a loose knot, and darted away down the street, swift and sinuous. Behind it a faint cloud of darker blue hung for a minute and dispersed, revealing again the carved figure above the door: the sea-flower, the cuttlefish, quick, great-eyed, graceful, evasive, the cherished sign, carved on a thousand walls, worked into the design of cornices, pavements, handles, lids of jewel boxes, canopies, tapestries, tabletops, gateways.

Down another street, about the level of the first-floor windows, came a flickering drift of hundreds of motes of silver. With a single motion all turned toward the cross street, and glittered off into the dark blue shadows.

There were shadows, now.

We looked up, up from the flight of silverfish, up from the streets where the jade-green currents flowed and the blue shadows fell. We moved and looked up, yearning, to the high towers of our city. They stood, the fallen towers. They glowed in the ever-brightening radiance, not blue or blue-green, up there, but gold. Far above them lay a vast, circular, trembling brightness: the sun's light on the surface of the sea.

We are here. When we break through the bright circle into life, the water will break and stream white down the white sides of the towers, and run down the steep streets back into the sea. The water will glitter in dark hair, on the eyelids of dark eyes, and dry to a thin white film of salt.

We are here.

Whose voice? Who called to us?

He was with me for twelve days. On January 28th the 'crats came from the Bureau of Health, Education and Welfare and said that since he was receiving Unemployment Compensation while suffering from an untreated illness, the government must look after him and restore him to health, because health is the inalienable right of the citizens of a democracy. He refused to sign the consent forms, so the chief health officer signed them. He refused to get up, so two of the policemen pulled him up off the bed. He started to try to fight them. The chief health officer pulled his gun and said that if he continued to struggle he would shoot him for resisting welfare, and arrest me for conspiracy to defraud the government. The man who was holding my arms behind my back said they could always arrest me for unreported pregnancy with intent to form a nuclear family. At that Simon stopped trying to get free. It was really all he was trying to do, not to fight them, just to get his arms free. He looked at me, and they took him out.

He is in the federal hospital in Salem. I have not been able to find out whether he is in the regular hospital or the mental wards.

It was on the radio again yesterday, about the rising land masses in the

South Atlantic and the Western Pacific. At Max's the other night I saw a TV special explaining about geophysical stresses and subsidence and faults. The U.S. Geodetic Service is doing a lot of advertising around town, the most common one is a big billboard that says IT'S NOT OUR FAULT! with a picture of a beaver pointing to a schematic map that shows how even if Oregon has a major earthquake and subsidence as California did last month, it will not affect Portland, or only the western suburbs perhaps. The news also said that they plan to halt the tidal waves in Florida by dropping nuclear bombs where Miami was. Then they will reattach Florida to the mainland with landfill. They are already advertising real estate for housing developments on the landfill. The president is staying at the Mile High White House in Aspen, Colorado. I don't think it will do him much good. Houseboats down on the Willamette are selling for $500,000. There are no trains or buses running south from Portland, because all the highways were badly damaged by the tremors and landslides last week, so I will have to see if I can get to Salem on foot. I still have the rucksack I bought for the Mount Hood Wilderness Week. I got some dry lima beans and raisins with my Federal Fair Share Super Value Green Stamp minimal ration book for February—it took the whole book—and Phil Drum made me a tiny camp stove powered with the solar cell. I didn't want to take the Primus, it's too bulky, and I did want to be able to carry the viola. Max gave me a half pint of brandy. When the brandy is gone I expect I will stuff this notebook into the bottle and put the cap on tight and leave it on a hillside somewhere between here and Salem. I like to think of it being lifted up little by little by the water, and rocking, and going out to the dark sea.

Where are you?
We are here. Where have you gone?

(1975)

JOANNA RUSS

A Few Things I Know About Whileaway

1

"Humanity is unnatural!" exclaimed the philosopher Dunyasha Bernadettesdaughter (A.C. 344–426), who suffered all her life from the slip of a genetic surgeon's hand which had given her one mother's jaw and the other mother's teeth—orthodontia is hardly ever necessary on Whileaway. Her daughter's teeth, however, were perfect. Plague came to Whileaway in P.C. 17 (Preceding Catastrophe) and ended in A.C. 03 with half the population dead; it had started so slowly that no one knew anything about it until it was too late. It attacked males only. Earth had been completely re-formed during the Golden Age (P.C. 300–ca. P.C. 180), and natural conditions presented considerably less difficulty than they might have during a similar catastrophe a millennium or so before. At the time of the Despair (as it is popularly called), Whileaway had two continents, called simply North and South Continents, both of which possessed many ideal bays or anchorages. Severe climatic conditions did not prevail below 72° S and 68° N latitudes. Conventional water traffic, at the time of the Catastrophe, was employed almost exclusively for freight, passengers using the smaller and more flexibly routed hovercraft. Houses were self-contained, with portable power sources, fuel-alcohol motors or solar cells replacing the earlier centralized power. The invention of practical matter-anti-matter reactors (K. Ansky, A.C. 239) produced great optimism for a decade or so, but these devices proved to be too bulky for personal use. Katharina Lucysdaughter Ansky (A.C. 201–282) was also responsible for the principles that made genetic surgery possible. (The merging of ova had been practiced for the previous century and a half.) Animal life had become scarce before the Golden Age; many species were reinvented by enthusiasts of the Ansky Period. In A.C. 280 there was an outbreak of coneys on Newland (an island off the neck of North Continent), a pandemic not without historical precedent. By A.C. 492, through the brilliant agitation of the great Betty Bettinasdaughter Murano (A.C. 453–A.C. 502), Terrestrial colonies were re-established on Mars, Ganymede, and among the Asteroids, the Selenic League assisting, according to the treaty of Mare Tenebrum (A.C. 240). Asked what she expected to find in space, Betty Murano made the immortal quip, "Nothing." By the third century A.C., intelligence was a controllable, heritable factor, though aptitudes and interests continued to elude the surgeons and intelligence itself could be raised only grossly. By the fifth century, clan organization had reached its present complex state and phosphorus was being almost completely recycled; by the seventh century, Jovian mining made it possible to replace a largely glass-and-ceramics technology with some metals (which were also recycled) and for the third time in four hundred years (fashions were sometimes cyclic, too) dueling became a serious social nuisance. By the beginning of the ninth century A.C., the induction helmet was a practical possibility, industry was being drastically altered, and the Selenic League had finally outproduced South Continent in kg. protein/person/annum. The induction helmet (which made it possible for one workwoman to have not only the brute force but the flexibility and control of thousands) allowed both South and North Continents to increase childbearing leave to five years. Historians of the period compared this custom to the ancient Chinese custom of three years' mourning for one's father; "A hiatus at the age of thirty" (as one has been quoted) "is just the right time." In A.C. 913, an obscure and discontented descendant of Katy Ansky put together various items of mathematical knowledge and thus discovered—or invented—probability mechanics, which offers the possibility (by looping into another continuum, exactly chosen) of teleportation. In the last hundred and twenty years, reorganization of industry consequent to the widespread introduction of the induction helmet has driven the Whileawayan workweek up to the unprecedented length of sixteen hours.

2

(Interview with a Whileawayan named Janet Evasdaughter)

MC: Our social scientists, as well as our physicists, tell us they will have to revise a great deal of theory in light of the information brought us by our fair visitor from the future. This is not *our* future, it seems, but only a possible future—Miss Evasdaughter, perhaps you had better explain about the existence of different probabilities in the future. You know, we were talking about that before.

JE: It's in the newspapers.

MC: But, Miss Evasdaughter, if you could, please explain it for the people watching the program.

JE: Let them read. Can't they read?

(A moment's silence)

MC: As you probably know, ladies and gentlemen, there have been no men on Whileaway for at least eight centuries—I don't mean no human beings, of course, but no men—and this society, run entirely by women, has naturally attracted a great deal of attention since the appearance last week of its representative and first ambassador, the lady on my left here. Miss Evasdaughter, can you tell us how you think your society in Whileaway will react to the appearance of men from Earth—I mean men from our present-day Earth, of course—after an isolation of eight hundred years?

JE: Nine hundred. What men?

MC: What men? Surely you expect men from our society to visit Whileaway.

JE: Why?

MC: For information, trade, ah—cultural contact, surely. (*Audience laughter*) I'm afraid you're making it rather difficult for me, Miss Evasdaughter. When the—ah—the plague you spoke of killed the men on Whileaway, weren't they missed? Weren't families broken up? Didn't the whole pattern of life change?

JE: Sure. People always miss what they are used to. Yes, they were missed. Even a whole set of words, like "he," "man," and so on—these are banned. Then the second generation, they use them to be daring, among themselves, and the third generation doesn't, to be polite, and by the fourth, who cares? Who remembers?

MC: But surely—that is—

JE: Excuse me, perhaps I'm mistaking what you intend to say, as this language we're speaking is only a hobby of mine; I am not as fluent as I would wish. What we speak is a pan-Russian even the Russians would not understand: it would be like Middle English to you, only vice versa.

MC: I see. But to get back to the question—

JE: Yes.

MC: Don't you want men to return to Whileaway, Miss Evasdaughter?

JE: Why?

MC: One sex is half a species, Miss Evasdaughter. Do you want to banish sex from Whileaway?

JE (*with massive dignity and complete naturalness*): Huh?

MC: I said, Do you want to banish sex from Whileaway?

JE: I'm married. I have two children. What the devil are you talking about?

MC: I—we—well, we know you form what you call "marriages," Miss Evasdaughter, that you reckon the descent of your children through both partners, and that you even have "tribes"—I'm calling them that—I know the translation isn't perfect—but I am not talking about economic institutions or even affectionate ones. I am talking about sexual love.

JE (*enlightened*): Oh! You mean copulation.

MC: Yes.

JE: Of course we have that.

MC: Ah?

(Great audience reaction)

JE: With each other. Allow me to—

(Commercial break. Later:)

MC: How do the women of Whileaway do their hair?

JE (*annoyed*): They hack it off with clam shells.

3

On Whileaway they have a saying: When the mother and child are separated they both howl, the child because it is separated from the mother, the mother because she has to go back to work. Whileawayans bear their children at thirty—singletons or twins, as the demographic pressures require. These children have as one genotypic parent the biological mother (the "body-mother") while the nonbearing parent contributes the other ovum ("other-mother"). A family of thirty persons may have as many as four mother-and-child pairs in the common nursery at one time. Food, cleanliness, and shelter are taken care of communally; they are not the mothers' business. At the age of four or five, these independent, blooming, pampered, extremely intelligent little girls are torn weeping and arguing from their thirty relatives and sent to the regional school, where some of them have been known to construct deadfalls or small bombs (having picked this knowledge up from their parents) in order to obliterate their instructors. Children are cared for in groups of five and taught in groups of differing sizes according to the subject under discussion. Their education at this point is heavily practical: how to run machines, how to get along without machines, law, geography, transportation, and so on. At puberty, they are invested with Middle Dignity and turned loose; children have the right of food and lodging wherever they go, up to the power of the particular community to support them.

Some go back home, but neither mother may be there, and the adults who were so kind to a four-year-old have little time for an almost-adult.

Some, wild with the desire for exploration, travel all around the world—usually in the company of other children. Bands of children going to visit this or that are a common sight on Whileaway.

The more profound may abandon all possessions and live off the land just above or below the forty-eighth parallel; they return with animal skins, scars, visions.

Some make a beeline for their callings and pester part-time actors, part-time musicians, part-time scholars, and so on.

At seventeen, they achieve Three-Quarters Dignity and are assimilated into the labor force. Groups of friends are kept together, if the members request it and if it is possible, but most adolescents go where they are sent, not where they wish. This is generally the worst time in a Whileawayan's life. None can join the Geographical Parliament or the Professions Parliament until she has entered a family and developed that network of informal associations of the like-minded which is Whileaway's substitute for everything else.

At twenty-two, they achieve Full Dignity and begin either to learn heretofore forbidden jobs or have their learning formally certified. They may marry into pre-existing families or form their own. Some signal this time of life by braiding their hair. By now, the typical Whileawayan is competent to do almost any job on the planet; by twenty-five, she has entered a family, which consists of twenty to thirty other persons, ranging in age from her own to the early fifties. Approximately every fourth person must begin a new or join a nearly new family.

Sexual relations—which have begun at puberty—continue both inside the family and outside it. Whileawayan psychology locates the basis of Whileawayan character in the early indulgence, pleasure, and flowering which is drastically curtailed by separation from the mothers. This (it says) gives Whileawayan life its characteristic independence, its dissatisfaction, its suspicion, and its tendency toward a rather irritable solipsism.

"Without which" (says Dunyasha Bernadettesdaughter, q.v.) "we would all become contented slobs, *nicht wahr*?"

The genuine flowering of Whileawayan life is in old age (i.e., after fifty-eight), for then the Whileawayan—no longer physically as strong and elastic as in youth—is allowed to join with computing machines in the state they say can't be described. Sedentary jobs are held by the old, who can use one-fiftieth of their brainpower for work while the other forty-nine parts riot in a freedom they haven't had since adolescence. The old can spend their days mapping, drawing, thinking, writing, collating, composing. In the libraries, old hands come out from beneath the induction helmets and give Whileawayan customers reproductions of the books they want; old feet twinkle below the computer shelves, hanging down like Humpty-Dumpty's; old ladies chuckle while composing such works as the *Blasphemous Cantata* (universally considered the greatest art work in Whileawayan history) or mad-moon cityscapes that turn out to be—surprisingly—doable after all.

On Whileaway it is the young who are priggish about the old; they don't approve of them.

Whileawayan taboos: sexual relations with anybody considerably older or younger than oneself, waste, ignorance, offending others without intending to.

No Whileawayan works more than three hours at a time on any one job, except in emergencies.

No Whileawayan marries monogamously. Some restrict their sexual relations to one other person—at least while that other person is nearby—but there is no legal bond. Whileawayan psychology again refers to the distrust of the mother and the reluctance to form a tie that will engage every level of emotion. Also, the necessity for artificial dissatisfactions.

"Without which" (Dunyasha Bernadettesdaughter, *op. cit.*) "we would become so happy we would sit down on our fat, pretty behinds and starve to death, *nyet*?"

4

A quiet country night. The hills east of Green Bay, the wet heat of August during the day. One woman reads; another sews; another smokes. Somebody takes from the wall a kind of whistle and plays on it the four notes of the major chord. This is repeated over and over again. We hold on to these four notes as long as we can; then we transform them by only one note; again we repeat these four notes. Slowly something tears itself away from the not-melody. Distances between the harmonics stretch wider and wider. How the lines open up! Three notes now. The playfulness and terror of the music written right on the air. Although the player is employing nearly the same dynamics throughout, the sounds have become painfully loud; the little instrument's guts are coming out. Too much to listen to, with its lips right against your ear. By dawn, it will stop; by dawn it will have gone through six or seven changes of notes, maybe two in an hour.

By dawn you'll have learned a little something about the major triad. You'll have celebrated a little something.

5

Etsuko Belin of the cave-dwelling Belins, stretched cruciform on a glider, shifts her weight and goes into a slow turn, seeing fifteen hundred feet below her the rising sun of Whileaway reflected in the glaciated lakes of Old Dirtyskirts. She flips the glider over and—sailing on her back—passes a hawk.

6

A troop of little girls contemplating three silver hoops welded to a silver cube are laughing so hard that some have fallen down into the autumn leaves on the plaza and are holding their stomachs. Their hip-packs lie around the edge of the plaza, near the fountains. Their reaction is not embarrassment or ignorant contempt for something new; they are genuine connoisseurs who have hiked for three days in order to experience just this moment.

7

An ancient statue outside the fuel-alcohol distillery at Ciudad Sierra: a man seated on a stone, his knees spread, both hands pressed against the pit of his stomach, a look of blind distress, his face blurred by time. Some wag has carved on the base the eight-lying-on-its-side that means infinity, and has added a straight line down the middle; this double-lollipop-on-a-stick is both the Whileawayan schematic of the male genital and the mathematical symbol for self-contradiction.

8

Some homes are extruded foam: white caves hung with veils of diamonds, indoor gardens, ceilings that weep. There are places in the Arctic to sit and meditate, invisible walls that shut in the same ice as outside, the same clouds. There is one rain forest, there is one shallow sea, there is one mountain chain, there is one desert. Rafts anchored in the blue eye of a dead volcano. Eyries built for nobody in particular, whose guests arrive by glider. There are more shelters than homes, more homes than persons; as the saying goes, "My home is in my shoes." Everything (they know) is eternally in transit. Everything is pointed toward death. Radar dish-ears listen for whispers from Outside. Whileaway is inhabited by the pervasive spirit of underpopulation, and alone at twilight in the permanently deserted city that is only a jungle of sculptured forms set on the Altiplano, attending to the rush of one's own breath in the respiratory mask, then—

9

I gambled for chores and breakfast with an old, old woman, in the middle of the night by the light of an alcohol lamp. Somewhere on the back roads of the swamp and pine flats of South Continent. Watching the shadows dance on her wrinkled face, I understood why other women speak with awe of seeing the withered legs dangling from the shell of a computer housing: Humpty-Dumptess on her way to the ultimate Inside of things.

(I lost. I carried her baggage and did her chores for a day.)

10

If you are so foolhardy as to ask a Whileawayan child to "be a good girl" and do something for you:

"What does running other people's errands have to do with being a good girl?

"Why can't you run your own errands?

"Are you crippled?"

(The double pairs of hard, dark children's eyes everywhere, like mating cats'.)

11

There is an unpolished white marble statue of God on Rabbit Island, all alone in a field of weeds and snow. She is seated, naked to the waist, an outsized female figure as awful as a classical Zeus. Her dead eyes staring into nothing. At first She is majestic; then I notice that Her cheekbones are too broad, Her eyes set at different levels, that Her whole figure is a jumble of badly matching planes, a mass of inhuman contradictions. There is also a distinct resemblance to Dunyasha Bernadettesdaughter, also known as the Playful Philosopher (A.C. 344–426), although God is older than Bernadettesdaughter and it's possible that Dunyasha's genetic surgeon modeled her after God instead of the other way round.

Persons who look at the statue longer than I did have reported that one cannot pin it down at all, that She is a constantly changing contradiction, that She becomes in turn gentle, terrifying, hateful, loving, "stupid" (or "dead"), and finally indescribable.

Persons who look at Her longer than that have been known to vanish right off the face of the Earth.

12

I study my Whileawayan hostess's blue-black hair and velvety brown eyes, her heavy, obstinate chin. Her waist is too long (like a flexible mermaid's), her solid thighs and buttocks surprisingly sturdy. She gets a lot of praise in Whileaway because of her big behind. She is modestly interesting, like everything else in this world formed for the long acquaintance and the close view; they work outdoors in their pink or gray pajamas and indoors in the nude until you know every wrinkle and fold of flesh, until your body's in a common medium with theirs, and there are no pictures made out of anybody or anything; everything becomes translated instantly into its own inside. Whileaway is the inside of everything else. I sleep in the Belins' common room for three weeks, surrounded by people with names like Nofretari Ylayesdaughter and Nguna Twasdaughter. One little girl decides I need a protector and sticks by me, trying to learn English. She takes me into the kitchen, which is a storytelling place.

My hostess translates, speaking softly and precisely:

"Once upon a time there was a child who was raised by bears. Her mother went up into the woods pregnant and gave birth there, for she had made an error in reckoning. Also, she had got lost. Why she was in the woods doesn't matter. It is not germane to this story.

"Well, if you must know, the mother was up there to shoot bears for a zoo. She had captured three bears and shot eighteen but she was running out of film; and when she went into labor she let the three bears go, for she didn't know how long the labor would last and there was nobody to feed the bears. They stayed around, though, because they had never seen a human being give birth before and they were curious. Everything went fine until the baby's head came out, and then the Spirit of Chance, who is very mischievous and clever, decided to have some fun. So right after the baby came out, it sent a rockslide down the mountain, cut the umbilical cord, and knocked the mother to one side. And then it made an earthquake which separated the mother and the baby by miles and miles, like the Great Canyon in South Continent."

"Isn't that going to a lot of trouble?" say I.

"Do you want to hear this story or don't you? *I* say they were separated by miles and miles. When the mother saw this, she said, 'Damn!' Then she went back to civilization to get a search party together, but by then the bears had adopted the baby and all of them were hidden up above the forty-ninth parallel. So the little girl grew up with the bears.

"When she was ten, there began to be trouble. She had some bear friends by then, although she didn't like to walk on all fours as the bears did and the bears didn't like that, because bears are very conservative. She argued that walking on all fours didn't suit her skeletal development. The bears said, 'Oh, but we have always walked this way.' They were pretty stupid. But nice, I mean. Anyway, she walked upright, the way it felt best, but when it came to copulation, that was another matter. The little girl wanted to try it with her male-best-bear-friend (for animals do not live the way people do, you know), but the he-bear would not even try. 'Alas,' he said (you can tell by that he is much more elegant than the other bears), 'I'm afraid I'd hurt you with my claws because you don't have the fur that she-bears have. And besides, you have trouble assuming the proper position because your back legs are too long. And besides *that*, you don't smell like a bear and I'm afraid my mother would say it was bestiality.' That's a joke. Actually it's race prejudice. Anyway, the little girl was very lonely and bored. Finally she browbeat her bear-mother into telling her about her origins, so she decided to go out and look for some people. So she said goodbye to her bear-friends and started south. The little girl was very hardy and woods-wise, since she had been taught by the bears. She traveled all day and slept all night. Finally she came to a settlement of people, just like this one, and they took her in. Of course she didn't speak people-talk" (with a sly glance at me), "and they didn't speak Bearish. This was a big problem. Eventually she learned their language so she could talk to them, and when they found out she had been raised by bears, they directed her to the Geddes Regional Park where she spent a great deal of time speaking Bearish to the scholars. She made friends and so had plenty of people to copulate with, but on moonlit nights she longed to be back with the bears, for she wanted to do the great bear dances, which bears do in the winter under the full moon. So eventually she went back north again. But the bears were a bore. So she decided to find her human mother. At the flats to Rabbit Island, she found a statue with an inscription that said, 'Go that way,' so she did. At the exit from the bridge to North Continent, she found an arrow sign that had been overturned, so she followed the new direction it pointed in. The Spirit of Chance was tracking her. At the entry to Green Bay, she found a huge goldfish bowl barring her way, which turned into the

Spirit of Chance, a very very old woman with tiny, dried-up legs, sitting on top of a wall. The wall stretched *all* the way across the forty-eighth parallel.

" 'Play cards with me,' said the Spirit of Chance.

" 'Not on your life,' said the little girl, who knew better.

"Then the Spirit of Chance winked and said, 'Aw, come on,' so the little girl thought it might be fun. She was just going to pick up her cards when she saw that the Spirit of Chance was wearing an induction helmet with a wire that stretched way back into the distance.

"The Spirit of Chance was connected to a computer!

" 'That's cheating!' cried the little girl angrily. She ran at the wall and they had an awful fight, but in the end everything melted away, leaving nothing but a lot of pebbles and sand, and afterward that melted away, too. Then the little girl went and found her real mother, who was a very smart, beautiful lady with fuzzy black hair combed out all round like electricity. But the mother had to go build a bridge (and fast, too), because the people couldn't get from one place to the other without the bridge. So the little girl went to school and had lots of lovers and friends, and practiced archery, and got into a family, and had lots of adventures, and saved everybody from a volcano by bombing it from the air in a glider, and achieved Enlightenment.

"Then one morning somebody told her there was a bear looking for her—"

"Wait a minute," I say, "this story doesn't have an end. It just goes on and on. What about the volcano? And the adventures? And the achieving Enlightenment—surely that takes some time, doesn't it?"

"I tell things," says my dignified little friend (through her interpreter), "the way they happen," and, slipping her head under her induction helmet, she goes back to stirring thirty bowls of blancmange.

She says, casually over her shoulder, "The story is about you, you know," and then (through my hostess, who finds this most amusing):

"Anyone who lives in two worlds at once is bound to lead a complicated life."

13

This is a story about a Whileawayan folk character called the Old Philosopher.

The Old Philosopher was sitting cross-legged among her disciples (as usual) when, without the slightest explanation, she put her fingers into her vagina, withdrew them, and asked, "What have I in my hand?"

The disciples all thought very deeply.

"Life," said one young woman.

"Power," said another.

"Housecleaning," said a third.

"The passing of time," said the fourth, "and the tragic irreversibility of organic truth."

The Old Whileawayan Philosopher hooted. She was immensely entertained by this passion for mythmaking. "Exercise your projective imaginations," she said, "on something that can't fight back," and, opening her hand, she showed them that her fingers were perfectly unstained by any blood whatever, partly because she was one hundred and three years old (and so long past the menopause) and partly because she had just died that morning. She then thumped her disciples severely about the head and shoulders with her crutch and vanished. Instantly two of the disciples achieved Enlightenment, the third became violently angry at the imposture and went to live as a hermit in the mountains, while the fourth—entirely disillusioned with philosophy, which she concluded was a game for crackpots—left philosophizing forever to undertake the dredging of silted-up harbors. Now, the moral of this story is that all images, ideals, pictures, and fanciful representations tend to vanish sooner or later unless they have the great good luck to be exuded from within, like bodily secretions or the bloom on the grape. That is, romance is bad for the mind.

Do not tell me about masculinity and femininity; do not tell me that enchanted frogs turn into princes, that frogesses under a spell turn into princesses. Why slander frogs? Princes and princesses are fools. They do nothing interesting in your stories. According to your history books, you passed through the stage of feudal social organization in Europe some time ago. Frogs, on the other hand, are covered with mucus, which they find delightful; they suffer agonies of passionate desire in the spring, in which the male will embrace a stick or your finger if he cannot get anything better; and they experience rapturous, metaphysical joy (of a froggy sort, to be sure) which shows plainly in their beautiful, chrysoberylline eyes.

How many princes or princesses can say as much?

14

I am a liar. I have never been to Whileaway.

Whileawayans breed into themselves an immunity to ticks, mosquitoes, midges, and parasites of all kinds. I have no such immunity. And the way into Whileaway is barred not by time, distance, or an angel with a flaming pen, but by a large cloud or crowd of gnats.

Two-legged, talking gnats.

(1975)

HARLAN ELLISON

STRANGE WINE

Two whipcord-lean California highway patrolmen supported Willis Kaw between them, leading him from the cruiser to the blanket-covered shape in the middle of the Pacific Coast Highway. The dark brown smear that began sixty yards west of the covered shape disappeared under the blanket. He heard one of the onlookers say, "She was thrown all that way, oh it's awful," and he didn't want them to show him his daughter.

But he had to make the identification, and one of the cops held him securely as the other went to one knee and pulled back the blanket. He recognized the jade pendant he had given her for graduation. It was all he recognized.

"That's Debbie," he said, and turned his head away.

Why is this happening to me, he thought. *I'm not from here; I'm not one of them. This should be happening to a human.*

"Did you take your shot?"

He looked up from the newspaper and had to ask her to repeat what she had said. "I asked you," Estelle said very softly, with as much kindness as she had left in her, "if you took your insulin." He smiled briefly, recognizing her concern and her attempt to avoid invading his sorrow, and he said he had taken the shot. His wife nodded and said, "Well, I think I'll go upstairs to bed. Are you coming?"

"Not right now. In a little, maybe."

"You'll fall asleep in front of the set again."

"Don't worry about it. I'll be up in a little while."

She stood watching him for a moment longer, then turned and climbed the stairs. He listened for the sounds of the upstairs ritual—the toilet flushing, the water moving through the pipes to the sink, the clothes closet door squeaking as it was opened, the bedsprings responding as Estelle put herself down for the night. And then he turned on the television set. He turned to Channel 30, one of the empty channels, and turned down the volume control so he did not have to hear the sound of coaxial "snow."

He sat in front of the set for several hours, his right hand flat against the picture tube, hoping the scanning pattern of the electron bombardment would reveal, through palm flesh grown transparent, the shape of alien bones.

In the middle of the week he asked Harvey Rothammer if he could have the day off Thursday so he could drive out to the hospital in Fontana to see his son. Rothammer was not particularly happy about it, but he didn't have the heart to refuse. Kaw had lost his daughter, and the son was still ninety-five percent incapacitated, lying in a therapy bed with virtually no hope of ever walking again. So he told Willis Kaw to take the day off, but not to forget that April was almost upon them and for a firm of certified public accountants it was rush season. Willis Kaw said he knew that.

The car broke down twenty miles east of San Dimas, and he sat behind the wheel, in the bludgeoning heat, staring at the desert and trying to remember what the surface of his home planet looked like.

His son, Gilvan, had gone on a vacation to visit friends in New Jersey the summer before. The friends had installed a free-standing swimming pool in the back yard. Gil had dived in and struck bottom; he had broken his back.

Fortunately, they had pulled him out before he could drown, but he was paralyzed from the waist down. He could move his arms, but not his hands. Willis had gone East, had arranged to have Gil flown back to California, and there he lay in a bed in Fontana.

He could remember only the color of the sky. It was a brilliant green, quite lovely. And things that were not birds, that skimmed instead of flying. More than that he could not remember.

The car was towed back to San Dimas, but the garage had to send off to Los Angeles for the necessary parts. He left the car and took a bus back home. He did not get to see Gil that week. The repair bill was two hundred and eighty-six dollars and forty-five cents.

That March the eleven-month drought in Southern California broke. Rain thundered down without end for a week; not as heavily as it does in Brazil, where the drops are so thick and come so close together that people have been known to suffocate if they walk out in the downpour. But heavily enough that the roof of the house sprang leaks. Willis Kaw and Estelle stayed up one entire night, stuffing towels against the baseboards in the living room; but the leaks from the roof apparently weren't over the outer walls but rather in low spots somewhere in the middle; the water was running down and triculating through.

The next morning, depressed beyond endurance, Willis Kaw began to cry. Estelle heard him as she was loading the soaking towels into the dryer, and ran into the living room. He was sitting on the wet carpet, the smell of mildew rising in the room, his hands over his face, still holding a wet bath towel. She knelt down beside him and took his head in her hands and kissed his forehead. He did not stop crying for a very long time, and when he did, his eyes burned.

"It only rains in the evening where I come from," he said to her. But she didn't know what he meant.

When she realized, later, she went for a walk, trying to decide if she could help her husband.

He went to the beach. He parked on the shoulder just off the Old Malibu Road, locked the car, and trotted down the embankment to the beach. He walked along the sand for an hour, picking up bits of milky glass worn smooth by the Pacific, and finally he lay down on the slope of a small, weed-thatched dune and went to sleep.

He dreamed of his home world and—perhaps because the sun was high and the ocean made eternal sounds—he was able to bring much of it back. The bright green sky, the skimmers swooping and rising overhead, the motes of pale yellow light that flamed and then floated up and were lost to sight. He felt himself in his real body, the movement of many legs working in unison, carrying him across the mist sands, the smell of alien flowers in his mind. He knew he had been born on that world, had been raised there, had grown to maturity and then . . .

Sent away.

In his human mind, Willis Kaw knew he had been sent away for doing something bad. He knew he had been condemned to this planet, this Earth, for having perhaps committed a crime. But he could not remember what it was. And in the dream he could feel no guilt.

But when he woke, his humanity came back and flooded over him and he felt guilt. And he longed to be back out there, where he belonged, not trapped in this terrible body.

"I didn't want to come to you," Willis Kaw said. "I think it's stupid. And if I come, then I admit there's room for doubt. And I don't doubt, so . . ."

The psychiatrist smiled and stirred the cup of cocoa. "And so . . . you came because your wife insisted."

"Yes." He stared at his shoes. They were brown shoes, he had owned them for three years. They had never fit properly; they pinched and made his big toe on each foot feel as if it were being pressed down by a knife edge, a dull knife edge.

The psychiatrist carefully placed the spoon on a piece of Kleenex, and sipped at his cocoa. "Look, Mr. Kaw, I'm open to suggestion. I don't want you to be here, nor do you *want* to be here, if it isn't going to help you. And," he added quickly, "by *help* you I don't mean convert you to any world view, any systematized belief, you choose to reject. I'm not entirely convinced, by Freud or Werner Erhard or Scientology or any other rigor, that there is such a thing as 'reality.' Codified reality. A given, an immutable, a constant. As long as what someone believes doesn't get him put in a madhouse or a prison, there's no reason why it should be less acceptable than what we, uh, 'straight folks' call reality. If it makes you happy, believe it. What I'd like to do is listen to what you have to say, perhaps offer a few comments, and then see if *your* reality is compatible with *straight folks'* reality.

"How does that sound to you?"

Willis Kaw tried to smile back. "It sounds fine. I'm a little nervous."

"Well, try not to be. That's easy for me to say and hard for you to do, but I mean you no harm; and I'm really quite interested."

Willis uncrossed his legs and stood up. "Is it all right if I just walk around the office a little? It'll help, I think." The psychiatrist nodded and smiled, and indicated the cocoa. Willis Kaw shook his head. He walked around the psychiatrist's office and finally said, "I don't belong in this body. I've been condemned to life as a human being, and it is killing me."

The psychiatrist asked him to explain.

Willis Kaw was a small man, with thinning brown hair and bad eyes. He had weak legs and constantly had need of a handkerchief. His face was set in lines of worry and sadness. He told the psychiatrist all this. Then he said, "I believe this planet is a place where bad people are sent to atone for their crimes. I believe that all of us come from other worlds; other planets where we have done something wrong. This Earth is a prison, and we're sent here to live in these awful bodies that decay and smell bad and run down and die. And that's our punishment."

"But why do *you* perceive such a condition, and no one else?" The psychiatrist had set aside the cocoa, and it was growing cold.

"This must be a defective body they've put me in," Willis Kaw said. "Just a little extra pain, knowing I'm an alien, knowing I'm serving a prison sentence for something I did, something I can't remember; but it must have been an awful thing for me to have drawn such a sentence."

"Have you ever read Franz Kafka, Mr. Kaw?"

"No."

"He wrote books about people who were on trial for crimes the nature of which they never learned. People who were guilty of sins they didn't know they had committed."

"Yes. I feel that way. Maybe Kafka felt that way; maybe he had a defective body, too."

"What you're feeling isn't that strange, Mr. Kaw," the psychiatrist said. "We have many people these days who are dissatisfied with their lives, who find out—perhaps too late—that they are transsexual, that they should have been living their days as something else, a man, a woman—"

"No, no! That isn't what I mean. I'm not a candidate for a sex change. I'm telling you I come from a world with a green sky, with mist sand and light motes that flame and then float up . . . I have many legs, and webs between the digits and they aren't fingers . . . " He stopped and looked embarrassed.

Then he sat down and spoke very softly. "Doctor, my life is like everyone else's life. I'm sick much of the time, I have bills I cannot pay, my daughter was struck by a car and killed and I cannot bear to think about it. My son was cut off in the prime of his life and he'll be a cripple from now on. My wife and I don't talk much, we don't love each other . . . if we ever did. I'm no better and no worse than anyone else on this planet and *that's* what I'm talking about: the pain, the anguish, the living in terror. Terror of each day. Hopeless. Empty. Is this the best a person can have, this terrible life here as a human being? I tell you there are better places, other worlds where the torture of being a human being doesn't exist!"

It was growing dark in the psychiatrist's office. Willis Kaw's wife had made the appointment for him at the last moment and the doctor had taken the little man with the thinning brown hair as a fill-in, at the end of the day.

"Mr. Kaw," the psychiatrist said, "I've listened to all you've said, and I want you to know that I'm very much in sympathy with your fears." Willis Kaw felt relieved. He felt at last someone might be able to help him. If not to relieve him of this terrible knowledge and its weight, at least to tell him he wasn't alone. "And frankly, Mr. Kaw," the psychiatrist said, "I think you're a man with a very serious problem. You're a sick man and you need intense psychiatric help. I'll talk to your wife if you like, but if you take my advice, you'll have yourself placed in a proper institution before this condition . . . "

Willis Kaw closed his eyes.

He pulled down the garage door tight and stuffed the cracks with rags. He could not find a hose long enough to feed back into the car from the tail pipe, so he merely opened the car windows and started the engine and let it run. He sat in the back seat and tried to read Dickens' *Dombey and Son,* a book Gil had once told him he would enjoy.

But he couldn't keep his attention on the story, on the elegant language, and after a while he let his head fall back, and he tried to sleep, to dream of the other world that had been stolen from him, the world he knew he would never again see. Finally, sleep took him, and he died.

The funeral service was held at Forest Lawn, and very few people came. It was a weekday. Estelle cried, and Harvey Rothammer held her and told her it was okay. But he was checking his wristwatch over her shoulder, because April was almost upon him.

And Willis Kaw was put down in the warm ground, and the dirt of an alien planet was dumped in on him by a Chicano with three children who was forced to moonlight as a dishwasher in a bar and grill because he simply couldn't meet the payments on his six-piece living room suite if he didn't.

The many-legged Consul greeted Willis Kaw when he returned. He turned over and looked up at the Consul and saw the bright green sky above. "Welcome back, Plydo," the Consul said.

He looked very sad.

Plydo, who had been Willis Kaw on a faraway world, got to his feet and looked around. Home.

But he could not keep silent and enjoy the moment. He had to know. "Consul, please . . . tell me . . . what did I do that was so terrible?"

"Terrible!" The Consul seemed stunned. "We owe you nothing but honor, your grace. Your name is valued above all others." There was deep reverence in his words.

"Then why was I condemned to live in anguish on that other world? Why was I sent away to exist in torment?"

The Consul shook his hairy head, and his mane billowed in the warm breeze. "No, your grace, no! Anguish is what *we* suffer. Torment is all *we* know. Only a few, only a very few honored and loved among all the races of the universe can go to that world. Life there is sweet compared to what passes for life everywhere else. You are still disoriented. It will all come back to you. You will remember. And you will understand."

And Plydo, who had been, in a better part of his almost eternal life of pain, Willis Kaw, *did* remember. As time passed, he recalled all the eternities of sadness that had been born in him, and he knew that they had given him the only gift of joy permitted to the races of beings who lived in the far galaxies. The gift of a few precious years on a world where anguish was so much less than that known everywhere else.

He remembered the rain, and the sleep, and the feel of beach sand beneath his feet, and ocean rolling in to whisper its eternal song, and on just such nights as those he had despised on Earth, he slept and dreamed good dreams.

Of life as Willis Kaw, life on the pleasure planet.

(1976)

JOHN VARLEY

Lollipop and the Tar Baby

"*Zzzz*ello. *Zzz.* Hello. Hello." Someone was speaking to Xanthia from the end of a ten-kilometer metal pipe, shouting to be heard across a roomful of gongs and cymbals being knocked over by angry giant bees. She had never heard such interference.

"Hello?" she repeated. "What are you doing on my wavelength?"

"Hello." The interference was still there, but the voice was slightly more distinct. "Wavelength. Searching, searching wavelength . . . get best reception with . . . Hello? Listening?"

"Yes, I'm listening. You're talking over . . . my radio isn't even . . ." She banged the radio panel with her palm in the ancient ritual humans employ when their creations are being balky. "My goddamn *radio* isn't even on. Did you know that?" It was a relief to feel anger boiling up inside her. Anything was preferable to feeling lost and silly.

"Not necessary."

"What do you mean, not—who *are* you?"

"Who. Having . . . *I'm,* pronoun, yes, I'm having difficulty. Bear with. Me? Yes, pronoun. Bear with me. I'm not who. What. *What* am I?"

"All right. *What* are you?"

"Spacetime phenomenon. I'm gravity and causality-sink. Black hole."

Xanthia did not need black holes explained to her. She had spent her entire eighteen years hunting them, along with her clone-sister, Zoetrope. But she was not used to having them talk to her.

"Assuming for the moment that you really are a black hole," she said, beginning to wonder if this might be some elaborate trick played on her by Zoe, "just taking that as a tentative hypothesis—how are you able to talk to me?"

There was a sound like an attitude thruster going off, a rumbling pop. It was repeated.

"I manipulate spacetime framework . . . no, please hold line . . . *the* line. I manipulate the spacetime framework with controlled gravity waves projected in narrow . . . a narrow cone. I direct at the speaker in your radio. You hear. Me."

"What was that again?" It sounded like a lot of crap to her.

"I elaborate. I will elaborate. I cut through space itself, through—hold the line, hold the line, reference." There was a sound like a tape reeling rapidly through playback heads. "This is the BBC," said a voice that was recognizably human, but blurred by static. The tape whirred again. "gust the third, in the year of our Lord nineteen fifty-seven. Today in—" Once again the tape hunted.

"chelson-Morley experiment disproved the existence of the ether, by ingeniously arranging a rotating prism—" Then the metallic voice was back.

"Ether. I cut through space itself, through a—hold the line." This time the process was shorter. She heard a fragment of what sounded like a video adventure serial. "Through a spacewarp made through the ductile etheric continuum—"

"Hold on there. That's not what you said before."

"I was elaborating."

"Go on. Wait, what were you doing? With that tape business?"

The voice paused, and when the answer came the line had cleared up quite a bit. But the voice still didn't sound human. Computer?

"I am not used to speech. No need for it. But I have learned your language by listening to radio transmissions. I speak to you through use of indeterminate statistical concatenations. Gravity waves and probability, which is not the same thing in a causality singularity, enables a nonrational event to take place."

"Zoe, this is really you, isn't it?"

Xanthia was only eighteen Earth-years old, on her first long orbit into the space beyond Pluto, the huge cometary zone where space is truly flat. Her whole life had been devoted to learning how to find and capture black holes, but one didn't come across them very often. Xanthia had been born a year after the beginning of the voyage and had another year to go before the end of it. In her whole life she had seen and talked to only one other human being, and that was Zoe, who was one hundred and thirty-five years old and her identical twin.

Their home was the *Shirley Temple,* a fifteen thousand tonne fusion-drive ship registered out of Lowell, Pluto. Zoe owned *Shirley* free and clear; on her first trip, many years ago, she had found a scale-five hole and had become instantly rich. Most hole hunters were not so lucky.

Zoe was also unusual in that she seemed to thrive on solitude. Most hunters who made a strike settled down to live in comfort, buy a large company or put the money into safe investments and live off the interest. They were unwilling or unable to face another twenty years alone. Zoe had gone out again, and a third time after the second trip had proved fruitless. She had found a hole on her third trip, and was now almost through her fifth.

But for some reason she had never adequately explained to Xanthia, she had wanted a companion this time. And what better company than herself? With the medical facilities aboard *Shirley* she had grown a copy of herself and raised the little girl as her daughter.

Xanthia squirmed around in the control cabin of *The Good Ship Lollipop,* stuck her head through the hatch leading to the aft exercise room, and found nothing. What she had expected, she didn't know. Now she crouched in midair with a screwdriver, attacking the service panels that protected the radio assembly.

"What are you doing by yourself?" the voice asked.

"Why don't *you* tell *me,* Zoe?" she said, lifting the panel off and tossing it angrily to one side. She peered into the gloomy interior, wrinkling her nose at the smell of oil and paraffin. She shone her pencil-beam into the space, flicking it from one component to the next, all as familiar to her as neighborhood corridors would be to a planet-born child. There was nothing out of place, nothing that shouldn't be there. Most of it was sealed into plastic blocks to prevent moisture or dust from getting to critical circuits. There were no signs of tampering.

"I am failing to communicate. I am not your mother, I am a gravity and causality—"

"She's not my mother," Xanthia snapped.

"My records show that she would dispute you."

Xanthia didn't like the way the voice said that. But she was admitting to herself that there was no way Zoe could have set this up. That left her with the alternative: she really was talking to a black hole.

"She's not my mother," Xanthia repeated. "And if you've been listening in, you *know* why I'm out here in a lifeboat. So why do you ask?"

"I wish to help you. I have heard tension building between the two of you these last years. You are growing up."

Xanthia settled back in the control chair. Her head did not feel so good.

Hole hunting was a delicate economic balance, a tightrope walked between the needs of survival and the limitations of mass. The initial investment was tremendous and the return was undependable, so the potential hole hunter had to have a line to a source of speculative credit or be independently wealthy.

No consortium or corporation had been able to turn a profit at the business by going at it in a big way. The government of Pluto maintained a monopoly on the use of one-way robot probes, but they had found over the years that when a probe succeeded in finding a hole, a race usually developed to see who would reach it and claim it first. Ships sent after such holes had a way of disappearing in the resulting fights, far from law and order.

The demand for holes was so great that an economic niche remained which was filled by the solitary prospector, backed by people with tax write-offs to gain. Prospectors had a ninety per cent bankruptcy rate. But as with gold and oil in earlier days, the potential profits were huge, so there was never a lack of speculators.

Hole hunters would depart Pluto and accelerate to the limits of engine power, then coast for ten to fifteen years, keeping an eye on the mass detector. Sometimes they would be half a light-year from Sol before they had to decelerate and turn around. Less mass equalled more range, so the solitary hunter was the rule.

Teaming of ships had been tried, but teams that discovered a hole seldom came back together. One of them tended to have an accident. Hole hunters were a greedy lot, self-centered and self-sufficient.

Equipment had to be reliable. Replacement parts were costly in terms of mass, so the hole hunter had to make an agonizing choice with each item. Would it be better to leave it behind and chance a possibly fatal failure, or take it along, decreasing the range, and maybe miss the glory hole that is sure to be lurking just one more AU away? Hole hunters learned to be handy at repairing, jury-rigging, and bashing, because in twenty years even fail-safe triplicates can be on their last legs.

Zoe had sweated over her faulty mass detector before she admitted it was beyond her skills. Her primary detector had failed ten years into the voyage, and the second one had begun to act up six years later. She tried to put together one functioning detector with parts cannibalized from both. She nursed it along for a year with the equivalents of bobby pins and bubblegum. It was hopeless.

But *Shirley Temple* was a palace among prospecting ships. Having found two holes in her career, Zoe had her own money. She had stocked spare parts, beefed up the drive, even included that incredible luxury, a lifeboat.

The lifeboat was sheer extravagance, except for one thing. It had a mass detector as part of its astrogational equipment. She had bought it mainly for that reason, since it had only an eighteen-month range and would be useless except at the beginning and end of the trip, when they were close to Pluto. It made extensive use of plug-in components, sealed in plastic to prevent tampering or accidents caused by inexperienced passengers. The mass detector on board did not have the range or accuracy of the one on *Shirley.* It could be removed or replaced, but not recalibrated.

They had begun a series of three-month loops out from the mother ship. Xanthia had flown most of them earlier, when Zoe did not trust her to run *Shirley.* Later they had alternated.

"And that's what I'm doing out here by myself," Xanthia said. "I have to get out beyond ten million kilometers from *Shirley* so its mass doesn't affect the detector. My instrument is calibrated to ignore only the mass of this ship, not *Shirley.* I stay out here for three months, which is a reasonably safe time for the life systems on *Lollipop,* and time to get pretty lonely. Then back for refueling and supplying."

"The *Lollipop*?"

Xanthia blushed. "Well, I named this lifeboat that, after I started spending so much time on it. We have a tape of Shirley Temple in the library, and she sang this song, see—"

"Yes, I've heard it. I've been listening to radio for a very long time. So you no longer believe this is a trick by your mother?"

"She's *not* . . . " Then she realized she had referred to Zoe in the third person again.

"I don't know what to think," she said, miserably. "Why are you doing this?"

"I sense that you are still confused. You'd like some proof that I am what I say I am. Since you'll think of it in a minute, I might as well ask you this question. Why do you suppose I haven't yet registered on your mass detector?"

Xanthia jerked in her seat, then was brought up short by the straps. It was true, there was not the slightest wiggle on the dials of the detector.

"All right, why haven't you?" She felt a sinking sensation. She was sure the punchline came now, after she'd shot off her mouth about *Lollipop*—her secret from Zoe—and made such a point of the fact that Zoe was not her mother. It was her own private rebellion, one that she had not had the nerve to face Zoe with. Now she's going to reveal herself and tell me how she did it, and I'll feel like a fool, she thought.

"It's simple," the voice said. "You weren't in range of me yet. But now you are. Take a look."

The needles were dancing, giving the reading of a scale-seven hole. A scale seven would mass about a tenth as much as the asteroid Ceres.

"Mommy, what *is* a black hole?"

The little girl was seven years old. One day she would call herself Xanthia, but she had not yet felt the need for a name and her mother had not seen fit to give her one. Zoe reasoned that you needed two of something before you needed names. There was only one other person on *Shirley.* There was no possible confusion. When the girl thought about it at all, she assumed her name must be Hey, or Darling.

She was a small child, as Zoe had been. She was recapitulating the growth Zoe had already been through a hundred years ago. Though she didn't know it, she was pretty: dark eyes with an oriental fold, dark skin, and kinky blond hair. She was a genetic mix of Chinese and Negro, with dabs of other races thrown in for seasoning.

"I've tried to explain that before," Zoe said. "You don't have the math for it yet. I'll get you started on spacetime equations, then in about a year you'll be able to understand."

"But I want to know now." Black holes were a problem for the child. From her earliest memories the two of them had done nothing but hunt them, yet they never found one. She'd been doing a lot of reading—there was little else to do—and was wondering if they might inhabit the same category where she had tentatively placed Santa Claus and leprechauns.

"If I try again, will you go to sleep?"

"I promise."

So Zoe launched into her story about the Big Bang, the time in the long-ago when little black holes could be formed.

"As far as we can tell, all the little black holes like the ones we hunt were made in that time. Nowadays other holes can be formed by the collapse of very large stars. When the fires burn low and the pressures that are trying to blow the star apart begin to fade, gravity takes over and starts to pull the star in on itself." Zoe waved her hands in the air, forming cups to show bending space, flailing out to indicate pressures of fusion. These explanations were almost as difficult for her as stories of sex had been for earlier generations. The truth was that she was no relativist and didn't really grasp the slightly incredible premises behind black-hole theory. She suspected that no one could really visualize one, and if you can't do that, where are you? But she was practical enough not to worry about it.

"And what's gravity? I forgot." The child was rubbing her eyes to stay awake. She struggled to understand but already knew she would miss the point yet another time.

"Gravity is the thing that holds the universe together. The glue, or the rivets. It pulls everything toward everything else, and it takes energy to fight it and overcome it. It feels like when we boost the ship, remember I pointed that out to you?"

"Like when everything wants to move in the same direction?"

"That's right. So we have to be careful, because we don't think about it much. We have to worry about where things are because when we boost, everything will head for the stern. People on planets have to worry about that all the time. They have to put something strong between themselves and the center of the planet, or they'll go down."

"Down." The girl mused over that word, one that had been giving her trouble as long as she could remember, and thought she might finally have understood it. She had seen pictures of places where down was always the same direction, and they were strange to the eye. They were full of tables to put things on, chairs to sit in, and funny containers with no tops. Five of the six walls of rooms on planets could hardly be used at all. One, the "floor," was called on to take all the use.

"So they use their legs to fight gravity with?" She was yawning now.

"Yes. You've seen pictures of the people with the funny legs. They're not so funny when you're in gravity. Those flat things on the ends are called feet. If they had peds like us, they wouldn't be able to walk so good. They always have to have one foot touching the floor, or they'd fall toward the surface of the planet."

Zoe tightened the strap that held the child to her bunk, and fastened the velcro patch on the blanket to the side of the sheet, tucking her in. Kids needed a warm snug place to sleep. Zoe preferred to float free in her own bedroom, tucked into a fetal position and drifting.

"G'night, Mommy."

"Good night. You get some sleep, and don't worry about black holes."

But the child dreamed of them, as she often did. They kept tugging at her, and she would wake breathing hard and convinced that she was going to fall into the wall in front of her.

"You don't mean it? I'm rich!"

Xanthia looked away from the screen. It was no good pointing out that Zoe had always spoken of the trip as a partnership. She owned *Shirley* and *Lollipop.*

"Well, you too, of course. Don't think you won't be getting a real big share of the money. I'm going to set you up so well that you'll be able to buy a ship of your own, and raise little copies of yourself if you want to."

Xanthia was not sure that was her idea of heaven, but said nothing.

"Zoe, there's a problem, and I . . . well, I was—" But she was interrupted again by Zoe, who would not hear Xanthia's comment for another thirty seconds.

"The first data is coming over the telemetry channel right now, and I'm feeding it into the computer. Hold on a second while I turn the ship. I'm going to start decelerating in about one minute, based on these figures. You get the refined data to me as soon as you have it."

There was a brief silence.

"What problem?"

"It's talking to me, Zoe. The hole is talking to me."

This time the silence was longer than the minute it took the radio signal to make the round trip between ships. Xanthia furtively thumbed the contrast knob, turning her sister-mother down until the screen was blank. She could look at the camera and Zoe wouldn't know the difference.

Damn, damn, she thinks I've flipped. But I *had* to tell her.

"I'm not sure what you mean."

"Just what I *said.* I don't understand it, either. But it's been talking to me for the last hour, and it says the *damnedest* things."

There was another silence.

"All right. When you get there, don't do anything, repeat, *anything,* until I arrive. Do you understand?"

"Zoe, I'm not crazy. I'm *not.*"

Then why am I crying?

"Of course you're not, baby, there's an explanation for this and I'll find out what it is as soon as I get there. You just hang on. My first rough estimate puts me alongside you about three hours after you're stationary relative to the hole."

Shirley and *Lollipop,* traveling parallel courses, would both be veering from their straight-line trajectories to reach the hole. But Xanthia was closer to it; Zoe would have to move at a more oblique angle and would be using more fuel. Xanthia thought four hours was more like it.

"I'm signing off," Zoe said. "I'll call you back as soon as I'm in the groove."

Xanthia hit the off button on the radio and furiously unbuckled her seatbelt. Damn Zoe, damn her, damn her, *damn her.* Just sit tight, she says. I'll be there to explain the unexplainable. It'll be all right.

She knew she should start her deceleration, but there was something she must do first.

She twisted easily in the air, grabbing at braces with all four hands, and dived through the hatch to the only other living space in *Lollipop*: the exercise area. It was cluttered with equipment that she had neglected to fold into the walls, but she didn't mind; she liked close places. She squirmed through the maze like a fish gliding through coral, until she reached the wall she was looking for. It had been taped over with discarded manual pages, the only paper she could find on *Lollipop.* She started ripping at the paper, wiping tears from her cheeks with one ped as she worked. Beneath the paper was a mirror.

How to test for sanity? Xanthia had not considered the question; the thing to do had simply presented itself and she had done it. Now she confronted the mirror and searched for . . . what? Wild eyes? Froth on the lips?

What she saw was her mother.

Xanthia's life had been a process of growing slowly into the mold Zoe represented. She had known her pug nose would eventually turn down. She had known what baby fat would melt away. Her breasts had grown just into the small cones she knew from her mother's body and no farther.

She hated looking in mirrors.

Xanthia and Zoe were small women. Their most striking feature was the frizzy dandelion of yellow hair, lighter than their bodies. When the time had come for naming, the young clone had almost opted for Dandelion until she came upon the word *xanthic* in a dictionary. The radio call-letters for *Lollipop* happened to be X-A-N, and the word was too good to resist. She knew, too, that Orientals were thought of as having yellow skin, though she could not see why.

Why had she come here, of all places? She strained toward the mirror, fighting her repulsion, searching her face for signs of insanity. The narrow eyes were a little puffy, and as deep and expressionless as ever. She put her hands to the glass, startled in the silence to hear the multiple clicks as the long nails just missed touching the ones on the other side. She was always forgetting to trim them.

Sometimes, in mirrors, she knew she was not seeing herself. She could twitch her mouth, and the image would not move. She could smile, and the image would frown. It had been happening for two years, as her body put the finishing touches on its eighteen-year process of duplicating Zoe. She had not spoken of it, because it scared her.

"And this is where I come to see if I'm sane," she said aloud, noting that the lips in the mirror did not move. "Is she going to start talking to me now?" She waved her arms wildly, and so did Zoe in the mirror. At least it wasn't that bad yet; it was only the details that failed to match: the small movements, and especially the facial expressions. Zoe was inspecting her dispassionately and did not seem to like what she saw. That small curl at the edge of the mouth, the almost brutal narrowing of the eyes . . .

Xanthia clapped her hands over her face, then peeked out through the fingers. Zoe was peeking out, too. Xanthia began rounding up the drifting scraps of paper and walling her twin in again with new bits of tape.

The beast with two backs and legs at each end writhed, came apart, and resolved into Xanthia and Zoe, drifting, breathing hard. They caromed off the walls like monkeys, giving up their energy, gradually getting breath back under control. Golden, wet hair and sweaty skin brushed against each other again and again as they came to rest.

Now the twins floated in the middle of the darkened bedroom. Zoe was already asleep, tumbling slowly with that total looseness possible only in free fall. Her leg rubbed against Xanthia's belly and her relative motion stopped. The leg was moist. The room was close, thick with the smell of passion. The recirculators whined quietly as they labored to clear the air.

Pushing one finger gently against Zoe's ankle, Xanthia turned her until they were face to face. Frizzy blonde hair tickled her nose, and she felt warm breath on her mouth.

Why can't it always be like this?

"You're not my mother," she whispered. Zoe had no reaction to this heresy. "You're *not.*"

Only in the last year had Zoe admitted the relationship was much closer. Xanthia was now fifteen.

And what was different? Something, there had to be something beyond the mere knowledge that they were not mother and child. There was a new quality in their relationship, growing as they came to the end of the voyage. Xanthia would look into those eyes where she had seen love and now see only blankness, coldness.

"Oriental inscrutability?" she asked herself, half-seriously. She knew she was hopelessly unsophisticated. She had spent her life in a society of two. The only other person she knew had her own face. But she had thought she knew Zoe. Now she felt less confident with every glance into Zoe's face and every kilometer passed on the way to Pluto.

Pluto.

Her thoughts turned gratefully away from immediate problems and toward that unimaginable place. She would be there in only four more years. The cultural adjustments she would have to make were staggering. Thinking about that, she felt a sensation in her chest that she guessed was her heart leaping in anticipation. That's what happened to characters in tapes when they got excited, anyway. Their hearts were forever leaping, thudding, aching, or skipping beats.

She pushed away from Zoe and drifted slowly to the viewport. Her old friends were all out there, the only friends she had ever known, the stars. She greeted them all one by one, reciting childhood mnemonic riddles and rhymes like bedtime prayers.

It was a funny thought that the view from her window would terrify many of those strangers she was going to meet on Pluto. She'd read that many tunnel-raised people could not stand open spaces. What it was that scared them, she could not understand. The things that scared her were crowds, gravity, males, and mirrors.

"Oh, damn. Damn! I'm going to be just *hopeless.* Poor little idiot girl from the sticks, visiting the big city." She brooded for a time on all the thousands of things she had never done, from swimming in the gigantic underground disneylands to seducing a boy.

"To *being* a boy." It had been the source of their first big argument. When Xanthia had reached adolescence, the time when children want to begin experimenting, she had learned from Zoe that *Shirley Temple* did not carry the medical equipment for sex changes. She was doomed to spend her critical formative years as a sexual deviate, a unisex.

"It'll stunt me forever," she had protested. She had been reading a lot of pop psychology at the time.

"Nonsense," Zoe had responded, hard-pressed to explain why she had not stocked a viro-genetic imprinter and the companion Y-alyzer. Which, as Xanthia pointed out, *any* self-respecting home surgery kit should have.

"The human race got along for millions of years without sex changing," Zoe had said. "Even after the Invasion. We were a highly technological race for hundreds of years before changing. Billions of people lived and died in the same sex."

"Yeah, and look what they were like."

Now, for another of what seemed like an endless series of nights, sleep was eluding her. There was the worry of Pluto, and the worry of Zoe and her strange behavior, and no way to explain anything in her small universe which had become unbearably complicated in the last years.

I wonder what it would be like with a man?

Three hours ago Xanthia had brought *Lollipop* to a careful rendezvous with the point in space her instruments indicated contained a black hole. She had long since understood that even if she ever found one she would never see it, but she could not restrain herself from squinting into the starfield for some evidence. It was silly; though the hole massed ten to the fifteenth tonnes (the original estimate had been off one order of magnitude) it was still only a fraction of a millimeter in diameter. She was staying a good safe hundred kilometers from it. Still, you ought to be able to sense something like that, you ought to be able to *feel* it.

It was no use. This hunk of space looked exactly like any other.

"There is a point I would like explained," the hole said. "What will be done with me after you have captured me?"

The question surprised her. She still had not got around to thinking of the voice as anything but some annoying aberration like her face in the mirror. How was she supposed to deal with it? Could she admit to herself that it existed, that it might even have feelings?

"I guess we'll just mark you, in the computer, that is. You're too big for us to haul back to Pluto. So we'll hang around you for a week or so, refining your trajectory until we know precisely where you're going to be, then we'll leave you. We'll make some maneuvers on the way in so no one could retrace our path and find out where you are, because they'll know we found a big one when we get back."

"How will they know that?"

"Because we'll be renting . . . well, *Zoe* will be chartering one of those bit monster tugs, and she'll come out here and put a charge on you and tow you . . . say, how do you feel about this?"

"Are you concerned with the answer?"

The more Xanthia thought about it, the less she liked it. If she really was not hallucinating this experience, then she was contemplating the capture and imprisonment of a sentient being. An innocent sentient being who had been wandering around the edge of the system, suddenly to find him or herself . . .

"Do you have a sex?"

"No."

"All right, I guess I've been kind of short with you. It's just because you *did* startle me, and I *didn't* expect it, and it was all a little alarming."

The hole said nothing.

"You're a strange sort of person, or whatever," she said.

Again there was a silence.

"Why don't you tell me more about yourself? What's it like being a black hole, and all that?" She still couldn't fight down the ridiculous feeling those words gave her.

"I live much as you do, from day to day. I travel from star to star, taking about ten million years for the trip. Upon arrival, I plunge through the core of the star. I do this as often as is necessary, then I depart by a slingshot maneuver through the heart of a massive planet. The Tunguska Meteorite, which hit Siberia in 1908, was a black hole gaining momentum on its way to Jupiter, where it could get the added push needed for solar escape velocity."

One thing was bothering Xanthia. "What do you mean, 'as often as is necessary'?"

"Usually five or six thousand passes is sufficient."

"No, no. What I meant is *why* is it necessary? What do you get out of it?"

"Mass," the hole said. "I need to replenish my mass. The Relativity Laws state that nothing can escape from a black hole, but the Quantum Laws, specifically the Heisenberg Uncertainty Principle, state that below a certain radius the position of a particle cannot be determined. I lose mass constantly through tunneling. It is not all wasted, as I am able to control the direction and form of the escaping mass, and to use the energy that results to perform functions that your present-day physics says are impossible."

"Such as?" Xanthia didn't know why, but she was getting nervous.

"I can exchange inertia for gravity, and create energy in a variety of ways."

"So you can move yourself."

"Slowly."

"And you eat . . . "

"Anything."

Xanthia felt a sudden panic, but she didn't know what was wrong. She glanced down at her instruments and felt her hair prickle from her wrists and ankles to the nape of her neck.

The hole was ten kilometers closer than it had been.

"How could you *do* that to me?" Xanthia raged. "I trusted you, and that's how you repaid me, by trying to sneak up on me and . . . and—"

"It was not intentional. I speak to you by means of controlled gravity waves. To speak to you at all, it is necessary to generate an attractive force between us. You were never in any danger."

"I don't believe that," Xanthia said angrily. "I think you're doubletalking me. I don't think gravity works like that, and I don't think you really tried very hard to tell me how you talk to me, back when we first started." It occurred to her now, also, that the hole was speaking much more fluently than in the beginning. Either it was a very fast learner, or that had been intentional.

The hole paused. "This is true," it said.

She pressed her advantage. "Then why did you do it?"

"It was a reflex, like blinking in a bright light, or drawing one's hand back from a fire. When I sense matter, I am attracted to it."

"The proper cliché would be 'like a moth to a flame.' But you're not a moth, and I'm not a flame. I don't believe you. I think you could have stopped yourself if you wanted to."

Again the hole hesitated. "You are correct."

"So you were trying to . . . ?"

"I was trying to eat you."

"Just like *that*? Eat someone you've been having a conversation with?"

"Matter is matter," the hole said, and Xanthia thought she detected a defensive note in its voice.

"What do you think of what I said we're going to do with you? You were going to tell me, but we got off on that story about where you came from."

"As I understand it, you propose to return for me. I will be towed to near Pluto's orbit, sold, and eventually come to rest in the heart of an orbital power station, where your species will feed matter into my gravity well, extracting power cheaply from the gravitational collapse."

"Yeah, that's pretty much it."

"It sounds ideal. My life is struggle. Failing to find matter to consume would mean loss of mass until I am smaller than an atomic nucleus. The loss rate would increase exponentially, and my universe would disappear. I do not know what would happen beyond that point. I have never wished to find out."

How much could she trust this thing? Could it move very rapidly? She toyed with the idea of backing off still further. The two of them were now motionless relative to each other, but they were both moving slowly away from the location she had given Zoe.

It didn't make sense to think it could move in on her fast. If it could, why hadn't it? Then it could eat her and wait for Zoe to arrive—Zoe, who was helpless to detect the hole with her broken mass detector.

She should relay the new vectors to Zoe. She tried to calculate where her twin would arrive, but was distracted by the hole speaking.

"I would like to speak to you now of what I initially contacted you for. Listening to Pluto radio, I have become aware of certain facts that you should know, if, as I suspect, you are not already aware of them. Do you know of Clone Control Regulations?"

"No, what are they?" Again, she was afraid without knowing why.

The genetic statutes, according to the hole, were the soul of simplicity. For three hundred years, people had been living just about forever. It had become necessary to limit the population. Even if everyone had only one child—the Birthright—population would still grow. For a while, clones had been a loophole. No more. Now, only one person had the right to any one set of genes. If two possessed them, one was excess, and was summarily executed.

"Zoe has prior property rights to her genetic code," the hole concluded. "This is backed up by a long series of court decisions."

"So I'm—"

"Excess."

Zoe met her at the airlock as Xanthia completed the docking maneuver. She was smiling, and Xanthia felt the way she always did when Zoe smiled these days: like a puppy being scratched behind the ears. They kissed, then Zoe held her at arm's length.

"Let me look at you. Can it only be three months? You've *grown,* my baby."

Xanthia blushed. "I'm not a baby anymore, Mother." But she was happy. Very happy.

"No, I should say not." She touched one of Xanthia's breasts, then turned her around slowly. "I should say not. Putting on a little weight in the hips, aren't we?"

"And the bosom. One inch while I was gone. I'm almost there." And it was true. At sixteen, the young clone was almost a woman.

"Almost there," Zoe repeated, and glanced away from her twin. But she hugged her again, and they kissed, and began to laugh as the tension was released.

They made love, not once and then to bed, but many times, feasting on each other. One of them remarked—Xanthia could not remember who because it seemed so accurate that either of them might have said it—that the only good thing about these three-month separations was the homecoming.

"You did very well," Zoe said, floating in the darkness and sweet exhausted atmosphere of their bedroom many hours later. "You handled the lifeboat like it was part of your body. I watched the docking. I *wanted* to see you make a mistake, I think, so I'd know I still have something on you." Her teeth showed in the starlight, rows of lights below the sparkles of her eyes and the great dim blossom of her hair.

"Ah, it wasn't that hard," Xanthia said, delighted, knowing full well that it *was* that hard.

"Well, I'm going to let you handle it again the next swing. From now on, you can think of the lifeboat as *your* ship. You're the skipper."

It didn't seem like the time to tell her that she already thought of it that way. Nor that she had christened the ship.

Zoe laughed quietly. Xanthia looked at her.

"I remember the day I first boarded my own ship," she said. "It was a big day for me. My own ship."

"This is the way to live," Xanthia agreed. "Who needs all those people? Just the two of us. And they say hole hunters are crazy. I . . . wanted to . . . " The words stuck in her throat, but Xanthia knew this was the time to get them out, if there ever would be a time. "I don't want to stay too long at Pluto, Mother. I'd like to get right back out here with you." There, she'd said it.

Zoe said nothing for a long time.

"We can talk about that later."

"I love you, Mother," Xanthia said, a little too loudly.

"I love you, too, baby," Zoe mumbled. "Let's get some sleep, okay?"

She tried to sleep, but it wouldn't happen. What was *wrong*?

Leaving the darkened room behind her, she drifted through the ship, looking for something she had lost, or was losing, she wasn't sure which. What had happened, after all? Certainly nothing she could put her finger on. She loved her mother, but all she knew was that she was choking on tears.

In the water closet, wrapped in the shower bag with warm water misting around her, she glanced in the mirror.

"Why? Why would she do a thing like that?"

"Loneliness. And insanity. They appear to go together. This is her solution. You are not the first clone she has made."

She had thought herself beyond shock, but the clarity that simple declarative sentence brought to her mind was explosive. Zoe had always needed the companionship Xanthia provided. She needed a child for diversion in the long, dragging years of a voyage; she needed someone to talk to. *Why couldn't she have brought a dog?* She saw herself now as a shipboard pet, and felt sick. The local leash laws would necessitate the destruction of the animal before landing. Regrettable, but there it was. Zoe had spent the last year working up the courage to do it.

How many little Xanthias? They might even have chosen that very name; they would have been that much like her. Three, four? She wept for her forgotten sisters. Unless . . .

"How do I know you're telling me the truth about this? How could she have kept it from me? I've seen tapes of Pluto. I never saw any mention of this."

"She edited those before you were born. She has been careful. Consider her position: there can be only one of you, but the law does not say which it has to be. With her death, you become legal. If you had known that, what would life have been like in *Shirley Temple*?"

"I don't believe you. You've got something in mind, I'm sure of it."

"Ask her when she gets here. But be careful. Think it out, all the way through."

She had thought it out. She had ignored the last three calls from Zoe while she thought. All the options must be considered, all the possibilities planned for. It was an impossible task; she knew she was far too emotional to think clearly, and there wasn't time to get herself under control.

But she had done what she could. Now *The Good Ship Lollipop,* outwardly unchanged, was a ship of war.

Zoe came backing in, riding the fusion torch and headed for a point dead in space relative to Xanthia. The fusion drive was too dangerous for *Shirley* to complete the rendezvous; the rest of the maneuver would be up to *Lollipop.*

Xanthia watched through the telescope as the drive went off. She could see *Shirley* clearly on her screen, though the ship was fifty kilometers away.

Her screen lit up again, and there was Zoe. Xanthia turned her own camera on.

"There you are," Zoe said. "Why wouldn't you talk to me?"

"I didn't think the time was ripe."

"Would you like to tell me how come this nonsense about talking black holes? What's gotten into you?"

"Never mind about that. There never was a hole, anyway. I just needed to talk to you about something you forgot to erase from the tape library in the *Lol*. . . in the lifeboat. You were pretty thorough with the tapes in *Shirley,* but you forgot to take the same care here. I guess you didn't think I'd ever be using it. Tell me, what are Clone Control Regulations?"

The face on the screen was immobile. Or was it a mirror, and was she smiling? Was it herself, or Zoe she watched? Frantically, Xanthia thumbed a switch to put her telescope image on the screen, wiping out the face. Would Zoe try to talk her way out of it? If she did, Xanthia was determined to do nothing at all. There was no way she could check out any lie Zoe might tell her, nothing she could confront Zoe with except a fantastic story from a talking black hole.

Please say something. Take the responsibility out of my hands. She was willing to die, tricked by Zoe's fast talk, rather than accept the hole's word against Zoe's.

But Zoe was acting, not talking, and the response was exactly what the hole had predicted. The attitude control jets were firing, *Shirley Temple* was pitching and yawing slowly, the nozzles at the stern hunting for a speck in the telescope screen. When the engines were aimed, they would surely be fired, and Xanthia and the whole ship would be vaporized.

But she was ready. Her hands had been poised over the thrust controls. *Lollipop* had a respectable acceleration, and every gee of it slammed her into the couch as she scooted away from the danger spot.

Shirley's fusion engines fired, and began a deadly hunt. Xanthia could see the thin, incredibly hot stream playing around her as Zoe made finer adjustments in her orientation. She could only evade it for a short time, but that was all she needed.

Then the light went out. She saw her screen flare up as the telescope circuit became overloaded with an intense burst of energy. And it was over. Her radar screen showed nothing at all.

"As I predicted," the hole said.

"Why don't you shut up?" Xanthia sat very still, and trembled.

"I shall, very soon. I did not expect to be thanked. But what you did, you did for yourself."

"And you, too, you . . . you *ghoul*! Damn you, damn you to hell." She was shouting through her tears. "Don't think you've fooled me, not completely, anyway. I know what you did, and I know how you did it."

"Do you?" The voice was unutterably cool and distant. She could see that now the hole was out of danger, it was rapidly losing interest in her.

"Yes, I do. Don't tell me it was coincidence that when you changed direction it was just enough to be near Zoe when she got here. You had this planned from the start."

"From much further back than you know," the hole said. "I tried to get you both, but it was impossible. The best I could do was take advantage of the situation as it was."

"Shut up, shut up."

The hole's voice was changing from the hollow, neutral tones to something that might have issued from a tank of liquid helium. She would never have mistaken it for human.

"What I did, I did for my own benefit. But I saved your life. She was going to try to kill you. I maneuvered her into such a position that, when she tried to turn her fusion drive on you, she was heading into a black hole she was powerless to detect."

"You *used* me."

"You used me. You were going to imprison me in a power station."

"But you said you wouldn't *mind*! You said it would be the perfect place."

"Do you believe that eating is all there is to life? There is more to do in the wide universe than you can even suspect. I am slow. It is easy to catch a hole if your mass detector is functioning; Zoe did it three times. But I am beyond your reach now."

"What do you mean? What are you going to do? What am *I* going to do?" That question hurt so much that Xanthia almost didn't hear the hole's reply.

"I am on my way out. I converted *Shirley* into energy; I absorbed very little mass from her. I beamed the energy very tightly, and am now on my way out of your system. You will not see me again. You have two options. You can go back to Pluto and tell everyone what happened out here. It would be necessary for scientists to rewrite natural laws if they believed you. It has been done before, but usually with more persuasive evidence. There will be questions asked concerning the fact that no black hole has ever evaded capture, spoken, or changed velocity in the past. You can explain that when a hole has a chance to defend itself, the hole hunter does not survive to tell the story."

"I will. I *will* tell them what happened!" Xanthia was eaten by a horrible doubt. Was it possible there had been a solution to her problem that did not involve Zoe's death? Just how badly had the hole tricked her?

"There is a second possibility," the hole went on, relentlessly. "Just what *are* you doing out here in a lifeboat?"

"What am I . . . I told you, we had . . . " Xanthia stopped. She felt herself choking.

"It would be easy to see you as crazy. You discovered something in *Lollipop*'s library that led you to know you must kill Zoe. This knowledge was too much for you. In defense, you invented me to trick you into doing what you had to do. Look in the mirror and tell me if you think your story will be believed. Look closely, and be honest with yourself."

She heard the voice laugh for the first time, from down in the bottom of its hole, like a voice from a well. It was an extremely unpleasant sound.

Maybe Zoe had died a month ago, strangled or poisoned or slashed with a knife. Xanthia had been sitting in her lifeboat, catatonic, all that time, and had constructed this episode to justify the murder. It *had* been self-defense, which was certainly a good excuse, and a very convenient one.

But she knew. She was sure, as sure as she had ever been of anything, that the hole was out there, that everything had happened as she had seen it happen. She saw the flash again in her mind, the awful flash that had turned Zoe into radiation. But she also knew that the other explanation would haunt her for the rest of her life.

"I advise you to forget it. Go to Pluto, tell everyone that your ship blew up and you escaped and you are Zoe. Take her place in the world, and never, *never* speak of talking black holes."

The voice faded from her radio. It did not speak again.

After days of numb despair and more tears and recriminations than she cared to remember, Xanthia did as the hole had predicted. But life on Pluto did not agree with her. There were too many people, and none of them looked very much like her. She stayed long enough to withdraw Zoe's money from the bank and buy a ship, which she named *Shirley Temple.* It was massive, with power to blast to the stars if necessary. She had left something out there, and she meant to search for it until she found it again.

(1977)

KATHERINE MACLEAN

Night-Rise

Now mercy.

Down certain dark and filthy alleys—

In fetid spots between the buildings of the best neighborhoods, by running water, and deep black pools, those who bring themselves to the altar joyfully—

They will be allowed to enter nothingness.

"——" Someone had been speaking. The sound of a voice lingered in my ears. I thought back. The meaning. Something religious and strange.

Nothingness? The world came partially into focus.

I felt the wood of a bar under my fingers. "I know some people who are already nothing, and they think someone in the sky knows what he is doing with them."

A voice beside me. "It can be reborn as a mindless animal, without responsibility or remorse. No need to think ever again. The Dark Christ is merciful, will give darkness as love."

I closed my hand around a smooth shot glass and looked to see if it was empty. It was half full. I looked into the mirror across the bar. Dark amber glass. The people relaxing here did not have to see those dim amber faces. Concealed, those faces watched them.

What was my excuse for being here? Only a little vacation, a drink between assignments and hard work. I was almost working, even here, for the bar smelled bad. It was a danger place, an international border, mixing refugees from law and logic, criminals and perverts and blind, bad-tempered tourists looking for glamour in evil. Stories might rise out of this muck.

Beside me in the mirror, clear-cut and almost visible, was the face of an adolescent Hindu boy, dark eyes, full sculptured lips. He looked familiar. I could almost guess which ambassadorial family he belonged to. They would not want him to be here in danger. He touched my elbow. I felt the touch, although I did not see it in the mirror.

"Are you all right, sair?" said the soft Indian voice.

"I don't know," I said, and did not turn to look at him yet. Everything was becoming too real. The amber mirror still held a little of unreality. "I think I'm sobering up."

The echo of a voice still lingered.

Something had hit me with a great gong of meaning recently, within ten minutes. Somewhere near me was a story. I had been out on my feet, "gone" into one of those blackouts where an experienced drinker can be unconscious and still walk and talk and sound alive. The sound of a story had brought me back.

The feeling of something important was still bringing me back. I climbed upward from under the sea of warm whiskey. The lights grew brighter and the sounds harsher and more shrill as I approached surface. Someone was repeating the details of a fight. A blurred voice was trying to make a point to a precise voice that questioned insistently and quietly, going after a purpose. Voice one should guard himself against voice two. Half-filled bottles before my eyes lined up against the back mirror. The smell of insect spray and odor killer, whiskey, fear, sweat . . . A beefy bartender, accustomed to trouble, stolidly refilled drinks for the drunks and ignored their attempts to converse with him.

"What were you saying?" I asked the Indian boy. "I think I missed some of it." I fumbled with my wallet on the bar checking my cash. Five dollars. I braced for reality and looked straight at the boy.

Quality, yes. Education, yes, but primitive, and overmuscled for his age. His face was smooth sculptured stone. Legally too young to drink and enter bars. My duty was to get him out of there, said the imagined voice of his family. I ignored it and listened again. The echo made real.

"There are two Christs, sair," the boy said, licking his lips and glancing away from my wallet. He turned his dark eyes on me with sincere earnestness as if even a strange bum with bloodshot eyes at a bar had a right to know.

He said, "There is a Dark Christ also. I mean a bad one. He is coming this time. He is a god also, like the other, but on the left hand now. He is in the souls of men, gaining shape, a thought by God slowly forming to become solid—I think strong enough to already be born in the flesh as a man, growing somewhere already. Have you not felt him coming all your life? He rises in the land of your soul, like a dark sun, slowly."

It hit me somewhere. I shuddered and kept shuddering. I thought I was going to break apart physically. I pulled out of it with my fingers gripping the edge of the bar hard enough to dent walnut.

I have felt that thing before, watching the first thread of smoke trickling upward from a volcano that was going to blow, but this was the first time I had had a sixty-mile-an-hour, head-on collision with words. I looked around for something to help me disconnect and forget it. On the other side of the boy a richly dressed slender man gave me a steady-eyed expressionless stare, then looked the Indian boy up and down as if I had offered him for sale.

People had vanished from this neighborhood.

"Does your family know where you are?" I asked the boy.

"I am where I choose to be, sir," he said. "I know judo, and I am armed." The children of diplomats must travel from country to country. If they learn to escape protection and explore each place, they may grow up in premature understanding of the ways of the world, even the ways of evil. I remembered that the men who go into the borderworld, and are destroyed and do not return, are usually deviates looking for companions for their strange tastes. Like the man on the other side of the Indian boy. He edged closer, but I did not feel any need to warn my young companion of his intentions. He must have met that sort of attention before.

The boy had been telling me of a young criminal gang. I remembered that now. It could have made a good story. Memory keeps slipping. I reached into a pocket, found a note pad. Better to write it down.

"Do you want me to take notes and write an article?"

He nodded. Again the sincere, earnest look. He wanted to help me, or the world, by telling it the truth. I did not want any more theology, only the events.

I said, "Go on with what you were telling me. The story I mean. How did it start?"

"About the stealing? The impulse came to me. I did not need the money—my parents are rich, but the impulse came to me, feeling like wisdom. I found poor gang boys for companions. I went into buildings, we stole, and sold, and gave away. I saw that I could go into anyplace. All doors are unlocked. I saw that the poor boys did not want to steal, did not want to give away what they had stolen and help each other; they wanted to destroy what they did not have and they wanted to destroy what they did not understand. They would smash beautiful obedient machines in offices, smear their offal on walls, hit each other with what they had stolen. The world lay open to them, but they could take nothing for themselves that would help them. They learned nothing. They were in pain, dry and hungry inside for they were never loved, and they could not love. Another impulse came to me, as if by wisdom. I was sure. I took them into a dark place and I returned them to the wheel of Karma, to be reborn as animals and birds and live with humbleness and beauty."

He took a white scarf from his pocket, a white scarf such as the murdering servants of Kali Durga, the destroyer goddess, had used in ritual street murder long ago. It was as if he had taken a knife out of his pocket. The memory of mankind is long. Voices faltered, and in the silence he said, "I shed no blood. And afterward I prayed for their souls."

If he had mentioned excrement and elimination in the presence of an old ladies' tea party he would have gotten the same polite pretense that he had said nothing, the same immediate resumption of general chatter on other topics. He had mentioned something that was done and accepted, but not openly talked about. Murder. The boy went on talking, but now no one else listened to him. The richly dressed deviate turned his back and began a cordial conversation with a skinny young man who had been crowding him from the other side. The skinny young man had mascaraed eyes and looked hungry.

Drunken voices rose about us, and a fight began near the door. The bartender lumbered in that direction.

The boy went on talking. I have interviewed great scientists and poets and there is always something in the way they talk. This poor damned kid had some crazy notion of Christ, and he had killed a whole peck of his fellow ragamuffins with his white scarf. But there was power in his voice and in his thinking. When he began to speak again, I heard the essential child savagery in the smooth young voice, but I still heard the power.

He said, "I found this scarf in the place where I first thought of returning them to darkness and I knew it was a sign." He folded up the white silk scarf and put it quietly back in his pocket.

"A sign of what?" An unsafe question. But one interviews with questions.

"Kali Durga has returned, I thought. But I was wrong. It is the sign of the other one. The Dark Christ asked for those souls. I know him now, for I have met others who know also. They do as I do. And we are sure who it is that we obey." Listening, I felt that shudder of recognition. This was the true group madness, contagious. It could inflame a nation to drown itself in instinct.

I am a reporter and a writer of articles. One does not turn the person one interviews over to the police. Making arrests is a job for the police. I get stories, write them, and get them into print.

In the phone booth it was close and sweaty, listening to the fan whir and the operator distantly speak, negotiating a reverse-charges call to *World Pix.* The phone line cleared and the editor answered.

"What's on your so-called mind, Tom? And where are you?"

I used to work for him on assignment, but steady work interfered with my drinking time, so I had quit and gone back to free lance. I knew what his magazine needed and liked.

"Brad, I've just run across a new religious cult of murderers. Would you buy a special?"

"Great. I'll bump a rehash of Nazi horrors for it. We're crying for good material. When can you get it to me? I need it yesterday. The galleys are at the printers already."

"Maybe tonight. I'm attending a meeting."

"Get at that typewriter! We'll make it a series. Never mind about facts for the first part. Just rehash Kali and Beal and Freud. Finish the first part and get it in tonight. Attend your meeting and get cooked and eaten next week. Okay?"

I laughed and hung up.

It was dark, it smelled of dead fish and harbor fog, and the oil of ships. The alley pavement was broken, and mud sucked at one foot when I shifted position. The boy Haran was a shadow on one side of me and two taller lads were shadows on the other side. I could hear them breathing, but they said nothing. I had not asked their names; one never asked names when reporting crime. They had assured me that I would see a service to the Dark Christ.

"How many worshipers are there?" I asked, wondering where the others were.

"Twenty here. Others in the city across the river."

"When are they coming here?"

"We only need three for service. Sometimes only one." I saw the flash of a white scarf dangling from a hand in the dark. The tallest one had answered.

It sounded like a killing. I said uneasily, "No rough stuff right in front of me, okay? I just want to see a service to the Dark Christ."

"It is the same Christ," said the tall one. "Christ and Krishna died to also show us the way to die. Our service is to him and all mankind. We serve anyone who comes to us for help."

It still sounded like a killing was scheduled for that night. I wondered who. "How do you pick them?"

"They volunteer."

"How do they volunteer?"

Haran's soft voice answered. "They come to the altar over there."

It looked something like a large block of stone, a lighter square against a black mass of the windowless warehouse wall.

"They can find their way."

Haran murmured, "The human soul is wise. It knows when it is weary of being clothed in flesh. It leads a man to us."

Far away a slot of light showed the entrance to the alley. People walked past that slot of light, auto headlights flashed by it, and in the distance a neon sign flickered. I saw a man stop at the entrance, hesitating. I hoped he would not come in.

"We help the weak who are too weak to taste fully of life, and continue on, without experience, only because they are afraid to die. Christ will open the door at which they stand too timid to knock. They will be able to leave without blame, offending no one, breaking no law against suicide, issued gently into nothing and nothing. They have passed their lives swaddled in safety and comfort for their bodies. They have found comfort without thought; their selves are washed clean and blank. Their bodies can pass into nothingness without pain and leave not a ripple of soul behind."

It was a clear, compelling picture. It made murder sound kind. Haran was a poet, a prophet, a Saint Paul of Death. He was starting here in the alleys of this city, but the worship he started could spread to engulf the world. The distant man at the entrance to the alley entered and began to walk toward us, his gait uncertain and stumbling.

"How did you choose this place for worship?" I asked.

"In any city we choose a stone in a dark place, a stone that looks like an altar. When the dark spirit says yes, it becomes his altar. We wait beside the altar and pray for the souls of who comes to us."

"Always the one who offers himself to the Dark Christ comes and stands beside the altar and waits."

I heard the others murmur agreement, but I protested. "But how do you know? Suppose a man is going somewhere else, and just stops. He's not offering himself for . . . for . . . "

The distant stranger still advanced toward us, away from the light. His gait was uncertain. He braced himself by one hand against the wall and groped with his feet for the pavement.

"This alley leads nowhere else."

The victim fumbled along the wall, going step by step into what must have seemed bottomless blackness. He did not know he was clearly outlined against the slot of light behind him. I thought of warning him. My companions on either side were killers. If I yelled they could overtake their victim even if he started to run, and they would kill me. I would die in the dark with no medals for heroism.

I decided not to yell, and hoped that the victim was some miserable bum dying of drink and malnutrition, with vomit on his clothes, for whom killing would be quick mercy.

The young killers were shadows on either side of me, saying nothing and waiting as the man advanced. The silhouetted figure advanced almost to us, then walked out of the light toward the altar. He coughed. He cleared his throat. He spoke nervously. "Where are you, kiddo? I saw you come in here. I'm not mad really. I won't hurt you. You can keep the money you took out of my money belt."

He took two more steps and stopped, with the altar a ghostly square of white stone behind him.

"Peace be with you," Haran said, and began to chant in a language I did not recognize.

The man was a shadow before the altar, his voice a lonely sound in the dark. "I know you're here, kiddo, I hear you singing. I won't hurt you. I liked you. You liked me, didn't you?"

One of my three companions left my side.

The silk scarf of Kali was used by the Thuggs as a killing weapon in the time two centuries ago when Thuggee was practiced as a religion. It was looped over the head of the victim and given a quick pull that broke the neck.

A tugboat whistled on the river, a liner hooted a reply. I heard the dull crack of bone breaking.

Far away the slot of light led to the orderly, busy parts of the city. No one else darkened that slot. No one entered.

The electric typewriter typed quietly and rapidly as if recording someone else's thoughts. I wrote, "Christ the Preserver has ruled long and long, and he has succeeded, there are many preserved, crowds and multitudes of humankind. They are protected and do not need either courage or wisdom, they do not struggle, they neither win nor lose. They feel neither challenge nor triumph, they do neither evil nor good. They seek comfort which is nothingness, and they fear hunger and live in satiety which is nothingness. They exist without experience, and fear experience. They deserve neither Heaven nor Hell; those alive enough to be afraid are in Hell, live on the edge of the avalanche, and are afraid to move. The protected have neither friends nor enemies, strangers protect them, because the preserving Christ commanded it. In all his names, as Krishna, as Buddha, he commanded that the strong protect and preserve strangers."

I stopped and read it back. It sounded like Haran's voice and his thinking. I typed, "The preserving Christ has accumulated these people on Earth. Earth is overladen. The destroying Christ is God's other hand and he has come to clear them away and make room.

"In the name of mercy. Down certain lonely alleys, in dark and secret places between buildings, those who do not know how to live and are afraid to die, they can find nothingness. The New Christ is merciful. He will not inflict eternal life on the weary. Nothingness is comfort."

Much later, in daylight, I was sleeping.

The phone rang in the hotel room. I rolled over and put the pillow on top of my head. The phone stopped ringing and then started again. I picked it up and brought it under the pillow and laid the receiver on the bed beside my ear and went back to sleep.

Sometime later the voice shouting in my ear brought me back.

"We can't print it like this. What are you trying to do, convert everyone to Thuggee? All the nancy pressure groups hate this kind of stuff!"

"It's the way they think," I said, remembering the young men with scarves waiting in the dark. "It's the way they think."

"You wrote it like it was the way you think, you boob."

"So add quote marks," I said. The pillow held the phone near my ear. The bed was soft against my face.

"Did you see a service?"

"Yes. They used a white scarf and killed a man, just like I wrote it. Look up Kali worship. Very same."

"*Who* did they kill?"

"Unidentified man." It didn't seem too important. "About five feet ten, weight about a hundred and forty, age about a tired thirty. Well off, good black suit, good shoes. Broken neck. He'll be raked out of the river today or tomorrow. Condolences. Not sure he volunteered. Sorry."

After a while the phone was buzzing the notices of an empty line.

I reached in under the mattress, almost falling over the edge of the bed, and felt a crumpled wad of oily paper that was money. The bundle of green stuff testified that they had trusted me and bought by counting the pages without even reading it. They would print my article. It would come out a little neater and more coherent than I had written it, with the statement of the Dark Christ Religion put neatly into quote marks. Someone else would add the Freudian crap, and the sociological crap, explaining the sources of murder within the person as suicide turned outward, the population pressure as a social source of the impulse to kill, felt within the crowded individual. They would frame the story with a long view of the history of other times killing had appeared as a religious impulse. They could do it as easily as I could. My interview with the young assassins, with what they said and thought, that would be unchanged, presented clearly as an interview. Interview by Thomas Barlan.

That was a name they would remember. The other photo journalists and pressmen knew me too well and made fun of my name but they did not make fun of my interviews. Tom of Lower Bar Country had struck again. With the bills clutched comfortably in my fingers I fell asleep.

I woke up at sundown in the expensive hotel room, with a golden haze of sunset over the city. I was hungry, empty, shaky, and happy; and sober. I showered and shaved, and went down to the most expensive restaurant in the hotel, started breakfast with a cafe royal, and then ordered the greatest breakfast that they had on the menu.

After the third cup of coffee the back of my neck began to prickle. The feeling of sitting next to a live volcano about to blow returned, and stood my fur up along my arms. Kali worship, Death worship, a match in a fireworks factory.

The world was overpopulated, and the needs of living quietly together had made violent men into mice. An explosion of Kali worship would spread. It would change to simple murder, by killers choosing the most helpless and easily felled victims, with "mercy" an excuse for murder. An explosion of this sort would solve the population problem but it would kill the mice and leave the wolves. People who had no taste for violent self-defense would die. Did I want a world of human wolves?

It would not be very different. Half the history of man is the history of wolf-man, which is why humanity has dominated all the other animals of the planet and his history is a history of blood.

Should I try to stop Haran and the others from spreading the worship of the Dark Christ? The decision was yes, but it tightened my breathing. It was already evening. The nightclub orchestra came on and began to play. Maybe it was the last time I would hear it if I decided to turn the Kali cult in to the police. They would kill me.

I ordered some stiff drinks and tried to see an easy answer. Was it stupid to think that one reporter could stop or spread this disease of Death worship? No. The source was Haran. Haran the Indian boy was a light of thought, a poet who spread the love of darkness. Lamp of darkness to the others. He was probably wrong. He was not waiting for the Messiah Christ to come, he was the Messiah of the new religion himself, the spokesman for Death who would make Death into a god.

If Haran died this young, he would be forgotten and the movement would stop. Murder would continue in the world, but not organized murder, and Death would not again become a god. I should kill Haran, the boy with beautiful dark eyes and the innocent sculptured mouth. The police would not arrest him. His family would protect him. His family was influential. If I forced an arrest he would be released on bail.

I would die.

I listened to the orchestra, ordered a steak and a double shot of good Irish. I needed to fill up with good food to make up for last week's concentration on drinking, and I needed to fill up on whiskey to change my line of thinking. Only sober thinking could get me so crazily involved with problems of responsibility and world history. As the drinks arrived I wondered what the effect of my article would be. *What are you trying to do, convert everyone to Thuggee?* I tossed the drinks down quickly before turning my attention to the steak.

Thomas Barlan was a good reporter. A reporter's job was to report. He had no responsibility for the effects of reporting. That was a problem for ministers and social scientists and policemen. Thomas of Lower Bar Country had one job, to go into Lower Bar Country and find news, and drink.

I watched the reporter that was connected with my body try to drown thought in drink and get back to the happy blind reporter.

The problem was easily taken care of. Drink. Never so great. Never so high before. The world was pretty and more pretty, shapes without meaning, a pattern of colors like clouds at sunset . . . Outside into cooler air . . . Dark outside, streetlights, colors of lights from neon signs. The shapes not solid.

The reporter, I, moved through the world of patterns trying to remember something he should be finding, something he should do when he found it. The shapes around him, the reporter, not solid, like letters, Egyptian picture language. The world is a message from God written in Egyptian picture letters in an unknown tongue. A language half remembered. The shapes whispered meanings, and they seemed to mean more away from the brightest lights.

I found a dark corner and stood swaying on the edge of the sidewalk, watching the distant neon signs reflected in a street made shiny by rain. Eventually the sidewalk and walls grew solid again and the lights were merely reflected advertisements, so I went into the nearest bar and had some more Irish whiskey and some Benedictine to celebrate the meal of the week. No one inside said anything that seemed to be a story.

When he/I came out the signs did not mean anything, just colors and meaninglessness was best, and he went floating along on legs that did not quite reach down to the sidewalk, away from lights that seemed too bright, toward the cool darkness and the sound of tugboats where I remembered there was a story.

Along a sidewalk, following the sound of tugboats, and the smell of fish as a faint sometimes smell whenever the wind shifted. Past a dark street entrance that led downhill into darkness. The tugboats hooted from that direction. I turned back and went cheerfully lurching and fumbling down the hill toward the tugboats.

"Shlow up go right into the river," I said and laughed at the idea going swimming and, laughing into the darkness around him, braced his hand against a table-sized block of stone and stopped.

Behind him he heard a boy's musical voice say something in a strange language, and then in English, Haran, saying, "We thank you, sair, for your offer of yourself. We were praying for you." He imagined he saw young, sympathetic faces around him, sympathetic but mistaken. But it was too black; he could see nothing.

Trying to speak, felt the caress of white silk around his neck.

(1978)

PHILIP K. DICK

Frozen Journey

After take-off, the ship routinely monitored the condition of the sixty people sleeping in its cryonic tanks. One malfunction showed, that of person nine. His EEG revealed brain activity.

Shit, the ship said to itself.

Complex homeostatic devices locked into circuit feed, and the ship contacted person nine.

"You are slightly awake," the ship said, utilizing the psychotronic route; there was no point in rousing person nine to full consciousness. After all, the flight would last a decade.

Virtually unconscious but, *unfortunately,* still able to think, person nine thought. Someone is addressing me. He said, "Where am I located? I don't see anything."

"You're in faulty cryonic suspension."

He said, "Then I shouldn't be able to hear you."

"Faulty, I said. That's the point; you can hear me. Do you know your name?"

"Victor Kemmings. Bring me out of this."

"We are in flight."

"Then put me under."

"Just a moment." The ship examined the cryonic mechanisms; it scanned and surveyed, and then it said, "I will try."

Time passed. Victor Kemmings, unable to see anything, unaware of his body, found himself still conscious. "Lower my temperature," he said. He could not hear his voice; perhaps he only imagined he spoke. Colors floated toward him and then rushed at him. He liked the colors; they reminded him of a child's paintbox, the semi-animated kind, an artificial life form. He had used them in school, 200 years ago.

"I can't put you under," the voice of the ship sounded inside Kemmings' head. "The malfunction is too elaborate; I can't correct it and I can't repair it. You will be conscious for ten years."

The semi-animated colors rushed toward him, but now they possessed a sinister quality, supplied to them by his own fear. "Oh, my God," he said. Ten years! The colors darkened.

As Victor Kemmings lay paralyzed, surrounded by dismal flickerings of light, the ship explained to him its strategy. This strategy did not represent a decision on its part; the ship had been programmed to seek this solution in case of a malfunction of this sort.

"What I will do," the voice of the ship came to him, "is feed you sensory stimulation. The peril to you is sensory deprivation. If you are conscious for ten years without sensory data, your mind will deteriorate. When we reach the LR4 system, you will be a vegetable."

"Well, what do you intend to feed me?" Kemmings said in panic. "What do you have in your information storage banks? All the video soap operas of the last century? Wake me up and I'll walk around."

"There is no air in me," the ship said. "Nothing for you to eat. No one to talk to, since everyone else is under."

Kemmings said, "I can talk to you. We can play chess."

"Not for ten years. Listen to me; I say, I have no food and no air. You must remain as you are . . . a bad compromise, but one forced on us. You are talking to me now. I have no particular information stored. Here is policy in these situations: I will feed you your own buried memories, emphasizing the pleasant ones. You possess 206 years of memories and most of them have sunk down into your unconscious. This is a splendid source of sensory data for you to receive. Be of good cheer. This situation, which you are in, is not unique. It has never happened within my domain before, but I am programmed to deal with it. Relax and trust me. I will see that you are provided with a world."

"They should have warned me," Kemmings said, "before I agreed to emigrate."

"Relax," the ship said.

He relaxed, but he was terribly frightened. Theoretically, he should have gone under, into the successful cryonic suspension, then awakened a moment later at his star of destination; or, rather, the planet, the colony-planet, of that star. Everyone else aboard the ship lay in an unknowing state; he was the exception, as if bad karma had attacked him for obscure reasons. Worst of all, he had to depend totally on the good will of the ship. Suppose it elected to feed him monsters. The ship could terrorize him for ten years—ten objective years and undoubtedly more from a subjective standpoint. He was, in effect, totally in the ship's power. Did interstellar ships enjoy such a situation? He knew little about interstellar ships; his field was microbiology. Let me think, he said to himself. My first wife, Martine; the lovely little French girl who wore jeans and a red shirt open to the waist and cooked delicious crepes.

"I hear," the ship said. "So be it."

The rushing colors resolved themselves into coherent, stable shapes. A building: a little old yellow wooden house that he had owned when he was nineteen years old, in Wyoming. "Wait," he said in panic. "The foundation was bad; it was on a mud sill. And the roof leaked." But he saw the kitchen, with the table that he had built himself. And he felt glad.

"You will not know, after a little while," the ship said, "that I am feeding you your own buried memories."

"I haven't thought of that house in a century," he said, wonderingly; entranced, he made out his old electric drip coffeepot with the box of paper filters beside it. This is the house where Martine and I lived, he realized. "Martine!" he said aloud.

"I'm on the phone," Martine said, from the living room.

The ship said, "I will cut in only when there is an emergency. I will be monitoring you, however, to be sure you are in a satisfactory state. Don't be afraid."

"Turn down the right rear burner on the stove," Martine called. He could hear her and yet not see her. He made his way from the kitchen through the dining room and into the living room. At the VF, Martine stood in rapt conversation with her brother; she wore shorts and she was barefoot. Through the front windows of the living room, he could see the street; a commercial vehicle was trying to park, without success.

It's a warm day, he thought. I should turn on the air conditioner.

He seated himself on the old sofa as Martine continued her VF conversation, and he found himself gazing at his most cherished possession, a framed poster on the wall above Martine: Gilbert Shelton's *Fat Freddy Says* drawing in which Freddy Freak sits with his cat on his lap and Fat Freddy is trying to say, "Speed kills," but he is so wired on speed—he holds in his hand every kind of amphetamine tablet, pill, Spansule and capsule that exists—that he can't say it, and the cat is gritting its teeth and wincing in a mixture of dismay and disgust. The poster is signed by Gilbert Shelton himself; Kemmings' best friend, Ray Torrance, gave it to him and Martine as a wedding present. It is worth thousands. It was signed by the artist back in the 1980s. Long before either Victor Kemmings or Martine lived.

If we ever run out of money, Kemmings thought to himself, we could sell the poster. It was not *a poster;* it was *the* poster. Martine adored it. The Fabulous Furry Freak Brothers—from the golden age of a long-ago society. No wonder he loved Martine so; she herself loved back, loved the beauties of the world, and treasured and cherished them as she treasured and cherished him; it was a protective love that nourished but did not stifle. It had been her idea to frame the poster; he would have tacked it up on the wall, so stupid was he.

"Hi," Martine said, off the VF now. "What are you thinking?"

"Just that you keep alive what you love," he said.

"I think that's what you're supposed to do," Martine said. "Are you ready for dinner? Open some red wine, a cabernet."

"Will an '07 do?" he said, standing up; he felt, then, like taking hold of his wife and hugging her.

"Either an '07 or a '12." She trotted past him, through the dining room and into the kitchen.

Going down into the cellar, he began to search among the bottles, which, of course, lay flat. Musty air and dampness; he liked the smell of the cellar, but then he noticed the redwood planks lying half-buried in the dirt and he thought, I know I've got to get a concrete slab poured. He forgot about the wine and went over to the far corner, where the dirt was piled highest; bending down, he poked at a board . . . he poked with a trowel and then he thought, Where did I get this trowel? I didn't have it a minute ago. The board crumbled against the trowel. This whole house is collapsing, he realized. Christ sake. I better tell Martine.

Going back upstairs, the wine forgotten, he started to say to her that the foundation of the house was dangerously decayed; but Martine was nowhere in sight. And nothing cooked on the stove, no pots, no pans. Amazed, he put his hand on the stove and found it cold. Wasn't she just now cooking? he asked himself.

"Martine!" he said loudly.

No response. Except for himself, the house was empty. Empty, he thought, and collapsing. Oh, my God. He seated himself at the kitchen table and felt the chair give slightly under him; it did not give much, but he felt it, he felt the sagging.

I'm afraid, he thought. Where did she go?

He returned to the living room. Maybe she went next door to borrow some spices or butter or something, he reasoned. Nonetheless, panic now filled him.

He looked at the poster. It was unframed. And the edges had been torn.

I know she framed it, he thought; he ran across the room to it, to examine it closely. Faded . . . the artist's signature had faded; he could scarcely make it out. She insisted on framing it and under glare-free, reflection-free glass. But it isn't framed and it's torn! The most precious thing we own!

Suddenly, he found himself crying. It amazed him, his tears. Martine is gone; the poster is deteriorated; the house is crumbling away; nothing is cooking on the stove. This is terrible, he thought. And I don't understand it.

The ship understood it. The ship had been carefully monitoring Victor Kemmings' brain wave patterns, and the ship knew that something had gone wrong. The wave forms showed agitation and pain. I must get him out of this feed circuit or I will kill him, the ship decided. Where does the flaw lie? it asked itself. Worry dormant in the man; underlying anxieties. Perhaps if I intensify the signal, I will use the same source but amp up the charge. What has happened is that massive subliminal insecurities have taken possession of him; the fault is not mine but lies, instead, in his psychological make-up.

I will try an earlier period in his life, the ship decided. Before the neurotic anxieties got laid down.

In the back yard, Victor scrutinized a bee that had gotten itself trapped in a spider's web. The spider wound up the bee with great care. That's wrong, Victor thought. I'll let the bee loose. Reaching up, he took hold of the encapsulated bee, drew it from the web and, scrutinizing it carefully, began to unwrap it.

The bee stung him; it felt like a little patch of flame.

Why did it sting me? he wondered. I was letting it go.

He went indoors to his mother and told her, but she did not listen; she was watching television. His finger hurt where the bee had stung it, but, more important, he did not understand why the bee would attack its rescuer. I won't do that again, he said to himself.

"Put some Bactine on it," his mother said at last, roused from watching the TV.

He had begun to cry. It was unfair. It made no sense. He was perplexed and dismayed and he felt a hatred toward small living things, because they were dumb. They didn't have any sense.

He left the house, played for a time on his swings, his slide, in his sandbox, and then he went into the garage, because he heard a strange flapping, whirring sound, like a kind of fan. Inside the gloomy garage, he found that a bird was fluttering against the cobwebbed rear window, trying to get out. Below it, the cat, Dorky, leaped and leaped, trying to reach the bird.

He picked up the cat; the cat extended its body and its front legs, it extended its jaws and bit into the bird. At once, the cat scrambled down and ran off with the still-fluttering bird.

Victor ran into the house. "Dorky caught a bird!" he told his mother.

"That goddamn cat." His mother took the broom from the closet in the kitchen and ran outside, trying to find Dorky. The cat had concealed itself under the bramblebushes; she could not reach it with the broom. "I'm going to get rid of that cat," his mother said.

Victor did not tell her that he had arranged for the cat to catch the bird; he watched in silence as his mother tried and tried to pry Dorky out from her hiding place; Dorky was crunching up the bird; he could hear the sound of breaking bones, small bones. He felt a strange feeling, as if he should tell his mother what he had done, and yet, if he told her, she would punish him. I won't do that again, he said to himself. His face, he realized, had turned red. What if his mother figured it out? What if she had some secret way of knowing? Dorky couldn't tell her and the bird was dead. No one would ever know. He was safe.

But he felt bad. That night, he could not eat his dinner. Both his parents noticed. They thought he was sick; they took his temperature. He said nothing about what he had done. His mother told his father about Dorky and they decided to get rid of Dorky. Seated at the table, listening, Victor began to cry.

"All right," his father said gently. "We won't get rid of her. It's natural for a cat to catch a bird."

The next day, he sat playing in his sandbox. Some plants grew up through the sand. He broke them off. Later, his mother told him that had been a wrong thing to do.

Alone in the back yard, in his sandbox, he sat with a pail of water, forming a small mound of wet sand. The sky, which had been blue and clear, became by degrees overcast. A shadow passed over him and he looked up. He sensed a presence around him, something vast that could think.

You are responsible for the death of the bird, the presence thought; he could understand its thoughts.

"I know," he said. He wished, then, that he could die. That he could replace the bird and die for it, leaving it as it had been, fluttering against the cobwebbed window of the garage.

The bird wanted to fly and eat and live, the presence thought.

"Yes," he said, miserably.

You must never do that again, the presence told him.

"I'm sorry," he said, and wept.

This is a very neurotic person, the ship realized. I am having an awful lot of trouble finding happy memories. There is too much fear in him and too much guilt. He has buried it all, and yet it is still there, worrying him like a dog worrying a rag. Where can I go in his memories to find him solace? I must come up with ten years of memories, or his mind will be lost.

Perhaps, the ship thought, the error that I am making is in the area of choice on my part; I should allow him to select his own memories. However, the ship realized, this will allow an element of fantasy to enter. And that is not usually good. Still . . .

I will try the segment dealing with his first marriage once again, the ship decided. He really loved Martine. Perhaps this time, if I keep the intensity of the memories at a greater level, the entropic factor can be abolished. What happened was a subtle vitiation of the remembered world, a decay of structure. I will try to compensate for that. So be it.

"Do you suppose Gilbert Shelton really signed this?" Martine said pensively; she stood before the poster, her arms folded; she rocked back and forth slightly, as if seeking a better perspective on the brightly colored drawing hanging on their living-room wall. "I mean, it could have been forged. By a dealer somewhere along the line. During Shelton's lifetime or after."

"The letter of authentication," Victor Kemmings reminded her.

"Oh, that's right!" She smiled her warm smile. "Ray gave us the letter that goes with it. But suppose the letter is a forgery? What we need is another letter certifying that the first letter is authentic." Laughing, she walked away from the poster.

"Ultimately," Kemmings said, "we would have to have Gilbert Shelton here to personally testify that he signed it."

"Maybe he wouldn't know. There's that story about the man taking the Picasso picture to Picasso and asking him if it was authentic, and Picasso immediately signed it and said, 'Now it's authentic.' " She put her arm around Kemmings and, standing on tiptoe, kissed him on the cheek. "It's genuine. Ray wouldn't have given us a forgery. He's the leading expert on counterculture art of the Twentieth Century. Do you know that he owns an actual lid of dope? It's preserved under—"

"Ray is dead," Victor said.

"What?" She gazed at him in astonishment. "Do you mean something happened to him since we last—"

"He's been dead two years," Kemmings said. "I was responsible. I was driving the buzz car. I wasn't cited by the police, but it was my fault."

"Ray is living on Mars!" She stared at him.

"I know I was responsible. I never told you. I never told anyone. I'm sorry. I didn't mean to do it. I saw it flapping against the window, and Dorky was trying to reach it, and I lifted Dorky up, and I don't know why, but Dorky grabbed it—"

"Sit down, Victor," Martine led him to the overstuffed chair and made him seat himself. "Something's wrong," she said.

"I know," he said. "Something terrible is wrong. I'm responsible for the taking of a life, a precious life that can never be replaced. I'm sorry. I wish I could make it OK, but I can't."

After a pause, Martine said, "Call Ray."

"The cat—" he said.

"What cat?"

"There." He pointed. "In the poster. On Fat Freddy's lap. That's Dorky. Dorky killed Ray."

Silence.

"The presence told me," Kemmings said. "It was God. I didn't realize it at the time, but God saw me commit the crime. The murder. And He will never forgive me."

His wife stared at him numbly.

"God sees everything you do," said Kemmings. "He sees even the falling sparrow. Only, in this case, it didn't fall; it was grabbed. Grabbed out of the air and torn down. God is tearing this house down which is my body, to pay me back for what I've done. We should have had a building contractor look this house over before we bought it. It's just falling goddamn to pieces. In a year, there won't be anything left of it. Don't you believe me?"

Martine faltered, "I—"

"Watch," Kemmings reached up his arms toward the ceiling; he stood; he reached; he could not touch the ceiling. He walked to the wall and then, after a pause, put his hand through the wall.

Martine screamed.

The ship aborted the memory retrieval instantly. But the harm had been done.

He has integrated his early fears and guilt into one interwoven grid, the ship said to itself. There is no way I can serve up a pleasant memory to him, because he instantly contaminates it. However pleasant the original experience in itself was. This is a serious situation, the ship decided. The man is already showing signs of psychosis. And we are hardly into the trip; years lie ahead of him.

After allowing itself time to think the situation through, the ship decided to contact Victor Kemmings once more.

"Mr. Kemmings," the ship said.

"I'm sorry," Kemmings said. "I didn't mean to foul up those retrievals. You did a good job, but I—"

"Just a moment," the ship said. "I am not equipped to do psychiatric reconstruction of you; I am a simple mechanism, that's all. What is it you want? Where do you want to be and what do you want to be doing?"

"I want to arrive at our destination," Kemmings said. "I want this trip to be over."

Ah, the ship thought. That is the solution.

One by one, the cryonic systems shut down. One by one, the people returned to life, among them Victor Kemmings. What amazed him was the lack of a sense of the passage of time. He had entered the chamber, lain down, had felt the membrane cover him and the temperature begin to drop—

And now he stood on the ship's external platform, the unloading platform, gazing down at a verdant planetary landscape. This, he realized, is LR4-six, the colony world to which I have come in order to begin a new life.

"Looks good," a heavy-set woman beside him said.

"Yes," he said, and felt the newness of the landscape rush up at him, its promise of a beginning. Something better than he had known the past 200 years. I am a fresh person in a fresh world, he thought. And he felt glad.

Colors raced at him, like those of a child's semi-animate kit. St. Elmo's fire, he realized. That's right; there is a great deal of ionization in this planet's atmosphere. A free light show, such as they had back in the 20th Century.

"Mr. Kemmings," a voice said. An elderly man had come up beside him, to speak to him. "Did you dream?"

"During the suspension?" Kemmings said. "No, not that I can remember."

"I think I dreamed," the elderly man said. "Would you take my arm on the descent ramp? I feel unsteady. The air seems thin. Do you find it thin?"

"Don't be afraid," Kemmings said to him. He took the elderly man's arm. "I'll help you down the ramp. Look; there's a guide coming this way. He'll arrange our processing for us; it's part of the package. We'll be taken to a resort hotel and given first-class accommodations. Read your brochure." He smiled at the uneasy older man to reassure him.

"You'd think our muscles would be nothing but flab after ten years in suspension," the elderly man said.

"It's just like freezing peas," Kemmings said. Holding on to the timid older man, he descended the ramp to the ground. "You can store them forever if you get them cold enough."

"My name's Shelton," the elderly man said.

"What?" Kemmings said, halting. A strange feeling moved through him.

"Don Shelton." The elderly man extended his hand; reflexively, Kemmings accepted it and they shook. "What's the matter, Mr. Kemmings? Are you all right?"

"Sure," he said. "I'm fine. But hungry. I'd like to get something to eat. I'd like to get to our hotel, where I can take a shower and change my clothes." He wondered where their baggage could be found. Probably it would take the ship an hour to unload it. The ship was not particularly intelligent.

In an intimate, confidential tone, elderly Mr. Shelton said, "You know what I brought with me? A bottle of Wild Turkey bourbon. The finest bourbon on Earth. I'll bring it over to your hotel room and we'll share it." He nudged Kemmings.

"I don't drink." Kemmings said. "Only wine." He wondered if there were any good wines here on this distant colony world. Not distant now, he reflected. It is Earth that's distant. I should have done like Mr. Shelton and brought a few bottles with me.

Shelton. What did the name remind him of? Something in his far past, in his early years. Something precious, along with good wine and a pretty, gentle young woman making crepes in an old-fashioned kitchen. Aching memories; memories that hurt.

Presently, he stood by the bed in his hotel room, his suitcase open; he had begun to hang up his clothes. In the corner of the room, a TV hologram showed a newscaster; he ignored it, but liking the sound of a human voice, he kept it on.

Did I have any dreams? he asked himself. During these past ten years?

His hand hurt. Gazing down, he saw a red welt, as if he had been stung. A bee stung me, he realized. But when? How? While I lay in cryonic suspension? Impossible. Yet he could see the welt and he could feel the pain. I'd better get something to put on it, he realized. There's undoubtedly a robot doctor in the hotel; it's a first-rate hotel.

When the robot doctor arrived and began treating the bee sting, Kemmings said, "I got this as punishment for killing the bird."

"Really?" the robot doctor said.

"Everything that ever meant anything to me has been taken away from me," Kemmings said. "Martine, the poster—my little old house with the wine cellar. We had everything and now it's gone. Martine left me because of the bird."

"The bird you killed?" the robot doctor said.

"God punished me. He took away all that was precious to me because of my sin. It wasn't Dorky's sin; it was my sin."

"But you were just a little boy," the robot doctor said.

"How did you know that?" Kemmings said. He pulled his hand away from the robot doctor's grasp. "Something's wrong. You shouldn't have known that."

"Your mother told me," the robot doctor said.

"My mother didn't know!"

The robot doctor said, "She figured it out. There was no way the cat could have reached the bird without your help."

"So all the time that I was growing up, she knew. But she never said anything."

"You can forget about it," the robot doctor said.

Kemmings said, "I don't think you exist. There is no possible way that you could know these things. I'm still in a cryonic suspension and the ship is still feeding me my own buried memories. So I won't become psychotic from sensory deprivation."

"You could hardly have a memory of completing the trip."

"Wish fulfillment, then. It's the same thing. I'll prove it to you. Do you have a screwdriver?"

"Why?"

Kemmings said, "I'll remove the back of the TV set and you'll see; there's nothing inside it, no components, no parts, no chassis—nothing."

"I don't have a screwdriver."

"A small knife, then. I can see one in your surgical-supply bag." Bending, Kemmings lifted up a small scalpel. "This will do. If I show you, will you believe me?"

"If there's nothing inside the TV cabinet—"

Squatting down, Kemmings removed the screws holding the back panel of the TV set in place. The panel came loose and he set it down on the floor.

There was nothing inside the TV cabinet. And yet the color hologram continued to fill a quarter of the hotel room and the voice of the newscaster issued forth from his three-dimensional image.

"Admit you're the ship," Kemmings said to the robot doctor.

"Oh, dear," the robot doctor said.

Oh, dear, the ship said to itself. And I've got almost ten years of this lying ahead of me. He is hopelessly contaminating his experiences with childhood guilt; he imagines that his wife left him because, when he was four years old, he helped a cat catch a bird. The only solution would be for Martine to return to him; but how am I going to arrange that? She may not still be alive. On the other hand, the ship reflected, maybe she *is* alive. Maybe she could be induced to do something to save her former husband's sanity. People by and large have very positive traits. And ten years from now, it will take a lot to save—or, rather, restore—his sanity; it will take something drastic, something I myself cannot do alone.

Meanwhile, there was nothing to be done but recycle the wish-fulfillment arrival of the ship at its destination. I will run him through the arrival, the ship decided, then wipe his conscious memory clean and run him through it again. The only positive aspect of this, it reflected, is that it will give me something to do, which may help preserve *my* sanity.

Lying in cryonic suspension—faulty cryonic suspension—Victor Kemmings imagined, once again, that the ship was touching down and he was being brought back to consciousness.

"Did you dream?" a heavy-set woman asked him as the group of passengers gathered on the outer platform. "I have the impression that I dreamed. Early scenes from my life . . . over a century ago."

"None that I can remember," Kemmings said. He was eager to reach his hotel; a shower and a change of clothes would do wonders for his morale. He felt slightly depressed and wondered why.

"There's our guide," an elderly lady said. "They're going to escort us to our accommodations."

"It's in the package," Kemmings said. His depression remained. The others seemed so spirited, so full of life, but over him only a weariness lay, a weighing down sensation, as if the gravity of this colony-planet were too much for him. Maybe that's it, he said to himself. But according to the brochure, the gravity here matched Earth's; that was one of the attractions.

Puzzled, he made his way slowly down the ramp, step by step, holding on to the rail. I don't really deserve a new chance at life anyhow, he realized. I'm just going through the motions . . . I am not like these other people. There is something wrong with me; I cannot remember what it is, but, nonetheless, it is there. In me. A bitter sense of pain. Of lack of worth.

An insect landed on the back of Kemmings' right hand, an old insect, weary with flight. He halted, watched it crawl across his knuckles. I could crush it, he thought. It's so obviously infirm; it won't live much longer anyhow.

He crushed it—and felt great inner horror. What have I done? he asked himself. My first moment here and I have wiped out a little life. Is this my new beginning?

Turning, he gazed back up at the ship. Maybe I ought to go back, he thought. Have them freeze me forever. I am a man of guilt, a man who destroys. Tears filled his eyes.

And within its sentient works, the interstellar ship moaned.

During the ten long years remaining of the trip to the LR4 system, the ship had plenty of time to track down Martine Kemmings. It explained the situation to her. She had emigrated to a vast orbiting dome in the Sirius system, found her situation unsatisfactory and was en route back to Earth. Roused from her own cryonic suspension, she listened intently and then agreed to be at the colony world at LR4 when her exhusband arrived—if it was at all possible.

Fortunately, it was possible.

"I don't think he'll recognize me," Martine said to the ship. "I've allowed myself to age. I don't really approve of entirely halting the aging process."

He'll be lucky if he recognizes anything, the ship thought.

At the intersystem spaceport on the colony world of LR4, Martine stood waiting for the people aboard the ship to appear on the outer platform. She wondered if she would recognize her former husband. She was a little afraid, but she was glad that she had gotten to LR4 in time. It had been close. Another week and his ship would have arrived before hers. Luck is on my side, she said to herself, and scrutinized the newly landed interstellar ship.

People appeared on the platform. She saw him. Victor had changed very little.

As he came down the ramp, holding on to the railing as if weary and hesitant, she went up to him, her hands thrust deep in the pockets of her coat; she felt *shy,* and when she spoke, she could hardly hear her own voice.

"Hi, Victor," she managed to say.

He halted, gazed at her. "I know you," he said.

"It's Martine," she said.

Holding out his hand, he said, smiling, "You heard about the trouble on the ship?"

"The ship contacted me." She took his hand and held it. "What an ordeal."

"Yeah," he said. "Recirculating memories forever. Did I ever tell you about a bee that I was trying to extricate from a spider's web when I was four years old? The idiotic bee stung me." He bent down and kissed her. "It's good to see you," he said.

"Did the ship—"

"It said it would try to have you here. But it wasn't sure if you could make it."

As they walked toward the terminal building, Martine said, "I was lucky; I managed to get a transfer to a military vehicle, a high-velocity-drive ship that just shot along like a mad thing. A new propulsion system entirely."

Victor Kemmings said, "I have spent more time in my own unconscious mind than any other human in history. Worse than early twentieth-century psychoanalysis. And the same material over and over again. Did you know I was scared of my mother?"

"*I* was scared of your mother," Martine said. They stood at the baggage depot, waiting for his luggage to appear. "This looks like a really nice little planet. Much better than where I was. . . . I haven't been happy at all."

"So maybe there's a cosmic plan," he said, grinning. "You look great."

"I'm old."

"Medical science—"

"It was my decision. I like older people." She surveyed him. He has been hurt a lot by the cryonic malfunction, she said to herself. I can see it in his eyes. They look broken. Broken eyes. Torn down into pieces by fatigue and—defeat. As if his buried, early memories swam up and destroyed him. But it's over, she thought. And I did get here in time.

At the bar in the terminal building, they sat having a drink.

"This old man got me to try Wild Turkey bourbon," Victor said. "It's amazing bourbon. He says it's the best on Earth. He brought a bottle with him from. . . . " His voice died in the silence.

"One of your fellow passengers," Martine finished.

"I guess so," he said.

"Well, you can stop thinking of the birds and the bees," Martine said.

"Sex?" he said, and laughed.

"Being stung by a bee; helping a cat catch a bird. That's all past."

"That cat," Victor said, "has been dead 182 years. I figured it out while they were bringing us out of suspension. Probably just as well. Dorky. Dorky the killer cat. Nothing like Fat Freddy's cat."

"I had to sell the poster," Martine said. "Finally."

He frowned.

"Remember?" she said. "You let me have it when we split up. Which I always thought was really good of you."

"How much did you get for it?"

"A lot. I should pay you something like. . . . " She calculated. "Taking inflation into account, I should pay you about two million dollars."

"Would you consider," he said, "instead, in place of the money, my share of the sale of the poster, spending some time with me? Until I get used to this planet?"

"Yes," she said. And she meant it. Very much.

They finished their drinks and then, with his luggage transported by robot spacecap, made their way to his hotel room.

"This is a nice room," Martine said, perched on the edge of the bed. "And it has a hologram TV. Turn it on."

"There's no use turning it on," Victor Kemmings said. He stood by the open closet, hanging up his shirts.

"Why not?"

Kemmings said, "There's nothing in it."

Going over to the TV set, Martine turned it on. A hockey game materialized, projected out into the room, in full color, and the sound of the game assailed her ears.

"It works fine," she said.

"I know," he said. "I can prove it. If you have a nail file or something, I'll unscrew the back plate and show you."

"But I can—"

"Look at this." He paused in his work of hanging up his clothes. "Watch me put my hand through the wall." He placed the palm of his right hand against the wall. "See?"

His hand did not go through the wall, because hands do not go through walls; his hand remained pressed against the wall, unmoving.

"And the foundation," he said, "is rotting away."

"Come and sit down by me," Martine said.

"I've lived this often enough to know," he said. "I've lived this over and over again. I come out of suspension; I walk down the ramp; I get my luggage; sometimes I have a drink at the bar and sometimes I come directly to my room. Usually, I turn on the TV and then. . . . " He went over and held his hand toward her. "See where the bee stung me?"

She saw no mark on his hand; she took his hand and held it.

"There is no bee sting there," she said.

"And when the robot doctor comes, I borrow a tool from him and take off the back plate of the TV set. To prove to him that it has no chassis, no components in it. And then the ship starts me over again."

"Victor," she said. "Look at your hand."

"This is the first time you've been here, though," he said.

"Sit down," she said.

"OK," he seated himself on the bed, beside her, but not too close to her.

"Won't you sit closer to me?" she said.

"It makes me too sad," he said. "Remembering you. I really loved you. I wish this was real."

Martine said, "I will sit with you until it is real for you."

"I'm going to try reliving the part with the cat," he said, "and this time *not* pick up the cat and *not* let it get the bird. If I do that, maybe my life will change so that it turns into something happy. Something that is real. My real mistake was separating from you. Here; I'll put my hand through you." He placed his hand against her arm. The pressure of his muscles was vigorous; she felt the weight, the physical presence of him, against her. "See?" he said. "It goes right through you."

"And all this," she said, "because you killed a bird when you were a little boy."

"No," he said. "All this because of a failure in the temperature-regulating assembly aboard the ship. I'm not down to the proper temperature. There's just enough warmth left in my brain cells to permit cerebral activity." He stood up, then, stretched, smiled at her. "Shall we go get some dinner?" he asked.

She said, "Im sorry. I'm not hungry."

"I am. I'm going to have some of the local seafood. The brochure says it's terrific. Come along, anyhow; maybe when you see the food and smell it, you'll change your mind."

Gathering up her coat and purse, she went with him.

"This is a beautiful little planet," he said. "I've explored it dozens of times. I know it thoroughly. We should stop downstairs at the pharmacy for some Bactine, though. For my hand. It's beginning to swell and it hurts like hell." He showed her his hand. "It hurts more this time than ever before."

"Do you want me to come back to you?" Martine said.

"Are you serious?"

"Yes," she said. "I'll stay with you as long as you want. I agree; we should never have been separated."

Victor Kemmings said, "The poster is torn."

"What?" she said.

"We should have framed it," he said. "We didn't have sense enough to take care of it. Now it's torn. And the artist is dead."

(1980)

EDWARD BRYANT

Precession

Broken free from time and space, I grabbed for anchored razor blades. I grimly held on to bits and pieces of continuum. And what if no one touched you again? I thought. I touched no one . . . I lost my concentration and time swung round . . .

I swiveled the chair back from the small, crosshatched panes; the summerscape wavered beyond. I forced my face toward the window. Trees bent nearly double in the sudden storm; branches lashed fitfully. Some broke, the wind whirling green swatches of leaves into the avenue where traffic had slowed to a near-stop. Hail chattered across the glass with each gust. Rain followed, a soft hiss. The late-afternoon sun still shone above the mountains. The range today was blue-gray.

My safe mechanical phase: tracking like the security camera in a department store, my stare returned to the interior of the apartment.

—her eyes were dark blue-gray—

I squinted, soft-focusing on the couch to my left. The topography of the aging green furniture—lumpy cushions reflected the hills and depressions of a form now absent. I panned along the wall to the surrealistic painting of an abandoned oil refinery; blinding white faded to blue, to green, to black. I began to rock back and forth in the chair with my hands in fists. I watched the diffraction-spiral mobile turning in the heat from the table lamp. Rainbow colors glittered. I thought the mobile was slowing. I continued to rock, sensing the proximity of a mood too leaden for directed action to affect. After a very long time I reached for the telephone.

I work with change the only ways I can.

—once—

From outside the noise of the weather ceased in dying whimpers of wind. The air in the apartment was stuffy—I tried to moisten my dry mouth with dry tongue. When I reached to unlatch and open one of the windows, I saw that autumn lay beyond. The sky had darkened. The leaves still hanging from the branches of the nearer elms were parched and brown. Mercury lights came on in the street.

—her hair shone metallic; copper in the street glow, gold in the sun—

I wasn't sure exactly how much time passed before I felt the slick plastic receiver in my hand. I dialed and she answered on the ninth ring. "Hello?" I tried to answer but my throat was still dry. "Who is it?"

"It's me."

"Cal?" Her voice sounded strained.

"Yes. Did I catch you in the tub?"

"No, I was right here by the phone. I'm expecting my parents to call."

"I let it go nine rings—"

"No, one," she said. "I picked it up on the first one."

"I counted. Nine."

"Maybe a bad circuit—"

"Nine," I said determinedly. "Elizabeth—"

"You feel okay? You don't, do you?"

"What do you mean?" I consciously loosened my grip on the receiver.

"I asked how you felt."

"I feel—"

—her flesh always seemed hotter than normal blood temperature. Her heart always beat stronger than mine—

"Okay, you're not all right," said Elizabeth.

"I don't feel—"

—soft voice, her words traced with a light finger against a mat of suede—

I didn't notice how long I said nothing. I concentrated on her presence; imagined the touch, recreated her face, her fingers. I love—

"Cal, are you there? Say something."

"I'm here, I'm here. Are—you?" Dreading the true answer, wondering if tears might be the cheapest release. No solution beyond the immediate. Nothing beyond the now—

"Want me to drive in?" said Elizabeth. "I can be there in half an hour."

"What good . . . "

"Cal? You sound like you're fading."

"I'm here, I'm here, I'm . . . " The words overlapped on the wire, echoed, diminishing.

"I'll come in," she said insistently. "It's no problem; I had the snow tires mounted yesterday."

Winter now? I thought. The phone cord stretched as I swiveled back to the window. Winter. I saw a snowy nimbus surrounding each street lamp. Snow treads crunched on the street; occasional truck chains rattled. "How long's it been snowing?" Silly question.

Elizabeth said, "Here? Just a couple of hours. What's it like in town?"

"I won't—don't know."

Hesitating, "I still don't have a definite answer."

"Okay. I mean yes; come in if you want. But it looks—cold." I saw an image of robins, brittle as the frozen grass, stricken untimely on my lawn.

"It *is* cold—hasn't been above zero all day. No problem. My Volvo's got a good heater. Shall I pick up some wine on the way?"

We should celebrate the passing of seasons? My elbow ached; I transferred the receiver to my left hand.

"Cal?"

It took another conscious decision to answer. "Sure. Make it something cheap and red that I can't spoil with mulled wine mix."

"Okay. See you in an hour."

I said, "It'll be all right?"

She paused too long. "It will. See you, love."

Thirty seconds after the circuit broke, the howler reminded me I was party to a dead line. I replaced the receiver. My apartment lightened. The western clouds reflected the reds and yellows of sunrise; my eyes tried to register the spectrum from ultraviolet to infrared. I reeled before the onslaught of spring as I heard the Easter cry of the robins.

Recall the immutable past?

Certainly I remembered abnormal, unnatural times:

As usual I got up with the alarm at seven, turned on the *Today Show,* immediately poured myself a glass of cold water, added two effervescent tablets, and drank it with six aspirin. My mouth felt the way my rumpled bed looked. I ritualistically flensed my gums with nylon bristles and green gel. My downstairs neighbor always got up before me; I waited for the hot-water tank (only one to the building) to refill so I could shower away the last foggy caul of sleep. I listened to the guest congresswoman on *Today* confidently list syllogistic answers to the food and fuel shortages.

"But are you sure about that?" said the interviewer.

"Logic stands behind us," said the guest. "It enables our system to function."

The interviewer did not look convinced. "Many administration critics seem to feel the present crises will irreversibly worsen."

The guest said, "That violates our national philosophy." She laughed. "In another year, that could qualify as treason."

I was not reassured; then I abandoned myself to shower spray and was grateful the water was at least at room temperature. By the time I'd toweled off, my stomach had settled and I felt like eating something more substantial than Alka-Seltzer and bran flakes. I had grape juice with my bran flakes.

The time and temperature number confirmed what I'd seen in a glance out the window. The late-autumn day would require a heavy sweater. Time to leave; promptness at school counted. I knew the average driving time to campus was seventeen minutes.

At nine-thirty I was in my office at the college. Disgruntled students were already queuing in the hallway. Every term it was the same; I could predict it all. At mid-term I'd give them the broad guidelines for the final project. After a week they'd come out of shock and start bitching. It's too demanding, they would say, eyes narrowed, jaws quivering. Well, I'd answer, you're partly right. It's demanding. Some students fell apart; some drew discipline and structure about themselves and accomplished the project. At least they had the choice. At the time, so did I.

At eleven I had the introduction to fiction course; at noon, the composition section; then a special session of office hours for more students who were worried about their little universe flying apart from its center. ("Listen, I don't know if I can *do* the project, and if I drop out now or if I flunk, I won't have the hours to get into nursing school, and then my parents'll kill me, but if I have to leave school they really *will* kill me, and I won't be able to get a job and then what'll I do?") Just do the project, I'd say. Develop an idea as best you can; be logically consistent; follow through; consider ramifications. Concentrate. The universe abhors chaos. If you want, I'll help you.

Today I could go home at four. Gratefully I arrived at the apartment and collapsed on the couch. As usual I turned on a *Star Trek* rerun and went to sleep for a half-hour nap. I woke up, turned off the TV, read whatever magazine had come in the day's mail. Today it was *New York.* Conscience reminded me I ought to grade last week's in-class essays. I did so for two hours until my body told me to eat. I obeyed that reassuring biological clock by fixing soup and a sandwich.

After supper I watched a made-for-television movie about a disastrous blizzard: an entire city ceased to function after a giant storm. All the inhabitants died. It was uncharacteristically pessimistic for commercial TV. Vaguely disturbed, I switched it off before the end credits. I knew I should get back to work. Again it was time. The routine must be obeyed.

I wished Elizabeth weren't visiting her parents in Michigan. I wanted to call her, see her, perhaps go out to a late film. We would return here and make love. In sleep we would touch each other all night, hip to hip, fingers on flank. But I couldn't call—it was another time zone. It was too late. I suddenly shivered. *Someone's walking across your grave,* my father would have said. I shivered again. *Someone's standing there . . . tapping a foot, tamping the fill.*

I graded essays for another three hours.

And went to bed; one more day spent.

Aberrant, logical times; I remember them.

The raucous objection of crows, as they argued with a Manx on the fire escape over an unidentifiable bit of carrion, echoed in my ears. The cat, ears laid back, yowled and scimitared the air with its paw.

The cat cry merged with the rasp of the door buzzer. Through the window, I saw the sparrow's breast explode in a puff of gray feathers. The ragged tomcat seized the prey between its jaws and trotted down the stairs.

Sunlight pooled around the blood on the step. It was a beautiful day.

I left the door to my apartment open and walked down the four flights to the side entrance; precisely thirty-one steps. Each time I descended, I counted.

"Good morning," said Elspeth when I opened the door. Her eyes seemed to fade to a lighter gray in the dim light of the entryway. She carried a brown grocery sack, obviously heavy: she shifted it to the other arm and smiled.

I smiled back tentatively. "Elizabeth, I'm glad—"

"Who?"

"Elizabeth, I—"

"Nobody calls me that," she said. "Elspeth."

I realized I knew that. "Elspeth," I said. "I'm glad you're here."

"Me too." She shook the long chestnut hair away from her eyes. The green irises seemed to glow. "I've got plenty of picnic things. The store had some Chenin Blanc in the cooler. I thought we could go to the park."

"It's Febr—"

"July," she said hurriedly. "A beautiful summer day. Can I use the john before we go?"

"Sure," I said, again defeated temporarily and temporally. "I left the door open; slam it when you come back down. I'll guard the wine."

She kissed my cheek lightly as she moved past me in the hall. A chill breeze from the open door made me shiver. But, for whatever reason, I felt strong this morning. For the time I was in command. From outside the light brightened and the wind warmed as though clouds were breaking, unmasking the sun.

I relaxed; I would get through *this* day. Considering tomorrow could wait.

Elspeth returned, breath broken. "I've got to start swimming again and get back into shape. Forty steps are killing me."

"Thirty-two," I said automatically. Thirty-two? Thirty-one? Sometimes the details were the worst part. "Close."

She ignored me. "Breath's gone—ought to stop smoking."

"You stopped smoking on your birthday."

"No," she said. "I *will.*" She took a pack of Marlboros from her handbag. "On my birthday I will."

I hefted the grocery sack. "Let's go to the park." A distant siren quavered.

"What a marvelous day," said Elspeth. The remark sounded forced. "How do you feel?"

"Better. Not good."

"I didn't think so." She and I walked west along the avenue toward a crosswalk. Elspeth balked at the extra distance. "We can just jaywalk."

"I thought you wanted real exercise." The siren screamed past, the sounds scratching furrows across our ears. The tires of the ambulance shrieked nearly as loud as the vehicle rocked and skidded into the park entrance. "There's another reason why not." We waited for the light.

The edge of the park was only two blocks from the avenue. "Can we eat by the lake?" said Elspeth.

"Sure."

"I suppose I know what's wrong." Elspeth took my elbow as we left the sidewalk for the grass between the trees. "Do you want to talk about it now?"

I nodded slowly. "That's why I called you."

She glanced sidewise at me. "More attacks—" She hesitated.

"Of reality, as you called them." I nodded again.

"Disorientation?"

"Our definitions differ," I said, "but yes."

"Depression?"

"More like fear. If this is the way things really are, I'm not sure I can handle them much longer." I looked at her skeptically. "You know what I mean?"

She said, "I'm not sure I really understand, but I'm trying. I trust you."

I felt her love, and was strengthened. The center ceased its fragmentation. For a time, I would live.

We approached the south neck of the lake, the centerpiece of the park. Directly ahead, a small frame building served as refreshment stand and headquarters for the rental boat concession. Segregated by a chain-link fence, brightly painted craft filled the boatyard. A crowd had gathered around the steel gate where the ambulance waited with idling engine.

Many of the spectators were children. "What's going on?" I asked an onlooker.

"Guy fell out of a boat in the middle," said the boy. "Drownded. Weeds got him right off."

"Weeds?" said Elspeth.

"There've always been two or three drownings a summer," I said. "People don't seem to be able to swim, they get careless and fall out of the boat, then they get caught in the weeds and panic."

"Hey, they found him!" someone in the crowd said. There was a surge of bodies toward the fence as people jockeyed for a good view. I saw distant wetsuited figures pulling a shapeless bundle over the side of the boat. Then, like adjusting the eyepiece of a telescope and suddenly altering scale, I saw something else.

"Let's not eat our picnic here," said Elspeth. Her voice sounded dry.

"Wait a second," I said. "Do you know what this looks like?"

She turned away from the crowd. "A circus."

"The lake," I said. "It looks like a goddamned brain."

She smiled wanly. "Or a cauliflower. So what?"

"No, it really does," I said. "Look at it. The whole thing copies the central nervous system. All the lobes are there. The medulla—that's the bulge down there." I gestured. "The brain stem . . . that spring-fed creek running past us. There's the spinal cord."

"Um," she said.

"Just *look.*"

I saw the neon letters *humor him* igniting in *her* brain. "Can we walk up to the temporal lobe, okay?" she said.

I stopped, still hugging the grocery bag, staring at her. "Why did you say that?"

Elspeth said, "No reason. I just picked a lobe." She ran her fingers through her short red hair. "Honestly." She shook her wrist. "The watch, it reminded me."

"Time sense," I said slowly. "It's partially controlled in the temporal lobe."

"Listen, I really didn't mean to say anything to upset you."

"Elspeth, I—"

"Elise," Elise said.

"Elise, let's get out of here before I—"

A police officer approached us, motioning with his nightstick. "You folks like to move back? Give the ambulance some room." The recovery boat lay alongside the small dock. Medics wheeled a litter to its side. The divers made sounds of exertion and passed them a tarpaulin-covered form, its face covered. The crowd pressed forward, unsatisfied.

Elise tugged at my fingers. "Okay, anywhere," she said. "Just not here." Her voice sounded determinedly cheerful. "We'll go to the hippocampus."

"That's worse," I said, starting to walk away from her. "The short-term memory is housed in the hippocampal region. Did you know there's a man institutionalized in the Midwest who had the wrong part of his hippocampus burned out twenty-five years ago when the doctors were trying to excise a lesion? So far as he's concerned, ever since, it's still twelve hours before the operation. It'll be that way endlessly. If he goes into a bathroom, he forgets why he's there while he's still in the doorway."

"Why are you talking about him?"

"At least he's found a kind of stability," I said. "I don't think you can understand."

Both her face and voice were frightened. "You've *never* had neurosurgery."

"Not with a knife. Not with a wire." I laughed mirthlessly. "Maybe it's the chemicals, Elise. Remember them? You lived through the sixties just as I did. Did you try everything? Did you become a mutant? Did you sample the Catastrophenol, the Entropine, the Chaozine-25? Strange conjunctions of pharmaceutical stars."

She looked at me as if I were crazy; and I suppose, briefly, I might have been. I took a few deep, shuddering breaths. "One theory," I said. "Or a joke."

Elise took my free hand tightly. "No picnic today; it's getting cold. Let's go back to the apartment."

As we started out of the park, the first powdery snow of autumn sifted down around us. Elise and Cal, changing yet unchanged. "We'll light a fire," said Elise.

"You know I don't have a fireplace."

"Then we'll turn up the radiator, mull the Burgundy, make up the bed."

I love you. More than before, the warmth flowed out. I let the grocery sack slip to the grass and hugged Elise. She framed my face with her fingers. "It will be all right," she said.

We heard the crowd shift disappointedly behind us. I turned my head back. The tarpaulin had fallen away as the man on the litter sat up. The covering over his face came free. The expression on his face transmuted from panic to bewilderment to relief. He stared at the faces looking back at him. A medic helped him to his feet.

"You're lucky, mister," said one of the police. "That was pretty close."

"Maybe . . ." I said.

"Cal?"

Can I stop the process? I thought. Even reverse it? Perhaps only for others, perhaps only temporarily, but perhaps for myself as well. I don't want only Pyrrhic victories.

But something's always lost. Already starting to blot the scene, snow clung to the lenses of my glasses. Elise's hand cooled in mine. Again I grabbed for anchored razor blades.

Life, returning; or at least in motion. "How pale your skin is," I said. "How light your eyes." She looked back at me, features expressionless. Beth, have you changed? The sick feeling returned.

"My eyes I was born with," said Beth. "My skin—I should have gotten out more last summer." With her fingers she urged my hands to touch her skin. "Does pallor offend your sense of aesthetics?"

I ran my fingers along the coolness of her flanks and felt no need to say anything. Now wordless as well, she offered me shelter. I shivered against her and Beth wrapped me close in her arms. I needed to touch her as I needed to be touched. I buried myself in her as though tapping submerged volcanic heat. She cried out and we rested, for the moment warm, for the second secure, cocooned in down-filled comforters.

After a time, she said, "I was reading Wilde today. I brought you something from that."

"Oscar Wilde? Doesn't seem entirely appropriate."

She didn't smile in return. "It's a paraphrase—I'm never any good with quotations. Anyway, he said that once you've loved somebody, you can do anything for them but love them that way again."

"It seems a little cynical," I said. "Do you take it literally and beyond? That the universe militates against loving anybody the same way, or to the same degree, twice?" Beth didn't answer. "Maybe it codifies some sort of second law of human dynamics?" I knew my smile had no warmth. I shivered. In the almost-darkness my fingertips proved she wasn't smiling either.

"I didn't say I understood all this. I only feel—"

"Do you want to understand?"

"I don't know that either." She paused. "Yes, no, I don't know."

Propped on an elbow, I looked down at her light champagne hair blending against the pillow, almost disappearing into its surface. Paler still were her eyes, shadowed and shading into darkness. "I'm out of phase with all this," I said. "Somehow I'm cut loose—"

"I know," said Liz, now tracing out my cheekbones with the side of her hand. I could barely feel her.

"Loving, but not enough." Had I really said that? Yes.

"No," she said. "You love me. I love you. But some processes you simply can't reverse. It has nothing to do with good or virtue or love."

I said, "It's all winding down."

"Cal." The gentle whisper faded in my ear. "I'm here."

I shook my head slowly, feeling the last resistance evaporating. It occurred to me—for perhaps an infinite time—that it's impossible to ascribe unfairness to impersonal process. It didn't help; not at all; no.

Winter, summer, autumn, spring. "Love?"

Yes.

"Liz, I can barely hear you." Light sheeted from the windows; photons flooded *away* from me, a vessel draining. Darkness overwhelmed shapes and forms with chiaroscuro.

Love? No strength, no energy, only a final railing against that which seemed inevitable; but I tried.

Starless night opened for me; a bed without heat. Emptiness champed at me; I jerked away. I reached out, grasped, groped, touching nothing, trying to secure my entropic lover.

"I'm here," she said.

And then that too changed.

(1980)

MARION ZIMMER BRADLEY

Elbow Room

Sometimes I feel the need to go to confession on my way to work.

It's quiet at firstdawn, with Aleph Prime not above the horizon yet; there's always some cognitive dissonance because, with the antigravs turned up high enough for comfort, you feel that the "days" ought to reflect a planet of human mass, not a mini-planetoid space station. So at first dawn you're set for an ordinary-sized day; twenty hours, or twenty-three, or something your circadian rhythms could compromise with. Thus when Prime sets again for firstdark you aren't prepared for it. With your mind, maybe, but not down where you need it, in your guts. By thirddawn you're gearing up for a whole day on Checkout Station again, and you can cope with thirddark and fifthdark and by twelfthdark you're ready to put on your sleep mask and draw the curtains and shut it all out again till firstdawn next day.

But at firstdawn you get that illusion, and I always enjoy it for a little while. It's like being really alone on a silent world, a real world. And even before I came here to Checkout I was always a loner, preferring my own company to anyone else's.

That's the kind they always pick for the Vortex stations, like Checkout. There isn't much company there. And we learn to give each other elbow room.

You'd think, with only five of us here—or is it only four; I've never been quite sure, for reasons I'll go into later—we'd do a lot of socializing. You'd think we would huddle together against the enormous agoraphobia of space. I really don't know why we don't. I guess, though, the kind of person who could really enjoy living on Checkout—and I do—would have to be a loner. And I go squirrelly when there are too many other people around.

Of course, I know I couldn't really live here alone, as much as I'd like to. They tried that, early in the days of the Vortex stations, sending one man or woman out alone. One after another, with monotonous regularity, they suicided. Then they tried sending well-adjusted couples, small groups, sociable types who would huddle together and socialize, and they all went nuts and did one another in. I know why, of course; they saw too much of each other, and began to rely on one another for their sanity and self-validation. And of course that solution didn't work. You have to be the kind of person who can be wholly self-reliant.

So now they do it this way. I always know I'm not alone. But I never have to *see* too much of the other people here; I never have to see them unless I *want* to. I don't know how much socializing the others do, but I suspect they're as much loners as I am. I don't really care, as long as they don't intrude on *my* privacy and as long as they take orders the way they're supposed to. I love them all, of course, all four or maybe five of them. They told me, back at Psych Conditioning, that this would happen. But I don't remember how it happened, whether it just happened or whether they *made* it happen. I don't ask too many questions. I'm glad that I love them; I'd hate to think that some Psych-tech *made* me love them! Because they're sweet, dear, wonderful, lovable people. All of them.

As long as I don't have to see them very often.

Because I'm the boss. I'm in control. It's *my* Station! Slight tendencies toward megalomania, they called it in Psych. It's good for a Station Programmer to have these mild megalomanic tendencies, they explained it all to me. If they put humble self-effacing types out here, they'd start thinking of themselves as wee little fleabites upon the vast face of the Universe, and sooner or later they'd be found with their throats cut, because they couldn't believe they were big enough to be in control of anything on the cosmic scale of the Vortex.

Lonely, yes. But I like it that way. I like being boss out here. And I like the way they've provided for my needs. I think I have the best chef in the galaxy. She cooks all my favorite foods—I suppose Psych gave her my profile. I wonder sometimes if the other people at the station have to eat what I like, or if they get to order their own favorites. I don't really care, as long as I get to order what I like. And then I have my own personal librarian, with all the music of the galaxy at her fingertips, the best sound-equipment known, state-of-the-art stuff I'd never be able to afford in any comparable job back Earthside. And my own gardener, and a technician to do the work I can't handle. And even my own personal priest. Can you imagine that? Sending a priest all the way out here, just to minister to my spiritual needs! Well, at least to a congregation of four. Or five.

Or is it six? I keep thinking I've forgotten somebody.

Firstdawn is rapidly giving way to firstnoon when I leave the garden and kneel in the little confessional booth. I whisper, "Bless me, Father, for I have sinned."

"Bless you, my child." Father Nicholas is there, although his Mass must be long over. I sometimes wonder if this doesn't violate the sanctity of the confessional, that he cannot help knowing which of his congregation is kneeling there; I am the only one who ever gets up before second-dawn. And I don't really know whether I have sinned or not. How could I sin against God or my fellow man, when I am thousands of millions of miles away from all but five or six of them? And I so seldom see the others, I have no chance to sin with them or against them. Maybe I only need to hear his voice; a human voice, a light, not particularly masculine voice. Deeper than mine, though, *different* from mine. That's the important thing; to hear a voice which *isn't* mine.

"Father, I have entertained doubts about the nature of God."

"Continue, my child."

"When I was out in the Wheel the other day, watching the Vortex, I found myself wondering if the Vortex was God. After all, God is unknowable, and the Vortex is so totally alien from human experience. Isn't this the closest thing that the human race has ever found, to the traditional view of God? Something totally beyond matter, energy, space or time?"

There is a moment of silence. Have I shocked the priest? But after a long time his soft voice comes quietly into the little confessional. Outside the light is already dimming toward firstdark.

"There is no harm in regarding the Vortex as a symbol of God's relationship to man, my child. After all, the Vortexes are perhaps the most glorious of God's works. It is written in scripture that the Heavens declare the glory of God, and the firmament proclaims the wonder of His work."

"But does this mean, then, that God is distant, incapable of loving mankind? I can't imagine the Vortex loving anyone or being conscious of anyone. Not even me."

"Is that a defect in God, or a defect in your own imagination, my child, in ascribing limits to God's power?"

I persist. "But does it matter if I say my prayers to the Vortex, and worship it?"

Behind the screen I hear a soft laugh. "God will hear your prayers wherever you say them, dear child, and whenever you find anything worthy of worship and admiration you are worshipping God, by whatever name you choose to call it. Is there anything else, my child?"

"I have been guilty of uncharitable thoughts about my cook, Father. Last night she didn't fix my dinner till late, and I wanted to tear her eyes out!"

"Did you harm her, child?"

"No. I just yelled through the screen that she was a lazy, selfish, stupid bitch. I wanted to go out and hit her, but I didn't."

"Then you exercised commendable self-restraint, did you not? What did she answer?"

"She didn't answer at all. And that made me madder than ever."

"You should love your neighbor—and I mean your chef, too—as yourself, child," he reproves, and I say, hanging my head, "I'm not loving myself very much these days, maybe that's the trouble."

Mind, now, I'm not sure there really is a Father Nicholas behind that screen. Maybe it's a relay system which puts me into touch with a priest Earthside. Or maybe Father Nicholas is only a special voice program on the main computer, which is why I sometimes ask the craziest questions, and play a game with myself to see how long it takes "Father Nicholas" to find the right program for an answer. As I said, it seems crazy to send a priest out here for five people. Or is it six?

But then, why not? We people at the Vortex stations keep the whole galaxy running. Nothing is too good for us, so why not my personal priest?

"Tell me what is troubling you, my child."

Always *my child.* Never by name. Does he even know it? He must. After all, I am in charge here; Checkout Programmer. The boss. Or is this just the manners of the confessional, a subtle way of reemphasizing that all of us are the same to him, equal in his sight and in the sight of God? I don't know if I like that. It's disquieting. Perhaps my chef runs to him and tells tales of me, how I shrieked foul names at her, and abused her through the kitchen hatch! I cover my face with my hands and sob, hearing him make soothing sounds.

I envy that priest, secure behind his curtain. Listening to the human faults of others, having none of his own. I almost became a priest myself. I tell him so.

"I know that, child, you told me. But I'm not clear in my mind why you chose not to be ordained."

I'm not clear either, and I tell him so, trying to remember. If I had been a man I would surely have gone through with it, but it is still not entirely easy to be ordained, for a woman, and the thought of seminary, with ninety or a hundred other priestlings and priestlets herded all together, even then the thought made me uneasy. I couldn't have endured the fight for a woman to be ordained. "I'm not a fighter, Father."

But I am disquieted when he agrees with me. "No. If you were, you wouldn't be out here, would you?" Again I feel uneasy; am I just running away? I choose to live here on the ragged rim of the Universe, tending the Vortex, literally at the back end of Beyond. I pour all this uncertainty out to him, knowing he will reassure me, understand me as always.

But his reassuring noises are too soothing, too calming, humoring me.

Damn it, is there anyone *there* behind that curtain? I want to tear it down, to see the priest's face, his human face, or else to be sure that it is only a bland computer console programmed to reassure and thus to mock me. My hand already extended, I draw it back. I don't really want to know. Let them laugh at me, if there is really a *they,* a priest Earthside listening over this unthinkable extension of the kilometers and the megakilometers, let them laugh. They deserve it, if they are really such clever programmers, making it possible for me to draw endless sympathy and reassurance from the sound of an alien voice.

Whatever we do, we do to make it possible for you to live and keep your sanity . . . "I think, Father, that I am—am a little lonely. The dreams are building up again."

"Perfectly natural," he says soothingly, and I know that he will arrange one of Julian's rare visits. Even now I hang my head, blush, cannot face him, but it is less embarrassing this way than if I had to take the initiative alone, unaided. It's part of being the kind of loner I am, that I could never endure it, to call Julian direct, have to take—perhaps—a rebuff or a downright rejection. Well, I never claimed to be a well-adjusted personality. A well-adjusted personality could not survive out here, at the rim of nowhere. Back on Earthside I probably wouldn't even *have* a love life, I avoid people too much. But here they provide for all my needs. All. Even this one, which, left to myself, I would probably neglect.

Ego te absolvo.

I kneel briefly to say my penance, knowing that the ritual is foolish. Comforting; but foolish. He reminds me to turn on the monitor in my room and he will say Mass for me tomorrow. And again I am certain that there is nobody there, that it is a program in the computer; is there any other reason we do not all assemble for Christian fellowship? Or do we all share this inability to tolerate one another's company?

But I feel soothed and comforted as I go down between the automatic sprinklers through the little patch of garden tended so carefully by my own gardener. I catch a glimpse, a shimmer in the air, of someone in the garden, turned away like a distant reflection, but no one is supposed to be here at this hour and I quickly look away.

Still it is comforting not to be alone and I call out a cheery good-morning to the invisible image, wondering, with a strange little cramp of excitement low in my body; *is it Julian?* I see him so briefly, so seldom, except in the half-darkness of my room on those rare occasions he comes to me. I'm not even sure what he does here. We don't talk about his work. We have better things to do. Thinking of that makes me tremble, squeeze my legs tight, thinking that it may not be long till I see him again. But I have a day's work to do, and with seconddawn brightening the sky, glinting on reflections from which I glance away . . . *you never look in mirrors* . . . I climb up into the seat that will take me up to the Wheel, out by the Vortex.

There is an exhilaration to that, shooting up toward the strange seething no-color of it. There is a ship already waiting. Waiting for *me,* for the Vortex to open. All that power and burning and fusion and raw energy, all waiting for *me,* and I enjoy my daily dose of megalomania as I push the speech button.

"Checkout speaking. Register your name and business."

It is always a shock to hear a voice from outside, a really strange voice. But I register the captain's voice, the name and registry number so that later they can match programs with Checkin, my opposite number on the far side of the Vortex—in a manner of speaking. Where the Vortex is concerned, of course, Near and Far, or Here and There, or Before and After, have no more meaning than—oh, than I and Thou. In one of the mirrors on the wheel I catch a glimpse of my technician, waiting, and I sit back and listen as she rattles off the coordinates in a sharp staccato. She and I have nothing to say to each other. I don't really think that girl is interested in anything except mathematics. I drift, watching myself in the mirror, listening to the ship's captain arguing with the technician, and I am irritated. How dare he argue, her conduct reflects on me and I am enraged by any hint of rudeness to my staff. So I speak the code which starts the Vortex into its strange nonspace whorl, the colors and swirls.

This could all be done by computers, of course.

I am here, almost literally, to push a button by hand if one gets stuck. From the earliest days of telemetered equipment, machinery has tended to go flukey and sometimes jam; and during the two hundred years that the Vortex stations have been in operation, they've found out that it's easier and cheaper to maintain the stations with their little crews of agoraphobic and solitary loners. They even provide us with chefs and gardeners and all our mental and spiritual comforts. We humans are just software which doesn't—all things considered—get out of order quite as often as the elaborate self-maintaining machineries do. Furthermore, we can be serviced more cheaply when we *do* get out of order. So we're there to make sure that if any of the buttons stick, we can unstick them before they cost the Galaxy more than the whole operating costs of Checkout for the next fifty years.

I watch the Vortex swirl, and my knowledge and judgment tell me the same thing as do my instruments. "Whenever you're ready," I say, receive their acknowledgment, and then the strange metal shape of the ship swirls with the Vortex, becomes nonshape, I almost see it vanish into amorphous nothingness, to come out—or so the theory is—at

Checkin Station, several hundred light-years away. Do these ships go anywhere at all, I wonder? Do they ever return? They vanish when I push those buttons, and they never come back. Am I sending them into oblivion, or to their proper prearranged destination? I don't know. And, if the truth be told, I don't really care. For all the difference it makes to me they could be going into another dimension, or to the theological Hell.

But I like it out here on the Wheel. There is *real* solitude up here. Down there on Checkout there is solitude with other people around, though I seldom see them. I realize I am still twitching from a brief encounter with the gardener this morning. Don't they know, these people, that they aren't supposed to be around when I am walking in the gardens? But even that brief surge of adrenaline has been good for me, I suppose. Do they arrange for me to get a glimpse of one of my fellow humans only when I *need* that kind of stirring up?

Back at Checkout—there will not be another ship today—I walk again through the garden, putter a little, cherish with my eyes the choice melon I am growing under glass, warn the gardener through the intercom not to touch it until I myself order it served up for my supper. I remember the satisfaction of the cargo ship waiting, metal tentacles silent against the black of space, waiting. Waiting for me, waiting for my good pleasure, gatekeeper to the Void, Cerberus at a new kind of hell.

Rank has its privileges. While I am in the garden none of the others come near; but I am a little fatigued, I leave the garden to the others and go to my room for deep meditation. I can sense them all around me, the gardener working with the plants like an extension of my own consciousness, I sit like a small spider at the center of a web and watch the others working as I sit back to meditate. My mind floats free, my alpha rhythms take over, I disappear . . .

Later, waiting for my supper, I wonder what kind of woman would become chef on a Checkout station. I *can* cook, I *have* done my own cooking, I am a damn good cook, but I wouldn't have taken a job like that. Is she completely without ambition? I don't see her very often. We wouldn't have much in common; what could I possibly have to say to a woman like that? Waiting, floating, spider in my web, I find I can imagine her going carefully through the motions and little soothing rituals, chopping fresh vegetables I fingered in the garden this morning, heating the trays, all the little soothing mindless things. But to spend her life like that? The woman must be a fool.

I come out of the meditative state to find my supper waiting for me. I call my thanks to her, eat. The food is good, it is always good, but the dishes are too hot, somehow I have burned my hand on them. But it doesn't matter, I have something more to look forward to, tonight. I delay, savoring the knowledge, listening to one of my operatic tapes, lost in a vague romantic reverie. Tonight, Julian is coming.

I wonder sometimes why we are not allowed to see one another more often. Surely, if he cares for me as much as he says, it would be proper to see each other casually now and then, to talk about our work. But I am sure Psych is right, that it is better for us not to see each other too often. On Earth, if we grew tired of one another, we could each find someone else. But here there *is* no one else—for either of us. A phrase floats through my mind from nowhere, *chains of mnemonic suggestion,* as I set the controls which will allow him to come, silent and alone, into my room after I have gone to bed.

He has come and gone.

I do not know why the rules are as they are. Perhaps to keep us from quarreling, to avoid the tragedies of the early days of the Vortex stations. Perhaps, simply, to avoid our growing bored with each other. As if I could ever be bored with Julian! To me, he is perfect, even his name. Julian has always seemed to me the most perfect name for a man, and Julian, *my* Julian, my lover, the perfect man to match the perfect name. So why is it we are not allowed to meet more often? Why can we meet like this, only in the silent dark?

Langorous, satisfied, exhausted, I muse drowsily, wondering if it is some obscure mystery of my inner Psych-profile, that one of us subconsciously desires the old myth of Psyche, who could retain her lover Eros only as long as she never saw his face? I see him only for a moment in the mirror, misty, never clearly perceived, over my shoulder; but I know he is handsome.

I am so sensitive to Julian's moods that I think sometimes I am developing special senses for my love; becoming a telepath, but only for him. When our bodies join it seems often as if I were one in mind with him, touching him, how else could I be so aware of his emotions, so completely secure of his tenderness and his concern? How else could he know so perfectly all my body's obscurer desires, when I myself can hardly bring myself to speak them, when I would be afraid or ashamed to voice them aloud? But he knows, he always knows, leaving me satisfied, worn, spent. I wish, with a longing so intense it is pain, that the regulations by which we live would let him lie here in my arms for the rest of the night, that I could feel myself held close and cherished, comforted against this vast, eternal loneliness; that he could cuddle me in his arms, that we could meet sometimes for a drink or share our dinner. Why not?

A terrible thought comes to me. They give me everything else. My own cook. My own gardener. My technician. My personal priest.

My very own male whore.

I cannot believe it. No, no. No. I do not believe it. Julian loves me, and I love him. Anyhow, it would not suit the Puritan consciences of our legislators. No, I can't see it; how would they justify it on the requisition forms? *Whore, male, one, Checkout Programmer, for the use of.* No, such a thing couldn't happen. Surely they just hired some male technician, determined by Psych-profile to have the maximum sexual compatibility with myself. That's bad enough, heaven knows.

Now an even more frightening thought surges up into my conscious mind. Can it be possible—oh, God, no!—that Julian, *my* Julian, is an android?

They have designed some of them, I know, with extremely sophisticated sex programs. I have seen them advertised in those catalogs we used to giggle over when we were little girls. I am sick with fear and dread at the thought that during those conditioning trances which I have been conditioned to forget, I gave up all that data about my secret dreams and desires and sexual fantasies, so that they might program them all into the computer of an android, and what emerged was . . . Julian.

Is he a multipurpose android, perhaps, then? Hardware, no more, both useful and economical; perhaps that gardener I see dimly sometimes, like a hologram, in the distance. He could, of course, be the gardener, though in the brief glimpses of the gardener I had the impression the gardener was a woman. Who can tell, with these coveralls we all wear, uniform, unisex? And it would look better on the congressional requisitions: *Android, one, multiprogrammed. Checkout Station, for the maintenance of.* And a special sexual program would only be a memo in the files of Psych. Nothing to embarrass anyone—anyone but me, that is, and I am not supposed to know. Just another piece of Station hardware. For maintenance of the Station. And of the Station Programmer. Hardware. Yes, very. Oh, God!

I have no time now for worrying about Julian, or what he is, or about my own dissatisfactions and fears. I cannot take any of these disquieting thoughts to that computerized priest, if he is indeed only a sophisticated computer, a mechanical priest-psychiatrist! Is he another android, perhaps? Or is he indeed the same android with still another program? Priest and male whore at the flip of a switch? Am I alone here with a multipurpose android serving all my functions? No time for that. A ship is out there, waiting for me; and my instruments tell me, as I ride out to the Wheel, even before I get the message; that ship is in trouble.

Perhaps all the signs, all my fears that I am going mad, are simply signs of developing telepathic potential; I never believed that I was even potentially an esper, yet somehow I am aware of nearly everything my technician said to the ship's captain. I did not understand it all, of course, I have no technical skill at all. My skills are all executive. I can barely manage to make my little pocket calculator figure out the tariffs for the ships I send into the Vortex; I joked with Central that they should allow me a bookkeeper, but they are too stingy. But even though I did not understand all of what the technician said, when I read the report she left for me, I know that if the ship went into the Vortex in this state, it might never emerge; worse, it might create spatial anomalies to disturb the fields for other ships and put the Vortex very badly out of commission. So I know that they dare not pass through that gate; I cannot follow the precise mathematics of the switch, though, and I feel like a fool. When I was in preparatory school I tested higher in all the groups, including mathematical ability. But I ended up with no technical skill. How, I wonder, did that happen?

Later I have leisure to visit the captain by screen. He is a big man, youthful, soft-spoken, his smile strangely stirring. And he asks me a strange question.

"You are the Programmer? Are you people a clone?"

"Why, no, nothing like that," I say to him, and ask why.

"The technician—she's very like you. Oh, of course, you are nothing alike otherwise, she's all business—a shame, in a lovely young woman! I could hardly get her to say a pleasant word to me!"

I tell him that I am an only child. Only children are best for work like this; the necessary isolation from peer groups. A child reared in a puppy-pack, under peer pressure from siblings and agemates, becomes other-directed; dependent upon the opinions and the approval of others, without the inner resources to tolerate the solitude which is the breath of life to me. I am even a little offended. "I can't see the slightest resemblance between us," I tell him, and he shakes his head and says diplomatically that perhaps it is a similarity of height and coloring which misled him.

"Anyway, I didn't like her much, she flayed me with her tongue, kept strictly to business—you'd think it was my *fault* the ship was out of commission! You're much, *much* pleasanter than she is!"

And that is as it should be, I am the one with leisure for reflection and conversation; it wouldn't be right for my technician to waste her time talking! So we talk, we even flirt a little. I am aware of it; I pose and preen a little for him, letting the animal woman surface from all the other faces I wear, and finally I agree to the hazardous step, to visit him on his ship.

So strange, so strange to think of being with one who is not carefully Psych-profiled to be agreeable to me. There is nothing in the regulations against it, of course, perhaps they believe our love of solitude will keep us away as it has always done before, for me. Even a little welcome, alien.

But when I am actually through the airlock I am shocked into silence by the strange faces, the alien smells, the different body-chemistry of strange male life. They say that men give off hormones, analogous to pheromones in the lower kingdoms, which they cannot smell on one another; which only a woman is chemically able to smell. I believe, it, it is true, the ship reeks of maleness. Ushered into a room where I may strip my suit I avoid the mirror. *Never look into a mirror, unless . . . unless* . . . why would Psych have imprinted that prohibition on me? I need to see that my hair is tidy, my coverall free of grease. Defiantly I look into it anyway, my head swims and I look away in haste.

Fear, fear of what I may see, my face dissolving, identity lost . . . stranger, not myself, unknown. . . .

A drink in my hand, flattery and compliments; I find I am hungry for this after long isolation. Of course I am selfish and vain, it is a professional necessity, like my little touch of daily megalomania. I accept this, and revel in seeing others, interacting with strange faces—*really* strange, not programmed to my personal needs and wishes. Yes, I know I need to be alone, I remember all the reasons, but I know also, too well, the terrible face of loneliness. All my carefully chosen companions are so dovetailed to my personality that talking to them is like . . . *like talking to myself, like looking in a mirror* . . .

Two drinks help me unwind, relax. I know all the dangers of alcohol, but tonight I am defiant; we are off duty, both the captain and myself, we need not guard ourselves. Before too long I find the captain's hands on me, touching me, rousing me in a way Julian has not done since his first visits. I give myself over to his kisses, and when he asks the inevitable question I brace myself for a moment, then shrug and ask myself *Why not?* His touch on me is welcome, I brush aside thoughts of Julian, even Julian has been too carefully adjusted, dovetailed, programmed to my own personality; perhaps even a little abrasiveness helps to alter the far-too-even tenor of the days, to create something of the necessary *otherness* of lovemaking. That is what I have missed, the otherness; Julian being too carefully selected and Psych-profiled to me.

If a love-partner is too similar to the self there is not the needed, satisfying *merging.* Even the amoeba which splits itself, infinitely reduplicating perfect analogies of its own personality and awareness, feels now and then the need to merge, to exchange its very protoplasm and cell-stuff with the *other;* too much of even the most necessary similarity is deadly, and makes of lovemaking only a more elaborate and ritualized masturbation. It is good to be touched by *another.*

Together, then, into his room. And our bodies merge abruptly into an unlovely struggle at the height of which he blurts out, as if in shock, "But you couldn't *possibly* be that inexperienced . . . " and then, seeing and sensing my shock, he is all gentleness again, apologetic, saying he had forgotten how young I was. I am confused and distressed; *I* inexperienced? Now I am on my mettle, to prove myself equal to passion, sophisticated and knowledgeable, tolerating discomfort and strangeness, to think longingly of Julian. It serves me right, to be unfaithful to him, Psych was right, Julian is exactly what I need; I know, even while the captain and I are lying close, afterward, all tenderness, that I will not do this again. The regulations are wise. Back to the Station, back to my quarters, blur the experience all away in sleep, all of it . . . *awkwardness, struggle that felt like rape* . . . no, I will not do this again, I know now why it is forbidden. I do not think I will confess it even to the priest, I have done penance enough. Seal it all away in some inaccessible part of my mind, the bruising and humiliation of the memory.

Flotsam in my mind from the vast amnesia of the training program, as I seek to forget, that conditioning they will never let us remember; that I am suitable for this work because I dissociate with abnormal rapidity. . . .

And next morning at firstdawn I go up even before breakfast to the Wheel; their repairs are made and they do not want to lose time. The captain wants to speak with me, but I let him speak with the technician while I watch out of sight. I do not want to look into his face again; I never want to see again in any face that mixture of tenderness, pity—contempt.

I am glad to see their ship dissolve into the vast nonshape of the Vortex. I do not care if their repairs have been made properly or if they lose themselves somewhere inside the Vortex and never return. Watching their shape vanish I see a face dissolving in a mirror and I am agitated and frightened, frightened . . . they are not part of my world, I have seen them go, I have perhaps destroyed them. I think of how easy it would have been, how glad I would have been if my technician had given them the wrong program and they had vanished into the Vortex and come out . . . nowhere. As I have destroyed everything not the self.

Julian has been destroyed for me too. . . .

Maybe there is nothing out there, no ship, no Vortex, nothing. Everything comes into the human mind through the filters of self, my priest created to absolve a self which is not there, or is it the priest who is not there at all? Maybe there is nothing out there, maybe I created it all out of my own inner needs, priest, ship, Station, Vortex, perhaps I am still lying in the conditioning trances down there on Earth, fantasizing people who would help me to survive the terrors of loneliness, perhaps these people whom I see, but never clearly, are all androids, or fantasies born of my own madness and my inner needs . . . a random phrase floats again through my mind, *always the danger of solipsism, in the dissociator, the feeling that only the self exists . . . eternal preoccupation with internal states is morbid and we take advantage . . .*

Was there ever a ship out there? Did my mind create it to break the vast monotony of solitude, the loneliness I find I cannot endure, did I even fantasize the captain's gross body lying on my own?

Or is it Julian that I created, my own hands on my body, fantasy . . . a half-lighted image in a mirror . . .

The terrible solitude, the solitude I need and yet cannot endure, the solitude that is madness. And yet I need the solitude, so that I will not kill them all, I could murder them as all the earlier Vortex stations murdered one another, or is it only suicide when there is nothing but myself?

Is the whole cosmos out there—stars, galaxies, Vortex—only an emanation of my own brain? If so, then I can unmake it with a thought as I made it. I can snatch up my cook's kitchen knife and plunge it into my throat and all the stars will go away and all the universes. What am I doing in the kitchen . . . the cook's knife in my hand . . . here where I never go? She will be angry; I am supposed to give her the same privacy I yield to myself, I call out an apology and leave. Or is that pointless, am I crying out apology or abuse to myself? I have had no breakfast, at this hour, near thirddawn, the cook always prepares, I always prepare breakfast, I meditate while breakfast is prepared and served to me on my tray, facing the mirror from which I emerge . . . I am the other, the one with leisure for meditation and reflection—the executive, creative, I am God creating all these universes inside and outside of my mind . . . dizzied, I catch at the mirror, the knife slips, my face dissolves, my hand bleeds and all the universes wobble and spin on their cosmic axes, the face in the mirror commands in the voice of Father Nicholas, "Go, my child, and meditate."

"No! No!" I refuse to be tranquilized again, to be deceived . . .

"Command over-ride!" A voice I do not remember. "Go and meditate, meditate . . . " *meditate, meditate . . .*

Like the tolling of a great bell, commanding, rising out of the deeps, the voice of God. I meditate, seeing my face dissolve and change. . . .

No wonder I can read the technician's mind, I am the technician . . .

There is no one here. There has never been anyone here.

Only myself, and I am all, I am the God, the maker and unmaker of all the universes, I am Brahma, I am the Cosmos and the Vortex, I am the slow unraveling . . .

. . . unraveling of the mind . . .

I stumble to the chapel, images dissolving in my mind like the cook's face with the knife, into the confessional, the confessional I have always known is empty, sob out a prayer to the empty shrine. *Oh, God, if there is a God, let there be a God, let there be somebody there . . . or is God too only an emanation of my mind . . .*

And the slow dissolve into the mirror, the priest's voice saying soothing things which I do not really hear, the mirror as my mind dissolves, the priest's voice soothing and calm, my own voice weeping, pleading, sobbing, begging . . .

But his words mean nothing, a fragment of my own disintegration, I want to die, I want to die, I am dying, gone, nowhere . . .

The phenomenon of selective attention, what used to be called hypnosis, a self-induced dissociation or fugue state, dissociational hysteria sometimes regarded as multiple personality when the fragmented self-organized chains of memory and personality sets organize themselves into different consciousness. There is always the danger of solipsism, but the personality defends itself with enormously complex coping mechanisms. For instance, although we knew she had briefly attended a seminary, we had not expected the priest. . . .

"Ego te absolvo. Make a good act of contrition, my child."

I murmur the foolish, comforting, ritual words. He says, gently, "Go and meditate, child, you will feel better."

He is right. He is always right. I think sometimes that Father Nicholas is my conscience. That, of course, is the function of a priest. I meditate. All the terrors dissolve while I sit quietly in meditation, spinning the threads of this web where I sit, happy at the center, conscious of all the others moving around me. I must be developing esper powers, there is no other explanation, for while I sit quietly here meditating in the chapel the soothing vibrations of the garden come up through my fingers while my gardener works quietly, detached and calm, in my garden, growing delicious things for my supper. I love them all, all my friends around me here, they are all so kind to me, protecting my precious solitude, my privacy. I cannot cook the lovely things he grows, so I sit in my cherished solitude while my cook creates all manner of delicious things for my supper. How kind she is to me, a sweet woman really, though I know that I would have nothing to say to a woman like that. I waken out of meditation to see supper in my tray. How quickly the day has gone, seventhdawn brightening into seventhnoon, and darkness will be upon all of us again soon. How good it is, how sweet and fresh the food from my own garden; I call my thanks to her, this cook who spends all her time thinking up delightful things for me to eat. She must have esper powers too, my prize melon is on my tray, she knew exactly what I wanted after such a day as this.

"Good-night, dear cook, thank you, God bless you, good-night."

She does not answer, I know she will not answer, she knows her place, but I know she hears and is pleased at my praise.

"Sleep well, my dear, good-night."

As I go to my room through the dimming of eighthdark, it crosses my mind that sometimes I am a little lonely here. But I am doing important work, and after all, the Psych people knew what they were doing. They knew that I need elbow room.

(1980)

PHYLLIS GOTLIEB

TAUF ALEPH

Samuel Zohar ben Reuven Begelman lived to a great age in the colony Pardes on Tau Ceti IV and in his last years he sent the same message with his annual request for supplies to Galactic Federation Central: *Kindly send one mourner/gravedigger so I can die in peace respectfully.*

And Sol III replied through GalFed Central with the unvarying answer: *Regret cannot find one Jew yours faithfully.*

Because there was not one other identifiable Jew in the known universe, for with the opening of space the people had scattered and intermarried, and though their descendants were as numerous, in the fulfillment of God's promise, as the sands on the shore and the stars in the heavens, there was not one called Jew, nor any other who could speak Hebrew and pray for the dead. The home of the ancestors was emptied: it was now a museum where perfect simulacra performed 7500 years of history in hundreds of languages for tourists from the breadth of the Galaxy.

In Central, Hrsipliy the Xiploid said to Castro-Ibanez the Solthree, "It is a pity we cannot spare one person to help that poor *juddar.*" She meant by this term: body/breath/spirit/sonofabitch, being a woman with three tender hearts.

Castro-Ibanez, who had one kind heart and one hard head, answered, "How can we? He is the last colonist on that world and refuses to be moved; we keep him alive at great expense already." He considered for some time and added, "I think perhaps we might send him a robot. One that can dig and speak recorded prayers. Not one of the new expensive ones. We ought to have some old machine good enough for last rites."

O/G5/842 had been resting in a very dark corner of Stores for 324 years, his four coiled arms retracted and his four hinged ones resting on his four wheeled feet. Two of his arms terminated in huge scoop shovels, for he had been an ore miner, and he was also fitted with treads and sucker-pods. He was very great in size; they made giant machines in those days. New technologies had left him useless; he was not even worthy of being dismantled for parts.

It happened that this machine was wheeled into the light, scoured of rust and lubricated. His ore-scoops were replaced with small ones retrieved from Stores and suitable for gravedigging, but in respect to Sam Begelman he was not given a recording: he was rewired and supplemented with an almost new logic and given orders and permission to go and learn. Once he had done so to the best of his judgment he would travel out with Begelman's supplies and land. This took great expense, but less than an irreplaceable person or a new machine; it fulfilled the Galactic-Colonial contract. O/G would not return, Begelman would rest in peace, no one would recolonize Tau Ceti IV.

O/G5/842 emerged from his corner. In the Library he caused little more stir than the seven members of the Khagodi embassy (650 kilos apiece) who were searching out a legal point of intra-Galactic law. He was too broad to occupy a cubicle, and let himself be stationed in a basement exhibit room where techs wired him to sensors, sockets, inlets, outlets, screens and tapes. Current flowed, light came, and he said, LET ME KNOW SAMUEL ZOHAR BEN REUVEN BEGELMAN DOCTOR OF MEDICINE AND WHAT IT MEANS THAT HE IS A JEW.

He recorded the life of Sam Begelman; he absorbed Hebrew, Aramaic, Greek; he learned Torah, which is Law: day one. He learned Writings, Prophets, and then Mishna, which is the first exegesis of Law: day the second. He learned Talmud (Palestinian and Babylonian), which is the completion of Law, and Tosefta, which are ancillary writings and divergent opinions in Law: day the third. He read 3500 years of Commentary and Responsa: day the fourth. He learned Syriac, Arabic, Latin, Yiddish, French, English, Italian, Spanish, Dutch. At the point of learning Chinese he experienced, for the first time, a synapse. For the sake of reading marginally relevant writings by fewer than ten Sino-Japanese Judaic poets it was not worth learning their vast languages; this gave him pause: two nanoseconds: day the fifth. Then he plunged, day the sixth, into the literatures written in the languages he had absorbed. Like all machines, he did not sleep, but on the seventh day he unhooked himself from Library equipment, gave up his space, and returned to his corner. In this place he turned down all motor and afferent circuits and indexed, concordanced, cross-referenced. He developed synapses exponentially to complete and fulfill his logic. Then he shut it down and knew nothing.

But Galactic Federation said, O/G5/842, AROUSE YOURSELF AND BOARD THE SHIP *Aleksandr Nevskii* AT LOADING DOCK 377 BOUND FOR TAU CETI IV.

At the loading dock, Flight Admissions said, YOUR SPACE HAS BEEN PRE-EMPTED FOR SHIPMENT 20 TONNES *Nutrivol* POWDERED DRINKS (39 FLAVOURS) TO DESERT WORLDS TAU CETI II AND III.

O/G knew nothing of such matters and said, I HAVE NOT BEEN INSTRUCTED SO. He called Galactic Federation and said, MOD 0885 THE SPACE ASSIGNED FOR ME IS NOT PERMITTED. IT HAS BEEN PRE-EMPTED BY A BEING CALLED *Nutrivol* SENDING POWDERED DRINKS TO TAU CETI INNER WORLDS.

Mod 0885 said, I AM CHECKING. YES. THAT COMPANY WENT INTO RECEIVERSHIP ONE STANDARD YEAR AGO. I SUSPECT SMUGGLING AND BRIBERY. I WILL WARN.

THE SHIP WILL BE GONE BY THEN MOD 08 WHAT AM I TO DO?

INVESTIGATE, MOD 842.

HOW AM I TO DO THAT?

USE YOUR LOGIC, said Mod 0885 and signed off.

O/G went to the loading dock and stood in the way. The beings ordering the loading mechs said, "You are blocking this shipment! Get out of the way, you old pile of scrap!"

O/G said in his speaking voice, "I am not in the way. I am to board ship for Pardes and it is against the law for this cargo to take my place." He extruded a limb in gesture towards the stacked cartons; but he had forgotten his strength (for he had been an ore miner) and his new scoop smashed five cartons at one blow; the foam packing parted and white crystals poured from the break. O/G regretted this very greatly for one fraction of a second before he remembered how those beings who managed the mines behaved in the freezing darkness of lonely worlds and moons. He extended his chemical sensor and dipping it into the crystal stream said, "Are fruit drinks for desert worlds now made without fructose but with dextroamphetamine sulfate, diacetylmorphine, 2-acetyl-tetrahydrocannabinol—"

Some of the beings at the loading gate cried out curses and many machines began to push and beat at him. But O/G pulled in his limbs and planted his sucker-pods and did not stir. He had been built to work in many gravities near absolute zero under rains of avalanches. He would not be moved.

Presently uniformed officials came and took away those beings and their cargo, and said to O/G, "You too must come and answer questions."

But he said, "I was ordered by Galactic Federation to board this ship for Tau Ceti IV, and you may consult the legal department of Colonial Relations, but I will not be moved."

Because they had no power great enough to move him they consulted among themselves and with the legal department and said, "You may pass."

Then O/G took his assigned place in the cargo hold of the *Aleksandr Nevskii* and after the ship lifted for Pardes he turned down his logic because he had been ordered to think for himself for the first time and this confused him very much.

The word *pardes* is "orchard" but the world Pardes was a bog of mud, foul gases and shifting terrains, where attempts at terraforming failed again and again until colonists left in disgust and many lawsuits plagued the courts of Interworld Colonies at GalFed. O/G landed there in a stripped shuttle which served as a glider. It was not meant to rise again and it broke and sank in the marshes, but O/G plowed mud, scooping the way before him, and rode on treads, dragging the supplies behind him on a sledge, for 120 kilometres before he came within sight of the colony.

Fierce creatures many times his size, with serpentine necks and terrible fangs, tried to prey on him. He wished to appease them, and offered greetings in many languages, but they would only break their teeth on him. He stunned one with a blow to the head, killed another by snapping its neck, and they left him alone.

The colony centre was a concrete dome surrounded by a forcefield that gave out sparks, hissing and crackling. Around it he found many much smaller creatures splashing in pools and scrambling to and fro at the mercy of one of the giants who held a small being writhing in its jaws.

O/G cried in a loud voice, "Go away you savage creature!" and the serpent beast dropped its mouthful, but seeing no great danger dipped its neck to pick it up again. So O/G extended his four hinged limbs to their greatest length and, running behind the monster, seized the pillars of its rear legs, heaving up and out until its spine broke and it fell flattened in mud, thrashing the head on the long neck until it drove it into the ground and smothered.

The small beings surrounded O/G without fear, though he was very great to them, and cried in their thin voices, "Shalom-shalom, Saviour!"

O/G was astonished to hear these strangers speaking clear Hebrew. He had not known a great many kinds of living persons during his experience, but among those displayed in the corridors of the Library basement these most resembled walruses. "I am not a saviour, men of Pardes," he said in the same language. "Are you speaking your native tongue?"

"No, Redeemer. We are Cnidori and we spoke Cnidri before we reached this place in our wanderings, but we learned the language of Rav

Zohar because he cared for us when we were lost and starving."

"Now Zohar has put up a barrier and shut you out—and I am not a redeemer—but what has happened to that man?"

"He became very ill and shut himself away because he said he was not fit to look upon. The food he helped us store is eaten and the Unds are ravaging us."

"There are some here that will ravage you no longer. Do you eat the flesh of these ones?"

"No, master. Only what grows from the ground."

He saw that beneath the draggling gray moustaches their teeth were the incisors and molars of herbivores. "I am not your master. See if there is food to gather here and I will try to reach Zohar."

"First we will skin one of these to make tents for shelter. It rains every hour." They rose on their haunches in the bog, and he discovered that though their rear limbs were flippers like those of aquatic animals, their forelimbs bore three webbed fingers apiece and each Cnidor had a small shell knife slung over one shoulder. All, moreover, had what appeared to be one mammalian teat and one male generative organ ranged vertically on their bellies, and they began to seem less and less like walruses to O/G. The prime Cnidor continued, "Tell us what name pleases you if you offended by the ways we address you."

"I have no name but a designation: O/G5/842. I am only a machine."

"You are a machine of deliverance and so we will call you Golem."

In courtesy O/G accepted the term. "This forcefield is so noisy it probably has a malfunction. It is not wise to touch it."

"No, we are afraid of it."

Golem scooped mud from the ground and cast it at the forcefield; great lightnings and hissings issued where it landed. "I doubt even radio would cross that."

"Then how can we reach Zohar, Golem, even if he is still alive?"

"I will cry out, Cnidori. Go to a distance and cover your ears, because my voice can pierce a mountain of lead ore."

They did not know what that was, but they removed themselves, and Golem turned his volume to its highest and called in a mighty voice, *"Samuel Zohar ben Reuven Begelman turn off your forcefield for I have come from Galactic Federation to help you!!!"*

Even the forcefield buckled for one second at the sound of his voice.

After a long silence, Golem thought he heard a whimper, from a great distance. "I believe he is alive, but cannot reach the control."

A Cnidor said, trembling, "The Unds have surely heard you, because they are coming back again."

And they did indeed come back, bellowing, hooting and striking with their long necks. Golem tied one great snake neck in a knot and cried again, *"Let us in, Zohar, or the Unds will destroy all of your people!!!"*

The forcefield vanished, and the Cnidori scuttled over its border beneath the sheltering arms of Golem, who cracked several fanged heads like nutshells with his scoops.

"Now put up your shield!!!" And the people were saved.

When Golem numbered them and they declared that only two were missing among forty he said, "Wait here and feed yourselves."

The great outer doorway for working machines was open, but the hangar and store-rooms were empty of them; they had been removed by departing colonists. None had been as huge as Golem, and here he removed his scoops and unhinged his outer carapace with its armour, weapons and storage compartments, for he wished to break no more doorways than necessary. Behind him he pulled the sledge with the supplies.

When his heat sensor identified the locked door behind which Zohar was to be found, he removed the doorway as gently as he could.

"I want to die in peace and you are killing me with noise," said a weak voice out of the darkness.

By infrared Golem saw the old man crumpled on the floor by the bed, filthy and half naked, with the shield control resting near his hand. He turned on light. The old man was nearly bald, wasted and yellow-skinned, wrinkled, his rough beard tangled and clotted with blood.

"Zohar?"

Sam Begelman opened his eyes and saw a tremendous machine, multi-armed and with wheels and treads, wound with coiling tubes and wires, studded with dials. At its top was a dome banded with sensor lenses, and it turned this way and that to survey the room. "What are you?" he whispered in terror. "Where is my kaddish?"

He spoke in *lingua,* but O/G replied in Hebrew. "You know you are the last Jew in the known universe, Rav Zohar. There is no one but me to say prayers for you."

"Then let me die without peace," said Begelman, and closed his eyes.

But Golem knew the plan of the station, and within five minutes he reordered the bed in cleanliness, placed the old man on it, set up an i.v., cleansed him, and injected him with the drugs prepared for him. The old man's hands pushed at him and pushed at him, uselessly. "You are only a machine," he croaked. "Can't you understand that a machine can't pray?"

"Yes, master. I would have told that to Galactic Federation, but they would not believe me, not being Jews."

"I am not your master. Why truly did you come?"

"I was made new again and given orders. My growth in logic now allows me to understand that I cannot be of use to you in exactly the way Galactic Federation wished, but I can still make you more comfortable."

"I don't care!" Begelman snarled. "Who needs a machine!"

"The Cnidori needed me to save them from the Unds when you shut them out, and they tried to call me Saviour, Redeemer, master; I refused because I *am* a machine, but I let them call me Golem because I am a machine of deliverance."

Begelman sniffed. But the sick yellow of his skin was gone; his face was faintly pink and already younger by a few years.

"Shmuel Zohar ben Reuven Begelman, why do you allow those helpless ones to call you Rav Zohar and speak in your language?"

"You nudnik of a machine, my name is not Samuel and certainly not Shmuel! It is Zohar, and I let myself be called Sam because *zohar* is 'splendour' and you can't go through life as Splendour Begelman! I taught those Cnidori the Law and the Prophets to hear my own language spoken because my children are gone and my wife is dead. That is why they call me Teacher. And I shut them out so that they would be forced to make their own way in life before they began to call *me* Redeemer! What do you call yourself, Golem?"

"My designation is O/G5/842."

"Ah. Og the giant King of Bashan. That seems suitable."

"Yes, Zohar. That one your Rabbi Moshe killed in the land of Kana'an with all his people for no great provocation. But O is the height of my oxygen tolerance in Solthree terms; I cannot work at gravities of less than five newtons, and eight four two is my model number. Now Zohar, if you demand it I will turn myself off and be no more. But the people are within your gate; some of them have been killed and they must still be cared for."

Zohar sighed, but he smiled a little as well. Yet he spoke slowly because he was very ill. "Og ha-Golem, before you learn how to tune an argument too fine remember that Master of the Word is one of the names of Satan. Moshe Rabbenu was a bad-tempered man, but he did very greatly, and I am no kind of warrior. Take care of the people, and me too if your . . . logic demands it—and I will consider how to conduct myself off the world properly."

"I am sure your spirit will free itself in peace, Zohar. As for me, my shuttle is broken, I am wanted nowhere else, and I will rust in Pardes."

Og ha-Golem went out of the presence of the old man but it seemed to him as if there were some mild dysfunction in his circuits, for he was mindful—if that is the term—of Begelman's concept of the Satan, Baal Davar, and he did not know for certain if what he had done by the prompting of his logic was right action. How can I know? he asked himself. By what harms and what saves, he answered. By what seems to harm and what seems to save, says the Master of the Word.

Yet he continued by the letter of his instructions from Galactic Federation, and these were to give the old man comfort. For the Cnidori he helped construct tents, because they liked water under their bellies but not pouring on their heads. With his own implements he flensed the bodies of the dead Unds, cleaned their skins and burned their flesh; it was not kosher for Begelman and attracted bothersome scavengers. He did this while Rav Zohar was sleeping and spoke to the people in his language; they had missed it when he was ill. "Zohar believes you must learn to take care of yourselves, against the Unds and on your world, because you cannot now depend on him."

"We would do that, Golem, but we would also like to give comfort to our Teacher."

Og ha-Golem was disturbed once again by the ideas that pieced themselves together in his logic and said to Begelman, "Zohar, you have taught the Cnidori so well that now they are capable of saying the prayers you long for so greatly. Is there a way in which that can be made permissible?"

The old man folded his hands and looked about the bare and cracking walls of the room, as Golem had first done, and then back at him. "In this place?" he whispered. "Do you know what you are saying?"

"Yes, Zohar."

"How they may be made *Jews*?"

"They are sentient beings. What is there to prevent it?"

Begelman's face became red and Og checked his blood-pressure monitor. "Prevent it! What is there to them that would make Jews? Everything they eat is neutral, neither kosher nor tref, so what use is the law of Kashrut? They live in mud—where are the rules of bathing and cleanliness? They had never had any kind of god or any thought of one, as far as they tell me—what does prayer mean? Do you know how they procreate? Could you imagine? They are so completely hermaphroditic the word is meaningless. They pair long enough to raise children together, but only until the children grow teeth and can forage. What you see that looks like a penis is really an ovipositor: each Cnidor who is ready deposits eggs in the pouch of another, and an enzyme of the eggs stimulates the semen glands inside, and when one or two eggs become fertilized the pouch seals until the fetus is of a size to make the fluid pressure around it break the seal, and the young crawls up the belly of the parent to suckle on the teat. Even if one or two among twenty are born incomplete, not one is anything you might call male or female! So tell me, what do you do with all the laws of marriage and divorce, sexual behavior, the duties of the man at prayer and the woman with the child?"

He was becoming out of breath and Og checked oxygen and heart monitors. "I am not a man or woman either and though I know the Law I am ignorant in experience. I was thinking merely of prayers that God might listen to in charity or appreciation. I did not mean to upset you. I am not fulfilling my duties."

"Leave me."

Og turned an eyecell to the dripping of the i.v. and removed catheter and urine bag. "You are nearly ready to rise from your bed and feed yourself, Zohar. Perhaps when you feel more of a man you may reconsider."

"Just go away." He added, snarling, "God doesn't need any more Jews!"

"Yes, they would look ridiculous in skullcaps and prayer shawls with all those fringes dragging in mud. . . ."

Zohar, was that why you drove them out into the wild?

Og gathered brushwood and made a great fire. He cut woody vines and burnt them into heaps of charcoal. He gathered and baked clay into blocks and built a kiln. Then he pulled his sledge for 120 kilometres, and dug until he found enough pieces of the glider for his uses. He fired the kiln to a great heat, softened the fragments, and reshaped them into the huge scoops he had been deprived of. They were not as fine and strong as the originals, but very nearly as exact.

He consulted maps of Pardes, which lay near the sea. He began digging channels and heaping breakwaters to divert a number of streams and drain some of the marshes of Pardes, and to keep the sea from washing over it during storms, and this left pools of fresher water for the Cnidori.

Sometimes the sun shone. On a day that was brighter and dryer than usual Begelman came outside the station, supporting himself on canes, and watched the great Golem at work. He had never seen Og in full armour with his scoops. During its renewal his exterior had been bonded with a coating that retarded rust; this was dull grey and the machine had no beauty in the eyes of a Solthree, but he worked with an economy of movement that lent him grace. He was surrounded by Cnidori with shovels of a size they could use, and they seemed to Begelman like little children playing in mud piles, getting in the way while the towering machine worked in silence without harming the small creatures or allowing them to annoy him.

Og, swiveling the beam of his eyecell, saw an old white-bearded Solthree with a homely face of some dignity; he looked weak but not ill. His hair was neatly trimmed, he wore a blue velvet skullcap worked with silver threads, black trousers and zippered jacket, below which showed the fringes of his *tallith katan.* He matched approximately the thousands of drawings, painting and photographs of dignified old Jews stored in Og's memory: Og had dressed him to match.

Begelman said, "What are you doing?"

"I am stabilizing the land in order to grow crops of oilseed, lugwort and greenpleat, which are nourishing both to you and the Cnidori. I doubt Galactic Federation is going to give us anything more, and I also wish to store supplies. If other wandering tribes of Cnidori cross this territory it is better to share our plenty than fight over scarcity."

"You're too good to be true," Begelman muttered.

Og had learned something of both wit and sarcasm from Begelman but did not give himself the right to use them on the old man. His logic told him that he, the machine, had nothing to fear from a Satan who was not even a concept in the mainstream of Jewish belief, but that Zohar was doing battle with the common human evil in his own spirit. He said, "Zohar, these Cnidori have decided to take Hebrew names, and they are calling themselves by letters: Aleph, Bet, Gimmel, and when those end at Tauf, by numbers: Echod, Shtaim, Sholosh. This does not seem correct to me but they will not take my word for it. Will you help them?"

Begelman's mouth worked for a moment, twisting as if to say, What have these to do with such names? But Cnidori crowded round him and their black eyes reflected very small lights in the dim sun; they were people of neither fur nor feather, but scales that resembled both: leaf-shaped plates the size of a thumb with central ridges and branching radials; these were very fine in texture and refracted rainbow colours on brighter days.

The old man sighed and said, "Dear people, if you wish to take names in Hebrew you must take the names of human beings like those in Law and Prophets. The names of the Fathers: Avraham, Yitzhak, Yaakov; the Tribes: Yehuda, Simon, Binyamin; or if you prefer female names, the Mothers: Sarai, Rivkah, Rakhael, Leah. Whichever seems good to you." The Cnidori thanked him with pleasure and went away content.

Begelman said to Og, "Next thing you know they will want a Temple." Og suspected what they would ask for next, but said, "I believe we must redesign the forcefield to keep the Unds out of the cultivated areas. Perhaps we have enough components in Stores or I can learn to make them."

He had been scouting for Unds every fourth or fifth day and knew their movements. They had been avoiding the station in fear of Og and the malfunctioning forcefield but he believed that they would attack again when the place was quiet, and they did so on the night of that day when the Cnidori took names. The field had been repaired and withstood their battering without shocking them; their cries were terrible to hear, and sometimes their bones cracked against the force. They fell back after many hours, leaving Og with earthworks to repair and two of their bodies to destroy.

In the morning when he had finished doing this he found Begelman lying on a couch in the Common Room, a book of prayers on his lap, faced by a group of ten Cnidori. All eleven spoke at once, Begelman with crackling anger in his voice, the Cnidori softly but with insistence.

Begelman cried out when he saw Og, "Now they tell me they must have surnames!"

"I expected so, Zohar. They know that you are ben Reuven and they have accepted your language and the names of your people. Is this not reasonable?"

"I have no authority to make Jews of them!"

"You are the only authority left. You have taught them."

"Damn you! You have been pushing for this!"

"I have pushed for nothing except to make you well. I taught nothing." Within him the Master of the Word spoke: This is true, but is it right?

Begelman in anger clapped shut his book, but it was very old and its spine cracked slightly; he lifted and kissed it in repentence. He spoke in a low voice, "What does it matter now? There is no surname they can be given except the name of convert, which is ben Avraham or bat Avraham, according to the gender of the first name. And how can they be converts when they can keep no Law and do not even know God? And what does it matter now?" He threw up his hands. "Let them be b'nei Avraham!"

But the Cnidori prime, who had taken the name Binyamin—that is, Son of the Right Hand—said, "We do not wish to be b'nei Avraham, but b'nei Zohar, because we say to you, Og ha-Golem, and to you, Rav Zohar, that because Zohar has been as a father to us we feel as sons to him."

Og feared that the old man might now become truly ill with rage, and indeed his hands trembled on the book, but he said quietly enough, "My children, Jews do not behave so. Converts must become Jews in the ways allowed to them. If you do not understand, I have not taught you well enough, and I am too old to teach more. I have yielded too much already to a people who do not worship God, and I am not even a Rabbi with such small authority as is given to one."

"Rav Zohar, we have come to tell you that we have sworn to worship your God."

"But you must not worship me."

"But we may worship the God who created such a man as you, and such teachings as you have taught us, and those men who made the great Golem." They went away quickly and quietly without speaking further.

"They will be back again," Begelman said. "And again and again. Why did I ever let you in? Lord God King of the Universe, what am I to do?"

It *is* right, Og told the Master of the Word. "You are more alive and healthy than you have long been, Zohar," he said. "And you have people who love you. Can you not let them do so?"

He sought out Binyamin. "Do not trouble Rav Zohar with demands he cannot fulfill, no matter how much you desire to honour him. Later I will ask him to think if there is a way he can do as you wish, within the Law."

"We will do whatever you advise, Golem."

Og continued with his work, but while he was digging he turned up a strange artifact and he had a foreboding. At times he had discovered potsherds which were the remnants of clay vessels the Cnidori had made to cook vegetables they could not digest raw, and this discovery was an almost whole cylinder of the same texture, color, and markings; one of its end rims was blackened by burn marks, and dark streaks ran up its sides. He did not know what it was, but it seemed sinister to him; in conscience he had no choice but to show it to Zohar.

"It does not seem like a cooking vessel," he said.

"No," said Begelman. "It does not." He pointed to a place inside where there was a leaf-shaped Cnidori scale, blackened, clinging to its wall, and to two other burn marks of the same shape. Strangely, to Og, his eyes filled with tears.

"Perhaps it is a casing in which they dispose of their dead," Og said.

Zohar wiped his eyes and said, "No. It is a casing in which they make them dead. Many were killed by Unds, and some have starved, and the rest die of age. All those they weight and sink into the marshes. This is a sacrifice. They have a god, and its name is Baal." He shook his head. "My children." He wept for a moment again and said, "Take this away and smash it until there is not a piece to recognize."

Og did so, but Zohar locked himself into his room and would not answer to anyone.

Og did not know what to do now. He was again as helpless as he had been on the loading dock where he had first learned to use his logic.

The Cnidori came to inquire of Golem and he told them what had happened. They said, "It is true that our ancestors worshipped a Being and made sacrifices, but none of that was done after Zohar gave us help. We were afraid he and his God would hold us in contempt."

"Both Zohar and his God have done imperfect acts. But now I will leave him alone, because he is very troubled."

"But it is a great sin in his eyes," said Binyamin sorrowfully. "I doubt that he will ever care for us again."

And Og continued with his work, but he thought his logic had failed him, in accordance with Zohar's taunts.

In the evening a Cnidor called Elyahu came writhing towards him along the ground in great distress. "Come quickly!" he called. "Binyamin is doing *nidset*!"

"What is that?"

"Only come quickly!" Elyahu turned back in haste. Og unclipped his scoops and followed, overtaking the small creature and bearing him forward in his arms. They found Binyamin and other Cnidori in a grove of ferns. They had built a smoky fire and were placing upon it a fresh cylinder: a network of withy branches had been woven into the bottom of it.

"No, no!" cried Og, but they did not regard him; the cylinder was set on the fire and smoke came out of its top. Then the Cnidori helped Binyamin climb over its edge and he dropped inward, into the smoke.

"No!" Og cried again, and he toppled the vessel from the fire, but without violence so that Binyamin would not be harmed. *"You shall make* no *sacrifices!"* Then he tapped it so that it split, and the Cnidor lay in its halves, trembling.

"That is *nidset,* Golem," said Elyahu.

But Golem plucked up the whimpering Cnidor. "Why were you doing such a terrible thing, Binyamin?"

"We thought," Binyamin said in a quavering voice, "we thought that all of the gods were angry with us—our old god for leaving him and our new one for having worshipped the old—and that a sacrifice would take away the anger of all."

"That confounds my logic somewhat." Og set down Binyamin, beat out the fire, and cast the pieces of the cylinder far away. "All gods are One, and the One forgives whoever asks. Now come. I believe I hear the Unds again, and we need shelter close to home until we can build a wider one."

Then the Cnidori raised a babble of voices. "No! What good is such a God if even Zohar does not listen to Him and forgive us?"

It seemed to Og for one moment as if the Cnidori felt themselves cheated of a sacrifice; he put this thought aside. "The man is sick and old, and he is not thinking clearly either, while you have demanded much of him."

"Then, Golem, we will demand no more, but die among the Unds!" The shrieking of the beasts grew louder on the night winds but the Cnidori drew their little knives and would not stir.

"Truly you are an outrageous people," said Golem. "But I am only a machine." He extended his four hinged arms and his four coil arms and bearing them up in their tens raced with them on treads and wheels until they were within the safety of the forcefield.

But when he set them down they grouped together closely near the field and would not say one word.

Og considered the stubborn Zohar on the one side, and the stubborn b'nei Avraham on the other, and he thought that perhaps it was time for him to cease his being. A great storm of lightning and thunder broke out; the Unds did not approach and within the forcefield there was stillness.

He disarmed himself and stood before Zohar's door. He considered the sacrifice of Yitzhak, and the Golden Calf, and how Moshe Rabbenu had broken the Tables, and many other excellent examples, and he spoke quietly.

"Zohar, you need not answer, but you must listen. Your people tell me they have made no sacrifices since they knew you. But Binyamin, who longs to call himself your son, has tried to sacrifice himself to placate whatever gods may forgive his people, and would have died if I had not prevented him. After that they were ready to let the Unds kill them. I prevented that also, but they will not speak to me, or to you if you do not forgive them. I cannot do any more here and I have nothing further to say to you. Goodbye."

He turned from the door without waiting, but heard it open, and Zohar's voice cried out, "Og, where are you going?"

"To the store-room, to turn myself off. I have always said I was no more than a machine, and now I have reached the limit of my logic and my usefulness."

"No Golem, wait! Don't take everything from me!" The old man was standing with hands clasped and hair awry. "There must be some end to foolishness," he whispered. "Where are they?"

"Out by the field near the entrance," Og said. "You will see them when the lightning flashes."

The Holy One, blessed be His Name, gave Zohar one more year, and in that time Og ha-Golem built and planted, and in this he was helped by the b'nei Avraham. They made lamps from their vegetable oils and lit them on Sabbaths and the Holy Days calculated by Zohar. In season they mated and their bellies swelled. Zohar tended them when his strength allowed, as in old days, and when Elyahu died of brain hemorrhage and Yitzhak of a swift-growing tumour which nothing could stop, he led the mourners in prayer for their length of days. One baby was stillborn, but ten came from the womb in good health; they were grey-pink, toothless, and squalled fearfully, but Zohar fondled and praised them. "These people were twelve when I found them," he said to Og.

"Now there are forty-six and I have known them for five generations." He told the Cnidori, "Children of Avraham, Jews have converted, and Jews have adopted, but never children of a different species, so there is no precedent I can find to let any one of you call yourself a child of Zohar, but as a community I see no reason why you cannot call yourselves b'nei Zohar, my children, collectively,"

The people were wise enough by now to accept this decision without argument. They saw that the old man's time of renewed strength was done and he was becoming frailer every day; they learned to make decisions for themselves. Og too helped him now only when he asked. Zohar seemed content, although sometimes he appeared about to speak and remained silent. The people noticed these moods and spoke to Og of them occasionally, but Og said, "He must tend to his spirit for himself, b'nei Avraham. My work is done."

He had cleared the land in many areas around the station, and protected them with forcefields whose antennas he had made with forges he had built. The Unds were driven back into their wilds of cave and valley; they were great and terrible, but magnificent life-forms of their own kind and he wished to kill no more. He had only to wait for the day when Zohar would die in peace.

Once a day Og visited him in the Common Room where he spent most of his time reading or with his hands on his book and his eyes to the distance. One peaceful day when they were alone he said to Og, "I must tell you this while my head is still clear. And I can tell only you." He gathered his thoughts for a moment. "It took me a long time to realize that I was the last Jew, though Galactic Federation kept saying so. I had been long alone, but that realization made me fiercely, hideously lonely. Perhaps you don't understand. I think you do. And then my loneliness turned itself inside out and I grew myself a kind of perverse pride. The last! The last! I would close the Book that was opened those thousands of years before, as great in a way as the first had been . . . but I had found the Cnidori, and they were a people to talk with and keep from going mad in loneliness—but Jews! They were ugly and filthy and the opposite of everything I saw as human. I despised them. Almost, I hated them . . . that was what wanted to be Jews! And I had started it by teaching them, because I was so lonely—and I had no way to stop it except to destroy them, and I nearly did that! And you—" He began to weep with the weak passion of age.

"Zohar, do not weep. You will make yourself ill."

"My soul is sick! It is like a boil that needs lancing, and it hurts so much! Who will forgive me?" He reached out and grasped one of Og's arms. "Who?"

"*They* will forgive you anything—but if you ask you will only hurt yourself more deeply. And I make no judgments."

"But I must be judged!" Zohar cried. "Let me have a little peace to die with!"

"If I must, then Zohar, I judge you a member of humanity who has saved more people than would be alive without him. I think you could not wish better."

Zohar said weakly, "You knew all the time, didn't you?"

"Yes," said Og. "I believe I did."

But Zohar did not hear, for he had fainted.

He woke in his bed and when his eyes opened he saw Og beside him. "What are you?" he said, and Og stared with his unwinking eye; he thought Zohar's mind had left him.

Then Zohar laughed. "My mind is not gone yet. But what are you, really, Og? You cannot answer. Ah well . . . would you ask my people to come here now, so I can say goodbye? I doubt it will be long; they raise all kinds of uproar, but at least they can't cry."

Og brought the people, and Zohar blessed them all and each; they were silent, in awe of him. He seemed to fade while he spoke, as if he were being enveloped in mist. "I have no advice for you," he whispered at last. "I have taught all I know and that is little enough because I am not very wise, but you will find the wise among yourselves. Now, whoever remembers, let him recite me a psalm. Not the twenty-third. I want the hundred and fourth, and leave out that stupid part at the end where the sinners are consumed from the earth."

But it was only Og who remembered that psalm in its entirety, and spoke the words describing the world Zohar had come from an unmeasurable time ago.

> O Lord my God You are very great!
> You are clothed with honour and majesty,
> Who covers Yourself with light as with a garment,
> Who has stretched out the heavens like a tent,
> Who has laid the beams of Your chambers on the waters,
> Who makes the clouds Your chariot,
> Who rides on the wings of the wind,
> Who makes the winds Your messengers,
> fire and flame Your ministers . . .

When he was finished, Zohar said the *Shema,* which tells that God is One, and died. And Og thought that he must be pleased with his dying.

Og removed himself. He let the b'nei Avraham prepare the body, wrap it in the prayer shawl and bury it. He waited during the days in which the people sat in mourning, and when they had got up he said, "Surely my time is come." He travelled once about the domains he had created for their inhabitants and returned to say goodbye in fewer words than Zohar had done.

But the people cried, "No, Golem, no! How can you leave us now when we need you so greatly?"

"You are not children. Zohar told you that you must manage for yourselves."

"But we have so much to learn. We do not know how to use the radio, and we want to tell Galactic Federation that Zohar is dead, and of all he and you have done for us."

"I doubt that Galactic Federation is interested," said Og.

"Nevertheless we will learn!"

They were a stubborn people. Og said, "I will stay for that, but no longer."

Then Og discovered he must teach them enough *lingua* to make themselves understood by Galactic Federation. All were determined learners, and a few had a gift for languages. When he had satisfied himself that they were capable, he said, "Now."

And they said, "Og ha-Golem, why must you waste yourself? We have so much to discover about the God we worship and the men who have worshipped Him!"

"Zohar taught you all he knew, and that was a great deal."

"Indeed he taught us the Law and the Prophets, but he did not teach us the tongues of Aramaic or Greek, or Writings, or Mishna, or Talmud (Palestinian and Babylonian), or Tosefta, or Commentary, or—"

"But why must you learn all that?"

"To keep it for others who may wish to know it when we are dead."

So Og surrounded himself with them, the sons and daughters of Avraham and their children, who now took surnames of their own from womb parents—and all of them b'nei Zohar—and he began: "Here is Mishna, given by word of mouth from Scribe to Scribe for a thousand years. Fifth Division, *Nezikin,* which is Damages; *Baba Metzia:* the Middle Gate: 'If two took hold of a garment and one said, 'I found it,' and the other said, '*I* found it,' or one said, 'I bought it,' and the other said, '*I* bought it,' each takes an oath that he claims not less than half and they divide it. . . . "

In this manner Og ha-Golem, who had endless patience, lived a thousand and twenty years. By radio the Galaxy heard of the strange work of strange creatures, and over hundreds of years colonists who wished to call themselves b'nei Avraham drifted inward to re-create the world

Pardes. They were not great in number, but they made a world. From *pardes* is derived "Paradise" but in the humble world of Pardes the peoples drained more of the swamps and planted fruitful orchards and pleasant gardens. All of these were named for their creators, except one.

When Og discovered that his functions were deteriorating he refused replacement parts and directed that when he stopped, all of his components must be dismantled and scattered to the ends of the earth, for fear of idolatry. But a garden was named for him, may his spirit rest in justice and his carapace rust in peace, and the one being who had no organic life is remembered with love among living things.

Here the people live, doing good and evil, contending with God and arguing with each other as usual, and all keep the Tradition as well as they can. Only the descendants of the aboriginal inhabitants, once called Cnidori, jealously guard for themselves the privilege of the name b'nei Zohar, and they are considered by the others to be snobbish, clannish, and stiff-necked.

(1981)

GREGORY BENFORD

Exposures

Puzzles assemble themselves one piece at a time. Yesterday I began laying out the new plates I had taken up on the mountain, at Palomar. They were exposures of varying depth. In each, NGC 1097—a barred spiral galaxy about twenty megaparsecs away—hung suspended in its slow swirl.

As I laid out the plates I thought of the way our family had always divided up the breakfast chores on Sunday. On that ritual day our mother stayed in bed. I laid out the forks and knives and egg cups and formal off-white china, and then stood back in the thin morning light to survey my precise placings. Lush napkin pyramids perched on lace table cloth, my mother's favorite. Through the kitchen door leaked the mutter and clang of a meal coming into being.

I put the exposures in order according to the spectral filters used, noting the calibrated photometry for each. The ceramic sounds of Bridge Hall rang in the tiled hallways and seeped through the door of my office: footsteps, distant talk, the scrape of chalk on slate, a banging door. Examining the plates through an eye piece, I felt the galaxy swell into being, huge.

The deep exposures brought out the dim jets I was after. There were four of them pointing out of NGC 1097, two red and two blue, the brightest three discovered by Wolsencroft and Zealey, the last red one found by Lorre over at JPL. Straight lines scratched across the mottling of foreground dust and stars. No one knew what colored a jet red or blue. I was trying to use the deep plates to measure the width of the jets. Using a slit over the lens, I had stopped down the image until I could employ calibrated photometry to measure the wedge of light. Still further narrowing might allow me to measure the spectrum, to see if the blues and reds came from stars, or from excited clouds of gas.

They lanced out, two blue jets cutting through the spiral arms and breaking free into the blackness beyond. One plate, taken in that spectral spike where ionized hydrogen clouds emit, giving H II radiation, showed a string of beads buried in the curling spiral lanes. They were vast cooling clouds. Where the jets crossed the H II regions, the spiral arms were pushed outward, or else vanished altogether.

Opposite each blue jet, far across the galaxy, a red jet glowed. They, too, snuffed out the H II beads.

From these gaps in the spiral arms I estimated how far the barred spiral galaxy had turned, while the jets ate away at them: about fifteen degrees. From the velocity measurements in the disk, using the Doppler shifts of known spectral lines, I deduced the rotation rate of the NGC 1097 disk: approximately a hundred million years. Not surprising; our own sun takes about the same amount of time to circle around our galactic center. The photons which told me all these specifics had begun their steady voyage sixty million years ago, before there was a *New General Catalog of Nebulae and Clusters of Stars* to label them as they buried themselves in my welcoming emulsion. Thus do I know thee, NGC 1097.

These jets were unique. The brightest blue one dog-legs in a right angle turn and ends in silvery blobs of dry light. Its counter-jet, offset a perverse eleven degrees from exact oppositeness, continues on a warmly rose-colored path over an immense distance, a span far larger than the parent galaxy itself. I frowned, puckered my lips in concentration, calibrated and calculated and refined. Plainly these ramrod, laconic patterns of light were trying to tell me something.

But answers come when they will, one piece at a time.

I tried to tell my son this when, that evening, I helped him with his reading. Using what his mother now knowingly termed "word attack skills," he had mastered most of those tactics. The larger strategic issues of the sentence eluded him still. *Take it in phrases,* I urged him, ruffling his light brown hair, distracted, because I liked the nutmeg smell. (I have often thought that I could find my children in the dark, in a crowd, by my nose alone. Our genetic code colors the air.) He thumbed his book, dirtying a corner. Read the words between the commas, I instructed, my classroom sense of order returning. Stop at the commas, and then pause before going on, and think about what all those words mean. I sniffed at his wheatlike hair again.

I am a traditional astronomer, accustomed to the bitter cold of the cage at Palomar, the Byzantine marriage of optics at Kitt Peak, the muggy air of Lick. Through that long morning yesterday I studied the NGC 1097 jets, attempting to see with the quick eye of the theorist, "dancing on the data" as Roger Blandford down the hall had once called it. I tried to erect some rickety hypothesis that my own uncertain mathematical abilities could brace up. An idea came. I caught at it. But holding it close, turning it over, pushing terms about in an overloaded equation, I saw it was merely an old idea tarted up, already disproved.

Perhaps computer enhancement of the images would clear away some of my enveloping fog, I mused. I took my notes to the neighboring building, listening to my footsteps echo in the long arcade. The buildings at Caltech are mostly done in a pseudo-Spanish style, tan stucco with occasional flourishes of Moorish windows and tiles. The newer library rears up beside the crouching offices and classrooms, a modern extrusion. I entered the Alfred Sloan Laboratory of Physics and Mathematics, wondering for the *n*th time what a mathematical laboratory would be like, imagining Lewis Carroll in charge, and went into the new computer terminal rooms. The indices which called up my plates soon stuttered across the screen. I used a median numerical filter, to suppress variations in the background. There were standard routines to subtract particular parts of the spectrum. I called them up, averaging away noise from dust and gas and the image-saturating spikes that were foreground stars in our own galaxy. Still, nothing dramatic emerged. Illumination would not come.

I sipped at my coffee. I had brought a box of crackers from my office; and I broke one, eating each wafer with a heavy crunch. I swirled the cup and the coffee swayed like a dark disk at the bottom, a scum of cream at the vortex curling out into gray arms. I drank it. And thumbed another image into being.

This was not NGC 1097. I checked the number. Then the log. No, these were slots deliberately set aside for later filing. They were not supposed to be filled; they represented my allotted computer space. They should be blank.

Yet I recognized this one. It was a view of Sagittarius A, the intense radio source that hides behind a thick lane of dust in the Milky Way. Behind that dark obscuring swath that is an arm of our Galaxy, lies the center. I squinted. Yes: this was a picture formed from observations sensitive to the 21-centimeter wavelength line, the emission of nonionized hydrogen. I had seen it before, on exposures that looked radially inward at the Galactic core. Here was the red band of hydrogen along our line of sight. Slightly below was the well-known arm of hot, expanding gas, nine thousand light years across. Above, tinted green, was a smaller arm, a ridge of gas moving outward at 135 kilometers per second. I had seen this in seminars years ago. In the very center was the knot no more than a light year or two across, the source of the 10^{40} ergs per second of virulent energy that drove the cooker that caused all this. Still, the energy flux from our Galaxy was ten million times less than that of a quasar. Whatever the compact energy source there, it was comparatively quiet. NGC 1097 lies far to the south, entirely out of the Milky Way. Could the aim of the satellite camera have strayed so much?

Curious, I thumbed forward. The next index number gave another scan of the Sagittarius region, this time seen by the spectral emissions from outward-moving clouds of ammonia. Random blobs. I thumbed again. A formaldehyde-emission view. But now the huge arm of expanding hydrogen was sprinkled with knots, denoting clouds which moved faster, Dopplered into blue.

I frowned. No, the Sagittarius A exposures were no aiming error. These slots were to be left open for my incoming data. Someone had co-opted the space. Who? I called up the identifying codes, but there were none. As far as the master log was concerned, these spaces were still empty.

I moved to erase them. My finger paused, hovered, went limp. This was obviously high-quality information, already processed. Someone would want it. They had carelessly dumped it into my territory, but. . . .

My pause was in part that of sheer appreciation. Peering at the color-coded encrustations of light, I recalled what all this had once been like: impossibly complicated, ornate in its terms, caked with the eccentric jargon of long-dead professors, choked with thickets of atomic physics and thermodynamics, a web of complexity that finally gave forth mental pictures of a whirling, furious past, of stars burned now into cinders, of whispering, turbulent hydrogen that filled the void between the suns. From such numbers came the starscape that we knew. From a sharp scratch on a strip of film we could catch the signature of an element, deduce velocity from the Doppler shift, and then measure the width of that scratch to give the random component of the velocity, the random jigglings due to thermal motion, and thus the temperature. All from a scratch. No, I could not erase it.

When I was a boy of nine I was brow-beaten into serving at the altar, during the unendurably long Episcopal services that my mother felt we should attend. I wore the simple robe and was the first to appear in the service, lighting the candles with an awkward long device and its sliding wick. The organ music was soft and did not call attention to itself, so the congregation could watch undistracted as I fumbled with the wick and tried to keep the precarious balance between feeding it too much (so that, engorged, it bristled into a ball of orange) and the even worse embarrassment of snuffing it into a final accusing puff of black. Through the service I would alternately kneel and stand, murmuring the worn phrases as I thought of the softball I would play in the afternoon, feeling the prickly gathering heat underneath my robes. On a bad day the sweat would accumulate and a drop would cling to my nose. I'd let it hang there in mute testimony. The minister never seemed to notice. I would often slip off into decidedly untheological daydreams, intoxicated by the pressing moist heat, and miss the telltale words of the litany which signalled the beginning of communion. A whisper would come skating across the layered air and I would surface, to see the minister turned with clotted face toward me, holding the implements of his forgiving trade, waiting for me to bring the wine and wafers to be blessed. I would surge upward, swearing under my breath with the ardor only those who have just learned the words can truly muster, unafraid to be muttering these things as I snatched up the chalice and sniffed the too-sweet murky wine, fetching the plates of wafers, swearing that once the polished walnut altar rail was emptied of its upturned and strangely blank faces, once the simpering organ had ebbed into silence and I had shrugged off these robes swarming with the stench of mothballs, I would have no more of it, I would erase it.

I asked Redman who the hell was logging their stuff into my inventory spaces. He checked. The answer was: nobody. There were no recorded intrusions into those sections of the memory system. *Then look further,* I said, and went back to work at the terminal.

They were still there. What's more, some index numbers that had been free before were now filled.

NGC 1097 still vexed me, but I delayed working on the problem. I studied these new pictures. They were processed, Doppler-coded, and filtered for noise. I switched back to the earlier plates, to be sure. Yes, it was clear: these were different.

Current theory held that the arm of expanding gas was on the outward phase of an oscillation. Several hundred million years ago, so the story went, a massive explosion at the galactic center had started the expansion: a billowing, spinning doughnut of gas swelled outward. Eventually its energy was matched by the gravitational attraction of the massive center. Then, as it slowed and finally fell back toward the center, it spun faster, storing energy in rotational motion, until centrifugal forces stopped its inward rush. Thus the hot cloud could oscillate in the potential well of gravity, cooling slowly.

These computer-transformed plates said otherwise. The Doppler shifts formed a cone. At the center of the plate, maximum values, far higher than any observed before, over a thousand kilometers per second. That exceeded escape velocity from the Galaxy itself. The values tapered off to the sides, coming smoothly down to the shifts that were on the earlier plates.

I called the programming director. He looked over the displays, understanding nothing of what it meant but everything about how it could have gotten there; and his verdict was clean, certain: human error. But further checks turned up no such mistake. "Must be comin' in on the transmission from orbit," he mused. He seemed half-asleep as he punched in commands, traced the intruders. These data had come in from the new combination optical, IR, and UV 'scope in orbit, and the JPL programs had obligingly performed the routine miracles of enhancement and analysis. But the orbital staff were sure no such data had been transmitted. In fact, the 'scope had been down for inspection, plus an alignment check, for over two days. The programming director shrugged and promised to look into it, fingering the innumerable pens clipped in his shirt pocket.

I stared at the Doppler cone, and thumbed to the next index number. The cone had grown, the shifts were larger. Another: still larger. And then I noticed something more; and a cold sensation seeped into me, banishing the casual talk and mechanical-printout stutter of the terminal room.

The point of view had shifted. All the earlier plates had shown a particular gas cloud at a certain angle of inclination. This latest plate was slightly cocked to the side, illuminating a clotted bunch of minor H II regions and obscuring a fraction of the hot, expanding arm. Some new features were revealed. If the JPL program had done such a rotation and shift, it would have left the new spaces blank, for there was no way of filling them in. These were not empty. They brimmed with specific shifts, detailed spectral indices. The JPL program would not have produced the field of numbers unless the raw data contained them. I stared at the screen for a long time.

That evening I drove home the long way, through the wide boulevards of Pasadena, in the gathering dusk. I remembered giving blood the month before, in the eggshell light of the Caltech dispensary. They took the blood away in a curious plastic sack, leaving me with a small bandage in the crook of my elbow. The skin was translucent, showing the riverwork of tributary blue veins, which—recently tapped—were nearly as pale as the skin. I had never looked at that part of me before and found it tender, vulnerable, an unexpected opening. I remembered my wife had liked being stroked there when we were dating, and that I had not touched her there for a long time. Now I had myself been pricked there, to pipe brimming life into a sack, and then to some other who could make use of it.

That evening I drove again, taking my son to Open House. The school bristled with light and seemed to command the neighborhood with its luminosity, drawing families out of their homes. My wife was taking my daughter to another school, and so I was unshielded by her ability to recognize people we knew. I could never sort out their names in time to answer the casual hellos. In our neighborhood the PTA nights draw a disproportionate fraction of technical types, like me. Tonight I saw them without the quicksilver verbal fluency of my wife. They had compact cars that seemed too small for their large families, wore shoes whose casualness offset the formal, just-come-from-work jackets and slacks, and carried creamy folders of their children's accumulated work, to use in conferring with the teachers. The wives were sun-darkened, wearing crisp, print dresses that looked recently put on, and spoke with ironic turns about PTA politics, bond issues, and class sizes. In his classroom my son tugged me from board to board, where he had contributed paragraphs on wildlife. The crowning exhibit was a model of Io, Jupiter's pizza-mocking moon, which he had made from a tennis ball and thick, sulphurous paint. It hung in a box painted black and looked remarkably, ethereally real. My son had won first prize in his class for the mockup moon, and his teacher stressed this as she went over the less welcome news that he was not doing well at his reading. Apparently he arranged the plausible phrases—A, then B, then C—into illogical combinations, C coming before A, despite the instructing commas and semicolons which should have guided him. It was a minor problem, his teacher assured me, but should be looked after. Perhaps a little more reading at home, under my eye? I nodded, sure that the children of the other scientists and computer programmers and engineers did not have this difficulty, and already knew what the instructing phrase of the next century would be, before the end of this one. My son took the news matter-of-factly, unafraid, and went off to help with the cake and Kool-aid. I watched him mingle with girls whose awkwardness was lovely, like giraffes'. I remembered that his teacher (I had learned from gossip) had a mother dying of cancer, which might explain the furrow between her eyebrows that would not go away. My son came bearing cake. I ate it with him, sitting with knees slanting upward in the small chair; and quite calmly and suddenly an idea came to me and would not go away. I turned it over and felt its shape, testing it in a preliminary fashion. Underneath I was both excited and fearful and yet sure that it would survive: it was right. Scraping up the last crumbs and icing, I looked down, and saw my son had drawn a crayon design, an enormous father playing ball with a son, running and catching, the scene carefully fitted into the small compass of the plastic, throwaway plate.

The next morning I finished the data reduction on the slit-image exposures. By carefully covering over the galaxy and background, I had managed to take successive plates which blocked out segments of the space parallel to the brightest blue jet. Photometry of the resulting weak signal could give a cross section of the jet's intensity. Pinpoint calibration then yielded the thickness of the central jet zone.

The data was somewhat scattered, the error bars were larger than I liked, but still—I was sure I had it. The jet had a fuzzy halo and a bright core. The core was less than a hundred light years across, a thin filament of highly ionized hydrogen, cut like a swath through the gauzy dust beyond the galaxy. The resolute, ruler-sharp path, its thinness, its profile of luminosity: all pointed toward a tempting picture. Some energetic object had carved each line, moving at high speeds. It swallowed some of the matter in its path; and in the act of engorgement the mass was heated to incandescent brilliance, spitting UV and X-rays into an immense surrounding volume. This radiation in turn ionized the galactic gas, leaving a scratch of light behind the object, like picnickers dumping luminous trash as they pass by.

The obvious candidates for the fast-moving sources of the jets were black holes. And as I traced the slim profiles of the NGC 1097 jets back into the galaxy, they all intersected at the precise geometrical center of the barred spiral pattern.

Last night, after returning from the Open House with a sleepy boy in tow, I talked with my wife as we undressed. I described my son's home room, his artistic achievements, his teacher. My wife let slip offhandedly some jarring news. I had, apparently, misheard the earlier gossip; perhaps I had mused over some problem while she related the story to me over breakfast. It was not the teacher's mother who had cancer, but the teacher herself. I felt an instant, settling guilt. I could scarcely remember the woman's face, though it was a mere hour later. I asked why she was still working. Because, my wife explained with straightforward New England sense, it was better than staring at a wall. The chemotherapy took only a small slice of her hours. And anyway, she probably needed the money. The night beyond our windows seemed solid, flinty, harder than the soft things inside. In the glass I watched my wife take off a print dress and stretch backward, breasts thinning into crescents, her nobbed spine describing a serene curve that anticipated bed. I went over to my chest of drawers and looked down at the polished walnut surface, scrupulously rectangular and arranged, across which I had tossed the residue of an hour's dutiful parenting: a scrawled essay on marmosets, my son's anthology of drawings, his reading list, and on top, the teacher's bland paragraph of assessment. It felt odd to have called these things into being, these signs of a forward tilt in a small life, by an act of love or at least lust, now years past. The angles appropriate to cradling my children still lived in my hands. I could feel clearly the tentative clutch of my son as he attempted some upright steps. Now my eye strayed to his essay. I could see him struggling with the notion of clauses, with ideas piled upon each other to build a point, and with the caged linearity of the sentence. On the page above, in the loops of the teacher's generous flow pen, I saw a hollow rotundity, a denial of any constriction in her life. She had to go on, this schoolgirl penmanship said, to forcefully forget a gnawing illness among a roomful of bustling children. Despite all the rest, she had to keep on doing.

What could be energetic enough to push black holes out of the galactic center, up the slopes of the deep gravitational potential well? Only another black hole. The dynamics had been worked out years before—as so often happens, in another context—by William Saslaw. Let a bee-swarm of black holes orbit about each other, all caught in a gravitational depression. Occasionally, they veer close together, deforming the space-time nearby, caroming off each other like billiard balls. If several undergo these near-miss collisions at once, a black hole can be ejected from the gravitational trap altogether. More complex collisions can throw pairs of black holes in opposite directions, conserving angular momentum: jets and counter-jets. But why did NGC 1097 display two blue jets and two red? Perhaps the blue ones glowed with the phosphorescent waste left by the largest, most energetic black holes; their counter-jets must be, by some detail of the dynamics, always smaller, weaker, redder.

I went to the jutting, air-conditioned library, and read Saslaw's papers. Given a buzzing hive of black holes in a gravitational well—partly of their own making—many things could happen. There were compact configurations, tightly orbiting and self-obsessed, which could be ejected as a body. These close-wound families could in turn be unstable, once they were isolated beyond the galaxy's tug, just as the group at the center had been. Caroming off each other, they could eject unwanted siblings. I frowned. This could explain the astonishing right-angle turn the long blue jet made. One black hole thrust sidewise and several smaller, less energetic black holes pushed the opposite way.

As the galactic center lost its warped children, the ejections would become less probable. Things would die down. But how long did that take? NGC 1007 was no younger than our own Galaxy; on the cosmic scale, a sixty-million-year difference was nothing.

In the waning of afternoon—it was only a bit more than twenty-four hours since I first laid out the plates of NGC 1097—the Operations report came in. There was no explanation for the Sagittarius A data. It had been received from the station in orbit and duly processed. But no command had made the scope swivel to that axis. Odd, Operations said, that it pointed in an interesting direction, but no more.

There were two added plates, fresh from processing. I did not mention to Redman in Operations that the resolution of these plates was astonishing, that details in the bloated, spilling clouds were unprecedented. Nor did I point out that the angle of view had tilted further, giving a better perspective on the outward-jutting inferno. With their polynomial percussion, the computers had given what was in the stream of downward-flowing data, numbers that spoke of something being banished from the pivot of our Galaxy.

Caltech is a compact campus. I went to the Athenaeum for coffee, ambling slowly beneath the palms and scented eucalyptus, and circumnavigated the campus on my return. In the varnished perspectives of these tiled hallways, the hammer of time was a set of Dopplered numbers, blue-shifted because the thing rushed toward us, a bulge in the sky. Silent numbers.

There were details to think about, calculations to do, long strings of hypothesis to unfurl like thin flags. I did not know the effect of a penetrating, ionizing flux on Earth. Perhaps it could affect the upper atmosphere and alter the ozone cap that drifts above our heedless heads. A long trail of disturbed, high-energy plasma could fan out through our benign spiral arm—odd, to think of bands of dust and rivers of stars as a neighborhood where you have grown up—churning, working, heating. After all, the jets of NGC 1097 had snuffed out the beaded H II regions as cleanly as an eraser passing across a blackboard, ending all the problems that life knows.

The NGC 1097 data was clean and firm. It would make a good paper, perhaps a letter to *Astrophysical Journal Letters.* But the rest—there was no crisp professional path. These plates had come from much nearer the Galactic center. The information had come outward at light speed, far faster than the pressing bulge, and tilted at a slight angle away from the radial vector that led to Earth.

I had checked the newest Palomar plates from Sagittarius A this afternoon. There were no signs of anything unusual. No Doppler bulge, no exiled mass. They flatly contradicted the satellite plates.

That was the key: old reliable Palomar, our biggest ground-based 'scope, showed nothing. Which meant that someone in high orbit had fed data into our satellite 'scope—exposures which had to be made nearer the Galactic center and then brought here and deftly slipped into our ordinary astronomical research. Exposures which spoke of something stirring where we could not yet see it, beyond the obscuring lanes of dust. The plumes of fiery gas would take a while longer to work through that dark cloak.

These plain facts had appeared on a screen, mute and undeniable, keyed to the data on NGC 1097. Keyed to a connection that another eye than mine could miss. Some astronomer laboring over plates of eclipsing binaries or globular clusters might well have impatiently erased the offending, multicolored spattering, not bothered to uncode the Dopplers, to note the persistent mottled red of the Galactic dust arm at the lower right, and so not known what the place must be. Only I could have made the connection to NGC 1097, and guessed what an onrushing black hole could do to a fragile planet: burn away the ozone layer, hammer the land with high-energy particles, mask the sun in gas and dust.

But to convey this information in this way was so strange, so—yes, that was the word—so alien. Perhaps this was the way they had to do it; quiet, subtle, indirect. Using an oblique analogy which only suggested, yet somehow disturbed more than a direct statement. And of course, this might be only a phrase in a longer message. Moving out from the Galactic center, they would not know we were here until they grazed the expanding bubble of radio noise that gave us away, and so their data would use what they had, views at a different slant. The data itself, raw and silent, would not necessarily call attention to itself. It had to be placed in context, beside NGC 1097. How had they managed to do that? Had they tried before? What odd logic dictated this approach? How. . . .

Take it in pieces. Some of the data I could use, some not. Perhaps a further check, a fresh look through the dusty Sagittarius arm, would show the beginnings of a ruddy swelling, could give a verification. I would have to look, try to find a bridge that would make plausible what I knew but could scarcely prove. The standards of science are austere, unforgiving—and who would have it differently? I would have to hedge, to take one step back for each two forward, to compare and suggest and contrast, always sticking close to the data. And despite what I thought I knew now, the data would have to lead, they would have to show the way.

There is a small Episcopal church, not far up Hill Street, which offers a Friday communion in early evening. Driving home through the surrounding neon consumer gumbo, musing, I saw the sign, and stopped. I had the NGC 1097 plates with me in a carrying case, ripe beneath my arm with their fractional visions, like thin sections of an exotic cell. I went in. The big oak door thumped solemnly shut behind me. In the nave two elderly men were passing woven baskets, taking up the offertory. I took a seat near the back. Idly I surveyed the people, distributed randomly like a field of unthinking stars, in the pews before me. A man came nearby and a pool of brassy light passed before me and I put something in, the debris at the bottom clinking and rustling as I stirred it. I watched the backs of heads as the familiar litany droned on, as devoid of meaning as before. I do not believe, but there is communion. Something tugged at my attention; one head turned a fraction. By a kind of triangulation I deduced the features of the other, closer to the ruddy light of the altar, and saw it was my son's teacher. She was listening raptly. I listened, too, watching her, but could only think of the gnawing at the center of a bustling, swirling galaxy. The lights seemed to dim. The organ had gone silent. *Take, eat. This is the body and blood of* and so it had begun. I waited my turn. I do not believe, but there is communion. The people went forward in their turns. The woman rose; yes, it was she, the kind of woman whose hand would give forth loops and spirals and who would dot her **i**'s with a small circle. The faint timbre of the organ seeped into the layered air. When it was time I was still thinking of NGC 1097, of how I would write the paper—fragments skittered across my mind, the pyramid of the argument was taking shape—and I very nearly missed the gesture of the elderly man at the end of my pew. Halfway to the altar rail I realized that I still carried the case of NGC 1097 exposures, crooked into my elbow, where the pressure caused a slight ache to spread: the spot where they had made the transfusion in the clinic, transferring a fraction of life, blood given. I put it beside me as I knelt. The robes of the approaching figure were cobalt blue and red, a change from the decades since I had been an acolyte. There were no acolytes at such a small service, of course. The blood would follow; first came the offered plate of wafers. Take, eat. Life calling out to life. I could feel the pressing weight of what lay ahead for me, the long roll of years carrying forward one hypothesis, and then, swallowing, knowing that I would never believe this and yet I would want it, I remembered my son, remembered that these events were only pieces, that the puzzle was not yet over, that I would never truly see it done, that as an astronomer I had to live with knowledge forever partial and provisional, that science was not final results but instead a continuing meditation carried on in the face of enormous facts—*take it in phrases*—let the sentences of our lives pile up.

(1981)

WILLIAM GIBSON

The Gernsback Continuum

Mercifully, the whole thing is starting to fade, to become an episode. When I do still catch the odd glimpse, it's peripheral; mere fragments of mad-doctor chrome, confining themselves to the corner of the eye. There was that flying-wing liner over San Francisco last week, but it was almost translucent. And the shark-fin roadsters have gotten scarcer, and freeways discreetly avoid unfolding themselves into the gleaming eighty-lane monsters I was forced to drive last month in my rented Toyota. And I know that none of it will follow me to New York; my vision is narrowing to a single wavelength of probability. I've worked hard for that. Television helped a lot.

I suppose it started in London, in that bogus Greek taverna in Battersea Park Road, with lunch on Cohen's corporate tab. Dead steam-table food and it took them thirty minutes to find an ice bucket for the retsina. Cohen works for Barris-Watford, who publish big, trendy "trade" paperbacks: illustrated histories of the neon sign, the pinball machine, the windup toys of Occupied Japan. I'd gone over to shoot a series of shoe ads; California girls with tanned legs and frisky Day-Glo jogging shoes had capered for me down the escalators of St. John's Wood and across the platforms of Tooting Bec. A lean and hungry young agency had decided that the mystery of London Transport would sell waffle-tread nylon runners. They decide; I shoot. And Cohen, whom I knew vaguely from the old days in New York, had invited me to lunch the day before I was due out of Heathrow. He brought along a very fashionably dressed young woman named Dialta Downes, who was virtually chinless and evidently a noted pop-art historian. In retrospect, I see her walking in beside Cohen under a floating neon sign that flashes THIS WAY LIES MADNESS in huge sans-serif capitals.

Cohen introduced us and explained that Dialta was the prime mover behind the latest Barris-Watford project, an illustrated history of what she called "American Streamlined Moderne." Cohen called it "raygun

Gothic." Their working title was *The Airstream Futuropolis: The Tomorrow That Never Was.*

There's a British obsession with the more baroque elements of American pop culture, something like the weird cowboys-and-Indians fetish of the West Germans or the aberrant French hunger for old Jerry Lewis films. In Dialta Downes this manifested itself in a mania for a uniquely American form of architecture that most Americans are scarcely aware of. At first I wasn't sure what she was talking about, but gradually it began to dawn on me. I found myself remembering Sunday morning television in the Fifties.

Sometimes they'd run old eroded newsreels as filler on the local station. You'd sit there with a peanut butter sandwich and a glass of milk, and a static-ridden Hollywood baritone would tell you that there was A Flying Car in Your Future. And three Detroit engineers would putter around with this big old Nash with wings, and you'd see it rumbling furiously down some deserted Michigan runway. You never actually saw it take off, but it flew away to Dialta Downes's never-never land, true home of a generation of completely uninhibited technophiles. She was talking about those odds and ends of "futuristic" Thirties and Forties architecture you pass daily in American cities without noticing; the movie marquees ribbed to radiate some mysterious energy, the dime stores faced with fluted aluminum, the chrome-tube chairs gathering dust in the lobbies of transient hotels. She saw these things as segments of a dreamworld, abandoned in the uncaring present; she wanted me to photograph them for her.

The Thirties had seen the first generation of American industrial designers; until the Thirties, all pencil sharpeners had looked like pencil sharpeners—your basic Victorian mechanism, perhaps with a curlicue of decorative trim. After the advent of the designers, some pencil sharpeners looked as though they'd been put together in wind tunnels. For the most part, the change was only skin-deep; under the streamlined chrome shell, you'd find the same Victorian mechanism. Which made a certain kind of sense, because the most successful American designers had been recruited from the ranks of Broadway theater designers. It was all a stage set, a series of elaborate props for playing at living in the future.

Over coffee, Cohen produced a fat manila envelope full of glossies. I saw the winged statues that guard the Hoover Dam, forty-foot concrete hood ornaments leaning steadfastly into an imaginary hurricane. I saw a dozen shots of Frank Lloyd Wright's Johnson's Wax Building, juxtaposed with the covers of old *Amazing Stories* pulps, by an artist named Frank R. Paul; the employees of Johnson's Wax must have felt as though they were walking into one of Paul's spray-paint pulp utopias. Wright's building looked as though it had been designed for people who wore white togas and Lucite sandals. I hesitated over one sketch of a particularly grandiose prop-driven airliner, all wing, like a fat symmetrical boomerang with windows in unlikely places. Labeled arrows indicated the locations of the grand ballroom and two squash courts. It was dated 1936.

"This thing couldn't have flown . . . ?" I looked at Dialta Downes.

"Oh, no, quite impossible, even with those twelve giant props; but they loved the look, don't you see? New York to London in less than two days, first-class dining rooms, private cabins, sun decks, dancing to jazz in the evening . . . The designers were populists, you see; they were trying to give the public what it wanted. What the public wanted was the future."

I'd been in Burbank for three days, trying to suffuse a really dull-looking rocker with charisma, when I got the package from Cohen. It is possible to photograph what isn't there; it's damned hard to do, and consequently a very marketable talent. While I'm not bad at it, I'm not exactly the best, either, and this poor guy strained my Nikon's credibility. I got out, depressed because I do like to do a good job, but not totally depressed, because I did make sure I'd gotten the check for the job, and I decided to restore myself with the sublime artiness of the Barris-Watford assignment. Cohen had sent me some books on Thirties design, more photos of streamlined buildings, and a list of Dialta Downes's fifty favorite examples of the style in California.

Architectural photography can involve a lot of waiting; the building becomes a kind of sundial, while you wait for a shadow to crawl away from a detail you want, or for the mass and balance of the structure to reveal itself in a certain way. While I was waiting, I thought myself in Dialta Downes's America. When I isolated a few of the factory buildings on the ground glass of the Hasselblad, they came across with a kind of sinister totalitarian dignity, like the stadiums Albert Speer built for Hitler. But the rest of it was relentlessly tacky: ephemeral stuff extruded by the collective American subconscious of the Thirties, tending mostly to survive along depressing strips lined with dusty motels, mattress wholesalers, and small used-car lots. I went for the gas stations in a big way.

During the high point of the Downes Age, they put Ming the Merciless in charge of designing California gas stations. Favoring the architecture of his native Mongo, he cruised up and down the coast erecting raygun emplacements in white stucco. Lots of them featured superfluous central towers ringed with those strange radiator flanges that were a signature motif of the style, and made them look as though they might generate potent bursts of raw technological enthusiasm, if you could only find the switch that turned them on. I shot one in San Jose an hour before the bulldozers arrived and drove right through the structural truth of plaster and lathing and cheap concrete.

"Think of it," Dialta Downes had said, "as a kind of alternate America: a 1980 that never happened. An architecture of broken dreams."

And that was my frame of mind as I made the stations of her convoluted socioarchitectural cross in my red Toyota—as I gradually tuned in to her image of a shadowy America-that-wasn't, of Coca-Cola plants like beached submarines, and fifth-run movie houses like the temples of some lost sect that had worshiped blue mirrors and geometry. And as I moved among these secret ruins, I found myself wondering what the inhabitants of that lost future world think of the world I lived in. The Thirties dreamed white marble and slipstream chrome, immortal crystal and burnished bronze, but the rockets on the covers of the Gernsback pulps had fallen on London in the dead of night, screaming. After the war, everyone had a car—no wings for it—and the promised superhighway to drive it down, so that the sky itself darkened, and the fumes ate the marble and pitted the miracle crystal. . . .

And one day, on the outskirts of Bolinas, when I was setting up to shoot a particularly lavish example of Ming's martial architecture, I penetrated a fine membrane, a membrane of probability. . . .

Ever so gently, I went over the Edge—

And looked up to see a twelve-engined thing like a bloated boomerang, all wing, thrumming its way east with an elephantine grace, so low that I could count the rivets in its dull silver skin, and hear—maybe—the echo of jazz.

I took it to Kihn.

Merv Kihn, free-lance journalist with an extensive line in Texas pterodactyls, redneck UFO contactees, bush-league Loch Ness monsters, and the Top Ten conspiracy theories in the loonier reaches of the American mass mind.

"It's good," said Kihn, polishing his yellow Polaroid shooting glasses on the hem of his Hawaiian shirt, "but it's not *mental;* lacks the true quill."

But I saw it, Mervyn." We were seated poolside in brilliant Arizona sunlight. He was in Tucson waiting for a group of retired Las Vegas civil servants whose leader received messages from Them on her microwave oven. I'd driven all night and was feeling it.

"Of course you did. Of course you saw it. You've read my stuff; haven't you grasped my blanket solution to the UFO problem? It's simple, plain and country simple: people"—he settled the glasses carefully on his long hawk nose and fixed me with his best basilisk glare—"*see* . . . things. People see these things. Nothing's there, but people *see* them anyway. Because they need to, probably. You've read Jung, you should know the score. . . . In your case, it's so obvious: You admit you were thinking about this crackpot architecture, having fantasies. . . . Look, Im sure you've taken your share of drugs, right? How many people survived the Sixties in California without having the odd hallucination? All those nights when you discovered that whole armies of Disney technicians had been employed to weave animated holograms of Egyptian hieroglyphs into the fabric of your jeans, say, or the times when—"

"But it wasn't like that."

"Of course not. It wasn't like that at all; it was 'in a setting of clear reality,' right? Everything normal, and then there's the monster, the mandala, the neon cigar. In your case, a giant Tom Swift airplane. It happens *all the time.* You aren't even crazy. You know that, don't you?" He fished a beer out of the battered foam cooler beside his deck chair.

"Last week I was in Virginia. Grayson County. I interviewed a sixteen-year-old girl who'd been assaulted by a *bar hade.*"

"A what?"

"A bear head. The severed head of a bear. This *bar hade,* see, was floating around on its own little flying saucer, looked kind of like the hubcaps on cousin Wayne's vintage Caddy. Had red, glowing eyes like two cigar stubs and telescoping chrome antennas poking up behind its ears." He burped.

"It assaulted her? How?"

"You don't want to know; you're obviously impressionable. 'It was cold' "—he lapsed into his bad southern accent—" 'and metallic.' It made electronic noises. Now that is the real thing, the straight goods from the mass unconscious, friend; that little girl is a witch. There's just no place for her to function in this society. She'd have seen the devil, if she hadn't been brought up on 'The Bionic Man' and all those 'Star Trek' reruns. She is clued into the main vein. And she knows that it happened to her. I got out ten minutes before the heavy UFO boys showed up with the polygraph."

I must have looked pained, because he set his beer down carefully beside the cooler and sat up.

"If you want a classier explanation, I'd say you saw a semiotic ghost. All these contactee stories, for instance, are framed in a kind of sci-fi imagery that permeates our culture. I could buy aliens, but not aliens that look like Fifties' comic art. They're semiotic phantoms, bits of deep cultural imagery that have split off and taken on a life of their own, like the Jules Verne airships that those old Kansas farmers were always seeing. But you saw a different kind of ghost, that's all. That plane was part of the mass unconscious, once. You picked up on that, somehow. The important thing is not to worry about it."

I did worry about it, though.

Kihn combed his thinning blond hair and went off to hear what They had had to say over the radar range lately, and I drew the curtains in my room and lay down in air-conditioned darkness to worry about it. I was still worrying about it when I woke up. Kihn had left a note on my door; he was flying up north in a chartered plane to check out a cattle-mutilation rumor ("muties," he called them; another of his journalistic specialties).

I had a meal, showered, took a crumbling diet pill that had been kicking around in the bottom of my shaving kit for three years, and headed back to Los Angeles.

The speed limited my vision to the tunnel of the Toyota's headlights. The body could drive, I told myself, while the mind maintained. Maintained and stayed away from the weird peripheral window dressing of amphetamine and exhaustion, the spectral, luminous vegetation that grows out of the corners of the mind's eye along late-night highways. But the mind had its own ideas, and Kihn's opinion of what I was already thinking of as my "sighting" rattled endlessly through my head in a tight, lopsided orbit. Semiotic ghosts. Fragments of the Mass Dream, whirling past in the wind of my passage. Somehow this feedback-loop aggravated the diet pill, and the speed-vegetation along the road began to assume the colors of infrared satellite images, glowing shreds blown apart in the Toyota's slipstream.

I pulled over, then, and a half-dozen aluminum beer cans winked goodnight as I killed the headlights. I wondered what time it was in London, and tried to imagine Dialta Downes having breakfast in her Hampstead flat, surrounded by streamlined chrome figurines and books on American culture.

Desert nights in that country are enormous; the moon is closer. I watched the moon for a long time and decided that Kihn was right. The main thing was not to worry. All across the continent, daily, people who were more normal than I'd ever aspired to be saw giant birds, Bigfeet, flying oil refineries; they kept Kihn busy and solvent. Why should I be upset by a glimpse of the 1930s pop imagination loose over Bolinas? I decided to go to sleep, with nothing worse to worry about than rattlesnakes and cannibal hippies, safe amid the friendly roadside garbage of my own familiar continuum. In the morning I'd drive down to Nogales and photograph the old brothels, something I'd intended to do for years. The diet pill had given up.

The light woke me, and then the voices.

The light came from somewhere behind me and threw shifting shadows inside the car. The voices were calm, indistinct, male and female, engaged in conversation.

My neck was stiff and my eyeballs felt gritty in their sockets. My leg had gone to sleep, pressed against the steering wheel. I fumbled for my glasses in the pocket of my work shirt and finally got them on.

Then I looked behind me and saw the city.

The books on Thirties design were in the trunk; one of them contained sketches of an idealized city that drew on *Metropolis* and *Things to Come,* but squared everything, soaring up through an architect's perfect clouds to zeppelin docks and mad neon spires. That city was a scale model of the one that rose behind me. Spire stood on spire in gleaming ziggurat steps that climbed to a central golden temple tower ringed with the crazy radiator flanges of the Mongo gas stations. You could hide the Empire State Building in the smallest of those towers. Roads of crystal soared between the spires, crossed and recrossed by smooth silver shapes like beads of running mercury. The air was thick with ships: giant wing-liners, little darting silver things (sometimes one of the quicksilver shapes from the sky bridges rose gracefully into the air and flew up to join the dance), mile-long blimps, hovering dragonfly things that were gyrocopters . . .

I closed my eyes tight and swung around in the seat. When I opened them, I willed myself to see the mileage meter, the pale road dust on the black plastic dashboard, the overflowing ashtray.

"Amphetamine psychosis," I said. I opened my eyes. The dash was still there, the dust, the crushed filtertips. Very carefully, without moving my head, I turned the headlights on.

And saw them.

They were blond. They were standing beside their car, an aluminum avocado with a central shark-fin rudder jutting up from its spine and smooth black tires like a child's toy. He had his arm around her waist and was gesturing toward the city. They were both in white: loose clothing, bare legs, spotless white sun shoes. Neither of them seemed aware of the beams of my headlights. He was saying something wise and strong, and she was nodding, and suddenly I was frightened, frightened in an entirely different way. Sanity had ceased to be an issue; I knew, somehow, that the city behind me was Tucson—a dream Tucson thrown up out of the collective yearning of an era. That it was real, entirely real. But the couple in front of me lived in it, and they frightened me.

They were the children of Dialta Downes's '80-that-wasn't; they were Heirs to the Dream. They were white, blond, and they probably had blue eyes. They were American. Dialta had said that the Future had come to America first, but had finally passed it by. But not here, in the heart of the Dream. Here, we'd gone on and on, in a dream logic that knew nothing of pollution, the finite bounds of fossil fuel, or foreign wars it was possible to lose. They were smug, happy, and utterly content with themselves and their world. And in the Dream, it was *their* world.

Behind me, the illuminated city: Searchlights swept the sky for the sheer joy of it. I imagined them thronging the plazas of white marble, orderly and alert, their bright eyes shining with enthusiasm for their floodlit avenues and silver cars.

It had all the sinister fruitiness of Hitler Youth propaganda.

I put the car in gear and drove forward slowly, until the bumper was within three feet of them. They still hadn't seen me. I rolled the window down and listened to what the man was saying. His words were bright and hollow as the pitch in some Chamber of Commerce brochure, and I knew that he believed in them absolutely.

"John," I heard the woman say, "we've forgotten to take our food pills." She clicked two bright wafers from a thing on her belt and passed one to him. I backed onto the highway and headed for Los Angeles, wincing and shaking my head.

I phoned Kihn from a gas station. A new one, in bad Spanish Modern. He was back from his expedition and didn't seem to mind the call.

"Yeah, that is a weird one. Did you try to get any pictures? Not that they ever come out, but it adds an interesting *frisson* to your story, not having the pictures turn out. . . ."

But what should I do?

"Watch lots of television, particularly game shows and soaps. Go to porn movies. Ever see *Nazi Love Motel*? They've got it on cable, here. Really awful. Just what you need."

What was he talking about?

"Quit yelling and listen to me. I'm letting you in on a trade secret: Really bad media can exorcise your semiotic ghosts. If it keeps the saucer people off my back, it can keep these Art Deco futuroids off yours. Try it. What have you got to lose?"

Then he begged off, pleading an early-morning date with the Elect.

"The who?"

"These oldsters from Vegas; the ones with the microwaves."

I considered putting a collect call through to London, getting Cohen at Barris-Watford and telling him his photographer was checked out for a protracted season in the Twilight Zone. In the end, I let a machine mix me a really impossible cup of black coffee and climbed back into the Toyota for the haul to Los Angeles.

Los Angeles was a bad idea, and I spent two weeks there. It was prime Downes country; too much of the Dream there, and too many fragments of the Dream waiting to snare me. I nearly wrecked the car on a stretch of overpass near Disneyland, when the road fanned out like an origami trick and left me swerving through a dozen minilanes of whizzing chrome teardrops with shark fins. Even worse, Hollywood was full of people who looked too much like the couple I'd seen in Arizona. I hired an Italian director who was making ends meet doing darkroom work and installing patio decks around swimming pools until his ship came in; he made prints of all the negatives I'd accumulated on the Downes job. I didn't want to look at the stuff myself. It didn't seem to bother Leonardo, though, and when he was finished I checked the prints, riffling through them like a deck of cards, sealed them up, and sent them air freight to London. Then I took a taxi to a theater that was showing *Nazi Love Motel,* and kept my eyes shut all the way.

Cohen's congratulatory wire was forwarded to me in San Francisco a week later. Dialta had loved the pictures. He admired the way I'd "really gotten into it," and looked forward to working with me again. That afternoon I spotted a flying wing over Castro Street, but there was something tenuous about it, as though it were only half there. I rushed into the nearest newsstand and gathered up as much as I could find on the petroleum crisis and the nuclear energy hazard. I'd just decided to buy a plane ticket for New York.

"Hell of a world we live in, huh?" The proprietor was a thin black man with bad teeth and an obvious wig. I nodded, fishing in my jeans for change, anxious to find a park bench where I could submerge myself in hard evidence of the human near-dystopia we live in. "But it could be worse, huh?"

"That's right," I said, "or even worse, it could be perfect."

He watched me as I headed down the street with my little bundle of condensed catastrophe.

(1981)

CAROL EMSHWILLER

The Start of the End of the World

First the distant sound of laughter. I thought it was laughter. Kind of chuckling . . . choking maybe . . . or spasms of some sort. Can't explain it. Scary laughter coming closer. Then they came in in a scary way, pale, with shiny raincoats and fogged glasses, sat down, and waited out the storm here. Asked only for warm water to sip. Crossed their legs with refined grace and watched late-night TV. They spoke of not wanting to end up in a museum . . . neither them nor their talismans nor their flags, their dripping flags. They looked so vulnerable and sad . . . chuckling, choking sad that I lost all fear of them. They left in the morning, most of them. All but three left. Klimp, their regional director, and two others stayed.

"It is important and salutary to speak of incomprehensible things," they said, and so we did till dawn. They also said that their love for this planet, "this splendid planet," knows no bounds, and that they could take over with just a tiny smidgen of violence, especially since we had been softening up the people ourselves as though in preparation for them. I believed them. I saw their love for this place in their eyes.

"But am I"—and I asked them this directly—"am I, a woman, and a woman of, should I say, a certain age, am I really to be included in the master plan?" They implied, yes, chuckling (choking), but then everyone has always tried to give me that impression (former husband especially) and it never was true before. It's nice, though, that they said they couldn't do it without me and others like me.

What they also say is, "As sun to earth, so kitchen is to house and so house is to the rest of the world. Politics," they say, "begins at home, and most especially in the kitchen, place of warmth, chemistry, and changes, means toward ends. Grandiose plans cooked up here. A house," they say, "hardly need be more than kitchen and a few good chairs." Where they come from that's the way it is. And I agree that if somebody wanted to take over the Earth, it's true: they could do worse than to do it from the kitchen.

They also say that it will be necessary to let the world lie fallow and recoup for fifteen years. That's about step number three of their plan.

"But first," they say (step number one), "it will be necessary to get rid of the cats."

Klimp! His kind did not, absolutely not descend from apelike creatures, but from higher beings. Sky folk. We can't understand that, he said. Their sex organs are, he told me, pure and unconnected to excretory organs in any way. Body hair in different patterns. None, and this is significant, under the arms, and, actually, what's on their head really isn't hair either. Just looks like it. They're a manifestation in living form of a kind of purity not to be achieved by any of us except by artificial means. They also say that, because of what they are, they will do a lot better with this world than we do. Klimp promises me that and I believe him. They're simply crazy about this world. "It's a treasure," Klimp keeps saying.

I ask, "How much time is there, actually, till doomsday, or whatever you call it?"

No special name, though Restoration Day or (even better) Resurrection Day might serve. No special time either. ("Might take a lifetime. Might not.") They live like that but without confusion.

But first, as they say, it is necessary to get rid of the cats, though I am trying to see both sides: (a) Klimp's and his friends' and (b) trying to come to terms with three hyperactive cats that I've had since the divorce. The white one is throwing up on the rug. Turns out to be a rubber band and a long piece of string.

Of the three, Klimp is clearly mine. He likes to pass his cool hands . . . his always-cold hands through my hair, but if I try to sit on his lap to confirm our relationship, he can't bear that. We've known each other almost two weeks now, shuffled along in the park (I name the trees), the shady side of streets, examined the different kinds of grasses. (I never noticed how many kinds there were.) He looks all right from every angle but one, and he always wears his raincoat so we don't have any trouble.

"I accept," I say, when he asks me a few days later, anthropomorphising as usual, and tired of falling in love with TV stars and newsmen or the equivalent. I put on my old wedding ring and start, then, to keep a record of the take-over, kitchen by kitchen by kitchen. . . .

Klimp says, "Let's get in bed and see what happens."

Something does, but I won't say what.

I haven't seen any of them, even Klimp, totally naked, though a couple of times I saw him wearing nothing but a teacup.

(They read our sex manuals before beginning their take-over.)

But willing servants (women are) of almost anything that looks or feels like male or has a raspy voice, regardless of the real sex whatever that may be, or if sex at all. And sometimes one had to make do (we older women do, anyway) with the peculiar, the alien or the partly alien, the egocentric, the disgruntled, the dissipated. . . . But also, and especially, willing servants of things that can fly, or things, rather, that may have descended from things that could fly once or things that could almost fly (though lots of things can *almost* fly). But I heard some woman say that someone told her that one had been seen actually vibrating himself into the sky, arched back, hands in pockets . . . had also, this person said, been seen throwing money off the Ambassador Bridge. The ultimate subversion.

Also I heard they may have already infiltrated the mayonnaise company. A great deal of harm can be done simply by loosening all the jar lids. Is this without violence! And when one of them comes up behind you on the street, grabs your arm with long, strong thumb and forefinger, quietly asking for money and your watch and promising not to hurt you . . . especially not to hurt you, then you give them. Afterward I hear they sometimes crumple the bills into their big, white pipes and smoke them on the spot. They flush the watches down toilets. This last I've seen myself.

But is all this without violence! Klimp takes the time to explain it to me. We're using the same word with two somewhat different meanings, as happens with people from different places. But then there's never any need to justify the already righteous. Sure of his own kindnesses, as look at him right now, Klimp, kiss to earlobe and one finger drawing tickly circles in the palm of my hand. He sees, he says, the Eastern Seaboard as it could be were it the kind of perfection that it should be. He says it will be splendid and these are means toward that end.

Random pats, now, in the region of the belly button. (His pats. My belly button.) Asks me if I ever saw a cat fly. It's important. "Not exactly," I say, "but I saw one fall six stories once and not get hurt, if that counts."

As we sit here, the white cat eats a twenty-dollar bill.

I was divorced, as I mentioned. We were, all of us women who are in this thing with them, all divorced. DIVORCE. A tearing word. I was divorced in the abdomen and in the chest. In those days I sometimes telephoned just to hear "Hello." I was divorced at and against sunsets, hills, fall leaves, and, later on in the spring, I was divorced from spring.

But now, suddenly, I have not failed everything. None of us has failed. And we want nothing for ourselves. Never have. We want to do what's best for the planet.

Sometimes lately, when the afternoon is perfect . . . a pale, humid day, the kind they like the most . . . cool . . . white sky . . . and Klimp or one of the others (it's hard to tell them apart sometimes, though Klimp usually wears the largest cap . . . yellow plastic cap) . . . when the one I think is Klimp is on the lawn chair figuring how to get rid of all the bees by too much spraying of fruit trees or how best to distribute guns to the quick tempered or some such problems, then I think that life has turned perfect already, though they keep telling me that comes later . . . but perfect right now, at least as far as I'm concerned. I like it with the take-over only half begun. Doing the job, it's been said, is half the fun. To me it's all the fun. And I especially like the importance of the kitchen for things other than mere food. Yesterday, for instance, I destroyed (at the self-cleaning setting) a bushel of important medical records plus several reference works and dictionaries, also textbooks and a bin of brand-new maps. When I see Klimp, then, on the lawn, or all three sometimes, and all three gauzy, pale blue flags unfurled, and they're chuckling and whispering and choking together, I feel as though the kitchen itself, by its several motors, will take off into the air . . . hum itself into the sunset riding smoothly on a warm updraft, all its engines turned to low. I want to tell them how I feel. "Perfect," I say. "Everything's perfect except for these three things: wet sand tracked into the vestibule, stepping on the tails of cats, and please don't look at me with such a steady, fishlike gaze, because when you do, I can't read the recipes you gave me for things that make people feel good, rot the brain, and cost a lot."

But I shouldn't have reminded them of the cats. They are saying again that I have to choose between the cats or them. They say their talismans are getting lost under the furniture, that some of their wafers have been found chewed on and spat out. They say I don't realize the politics of the situation and I suppose I don't. I never did pay much attention to politics. "You have to realize everything is political," they say, "even cats."

I'm thinking perhaps I'll take them to the state park outside of town. They'll do all right. Cats do. Get rid of them in some nice place I'd like to be in myself, by a river, near some hills. . . . Leave them with full stomachs. Be up there and back by evening. Klimp will be pleased.

But look what's coming true now! Dead cats . . . drowned cats washed up on the beaches. I saw the pictures on the news. Great flocks of cats, as though they had been caught at sea in a storm, or as though they had flown too far from shore and fallen into the ocean from exhaustion.

Perhaps I understand even less about politics than I thought.

I decide to please my cats with a big dish of fresh fish. (Klimp is out tonight turning up amplifiers in order to impair hearing, while the others are out pulling the hands off clocks.)

The house has a sort of air space above the attic. There's a little vent which, if removed, a cat could live up there quite comfortably, climbing up and down by way of the roof of the garage and a tree near it. A cat could be fed secretly outside and might not be recognized as one who lived here. It isn't that I don't dedicate myself to Klimp and the others. I do, but, as for the cats, I also dedicate myself to them.

Klimp and the others come back at dawn, flags furled, tired but happy. "Job's well done," they say. I fill the bathtub, boil water for them to dip their wafers in. They chuckle, pat me. (They're so demonstrative. Not at all like my husband used to be.) They move their hands in cryptic signals, or perhaps it's just nervousness. They blink at each other. They even blink at me. I'm thinking this is pure joy. Must never end. And now I have the cats and them also. I love. I love. Luff . . . loove . . . loofe . . . they can't pronounce it, but they use the word all the time. Sometimes I wonder exactly what they mean by it, it comes so easily to their lips.

At least I know what *I* mean by "love," and I know I've gone from having nothing and nobody (I had the cats, of course, but I have people now) to having all the best things in life: love and a kind of family and meaningful work to do . . . world-shaking work. . . . All of us useless old women, now part of a vast international kitchen network and I'm wondering if we can go even further. Get to be sort of a world-watching crew while the earth lies fallow. "Listen, what about us in all this?" I ask, my arm across Klimp's barrel chest. "We're no harm. We're all over child-bearing age. What about if we watch over things for you during the time the Earth rests up?"

He answers, "Is as does. Does as is." (If he really loves me, he'll do it.)

"Listen, we could see to it that no smart ape would start leveling out hills."

"What we need," he says, "are a lot of little, warm, wet places." He tells me he's glad the cats are no longer here. He says, "I know you love ('luff') me now," and wants me to eat a big pink wafer. I try to get out of it politely. Who knows what's in it? And the ones they always eat are white. But what has made me worthy of this honor, just that the cats are no longer in view?

"All right," I say, "but just one tiny bite." Tastes dry and chalky and sweet . . . too sweet. Klimp . . . but I see it's not Klimp this time . . . one of the others . . . urges another bite. "Where's Klimp?" "I also love ('luff') you," he says and "Time to find lots of little dark, wet places. We told you already."

I'm wondering what sort of misunderstanding is happening right now.

I have a vision of a skyful of minnows . . . silver schools of minnows . . . the buzz of air . . . the tinkling . . . the glitter . . . *my* minnows flashing by. Why not? And then more and more until the sky is bursting with them. I can't tell anymore which are mine. Somewhere a group of thirty-six . . . no, lots more than that . . . eighty-four . . . I'm not sure. One hundred and eight? Yes, my group among the others. They, my own, swim back to me, then swirl up and away. Forever. And forever mine. Why not?

I wake to the sounds of sheep. I have a backyard full of them. Ewes, it turns out. They are contented. As am I. I watch the setting moon, eat the oranges and onions Klimp brings me, sip mint tea, feel slightly nauseous, get a call from a friend. Seems she's had sheep for a couple of weeks now. Took her cats up to the state park just as I'd thought of doing and had sheep the next day, though she wishes now she had put those cats in the attic as I've done, but she's wondering will I get away with it? She wants me to come over, secretly if I can. She says it's important. But there's a lot of work to be done here. Klimp is talking, even now, about important projects such as opening the wild animal cages at the zoo and the best way to drop water into mailboxes and how about digging pot-holes in the roads? How about handing out free cartons of cigarettes especially those high in tars? He hangs up the phone for me and brings me another onion. I don't need any other friends.

She calls me again a few days later. She says she thinks she's pregnant, but we both know that can't be true. I say to see a doctor. It's probably a tumor. She says they don't want her to, that they drove her car away somewhere. She thinks they pushed it off the pier along with a lot of others. I say I thought they were doing just the opposite. Switching road signs and such to get people to drive around wasting gas. Anyway, she says, they won't let her out of the house. Well, I can't be bothered with the illusions of every old lady around. I have enough troubles of my own and I haven't been feeling so well lately either, tired all the time and a little sick. Irritable. Too irritable to talk with her.

The ewes in the backyard are all obviously pregnant. They swell up fast. The bitch dog next door seems pregnant, too, which is funny because I though she was a spay. It makes you stop and think. I wonder, what if *I* wanted to go out? And is my old car still in the garage? They've been watching me all the time lately. I can't even go to the bathroom without one of them listening outside the door. I haven't been able to feed the cats lately. I used to hate it when they killed birds, but now I hope there are some winter birds around. I think I will put up a bird feeder. I think spring is coming. I've lost track, but I'm sure we're well into March now. Klimp says, "I luff, I luff," and wants to rub my back, but I won't let him . . . not anymore . . . or not right now. Why won't they all three go out at the same time as they used to?

What's wrong with me lately? Can't sleep . . . itch all over . . . angry at nothing. . . . They're not so bad, Klimp and the others. Actually better than most. Always squeeze the toothpaste from the bottom, leave the toilet seat down . . . they don't cut their toenails and leave them in little piles on the night table, use their own towels usually, listen to me when I talk. Why be so angry?

I must try harder. I will tell Klimp that he can rub my back later. I'll apologize for being angry and I'll try to do it in a nice way. Then I'll go into the bedroom, shut the door, brace it with a chair and be really alone for a while. Lie down and relax. I know I'll miss cooking up some important concoctions, but I've missed a lot of things lately.

Next thing I know I wake up and it's dark outside. I have a terrible stomachache like a lot of gas rolling around inside. I feel very strange. I have to get out of here.

I can hear one of them moving outside the door. I hear him brush against it . . . a chitinous scraping. "Let me in. I loofe you." Then there's that kind of giggle. He can't help it, I know, but it's getting on my nerves. "Is as does," he says. "Now you see that." I put on my sneakers and grab my old sweatshirt. "Just a minute, dear"—I try to say it sweetly—"I just woke up. I'll let you in in a minute. I need a cup of tea. I'd love if you'd get one for me." (I really do need one, but I'm not going to wait around for it.) I open the window and step out on the garage roof, cross to the tree, and climb down. Not hard. I'm a chubby old woman, but I'm in pretty good shape. The cats follow me. All three.

As I trot by, I see all the ewes in the backyard lying down and panting. God! I have to get out of here. I run, holding my stomach. I know of an empty lot with an old Norway spruce tree that comes down to the ground all around. I think I can make that. I see cats all around me, more than just my own. Maybe six or eight. Maybe more. Hard to see but, thank God, Klimp has broken all the streetlights. I cross vacant lots, tear through brambles, finally crawl under the spruce branches and lie down panting . . . panting. It feels right to pant. I saw my cat do that under similar circumstances.

I have them. I give birth to them, the little silvery ones squeaking

. . . sparkling. I'll surprise Klimp with eighty-four . . . ninety-six . . . one hundred and eight? Look what we did together! But it wasn't Klimp and I. Suddenly I realize it. It was Klimp and that other. Through me. And all those ewes . . . fourteen ewes and one bitch dog times eighty-four or one hundred and eight. That's well over a thousand of them that I know about already.

My little ones cough and flutter, try to swim into the air, but only raise themselves an inch or so . . . hardly that. They smell of fish. They slither over each other as though looking for a stream. They are covered with a shiny, clear kind of slime. Do I love them or hate them?

So that's the way it is. As with us humans, it takes two, only I wasn't one of them. I might just as well have been a bitch or a ewe . . . better, in fact, to have been some dumb animal. "Lots of little warm, wet places!" It must have been a big night, that night. Some sacred sort of higher beings they turned out to be. That's not love . . . nor luff nor loove. Whatever they mean by those words, this can't be it.

But look what all those hungry cats are doing. Eating up my minnows. I try to gather the little things up, but they're too slippery. I can't even get one. I try to push the cats away, but there are too many of them and they all seem very hungry. And then, suddenly, Klimp is there helping me, kicking out at the cats in a fury and gathering up minnows at the same time. For him it's easy. They stick to him wherever he touches them. He's up to his elbows in them. They cluster on his ankles like barnacles, but I'm afraid lots are eaten up already. And now he's kicking out at me. Hits me hard on the cheek and shoulder. Stamps on my hand.

"I'm confused," I say, getting up, thinking he can explain all this in a fatherly way, but now he stamps on my foot and knocks me down with his elbow. Then I see him give a kind of hop step, the standard dance way of getting from one foot to the other. He was going to lift. I don't know how I know, but I do. He has that look on his face, too, eyes half closed . . . ecstasy. I see it now—flying, or almost flying, is their ultimate orgasm . . . their true love (or loofe) . . . if this *is* flying. Yes, he's up, but only inches, and struggling . . . pulling at my fingers. This is *not* flying.

"You call this flying!" I yell. "And you call this whole thing being a pure aerial being! I say, cloaca . . . cloaca, I say, is your only orifice." I have, by now, one knee hooked around his neck and both hands grabbing his elbow, and he's not really more than one foot off the ground at the very highest, if that, and struggling for every inch. "Cloaca! You and your 'luff'!" The slime and minnows are all over him. He seems dressed in them . . . sparkling like sequins. He's too slippery with them. I can't hang on. I slip off and drop lightly into the brambles. Klimp slides away at a diagonal, right shoulder leading, and glides, luminous with slime, just off the ground. Disappears in a few seconds behind the trees. "Cloaca!" I shout after him. It's the worst I've ever said to anyone. "Filthy fish thing! Call that flying!"

Everything is going wrong. It always does, I should know that by now. I'm thinking that my former husband slipped away in almost exactly the same way. He was slippery too, sneaked out first with younger women and then left for one of them later on. I tried to grab at him the same way I grabbed at Klimp. Tried to hold him back. I even tried to change my ways to suit him. I know I've got faults. I talk too much. I worry about things that never happen (though they did finally happen, almost all of them, and *now* look).

I hobble back (with cats), too angry to feel the pain of my bruises. No sign of the ewes or the dog, but the backyard looks all silvery. No minnows left there, though, just slime. I have to admit it's lovely. Makes me feel romantic feelings for Klimp in spite of myself. I wonder if he saw it. They're so sensitive to beautiful things and they love glitter. I can see why.

The house is dark. I open the door cautiously. I let in all eight . . . no, nine, maybe ten cats. I call. No answer. I lock all the windows and the doors. I check under the beds and in the closets. Nobody. I go into the bathroom and lock that door too. Fill tub. Take off my clothes. Find two minnows stuck inside my sweatshirt. One is dead. The other very weak. I put him in the tub and he seems to revive a little. He has big eyes, four fins where legs and arms would be, a tail . . . a minnow's tail . . . actually big blue eyes . . . pale blue, like Klimp's. He looks at me with such pleading. He comes to the surface to breathe and squeaks now and then. I keep making reassuring sounds as if I were talking to the cats. Then I decide to get in the tub with him myself. Carefully, though. With me in the tub, the creature seems happier. Swims around making a kind of humming sound and blowing bubbles. Follows my hand. Lets me pick it up. I'm thinking it's a clear case of bonding, perhaps for both of us.

Now that I'm relaxing in the water, I'm feeling a lot better. And nothing like a helpless little blue-eyed creature of some sort to care for to bring brightness back into life. The thing needs me. And so do all those cats.

I lie quietly, cats miawing outside the door, but I just lie here and Charles (Charles was my father's name) . . . Charles? Howard? Henry? He falls asleep in the shallows between my breasts. I don't dare move. The phone rings and there's the thunk of something knocked over by cats. I don't move. I don't care.

So what about ecology? What about our favorite planet, Klimp's and mine? How best save it? And who for? Make it safe for this thing on my chest? (Charles Bird? Henry Fishman?) Quietly breathing. Blue eyes shut. And what about all those thousands of others? Department of fisheries? Department of lakes and streams? Gelatin factory? Or the damp basements of those housing developments built in former swamps?

I blame myself. I really do. Perhaps if I'd been more understanding of their problems . . . accepted them as they are. Not criticized all that sand tracked in. And so what if they did step on the tails of cats? I've been so irritable these last few days. No wonder Klimp kicked out at me. If only I had controlled myself and thought about what *they* were going through. It was a crucial time for them too. But all I thought about was myself and my blowing-up stomach. Me, me, me! No wonder my former husband walked out. And now the same old pattern. Another breakup, another identity crisis. It shows I haven't learned a thing.

I almost fall asleep lying here, but when the water begins to get cold we both wake up, Charles and I. I rig up a system, then, with the electric frying pan on the lowest setting and two inches of water on top of a piece of flannel. Put Charles . . . Henry? . . . inside, sprinkle in crumbs of wafer. Lid on. Vent open. Lock the whole business in my bedroom on top of the knickknack shelves. Then I check out their room, Klimp's and the others. It's a mess, wafers scattered around . . . several pink ones, bed not made. If they were, all three, men, I'd understand it, but that can't be. I wonder if they used servants where they come from . . . or slaves? Well, Charles will be brought up differently. Learn to pick up his underwear and help out around the house, cook something besides telephone books and such. I find a talisman under the bed. I shut my eyes, squeeze hard, wondering can I lift with it? Maybe, on the other hand, it's some sort of anchor to stop with or to be let down by. Something thrown out to keep *from* flying. I'll save it for Charles.

I sit down to rest with a cup of tea, two cats on my lap and one across my shoulders. All the cats seem fat and happy, and I really feel pretty happy too . . . considering.

The telephone rings again and this time I answer it. It's a love call. I think I recognize Klimp's voice, but he won't say if it's him and they do all sound a lot alike, sort of muffled and slurred. Anyway, he says he wants to do all those things with me, things, actually, he already did. I suppose this call is part of a new campaign. I don't think much of it and I tell him so. "How about breaking school windows and stealing library books?" I say. But whose side am I on now? "Listen," I say, "I know of a nice wet place devoid of cats. It's called The Love Canal and you'll love it. Lots of empty houses. And there's another place in New Jersey that I know of. Call me back and I'll have the exact address for you." I think he believes me. (Evidently they haven't read *all* the books about women.)

Political appointees. I'll bet that's what they are. Makes a lot of sense. I could do as well myself. And who was it sent them out with spray-paint cans? Who told them how to cause static on TV? Who had thousands of stickers made up reading: NO DANGER, NONTOXIC, and GENERALLY REGARDED AS SAFE?

We can do all this by ourselves. Let's see: number 1, day-care-aquarium centers; number 2, separate cat-breeding facilities; number 3, the take-over proper; number 4, the lying-fallow period. And we have time . . . plenty of time. Our numbers keep increasing, too, though slowly . . . the rejected, the divorced, the growing older, the left out. . . . Maybe they've already started it. I can't be the only one thinking this way. Maybe they're out there just waiting for my call, kitchens all warmed up. I'll dial my old friend. "Include me in," I'll say.

Everything perfect, and I even have Charles. We don't need them. Bunch of bureaucrats. *That* wasn't flying.

(1981)

GREG BEAR

Schrödinger's Plague

Interdepartmental Memo—Werner Dietrich to Carl Kranz

Carl: I'm not sure what we should do about the Lambert journal. We know so little about the whole affair—but there's no doubt in my mind we should hand it over to the police. Incredible as the entries are, they directly relate to the murders and suicides, and they even touch on the destruction of the lab. Just reading them in your office isn't enough: I'll need copies of the journal. And how long did it circulate in the system before you noticed it?

Kranz to Dietrich

Werner: It must have been in the system since just before the events, so a month at least. Copies enclosed of the appropriate entries. The rest, I think, is irrelevant and private. I'd like to return the journal to Richard's estate. The police would probably hold it. And—well, I have other reasons for wanting to keep it to ourselves. For the moment, anyway. Examine the papers carefully. As a physicist, tell me if there's anything in them you find completely unbelievable. If not, more thought should be applied to the whole problem.

P.S. I'm verifying the loss from Bernard's lab now. Lots of hush-hush over there. It's definite Bernard was working on a government CBW contract, apparently in defiance of the university's guidelines. ?—How did Goa get access to the materials? Tight security over there.

Enc.: five pages.

The Journal

April 15, 1981

Today has been a puzzler. Marty convened an informal meeting of the Hydroxyl Radicals for lunch—on him. In attendance, the physics contingent: Martin Goa himself, Frederik Newman, and the new member, Kaye (pr: *Kie*) Parkes; the biologists, Oscar Bernard and yours truly; and the sociologist, Thomas Fauch. We met outside the lounge, and Marty took us to the auxiliary physics building to give us a brief tour of an experiment. Nothing spectacular. Then back to the lounge for lunch. Why he should waste our time thus is beyond me. Call it intuition, but something is up. Bernard is a bit upset for reason or reasons unknown.

May 14, 1981

Radicals convened again today, at lunch. Some of the most absurd shit I've ever heard in my life. Marty at it again. The detail is important here.

"Gentlemen," Marty said in the private lounge, after we had eaten. "I have just destroyed an important experiment. And I have just resigned my position with the university. I'm to have all my papers and materials off campus by this date next month."

Pole-axed silence.

"I have my reasons. I'm going to establish something once and for all."

"What's that, Marty?" Frederik asked, looking irritated. None of us approve of theatrics.

"I'm putting mankind's money where our mouth is. Our veritable collective scientific mouth. Frederik, you can help me explain. You are all aware how good a physicist Frederik is. Better at grants, better at subtleties. Much better than I am. Frederik, what is the most generally accepted theory in physics today?"

"Special relativity," Frederik said without hesitating.

"And the next?"

"Quantum electrodynamics."

"Would you explain Schrödinger's cat to us?"

Frederik looked around the table, obviously a bit put-upon, then shrugged his shoulders. "The final state of a quantum event—an event on a microcosmic scale—appears to be defined by the making of an observation. That is, the event is indeterminate until it is measured. Then it assumes one of a variety of possible states. Schrödinger proposed linking quantum events to macrocosmic events. He suggested putting a cat in an enclosed box, and also a device which would detect the decay of a single radioactive nucleus. Let's say the nucleus has a fifty-fifty chance of decaying in an arbitrary length of time. If it does decay, it triggers the device, which drops a hammer on a vial of cyanide, releasing the gas into the box and killing the cat. The scientist conducting this experiment has no way of knowing whether the nucleus decayed or not without opening the box. Since the final state of the nucleus is not determined without first making a measurement, and the measurement in this case is the opening of the box to discover whether the cat is dead, Schrödinger suggested that the cat would find itself in an undetermined state, neither alive nor dead, but somewhere in between. Its fate is uncertain until a qualified observer opens the box."

"And could you explain some of the implications of this thought experiment?" Marty looked a bit like a cat himself—one who has swallowed a canary.

"Well," Frederik continued, "if we dismiss the cat as a qualified observer, there doesn't seem to be any way around the conclusion that the cat is neither alive nor dead until the box is opened."

"Why not?" Fauch, the sociologist, asked. "I mean, it seems obvious that only one state is possible."

"Ah," Frederik said, warming to the subject, "but we have linked a quantum event to the macrocosm, and quantum events are tricky. We have amassed a great deal of experimental evidence to show that quantum states are not definite until they are observed, that in fact they fluctuate, interact, as if two or more universes—each containing a potential outcome—are meshed together, until the physicist causes the collapse into the final state by observing. Measuring."

"Doesn't that give consciousness a godlike importance?" Fauch asked.

"It does indeed," said Frederik. "Modern physics is on a heavy power trip."

"It's all just theoretical, isn't it?" I asked, slightly bored.

"Not at all," Frederik said. "Established experimentally."

"Wouldn't a machine—or a cat—serve just as well to make the measurement?" Oscar, my fellow biologist, asked.

"That depends on how conscious you regard a cat as being. A machine—no, because its state would not be certain until the physicist looked over the record it had made."

"Commonly," said Parkes, his youthful interest piqued, "we substitute Wigner's friend for the cat. Wigner was a physicist who suggested putting a man in the box. Wigner's friend would presumably be conscious enough to know whether he was alive or dead, and to properly interpret the fall of the hammer and the breaking of the vial to indicate that the nucleus has, in fact, decayed."

"Wonderful," Goa said. "And this neat little fable reflects the attitudes of those who work with one of the most accepted theories in modern science."

"Well, there are elaborations," Frederik said.

"Indeed, and I'm about to add another. What I'm about to say will probably be interpreted as a joke. It isn't. I'm not joking. I've been working with quantum mechanics for twenty years now, and I've always been uncertain—pardon the pun—whether I could accept the foundations of the very discipline which provided my livelihood. The dilemma has bothered me deeply. It's more than bothered me—it's caused sleepless nights, nervous distress, made me go to a psychiatrist. None of what Frederik calls 'elaborations' have provided any relief. So I've used my influence—and my contacts—to somewhat crooked advantage. I've begun an experiment. Not being happy with just a cat, or with Wigner's friend, I've involved all of you in the experiment, and myself, as well. Ultimately, many more people—conscious observers—will be involved."

Oscar smiled, trying to keep from laughing. "I do believe you've gone mad, Martin."

"Have I? Have I indeed, my *dear* Oscar? While I have been driven to distraction by intellectual considerations, why haven't you been driven to distraction by ethical ones?"

"What?" Oscar asked, frowning.

"You are, I believe, trying to locate a vial labeled DERVM-74."

"How did you—"

"Because I stole the vial while looking over your lab. And I cribbed a few of your notes. Now. You're among friends, Oscar. Tell us about DERVM-74. Tell them, or I will."

Oscar looked like a carp out of water for a few seconds. "That's classified," he said. "I refuse."

"DERVM-74," Marty said, "stands for Dangerous Experimental Rhino Virus, Mutation 74. Oscar does some moonlighting on contract for the government. This is one of his toys. Tell us about its nature, Oscar."

"You have the vial?"

"Not anymore," Marty said.

"You idiot! That virus is deadly. I was about to destroy it when the culture disappeared. It's of no use to anybody!"

"How does it work, Oscar?"

"It has a very long gestation period—about 330 days. Much too long for military uses. After that time, death is certain in ninety-eight percent of those who have contracted it. It can be spread by simple contact, by breathing the air around a contaminated subject." Oscar stood. "I must report this, Martin."

"Sit down." Marty pulled a broken glass tube out of his pocket, with a singed label still wrapped around it. He handed it to Oscar, who paled. "Here's my proof. You're much too late to stop the experiment."

"Is this all true?" Parkes asked.

"That's the vial," Oscar said.

"What in *hell* have you done?" I asked, loudly.

The other Radicals were as still as cold agar.

"I made a device which measures a quantum event, in this case the decay of a particle of radioactive Americium. Over a small period of time, I exposed an instrument much like a Geiger counter to the possible effects of this decay. In that time, there was exactly a fifty-fifty chance that a nucleus in the particle would decay, triggering the Geiger counter. If the Geiger counter was triggered, it released the virus contained in this vial into a tightly sealed area. Immediately afterward, I entered the area, and an hour later, I gave all five of you a tour through the same area. The device was then destroyed, and everything in the chamber sterilized, including the vial. If the virus was not released, it was destroyed along with the experimental equipment. If it was released, then we have all been exposed."

"Was it released?" Fauch asked.

"I don't know. It's impossible to tell—yet."

"Oscar," I said, "it's been a month since Marty did all this. We're all influential people—giving talks, attending meetings, we all travel a fair amount. How many people have been exposed—potentially?"

"It's very contagious," Oscar said. "Simple contact guarantees passage from one vector . . . to another."

Fauch took out his calculator. "If we exposed five people each day, and they went on to expose five more . . . Jesus Christ. By now, everyone on Earth could have it."

"Why did you do this, Marty?" Frederik asked.

"Because if the best mankind can do is come up with an infuriating theory like this to explain the universe, then we should be willing to live or die by our belief in the theory."

"I don't get you," Frederik said.

"You know as well as I. Oscar, is there any way to detect contamination by the virus?"

"None. Marty, that virus was a mistake—useless to everybody. Even my notes were going to be destroyed."

"Not useless to me. That's unimportant now, anyway. Frederik, what I'm saying is, according to theory, nothing has been determined yet. The nucleus may or may not have decayed, but that hasn't been decided. We may have better than a fifty-fifty chance—if we truly believe in the theory."

Parkes stood up and looked out the window. "You should have been more thorough, Marty. You should have researched this thing more completely."

"Why?"

"Because I'm a hypochondriac, you bastard. I have a very difficult time telling whether I'm sick or not."

"What does that have to do with anything?" Oscar asked.

Frederik leaned forward. "What Marty is implying is, since the quantum event hasn't been determined yet, the measurement that will flip it into one state or another is our sickness, or health, about three hundred days from now."

I picked up on the chain of reasoning. "And since Parkes is a hypochondriac, if he believes he's ill, that will flip the event into certainty. It will determine the decay, after the fact—" My head began to ache. "Even after the particle has been destroyed, and all other records?"

"If he truly believes he's ill," Marty said. "Or if any of us truly believes. Or if we actually become ill. I'm not sure there's any real difference, in this case."

"So you're going to jeopardize the entire world—" Fauch began, then he started to laugh. "This is a diabolical joke, Martin. You can stop it right here."

"He's not joking," Oscar said, holding up the vial. "That's my handwriting on the label."

"Isn't it a beautiful experiment?" Marty asked, grinning. "It determines so many things. It tells us whether our theory of quantum events is correct, it tells us the rôle of consciousness in determining the universe, and, in Parkes's case, it—"

"Stop it!" Oscar shouted. At that point, we had to restrain the biologist from attacking Marty, who danced away, laughing.

May 17, 1981

Today all of us—except Marty—convened. Frederik and Parkes presented documentary evidence to support the validity of quantum theory, and, perversely enough, the validity of Marty's experiment. The evidence was impressive, but I'm not convinced. Still, it was a marathon session, and we now know more than we ever cared to know about the strange world of quantum physics.

The physicists—and Fauch, and Oscar, who is very quiet nowadays—

are completely convinced that Marty's nucleus is—or was—in an undetermined state, and that all the casual chains leading to the potential release of the rhinovirus mutation are also in a state of flux. Whether the human race will live or die has not been decided yet.

And Parkes is equally convinced that, as soon as the gestation period passes, he will begin having symptoms, and he will feel—however irrationally—that he has contracted the disease. We cannot convince him otherwise.

In one way, we were very stupid. We had Oscar describe the symptoms—the early signs—of the disease to us. If we had thought things out more carefully, we would have withheld the information, at least from Parkes. But since Oscar knows, if he became convinced he had the disease, that would be enough to flip the state, Frederik believes. Or would it? We don't know yet how many of us will need to be convinced. Would Marty alone suffice? Is a consensus necessary? A two-thirds majority?

It all seemed—seems—totally preposterous to me. I've always been suspicious of physicists, and now I know why.

Then Frederik made a horrible proposal.

May 23, 1981

Frederik made the proposal again at today's meeting.

The others considered the proposal seriously. Seeing how serious they were, I tried to make objections but got nowhere. I am completely convinced that there is nothing we can do, that if the nucleus decayed, then we are doomed. In three hundred days, the first signs will appear—backache, headache, sweaty palms, piercing pains behind the eyes. If they don't, we won't. Even Frederik saw the ridiculous nature of his proposal, but he added, "The symptoms aren't that much different from flu, you know. And if just one of us becomes convinced . . ."

Indicating that the flipping of the state, because of human frailty, was almost certainly going to result in release of the virus. Had resulted.

His proposal—I write it down with great difficulty—is that we should all commit suicide, all six of us. Since we are the only ones who know about the experiment, we are the only ones, he feels, who can flip the state, make things certain. Parkes, he says, is particularly dangerous, but we are all potential hypochondriacs. With the strain of almost ten months waiting between now and the potential appearance of symptoms, we may all be near the breaking point.

May 30, 1981

I have refused to go along with them. Everyone has been extremely quiet, stayed away from each other. But I suspect Parkes and Frederik are doing something. Oscar is morose—he seems suicidal anyway, but is too much of a coward to go it alone. Fauch . . . I can't reach him.

—Ah, Christ. Frederik called. He said I can't hold out. They've killed Marty and destroyed the lab building to wipe out all traces of the experiment, so that no one will know it ever took place. The group is coming over to my apartment now. I just have time to put this in the university pick-up box. What can I do, run?

They're too close.

Dietrich to Kranz

Carl: I've read the journal, although I'm not sure I've assimilated it. What have you found out about Bernard?

Kranz to Dietrich

Werner: Oscar Bernard was indeed working on a rhinovirus mutation around the time of the incident. I haven't been able to find out much—lots of people in gray suits wandering through the corridors over there. But the rumor is that all his notes on certain projects are missing.

Do you believe it? I mean—do you believe the theory enough to agree with me, that word about the journal should end here? I feel both scared and silly.

Dietrich to Kranz

Carl: We have to find out the complete list of symptoms—besides headache, sweaty palms, backache, pains behind the eyes.

Yes. I'm a firm believer in the theory. And if Goa did what the journal says . . . you and I can flip the state.

Anyone who reads this can flip the state.

What in God's name are we going to do?

(1982)

HOWARD WALDROP

"... THE WORLD, AS WE KNOW 'T"

The neptunists and vulcanists were going at it hammer and tongs.

The fight had begun just after Curwell's demonstration on counteracting the effects of garlic on the compass. His methods, which would open the seas to safe passage of condiments and spices, had been wildly applauded by his peers in the Lunatick Society.

He had graciously accepted their accolades, and was making a few extemporary remarks. He seemed the essence of charm and grace as he answered questions from the audience, until he made the unfortunate mistake of mentioning the age of the earth.

Canes had begun rapping on the floor, there were whistles, words of dispute, and then the yelling had begun.

The president of the Society gaveled for quiet. Fists were brandished in faces. "Gentlemen! Order, please. Order."

This only infuriated them the more.

"I maintain," someone shouted from the back of the hall, "that the earth is no less than . . ."

They yelled him down.

To make matters worse, the argument began to eddy and splinter around the main one. The gradualist uniformitarians, who thought the land masses had been uncovered from a once all-pervading ocean, were yelling at the catastrophic vulcanists who were gathered in one corner of the hall.

" . . . The earth has been made over," yelled one of the latter in the face of one of the former, "by terrible volcanic upheavals something approaching twenty-seven consecutive times!"

"Faddle."

"Hear, hear!"

Across the aisle, a catastrophic neptunist climbed atop his chair and shouted at both groups. "You people can't use your own eyes to see that the rocks of the Northwest Territory were carried there by the action of a series of deluges, more than seven, but no more than ten in number, as has . . ."

Instantly, members of *all* the other factions turned on him.

The president kept gaveling for order.

Sir Robert Athole, mounting the platform, shook hands with Curwell, who was smiling and watching the uproar he had caused.

"They really are in some mood tonight," said Lawrence Curwell, who was a young man with a broad handsome face.

"It's really too bad you gave them no points to dispute in your presentation, which was quite remarkable," said Sir Robert.

They were bumped from behind by a black man who was taking models and equipment to the raised stage, where the gavel kept pounding and having absolutely no effect on the turmoil.

"Sorry, sir, so sorry," said the black.

Curwell took no notice.

"Thank you for the compliment," said Curwell. "I've already turned the results over to your Maritime Commission. I hope no more tragedies of the kind which took the *Bon Apetit* and the *Lucie Marie* to their watery graves will occur again because of my researches."

There were dull thuds from the back of the room. The two men turned to watch cane-brandishing men be pulled apart by their friends to the uttering of great vile oaths and epithets.

"Shall you be visiting the States long?" asked Sir Robert of Curwell. "If it's at all possible, I should like you to come visit and see the progress of my researches. They might interest you."

"I'd love to. I hear you're doing splendid things. I look forward to your presentation tonight."

Sir Robert Athole began to bow, but paused to turn and watch as one of the more elderly philosophs bounded across the aisle and began to vigorously choke a younger man. They were absorbed in the crowd.

Then "oohs" and "ahhs" raced from the front of the room toward the back. It became very quiet and somber, and some bowed their heads.

For up on the dais, the president of the Society had signaled for the sergeant-at-arms to bring in a small square box and place it in the center of the president's desk.

"Franklin's spectacles," whispered someone. The whisper susurrated through the room. Persons righted their overturned chairs, straightened their wigs, took their seats.

"Order," said the president. The two raps of his small gavel now sounded like the slamming of the great gates of a fort in the still hall.

"The next item on the agenda," he said, "will be a presentation by Sir Robert Athole on the absolute nature of phlogiston."

The room itself was old, huge, and dark. It was lit by chandeliers and by candle sconces along the walls. The odor of wig powder, soot, and sweat filled the hall. Through several doors leading in, household servants could be seen coming and going, preparing the traditional meal which would end the monthly meeting of the Lunatick Society.

Velvet and brocade rustled as the men moved about in their upholstered chairs. A snort, sniff and occasional sneeze broke the quiet as one or another of them took snuff. A cane rolled from a lap and clattered loudly to the floor.

The black man indicated to Sir Robert that the models were ready. He came a little closer. "Go easy on the cylinder," he said. "I think it might have cracked a little on the way over in the wagon."

"Very good, Hamp," said Sir Robert, and nodded to the president. There was polite applause for him as he stepped to the rostrum, on which sat a whale-oil lamp smoking quietly.

He looked out at the mass of faces and wigs flickering slowly in the dim light, and saw them as bubbles in the darkening pudding that was the world. No matter. He smiled and began.

He started with the history of combustion and with mention of the works of Becher and Stahl.

"Phlogiston is thought to permeate all things in finely inseparable parts. It is characterized by setting up a violent motion within substances in the presence of heat. This motion results in flame, and as long as the air is not kept from it, the motion will continue until only earthy ash remains."

He then described *terra pinguis* and the fatty earths, and the search for the phlogistic principle itself. His audience continued to listen intently, even a little restlessly. So far he had told them nothing new.

"Recently Cavendish thought he had found the most highly phlogiston-charged substance in his inflammable gas, which is lighter than common air, and is used to lift aerostatic vehicles to heretofore unheard-of heights. Inflammable gas burns violently in air, sometimes to the point of detonation. But, as others, including Dr. Priestley, have shown, a mixture of inflammable gas and eminently respirable air explodes, but leaves as residue a wet liquid, indistinguishable from common water.

"And water, as you know, is the enemy of phlogiston. It seems to me therefore, that a mixture of phlogiston and any other substance *could not* give a residue of its exact opposite. Cavendish, however . . ."

"Question!"

Sir Robert looked up.

"Yes?"

"According to the leading French theorists, eminently respirable air is . . ."

"The French," said someone else, "are a bunch of rabble who cannot even carry out a revolution in the accepted manner, as did we."

There was a matter of agreement.

"You were going to say," said Sir Robert to his questioner, "that the French New Chemistry, which denies the phlogistic principle, attributes other causes to combustion and calcination. Most of these concern the properties of the eminently respirable air, or oxygine, as it is named. Instead of phlogiston being given off by substances in combustion, the New Chemistry says substances combine with this oxygine in the presence of heat. And you are asking what I think of this theory?"

"Yes."

"Not much," said Sir Robert. "I *have* read in the French Chemistry. If you must deal with the devil, first you must know him." There was hearty applause from the back. "I have decided to ignore most of these theories, insofar as is possible. For I believe it is now within the power of science to isolate phlogiston itself."

"No! No! Impossible! Wrong!" they shouted.

Oaths crossed the air again as others took his side.

Sir Robert raised his hand for quiet.

"I have come here tonight to outline my plans and to show you models of the operations by which I intend to carry out . . ."

"Phlogiston . . .," said a voice, " . . . is present to some extent in all matter, and indivisible. Might as well try and weigh or separate sunlight itself!"

"Hear! Hear!"

Sir Robert looked them down. A tremor passed through his hand then, something he had noticed as happening more often since he began experimenting with his mercuric pneumatic troughs. He raised it as the tremor passed. "Some say phlogiston drifts down from the shooting stars through the aether. Others say it *comes* from the very sun. Perhaps if I succeed in isolating the phlogistic principle, we shall find, indeed, the true nature of even that great sun overhead."

That was too much for even the devout phlogistians in the audience. They came to their feet, arguing against him.

"Nevertheless," said Sir Robert, rolling up his manuscript. "Nevertheless, I have had special equipment ordered, and will carry through . . ." The president stood up and pounded with his gavel. " . . . I will prevail in my work, and expect within a fortnight to have all ready. Such of you as may want shall be invited to witness . . . " The roar rose above his words for a space and he paused, " . . . to witness this great thing, and those of you who don't can go to the very devil himself!"

He stomped from the dais. Hamp drove home in the wagon down the snow-covered ruts which passed for a road. The ground was lit by the cold still glow of the full moon, on whose closest Monday night the Lunatick Society sat, and for whose shining light it was named.

At noon two days later, Lawrence Curwell arrived. Sir Robert and Lady Margurite Athole met him on the wide carriage porch in the light of a bright cold sun.

Curwell bowed to Lady Margurite. "Your servant, madam."

"Sorry Hamp isn't here, too," said Sir Robert. "He's out in the laboratory, unpacking the new globe which arrived this forenoon from Philadelphia."

"I'm sure my note arrived rather late the night of the meeting," said Curwell. "I was surrounded by disputants during your speech. It's only luck we kept Hazzard from plunging his pen-knife into Revecher. What a contentious lot!"

Lawrence Curwell, like Sir Robert, was from Britain. Unlike the elder scientist, he could return, being in America to check on his brother's tobacco holdings. This was possible only because the new Constitution had been adopted, and relations between the two countries were normalizing again after the shaky years of the Confederation.

Sir Robert, who had once been a notorious supporter of the Colonies in their rebellion, had been hounded to the States, much like his contemporary Priestley who now lived in Pennsylvania.

Curwell, who was young and still loyal to Britain, and Sir Robert, in his fifties, experienced, but now apolitical, met only on the common ground of a devotion to knowledge and the empire of science. They shared another opinion that the American philosophs were hotheaded, opinionated, prejudiced, and had no science to match the new country's ideals. With a few exceptions: the late, lamented Franklin, Priestley, who really didn't count, Bartram of Carolina.

"I trust they'll sing another tune if you succeed," said Curwell.

"They'll have to," said Lady Margurite.

"Do we have time to see how Hamp's getting on before lunch?" asked Sir Robert.

Lady Margurite gave a knowing smile. "Surely," she said.

"Will you come with us?" asked Curwell, who was very taken with her beauty.

"Not presently. I have to see to the servants," she said, and turned to go into the house, which was an imposing, square, white three-story structure with a green roof.

"This way," said Sir Robert.

They followed a flagstone path around the house. A vista opened up to the flat rolling hills toward the west. Here was a barn, there poultry houses, stables and servant quarters larger than the cottage Curwell lived in. Past those was a wide field and beyond that a low squat edifice of fieldstones with many smokestacks and chimneys protruding from it. As Curwell neared it, he saw a huge pile of sand under the fire bell tower which stood near the doorway. One of the many large windows showed blackened signs of scorching.

"An accident late last year," said Sir Robert.

There were still a few patches of snow here and there in the shadows of the building and trees across the field. The wind was from the north but spring was in the air.

"This is quite a marvelous globe flask," said Sir Robert as they entered the building through a low rickety door. Several white servants and the black man were busy with crates and boxes. "It has a diameter of three feet, its sides are two and one-half inches in thickness, stoppable ports and conduits for sparking. I had it made especially for the grand experiment."

"Hamp," said Sir Robert. The black man looked up from his work, rubbed his hands on a chamois, came over. "Hamp. Lawrence Curwell. Lawrence, Hampton Hamilton."

"Pleased, indeed," said Hampton, and offered his hand.

It was the first time Lawrence Curwell had been offered the hand of a black man. He shook it nonetheless. He had assumed at the meeting that the man had been Sir Robert's slave.

"Hamp runs the laboratory for me, and is in charge of all the equipment and requisitioning. How's the globe, Hamp?"

"Excellent, indeed," said Hamp. Turning to the great transparent globe before them supported on sawhorses, he said, "The ports fit so tightly that I doubt we shall need wax and quicklime to seal the joints tight."

"Good, good," said Sir Robert. "Let me see the bill of lading, will you? Excuse me, Lawrence . . ."

While they put their heads together, Lawrence Curwell looked around the laboratory. He was struck by the spaciousness and cleanliness of the place and its supplies. Where most chemists got on with two or three small furnaces, Sir Robert had no less than seven—three of them large reverberatory cones, two forced-draft furnaces,, two smaller ones spread down the length of the room, each with its own stack or chimney.

At one end stood large jugs—gallons of ether, vitriol, spirit of wine, acid, distilled waters. In other places were ceramic buckets marked sulfur, antimony, lead, earth of rhubarb, Mohr's salt.

Shelf after shelf stretched across the walls with tins, vials and flasks—

the most completely stocked workroom Curwell had ever seen—syrup of violets, oil of Dippel, ley of oxblood, Icy Butter, Starkeys Soap, salt of Gall, Glauber's salt, liquor of flints, Minderer's spirit. Numberless others.

At the far end of the laboratory were pumps and basins for washing. Near each end were large workbenches covered with experiments in progress.

In the center of the room were pneumatic troughs for the recovery of gases. Two were filled with water, the third with four inches of mercury. Several glass bottles, some filled with a reddish air, stood upside down in each.

Curwell walked to the workbench where retorts and a Woulfe bottle caught his eye. In a few seconds he recognized it as the cohobation of some solid. At another spot he found lixiviation in process—how long it had been going on he did not know. He had seen some last for half a year, with virtually no result.

He followed to another spot where some matter was being edulcorated from acid by a water bath.

There seemed no order to the experiments, nowhere they should be leading. There was no thread holding them together, except perhaps that of refinement. Maybe Sir Robert was getting the best possible metals and calxes together before using them in his actual work.

"Lawrence," said Sir Robert. "Here, come over here." He was now standing near one of his pneumatic troughs, while behind him Hamp and the others busied themselves once more with the boxes.

"Here." He pointed at one of the inverted bottles. "I've been doing things with a gas collected over sulfur and nitre. Would you like to see?"

He began by showing Curwell some of the properties of the gas, talking occasionally of how it would be a part of the great experiment. They began moving from table to trough to bench as one or another thing they should try came to them. At one point they took off their frock coats, and sometime later their wigs. Curwell suggested other properties, other processes. They took bottles from workbench to crucible to mortar and pestle. The workmen came and left, came again. They ignored the two men huddling over the trough.

At some time Hamp lit candles in the room, finished the unpacking. Then he left. The candles burned down.

At 11 P.M. the two scientists stumbled back to the house, talking, gesturing, happy as mice and famished as wolves. Everyone was asleep.

It was the second week of Curwell's stay. Something was bothering Sir Robert, and both Margurite and Hampton could tell. Sir Robert seemed distracted in the middle of conversation or experiments. He drew plans on sheets of foolscap with a thick graphite pencil, then discarded them in lumps around the house or the laboratory.

Most of them dealt with clockwork devices, cogs, fuses. None seemed to satisfy him.

Curwell had begun to see that all the experiments and processes in the laboratory were coming together in a great design. It was ambitious, complicated, and to Curwell's mind it would probably not work. Most of it centered on fixing the phlogiston, much as fixed air is obtained from common air. He thought there were too many variables, and it depended on timing of at least four major processes. But Sir Robert's enthusiasm stirred him, and he and Hamp set about putting together minor portions of the apparatus and materials. Sir Robert talked less and less, worked more and more, and became still more dissatisfied.

One morning as he and Curwell walked toward the laboratory, they were interrupted by a halloo. Turning, they saw Athole's gamekeeper riding slowly toward them down the road. On the wagon-rut before him walked a trussed man dressed in deerskin trousers and jacket who seemed much the worse for wear.

"Caught a live one, Your Lordship," said the gamekeeper, who was Irish. "He made the best shot I've ever seen. Right into one of your heath hens," he continued, and produced the feathered evidence from his saddlepack. "Am I to take him to the constable, or shall I pummel him unmercifully?"

"As if you haven't already!" grumbled the man in leather.

"Quiet, you!" said the gamekeeper, and yanked on the rope.

Sir Robert was staring as if transfixed. "What rifle did he use?"

"Here," said the gamekeeper, and handed down a Kentucky rifle.

"I didn't do anything," said the man.

"Quite right," said the gamekeeper, and dealt him a smart blow behind the ear with his own rifle butt.

"No need for that, McCartney," said Sir Robert.

"Ow Ow Ow!" said the man, who had fallen to the ground.

"How far was the hen?" asked Sir Robert.

"Between eighty and a hundred paces, my lord," said McCartney.

"It was a hundred or I'm damned," said the man on the road.

"And could you make a shot at a quarter mile?"

"How big a target, and with what gun?" asked the man.

Sir Robert thought a moment. "A target two feet across, and with whatever weapon you need."

"It'd take a Philadelphia rifle of .60 caliber," said the man, "and I could do it."

"Done!" said Sir Robert. "Be here at dawn on the twenty-first of the month. You shall have the Philadelphia rifle, and yours to keep, and a gold crown for making the shot."

"What's the catch?" asked the man.

"None whatever. You've solved a problem of great weight for me."

"I'm not going to have to kill a man, am I?"

"No, no! What's your name, man?"

"Bumppo," he said.

"Well, Bumppo, make this shot, you have all I named before and free hunting on my land besides, in perpetuity. What say?"

"But, sir—" said McCartney.

"Untie the man, McCartney," said Sir Robert, "so he can shake hands on the deal." Then he danced a little jig on the edge of the road.

The ropes came off. Humbly, Bumppo shook Sir Robert's hand.

They set up the apparatus for the Great Experiment in a field near the woods two miles from the house. It was a quarter mile from an old Indian mound which Sir Robert thought would serve as an excellent vantage point for the spectators.

The experiment had many stops, all leading to the great glass globe which was at the center of the setup. It was surrounded by charcoal buckets, basins and jars. Over all they had erected canvas to protect it from the elements.

The invitations had been posted for the morning of the twenty-first, weather permitting.

On the afternoon of the nineteenth, they were linking the last of the equipment in place. There came to them a far-off noise, like low thunder or fireworks on the Fourth of July.

Sir Robert came out from under a basin he was installing. "What's that?"

Hampton turned to the south, from where the noise rose.

He smiled. "Pigeons," he said.

The rumble heightened like a great wind from a storm.

"Here they come," said Hamp.

To the south was a ragged blot on the horizon which wound in on itself, then spread.

"Pigeons?" asked Curwell, his face covered with soot from a charcoal bucket. "That noise?"

He stood beside the black man, who pointed.

"Passenger pigeons," he said. "Coming north again to nest. This time every year."

The line covered a quarter of the southern horizon. The sound was like a droning flutter, and the shape moved toward them with the inexorability of the rising tide. It seemed a solid mass which only resolved itself as they drew near the zenith.

They were brown and blue specks which flashed pink. They were packed more densely than Curwell had ever seen birds, ten or twenty sleek shapes to the cubic yard. They flew in a column thirty feet thick and two miles wide and—Curwell tried to count. "What's their rate of flight?"

"A mile to the minute," said Hamp, who watched a hawk diving at one of the edges of the flock. Where the predator flew the pigeons eddied and swirled, but still the column came on.

Curwell looked at his watch. The sun was blotted out as the pigeons passed over, and the fluttering roar was omnipresent.

"Under the awning!" said Hamp, and pulled Curwell back. White flashes like snow, and occasional feathers began to drift down. Passenger pigeon excrement dotted the ground in spots, then more, and fell like a gentle white rain.

Through the flutter of wings, shots could be heard from the neighboring estates. Curwell saw great clumps of pigeons drop a mile away on a surrounding farm.

Then one fell a few feet outside the canvas, struggled and lay still. It must have been hit some distance away and flow this far.

Curwell ran out, picked it up and brought it inside the tent.

It was the most beautiful bird he had ever seen, even in death. Its back was blue, its neck and stomach bronze, its chest pink and dull red, with an iridescent sheen to all the feathers. Its beak was dark, and its legs, feet and eyes were a brilliant orange-red. He placed it on the bench and examined it minutely.

Still the fluttering roared overhead, and the ground was as white as in a snow flurry. The sky outside was an interrupted play of darkness and light where the cloud of birds went in transit across the sun.

Curwell went back to work in the artificial gloom, occasionally looking out to make sure the flock was still traveling. Gunshots came more frequently from the nearby roads and fields.

Sometime later, the sound subsided. Curwell came out of the tent in time to see the last of the flock rocket overhead. The late evening sun began to shine again.

He looked at his watch. Two hours and forty minutes had elapsed. The column had been one hundred and sixty miles long. At ten birds to the yard, ten yards thick, 1,700 yards to the mile, two miles wide . . .

Sir Robert looked at Curwell. "About sixteen million birds, I'd say."

"I've seen more," said Hamp. "When I was a boy I saw a flock that took from noon to dusk to pass. It got dark at midday, and we never saw the sun go down. We had only morning that day." He pounded a copper pipe in place with a maul. He stopped to look at the encrusted ground for a moment.

Then they all went back to work.

All was in readiness.

The spectators, scientific men for the most part, had begun arriving in the early hours of the morn. Dawn was approaching. Then men on the Indian mound waited while Curwell, Hampton and Sir Robert Athole walked up the intervening field from the apparatus, which looked to be a jumble of metal and glass to the unaided eye at this distance.

Bumppo stood well back from the others. McCartney kept an eye on him. The leather-clad man was testing the feel of his new Philadelphia rifle, swinging it up and down from his shoulder.

Sir Robert came to the top of the mound and stood beside Lady Margurite.

"Gentlemen," he said. "Lady. Others.

"You are here to witness what I hope is a grand event in scientific progress. On yonder field," he pointed, "are working apparatus for the generation of gases and air—of dephlogisticated, or eminently respirable, air; of flammable gas, of sulfur air, of phosphorus. They are all working and generating as we stand here, and shall be in fruition soon.

"They enter into conduits taken to the glass globe which you see at the center. They will enter the glass when Mr. Bumppo . . ." Here Bumppo held up his hand shyly, and a ragged cheer went up from the spectators, " . . . fires at his target disk. These phlogiston-rich gases and liquids will rush together. They should produce the essence of fire, of combustion, of calcination, viz. phlogiston itself. A clockwork will then be put in motion, and fifteen seconds later, the mixture will be sparked by means of a circuit from a Leyden jar. This should fix the phlogiston itself, much as common air becomes fixed air in the presence of the electric principle, and allow us the examination for the first time, of one of the principles, of one of the elements itself.

"That is my Great Experiment."

Some applauded.

"Question?"

"Yes?"

"You're mixing inflammable air, dephlogisticated air and phosphorus in the presence of common air, and sparking it?"

"That is my plan."

"Then what you'll get," said the voice, after a moment's reckoning, "is a gentle explosion, a small quantity of fixed air, and a small field fire to fight."

Some laughed.

"I doubt that," said Sir Robert Athole. "I have taken the precaution of removing us to this distance in case of some apparatus failure, and the leakage of noxious fumes."

The sun topped the small ridge to the east, and the field and mound were bathed in a frosty light.

"Win or lose," said Sir Robert, "I feel on the edge of great things."

"And I," said Curwell.

"I, too," said Lady Margurite, and took her husband's hand.

"Mr. Bumppo," said Sir Robert. "You see your target?"

"That I do," said Bumppo.

"Then earn your crown, man!"

The leather-clad man stepped to the front of the mound. Smoothly he raised the weapon as if it were part of him, pulled back the dog-ear hammer, aimed and fired.

The smoke from the muzzle wafted away.

Even without his spy-glass, Sir Robert saw the great globe turn milky white. But it was not the milk-white of residue gases. It roiled and swirled slowly. An "ooh" went up from the small crowd. Winks of light seemed to play across the equipment from the globe. All the apparatus was bathed in a white light.

Sir Robert felt the muscles of his stomach twitch.

For the requisite few more seconds, nothing happened.

Then it did.

Shaken and dazed, Sir Robert pulled himself from the ground in the blinding light. He was near the bottom of the mound. Some of the others were getting up as well as they could. One man lay with a branch through his chest. A few lay unmarked but unmoving. Hampton, near him, held his arm crookedly the wrong way.

There was a roaring in their ears, and it did not subside. Sir Robert stumbled back to the top of the mound, shielding his eyes.

To the west was a great roiling white cloud, too bright to be looked at directly. Bright blooms and bursts of light flew out from it like those from a pan of burning phosphorus. Sir Robert could tell that it was moving slowly away from him to the westward.

He turned. The cloud stretched to north and south, horizon to horizon, moving laterally to its progress westward. Ribbons of red flame shot through the bright white wall.

The smell of burnt wood permeated all the air. As the cloud moved away, it continued to grow in height.

The wind rose from the east, first gently, then in gusts, then faster and faster. The earth to the west was charred to the surface. Matchstick trees poked up. As Sir Robert watched, a puff of wind blew them to ash before his eyes.

The numbed scientists were milling around behind the mound. The wind rose to gale force.

"It's moving west with the rotation of the earth," said Hampton Hamilton. He knew, as did any schoolboy, that the air moves with the surface under it falling behind, from whence rise winds.

Sir Robert turned to see Curwell helping Lady Margurite up. They both seemed safe, though Lady Margurite's skirts flapped immodestly in the racking wind. Sir Robert noticed his wig was gone just as he saw Hamp's wig blow off and be lost in the western distance toward the bright cloud. They climbed down the Indian mound against the force of the wind.

"How long will it burn?" asked Curwell.

"I have no idea," said Sir Robert. "It was not supposed to burn at all. It was supposed to fix in the globe. I just don't understand."

"It may burn until it reaches the Western Ocean," said Hampton, and he had voiced all their fears.

"Surely, surely not," said Athole, yelling to be heard above the wind.

"But you must have succeeded," said someone else. "You *must* have released all the phlogiston in the mixed matter. There's no telling what will happen with it. It could burn that far!"

"Then the water will put it out. The water!" said Sir Robert. He felt a spasm go through him and he lost consciousness.

He awakened with smoke and the smell of soot in his nostrils. The light outside was murky. A wind whistled around the rafters outside the house, but it was no longer the gale it had been. A brown darkness of smoke lapped against the windows.

He sat up on the couch where they had lain him.

Lady Margurite was crying on the sofa opposite.

"Everything to the west is gone, Robert," she said quietly when she saw him rouse.

"Everything?"

"As far as a horse and man can ride, before it becomes too hot to continue. And that was hours ago, when the scout from the township came back from his reconnoiter."

"The barometer," said Lawrence Curwell, tapping the great Dresden instrument atop the mantelpiece. "The barometer has dropped a full six inches since this morning, and is still falling."

"Oh, great Jehovah!" said Sir Robert. "What have I done?"

"Nothing any of us wouldn't have done," said Hampton Hamilton tiredly from another chair. "It only seems you succeeded much better than you had planned."

"Why didn't you stop me?"

"I don't know," said Hampton. "I doubt you would have stopped me."

"What time is it?"

"A little after five."

"We'll know in fourteen hours, then," said Curwell. He continued to stare at the barometer, as if to drag secrets from it.

They tried to eat after darkness fell, but no one was hungry. Tins of molasses had begun to pop their lids in the pantry. Sir Robert imagined it was harder to breathe, but knew better.

They sat in the parlor until no one could stand the waiting and the heat any longer.

"Damn it!" Sir Robert jumped to his feet. "If it's going to happen, I want to look it in the face. We'll go to the ocean."

They looked at him a moment, then climbed from their chairs. It was better than waiting here, where each ticking of the clock sounded loud as a carpenter's hammer to them.

The wagon bounced on the rutted road. The horse labored.

Sir Robert drove in front with Hampton; Curwell and Lady Margurite were in back with a picnic basket and blankets.

It was nearing midnight. The air was filled with the odors of burning—of a thousand things, burnt wood, grass, feathers, calcined metals, gunpowder smells. The wind brought warmth. Through rifts in the smoky sky they saw the stars—larger and colder than they had ever looked before, and they hardly twinkled.

The temperature was still rising, and the barometer had bottomed out an hour ago. It was now decidedly harder to breathe.

They topped the hill overlooking the port town of New Sharpton. Candles burned in the houses, torches moved in the streets as knots of people formed together and dispersed. An occasional rider left on the road down the coast.

"Over here will be fine," said Sir Robert, guiding the horse to a spot beneath a group of trees atop the hill.

They spread the blankets on the seaward side of the hill and lay back, watching the still Atlantic.

Sir Robert drifted in and out of sleep as from fatigue. The air was hot and close, as if he were shut up in a chimney in the middle of summer.

Curwell had gone down the hill toward the bay. It had taken him a long time to go the few hundred yards. He had stopped frequently and rested.

The horse, which had been unhitched from the wagon, was in distress, as if it had been galloped miles, instead of being walked the few from the estate to the sea.

"The water temperature is rising, and the streams coming to it are out of their banks from melted snow," said Curwell, when he had labored up the hill and lay down. "There are shoals of dead fish away from the stream outlet. There are so many we could smell them from here were it not for this infernal smoke."

"It just can't be true," said Sir Robert. "It just cannot. Water *will not* burn!"

"Maybe," said Hampton, where he lay on the ground above them, holding his splinted and broken arm. "Maybe the New Chemistry has some truths. Perhaps water is *not* an element. Perhaps it, too, contains phlogiston, or inflammable gas, which . . . " For the first time in his life, Hampton was having trouble following a line of thought. He shook his head to clear it. " . . . Inflammable gas. Perhaps a constituent like the oxygine principle. Perhaps it was separated by the heat from the land. Perhaps the fire is fueled from it. Maybe it will have to pass over the Earth innumerable times before it is all combusted with phlogiston . . ."

Sir Robert lay back on the blanket. He held Lady Margurite's hand.

"All gone," he said at last.

"The buffalo. The Indians," said Margurite.

"The Chinese. The bold Russians. The Turks," said Hampton.

"The French. *Britain!*" said Curwell.

"Now us," said Hampton Hamilton, and pointed.

The east was beginning to lighten, though it was still an hour before dawn. The wind blew toward the sea, but it was still a gentle wind, a thin wind. It had very little force.

From north to south the bright white boiling line appeared, like the sun breaking through under a late afternoon storm. But much brighter.

"Shall we be burned?" asked Lady Margurite. Her arm sprouted gooseflesh. "The thought of burning is the worst."

"I think not," said Curwell. "Like the martyrs, I think the air will be too saturated with phlogiston for us to breathe before the fire reaches us." He paused as a great tongue of flame licked out of the roil toward them.

The hill and the village were bathed in the glaring artificial dawn. Screams came from the town from those who were still able to scream.

The thin wind rose more.

They watched the burning line quietly, each locked in their thoughts.

The edge of the great combusting cloud was still more than two hundred miles away.

"Phlogiston!" said Sir Robert Athole and turned and passed away.

"I want to stand up," said Hamp. They heard him stir and fall behind them.

"The French *were* right, partly . . ." said Curwell.

"Robert . . . ?" asked Lady Margurite.

Curwell looked at the enormous burning wall.

"It's the end of . . ."

The sentence was the only thing left unfinished.

(1982)

MICHAEL G. CONEY

The Byrds

Gran started it all.

Late one afternoon in the hottest summer in living memory, she took off all her clothes, carefully painted red around her eyes and down her cheeks, chin and throat, painted the rest of her body a contrasting black with the exception of her armpits and the inside of her wrists which she painted white, strapped on her new antigravity belt, flapped her arms and rose into the nearest tree, a garry oak, where she perched.

She informed us that, as of now, she was Rufous-necked Hornbill, of India.

"She always wanted to visit India," Gramps told us.

Gran said no more, for the logical reason that Hornbills are not talking birds.

"Come down, Gran!" called Mother. "You'll catch your death of cold."

Gran remained silent. She stretched her neck and gazed at the horizon.

"She's crazy," said Father. "She's crazy. I always said she was. I'll call the asylum."

"You'll do no such thing!" Mother was always very sensitive about Gran's occasional peculiarities. "She'll be down soon. The evenings are drawing in. She'll get cold."

"What's an old fool her age doing with an antigravity unit anyway, that's what I want to know," said Father.

The Water Department was restricting supply and the weatherman was predicting floods. The Energy Department was warning of depleted stocks, the Department of Rest had announced that the population must fall by one-point-eight per cent by November or else, the Mailgift was spewing out a deluge of application forms, tax forms and final reminders, the Tidy Mice were malfunctioning so that the house stank. . . .

And now this.

It was humiliating and embarrassing. Gran up a tree, naked and painted. She stayed there all evening, and I knew that my girlfriend Pandora would be dropping by soon and would be sure to ask questions.

Humanity was at that point in the morality cycle when nudity was considered indecent. Gran was probably thirty years before her time. There was something lonely and anachronistic about her, perched there, balancing unsteadily in a squatting position, occasionally grabbing at the trunk for support then flapping her arms to re-establish the birdlike impression. She looked like some horrible mutation. Her resemblance to a Rufous-necked Hornbill was slight.

"Talk her down, Gramps," said Father.

"She'll come down when she's hungry."

He was wrong. Late in the evening Gran winged her way to a vacant lot where an ancient tree stood. She began to eat unsterilized apples, juice flowing down her chin. It was a grotesque sight.

"She'll be poisoned!" cried Mother.

"So, she's made her choice at last," said Father.

He was referring to Your Choice for Peace, the brochure which Gran and Gramps received monthly from the Department of Rest. Accompanying the brochure is a six-page form on which senior citizens describe all that is good about their life, and a few of the things which bug them. At the end of the form is a box in which the oldster indicates his preference for Life or Peace. If he does not check the box, or if he fails to complete the form, it is assumed that he has chosen Peace, and they send the Wagon for him.

Now Gran was cutting a picturesque silhouette against the pale blue of the evening sky as she circled the rooftops uttering harsh cries. She flew with arms outstretched, legs trailing, and we all had to admit to the beauty of the sight; that is, until a flock of starlings began to mob her. Losing directional control she spiralled downward, recovered, levelled out and skimmed towards us, outpacing the starlings and regaining her perch in the garry oak. She made preening motions and settled down for the night. The family Pesterminator, zapping bugs with its tiny laser, considered her electronically for a second but held its fire.

We were indoors by the time Pandora arrived. She was nervous, complaining that there was a huge mutation in the tree outside, and it had cawed at her.

Mother said quickly, "It's only a Rufous-necked Hornbill."

"A rare visitor to these shores," added Father.

"Why couldn't she have been a sparrow?" asked Mother. "Or something else inconspicuous." Things were not going well for her. The little robot Tidy Mice still sulked behind the wainscoting and she'd had to clean the house by hand.

The garish Gran shone like a beacon in the morning sunlight. There was no concealing the family's degradation. A small crowd had gathered and people were trying to tempt Gran down with breadcrumbs. She looked none the worse for her night out, and was greeting the morning with shrill yells.

Gramps was strapping on an antigravity belt. "I'm going up to fetch her down. This has gone far enough."

I said, "Be careful. She may attack you."

"Don't be a damned fool." Nevertheless Gramps went into the toolshed, later emerging nude and freshly painted. Mother uttered a small scream of distress, suspecting that Gramps, too, had become involved in the conspiracy to diminish the family's social standing.

I reassured her. "She's more likely to listen to one of her own kind."

"Has everyone gone totally insane?" asked Mother.

Gramps rose gracefully into the garry oak, hovered, then settled beside Gran. He spoke to her quietly for a moment and she listened, head cocked attentively.

Then she made low gobbling noises and leaned against him.

He called down, "This may take longer than I thought."

"Oh, my God," said Mother.

"That does it," said Father. "I'm calling the shrink."

Dr. Pratt was tall and dignified, and he took in the situation at a glance. "Has your mother exhibited birdish tendencies before?"

Father answered for Mother. "No more than anyone else. Although, in many other ways, she was—"

"Gran has always been the soul of conformity," said Mother quickly, beginning to weep. "If our neighbours have been saying otherwise I'll remind them of the slander laws. No—she did it to shame us. She always said she hated the colours we painted the house—she said it looked like a strutting peacock."

"Rutting peacock," said Father. "She said rutting peacock. Those were her exact words."

"Peacock, eh?" Dr. Pratt looked thoughtful. There was a definite avian thread running through this. "So you feel she may be acting in retaliation. She thinks you have made a public spectacle of the house in which she lives, so now she is going to make a public spectacle of you."

"Makes sense," said Father.

"Gran!" called Dr. Pratt. She looked down at us, beady little eyes ringed with red. "I have the personal undertaking of your daughter and son-in-law that the house will be repainted in colours of your own choosing." He spoke on for a few minutes in soothing tones. "That should do it," he said to us finally, picking up his bag. "Put her to bed and keep her off berries, seeds, anything like that. And don't leave any antigravity belts lying around. They can arouse all kinds of prurient interests in older people."

"She still isn't coming down," said Father. "I don't think she understood."

"Then I advise you to fell the tree," said Dr. Pratt coldly, his patience evaporated. "She's a disgusting old exhibitionist who needs to be taught a lesson. Just because she chooses to act out her fantasies in an unusual way doesn't make her any different from anyone else. And what's *he* doing up there, anyway? Does he resent the house paint as well?"

"He *chose* the paint. He's there to bring her down."

We watched them in perplexity. The pair huddled together on the branch, engaged in mutual grooming. The crowd outside the gate had swollen to over a hundred.

On the following morning Gran and Gramps greeted the dawn with a cacophony of gobbling and screeching.

I heard Father throw open his bedroom window and threaten to blast them right out of that goddamned tree and into the hereafter if they didn't keep it down. I heard the metallic click as he cocked his twelve-bore. I heard Mother squeal with apprehension, and the muffled thumping of a physical struggle in the next room.

I was saddened by the strain it puts on marriages when inlaws live in the house—or, in our case, outside the window.

The crowds gathered early and it was quickly apparent that Gramps was through with trying to talk Gran down; in fact, he was through with talking altogether. He perched beside his mate in spry fashion, jerking his head this way and that as he scanned the sky for hawks, cocking an eye at the crowd, shuddering suddenly as though shaking feathers into position.

Dr. Pratt arrived at noon, shortly before the media.

"A classic case of regression to the childlike state," he told us. "The signs are all there: the unashamed nakedness, the bright colours, the speechlessness, the favourite toy, in this case the antigravity belt. I have brought a surrogate toy which I think will solve our problem. Try luring them down with this."

He handed Mother a bright red plastic baby's rattle.

Gran fastened a beady eye on it, shuffled her arms, then launched herself from the tree in a swooping glide. As Mother ducked in alarm,

Gran caught the rattle neatly in her bony old toes, wheeled and flapped back to her perch. Heads close, she and Gramps examined the toy.

We waited breathlessly.

Then Gran stomped it against the branch and the shattered remnants fell to the ground.

The crowd applauded. For the first time we noticed the Newspocket van, and the crew with cameras. The effect on Dr. Pratt was instantaneous. He strode towards them and introduced himself to a red-haired woman with a microphone.

"Tell me, Dr. Pratt, to what do you attribute this phenomenon?"

"The manifestation of birdishness in the elderly is a subject which has received very little study up to the present date. Indeed, I would say that it has been virtually ignored. Apart from my own paper—still in draft form—you could search the psychiatric archives in vain for mention of Pratt's Syndrome."

"And why is that, Dr. Pratt?"

"Basically, fear. The fear in each and every one of us of admitting that something primitive and atavistic can lurk within our very genes. For what is more primitive than a bird, the only survivor of the age of dinosaurs?"

"What indeed, Dr. Pratt?"

"You see in that tree two pathetic human creatures who have reverted to a state which existed long before Man took his first step on Earth, a state which can only have been passed on as a tiny coded message in their very flesh and the flesh of their ancestors, through a million years of Time."

"And how long do you expect their condition to last, Dr. Pratt?"

"Until the fall. The winters in these parts are hard, and they'll be out of that tree come the first frost, if they've got any sense left at all."

"Well, thank you, Dr.—"

A raucous screaming cut her short. A group of shapes appeared in the eastern sky, low over the rooftops. They were too big for birds, yet too small for aircraft, and there was a moment's shocked incomprehension before we recognized them for what they were. Then they wheeled over the Newspocket van with a bedlam of yells and revealed themselves as teenagers of both sexes, unclothed, but painted a simple black semi-matt exterior latex. There were nine of them.

In the weeks following, we came to know them as the Crows. They flew overhead, circled, then settled all over the garry oak and the roof of our house.

They made no attempt to harass Gran or Gramps. Indeed, they seemed almost reverential in their attitude towards the old people.

It seemed that Gran had unlocked some kind of floodgate in the human unconscious, and people took to the air in increasing numbers. The manufacturers of antigravity belts became millionaires overnight, and the skies became a bright tapestry of wheeling, screeching figures in rainbow colours and startling nakedness.

The media named them the Byrds.

"I view it as a protest against today's moral code," said Dr. Pratt, who spent most of his time on panels or giving interviews. "For more years than I care to remember, people have been repressed, their honest desires cloaked in conformity just as tightly as their bodies have been swathed in concealing garb. Now, suddenly, people are saying they've had enough. They're pleasing themselves. It shouldn't surprise us. It's healthy. It's good."

It was curious, the way the doctor had become pro-Byrd. These days he seemed to be acting in the capacity of press-agent for Gran—who herself had become a cult-figure. In addition, he was working on his learned paper, The Origins and Spread of Avian Tendencies in Humans.

Pandora and I reckoned he was in the pay of the belt people.

"But it's fun to be in the centre of things," she said one evening, as the Crows came in to roost, and the garry oak creaked under the weight of a flock of Glaucous Gulls, come to pay homage to Gran. "It's put the town on the map—and your family too." She took my hand, smiling at me proudly.

There were the Pelicans, who specialized in high dives into the sea, deactivating their belts in mid-air, then reactivating them underwater to rocket Polaris-like from the depths. They rarely caught fish, though; and frequently had to be treated for an ailment known as Pelicans' Balloon, caused by travelling through water at speed with open mouth.

There were the Darwin's Tree Finches, a retiring sect whose existence went unsuspected for some weeks, because they spent so much time in the depths of forests with cactus spines held between their teeth, trying to extract bugs from holes in dead trees. They were a brooding and introspective group.

Virtually every species of bird was represented. And because every cult must have its lunatic fringe, there were the Pigeons. They flocked to the downtown city streets and mingled with the crowds hurrying to and fro. From the shoulders up they looked much like anyone else, only greyer, and with a curious habit of jerking their heads while walking. Bodily, though, they were like any other Byrd: proudly unclothed.

Their roosting habits triggered the first open clash between Byrds and Man. There were complaints that they kept people awake at night, and fouled the rooftops. People began to string electrified wires around their ridges and guttering, and to put poison out.

The Pigeons' retaliation took place early one evening, when the commuting crowds jammed the streets. It was simple and graphic, and well-coordinated. Afterwards, people referred to it obliquely as the Great Deluge, because it was not the kind of event which is discussed openly, in proper society.

There were other sects, many of them; and perhaps the strangest was a group who eschewed the use of antigravity belts altogether. From time to time we would catch sight of them sitting on the concrete abutments of abandoned motorways, searching one another for parasites. Their bodies were painted a uniform brown except for their private parts, which were a luminous red. They called themselves Hamadryas Baboons.

People thought they had missed the point of the whole thing, somehow.

Inevitably when there are large numbers of people involved, there are tragedies. Sometimes an elderly Byrd would succumb to cardiac arrest in mid-air, and drift away on the winds. Others would suffer belt malfunctions and plummet to the ground. As the first chill nights began to grip the country, some of the older Byrds died of exposure and fell from their perches. Courageously they maintained their role until the end, and when daylight came they would be found in the ritualistic "Dead Byrd" posture, on their backs with legs in the air.

"All good things come to an end," said Dr. Pratt one evening as the russet leaves drifted from the trees. It had been a busy day, dozens of groups having come to pay homage to Gran. There was a sense of wrapping up, of things coming to a climax. "We will stage a mass rally," said Dr. Pratt to the Newspocket reporter. "There will be such a gathering of Byrds as the country has never known. Gran will address the multitude at the Great Coming Down."

Mother said, "So long as it's soon. I don't think Gran can take any more frosts."

I went to invite Pandora to the Great Coming Down, but she was not at home. I was about to return when I caught sight of a monstrous thing sitting on the backyard fence. It was bright green except around the eyes, which were grey, and the hair, which was a vivid yellow. It looked at me. It blinked in oddly reptilian fashion. It was Pandora.

She said, "Who's a pretty boy, then?"

The very next day Gran swooped down from the garry oak and seized Mother's scarf with her toes, and a grim tug-of-war ensued.

"Let go, you crazy old fool!" shouted Mother.

Gran cranked her belt up to maximum lift and took a quick twist of the scarf around her ankles. The other end was wrapped snugly around

Mother's neck and tucked into her heavy winter coat. Mother left the ground, feet kicking. Her shouts degenerated into strangled grunts.

Father got a grip of Mother's knees as she passed overhead and Gran, with a harsh screech of frustration, found herself descending again; whereupon Gramps, having observed the scene with bright interest, came winging in and took hold of her, adding the power of his belt to hers.

Father's feet left the ground.

Mother by now had assumed the basic hanging attitude: arms dangling limply, head lolling, tongue protruding, face empurpled. I jumped and got hold of Father's ankles. There was a short, sharp rending sound and we fell back to earth in a heap, Mother on top. Gran and Gramps flew back to the garry oak with their half of the scarf, and began to pull it apart with their teeth. Father pried the other half away from Mother's neck. She was still breathing.

"Most fascinating," said Dr. Pratt.

"My wife nearly strangled by those goddamned brutes and he calls it fascinating?"

"No—look at the Hornbills."

"So they're eating the scarf. So they're crazy. What's new?"

"They're not eating it. If you will observe closely, you will see them shredding it. And see—the female is working the strands around that clump of twigs. It's crystal clear what they're doing, of course. This is a classic example of nest-building."

The effect on Father was instantaneous. He jumped up, seized Dr. Pratt by the throat and, shaking him back and forth, shouted, "Any fool knows birds only nest in the spring!" He was overwrought, of course. He apologized the next day.

By that time the Byrds were nesting all over town. They used a variety of materials and in many instances their craftsmanship was pretty to see. The local Newspocket station ran a competition for The Nest I Would Be Happiest To Join My Mate In, treating the matter as a great joke; although some of the inhabitants who had been forcibly undressed in the street thought otherwise. The Byrds wasted nothing. Their nests were intricately-woven collections of whatever could be stolen from below: overcoats, shirts, pants, clothesline, undergarments, hearing-aids, wigs.

"The nesting phenomenon has a two-fold significance," Dr. Pratt informed the media. "On the one hand, we have the desire of the Byrds to emulate the instinctive behavioural patterns of their avian counterparts. On the other hand, there is undoubtedly a suggestion of—how can I say it?—aggression towards the earthbound folk. The Byrds are saying, in their own way: join us. Be natural. Take your clothes off. Otherwise we'll do it for you."

"You don't think they're, uh, sexually *warped?*" asked the reporter.

"Sexually liberated," insisted Dr. Pratt.

The Byrds proved his point the next day, when they began to copulate all over the sky.

It was the biggest sensation since the Great Deluge. Writhing figures filled the heavens and parents locked their children indoors and drew the drapes. It was a fine day for love; the sun glinted on sweat-bedewed flesh, and in the unseasonable warmth the still air rang with cries of delight. The Byrds looped and zoomed and chased one another, and when they met they coupled. Artificial barriers of species were cast aside and Eagle mated with Chaffinch, Robin with Albatross.

"Clearly a visual parable," said Dr. Pratt. "The—"

"Shut up," said Mother. "Shut up, shut up, shut *up*!"

In the garry oak, Rufous-necked Hornbill mated with Rufous-necked Hornbill, then with Crow; then, rising joyously into the sky, with Skua, with Lark, and finally with Hamadryas Baboon, who had at last realized what it was all about and strapped on a belt.

"She's eighty-six years old! What is she thinking of?"

"She's an Earth Mother to them," said Dr. Pratt.

"Earth Mother my ass," said Father. "She's stark, staring mad, and it's about time we faced up to it."

"It's true, it's true!" wailed Mother, a broken woman. "She's crazy! She's been crazy for years! She's old and useless, and yet she keeps filling in all that stuff on her Peace form, instead of forgetting, like any normal old woman!"

"Winter is coming," said Dr. Pratt, "and we are witnessing the symbolic Preservation of the Species. Look at that nice young Tern up there. Tomorrow they must come back to earth, but in the wombs of the females the memory of this glorious September will live on!"

"She's senile and filthy! I've seen her eating roots from out of the ground, and do you know what she did to the Everattentive Waiter? She cross-wired it with the Mailgift chute and filled the kitchen with self-adhesive cookies!"

"She did?"

And the first shadow of doubt crossed Dr. Pratt's face. The leader of the Byrds crazy?

"And one day a Gameshow called on the visiphone and asked her a skill-testing question which would have set us all up for life—and she did the most disgusting thing, and it went out live and the whole town saw it!"

"I'm sure she has sound psychological reasons for her behaviour," said Dr. Pratt desperately.

"She doesn't! She's insane! She walks to town rather than fill out a Busquest form! She brews wine in a horrible jar under the bed! She was once sentenced to one week's community service for indecent exposure! She trespasses in the Department of Agriculture's fields! You want to know why the house stinks? She programmed the Pesterminator to zap the Tidy Mice!"

"But I thought. . . . Why didn't you tell me before? My God, when I think of the things I've said on Newspocket! If this comes out, my reputation, all I've worked for, all. . . ." He was becoming incoherent. "Why didn't you tell me?" he asked again.

"Well, Jesus Christ, it's obvious, isn't it?" snapped Father. "Look at her. She's up in the sky mating with a Hamadryas Baboon, or something very much like one. Now, that's what I call crazy."

"But it's a *Movement*. . . . It's free and vibrant and so basic, so—"

"A nut cult," said Father. "Started by a loonie and encouraged by a quack. Nothing more, nothing less. And the forecast for tonight is twenty below. It'll wipe out the whole lot of them. You'd better get them all down, Pratt, or you'll have a few thousand deaths on your conscience."

But the Byrds came down of their own accord, later that day. As though sensing the end of the Indian summer and the bitter nights to come, they drifted out of the sky in groups, heading for earth, heading for us. Gran alighted in the garry oak with whirling arms, followed by Gramps. They sat close together on their accustomed branch, gobbling quietly to each other. More Byrds came; the Crows, the Pelicans. They filled the tree, spread along the ridge of the roof and squatted on the guttering. They began to perch on fences and posts, even on the ground, all species intermingled. They were all around us, converging, covering the neighbouring roofs and trees, a great final gathering of humans who, just for a few weeks, had gone a little silly. They looked happy although tired, and a few were shivering as the afternoon shortened into evening. They made a great noise at first, a rustling and screeching and fluid piping, but after a while they quietened down. I saw Pandora amidst them, painted and pretty, but her gaze passed right through me. They were still Byrds, playing their role until the end.

And they all faced Gran.

They were awaiting the word to Come Down, but Gran remained silent, living every last moment.

It was like standing in the centre of a vast amphitheatre, with all those heads turned towards us, all those beady eyes watching us. The Newspocket crew were nowhere to be seen; they probably couldn't get through the crowd.

Finally Dr. Pratt strode forward. He was in the grip of a great despondency. He was going to come clean.

"Fools!" he shouted. A murmur of birdlike sounds arose, but soon died. "All through history there have been fools like you, and they've caused wars and disasters and misery. Fools without minds of their own, who follow their leader without thought, without stopping to ask if their leader knows what he is doing. Leaders like Genghis Khan, like Starbusch, like Hitler, leaders who manipulate their followers like puppets in pursuit of their own crazy ends. Crazy leaders drunk with power. Leaders like Gran here.

"Yes, Gran is crazy! I mean certifiably crazy, ready for Peace. Irrational and insane and a burden to the State and to herself. She had me fooled at first." He uttered a short, bitter laugh, not unlike the mating cry of Forster's Tern. "I thought I found logic in what she did. Such was the cunning nature of her madness. It was only recently, when I investigated Gran's past record, that I unmasked her for what she is: a mentally unbalanced old woman with marked antisocial tendencies. I could give you chapter and verse of Gran's past misdemeanors—and I can tell you right now, this isn't the first time she's taken her clothes off in public—but I will refrain, out of consideration for her family, who have suffered enough.

"It will suffice to say that I have recommended her committal and the Peace Wagon is on its way. The whole affair is best forgotten. Now, come down out of those trees and scrub off, and go home to your families, all of you."

He turned away, shoulders drooping. It was nothing like the Great Coming Down he'd pictured. It was a slinking thing, a creeping home, an abashed admission of stupidity.

Except that the Byrds weren't coming down.

They sat silently on their perches, awaiting the word from Gran.

All through Dr. Pratt's oration she'd been quiet, staring fixedly at the sky. Now, at last, she looked around. Her eyes were bright, but it was an almost-human brightness, a different thing from the beady stare of the past weeks. And she half-smiled through the paint, but she didn't utter a word.

She activated her belt and, flapping her arms, rose into the darkening sky.

And the Byrds rose after her.

They filled the sky, a vast multitude of rising figures, and Pandora was with them. Gran led, Gramps close behind, and then came Coot and Skua and Hawk, and the whole thousand-strong mob. They wheeled once over the town and filled the evening with a great and lonely cry. Then they headed off in V-formations, loose flocks, tight echelons, a pattern of dwindling black forms against the pale duck-egg blue of nightfall.

"Where in hell are they going?" shouted Dr. Pratt as I emerged from the shed, naked and painted. It was cold, but I would soon get used to it.

"South," I said.

"Why the hell south? What's wrong with here, for God's sake?"

"It's warmer, south. We're migrating."

So I activated my belt and lifted into the air, and watched the house fall away below me, and the tiny bolts of light as the Pesterminator hunted things. The sky seemed empty now but there was still a pink glow to the west. Hurrying south, I saw something winking like a red star and, before long, I was homing in on the gleaming hindquarters of a Hamadryas Baboon.

(1982)

OCTAVIA BUTLER

Speech Sounds

There was trouble aboard the Washington Boulevard bus. Rye had expected trouble sooner or later in her journey. She had put off going until loneliness and hopelessness drove her out. She believed she might have one group of relatives left alive—a brother and his two children twenty miles away in Pasadena. That was a day's journey one-way, if she were lucky. The unexpected arrival of the bus as she left her Virginia Road home had seemed to be a piece of luck—until the trouble began.

Two young men were involved in a disagreement of some kind, or, more likely, a misunderstanding. They stood in the aisle, grunting and gesturing at each other, each in his own uncertain T stance as the bus lurched over the potholes. The driver seemed to be putting some effort into keeping them off balance. Still, their gestures stopped just short of contact—mock punches, hand games of intimidation to replace lost curses.

People watched the pair, then looked at one another and made small anxious sounds. Two children whimpered.

Rye sat a few feet behind the disputants and across from the back door. She watched the two carefully, knowing the fight would begin when someone's nerve broke or someone's hand slipped or someone came to the end of his limited ability to communicate. These things could happen anytime.

One of them happened as the bus hit an especially large pothole and one man, tall, thin, and sneering, was thrown into his shorter opponent.

Instantly, the shorter man drove his left fist into the disintegrating sneer. He hammered his larger opponent as though he neither had nor needed any weapon other than his left fist. He hit quickly enough, hard enough to batter his opponent down before the taller man could regain his balance or hit back even once.

People screamed or squawked in fear. Those nearby scrambled to get out of the way. Three more young men roared in excitement and gestured wildly. Then, somehow, a second dispute broke out between two of these three—probably because one inadvertently touched or hit the other.

As the second fight scattered frightened passengers, a woman shook the driver's shoulder and grunted as she gestured toward the fighting.

The driver grunted back through bared teeth. Frightened, the woman drew away.

Rye, knowing the methods of bus drivers, braced herself and held on to the crossbar of the seat in front of her. When the driver hit the brakes, she was ready and the combatants were not. They fell over seats and onto screaming passengers, creating even more confusion. At least one more fight started.

The instant the bus came to a full stop, Rye was on her feet, pushing the back door. At the second push, it opened and she jumped out, holding her pack in one arm. Several other passengers followed, but some stayed on the bus. Buses were so rare and irregular now, people rode when they could, no matter what. There might not be another bus today—or tomorrow. People started walking, and if they saw a bus they flagged it down. People making intercity trips like Rye's from Los Angeles to Pasadena made plans to camp out, or risked seeking shelter with locals who might rob or murder them.

The bus did not move, but Rye moved away from it. She intended to wait until the trouble was over and get on again, but if there was shooting, she wanted the protection of a tree. Thus, she was near the curb when a battered blue Ford on the other side of the street made a U-turn and pulled up in front of the bus. Cars were rare these days—as rare as a severe shortage of fuel and of relatively unimpaired mechanics could make them. Cars that still ran were as likely to be used as weapons as they were to serve as transportation. Thus, when the driver of the Ford beckoned to Rye, she moved away warily. The driver got out—a big man, young, neatly bearded with dark, thick hair. He wore a long overcoat and a look of wariness that matched Rye's. She stood several feet from him, waiting to see what he would do. He looked at the bus, now rocking with the combat inside, then at the small cluster of passengers who had gotten off. Finally he looked at Rye again.

She returned his gaze, very much aware of the old forty-five automatic her jacket concealed. She watched his hands.

He pointed with his left hand toward the bus. The dark-tinted windows prevented him from seeing what was happening inside.

His use of the left hand interested Rye more than his obvious question. Left-handed people tended to be less impaired, more reasonable and comprehending, less driven by frustration, confusion, and anger.

She imitated his gesture, pointing toward the bus with her own left hand, then punching the air with both fists.

The man took off his coat revealing a Los Angeles Police Department uniform complete with baton and service revolver.

Rye took another step back from him. There was no more LAPD, no more *any* large organization, governmental or private. There were neighborhood patrols and armed individuals. That was all.

The man took something from his coat pocket, then threw the coat into the car. Then he gestured Rye back, back toward the rear of the bus. He had something made of plastic in his hand. Rye did not understand what he wanted until he went to the rear door of the bus and beckoned her to stand there. She obeyed mainly out of curiosity. Cop or not, maybe he could do something to stop the stupid fighting.

He walked around the front of the bus, to the street side where the driver's window was open. There, she thought she saw him throw something into the bus. She was still trying to peer through the tinted glass when people began stumbling out the rear door, choking and weeping. Gas.

Rye caught an old woman who would have fallen, lifted two little children down when they were in danger of being knocked down and trampled. She could see the bearded man helping people at the front door. She caught a thin old man shoved out by one of the combatants. Staggered by the old man's weight, she was barely able to get out of the way as the last of the young men pushed his way out. This one, bleeding from nose and mouth, stumbled into another and they grappled blindly, still sobbing from the gas.

The bearded man helped the bus driver out through the front door, though the driver did not seem to appreciate his help. For a moment, Rye thought there would be another fight. The bearded man stepped back and watched the driver gesture threateningly, watched him shout in wordless anger.

The bearded man stood still, made no sound, refused to respond to clearly obscene gestures. The least impaired people tended to do this—stand back unless they were physically threatened and let those with less control scream and jump around. It was as though they felt it beneath them to be as touchy as the less comprehending. This was an attitude of superiority and that was the way people like the bus driver perceived it. Such "superiority" was frequently punished by beatings, even by death. Rye had had close calls of her own. As a result, she never went unarmed. And in this world where the only likely common language was body language, being armed was often enough. She had rarely had to draw her gun or even display it.

The bearded man's revolver was on constant display. Apparently that was enough for the bus driver. The driver spat in disgust, glared at the bearded man for a moment longer, then strode back to his gas-filled bus.

He stared at it for a moment, clearly wanting to get in, but the gas was still too strong. Of the windows, only his tiny driver's window actually opened. The front door was open, but the rear door would not stay open unless someone held it. Of course, the air conditioning had failed long ago. The bus would take some time to clear. It was the driver's property, his livelihood. He had pasted old magazine pictures of items he would accept as fare on its sides. Then he would use what he collected to feed his family or to trade. If his bus did not run, he did not eat. On the other hand, if the inside of his bus was torn apart by senseless fighting, he would not eat very well either. He was apparently unable to perceive this. All he could see was that it would be some time before he could use his bus again. He shook his fist at the bearded man and shouted. There seemed to be words in his shout, but Rye could not understand them. She did not know whether this was his fault or hers. She had heard so little coherent human speech for the past three years, she was no longer certain how well she recognized it, no longer certain of the degree of her own impairment.

The bearded man sighed. He glanced toward his car, then beckoned to Rye. He was ready to leave, but he wanted something from her first. No. No, he wanted her to leave with him. Risk getting into his car when, in spite of his uniform, law and order were nothing—not even words any longer.

She shook her head in a universally understood negative, but the man continued to beckon.

She waved him away. He was doing what the less-impaired rarely did—drawing potentially negative attention to another of his kind. People from the bus had begun to look at her.

One of the men who had been fighting tapped another on the arm, then pointed from the bearded man to Rye, and finally held up the first two fingers of his right hand as though giving two-thirds of a Boy Scout salute. The gesture was very quick, its meaning obvious even at a distance. She had been grouped with the bearded man. Now what?

The man who had made the gesture started toward her.

She had no idea what he intended, but she stood her ground. The man was half a foot taller than she was and perhaps ten years younger. She did not imagine she could outrun him. Nor did she expect anyone to help her if she needed help. The people around her were all strangers.

She gestured once—a clear indication to the man to stop. She did not intend to repeat the gesture. Fortunately, the man obeyed. He gestured obscenely and several other men laughed. Loss of verbal language had spawned a whole new set of obscene gestures. The man, with stark simplicity, had accused her of sex with the bearded man and had suggested she accommodate the other men present—beginning with him.

Rye watched him wearily. People might very well stand by and watch if he tried to rape her. They would also stand and watch her shoot him. Would he push things that far?

He did not. After a series of obscene gestures that brought him no closer to her, he turned contemptuously and walked away.

And the bearded man still waited. He had removed his service revolver, holster and all. He beckoned again, both hands empty. No doubt his gun was in the car and within easy reach, but his taking it off impressed her. Maybe he was all right. Maybe he was just alone. She had been alone herself for three years. The illness had stripped her, killing her children one by one, killing her husband, her sister, her parents . . .

The illness, if it was an illness, had cut even the living off from one another. As it swept over the country, people hardly had time to lay blame on the Soviets (though they were falling silent along with the rest of the world), on a new virus, a new pollutant, radiation, divine retribution. . . . The illness was stroke-swift in the way it cut people down and stroke-like in some of its effects. But it was highly specific. Language was always lost or severely impaired. It was never regained. Often there was also paralysis, intellectual impairment, death.

Rye walked toward the bearded man, ignoring the whistling and applauding of two of the young men and their thumbs-up signs to the bearded man. If he had smiled at them or acknowledged them in any way, she would almost certainly have changed her mind. If she had let herself think of the possible deadly consequences of getting into a stranger's car, she would have changed her mind. Instead, she thought of the man who lived across the street from her. He rarely washed since his bout with the illness. And he had gotten into the habit of urinating wherever he happened to be. He had two women already—one tending each of his large gardens. They put up with him in exchange for his protection. He had made it clear that he wanted Rye to become his third woman.

She got into the car and the bearded man shut the door. She watched as he walked around to the driver's door—watched for his sake because his gun was on the seat beside her. And the bus driver and a pair of young men had come a few steps closer. They did nothing, though, until the bearded man was in the car. Then one of them threw a rock. Others followed his example, and as the car drove away, several rocks bounced off harmlessly.

When the bus was some distance behind them, Rye wiped sweat from her forehead and longed to relax. The bus would have taken her more than halfway to Pasadena. She would have had only ten miles to walk. She wondered how far she would have to walk now—and wondered if walking a long distance would be her only problem.

At Figueroa and Washington where the bus normally made a left turn, the bearded man stopped, looked at her, and indicated that she should choose a direction. When she directed him left and he actually turned left, she began to relax. If he was willing to go where she directed, perhaps he was safe.

As they passed blocks of burned, abandoned buildings, empty lots, and wrecked or stripped cars, he slipped a gold chain over his head and handed it to her. The pendant attached to it was a smooth, glassy, black rock. Obsidian. His name might be Rock or Peter or Black, but she decided to think of him as Obsidian. Even her sometimes useless memory would retain a name like Obsidian.

She handed him her own name symbol—a pin in the shape of a large golden stalk of wheat. She had bought it long before the illness and the silence began. Now she wore it, thinking it was as close as she was likely to come to Rye. People like Obsidian who had not known her before probably thought of her as Wheat. Not that it mattered. She would never hear her name spoken again.

Obsidian handed her pin back to her. He caught her hand as she reached for it and rubbed his thumb over her calluses.

He stopped at First-Street and asked which way again. Then, after turning right as she had indicated, he parked near the Music Center. There, he took a folded paper from the dashboard and unfolded it. Rye recognized it as a street map, though the writing on it meant nothing to her. He flattened the map, took her hand again, and put her index finger on one spot. He touched her, touched himself, pointed toward the floor. In effect, "We are here." She knew he wanted to know where she was going. She wanted to tell him, but she shook her head sadly. She had lost reading and writing. That was her most serious impairment and her most painful. She had taught history at UCLA. She had done freelance writing. Now she could not even read her own manuscripts. She had a houseful of books that she could neither read nor bring herself to use as fuel. And she had a memory that would not bring back to her much of what she had read before.

She stared at the map, trying to calculate. She had been born in Pasadena, had lived for fifteen years in Los Angeles. Now she was near L.A. Civic Center. She knew the relative positions of the two cities, knew streets, directions, even knew to stay away from freeways which might be blocked by wrecked cars and destroyed overpasses. She ought to know how to point out Pasadena even though she could not recognize the word.

Hesitantly, she placed her hand over a pale orange patch in the upper right corner of the map. That should be right. Pasadena.

Obsidian lifted her hand and looked under it, then folded the map and put it back on the dashboard. He could read, she realized belatedly. He could probably write, too. Abruptly, she hated him—deep, bitter hatred. What did literacy mean to him—a grown man who played cops and robbers? But he was literate and she was not. She never would be. She felt sick to her stomach with hatred, frustration, and jealousy. And only a few inches from her hand was a loaded gun.

She held herself still, staring at him, almost seeing his blood. But her rage crested and ebbed and she did nothing.

Obsidian reached for her hand with hesitant familiarity. She looked at him. Her face had already revealed too much. No person still living in what was left of human society could fail to recognize that expression, that jealousy.

She closed her eyes wearily, drew a deep breath. She had experienced longing for the past, hatred of the present, growing hopelessness, purposelessness, but she had never experienced such a powerful urge to kill another person. She had left her home, finally, because she had come near to killing herself. She had found no reason to stay alive. Perhaps that was why she had gotten into Obsidian's car. She had never before done such a thing.

He touched her mouth and made chatter motions with thumb and fingers. Could she speak?

She nodded and watched his milder envy come and go. Now both had admitted what it was not safe to admit, and there had been no violence. He tapped his mouth and forehead and shook his head. He did not speak or comprehend spoken language. The illness had played with them, taking away, she suspected, what each valued most.

She plucked at his sleeve, wondering why he had decided on his own to keep the LAPD alive with what he had left. He was sane enough otherwise. Why wasn't he at home raising corn, rabbits, and children? But she did not know how to ask. Then he put his hand on her thigh and she had another question to deal with.

She shook her head. Disease, pregnancy, helpless, solitary agony . . . no.

He massaged her thigh gently and smiled in obvious disbelief.

No one had touched her for three years. She had not wanted anyone to touch her. What kind of world was this to chance bringing a child into even if the father were willing to stay and help raise it? It was too bad, though. Obsidian could not know how attractive he was to her—young, probably younger than she was, clean, asking for what he wanted rather than demanding it. But none of that mattered. What were a few moments of pleasure measured against a lifetime of consequences?

He pulled her closer to him and for a moment she let herself enjoy the closeness. He smelled good—male and good. She pulled away reluctantly.

He sighed, reached toward the glove compartment. She stiffened, not knowing what to expect, but all he took out was a small box. The writing on it meant nothing to her. She did not understand until he broke the seal, opened the box, and took out a condom. He looked at her and she first looked away in surprise. Then she giggled. She could not remember when she had last giggled.

He grinned, gestured toward the backseat, and she laughed aloud. Even in her teens, she had disliked backseats of cars. But she looked around at the empty streets and ruined buildings, then she got out and into the backseat. He let her put the condom on him, then seemed surprised at her eagerness.

Sometime later, they sat together, covered by his coat, unwilling to become clothed near-strangers again just yet. He made rock-the-baby gestures and looked questioningly at her.

She swallowed, shook her head. She did not know how to tell him her children were dead.

He took her hand and drew a cross in it with his index finger, then made his baby-rocking gesture again.

She nodded, held up three fingers, then turned away, trying to shut out a sudden flood of memories. She had told herself that the children growing up now were to be pitied. They would run through the downtown canyons with no real memory of what the buildings had been or even how they had come to be. Today's children gathered books as well as wood to be burned as fuel. They ran through the streets chasing one another and hooting like chimpanzees. They had no future. They were now all they would ever be.

He put his hand on her shoulder and she turned suddenly, fumbling for his small box, then urging him to make love to her again. He could give her forgetfulness and pleasure. Until now, nothing had been able to do that. Until now, every day had brought her closer to the time when she would do what she had left home to avoid doing: putting her gun in her mouth and pulling the trigger.

She asked Obsidian if he would come home with her, stay with her.

He looked surprised and pleased once he understood. But he did not answer at once. Finally he shook his head as she had feared he might. He was probably having too much fun playing cops and robbers and picking up women.

She dressed in silent disappointment, unable to feel any anger toward him. Perhaps he already had a wife and a home. That was likely. The illness had been harder on men than on women—had killed more men, had left male survivors more severely impaired. Men like Obsidian were rare. Women either settled for less or stayed alone. If they found an Obsidian, they did what they could to keep him. Rye suspected he had someone younger, prettier keeping him.

He touched her while she was strapping her gun on and asked with a complicated series of gestures whether it was loaded.

She nodded grimly.

He patted her arm.

She asked once more if he would come home with her, this time using a different series of gestures. He had seemed hesitant. Perhaps he could be courted.

He got out and into the front seat without responding.

She took her place in front again, watching him. Now he plucked at his uniform and looked at her. She thought she was being asked something, but did not know what it was.

He took off his badge, tapped it with one finger, then tapped his chest. Of course.

She took the badge from his hand and pinned her wheat stalk to it. If playing cops and robbers was his only insanity, let him play. She would take him, uniform and all. It occurred to her that she might eventually lose him to someone he would meet as he had met her. But she would have him for a while.

He took the street map down again, tapped it, pointed vaguely northeast toward Pasadena, then looked at her.

She shrugged, tapped his shoulder, then her own, and held up her index and second fingers tight together, just to be sure.

He grasped the two fingers and nodded. He was with her.

She took the map from him and threw it onto the dashboard. She pointed back southwest—back toward home. Now she did not have to go to Pasadena. Now she could go on having a brother there and two nephews—three right-handed males. Now she did not have to find out for certain whether she was as alone as she feared. Now she was not alone.

Obsidian took Hill Street south, then Washington west, and she leaned back, wondering what it would be like to have someone again. With what she had scavenged, what she had preserved, and what she grew, there was easily enough food for them. There was certainly room enough in a four-bedroom house. He could move his possessions in. Best of all, the animal across the street would pull back and possibly not force her to kill him.

Obsidian had drawn her closer to him and she had put her head on his shoulder when suddenly he braked hard, almost throwing her off the seat. Out of the corner of her eye, she saw that someone had run across the street in front of the car. One car on the street and someone had to run in front of it.

Straightening up, Rye saw that the runner was a woman, fleeing from an old frame house to a boarded-up storefront. She ran silently, but the man who followed her a moment later shouted what sounded like garbled words as he ran. He had something in his hand. Not a gun. A knife, perhaps.

The woman tried a door, found it locked, looked around desperately, finally snatched up a fragment of glass broken from the storefront window. With this she turned to face her pursuer. Rye thought she would be more likely to cut her own hand than to hurt anyone else with the glass.

Obsidian jumped from the car, shouting. It was the first time Rye had heard his voice—deep and hoarse from disuse. He made the same sound over and over the way some speechless people did, "Da, da, da!"

Rye got out of the car as Obsidian ran toward the couple. He had drawn his gun. Fearful, she drew her own and released the safety. She looked around to see who else might be attracted to the scene. She saw the man glance at Obsidian, then suddenly lunge at the woman. The woman jabbed his face with her glass, but he caught her arm and managed to stab her twice before Obsidian shot him.

The man doubled, then toppled, clutching his abdomen. Obsidian shouted, then gestured Rye over to help the woman.

Rye moved to the woman's side, remembering that she had little more than bandages and antiseptic in her pack. But the woman was beyond help. She had been stabbed with a long, slender boning knife.

She touched Obsidian to let him know the woman was dead. He had bent to check the wounded man who lay still and also seemed dead. But as Obsidian looked around to see what Rye wanted, the man opened his eyes. Face contorted, he seized Obsidian's just-holstered revolver and fired. The bullet caught Obsidian in the temple and he collapsed.

It happened just that simply, just that fast. An instant later, Rye shot the wounded man as he was turning the gun on her.

And Rye was alone—with three corpses.

She knelt beside Obsidian, dry-eyed, frowning, trying to understand why everything had suddenly changed. Obsidian was gone. He had died and left her—like everyone else.

Two very small children came out of the house from which the man and woman had run—a boy and girl perhaps three years old. Holding hands, they crossed the street toward Rye. They stared at her, then edged past her and went to the dead woman. The girl shook the woman's arm as though trying to wake her.

This was too much. Rye got up, feeling sick to her stomach with grief and anger. If the children began to cry, she thought she would vomit.

They were on their own, those two kids. They were old enough to scavenge. She did not need any more grief. She did not need a stranger's children who would grow up to be hairless chimps.

She went back to the car. She could drive home, at least. She remembered how to drive.

The thought that Obsidian should be buried occurred to her before she reached the car, and she did vomit.

She had found and lost the man so quickly. It was as though she had been snatched from comfort and security and given a sudden, inexplicable beating. Her head would not clear. She could not think.

Somehow, she made herself go back to him, look at him. She found herself on her knees beside him with no memory of having knelt. She stroked his face, his beard. One of the children made a noise and she looked at them, at the woman who was probably their mother. The children looked back at her, obviously frightened. Perhaps it was their fear that reached her finally.

She had been about to drive away and leave them. She had almost done it, almost left two toddlers to die. Surely there had been enough dying. She would have to take the children home with her. She would not be able to live with any other decision. She looked around for a place to bury three bodies. Or two. She wondered if the murderer were the children's father. Before the silence, the police had always said some of the most dangerous calls they went out on were domestic disturbance calls. Obsidian should have known that—not that the knowledge would have kept him in the car. It would not have held her back either. She could not have watched the woman murdered and done nothing.

She dragged Obsidian toward the car. She had nothing to dig with her, and no one to guard for her while she dug. Better to take the bodies with her and bury them next to her husband and her children. Obsidian would come home with her after all.

When she had gotten him onto the floor in the back, she returned for the woman. The little girl, thin, dirty, solemn, stood up and unknowingly gave Rye a gift. As Rye began to drag the woman by her arms, the little girl screamed, "No!"

Rye dropped the woman and stared at the girl.

"No!" the girl repeated. She came to stand beside the woman. "Go away!" she told Rye.

"Don't talk," the little boy said to her. There was no blurring or confusing of sounds. Both children had spoken and Rye had understood. They boy looked at the dead murderer and moved further from him. He took the girl's hand. "Be quiet," he whispered.

Fluent speech! Had the woman died because she could talk and had taught her children to talk? Had she been killed by a husband's festering anger or by a stranger's jealous rage? And the children . . . they must have been born after the silence. Had the disease run its course, then? Or were these children simply immune? Certainly they had had time to fall sick and silent. Rye's mind leaped ahead. What if children of three of fewer years were safe and able to learn language? What if all they needed were teachers? Teachers and protectors.

Rye glanced at the dead murderer. To her shame, she thought she could understand some of the passions that must have driven him, whoever he was. Anger, frustration, hopelessness, insane jealousy . . . how many more of him were there—people willing to destroy what they could not have?

Obsidian had been the protector, had chosen that role for who knew what reason. Perhaps putting on an obsolete uniform and patrolling the empty streets had been what he did instead of putting a gun into his mouth. And now that there was something worth protecting, he was gone.

She had been a teacher. A good one. She had been a protector, too, though only of herself. She had kept herself alive when she had no reason to live. If the illness let these children alone, she could keep them alive.

Somehow she lifted the dead woman into her arms and placed her on the backseat of the car. The children began to cry, but she knelt on the broken pavement and whispered to them, fearful of frightening them with the harshness of her long unused voice.

"It's all right," she told them. "You're going with us, too. Come on." She lifted them both, one in each arm. They were so light. Had they been getting enough to eat?

The boy covered her mouth with his hand, but she moved her face away. "It's all right for me to talk," she told him. "As long as no one's around, it's all right." She put the boy down on the front seat of the car and he moved over without being told to, to make room for the girl. When they were both in the car Rye leaned against the window, looking at them, seeing that they were less afraid now, that they watched her with at least as much curiosity as fear.

"I'm Valerie Rye," she said, savoring the words. "It's all right for you to talk to me."

(1983)

ANDREW WEINER

Distant Signals

There was something not quite right about the young man.

His suit appeared brand new. Indeed, it glistened with an almost unnatural freshness and sharpness of definition. Yet it was made in a style that had not been fashionable since the late 1950s. The lapels were too wide, the trousers too baggy; the trouser legs terminated in one-inch cuffs. The young man's hair was short—too short. It was parted neatly on the left-hand side and plastered down with some sort of grease. And his smile was too wide. Too wide, at least, for nine o'clock on a Monday morning at the Parkdale Public Library.

Out for the day, was the librarian's first and last thought on the matter. Out, that is, from the state-run mental health centre just three blocks away.

"I would like," said the young man, "to be directed to the TV and film section."

His voice, too, had an unnatural definition, as if he were speaking through some hidden microphone. It projected right across the library. Several patrons turned their heads to peer at him.

"Over there," said the librarian, in a very pointed whisper. "Just over there."

STRANGER IN TOWN. Series, 1960. Northstar Studios for NBC-TV. Produced by KEN ODELL. From an original idea by BILL HURN. Directors included JASON ALTBERG, NICK BALL, and JIM SPEIGEL. 26 b/w episodes. Running time: 50 minutes.

Horse opera following the exploits of Cooper aka The Stranger (VANCE MACCOBY), an amnesiacal gunslinger who wanders from town to town in search of his lost identity, stalked always by the mysterious limping loner Loomis (TERRY WHITE) who may or may not know his real name. Despite this promisingly mythic premise, the series quickly degenerated into a formulaic pattern, with Cooper as a Shane-style savior of widows and orphans.

The show won mediocre ratings, and NBC declined to pick up its option for a second season. The identity of Cooper was never revealed.
See also: GUNSLINGERS; HOLLYWOOD EXISTENTIALISM; LAW AND ORDER; WESTERNS.

MACCOBY, VANCE (1938?–). Actor. Born Henry Mulvin in Salt Lake City, Utah. Frequent guest spots in WAGON TRAIN, RIVERBOAT, CAPTAIN CHRONOS, THE ZONE BEYOND, etc. 1957–59. Lead in the 1960 oater STRANGER IN TOWN and the short-lived 1961 private eye show MAC PARADISE, canceled after 6 episodes. Subsequent activities unknown. One of dozens of nearly interchangeable identikit male stars of the first period of episodic TV drama. Maccoby had a certain brooding quality, particularly in b/w, that carried him far, but apparently lacked the resources for the long haul.
See also STARS AND STARDOM

—From *The Complete TV Encyclopedia,* Chuck Gingle, editor.

There was something distinctly odd about the young man in the white loafers and pompadour hair-style, the young man who had been haunting the ante-room of his office all day.

Had the Kookie look come back? Feldman wondered.

"Look, kid," he said, not unkindly, "as my secretary told you, I'm not taking on any more clients. I have a full roster right now. You'd really be much better off going to Talentmart, or one of those places. They specialize in, you know, unknowns."

"And as I told your secretary," the young man said, "I don't want to be an actor, I want to hire one. One of your clients. This is strictly a business proposition."

Business proposition my ass, Feldman thought. *Autograph hunter, more like.* But he said wearily, "Which one would that be? Lola Banks? Dirk Raymond?"

"Vance Maccoby."

"Vance Maccoby?" For a moment he had to struggle to place the name. "Vance Maccoby?" he said again. "That bum? What the hell do you want with Vance Maccoby?"

"Mr. Feldman, I represent a group of overseas investors interested in independently producing a TV series for syndicated sale. We want Mr. Maccoby to star. However, we have so far been unable to locate him."

"I haven't represented him in years. No one has. He hasn't *worked* in years. Not since . . . what was that piece of crap called? *Max Paradise?* I don't like to speak ill of former clients, but the man was impossible, you know. A drunk. Quite impossible. No one could work with him."

"We're aware of that," the young man said. "We've taken all that into consideration, and we are still interested in talking to Mr. Maccoby. We think he is the only man for the part. And we believe that if anyone can find him, you can."

The young man opened his briefcase and fumbled inside it. "We would like," he continued, "to retain your services toward that end. And we are prepared to make suitable remuneration whether or not a contract should be signed with Mr. Maccoby and whether or not you choose to represent him as agent of record in that transaction."

"Kid," Feldman began, "what you need is a private detective—" He stopped and stared at the bar-shaped object in the young man's hand. "Is that gold?"

"It certainly is, Mr. Feldman. It certainly is."

The young man laid the bar on the desk between them.

"An ounce of gold?"

"One point three four ounces," said the young man. "We apologize for the unusual denomination."

He held open the briefcase. "I have twenty-four more such bars here. At the New York spot price this morning, this represents a value of approximately fifteen thousand dollars."

"Fifteen thousand dollars to find Vance Maccoby?" Feldman said.

He got up and paced around the desk.

"Is this stuff hot?" he asked, pointing to the briefcase, feeling like a character in one of the more banal TV shows into which he booked his clients.

"Hot?" echoed the young man. He reached out and touched the gold bar on the desk. "A few degrees below room temperature, I would say."

"Cute," Feldman said. "Don't be cute. Just tell me, is this on the level?"

"Oh, I see," said the young man. "Yes, absolutely. We have a property which we wish to develop, to which we have recently purchased the rights from the estate of the late Mr. Kenneth Odell. There is only one man who can star in this show, and that is Vance Maccoby."

"What property?"

"*Stranger in Town*," said the young man.

"I knew it," she said. "I knew you would come back."

"You knew more than I did," Cooper said. "I was five miles out of town and heading west. But something . . . something made me turn around and come back here and face the Kerraway Brothers."

"You're a good man," she said. "You couldn't help yourself."

"I don't know if I'm a good man," Cooper said. "I don't know what kind of man I am." He stared morosely at the corpses strewn out on the

ground around the ranch house. "I just couldn't let the Kerraways take your land."

He mounted his horse. "Time to be moving on," he said. "You take good care of yourself and little Billy now."

"Will you ever come back?"

"Maybe," he said. "Maybe after I find what I'm looking for."

"I think you found it already," she said. "You just don't know it yet. You found yourself."

"That may be so," Cooper said. "But I still gotta put a name to it."

He rode off into a rapidly setting sun.

The video picture flickered, then resolved itself into an antique Tide commercial. Hurn cut the controls. He turned to the strange young man in the too-tweedy jacket and the heavy horn-rimmed glasses.

"That?" he said, gesturing at the screen. "You want to remake that . . . *garbage?*"

"Not remake," the young man said. "Revive. Continue. Conclude. Tell the remainder of the story of the stranger Cooper, and the re-acquisition of his memory and identity."

"Who cares?" Hurn asked. "Who the hell cares who Cooper is or what he did? Certainly not the viewers. Do you know how many letters we got after we cancelled the series? Sixteen. Sixteen letters. That's how many people cared."

"That is our concern, Mr. Hurn. We believe that we do have a market for this property. That is why we are making this proposition. We are prepared to go ahead with or without you. But certainly we would much rather have you with us. As the main creative force behind the original series—"

"Creative?" Hurn said. "Frankly, that whole show to me was nothing but an embarrassment. And I was glad when they cancelled it, actually. I wrote those scripts for one reason and one reason alone. Money."

"We can offer you a great deal of money, Mr. Hurn."

Hurn gestured, as though to indicate the oriental rugs on the floor, the rare books in the shelves on the wall, the sculptures and the paintings, the several-million-dollar Beverly Hills home that contained all this.

"I don't need money, Mr.—what did you say your name was?"

"Smith."

"Mr. Smith, I have all the money I could ever want. I have done well in this business, Mr. Smith. Quite well. I am no longer the struggling writer who conceived *Stranger in Town.* These days I choose my projects on the basis of quality."

"You disparage yourself unnecessarily, Mr. Hurn. We believe that *Stranger in Town* was a series of the highest quality. In some ways, in fact, it represented the very peak of televisual art. The existential dilemma of the protagonist, the picaresque nature of his journeyings, the obsessive fascination with the nature of memory . . . That scene . . ." The young man's eyes came alive. "That scene when Cooper bites into a watermelon and says, *"I remember a watermelon like this. I remember summer days, summer nights, a cool breeze on the porch, the river rushing by. I remember a woman's lips, her eyes, her deep blue eyes. But where, damn it? Where?"*

Hurn stared, open-mouthed. "You remember *that*? Word for word? Oh, my God."

"Art, Mr. Hurn. Unabashed art."

"Adolescent pretension. Fakery. Bullshit," Hurn said. "Embarrassing. Oh, my God, how embarrassing."

"In some ways trite," the young man conceded. "Brash. Even clumsy sometimes. But burning with an inner conviction. Mr. Hurn, you must help us. You must help us bring back *Stranger in Town.*"

"You can't," Hurn said. "You can't bring it back. Even if I agreed it was worth bringing back—and I'll admit to you that I've thought about it on occasion, though not in many years. I've always had a sense of it as a piece of unfinished business. . . . But even if I wanted to help you, it couldn't be done. Not now. It's too late, much too late. You can't repeat the past, Smith. You can't bring it back. It's over, finished, a dead mackerel."

"Of course you can," Smith said. "Of course you can repeat the past. We have absolutely no doubt on that question."

"Boats against the current," Hurn said. "But no, no. I can't agree. It's like when those promoters wanted to reunite the Beatles."

"Beetles?" Smith asked. "What beetles?"

"The Beatles," Hurn said, astonished. " 'She Loves You.' 'I Want to Hold Your Hand.' Like that."

"Oh, yes," Smith said vaguely.

Where is this guy from? Hurn wondered. *Mongolia?*

"What exactly is your proposition, Mr. Smith?"

The young man became business-like. He pulled a sheaf of notes from his briefcase. "One episode of *Stranger* was completed but not edited when the cancellation notice came from the network. We have acquired that footage, and it would be a simple matter to put it together. We have also acquired five scripts for the second season, commissioned prior to the cancellation. And we have an outline of your proposal for subsequent episodes, including a concluding episode in which the identity of Cooper is finally revealed. We would like you to supervise the preparation of these unwritten scripts and to write the final episode yourself. We are looking at a season of twenty-six fifty-minute episodes. For these services we are prepared to pay you the equivalent of two million dollars."

"The equivalent, Mr. Smith?"

"In gold, Mr. Hurn." The young man picked up the large suitcase he had brought with him into the writer's house. He opened it up. It was packed with yellowish metallic bars.

"My God," Hurn said. "That suitcase must weigh a hundred pounds."

"About one hundred and twenty-five pounds," said Mr. Smith. "Or the equivalent of about one million dollars at this morning's London gold fixing."

The young man, Hurn recalled, had carried in this suitcase without the slightest sign of exertion. He hefted it now as though it were full of feathers. Obviously he was not as frail as he looked.

"Tell me, Mr. Smith. Who is going to star in this show?"

"Oh. Vance Maccoby. Of course."

"Vance Maccoby, if he is even still alive, is a hopeless alcoholic, Mr. Smith. He hasn't worked in this town in twenty years. I don't even know where he is. Have you signed up Vance Maccoby, Mr. Smith?"

"Not yet," the young man said. "But we will. We will."

"My name's Loomis," said the tall man with the limp, as he stood beside Cooper at the bar. He picked up the shot glass and stared into it thoughtfully.

"First or last?" Cooper asked.

"Just Loomis," said the man.

"I'm Cooper," said the other. "Or at least that's what I call myself. One name's as good as another. There was a book in my saddle-bag by a man named Cooper. . . ."

"You forgot your name?"

"I forgot everything," he said. "Except how to speak and ride and shoot."

Loomis drained his drink. "Some things a man don't forget," he said.

Cooper stared at him intently. "Have I seen you in here before? There's something familiar. . . ."

"I don't think so," Loomis said. "I'm a stranger here myself."

The edges of the TV screen grew misty, then blurred. The picture dissolved. Another took shape. A bright, almost hallucinatory bright summer day. A farm house. Chickens in a coop. The door of the house open, banging in the wind.

The camera moved through the door, into a parlour. Signs of struggle, furniture up-ended, a broken dish on the floor. A man stopped to pick up the fragments.

"Aimee?" he called. "Aimee?"

The camera moved on, into a bedroom. A woman's body sprawled brokenly across the bed. The window open, the curtain blowing. And then a face, a man's face, staring into the room. His arm, holding a gun. A gunshot.

Darkness closed in. Outside, the shadow of a man running away. A shadow with a kind of limp.

And back, suddenly, to the bar.

"You all right, Cooper?"

"I'm all right," he said, gripping the bar tightly. "I'm all right."

"Yehh," said the fat bald man in the armchair. "Let's hear it for the strong silent ones."

He picked up his glass from the TV table in front of him, made a mocking toast to the blank screen, then winked to his old agent, Feldman, sitting on the couch next to the young man. There was something a little odd about the young man, but the fat man was too drunk to put his finger on it. Maybe it was the Desi Arnaz hair cut. . . .

"Vance," Feldman said. "Vance I—I hate to see you like this."

"Like what?" said the fat man who had once been Vance Maccoby. "And the name is Henry. Henry Mulvin."

He raised his bulk from the armchair and waddled into the tiny kitchen of the trailer to refreshen his drink.

Feldman looked helplessly at the young man.

"I told you, Smith. I told you this was pointless. You're going to have to find yourself another boy. Jesus, there must be hundreds in this town."

"There's only one Vance Maccoby," the young man said firmly. "Mr. Feldman, would you leave us together for a while? I promise you that I'll be in touch in the morning with regard to contractual arrangements."

"Contractual arrangements? You're whistling in the wind."

"I can be quite persuasive, Mr. Feldman. Believe me."

I believe you, Feldman thought. *Or what would I be doing in this stinking trailer?*

When the sound of Feldman's Mercedes had disappeared into the distance, the young man turned to Vance Maccoby.

"Mr. Maccoby," he said almost apologetically, "we have to have a serious talk. And in order to do that you will have to be sober."

"Sober?" The fat man laughed. "Never heard of it."

"This won't hurt," the young man said, producing a flat, boxlike device from his pocket and pointing it at the fat man. "It will merely accelerate the metabolization of the alcohol in your bloodstream." He pushed a button.

"But I don't *want* to be sober," the fat man said. He began to cry.

"When this is all over, Mr. Maccoby," the young man said soothingly, "you need never be sober nor unhappy ever again."

"Guess I should ride on," Cooper said. "You got a nice little town here and I could easily settle in it. Easily. But a man can't settle anyplace until he knows who he is."

"You think he knows?" the girl asked. "You think that limping man knows who you are?"

"Yes, he does," Cooper said. "He knows, and he's going to tell me. Fact is, he's itching to tell me. He thinks he just wants to kill me, but first of all he wants to tell me. Otherwise he would have just finished me off back at Oscar's barn. Him and me, reckon we got ourselves a piece of unfinished business. But he's got the better of me, because he knows what it is."

"He may kill you yet," the girl said, dabbing at the tears that had begun to well up in her eyes.

"I can take care of myself."

"Will you come back?" she asked. "Afterward?"

"Maybe so," he said. "Maybe so."

He rode off into the distance.

"Print it," said the director. "And see you all tomorrow."

Carefully, Vance Maccoby dismounted from his horse and began to walk back to his dressing room. Bill Hurn fell in step with him.

"That was good stuff, Vance," he said.

Maccoby smiled, although it was more like a tic. The skin of his face had been stretched tight by the face-lift operations, so that his usual expression was even blanker than it had been in his heyday. He took off his hat and ran his hand through his recently transplanted hair. Under the supervision of the strange young man called Smith, he had lost close to a hundred pounds in the three months prior to shooting.

For all of these changes, Maccoby close up looked every one of his forty-six years. The doctors could do little about the lines around his eyes, and nothing at all about the weariness in them. And yet the camera was still good to him, particularly in black and white. Hurn had argued fiercely on the subject of film stock, but Smith had been adamant. "It must be black and white. Just like the original. Cost is not the question. This is a matter of aesthetics."

Black and white helped hide the ravages of time. It just made Maccoby look more intense, more haunted. Perhaps that was why Smith had been so insistent. But Hurn doubted that. In many ways Smith was astonishingly ignorant of the mechanics of filmmaking.

"I didn't know," Maccoby said, "that *he* was still in here." He pointed to his chest.

"Cooper?"

"Maccoby," he said. "Vance Maccoby. Inside me, Henry Mulvin. Still there, after all these years. I thought I'd finished him off for good. But he was still in there."

Maccoby had not, to Hurn's knowledge, touched a drop of alcohol in six months. He was functioning well on the set, with none of the moodiness or tantrums that had marked his final days in Hollywood. But the stripping away of that alcoholic haze had only revealed the deeper sickness beneath: his unbearable discomfort with himself, or rather with the fictional person he had become—Vance Maccoby, TV star. Isolated, cut off, torn away from his roots, existing only on a million TV screens and in the pages of mass-circulation magazines.

Was that, Hurn wondered—and not for the first time—why he had made such a great Cooper? Despite his mediocrity as an actor, there had never been anyone else to play the role.

"Vance," he said. "Henry. . . ."

"Call me Vance. You always did. That's who I am here. For this little command performance."

"Vance, why did you agree to do this?"

"Why did you agree, Bill? And don't tell me it was the money. You don't care about the money any more than I do. You have all you want. I had all I needed to stay drunk."

"I don't know," Hurn said. "Smith . . . He just made it seem so *important.* Like there were millions of people just sitting around waiting for a new season of *Stranger in Town.* He flattered me. And he tempted me. This was my baby, remember, and the network killed it. And I suppose there was a part of me that always wanted to do this. Finish it properly, tie up all those loose ends . . . And yet I know the whole thing is crazy. This show will never run on a U.S. network. Not in black and white. Unless we put it straight into reruns." He snickered. "Maybe that's the plan. I mean, who would even know the difference? This whole thing is so—1960."

They had reached Maccoby's dressing room.

"Well," Maccoby said, "Smith is telling the truth, in a way. There *are* millions of people waiting for this."

"In Hong Kong? North Korea? I mean, where does he expect to sell this stuff? Who are these overseas investors of his? How can he piss so much money away like water, and how does he expect to ever recoup it? The whole thing is bizarre."

"Oh, it's bizarre all right," Maccoby said. "It sure is bizarre." He glanced up briefly into the hard blue sky. Then he said, "Well, I better get cleaned up."

"You killed her," Cooper said. "You killed her and you tried to kill me. But somehow I survived. And I crawled out of there, halfway out of my mind. And I crawled into the desert. And a wagon train found me. And they carried me along with them, and nursed me. And when I woke up I didn't even know my name. You took it. You took away my name."

"Stevens," Loomis said. "Brad Stevens." His hand did not waver on the gun.

"Oh, I remember that now," he said. "I remember it all. I remember Aimee . . . I remember it all."

"I'm glad about that," Loomis said. "I truly am. I've been waiting for you to remember for the most wearisome time. Not much sense in killing a person when he doesn't even know why."

He tightened his grip on the trigger. "But there's something more," he said. "More than that. Something you couldn't remember, because you never knew. Something I have been meaning to tell you for a long time. Longer than you could imagine."

"Make sense," said the man who called himself Cooper. "Make some kind of sense."

"Your name," Loomis said. "It ain't really Stevens. Not really. The name you've been trying so hard to remember isn't even your real name. Isn't that a hoot? Isn't that the funniest thing you ever heard?" He laughed.

"Make sense," said the man on the ground. "You're still not making any."

"Stevens," Loomis said. "That's just a name they gave you. The folks who picked you out at the orphanage. Picked out the pretty little baby. That was their name. Good God-fearing folks. But they only wanted the one, and they wanted a baby, not a full-grown child. And for sure they didn't want a gimp."

"I was adopted? You're saying I was adopted? How could you know that?"

"I was there, little brother. I was there. I was the gimp they passed over for the pretty little baby. I was only four years old at the time. But some things you really don't forget."

"Brother?"

"Right," Loomis said. "You and me, we're children of the very same flesh. Arnold and Mary Jane Loomis. Nobody ever changed my name. Nobody wanted the poor little cripple boy."

"Our parents. . . ."

"Dead," Loomis said. "Indians. They killed Pa. Killed Ma, too, after

they were through with her. Would have killed us, too, except they got interrupted."

Slowly, deliberately, the man who had been called Cooper climbed to his feet. "We were separated?" he said.

"For nearly thirty years. You eating your good home cooking and me eating the poor-house gruel. You growing into a solid citizen and marrying and farming. And me drifting from town to town like a piece of dried-up horse dung blown around by the wind. Never finding a place I could call home. And looking, looking for my little brother. And finally I found you. . . ."

"Why?" he asked. "Why did you do it?"

"I didn't mean to . . ." Loomis faltered. "It was like a kind of madness came over me. Seeing your house and your farm and your wife, everything you had and I didn't, everything I hated you for having . . . But I don't know. Maybe that was what I was intending all along, intending to make you suffer just a little of what I had to suffer. I don't know. I don't think I meant to kill Aimee, but when I did I knew I would have to kill you, too. And I thought I did. And then I saw you alive. And I realized that you didn't remember, didn't remember a single thing. So I just waited, watched and waited, until you did start to remember. So you would know why I had to kill you. And now it's time. It's time."

"You can't stand yourself, brother, can you?" said the man who had been called Cooper. "You and you, they don't get along at all. I can understand that. I been through a little of that myself. Not knowing who the hell I was or what I might have done or what I should be doing. But you find out. Maybe not your name, but how you should be living. If you're any good at all, you find that out."

He took a step toward Loomis. "But you're not any good, brother, and you never were. Sure, you had some lousy breaks, sure you did. But that isn't any kind of excuse for what you did. You're just no good to anyone, not even yourself. And if you kill me, you'll have nothing to live for. Nothing. Because nobody will know your name and nobody will care."

Another step.

"But I care, brother. I care in the worst way. You made me care. Buzzing around me like some house-fly waiting to be swatted. Waiting for me to remember. Trying to make me remember. Remember you."

Another step. He was only a few paces from Loomis now. He glanced down to his own gun on the floor of the stable. It was nearly within reach.

"Stay there," Loomis said. "Stay right where you are."

He took another step.

"I remember you, brother. For what you did to me. No one else will. Kill me and you'll be alone again, alone with yourself, the way you always were. Run away now and you'll have something to keep you going. Fear,

brother. Fear. That's a kind of something. Something to make you feel alive. And me, too. I'll have something to keep me going, too."

Loomis took a step backward. "Don't move," he said. "Don't move or I'll kill you now."

"What are you waiting for?" his brother asked him.

The gun wavered in his hand.

The man who had called himself Cooper stooped swiftly and scooped up his own gun from the floor.

Two guns blared.

Loomis stood straight for a moment. A strange smile spread over his face. And then, slowly, he crumpled to the floor of the stable.

The other continued to stand, in the clearing smoke, holding his wounded left arm.

"Damn," he said softly. "Damn."

The lights in the screening room came up. One man was applauding vigorously. Smith. All heads turned toward him.

"Bit of an anticlimax," Hurn said, "don't you think? We were afraid it might be. I think, in a way, we were afraid of having to finish it."

"On the contrary, Mr. Hurn," Smith said. "On the contrary. It's absolutely perfect. Perfect. Real mythic power. A glimpse into the human condition. Into a world in which brother must slay brother, even as Cain slew Abel. *Archetypal,* Mr. Hurn. Archetypal."

He stood up and addressed the small crowd.

"I want to thank all of you," he said, "for making this possible. In particular I want to thank Mr. Hurn and the one and only Vance Maccoby, without whom none of this would have been possible."

Maccoby grinned in a spaced-out way. Hurn could smell the drink on his breath from two rows away.

The cure didn't take, he thought. *Well, it took for long enough.*

"I will be leaving town tomorrow," Smith said, "and I will not be returning in the near future. So let me just say what a wonderful group of people you have been to work with, and what a great, great privilege this has been for me."

There was still, Hurn reflected, something rather odd about the young man. He was dressed now in what could pass as the uniform of the young Hollywood executive—safari jacket, open-collar sports shirt, gold medallion, aviator shades—and yet there was still something not quite *right* about it. He looked as if he had just stepped out of central casting.

"The show," Hurn said, as Smith headed toward the door. "When is the show going to run?"

"Oh, soon," Smith said. "Not in this country, at the present time, but we have plenty of interest overseas."

A Canadian tax shelter? Hurn wondered. *One of those productions that never actually play anywhere? But surely they would not have gone to so much trouble.*

"Where?" he persisted. "Where will it run?"

"Oh, faraway places," Smith said, fingering his aviator shades. "Far, far away." He disappeared through the door. Hurn would not see him again.

"Far away," Hurn repeated to himself.

"Very far," Maccoby said, staggering a little as he rose from his seat in the back row. He was quite drunk.

"You know something I don't know?" Hurn asked, following him from the screening room.

"Very far," Maccoby repeated, as they stepped into the parking lot. The smog was thin that night. Stars twinkled faintly in the sky. "About twenty light-years," he said, looking up.

"What?"

"Twenty light-years," he repeated. "Twenty years for the signals to reach them. Distant, distant signals. And then they stop. The signals stop. Before the story ends. And they don't like that."

"They?"

"Smith's people. Our overseas investors. Our faraway fans."

"Wait a minute," Hurn said. "You're telling me that our show was picked up . . . out there?"

Now he, too, craned his head to look up into the night sky. He shivered.

"I don't believe it," he said.

"Sure you do," Maccoby said.

"But it's crazy," Hurn said. "The whole thing is incredible. Up to and including the fact that they picked on our show."

"I wondered about that myself," Maccoby said. "But you've got to figure that their tastes are going to be, well . . . *different.*"

"Then he really meant it," Hurn said. "When he said that our show was—what did he call it? The peak of televisual art."

Maccoby nodded. "He really meant it."

"Art." Hurn tested the word on his tongue. "Life is short but art is long. Isn't that what they say? Something like that, at any rate."

"Right," Maccoby said absently. "Art. Or something like that."

He was staring now at the great mast of the TV antenna on the hill above the studio.

"Signals," he said again. "Distant, distant signals."

(1984)

KIM STANLEY ROBINSON

THE LUCKY STRIKE

War breeds strange pastimes. In July of 1945 on Tinian Island in the North Pacific, Captain Frank January had taken to piling pebble cairns on the crown of Mount Lasso—one pebble for each B-29 takeoff, one cairn for each mission. The largest cairn had four hundred stones in it. It was a mindless pastime, but so was poker. The men of the 509th had played a million hands of poker, sitting in the shade of a palm around an upturned crate sweating in their skivvies, swearing and betting all their pay and cigarettes, playing hand after hand after hand, until the cards got so soft and dog-eared you could have used them for toilet paper. Captain January had gotten sick of it, and after he lit out for the hilltop a few times some of his crewmates started trailing him. When their pilot Jim Fitch joined them it became a official pastime, like throwing flares into the compound or going hunting for stray Japs. What Captain January thought of the development he didn't say. The others grouped near Captain Fitch, who passed around his battered flask. "Hey, January," Fitch called. "Come have a shot."

January wandered over and took the flask. Fitch laughed at his pebble. "Practising your bombing up here, eh, Professor?"

"Yah," January said sullenly. Anyone who read more than the funnies was Professor to Fitch. Thirstily January knocked back some rum. He could drink it any way he pleased up here, out from under the eye of the group psychiatrist. He passed the flask on to Lieutenant Matthews, their navigator.

"That's why he's the best," Matthews joked. "Always practising."

Fitch laughed. "He's best because I make him be best, right, Professor?"

January frowned. Fitch was a bulky youth, thick-featured, pig-eyed—a thug, in January's opinion. The rest of the crew were all in their mid-twenties like Fitch, and they liked the captain's bossy roughhouse style. January, who was thirty-seven, didn't go for it. He wandered away, back to the cairn he had been building. From Mount Lasso they had an overview of the whole island, from the harbor at Wall Street to the north field in Harlem. January had observed hundreds of B-29s roar off the four parallel runways of the north field and head for Japan. The last quartet of this particular mission buzzed across the width of the island, and January dropped four more pebbles, aiming for crevices in the pile. One of them stuck nicely.

"There they are!" said Matthews. "They're on the taxing strip."

January located the 509th's first plane. Today, the first of August, there was something more interesting to watch than the usual Superfortress parade. Word was out that General Le May wanted to take the 509th's mission away from it. Their commander Colonel Tibbets had gone and bitched to Le May in person, and the general had agreed the mission was theirs, but on one condition: one of the general's men was to make a test flight with the 509th, to make sure they were fit for combat over Japan. The general's man had arrived, and now he was down there in the strike plane, with Tibbets and the whole first team. January sidled back to his mates to view the takeoff with them.

"Why don't the strike plane have a name, though?" Haddock was saying.

Fitch said, "Lewis won't give it a name because it's not his plane, and he knows it." The others laughed. Lewis and his crew were naturally unpopular, being Tibbets' favorites.

"What do you think he'll do to the general's man?" Matthews asked.

The others laughed at the very idea. "He'll kill an engine at takeoff, I bet you anything," Fitch said. He pointed at the wrecked B-29s that marked the end of every runway, planes whose engines had given out on takeoff. "He'll want to show that he wouldn't go down if it happened to him."

"Course he wouldn't!" Matthews said.

"You hope," January said under his breath.

"They let those Wright engines out too soon," Haddock said seriously. "They keep busting under the takeoff load."

"Won't matter to the old bull," Matthews said. Then they all started in about Tibbets' flying ability, even Fitch. They all thought Tibbets was the greatest. January, on the other hand, liked Tibbets even less than he liked Fitch. That had started right after he was assigned to the 509th. He had been told he was part of the most important group in the war, and then given a leave. In Vicksburg a couple of fliers just back from England had bought him a lot of whiskies, and since January had spent several months stationed near London they had talked for a good long time and gotten pretty drunk. The two were really curious about what January was up to now, but he had stayed vague on it and kept returning the talk to the blitz. He had been seeing an English nurse, for instance, whose flat had been bombed, family and neighbors killed. . . . But they had really wanted to know. So he had told them he was onto something special, and they had flipped out their badges and told him they were Army Intelligence, and that if he ever broke security like that again he'd be transferred to Alaska. It was a dirty trick. January had gone back to Wendover and told Tibbets so to his face, and Tibbets had turned red and threatened him some more. January despised him for that. The upshot was that January was effectively out of the war, because Tibbets really played his favorites. January wasn't sure he really minded, but during their year's training he had bombed better than ever, as a way of showing the old bull he was wrong to write January off. Every time their eyes had met it was clear what was going on. But Tibbets never backed off no matter how precise January's bombing got. Just thinking about it was enough to cause January to line up a pebble over an ant and drop it.

"Will you cut that out?" Fitch complained. "I swear you must hang from the ceiling when you take a shit so you can practice aiming for the toilet." The men laughed.

"Don't I bunk over you?" January asked. Then he pointed. "They're going."

Tibbets' plane had taxied to runway Baker. Fitch passed the flask around again. The tropical sun beat on them, and the ocean surrounding the island blazed white. January put up a sweaty hand to aid the bill of his baseball cap.

The four props cut in hard, and the sleek Superfortress quickly trundled up to speed and roared down Baker. Three-quarters of the way down the strip the outside right prop feathered.

"Yow!" Fitch crowed. "I told you he'd do it!"

The plane nosed off the ground and slewed right, then pulled back on course to cheers from the four young men around January. January pointed again. "He's cut number three, too."

The inside right prop feathered, and now the plane was pulled up by the left wing only, while the two right props windmilled uselessly. "Holy smoke!" Haddock cried. "Ain't the old bull something?"

They whooped to see the plane's power, and Tibbets' nervy arrogance.

"By God, Le May's man will remember this flight," Fitch hooted. "Why, look at that! He's banking!"

Apparently taking off on two engines wasn't enough for Tibbets; he banked the plane right until it was standing on its dead wing, and it curved back toward Tinian.

Then the inside left engine feathered.

War tears at the imagination. For three years Frank January had kept his imagination trapped, refusing to give it any play whatsoever. The dangers threatening him, the effects of the bombs, the fate of the other participants in the war, he had refused to think about any of it. But the war tore at his control. That English nurse's flat. The missions over the Ruhr. The bomber just below him blown apart by flak. And then there had been a year in Utah, and the vise-like grip that he had once kept on his imagination had slipped away.

So when he saw the number two prop feather, his heart gave a little jump against his sternum and helplessly he was up there with Ferebee, the first team bombardier. He would be looking over the pilots' shoulders. . . .

"Only one engine?" Fitch said.

"That one's for real," January said harshly. Despite himself he *saw* the panic in the cockpit, the frantic rush to power the two right engines. The plane was dropping fast and Tibbets leveled it off, leaving them on a course back toward the island. The two right props spun, blurred to a shimmer. January held his breath. They needed more lift; Tibbets was trying to pull it over the island. Maybe he was trying for the short runway on the south half of the island.

But Tinian was too tall, the plane too heavy. It roared right into the jungle above the beach, where 42nd Street met their East River. It exploded in a bloom of fire. By the time the sound of the explosion struck them they knew no one in the plane had survived.

Black smoke towered into white sky. In the shocked silence on Mount Lasso insects buzzed and creaked. The air left January's lungs with a gulp. He had been with Ferebee there at the end, he had heard the desperate shouts, seen the last green rush, been stunned by the dentist-drill-all-over pain of the impact.

"Oh my God," Fitch was saying. "Oh my God." Matthews was sitting. January picked up the flask, tossed it at Fitch.

"C-come on," he stuttered. He hadn't stuttered since he was sixteen. He led the others in a rush down the hill. When they got to Broadway a jeep careened toward them and skidded to a halt. It was Colonel Scholes, the old bull's exec. "What happened?"

Fitch told him.

"Those damned Wrights," Scholes said as the men piled in. This time one had failed at just the wrong moment; some welder stateside had kept flame to metal a second less than usual—or something equally minor, equally trivial—and that had made all the difference.

They left the jeep at 42nd and Broadway and hiked east over a narrow track to the shore. A fairly large circle of trees was burning. The fire trucks were already there.

Scholes stood besides January, his expression bleak. "That was the whole first team," he said.

"I know," said January. He was still in shock, in imagination crushed, incinerated, destroyed. Once as a kid he had tied sheets to his arms and waist, jumped off the roof and landed right on his chest; this felt like that had. He had no way of knowing what would come of this crash, but he had a suspicion that he had indeed smacked into something hard.

Scholes shook his head. A half-hour had passed, the fire was nearly out. January's four mates were over chattering with the Seabees. "He was going to name the plane after his mother," Scholes said to the ground. "He told me that just this morning. He was going to call it *Enola Gay.*"

At night the jungle breathed, and its hot wet breath washed over the 509th's compound. January stood in the doorway of his Quonset barracks hoping for a real breeze. No poker tonight. Voices were hushed, faces solemn. Some of the men had helped box up the dead crew's gear. Now most lay on their bunks. January gave up on the breeze, climbed onto his top bunk to stare at the ceiling.

He observed the corrugated arch over him. Cricketsong sawed through his thoughts. Below him a rapid conversation was being carried on in guilty undertones, Fitch at its center. "January is the best bombardier left," he said. "And I'm as good as Lewis was."

"But so is Sweeney," Matthews said. "And he's in with Scholes."

They were figuring out who would take over the strike. January scowled. Tibbets and the rest were less than twelve hours dead, and they were squabbling over who would replace them.

January grabbed a shirt, rolled off his bunk, put the shirt on.

"Hey, Professor," Fitch said. "Where you going?"

"Out."

Though midnight was near it was still sweltering. Crickets shut up as he walked by, started again behind him. He lit a cigarette. In the dark the MPs patrolling their fenced-in compound were like pairs of walking armbands. The 509th, prisoners in their own army. Fliers from other groups had taken to throwing rocks over the fence. Forcefully January expelled smoke, as if he could expel his disgust with it. They were only kids, he told himself. Their minds had been shaped in the war, by the war, and for the war. They knew you couldn't mourn the dead for long; carry around a load like that and your own engines might fail. That was all right with January. It was an attitude that Tibbets had helped to form, so it was what he deserved. Tibbets would *want* to be forgotten in favor of the mission, all he had lived for was to drop the gimmick on the Japs, he was oblivious to anything else, men, wife, family, anything.

So it wasn't the lack of feeling in his mates that bothered January.

And it was natural of them to want to fly the strike they had been training a year for. Natural, that is, if you were a kid with a mind shaped by fanatics like Tibbets, shaped to take orders and never imagine consequences. But January was not a kid, and he wasn't going to let men like Tibbets do a thing to his mind. And the gimmick . . . the gimmick was not natural. A chemical bomb of some sort, he guessed. Against the Geneva Convention. He stubbed his cigarette against the sole of his sneaker, tossed the butt over the fence. The tropical night breathed over him. He had a headache.

For months now he had been sure he would never fly a strike. The dislike Tibbets and he had exchanged in their looks (January was acutely aware of looks) had been real and strong. Tibbets had understood that January's record of pinpoint accuracy in the runs over the Salton Sea had been a way of showing contempt, a way of saying *you can't get rid of me even though you hate me and I hate you.* The record had forced Tibbets to keep January on one of the four second-string teams, but with the fuss they were making over the gimmick January had figured that would be far enough down the ladder to keep him out of things.

Now he wasn't so sure. Tibbets was dead. He lit another cigarette, found his hand shaking. The Camel tasted bitter. He threw it over the fence at a receding armband, and regretted it instantly. A waste. He went back inside.

Before climbing onto his bunk he got a paperback out of his footlocker. "Hey, Professor, what you reading now?" Fitch said, grinning.

January showed him the blue cover. *Winter's Tales,* by an Isak Dinesen. Fitch examined the little wartime edition. "Pretty racy, eh?"

"You bet," January said heavily. "This guy puts sex on every page." He climbed onto his bunk, opened the book. The stories were strange, hard to follow. The voices below bothered him. He concentrated harder.

As a boy on the farm in Arkansas, January had read everything he could lay his hands on. On Saturday afternoons he would race his father down the muddy lane to the mailbox (his father was a reader too), grab the *Saturday Evening Post* and run off to devour every word of it. That meant he had another week with nothing new to read, but he couldn't help it. His favorites were the Hornblower stories, but anything would do. It was a way off the farm, a way into the world. He had become a man who could slip between the covers of a book whenever he chose.

But not on this night.

• • •

The next day the chaplain gave a memorial service, and on the morning after that Colonel Scholes looked in the door of their hut right after mess. "Briefing at eleven," he announced. His face was haggard. "Be there early." He looked at Fitch with bloodshot eyes, crooked a finger. "Fitch, January, Matthews—come with me."

January put on his shoes. The rest of the men sat on their bunks and watched them wordlessly. January followed Fitch and Matthews out of the hut.

"I've spent most of the night on the radio with General Le May," Scholes said. He looked them each in the eye. "We've decided you're to be the first crew to make a strike."

Fitch was nodding, as if he had expected it.

"Think you can do it?" Scholes said.

"Of course," Fitch replied. Watching him January understood why they had chosen him to replace Tibbets: Fitch was like the old bull, he had that same ruthlessness. The young bull.

"Yes, sir," Matthews said.

Scholes was looking at him. "Sure," January said, not wanting to think about it. "Sure." His heart was pounding directly on his sternum. But Fitch and Matthews looked serious as owls, so he wasn't going to stick out by looking odd. It was big news, after all; anyone would be taken aback by it. Nevertheless, January made an effort to nod.

"Okay," Scholes said. "McDonald will be flying with you as co-pilot." Fitch frowned. "I've got to go tell those British officers that Le May doesn't want them on the strike with you. See you at the briefing."

"Yes, sir."

As soon as Scholes was around the corner Fitch swung a fist at the sky. "Yow!" Matthews cried. He and Fitch shook hands. "We did it!" Matthews took January's hand and wrung it, his face plastered with a goofy grin. "We did it!"

"Somebody did it, anyway," January said.

"Ah, Frank," Matthews said. "Show some spunk. You're always so cool."

"Old Professor Stoneface," Fitch said, glancing at January with a trace of amused contempt. "Come on, let's get to the briefing."

The briefing hut, one of the longer Quonsets, was completely surrounded by MPs holding carbines. "Gosh," Matthews said, subdued by the sight. Inside it was already smoky. The walls were covered by the usual maps of Japan. Two blackboards at the front were draped with sheets. Captain Shepard, the naval officer who worked with the scientists on the gimmick, was in back with his assistant Lieutenant Stone, winding a reel of film onto a projector. Dr. Nelson, the group psychiatrist, was already seated on a front bench near the wall. Tibbets had recently sicced the psychiatrist on the group—another one of his great ideas, like the spies in the bar. The man's questions had struck January as stupid.

He hadn't even been able to figure out that Easterly was a flake, something that was clear to anybody who flew with him, or even played him in a single round of poker. January slid onto a bench beside his mates.

The two Brits entered, looking furious in their stiff-upper-lip way. They sat on the bench behind January. Sweeney's and Easterly's crew filed in, followed by the other men, and soon the room was full. Fitch and the rest pulled out Lucky Strikes and lit up; since they had named the plane only January had stuck with Camels.

Scholes came in with several men January didn't recognize, and went to the front. The chatter died, and all the smoke plumes ribboned steadily into the air.

Scholes nodded, and two intelligence officers took the sheets off the blackboards, revealing aerial reconnaissance photos.

"Men," Scholes said, "these are the target cities."

Someone cleared his throat.

"In order of priority they are Hiroshima, Kokura, and Nagasaki. There will be three weather scouts: *Straight Flush* to Hiroshima, *Strange Cargo* to Kokura, and *Full House* to Nagasaki. *The Great Artiste* and *Number 91* will be accompanying the mission to take photos. And *Lucky Strike* will fly the bomb."

There were rustles, coughs. Men turned to look at January and his mates, and they all sat up straight. Sweeney stretched back to shake Fitch's hand, and there were some quick laughs. Fitch grinned.

"Now listen up," Scholes went on. "The weapon we are going to deliver was successfully tested stateside a couple of weeks ago. And now we've got orders to drop it on the enemy." He paused to let that sink in. "I'll let Captain Shepard tell you more."

Shepard walked to the blackboard slowly, savoring his entrance. His forehead was shiny with sweat, and January realized he was excited or nervous. He wondered what the shrink would make of that.

"I'm going to come right to the point," Shepard said. "The bomb you are going to drop is something new in history. We think it will knock out everything within four miles."

Now the room was completely still. January noticed that he could see a great deal of his nose, eyebrows, and cheeks; it was as if he were receding back into his body, like a fox into its hole. He kept his gaze rigidly on Shepard, steadfastly ignoring the feeling. Shepard pulled a sheet back over a blackboard while someone else turned down the lights.

"This is a film of the only test we have made," Shepard said. The film started, caught, started again. A wavery cone of bright cigarette smoke speared the length of the room, and on the sheet sprang a dead gray landscape: a lot of sky, a smooth desert floor, hills in the distance. The projector went *click-click-click-click, click-click-click-click.* "The bomb is on top of the tower," Shepard said, and January focused on the pin-like object sticking out of the desert floor, off against the hills. It was between eight and ten miles from the camera, he judged; he had gotten good at calculating distances. He was still distracted by his face.

Click-click-click-click, click—then the screen went white for a second, filling even their room with light. When the picture returned the desert floor was filled with a white bloom of fire. The fireball coalesced and then quite suddenly it leaped off the earth all the way into the *stratosphere,* by God, like a tracer bullet leaving a machine-gun, trailing a whitish pillar of smoke behind it. The pillar gushed up and a growing ball of smoke billowed outward, capping the pillar. January calculated the size of the cloud, but was sure he got it wrong. There it stood. The picture flickered, and then the screen went white again, as if the camera had melted or that part of the world had come apart. But the flapping from the projector told them it was the end of the film.

January felt the air suck in and out of his open mouth. The lights came on in the smoky room and for a second he panicked, he struggled to shove his features into an accepted pattern, the shrink would be looking around at them all—and then he glanced around and realized he needn't have worried, that he wasn't alone. Faces were bloodless, eyes were blinky or bug-eyed with shock, mouths hung open or were clamped whitely shut. For a few moments they all had to acknowledge what they were doing. January, scaring himself, felt an urge to say, "Play it again, will you?" Fitch was pulling his curled black hair off his thug's forehead uneasily. Beyond him January saw that one of the Limeys had already reconsidered how mad he was about missing the flight. Now he looked sick. Someone let out a long *whew,* another whistled. January looked to the front again, where the shrink watched them, undisturbed.

Shepard said, "It's big, all right. And no one knows what will happen when it's dropped from the air. But the mushroom cloud you saw will go to at least thirty thousand feet, probably sixty. And the flash you saw at the beginning was hotter than the sun."

Hotter than the sun. More licked lips, hard swallows, readjusted baseball caps. One of the intelligence officers passed out tinted goggles like welder's glasses. January took his and twiddled the opacity dial.

Scholes said, "You're the hottest thing in the armed forces, now. So no talking, even among yourselves." He took a deep breath. "Let's do it the way Colonel Tibbets would have wanted us to. He picked every one of you because you were the best, and now's the time to show he was right. So—so let's make the old man proud."

The briefing was over. Men filed out into the sudden sunlight. Into the heat and glare. Captain Shepard approached Fitch. "Stone and I will be flying with you to take care of the bomb," he said.

Fitch nodded. "Do you know how many strikes we'll fly?"

"As many as it takes to make them quit." Shepard stared hard at all of them. "But it will only take one."

War breeds strange dreams. That night January writhed over his sheets in the hot wet vegetable darkness, in that frightening half-sleep when you sometimes know you are dreaming but can do nothing about it, and he dreamed he was walking . . .

. . . walking through the streets when suddenly the sun swoops down, the sun touches down and everything is instantly darkness and smoke and silence, a deaf roaring. Walls of fire. His head hurts and in the middle of his vision is a bluewhite blur as if God's camera went off in his face. Ah—the sun fell, he thinks. His arm is burned. Blinking is painful. People stumbling by, mouths open, horribly burned—

He is a priest, he can feel the clerical collar, and the wounded ask him for help. He points to his ears, tries to touch them but can't. Pall of black smoke over everything, the city has fallen into the streets. Ah, it's the end of the world. In a park he finds shade and cleared ground. People crouch under bushes like frightened animals. Where the park meets the river red and black figures crowd into steaming water. A figure gestures from a copse of bamboo. He enters it, finds five or six faceless soldiers huddling. Their eyes have melted, their mouths are holes. Deafness spares him their words. The sighted soldier mimes drinking. The soldiers are thirsty. He nods and goes to the river in search of a container. Bodies float downstream.

Hours pass as he hunts fruitlessly for a bucket. He pulls people from the rubble. He hears a bird screeching and he realizes that his deafness is the roar of the city burning, a roar like the blood in his ears but he is not deaf, he only thought he was deaf because there are no human cries. The people are suffering in silence. Through the dusky night he stumbles back to the river, pain crashing through his head. In a field men are pulling potatoes out of the ground that have been baked well enough to eat. He shares one with them. At the river everyone is dead—

—and he struggled out of the nightmare drenched in rank sweat, the taste of dirt in his mouth, his stomach knotted with horror. He sat up and the wet rough sheet clung to his skin. His heart felt crushed between lungs desperate for air. The flowery rotting jungle smell filled him and images from the dream flashed before him so vividly that in the dim hut he saw nothing else. He grabbed his cigarettes and jumped off the bunk, hurried out into the compound. Trembling he lit up, started pacing around. For a moment he worried that the idiot psychiatrist might see him, but then he dismissed the idea. Nelson would be asleep. They were all asleep. He shook his head, looked down at his right arm and almost dropped his cigarette—but it was just his stove scar, an old scar, he'd had it most of his life, since the day he'd pulled the frypan off the stove and onto his arm, burning it with oil. He could still remember the round O of fear that his mother's mouth had made as she rushed in to see what was wrong. Just an old burn scar, he thought, let's not go overboard here. He pulled his sleeve down.

For the rest of the night he tried to walk it off, cigarette after cigarette. The dome of the sky lightened until all the compound and the jungle beyond it was visible. He was forced by the light of day to walk back into his hut and lie down as if nothing had happened.

Two days later Scholes ordered them to take one of Le May's men over Rota for a test run. This new lieutenant colonel ordered Fitch not to play with the engines on takeoff. They flew a perfect run. January put the dummy gimmick right on the aiming point just as he had so often in the Salton Sea, and Fitch powered the plane down into the violent bank that started their 150-degree turn and flight for safety. Back on Tinian the lieutenant colonel congratulated them and shook each of their hands. January smiled with the rest, palms cool, heart steady. It was as if his body were a shell, something he could manipulate from without, like a bombsight. He ate well, he chatted as much as he ever had, and when the psychiatrist ran him to earth for some questions he was friendly and seemed open.

"Hello, doc."

"How do you feel about all this, Frank?"

"Just like I always have, sir. Fine."

"Eating well?"

"Better than ever."

"Sleeping well?"

"As well as I can in this humidity. I got used to Utah, I'm afraid." Dr. Nelson laughed. Actually January had hardly slept since his dream. He was afraid of sleep. Couldn't the man see that?

"And how do you feel about being part of the crew chosen to make the first strike?"

"Well, it was the right choice, I reckon. We're the b—the best crew left."

"Do you feel sorry about Tibbets' crew's accident?"

"Yes, sir, I do." You better believe it.

After the jokes and firm handshakes that ended the interview January walked out into the blaze of the tropical noon and lit a cigarette. He allowed himself to feel how much he despised the psychiatrist and his blind profession at the same time he was waving good-bye to the man. Ounce brain. Why couldn't he have seen? Whatever happened it would be his fault. . . . With a rush of smoke out of him January realized how painfully easy it was to fool someone if you wanted to. All action was no more than a mask that could be perfectly manipulated from somewhere else. And all the while in that somewhere else January lived in a *click-click-click* of film, in the silent roaring of a dream, struggling against images he couldn't dispel. The heat of the tropical sun—ninety-three million miles away, wasn't it?—pulsed painfully on the back of his neck.

As he watched the psychiatrist collar their tail-gunner Kochenski, he thought of walking up to the man and saying *I quit.* I don't want to do this. In imagination he saw the look that would form in the man's eye, in Fitch's eye, in Tibbets' eye, and his mind recoiled from the idea. He felt too much contempt for them. He wouldn't for anything give them a means to despise him, a reason to call him coward. Stubbornly he banished the whole complext of thought. Easier to go along with it.

And so a couple of disjointed days later, just after midnight of August 9th, he found himself preparing for the strike. Around him Fitch and Matthews and Haddock were doing the same. How odd were the everyday motions of getting dressed when you were off to demolish a city, to end a hundred thousand lives! January found himself examining his hands, his boots, the cracks in the linoleum. He put on his survival vest, checked the pockets abstractedly for fish-hooks, water kit, first aid package, emergency rations. Then the parachute harness, and his coveralls over it all. Tying his bootlaces took minutes; he couldn't do it when watching his fingers so closely.

"Come on, Professor!" Fitch's voice was tight. "The big day is here."

He followed the others into the night. A cool wind was blowing. The chaplain said a prayer for them. They took jeeps down Broadway to runway Able. *Lucky Strike* stood in a circle of spotlights and men, half of them with cameras, the rest with reporter's pads. They surrounded the crew; it reminded January of a Hollywood premiere. Eventually he escaped up the hatch and into the plane. Others followed. Half an hour passed before Fitch joined them, grinning like a movie star. They started the engines, and January was thankful for their vibrating, thought-smothering roar. They taxied away from the Hollywood scene and January felt relief for a moment, until he remembered where they were going. On runway Able the engines pitched up to their twenty-three hundred rpm whine, and looking out the clear windscreen he saw the runway paintmarks move by ever faster. Fitch kept them on the runway till Tinian had run out from under them, then quickly pulled up. They were on their way.

When they got to altitude January climbed past Fitch and McDonald to the bombardier's seat and placed his parachute on it. He leaned back. The roar of the four engines packed around him like cotton batting. He was on the flight, nothing to be done about it now. The heavy vibration was a comfort, he liked the feel of it there in the nose of the plane. A drowsy, sad acceptance hummed through him.

Against his closed eyelids flashed a black eyeless face and he jerked awake, heart racing. He was on the flight, no way out. Now he realized how easy it would have been to get out of it. He could have just said he didn't want to. The simplicity of it appalled him. Who gave a damn what the psychiatrist or Tibbets or anyone else thought, compared to this? Now there was no way out. It was a comfort, in a way. Now he could stop worrying, stop thinking he had any choice.

Sitting there with his knees bracketing the bombsight January dozed, and as he dozed he daydreamed his way out. He could climb the step to Fitch and McDonald and declare he had been secretly promoted to Major and ordered to re-direct the mission. They were to go to Tokyo and drop the bomb in the bay. The Jap war cabinet had been told to watch this demonstration of the new weapon, and when they saw that fireball boil the bay and bounce into heaven they'd run and sign surrender papers as fast as they could write, kamikazes or not. They weren't crazy, after all. No need to murder a whole city. It was such a good plan that the generals back home were no doubt changing the mission at this very minute, desperately radioing their instructions to Tinian, only to find out it was too late . . . so that when they returned to Tinian January would become a hero for guessing what the generals really wanted, and for risking all to do it. It would be like one of the Hornblower stories in the *Saturday Evening Post.*

Once again January jerked awake. The drowsy pleasure of the fantasy was replaced with desperate scorn. There wasn't a chance in hell that he could convince Fitch and the rest that he had secret orders superseding theirs. And he couldn't go up there and wave his pistol around and *order* them to drop the bomb in Tokyo Bay, because he was the one who had to actually drop it, and he couldn't be down in front dropping the bomb and up ordering the others around at the same time. Pipe dreams.

Time swept on, slow as a second hand. January's thoughts, however, matched the spin of the props; desperately they cast about, now this way now that, like an animal caught by the leg in a trap. The crew was silent. The clouds below were a white scree on the black ocean. January's knee vibrated against the squat stand of the bombsight. He was the one who had to drop the bomb. No matter where his thoughts lunged they were brought up short by that. He was the one, not Fitch or the crew, not Le May, not the generals and scientists back home, not Truman and his advisors. Truman—suddenly January hated him. Roosevelt would have done it differently. If only Roosevelt had lived! The grief that had filled January when he learned of Roosevelt's death reverberated through him again, more strongly than ever. It was unfair to have worked so hard and then not see the war's end. And FDR would have ended it differently. Back at the start of it all he had declared that civilian centers were never to be bombed, and if he had lived, if, if, if. But he hadn't. And now it was smiling bastard Harry Truman, ordering *him,* Frank January, to drop the sun on two hundred thousand women and children. Once his father had taken him to see the Browns play before twenty thousand, a giant crowd—"I never voted for you," January whispered viciously, and jerked to realize he had spoken aloud. Luckily his microphone was off. And Roosevelt would have done it differently, he *would have.*

The bombsight rose before him, spearing the black sky and blocking some of the hundreds of little cruciform stars. *Lucky Strike* ground on toward Iwo Jima, minute by minute flying four miles closer to their target. January leaned forward and put his face in the cool headrest of the bombsight, hoping that its grasp might hold his thoughts as well as his forehead. It worked surprisingly well.

His earphones crackled and he sat up. "Captain January." It was Shepard. "We're going to arm the bomb now, want to watch?"

"Sure thing." He shook his head, surprised at his own duplicity. Stepping up between the pilots, he moved stiffly to the roomy cabin behind the cockpit. Matthews was at his desk taking a navigational fix on the radio signals from Iwo Jima and Okinawa, and Haddock stood beside him. At the back of the compartment was a small circular hatch, below the larger tunnel leading to the rear of the plane. January opened it, sat down and swung himself feet first through the hole.

The bomb bay was unheated, and the cold air felt good. He stood facing the bomb. Stone was sitting on the floor of the bay; Shepard was laid out under the bomb, reaching into it. On a rubber pad next to Stone were tools, plates, several cylindrical blocks. Shepard pulled back, sat up, sucked a scraped knuckle. He shook his head ruefully: "I don't dare wear gloves with this one."

"I'd be just as happy myself if you didn't let something slip," January joked nervously. The two men laughed.

"Nothing can blow till I change those green wires to the red ones," Stone said.

"Give me the wrench," Shepard said. Stone handed it to him, and he stretched under the bomb again. After some awkward wrenching inside it he lifted out a cylindrical plug. "Breech plug," he said, and set it on the mat.

January found his skin goose-pimpling in the cold air. Stone handed

Shepard one of the blocks. Shepard extended under the bomb again. "Red ends toward the breech." "I know." Watching them January was reminded of auto mechanics on the oily floor of a garage, working under a car. He had spent a few years doing that himself, after his family moved to Vicksburg. Hiroshima was a river town. One time a flat-bed truck carrying bags of cement powder down Fourth Street hill had lost its brakes and careened into the intersection with River Road, where despite the driver's efforts to turn it smashed into a passing car. Frank had been out in the yard playing, had heard the crash and saw the cement dust rising. He had been one of the first there. The woman and child in the passenger seat of the Model T had been killed. The woman driving was okay. They were from Chicago. A group of folks subdued the driver of the truck, who kept trying to help at the Model T, though he had a bad cut on his head and was covered with white dust.

"Okay, let's tighten the breech plug." Stone gave Shepard the wrench. "Sixteen turns exactly," Shepard said. He was sweating even in the bay's chill, and he paused to wipe his forehead. "Let's hope we don't get hit by lightning." He put the wrench down and shifted onto his knees, picked up a circular plate. Hubcap, January thought. Stone connected wires, then helped Shepard install two more plates. Good old American know-how, January thought, goose-pimples rippling across his skin like cat's-paws over water. There was Shepard, a scientist, putting together a bomb like he was an auto mechanic changing oil and plugs. January felt a tight rush of rage at the scientists who had designed the bomb. They had worked on it for over a year down there in New Mexico, had none of them in all that time ever stopped to think what they were doing?

But none of them had to drop it. January turned to hide his face from Shepard, stepped down the bay. The bomb looked like a big long trashcan, with fins at one end and little antennae at the other. Just a bomb, he thought, damn it, it's just another bomb.

Shepard stood and patted the bomb gently. "We've got a live one now." Never a thought about what it would do. January hurried by the man, afraid that hatred would crack his shell and give him away. The pistol strapped to his belt caught on the hatchway and he imagined shooting Shepard—shooting Fitch and McDonald and plunging the controls forward so that *Lucky Strike* tilted and spun down into the sea like a spent tracer bullet, like a plane broken by flak, following the arc of all human ambition. Nobody would ever know what had happened to them, and their trashcan would be dumped at the bottom of the Pacific where it belonged. He could even shoot everyone and parachute out, and perhaps be rescued by one of the Superdumbos following them. . . .

The thought passed and remembering it January squinted with disgust. But another part of him agreed that it was a possibility. It could be done. It would solve his problem. His fingers explored his holster snap.

"Want some coffee?" Matthews asked.

"Sure," January said, and took his hand from the gun to reach for the cup. He sipped: hot. He watched Matthews and Benton tune the loran equipment. As the beeps came in Matthews took a straightedge and drew lines from Okinawa and Iwo Jima on his map table. He tapped a finger on the intersection. "They've taken the art out of navigation," he said to January. "They might as well stop making the navigator's dome," thumbing up at the little bubble over them.

"Good old American know-how," January said.

Matthews nodded. With two fingers he measured the distance between their position and Iwo Jima. Benton measured with a ruler.

"Rendezvous at five thirty-five, eh?" Matthews said. They were to rendezvous with the two trailing planes over Iwo.

Benton disagreed: "I'd say five-fifty."

"What? Check again, guy, we're not in no tugboat here."

"The wind—"

"Yah, the wind. Frank, you want to add a bet to the pool?"

"Five thirty-six," January said promptly.

They laughed. "See, he's got more confidence in me," Matthews said with a dopey grin.

January recalled his plan to shoot the crew and tip the plane into the sea, and he pursed his lips, repelled. Not for anything would he be able to shoot these men, who, if not friends, were at least companions. They passed for friends. They meant no harm.

Shepard and Stone climbed into the cabin. Matthews offered them coffee. "The gimmick's ready to kick their ass, eh?" Shepard nodded and drank.

January moved forward, past Haddock's console. Another plan that wouldn't work. What to do? All the flight engineer's dials and gauges showed conditions were normal. Maybe he could sabotage something? Cut a line somewhere?

Fitch looked back at him and said, "When are we due over Iwo?"

"Five forty, Matthews says."

"He better be right."

A thug. In peacetime Fitch would be hanging around a pool table giving the cops trouble. He was perfect for war. Tibbets had chosen his men well—most of them, anyway. Moving back past Haddock January stopped to stare at the group of men in the navigation cabin. They joked, drank coffee. They were all a bit like Fitch: young toughs, capable and thoughtless. They were having a good time, an adventure. That was January's dominant impression of his companions in the 509th; despite all the bitching and the occasional moments of overmastering fear, they were having a good time. His mind spun forward and he saw what these young men would grow up to be like as clearly as if they stood before him in businessmen's suits, prosperous and balding. They would be tough and capable and thoughtless, and as the years passed and the great war receded in time they would look back on it with ever-increasing nostalgia, for they would be the survivors and not the dead. Every year of this war would feel like ten in their memories, so that the war would always remain the central experience of their lives—a time when history lay palpable in their hands, when each of their daily acts affected it, when moral issues were simple, and others told them what to do—so that as more years passed and the survivors aged, bodies falling apart, lives in one rut or another, they would unconsciously push harder and harder to thrust the world into war again, thinking somewhere inside themselves that if they could only return to world war then they would magically be again as they were in the last one—young, and free, and happy. And by that time they would hold the positions of power, they would be capable of doing it.

So there would be more wars, January saw. He heard it in Matthews' laughter, saw it in their excited eyes. "There's Iwo, and it's five thirty-one. Pay up! I win!" And in future wars they'd have more bombs like the gimmick, hundreds of them no doubt. He saw more planes, more young crews like this one, flying to Moscow no doubt or to wherever, fireballs in every capital, why not? And to what end? To what end? So that the old men could hope to become magically young again. Nothing more sane than that.

They were over Iwo Jima. Three more hours to Japan. Voices from *The Great Artiste* and *Number 91* crackled on the radio. Rendezvous accomplished, the three planes flew northwest, toward Shikoku, the first Japanese island in their path. January went aft to use the toilet. "You okay, Frank?" Matthews asked. "Sure. Terrible coffee, though." "Ain't it always," January tugged at his baseball cap and hurried away. Kochenski and the other gunners were playing poker. When he was done he returned forward. Matthews sat on the stool before his maps, readying his equipment for the constant monitoring of drift that would now be required. Haddock and Benton were also busy at their stations. January maneuvered between the pilots down into the nose. "Good shooting," Matthews called after him.

Forward it seemed quieter. January got settled, put his headphones on and leaned forward to look out the ribbed Plexiglas.

Dawn had turned the whole vault of the sky pink. Slowly the radiant shade shifted through lavender to blue, pulse by pulse a different color. The ocean below was a glittering blue plane, marbled by a pattern of puffy pink cloud. The sky above was a vast dome, darker above than on the horizon. January had always thought that dawn was the time when you could see most clearly how big the earth was, and how high above it they flew. It seemed they flew at the very upper edge of the atmosphere, and January saw how thin it was, how it was just a skin of air really, so that even if you flew up to its top the earth still extended away infinitely in every direction. The coffee had warmed January, he was sweating. Sunlight blinked off the Plexiglas. His watch said six. Plane and hemisphere of blue were split down the middle by the bombsight. His earphones crackled and he listened in to the reports from the lead planes flying over the target cities. Kokura, Nagasaki, Hiroshima, all of them had six-tenths cloud cover. Maybe they would have to cancel the whole mission because of weather. "We'll look at Hiroshima first," Fitch said. January peered down at the fields of miniature clouds with renewed interest. His parachute slipped under him. Readjusting it he imagined putting it on, sneaking back to the central escape hatch under the navigator's cabin, opening the hatch . . . he could be out of the plane and gone before anyone noticed. Leave it up to them. They could bomb or not but it wouldn't be January's doing. He could float down onto the world like a puff of dandelion, feel cool air rush around him, watch the silk canopy dome hang over him like a miniature sky, a private world.

An eyeless black face. January shuddered; it was as though the nightmare could return any time. If he jumped nothing would change, the bomb would still fall—would he feel any better, floating on his Inland Sea? Sure, one part of him shouted; maybe, another conceded; the rest of him saw that face. . . .

Earphones crackled. Shepard said, "Lieutenant Stone has now armed the bomb, and I can tell you all what we are carrying. Aboard with us is the world's first atomic bomb."

Not exactly, January thought. Whistles squeaked in his earphones. The first one went off in New Mexico. Splitting atoms: January had heard the term before. Tremendous energy in every atom, Einstein had said. Break one, and—he had seen the result on film. Shepard was talking about radiation, which brought back more to January. Energy released in the form of X-rays. Killed by X-rays! It would be against the Geneva Convention if they had thought of it.

Fitch cut in. "When the bomb is dropped Lieutenant Benton will record our reaction to what we see. This recording is being made for history, so watch your language." Watch your language! January choked back a laugh. Don't curse or blaspheme God at the sight of the first atomic bomb incinerating a city and all its inhabitants with X-rays!

Six twenty. January found his hands clenched together on the headrest of the bombsight. He felt as if he had a fever. In the harsh wash of morning light the skin on the backs of his hands appeared slightly translucent. The whorls in the skin looked like the delicate patterning of waves on the sea's surface. His hands were made of atoms. Atoms were the smallest building block of matter, it took billions of them to make those tense, trembling hands. Split one atom and you had the fireball. That meant that the energy contained in even one hand . . . he turned up a palm to look at the lines and the mottled flesh under the transparent skin. A person was a bomb that could blow up the world. January felt that latent power stir in him, pulsing with every hard heart-knock. What beings they were, and in what a blue expanse of a world!—And here they spun on to drop a bomb and kill a hundred thousand of these astonishing beings.

When a fox or raccoon is caught by the leg in a trap, it lunges until the leg is frayed, twisted, perhaps broken, and only then does the animal's pain and exhaustion force it to quit. Now in the same way January wanted to quit. His mind hurt. His plans to escape were so much crap—stupid, useless. Better to quit. He tried to stop thinking, but it was hopeless. How could he stop? As long as he was conscious he would be thinking. The mind struggles longer in its traps than any fox.

Lucky Strike tilted up and began the long climb to bombing altitude. On the horizon the clouds lay over a green island. Japan. Surely it had gotten hotter, the heater must be broken, he thought. Don't think. Every few minutes Matthews gave Fitch small course adjustments. "Two seventy-five, now. That's it." To escape the moment January recalled his childhood. Following a mule and plow. Moving to Vicksburg (rivers). For a while there in Vicksburg, since his stutter made it hard to gain friends, he had played a game with himself. He had passed the time by imagining that everything he did was vitally important and determined the fate of the world. If he crossed a road in front of a certain car, for instance, then the car wouldn't make it through the next intersection before a truck hit it, and so the man driving would be killed and wouldn't be able to invent the flying boat that would save President Wilson from kidnappers—so he had to wait for that car because everything afterward depended on it. Oh damn it, he thought, damn it, think of something *different.* The last Hornblower story he had read—how would *he* get out of this? The round O of his mother's face as she ran in and saw his arm—The Mississippi, mud-brown behind its levees—Abruptly he shook his head, face twisted in frustration and despair, aware at last that no possible avenue of memory would serve as an escape for him now, for now there was no part of his life that did not apply to the situation he was in, and no matter where he cast his mind it was going to shore up against the hour facing him.

Less than an hour. They were at thirty thousand feet, bombing altitude. Fitch gave him altimeter readings to dial into the bombsight. Matthews gave him windspeeds. Sweat got in his eye and he blinked furiously. The sun rose behind them like an atomic bomb, glinting off every corner and edge of the Plexiglas, illuminating his bubble compartment with a fierce blare. Broken plans jumbled together in his mind, his breath was short, his throat dry. Uselessly and repeatedly he damned the scientists, damned Truman. Damned the Japanese for causing the whole mess in the first place, damned yellow killers, they had brought this on themselves. Remember Pearl. American men had died under bombs when no war had been declared; they had started it and now it was coming back to them with a vengeance. And they deserved it. And an invasion of Japan would take years, cost millions of lives—end it now, end it, they deserved it, they deserved it steaming river full of charcoal people silently dying damned stubborn race of maniacs!

"There's Honshu," Fitch said, and January returned to the world of the plane. They were over the Inland Sea. Soon they would pass the secondary target Kokura, a bit to the south. Seven thirty. The island was draped more heavily than the sea by clouds, and again January's heart leaped with the idea that weather would cancel the mission. But they did deserve it. It was a mission like any other mission. He had dropped bombs on Africa, Sicily, Italy, all Germany. . . . He leaned forward to take a look through the sight. Under the X of the crosshairs was the sea, but at the lead edge of the sight was land. Honshu. At two hundred and thirty miles an hour that gave them about a half hour to Hiroshima. Maybe less. He wondered if his heart could beat so hard for that long.

Fitch said, "Matthews, I'm giving over guidance to you. Just tell us what to do."

"Bear south two degrees," was all Matthews said. At last their voices had taken on a touch of awareness, even fear.

"January, are you ready?" Fitch asked.

"I'm just waiting," January said. He sat up, so Fitch could see the back of his head. The bombsight stood between his legs. A switch on its side would start the bombing sequence; the bomb would not leave the plane immediately upon the flick of the switch, but would drop after a fifteen-second radio tone warned the following planes. The sight was adjusted accordingly.

"Adjust to a heading of two sixty-five," Matthews said. "We're coming in directly upwind." This was to make any side-drift adjustments for the bomb unnecessary. "January, dial it down to two hundred and thirty-one miles per hour."

"Two thirty-one."

Fitch said, "Everyone but January and Matthews, get your goggles on."

January took the darkened goggles from the floor. One needed to protect one's eyes or they might melt. He put them on, put his forehead on the headrest. They were in the way. He took them off. When he looked through the sight again there was land under the crosshairs. He checked his watch. Eight o'clock. Up and reading the papers, drinking tea.

"Ten minutes to AP," Matthews said. The aiming point was Aioi Bridge, a T-shaped bridge in the middle of the delta-straddling city. Easy to recognize.

"There's a lot of cloud down there," Fitch noted. "Are you going to be able to see?"

"I won't be sure until we try it," January said.

"We can make another pass and use radar if we need to," Matthews said.

Fitch said, "Don't drop it unless you're sure, January."

"Yes, sir."

Through the sight a grouping of rooftops and gray roads was just visible between broken clouds. Around it green forest. "All right," Matthews exclaimed, "here we go! Keep it right on this heading, Captain! January, we'll stay at two thirty-one."

"And same heading," Fitch said. "January, she's all yours. Everyone make sure your goggles are on. And be ready for the turn."

January's world contracted to the view through the bombsight. A stippled field of cloud and forest. Over a small range of hills and into Hiroshima's watershed. The broad river was mud brown, the land pale hazy green, the growing network of roads flat gray. Now the tiny rectangular shapes of buildings covered almost all the land, and swimming into the sight came the city proper, narrow islands thrusting into a dark blue bay. Under the crosshairs the city moved island by island, cloud by cloud. January had stopped breathing, his fingers were rigid as stone on the switch. And there was Aioi Bridge. It slid right under the crosshairs, a tiny T right in a gap in the clouds. January's fingers crushed the switch. Deliberately he took a breath, held it. Clouds swam under the crosshairs, then the next island. "Almost there," he said calmly into his microphone. "Steady." Now that he was committed his heart was humming like the Wrights. He counted to ten. Now flowing under the crosshairs were clouds alternating with green forest, leaden roads. "I've turned the switch, but I'm not getting a tone!" he croaked into the mike. His right hand held the switch firmly in place. Fitch was shouting something—Matthews' voice cracked across it—"Flipping it b-back and forth," January shouted, shielding the bombsight with his body from the eyes of the pilots. "But *still*—wait a second—"

He pushed the switch down. A low hum filled his ears. "That's it! It started!"

"But where will it land?" Matthews cried.

"Hold steady!" January shouted.

Lucky Strike shuddered and lofted up ten or twenty feet. January twisted to look down and there was the bomb, flying just below the plane. Then with a wobble it fell away.

The plane banked right and dove so hard that the centrifugal force threw January against the Plexiglas. Several thousand feet lower Fitch leveled it out and they hurtled north.

"Do you see anything?" Fitch cried.

From the tailgun Kochenski gasped "Nothing." January struggled upright. He reached for the welder's goggles, but they were no longer on his head. He couldn't find them. "How long has it been?" he said.

"Thirty seconds," Matthews replied.

January clamped his eyes shut.

The blood in his eyelids lit up red, then white.

On the earphones a clutter of voices: "Oh my God. Oh my God." The plane bounced and tumbled, metallically shrieking. January pressed himself off the Plexiglas. "Nother shockwave!" Kockenski yelled. The plane rocked again, bounced out of control, this is it, January thought, end of the world, I guess that solves my problem.

He opened his eyes and found he could still see. The engines still roared, the props spun. "Those were the shockwaves from the bomb," Fitch called. "We're okay now. Look at that! Will you look at that sonofabitch go!"

January looked. The cloud layer below had burst apart, and a black column of smoke billowed up from a core of red fire. Already the top of the column was at their height. Exclamations of shock clattered painfully in January's ears. He stared at the fiery base of the cloud, at the scores of fires feeding into it. Suddenly he could see past the cloud, and his fingernails cut into his palms. Through a gap in the clouds he saw it clearly, the delta, the six rivers, there off to the left of the tower of smoke: the city of Hiroshima, untouched.

"We missed!" Kochenski yelled. "We missed it!"

January turned to hide his face from the pilots; on it was a grin like a rictus. He sat back in his seat and let the relief fill him.

Then it was back to it. "God damn it!" Fitch shouted down at him. McDonald was trying to restrain him. "January, get up here!"

"Yes, sir." Now there was a new set of problems.

January stood and turned, legs weak. His right fingertips throbbed painfully. The men were crowded forward to look out the Plexiglas. January looked with them.

The mushroom cloud was forming. It roiled out as if it might continue to extend forever, fed by the inferno and the black stalk below it. It looked about two miles wide, and half a mile tall, and it extended well above the height they flew at, dwarfing their plane entirely. "Do you think we'll all be sterile?" Matthews said.

"I can taste the radiation," McDonald declared. "Can you? It tastes like lead."

Bursts of flame shot up into the cloud from below, giving a purplish tint to the stalk. There it stood: lifelike, malignant, sixty thousand feet tall. One bomb. January shoved past the pilots into the navigation cabin, overwhelmed.

"Should I start recording everyone's reactions, Captain?" asked Benton.

"To hell with that," Fitch said, following January back. But Shepard got there first, descending quickly from the navigation dome. He rushed across the cabin, caught January on the shoulder. "You bastard!" he screamed as January stumbled back. "You lost your nerve, coward!"

January went for Shepard, happy to have a target at last, but Fitch cut in and grabbed him by the collar, pulled him around until they were face to face—

"Is that right?" Fitch cried, as angry as Shepard. "Did you screw up on purpose?"

"No," January grunted, and knocked Fitch's hands away from his neck. He swung and smacked Fitch on the mouth, caught him solid. Fitch staggered back, recovered, and no doubt would have beaten January up, but Matthews and Benton and Stone leaped in and held him back, shouting for order. "Shut up! Shut up!" McDonald screamed from the cockpit, and for a moment it was bedlam, but Fitch let himself be restrained, and soon only McDonald's shouts for quiet were heard. January retreated to between the pilot seats, right hand on his pistol holster.

"The city was in the crosshairs when I flipped the switch," he said. "But the first couple of times I flipped it nothing happened—"

"That's a lie!" Shepard shouted. "There was nothing wrong with the switch, I checked it myself. Besides, the bomb exploded *miles* beyond Hiroshima, look for yourself! That's *minutes.*" He wiped spit from his chin and pointed at January. "You did it."

"You don't know that," January said. But he could see the men had been convinced by Shepard, and he took a step back. "You just get me to a board of inquiry, quick. And leave me alone till then. If you touch me again," glaring venomously at Fitch and then Shepard, "I'll shoot you."

He turned and hopped down to his seat, feeling exposed and vulnerable, like a treed raccoon.

"They'll shoot *you* for this," Shepard screamed after him. "Disobeying orders—treason—" Matthews and Stone were shutting him up.

"Let's get out of here," he heard McDonald say. "I can taste the lead, can't you?"

January looked out the Plexiglas. The giant cloud still burned and roiled. One atom. . . . Well, they had really done it to that forest. He almost laughed but stopped himself, afraid of hysteria. Through a break in the clouds he got a clear view of Hiroshima for the first time. It lay spread over its islands like a map, unharmed. Well, that was that. The inferno at the base of the mushroom cloud was eight or ten miles around the shore of the bay, and a mile or two inland. A certain patch of forest would be gone, destroyed—utterly blasted from the face of the earth. The Japs would be able to go out and investigate the damage. And if they were told it was a demonstration, a warning—and if they acted fast—well, they had their chance. Maybe it would work.

The release of tension made January feel sick. Then he recalled Shepard's words and he knew that whether his plan worked or not he was still in trouble. In trouble! It was worse than that. Bitterly he cursed the Japanese, he even wished for a moment that he *had* dropped it on them. Wearily he let his despair empty him.

A long while later he sat up straight. Once again he was a trapped animal. He began lunging for escape, casting about for plans. One alternative after another. All during the long grim flight home he considered it, mind spinning at the speed of the props and beyond. And when they came down on Tinian he had a plan. It was a long shot, he reckoned, but it was the best he could do.

The briefing hut was surrounded by MPs again. January stumbled from the truck with the rest and walked inside. He was more than ever aware of the looks given him, and they were hard, accusatory. He was too tired to care. He hadn't slept in more than thirty-six hours, and had slept very little since the last time he had been in the hut, a week before. Now the room quivered with the lack of engine vibration to stabilize it, and the silence roared. It was all he could do to hold on to the bare essentials of his plan. The glares of Fitch and Shepard, the hurt incomprehension of Matthews, they had to be thrust out of his focus. Thankfully, he lit a cigarette.

In a clamor of question and argument the others described the strike. Then the haggard Scholes and an intelligence officer led them through the bombing run. January's plan made it necessary to hold to his story: ". . . and when the AP was under the crosshairs I pushed down the switch, but got no signal. I flipped it up and down repeatedly until the tone kicked in. At that point there was still fifteen seconds to the release."

"Was there anything that may have caused the tone to start when it did?"

"Not that I noticed immediately, but—"

"It's impossible," Shepard interrupted, face red. "I checked the switch before we flew and there was nothing wrong with it. Besides, the drop occurred over a minute—"

"Captain Shepard," Scholes said. "We'll hear from you presently."

"But he's obviously lying—"

"Captain Shepard! It's not at all obvious. Don't speak unless questioned."

"Anyway," January said, hoping to shift the questions away from the issue of the long delay, "I noticed something about the bomb when it was falling that could explain why it stuck. I need to discuss it with one of the scientists familiar with the bomb's design."

"What was that?" Scholes asked suspiciously.

January hesitated. "There's going to be an inquiry, right?"

Scholes frowned. "This is the inquiry, Captain January. Tell us what you saw."

"But there will be some proceeding beyond this one?"

"It looks like there's going to be a court-martial, yes, Captain."

"That's what I thought. I don't want to talk to anyone but my counsel, and some scientist familiar with the bomb."

"*I'm* a scientist familiar with the bomb," Shepard burst out. "You could tell me if you really had anything, you—"

"I said I need a scientist!" January exclaimed, rising to face the scarlet Shepard across the table. "Not a G-God damned mechanic." Shepard started to shout, others joined in and the room rang with argument. While Scholes restored order January sat down, and he refused to be drawn out again.

"I'll see you're assigned counsel, and initiate the court-martial," Scholes said, clearly at a loss. "Meanwhile you are under arrest, on suspicion of disobeying orders in combat." January nodded, and Scholes gave him over to MPs.

"One last thing," January said, fighting exhaustion. "Tell General Le May that if the Japs are told this drop was a warning, it might have the same effect as—"

"I told you!" Shepard shouted. "I told you he did it on purpose!"

Men around Shepard restrained him. But he had convinced most of them, and even Matthews stared at him with surprised anger.

January shook his head wearily. He had the dull feeling that his plan, while it had succeeded so far, was ultimately not a good one. "Just trying to make the best of it." It took all of his remaining will to force his legs to carry him in a dignified manner out of the hut.

His cell was an empty NCO's office. MPs brought his meals. For the first couple of days he did little but sleep. On the third day he glanced out the office's barred window, and saw a tractor pulling a tarpaulin-draped trolley out of the compound, followed by jeeps filled with MPs. It looked like a military funeral. January rushed to the door and banged on it until one of the young MPs came.

"What's that they're doing out there?" January demanded.

Eyes cold and mouth twisted, the MP said, "They're making another strike. They're going to do it right this time."

"No!" January cried. "No!" He rushed the MP, who knocked him back and locked the door. *"No!"* He beat the door until his hands hurt, cursing wildly. "You don't *need* to do it, it isn't *necessary.*" Shell shattered at last, he collapsed on the bed and wept. Now everything he had done would be rendered meaningless. He had sacrificed himself for nothing.

A day or two after that the MPs led in a colonel, an iron-haired man who stood stiffly and crushed January's hand when he shook it. His eyes were a pale, icy blue.

"I am Colonel Dray," he said. "I have been ordered to defend you in court-martial." January could feel the dislike pouring from the man. "To do that I'm going to need every fact you have, so let's get started."

"I'm not talking to anybody until I've seen an atomic scientist."

"I am your *defense* counsel—"

"I don't care who you are," January said. "Your defense of me depends on you getting one of the scientists *here.* The higher up he is, the better. And I want to speak to him alone."

"I will have to be present."

So he would do it. But now January's counsel, too, was an enemy.

"Naturally," January said. "You're my counsel. But no one else. Our atomic secrecy may depend on it."

"You saw evidence of sabotage?"

"Not one word more until that scientist is here."

Angrily the colonel nodded and left.

Late the next day the colonel returned with another man. "This is Dr. Forest."

"I helped develop the bomb," Forest said. He had a crew-cut and dressed in fatigues, and to January he looked more Army than the colonel. Suspiciously he stared back and forth at the two men.

"You'll vouch for this man's identity on your word as an officer?" he asked Dray.

"Of course," the colonel said stiffly, offended.

"So," Dr. Forest said. "You had some trouble getting it off when you wanted to. Tell me what you saw."

"I saw nothing," January said harshly. He took a deep breath; it was time to commit himself. "I want you to take a message back to the scientists. You folks have been working on this thing for years, and you must have had time to consider how the bomb should have been used. You know we could have convinced the Japs to surrender by showing them a demonstration—"

"Wait a minute," Forest said. "You're saying you didn't see anything? There wasn't a malfunction?"

"That's right," January said, and cleared his throat. "It wasn't *necessary,* do you understand?"

Forest was looking at Colonel Dray. Dray gave him a disgusted shrug. "He told he saw evidence of sabotage."

"I want you to go back and ask the scientists to intercede for me," January said, raising his voice to get the man's attention. "I haven't got a chance in that court-martial. But if the scientists defend me then maybe they'll let me live, see? I don't want to get shot for doing something every one of you scientists would have done."

Dr. Forest had backed away. Color rising, he said, "What makes you think that's what we would have done? Don't you think we considered it? Don't you think men better qualified than you made the decision?" He waved a hand—"God damn it—what made you think you were competent to decide something as important as that!"

January was appalled at the man's reaction; in his plan it had gone differently. Angrily he jabbed a finger at Forest. "Because *I* was the man doing it, *Doctor* Forest. You take even one step back from that and suddenly you can pretend it's not your doing. Fine for you, but *I was there.*"

At every word the man's color was rising. It looked like he might pop a vein in his neck. January tried once more. "Have you ever tried to imagine what one of your bombs would do to a city full of people?"

"I've had enough!" the man exploded. He turned to Dray. "I'm under no obligation to keep what I've heard here confidential. You can be sure it will be used as evidence in Captain January's court-martial." He turned and gave January a look of such blazing hatred that January understood it. For these men to admit he was right would mean admitting that they were wrong—that every one of them was responsible for his part in the construction of the weapon January had refused to use.

Understanding that, January knew he was doomed.

The bang of Dr. Forest's departure still shook the little office. January sat on his cot, got out a smoke. Under Colonel Dray's cold gaze he lit one shakily, took a drag. He looked up at the colonel, shrugged. "It was my best chance," he explained. That did something—for the first and only time the cold disdain in the colonel's eyes shifted to a little, hard, lawyerly gleam of respect.

The court-martial lasted two days. The verdict was guilty of disobeying orders in combat, and of giving aid and comfort to the enemy. The sentence was death by firing squad.

For most of his remaining days January rarely spoke, drawing ever further behind the mask that had hidden him for so long. A clergyman came to see him, but it was the 509th's chaplain, the one who had said the prayer blessing the *Lucky Strike's* mission before they took off. Angrily January sent him packing.

Later, however, a young Catholic priest dropped by. His name was Patrick Getty. He was a little pudgy man, bespectacled and, it seemed, somewhat afraid of January. January let the man talk to him. When he returned the next day January talked back a bit, and on the day after that he talked some more. It became a habit.

Usually January talked about his childhood. He talked of plowing mucky black bottom land behind a mule. Of running down the lane to the mailbox. Of reading books by the light of the moon after he had been ordered to sleep, and of being beaten by his mother for it with a high-heeled shoe. He told the priest the story of the time his arm had been burnt, and about the car crash at the bottom of Fourth Street. "It's the truck driver's face I remember, do you see, Father?"

"Yes," the young priest said. "Yes."

And he told him about the game he had played in which every action he took tipped the balance of world affairs. "When I remembered that game I thought it was dumb. Step on a sidewalk crack and cause an earthquake—you know, it's stupid. Kids are like that." The priest nodded. "But now I've been thinking that if everybody were to live their whole lives like that, thinking that every move they made really was important, then . . . it might make a difference." He waved a hand vaguely, expelled cigarette smoke. "You're accountable for what you do."

"Yes," the priest said. "Yes, you are."

"And if you're given orders to do something wrong, you're still accountable, right? The orders don't change it."

"That's right."

"Hmph." January smoked a while. "So they say, anyway. But look what happens." He waved at the office. "I'm like the guy in a story I read—he thought everything in books was true, and after reading a bunch of westerns he tried to rob a train. They tossed him in jail." He laughed shortly. "Books are full of crap."

"Not all of them," the priest said. "Besides, you weren't trying to rob a train."

They laughed at the notion. "Did you read that story?"

"No."

"It was the strangest book—there were two stories in it, and they alternated chapter by chapter, but they didn't have a thing to do with each other! I didn't get it."

". . . Maybe the writer was trying to say that everything connects to everything else."

"Maybe. But it's a funny way to say it."

"I like it."

And so they passed the time, talking.

So it was the priest who was the one to come by and tell January that his request for a Presidential pardon had been refused. Getty said awkwardly, "It seems the President approves the sentence."

"That bastard," January said weakly. He sat on his cot.

Time passed. It was another hot, humid day.

"Well," the priest said. "Let me give you some better news. Given your situation I don't think telling you matters, though I've been told not to. The second mission—you know there was a second strike?"

"Yes."

"Well, they missed too."

"What?" January cried, and bounced to his feet. "You're kidding!"

"No. They flew to Kokura, but found it covered by clouds. It was the same over Nagasaki and Hiroshima, so they flew back to Kokura and tried to drop the bomb using radar to guide it, but apparently there was a—a genuine equipment failure this time, and the bomb fell on an island."

January was hopping up and down, mouth hanging open. "So we n-never—"

"We never dropped an atom bomb on a Japanese city. That's right." Getty grinned. "And get this—I heard this from my superior—they sent a message to the Japanese government telling them that the two explosions were warnings, and that if they didn't surrender by September first we would drop bombs on Kyoto and Tokyo, and then wherever else we had to. Word is that the Emperor went to Hiroshima to survey the damage, and when he saw it he ordered the Cabinet to surrender. So. . . ."

"So it worked," January said. He hopped around, "It worked, it worked!"

"Yes."

"Just like I said it would!" he cried, and hopping before the priest he laughed.

Getty was jumping around a little too, and the sight of the priest bouncing was too much for January. He sat on his cot and laughed till the tears ran down his cheeks.

"So—" he sobered quickly. "So Truman's going to shoot me anyway, eh?"

"Yes," the priest said unhappily. "I guess that's right."

This time January's laugh was bitter. "He's a bastard, all right. And proud of being a bastard, which makes it worse." He shook his head. "If Roosevelt had lived. . . ."

"It would have been different," Getty finished. "Yes. Maybe so. But he didn't." He sat beside January. "Cigarette?" He held out a pack, and January noticed the white wartime wrapper. He frowned.

"You haven't got a Camel?"

"Oh. Sorry."

"Oh well. That's all right." January took one of the Lucky Strikes, lit up. "That's awfully good news." He breathed out. "I never believed Truman would pardon me anyway, so mostly you've brought good news. Ha. They *missed.* You have no idea how much better that makes me feel."

"I think I do."

January smoked the cigarette.

". . . So I'm a good American after all. I *am* a good American," he insisted, "no matter what Truman says."

"Yes," Getty replied, and coughed. "You're better than Truman any day."

"Better watch what you say, Father." He looked into the eyes behind the glasses, and the expression he saw there gave him pause. Since the drop every look directed at him had been filled with contempt. He'd seen it so often during the court-martial that he'd learned to stop looking; and now he had to teach himself to see again. The priest looked at him as if he were . . . as if he were some kind of hero. That wasn't exactly right. But seeing it. . . .

January would not live to see the years that followed, so he would never know what came of his action. He had given up casting his mind forward and imagining possibilities, because there was no point to it. His planning was ended. In any case he would not have been able to imagine the course of the post-war years. That the world would quickly become an armed camp pitched on the edge of atomic war, he might have predicted. But he never would have guessed that so many people would join a January Society. He would never know of the effect the Society had on Dewey during the Korean crisis, never know of the Society's successful campaign for the test ban treaty, and never learn that thanks in part to the Society and its allies, a treaty would be signed by the great powers that would reduce the number of atomic bombs year by year, until there were none left.

Frank January would never know any of that. But in that moment on his cot looking into the eyes of young Patrick Getty, he guessed an inkling of it—he felt, just for an instant, the impact on history.

And with that he relaxed. In his last week everyone who met him carried away the same impression, that of a calm, quiet man, angry at Truman and others, but in a withdrawn, matter-of-fact way. Patrick Getty, a strong force in the January Society ever after, said January was talkative for some time after he learned of the missed attack on Kokura. Then he became quieter and quieter, as the day approached. On the morning that they woke him at dawn to march him out to a hastily constructed execution shed, his MPs shook his hand. The priest was with him as he smoked a final cigarette, and they prepared to put the hood over his head. January looked at him calmly. "They load one of the guns with a blank cartridge, right?"

"Yes," Getty said.

"So each man in the squad can imagine he may not have shot me?"

"Yes. That's right."

A tight, unhumorous smile was January's last expression. He threw down the cigarette, ground it out, poked the priest in the arm. "But I *know.*" Then the mask slipped back into place for good, making the hood redundant, and with a firm step January went to the wall. One might have said he was at peace.

(1984)

ROBERT SHECKLEY

THE LIFE OF ANYBODY

Last night, as I lay on the couch watching "The Late Show," a camera and sound crew came to my apartment to film a segment of a TV series called "The Life of Anybody." I can't say I was completely surprised, although I had not anticipated this. I knew the rules; I went on with my life exactly as if they were not there. After a few minutes, the camera and recording crew seemed to fade into the wallpaper. They are specially trained for that.

My TV was on, of course; I usually have it on. I could almost hear the groans of the critics: "Another goddamned segment of a guy watching the tube. Doesn't anybody in this country do anything but watch the tube?" That upset me, but there was nothing I could do about it. That's the way it goes.

So the cameras whizzed along, and I lay on the couch like a dummy and watched two cowboys play the macho game. After a while my wife came out of the bathroom, looked at the crew, and groaned, "Oh, Christ, not *tonight.*" She was wearing my CCNY sweatshirt on top, nothing on the bottom. She'd just washed her hair and she had a towel tied around her head. She had no makeup on. She looked like hell. Of all nights, they had to pick this one. She was probably imagining the reviews: "The wife in last night's turgid farce . . ."

I could see that she wanted badly to do something—to inject a little humor into our segment, to make it into a domestic farce. But she didn't. She knew as well as I did that anyone caught acting, fabricating, exaggerating, diminishing, or otherwise distorting his life, would be instantly cut off the air. She didn't want that. A bad appearance was better than no appearance at all. She sat down on a chair and picked up her crocheting hook. I picked up my magazine. Our movie went on.

You can't believe it when it happens to you. Even though you watch the show every evening and see it happen, you can't believe it's happening to you. I mean, it's suddenly *you* there, lying on the couch doing your nothing number, and there they are, filming it and implying that the segment represents *you.*

I prayed for something to happen. Air raid—sneak Commie attack—us a typical American family caught in the onrush of great events. Or a burglar breaks in, only he's not just a burglar, he's something else, and a whole fascinating sequence begins. Or a beautiful woman knocks at the door, claiming that only I can help her. Hell, I would have settled for a phone call.

But nothing happened. I actually started to get interested in that movie on TV, and I put down my magazine and actually watched it. I thought they might be interested in that.

The next day my wife and I waited hopefully, even though we knew we had bombed out. Still, you can never tell. Sometimes the public wants to see more of a person's life. Sometimes a face strikes their fancy and you get signed for a series. I didn't really expect that anyone would want to see a series about my wife and me, but you can never tell. Stranger things have happened.

Nowadays my wife and I spend our evenings in very interesting ways. Our sexual escapades are the talk of the neighborhood, my crazy cousin Zoe has come to stay with us, and regularly an undead thing crawls upstairs from the cellar.

Practically speaking, you never get another chance. But you can never tell. If they do decide to do a follow-up segment, we're ready.

(1984)

MOLLY GLOSS

INTERLOCKING PIECES

For Teo, there was never a question of abandoning the effort. After the last refusal—the East European Minister of Health sent her his personal explanation and regrets—it became a matter of patience and readiness and rather careful timing.

A uniformed policeman had been posted beside her door for reasons, apparently, of protocol. At eight-thirty, when he went down the corridor to the public lavatory, Teo was dressed and waiting, and she walked out past the nurses' station. It stood empty. The robo-nurse was still making the eight-o'clock rounds of the wing's seventy or eighty rooms. The organic nurse, just come on duty, was leaning over the vid displays in the alcove behind the station, familiarizing herself with the day's new admissions.

Because it was the nearest point of escape, Teo used the staircase. But the complex skill of descending stairs had lately deserted her, so she stepped down like a child, one leg at a time, grimly clutching the metal bannister with both hands. After a couple of floors she went in again to find a public data terminal in a ward that was too busy to notice her.

They had not told her even the donor's name, and a straightforward computer request met a built-in resistance: DATA RESTRICTED***KEY IN PHYSICIAN IDENT CODE. So she asked the machine for the names of organ donors on contract with the regional Ministry of Health, then a list of the hospital's terminal patients, the causes and projected times of their deaths, and the postmortem neurosurgeries scheduled for the next morning. And, finally, the names of patients about whom information was media-restricted. Teo's own name appeared on the last list. She should have been ready for that but found she was not, and she sat staring until the letters grew unfamiliar, assumed strange juxtapositions, became detached and meaningless—the name of a stranger.

The computer scanned and compared the lists for her, extrapolated from the known data, and delivered only one name. She did not ask for hard copy. She looked at the vid display a moment, maybe longer than a moment, and then punched it off and sat staring at the blank screen.

Perhaps not consciously, she had expected a woman. The name, a man's name, threw her off balance a little. She would have liked a little time to get used to the sound of it, the sound it made in her head and on her lips. She would have liked to know the name before she knew the man. But he would be dead in the morning. So she spoke it once, only once. Out loud. With exactness and with care. "Dhavir Stahl," she said. And then went to a pneumo-tube and rode up.

In the tube there were at first several others, finally only one. Not European, perhaps North African, a man with eyebrows in a thick straight line across a beetled brow. He watched her sidelong—clearly recognized her—and he wore a physician's ID badge. In a workplace as large as this one the rumor apparatus would be well established. He would know of her admission, maybe even the surgery that had been scheduled. Would, at the very least, see the incongruity of a VIP patient, street-dressed and unaccompanied, riding up in the public pneumo-tube. So Teo stood imperiously beside him with hands cupped together behind her back and eyes focused on the smooth center seam of the door while she waited for him to speak, or not. When the tube opened at the seventy-eighth floor he started out, then half turned toward her, made a stiff little bow, and said, "Good health, Madame Minister," and finally exited. If he reported straightaway to security, she might have five minutes, or ten, before they reasoned out where she had gone. And standing alone now in the pneumo-tube, she began to feel the first sour leaking of despair—what could be said, learned, shared in that little time?

There was a vid map beside the portal on the ninety-first floor. She searched it until she found the room and the straightest route, then went deliberately down the endless corridors, past the little tableaux of sickness framed where a door here or there stood open, and finally to Stahl's door, closed, where there was no special feel of death, only the numbered code posted alongside the name to denote a life that was ending.

She would have waited. She wanted to wait, to gather up a few dangling threads, reweave a place or two that had lately worn through. But the physician in the pneumo-tube had stolen that possibility. So she took in a thin new breath and touched one thumb to the admit disk. The door hushed aside, waited for her, closed behind her. She stood just inside, stood very straight, with her hands open beside her thighs.

The man whose name was Dhavir Stahl was fitting together the pieces of a masters-level holoplex, sitting cross-legged, bare-kneed, on his bed, with the scaffolding of the puzzle in front of him on the bed table and its thousands of tiny elements jumbled around him on the sheets. He looked at Teo from under the ledge of his eyebrows while he worked. He had that vaguely anxious quality all East Europeans seem to carry about their eyes. But his mouth was good, a wide mouth with creases lapping around its corners, showing the places where his smile would fit. And he worked silently, patiently.

"I . . . would speak with you," Teo said.

He was tolerant, even faintly apologetic. "Did you look at the file, or just the door code? I've already turned down offers from a priest and a psychiatrist and, this morning, from somebody in narcotics. I just don't seem to need any deathbed comforting."

"I am Teo."

"What is that? One of the research divisions?"

"My name."

His mouth moved, a near smile, perhaps embarrassment.

"They hadn't told you my name, then."

And finally he took it in. His face seemed to tighten, all of it pulling back toward his scalp as the skin shrinks from the skull of a corpse, so that his mouth was too wide and there was no space for smiling. Or too much.

"They . . . seem to have a good many arbitrary rules," Teo said. "They refused me this meeting, your name even. And you mine, it appears. I could not—I had a need to know."

She waited raggedly through a very long silence. Her palms were faintly damp, but she continued to hold them open beside her legs. Finally Dhavir Stahl moved, straightened a little, perhaps took a breath. But his eyes stayed with Teo.

"You look healthy," he said. It seemed a question.

She made a slight gesture with one shoulder, a sort of shrugging off. "I have . . . lost a couple of motor skills." And in a moment, because he continued to wait, she added, "The cerebellum is evidently quite diseased. They first told me I would die. Then they said no, maybe not, and they sent me here. 'The state of the art,' or something to that effect."

He had not moved his eyes from her. One of his hands lightly touched the framework of the puzzle as a blind man would touch a new face, but he never took his eyes from Teo. Finally she could not bear that, and her own eyes skipped out to the window and the dark sheets of rain flapping beneath the overcast.

"You are . . . not what I expected," he said. When her eyes came round to him again, he made that near smile and forced air from his mouth—not a laugh, a hard sound of bleak amusement. "Don't ask! God, I don't know what I expected." He let go the puzzle and looked away finally, looked down at his hands, then out to the blank vid screen on the wall, the aseptic toilet in the corner. When he lifted his face to her again, his eyes were very dark, very bright. She thought he might weep, or that she would. But he said only, "You are Asian." He was not quite asking it.

"Yes."

"Pakistani?"

"Nepalese."

He nodded without surprise or interest. "Do you climb?"

She lifted her shoulders again, shrugging. "We are not all Sherpa bearers," she said with a prickly edge of impatience. There was no change at his mouth, but he fell silent and looked away from her. Belatedly she felt she might have shown more tolerance. Her head began to ache a little from a point at the base of the skull. She would have liked to knead the muscles along her shoulders. But she waited, standing erect and stiff and dismal, with her hands hanging, while the time they had went away quickly and ill used.

Finally Dhavir Stahl raised his arms, made a loose, meaningless gesture in the air, then combed back his hair with the fingers of both hands. His hair and his hands seemed very fine. "Why did you come?" he said, and his eyelashes drew closed, shielding him as he spoke.

There were answers that would have hurt him again. She sorted through for one that would not. "To befriend you," she said, and saw his eyes open slowly. In a moment he sighed. It was a small sound, dry and sliding, the sound a bare foot makes in sand. He looked at the puzzle, touched an element lying loose on the bed, turned it round with a fingertip. And round.

Without looking toward her, he said, "Their computer has me dead at four-oh-seven-fourteen. They've told you that, I guess. There's a two percent chance of miscalculation. Two or three, I forget. So anyway, by four-thirty—" His mouth was drawn out thin.

"They would have given you another artificial heart."

He lifted his face, nearly smiled again. "They told you that? Yes. Another one. I wore out my own and one of theirs." He did not explain or justify. He simply raised his shoulders, perhaps shrugging, and said, "That's enough." He was looking toward her, but his eyes saw only inward. She waited for him. Finally he stirred, turned his hands palms up, studied them.

"Did they—I wasn't expecting a woman. Men and women move differently. I didn't think they'd give a man's cerebellum to a woman." He glanced at Teo, at her body. "And you're small. I'm, what, twenty kilos heavier, half a meter taller? I'd think you'd have some trouble getting used to . . . the way I move. Or anyway the way my brain tells my body to move." He was already looking at his hands again, rubbing them against one another with a slight papery sound.

"They told me I would adapt to it," Teo said. "Or the . . . new cerebellum could be retaught."

His eyes skipped up to her as if she had startled or frightened him. His mouth moved too, sliding out wide to show the sharp edge of his teeth. "They didn't tell me that," he said from a rigid grin.

It was a moment before she was able to find a reason for his agitation. "It won't—They said it wouldn't . . . reduce the donor's . . . sense of self."

After a while, after quite a while, he said, "What word did they use? They wouldn't have said 'reduce.' Maybe 'correct' or 'edit out.' " His eyes slid sideways, away from her, then back again. His mouth was still tight, grimacing, shaping a smile that wasn't there. "They were at least frank about it. They said the cerebellum only runs the automatic motor functions, the skilled body movements. They said they would have expected—no, they said they would have liked—a transplanted cerebellum to be mechanical. A part, like a lung or a kidney. The 'mind' ought to be all in the forebrain. They told me there wouldn't be any donor consciousness, none at all, if they could figure out how to stop it."

In the silence after, as if speaking had dressed the wound, his mouth began to heal. In a moment he was able to drop his eyes from Teo. He sat with his long, narrow hands cupped on his knees and stared at the scaffolding of his puzzle. She could hear his breath sliding in and out, a contained and careful sound. Finally he selected an element from among the thousands around him on the bed, turned it solemnly in his hands, turned it again, then reached to fit it into the puzzle, deftly finding a place for it among the multitude of interlocking pieces. He did not look at Teo. But in a moment he said, "You don't look scared. I'd be scared if they were putting bits of somebody else inside my head." He slurred the words a little at the end and jumped his eyes white-edged to Teo.

She made a motion to open her hands, to shrug, but then, irresistibly, turned her palms in, chafed them harshly against her pants legs. She chose a word from among several possible. "Yes," she said. And felt it was she who now wore the armored faceplate with its stiff and fearful grin.

Dhavir's eyes came up to her again with something like surprise, and certainly with tenderness. And then Teo felt the door behind her, its cushioned quiet sliding sideways, and there were three security people there, diminishing the size of the room with their small crowd, their turbulence. The first one extended her hand but did not quite touch Teo's arm. "Minister Teo," she said. Formal. Irritated.

Dhavir seemed not to register the address. Maybe he would remember it later, maybe not, and Teo thought probably it wouldn't matter. They watched each other silently, Teo standing carefully erect with her hands, the hands that no longer brushed teeth nor wrote cursive script, the hands she had learned to distrust, hanging open beside her thighs, and Dhavir sitting crosslegged amid his puzzle, with his forearms resting across those frail, naked knees. Teo waited. The security person touched her elbow, drew her firmly toward the door, and then finally Dhavir spoke her name. "Teo," he said. And she pulled her arm free, turned to stand on the door threshold, facing him.

"I run lopsided," he said, as if he apologized for more than that. "I throw my heels out or something." There were creases beside his mouth and his eyes, but he did not smile.

In a moment, with infinite, excruciating care, Teo opened her hands palms outward, lifted them in a gesture of dismissal. "I believe I can live with that," she said.

(1984)

LEWIS SHINER

The War at Home

Ten of us in the back of a Huey, assholes clenched like fists, C-rations turned to sno-cones in our bellies. Tracers float up at us, swollen, sizzling with orange light, like one dud firecracker after another. Ahead of us the gunships pound Landing Zone Dog with everything they have, flex guns, rockets, and 50-calibers, while the artillery screams overhead and the Air Force A1-Es strafe the clearing into kindling.

We hover over the LZ in the sudden phosphorus dawn of a flare, screaming, "Land, you fucker, land!" while the tracers close in, the shell of the copter ticking like a clock as the thumb-sized rounds go through her, ripping the steel like paper, spattering somebody's brains across the aft bulkhead.

Then falling into the knee-high grass, the air humming with bullets and stinking of swamp ooze and gasoline and human shit and blood. Spinning wildly, my finger jamming down the trigger of the M-16, not caring anymore where the bullets go.

And waking up in my own bed, Clare beside me, shaking me, hissing, "Wake up, wake up for Christ's sake."

I sat up, the taste of it still in my lungs, hands twitching with berserker frenzy. " 'M okay," I mumbled. "Nightmare. I was back in Nam."

"What?"

"Flashback," I said. "The war."

"What are you talking about? You weren't in the war."

I looked at my hands and remembered. It was true. I'd never even been in the Army, never set foot in Vietnam.

Three months earlier we'd been shooting an Eyewitness News series on Vietnamese refugees. His name was Nguyen Ky Duk, former ARVN colonel, now a fry cook at Jack in the Box. "You killed my country," he said. "All of you. Americans, French, Japanese. Like you would kill a dog because you thought it might have, you know, rabies. Just kill it and throw it in a ditch. It was a living thing, and now it is dead."

The afternoon of the massacre we got raw footage over the wire. About a dozen of us crowded the monitor and stared at the shattered windows of the Safeway, the mounds of cartridges, the bloodstains and the puddles of congealing food.

"What was it he said?"

"Something about 'gooks.' 'You're all fucking gooks, just like the others, and now I'll kill you too,' something like that."

"But he wasn't in Nam. They talked to his wife."

"So why'd he do it?"

"He was a gun nut. Black market shit, like that M-16 he had. Camo clothes, the whole nine yards. A nut."

I walked down the hall, past the lines of potted ferns and bamboo, and bought a Coke from the machine. I could still remember the dream, the feel of the M-16 in my hands, the rage, the fear.

"Like it?" Clare asked. She turned slowly, the loose folds of her black cotton pajamas fluttering, her face hidden by the conical straw hat.

"No," I said. "I don't know. It makes me feel weird."

"It's fashion," she said. "Fashion's supposed to make you feel weird."

I walked away from her, through the sliding glass door and into the back yard. The grass had grown a foot or more without my noticing, and strange plants had come up between the flowers, suffocating them in sharp fronds and broad green leaves.

"Did you go?"

"No," I said. "I was I-Y. Underweight, if you can believe that." But in fact I was losing weight again, the muscles turning stringy under sallow skin.

"Me either. My dad got a shrink to write me a letter. I did the marches, Washington and all that. But you know something? I feel weird about not going. Kind of guilty, somehow. Even though we shouldn't ever have been there, even though we were burning villages and fragging our own guys. I feel like . . . I don't know. Like I missed something. Something important."

"Maybe not," I said. Through cracked glass I could see the sunset thickening the trees.

"What do you mean?"

I shrugged. I wasn't sure myself. "Maybe it's not too late," I said.

I walk through the haunted streets of my town, sweltering in the January heat. The jungle arches over me; children's voices in the distance chatter in their weird pidgin Vietnamese. The TV station is a crumbling ruin and none of us feel comfortable there any longer. We work now in a thatched hut with a mimeo machine.

The air is humid, fragrant with anticipation. Soon the planes will come and it will begin in earnest.

(1985)

KAREN JOY FOWLER

The Lake Was Full of Artificial Things

Daniel was older than Miranda had expected. In 1970, when they had said good-bye, he had been twenty-two. Two years later he was dead, but now, approaching her with the bouncing walk which had suited his personality so well, he appeared as a middle-aged man and quite gray, though solid and muscular. She noted with relief that he was smiling. "Randy!" he said. He laughed delightedly. "You look wonderful."

Miranda glanced down at herself, wondering what, in fact, she did look like or if she had any form at all. She saw the flesh of her arms firm again and the skin smooth and tight. So *she* was the twenty-year old. Isn't that odd, she thought, turning her hands palms up to examine them. Then Daniel reached her. The sun was bright in the sky behind him, obscuring his face, giving him a halo. He put his arms around her. I feel him, she thought in astonishment. I smell him. She breathed in slowly. "Hello, Daniel," she said.

He squeezed her slightly, then dropped his arms and looked around. Miranda looked outward, too. They were on the college campus. Surely this was not the setting she would have chosen. It unsettled her, as if she had been sent backward in time and gifted with prescience, but remained powerless to make any changes, was doomed to see it all again, moving to its inevitable conclusion. Daniel, however, seemed pleased.

He pointed off to the right. "There's the creek," he said, and suddenly she could hear it. "Memories there, right?" and she remembered lying beneath him on the grass by the water. She put her hands on his shoulders now; his clothes were rough against her palms and military—like his hair. He gestured to the round brick building behind her. "Tollman Hall," he said. "Am I right? God, this is great, Randy. I remember *everything.* Total recall. I had Physics 10 there with Dr. Fielding. Physics for nonmajors. I couldn't manage my vectors and I got a B." He laughed again, throwing an arm around Miranda. "It's great to be back."

They began to walk together toward the center of campus, slow walking with no destination, designed for conversation. They were all alone,

Miranda noticed. The campus was deserted, then suddenly it wasn't. Students appeared on the pathways. Long-hairs with headbands and straights with slide rules. Just what she remembered. "Tell me what everyone's been doing," Daniel said. "It's been what? Thirty years? Don't leave out a thing."

Miranda stooped and picked a small daisy out of the grass. She twirled it absentmindedly in her fingers. It left a green stain on her thumb. Daniel stopped walking and waited beside her. "Well," Miranda said. "I've lost touch with most of them. Gail got a job on *Le Monde.* She went to Germany for the re-unification. I heard she was living there. The antinuclear movement was her permanent beat. She could still be there, I suppose."

"So she's still a radical," said Daniel. "What stamina."

"Margaret bought a bakery in San Francisco. Sixties cuisine. Whole grains. Tofu brownies. Heaviest cookies west of the Rockies. We're in the same cable chapter so I keep up with her better. I saw her last marriage on T.V. She's been married three times now, every one a loser."

"What about Allen?" Daniel asked.

"Allen," repeated Miranda. "Well, Allen had a promising career in jogging shoes. He was making great strides." She glanced at Daniel's face. "Sorry," she said. "Allen always brought out the worst in me. He lost his father in an air collision over Kennedy. Sued the airline and discovered he never had to work again. In short, Allen is rich. Last I heard, and this was maybe twenty years ago, he was headed to the Philippines to buy himself a submissive bride." She saw Daniel smile, the lines in his face deepening with his expression. "Oh, you'd like to blame me for Allen, wouldn't you?" she said. "But it wouldn't be fair. I dated him maybe three times, tops." Miranda shook her head. "Such an enthusiastic participant in the sexual revolution. And then it all turned to women's liberation on him. Poor Allen. We can only hope his tiny wife divorced him and won a large settlement when you could still get alimony."

Daniel moved closer to her and they began to walk again, passing under the shade of a redwood grove. The grass changed to needles under their feet. "You needn't be so hard on Allen," he said. "I never minded about him. I always knew you loved me."

"Did you?" asked Miranda anxiously. She looked at her feet, afraid to examine Daniel's face. My god, she was wearing moccasins. Had she ever worn moccasins? "I did get married, Daniel," she said. "I married a mathematician. His name was Michael." Miranda dropped her daisy, petals intact.

Daniel continued to walk, swinging his arms easily. "Well, you were always hot for mathematics. I didn't expect you to mourn me forever."

"So it's all right?"

Daniel stopped, turning to face her. He was still smiling, though it was not quite the smile she expected, not quite the easy, happy smile she remembered. "It's all right that you got married, Randy," he said softly. Something passed over his face and left it. "Hey!" he laughed again. "I remember something else from Physics 10. Zeno's paradox. You know what that is?"

"No," said Miranda.

"It's an argument. Zeno argued that motion was impossible because it required an object to pass through an infinite number of points in a finite amount of time." Daniel swung his arms energetically. "Think about it for a minute, Randy. Can you fault it? Then think about how far I came to be here with you."

"Miranda. Miranda." It was her mother's voice, rousing her for school. Only then it wasn't. It was Dr. Matsui who merely sounded maternal, despite the fact that she had no children of her own and was not yet thirty. Miranda felt her chair returning slowly to its upright position. "Are you back?" Dr. Matsui asked. "How did it go?"

"It was short," Miranda told her. She pulled the taped wires gently from her lids and opened her eyes. Dr. Matsui was seated beside her, reaching into Miranda's hair to detach the clips which touched her scalp.

"Perhaps we recalled you too early," she conceded. "Matthew spotted an apex so we pulled the plug. We just wanted a happy ending. It was happy, wasn't it?"

"Yes." Dr. Matsui's hair, parted on one side and curving smoothly under her chin, bobbed before Miranda's face. Miranda touched it briefly, then her own hair, her cheeks, and her nose. They felt solid under her hand, real, but no more so than Daniel had been. "Yes, it was," she repeated. "He was so happy to see me. So glad to be back. But, Anna, he was so real. I thought you said it would be like a dream."

"No," Dr. Matsui told her. "I said it *wouldn't* be. I said it was a memory of something that never happened and in that respect was like a dream. I wasn't speaking to the quality of the experience." She rolled her chair to the monitor and stripped the long feed-out sheet from it, tracing the curves quickly with one finger. Matthew, her technician, came to stand behind her. He leaned over her left shoulder, pointing. "There," he said. "That's Daniel. That's what I put in."

Dr. Matsui returned her chair to Miranda's side. "Here's the map," she said. "Maybe I can explain better."

Miranda tried to sit forward. One remaining clip pulled her hair and made her inhale sharply. She reached up to detach herself. "Sorry," said Dr. Matsui sheepishly. She held out the paper for Miranda to see. "The dark waves is the Daniel we recorded off your memories earlier. Happy memories, right? You can see the fainter echo here as you responded to it with the original memories. Think of it as memory squared. Naturally, it's going to be intense. Then, everything else here is the record of the additional activity you brought to this particular session. Look at these sharp peaks at the beginning. They indicate stress. You'll see that nowhere else do they recur. On paper it looks to have been an entirely successful session. Of course, only you know the content of the experience." Her dark eyes were searching and sympathetic. "Well," she said. "Do you feel better about him?"

"Yes," said Miranda. "I feel better."

"Wonderful." Dr. Matsui handed the feedback to Matthew. "Store it," she told him.

Miranda spoke hesitatingly. "I had other things I wanted to say to him," she said. "It doesn't feel resolved."

"I don't think the sessions ever resolve things," Dr. Matsui said. "The best they can do is open the mind to resolution. The resolution still has to be found in the real world."

"Can I see him again?" Miranda asked.

Dr. Matsui interlaced her fingers and pressed them to her chest. "A repeat would be less expensive, of course," she said. "Since we've already got Daniel. We could just run him through again. Still, I'm reluctant to advise it. I wonder what else we could possibly gain."

"Please, Anna," said Miranda. She was looking down at her arms, remembering how firmly fleshed they had seemed.

"Let's wait and see how you're feeling after our next couple regular visits. If the old regrets persist and, more importantly, if they're still interfering with your ability to get on with things, then ask me again."

She was standing. Miranda swung her legs over the side of the chair and stood, too. Matthew walked with her to the door of the office. "We've got a goalie coming in next," he confided. "She stepped into the goal while holding the ball; she wants to remember it the way it didn't happen. Self-indulgent if you ask me. But then, athletes make the money, right?" He held the door open, his arm stretched in front of Miranda. "You feel better, don't you?" he asked.

"Yes," she reassured him.

She met Daniel for lunch at Frank Fats Cafe. They ordered fried clams and scallops, but the food never came. Daniel was twenty again and luminescent with youth. His hair was blond and his face was smooth. Had he really been so beautiful? Miranda wondered.

"I'd love a Coke," he said. "I haven't had one in thirty years."

"You're kidding," said Miranda. "They don't have the real thing in heaven?"

Daniel looked puzzled.

"Skip it," she told him. "I was just wondering what it was like being dead. You could tell me."

"It's classified," said Daniel. "On a need to know basis."

Miranda picked up her fork which was heavy and cold. "This time it's you who looks wonderful. Positively beatific. Last time you looked so—" she started to say *old,* but amended it. After all, he had looked no older than she did these days. Such things were relative. "Tired," she finished.

"No, I wasn't tired," Daniel told her. "It was the war."

"The war's over now," Miranda said and this time his smile was decidedly unpleasant.

"Is it?" he asked. "Just because you don't read about it in the paper now? Just because you watch the evening news and there's no body count in the corner of the screen?"

"Television's not like that now," Miranda began, but Daniel hadn't stopped talking.

"What's really going on in Southeast Asia? Do you even know?" Daniel shook his head. "Wars never end," he said. He leaned threateningly over the table. "Do you imagine for one minute that it's over for me?"

Miranda slammed her fork down. "Don't do that," she said. "Don't try to make me guilty of that, too. You didn't have to go. I begged you not to. Jesus, you knew what the war was. If you'd gone off to save the world from communist aggression, I would have disagreed, but I could have understood. But you knew better than that. I never forgave you for going."

"It was so easy for you to see what was right," Daniel responded angrily. "You were completely safe. You women could graduate without losing your deferment. Your goddamn birthday wasn't drawn twelfth in the draft lottery and if it had been you wouldn't have cared. When was your birthday drawn? You don't even know." Daniel leaned back and looked out the window. People appeared on the street. A woman in a red mini-skirt got into a blue car. Then Daniel faced her again, large before Miranda. She couldn't shut him out. "Go to Canada," you said. "That's what I'd do.' I wonder. Could you have married your mathematician in Canada? I can just picture you saying good-bye to your mother forever."

"My mother's dead now," said Miranda. A knot of tears tightened about her throat.

"And so the hell am I." Daniel reached for her wrists, holding them too hard, hurting her deliberately. "But you're not, are you? You're just fine."

There was a voice behind Daniel. "Miranda. Miranda," it called.

"Mother," cried Miranda. But, of course it wasn't, it was Anna Matsui, gripping her wrists, bringing her back. Miranda gasped for breath and Dr. Matsui let go of her. "It was awful," said Miranda. She began to cry. "He accused me . . ." She pulled the wires from her eyes recklessly. Tears spilled out of them. Miranda ached all over.

"He accused you of nothing." Dr. Matsui's voice was sharp and disappointed. "You accused yourself. The same old accusations. We made Daniel out of you, remember?" She rolled her chair backward, moved to the monitor for the feedback. Matthew handed it to her and she read it, shaking her head. Her short black hair flew against her cheeks. "It shouldn't have happened," she said. "We used only the memories that made you happy. And with your gift for lucid dreaming—well, I didn't think there was a risk." Her face was apologetic as she handed Miranda a tissue and waited for the crying to stop. "Matthew wanted to recall you earlier," she confessed, "but I didn't want it to end this way."

"No!" said Miranda. "We can't stop now. I never answered him."

"You only need to answer yourself. It's your memory and imagination confronting you. He speaks only with your voice, he behaves only as you expect him to." Dr. Matsui examined the feedback map again. "I should never have agreed to a repeat. I certainly won't send you back." She looked at Miranda and softened her voice. "Lie still. Lie still until you feel better."

"Like in another thirty years?" asked Miranda. She closed her eyes; her head hurt from the crying and the wires. She reached up to detach one close to her ear. "Everything he said to me was true," she added tonelessly.

"Many things he didn't say are bound to be true as well," Dr. Matsui pointed out. "Therapy is not really concerned with truth, which is almost always merely a matter of perspective. Therapy is concerned with adjustment—adjustment to an unchangeable situation or to a changing truth." She lifted a pen from her collar, clicking the point in and out absentmindedly. "In any given case," she continued, "we face a number of elements within our control and a far greater number beyond it. In a case such as yours, where the patient has felt profoundly and morbidly guilty over an extended period of time, it is because she is focusing almost exclusively on her own behavior. 'If only I hadn't done x,' she thinks, 'then y would never have happened.' Do you understand what I'm saying, Miranda?"

"No."

"In these sessions we try to show you what might have happened if the elements you couldn't control were changed. In your case we let you experience a continued relationship with Daniel. You see that you bore him no malice. You wished him nothing ill. If he had come back the bitterness of your last meeting would have been unimportant."

"He asked me to marry him," said Miranda. "He asked me to wait for him. I told you that. And I said that I was seeing Allen. Allen! I said as far as I was concerned he was already gone."

"You wish you could change that, of course. But what you really want to change is his death and that was beyond your control" Dr. Matsui's face was sweet and intense.

Miranda shook her head. "You're not listening to me, Anna. I told you what happened, but I lied about why it happened. I pretended we had political differences. I thought my behavior would be palatable if it looked like a matter of conscience. But really I dated Allen for the first time before Daniel had even been drafted. Because I knew what was coming. I saw that his life was about to get complicated and messy. And I saw a way out of it. For me, of course. Not for him." Miranda began to pick unhappily at the loose skin around her nails. "What do you think of that?" she asked. "What do you think of me now?"

"What do *you* think?" Dr. Matsui said and Miranda responded in disgust.

"I know what *I* think. I think I'm sick of talking to myself. Is that the best you therapists can manage? I think I'll stay home and talk to the mirrors." She pulled off the remaining connections to her scalp and sat up. "Matthew," she said. "Matthew!"

Matthew came to the side of her chair. He looked thin, concerned, and awkward. What a baby he was, really, she thought. He couldn't be more than twenty-five. "How old are you, Matthew?" she asked.

"Twenty-seven."

"Be a hell of a time to die, wouldn't it?" She watched Matthew put a nervous hand on his short brown hair and run it backward. "I want your opinion about something, Matthew. A hypothetical case. I'm trusting you to answer honestly."

Matthew glanced at Dr. Matsui who gestured with her pen for him to go ahead. He turned back to Miranda. "What would you think of a woman who deserted her lover, a man she really claimed to love, because he got sick and she didn't want to face the unpleasantness of it?"

Matthew spoke carefully. "I would imagine that it was motivated by cowardice rather than cruelty," he said. "I think we should always forgive sins of cowardice. Even our own." He stood looking at Miranda with his earnest, innocent face.

"All right, Matthew," she said. "Thank you." She lay back down in the chair and listened to the hum of the idle machines. "Anna," she said. "He didn't behave as I expected. I mean, sometimes he did and sometimes he didn't. Even the first time."

"Tell me about it," said Dr. Matsui.

"The first session he was older than I expected. Like he hadn't died, but had continued to age along with me."

"Wish fulfillment."

"Yes, but I was *surprised* by it. And I was surprised by the setting. And he said something very odd right at the end. He quoted me Zeno's paradox and it really exists, but I never heard it before. It didn't sound like something Daniel would say, either. It sounded more like my husband, Michael. Where did it come from?"

"Probably from just where you said," Dr. Matsui told her. "Michael. You don't think you remember it, but obviously you did. And husbands and lovers are bound to resemble each other, don't you think? We often get bits of overlap. Our parents show up one way or another in almost all our memories." Dr. Matsui stood. "Come in Tuesday," she said. "We'll talk some more."

"I'd like to see him one more time," said Miranda.

"Absolutely not," Dr. Matsui answered, returning Miranda's chair to its upright position.

"Where are we, Daniel?" Miranda asked. She couldn't see anything.

"Camp Pendleton," he answered. "On the beach. I used to run here mornings. Guys would bring their girlfriends. Not me, of course."

Miranda watched the landscape fill in as he spoke. Fog remained. It was early and overcast. She heard the ocean and felt the wet, heavy air begin to curl her hair. She was barefoot on the sand and a little cold. "I'm so sorry, Daniel," she said. "That's all I ever really wanted to tell you. I loved you."

"I know you did." He put his arm around her. She leaned against him. I must look like his mother, she thought; in fact, her own son was older than Daniel now. She looked up at him carefully. He must have just arrived at camp. The hair had been all but shaved from his head.

"Maybe you were right, anyway," Daniel told her. "Maybe I just shouldn't have gone. I was so angry at you by then I didn't care anymore. I even thought about dying with some sense of anticipation. Petulant, you know, like a little kid. I'll go and get killed and *then* she'll be sorry."

"And she was," said Miranda. "God, was she." She turned to face him, pressed her lined cheek against his chest, smelled his clothes. He must have started smoking again. Daniel put both arms around her. She heard a gull cry out ecstatically.

"But when the time came I really didn't want to die," Daniel's voice took on an unfamiliar edge, frightened, slightly hoarse. "When the time came I was willing to do *anything* rather than die." He hid his face in her neck. "Do you have kids?" he asked. "Did you and Michael ever?"

"A son," she said.

"How old? About six?"

Miranda wasn't sure how old Jeremy was now. It changed every year. But she told him, wonderingly, "Of course not, Daniel. He's all grown up. He owns a pizza franchise, can you believe it? He thinks I'm a bore."

"Because I killed a kid during the war. A kid about six years old. I figured it was him or me. I shot him." Miranda pushed back from Daniel, trying to get a good look at his face. "They used kids, you know," he said. "They counted on us not being able to kill them. I saw this little boy coming for me with his hands behind his back. I told him to stop. I shouted at him to stop. I pointed my rifle and said I was going to kill him. But he kept coming."

"Oh, Daniel," said Miranda. "Maybe he didn't speak English."

"A pointed rifle is universal. He walked into the bullet."

"What was he carrying?"

"Nothing," said Daniel. "How could I know?"

"Daniel," Miranda said. "I don't believe you. You wouldn't do that." Her words unsettled her even more. "Not the way I remember you," she said. "This is not the way I remember you."

"It's so easy for you to see what's right," said Daniel.

I'm going back, thought Miranda. Where am I really? I must be with Anna, but then she remembered that she was not. She was in her own study. She worked to feel the study chair beneath her, the ache in her back as she curved over her desk. Her feet dangled by the wheels, she concentrated until she could feel them. She saw her own hand, still holding her pencil, and she put it down. She walked to the bedroom and summoned Dr. Matsui over the console. She waited perhaps fifteen minutes before Anna appeared.

"Daniel's the one with the problem," Miranda said. "It's not me, after all."

"There is no Daniel." Dr. Matsui's voice betrayed a startled concern. "Except in your mind and on my tapes. Apart from you, no Daniel."

"No. He came for me again. Just like in our sessions. Just as intense. Do you understand? Not a dream," she cut off Dr. Matsui's protest. "It was not a dream, because I wasn't asleep. I was working and then I was with him. I could feel him. I could smell him. He told me an absolutely horrible story about killing a child during the war. Where would I have gotten that? Not the sort of thing they send home in their letters to the bereaved."

"There were a thousand ugly stories out of Vietnam," said Dr. Matsui. "I know some and I wasn't even born yet. Or just barely born. Remember My Lai?" Miranda watched her image clasp its hands. "You heard this story somewhere. It became part of your concept of the war. So you put it together now with Daniel." Dr. Matsui's voice took on its professional patina. "I'd like you to come in, Miranda. Immediately. I'd like to take a complete read-out and keep you monitored a while. Maybe overnight. I don't like the turn this is taking."

"All right," said Miranda. "I don't want to be alone anyway. Because he's going to come again."

"No," said Dr. Matsui firmly. "He's not."

Miranda took the elevator to the garage and unlocked her bicycle. She was not frightened and wondered why not. She felt unhappy and uncertain, but in complete control of herself. She pushed out into the bike lane. When the helicopter appeared overhead, Miranda knew immediately where she was. A banana tree sketched itself in on her right. There was a smell in the air which was strange to her. Old diesel engines, which she recognized, but also something organic. A lushness almost turned to rot. In the distance the breathtaking green of rice growing. But the dirt at her feet was bare.

Miranda had never imagined a war could be so quiet. Then she heard the helicopter. And she heard Daniel. He was screaming. He stood right next to her, beside a pile of sandbags, his rifle stretched out before him. A small, delicately featured child was just walking into Miranda's view, his arms held behind him. All Miranda had to do was lift her hand.

"No, Daniel," she said. "His hands are empty."

Daniel didn't move. The war stopped. "I killed him, Randy," said Daniel. "You can't change that."

Miranda looked at the boy. His eyes were dark, a streak of dust ran all the way up one shoulder and onto his face. He was barefoot. "I know," she said. "I can't help him." The child faded and disappeared. "I'm trying to help you." The boy reappeared again, back further, at the very edge of her vision. He was beautiful, unbearably young. He began to walk to them once more.

"*Can* you help me?" Daniel asked.

Miranda pressed her palm into his back. He wore no shirt and was slick and sweaty. "I don't know," she said. "Was it a crime of cowardice or of cruelty? I'm told you can be forgiven the one, but not the other."

Daniel dropped his rifle into the dirt. The landscape turned slowly about them, became mountainous. The air smelled cleaner and was cold.

A bird flew over them in a beautiful arc, and then it became a baseball and began to fall in slow motion, and then it became death and she could plot its trajectory. It was aimed at Daniel whose rifle had reappeared in his hands. Now, Miranda thought. She could stay and die with Daniel the way she'd always believed she should. Death moved so slowly in the sky. She could see it, moment to moment, descending like a series of scarcely differentiated still frames. "Look, Daniel," she said. "It's Zeno's paradox in reverse. Finite points. Infinite time." How long did she have to make this decision? A lifetime. Her lifetime.

Daniel would not look up. He reached out his hand to touch her hair. Gray, she knew. Her gray under his young hand. He was twenty-four. "Don't stay," he said. "Do you think I would have wanted you to? I would never have wanted that."

So Miranda moved from his hand and found she was glad to do so. "I always loved you," she said as if it mattered. "Good-bye, Daniel," but he had already looked away. Other soldiers materialized beside him and death grew to accommodate them. But they wouldn't all die. Some would survive in pieces, she thought. And some would survive whole. Wouldn't they?

(1985)

JOHN CROWLEY

Snow

I don't think Georgie would ever have got one for herself: she was at once unsentimental and a little in awe of death. No, it was her first husband—an immensely rich and (from Georgie's description) a strangely weepy guy, who had got it for her. Or for himself, actually, of course. He was to be the beneficiary. Only he died himself shortly after it was installed. If *installed* is the right word. After he died, Georgie got rid of most of what she'd inherited from him, liquidated it. It was cash that she had liked best about that marriage anyway; but the Wasp couldn't really be got rid of. Georgie ignored it.

In fact the thing really was about the size of a wasp of the largest kind, and it had the same lazy and mindless flight. And of course it really was a bug, not of the insect kind but of the surveillance kind. And so its name fit all around: one of those bits of accidental poetry the world generates without thinking. O Death where is thy sting.

Georgie ignored it, but it was hard to avoid; you had to be a little careful around it, it followed Georgie at a variable distance, depending on her motions and the number of other people around her, the level of light and the tone of her voice, and there was always the danger you might shut it in a door or knock it down with a tennis racket. It cost a fortune (if you count in the access and the perpetual-care contract, all prepaid) and though it wasn't really fragile, it made you nervous.

It wasn't recording all the time. There had to be a certain amount of light, though not much. Darkness shut it off. And then sometimes it would get lost. Once when we hadn't seen it hovering around for a time, I opened a closet door and it flew out, unchanged, and went off looking for her, humming softly. It must have been shut in there for days.

Eventually it ran out, or down. A lot could go wrong, I suppose, with circuits that small, controlling that many functions. It ended up spending a lot of time bumping gently against the bedroom ceiling, over and over, like a winter fly. Then one day the maid swept it out from under the bureau, a husk. By that time it had transmitted at least eight thousand hours (eight thousand was the minimum guarantee) of Georgie: of her days and hours, her comings in and her goings out, her speech and motion, her living self: all on file, taking up next to no room, at The Park.

And then when the time came, you could go there, to The Park, say on a Sunday afternoon; and in quiet landscaped surroundings (as The Park described it) you would find her personal resting chamber; and there, in privacy, through the miracle of modern information storage and retrieval systems, you could access her: her alive, her as she was in every way, never changing or growing any older: fresher (as The Park's brochure said) than in memory—ever green.

I married Georgie for her money, the same reason she married her first, the one who took out The Park's contract for her. She married me, I think, for my looks; she always had a taste for looks in men. I wanted to write. I made a calculation that more women than men make, and decided that to be supported and paid for by a rich wife would give me freedom to do so, to "develop." The calculation worked out no better for me than it does for most women who make it. I carried a typewriter and a case of miscellaneous paper from Ibiza to Gstaad to Bali to London, and typed on beaches, and learned to ski. Georgie liked me in ski clothes.

Now that those looks are all but gone, I can look back on myself as a young hunk, and see that I was in a way a rarity, a type that you run into often among women, far less often among men, the beauty unaware of his beauty, aware that he affects women profoundly and more or less instantly but doesn't know why; thinks he is being listened to and understood, that his soul is being seen, when all that's being seen is long-lashed eyes and a strong square tanned wrist turning in a lovely gesture, stubbing out a cigarette. Confusing. By the time I figured out why I had for so long been indulged and cared for and listened to, why I was interesting, I wasn't as interesting as I had been. At about the same time I realized I wasn't a writer at all. Georgie's investment stopped looking as good to her, and my calculation had ceased to add up; only by that time I had come, pretty unexpectedly, to love Georgie a lot, and she just as unexpectedly had come to love and need me too, as much as she needed anybody. We never really parted, even though when she died I hadn't seen her for years. Phone calls, at dawn or four A.M. because she never, for all her travel, really grasped that the world turns and cocktail hour travels around with it.

She was a crazy, wasteful, happy woman, without a trace of malice or permanence or ambition in her; easily pleased and easily bored, and strangely serene despite the hectic pace she kept up. She cherished things and lost them and forgot them: things, days, people. She had fun, though, and I had fun with her; that was her talent, and her destiny, not always an easy one. Once, hungover in a New York hotel, watching a sudden snowfall out the immense window, she said to me: "Charlie, I'm going to die of fun."

And she did. Snow-foiling in Austria; she was among the first to get one of those Snow Leopards, silent beasts as fast as speedboats. Alfredo called me in California to tell me, but with the distance and his accent and his eagerness to tell me *he* wasn't to blame, I never grasped the details. I was still her husband, her closest relative, heir to the little she had left by that time, and beneficiary too of The Park's access concept. Fortunately The Park's services included collecting her from the morgue in Gstaad and installing her in her chamber at The Park's California unit. Beyond signing papers and taking delivery when Georgie arrived by freight airship at Van Nuys, there was nothing for me to do. The Park's representative was solicitous, and made sure I understood how to go about accessing Georgie, but I wasn't listening. I am only a child of my time, I suppose. Everything about death, the fact of it, the fate of the remains, and the situation of the living faced with it, seems grotesque to me, embarrassing, useless. And everything done about it only makes it more grotesque, more useless: someone I loved is dead, let me therefore dress in clown's clothes, talk backwards, and buy expensive machinery to make up for it. I went back to L.A.

A year or more later, the contents of some safe-deposit boxes of Georgie's arrived from the lawyer's: some bonds and such stuff, and a small steel case, velvet-lined, that contained a key, a key deeply notched on both sides and headed with smooth plastic, like the key to an expensive car.

Why did I go to The Park that first time? Mostly because I had forgotten about it: getting that key in the mail was like coming across a pile of old snapshots you hadn't cared to look at when they were new, but which after they have aged come to contain the past, as they did not contain the present. I was curious.

I understood very well that The Park and its access concept were very probably only another cruel joke on the rich, preserving the illusion that they can buy what can't be bought, like the cryonics fad of thirty years before. Once in Ibiza Georgie and I met a German couple who also had a contract with The Park; their Wasp hovered over them like a paraclete, and made them self-conscious in the extreme—they seemed to be constantly rehearsing the eternal show being stored up for their descendants. Their deaths had taken over their lives, as though they were pharaohs. Did they, Georgie wondered, exclude the Wasp from their bedroom? Or did its presence there stir them to greater efforts, proofs of undying love and admirable vigor for the unborn to see?

No, death wasn't to be cheated that way, any more than by pyramids, by masses said in perpetuity; it wasn't Georgie saved from death that I would find. But there were eight thousand hours of her life with me, genuine hours, stored there more carefully than they could be in my porous memory; Georgie hadn't excluded the Wasp from her bedroom, our bedroom, and she who had never performed for anybody could not have conceived of performing for it. And there would be me, too, undoubtedly, caught unintentionally by the Wasp's attention: out of those thousands of hours there would be hundreds of myself, and myself had just then begun to be problematic to me, something that had to be figured out, something about which evidence had to be gathered and weighed. I was thirty-eight years old.

That summer, then, I borrowed a Highway Access Permit (the old HAPpy cards of those days) from a county lawyer I knew, and drove the coast highway up to where The Park was, at the end of a pretty beach road, all alone above the sea. It looked from the outside like the best, most peaceful kind of Italian country cemetery, a low stucco wall topped with urns, amid cypresses, an arched gate in the center. A small brass plaque on the gate: Please Use Your Key. The gate opened, not to a square of shaded tombstones but onto a ramped corridor going down: the cemetery wall was an illusion, the works were underground. Silence, or nameless muzak like silence; solitude—either the necessary technicians were discreetly hidden, or none were needed. Certainly the access concept turned out to be simplicity itself, in operation anyway. Even I, who am an idiot about information technology, could tell that. The Wasp was genuine state-of-the-art stuff, but what we mourners got was as ordinary as home movies, as old letters tied up in ribbon.

A display screen near the entrance told me down which corridor to find Georgie, and my key let me into a small screening room where there was a moderate-sized TV monitor and two comfortable chairs; dark walls of chocolate-brown carpeting. The sweet-sad muzak. Georgie herself was evidently somewhere in the vicinity, in the wall or under the floor, they weren't specific about the charnel-house aspect of the place. In the control panel before the TV were a keyhole for my key, and two bars: ACCESS and RESET.

I sat, feeling foolish and a little afraid too, made more uncomfortable by being so deliberately soothed by neutral furnishings and sober tools. I imagined, around me, down other corridors, in other chambers, others communed with their dead as I was about to do, that the dead were murmuring to them beneath the stream of muzak; that they wept to see and hear, as I might. But I could hear nothing. I turned my key in its slot, and the screen lit up; the dim lights dimmed further, and the muzak ceased. I pushed ACCESS, obviously the next step. No doubt all these procedures had been explained to me long ago at the dock when Georgie in her aluminum box was being offloaded, and I hadn't listened. And on the screen she turned to look at me—only not at me, though I started and drew breath—at the Wasp that watched her.

She was in midsentence, midgesture. Where? When? *Or put it on the same card with the others,* she said, turning away. Someone said something, Georgie answered, and stood up, the Wasp panning and moving erratically with her, like an amateur with a home-video camera. A white room, sunlight, wicker. Ibiza. Georgie wore a cotton blouse, open; from a table she picked up lotion, poured some on her hand, and rubbed it across her freckled breastbone. The meaningless conversation about putting something on a card went on, ceased. I watched the room, wondering what year, what season I had stumbled into. Georgie pulled off her shirt—her small round breasts tipped with large childish nipples, child's breasts she still had at forty, shook delicately—and she went out onto the balcony, the Wasp following, blinded for a moment by sun, adjusting. *If you want to do it that way,* someone said. The someone crossed the screen, a brown blur, naked. It was me. Georgie said: *Oh, look, hummingbirds.*

She watched them, rapt, and the Wasp crept close to her cropped blond head, rapt too, and I watched her watch. She turned away, rested her elbows on the balustrade. I couldn't remember this day. How should I? One of hundreds, of thousands . . . She looked out to the bright sea, wearing her sleepwalking face, mouth partly open, and absently stroked her breast with her oiled hand. An iridescent glitter among the flowers was the hummingbird.

Without really knowing what I did—I felt hungry, suddenly, hungry for pastness, for more—I touched the RESET bar. The balcony in Ibiza vanished, the screen glowed emptily. I touched ACCESS.

At first there was darkness, a murmur; then a dark back moved away from before the Wasp's eye, and a dim scene of people resolved itself. Jump. Other people, or the same people, a party? Jump. Apparently the Wasp was turning itself on and off according to the changes in light levels here, wherever here was. Georgie in a dark dress having her cigarette lit: brief flare of the lighter. She said *Thanks.* Jump. A foyer or hotel lounge. Paris? The Wasp jerkily sought for her among people coming and going; it couldn't make a movie, establishing shots, cutaways—it could only doggedly follow Georgie, like a jealous husband, seeing nothing else. This was frustrating. I pushed RESET. ACCESS. Georgie brushed her teeth, somewhere, somewhen.

I understood, after one or two more of these terrible leaps. Access was random. There was no way to dial up a year, a day, a scene. The Park had supplied no program, none; the eight thousand hours weren't filed at all, they were a jumble like a lunatic's memory, like a deck of shuffled cards. I had supposed, without thinking about it, that they would begin at the beginning and go on till they reached the end. Why didn't they?

I also understood something else. If access was truly random, if I truly had no control, then I had lost as good as forever those scenes I had seen. Odds were on the order of eight thousand to one (more? far more? probabilities are opaque to me) that I would never light on them again by pressing this bar. I felt a pang of loss for that afternoon in Ibiza. It was doubly gone now. I sat before the empty screen, afraid to touch ACCESS again, afraid of what I would lose.

I shut down the machine (the light-level in the room rose, the muzak poured softly back in) and went out into the halls, back to the display screen in the entranceway. The list of names slowly, greenly rolled over like the list of departing flights at an airport: code numbers were missing from beside many, indicating perhaps that they weren't yet in residence, only awaited. In the D's, three names, and Director: hidden among them as though he were only another of the dead. A chamber number. I went to find it, and went in.

The Director looked more like a janitor, or a night watchman, the semi-retired type you often see caretaking little-visited places. He wore a brown smock like a monk's robe and was making coffee in a corner of his small office, out of which little business seemed to be done. He looked up startled, caught out, when I entered.

"Sorry," I said, "but I don't think I understand this system right."

"A problem?" he said. "Shouldn't be a problem." He looked at me a little wide-eyed and shy, hoping not to be called on for anything difficult. "Equipment's all working?"

"I don't know," I said. "It doesn't seem that it could be." I described what I thought I had learned about The Park's access concept. "That can't be right, can it?" I said. "That access is totally random . . . "

He was nodding, still wide-eyed, paying close attention.

"Is it?" I asked.

"Is it what?"

"Random."

"Oh, yes. Yes, sure. If everything's in working order."

I could think of nothing to say for a moment, watching him nod reassuringly. Then: "Why?" I asked. "I mean why is there no way at all to, to organize, to have some kind of organized access to the, to the material?" I had begun to feel that sense of grotesque foolishness in the presence of death, as though I were haggling over dead Georgie's effects. "That seems stupid, if you'll pardon me."

"Oh no, oh no," he said. "You've read your literature? You've read all your literature?"

"Well, to tell the truth . . . "

"It's all just as described," the Director said. "I can promise you. If there's any problem at all . . . "

"Do you mind," I said, "if I sit down?" I smiled—he seemed so afraid of me and my complaint, of me as mourner, possibly grief-crazed and unable to grasp the simple limits of his responsibilities to me, that he needed soothing himself. "I'm sure everything's fine," I said. "I just don't think I understand. I'm kind of dumb about these things."

"Sure. Sure. Sure." He regretfully put away his coffee makings and sat behind his desk, lacing his fingers together like a consultant. "People get a lot of satisfaction out of the access here," he said, "a lot of comfort, if they take it in the right spirit." He tried a smile. I wondered what qualifications he had had to show to get this job. "The random part. Now it's all in the literature. There's the legal aspect, you're not a lawyer are you, no no sure, no offense. You see, the material here isn't *for* anything, except, well, except for communing. But suppose the stuff *were* programmed, searchable. Suppose there was a problem about taxes or inheritance or so on. There could be subpoenas, lawyers all over the place, destroying the memorial concept completely."

I really hadn't thought of that. Built-in randomness saved past lives from being searched in any systematic way. And no doubt saved The Park from being in the records business, and at the wrong end of a lot of suits. "You'd have to watch the whole eight thousand hours," I said, "right, and even if you found what you were looking for there'd be no way to replay it after you'd seen it. It would have gone by." It would slide into the random past even as you watched it, like that afternoon in Ibiza, that party in Paris. Lost.

He smiled and nodded. I smiled and nodded.

"I'll tell you something," he said. "They didn't predict that. The randomness. It was a side effect, an effect of the storage process. Just luck." His grin turned down, his brows knitted seriously. "See, we're storing here at the molecular level. We have to go that small, for space problems. I mean your eight thousand hours guarantee, if we had gone tape or conventional, how much room would it take up? If the access concept caught on. A lot of room. So we went vapor-trap and endless-tracking. Size of my thumbnail. It's all in the literature." He looked at me strangely. I had a sudden intense sensation that I was being fooled, tricked, that the man before me in his smock was no expert, no technician, he was a charlatan, or maybe a madman impersonating a Director and not belonging here at all. It raised the hair on my neck, and passed. "So the randomness," he was saying. "It was an effect of going molecular. Brownian movement. All you do is lift the endless-tracking for a microsecond, and you get a rearrangement at the molecular level. We don't randomize. The molecules do it for us."

I remembered Brownian movement, just barely, from physics class. The random movement of molecules, the teacher said; it has a mathematical description; it's like the movement of dust motes you see swimming in a shaft of sunlight, like the swirl of snowflakes in a glass paperweight that shows a cottage being snowed on. "I see," I said. "I guess I see."

"Is there," he said, "any other problem?" He said it as though there might be some other problem, and that he knew what it might be, and that he hoped I didn't have it. "You understand the system, key lock, two bars, ACCESS, RESET . . . "

"I understand," I said. "I understand now."

"Communing," he said, standing, relieved, sure I would be gone soon. "I understand. It takes a while to relax into the communing concept."

"Yes," I said. "It does."

I wouldn't learn what I had come to learn, whatever that was. The Wasp had not been good at storage after all, no, no better than my young soul had been; days and weeks had been missed by its tiny eye, it hadn't seen well and in what it had seen it had been no more able to distinguish the just-as-well-forgotten from the unforgettable than my own eye had been: no better and no worse: the same.

And yet, and yet—she stood up in Ibiza and dressed her breasts with lotion, and spoke to me: *Oh look, hummingbirds.* I had forgotten, and the Wasp had not; and I owned once again what I hadn't known I had lost, hadn't known was precious to me.

The sun was setting when I left The Park, the satin sea foaming softly, randomly around the rocks.

I had spent my life waiting for something, not knowing what, not even knowing I waited. Killing time. I was still waiting. But what I had been waiting for had already occurred, and was past.

It was two years, nearly, since Georgie had died: two years until, for the first and last time, I wept for her; for her, and for myself.

Of course I went back. After a lot of work and correctly-placed dollars, I netted a HAPpy card of my own. I had time to spare, like a lot of people then, and often on empty afternoons (never on Sunday) I would get out onto the unpatched and weedgrown freeway and glide up the Coast. The Park was always open. I relaxed into the communing concept.

Now, after some hundreds of hours spent there underground, now when I have long ceased to go through those doors (I have lost my key, I think, anyway I don't know where to look for it), I know that the solitude I felt myself to be in was real; the watchers around me, the listeners I sensed in other chambers, were mostly my imagination. There was rarely anyone there. These tombs were as neglected as any tombs anywhere usually are. Either the living did not care to attend much on the dead—when have they ever?—or the hopeful buyers of the contracts had come to discover the flaw in the access concept: as I discovered it, in the end.

ACCESS and she takes dresses one by one from her closet, and holds them against her body, and studies the effect in a tall mirror, and puts them back again. She had a funny face which she never made except when looking at herself in the mirror, a face made for no one but herself, that was actually quite unlike her. The mirror Georgie.

RESET.

ACCESS. By a bizarre coincidence here she is looking in another mirror. I think the Wasp could be confused by mirrors. She turns away, the Wasp adjusts; there is someone asleep, tangled in bedclothes on a big hotel bed, morning, a room-service cart. Oh: the Algonquin: myself. Winter. Snow is falling outside the tall window. She searches her handbag, takes out a small vial, swallows a pill with coffee, holding the cup by its body and not its handle. I stir, show a tousled head of hair. Conversation: unintelligible. Gray room, whitish snow-light, color degraded. Would I now (I thought, watching us) reach out for her? Would I in the next take her, or she me, push aside the bedclothes, open her pale pajamas? She goes into the john, shuts the door. The Wasp watches stupidly, excluded, transmitting the door.

RESET, finally.

But what (I would wonder) if I had been patient, what if I had watched and waited?

Time, it turns out, takes an unconscionable time. The waste, the footless waste—it's no spectator sport; whatever fun there is in sitting idly looking at nothing and tasting your own being for a whole afternoon, there is no fun in replaying it, the waiting is excruciating. How often, in five years, in eight thousand hours of daylight or lamplight, might we have coupled, how much time expended in lovemaking? A hundred hours, two hundred? Odds were not high of my coming on such a scene, darkness swallowed most of them and the others were lost in the interstices of endless hours spent shopping, reading, on planes and in cars, asleep, apart. Hopeless.

ACCESS. She has turned on a bedside lamp. Alone. She hunts amid the Kleenex and magazines on the bedside table, finds a watch, looks at it dully, turns it right-side-up, looks again and puts it down. Cold. She burrows in the blankets, yawning, staring, then puts out a hand for the phone, but only rests her hand on it, thinking. Thinking at four A.M. She withdraws her hand, shivers a child's deep sleepy shiver, and shuts off the light. A bad dream. In an instant it's morning, dawn, the Wasp slept too. She sleeps soundly, unmoving, only the top of her blond head showing out of the quilt: and will no doubt sleep so for hours, watched over more attentively, more fixedly, than any peeping Tom could ever have watched over her.

RESET.

ACCESS.

"I can't hear as well as I did at first," I told the Director. "And the definition is getting softer."

"Oh sure, yes sure," the Director said. "That's really in the literature. We have to explain that very carefully. That this might be a problem."

"It isn't just my monitor?" I asked. "I thought it was probably only the monitor."

"No, no, not really, no," he said. He gave me coffee. We'd gotten to be friendly over the months. I think, as well as being afraid of me, he was glad I came around now and then; at least one of the living came here, one at least was using the services. "There's a *slight* degeneration that does occur."

"Everything seems to be getting gray."

His face had shifted into intense concern, no belittling this problem. "Mm-hm, mm-hm, see, at the molecular level where we're at, there *is* degeneration. It's just in the physics. It randomizes a little over time. So you lose—you don't lose a minute of what you've got—but you lose a little definition. A little color. But it levels off."

"It does."

"We think it does. Sure it does, we promise it does. We *predict* that it will."

"But you don't know."

"Well, well you see we've only been in this business a short while. This concept is new. There were things we couldn't know." He still looked at me, but seemed at the same time to have forgotten me. Tired. He seemed to have grown colorless himself lately, old, losing definition. "You might start getting some snow," he said softly.

ACCESS. RESET. ACCESS.

A gray plaza of herringbone-laid stones; gray, clicking palms. She turns up the collar of her sweater, narrowing her eyes in a stern wind. Buys magazines at a kiosk: *Vogue, Harper's, La Moda. Cold,* she says to the kiosk girl. *Frío.* The young man I was takes her arm; they walk back along the beach, which is deserted and strung with cast seaweed, washed by a dirty sea. Winter in Ibiza. We talk, but the Wasp can't hear, the sea's sound confuses it, it seems bored by its duties, and lags behind us.

RESET.

ACCESS. The Algonquin, terribly familiar; morning, winter. She turns away from the snowy window, I am in bed, and for a moment watching this I felt suspended between two mirrors, reflected endlessly. I had seen this before; I had lived it once, and remembered it once, and remembered the memory, and here it was again, or could it be nothing but another morning, a similar morning, there were far more than one like this, in this place. But no; she turns from the window, she gets out her vial of pills, picks up the coffee cup by its body: I had seen this moment before, not months before, weeks before, here in this chamber. I had come upon the same scene twice.

What are the odds of it, I wondered, what are the odds of coming upon the same minutes again, these minutes.

I stir within the bedclothes.

I leaned forward to hear, this time, what I would say; it was something like *but fun anyway,* or something.

Fun, she says, laughing, harrowed, the degraded sound a ghost's twittering. *Charlie someday I'm going to die of fun.*

She takes her pill. The Wasp follows her to the john, and is shut out.

Why am I here? I thought, and my heart was beating hard and slow. What am I here for? What?

RESET.

ACCESS.

Silvered icy streets, New York. Fifth Avenue. She is climbing shouting from a cab's dark interior: *just don't shout at me,* she shouts at someone, her mother I never met, a dragon. She is out and hurrying away down the sleety street with her bundles, the Wasp at her shoulder. I could reach out, and touch her shoulder, and make her turn, and follow me out.

Walking away, lost in the colorless press of traffic and people, impossible to discern, within the softened snowy image.

Something was very wrong.

Georgie hated winter, she escaped it most of the time we were together, about the first of the year beginning to long for the sun that had gone elsewhere; Austria was all right for a few weeks, the toy villages and sugar snow and bright sleek skiers was not really the winter she feared, though even in firewarmed chalets it was hard to get her naked without gooseflesh and shudders from some draft only she could feel. We were chaste in winter. So Georgie escaped it: Antigua and Bali and two months in Ibiza when the almonds blossomed, it was a continual false flavorless spring all winter long.

How often could snow have fallen when the Wasp was watching her?

Not often; countable times, times I could count up myself if I could remember as the Wasp could. Not often: not always.

"There's a problem," I said to the Director.

"It's peaked out, has it?" he said. "That definition problem?"

"Well, no," I said. "Actually, it's gotten worse."

He was sitting behind his desk, arms spread wide across his chair's back, and a false pinkish flush to his cheeks like undertaker's makeup. Drinking.

"Hasn't peaked out, huh," he said.

"That's not the problem," I said. "The problem is the access. It's not random like you said."

"Molecular level," he said. "It's in the physics."

"You don't understand. It's not getting more random. It's getting less random. It's getting selective. It's freezing up."

"No no no," he said dreamily. "Access is random. Life isn't all summer and fun, you know. Into each life some rain must fall."

I sputtered, trying to explain. "But but but . . . "

"You know," he said, "I've been thinking of getting out of access." He pulled open a drawer in the desk before him; it made an empty sound. He stared within it dully for a moment, and shut it. "The Park's been good for me, but I'm just not used to this. Used to be you thought you could render a service, you know? Well, hell, you know, you've had fun, what do you care."

He *was* mad. For an instant I heard the dead around me; I tasted on my tongue the stale air of underground.

"I remember," he said, tilting back in his chair and looking elsewhere, "many years ago, I got into access. Only we didn't call it that then. What I did was, I worked for a stock-footage house. It was going out of business like they all did, like this place here is going to do, shouldn't say that but you didn't hear it. Anyway. It was a big warehouse with steel shelves for miles, filled with film cans, film cans filled with old plastic film, you know? Film of every kind. And movie people, if they wanted old scenes of past time in their movies, would call up and ask for what they wanted, find me this, find me that. And we had everything, every kind of scene, but you know what the hardest thing to find was? Just ordinary scenes of daily life. I mean people just doing things and living their lives. You know what we *did* have? Speeches. People giving speeches. Like presidents. You could have hours of speeches, but not just people, whatchacallit, oh washing clothes, sitting in a park . . . "

"It might just be the reception," I said. "Somehow."

He looked at me for a long moment as though I had just arrived. "Anyway," he said at last, turning away again, "I was there a while learning the ropes. And producers called and said get me this, get me that. And one producer was making a film, some film of the past, and he wanted old scenes, *old*, of people long ago, in the summer; having fun; eating ice-cream. Swimming in bathing suits. Riding in convertibles. Fifty years ago. Eighty years ago."

He opened his empty drawer again, found a toothpick, and began to use it.

"So I accessed the earliest stuff. Speeches. More speeches. But I found a scene here and there: people in the street, fur coats, window-shopping, traffic. Old people, I mean they were young then, but people of the past; they have these pinched kind of faces, you get to know them. Sad, a little. On city streets, hurrying, holding their hats. Cities were sort of black then, in film; black cars in the streets, black derby hats. Stone.

"Well it wasn't what they wanted. I found summer for them, color summer, but new. They wanted old. I kept looking back. I kept looking. I did. The farther back I went, the more I saw these pinched faces, black cars, black streets of stone. Snow. There isn't any summer there."

With slow gravity he rose, and found a brown bottle and two coffee cups. He poured sloppily. "So it's not your reception," he said. "Film takes longer, I guess, but it's in the physics. All in the physics. A word to the wise is sufficient."

The liquor was harsh, a cold distillate of past sunlight. I wanted to go, get out, not look back. I would not stay watching until there was only snow.

"So I'm getting out of access," the Director said. "Let the dead bury the dead, right? Let the dead bury the dead."

I didn't go back; I never went back, though the highways opened again and The Park isn't far from the town I've settled in. Settled: the right word. It restores your balance, in the end, even in a funny way your cheerfulness, when you come to know, without regrets, that the best thing that's going to happen in your life has already happened. And I still have some summer left to me.

I think there are two different kinds of memory, and only one kind gets worse as I get older: the kind where by an effort of will you can reconstruct your first car or your serial number or the name and figure of your high-school physics teacher: a Mr. Holm, in a gray suit, a bearded guy, skinny, about thirty. The other kind doesn't worsen, if anything it grows more intense: the sleepwalking kind, the kind you stumble into as into rooms with secret doors to suddenly find yourself sitting not on your front porch but in a classroom, you can't at first think where or when, and a bearded smiling man is turning in his hand a glass paperweight inside which a little cottage stands in a swirl of snow.

There is no access to Georgie: except that now and then, unpredictably, when I'm sitting on the porch or pushing a grocery cart or standing at the sink, a memory of that kind will visit me, vivid and startling, like a hypnotist's snap of fingers, or like that funny experience you sometimes have, on the point of sleep, of hearing your name called softly and distinctly by someone who is not there.

(1985)

PAT CADIGAN

After the Days of Dead-Eye 'Dee

The third night Brett was gone, Merridee put out all the downstairs lights and waited at the window by the kitchen table, the shotgun loaded and ready. She'd left all the upstairs lights burning; the glow they threw down let her see the backyard pretty well, considering. At fifty-eight her eyesight wasn't as dependable as it had once been—thus, the shotgun and not the rifle. You didn't have to be a crackshot with a shotgun, though at one time she'd been handy with either weapon. Dead-Eye 'Dee, her brothers had called her back in her target shooting days. They should have seen old Dead-Eye 'Dee now, she thought, crouched on a chair in a dark kitchen with a shotgun, waiting for God-knew-what.

A hundred yards beyond the house, she could just make out the silhouette of the stand of trees near the well Brett had sunk twenty years ago, only to have it dry up a year later. That was where it came out of, those trees. Maybe it was actually holed up in the old well. If it were, she couldn't imagine how it was getting out. She shifted position on the chair and carefully set the shotgun on the table. A moth hurled itself against the screen and fluttered away, up toward the light. Awfully late in the year for moths, Merridee thought idly; maybe it wouldn't come tonight. Maybe it had wandered off or died or something.

There was a rustle of leaves; a small puff of chill October air came through the window. Merridee blinked, adjusting her glasses. Uh-huh, she thought. Dead leaves danced across the yard as the shadow detached itself from the stand of trees and approached the house. Would it think she was upstairs (if it thought at all)? Or could it sense her waiting in the dark?

The thing moved awkwardly, as though it were used to much different terrain. She could see it a lot better from the kitchen window than from upstairs, where she'd watched it the previous two nights. She hadn't been able to tell much about it at all, not even whether it was worth creeping downstairs to phone the sheriff about. But tonight she'd get a good look at it, see if it were man or beast, and then she'd know what to do. Maybe.

Just out of the range of light, it stopped and she thought she saw it hunker over, as though examining the ground. It was man-sized but she could tell the limbs were all wrong, the one arm she could make out was too long even for an ape. Maybe it was some poor freak, simple-minded as well as deformed, looking for shelter and food.

It made a strange sound and she jumped slightly, putting one hand on the shotgun. It wasn't a very fierce noise, something between a sigh and a growl, or maybe a sigh and a snore. Not very animal-sounding, but not human, either.

She peered through the screen, wanting to call to it just to make it step into the light. It sigh-growled again and shuffled along the grass and dead leaves, stopping when it was opposite the window.

It knew she was there. The thought gave her a sudden flash of panic. An image of Brett popped into her head. He knew she was here, too, here in the house alone while he was days away, fishing and hunting in Oklahoma with his friends. His friends knew where she was, too, and his friends' wives, and her son and daughter-in-law; they all knew. But none of them knew the way this thing knew. The thoughts chased each other around in spirals in her mind as panic passed, leaving behind a rationally cold fear.

She picked up the shotgun. Weeks ago, she had hinted to Brett she'd have enjoyed a camping trip. It had been a long time since they'd taken one together. He'd only reminded her of the rheumatism in her shoulders and knees, that she'd just be in pain the whole time. So he was gone with his friends now and she was safely at home, no rheumatism acting up, watching this shadow. She wished she were anywhere else. Then this thing, whatever it was, could have had the run of the whole place and she wouldn't have had to know about it, she wouldn't have been trapped in the kitchen, wondering if she should shoot it.

It didn't move again for a long time. Because it could see in the dark, she thought, and it was looking her over. She imagined how she must look to it, wide-eyed behind her glasses, her loose, broad face homely with old-lady worry, a shotgun in her thick hands like a rolling-pin. Not much of a damsel in distress. Somewhere in the back of her mind was the irrational idea that every bit of her life had been pointing toward this moment and whatever happened afterwards would be mere time-keeping till the grave.

She untensed the tiniest bit, her fear smoothing into puzzlement. All right, now what did the thing want? Was it going to attack or not? Should she phone the sheriff and let him come take care of it? Puzzlement mixed with impatience. Suppose she just walked out there, walked right out there and said *What do you want?* as bold as you please? With the shotgun, of course. Would that goad it into doing something? Anything was better than this cowering in the dark.

The notion of going out to it blossomed suddenly into a powerful urge. Yes, she would go out to it, get a good look, confront it. It certainly wasn't going to come in for examination. She thought of Brett sound asleep in the camper. He might think to call her and he might not. It wouldn't enter his head that anything could possibly happen to dull old dependable Merridee securely at home. She was always securely at home as far as he was concerned, him and everyone else. Except that thing, waiting for her in the dark.

Maybe, she thought as she slid quietly off the chair, it just wanted some food and she should throw it some stale bread.

Hunger. That idea took her as strongly as the notion to go outside. She paused with her hand on the deadbolt. *Hunger.* One-handed, she fumbled a loaf of that tasteless white stuff Brett was so partial to out of the breadbox on the counter, the shotgun seesawing in the crook of her other arm. Maybe it wouldn't like the stuff. No; rubbish, she thought. If it were hungry enough, it would eat anything.

She opened the door slowly and poked the screen door with the shotgun. Well, she couldn't fool it into thinking she was upstairs any more, she thought. But deep down, she knew she hadn't fooled it at all. *Go out. Hunger.* She wavered a little before she stepped over the threshold and let the screen door flap shut behind her.

The thing shuffled along in the grass and leaves again. Her coming out hadn't stampeded it; the knowledge made her feel satisfied and bold. She stood up a little straighter as she hurled the bread in the thing's general direction. The package landed just inside the lighted area where it lay like litter thrown from some out-of-towner's car.

Go on; take it, you blamed thing, it's for you. She wanted to say it out loud but the words stuck in her throat. She heard the hesitant rustling of grass and leaves; the trees on the north side of the house seemed to echo it. Leaves swirled down between herself and the thing. Its shadow stood out a little more clearly to her now and yes, it was all wrong for any man or beast.

It approached the bread with excruciating slowness, like an old fox coming upon a baited trap. Maybe she should have taken the bread out of the bag, Merridee thought. There was a sound like a grunt and she heard something slither along the ground. A lump appeared in the dead leaves beside the bread. Then fingers, big and thick, much thicker than her own or Brett's or anyone else's, broke through and clutched the package. Big, thick fingers, the color of a thunderhead about to let go, and only three of them, only three big, thick, blue-grey fingers. Merridee stared owlishly, unable to holler or run, the shotgun a meaningless weight in her hands. In some part of her mind, she was screaming her head off but it was so far removed it might as well have been someone else.

One of the all-wrong fingers pierced the plastic and tore into the bread, shredding it. And then . . . she blinked, her eyes watering madly. Something else strange, as though the arm belonging to those fingers had telescoped as the body came closer. Then the arm showed in the light and she saw it was exactly that way, not jointed but extendable, exactly like a telescope.

Without warning, it thrust its face into the light. Merridee stepped back, bringing one hand up defensively, the shotgun forgotten. At last she found voice enough to gasp; screaming was way beyond her. The face hung over the package of bread, refusing to go away. *Come out. Hunger.*

She hadn't had it quite right. It had wanted her to come out and it was hungry, but not for bread.

Merridee fled into the house.

She woke just after dawn, lying on top of the bed fully clothed with the shotgun beside her, the stock resting on Brett's pillow. For a moment she stared at it, not remembering. Then she sat up quickly, looking around the bedroom. *The thing*—well, it wasn't here with her unless it was hiding in the closet. The closet door was wide open, exposing thirty-four years' accumulation of clothes and personal belongings. No room for a *thing* in there. She flashed back to her childhood, a million years ago it felt like, the days of monsters in closets. Not her, but her brothers, Charlie and David. Her mother had always been soothing their night-time terrors, turning on the lights, showing them there was nothing in the closet but the most mundane items of clothing and shoes, while she lay in her own room listening, not a bit afraid. There had never been monsters in the dark for Merridee Dunham. Nor for Merridee Percy, married to Brett and living in this house for 500,000 years, nor for their one child, who was more of Brett than of herself.

She rubbed her hands over her face, feeling as unwashed and weary as a hobo. It was hard to believe in the thing in the daylight, the same way it had been hard to believe in her brothers' closet monsters. Now she could only vaguely remember the face it had shown her; she remembered her fear and she remembered running from it. But she remembered nothing after that.

Well, obviously, she'd been so tired from staying up that late she'd gone right to bed without even bothering to undress, just like some old man (*Brett;* who else) who'd spent all day and half the night in a duck blind.

She looked at the shotgun lying on Brett's side of the bed. If that wasn't the silliest thing in the world and dangerous besides, sleeping with a shotgun. She left it there while she went to wash.

Later, sitting at the kitchen table with a cup of coffee and two pieces of sourdough toast, she looked out the window at the stand of trees. All the leaves had blown off them now; the bare branches clawed at the sky in the wind. She tried to imagine how it would look, that creature coming through the trees and shuffling towards the house. It was like trying to picture the shirts and coats in her brothers' closet congealing into a monster. She couldn't do it. Shaking her head, she smiled to herself. Like two different worlds people lived in, one filled with strange, inexplicable shadows, one utterly prosaic, and she had never doubted once in her million-years-long life that she existed in the latter.

As she was getting up to refill her coffee cup, she caught sight of the spot where she had thrown the bread. It was gone; not even a shred of the plastic wrapper remained. Squirrels, she thought. And birds, the tough little sparrows who hopped through the bitter snows. And the wind had blown away whatever had been left behind.

In the early afternoon, she bundled herself up in two sweaters and one of Brett's old hunting jackets and went for a walk. The phone had not rung all day and she was tired of waiting for a call that probably wouldn't come. The house was clean—the house was always clean—and there was nothing that needed doing urgently. Brett could recaulk the windows and put up plastic himself after he came back. He was expecting her to do it while he was gone, she knew, but she didn't feel like it. Let him grumble over it. She would just tell him: *I didn't feel like doing it.* What would he make of that? She didn't know and didn't care. *I'm apathetic but who cares,* she thought, and giggled, still tickled at the old joke.

She walked the quarter mile down the dirt drive to the mailbox. The October wind tore at her hair and made her eyes water behind her glasses. She took the glasses off and tucked them into her jacket pocket. There wasn't much to look at. It was very pretty country but she'd seen it and seen it. Seen it for a million years.

The mailbox leaned forward over the paved road as though it might have been watching for oncoming traffic, of which there was very little on any given day. The mailman had left only one envelope, a brown and green announcement that she, Mrs. Merridee Percy, had another chance to enter the biggest sweepstakes of the year. A quarter-mile hike for a piece of junk mail. But she didn't begrudge the time or effort. She put her glasses back on and examined the brightly colored enclosures on the walk back. A $100,000 dream house, a yacht, a brand-new Lincoln-Continental (she could just picture it destroying its suspension on the dirt drive), a full-length mink, a home entertainment system with a big screen TV and a record player that took funny-looking little records—compact discs, the brochure called them—a video-recorder and lots of other things. Any of them might be hers already. There was also a sheet of little stamps offering cut-rate subscriptions to magazines. No purchase was necessary to enter this wonderful sweepstakes but she examined the stamps anyway. Maybe she might order a magazine or two, something that had articles on foreign places or one of those science magazines if they had one that wasn't too technical to understand. Brett had given her the *Ladies' Home Journal* once, years before, but she'd found little in it to pique her curiosity. She'd already been living in the *Ladies' Home Journal* for a quarter of a million years by then.

She reached the house, paused, and then walked around the back. The trip to the mailbox had not been sufficient to relieve her cooped-up feeling. The sweepstakes announcement was crammed into a pocket. She kept her hand on it while she approached the stand of trees. She wasn't looking for the creature, she told herself, absolutely not. It was getting harder and harder to believe in it as the day wore on. But if anything unlikely did pop out at her from somewhere, she'd pull the sweepstakes announcement out and throw the brochures right in its face. *All right,* she'd say, *you tell me how you can be real in a world that has sweepstakes and cut-rate magazine subscriptions!* Well, it wouldn't be able to, that was all there was to it, and the thing would just melt away into thin air, and that would be the end of the matter. A $100,000 dream house didn't come with monsters in the closets. Reality would take care of any old thing better than a shotgun would.

She found the package of bread lying torn up on the boards Brett had nailed down over the dried-up well. Some of it had been nibbled at. *Squirrels,* she thought firmly. And birds. Squirrels and birds for certain and apparently they didn't like that bland white stuff any better than she did. And monsters didn't eat Wonder Bread, whether they lived in closets or dried-up wells.

She left the enclosure describing the $100,000 dream house crumpled up next to the bread and walked back to her own house.

When evening came, she went upstairs to the bedroom and looked at the shotgun still lying on the bed.

"Slept all day, did you?" she said aloud and laughed at the absurdity of the statement and the sound of her own voice. She'd hardly ever spoken out loud in an empty house; unlike some people, she wasn't in the habit of talking to herself, never had been. Oh, when that Brett called—*if* he called— she'd give him what her grandfather had called Billy Blue Hill. *You go off shooting up half of Oklahoma and what happens to your stay-at-home wife but she becomes a babbling idiot, talking to shotguns and sundry. And seeing shadows in the back yard.*

She cradled the shotgun in her arms. Not thinking, not feeling anything at all, she took it downstairs to the kitchen and stood it against the wall next to the table while she made supper.

She ate staring at the barrel. *No,* she imagined herself saying to someone who didn't know anything about how people lived (and she couldn't think who that might be), *no, we generally don't eat supper with our shotguns handy, or sleep with them either. It's just a funny kind of thing I'm doing here and I don't know what for.*

A funny kind of thing. Come to think of it, there was lots of room in her life for funny kinds of things. She could set down her spoon, get up, walk around to the shotgun, pick it up and blow a hole right through any one of the four walls, or all of them. She could shoot up the whole house and dance naked in the ruins until Brett came home, if she wanted to. Or she could run upstairs, pack a bag and take off to see the world. She could fling her plate of pork and beans on the floor and roll around in the mess singing; she could phone the fire department and say there was a brush fire raging out of control behind the house; she could start the fire herself and not phone anyone. She could have done anything that came into her head no matter how foolish or malign, and there were plenty of people whose lives were so crowded up with such things that there was barely room for the things they hadn't done yet. But her life was spacious enough to accommodate a Sears-sized catalogue of antics. Even in the days of Dead-Eye 'Dee, there'd been plenty of latitude and a look down the coming longitude would have shown nothing but the traditional, famed, proverbial and inescapable straight-and-narrow.

I see, said the imaginary person she had been relating all this to. She froze, bent over her plate. A tingle crept along her scalp from neck to crown. She had forgotten this imaginary person, the one who didn't know anything about how people lived. She had done with that stray notion but here it was hanging on in her head as though she didn't know her own mind.

She turned her head to the window; it was closed and she saw only her own reflection against the night. Her reflection nodded at her slowly, with great certainty.

She didn't hurry. She scraped the rest of the pork and beans into the garbage pail and washed the bowl thoroughly, leaving it to drain in the dishrack. Then she slipped on the two sweaters and the jacket, taking time to adjust the rumples and pull the sleeves down. The shotgun—

well, of course, she would take it. She found extra shells in the utility drawer and put them in the empty pocket in the jacket.

Light? She went upstairs and put all the lights on again but she didn't turn off the kitchen light. There was no more bread to offer it except her own sourdough and she wasn't going to give it that—that was the good stuff. Tonight she'd fling the rest of the contest brochures at it if it got too active. Maybe then it would get the hint. And if it didn't, there was the shotgun.

Prepared, she stood in the middle of the kitchen and counted to thirty before she picked up the shotgun and went outside.

There was the smell of coming rain or snow in the chill air and the wind had picked up. Merridee walked forward a few steps, her feet crunching on the newest layer of dead leaves. She'd just keep going until there was some sign that she should stop.

The sign came as a feeling of pressure high on her chest, as if the wind pushing against her had suddenly become deep water. All right, she'd stop. She hefted the shotgun impatiently, wanting to get this whatever it was going to be over with, just as if she didn't have what amounted to all the time in the world.

She could practically feel all that time all around her, stretching away from her in every direction, past, present and future. Far, far away, almost too far to see was Dead-Eye 'Dee, still shooting and hitting nearly every bull's eye. You could only see her from behind; maybe she'd known even then there were no targets to shoot at ahead of her. After Dead-Eye 'Dee there was a big patch of present, forty years of Now, one day almost interchangeable with any before or behind it. And then an area that rose up unseeable into the dark, into the night sky for all she knew, but if it had been steps, she would have liked to climb them.

And if she did climb them, what might she find? Nothing so prosaic as, say, a $100,000 castle in the air or heaven. No, something else, something *really* else, that couldn't be weighed or measured by the standards of white bread or shotguns or sweepstakes. There would be closet monsters and strange, inexplicable moving shadows and ideas you'd have liked to have in your head to do if you could even have conceived of them, and things—

and things that moved in an atmosphere neither air nor water but something in between. They didn't eat anything like pork and beans or sourdough; they didn't eat. They were consumed themselves by something that might have been food in the real world of shotguns and somehow they emerged not just whole but more than they had been before, and they didn't take notions to do this or that, notions took them and they found themselves in this notion or that one. It was a world where they did not dream; the world dreamed them and lived through them as instruments. And as instruments, their limbs bent in odd angles and directions, and their joints telescoped—

And their faces. She looked at its face now without fear, without anything. Their faces were an asymmetrical arrangement on an oval of puckered openings, none of which were eyes and at the top a large irregular dark pad crisscrossed with tiny lines, like a picture in a science book of human skin enlarged a hundred times to show detail. It would be sensitive, that pad, like sight and smell and taste and touch and hearing all run together and enlarged a hundred times as well, and the size and shape of the patch would determine what the creature it belonged to was like—

"I see," Merridee said, even though there was no need to speak out loud. But she wanted to tell it the same thing it had told her. She lowered the shotgun, resting the stock on the ground.

The thing bowed its head, aiming the dark pad at her and its arm telescoped out, sliding through the grass and leaves until the three-fingered hand lay within six feet of her. The thing crouched and its arm telescoped inward, dragging the creature's body closer to her. The pressure against her chest increased.

Poor thing, she thought. It was hungry for its home. And where it touched her mind, it let her know that she was right. Yes, hungry to be home and it was going home soon.

Going home with her help . . .

Merridee's nerves gave a jump and she wasn't sure she had understood it that time. But it prodded her gently in her mind again (she still didn't think to wonder how it could do that) and she knew she had understood. Going home with her help. She would take it home.

"Me?" she whispered. "I can do that?"

Yes. She could.

She put a hand to her mouth. It was too—All her life—Nothing ever—The thoughts came and went in flashes. She looked back at the house (half a million years of nothing and he couldn't even find heart enough to take you on a camping trip, leave you behind with the rest of the furniture) and back at her life (Dead-Eye 'Dee shooting bull's-eyes with her back to the future because she knew nothing would come to a girl who didn't even get monsters in her closets) and back at her world (where sweepstakes announcements came solely to show her what other people would be having, at her correct address) and then she turned back to the creature with her eyes tearing in the cold October wind, a million years of life with all that room in it falling away from her old lady body like a worn-out skin. Yes, yes, she would take it home and gladly, if she had to carry it on her back, she would take it home if the effort tore her into a million bloody pieces. She would take it home. Yes.

No.

The negation in her mind was strong and deep enough to make her reel. She caught herself, leaning on the shotgun until the dizziness passed. The thing shimmered in her watery vision. Panting a little, she wiped her eyes and leaned toward the creature with pained confusion. "No?" she whispered. "But I thought—I thought you—" She remembered the thickened medium it lived in, the way its nourishment consumed it (what a bad time it would have had trying to get bread to eat it rather than vice versa); she remembered all the wonderful strangeness it had showed her and thought a question mark at the end. *I thought you wanted me to take you home?*

Its home receded in her mind and was replaced by the house behind her.

"What?" she asked and even as she spoke, the answer was forming. The dark pad, touched to her open mouth. She tasted something thick. The all-wrong limbs collapsed, the body shrank in on itself, the head going down like a deflating balloon. Gone home, at home in her and in her house and her world, where they would stay together, its own world only in their joint memory. She would remember what it remembered, know the things it knew. But she would remain in the house, waiting for Brett, and it would be home.

"Going home . . . to me? In me?" she said, incredulous.

The image of her open mouth pressed to the pad flashed in her brain again. No pain. No fear. No difference.

"You son of a bitch." She raised the shotgun and pulled the trigger.

The explosion seemed to echo for hours. She wasn't used to the noise of a shotgun; it had been years. The shotgun had bucked in her hands but Dead-Eye 'Dee had always been able to stand up to any kind of recoil. She waited until the ringing in her ears began to fade before she walked over to examine the thing.

She had literally blown it to pieces. There was hardly a fragment larger than the palm of her hand, except for its arm, which had still been extended. It lay like a forgotten pole in the leaves, the fingers limp and boneless. There wasn't blood, just a kind of syrupy jelly glistening on the dead leaves. She had a crazy urge to swoop the jelly up and touch it to her mouth, but the urge died quickly.

Even as she watched, the pieces of the thing were melting. Like snow. She poked one of the fragments with the barrel of the shotgun and made a face at the slime it left on the metal.

Here it had come creeping around the house, peering into her mind, showing her things, showing her all those wonderful things, touching her, making her feel different and letting her believe it would take her away, take her out of the house of white bread and Brett and sweepstakes—and all it wanted was for her to stay right where she was, knowing what was out there and not being allowed to go to any of it. Just like Brett and everybody else.

"You son of a bitch," she said again. "To hell with you." She kicked some leaves over the remains and turned back toward the house. The sight of the hand, melting like all the rest of it, stopped her for a moment. Then she walked on, hoping it had known at the end just what it was like to have a last chance snatched away from it.

It melted away completely during the night in spite of the cold temperatures. There was no trace of it at all in the morning, not even in the frost.

(1985)

MICHAEL BISHOP

The Bob Dylan Tambourine Software & Satori Support Services Consortium, Ltd.

"Gonna Change My Way of Thinking"

That Dylan would give up his career in music to become a computer-software impresario, few of us could have guessed. Not that this world-famous figure—in his various self-conscious guises as tubercular poet, blues guitarist, Chaplinesque tramp, folk-rock hero, civil-rights and anti-war activist, electronic surrealist, country-and-western troubadour, self-proclaimed heir to Elvis, charismatic Christian balladeer, and repentant Jew—had failed to experience changes aplenty in his astonishing forty-plus years. No, of course not, for Dylan had already remade himself a dozen times, always in ways that indisputably, if maybe somewhat mysteriously, bespoke his ongoing search for self-definition, meaning, and ultimate purpose; that bespoke, in short, his search for both sainthood and God.

Now, though, Dylan was apparently looking for all these things in the modern *terra incognita* of the microchip. Or, if that is too hyperbolic, in the new spiritual aesthetic of a software developer with almost unlimited capital, an unparalleled publicity and distribution network, and the kind of personal magnetism that even a dynamic commercial veep, not to mention an upwardly mobile young salesman, would kill for.

But Dylan's latest turnabout caught the doyens of contemporary popular culture even more off guard than had his shift from acoustic folkiness to hard-driving electronic music documented by the appearance of the 1965 album *Bringing It All Back Home.* It startled them even more than had his metamorphosis in 1969 into a kind of froggy-throated upstart Ernest Tubbs. (Listen to Dylan's inharmonious opening duet with Johnny Cash on "Girl From the North Country" on *Nashville Skyline.*) It certainly surprised them more than had his reemergence in the mid-

1970s, on such albums as *Blood on the Tracks* and *Desire,* as a stinging social critic and an image-making cartographer of the human heart. It even shocked, discomfited, and outraged them more than had Dylan's adoption of a fervent religious fundamentalism, which mind-boggling change in protective coloring our chameleon revealed to the world on his 1979 album *Slow Train Coming.*

After all, the foregoing transformations had taken place within the context of his career as a musician, or, at least, had found gratifying expression within that context.

Now, however, he seems to have abandoned his music—his chief and most eloquent means of defining the Dylan persona—to become just another foot soldier in the Computer Revolution. Today, as nearly everyone knows, would-be programmers are more plentiful than either would-be guitarists or novice harmonica players. Why, then, would this unique talent in American music forfeit his birthright to commit himself to a technological enterprise seemingly too well established for him to master and then to point in more fulfilling directions? The answer, of course, lies in Dylan's assessment of this enterprise as a route to spiritual discovery—to sainthood and God—potentially more viable and rewarding than either songwriting or on-stage self-sacrifice. And, of course, only a fool would fail to warn skeptics that in no endeavor that Dylan undertakes can he for long remain a cipher. In only a year, in fact, he had gone from a (granted, well-financed) foot soldier in the Computer Revolution to a (truly innovative) field marshal in this country's ever-expanding Software Wars.

"All Along the Watchtower"

Born in Duluth, Minnesota, but a resident of upstate New York before moving to the warmer West, Dylan has now renounced not only musicianship but also California's mellow milieu to relocate in the Peach State. Although many, I suppose, would have expected him to found his fledgling software firm near his former home in Malibu, he has chosen to headquarter the company in Atlanta, Georgia, not solely for its dogwood-blossom Aprils and often lamblike Februarys, but also for the attractive commercial incentives held out to him by both the city's black political hierarchy and its white business community. (The mayor's civil-rights activity with Martin Luther King during the 1960s is said to have counted as much with Dylan as the promised financial support of the Coca-Cola Company.) Dylan himself lives in the small town of *Duluth*—an instance of the sort of gentle self-mockery that he has always enjoyed—several miles northeast of Atlanta. He drives into the city every day with his car-pool partners, two of whom are management-level employees of his own company and the other of whom writes a regular column for the Business Monday section of the *Atlanta Constitution.*

Dylan christened—the term has a certain legitimacy—his firm Tambourine Software & Satori Support Services (or TS/3S, to give it its official stock-market abbreviation). He was himself the author of its first ten or twelve programs, which became such popular additions to our universal software library that they still sell briskly. (More about the programs themselves in a later part of my report.) The success of these early packages encouraged Dylan to hire creative assistants, a small brigade of program refiners and debuggers, an enthusiastic sales force, and a host of talent scouts ever on the alert for young men and women with programmable insights into the BASIC God-to-Person, Person-to-God relationship.

The company's first three creative assistants (all necessarily on part-time hire because of their commitments elsewhere) were Switzerland's Hans Küng, the controversial Catholic theologian; Lewis Thomas, physician, author, and former chancellor of the Sloan-Kettering Cancer Center; and Sherry Turkle, a sociologist and psychologist best known for her study of computers and human spirituality, *The Second Self.* Former Dallas Cowboy quarterback Roger Staubach also gave TS/3S valuable imaginative input, while singer Emmylou Harris acted throughout the early stages of the firm's organization as a calming influence on all those susceptible to panic.

For the most part, Dylan declined to use professionally trained computer people in his upstart company. As foolish as this tactic seemed at the time, it paid immediate dividends; and today, of course, Dylan's original company has affiliates or franchises all across the nation. In retrospect, we can see that although he may have abandoned music as a career, he had not really abandoned the improvisational techniques and the associational leaps of faith that typified his artistry—his genius, if you will—as both songwriter and performer.

It seems reasonable to conclude, in fact, that Dylan first detected his dormant passion for programming in a recording studio, where master tapes, synthesizers, and sophisticated sound-making equipment gave him a profound subliminal clue to the likelihood of effectively tapping into God by means of advanced twentieth-century technologies. It may have made him wonder what Jesus might have accomplished if the Son of God had been able to cut a record of the Sermon on the Mount, or what greater impact St. Francis of Assisi might have had if his prayer "Make Me an Instrument of Thy Peace" had had even the remotest chance to go platinum.

But of late, worldwide, either a terrible secularization or a dehumanizing cultification of young people had been going forward, and few of those with access to commercial recording equipment—"Do They Know It's Christmas?" and "We Are the World" aside—had consciously made use of it to stem the rising tides of materialism and narcissism. Ronald Reagan and the Moral Majority hadn't done the trick; nor had the Ayatollah Khomeini and his Islamic cohorts; nor had various Hindu swamis, Marxist priests, self-proclaimed Oriental messiahs, and reclusive ex-sci-fi writers who were also tax-finessing founders of various "rational" "religions." That most of what passed for contemporary Christian music struck Dylan as happy-talk spiritual Pablum, and that some of the biggest fans of the 1980s' sanctified superstar, Michael Jackson, actually regarded their androgynous moon-walker as the Archangel Michael come to announce Armageddon, so dismayed and demoralized Dylan that he could not in good conscience stay in the recording industry. To have stood pat would have been to profane both his own demanding hunger for God and his equally demanding need to nourish those with similar cravings.

"I Dreamed I Saw St. Augustine"

Hence the midlife career change. Hence the revelation that he might be able to move toward his own self-fulfillment, and even that of people who did not yet comprehend the real nature of their private hungers, by writing innovative sacramental software for TS/3S, his own company. Hence, in short, the astonishing growth of the Tambourine Consortium and the rapidly proliferating sale of game programs such as *Pilgrims on the Path to Grace*™ and *Spiritfall*™, domestic programs such as *Recipes for Would-be Believers*™ and *Household Shrines*™, educational programs like *Become As Children*™ and *Enlightenment Now!*™, and business programs of the popularity and usefulness of *Render Unto Caesar*™ and *SanctiCalc*™.

Indeed, the success of Tambourine Software & Satori Support Services has to a large extent come about because of (1) the interdependence of all the original programs in the consortium's software library and (2) the continually self-renewing Quest Reinforcement available to users from Dylan's dedicated support personnel. (Nationwide, the firm has *ten* toll-free 800 numbers to which confused customers may apply for on-line help with balky software, honest misconceptions about what Tambourine programs can and can't do, and even the technical resuscitation of crashed belief systems.) Because buyers benefit enormously from the interdependence of the firm's programs, augmenting their capability for spiritual growth with each new acquisition, TS/3S depends on, and earns, the zealous loyalty of its customers.

On the other hand, honesty and a hard-won distaste for guruism have led Dylan to insist that at the end of the Program License Agreement in the documentation issued with each Tambourine program, the following message must always appear:

BUYER BEWARE

> although i am convinced that all souls/have some superior t deal with/i reject the notion that anybody's superior is ever of mere human origin/no mortal can promise that if you only do so and so you'll touch God's face, or reach satori, or mend your tattered soul/no computer program can do those things either/we at Tambourine Software believe . . . an that means me an all the TS/3S gang . . . that one kind of enlightenment consists in *seeing*/in seeing that only by continually renewing the quest for Ultimate Meaning does anybody have a chance t actually get there/so my products're designed t keep you always heading in the right direction and refreshed on your road/that's all/but that's a lot/so keep booting up with Tambourine an those boots'll carry you on your jingle-jangle way t wherever you want an maybe even deserve t get
>
> —bob dylan

"With God on Our Side"

One program in the Tambourine Software arsenal—or *reliquary,* if a less warlike and more paradoxical metaphor is desired—both deserves and requires extended mention. This package, complete with one of the heftiest and most poetic instruction manuals ever released, is *Orphilodeon*™. Despite the above addendum to every TS/3S Program License Agreement, Dylan believes that *Orphilodeon* is the best single investment in software that the dedicated but less-than-affluent spiritual pilgrim can now make.

Why?

Because you can use it effectively without recourse to other programs on the Tambourine list. It is so powerful that the almost automatic trance state triggered by one's holistic interfacing with the program carries over into periods of heightened spirituality and God-consciousness *away from the computer.* A music-writing and -synthesizing program designed for compatibility with nearly every type of hardware system available today, *Orphilodeon,* in only six months, has become the standard against which pragmatists and pilgrims alike judge the competition.

A few important points about this state-of-the-art God-quest software.

First, it reminds us of some nifty Dylan doggerel on an insert in his 1964 album *The Times They Are A-Changin'*: "there's a movie called / *Shoot the Piano Player* / the last line proclaimin / 'music, man, that's where it's at' / it is a religious line" Well, *Orphilodeon* constitutes further proof, if anyone needs it, that everything Dylan does has either a religious or a musical dimension, if not both at once.

Second, a pair of eloquent lines in the program's 783 pages of documentation (its mind-blowing length a function of the fact that the author has displayed it all as verse) boldly declares that "the world all about us, t see an t touch, is frozen music / proud weepin architectures of unheard sound" (The absence of terminal punctuation both here and above follows Dylan himself.) Although not original with Dylan, this idea has probably never been more clearly demonstrated than in *Orphilodeon,* where its implementation in the software enables even musical illiterates—pilgrims with tin ears—to compose sublime oratorios and equally sublime (quasi-psychedelic) graphics. Those transported by Bach enter a Bach mode of exponentially heightened creativity, while those lifted by Mahler, Monk, or McCartney enter superscript versions of those exemplary mind-sets.

Third, in an interview in *Byte,* Dylan has said that in writing this particular program he felt that the Holy Spirit had settled upon him, much as it had upon the men and women who composed the books of both testaments of the Bible.

And, finally, the cost of *Orphilodeon* varies from about $560 to $720, depending on whether one orders through Tambourine Software as a preferred customer or tries to buy the program in one of the pricey big-city branches of Soft Warehouse™ or CompuMall™. Dylan admits that for individuals, as against large corporations with their own interface-worship facilities, the cost may seem steep, either way. He adds, however, that even with supernatural help *Orphilodeon* took him longer to write than any other single piece of work from either his recording or his programming career (with the possible exception of "Sad-Eyed Lady of the Lowlands" from *Blonde on Blonde*), and that no one who buys this package has to invest in other Tambourine products to achieve a satisfying modicum of enlightenment. *Recipes for Would-be Believers* and *Become As Children* might prove helpful to the neophyte saint, but neither they nor any other titles in the consortium's library are essential to a successful or, at least, an acceptable God-quest. So saith Dylan himself, and the vast majority of initial reviews bears out his witness.

"Mr. Tambourine Man"

And what of the former troubadour? How has Dylan's latest change of direction impacted on his own spiritual explorations? On the powerful, protean personality of the searcher himself? How, in short, has the change changed Dylan?

"I'm closer," he told me in a recent interview in the offices of TS/3S on Peachtree Street in downtown Atlanta. "Unlike Tricky Dick and Unlucky Lyndon, I can't see any all-redemptive light at the end of the tunnel, but I'm definitely closer to where I want to be and there's a kinduva glow shinin' right off the very top of the road itself. It's the traveling that counts, but the stops you make along the way mean something, too. I just don't like to get stuck too long at any one stop. That's death. It's a worse death than your old-fashioned bodily dying. 'Course, getting stuck's just as old-fashioned, isn't it?"

Dylan looks good. Although he used to verge on emaciation, his slenderness now suggests that of an upwardly mobile ad executive rather than that of an Ethiopian famine victim. He has shaved his scraggly rabbinical beard and trimmed his flyaway satyr tresses. When I spoke to him, he wore a Brooks Brothers suit, Gucci shoes, a Seiko watch. He refused to sit at his desk, but paced his office like a serenely anxious leopard at feeding time. He was as light on his feet and as deftly menacing. The menace, though, seemed less an implicit physical threat than a postural gloss on my fear that at any moment he might undergo a metamorphosis unlike any he has yet shown us. His bad teeth, always his worst feature, stayed hidden behind his pursed lips or, on those occasions when he spoke, an upraised hand.

"I useta say that square dress like this was a uniform, a well-bred badge of conventionality. Membership in the club, ya know. Conformity. Well, it works the other way, too. Motorcycle jackets, Mad Hatter hats, Jesus sandals, even secular yarmulkes. It's all vanity, isn't it? Every bit of it. Well, I might as well be hung for a tycoon as a typhoid carrier." He smiled. "What's important, *really* important, 's servin' my Somebody by gettin' my software around. That serves my neighbor as well as the Lord, and that's all I can foresee myself doing—or *wantin'* to do—from now till either the Rapture, or the Coming of the Hebrew Messiah, or the pop of our homemade nuclear Big Bang. But who knows? It's a stop, and even stops must have a stop." He smiled again. "It's nothing to do with money, though, I can tell ya that. Bein' beyond money's made it possible for me to, uh, song-write and program, and the programming's reopened a door I was sorta beginning to think I'd never go through again."

Even though Dylan had granted me thirty minutes, our talk was repeatedly interrupted by secretarial messages, telephone calls, or Federal Express deliveries. Somehow, he managed to slide around these distractions, imparting continuity to what could have been a totally helter-skelter conversation. I used the interruptions to take notes on the layout, décor, and personality of his work space, a few of which I'll share with the reader in a moment.

"What's happening to us as a people is that after millions of defections from our name-brand faiths and denominations, and some sad and desperate reachin'-out to false faiths and pseudo-messiahs, well, what's happening is we're actually beginning to get more religious and spirit-oriented. *Really,* I mean. It's something that's gonna go deep, right to the roots of our souls, and this amazing Spiritual Revolution is comin' at us in the long shadow of the Computer Revolution. No one expected it, but it's happenin', and that's why I had to jump in."

(It occurred to me that the unpredictability of Dylan's many career-course changes has an analog in the seemingly random way he chooses between endings when he pronounces a present participle aloud. Of course, this random observation fails to credit the sincere *intentionality* of the career changes.)

"I useta think that it'd be music that finally woke up our consciences and set our souls on the path to grace. That belief accounts for 'Blowing in the Wind,' early on, and for *Slow Train Coming* and *Shot of Love* when I started pushin' forty. Youthful illusions die hard, 'specially when you got a talent. But it was a stupid way to think. If music were *that* powerful, Alexander Pope and Max Davis to the contrary, you'd have to be amazed that Bach—I mean, Papa Johann and all the little Bachs—hadn't already won the whole world for Jesus. That Ravi Shankar never persuaded us to rename California Hindustan. That Itzhak Perlman hasn't been able to get Syria and Israel to kiss and make up. That Columbia Records haven't gained total control of the world commodities market."

"They haven't?"

Dylan sighted along his forefinger and dropped the hammer of his thumb—but to signal wry agreement rather than the obligatory pique of a former employee. (Weird gesture.)

Then he started pacing again and philosophically reminiscing as he paced: "Lots of times, it made *me* feel better, the music. The songs. But it proved a dead end, didn't it? A cul-de-sac with a brick wall waitin' at the end for me to bang my head against, if I was still insane enough to keep at it.

"Which is how I came to see that there had to be another way. *This* way. The way of the computer, the program, and interfaced would-be believers at their own terminals. Finally, a technology that's made the rudiments of religion user-friendly. It's a little like the Japanese, with their accessible Shinto shrines. Practically every household has one. Well, that's the way we're goin' with the personal computer. The Japanese, too. *Everyone,* nearly. People can get lost in a church or a synagogue, they can find themselves feelin' crushed by the weight of ritual and tradition. But not in front of a home computer. It's your altar and your shrine, and you can go to it to interface with the spirituality hidden in its microchips, which in turn're gonna boot you on up to God. Every hacker a penitent, every homemaker a communicant. We'll pray with our fingers on the keyboards of our Apples and IBMs. We'll go into our machines to go into ourselves, and it's the inside—not this suit or these shoes—that God sees. My programs—*Orphilodeon*'s the best example—let the computer mediate between the pilgrim user and our truest concepts of Deity. Each one of us is a church, and we worship alone at our reflexively responsive altars."

"Isn't this just another kind of narcissism?" I asked. "And if everyone's worshiping alone, what about fellowship?"

"Are prayer, meditation, and study narcissistic? Not usually. As for fellowship, haven't you ever heard of networking? Of user groups? Of computer clubs? Of software conventions and computer fairs? A new culture's growin' up, one with strong communal ties among its members, and they've begun to reclaim their spiritual heritage by tapping into the power of the microprocessor and the scriptural strength of inspired programs."

A tambourine, emblem of the company, hung from a peg on the wall behind Dylan's desk. He removed it and banged it on his hip, a series of exclamation points after his final comment.

" 'Mr. Tambourine Man,' " I said. "My favorite song on *Bringing It All Back Home.*"

"Well, there's that," Dylan said, examining the tambourine as if he'd never seen one before. "But something else, too." He gave the instrument a shake and said, "One o' the failings of middle-age is that you start explainin' yourself. You see, it's a kinduva musical floppy disk."

"In My Time of Dyin' "

After that, our interview almost over, he showed me the gallery of computer-graphic self-portraits on the wall next to the picture window. What disconcerted me about these colorful renderings—one suggestive of a Bosch, one of a Goya, one of an El Greco, one of Picasso's *Guernica,* one of a drawing by Escher, one of an early Mark Rothko, and one of an outlandish collaboration between René Magritte and Peter Max—was their deliberate morbidity. Each one showed the artist either dead or in the throes of dying, but no two depicted the same sort of farewell appearance.

"My God," I said.

"At least I didn't do a Buddy Holly plane crash."

However, he *had* done—with the aid of a computer, a 21-color jet-ink printer, and an art program of his own devising called *Stipple Genesis*™—portraits of Bob Dylan undergoing Karloffian electrocution on a concert stage, bursting into napalm flames on the edge of a Vietnamese rice paddy, going hell for Spanish leather over a Pacific-coast cliff on his motorcycle, reflecting himself unto annihilation in a hall of mirrors, hanging half-naked on a cross on a hill above Jerusalem, and suffering cardiac arrest on a jog through a crowd of white-faced mummers in Central Park.

"Visually attractive," I conceded. "But not very uplifting."

"Okay. You're entitled to pass that kind of judgment. But *Stipple-Genesis* is at least as helpful to the would-be believer as, say, our domestic programs. Dying's always fascinated me. What I was doing here was tryin' to work out my belief that our awareness of mortality triggers the religious impulse and invests our quests for satori or God with a hotfoot urgency." He hopped from Gucci to Gucci. "Ow, ow, ow, ow," he sang in his peculiarly nasal way.

I said, "In Dostoevski's *The Idiot,* a portrait of the dead Christ by Holbein prompts Prince Myshkin to exclaim, 'That picture might make some people lose their faith!' "

Dylan grew solemn again. He told me that he knew what I meant. If a painting of the crucified Jesus could do that, how unlikely it was that some computer graphics of an erstwhile rock 'n' roller's dying would either seed or fertilize anybody's faith. Well, they weren't intended for public viewing, and my seeing them had been an accident of our interview. Anyway, his private purpose had been different. To remind himself of his youthful preoccupation with death, and to commemorate how it had led him to seek to rediscover God, and to declare in primary colors and pastels that both faith and computer technology were viable avenues to immortality.

"Immortality?"

"Once, I thought the songs'd do it. Now I'm dichotomized on the question. If there's a soul in this body, it belongs to God, and he's the Man who'll get it. But my personality—every nuance of the Dylan persona and the Zimmerman nugget at its core—well, that'll survive in my software. It won't be me, not so I'll know it, but it'll still be me, with the solitary disadvantage that I won't. You take what you can get and give the glory to the Lord. I'll still be writin' songs, composin' programs, and puttin' on my boots to search for satori—but only in magnetic guise as a complex series of instructions to a microprocessor."

The president, chairman of the board, and foremost creative intellect of TS/3S took me to a bookshelf at the end of the computer-graphics gallery and showed me the vinyl-padded folder containing the documentation for the latest program from Tambourine Software. The title on the spine of the folder was *Bob Dylan*™, *1.00,* his prototype personality-duplicator and the first piece of software ever to essay quasi-immortality for its programmer. The cover on the folder reproduced the artwork from his Columbia double album *Self-Portrait* from the early 1970s.

"Are you going to market it?" I asked him.

"Oh, no. Not this one. Never."

"Why not?"

"You don't sell yourself. I mean, you do, but not this way, not so you're merchandising' your soul."

"Then *what?*"

"It's gonna go in a time capsule. A *copy* of it, of course. To be resurrected without benefit of body somewhere down the line when it might do some good."

My time was up. "You've been the victim of pirating before," I said, hurrying to put to Dylan the question that two of my editors had directed me to ask. "The Basement Tapes with The Band. Lots of others. How do you feel about software piracy?"

The question troubled him. Furrowing his brow, he put the *Bob Dylan* program back on the shelf. He hiked up his suit jacket and slid his hands into the hip pockets of his trousers. "One day," he said carefully, "we're gonna set up a booth in the middle o' town and hand out our software for free. When it's completely debugged, I mean. Nobody ought to hafta pirate God-consciousness. Nobody. Not even Ronnie Reagan."

I was hurrying to get these remarks into my notepad.

"That's off the record. Totally."

I stashed my pen. *Off* the record, I thought, but permanently *on* the software of my reportorial instincts. It was a quote too good to deep-six in the waters of oblivion. Therefore, it was the quote with which I ended my story:

"Nobody ought to hafta pirate God-consciousness."

"Most Likely You Go Your Way and I'll Go Mine"

Tonight I sit at my computer keyboard with pirated diskettes of *Spiritfall, Enlightenment Now!,* and *Orphilodeon.* I am trying to interface in a meditative way with the phosphor dots continuously refreshing themselves on my microprocessor's screen. I am also trying to anticipate Dylan's next career move. Maybe, in hopes of touching the face of God during a spacewalk on one of our shuttle flights, he plans to apply to NASA for astronaut training. Maybe, in hopes of parsing the enzyme-coded melodies of our genes and extracting from this cellular music the grace notes slotted there by the Ancient of Days, he plans to re-enroll in the University of Minnesota—in a program leading to a degree in recombinant-DNA research.

Who knows? God knows. I pray to God through my fingertips, through this machine. I pray for a brief burst of enlightenment about the intentions of His most mercurial contemporary prophet. After all, it's one of the ways I make my living.

(1985)

PAT MURPHY

His Vegetable Wife

Fynn planted her with the tomatoes in the greenhouse on the first day of spring. The instructions on the package were similar to the instructions on any seed envelope. Vegetable Wife: Prefers sandy soil, sunny conditions. Plant two inches deep after all danger of frost has passed. When seedling is two feet tall, transplant. Water frequently.

A week later, a fragile seedling sprouted in the plastic basin beside the tomatoes: two strong shoots that grew straight with little branching. The seedling grew quickly and when the shoots were two feet tall, Fynn transplanted the seedling to a sunny spot near the entrance to his living dome, where he would pass it on his way to the fields each day.

After transplanting the seedling, he stood beneath the green sky and surveyed his empire: a hastily assembled pre-fabricated living dome that marked the center of his homestead; a greenhouse built of Plexiglas slabs, tilted to catch the sun; and the fields, four fertile acres which he had tilled and planted himself. Most of the farm's tilled area was given over to cash crops: he was growing cimmeg, a plant that bore seeds valued for their flavor and medicinal properties. Row after row of dark green seedlings raised their pointed leaves to the pale sky.

Beyond the fields grew the tall grasses native to the planet, a vast expanse of swaying stalks. When the wind blew, the stalks shifted and moved and the grasses hissed. The soft sound of the wind in the grasses irritated Fynn; he thought it sounded like people whispering secrets. He had enjoyed hacking down the grass that had surrounded the living dome, churning its roots beneath the mechanical tiller, planting the straight rows of cimmeg.

Fynn was a square-jawed man with coarse brown hair and stubby, unimaginative fingers. He was a methodical man. He liked living alone, but he thought that a man should have a wife. He had chosen the seed carefully, selecting a hardy stock, bypassing the more delicate Vegetable Maiden and Vegetable Bride, selecting a variety noted for its ability to thrive under any conditions.

The seedling grew quickly. The two shoots met and joined forming a thicker trunk. By the time the cimmeg was knee-high, the wife had reached the height of his shoulders, a pale green plant with broad soft leaves and a trunk covered with downy hairs. The sun rose earlier each morning, the cimmeg grew to waist high, filling the air with an exotic spicy scent, and the Vegetable Wife's stem thickened and darkened to olive green. The curves of her body began to emerge: swelling hips pinching in to form a thin waist; rounded breasts covered with fine pale down; a willowy neck supporting the rounded knob that would become her head. Each morning, Fynn checked the dampness of the soil around the seedling and peered through the leaves at the ripening trunk.

In late spring, he first saw her pubic hair, a dark triangle just above where the twin trunks joined to form her body. Hesitantly, he parted the leaves and reached into the dimness to stroke the new growth. The smell of her excited him: rich and earthy and warm, like the smell of the greenhouse. The wood was warm beneath the hair and it yielded slightly to his touch. He moved closer, moving his hands up to cup the breasts, running his thumbs over the unevenness that promised to become nipples. The rustle of the wind in her leaves made him look up.

She was watching him: dark eyes, a suggestion of a nose, a mouth that was little more than a slit, lips barely parted.

He backed away hastily, noticing only then that he had broken the stalks of several leaves when he stepped in to fondle the trunk. He touched the broken leaves guiltily, then reminded himself that she was only a plant, she felt no pain. Still, he watered the wife generously that day, and when he went to work in the cimmeg fields, he hummed to himself so that he would not hear the grasses whispering.

The instructions had said that she would ripen at two months. Each morning, he checked on her progress, parting the leaves to admire the curves of her body, the willowy stalk of her neck, the fine bright gleam of her eyes. She had a full body and a softly rounded face. Though her eyes were open, her expression was that of a sleep-walker, an innocent young girl who wanders in the darkness unawares.

The expression excited him as much as her body, and sometimes he could not resist pushing close to her, running his hands along the gentle curve of her buttocks and back, stroking the fine dark hair that topped her head, still short like a little boy's hair, but growing, maturing like the rest of her.

It was late spring when he first felt her move under his touch. His hand was on her breast, and he felt her body shift as if she were trying to pull away. "Ah," he said with anticipation. "It won't be long." Her hand, which had formed recently from a thickened stalk, fluttered in the wind as if to push him away. He smiled, as she swayed in a puff of wind and her leaves rustled.

That afternoon, he brought a thick rope, looped it around her ankle, and knotted it carefully in place. Smiling at her angelic face, framed in dark hair, he spoke softly. "Can't have you running off. Not now that you're almost ripe." He tied the other end of the rope firmly to the frame of the dome, and after that he checked on her three times each day, rather than just once.

He cleaned the inside of the dome for the first time in months, washing the blankets of his bachelor bed, opening the windows to banish the mustiness. He could look out the open window and see her swaying in the breeze. Sometimes, she seemed to be struggling against the rope, and when she did that he checked the knots to make sure they were secure.

The cimmeg grew tall, its sharp glossy leaves catching the sunlight and glittering like obsidian blades. Her leaves withered and fell away, leaving her naked olive-green body exposed to the sun and to his gaze. He watched her carefully, returning from the fields several times each afternoon to check the knots.

He woke one morning to find her crouched at the end of her tether, pulling at the knot with soft fingers that bled pale sap where the coarse rope had cut her. "Now, now," he said, "leave that alone." He squatted beside her in the dust and put his hand on her sun-warmed shoulder, thinking to reassure her. She turned her head toward him slowly, majestically, with the stately grace of a flower turning to face the sun. Her face was blank; her eyes, expressionless. When he tried to embrace her, she did not respond except to push at his shoulders weakly with her hands.

Excitement washed over him, and he pushed her back on the hard ground, his mouth seeking her breast where the rough nipple tasted like vanilla, his hand parting her legs to open the mysteries of that dark downy triangle of hair.

When he was done, she was crying softly, a high faint sound like the singing of the small birds that nested in the tall grass. The sound woke compassion in him. He rolled off her and buttoned his pants, wishing that he could have been less hasty.

She lay in the dust, her dark hair falling to hide her face. She was silent, and he could hear the wind in her hair, like the wind in the tall grass.

"Come now," he said, torn between sympathy and annoyance. "You are my wife. It can't be that bad."

She did not look at him.

He cupped her chin in one hand and tilted her head so that he could see her expression. Her face was serene, expressionless, blank. He patted her shoulder, reassured by her expression. He knew she felt no pain; the instructions had said so.

He untied the rope from the frame of the dome and brought her inside. By the window, he set a basin of water for her. He secured the rope to the leg of the bed, leaving the tether long enough so that she could stand in the window or the doorway and watch him work in the fields.

She was not quite what he expected in a wife. She did not understand language. She did not speak language. She paid little attention to him unless he forced her to look at him, to see him. He tried being pleasant to her—bringing her flowers from the fields and refilling her basin with cool clean water. She took no notice. Day and night, she stood in the window, her feet in the basin of water. According to the instructions, she took her nourishment from the sun and the air and the water that she absorbed through pores in her skin.

She seemed to react only to violence, to immediate threats. When he made love to her, she struggled to escape, and sometimes she cried, a wordless sound like the babble of the irrigation water flowing in a ditch. After a time, her crying came to excite him—any response was better than no response.

She would not sleep with him. If he dragged her to bed, she would struggle free in the night, and when he woke she was always at the window, gazing out at the world.

He beat her one afternoon, when he returned from the fields and caught her sawing at the rope with a kitchen knife. He struck her on the back and shoulders with his belt. Her cries and the sight of the pale sap excited him and he made love to her afterwards. The rough blankets of his bed were sticky with her sap and his sperm.

He kept her as a man keeps a Vegetable Wife, as a man keeps a wild thing that he has taken into his home. Sometimes, he sat in the dome and watched darkness creep over his homestead as he listened to the wind in the grasses. He watched his Vegetable Wife and brooded about all the women who had ever left him. It was a long list, starting with his mother, who had given him up for adoption.

One day, a government agent came in a copter to inspect the cimmeg fields. Fynn did not like the man. Though Fynn directed his attention to the cimmeg, the government agent kept glancing toward the dome. The wife stood in the window, her naked skin glistening in the sun, smooth and clear and inviting. "You have good taste," said the agent, a young man dressed in khaki and leather. "Your wife is beautiful."

Fynn kept his temper with an effort.

"They're quite sensitive, I hear," said the young man.

Fynn shrugged.

The apple tree that he had planted near the dome entrance bore fruit: a basketful of small hard green apples. Fynn had crushed them into a mash and fermented a kind of applejack, a potent liquor smelling of rotten apples. Late in the afternoon after the agent had left, he sat beneath the apple tree and drank until he could barely stand. Then he went to his wife and dragged her away from the window.

Fynn whipped his wife for flaunting her nakedness. He called her a tramp, a whore, a filthy prostitute. Though the sap flowed from the welts on her back, her eyes were dry. She did not fight back, and her passivity inflamed him. "Goddamn you!" he cried, striking her repeatedly. "Goddamn you."

He grew tired and his blows grew softer, but his fury was not abated. She turned on the bed to face him, and his hands found her throat. He pressed on her soft skin, thinking somehow, in the confusion of drunkenness, that strangling her would stop the whispers that he heard, the secrets that were everywhere.

She watched him, impassive. Since she absorbed air through the skin, the pressure at her throat did not disturb her. Nevertheless, she lifted her hands and put them to his throat, applying slow steady pressure. He struggled drunkenly, but she clung to him until his struggles stopped.

He was quiet at last, quiet like a plant, like a tree, like the grasses outside. She groped in his pocket and found a jackknife. With it, she cut away the rope that bound her. The skin of her ankle was scarred and hardened where the rope had rubbed her.

She stood in the window, waiting for the sun. When it warmed the earth, she would plant the man, as she had seen him plant seeds. She would stand with her ankles in the mud and the wind in her hair and she would see what grew.

(1985)

MICHAEL BLUMLEIN

The Brains of Rats

There is evidence that Joan of Arc was a man. Accounts of her trial state that she did not suffer the infirmity of women. When examined by the prelates prior to her incarceration it was found that she lacked the characteristic escutcheon of women. Her pubic area, in fact, was as smooth and hairless as a child's.[1]

There is a condition of men, of males, called testicular feminization. The infants are born without a penis, and the testicles are hidden. The external genitalia are those of a female. Raised as women, these men at puberty develop breasts. Their voices do not deepen. They do not menstruate because they lack a uterus. They have no pubic hair.

These people carry a normal complement of chromosomes. The twenty-third pair, the so-called sex chromosome pair, is unmistakably male. XY. Declared a witch in 1431 and burned at the stake at the age of nineteen, Joan of Arc was quite likely one of these.

Herculine Barbin was born in 1838 in France; she was reared as a female. She spent her childhood in a convent and in boarding schools for girls and later became a schoolmistress. Despite her rearing, she had the sexual inclination of a male. She had already taken a female lover, when, on account of severe pain in her left groin, she sought the advice of a physician. Partly as a result of his examination her sex was redesignated, and in 1860 she was given the civil status of a male. The transformation brought shame and disgrace upon her. Her existence as a male was wretched, and in 1868 she took her own life.[2]

I have a daughter. I am married to a blond-haired, muscular woman. We live in enlightened times. But daily I wonder who is who and what is what. I am baffled by our choices; my mind is unclear. Especially now that I have the means to ensure that every child born on this earth is male.

A patient once came to me, a man with a painful drip from the end of his penis. He had had it for several days; neither excessive bathing nor drugstore remedies had proven helpful. About a week and a half before, on a business trip, he had spent time with a prostitute. I asked if he had enjoyed himself. In a roundabout way he said it was natural for a man.

Several days later, at home, his daughter tucked safely in bed, he had made love to his wife. He said that she got very excited. The way he said it made me think she was the only one in the room.

The two of them are both rather young. While he was in the examining room, she sat quietly in the waiting room. She stared ahead, fatigue and ignorance making her face impassive. In her lap her daughter was curled asleep.

In the room the man milked his penis, squeezing out a large amount of creamy material, which I smeared on a glass slide. In an hour the laboratory told me he had gonorrhea. When I conveyed the news to him, he was surprised and worried.

"What is that?" he asked.

"An infection," I said. "A venereal disease. It's spread through sexual contact."

He nodded slowly. "My wife, she got too excited."

"Most likely you got it from the prostitute."

He looked at me blankly and said it again. "She got too excited."

I was fascinated that he could hold such a notion and calmly repeated what I had said. I recommended treatment for both him and his wife. How he would explain the situation to her was up to him. A man with his beliefs would probably not have too hard a time.

I admit that I have conflicting thoughts. I am intrigued by hypnotism and the relations of power. For years I have wanted to be a woman, with small, firm breasts held even firmer by a brassiere. My hair would be shoulder-length and soft. It would pick up highlights and sweep down over one ear. The other side of my head would be bare, save for some wisps of hair at the nape and around my ear. I would have a smooth cheek.

I used to brush it this way, posing before my closet mirror in dark tights and high-heeled boots. The velveteen dress I wore was designed for a small person, and I split the seams the first time I pulled it over my head. My arms and shoulders are large; they were choked by the narrow sleeves. I could hardly move, the dress was so tight. But I was pretty. A very pretty thing.

I never dream of having men. I dream of women. I am a woman and I want women. I think of being simultaneously on the top and on the bottom. I want the power and I want it taken from me.

I should mention that I also have the means to make every conceptus a female. The thought is as disturbing as making them all male. But I think it shall have to be one or the other.

The genes that determine sex lie on the twenty-third pair of chromosomes. They are composed of a finite and relatively short sequence of nucleic acids on the X chromosome and one on the Y. For the most part these sequences have been mapped. Comparisons have been made between species. The sex-determining gene is remarkably similar in animals as diverse as the wasp, the turtle and the cow. Recently it has been found that the male banded krait, a poisonous snake of India separated evolutionarily from man by many millions of years, has a genetic sequence nearly identical to that of the human male.

The Y gene turns on other genes. A molecule is produced, a complex protein, which is present on the surface of virtually all cells in the male. It is absent in the female. Its presence makes cells and environments of cells develop in particular ways. These ways have not changed much in millions of years.

Certain regions of the brain in rats show marked sexual specificity. Cell density, dendritic formation, synaptic configuration of the male are different from the female. When presented with two solutions of water, one pure, the other heavily sweetened with saccharin, the female rat consistently chooses the latter. The male does just the opposite. Female chimpanzee infants exposed to high levels of male hormones in utero exhibit patterns of play different than their sisters. They initiate more, are rougher and more threatening. They tend to snarl a lot.

Sexual differences of the human brain exist, but they have been obscured by the profound evolution of this organ in the past half-million years. We have speech and foresight, consciousness and self-consciousness. We have art, physics and religion. In a language whose meaning men and women seem to share, we say we are different, but equal.

The struggles between sexes, the battles for power are a reflection of the schism between thought and function, between the power of our minds and powerlessness in the face of our design. Sexual equality, an idea present for hundreds of years, is subverted by instincts present for millions. The genes determining mental capacity have evolved rapidly; those determining sex have been stable for eons. Humankind suffers the consequences of this disparity, the ambiguities of identity, the violence between the sexes. This can be changed. It can be ended. I have the means to do it.

All my life I have watched men fight with women. Women with men. Women come to the clinic with bruised and swollen cheeks, where they have been slapped and beaten by their lovers. Not long ago an attractive middle-aged lady came in with a bloody nose, bruises on her arms and a cut beneath her eye, where the cheek bone rises up in a ridge. She was shaking uncontrollably, sobbing in spasms so that it was impossible to understand what she was saying. Her sister had to speak for her.

Her boss had beat her up. He had thrown her against the filing cabinets and kicked her on the floor. She had cried for him to stop, but he had kept on kicking. She had worked for him for ten years. Nothing like this had ever happened before.

Another time a young man came in. He wore a tank-top and had big muscles in his shoulders and arms. On one bicep was a tattoo of the upper torso and head of a woman, her huge breasts bursting out of a ragged garment. On his forearm beneath this picture were three long and deep tracks in the skin, oozing blood. I imagined the swipe of a large cat, a lynx or a mountain lion. He told me he had hurt himself working on his car.

I cleaned the scratches, cut off the dead pieces of skin bunched up at the end of the tracks. I asked again. It was his girlfriend, he said, smiling now a little, gazing proudly at the marks on his arm. They had had a fight, she had scratched him with her nails. He looked at me, turning more serious, trying to act like a man but sounding like a boy, and asked, you think I should have a shot for rabies?

Sexual differentiation in humans occurs at about the fifth week of gestation. Prior to this time the fetus is sexless, or more precisely, it has the potential to become either (or both) sex. Around the fifth week a single gene turns on, initiating a cascade of events that ultimately gives rise to testicle or ovary. In the male this gene is associated with the Y chromosome; in the female, with the X. An XY pair normally gives rise to a male; an XX pair, to a female.

The two genes have been identified and produced by artificial means. Despite a general reluctance in the scientific community as a whole, our laboratory has taken this research further. Recently, we have devised a method to attach either gene to a common rhinovirus. The virus is ubiquitous; among humans it is highly contagious. It spreads primarily through water droplets (sneezing, coughing), but also through other bodily fluids (sweat, urine, saliva, semen). We have attenuated the virus so that it is harmless to mammalian tissue. It incites little, if any, immune response, resting dormantly inside cells. It causes no apparent disruption of function.

When an infected female becomes pregnant, the virus rapidly crosses the placenta, infecting cells of the developing fetus. If the virus carries the X gene, the fetus will become a female; if it carries the Y, a male. In mice and rabbits we have been able to produce entire litters of male or female. Experiments in simians have been similarly successful. It is not premature to conclude that we have the capability to do the same for humans.

Imagine whole families of male or female. Districts, towns, even countries. So simple, it is as though it was always meant to be.

My daughter is a beautiful girl. She knows enough about sex, I think, to satisfy her for the present. She plays with herself often at night, sometimes during the day. She is very happy not to have to wear diapers anymore. She used to look at my penis a lot, and once in a while she would touch it. Now she doesn't seem to care.

Once maybe every three or four months she'll put on a pair of pants. The rest of the time she wears skirts or dresses. My wife, a laborer, wears only pants. She drives a truck.

One of our daughter's school teachers, a Church woman, told her that Christian girls don't wear pants. I had a dream last night that our next child is a boy.

I admit I am confused. In the ninth century there was a German woman with a name no one remembers. Call her Katrin. She met and fell in love with a man, a scholar. Presumably, the love was mutual. The man travelled to Athens to study and Katrin went with him. She disguised herself as a man so that they could live together.

In Athens the man died. Katrin stayed on. She had learned much from him, had become something of a scholar herself. She continued her studies and over time gained renown for her learning. She kept her disguise as a man.

Sometime later she was called to Rome to study and teach at the offices of Pope Leo IV. Her reputation grew, and when Leo died in 855, Katrin was elected Pope.

Her reign ended abruptly two and a half years later. In the midst of a papal procession through the streets of Rome, her cloak hanging loose, obscuring the contours of her body, Katrin squatted on the ground, uttered a series of cries and delivered a baby. Soon after, she was thrown in a dungeon, and later banished to an impoverished land to the north. From that time on, all popes, prior to confirmation, have been examined by two reliable clerics. Before an assembled audience they feel under his robes.

"Testiculos habet," they declare, at which point the congregation heaves a sigh of relief.

"Deo gratias," it chants back. "Deo gratias."[3]

I was at a benefit luncheon the other day, a celebration of regional women writers. Of five hundred people I was one of a handful of men. I went at the invitation of a friend because I like the friend and I like the writers who were being honored. I wore a sports coat and slacks and had a neatly trimmed four day growth of beard. I waited in a long line at the door, surrounded by women. Some were taller than me, but I was taller than most. All were dressed fashionably; most wore jewelry and makeup. I was uncomfortable in the crowd, not profoundly, but enough that my manner turned meek. I was ready for a fight.

A loud woman butted in front of me and I said nothing. At the registration desk I spoke softly, demurely. The woman at the desk smiled and said something nice. I felt a little better, took my card and went in.

It was a large and fancy room, packed with tables draped with white cloths. The luncheon was being catered by a culinary school located in the same building. There was a kitchen on the ground floor, to the left of the large room. Another was at the mezzanine level above the stage at the front of the room. This one was enclosed in glass, and during the luncheon there was a class going on. Students in white coats and a chef with a tall white hat passed back and forth in front of the glass. Their lips moved, but from below we didn't hear any sounds.

Mid-way through the luncheon the program started. The main organizer spoke about the foundation for which the luncheon was a benefit. It is an organization dedicated to the empowerment of women, to the rights of women and girls. My mind drifted.

I have been a feminist for years. I was in the room next door when my first wife formed a coven. I applauded her resolve. I celebrated with her the publication of Valerie Solanas's *The S.C.U.M. Manifesto.* The sisters made a slide show, using some of Valerie's words. It was shown around the East Coast. I helped them out by providing a man's voice. I am a turd, the man said. A lowly, abject turd.

My daughter is four. She is a beautiful child. I want her to be able to choose. I want her to feel her power. I will tear down the door that is slammed in her face because she is a woman.

The first honoree came to the podium, reading a story about the bond between a wealthy woman traveler and a poor Mexican room-maid. After two paragraphs a noise interrupted her. It was a dull, beating sound, went on for half a minute, stopped, started up again. It came from the glassed-in teaching kitchen above the stage. The white-capped chef was pounding a piece of meat, oblivious to the scene below. Obviously he could not hear.

The woman tried to keep reading but could not. She made one or two frivolous comments to the audience. We were all a little nervous, and there were scattered titters while we waited for something to be done.

The chef kept pounding the meat. Behind me a woman whispered loudly, male chauvinist.

I was not surprised, had, in fact, been waiting from the beginning for someone to say something like that. It made me mad. The man was innocent. The woman was a fool. A robot. I wanted to shake her, shake her up and make her pay.

I have a friend, a man with a narrow face and cheeks that always look unshaven. His eyes are quick; when he is with me, they always seem to be looking someplace else. He is facile with speech and quite particular about the words he chooses. He is not unattractive.

I like this man for the same reasons I dislike him. He is opportunistic and assertive. He is clever, in the way that being detached allows one to be. And fiercely competitive. He values those who rise to his challenges.

I think of him as a predator, as a man looking for an advantage. This would surprise, even bewilder him, for he carries the innocence of self-absorption. When he laughs at himself, he is so proud to be able to do so.

He has a peculiar attitude toward women. He does not like those who are his intellectual equal. He does not respect those who are not. And yet he loves women. He loves to make them. Especially he loves the ones who need to be convinced. I sometimes play tennis with him. I apologize if I hit a bad shot. I apologize if I am not adequate competition. I want to please him, and I lose every time we play. I am afraid to win, afraid that he might get angry, violent. He could explode.

I want to win. I want to win bad. I want to drive him into the net, into the concrete itself and beneath it with the force of my victory.

I admit I am perplexed. A man is aggressive, tender, strong, compassionate, hostile, moody, loyal, competent, funny, generous, searching, selfish, powerful, self-destructive, shy, shameful, hard, soft, duplicitous, faithful, honest, bold, foolhardy, vain, vulnerable and proud. Struggling to keep his instincts in check, he is both abused and blessed by his maleness:

Dr. P, a biologist, husband and father, never knew how much of his behavior to attribute to the involuntary release of chemicals, to the flow of electricity through synapses stamped male as early as sixty days after conception, and how much to reckon under his control. He did not want to dilute his potency as a scientist, as a man, by struggling too hard against his impulses, and yet the glimpses he had of another way of life were often too compelling to disregard. The bond between his wife and daughter sometimes brought tears to his eyes. The thought of his wife carrying the child in her belly for nine months and pushing her out through the tight gap between her legs sometimes settled in his mind like a hypnotic suggestion, like something so sweet and pure that he would wither without it.[4]

I asked another friend what it was to him to be a man. He laughed nervously and said the question was too hard. Okay, I said, what is it you like best? He shied away but I pressed him. Having a penis, he said. I nodded. Having it sucked, putting it in a warm place. Coming. He smiled and looked beatific. Oh God, he said, it's so good to come.

Later on he said, I like the authority I have, the subtle edge. I like the respect. A man, just by being a man, gets respect. When I get an erection, when I get very hard, I feel strong. I take on power that at other times is hidden. Impossibilities seem to melt away.

(A world like that, I think. A world of men. How wondrous! The Y virus then. I think it must be the Y.)

In the summer of our marriage I was sitting with my first wife in the mountains. She was on one side of a dirt road that wound up to a pass and I was on the other. Scattered on the mountain slope were big chunks of granite and around them stands of aspen and a few solitary pines. The sky was a deep blue, the kind that makes you suck in your breath. The air was crisp.

She was throwing rocks at me, and arguing. Some of the rocks were quite big, as big as you could hold in a palm. They landed close, throwing up clouds of dust in the roadbed. She was telling me why we should get married.

"I'll get more respect," she said. "Once we get married then we can get divorced. A divorced woman gets respect."

I asked her to stop throwing rocks. She was mad because she wasn't getting her way. Because I was being truculent. Because she was working a man's job cleaning out the insides of ships, scaling off the plaque and grime, and she was being treated like a woman. She wanted to be treated like a man, be tough like a man, dirty and tough. She wanted to smoke in bars, get drunk, shoot pool. In the bars she wanted to act like a man, be loud, not take shit. She wanted to do this and also she wanted to look sharp, she wanted to dress sexy, in tight blouses and pants. She wanted men to come on to her, she wanted them to fawn a little. She wanted the power.

"A woman who's been married once, they know she knows something. She's not innocent. She's gotten rid of one, she can get rid of another. They show a little respect."

She stopped throwing rocks and came over to me. I was a little cowed. She said that if I loved her I would marry her so she could divorce me. She was tender and insistent. I did love her, and I understood the importance of respect. But also I was mixed-up. I couldn't make up my mind.

"You see," she said, angry again, "you're the one who gets to decide. It's always you who's in control."

"I am a turd," I replied. "A lowly, abject turd."

A woman came to me the other day. She knew my name, was aware of the thrust of my research but not the particulars. She did not know that in the blink of an eye her kind, or mine, could be gone from the face of the earth. She did not know, but it did not seem to matter.

She was dressed simply; her face was plain. She seemed at ease when she spoke, though she could not conceal (nor did she try) a certain intensity of feeling. She said that as a woman she could not trust a man to make decisions regarding her future. To my surprise I told her that I am not a man at all.

"I am a mother," I said. "When my daughter was an infant, I let her suckle my breast."

"You have no breasts," she said scornfully.

"Only no milk." I unbuttoned my shirt and pulled it to the side. I squeezed a nipple. "She wouldn't stay on because it was dry."

"You are a man," she said, unaffected. "You look like one. I've seen you walk, you walk like one."

"How does a man walk?"

"Isn't it obvious?"

"I am courteous. I step aside in crowds, wait for others to pass."

"Courtesy is the manner the strong adopt toward the weak. It is the recognition of their dominance."

"Sometimes I am meek," I said. "Sometimes I'm quite shy."

She gave me an exasperated look, as though I were a child who had strained the limits of her patience. "You are a man, and men are outcasts. You are outcasts from the very world you made. The world you built on the bodies of other species. Of women."

I did not want to argue with her. In a way she was right. Men have tamed the world.

"You think you rise above," she went on, less stridently. "It is the folly of comparison. There's no one below. No one but yourselves."

"I don't look down," I said.

"Men don't look at all. If you did, you'd see that certain parts of your bodies are missing."

"What does that mean?"

She looked at me quietly. "Don't you think it's time women had a chance?"

"Let me tell you something," I said. "I have always wanted to be a woman. I used to dress like one whenever I had the chance. I was too frightened to keep women's clothes in my own apartment, and I used to borrow my neighbor's. She was a tall woman, bigger than me, and she worked evenings. I had the key to her apartment, and at night after work, before she came home, I would sneak into her place and go through her drawers. Because of her size, most of her clothes fit. She had a pair of boots, knee-high soft leather boots which I especially liked."

"Why are you telling me this?" she asked suspiciously.

"I want to. It's important that you understand."

"Listen, no man wants to be a woman. Not really. Not deep down."

"Men are beautiful." I made a fist. "Our bodies are powerful, like the ocean, and strong. Our muscles swell and tuck into each other like waves.

"There is nothing so pure as a man. Nothing like the face of a boy. The smooth and innocent cheek. The promise in the eyes.

"I love men. I love to trace our hard parts, our soft ones with my eyes, my imagination. I love to see us naked, but I am not aroused. I never have thoughts of having men.

"One night, though, I did. I was coming from my neighbor's apartment, where I had dressed up pretty in dark tights, those high boots of hers, and a short, belted dress. I had stuffed socks in the cups of her bra and was a very stacked lady. When I was done, I took everything off, folded it and put it neatly back in the drawers. I got dressed in my own pants and shirt, a leather jacket on top, and left. I was going to spend the night with my wife.

"On the street I still felt aroused. I had not relieved the tension and needed some release. As I walked, I alternated between feeling like a man on the prowl and a woman wanting to grab something between her legs. I think I felt more the latter, because I wanted something to be done to me. I wanted someone else to be boss.

"I started down the other side of the hill that separated my house from my wife's. It was late and the street was dark. A single car, a Cadillac, crept down the hill. When it came to me, it slowed. The driver motioned me over and I moved away. My heart skittered. He did it again and I swallowed and went to him.

"He was a burly black man, smelled of alcohol. I sat far away from him, against the door, and stared out the windshield. He asked where was my place. I said I had none. He grunted and drove up a steep hill and several more. He pulled the big car into the basement lot of an apartment complex. 'A ladyfriend's,' he said, and I followed him up some flights of stairs and down a corridor to the door of the apartment. I was aroused, frightened, determined. I don't think he touched me that whole time.

"He opened the door and we went in. The living room was bare, except for a record player on the floor and a scattered bunch of records. There was a record on, about two-thirds done, and I expected to see someone else in the apartment. But it was empty.

"The man went into another room, maybe the kitchen, and fixed himself a drink. He wasn't friendly to me, wasn't cruel. I think he was a little nervous to have me there, but otherwise acted as if I were a piece of something to deal with in his own way at his own time. I did not feel that I needed to be treated any differently than that.

"He took me into the bedroom, put me on the bed. That was in the beginning: later I remember only the floor. He took off his shirt and his pants and pulled my pants down. He settled on me, his front to my front. He was barrelchested, big and heavy. I wrapped my legs around him and he began to rub up and down on me. His lips were fat, and he kissed me hard and tongued me. He smelled very strong, full of drugs and liquor. His beard was rough on my cheek. I liked the way it felt but not the way it scratched. He began to talk to himself.

" 'The swimmin' gates,' he muttered. 'Let me in the swimmin' gates. The swimmin' gates.'

"He said these words over and over, drunkenly, getting more and more turned on. He rolled me over, made me squat on my knees with my butt in the air. He grabbed me with his arms, tried to enter me. I was very dry and it hurt. I let him do it despite the pain because I wanted to feel it, I wanted to know what it was like. I didn't want to let him down.

"Even before then, before the pain, I had withdrawn. I was no longer aroused, or not much. I liked his being strong because I wanted to be dominated, but as he got more and more excited, I lost a sense that I was anything at all. I was a man, but I might just as easily have been a woman, or a dog, or even a tube lined with fur. I felt like nothing; I was out of my body and growing cold. I did not even feel the power of having brought him to his climax. If it wasn't me, it would have been something else . . ."

I stopped. The woman was quiet for awhile.

"So what's your point?" she asked.

"I'm wrong to think he didn't need me. Or someone, to do what he wanted. To take it without question."

"He hurt you."

"In a way I pity him. But also, I admire his determination."

She was upset. "So you think you know what it's like to be a woman? Because of that you think you know?"

"I don't know anything," I said. "Except that when I think about it I always seem to know more about what it is to be a woman than what it is to be a man."

Having a penis, my friend said. That's what I like best. It reminds me of a patient I once had, a middle-aged man with diabetes. He took insulin injections twice a day, was careful with his diet, and still he suffered the consequences of that disease. Most debilitating to him was the loss of his sex life.

"I can't get it up," he told me. "Not for more than a minute or two."

I asked if he came. Diabetes can be quite selective in which nerves it destroys.

"Sometimes. But it's not the same. It feels all right, it feels good, but it's not the same. A man should get hard."

I nodded, thinking that he should be grateful, it could be worse. "At least you can come. Some people can't even do that."

"Don't you have some shot, Doc? Something so I can get it up."

I said no, I didn't, it wasn't a question of some shot, it was a question of his diabetes. We agreed to work harder at keeping it under control, and we did, but his inability to get an erection remained. He didn't become depressed, as many do, nor did he get angry. He was matter-of-fact, candid, even funny at times. He told me that his wife liked him better the way he was.

"I don't run around," he explained. "It's not that I can't . . . the ladies, they don't seem to mind the way I am. In fact, they seem to like it. I just don't want to, I don't feel like a man."

"So the marriage is better?"

He shrugged. "She's a prude. She'd rather not have sex anyway. So how about a hormone shot, Doc? What do we got to lose?"

His optimism was infectious, and I gave him a shot of testosterone. And another a few weeks later. It didn't change anything. The next time I saw him he was carrying a newspaper clipping.

"I heard about this operation," he said, handing me the article. "They got something they put in your penis to make it hard. A metal rod, something like that. They also got this tube they can put in. With a pump, so you can pump it up when you're ready and let it down when you're finished. What do you think, Doc?"

I knew a little about the implants. The rods were okay, except the penis stayed stiff all the time. It was a nuisance, and sometimes it hurt if it got bent the wrong way. The inflatable tubes were unreliable, sometimes breaking open, other times not deflating when they were supposed to. I told him this.

"It's worth a try," he said. "What do I got to lose?"

It was four or five months before I saw him again. He couldn't wait to get me in the examining room, pulling down his pants almost as soon as I shut the door. Through the slit in his underwear his penis pointed at me like a finger. His face beamed.

"I can go for hours now, Doc," he said proudly. "Six, eight, all night if I want. And look at this . . . " He bent it to the right, where it stayed, nearly touching his leg. Then to the left. Then straight up, then down. "Any position, for as long as I want. The women, they love it."

I sat there, marvelling. "That's great."

"You should see them," he said, bending it down in the shape of a question mark and stuffing it back in his pants. "They go crazy. I'm like a kid, Doc. They can't keep up with me."

I thought of him, sixty-two years old, happy, stiff, rolling back and forth on an old mattress, stopping every so often to ask his companion that night which way she wanted it. Did she like it better left or right, curved or straight, up or down? He was a man now, and he loved women. I asked about his wife.

"She wants to divorce me," he said. "I got too many women now."

The question, I think, is not so much what I have in common with the banded krait of India, him slithering through the mud of that ancient country's monsoon-swollen rivers, me sitting pensively in a cardigan at my desk. We share that certain sequence of nucleic acids, that gene on the Y chromosome that makes us male. The snake is aggressive; I am loyal and dependable. He is territorial; I am a faithful family man. He dominates the female of his species; I am strong, reliable, a good lover.

The question really is how I differ from my wife. We lay in bed, our long bodies pressed together as though each of us were trying to become the other. We talk, sometimes of love, mostly of problems. She says, my job, it is so hard, I am so tired my body aches. And I think, that is too bad, I am so sorry, where is the money to come from, be tough, buck up. I say, I am insecure at work, worried about being a good father, a husband. And she says, you are good, I love you, which washes off me as though she had said the sky is blue. She strokes my head and I feel trapped; I stroke hers and she purrs like a cat. What is this? I ask, nervous, frightened. Love, she says. Kiss me.

I am still so baffled. It is not as simple as the brains of rats. As a claw, a fang, a battlefield scarred with bodies. I want to possess, and be possessed.

One night she said to me, "I think men and women are two different species."

It was late. We were close, not quite touching. "Maybe soon," I said. "Not yet."

"It might be better." She yawned. "It would certainly be easier."

I took her hand and squeezed it. "That's why we cling so hard to one another."

She snuggled up to me. "We like it."

I sighed. "It's because we know someday we may not want to cling at all."

References

1. Wachtel, Stephen: *H-Y Antigen and the Biology of Sex Determination* (New York: Grune & Stratton, 1983), p. 170.
2. Ibid., p. 172.
3. Gordon, H., in Vallet, H. L., and I. H. Porter (eds): *Genetic Mechanisms of Sexual Development* (New York: Academic Press, 1979), p. 18.
4. Rudolf, I. E., et al.: *Whither the Male?: Studies in Functionally Split Identities* (Philadelphia: Ova Press, 1982).

(1986)

NANCY KRESS

Out of All Them Bright Stars

So I'm filling the catsup bottles at the end of the night, and I'm listening to the radio Charlie has stuck up on top of the movable panel in the ceiling, when the door opens and one of them walks in. I know right away it's one of them—no chance to make a mistake about *that*—even though it's got on a nice-cut suit and a brim hat like Humphrey Bogart used to wear in *Casablanca.* But there's nobody with it, no professor from the college or government men like on the TV show from the college or even any students. It's all alone. And we're a long way out on the highway from the college.

It stands in the doorway, blinking a little, with rain dripping off its hat. Kathy, who's supposed to be cleaning the coffee machine behind the counter, freezes and stares with one hand still holding the used filter up in the air like she's never going to move again. Just then Charlie calls out from the kitchen, "Hey, Kathy, you ask anybody who won the trifecta?" and she doesn't even answer him. Just goes on staring with her mouth open like she's thinking of screaming but forgot how. And the old couple in the corner booth, the only ones left from the crowd after the movie got out, stop chewing their chocolate cream pie and stare, too. Kathy closes her mouth and opens it again, and a noise comes out like "Uh—errrgh. . . ."

Well, that made me annoyed. Maybe she tried to say "ugh" and maybe she didn't, but here it is standing in the doorway with rain falling around it in little drops and we're staring like it's a clothes dummy and not a customer. So I think that's not right and maybe we're even making it feel a little bad. *I* wouldn't like Kathy staring at me like that, and I dry my hands on my towel and go over.

"Yes, sir, can I help you?" I say.

"Table for one," it says, like Charlie's was some nice steak house in town. But I suppose that's the kind of place the government people mostly take them to. And besides, its voice is polite and easy to understand, with a sort of accent but not as bad as some we get from the college. I can tell what it's saying. I lead him to a booth in the corner opposite the old couple, who come in every Friday night and haven't left a tip yet.

He sits down slowly. I notice he keeps his hands on his lap, but I can't tell if that's because he doesn't know what to do with them or because he thinks I won't want to see them. But I've seen the closeups on TV—they don't look so weird to me like they do to some. Charlie says they make his stomach turn, but I can't see it. You'd think he'd of seen worse meat in Vietnam. He talks enough like he did, on and on, and sometimes we even believe him.

I say, "Coffee, sir?"

He makes a sort of movement with his eyes. I can't tell what the movement means, but he says in that polite voice, "No, thank you. I am unable to drink coffee," and I think that's a good thing, because I suddenly remember that Kathy's got the filter out. But then he says, "May I have a green salad, please? With no dressing, please."

The rain is still dripping off his hat. I figure the government people never told him to take off his hat in a restaurant, and for some reason that tickles me and makes me feel real bold. This polite blue guy isn't going to bother anybody, and that fool Charlie was just spouting off his mouth again.

"The salad's not too fresh, sir," I say, experimental-like, just to see what he'll say next. And it's the truth—the salad is left over from yesterday. But the guy answers like I asked him something else.

"What is your name?" he says, so polite I know he's curious and not starting anything. And what could he start anyway, blue and with those hands? Still, you never know.

"Sally," I say. "Sally Gourley."

"I am John," he says, and makes that movement with his eyes again. All of a sudden it tickles me—"John!" For this blue guy! So I laugh, and right away I feel sorry, like I might have hurt his feelings or something. How could you tell?

"Hey, I'm sorry," I say, and he takes off his hat. He does it real slow, like taking off the hat is important and means something, but all there is underneath is a bald blue head. Nothing weird like with the hands.

"Do not apologize," John says. "I have another name, of course, but in my own language."

"What is it?" I say, bold as brass, because all of a sudden I picture myself telling all this to my sister Mary Ellen and her listening real hard.

John makes some noise with his mouth, and I feel my own mouth open because it's not like a word he says at all, it's a beautiful sound—like a birdcall, only sadder. It's just that I wasn't expecting it, that beautiful sound right here in Charlie's diner. It surprised me, coming out of that bald blue head. That's all it was: surprise.

I don't say anything. John looks at me and says, "It has a meaning that can be translated. It means—" But before he can say what it means, Charlie comes charging out of the kitchen, Kathy right behind him. He's still got the racing form in one hand, like he's been studying the trifecta, and he pushes right up against the booth and looks red and furious. Then I see the old couple scuttling out the door, their jackets clutched to their fronts, and the chocolate cream pie not half-eaten on their plates. I see they're going to stiff me for the check, but before I can stop them, Charlie grabs my arm and squeezes so hard his nails slice into my skin.

"What the hell do you think you're doing?" he says right to me. Not so much as a look at John, but Kathy can't stop looking and her fist is pushed up to her mouth.

I drag my arm away and rub it. Once I saw Charlie push his wife so hard she went down and hit her head and had to have four stitches. It was me that drove her to the emergency room.

Charlie says again, "What the hell do you think you're doing?"

"I'm serving my table. He wants a salad. Large." I can't remember if John'd said a large or a small salad, but I figure a large order would make Charlie feel better. But Charlie doesn't want to feel better.

"You get him out of here," Charlie hisses. He still doesn't look at John. "You hear me, Sally? You get him *out.* The government says I gotta serve spiks and niggers, but it don't say I gotta serve *him!*"

I look at John. He's putting on his hat, ramming it onto his bald head, and half-standing in the booth. He can't get out because Charlie and me are both in the way. I expect John to look mad or upset, but except that he's holding the muscles in his face in some different way, I can't see any change of expression. But I figure he's got to feel something bad, and all of a sudden I'm mad at Charlie, who's a bully and who's got the feelings of a scumbag. I open my mouth to tell him so, plus one or two other little things I been saving up, when the door flies open and in burst four men, and damn if they aren't *all* wearing hats like Humphrey Bogart in *Casablanca.* As soon as the first guy sees John, his walk changes and he comes over slower but more purposeful-like, and he's talking to John and to Charlie in a sincere voice like a TV anchorman giving out the news.

I see the situation now belongs to him, so I go back to the catsup bottles. I'm still plenty burned, though, about Charlie manhandling me and about Kathy rushing so stupid into the kitchen to get Charlie. She's a flake and always has been.

Charlie is scowling and nodding. The harder he scowls, the nicer the government guy's voice gets. Pretty soon the government man is smiling sweet as pie. Charlie slinks back into the kitchen, and the four men move toward the door with John in the middle of them like some high school football huddle. Next to the real men, he looks stranger than he did before, and I see how really flat his face is. But then when the huddle's right opposite the table with my catsup bottles, John breaks away and comes over to me.

"I am sorry, Sally Gourley," he says. And then: "I seldom have the chance to show our friendliness to an ordinary Earth person. I make so little difference!"

Well, that throws me. His voice sounds so sad, and besides, I never thought of myself as an ordinary Earth person. Who would? So I just shrug and wipe off a catsup bottle with my towel. But then John does a weird thing. He just touches my arm where Charlie squeezed it, just touches it with the palm of those hands. And the palm's not slimy at all—dry, and sort of cool, and I don't jump or anything. Instead, I remember that beautiful noise when he said his other name. Then he goes out with three of the men, and the door bangs behind them on a gust of rain because Charlie never fixed the air-stop from when some kids horsing around broke it last spring.

The fourth man stays and questions me: What did the alien say, what did I say. I tell him, but then he starts asking the same exact questions all over again, like he didn't believe me the first time, and that gets me mad. Also, he has this snotty voice, and I see how his eyebrows move when I slip once and accidentally say, "he don't." I might not know what John's muscles mean, but I sure the hell can read those eyebrows. So I get miffed, and pretty soon he leaves and the door bangs behind him.

I finish the catsup and mustard bottles, and Kathy finishes the coffee machine. The radio in the ceiling plays something instrumental, no words, real sad. Kathy and me start to wash down the booths with disinfectant, and because we're doing the same work together and nobody comes in, I finally say to her, "It's funny."

She says, "What's funny?"

"Charlie called that guy 'him' right off. 'I don't got to serve him,' he said. And I thought of him as 'it' at first, least until I had a name to use. But Charlie's the one who threw him out."

Kathy swipes at the back of her booth. "And Charlie's right. That thing scared me half to death, coming in here like that. And where there's food being served, too." She snorts and sprays on more disinfectant.

Well, she's a flake. Always has been.

"*The National Enquirer,*" Kathy goes on, "told how they have all this firepower up there in the big ship that hasn't landed yet. My husband says they could blow us all to smithereens, they're so powerful. I don't know why they even came here. *We* don't want them. I don't even know why they came, all that way."

"They want to make a difference," I say, but Kathy barrels on ahead, not listening.

"The Pentagon will hold them off, it doesn't matter what weapons they got up there or how much they insist on seeing about our defenses, the Pentagon won't let them get any toeholds on Earth. That's what my husband says. Blue bastards."

I say, "Will you please shut up?"

She gives me a dirty look and flounces off. I don't care. None of it is anything to me. Only, standing there with the disinfectant in my hand, looking at the dark windows and listening to the music wordless and slow on the radio, I remember that touch on my arm, so light and cool. And I think they didn't come here with any firepower to blow us all to smithereens. I just don't believe it. But then why did they come? Why come all that way from another star to walk into Charlie's diner and order a green salad with no dressing from an ordinary Earth person?

Charlie comes out with his keys to unlock the cash register and go over the tapes. I remember the old couple who stiffed me and I curse to myself. Only pie and coffee, but it still comes off my salary. The radio in the ceiling starts playing something else, not the sad song, but nothing snappy neither. It's a love song, about some guy giving and giving and getting treated like dirt. I don't like it.

"Charlie," I say, "what did those government men say to you?"

He looks up from his tapes and scowls, "What do you care?"

"I just want to know."

"And maybe I don't want you to know," he says, and smiles nasty-like. Me asking him has put him in a better mood, the creep. All of a sudden I remember what his wife said when she got the stitches, "The only way to get something from Charlie is to let him smack me around a little, and then ask him when I'm down. He'll give me anything when I'm down. He gives me shit if he thinks I'm on top."

I do the rest of the cleanup without saying anything. Charlie swears at the night's take—I know from my tips that it's not much. Kathy teases her hair in front of the mirror behind the doughnuts and pies, and I put down the breakfast menus. But all the time I'm thinking, and I don't much like my thoughts.

Charlie locks up and we all leave. Outside it's stopped raining, but it's still misty and soft, real pretty but too cold. I pull my sweater around myself and in the parking lot, after Kathy's gone, I say, "Charlie."

He stops walking toward his truck. "Yeah?"

I lick my lips. They're all of a sudden dry. It's an experiment, like, what I'm going to say. It's an experiment.

"Charlie. What if those government guys hadn't come just then and the . . . blue guy hadn't been willing to leave? What would you have done?"

"What do you care?"

I shrug. "I don't care. Just curious. It's *your* place."

"Damn right it's my place!" I could see him scowl, through the mist. "I'd of squashed him flat!"

"And then what? After you squashed him flat, what if the men came then and made a stink?"

"Too bad. It'd be too late by then, huh?" He laughs, and I can see how he's seeing it: the blue guy bleeding on the linoleum, and Charlie standing over him, dusting his hands together.

Charlie laughs again and goes off to his truck, whistling. He has a little bounce to his step. He's still seeing it all, almost like it really *had* happened. Over his shoulder he calls to me, "They're built like wimps. Or girls. All bone, no muscle. Even *you* must of seen that," and his voice is cheerful. It doesn't have any more anger in it, or hatred, or anything but a sort of friendliness. I hear him whistle some more, until the truck engine starts up and he peels out of the parking lot, laying rubber like a kid.

I unlock my Chevy. But before I get in, I look up at the sky. Which is really stupid because of course I can't see anything, with all the mists and clouds. No stars.

Maybe Kathy's husband is right. Maybe they do want to blow us all to smithereens. I don't think so, but what the hell difference does it ever make what I think? And all at once I'm furious at John, furiously mad, as furious as I've ever been in my life.

Why does he have to come here, with his birdcalls and his politeness? Why can't they all go someplace else besides here? There must be lots of other places they can go, out of all them bright stars up there behind the clouds. They don't need to come here, here where I need this job and that means I need Charlie. He's a bully, but I want to look at him and see nothing else but a bully. Nothing else but that. That's all I want to see in

Charlie, in the government men—just small-time bullies, nothing special, not a mirror of anything, not a future of anything. Just Charlie. That's all. I won't see anything else.

I won't.

"I make so little difference," he says.

Yeah. Sure.

(1986)

JAMES PATRICK KELLY

RAT

Rat had stashed the dust in four plastic capsules and then swallowed them. From the stinging at the base of his ribs, he guessed they were now squeezing into his duodenum. Still plenty of time. The bullet train had been shooting through the vacuum of the TransAtlantic tunnel for almost two hours now; they would arrive at Port Authority/Koch soon. Customs had already been fixed, according to the maréchal. All Rat had to do was to get back to his nest, lock the smart door behind him, and put the word out on his protected nets. He had enough Algerian Yellow to dust at least half the cerebrums on the East Side. If he could turn this deal, he would be rich enough to bathe in Dom Pérignon and dry himself with Gromaire tapestries. Another pang shot down his left flank. Instinctively his hind leg came off the seat and scratched at air.

There was only one problem; Rat had decided to cut the maréchal out. That meant he had to lose the old man's spook before he got home.

The spook had attached herself to him at Marseilles. She braided her blonde hair in pigtails. She had freckles, wore braces on her teeth. Tiny breasts nudged a modest silk turtleneck. She looked to be between twelve and fourteen. Cute. She had probably looked that way for twenty years, would stay the same another twenty if she did not stop a slug first or get cut in half by some automated security laser that tracked only heat and could not read—or be troubled by—cuteness. Their passports said they were Mr. Sterling Jaynes and daughter Jessalynn, of Forest Hills, New York. She was typing in her notebook, chubby fingers curled over the keys. Homework? A letter to a boyfriend? More likely she was operating on some corporate database with scalpel code of her own devising.

"Ne fais pas semblant d'étudier, ma petite," Rat said, *"Que fais-tu?"*

"Oh, Daddy," she said, pouting, "can't we go back to plain old English? After all, we're almost home." She tilted her notebook so that he could see the display. It read: "Two rows back, second seat from aisle. Fed. If he knew you were carrying, he'd cut the dust out of you and wipe his ass with your pelt." She tapped the Return key, and the message disappeared.

"All right, dear." He arched his back, fighting a surge of adrenaline that made his incisors click. "You know, all of a sudden I feel hungry. Should we do something here on the train or wait until we get to New York?" Only the spook saw him gesture back toward the fed.

"Why don't we wait for the station? More choice there."

"As you wish, dear." He wanted her to take the fed out *now,* but there was nothing more he dared say. He licked his hands nervously and groomed the fur behind his short, thick ears to pass the time.

The International Arrivals Hall at Koch Terminal was unusually quiet for a Thursday night. It smelled to Rat like a setup. The passengers from the bullet shuffled through the echoing marble vastness toward the row of customs stations. Rat was unarmed; if they were going to put up a fight, the spook would have to provide the firepower. But Rat was not a fighter, he was a runner. Their instructions were to pass through Station Number Four. As they waited in line, Rat spotted the federally appointed vigilante behind them. The classic invisible man: neither handsome nor ugly, five-ten, about one-seventy, brown hair, dark suit, white shirt. He looked bored.

"Do you have anything to declare?" The customs agent looked bored, too. Everybody looked bored except Rat, who had two million new dollars' worth of illegal drugs in his gut and a fed ready to carve them out of him.

"We hold these truths to be self-evident," said Rat, "that all men are created equal." He managed a feeble grin—as if this were a witticism and not the password.

"Daddy, please!" The spook feigned embarrassment. "I'm sorry, ma'am; it's his idea of a joke. It's the declaration of Independence, you know."

The customs agent smiled as she tousled the spook's hair. "I know that, dear. Please put your luggage on the conveyor." She gave a perfunctory glance at her monitor as their suitcases passed through the scanner, and then nodded at Rat. "Thank you, sir, and have a pleasant . . ." The insincere thought died on her lips as she noticed the fed pushing through the line toward them. Rat saw her spin toward the exit at the same moment that the spook thrust her notebook computer into the scanner. The notebook stretched a blue finger of point discharge toward the magnetic lens just before the overhead lights novaed and went dark. The emergency backup failed as well. Rat's snout filled with the acrid smell of electrical fire. Through the darkness came shouts and screams, thumps and cracks—the crazed pounding of a stampede gathering momentum.

He dropped to all fours and skittered across the floor. Koch Terminal was his territory. He had crisscrossed its many levels with scent trails. Even in total darkness he could find his way. But in his haste he cracked his head against a pair of stockinged knees, and a squawking weight fell across him, crushing the breath from his lungs. He felt an icy stab on his hindquarters and scrabbled at it with his hind leg. His toes came away wet and he squealed. There was an answering scream, and the point of a shoe drove into him, propelling him across the floor. He rolled left and came up running. Up a dead escalator, down a carpeted hall. He stood upright and stretched to his full twenty-six inches, hands scratching until they found the emergency bar across the fire door. He hurled himself at it, a siren shrieked, and with a whoosh the door opened, dumping him into an alley. He lay there for a moment, gasping, half in and half out of Koch Terminal. With the certain knowledge that he was bleeding to death, he touched the coldness on his back. A sticky purple substance; he sniffed, then tasted it. Ice cream. Rat threw back his head and laughed. The high squeaky sound echoed in the deserted alley.

But there was no time to waste. He could already hear the buzz of police hovers swooping down from the night sky. The blackout might keep them busy for a while; Rat was more worried about the fed. And the spook. They would be out soon enough, looking for him. Rat scurried down the alley toward the street. He glanced quickly at the terminal, now a black hole in the galaxy of bright holographic sleaze that was Forty-second Street. A few cops with flashlights were trying to fight against the flow of panicky travelers pouring from its open doors. Rat smoothed his ruffled fur and turned away from the disaster, walking crosstown. His instincts said to run, but Rat forced himself to dawdle like a hick shopping for big-city excitement. He grinned at the pimps and windowshopped the hardware stores. He paused in front of a pair of mirror-image sex stops—GIRLS! LIVE! GIRLS! and LIVE! GIRLS! LIVE!—to sniff the pheromone-scented sweat pouring off an androgynous robot shill that was working the sidewalk. The robot obligingly put its hand to Rat's crotch, but he pushed it away with a hiss and continued on. At last, sure that he was not being followed, he powered up his wallet and tapped into the transnet to summon a hovercab. The wallet informed him that the city had cordoned off midtown airspace to facilitate rescue operations at Koch Terminal. It advised trying the subway or a taxi. Since he had no intention of sticking an ID chip—even a false one!—into a subway turnstyle, he stepped to the curb and began watching the traffic.

The rebuilt Checker that rattled to a stop beside him was a patchwork of orange ABS and stainless-steel armor. "No we leave Manhattan," said a speaker on the roof light. "No we north of a hundred and ten." Rat nodded and the door locks popped. The passenger compartment smelled of chlorobenzyl-malononitrile and urine.

"First Avenue Bunker," said Rat, sniffing. "Christ, it stinks back here. Who was your last fare—the circus?"

"Troubleman." The speaker connections were loose, giving a scratchy edge to the cabbie's voice. The locks reengaged as the Checker pulled away from the curb. "Ha-has get a full snoot of tear gas in this hack."

Rat had already spotted the pressure vents in the floor. He peered through the gloom at the registration. A slogan had been lased in over it—probably by one of the new Mitsubishi penlights. "Free the dead." Rat smiled: the dead were his customers. People who had chosen the dust road. Twelve to eighteen months of glorious addiction: synthetic orgasms, recursive hallucinations leading to a total sensory overload and an ecstatic death experience. One dose was all it took to start down the dust road. The feds were trying to cut off the supply—with dire consequences for the dead. They could live a few months longer without dust, but their joyride down the dusty road was transformed into a grueling marathon of withdrawal pangs and madness. Either way, they were dead. Rat settled back onto the seat. The penlight graffito was a good omen. He reached into his pocket and pulled out a leather strip that had been soaked with a private blend of fat-soluble amphetamines and began to gnaw at it.

From time to time he could hear the cabbie monitoring NYPD net for flameouts or wildcat tolls set up by street gangs. They had to detour to heavily guarded Park Avenue all the way uptown to Fifty-ninth before doubling back toward the bunker. Originally built to protect U.N. diplomats from terrorists, the bunker had gone condo after the dissolution of the United Nations. Its hype was that it was the "safest address in the city." Rat knew better, which is why he had had a state-of-the-art smart door installed. Its rep was that most of the owners' association were candidates either for a mindwipe or an extended vacation on a fed punkfarm.

"Hey, Fare," said the cabbie, "Net says the dead be rioting front of your door. Crash through or roll away?"

The fur along Rat's backbone went erect. "Cops?"

"Letting them play for now."

"You've got armor for a crash?"

"Shit, yes. Park this hack to ground zero for the right fare." The cabbie's laugh was static. "Don't worry, bunkerman. Give those deadboys a shot of old CS gas and they be too busy scratching they eyes out to bother us much."

Rat tried to smooth his fur. He could crash the riot and get stuck. But if he waited, either the spook or the fed would be stepping on his tail before long. Rat had no doubt that both had managed to plant locator bugs on him.

" 'Course, riot crashing don't come cheap," said the cabbie.

"Triple the meter." The fare was already over two hundred dollars for the fifteen-minute ride. "Shoot for Bay Two—the one with the yellow door." He pulled out his wallet and started tapping its luminescent keys. "I'm sending recognition code now."

He heard the cabbie notify the cops that they were coming through. Rat could feel the Checker accelerate as they passed the cordon, and he had a glimpse of strobing lights, cops in blue body armor, a tank studded with water cannons. Suddenly the cabbie braked, and Rat pitched forward against his shoulder harness. The Checker's solid rubber tires squealed, and there was the thump of something bouncing off the hood. They had slowed to a crawl, and the dead closed around them.

Rat could not see out the front because the cabbie was protected from his passengers by steel plate. But the side windows filled with faces streaming with sweat and tears and blood. Twisted faces, screaming faces, faces etched by the agonies of withdrawal. The soundproofing muffled their howls. Fear and exhilaration filled Rat as he watched them pass. If only they knew how close they were to dust, he thought. He imagined the dead faces gnawing through the cab's armor in a frenzy, pausing only to spit out broken teeth. It was wonderful. The riot was proof that the dust market was still white-hot. The dead must be desperate to attack the bunker like this looking for a flash. He decided to bump the price of his dust another ten percent.

Rat heard a clatter on the roof; then someone began to jump up and down. It was like being inside a kettledrum. Rat sank claws into the seat and arched his back. "What are you waiting for? Gas them, damn it!"

"Hey, Fare. Stuff ain't cheap. We be fine—almost there."

A woman with bloody red hair matted to her head pressed her mouth against the window and screamed. Rat reared up on his hind legs and made biting feints at her. Then he saw the penlight in her hand. At the last moment Rat threw himself backward. The penlight flared, and the passenger compartment filled with the stench of melting plastic. A needle of coherent light singed the fur on Rat's left flank; he squealed and flopped onto the floor, twitching.

The cabbie opened the external gas vents, and abruptly the faces dropped away from the windows. The cab accelerated, bouncing as it ran over the fallen dead. There was a dazzling transition from the darkness of the violent night to the floodlit calm of Bay Number Two. Rat scrambled back onto the seat and looked out the back window in time to see the hydraulic doors of the outer lock swing shut. Something was caught between them—something that popped and spattered. The inner door rolled down on its track like a curtain coming down on a bloody final act.

Rat was almost home. Two security guards in armor approached. The door locks popped, and Rat climbed out of the cab. One of the guards leveled a burster at his head; the other wordlessly offered him a print-reader. He thumbed it, and bunker's computer verfied him immediately.

"Good evening, sir," said one of the guards. "Little rough out there tonight. Did you have luggage?"

The front door of the cab opened, and Rat heard the low whine of electric motors as a mechanical arm lowered the cabbie's wheelchair onto the floor of the bay. She was a gray-haired woman with a rheumy stare who looked like she belonged in a rest home in New Jersey. A knitted shawl covered her withered legs. "You said triple." The cab's hoist clicked and released the chair; she rolled toward him. "Six hundred and sixty-nine dollars."

"No luggage, no." Now that he was safe inside the bunker, Rat regretted his panic-stricken generosity. A credit transfer from one of his own accounts was out of the question. He slipped his last thousand-dollar bubble chip into his wallet's card reader, dumped $331 from it into a Bahamian laundry loop, and then dropped the chip into her outstretched hand. She accepted it dubiously: for a minute he expected her to bite into it like they did sometimes on fossil TV. Old people made him nervous. Instead she inserted the chip into her own card reader and frowned at him.

"How about a tip?"

Rat sniffed. "Don't pick up strangers."

One of the guards guffawed obligingly. The other pointed, but Rat saw the skunk port in the wheelchair a millisecond too late. With a wet *plot* the chair emitted a gaseous stinkball that bloomed like an evil flower beneath Rat's whiskers. One guard tried to grab at the rear of the chair, but the old cabbie backed suddenly over his foot. The other guard aimed his burster.

The cabbie smiled like a grandmother from hell. "Under the pollution index. No law against sharing a little scent, boys. And you wouldn't want to hurt me anyway. The hack monitors my EEG. I go flat and it goes berserk."

The guard with the bad foot stopped hopping. The guard with the gun shrugged. "It's up to you, sir."

Rat batted the side of his head several times and then buried his snout beneath his armpit. All he could smell was rancid burger topped with sulphur sauce. "Forget it. I haven't got time."

"You know," said the cabbie. "I never get out of the hack, but I just wanted to see what kind of person would live in a place like this." The lifts whined as the arm fitted its fingers into the chair. "And now I know." She cackled as the arm gathered her back into the cab. "I'll park it by the door. The cops say they're ready to sweep the street."

The guards led Rat to the bank of elevators. He entered the one with the open door, thumbed the printreader, and spoke his access code.

"Good evening, sir," said the elevator. "Will you be going straight to your rooms?"

"Yes."

"Very good, sir. Would you like a list of the communal facilities currently open to serve you?"

There was no shutting the sales pitch off, so Rat ignored it and began to lick the stink from his fur.

"The pool is open for lap swimmers only," said the elevator as the doors closed. "All environments except for the weightless room are currently in use. The sensory deprivation tanks will be occupied until eleven. The surrogatorium is temporarily out of female chassis; we apologize for any inconvenience . . ."

The cab moved down two and a half floors and then stopped just above the subbasement. Rat glanced up and saw a dark gap opening in the array of light diffuser panels. The spook dropped through it.

". . . the holo therapist is off-line until eight tomorrow morning, but the interactive sex booths will stay open until midnight. The drug dispensary . . ."

She looked as if she had been water-skiing through the sewer. Her blonde hair was wet and smeared with dirt; she had lost the ribbons from her pigtails. Her jeans were torn at the knees, and there was an ugly scrape on the side of her face. The silk turtleneck clung wetly to her. Yet despite her dishevelment, the hand that held the penlight was as steady as a jewel cutter's.

"There seems to be a minor problem," said the elevator in a soothing voice. "There is no cause for alarm. This unit is temporarily nonfunctional. Maintenance has been notified and is now working to correct the problem. In case of emergency, please contact Security. We regret this temporary inconvenience."

The spook fired a burst of light at the floor selector panel; it spat fire at them and went dark. "Where the hell were you?" said the spook. "You said the McDonald's in Time Square if we got separated."

"Where were *you*?" Rat rose up on his hind legs. "When I got there the place was swarming with cops."

He froze as the tip of the penlight flared. The spook traced a rough outline of Rat on the stainless-steel door behind him. "Fuck your lies," she said. The beam came so close that Rat could smell his fur curling away from it. "I want the dust."

"Trespass alert!" screeched the wounded elevator. A note of urgency had crept into its artificial voice. "Security reports unauthorized persons within the complex. Residents are urged to return immediately to their apartments and engage all personal security devices. Do not be alarmed. We regret this temporary inconvenience."

The scales on Rat's tail fluffed. "We have a deal. The maréchal needs my networks to move his product. So let's get out of here before . . ."

"The dust."

Rat sprang at her with a squeal of hatred. His claws caught on her turtleneck and he struck repeatedly at her open collar, gashing her neck with his long red incisors. Taken aback by the swiftness and ferocity of his attack, she dropped the penlight and tried to fling him against the wall. He held fast, worrying at her and chittering rabidly. When she stumbled under the open emergency exit in the ceiling, he leaped again. He cleared the suspended ceiling, caught himself on the inductor, and scrabbled up onto the hoist cables. Light was pouring into the shaft from above; armored guards had forced the door open and were climbing down toward the stalled car. Rat jumped from the cables across five feet of open space to the counterweight and huddled there, trying to use its bulk to shield himself from the spook's fire. Her stand was short and inglorious. She threw a dazzler out of the hatch, hoping to blind the guards, then tried to pull herself through. Rat could hear the shriek of burster fire. He waited until he could smell the aroma of broiling meat and scorched plastic before he emerged from the shadows and signaled to the security team.

A squad of apologetic guards rode the service elevator with Rat down to the storage subbasement where he lived. When he had first looked at the bunker, the broker had been reluctant to rent him the abandoned rooms, insisting that he live above-ground with the other residents. But all of the suites they showed him were unacceptably open, clean, and uncluttered. Rat much preferred his musty dungeon, where odors lingered in the still air. He liked to fall asleep to the booming of the ventilation system on the level above him, and slept easier knowing that he was as far away from the stink of other people as he could get in the city.

The guards escorted him to the gleaming brass smart door and looked away discreetly as he entered his passcode on the key-pad. He had ordered it custom-built from Mosler so that it would recognize high-frequency squeals well beyond the range of human hearing. He called to it and then pressed trembling fingers onto the printreader. His bowels had loosened in terror during the firefight, and the capsules had begun to sting terribly. It was all he could do to keep from defecating right there in the hallway. The door sensed the guards and beeped to warn him of their presence. He punched in the override sequence impatiently, and the seals broke with a sigh.

"Have a pleasant evening, sir," said one of the guards as he scurried inside. "And don't worry ab—" The door cut him off as it swung shut.

Against all odds, Rat had made it. For a moment he stood, tail switching against the inside of the door, and let the magnificent chaos of his apartment soothe his jangled nerves. He had earned his reward—the dust was all his now. No one could take it away from him. He saw himself in a shard of mirror propped up against an empty THC aerosol and wriggled in self-congratulation. He was the richest rat on the East Side, perhaps in the entire city.

He picked his way through a maze formed by a jumble of overburdened steel shelving left behind years, perhaps decades, ago. The managers of the bunker had offered to remove them and their contents before he moved in; Rat had insisted that they stay. When the fire inspector had come to approve his newly installed sprinkler system, she had been horrified at the clutter on the shelves and had threatened to condemn the place. It had cost him plenty to buy her off, but it had been worth it. Since then Rat's trove of junk had at least doubled in size. For years no one had seen it but Rat and the occasional cockroach.

Relaxing at last, Rat stopped to pull a mildewed wing tip down from the huge collection of shoes; he loved the bouquet of fine old leather and gnawed and gnawed it whenever he could. Next to the shoes was a heap of books: his private library. One of Rat's favorite delicacies was the first edition of *Leaves of Grass* that he had pilfered from the rare book collection at the New York Public Library. To celebrate his safe arrival, he ripped out page 43 for a snack and stuffed it into the wing tip. He dragged the shoe over a pile of broken sheetrock and past shelves filled with scrap electronics: shattered monitors and dead typewriters, microwaves and robot vacuums. He had almost reached his nest when the fed stepped from behind a dirty Hungarian flag that hung from a broken fluorescent light fixture.

Startled, Rat instinctively hurled himself at the crack in the wall where he had built his nest. But the fed was too quick. Rat did not recognize the weapon; all he knew was that when it hissed, Rat lost all feeling in his hindquarters. He landed in a heap but continued to crawl, slowly, painfully.

"You have something I want." The fed kicked him. Rat skidded across the concrete floor toward the crack, leaving a thin gruel of excrement in his wake. Rat continued to crawl until the fed stepped on his tail, pinning him.

"Where's the dust?"

"I . . . I don't . . . "

The fed stepped again; Rat's left fibula snapped like cheap plastic. He felt no pain.

"The dust." The fed's voice quavered strangely.

"Not here. Too dangerous."

"Where?" The fed released him. "Where?"

Rat was surprised to see that the fed's gun hand was shaking. For the first time he looked up at the man's eyes and recognized the telltale yellow tint. Rat realized then how badly he had misinterpreted the fed's expression back at Koch. Not bored. *Empty.* For an instant he could not believe his extraordinary good fortune. Bargain for time, he told himself. There's still a chance. Even though he was cornered, he knew his instinct to fight was wrong.

"I can get it for you fast if you let me go," said Rat. "Ten minutes, fifteen. You look like you need it."

"What are you talking about?" The fed's bravado started to crumble, and Rat knew he had the man. The fed wanted the dust for himself. He was one of the dead.

"Don't make it hard on yourself," said Rat. "There's a terminal in my nest. By the crack. Ten minutes." He started to pull himself toward the nest. He knew the fed would not dare stop him; the man was already deep into withdrawal. "Only ten minutes and you can have all the dust you want." The poor fool could not hope to fight the flood of neuroregulators pumping crazily across his synapses. He might break any minute, let his weapon slip from trembling hands. Rat reached the crack and scrambled through into comforting darkness.

The nest was built around a century-old shopping cart and a stripped subway bench. Rat had filled the gaps in with pieces of synthetic rubber, a hubcap, plastic greeting cards, barbed wire, disk casings, Baggies, a No Parking sign, and an assortment of bones. Rat climbed in and lowered himself onto the soft bed of shredded thousand-dollar bills. The profits of six years of deals and betrayals, a few dozen murders, and several thousand dusty deaths.

The fed sniffled as Rat powered up his terminal to notify Security. "Someone set me up some vicious bastard slipped it to me I don't know when I think it was Barcelona . . . it would kill Sarah to see . . . " He began to weep. "I wanted to turn myself in . . . they keep working on new treatments you know but it's not fair damn it! The success rate is less than . . . I made my first buy two weeks only two God it seems . . . killed a man to get some lousy dust . . . but they're right it's, it's, I can't begin to describe what it's like . . . "

Rat's fingers flew over the glowing keyboard, describing his situation, the layout of the rooms, a strategy for the assault. He had overridden the smart door's recognition sequence. It would be tricky, but Security could take the fed out if they were quick and careful. Better risk a surprise attack than to dicker with an armed and unraveling dead man.

"I really ought to kill myself . . . would be best but it's not only me . . . I've seen ten-year olds . . . what kind of animal sells dust to kids . . . I should kill myself and you." Something changed in the fed's voice as Rat signed off. "And you." He stooped and reached through the crack.

"It's coming," said Rat quickly. "By messenger. Ten doses. By the time you get to the door, it should be here." He could see the fed's hand and burrowed into the rotting pile of money. "You wait by the door, you hear? It's coming any minute."

"I don't want it." The hand was so large it blocked the light. Rat's fur went erect and he arched his spine. "Keep your fucking dust."

Rat could hear the guards fighting their way through the clutter. Shelves crashed. So clumsy, these men.

"It's you I want." The hand sifted through the shredded bills, searching for Rat. He had no doubt that the fed could crush the life from him—the hand was huge now. In the darkness he could count the lines on the palm, follow the whorls on the fingertips. They seemed to spin in Rat's brain—he was losing control. He realized then that one of the capsules must have broken, spilling a megadose of first-quality Algerian Yellow dust into his gut. With a hallucinatory clarity, he imagined sparks streaming through his blood, igniting neurons like tinder. Suddenly the guards did not matter. Nothing mattered except that he was cornered. When he could no longer fight the instinct to strike, the fed's hand closed around him. The man was stronger than Rat could have imagined. As the fed hauled him—clawing and biting—back into the light, Rat's only thought was of how terrifyingly large a man was. So much larger than a rat.

(1986)

ORSON SCOTT CARD

America

Sam Monson and Anamari Boagente had two encounters in their lives, forty years apart. The first encounter lasted for several weeks in the high Amazon jungle, the village of Agualinda. The second was for only an hour near the ruins of the Glen Canyon Dam, on the border between Navaho country and the State of Deseret.

When they met the first time, Sam was a scrawny teenager from Utah and Anamari was a middle-aged spinster Indian from Brazil. When they met the second time, he was governor of Deseret, the last European state in America, and she was, to some people's way of thinking, the mother of God. It never occurred to anyone that they had ever met before, except me. I saw it plain as day, and pestered Sam until he told me the whole story. Now Sam is dead, and she's long gone, and I'm the only one who knows the truth. I thought for a long time that I'd take this story untold to my grave, but I see now that I can't do that. The way I see it, I won't be allowed to die until I write this down. All my real work was done long since, so why else am I alive? I figure the land has kept me breathing so I can tell the story of its victory, and it has kept *you* alive so you can hear it. Gods are like that. It isn't enough for them to run everything. They want to be famous, too.

Agualinda, Amazonas

Passengers were nothing to her. Anamari only cared about helicopters when they brought medical supplies. This chopper carried a precious packet of benaxidene; Anamari barely noticed the skinny, awkward boy who sat by the crates, looking hostile. Another Yanqui who doesn't want to be stuck out in the jungle. Nothing new about that. Norteamericanos were almost invisible to Anamari by now. They came and went.

It was the Brazilian government people she had to worry about, the petty bureaucrats suffering through years of virtual exile in Manaus, working out their frustrations by being petty tyrants over the helpless Indians. No I'm sorry we don't have any more penicillin, no more syringes, what did you do with the AIDS vaccine we gave you three years ago? Do you think we're made of money here? Let them come to town if they want to get well. There's a hospital in São Paulo de Olivença, send them there, we're not going to turn you into a second hospital out there in the middle of nowhere, not for a village of a hundred filthy Baniwas, it's not as if you're a doctor, you're just an old withered up Indian woman yourself, you never graduated from the medical schools, we can't spare medicines for you. It made them feel so important, to decide whether or not an Indian child would live or die. As often as not they passed sentence of death by refusing to send supplies. It made them feel powerful as God.

Anamari knew better than to protest or argue—it would only make that bureaucrat likelier to kill again in the future. But sometimes, when the need was great and the medicine was common, Anamari would go to the Yanqui geologists and ask if they had this or that. Sometimes they did. What she knew about Yanquis was that if they had some extra, they would share, but if they didn't, they wouldn't lift a finger to get any. They were not tyrants like the Brazilian bureaucrats. They just didn't give a damn. They were there to make money.

That was what Anamari saw when she looked at the sullen light-haired boy in the helicopter—another Norteamericano, just like all the other Norteamericanos, only younger.

She had the benaxidene, and so she immediately began spreading word that all the Baniwas should come for injections. It was a disease that had been introduced during the war between Guyana and Venezuela two years ago; as usual, most of the victims were not citizens of either country, just the Indios of the jungle, waking up one morning with their joints stiffening, hardening until no movement was possible. Benaxidene was the antidote, but you had to have it every few months or your joints would stiffen up again. As usual, the bureaucrats had diverted a shipment and there were a dozen Baniwas bedridden in the village. As usual, one or two of the Indians would be too far gone for the cure; one or two of their joints would be stiff for the rest of their lives. As usual, Anamari said little as she gave the injections, and the Baniwas said less to her.

It was not until the next day that Anamari had time to notice the young Yanqui boy wandering around the village. He was wearing rumpled white clothing, already somewhat soiled with the greens and browns of life along the rivers of the Amazon jungle. He showed no sign of being interested in anything, but an hour into her rounds, checking on the results of yesterday's benaxidene treatments, she became aware that he was following her.

She turned around in the doorway of the government-built hovel and faced him. "O que é?" she demanded. What do you want?

To her surprise, he answered in halting Portuguese. Most of these Yanquis never bothered to learn the language at all, expecting her and everybody else to speak English. "Posso ajudar?" he asked. Can I help?

"Não," she said. "Mas pode olhar." You can watch.

He looked at her in bafflement.

She repeated her sentence slowly, enunciating clearly. "Pode olhar."

"Eu?" Me?

"Você, sim. And I can speak English."

"I don't want to speak English."

"Tanto faz," she said. Makes no difference.

He followed her into the hut. It was a little girl, lying naked in her own feces. She had palsy from a bout with meningitis years ago, when she was an infant, and Anamari figured that the girl would probably be one of the ones for whom the benaxidene came too late. That's how things usually worked—the weak suffer most. But no, her joints were flexing again, and the girl smiled at them, that heartbreakingly happy smile that made palsy victims so beautiful at times.

So. Some luck after all, the benaxidene had been in time for her. Anamari took the lid off the clay waterjar that stood on the one table in the room, and dipped one of her clean rags in it. She used it to wipe the girl, then lifted her frail, atrophied body and pulled the soiled sheet out from under her. On impulse, she handed the sheet to the boy.

"Leva fora," she said. And, when he didn't understand, "Take it outside."

He did not hesitate to take it, which surprised her. "Do you want me to wash it?"

"You could shake off the worst of it," she said. "Out over the garden in back. I'll wash it later."

He came back in, carrying the wadded-up sheet, just as she was leaving. "All done here," she said. "We'll stop by my house to start that soaking. I'll carry it now."

He didn't hand it to her. "I've got it," he said. "Aren't you going to give her a clean sheet?"

"There are only four sheets in the village," she said. "Two of them are on my bed. She won't mind lying on the mat. I'm the only one in the village who cares about linens. I'm also the only one who cares about this girl."

"She likes you," he said.

"She smiles like that at everybody."

"So maybe she likes everybody."

Anamari grunted and led the way to her house. It was two government hovels pushed together. The one served as her clinic, the other as her home. Out back she had two metal washtubs. She handed one of them to the Yanqui boy, pointed at the rainwater tank, and told him to fill it. He did. It made her furious.

"What do you want!" she demanded.

"Nothing," he said.

"Why do you keep hanging around!"

"I thought I was helping." His voice was full of injured pride.

"I don't need your help." She forgot that she had meant to leave the sheet to soak. She began rubbing it on the washboard.

"Then why did you ask me to . . . "

She did not answer him, and he did not complete the question.

After a long time he said, "You were trying to get rid of me, weren't you?"

"What do you want here?" she said. "Don't I have enough to do, without a Norteamericano *boy* to look after?"

Anger flashed in his eyes, but he did not answer until the anger was gone. "If you're tired of scrubbing, I can take over."

She reached out and took his hand, examined it for a moment. "Soft hands," she said. "Lady hands. You'd scrape your knuckles on the washboard and bleed all over the sheet."

Ashamed, he put his hands in his pockets. A parrot flew past him, dazzling green and red; he turned in surprise to look at it. It landed on the rainwater tank. "Those sell for a thousand dollars in the States," he said.

Of course the Yanqui boy evaluates everything by price. "Here they're free," she said. "The Baniwas eat them. And wear the feathers."

He looked around at the other huts, the scraggly gardens. "The people are very poor here," he said. "The jungle life must be hard."

"Do you think so?" she snapped. "The jungle is very kind to these people. It has plenty for them to eat, all year. The Indians of the Amazon did not know they were poor until Europeans came and made them buy pants, which they couldn't afford, and build houses, which they couldn't keep up, and plant gardens. Plant gardens! In the midst of this magnificent Eden. The jungle life was good. The Europeans made them poor."

"Europeans?" asked the boy.

"Brazilians. They're all Europeans. Even the black ones have turned European. Brazil is just another European country, speaking a European language. Just like you Norteamericanos. You're Europeans too."

"I was born in America," he said. "So were my parents and grandparents and great-grandparents."

"But your bis-bis-avós, they came on a boat."

"That was a long time ago," he said.

"A long time!" She laughed. "I am a pure Indian. For ten thousand generations I belong to this land. You are a stranger here. A fourth-generation stranger."

"But I'm a stranger who isn't afraid to touch a dirty sheet," he said. He was grinning defiantly.

That was when she started to like him. "How old are you?" she asked.

"Fifteen," he said.

"Your father's a geologist?"

"No. He heads up the drilling team. They're going to sink a test well here. He doesn't think they'll find anything, though."

"They will find plenty of oil," she said.

"How do you know?"

"Because I dreamed it," she said. "Bulldozers cutting down the trees, making an airstrip, and planes coming and going. They'd never do that, unless they found oil. Lots of oil."

She waited for him to make fun of the idea of dreaming true dreams. But he didn't. He just looked at her.

So she was the one who broke the silence. "You came to this village to kill time while your father is away from you, on the job, right?"

"No," he said. "I came here because he hasn't started to work yet. The choppers start bringing in equipment tomorrow."

"You would rather be away from your father?"

He looked away. "I'd rather see him in hell."

"This *is* hell," she said, and the boy laughed. "Why did you come here with him?"

"Because I'm only fifteen years old, and he has custody of me this summer."

"Custody," she said. "Like a criminal."

"He's the criminal," he said bitterly.

"And his crime?"

He waited a moment, as if deciding whether to answer. When he spoke, he spoke quietly and looked away. Ashamed. Of his father's crime. "Adultery," he said. The word hung in the air. The boy turned back and looked her in the face again. His face was tinged with red.

Europeans have such transparent skin, she thought. All their emotions show through. She guessed a whole story from his word—a beloved mother betrayed, and now he had to spend the summer with her betrayer. "Is that a *crime*?"

He shrugged. "Maybe not to Catholics."

"You're Protestant?"

He shook his head. "Mormon. But I'm a heretic."

She laughed. "You're a heretic, and your father is an adulterer."

He didn't like her laughter. "And you're a virgin," he said. His words seemed calculated to hurt her.

She stopped scrubbing, stood there looking at her hands. "Also a crime?" she murmured.

"I had a dream last night," he said. "In my dream your name was Anna Marie, but when I tried to call you that, I couldn't. I could only call you by another name."

"What name?" she asked.

"What does it matter? It was only a dream." He was taunting her. He knew she trusted in dreams.

"You dreamed of me, and in the dream my name was Anamari?"

"It's true, isn't it? That *is* your name, isn't it?" He didn't have to add the other half of the question: You *are* a virgin, aren't you?

She lifted the sheet from the water, wrung it out and tossed it to him. He caught it, vile water spattering his face. He grimaced. She poured the washwater onto the dirt. It spattered mud all over his trousers. He did not step back. Then she carried the tub to the water tank and began to fill it with clean water. "Time to rinse," she said.

"You dreamed about an airstrip," he said. "And I dreamed about you."

"In your dreams you better start to mind your own business," she said.

"I didn't ask for it, you know," he said. "But I followed the dream out to this village, and you turned out to be a dreamer, too."

"That doesn't mean you're going to end up with your pinto between my legs, so you can forget it," she said.

He looked genuinely horrified. "Geez, what are you talking about! That would be fornication! Plus you've got to be old enough to be my mother!"

"I'm forty-two," she said. "If it's any of your business."

"You're *older* than my mother," he said. "I couldn't possibly think of you sexually. I'm sorry if I gave that impression."

She giggled. "You are a very funny boy, Yanqui. First you say I'm a virgin—"

"That was in the dream," he said.

"And then you tell me I'm older than your mother and too ugly to think of me sexually."

He looked ashen with shame. "I'm sorry, I was just trying to make sure you knew that I would never—"

"You're trying to tell me that you're a good boy."

"Yes," he said.

She giggled again. "You probably don't even play with yourself," she said.

His face went red. He struggled to find something to say. Then he threw the wet sheet back at her and walked furiously away. She laughed and laughed. She liked this boy very much.

The next morning he came back and helped her in the clinic all day. His name was Sam Monson, and he was the first European she ever knew who dreamed true dreams. She had thought only Indios could do that. Whatever god it was that gave her dreams to her, perhaps it was the same god giving dreams to Sam. Perhaps that god brought them together here in the jungle. Perhaps it was that god who would lead the drill to oil, so that Sam's father would have to keep him here long enough to accomplish whatever the god had in mind.

It annoyed her that the god had mentioned she was a virgin. That was nobody's business but her own.

Life in the jungle was better than Sam ever expected. Back in Utah, when Mother first told him that he had to go to the Amazon with the old bastard, he had feared the worst. Hacking through thick viney jungles with a machete, crossing rivers of piranha in tick-infested dugouts, and always sweat and mosquitos and thick, heavy air. Instead the American oilmen lived in a pretty decent camp, with a generator for electric light. Even though it rained all the time and when it didn't it was so hot you wished it would, it wasn't constant danger as he had feared, and he never had to hack through jungle at all. There were paths, sometimes almost roads, and the thick, vivid green of the jungle was more beautiful than he had ever imagined. He had not realized that the American West was such a desert. Even California, where the old bastard lived when he wasn't traveling to drill wells, even those wooded hills and mountains were grey compared to the jungle green.

The Indians were quiet little people, not headhunters. Instead of avoiding them, like the adult Americans did, Sam found that he could be with them, come to know them, even help them by working with Anamari. The old bastard could sit around and drink his beer with the guys—adultery *and* beer, as if one contemptible sin of the flesh weren't enough—but Sam was actually doing some good here. If there was anything Sam could do to prove he was the opposite of his father, he would do it; and because his father was a weak, carnal, earthy man with no self-control, then Sam had to be a strong, spiritual, intellectual man who did not let any passions of the body rule him. Watching his father succumb to alcohol, remembering how his father could not even last a month away from Mother without having to get some whore into his bed, Sam was proud of his self-discipline. He ruled his body; his body did not rule him.

He was also proud to have passed Anamari's test on the first day. What did he care if human excrement touched his body? He was not afraid to breathe the hot stink of suffering, he was not afraid of the innocent dirt of a crippled child. Didn't Jesus touch lepers? Dirt of the body did not disgust him. Only dirt of the soul.

Which was why his dreams of Anamari troubled him. During the day they were friends. They talked about important ideas, and she told him stories of the Indians of the Amazon, and about her education as a teacher in São Paulo. She listened when he talked about history and religion and evolution and all the theories and ideas that danced in his head. Even Mother never had time for that, always taking care of the younger kids or doing her endless jobs for the church. Anamari treated him like his ideas mattered.

But at night, when he dreamed, it was something else entirely. In those dreams he kept seeing her naked, and the voice kept calling her "Virgem America." What her virginity had to do with America he had no idea—even true dreams didn't always make sense—but he knew this much: when he dreamed of Anamari naked, she was always reaching out to him, and he was filled with such strong passions that more than once he awoke from the dream to find himself throbbing with imaginary pleasure, like Onan in the Bible, Judah's son, who spilled his seed upon the ground and was struck dead for it.

Sam lay awake for a long time each time this happened, trembling, fearful. Not because he thought God would strike him down—he knew that if God hadn't struck his father dead for adultery, Sam was certainly in no danger because of an erotic dream. He was afraid because he knew that in these dreams he revealed himself to be exactly as lustful and evil as his father. He did not want to feel any sexual desire for Anamari. She was old and lean and tough, and he was afraid of her, but most of all Sam didn't want to desire her because he was not like his father, he would never have sexual intercourse with a woman who was not his wife.

Yet when he walked into the village of Agualinda, he felt eager to see her again, and when he found her—the village was small, it never took long—he could not erase from his mind the vivid memory of how she looked in the dreams, reaching out to him, her breasts loose and jostling, her slim hips rolling toward him—and he would bite his cheek for the pain of it, to distract him from desire.

It was because he was living with Father; the old bastard's goatishness was rubbing off on him, that's all. So he spent as little time with his father as possible, going home only to sleep at night.

The harder he worked at the jobs Anamari gave him to do, the easier it was to keep himself from remembering his dream of her kneeling over him, touching him, sliding along his body. Hoe the weeds out of the corn until your back is on fire with pain! Wash the Baniwa hunter's wound and replace the bandage! Sterilize the instruments in the alcohol! Above all, do not, even accidentally, let any part of your body brush against hers; pull away when she is near you, turn away so you don't feel her warm breath as she leans over your shoulder, start a bright conversation whenever there is a silence filled only with the sound of insects and the sight of a bead of sweat slowly etching its way from her neck down her chest to disappear between her breasts where she only tied her shirt instead of buttoning it.

How could she possibly be a virgin, after the way she acted in his dreams?

"Where do you think the dreams come from?" she asked.

He blushed, even though she could not have guessed what he was thinking. Could she?

"The dreams," she said. "Why do you think we have dreams that come true?"

It was nearly dark. "I have to get home," he said. She was holding his hand. When had she taken his hand like that, and why?

"I have the strangest dream," she said. "I dream of a huge snake, covered with bright green and red feathers."

"Not all the dreams come true," he said.

"I hope not," she answered. "Because this snake comes out of—I give birth to this snake."

"Quetzal," he said.

"What does that mean?"

"The feathered serpent god of the Aztecs. Or maybe the Mayas. Mexican, anyway. I have to go home."

"But what does it mean?"

"It's almost dark," he said.

"Stay and talk to me!" she demanded. "I have room, you can stay the night."

But Sam had to get back. Much as he hated staying with his father, he dared not spend a night in this place. Even her invitation aroused him. He would never last a night in the same house with her. The dream would be too strong for him. So he left her and headed back along the path through the jungle. All during the walk he couldn't get Anamari out of his mind. It was as if the plants were sending him the vision of her, so his desire was even stronger than when he was with her.

The leaves gradually turned from green to black in the seeping dark. The hot darkness did not frighten him; it seemed to invite him to step away from the path into the shadows, where he would find the moist relief, the cool release of all his tension. He stayed on the path, and hurried faster.

He came at last to the oilmen's town. The generator was loud, but the insects were louder, swarming around the huge area light, casting shadows of their demonic dance. He and his father shared a large one-room house on the far edge of the compound. The oil company provided much nicer hovels than the Brazilian government.

A few men called out to greet him. He waved, even answered once or twice, but hurried on. His groin felt so hot and tight with desire that he was sure that only the shadows and his quick stride kept everyone from seeing. It was maddening: the more he thought of trying to calm himself, the more visions of Anamari slipped in and out of his waking mind, almost to the point of hallucination. His body would not relax. He was almost running when he burst into the house.

Inside, Father was washing his dinner plate. He glanced up, but Sam was already past him. "I'll heat up your dinner."

Sam flopped down on his bed. "Not hungry."

"Why are you so late?" asked his father.

"We got to talking."

"It's dangerous in the jungle at night. You think it's safe because nothing bad ever happens to you in the daytime, but it's dangerous."

"Sure, Dad. I know." Sam got up, turned his back to take off his pants. Maddeningly, he was still aroused; he didn't want his father to see.

But with the unerring instinct of prying parents, the old bastard must have sensed that Sam was hiding something. When Sam was buck naked, Father walked around and *looked,* just as if he never heard of privacy. Sam blushed in spite of himself. His father's eyes went small and hard. I hope I don't ever look like that, thought Sam. I hope my face doesn't get that ugly suspicious expression on it. I'd rather die than look like that.

"Well, put on your pajamas," Father said. "I don't want to look at that forever."

Sam pulled on his sleeping shorts.

"What's going on over there?" asked Father.

"Nothing," said Sam.

"You must do *something* all day."

"I told you, I help her. She runs a clinic, and she also tends a garden. She's got no electricity, so it takes a lot of work."

"I've done a lot of work in my time, Sam, but I don't come home like *that.*"

"No, you always stopped and got it off with some whore along the way."

The old bastard whipped out his hand and slapped Sam across the face. It stung, and the surprise of it wrung tears from Sam before he had time to decide not to cry.

"I never slept with a whore in my life," said the old bastard.

"You only slept with one woman who wasn't," said Sam.

Father slapped him again, only this time Sam was ready, and he bore the slap stoically, almost without flinching.

"I had one affair," said Father.

"You got caught once," said Sam. "There were dozens of women."

Father laughed derisively. "What did you do, hire a detective? There was only the one."

But Sam knew better. He had dreamed these women for years. Laughing, lascivious women. It wasn't until he was twelve years old that he found out enough about sex to know what it all meant. By then he had long since learned that any dream he had more than once was true. So when he had a dream of Father with one of the laughing women, he woke up, holding the dream in his memory. He thought through it from beginning to end, remembering all the details he could. The name of the motel. The room number. It was midnight, but Father was in California, so it was an hour earlier. Sam got out of bed and walked quietly into the kitchen and dialed directory assistance. There was such a motel. He wrote down the number. Then Mother was there, asking him what he was doing.

"This is the number of the Seaview Motor Inn," he said. "Call this number and ask for room twenty-one twelve and then ask for Dad."

Mother looked at him strangely, like she was about to scream or cry or hit him or throw up. "Your father is at the Hilton," she said.

But he just looked right back at her and said, "No matter who answers the phone, ask for Dad."

So she did. A woman answered, and Mom asked for Dad by name, and he was there. "I wonder how we can afford to pay for two motel rooms on the same night," Mom said coldly. "Or are you splitting the cost with your friend?" Then she hung up the phone and burst into tears.

She cried all night as she packed up everything the old bastard owned. By the time Dad got home two days later, all his things were in storage. Mom moved fast when she made up her mind. Dad found himself divorced and excommunicated all in the same week, not two months later.

Mother never asked Sam how he knew where Dad was that night. Never even hinted at wanting to know. Dad never asked him how Mom knew to call that number, either. An amazing lack of curiosity, Sam thought sometimes. Perhaps they just took it as fate. For a while it was secret, then it stopped being secret, and it didn't matter how the change happened. But one thing Sam knew for sure—the woman at the Seaview Motor Inn was not the first woman, and the Seaview was not the first motel. Dad had been an adulterer for years, and it was ridiculous for him to lie about it now.

But there was no point in arguing with him, especially when he was in the mood to slap Sam around.

"I don't like the idea of you spending so much time with an older woman," said Father.

"She's the closest thing to a doctor these people have. She needs my help and I'm going to keep helping her," said Sam.

"Don't talk to me like that, little boy."

"You don't know anything about this, so just mind your own business."

Another slap. "You're going to get tired of this before I do, Sammy."

"I love it when you slap me, Dad. It confirms my moral superiority."

Another slap, this time so hard that Sam stumbled under the blow, and he tasted blood inside his mouth. "How hard next time, Dad?" he said. "You going to knock me down? Kick me around a little? Show me who's boss?"

"You've been asking for a beating ever since we got here."

"I've been asking to be left alone."

"I know women, Sam. You have no business getting involved with an older woman like that."

"I help her wash a little girl who has bowel movements in bed, Father. I empty pails of vomit. I wash clothes and help patch leaking roofs and while I'm doing all these things we talk. Just talk. I don't imagine you have much experience with that, Dad. You probably never talk at all with the women *you* know, at least not after the price is set."

It was going to be the biggest slap of all, enough to knock him down, enough to bruise his face and black his eye. But the old bastard held it in. Didn't hit him. Just stood there, breathing hard, his face red, his eyes tight and piggish.

"You're not as pure as you think," the old bastard finally whispered. "You've got every desire you despise in me."

"I don't despise you for *desire,*" said Sam.

"The guys on the crew have been talking about you and this Indian bitch, Sammy. You may not like it, but I'm your father and it's my job to warn you. These Indian women are easy, and they'll give you a disease."

"The guys on the crew," said Sam. "What do they know about Indian women? They're all fags or jerk-offs."

"I hope someday you say that where they can hear you, Sam. And I hope when it happens I'm not there to stop what they do to you."

"I would never *be* around men like that, Daddy, if the court hadn't given you shared custody. A no-fault divorce. What a joke."

More than anything else, those words stung the old bastard. Hurt him enough to shut him up. He walked out of the house and didn't come back until Sam was long since asleep.

Asleep and dreaming.

Anamari knew what was on Sam's mind, and to her surprise she found it vaguely flattering. She had never known the shy affection of a boy. When she was a teenager, she was the one Indian girl in the schools in São Paulo. Indians were so rare in the Europeanized parts of Brazil that she might have seemed exotic, but in those days she was still so frightened. The city was sterile, all concrete and harsh light, not at all like the deep soft meadows and woods of Xingu Park. Her tribe, the Kuikuru, were much more Europeanized than the jungle Indians—she had seen cars all her life, and spoke Portuguese before she went to school. But the city made her hungry for the land, the cobblestones hurt her feet, and these intense, competitive children made her afraid. Worst of all, true dreams stopped in the city. She hardly knew who she was, if she was not a true dreamer. So if any boy desired her then, she would not have known it. She would have rebuffed him inadvertently. And then the time for such things had passed. Until now.

"Last night I dreamed of a great bird, flying west, away from land. Only its right wing was twice as large as its left wing. It had great bleeding wounds along the edges of its wings, and the right wing was the sickest of all, rotting in the air, the feathers dropping off."

"Very pretty dream," said Sam. Then he translated, to keep in practice. "Que sonho lindo."

"Ah, but what does it mean?"

"What happened next?"

"I was riding on the bird. I was very small, and I held a small snake in my hands—"

"The feathered snake."

"Yes. And I turned it loose, and it went and ate up all the corruption, and the bird was clean. And that's all. You've got a bubble in that syringe. The idea is to inject medicine, not air. What does the dream mean?"

"What, you think I'm a Joseph? A Daniel?"

"How about a Sam?"

"Actually, your dream is easy. Piece of cake."

"What?"

"Piece of cake. Easy as pie. That's how the cookie crumbles. Man shall not live by bread alone. All I can think of are bakery sayings. I must be hungry."

"Tell me the dream or I'll poke this needle into your eye."

"That's what I like about you Indians. Always you have torture on your mind."

She planted her foot against him and knocked him off his stool onto the packed dirt floor. A beetle skittered away. Sam held up the syringe he had been working with; it was undamaged. He got up, set it aside. "The bird," he said, "is North and South America. Like wings, flying west. Only the right wing is bigger." He sketched out a rough map with his toe on the floor.

"That's the shape, maybe," she said. "It could be."

"And the corruption—show me where it was."

With her toe, she smeared the map here, there.

"It's obvious," said Sam.

"Yes," she said. "Once you think of it as a map. The corruption is all the Europeanized land. And the only healthy places are where the Indians still live."

"Indians or half-Indians," said Sam. "All your dreams are about the same thing, Anamari. Removing the Europeans from North and South America. Let's face it. You're an Indian chauvinist. You give birth to the resurrection god of the Aztecs, and then you send it out to destroy the Europeans."

"But why do I dream this?"

"Because you hate Europeans."

"No," she said. "That isn't true."

"Sure it is."

"I don't hate *you.*"

"Because you know me. I'm not a European anymore, I'm a person. Obviously you've got to keep that from happening anymore, so you can keep your bigotry alive."

"You're making fun of me, Sam."

He shook his head. "No, I'm not. These are true dreams, Anamari. They tell you your destiny."

She giggled. "If I give birth to a feathered snake, I'll know the dream was true."

"To drive the Europeans out of America."

"No," she said. "I don't care what the dream says. I won't do that. Besides, what about the dream of the flowering weed?"

"Little weed in the garden, almost dead, and then you water it and it grows larger and larger and more beautiful—"

"And something else," she said. "At the very end of the dream, all the other flowers in the garden have changed. To be just like the flowering weed." She reached out and rested her hand on his arm. "Tell me *that* dream."

His arm became still, lifeless under her hand. "Black is beautiful," he said.

"What does *that* mean?"

"In America. The U.S., I mean. For the longest time, the blacks, the former slaves, they were ashamed to be black. The whiter you were, the more status you had—the more honor. But when they had their revolution in the sixties—"

"You don't remember the sixties, little boy."

"Heck, I barely remember the seventies. But I read books. One of the big changes, and it made a huge difference, was that slogan. Black is beautiful. The blacker the better. They said it over and over. Be proud of blackness, not ashamed of it. And in just a few years, they turned the whole status system upside down."

She nodded. "The weed came into flower."

"So. All through Latin America, Indians are very low status. If you want a Bolivian to pull a knife on you, just call him an Indian. Everybody who possibly can, pretends to be of pure Spanish blood. Pure-blooded Indians are slaughtered wherever there's the slightest excuse. Only in Mexico is it a little bit different."

"What you tell me from my dreams, Sam, this is no small job to do. I'm one middle-aged Indian woman, living in the jungle. I'm supposed to tell all the Indians of America to be proud? When they're the poorest of the poor and the lowest of the low?"

"When you give them a name, you create them. Benjamin Franklin did it, when he coined the name *American* for the people of the English colonies. They weren't New Yorkers or Virginians, they were Americans. Same thing for you. It isn't Latin Americans against Norteamericanos. It's Indians and Europeans. Somos todos indios. We're all Indians. Think that would work as a slogan?"

"Me. A revolutionary."

"Nós somos os americanos. Vai fora, Europa! America p'ra americanos! All kinds of slogans."

"I'd have to translate them into Spanish."

"Indios moram na India. Americanos moram na America. America nossa! No, better still: Nossa America! Nuestra America! It translates. Our America."

"You're a very fine slogan maker."

He shivered as she traced her finger along his shoulder and down the sensitive skin of his chest. She made a circle on his nipple and it shriveled and hardened, as if he were cold.

"Why are you silent now?" She laid her hand flat on his abdomen, just above his shorts, just below his navel. "You never tell me your own dreams," she said. "But I know what they are."

He blushed.

"See? Your skin tells me, even when your mouth says nothing. I have dreamed these dreams all my life, and they troubled me, all the time, but now you tell me what they mean, a white-skinned dream-teller, you tell me that I must go among the Indians and make them proud, make them strong, so that everyone with a drop of Indian blood will call himself an Indian, and Europeans will lie and claim native ancestors, until America is all Indian. You tell me that I will give birth to the new Quetzalcoatl, and he will unify and heal the land of its sickness. But what you never tell me is this: Who will be the father of my feathered snake?"

Abruptly he got up and walked stiffly away. To the door, keeping his back to her, so she couldn't see how alert his body was. But she knew.

"I'm fifteen," said Sam, finally.

"And I'm very old. The land is older. Twenty million years. What does it care of the quarter-century between us?"

"I should never have come to this place."

"You never had a choice," she said. "My people have always known the god of the land. Once there was a perfect balance in this place. All the people loved the land and tended it. Like the garden of Eden. And the land fed them. It gave them maize and bananas. They took only what they needed to eat, and they did not kill animals for sport or humans for hate. But then the Incas turned away from the land and worshipped gold and the bright golden sun. The Aztecs soaked the ground in the blood of their human sacrifices. The Pueblos cut down the forests of Utah and Arizona and turned them into red-rock deserts. The Iroquois tortured their enemies and filled the forests with their screams of agony. We found tobacco and coca and peyote and coffee and forgot the dreams the land gave us in our sleep. And so the land rejected us. The land called to Columbus and told him lies and seduced him and he never had a chance, did he? Never had a choice. The land brought the Europeans to punish us. Disease and slavery and warfare killed most of us, and the rest of us tried to pretend we were Europeans rather than endure any more of the punishment. The land was our jealous lover, and it hated us for a while."

"Some Catholic you are," said Sam. "I don't believe in your Indian gods."

"Say *Deus* or *Cristo* instead of *the land* and the story is the same," she said. "But now the Europeans are worse than we Indians ever were. The land is suffering from a thousand different poisons, and you threaten to kill all of life with your weapons of war. We Indians have been punished enough, and now it's our turn to have the land again. The land chose Columbus exactly five centuries ago. Now you and I dream our dreams, the way he dreamed."

"That's a good story," Sam said, still looking out the door. It sounded so close to what the old prophets in the Book of Mormon said would happen to America; close, but dangerously different. As if there were no hope for the Europeans anymore. As if their chance had already been lost, as if no repentance would be allowed. They would not be able to pass the land on to the next generation. Someone else would inherit. It made him sick at heart, to realize what the white man had lost, had thrown away, had torn up and destroyed.

"But what should I do with my story?" she asked. He could hear her coming closer, walking up behind him. He could almost feel her breath on his shoulder. "How can I fulfill it?"

By yourself. Or at least without me. "Tell it to the Indians. You can cross all these borders in a thousand different places, and you speak Portuguese and Spanish and Arawak and Carib, and you'll be able to tell your story in Quechua, too, no doubt, crossing back and forth between Brazil and Colombia and Bolivia and Peru and Venezuela, all close together here, until every Indian knows about you and calls you by the name you were given in my dream."

"Tell me my name."

"Virgem America. See? The land or god or whatever it is wants you to be a virgin."

She giggled. "Nossa senhora," she said. "Don't you see? I'm the new Virgin *Mother.* It wants me to be a *mother,* all the old legends of the Holy Mother will transfer to me; they'll call me virgin no matter what the truth is. How the priests will hate me. How they'll try to kill my son. But he will live and become Quetzalcoatl, and he will restore America to the true Americans. That is the meaning of my dreams. My dreams and yours."

"Not me," he said. "Not for any dream or any god." He turned to face her. His fist was pressed against his groin, as if to crush out all rebellion there. "My body doesn't rule me," he said. "Nobody controls me but myself."

"That's very sick," she said cheerfully. "All because you hate your father. Forget that hate, and love me instead."

His face became a mask of anguish, and then he turned and fled.

He even thought of castrating himself, that's the kind of madness that drove him through the jungle. He could hear the bulldozers carving out the airstrip, the screams of falling timbers, the calls of birds and cries of animals displaced. It was the terror of the tortured land, and it maddened him even more as he ran between thick walls of green. The rig was sucking oil like heartblood from the forest floor. The ground was wan and trembling under his feet. And when he got home he was grateful to lift his feet off the ground and lie on his mattress, clutching his pillow, panting or perhaps sobbing from the exertion of his run.

He slept, soaking his pillow in afternoon sweat, and in his sleep the voice of the land came to him like whispered lullabies. I did not choose you, said the land. I cannot speak except to those who hear me, and because it is in your nature to hear and listen, I spoke to you and led you here to save me, save me, save me. Do you know the desert they will make of me? Encased in burning dust or layers of ice, either way I'll be dead. My whole purpose is to thrust life upward out of my soils, and feel the press of living feet, and hear the songs of birds and the low music of the animals, growling, lowing, chittering, whatever voice they choose. That's what I ask of you, the dance of life, just once to make the man whose mother will teach him to be Quetzalcoatl and save me, save me, save me.

He heard that whisper and he dreamed a dream. In his dream he got up and walked back to Agualinda, not along the path, but through the deep jungle itself. A longer way, but the leaves touched his face, the spiders climbed on him, the tree lizards tangled in his hair, the monkeys dunged him and pinched him and jabbered in his ear, the snakes entwined around his feet; he waded streams and fish caressed his naked ankles, and all the way they sang to him, songs that celebrants might sing at the wedding of a king. Somehow, in the way of dreams, he lost his clothing without removing it, so that he emerged from the jungle naked, and walked through Agualinda as the sun was setting, all the Baniwas peering at him from their doorways, making clicking noises with their teeth.

He awoke in darkness. He heard his father breathing. He must have slept through the afternoon. What a dream, what a dream. He was exhausted.

He moved, thinking of getting up to use the toilet. Only then did he realize that he was not alone on the bed, and it was not his bed. She stirred and nestled against him, and he cried out in fear and anger.

It startled her awake. "What is it?" she asked.

"It was a dream," he insisted. "All a dream."

"Ah yes," she said, "it was. But last night, Sam, we dreamed the same dream." She giggled. "All night long."

In his sleep. It happened in his sleep. And it did not fade like common dreams, the memory was clear, pouring himself into her again and again, her fingers gripping him, her breath against his cheek, whispering the same thing, over and over: "Aceito, aceito-te, aceito." Not love, no, not when he came with the land controlling him, she did not love him, she merely accepted the burden he placed within her. Before tonight she had been a virgin, and so had he. Now she was even purer than before,

Virgem America, but his purity was hopelessly, irredeemably gone, wasted, poured out into this old woman who had haunted his dreams. "I hate you," he said. "What you stole from me."

He got up, looking for his clothing, ashamed that she was watching him.

"No one can blame you," she said. "The land married us, gave us to each other. There's no sin in that."

"Yeah," he said.

"One time. Now I am whole. Now I can begin."

"And now I'm finished."

"I didn't mean to rob you," she said. "I didn't know you were dreaming."

"I thought I was dreaming," he said, "but I loved the dream. I dreamed I was fornicating and it made me glad." He spoke the words with all the poison in his heart. "Where are my clothes?"

"You arrived without them," she said. "It was my first hint that you wanted me."

There was a moon outside. Not yet dawn. "I did what you wanted," he said. "Now can I go home?"

"Do what you want," she said. "I didn't plan this."

"I know. I wasn't talking to you." And when he spoke of home, he didn't mean the shack where his father would be snoring and the air would stink of beer.

"When you woke me, I was dreaming," she said.

"I don't want to hear it."

"I have him now," she said, "a boy inside me. A lovely boy. But you will never see him in all your life, I think."

"Will you tell him? Who I am?"

She giggled. "Tell Quetzalcoatl that his father is a European? A man who blushes? A man who burns in the sun? No, I won't tell him. Unless someday he becomes cruel, and wants to punish the Europeans even after they are defeated. Then I will tell him that the first European he must punish is himself. Here, write your name. On this paper write your name, and give me your fingerprint, and write the date."

"I don't know what day it is."

"October twelfth," she said.

"It's August."

"Write October twelfth," she said. "I'm in the legend business now."

"August twenty-fourth," he murmured, but he wrote the date she asked for.

"The helicopter comes this morning," she said.

"Good-bye," he said. He started for the door.

Her hands caught at him, held his arm, pulled him back. She embraced him, this time not in a dream, cool bodies together in the doorway of the house. The geis was off him now, or else he was worn out; her body had no power over his anymore.

"I did love you," she murmured. "It was not just the god that brought you."

Suddenly he felt very young, even younger than fifteen, and he broke away from her and walked quickly away through the sleeping village. He did not try to retrace his wandering route through the jungle; he stayed on the moonlit path and soon was at his father's hut. The old bastard woke up as Sam came in.

"I knew it'd happen," Father said.

Sam rummaged for underwear and pulled it on.

"There's no man born who can keep his zipper up when a woman wants it." Father laughed. A laugh of malice and triumph. "You're no better than I am, boy."

Sam walked to where his father sat on the bed and imagined hitting him across the face. Once, twice, three times.

"Go ahead, boy, hit me. It won't make you a virgin again."

"I'm not like you," Sam whispered.

"No?" asked Father. "For you it's a sacrament or something? As my daddy used to say, it don't matter who squeezes the toothpaste, boy, it all squirts out the same."

"Then your daddy must have been as dumb a jackass as mine." Sam went back to the chest they shared, began packing his clothes and books into one big suitcase. "I'm going out with the chopper today. Mom will wire me the money to come home from Manaus."

"She doesn't have to. I'll give you a check."

"I don't want your money. I just want my passport."

"It's in the top drawer." Father laughed again. "At least I always wore my clothes home."

In a few minutes Sam had finished packing. He picked up the bag, started for the door.

"Son," said Father, and because his voice was quiet, not derisive, Sam stopped and listened. "Son," he said, "once is once. It doesn't mean you're evil, it doesn't even mean you're weak. It just means you're human." He was breathing deeply. Sam hadn't heard him so emotional in a long time. "You aren't a thing like me, son," he said. "That should make you glad."

Years later Sam would think of all kinds of things he should have said. Forgiveness. Apology. Affection. Something. But he said nothing, just left and went out to the clearing and waited for the helicopter. Father didn't come to try to say good-bye. The chopper pilot came, unloaded, left the chopper to talk to some people. He must have talked to Father because when he came back he handed Sam a check. Plenty to fly home, and stay in good places during the layovers, and buy some new clothes that didn't have jungle stains on them. The check was the last thing Sam had from his father. Before he came home from that rig, the Venezuelans bought a hardy and virulent strain of syphilis on the black market, one that could be passed by casual contact, and released it in Guyana. Sam's father was one of the first million to die, so fast that he didn't even write.

Page, Arizona

The State of Deseret had only sixteen helicopters, all desperately needed for surveying, spraying, and medical emergencies. So Governor Sam Monson rarely risked them on government business. This time, though, he had no choice. He was only fifty-five, and in good shape, so maybe he could have made the climb down into Glen Canyon and back up the other side. But Carpenter wouldn't have made it, not in a wheelchair, and Carpenter had a right to be here. He had a right to see what the red-rock Navaho desert had become.

Deciduous forest, as far as the eye could see.

They stood on the bluff where the old town of Page had once been, before the dam was blown up. The Navahos hadn't tried to reforest here. It was their standard practice. They left all the old European towns unplanted, like pink scars in the green of the forest. Still, the Navahos weren't stupid. They had come to the last stronghold of European science, the University of Desert at Zarahemla, to find out how to use the heavy rainfalls to give them something better than perpetual floods and erosion. It was Carpenter who gave them the plan for these forests, just as it was Carpenter whose program had turned the old Utah deserts into the richest farmland in America. The Navahos filled their forests with bison, deer, and bears. The Mormons raised crops enough to feed five times their population. That was the European mindset, still in place: enough is never enough. Plant more, grow more, you'll need it tomorrow.

"They say he has two hundred thousand soldiers," said Carpenter's computer voice. Carpenter *could* speak, Sam had heard, but he never did. Preferred the synthesized voice. "They could all be right down there, and we'd never see them."

"They're much farther south and east. Strung out from Phoenix to Santa Fe, so they aren't too much of a burden on the Navahos."

"Do you think they'll buy supplies from us? Or send an army in to take them?"

"Neither," said Sam. "We'll give our surplus grain as a gift."

"He rules all of Latin America, and he needs *gifts* from a little remnant of the U.S. in the Rockies?"

"We'll give it as a gift, and be grateful if he takes it that way."

"How else might he take it?"

"As tribute. As taxes. As ransom. The land is his now, not ours."

"We made the desert live, Sam. That makes it ours."

"There they are."

They watched in silence as four horses walked slowly from the edge of the woods, out onto the open ground of an ancient gas station. They bore a litter between them, and were led by two—not Indians—Americans. Sam had schooled himself long ago to use the word *American* to refer only to what had once been known as Indians, and to call himself and his own people Europeans. But in his heart he had never forgiven them for stealing his identity, even though he remembered very clearly where and when that change began.

It took fifteen minutes for the horses to bring the litter to him, but Sam made no move to meet them, no sign that he was in a hurry. That was also the American way now, to take time, never to hurry, never to rush. Let the Europeans wear their watches. Americans told time by the sun and stars.

Finally the litter stopped, and the men opened the litter door and helped her out. She was smaller than before, and her face was tightly wrinkled, her hair steel-white.

She gave no sign that she knew him, though he said his name. The Americans introduced her as Nuestra Señora. Our Lady. Never speaking her most sacred name: Virgem America.

The negotiations were delicate but simple. Sam had authority to speak for Deseret, and she obviously had authority to speak for her son. The grain was refused as a gift, but accepted as taxes from a federated state. Deseret would be allowed to keep its own government, and the borders negotiated between the Navahos and the Mormons eleven years before were allowed to stand.

Sam went further. He praised Quetzalcoatl for coming to pacify the chaotic lands that had been ruined by the Europeans. He gave her maps that his scouts had prepared, showing strongholds of the prairie raiders, decommissioned nuclear missiles, and the few places where stable governments had been formed. He offered, and she accepted, a hundred experienced scouts to travel with Quetzalcoatl at Deseret's expense, and promised that when he chose the site of his North American capital, Deseret would provide architects and engineers and builders to teach his American workmen how to build the place themselves.

She was generous in return. She granted all citizens of Deseret conditional status as adopted Americans, and she promised that Quetzalcoatl's armies would stick to the roads through the northwest Texas panhandle, where the grasslands of the newest New Lands project were still so fragile that an army could destroy five years of labor just by marching through. Carpenter printed out two copies of the agreement in English and Spanish, and Sam and Virgem America signed both.

Only then, when their official work was done, did the old woman look up into Sam's eyes and smile. "Are you still a heretic, Sam?"

"No," he said. "I grew up. Are you still a virgin?"

She giggled, and even though it was an old lady's broken voice, he remembered the laughter he had heard so often in the village of Agualinda, and his heart ached for the boy he was then, and the girl she was. He remembered thinking then that forty-two was old.

"Yes, I'm still a virgin," she said. "God gave me my child. God sent me an angel, to put the child in my womb. I thought you would have heard the story by now."

"I heard it," he said.

She leaned closer to him, her voice a whisper. "Do you dream, these days?"

"Many dreams. But the only ones that come true are the ones I dream in daylight."

"Ah," she sighed. "My sleep is also silent."

She seemed distant, sad, distracted. Sam also; then, as if by conscious decision, he brightened, smiled, spoke cheerfully. "I have grandchildren now."

"And a wife you love," she said, reflecting his brightening mood. "I have grandchildren, too." Then she became wistful again. "But no husband. Just memories of an angel."

"Will I see Quetzalcoatl?"

"No," she said, very quickly. A decision she had long since made and would not reconsider. "It would not be good for you to meet face to face, or stand side by side. Quetzalcoatl also asks that in the next election, you refuse to be a candidate."

"Have I displeased him?" asked Sam.

"He asks this at my advice," she said. "It is better, now that his face will be seen in this land, that your face stay behind closed doors."

Sam nodded. "Tell me," he said. "Does he look like the angel?"

"He is as beautiful," she said. "But not as pure."

They embraced each other and wept. Only for a moment. Then her men lifted her back into her litter, and Sam returned with Carpenter to the helicopter. They never met again.

In retirement, I came to visit Sam, full of questions lingering from his meeting with Virgem America. "You knew each other," I insisted. "You had met before." He told me all this story then.

That was thirty years ago. She is dead now, he is dead, and I am old, my fingers slapping these keys with all the grace of wooden blocks. But I write this sitting in the shade of a tree on the brow of a hill, looking out across woodlands and orchards, fields and rivers and roads, where once the land was rock and grit and sagebrush. This is what America wanted, what it bent our lives to accomplish. Even if we took twisted roads and got lost or injured on the way, even if we came limping to this place, it is a good place, it is worth the journey, it is the promised, the promising land.

(1987)

CONNIE WILLIS

Schwarzschild Radius

"When a star collapses, it sort of falls in on itself." Travers curved his hand into a semicircle and then brought the fingers in, "and sometimes it reaches a kind of point of no return where the gravity pulling in on it is stronger than the nuclear and electric forces, and when it reaches that point nothing can stop it from collapsing and it becomes a black hole." He closed his hand into a fist. "And that critical diameter, that point where there's no turning back, is called the Schwarzschild radius." Travers paused, waiting for me to say something.

He had come to see me every day for a week, sitting stiffly on one of my chairs in an unaccustomed shirt and tie, and talked to me about black holes and relativity, even though I taught biology at the university before my retirement, not physics. Someone had told him I knew Schwarzschild, of course.

"The Schwarzschild radius?" I said in my quavery, old man's voice, as if I could not remember ever hearing the phrase before, and Travers looked disgusted. He wanted me to say, "The Schwarzschild radius! Ah, yes, I served with Karl Schwarzschild on the Russian front in World War I!" and tell him all about how he had formulated his theory of black holes while serving with the artillery, but I had not decided yet what to tell him. "The event horizon," I said.

"Yeah. It was named after Schwarzschild because he was the one who worked out the theory," Travers said. He reminded me of Muller with his talk of theories. He was the same age as Muller, with the same shock of stiff yellow hair and the same insatiable curiosity, and perhaps that was why I let him come every day to talk to me, though it was dangerous to let him get so close.

"I have drawn up a theory of the stars," Muller says while we warm our hands over the Primus stove so that they will get enough feeling in them to be able to hold the liquid barretter without dropping it. "They are not balls of fire, as the scientists say. They are frozen."

"How can we see them if they are frozen?" I say. Muller is insulted if I do not argue with him. The arguing is part of the theory.

"Look at the wireless!" he says, pointing to it sitting disemboweled on the table. We have the back off the wireless again, and in the barretter's glass tube is a red reflection of the stove's flame. "The light is a reflection off the ice of the star."

"A reflection of what?"

"Of the shells, of course."

I do not say that there were stars before there was this war, because Muller will not have an answer to this, and I have no desire to destroy his theory, and besides, I do not really believe there was a time when this war did not exist. The star shells have always exploded over the snow-covered craters of No Man's Land, shattering in a spray of white and red, and perhaps Muller's theory is true.

"At that point," Travers said, "at the event horizon, no more information can be transmitted out of the black hole because gravity has become so strong, and so the collapse appears frozen at the Schwarzschild radius."

"Frozen," I said, thinking of Muller.

"Yeah. As a matter of fact, the Russians call black holes 'frozen stars.' You were at the Russian front, weren't you?"

"What?"

"In World War I."

"But the star doesn't really freeze," I said. "It goes on collapsing."

"Yeah, sure," Travers said. "It keeps collapsing in on itself until even the atoms are stripped of their electrons and there's nothing left except what they call a naked singularity, but we can't see past the Schwarzschild radius, and nobody inside a black hole can tell us what it's like in there because they can't get messages out, so nobody can ever know what it's like inside a black hole."

"I know," I said, but he didn't hear me.

He leaned forward. "What was it like at the front?"

It is so cold we can only work on the wireless a few minutes at a time before our hands stiffen and grow clumsy, and we are afraid of dropping the liquid barretter. Muller holds his gloves over the Primus stove and then puts them on. I jam my hands in my ice-stiff pockets.

We are fixing the wireless set. Eisner, who had been delivering messages between the sectors, got sent up to the front when he could not fix his motorcycle. If we cannot fix the wireless we will cease to be telegraphists and become soldiers and we will be sent to the front lines.

We are already nearly there. If it were not snowing we could see the barbed wire and pitted snow of No Man's Land, and the big Russian coalboxes sometimes land in the communication trenches. A shell hit our wireless hut two weeks ago. We are ahead of our own artillery lines, and some of the shells from our guns fall on us, too, because the muzzles are worn out. But it is not the front, and we guard the liquid barretter with our lives.

"Eisner's unit was sent up on wiring fatigue last night," Muller says, "and they have not come back. I have a theory about what happened to them."

"Has the mail come?" I say, rubbing my sore eyes and then putting my cold hands immediately back in my pockets. I must get some new gloves, but the quartermaster has none to issue. I have written my mother three times to knit me a pair, but she has not sent them yet.

"I have a theory about Eisner's unit," he says doggedly. "The Russians have a magnet that has pulled them into the front."

"Magnets pull iron, not people," I say.

I have a theory about Muller's theories. Littering the communications trenches are things that the soldiers going up to the front have discarded: water bottles and haversacks and bayonets. Hans and I sometimes tried to puzzle out why they would discard such important things.

"Perhaps they were too heavy," I would say, though that did not explain the bayonets or the boots.

"Perhaps they know they are going to die," Hans would say, picking up a helmet.

I would try to cheer him up. "My gloves fell out of my pocket yesterday when I went to the quartermaster's. I never found them. They are in this trench somewhere."

"Yes," he would say, turning the helmet round and round in his hands, "perhaps as they near the front, these things simply drop away from them."

My theory is that what happens to the water bottles and helmets and bayonets is what has happened to Muller. He was a student in university before the war, but his knowledge of science and his intelligence have fallen away from him, and now we are so close to the front, all he has left are his theories. And his curiosity, which is a dangerous thing to have kept.

"Exactly. Magnets pull iron, but *they* were carrying barbed wire!" he says triumphantly, "and so they were pulled in to the magnet."

I put my hands practically into the Primus flame and rub them together, trying to get rid of the numbness. "We had better get the barretter in the wireless again or this magnet of yours will suck it in, too."

I go back to the wireless. Muller stays by the stove, thinking about his magnet. The door bangs open. It is not a real door, only an iron humpie tied to the beam that reinforces the dugout and held with a wedge, and when someone pushes against it, it flies inward, bringing the snow with it.

Snow swirls in, and light, and the sound from the front, a low rumble like a dog growling. I clutch the liquid barretter to my chest and Muller flings himself over the wireless as if it were a wounded comrade. Someone bundled in a wool coat and mittens, with a wool cap pulled over his ears, stands silhouetted against the reddish light in the doorway, blinking at us.

"Is Private Rottschieben here? I have come to see him about his eyes," he says, and I see it is Dr. Funkenheld.

"Come in and shut the door," I say, still carefully protecting the liquid barretter, but Muller has already jammed the metal back against the beam.

"Do you have news?" Muller says to the doctor, eager for new facts to spin his theories from. "Has the wiring fatigue come back? Is there going to be a bombardment tonight?"

Dr. Funkenheld takes off his mittens. "I have come to examine your eyes," he says to me. His voice frightens me. All through the war he has kept his quiet bedside voice, speaking to the wounded in the dressing station and at the stretcher bearer's posts as if they were in his surgery in Stuttgart, but now he sounds agitated and I am afraid it means a bombardment is coming and he will need me at the front.

When I went to the dressing station for medicine for my eyes, I foolishly told him I had studied medicine with Dr. Zuschauer in Jena. Now I am afraid he will ask me to assist him, which will mean going up to the front. "Do your eyes still hurt?" he says.

I hand the barretter to Muller and go over to stand by the lantern that hangs from a nail in the beam.

"I think he should be invalided home, Herr Doktor," Muller says. He knows it is impossible, of course. He was at the wireless the day the message came through that no one was to be invalided out for frostbite or "other noncontagious diseases."

"Can you find me a better light?" the doctor says to him.

Muller's curiosity is so strong that he cannot bear to leave any place where something interesting is happening. If he went up to the front I do not think he would be able to pull himself away, and now I expect him to make some excuse to stay, but I have forgotten that he is even more curious about the wiring fatigue. "I will go see what has happened to Eisner's unit," he says, and opens the door. Snow flies in, as if it had been beating against the door to get in, and the doctor and I have to push against the door to get it shut again.

"My eyes have been hurting," I say, while we are still pushing the metal into place, so that he cannot ask me to assist him. "They feel like sand has gotten into them."

"I have a patient with a disease I do not recognize," he says. I am relieved, though disease can kill us as easily as a trench mortar. Soldiers die of pneumonia and dysentery and blood poisoning every day in the dressing station, but we do not fear it the way we fear the front.

"The patient has fever, excoriated lesions, and suppurating bullae," Dr. Funkenheld says.

"Could it be boils?" I say, though of course he would recognize something so simple as boils, but he is not listening to me, and I realize that it is not a diagnosis from me that he has come for.

"The man is a scientist, a Jew named Schwarzschild, attached to the artillery," he says, and because the artillery are even farther back from the front lines than we are, I volunteer to go and look at the patient, but he does not want that either.

"I must talk to the medical headquarters in Bialystok," he says.

"Our wireless is broken," I say, because I do not want to have to tell him why it is impossible for me to send a message for him. We are allowed to send only military messages, and they must be sent in code, tapped out on the telegraph key. It would take hours to send his message, even if it were possible. I hold up the dangling wire. "At any rate, you must clear it with the commandant," but he is already writing out the name and address on a piece of paper, as if this were a telegraph office.

"You can send the message when you get the wireless fixed. I have written out the symptoms."

I put the back on the wireless. Muller comes in, kicking the door open, and snow flies everywhere, picking up Dr. Funkenheld's message and sending it circling around the dugout. I catch it before it spirals into the flame of the Primus stove.

"The wiring fatigue was pinned down all night," Muller says, setting down a hand lamp. He must have gotten it from the dressing station. "Five of them frozen to death, the other eight have frostbite. The commandant thinks there may be a bombardment tonight." He does not mention Eisner, and he does not say what has happened to the rest of the thirty men in Eisner's unit, though I know. The front has gotten them. I wait, holding the message in my stiff fingers, hoping Dr. Funkenheld will say, "I must go attend to their frostbite."

"Let me examine your eyes," the doctor says, and shows Muller how to hold the hand lamp. Both of them peer into my eyes. "I have an ointment for you to use twice daily," he says, getting a flat jar out of his bag. "It will burn a little."

"I will rub it on my hands then. It will warm them," I say, thinking of Eisner frozen at the front, still holding the roll of barbed wire, perhaps.

He pulls my bottom eyelid down and rubs the ointment on with his little finger. It does not sting, but when I have blinked it into my eye, everything has a reddish tinge. "Will you have the wireless fixed by tomorrow?" he says.

"I don't know. Perhaps."

Muller has not put down the hand lamp. I can see by its light that he has forgotten all about the wiring fatigue and the Russian magnet and is wondering what the doctor wants with the wireless.

The doctor puts on his mittens and picks up his bag. I realize too late I should have told him I would send the message in exchange for them. "I will come check your eyes tomorrow," he says and opens the door to the snow. The sound of the front is very close.

As soon as he is gone, I tell Muller about Schwarzschild and the message the doctor wants to send. He will not let me rest until I have told him, and we do not have time for his curiosity. We must fix the wireless.

"If you were on the wireless, you must have sent messages for Schwarzschild," Travers said eagerly. "Did you ever send a message to Einstein? They've got the letter Einstein sent to him after he wrote him his theory, but if Schwarzschild sent him some kind of message, too, that would be great. It would make my paper."

"You said that no message can escape a black hole?" I said. "But they could escape a collapsing star. Is that not so?"

"Okay," Travers said impatiently and made his fingers into a semicircle again. "Suppose you have a fixed observer over here." He pulled his curved hand back and held the forefinger of his other hand up to represent the fixed observer, "and you have somebody in the star. Say when the star starts to collapse, the person in it shines a light at the fixed observer. If the star hasn't reached the Schwarzschild radius, the fixed observer will be able to see the light, but it will take longer to reach him because the gravity of the black hole is pulling on the light, so it will seem as if time on the star has slowed down and the wavelengths will have been lengthened, so the light will be redder. Of course that's just a thought problem. There couldn't really be anybody in a collapsing star to send the messages."

"We sent messages," I said. "I wrote my mother asking her to knit me a pair of gloves."

There is still something wrong with the wireless. We have received only one message in two weeks. It said, "Russian opposition collapsing," and there was so much static we could not make out the rest of it. We have taken the wireless apart twice. The first time we found a loose wire but the second time we could not find anything. If Hans were here he would be able to find the trouble immediately.

"I have a theory about the wireless," Muller says. He has had ten theories in as many days: The magnet of the Russians is pulling our signals in to it; the northern lights, which have been shifting uneasily on the horizon, make a curtain the wireless signals cannot get through; the Russian opposition is not collapsing at all. They are drawing us deeper and deeper into a trap.

I say, "I am going to try again. Perhaps the trouble has cleared up," and put the headphones on so I do not have to listen to his new theory. I can hear nothing but a rumbling roar that sounds like the front.

I take out the folded piece of paper Dr. Funkenheld gave me and lay it on the wireless. He comes nearly every night to see if I have gotten an answer to his message, and I take off the headphones and let him listen to the static. I tell him that we cannot get through, but even though that is true, it is not the real reason I have not sent the message. I am afraid of the commandant finding out. I am afraid of being sent to the front.

I have compromised by writing a letter to the professor that I studied medicine with in Jena, but I have not gotten an answer from him yet, and so I must go on pretending to the doctor.

"You don't have to do that," Muller says. He sits on the wireless, swinging his leg. He picks up the paper with the symptoms on it and holds it to the flame of the Primus stove. I grab for it, but it is already burning redly. "I have sent the message for you."

"I don't believe you. Nothing has been getting out."

"Didn't you notice the northern lights did not appear last night?"

I have not noticed. The ointment the doctor gave to me makes everything look red at night, and I do not believe in Muller's theories. "Nothing is getting out now," I say, and hold the headphones out to him so he can hear the static. He listens, still swinging his leg. "You will get us both in trouble. Why did you do it?"

"I was curious about it." If we are sent up to the front, his curiosity will kill us. He will take apart a land mine to see how it works. "We cannot get in trouble for sending military messages. I said the commandant was afraid it was a poisonous gas the Russians were using." He swings his leg and grins because now I am the curious one.

"Well, did you get an answer?"

"Yes," he says maddeningly and puts the headphones on. "It is not a poisonous gas."

I shrug as if I do not care whether I get an answer or not. I put on my cap and the muffler my mother knitted for me and open the door, "I am going out to see if the mail has come. Perhaps there will be a letter there from my professor."

"Nature of disease unknown," Muller shouts against the sudden force of the snow. "Possibly impetigo or glandular disorder."

I grin back at him and say, "If there is a package from my mother I will give you half of what is in it."

"Even if it is your gloves?"

"No, not if it is my gloves," I say, and go to find the doctor.

At the dressing station they tell me he has gone to see Schwarzschild and give me directions to the artillery staff's headquarters. It is not very far, but it is snowing and my hands are already cold. I go to the quartermaster's and ask him if the mail has come in.

There is a new recruit there, trying to fix Eisner's motorcycle. He has parts spread out on the ground all around him in a circle. He points to a burlap sack and says, "That is all the mail there is. Look through it yourself."

Snow has gotten into the sack and melted. The ink on the envelopes has run, and I squint at them, trying to make out the names. My eyes begin to hurt. There is not a package from my mother or a letter from my professor, but there is a letter for Lieutenant Schwarzschild. The return address says *Doctor.* Perhaps he has written to a doctor himself.

"I am delivering a message to the artillery headquarters," I say, showing the letter to the recruit. "I will take this up, too." The recruit nods and goes on working.

It has gotten dark while I was inside, and it is snowing harder. I jam my hands in the ice-stiff pockets of my coat and start to the artillery headquarters in the rear. It is pitch-dark in the communication trenches, and the wind twists the snow and funnels it howling along them. I take off my muffler and wrap it around my hands like a girl's muff.

A band of red shifts uneasily all along the horizon, but I do not know if it is the front or Muller's northern lights, and there is no shelling to guide me. We are running out of shells, so we do not usually begin shelling until nine o'clock. The Russians start even later. Sometimes I hear machine-gun fire, but it is distorted by the wind and the snow, and I cannot tell what direction it is coming from.

The communication trench seems narrower and deeper than I remember it from when Hans and I first brought the wireless up. It takes me longer than I think it should to get to the branching that will lead north to the headquarters. The front has been contracting, the ammunition dumps and officer's billets and clearing stations moving up closer and closer behind us. The artillery headquarters has been moved up from the village to a dugout near the artillery line, not half a mile behind us. The nightly firing is starting. I hear a low rumble, like thunder.

The roar seems to be ahead of me, and I stop and look around, wondering if I can have gotten somehow turned around, though I have not left the trenches. I start again, and almost immediately I see the branching and the headquarters.

It has no door, only a blanket across the opening, and I pull my hands free of the muffler and duck through it into a tiny space like a rabbit hole, the timber balks of the earthen ceiling so low I have to stoop. Now that I am out of the roar of the snow, the sound of the front separates itself into the individual crack of a four-pounder, the whine of a star shell, and under it the almost continuous rattle of machine guns. The trenches must not be as deep here. Muller and I can hardly hear the front at all in our wireless hut.

A man is sitting at an uneven table spread with papers and books. There is a candle on the table with a red glass chimney, or perhaps it only looks that way to me. Everything in the dugout, even the man, looks faintly red. He is wearing a uniform but no coat, and gloves with the finger ends cut off, even though there is no stove here. My hands are already cold.

A trench mortar roars, and clods of frozen dirt clatter from the roof onto the table. The man brushes the dirt from the papers and looks up.

"I am looking for Dr. Funkenheld," I say.

"He is not here." He stands up and comes around the table, moving stiffly, like an old man, though he does not look older than forty. He has a moustache, and his face looks dirty in the red light.

"I have a message for him."

An eight-pounder roars, and more dirt falls on us. The man raises his arm to brush the dirt off his shoulder. The sleeve of his uniform has been slit into ribbons. All along the back of his raised hand and the side of his arm are red sores running with pus. I look back at his face. The sores in his moustache and around his nose and mouth have dried and are covered with a crust. Excoriated lesions. Suppurating bullae. The gun roars again, and dirt rains down on his raw hands.

"I have a message for him," I say, backing away from him. I reach in the pocket of my coat to show him the message, but I pull out the letter instead. "There was a letter for you, Lieutenant Schwarzschild." I hold it out to him by one corner so he will not touch me when he takes it.

He comes toward me to take the letter, the muscles in his jaw tightening, and I think in horror that the sores must be on his legs as well. "Who is it from?" he says. "Ah, Herr Professor Einstein. Good," and turns it over. He puts his fingers on the flap to open the letter, and cries out in pain. He drops the letter.

"Would you read it to me?" he says and sinks down into the chair, cradling his hand against his chest. I can see there are sores in his fingernails.

I do not have any feeling in my hands. I pick the envelope up by its corners and turn it over. The skin of his finger is still on the flap. I back away from the table. "I must find the doctor. It is an emergency."

"You would not be able to find him," he says. Blood oozes out of the tip of his finger and down over the blister in his fingernail. "He has gone up to the front."

"What?" I say, backing and backing until I run into the blanket. "I cannot understand you."

"He has gone up to the front," he says, more slowly, and this time I can puzzle out the words, but they make no sense. How can the doctor be at the front? This is the front.

He pushes the candle toward me. "I order you to read me the letter."

I do not have any feeling in my fingers. I open it from the top, tearing the letter almost in two. It is a long letter, full of equations and numbers, but the words are warped and blurred. " 'My Esteemed Colleague! I have read your paper with the greatest interest. I had not expected that one could formulate the exact solution of the problem so simply. The analytical treatment of the problem appears to me splendid. Next Thursday I will present the work with several explanatory words, to the Academy!' "

"Formulated so simply," Schwarzschild says, as if he is in pain. "That is enough. Put the letter down. I will read the rest of it."

I lay the letter on the table in front of him, and then I am running down the trench in the dark with the sound of the front all around me, roaring and shaking the ground. At the first turning, Muller grabs my arm and stops me. "What are you doing here?" I shout. "Go back! Go back!"

"Go back?" he says. "The front's that way." He points in the direction he came from. But the front is not that way. It is behind me, in the artillery headquarters. "I told you there would be a bombardment tonight. Did you see the doctor? Did you give him the message? What did he say?"

"So you actually held the letter from Einstein?" Travers said. "How exciting that must have been! Only two months after Einstein had published his theory of general relativity. And years before they realized black holes really existed. When was this exactly?" He took out a notebook and began to scribble notes. "My esteemed colleague . . . " he muttered to himself. "Formulated so simply. This is great stuff. I mean, I've been trying to find out stuff on Schwarzschild for my paper for months, but there's hardly any information on him. I guess because of the war."

"No information can get out of a black hole once the Schwarzschild radius has been passed," I said.

"Hey, that's great!" he said, scribbling. "Can I use that in my paper?"

Now I am the one who sits endlessly in front of the wireless sending out messages to the Red Cross, to my professor in Jena, to Dr. Einstein. I have frostbitten the forefinger and thumb of my right hand and have to tap out the letters with my left. But nothing is getting out, and I must get a message out. I must find someone to tell me the name of Schwarzschild's disease.

"I have a theory," Muller says. "The Jews have seized power and have signed a treaty with the Russians. We are completely cut off."

"I am going to see if the mail has come," I say, so that I do not have to listen to any more of his theories, but the doctor stops me on my way out the hut.

I tell him what the message said. "Impetigo!" the doctor shouts. "You saw him! Did that look like impetigo to you?"

I shake my head, unable to tell him what I think it looks like.

"What are his symptoms?" Muller asks, burning with curiosity. I have not told him about Schwarzschild. I am afraid that if I tell him, he will only become more curious and will insist on going up to the front to see Schwarzschild himself.

"Let me see your eyes," the doctor says in his beautiful calm voice. I wish he would ask Muller to go for a hand lamp again so that I could ask him how Schwarzschild is, but he has brought a candle with him. He holds it so close to my face that I cannot see anything but the red flame.

"Is Lieutenant Schwarzschild worse? What are his symptoms?" Muller says, leaning forward.

His symptoms are craters and shell holes, I think. I am sorry I have not told Muller, for it has only made him more curious. Until now I have told him everything, even how Hans died when the wireless hut was hit, how he laid the liquid barretter carefully down on top of the wireless before he tried to cough up what was left of his chest and catch it in his hands. But I cannot tell him this.

"What symptoms does he have?" Muller says again, his nose almost in the candle's flame, but the doctor turns from him as if he cannot hear him and blows the candle out. The doctor unwraps the dressing and looks at my fingers. They are swollen and red. Muller leans over the doctor's shoulder. "I have a theory about Lieutenant Schwarzschild's disease," he says.

"Shut up," I say. "I don't want to hear any more of your stupid theories," and do not even care about the wounded look on Muller's face or the way he goes and sits by the wireless. For now I have a theory, and it is more horrible than anything Muller could have dreamt of.

We are all of us—Muller, and the recruit who is trying to put together Eisner's motorcycle, and perhaps even the doctor with his steady bedside voice—afraid of the front. But our fear is not complete, because unspoken in it is our belief that the front is something separate from us, something we can keep away from by keeping the wireless or the motorcycle fixed, something we can survive by flattening our faces into the frozen earth, something we can escape altogether by being invalided out.

But the front is not separate. It is inside Schwarzschild, and the symptoms I have been sending out, suppurative bullae and excoriated lesions, are not what is wrong with him at all. The lesions on his skin are only the barbed wire and shell holes and connecting trenches of a front that is somewhere farther in.

The doctor puts a new dressing of crepe paper on my hand. "I have tried to invalid Schwarzschild out," the doctor says, and Muller looks at him, astounded. "The supply lines are blocked with snow."

"Schwarzschild cannot be invalided out," I say. "The front is inside him."

The doctor puts the roll of crepe paper back in his kit and closes it. "When the roads open again, I will invalid you out for frostbite. And Muller too."

Muller is so surprised he blurts, "I do not have frostbite."

But the doctor is no longer listening. "You must both escape," he says—and I am not sure he is even listening to himself—"while you can."

"I have a theory about why you have not told me what is wrong with Schwarzschild," Muller says as soon as the doctor is gone.

"I am going for the mail."

"There will not be any mail," Muller shouts after me. "The supply lines are blocked," but the mail is there, scattered among the motorcycle parts. There are only a few parts left. As soon as the roads are cleared, the recruit will be able to climb on the motorcycle and ride away.

I gather up the letters and take them over to the lantern to try to read them, but my eyes are so bad I cannot see anything but a red blur. "I am taking them back to the wireless hut," I say, and the recruit nods without looking up.

It is starting to snow. Muller meets me at the door, but I brush past him and turn the flame of the Primus stove up as high as it will go and hold the letters up behind it.

"I will read them for you," Muller says eagerly, looking through the envelopes I have discarded. "Look, here is a letter from your mother. Perhaps she has sent your gloves."

I squint at the letters one by one while he tears open my mother's letter to me. Even though I hold them so close to the flame that the paper scorches, I cannot make out the names.

" 'Dear son,' " Muller reads, 'I have not heard from you in three months. Are you hurt? Are you ill? Do you need anything?' "

The last letter is from Professor Zuschauer in Jena. I can see his name quite clearly in the corner of the envelope, though mine is blurred beyond recognition. I tear it open. There is nothing written on the red paper.

I thrust it at Muller. "Read this," I say.

"I have not finished with your mother's letter yet," Muller says, but he takes the letter and reads: " 'Dear Herr Rottschieben, I received your letter yesterday. I could hardly decipher your writing. Do you not have decent pens at the front? The disease you describe is called Neumann's disease or pemphigus—' "

I snatch the letter out of Muller's hands and run out the door. "Let me come with you!" Muller shouts.

"You must stay and watch the wireless!" I say joyously, running along the communication trench. Schwarzschild does not have the front inside him. He has pemphigus, he has Neumann's disease, and now he can be invalided home to hospital.

I go down and think I have tripped over a discarded helmet or a tin of beef, but there is a crash, and dirt and revetting fall all around me. I hear the low buzz of a daisy cutter and flatten myself into the trench, but the buzz does not become a whine. It stops, and there is another crash and the trench caves in.

I scramble out of the trench before it can suffocate me and crawl along the edge toward Schwarzschild's dugout, but the trench has caved in all along its length, and when I crawl up and over the loose dirt, I lose it in the swirling snow.

I cannot tell which way the front lies, but I know it is very close. The sound comes at me from all directions, a deafening roar in which no individual sounds can be distinguished. The snow is so thick I cannot see the burst of flame from the muzzles as the guns fire, and no part of the horizon looks redder than any other. It is all red, even the snow.

I crawl in what I think is the direction of the trench, but as soon as I do, I am in barbed wire. I stop, breathing hard, my face and hands pressed into the snow. I have come the wrong way. I am at the front. I hear a sound out of the barrage of sound, the sound of tires on the snow, and I think it is a tank, and cannot breathe at all. The sound comes closer, and in spite of myself I look up and it is the recruit who was at the quartermaster's.

He is a long way away, behind a coiled line of barbed wire, but I can see him quite clearly in spite of the snow. He has the motorcycle fixed, and as I watch, he flings his leg over it and presses his foot down. "Go!" I shout. "Get out!" The motorcycle jumps forward. "Go!"

The motorcycle comes toward me, picking up speed. It rears up, and I think it is going to jump the barbed wire, but it falls instead, the motorcycle first and then the recruit, spiraling slowly down into the iron spikes. The ground heaves, and I fall too.

I have fallen into Schwarzschild's dugout. Half of it has caved in, the timber balks sticking out at angles from the heap of dirt and snow, but the blanket is still over the door, and Schwarzschild is propped in a chair. The doctor is bending over him. Schwarzschild has his shirt off. His chest looks like Hans's did.

The front roars and more of the roof crumbles. "It's all right! It's a disease!" I shout over it. "I have brought you a letter to prove it," and hand him the letter which I have been clutching in my unfeeling hand.

The doctor grabs the letter from me. Snow whirls down through the ruined roof, but Schwarzschild does not put on his shirt. He watches uninterestedly as the doctor reads the letter.

" 'The symptoms you describe are almost certainly those of Neumann's disease, or pemphigus vulgaris. I have treated two patients with the disease, both Jews. It is a disease of the mucous membranes and is not contagious. Its cause is unknown. It always ends in death.' " Dr. Funkenheld crumples up the paper. "You came all this way in the middle of a bombardment to tell me there is no hope?" he shouts in a voice I do not even recognize, it is so unlike his steady doctor's voice. 'You should have tried to get away. You should have—" and then he is gone under a crashing of dirt and splintered timbers.

I struggle toward Schwarzschild through the maelstrom of red dust and snow. "Put your shirt on!" I shout at him. "We must get out of here!" I crawl to the door to see if we can get out through the communication trench.

Muller bursts through the blanket. He is carrying, impossibly, the wireless. The headphones trail behind him in the snow. "I came to see what had happened to you. I thought you were dead. The communication trenches are shot to pieces."

It is as I had feared. His curiosity has got the best of him, and now he is trapped, too, though he seems not to know it. He hoists the wireless onto the table without looking at it. His eyes are on Schwarzschild, who leans against the remaining wall of the dugout, his shirt in his hands.

"Your shirt!" I shout and come around to help Schwarzschild put it on over the craters and shell holes of his blasted skin. The air screams and the mouth of the dugout blows in. I grab at Schwarzschild's arm, and the skin of it comes off in my hands. He falls against the table, and the wireless goes over. I can hear the splintering tinkle of the liquid barretter breaking, and then the whole dugout is caving in and we are under the table. I cannot see anything.

"Muller!" I shout. "Where are you?"

"I'm hit," he says.

I try to find him in the darkness, but I am crushed against Schwarzschild. I cannot move. "Where are you hit?"

"In the arm," he says, and I hear him try to move it. The movement dislodges more dirt, and it falls around us, shutting out all sound of the front. I can hear the creak of wood as the table legs give way.

"Schwarzschild?" I say. He doesn't answer, but I know he is not dead. His body is as hot as the Primus stove flame. My hand is underneath his body, and I try to shift it, but I cannot. The dirt falls like snow, piling up around us. The darkness is red for a while, and then I cannot see even that.

"I have a theory," Muller says in a voice so close and so devoid of curiosity it might be mine. "It is the end of the world."

"Was that when Schwarzschild was sent home on sick leave?" Travers said.

"Or validated, or whatever you Germans call it? Well, yeah, it had to be, because he died in March. What happened to Muller?"

I had hoped he would go away as soon as I had told him what had happened to Schwarzschild, but he made no move to get up. "Muller was invalided out with a broken arm. He became a scientist."

"The way you did." He opened his notebook again. "Did you see Schwarzschild after that?"

The question makes no sense.

"After you got out? Before he died?"

It seems to take a long time for his words to get to me. The message bends and curves, shifting into the red, and I can hardly make it out. "No," I say, though that is a lie.

Travers scribbles. "I really do appreciate this, Dr. Rottschieben. I've always been curious about Schwarzschild, and now that you've told me all this stuff I'm even more interested," Travers says, or seems to say. Messages coming in are warped by the gravitational blizzard into something that no longer resembles speech. "If you'd be willing to help me, I'd like to write my thesis on him."

Go. Get out. "It was a lie," I say. "I never knew Schwarzschild. I saw him once, from a distance—your fixed observer."

Travers looks up expectantly from his notes as if he is still waiting for me to answer him.

"Schwarzschild was never even in Russia," I lie. "He spent the whole winter in hospital in Göttingen. I lied to you. It was nothing but a thought problem."

He waits, pencil ready.

"You can't stay here!" I shout. "You have to get away. There is no safe distance from which a fixed observer can watch without being drawn in, and once you are inside the Schwarzschild radius you can't get out. Don't you understand? We are still there!"

We are still there, trapped in the trenches of the Russian front, while the dying star burns itself out, spiraling down into that center where time ceases to exist, where everything ceases to exist except the naked singularity that is somehow Schwarzschild.

Muller tries to dig the wireless out with his crushed arm so he can send a message that nobody can hear—"Help us! Help us!"—and I struggle to free the hands that in spite of Schwarzschild's warmth are now so cold I cannot feel them, and in the very center Schwarzschild burns himself out, the black hole at his center imploding him cell by cell, carrying him down into darkness, and us with him.

"It is a trap!" I shout at Travers from the center, and the message struggles to escape and then falls back.

"I wonder how he figured it out?" Travers says, and now I can hear him clearly. "I mean, can you imagine trying to figure out something like the theory of black holes in the middle of a war and while you were suffering from a fatal disease? And just think, when he came up with the theory, he didn't have any idea that black holes even existed."

(1987)

EILEEN GUNN

Stable Strategies for Middle Management

Our cousin the insect has an external skeleton made of shiny brown chitin, a material that is particularly responsive to the demands of evolution. Just as bioengineering has sculpted our bodies into new forms, so evolution has shaped the early insect's chewing mouthparts into her descendants' chisels, siphons, and stilettos, and has molded from the chitin special tools—pockets to carry pollen, combs to clean her compound eyes, notches on which she can fiddle a song.

—*From the popular science program* Insect People!

I awoke this morning to discover that bioengineering had made demands upon me during the night. My tongue had turned into a stiletto, and my left hand now contained a small chitinous comb, as if for cleaning a compound eye. Since I didn't have compound eyes, I thought that perhaps this presaged some change to come.

I dragged myself out of bed, wondering how I was going to drink my coffee through a stiletto. Was I now expected to kill my breakfast, and dispense with coffee entirely? I hoped I was not evolving into a creature whose survival depended on early-morning alertness. My circadian rhythms would no doubt keep pace with any physical changes, but my unevolved soul was repulsed at the thought of my waking cheerfully at dawn, ravenous for some wriggly little creature that had arisen even earlier.

I looked down at Greg, still asleep, the edge of our red and white quilt pulled up under his chin. His mouth had changed during the night too, and seemed to contain some sort of a long probe. Were we growing apart?

I reached down with my unchanged hand and touched his hair. It was still shiny brown, soft and thick, luxurious. But along his cheek, under his beard, I could feel patches of sclerotin, as the flexible chitin in his skin was slowly hardening to an impermeable armor.

He opened his eyes, staring blearily forward without moving his head. I could see him move his mouth cautiously, examining its internal changes. He turned his head and looked up at me, rubbing his hair slightly into my hand.

"Time to get up?" he asked. I nodded. "Oh, God," he said. He said this every morning. It was like a prayer.

"I'll make coffee," I said. "Do you want some?"

He shook his head slowly. "Just a glass of apricot nectar," he said. He unrolled his long, rough tongue and looked at it, slightly cross-eyed. "This is real interesting, but it wasn't in the catalog. I'll be sipping lunch from flowers pretty soon. That ought to draw a second glance at Duke's."

"I thought account execs were expected to sip their lunches," I said.

"Not from the flower arrangements . . . " he said, still exploring the odd shape of his mouth. Then he looked up at me and reached up from under the covers. "Come here."

It had been a while, I thought, and I had to get to work. But he did smell terribly attractive. Perhaps he was developing aphrodisiac scent glands. I climbed back under the covers and stretched my body against his. We were both developing chitinous knobs and odd lumps that made this less than comfortable. "How am I supposed to kiss you with a stiletto in my mouth?" I asked.

"There are other things to do. New equipment presents new possibilities." He pushed the covers back and ran his unchanged hands down my body from shoulder to thigh. "Let me know if my tongue is too rough."

It was not.

Fuzzy-minded, I got out of bed for the second time and drifted into the kitchen.

Measuring the coffee into the grinder, I realized that I was no longer interested in drinking it, although it was diverting for a moment to spear the beans with my stiletto. What was the damn thing for, anyhow? I wasn't sure I wanted to find out.

Putting the grinder aside, I poured a can of apricot nectar into a tulip glass. Shallow glasses were going to be a problem for Greg in the future, I thought. Not to mention solid food.

My particular problem, however, if I could figure out what I was supposed to eat for breakfast, was getting to the office in time for my ten A.M. meeting. Maybe I'd just skip breakfast. I dressed quickly and dashed out the door before Greg was even out of bed.

Thirty minutes later, I was more or less awake and sitting in the small conference room with the new marketing manager, listening to him lay out his plan for the Model 2000 launch.

In signing up for his bioengineering program, Harry had chosen specialized primate adaptation, B-E Option No. 4. He had evolved into a textbook example: small and long-limbed, with forward-facing eyes for judging distances and long, grasping fingers to keep him from falling out of his tree.

He was dressed for success in a pin-striped three-piece suit that fit his simian proportions perfectly. I wondered what premium he paid for custom-made. Or did he patronize a ready-to-wear shop that catered especially to primates?

I listened as he leaped agilely from one ridiculous marketing premise to the next. Trying to borrow credibility from mathematics and engineering, he used wildly metaphoric bizspeak, "factoring in the need for pipeline throughout," "fine-tuning the media mix," without even cracking a smile.

Harry had been with the company only a few months, straight from business school. He saw himself as a much-needed infusion of talent. I didn't like him, but I envied his ability to root through his subconscious and toss out one half-formed idea after another. I know he felt it reflected badly on me that I didn't join in and spew forth a random selection of promotional suggestions.

I didn't think much of his marketing plan. The advertising section was a textbook application of theory with no practical basis. I had two options: I could force him to accept a solution that would work, or I could yes him to death, making sure everybody understood it was his idea. I knew which path I'd take.

"Yeah, we can do that for you," I told him. "No problem." We'd see which of us would survive and which was hurtling to an evolutionary dead end.

Although Harry had won his point, he continued to belabor it. My attention wandered—I'd heard it all before. His voice was the hum of an air conditioner, a familiar, easily ignored background noise. I drowsed and new emotions stirred in me, yearnings to float through moist air currents, to land on bright surfaces, to engorge myself with warm, wet food.

Adrift in insect dreams, I became sharply aware of the bare skin of Harry's arm, between his gold-plated watchband and his rolled-up sleeve, as he manipulated papers on the conference room table. He smelled greasily delicious, like a pepperoni pizza or a charcoal-broiled hamburger. I realized he probably wouldn't taste as good as he smelled, but I was hungry. My stiletto-like tongue was there for a purpose, and it wasn't to skewer cubes of tofu. I leaned over his arm and braced myself against the back of his hand, probing with my styles to find a capillary.

Harry noticed what I was doing and swatted me sharply on the side of the head. I pulled away before he could hit me again.

"We were discussing the Model 2000 launch. Or have you forgotten?" he said, rubbing his arm.

"Sorry. I skipped breakfast this morning." I was embarrassed.

"Well, get your hormones adjusted, for chrissake." He was annoyed, and I couldn't really blame him. "Let's get back to the media allocation issue, if you can keep your mind on it. I've got another meeting at eleven in Building Two."

Inappropriate feeding behavior was not unusual in the company, and corporate etiquette sometimes allowed minor lapses to pass without pursuit. Of course, I could no longer hope that he would support me on moving some money out of the direct-mail budget. . . .

During the remainder of the meeting, my glance kept drifting through the open door of the conference room, toward a large decorative plant in the hall, one of those oases of generic greenery that dot the corporate landscape. It didn't look succulent exactly—it obviously wasn't what I would have preferred to eat if I hadn't been so hungry—but I wondered if I swung both ways?

I grabbed a handful of the broad leaves as I left the room and carried them back to my office. With my tongue, I probed a vein in the thickest part of a leaf. It wasn't so bad. Tasted green. I sucked them dry and tossed the husks in the wastebasket.

I was still omnivorous, at least—female mosquitoes don't eat plants. So the process wasn't complete. . . .

I got a cup of coffee, for company, from the kitchenette and sat in my office with the door closed and wondered what was happening. The incident with Harry disturbed me. Was I turning into a mosquito? If so, what the hell kind of good was that supposed to do me? The company didn't have any use for a whining loner.

There was a knock at the door, and my boss stuck his head in. I nodded and gestured him into my office. He sat down in the visitor's chair on the other side of my desk. From the look on his face, I could tell Harry had talked to him already.

Tom Samson was an older guy, pre-bioengineering. He was well versed in stimulus-response techniques, but had somehow never made it to the top job. I liked him, but then that was what he intended. Without sacrificing authority, he had pitched his appearance, his gestures, the tone of his voice, to the warm end of the spectrum. Even though I knew what he was doing, it worked.

He looked at me with what appeared to be sympathy, but was actually a practiced sign stimulus, intended to defuse any fight-or-flight response. "Is there something bothering you, Margaret?"

"Bothering me? I'm hungry, that's all. I get short-tempered when I'm hungry."

Watch it, I thought. He hasn't referred to the incident; leave it for him to bring up. I made my mind go bland and forced myself to meet his eyes. A shifty gaze is a guilty gaze.

Tom just looked at me, biding his time, waiting for me to put myself on the spot. My coffee smelt burnt, but I stuck my tongue in it and pretended to drink. "I'm just not human until I've had my coffee in the morning." Sounded phony. Shut up, I thought.

This was the opening that Tom was waiting for. "That's what I wanted to speak to you about, Margaret." He sat there, hunched over in a relaxed way, like a mountain gorilla, unthreatened by natural enemies. "I just talked to Harry Winthrop, and he said you were trying to suck his blood during a meeting on marketing strategy." He paused for a moment to check my reaction, but the neutral expression was fixed on my face and I said nothing. His face changed to project disappointment. "You know, when we noticed you were developing three distinct body segments, we had great hopes for you. But your actions just don't reflect the social and organizational development we expected."

He paused, and it was my turn to say something in my defense. "Most insects are solitary, you know. Perhaps the company erred in hoping for a termite or an ant. I'm not responsible for that."

"Now, Margaret," he said, his voice simulating genial reprimand. "This isn't the jungle, you know. When you signed those consent forms, you agreed to let the B-E staff mold you into a more useful corporate organism. But this isn't nature, this is man reshaping nature. It doesn't follow the old rules. You can truly be anything you want to be. But you have to cooperate."

"I'm doing the best I can," I said, cooperatively. "I'm putting in eighty hours a week."

"Margaret, the quality of your work is not an issue. It's your interactions with others that you have to work on. You have to learn to work as part of the group. I just cannot permit such backbiting to continue. I'll have Arthur get you an appointment this afternoon with the B-E counselor." Arthur was his secretary. He knew everything that happened in the department and mostly kept his mouth shut.

"I'd be a social insect if I could manage it," I muttered as Tom left my office. "But I've never known what to say to people in bars."

For lunch I met Greg and our friend David Detlor at a health-food restaurant that advertises fifty different kinds of fruit nectar. We'd never eaten there before, but Greg knew he'd love the place. It was already a favorite of David's, and he still has all his teeth, so I figured it would be okay with me.

David was there when I arrived, but not Greg. David works for the company too, in a different department. He, however, has proved remarkably resistant to corporate blandishment. Not only has he never undertaken B-E, he hasn't even bought a three-piece suit. Today he was wearing chewed-up blue jeans and a flashy Hawaiian shirt, of a type that was cool about ten years ago.

"Your boss lets you dress like that?" I asked.

"We have this agreement. I don't tell her she has to give me a job, and she doesn't tell me what to wear."

David's perspective on life is very different from mine. And I don't think it's just that he's in R&D and I'm in Advertising—it's more basic than that. Where he sees the world as a bunch of really neat but optional puzzles put there for his enjoyment, I see it as . . . well, as a series of SATs.

"So what's new with you guys?" he asked, while we stood around waiting for a table.

"Greg's turning into a goddamn butterfly. He went out last week and bought a dozen Italian silk sweaters. It's not a corporate look."

"He's not a corporate *guy,* Margaret."

"Then why is he having all this B-E done if he's not even going to use it?"

"He's dressing up a little. He just wants to look nice. Like Michael Jackson, you know?"

I couldn't tell whether David was kidding me or not. Then he started telling me about his music, this barbershop quartet that he sings in. They were going to dress in black leather for the next competition and sing Shel Silverstein's "Come to Me, My Masochistic Baby."

"It'll knock them on their tails," he said gleefully. "We've already got a great arrangement."

"Do you think it will win, David?" It seemed too weird to please the judges in that sort of a show.

"Who cares?" said David. He didn't look worried.

Just then Greg showed up. He was wearing a cobalt blue silk sweater with a copper green design on it. Italian. He was also wearing a pair of dangly earrings shaped like bright blue airplanes. We were shown to a table near a display of carved vegetables.

"This is great," said David. "Everybody wants to sit near the vegetables. It's where you sit to be *seen* in this place." He nodded to Greg. "I think it's your sweater."

"It's the butterfly in my personality," said Greg. "Headwaiters never used to do stuff like this for me. I always got the table next to the espresso machine."

If Greg was going to go on about the perks that come with being a butterfly, I was going to change the subject.

"David, how come you still haven't signed up for B-E?" I asked. "The company pays half the cost, and they don't ask questions."

David screwed up his mouth, raised his hands to his face, and made small, twitching, insect gestures, as if grooming his nose and eyes. "I'm doing okay the way I am."

Greg chuckled at this, but I was serious. "You'll get ahead faster with a little adjustment. Plus you're showing a good attitude, you know, if you do it."

"I'm getting ahead faster than I want to right now—it looks like I won't be able to take the three months off that I wanted this summer."

"Three months?" I was astonished. "Aren't you afraid you won't have a job to come back to?"

"I could live with that," said David calmly, opening his menu.

The waiter took our orders. We sat for a moment in a companionable silence, the self-congratulation that follows ordering high-fiber foodstuffs. Then I told them the story of my encounter with Harry Winthrop.

"There's something wrong with me," I said. "Why suck his blood? What good is that supposed to do me?"

"Well," said David, "*you* chose this schedule of treatments. Where did you want it to go?"

"According to the catalog," I said, "the No. 2 Insect Option is supposed to make me into a successful competitor for a middle-management niche, with triggerable responses that can be useful in gaining entry to upper hierarchical levels. Unquote." Of course, that was just ad talk—I didn't really expect it to do all that. "That's what I want. I want to be in charge. I want to be the boss."

"Maybe you should go back to BioEngineering and try again," said Greg. "Sometimes the hormones don't do what you expect. Look at my tongue, for instance." He unfurled it gently and rolled it back into his mouth. "Though I'm sort of getting to like it." He sucked at his drink, making disgusting slurping sounds. He didn't need a straw.

"Don't bother with it, Margaret," said David firmly, taking a cup of rosehip tea from the waiter. "Bioengineering is a waste of time and money and millions of years of evolution. If human beings were intended to be managers, we'd have evolved pin-striped body covering."

"That's cleverly put," I said, "but it's dead wrong."

The waiter brought our lunches, and we stopped talking as he put them in front of us. It seemed like the anticipatory silence of three very hungry people, but was in fact the polite silence of three people who have been brought up not to argue in front of disinterested bystanders. As soon as he left, we resumed the discussion.

"I mean it," David said. "The dubious survival benefits of management aside, bioengineering is a waste of effort. Harry Winthrop, for instance, doesn't need B-E at all. Here he is, fresh out of business school, audibly buzzing with lust for a high-level management position. Basically he's just marking time until a presidency opens up somewhere. And what gives him the edge over you is his youth and inexperience, not some specialized primate adaptation."

"Well," I said with some asperity, "he's not constrained by a knowledge of what's failed in the past, that's for sure. But saying that doesn't solve my problem, David. Harry's signed up. I've signed up. The changes are under way and I don't have any choice."

I squeezed a huge glob of honey into my tea from a plastic bottle shaped like a teddy bear. I took a sip of the tea; it was minty and very sweet. "And now I'm turning into the wrong kind of insect. It's ruined my ability to deal with Product Marketing."

"Oh, give it a rest!" said Greg suddenly. "This is *so* boring. I don't want to hear any more about corporate hugger-mugger. Let's talk about something that's fun."

I had had enough of Greg's lepidopterate lack of concentration. "Something that's *fun*? I've invested all my time and most of my genetic material in this job. This is all the goddamn fun there is."

The honeyed tea made me feel hot. My stomach itched—I wondered if I was having an allergic reaction. I scratched, and not discreetly. My hand came out from under my shirt full of little waxy scales. What the hell was going on under there? I tasted one of the scales; it was wax all right. Worker bee changes? I couldn't help myself—I stuffed the wax into my mouth.

David was busying himself with his alfalfa sprouts, but Greg looked disgusted. "That's gross, Margaret," he said. He made a face, sticking his tongue part way out. Talk about gross. "Can't you wait until after lunch?"

I was doing what came naturally, and did not dignify his statement with a response. There was a side dish of bee pollen on the table. I took a spoonful and mixed it with the wax, chewing noisily. I'd had a rough morning, and bickering with Greg wasn't making the day more pleasant.

Besides, neither he nor David has any real respect for my position in the company. Greg doesn't take my job seriously at all. And David simply does what he wants to do, regardless of whether it makes any money, for himself or anyone else. He was giving me a back-to-nature lecture, and it was far too late for that.

This whole lunch was a waste of time. I was tired of listening to them, and felt an intense urge to get back to work. A couple of quick stings distracted them both: I had the advantage of surprise. I ate some more honey and quickly waxed them over. They were soon hibernating side by side in two large octagonal cells.

I looked around the restaurant. People were rather nervously pretending not to have noticed. I called the waiter over and handed him my credit card. He signaled to several bus boys, who brought a covered cart and took Greg and David away. "They'll eat themselves out of that by Thursday afternoon," I told him. "Store them on their sides in a warm, dry place, away from direct heat." I left a large tip.

I walked back to the office, feeling a bit ashamed of myself. A couple days of hibernation weren't going to make Greg or David more sympathetic to my problems. And they'd be real mad when they got out.

I didn't use to do things like that. I used to be more patient, didn't I? More appreciative of the diverse spectrum of human possibility. More interested in sex and television.

This job was not doing much for me as a warm, personable human being. At the very least, it was turning me into an unpleasant lunch companion. Whatever had made me think I wanted to get into management anyway?

The money, maybe.

But that wasn't all. It was the challenge, the chance to do something new, to control the total effort instead of just doing part of a project. . . .

The money too, though. There were other ways to get money. Maybe I should just kick the supports out from under the damn job and start over again.

I saw myself sauntering into Tom's office, twirling his visitor's chair around and falling into it. The words "I quit" would force their way out, almost against my will. His face would show surprise—feigned, of course. By then I'd have to go through with it. Maybe I'd put my feet up on his desk. And then—

But was it possible to just quit, to go back to being the person I used to be? No, I wouldn't be able to do it. I'd never be a management virgin again.

I walked up to the employee entrance at the rear of the building. A suction device next to the door sniffed at me, recognized my scent, and clicked the door open. Inside, a group of new employees, trainees, were clustered near the door, while a personnel officer introduced them to the lock and let it familiarize itself with their pheromones.

On the way down the hall, I passed Tom's office. The door was open. He was at his desk, bowed over some papers, and looked up as I went by.

"Ah, Margaret," he said. "Just the person I want to talk to. Come in for a minute, would you." He moved a large file folder onto the papers in front of him on his desk, and folded his hands on top of them. "So glad you were passing by." He nodded toward a large, comfortable chair. "Sit down."

"We're going to be doing a bit of restructuring in the department," he began, "and I'll need your input, so I want to fill you in now on what will be happening."

I was immediately suspicious. Whenever Tom said "I'll need your input," he meant everything was decided already.

"We'll be reorganizing the whole division, of course," he continued, drawing little boxes on a blank piece of paper. He'd mentioned this at the department meeting last week.

"Now, your group subdivides functionally into two separate areas, wouldn't you say?"

"Well—"

"Yes," he said thoughtfully, nodding his head as though in agreement. "That would be the way to do it." He added a few lines and a few more boxes. From what I could see, it meant that Harry would do all the interesting stuff and I'd sweep up afterwards.

"Looks to me as if you've cut the balls out of my area and put them over into Harry Winthrop's," I said.

"Ah, but your area is still very important, my dear. That's why I don't have you actually reporting to Harry." He gave me a smile like a lie.

He had put me in a tidy little bind. After all, he was my boss. If he was going to take most of my area away from me, as it seemed he was, there wasn't much I could do to stop him. And I would be better off if we both pretended that I hadn't experienced any loss of status. That way I kept my title and my salary.

"Oh, I see." I said. "Right."

It dawned on me that this whole thing had been decided already, and that Harry Winthrop probably knew all about it. He'd probably even wangled a raise out of it. Tom had called me in here to make it look casual, to make it look as though I had something to say about it. I'd been set up.

This made me mad. There was no question of quitting now. I'd stick around and fight. My eyes blurred, unfocused, refocused again. Compound eyes! The promise of the small comb in my hand was fulfilled! I felt a deep chemical understanding of the ecological system I was now a part of. I knew where I fit in. And I knew what I was going to do. It was inevitable now, hardwired in at the DNA level.

The strength of this conviction triggered another change in the chitin, and for the first time I could actually feel the rearrangement of my mouth and nose, a numb tickling like inhaling seltzer water. The stiletto receded and mandibles jutted forth, rather like Katharine Hepburn. Form and function achieved an orgasmic synchronicity. As my jaw pushed forward, mantis-like, it also opened, and I pounced on Tom and bit his head off.

He leaped from his desk and danced headless about the office.

I felt in complete control of myself as I watched him and continued the conversation. "About the Model 2000 launch," I said. "If we factor in the demand for pipeline throughput and adjust the media mix just a bit, I think we can present a very tasty little package to Product Marketing by the end of the week."

Tom continued to strut spasmodically, making vulgar copulative motions. Was I responsible for evoking these mantid reactions? I was unaware of a sexual component in our relationship.

I got up from the visitor's chair and sat behind his desk, thinking about what had just happened. It goes without saying that I was surprised at my own actions. I mean, irritable is one thing, but biting people's heads off is quite another. But I have to admit that my second thought was, well, this certainly is a useful strategy, and should make a considerable difference in my ability to advance myself. Hell of a lot more productive than sucking people's blood.

Maybe there was something after all to Tom's talk about having the proper attitude.

And, of course, thinking of Tom, my third reaction was regret. He really had been a likeable guy, for the most part. But what's done is done, you know, and there's no use chewing on it after the fact.

I buzzed his assistant on the intercom. "Arthur," I said, "Mr. Samson and I have come to an evolutionary parting of the ways. Please have him re-engineered. And charge it to Personnel."

Now I feel an odd itching on my forearms and thighs. Notches on which I might fiddle a song?

(1988)

MIKE RESNICK

Kirinyaga

In the beginning, Ngai lived alone atop the mountain called Kirinyaga. In the fullness of time He created three sons, who became the fathers of the Masai, the Kamba, and the Kikuyu races, and to each son He offered a spear, a bow, and a digging-stick. The Masai chose the spear, and was told to tend herds on the vast savannah. The Kamba chose the bow, and was sent to the dense forests to hunt for game. But Gikuyu, the first Kikuyu, knew that Ngai loved the earth and the seasons, and chose the digging-stick. To reward him for this Ngai not only taught him the secrets of the seed and the harvest, but gave him Kirinyaga, with its holy fig tree and rich lands.

The sons and daughters of Gikuyu remained on Kirinyaga until the white man came and took their lands away, and even when the white man had been banished they did not return, but chose to remain in the cities, wearing Western clothes and using Western machines and living Western lives. Even I, who am a *mundumugu*—a witch doctor— was born in the city. I have never seen the lion or the elephant or the rhinoceros, for all of them were extinct before my birth; nor have I seen Kirinyaga as Ngai meant it to be seen, for a bustling, overcrowded city of three million inhabitants covers its slopes, every year approaching closer and closer to Ngai's throne at the summit. Even the Kikuyu have forgotten its true name, and now know it only as Mount Kenya.

To be thrown out of Paradise, as were the Christian Adam and Eve, is a terrible fate, but to live beside a debased Paradise is infinitely worse. I think about them frequently, the descendants of Gikuyu who have forgotten their origin and their traditions and are now merely Kenyans, and I wonder why more of them did not join with us when we created the Eutopian world of Kirinyaga.

True, it is a harsh life, for Ngai never meant life to be easy; but it is also a satisfying life. We live in harmony with our environment, we offer sacrifices when Ngai's tears of compassion fall upon our fields and give sustenance to our crops, we slaughter a goat to thank him for the harvest.

Our pleasures are simple: a gourd of *pombe* to drink, the warmth of a *boma* when the sun has gone down, the wail of a newborn son or daughter, the foot-races and spear-throwing and other contests, the nightly singing and dancing.

Maintenance watches Kirinyaga discreetly, making minor orbital adjustments when necessary, assuring that our tropical climate remains constant. From time to time they have subtly suggested that we might wish to draw upon their medical expertise, or perhaps allow our children to make use of their educational facilities, but they have taken our refusal with good grace, and have never shown any desire to interfere in our affairs.

Until I strangled the baby.

It was less than an hour later that Koinnage, our paramount chief, sought me out.

"That was an unwise thing to do, Koriba," he said grimly.

"It was not a matter of choice," I replied. "You know that."

"Of course you had a choice," he responded. "You could have let the infant live." He paused, trying to control his anger and his fear. "Maintenance has never set foot on Kirinyaga before, but now they will come."

"Let them," I said with a shrug. "No law has been broken."

"We have killed a baby," he replied. "They will come, and they will revoke our charter!"

I shook my head. "No one will revoke our charter."

"Do not be too certain of that, Koriba," he warned me. "You can bury a goat alive, and they will monitor us and shake their heads and speak contemptuously among themselves about our religion. You can leave the aged and the infirm out for the hyenas to eat, and they will look upon us with disgust and call us godless heathens. But I tell you that killing a newborn infant is another matter. They will not sit idly by; they will come."

"If they do, I shall explain why I killed it," I replied calmly.

"They will not accept your answers," said Koinnage. "They will not understand."

"They will have no choice but to accept my answers," I said. "This is Kirinyaga, and they are not permitted to interfere."

"They will find a way," he said with an air of certainty. "We must apologize and tell them that it will not happen again."

"We will not apologize," I said sternly. "Nor can we promise that it will not happen again."

"Then, as paramount chief, *I* will apologize."

I stared at him for a long moment, then shrugged. "Do what you must do," I said.

Suddenly I could see the terror in his eyes.

"What will you do to me?" he asked fearfully.

"I? Nothing at all," I said. "Are you not my chief?" As he relaxed, I added: "But if I were you, I would beware of insects."

"Insects?" he repeated. "Why?"

"Because the next insect that bites you, be it spider or mosquito or fly, will surely kill you," I said. "Your blood will boil within your body, and your bones will melt. You will want to scream out your agony, yet you will be unable to utter a sound." I paused. "It is not a death I would wish on a friend," I added seriously.

"Are we not friends, Koriba?" he said, his ebony face turning an ash gray.

"I thought we were," I said. "But my friends honor our traditions. They do not apologize for them to the white man."

"I will not apologize!" he promised fervently. He spat on both his hands as a gesture of his sincerity.

I opened one of the pouches I kept around my waist and withdrew a small polished stone from the shore of our nearby river. "Wear this around your neck," I said, handing it to him, "and it shall protect you from the bites of insects."

"Thank you, Koriba!" he said with sincere gratitude, and another crisis had been averted.

We spoke about the affairs of the village for a few more minutes, and finally he left me. I sent for Wambu, the infant's mother, and led her through the ritual of purification, so that she might conceive again. I also gave her an ointment to relieve the pain in her breasts, since they were heavy with milk. Then I sat down by the fire before my *boma* and made myself available to my people, settling disputes over the ownership of chickens and goats, and supplying charms against demons, and instructing my people in the ancient ways.

By the time of the evening meal, no one had a thought for the dead baby. I ate alone in my *boma,* as befitted my status, for the *mundumugu* always lives and eats apart from his people. When I had finished I wrapped a blanket around my body to protect me from the cold and walked down the dirt path to where all the other *bomas* were clustered. The cattle and goats and chickens were penned up for the night, and my people, who had slaughtered and eaten a cow, were now singing and dancing and drinking great quantities of *pombe.* As they made way for me, I walked over to the caldron and took a drink of *pombe,* and then, at Kanjara's request, I slit open a goat and read its entrails and saw that his youngest wife would soon conceive, which was cause for more celebration. Finally the children urged me to tell them a story.

"But not a story of Earth," complained one of the taller boys. "We hear those all the time. This must be a story about Kirinyaga."

"All right," I said. "If you will all gather around, I will tell you a story of Kirinyaga." The youngsters all moved closer. "This," I said, "is the story of the Lion and the Hare." I paused until I was sure that I had everyone's attention, especially that of the adults. "A hare was chosen by his people to be sacrificed to a lion, so that the lion would not bring disaster to their village. The hare might have run away, but he knew that sooner or later the lion would catch him, so instead he sought out the lion and walked right up to him, and as the lion opened his mouth to swallow him, the hare said, 'I apologize, Great Lion.'

" 'For what?' asked the lion curiously.

" 'Because I am such a small meal,' answered the hare. 'For that reason, I brought honey for you as well.'

" 'I see no honey,' said the lion.

" 'That is why I apologized,' answered the hare. 'Another lion stole it from me. He is a ferocious creature, and says that he is not afraid of you.'

"The lion rose to his feet. 'Where is this other lion?' he roared.

"The hare pointed to a hole in the earth. 'Down there,' he said, 'but he will not give you back your honey.'

" 'We shall see about that!' growled the lion.

"He jumped into the hole, roaring furiously, and was never seen again, for the hare had chosen a very deep hole indeed. Then the hare went home to his people and told them that the lion would never bother them again."

Most of the children laughed and clapped their hands in delight, but the same young boy voiced his objection.

"That is not a story of Kirinyaga," he said scornfully. "We have no lions here."

"It *is* a story of Kirinyaga," I replied. "What is important about the story is not that it concerned a lion and a hare, but that it shows that the weaker can defeat the stronger if he uses his intelligence."

"What has that to do with Kirinyaga?" asked the boy.

"What if we pretend that the men of Maintenance, who have ships and weapons, are the lion, and the Kikuyu are the hares?" I suggested. "What shall the hares do if the lion demands a sacrifice?"

The boy suddenly grinned. "Now I understand! We shall throw the lion down a hole!"

"But we have no holes here," I pointed out.

"Then what shall we do?"

"The hare did not know that he would find the lion near a hole," I replied. "Had he found him by a deep lake, he would have said that a large fish took the honey."

"We have no deep lakes."

"But we do have intelligence," I said. "And if Maintenance ever interferes with us, we will use our intelligence to destroy the lion of Maintenance, just as the hare used his intelligence to destroy the lion of the fable."

"Let us think how to destroy Maintenance right now!" cried the boy. He picked up a stick and brandished it at an imaginary lion as if it were a spear and he a great hunter.

I shook my head. "The hare does not hunt the lion, and the Kikuyu do not make war. The hare merely protects himself, and the Kikuyu do the same."

"Why would Maintenance interfere with us?" asked another boy, pushing his way to the front of the group. "They are our friends."

"Perhaps they will not," I answered reassuringly. "But you must always remember that the Kikuyu have no true friends except themselves."

"Tell us another story, Koriba!" cried a young girl.

"I am an old man," I said. "The night has turned cold, and I must have my sleep."

"Tomorrow?" she asked. "Will you tell us another tomorrow?"

I smiled. "Ask me tomorrow, after all the fields are planted and the cattle and goats are in their enclosures and the food has been made and the fabrics have been woven."

"But girls do not herd the cattle and goats," she protested. "What if my brothers do not bring all their animals to the enclosure?"

"Then I will tell a story just to the girls," I said.

"It must be a long story," she insisted seriously, "for we work much hard than the boys."

"I will watch you in particular, little one," I replied, "and the story will be as long or as short as your work merits."

The adults all laughed and suddenly she looked very uncomfortable, but then I chuckled and hugged her and patted her head, for it was necessary that the children learned to love their *mundumugu* as well as hold him in awe, and finally she ran off to play and dance with the other girls, while I retired to my *boma.*

Once inside, I activated my computer and discovered that a message was waiting for me from Maintenance, informing me that one of their number would be visiting me the following morning. I made a very brief reply—"Article II, Paragraph 5," which is the ordinance forbidding intervention—and lay down on my sleeping blanket, letting the rhythmic chanting of the singers carry me off to sleep.

I awoke with the sun the next morning and instructed my computer to let me know when the Maintenance ship had landed. Then I inspected my cattle and my goats—I, alone of my people, planted no crops, for the Kikuyu feed their *mundumugu,* just as they tend his herds and weave his blankets and keep his *boma* clean—and stopped by Simani's *boma* to deliver a balm to fight the disease that was afflicting his joints. Then, as the sun began warming the earth, I returned to my own *boma,* skirting the pastures where the young men were tending their animals. When I arrived, I knew the ship had landed, for I found the droppings of a hyena on the ground near my hut, and that is the surest sign of a curse.

I learned what I could from the computer, then walked outside and scanned the horizon while two naked children took turns chasing a small dog and running away from it. When they began frightening my chickens, I gently sent them back to their own *boma,* and then seated myself beside my fire. At last I saw my visitor from Maintenance, coming up the path from Haven. She was obviously uncomfortable in the heat, and she slapped futilely at the flies that circled her head. Her blond hair was starting to turn grey, and I could tell by the ungainly way she negotiated the steep, rocky path that she was unused to such terrain. She almost lost her balance a number of times, and it was obvious that her proximity to so many animals frightened her, but she never slowed her pace, and within another ten minutes she stood before me.

"Good morning," she said.

"*Jambo,* Memsahib," I replied.

"You are Koriba, are you not?"

I briefly studied the face of my enemy; middle-aged and weary, it did not appear formidable. "I am Koriba," I replied.

"Good," she said. "My name is—"

"I know who you are," I said, for it is best, if conflict cannot be avoided, to take the offensive.

"You do?"

I pulled the bones out of my pouch and cast them on the dirt. "You are Barbara Eaton, born of Earth," I intoned, studying her reactions as I picked up the bones and cast them again. "You are married to Robert Eaton, and you have worked for Maintenance for nine years." A final cast of the bones. "You are forty-one years old, and you are barren."

"How did you know all that?" she asked with an expression of surprise.

"Am I not the *mundumugu?*"

She stared at me for a long minute. "You read my biography on your computer," she concluded at last.

"As long as the facts are correct, what difference does it make whether I read them from the bones or the computer?" I responded, refusing to confirm her statement. "Please sit down, Memsahib Eaton."

She lowered herself awkwardly to the ground, wrinkling her face as she raised a cloud of dust.

"It's very hot," she noted uncomfortably.

"It is very hot in Kenya," I replied.

"You could have created any climate you desired," she pointed out.

"We *did* create the climate we desired," I answered.

"Are there predators out there?" she asked, looking out over the savannah.

"A few," I replied.

"What kind?"

"Hyenas."

"Nothing larger?" she asked.

"There *is* nothing larger anymore," I said.

"I wonder why they didn't attack me?"

"Perhaps because you are an intruder," I suggested.

"Will they leave me alone on my way back to Haven?" she asked nervously, ignoring my comment.

"I will give you a charm to keep them away."

"I'd prefer an escort."

"Very well," I said.

"They're such ugly animals," she said with a shudder. "I saw them once when we were monitoring your world."

"They are very useful animals," I answered, "for they bring many omens, both good and bad."

"Really?"

I nodded. "A hyena left me an evil omen this morning."

"And?" she asked curiously.

"And here you are," I said.

She laughed. "They told me you were a sharp old man."

"They were mistaken," I replied. "I am a feeble old man who sits in front of his *boma* and watches younger men tend his cattle and goats."

"You are a feeble old man who graduated with honors from Cambridge and then acquired two postgraduate degrees from Yale," she replied.

"Who told you that?"

She smiled. "You're not the only one who reads biographies."

I shrugged. "My degrees did not help me become a better *mundumugu,*" I said. "The time was wasted."

"You keep using that world. What, exactly, *is* a *mundumugu?*"

"You would call him a witch doctor," I answered. "But in truth the *mundumugu,* while he occasionally casts spells and interprets omens, is more a repository of the collected wisdom and traditions of his race."

"It sounds like an interesting occupation," she said.

"It is not without its compensations."

"And *such* compensations!" she said with false enthusiasm as a goat bleated in the distance and a young man yelled at it in Swahili. "Imagine having the power of life and death over an entire Eutopian world!"

So now it comes, I thought. Aloud I said: "It is not a matter of exercising power, Memsahib Eaton, but of maintaining traditions."

"I rather doubt that," she said bluntly.

"Why should you doubt what I say?" I asked.

"Because if it were traditional to kill newborn infants, the Kikuyus would have died out after a single generation."

"If the slaying of the infant arouses your disapproval," I said calmly, "I am surprised Maintenance has not previously asked about our custom of leaving the old and the feeble out for the hyenas."

"We know that the elderly and the infirm have consented to your treatment of them, much as we may disapprove of it," she replied. "We also know that a newborn infant could not possibly consent to its own death." She paused, staring at me. "May I ask why this particular baby was killed?"

"That *is* why you have come here, is it not?"

"I have been sent here to evaluate the situation," she replied, brushing an insect from her cheek and shifting her position on the ground. "A newborn child was killed. We would like to know why."

I shrugged. "It was killed because it was born with a terrible *thahu* upon it."

She frowned. "A *thahu*? What is that?"

"A curse."

"Do you mean that it was deformed?" she asked.

"It was not deformed."

"Then what was this curse that you refer to?"

"It was born feet-first," I said.

"That's it?" she asked, surprised. "That's the curse?"

"Yes."

"It was murdered simply because it came out feet-first?"

"It is not murder to put a demon to death," I explained patiently. "Our tradition tells us that a child born in this manner is actually a demon."

"You are an educated man, Koriba," she said. "How can you kill a perfectly healthy infant and blame it on some primitive tradition?"

"You must never underestimate the power of tradition, Memsahib Eaton," I said. "The Kikuyu turned their backs on their traditions once; the result is a mechanized, impoverished, overcrowded country that is no longer populated by Kikuyu, or Masai, or Luo, or Wakamba, but by a new, artificial tribe known only as Kenyans. We here on Kirinyaga are true Kikuyu, and we will not make that mistake again. If the rains are late, a ram must be sacrificed. If a man's veracity is questioned, he must undergo the ordeal of the *githani* trial. If an infant is born with a *thahu* upon it, it must be put to death."

"Then you intened to continue to kill any children that are born feet-first?" she asked.

"That is correct," I responded.

A drop of sweat rolled down her face as she looked directly at me and said: "I don't know what Maintenance's reaction will be."

"According to our charter, Maintenance is not permitted to interfere with us," I reminded her.

"It's not that simple, Koriba," she said. "According to your charter, any member of your community who wishes to leave your world is allowed free passage to Haven, from which he or she can board a ship to Earth." She paused. "Was the baby you killed given such a choice?"

"I did not kill a baby, but a demon," I replied, turning my head slightly as a hot breeze stirred up the dust around us.

She waited until the breeze died down, then coughed before speaking. "You do understand that not everyone in Maintenance may share that opinion?"

"What Maintenance thinks is of no concern to us," I said.

"When innocent children are murdered, what Maintenance thinks is of supreme importance to you," she responded. "I am sure you do not want to defend your practices in the Eutopian Court."

"Are you here to evaluate the situation, as you said, or to threaten us?" I asked calmly.

"To evaluate the situation," she replied. "But there seems to be only one conclusion that I can draw from the facts that you have presented to me."

"Then you have not been listening to me," I said, briefly closing my eyes as another, stronger breeze swept past us.

"Koriba, I know that Kirinyaga was created so that you could emulate the ways of your forefathers—but surely you must see the difference between the torture of animals as a religious ritual and the murder of a human baby."

I shook my head. "They are one and the same," I replied. "We cannot change our way of life because it makes *you* uncomfortable. We did that once before, and within a mere handful of years your culture had corrupted our society. With every factory we built, with every job we created, with every bit of Western technology we accepted, with every Kikuyu who converted to Christianity, we became something we were not meant to be." I stared directly into her eyes. "I am the *mundumugu*, entrusted with preserving all that makes us Kikuyu, and I will not allow that to happen again."

"There are alternatives," she said.

"Not for the Kikuyu," I replied adamantly.

"There *are,*" she insisted, so intent upon what she had to say that she paid no attention to a black-and-gold centipede that crawled over her boot. "For example, years spent in space can cause certain physiological and hormonal changes in humans. You noted when I arrived that I am forty-one years old and childless. That is true. In fact, many of the women in Maintenance are childless. If you will turn the babies over to us, I am sure we can find families for them. This would effectively remove them from your society without the necessity of killing them. I could speak to my superiors about it; I think that there is an excellent chance that they would approve."

"That is a thoughtful and innovative suggestion, Memsahib Eaton," I said truthfully. "I am sorry that I must reject it."

"But why?" she demanded.

"Because the first time we betray our traditions this world will cease to be Kirinyaga, and will become merely another Kenya, a nation of men awkwardly pretending to be something they are not."

"I could speak to Koinnage and the other chiefs about it," she suggested meaningfully.

"They will not disobey my instructions," I replied confidently.

"You hold that much power?"

"I hold that much respect," I answered. "A chief may enforce the law, but it is the *mundumugu* who interprets it."

"Then let us consider other alternatives."

"No."

"I am trying to avoid a conflict between Maintenance and your people," she said, her voice heavy with frustration. "It seems to me that you could at least make the effort to meet me halfway."

"I do not question your motives, Memsahib Eaton," I replied, "but you are an intruder representing an organization that has no legal right to interfere with our culture. We do not impose our religion or our morality upon Maintenance, and Maintenance may not impose its religion or morality upon us."

"It's not that simple."

"It is precisely that simple," I said.

"That is your last word on the subject?" she asked.

"Yes."

She stood up. "Then I think it is time for me to leave and make my report."

I stood up as well, and a shift in the wind brought the odors of the village: the scent of bananas, the smell of a fresh caldron of *pombe,* even the pungent odor of a bull that had been slaughtered that morning.

"As you wish, Memsahib Eaton," I said. "I will arrange for your escort." I signalled to a small boy who was tending three goats and instructed him to go to the village and send back two young men.

"Thank you," she said. "I know it's an inconvenience, but I just don't feel safe with hyenas roaming loose out there."

"You are welcome," I said. "Perhaps, while we are waiting for the men who will accompany you, you would like to hear a story about the hyena."

She shuddered involuntarily. "They are such ugly beasts!" she said distastefully. "Their hind legs seem almost deformed." She shook her head. "No, I don't think I'd be interested in hearing a story about a hyena."

"You will be interested in *this* story," I told her.

She stared at me curiously, then shrugged. "All right," she said. "Go ahead."

"It is true that hyenas are deformed, ugly animals," I began, "but once, a long time ago, they were as lovely and graceful as the impala. Then one day a Kikuyu chief gave a hyena a young goat to take as a gift to Ngai, who lived atop the holy mountain Kirinyaga. The hyena took the goat between his powerful jaws and headed toward the distant mountain—but on the way he passed a settlement filled with Europeans and Arabs. It abounded in guns and machines and other wonders he had never seen before, and he stopped to look, fascinated. Finally an Arab noticed him staring intently and asked if he, too, would like to become a civilized man—and as he opened his mouth to say that he would, the goat fell to the ground and ran away. As the goat raced out of sight, the Arab laughed and explained that he was only joking, that of course no hyena could become a man." I paused for a moment, and then continued. "So the hyena proceeded to Kirinyaga, and when he reached the summit, Ngai asked him what had become of the goat. When the hyena told him, Ngai hurled him off the mountaintop for having the audacity to believe he could become a man. He did not die from the fall, but his rear legs were crippled, and Ngai declared that from that day forward, all hyenas would appear thus—and to remind them of the foolishness of trying to become something that they were not, He also gave them a fool's laugh." I paused again, and stared at her. "Memsahib Eaton, you do not hear the Kikuyu laugh like fools, and I will not let them become crippled like the hyena. Do you understand what I am saying?"

She considered my statement for a moment, then looked into my eyes. "I think we understand each other perfectly, Koriba," she said.

The two young men I had sent for arrived just then, and I instructed them to accompany her to Haven. A moment later they set off across the dry savannah, and I returned to my duties.

I began by walking through the fields, blessing the scarecrows. Since a number of the smaller children followed me, I rested beneath the trees more often than was necessary, and always, whenever we paused, they begged me to tell them more stories. I told them the tale of the Elephant and the Buffalo, and how the Masai *elmoran* cut the rainbow with his spear so that it never again came to rest upon the earth, and why the nine Kikuyu tribes are named after Gikuyu's nine daughters, and when the sun became too hot I led them back to the village.

Then, in the afternoon, I gathered the older boys about me and explained once more how they must paint their faces and bodies for their forthcoming circumcision ceremony. Ndemi, the boy who had insisted upon a story about Kirinyaga the night before, sought me out privately to complain that he had been unable to slay a small gazelle with his spear, and asked for a charm to make its flight more accurate. I explained to him that there would come a day when he faced a buffalo or a hyena with no charm, and that he must practice more before he came to me again. He was one to watch, this little Ndemi, for he was impetuous and totally without fear; in the old days, he would have made a great warrior, but on Kirinyaga we had no warriors. If we remained fruitful and fecund, however, we would someday need more chiefs and even another *mundumugu,* and I made up my mind to observe him closely.

In the evening, after I ate my solitary meal, I returned to the village, for Njogu, one of our young men, was to marry Kamiri, a girl from the next village. The bride-price had been decided upon, and the two families were waiting for me to preside at the ceremony.

Njogu, his faced streaked with paint, wore an ostrich-feather headdress, and looked very uneasy as he and his betrothed stood before me. I slit the throat of a fat ram that Kamiri's father had brought for the occasion, and then I turned to Njogu.

"What have you to say?" I asked.

He took a step forward. "I want Kamiri to come and till the fields of my *shamba,*" he said, his voice cracking with nervousness as he spoke the prescribed words, "for I am a man, and I need a woman to tend to my *shamba* and dig deep around the roots of my plantings, that they may grow well and bring prosperity to my house."

He spit on both his hands to show his sincerity, and then, exhaling deeply with relief, he stepped back.

I turned to Kamiri.

"Do you consent to till the *shamba* of Njogu, son of Muchiri?" I asked her.

"Yes," she said softly, bowing her head. "I consent."

I held out my right hand, and the bride's mother placed a gourd of *pombe* in it.

"If this man does not please you," I said to Kamiri, "I will spill the *pombe* upon the ground."

"Do not spill it," she replied.

"Then drink," I said, handing the gourd to her.

She lifted it to her lips and took a swallow, then handed it to Njogu, who did the same.

When the gourd was empty, the parents of Njogu and Kamiri stuffed it with grass, signifying the friendship between the two clans.

Then a cheer rose from the onlookers, the ram was carried off to be roasted, more *pombe* appeared as if by magic, and while the groom took the bride off to his *boma,* the remainder of the people celebrated far into the night. They stopped only when the bleating of the goats told them that some hyenas were nearby, and then the women and children went off to their *bomas* while the men took their spears and went into the fields to frighten the hyenas away.

Koinnage came up to me as I was about to leave.

"Did you speak to the woman from Maintenance?" he asked.

"I did," I replied.

"What did she say?"

"She said that they do not approve of killing babies who are born feet-first."

"And what did *you* say?" he asked nervously.

"I told her that we did not need the approval of Maintenance to practice our religion," I replied.

"Will Maintenance listen?"

"They have no choice," I said. "And *we* have no choice, either," I added. "Let them dictate one thing that we must or must not do, and soon they will dictate all things. Give them their way, and Njogu and Kamiri would have recited wedding vows from the Bible or the Koran. It happened to us in Kenya; we cannot permit it to happen on Kirinyaga."

"But they will not punish us?" he persisted.

"They will not punish us," I replied.

Satisfied, he walked off to his *boma* while I took the narrow, winding path to my own. I stopped by the enclosure where my animals were kept and saw that there were two new goats there, gifts from the bride's and groom's families in gratitude for my services. A few minutes later I was asleep within the walls of my own *boma.*

The computer woke me a few minutes before sunrise. I stood up, splashed my face with water from the gourd I keep by my sleeping blanket, and walked over to the terminal.

There was a message for me from Barbara Eaton, brief and to the point:

> It is the preliminary finding of Maintenance that infanticide, for any reason, is a direct violation of Kirinyaga's charter. No action will be taken for past offenses.
>
> We are also evaluating your practice of euthanasia, and may require further testimony from you at some point in the future.
>
> Barbara Eaton

A runner from Koinnage arrived a moment later, asking me to attend a meeting of the Council of Elders, and I knew that he had received the same message.

I wrapped my blanket around my shoulders and began walking to Koinnage's *shamba,* which consisted of his *boma,* as well as those of his three sons and their wives. When I arrived I found not only the local elders waiting for me, but also two chiefs from neighboring villages.

"Did you receive the message from Maintenance?" demanded Koinnage, as I seated myself opposite him.

"I did."

"I warned you that this would happen!" he said. "What will we do now?"

"We will do what we have always done," I answered calmly.

"We cannot," said one of the neighboring chiefs. "They have forbidden it."

"They have no right to forbid it," I replied.

"There is a woman in my village whose time is near," continued the chief, "and all of the signs and omens point to the birth of twins. We have been taught that the firstborn must be killed, for one mother cannot produce two souls—but now Maintenance has forbidden it. What are we to do?"

"We must kill the firstborn," I said, "for it will be a demon."

"And then Maintenance will make us leave Kirinyaga!" said Koinnage bitterly.

"Perhaps we could let the child live," said the chief. "That might satisfy them, and then they might leave us alone."

I shook my head. "They will not leave you alone. Already they speak about the way we leave the old and the feeble out for the hyenas, as if this were some enormous sin against their God. If you give in on the one, the day will come when you must give in on the other."

"Would that be so terrible?" persisted the chief. "They have medicines that we do not possess; perhaps they could make the old young again."

"You do not understand," I said, rising to my feet. "Our society is not a collection of separate people and customs and traditions. No, it is a complex system, with all the pieces as dependent upon each other as the animals and vegetation of the savannah. If you burn the grass, you will not only kill the impala who feeds upon it, but the predator who feeds upon the impala, and the ticks and flies who live upon the predator, and the vultures and maribou storks who feed upon his remains when he dies. You cannot destroy the part without destroying the whole."

I paused to let them consider what I had said, and then continued speaking: "Kirinyaga is like the savannah. If we do not leave the old and the feeble out for the hyenas, the hyenas will starve. If the hyenas starve, the grass eaters will become so numerous that there is no land left for our cattle and goats to graze. If the old and the feeble do not die when Ngai decrees it, then soon we will not have enough food to go around."

I picked up a stick and balanced it precariously on my forefinger.

"This stick," I said, "is the Kikuyu people, and my finger is Kirinyaga. They are in perfect balance." I stared at the neighboring chief. "But what will happen if I alter the balance, and put my finger *here*?" I asked, gesturing to the end of the stick.

"The stick will fall to the ground."

"And here?" I asked, pointing to a stop an inch away from the center.

"It will fall."

"Thus is it with us," I explained. "Whether we yield on one point or all points, the result will be the same: the Kikuyu will fall as surely as the stick will fall. Have we learned nothing from our past? We *must* adhere to our traditions; they are all that we have!"

"But Maintenance will not allow us to do so!" protested Koinnage.

"They are not warriors, but civilized men," I said, allowing a touch of contempt to creep into my voice. "Their chiefs and their *mundumugus* will not send them to Kirinyaga with guns and spears. They will issue warnings and findings and declarations, and finally, when that fails, they will go to the Eutopian Court and plead their case, and the trial will be postponed many times and reheard many more times." I could see them finally relaxing, and I smiled confidently at them. "Each of you will have died from the burden of your years before Maintenance does anything other than talk. I am your *mundumugu;* I have lived among civilized men, and I tell you that this is the truth."

The neighboring chief stood up and faced me. "I will send for you when the twins are born," he pledged.

"I will come," I promised him.

We spoke further, and then the meeting ended and the old men began wandering off to their *bomas,* while I looked to the future, which I could see more clearly than Koinnage or the elders.

I walked through the village until I found the bold young Ndemi, brandishing his spear and hurling it at a buffalo he had constructed out of dried grasses.

"*Jambo,* Koriba!" he greeted me.

"*Jambo,* my brave young warrior," I replied.

"I have been practicing, as you ordered."

"I thought you wanted to hunt the gazelle," I noted.

"Gazelles are for children," he answered. "I will slay *mbogo,* the buffalo."

"*Mbogo* may feel differently about it," I said.

"So much the better," he said confidently. "I have no wish to kill an animal as it runs away from me."

"And when will you go out to slay the fierce *mbogo*?"

He shrugged. "When I am more accurate." He smiled up at me. "Perhaps tomorrow."

I stared at him thoughtfully for a moment, and then spoke: "Tomorrow is a long time away. We have business tonight."

"What business?" he asked.

"You must find ten friends, none of them yet of circumcision age, and tell them to come to the pond within the forest to the south. They must come after the sun has set, and you must tell them that Koriba the *mundumugu* commands that they tell no one, not even their parents, that they are coming." I paused. "Do you understand, Ndemi?"

"I understand."

"Then go," I said. "Bring my message to them."

He retrieved his spear from the straw buffalo and set off at a trot, young and tall and strong and fearless.

You are the future, I thought, as I watched him run toward the village. *Not Koinnage, not myself, not even the young bridegroom Njogu, for their time will have come and gone before the battle is joined. It is you, Ndemi, upon whom Kirinyaga must depend if it is to survive.*

Once before the Kikuyu have had to fight for their freedom. Under the leadership of Jomo Kenyatta, whose name has been forgotten by most of your parents, we took the terrible oath of Mau Mau, and we maimed and we killed and we committed such atrocities that finally we achieved Uhuru, for against such butchery civilized men have no defense but to depart.

And tonight, young Ndemi, while your parents are asleep, you and your companions will meet me deep in the woods, and you in your turn and they in theirs will learn one last tradition of the Kikuyu, for I will invoke not only the strength of Ngai but also the indomitable spirit of Jomo Kenyatta. I will administer a hideous oath and force you to do unspeakable things to prove your fealty, and I will teach each of you, in turn, how to administer the oath to those who come after you.

There is a season for all things: for birth, for growth, for death. There is unquestionably a season for Utopia, but it will have to wait.

For the season of Uhuru is upon us.

(1988)

MICHAEL SWANWICK

A Midwinter's Tale

Maybe I shouldn't tell you about that childhood Christmas Eve in the Stone House, so long ago. My memory is no longer reliable, not since I contracted the brain fever. Soon I'll be strong enough to be reposted offplanet, to some obscure star light-years beyond that plangent moon rising over your father's barn, but how much has been burned from my mind! Perhaps none of this actually happened.

Sit on my lap and I'll tell you all. Well then, my knee. No woman was ever ruined by a knee. You laugh, but it's true. Would that it were so easy!

The hell of war as it's now practiced is that its purpose is not so much to gain territory as to deplete the enemy, and thus it's always better to maim than to kill. A corpse can be bagged, burned, and forgotten, but the wounded need special care. Regrowth tanks, false skin, medical personnel, a long convalescent stay on your parents' farm. That's why they will vary their weapons, hit you with obsolete stone axes or toxins or radiation, to force your Command to stock the proper prophylaxes, specialized medicines, obscure skills. Mustard gas is excellent for that purpose, and so was the brain fever.

All those months I lay in the hospital, awash in pain, sometimes hallucinating. Dreaming of ice. When I awoke, weak and not really believing I was alive, parts of my life were gone, randomly burned from my memory. I recall standing at the very top of the iron bridge over the Izveltaya, laughing and throwing my books one by one into the river, while my best friend Fennwolf tried to coax me down. "I'll join the militia! I'll be a soldier!" I shouted hysterically. And so I did. I remember that clearly, but just what led up to that preposterous instant is utterly beyond me. Nor can I remember the name of my second-eldest sister, though her face is as plain to me as yours is now. There are odd holes in my memory.

That Christmas Eve is an island of stability in my seachanging memories, as solid in my mind as the Stone House itself, that neolithic cavern in which we led such basic lives that I was never quite sure in which era of history we dwelt. Sometimes the men came in from the hunt, a larl or two pacing ahead content and sleepy-eyed, to lean bloody spears against the walls, and it might be that we lived on Old Earth itself then. Other times, as when they brought in projectors to fill the common room with colored lights, scintillae nesting in the branches of the season's tree, and cool, harmless flames dancing atop the presents, we seemed to belong to a much later age, in some mythologized province of the future.

The house was abustle, the five families all together for this one time of the year, and outlying kin and even a few strangers staying over, so that we had to put bedding in places normally kept closed during the winter, moving furniture into attic lumber rooms, and even at that there were cots and thick bolsters set up in the blind ends of hallways. The women scurried through the passages, scattering uncles here and there, now settling one in an armchair and plumping him up like a cushion, now draping one over a table, cocking up a mustachio for effect. A pleasant time.

Coming back from a visit to the kitchens, where a huge woman I did not know, with flour powdering her big-freckled arms up to the elbows, had shooed me away, I surprised Suki and Georg kissing in the nook behind the great hearth. They had their arms about each other, and I stood watching them. Suki was smiling, cheeks red and round. She brushed her hair back with one hand so Georg could nuzzle her ear, turning slightly as she did so, and saw me. She gasped and they broke apart, flushed and startled.

Suki gave me a cookie, dark with molasses and a single stingy crystallized raisin on top, while Georg sulked. Then she pushed me away, and I heard her laugh as she took Georg's hand to lead him to some darker forest recess of the house.

Father came in, boots all muddy, to sling a brace of game birds down on the hunt cabinet. He set his unstrung bow and quiver of arrows on their pegs, then hooked an elbow atop the cabinet to accept admiration and a hot drink from Mother. The larl padded by, quiet and heavy and content. I followed it around a corner, ancient ambitions of riding the beast rising up within. I could see myself, triumphant before my cousins, high atop the black carnivore. "Flip!" my father called sternly. "Leave Samson alone! He is a bold and noble creature, and I will not have you pestering him."

He had eyes in the back of his head, had my father.

Before I could grow angry, my cousins hurried by, on their way to hoist the straw men into the trees out front, and swept me up along with them. Uncle Chittagong, who looked like a lizard and had to stay in a glass tank for reasons of health, winked at me as I skirled past. From the corner of my eye I saw my second-eldest sister beside him, limned in blue fire.

Forgive me. So little of my childhood remains; vast stretches were lost in the blue icefields I wandered in my illness. My past is like a sunken continent with only mountaintops remaining unsubmerged, a scattered archipelago of events from which to guess the shape of what was lost. Those remaining fragments I treasure all the more, and must pass my hands over them periodically to reassure myself that something remains.

So where was I? Ah, yes: I was in the north bell tower, my hidey-place in those days, huddled behind Old Blind Pew, the bass of our triad of bells, crying because I had been deemed too young to light one of the yule torches. "Hallo!" cried a voice, and then, "Out here, stupid!" I ran to the window, tears forgotten in my astonishment at the sight of my brother Karl silhouetted against the yellowing sky, arms out, treading the roof gables like a tightrope walker.

"You're going to get in trouble for that!" I cried.

"Not if you don't tell!" Knowing full well how I worshiped him. "Come on down! I've emptied out one of the upper kitchen cupboards. We can crawl in from the pantry. There's a space under the door—we'll see everything!"

Karl turned and his legs tangled under him. He fell. Feetfirst, he slid down the roof.

I screamed. Karl caught the guttering and swung himself into an open window underneath. His sharp face rematerialized in the gloom, grinning. "Race you to the jade ibis!"

He disappeared, and then I was spinning wildly down the spiral stairs, mad to reach the goal first.

It was not my fault we were caught, for I would never have giggled if Karl hadn't been tickling me to see just how long I could keep silent. I was frightened, but not Karl. He threw his head back and laughed until he cried, even as he was being hauled off by three very angry grandmothers, pleased more by his own roguery than by anything he might have seen.

I myself was led away by an indulgent Katrina, who graphically described the caning I was to receive and then contrived to lose me in the crush of bodies in the common room. I hid behind the goat tapestry until I got bored—not long!—and then Chubkin, Kosmonaut, and Pew rang, and the room emptied.

I tagged along, ignored, among the moving legs, like a marsh bird scuttling through waving grasses. Voices clangoring in the east stairway, we climbed to the highest balcony, to watch the solstice dance. I hooked hands over the crumbling balustrade and pulled myself up on tiptoe so I could look down on the procession as it left the house. For a long time nothing happened, and I remember being annoyed at how casually the adults were taking all this, standing about with drinks, not one in ten glancing away from themselves. Pheidre and Valerian (the younger children had been put to bed, complaining, an hour ago) began a game of tag, running through the adults, until they were chastened and ordered with angry shakes of their arms to be still.

Then the door below opened. The women who were witches walked solemnly out, clad in hooded terrycloth robes as if they'd just stepped from the bath. But they were so silent I was struck with fear. It seemed as if something cold had reached into the pink giggling women I had seen preparing themselves in the kitchen and taken away some warmth or laughter from them. "Katrina!" I cried in panic, and she lifted a moon-cold face toward me. Several of the men exploded in laughter, white steam puffing from bearded mouths, and one rubbed his knuckles in my hair. My second-eldest sister drew me away from the balustrade and hissed at me that I was not to cry out to the witches, that this was important, that when I was older I would understand, and in the meantime if I did not behave myself I would be beaten. To soften her words, she offered me a sugar crystal, but I turned away stern and unappeased.

Single-file the women walked out on the rocks to the east of the house, where all was barren slate swept free of snow by the wind from the sea, and at a great distance—you could not make out their faces—doffed their robes. For a moment they stood motionless in a circle, looking at one another. Then they began the dance, each wearing nothing but a red ribbon tied about one upper thigh, the long end blowing free in the breeze.

As they danced their circular dance, the families watched, largely in silence. Sometimes there was a muffled burst of laughter as one of the younger men muttered a racy comment, but mostly they watched with great respect, even a kind of fear. The gusty sky was dark, and flocked with small clouds like purple-headed rams. It was chilly on the roof, and I could not imagine how the women withstood it. They danced faster and faster, and the families grew quieter, packing the edges more tightly, until I was forced away from the railing. Cold and bored, I went downstairs, nobody turning to watch me leave, back to the main room, where a fire still smoldered in the hearth.

The room was stuffy when I'd left, and cooler now. I lay down on my stomach before the fireplace. The flagstones smelled of ashes and were gritty to the touch, staining my fingertips as I trailed them in idle little circles. The stones were cold at the edges, slowly growing warmer, and then suddenly too hot and I had to snatch my hand away. The back of the fireplace was black with soot, and I watched the fire-worms crawl over the stone heart-and-hands carved there, as the carbon caught fire and burned out. The log was all embers and would burn for hours.

Something coughed.

I turned and saw something moving in the shadows, an animal. The larl was blacker than black, a hole in the darkness, and my eyes swam to look at him. Slowly, lazily, he strode out onto the stones, stretched his back, yawned a tongue-curling yawn, and then stared at me with those great green eyes.

He spoke.

I was astonished, of course, but not in the way my father would have been. So much is inexplicable to a child! "Merry Christmas, Flip," the creature said, in a quiet, breathy voice. I could not describe its accent; I have heard nothing quite like it before or since. There was a vast alien amusement in his glance.

"And to you," I said politely.

The larl sat down, curling his body heavily about me. If I had wanted to run, I could not have gotten past him, though that thought did not occur to me then. "There is an ancient legend, Flip, I wonder if you have heard of it, that on Christmas Eve the beasts can speak in human tongue. Have your elders told you that?"

I shook my head.

"They are neglecting you." Such strange humor dwelt in that voice. "There is truth to some of those old legends, if only you knew how to get at it. Though perhaps not all. Some are just stories. Perhaps this is not happening now; perhaps I am not speaking to you at all?"

I shook my head. I did not understand. I said so.

"That is the difference between your kind and mine. My kind understands everything about yours, and yours knows next to nothing about mine. I would like to tell you a story, little one. Would you like that?"

"Yes," I said, for I was young and I liked stories very much.

He began:

When the great ships landed—

Oh, God. When—no, no, no, wait. Excuse me. I'm shaken. I just this instant had a vision. It seemed to me that it was night and I was standing at the gates of a cemetery. And suddenly the air was full of light, planes and cones of light that burst from the ground and nested twittering in the trees. Fracturing the sky. I wanted to dance for joy. But the ground crumbled underfoot and when I looked down the shadow of the gates touched my toes, a cold rectangle of profoundest black, deep as all eternity, and I was dizzy and about to fall and I, and I . . .

Enough! I have had this vision before, many times. It must have been something that impressed me strongly in my youth, the moist smell of newly opened earth, the chalky whitewash on the picket fence. It must be. I do not believe in hobgoblins, ghosts, or premonitions. No, it does not bear thinking about. Foolishness! Let me get on with my story.

—When the great ships landed, I was feasting on my grandfather's brains. All his descendants gathered respectfully about him, and I, as youngest, had first bite. His wisdom flowed through me, and the wisdom of his ancestors and the intimate knowledge of those animals he had eaten for food, and the spirit of valiant enemies who had been killed and then honored by being eaten, even as if they were family. I don't suppose you understand this, little one.

I shook my head.

People never die, you see. Only humans die. Sometimes a minor part of a Person is lost, the doings of a few decades, but the bulk of his life is preserved, if not in this body, then in another. Or sometimes a Person will dishonor himself, and his descendants will refuse to eat him. This is a great shame, and the Person will go off to die somewhere alone.

The ships descended bright as newborn suns. The People had never seen such a thing. We watched in inarticulate wonder, for we had no language then. You have seen the pictures, the baroque swirls of colored metal, the proud humans stepping down onto the land. But I was there, and I can tell you, your people were ill. They stumbled down the gangplanks with the stench of radiation sickness about them. We could have destroyed them all then and there.

Your people built a village at Landfall and planted crops over the bodies of their dead. We left them alone. They did not look like good game. They were too strange and too slow, and we had not yet come to savor your smell. So we went away, in baffled ignorance.

That was in early spring.

Half the survivors were dead by midwinter, some of disease but most because they did not have enough food. It was of no concern to us. But then the woman in the wilderness came to change our universe forever.

When you're older you'll be taught the woman's tale, and what desperation drove her into the wilderness. It's part of your history. But to myself, out in the mountains and winter-lean, the sight of her striding through the snows in her furs was like a vision of winter's queen herself. A gift of meat for the hungering season, life's blood for the solstice.

I first saw the woman while I was eating her mate. He had emerged from his cabin that evening as he did every sunset, gun in hand, without looking up. I had observed him over the course of five days, and his behavior never varied. On that sixth nightfall I was crouched on his roof when he came out. I let him go a few steps from the door, then leapt. I felt his neck break on impact, tore open his throat to be sure, and ripped through his parka to taste his innards. There was no sport in it, but in winter we will take game whose brains we would never eat.

My mouth was full and my muzzle pleasantly, warmly moist with blood when the woman appeared. I looked up, and she was topping the rise, riding one of your incomprehensible machines, what I know now to be a snowstrider. The setting sun broke through the clouds behind her, and for an instant she was embedded in glory. Her shadow stretched narrow before her and touched me, a bridge of darkness between us. We looked in one another's eyes . . .

Magda topped the rise with a kind of grim, joyless satisfaction. I am now a hunter's woman, she thought to herself. We will always be welcome at Landfall for the meat we bring, but they will never speak civilly to me again. Good. I would choke on their sweet talk anyway. The baby stirred, and without looking down she stroked him through the furs, murmuring, "Just a little longer, my brave little boo, and we'll be at our new home. Will you like that, eh?"

The sun broke through the clouds to her back, making the snow a red dazzle. Then her eyes adjusted, and she saw the black shape crouched over her lover's body. A very great distance away, her hands throttled down the snowstrider and brought it to a halt. The shallow bowl of land before her was barren, the snow about the corpse black with blood. A last curl of smoke lazily separated from the hut's chimney. The brute lifted its bloody muzzle and looked at her.

Time froze and knotted in black agony.

The larl screamed. It ran straight at her, faster than thought. Clumsily, hampered by the infant strapped to her stomach, Magda clawed the rifle from its boot behind the saddle. She shucked her mittens, fitted hands to metal that stung like hornets, flicked off the safety, and brought the stock to her shoulder. The larl was halfway to her. She aimed and fired.

The larl went down. One shoulder shattered, slamming it to the side. It tumbled and rolled in the snow. "You sonofabitch!" Magda cried in triumph. But almost immediately the beast struggled to its feet, turned and fled.

The baby began to cry, outraged by the rifle's roar. Magda powered up the engine. "Hush, small warrior." A kind of madness filled her, a blind anesthetizing rage. "This won't take long." She flung her machine downhill, after the larl.

Even wounded, the creature was fast. She could barely keep up. As it entered the spare stand of trees to the far end of the meadow, Magda paused to fire again, burning a bullet by its head. The larl leaped away.

From then on it varied its flight with sudden changes of direction and unexpected jogs to the side. It was a fast learner. But it could not escape Magda. She had always been a hothead, and now her blood was up. She was not about to return to her lover's gutted body with his killer still alive.

The sun set, and in the darkening light she lost sight of the larl. But she was able to follow its trail by two-shadowed moonlight, the deep, purple footprints, the darker spatter of blood it left, drop by drop, in the snow.

It was the solstice, and the moons were full—a holy time. I felt it even as I fled the woman through the wilderness. The moons were bright on the snow. I felt the dread of being hunted descend on me, and in my inarticulate way I felt blessed.

But I also felt a great fear for my kind. We had dismissed the humans as incomprehensible, not very interesting creatures, slow-moving, bad-smelling, and dull-witted. Now, pursued by this madwoman on her fast machine, brandishing a weapon that killed from afar, I felt all natural order betrayed. She was a goddess of the hunt, and I was her prey.

The People had to be told.

I gained distance from her, but I knew the woman would catch up. She was a hunter, and a hunter never abandons wounded prey. One way or another, she would have me.

In the winter, all who are injured or too old must offer themselves to the community. The sacrifice rock was not far, by a hill riddled from time beyond memory with our burrows. My knowledge must be shared: the humans were dangerous. They would make good prey.

I reached my goal when the moons were highest. The flat rock was bare of snow when I ran limping in. Awakened by the scent of my blood, several People emerged from their dens. I laid myself down on the sacrifice rock. A grandmother of the People came forward, licked my wound, tasting, considering. Then she nudged me away with her forehead. The wound would heal, she thought, and winter was young; my flesh was not yet needed.

But I stayed. Again she nudged me away. I refused to go. She whined in puzzlement. I licked the rock.

That was understood. Two of the People came forward and placed their weight on me. A third lifted a paw. He shattered my skull, and they ate.

Magda watched through power binoculars from atop a nearby ridge. She saw everything. The rock swarmed with lean black horrors. It would be dangerous to go down among them, so she waited and watched the puzzling tableau below. The larl had wanted to die, she'd swear it, and now the beasts came forward daintily, almost ritualistically, to taste the brains, the young first and then the old. She raised her rifle, thinking to exterminate a few of the brutes from afar.

A curious thing happened then. All the larls that had eaten of her prey's brain leaped away, scattering. Those that had not eaten waited, easy targets, not understanding. Then another dipped to lap up a fragment of brain, and looked up with sudden comprehension. Fear touched her.

The hunter had spoken often of the larls, had said that they were so elusive he sometimes thought them intelligent. "Come spring, when I can afford to waste ammunition on carnivores, I look forward to harvesting a few of these beauties," he'd said. He was the colony's xenobiologist, and he loved the animals he killed, treasured them even as he smoked their flesh, tanned their hides, and drew detailed pictures of their internal organs. Magda had always scoffed at his theory that larls gained insight into the habits of their prey by eating their brains, even though he'd spent much time observing the animals minutely from afar, gathering evidence. Now she wondered if he were right.

Her baby whimpered, and she slid a hand inside her furs to give him a breast. Suddenly the night seemed cold and dangerous, and she thought: What am I doing here? Sanity returned to her all at once, her anger collapsing to nothing, like an ice tower shattering in the wind. Below, sleek black shapes sped toward her, across the snow. They changed direction every few leaps, running evasive patterns to avoid her fire.

"Hang on, kid," she muttered, and turned her strider around. She opened up the throttle.

Magda kept to the open as much as she could, the creatures following her from a distance. Twice she stopped abruptly and turned her rifle on her pursuers. Instantly they disappeared in puffs of snow, crouching belly-down but not stopping, burrowing toward her under the surface. In the eerie night silence, she could hear the whispering sound of the brutes tunneling. She fled.

Some frantic timeless period later—the sky had still not lightened in the east—Magda was leaping a frozen stream when the strider's left ski struck a rock. The machine was knocked glancingly upward, cybernetics screaming as they fought to regain balance. With a sickening crunch, the strider slammed to earth, one ski twisted and bent. It would take extensive work before the strider could move again.

Magda dismounted. She opened her robe and looked down on her child. He smiled up at her and made a gurgling noise.

Something went dead in her.

A fool. I've been a criminal fool, she thought. Magda was a proud woman who had always refused to regret, even privately, anything she had done. Now she regretted everything: her anger, the hunter, her entire life, all that had brought her to this point, the cumulative madness that threatened to kill her child.

A larl topped the ridge.

Magda raised her rifle, and it ducked down. She began walking downslope, parallel to the stream. The snow was knee deep, and she had to walk carefully not to slip and fall. Small pellets of snow rolled down ahead of her, were overtaken by other pellets. She strode ahead, pushing up a wake.

The hunter's cabin was not many miles distant; if she could reach it, they would live. But a mile was a long way in winter. She could hear the larls calling to each other, soft coughlike noises, to either side of the ravine. They were following the sound of her passage through the snow. Well, let them. She still had the rifle, and if it had few bullets left, *they* didn't know that. They were only animals.

This high in the mountains, the trees were sparse. Magda descended a good quarter-mile before the ravine choked with scrub and she had to climb up and out or risk being ambushed. Which way? she wondered. She heard three coughs to her right, and climbed the left slope, alert and wary.

We herded her. Through the long night we gave her fleeting glimpses of our bodies whenever she started to turn to the side she must not go, and let her pass unmolested the other way. We let her see us dig into the distant snow and wait motionless, undetectable. We filled the woods with our shadows. Slowly, slowly, we turned her around. She struggled to return to the cabin, but she could not. In what haze of fear and despair she walked! We could smell it. Sometimes her baby cried, and she hushed the milky-scented creature in a voice gone flat with futility. The night deepened as the moons sank in the sky. We forced the woman back up into the mountains. Toward the end, her legs failed her several times; she lacked our strength and stamina. But her patience and guile were every bit our match. Once we approached her still form, and she killed two of us before the rest could retreat. How we loved her! We paced her, confident that sooner or later she'd drop.

It was at night's darkest hour that the woman was forced back to the burrowed hillside, the sacred place of the People where stood the sacrifice rock. She topped the same rise for the second time that night, and saw it. For a moment she stood helpless, and then she burst into tears.

We waited, for this was the holiest moment of the hunt, the point when the prey recognizes and accepts her destiny. After a time, the

woman's sobs ceased. She raised her head and straightened her back.
Slowly, steadily, she walked downhill.

She knew what to do.

Larls retreated into their burrows at the sight of her, gleaming eyes dissolving into darkness. Magda ignored them. Numb and aching, weary to death, she walked to the sacrifice rock. It had to be this way.

Magda opened her coat, unstrapped her baby. She wrapped him deep in the furs and laid the bundle down to one side of the rock. Dizzily, she opened the bundle to kiss the top of his sweet head, and he made an angry sound. "Good for you, kid," she said hoarsely. "Keep that attitude." She was so tired.

She took off her sweaters, her vest, her blouse. The raw cold nipped at her flesh with teeth of ice. She stretched slightly, body aching with motion. God, it felt good. She laid down the rifle. She knelt.

The rock was black with dried blood. She lay down flat, as she had earlier seen her larl do. The stone was cold, so cold it almost blanked out the pain. Her pursuers waited nearby, curious to see what she was doing; she could hear the soft panting noise of their breathing. One padded noiselessly to her side. She could smell the brute. It whined questioningly.

She licked the rock.

Once it was understood what the woman wanted, her sacrifice went quickly. I raised a paw, smashed her skull. Again I was youngest. Innocent, I bent to taste.

The neighbors were gathering, hammering at the door, climbing over one another to peer through the windows, making the walls bulge and breathe with their eagerness. I grunted and bellowed, and the clash of silver and clink of plates next door grew louder. Like peasant animals, my husband's people tried to drown out the sound of my pain with toasts and drunken jokes.

Through the window I saw Tevin-the-Fool's bonewhite skin gaunt on his skull, and behind him a slice of face—sharp nose, white cheeks—like a mask. The doors and walls pulsed with the weight of those outside. In the next room, children fought and wrestled, and elders pulled at their long white beards, staring anxiously at the closed door.

The midwife shook her head, red lines running from the corners of her mouth down either side of her stern chin. Her eye sockets were shadowy pools of dust. "Now push!" she cried. "Don't be a lazy sow!"

I groaned and arched my back. I shoved my head back and it grew smaller, eaten up by the pillows. The bedframe skewed as one leg slowly buckled under it. My husband glanced over his shoulder at me, an angry look, his fingers knotted behind his back.

All of Landfall shouted and hovered on the walls.

"Here it comes!" shrieked the midwife. She reached down to my bloody crotch, and eased out a tiny head, purple and angry, like a goblin.

And then all the walls glowed red and green and sprouted large flowers. The door turned orange and burst open, and the neighbors and crew flooded in. The ceiling billowed up, and aerialists tumbled through the rafters. A boy who had been hiding beneath the bed flew up laughing to where the ancient sky and stars shone through the roof.

They held up the child, bloody on a platter.

Here the larl touched me for the first time, that heavy black paw like velvet on my knee, talons sheathed. "Are you following this?" he asked. "Can you separate truth from fantasy, tell what is fact and what the mad imagery of emotions we did not share? No more could I. All that, the first birth of human young on this planet, I experienced in an instant. Blind with awe, I understood the personal tragedy and the communal triumph of that event, and the meaning of the lives and culture behind it. A second before, I lived as an animal, with an animal's simple thoughts and hopes. Then I ate of your ancestor and was lifted all in an instant halfway to godhood.

"As the woman had intended. She had died thinking of the child's birth, in order that we might share in it. She gave us that. She gave us more. She gave us *language.* We were wise animals before we ate her brain, and we were People afterward. We owed her so much. And we knew what she wanted from us." The larl stroked my cheek with his great smooth paw, the ivory claws hooded but quivering slightly, as if about to awake.

I hardly dared breathe.

"That morning I entered Landfall, carrying the baby's sling in my mouth. It slept through most of the journey. At dawn I passed through the empty street as silently as I knew how. I came to the First Captain's house. I heard the murmur of voices within, the entire village assembled for worship. I tapped the door with one paw. There was sudden, astonished silence. Then slowly, fearfully, the door opened."

The larl was silent for a moment. "That was the beginning of the association of People with humans. We were welcomed into your homes, and we helped with the hunting. It was a fair trade. Our food saved many lives that first winter. No one needed know how the woman had perished, or how well we understood your kind.

"That child, Flip, was your ancestor. Every few generations we take one of your family out hunting, and taste his brains, to maintain our closeness with your line. If you are a good boy and grow up to be as bold and honest, as intelligent and noble, a man as your father, then perhaps it will be you we eat."

The larl presented his blunt muzzle to me in what might have been meant as a friendly smile. Perhaps not; the expression hangs unreadable, ambiguous in my mind even now. Then he stood and padded away into the friendly dark shadows of the Stone House.

I was sitting staring into the coals a few minutes later when my second-eldest sister—her face a featureless blaze of light, like an angel's—came into the room and saw me. She held out a hand, saying, "Come on, Flip, you're missing everything." And I went with her.

Did any of this actually happen? Sometimes I wonder. But it's growing late, and your parents are away. My room is small but snug, my bed warm but empty. We can burrow deep in the blankets and scare away the cave-bears by playing the oldest winter games there are.

You're blushing! Don't tug away your hand. I'll be gone soon to some distant world to fight in a war for people who are as unknown to you as they are to me. Soldiers grow old slowly, you know. We're shipped frozen between the stars. When you are old and plump and happily surrounded by grandchildren, I'll still be young, and thinking of you. You'll remember me then, and our thoughts will touch in the void. Will you have nothing to regret? Is that really what you want?

I thought once that I could outrun the darkness. I thought—I must have thought—that by joining the militia I could escape my fate. But for all that I gave up my home and family, in the end the beast came anyway to eat my brain. Now I am alone. A month from now, in all this world, only you will remember my name. Let me live in your memory.

Come, don't be shy. Let's put the past aside and get on with our lives. That's better. Blow the candle out, love, and there's an end to my tale.

All this happened long ago, on a planet whose name has been burned from my memory.

(1988)

CANDAS JANE DORSEY

(Learning About) Machine Sex

A naked woman working at a computer. Which attracts you most? It was a measure of Whitman that, as he entered the room, his eyes went first to the unfolded machine gleaming small and awkward in the light of the long-armed desk lamp; he'd seen the woman before.

Angel was the woman. Thin and pale-skinned, with dark nipples and black pubic hair, and her face hidden by a dark unkempt mane of long hair as she leaned over her work.

A woman complete with her work. It was a measure of Angel that she never acted naked, even when she was. Perhaps especially when she was.

So she has a new board, thought Whitman, and felt his guts stir the way they stirred when he first contemplated taking her to bed. That was a long time ago. And she knew it, felt without turning her head the desire, and behind the screen of her straight dark hair, uncombed and tumbled in front of her eyes, she smiled her anger down.

"Where have you been?" he asked, and she shook her hair back, leaned backward to ease her tense neck.

"What is that thing?" he went on insistently, and Angel turned her face to him, half-scowling. The board on the desk had thin irregular wings spreading from a small central module. Her fingers didn't slow their keyboard dance.

"None of your business," she said.

She saved the input, and he watched her fold the board into a smaller and smaller rectangle. Finally she shook her hair back from her face.

"I've got the option on your bioware," he said.

"Pay as you go," she said. "New house rule."

And found herself on her ass on the floor from his reflexive, furious blow. And his hand in her hair, pulling her up and against the wall. Hard. Astonishing her with how quickly she could hurt how much. Then she hurt too much to analyse it.

"You are a bitch," he said.

"So what?" she said. "When I was nicer, you were still an asshole."

Her head back against the wall, crack. Ouch.

Breathless, Angel: "Once more and you never see this bioware." And Whitman slowly draws breath, draws back, and looks at her the way she knew he always felt.

"Get out," she said. "I'll bring it to Kozyk's office when it's ready."

So he went. She slumped back in the chair, and tears began to blur her vision, but hate cleared them up fast enough, as she unfolded the board again, so that despite the pain she hardly missed a moment of programming time.

Assault only a distraction now, betrayal only a detail: Angel was on a roll. She had her revenge well in hand, though it took a subtle mind to recognise it.

Again: "I have the option on any of your bioware." This time, in the office, Whitman wore the nostalgic denims he now affected, and Angel her street-silks and leather.

"This is mine, but I made one for you." She pulled it out of the bag. Where her board looked jerry-built, this one was sleek. Her board looked interesting; this one packaged. "I made it before you sold our company," she said. "I put my best into it. You may as well have it. I suppose you own the option anyway, eh?"

She stood. Whitman was unconsciously restless before her.

"When you pay me for this," she said, "make it in MannComp stock." She tossed him the board. "But be careful. If you take it apart wrong, you'll break it. Then you'll have to ask me to fix it, and from now on, my tech rate goes up."

As she walked by him, he reached for her, hooked one arm around her waist. She looked at him, totally expressionless. "Max," she said, "it's like I told you last night. From now on, if you want it, you pay. Just like everyone else." He let her go. She pulled the soft dirty white silk shirt on over the black leather jacket. The compleat rebel now.

"It's a little going away present. When you're a big shot in MannComp, remember that I made it. And that you couldn't even take it apart right. I guarantee."

He wasn't going to watch her leave. He was already studying the board. Hardly listening, either.

"Call it the Mannboard," she said. "It gets big if you stroke it." She shut the door quietly behind herself.

It would be easier if this were a story about sex, or about machines. It is true that the subject is Angel, a woman who builds computers like they have never been built before outside the human skull. Angel, like everyone else, comes from somewhere and goes somewhere else. She lives in that linear and binary universe. However, like everyone else, she lives concurrently in another universe less simple. Trivalent, quadrivalent, multivalent. World without end, with no amen. And so, on.

They say a hacker's burned out before he's twenty-one. Note the pronoun: he. Not many young women in that heady realm of the chip.

Before Angel was twenty-one—long before—she had taken the cybernetic chip out of a Wm Kuhns fantasy and patented it; she had written the program for the self-taught AI the Bronfmanns had bought and used to gain world prominence for their MannComp lapboard; somewhere in there, she'd lost innocence, and when her clever additions to that AI turned it into something the military wanted, she dropped out of sight in Toronto and went back to Rocky Mountain House, Alberta on a Greyhound bus.

It was while she was thinking about something else—cash, and how to get some—that she had looked out of the bus window in Winnipeg into the display window of a sex shop. Garter belts, sleazy magazines on cheap coated paper with Day-Glo orange stickers over the genitals of bored sex kings and queens, a variety of ornamental vibrators. She had too many memories of Max to take it lightly, though she heard the laughter of the roughnecks in the back of the bus as they topped each others' dirty jokes, and thought perhaps their humour was worth emulating. If only she could.

She passed her twentieth birthday in a hotel in Regina, where she stopped to take a shower and tap into the phone lines, checking for pursuit. Armed with the money she got through automatic transfer from a dummy account in Medicine Hat, she rode the bus the rest of the way ignoring the rolling of beer bottles under the seats, the acrid stink of the onboard toilet. She was thinking about sex.

As the bus roared across the long flat prairie she kept one hand on the roll of bills in her pocket, but with the other she made the first notes on the program that would eventually make her famous.

She made the notes on an antique NEC lapboard which had been her aunt's, in old-fashioned BASIC—all the machine would support—but she unravelled it and knitted it into that artificial trivalent language when she got to the place at Rocky and plugged the idea into her Mannboard. She had it written in a little over four hours on-time, but that counted an hour and a half she took to write a new loop into the AI. (She would patent that loop later the same year and put the royalties into a blind trust for her brother, Brian, brain damaged from birth. He was in Michener Centre in Red Deer, not educable; no one at Bronfmann knew about her family, and she kept it that way.)

She called it Machine Sex; working title.

Working title for a life: born in Innisfail General Hospital, father a rodeo cowboy who raised rodeo horses, did enough mixed farming out near Caroline to build his young second wife a big log house facing the mountain view. The first baby came within a year, ending her mother's tenure as teller at the local bank. Her aunt was a programmer for the University of Lethbridge, chemical molecular model analysis on the University of Calgary mainframe through a modem link.

From her aunt she learned BASIC, Pascal, COBOL and C; in school she played the usual turtle games on the Apple IIe; when she was fourteen she took a bus to Toronto, changed her name to Angel, affected a punk hairstyle and the insolent all-white costume of that year's youth, and eventually walked into Northern Systems, the company struggling most successfully with bionics at the time, with the perfected biochip, grinning at the proper young men in their grey three-piece suits as they tried to find a bug in it anywhere. For the first million she let them open it up; for the next five she told them how she did it. Eighteen years old by the phony records she'd cooked on her arrival in Toronto, she was free to negotiate her own contracts.

But no one got her away from Northern until Bronfmann bought Northern lock, stock and climate-controlled workshop. She had been sleeping with Northern's boy-wonder president by then for about a year, had yet to have an orgasm though she'd learned a lot about kinky sex toys. Figured she'd been screwed by him for the last time when he sold the company without telling her; spent the next two weeks doing a lot of drugs and having a lot of cheap sex in the degenerate punk underground; came up with the AI education program.

Came up indeed, came swaggering into Ted Kozyk's office, president of Bronfmann's MannComp subsidiary, with that jury-rigged Mannboard tied into two black-box add-ons no bigger than a bar of soap, and said, "Watch this."

Took out the power supply first, wiped the memory, plugged into a wall outlet and turned it on.

The bootstrap greeting sounded a lot like Goo.

"Okay," she said, "it's ready."

"Ready for what?"

"Anything you want," she said. By then he knew her, knew her rep, knew that the sweaty-smelling, disheveled, anorectic-looking waif in the filthy, oversized silk shirt (the rebels had affected natural fabrics the year she left home, and she always did after that, even later when the silk was cleaner, more upmarket, and black instead of white) had something.

Two weeks ago he'd bought a company on the strength of that something, and the board Whitman had brought him yesterday, even without the software to run on it, had been enough to convince him he'd been right.

He sat down to work, and hours later he was playing Go with an AI he'd taught to talk back, play games, and predict horse races and the stock market.

He sat back, flicked the power switch and pulled the plug, and stared at her.

"Congratulations," she said.

"What for?" he said; "you're the genius."

"No, congratulations, you just murdered your first baby," she said, and plugged it back in. "Want to try for two?"

"Goo," said the deck. "Dada."

It was her little joke. It was never a feature on the MannComp A-One they sold across every MannComp counter in the world.

But now she's all grown up, she's sitting in a log house near Rocky Mountain house, watching the late summer sunset from the big front windows, while the computer runs Machine Sex to its logical conclusion, orgasm.

She had her first orgasm at nineteen. According to her false identity, she was twenty-three. Her lover was a delegate to MannComp's annual sales convention; she picked him up after the speech she gave on the ethics of selling AIs to high school students in Thailand. Or whatever, she didn't care. Kozyk used to write her speeches but she usually changed them to suit her mood. This night she'd been circumspect, only a few expletives, enough to amuse the younger sales representatives and reassure the older ones.

The one she chose was smooth in his approach and she thought, well, we'll see. They went up to the suite MannComp provided, all mod cons and king-size bed, and as she undressed she looked at him and thought, he's ambitious, this boy, better not give him an inch.

He surprised her in bed. Ambitious maybe, but he paid a lot of attention to detail.

After he spread her across the universe in a way she had never felt before, he turned to her and said, "That was pretty good, eh, baby?" and smiled a smooth little grin. "Sure," she said, "it was okay," and was glad she hadn't said more while she was out in the ozone.

By then she thought she was over what Whitman had done to her. And after all, it had been simple enough, what he did. Back in that loft she had in Hull, upstairs of a shop, where she covered the windows with opaque mylar and worked night and day in that twilight. That night as she worked he stood behind her, hands on her shoulders, massaging her into further tenseness.

"Hey, Max, you know I don't like it when people look over my shoulder when I'm working."

"Sorry, baby." He moved away, and she felt her shoulders relax just to have his hands fall away.

"Come on to bed," he said. "You know you can pick that up whenever."

She had to admit he was being pleasant tonight. Maybe he too was tired of the constant scrapping, disguised as jokes, that wore at her nerves so much. All his efforts to make her stop working, slow her down so he could stay up. The sharp edges that couldn't be disguised. Her bravado made her answer in the same vein, but in the mornings, when he was gone to Northern, she paced and muttered to herself, reworking the previous day until it was done with, enough that she could go on. And after all what was missing? She had no idea how to debug it.

Tonight he'd even made some dinner, and touched her kindly. Should she be grateful? Maybe the conversations, such as they were, where she tried to work it out, had just made it worse—

"Ah, shit," she said, and pushed the board away. "You're right, I'm too tired for this. *Demain.*" She was learning French in her spare time.

He began with hugging her, and stroking the long line along her back, something he knew she liked, like a cat likes it, arches its back at the end of the stroke. He knew she got turned on by it. And she did. When they had sex at her house he was without the paraphernalia he preferred, but he seemed to manage, buoyed up by some mood she couldn't share; nor could she share his release.

Afterward, she lay beside him, tense and dissatisfied in the big bed, not admitting it, or she'd have to admit she didn't know what would help. He seemed to be okay, stretched, relaxed and smiling.

"Had a big day," he said.

"Yeah?"

"Big deal went through."

"Yeah?"

"Yeah, I sold the company."

"You what?" Reflexively moving herself so that none of her body touched his.

"Northern. I put it to Bronfmann. Megabucks."

"Are you joking?" but she saw he was not. "You didn't, I didn't. . . . Northern's *our* company."

"My company. I started it."

"I made it big for you."

"Oh, and I paid you well for every bit of that."

She got up. He was smiling a little, trying on the little-boy grin. No, baby, she thought, not tonight.

"Well," she said, "I know for sure that this is my bed. Get out of it."

"Now, I knew you might take this badly. But it really was the best thing. The R&D costs were killing us. Bronfmann can eat them for breakfast."

R&D costs meant her. "Maybe. Your clothes are here." She tossed them on the bed, went into the other room.

As well as sex, she hadn't figured out betrayal yet either; on the street, she thought, people fucked you over openly, not in secret.

This, even as she said it to herself, she recognised as romantic and certainly not based on experience. She was street-wise in every way but one: Max had been her first lover.

She unfolded the new board. It had taken her some time to figure out how to make it expand like that, to fit the program it was going to run. This idea of shaping the hardware to the software had been with her since she made the biochip, and thus made it possible and much more interesting than the other way around. But making the hardware to fit her new idea had involved a great deal of study and technique, and so far she had had limited success.

This reminded her again of sex, and, she supposed, relationships, although it seemed to her that before sex everything had been on surfaces, very easy. Now she had sex, she had had Max, and now she had no way to realize the results of any of that. Especially now, when Northern had just vanished into Bronfmann's computer empire, putting her in the position again of having to prove herself. What had Max used to make Bronfmann take the bait? She knew very clearly: Angel, the Northern Angel, would now become the MannComp Angel. The rest of the bait would have been the AI; she was making more of it every day, but couldn't yet bring it together. Could it be done at all? Bronfmann had paid high for an affirmative answer.

Certainly this time the bioware was working together. She began to smile a little to herself, almost unaware of it, as she saw how she could interconnect the loops to make a solid net to support the program's full and growing weight. Because, of course, it would have to learn as it went along—that was basic.

Angel as metaphor; she had to laugh at herself when she woke from programming hours later, Max still sleeping in her bed, ignoring her eviction notice. He'll have to get up to piss anyway, she thought; that's when I'll get him out. She went herself to the bathroom in the half-dawn light, stretching her cramped back muscles and thinking remotely, well, I got some satisfaction out of last night after all: the beginnings of the idea that might break this impasse. While it's still inside my head, this one is mine. How can I keep it that way?

New fiscal controls, she thought grimly. New contracts, now that Northern doesn't exist any more. Max can't have this, whatever it turns into, for my dowry to MannComp.

When she put on her white silks—leather jacket underneath, against the skin as street fashion would have it—she hardly knew herself what she would do. The little board went into her bag with the boxes of pills the pharmaceutical tailor had made for her. If there was nothing there to suit, she'd buy something new. In the end, she left Max sleeping in her bed; so what? she thought as she reached the highway. The first ride she hitched took her to Toronto, not without a little tariff, but she no longer gave a damn about any of that.

By then the drugs in her system had lifted her out of a body that could be betrayed, and she didn't return to it for two weeks, two weeks of floating in a soup of disjointed noise, and always the program running, unfolding, running again, unfolding inside her relentless mind. She kept it running to drown anything she might remember about trust or the dream of happiness.

When she came home two weeks later, on a hot day in summer with the Ottawa Valley humidity unbearable and her body tired, sore and bruised, and very dirty, she stepped out of her filthy silks in a room messy with Whitman's continued inhabitation; furious, she popped a system cleanser and unfolded the board on her desk. When he came back in she was there, naked, angry, working.

A naked woman working at a computer. What good were cover-ups? Watching Max after she took the new AI up to Kozyk, she was only triumphant because she'd done something Max could never do, however much he might be able to sell her out. Watching them fit it to the bioboard, the strange unfolding machine she had made to fit the ideas only she could have, she began to be afraid. The system cleanser she'd taken made the clarity inescapable. Over the next few months, as she kept adding clever loops and twists, she watched their glee and she looked at what telephone numbers were in the top ten on their modem memories and she began to realise that it was not only business and science that would pay high for a truly thinking machine.

She knew that ten years before there had been Pentagon programmers working to model predatory behaviour in AIs using Prolog and its like. That was old hat. None of them, however, knew what they needed to know to write for her bioware yet. No one but Angel could do that. So, by the end of her nineteenth year, that made Angel one of the most sought-after, endangered ex-anorectics on the block.

She went to conferences and talked about the ethics of selling AIs to teenagers in Nepal. Or something. And took a smooth salesman to bed, and thought all the time about when they were going to make their approach. It would be Whitman again, not Kozyk, she thought; Ted wouldn't get his hands dirty, while Max was born with grime under his nails.

She thought also about metaphors. How, even in the new street slang which she could speak as easily as her native tongue, being screwed, knocked, fucked over, jossed, dragged all meant the same thing: hurt to the core. And this was what people sought out, what they spent their time seeking in pick-up joints, to the beat of bad old headbanger bands, that nostalgia shit. Now, as well as the biochip, Max, the AI breakthrough, and all the tailored drugs she could eat, she'd had orgasm too.

Well, she supposed it passed the time.

What interested her intellectually about orgasm was not the lovely illusion of transcendence it brought, but the absolute binary predictability of it. When you learn what to do to the nerve endings, and they are in a receptive state, the program runs like kismet. Warm boot. She'd known a hacker once who'd altered his bootstrap messages to read "Warm pussy." She knew where most hackers were at; they played with their computers more than they played with themselves. She was the same, otherwise why would it have taken a pretty-boy salesman in a three-piece to show her the simple answer? All the others, just like trying to use an old MS-DOS disc to boot up one of her Mann lapboards with crystal RO/RAM.

Angel forgets she's only twenty. Genius is uneven. There's no substitute for time, that relentless shaper of understanding. Etc. Etc. Angel paces with the knowledge that everything is a phase, even this. Life is hard and then you die, and so on. And so, on.

One day it occurred to her that she could simply run away.

This should have seemed elementary but to Angel it was a revelation. She spent her life fatalistically; her only successful escape had been from the people she loved. Her lovely, crazy grandfather; her generous and slightly avaricious aunt; and her beloved imbecile brother: they were buried deep in a carefully forgotten past. But she kept coming back to Whitman, to Kozyk and Bronfmann, as if she liked them.

As if, like a shocked dog in a learned helplessness experiment, she could not believe that the cage had a door, and the door was open.

She went out the door. For old times' sake, it was the bus she chose; the steamy chill of an air-conditioned Greyhound hadn't changed at all.

Bottles—pop and beer—rolling under the seats and the stench of chemicals filling the air whenever someone sneaked down to smoke a cigarette or a reef in the toilet. Did anyone ever use it to piss in? She liked the triple seat near the back, but the combined smells forced her to the front, behind the driver, where she was joined, across the country, by an endless succession of old women, immaculate in their fortrels, who started conversations and shared peppermints and gum.

She didn't get stoned once.

The country unrolled strangely: sex shop in Winnipeg, bank machine in Regina, and hours of programming alternating with polite responses to the old women, until eventually she arrived, creased and exhausted, in Rocky Mountain House.

Rocky Mountain House: a comfortable model of a small town, from which no self-respecting hacker should originate. But these days, the world a net of wire and wireless, it doesn't matter where you are, as long as you have the information people want. Luckily for Angel's secret past, however, this was not a place she would be expected to live—or to go—or to come from.

An atavism she hadn't controlled had brought her this far. A rented car took her the rest of the way to the ranch. She thought only to look around, but when she found the tenants packing for a month's holiday, she couldn't resist the opportunity. She carried her leather satchel into their crocheted, frilled guest room—it had been her room fifteen years before—with a remote kind of satisfaction.

That night, she slept like the dead—except for some dreams. But there was nothing she could do about them.

Lightning and thunder. I should stop now, she thought, wary of power surges through the new board which she was charging as she worked. She saved her file, unplugged the power, stood, stretched, and walked to the window to look at the mountains.

The storm illuminated the closer slopes erratically, the rain hid the distances. She felt some heaviness lift. The cool wind through the window refreshed her. She heard the program stop, and turned off the machine. Sliding out the backup capsule, she smiled her angry smile unconsciously. When I get back to the Ottawa Valley, she thought, where weather never comes from the west like it's supposed to, I'll make those fuckers eat this.

Out in the corrals where the tenants kept their rodeo horses, there was animal noise, and she turned off the light to go and look out the side window. A young man was leaning his weight against the reins-length pull of a rearing, terrified horse. Angel watched as flashes of lightning strobed the hackneyed scene. This was where she came from. She remembered her father in the same struggle. And her mother at this window with her, both of them watching the man. Her mother's anger she never understood until now. Her father's abandonment of all that was in the house, including her brother, Brian, inert and restless in his oversized crib.

Angel walked back through the house, furnished now in the kitschy western style of every trailer and bungalow in this countryside. She was lucky to stay, invited on a generous impulse, while all but their son were away. She felt vaguely guilty at her implicit criticism.

Angel invited the young rancher into the house only because this is what her mother and her grandmother would have done. Even Angel's great-grandmother, whose father kept the stopping house, which meant she kept the travellers fed, even her spirit infused in Angel the unwilling act. She watched him almost sullenly as he left his rain gear in the wide porch.

He was big, sitting in the big farm kitchen. His hair was wet, and he swore almost as much as she did. He told her how he had put a trailer on the north forty, and lived there now, instead of in the little room where she'd been invited to sleep. He told her about the stock he'd accumulated riding the rodeo. They drank Glenfiddich. She told him her father had been a rodeo cowboy. He told her about his university degree in agriculture. She told him she'd never been to university. They drank more whiskey and he told her he couldn't drink that other rot gut any more since he tasted real Scotch. He invited her to see his computer. She went with him across the yard and through the trees in the rain, her bag over her shoulder, board hidden in it, and he showed her his computer. It turned out to be the first machine she designed for Northern—archaic now, compared with the one she'd just invented.

Fair is fair, she thought drunkenly, and she pulled out her board and unfolded it.

"You showed me yours, I'll show you mine," she said.

He liked the board. He was amazed that she had made it. They finished the Scotch.

"I like you," she said. "Let me show you something. You can be the first." And she ran Machine Sex for him.

He was the first to see it: before Whitman and Kozyk who bought it to sell to people who already have had and done everything; before David and Jonathan, the Hardware Twins in MannComp's Gulf Islands shop, who made the touchpad devices necessary to run it properly; before a world market hungry for the kind of glossy degradation Machine Sex could give them bought it in droves from a hastily-created—MannComp-subsidiary—numbered company. She ran it for him with just the automouse on her board, and a description of what it would do when the hardware was upgraded to fit.

It was very simple, really. If orgasm was binary, it could be programmed. Feed back the sensation through one or more touchpads to program the body. The other thing she knew about human sex was that it was as much cortical as genital, or more so: touch is optional for the turn-on. Also easy, then, to produce cortical stimuli by programmed input. The rest was a cosmetic elaboration of the premise.

At first it did turn him on, then off, then it made his blood run cold. She was pleased by that: her work had chilled her too.

"You can't market that thing!" he said.

"Why not. It's a fucking good program. Hey, get it? Fucking good."

"It's not real."

"Of course it isn't. So what?"

"So, people don't need that kind of stuff to get turned on."

She told him about people. More people than he'd known were in the world. People who made her those designer drugs, given in return for favours she never granted until after Whitman sold her like a used car. People like Whitman, teaching her about sexual equipment while dealing with the Pentagon and CSIS to sell them Angel's sharp angry mind, as if she'd work on killing others as eagerly as she was trying to kill herself. People who would hire a woman on the street, as they had her during that two-week nightmare almost a year before, and use her as casually as their own hand, without giving a damn.

"One night," she said, "just to see, I told all the johns I was fourteen. I was skinny enough, even then, to get away with it. And they all loved it. Every single one gave me a bonus, and took me anyway."

The whiskey fog was wearing a little thin. More time had passed than she thought, and more had been said than she had intended. She went to her bag, rummaged, but she'd left her drugs in Toronto, some dim idea at the time that she should clean up her act. All that had happened was that she had spent the days so tight with rage that she couldn't eat, and she'd already cured herself of that once; for the record, she thought, she'd rather be stoned.

"Do you have any more booze?" she said, and he went to look. She followed him around his kitchen.

"Furthermore," she said, "I rolled every one of them that I could, and all but one had pictures of his kids in his wallet, and all of them were teenagers. Boys and girls together. And their saintly dads out fucking someone who looked just like them. Just like them."

Luckily, he had another bottle. Not quite the same quality, but she wasn't fussy.

"So I figure," she finished, "that they don't care who they fuck. Why not the computer in the den? Or the office system at lunch hour?"

"It's not like that," he said. "It's nothing like that. People deserve better." He had the neck of the bottle in his big hand, was seriously, carefully pouring himself another shot. He gestured with both bottle and glass. "People deserve to have—love."

"Love?"

"Yeah, love. You think I'm stupid, you think I watched too much TV as a kid, but I know it's out there. Somewhere. Other people think so too. Don't you? Didn't you, even if you won't admit it now, fall in love with that guy Max at first? You never said what he did at the beginning, how he talked you into being his lover. Something must have happened. Well, that's what I mean: love."

"Let me tell you about love. Love is a guy who talks real smooth taking me out to the woods and telling me he just loves my smile. And then taking me home and putting me in leather handcuffs so he can come. And if I hurt he likes it, because he likes it to hurt a little and he thinks I must like it like he does. And if I moan he thinks I'm coming. And if I cry he thinks it's love. And so do I. Until one evening—not too long after my *last* birthday, as I recall—he tells me that he has sold me to another company. And this only after he fucks me one last time. Even though I don't belong to him any more. After all, he had the option on all my bioware."

"All that is just politics." He was sharp, she had to grant him that.

"Politics," she said, "give me a break. Was it politics made Max able to sell me with the stock: hardware, software, liveware?"

"I've met guys like that. Women too. You have to understand that it wasn't personal to him, it was just politics." Also stubborn. "Sure, you were naive, but you weren't wrong. You just didn't understand company politics."

"Oh, sure I did. I always have. Why do you think I changed my name? Why do you think I dress in natural fibres and go through all the rest of this bullshit? I know how to set up power blocs. Except in mine there is only one party—me. And that's the way it's going to stay. Me against them from now on."

"It's not always like that. There are assholes in the world, and there are other people too. Everyone around here still remembers your grandfather, even though he's been retired in Camrose for fifteen years. They still talk about the way he and his wife used to waltz at the Legion Hall. What about him? There are more people like him than there are Whitmans."

"Charlotte doesn't waltz much since her stroke."

"That's a cheap shot. You can't get away with cheap shots. Speaking of shots, have another."

"Don't mind if I do. Okay, I give you Eric and Charlotte. But one half-happy ending doesn't balance out the people who go through their lives with their teeth clenched, trying to make it come out the same as a True Romance comic, and always wondering what's missing. They read those bodice-ripper novels, and make that do for the love you believe in so naively." Call her naive, would he? Two could play at that game. "That's why they'll all go crazy for Machine Sex. So simple. So linear. So fast. So uncomplicated."

"You underestimate people's ability to be happy. People are better at loving than you think."

"You think so? Wait until you have your own little piece of land and some sweetheart takes you out in the trees on a moonlit night and gives you head until you think your heart will break. So you marry her and have some kids. She furnishes the trailer in a five-room sale grouping. You have to quit drinking Glenfiddich because she hates it when you talk too loud. She gets an allowance every month and crochets a cozy for the TV. You work all day out in the rain and all evening in the back room making the books balance on the outdated computer. After the kids come she gains weight and sells real estate if you're lucky. If not she makes things out of recycled bleach bottles and hangs them in the yard. Pretty soon she wears a nightgown to bed and turns her back when you slip in after a hard night at the keyboard. So you take up drinking again and teach the kids about the rodeo. And you find some square-dancing chick who gives you head out behind the bleachers one night in Trochu, so sweet you think your heart will break. What you gonna do then, mountain man?"

"Okay, we can tell stories until the sun comes up. Which won't be too long, look at the time; but no matter how many stories you tell, you can't make me forget about that thing." He pointed to the computer with loathing.

"It's just a machine."

"You know what I mean. That thing in it. And besides, I'm gay. Your little scenario wouldn't work."

She laughed and laughed. "So that's why you haven't made a pass at me yet," she said archly, knowing it wasn't that simple, and he grinned. She wondered coldly how gay he was, but she was tired, so tired of proving power. His virtue was safe with her; so, she thought suddenly, strangely, was hers with him. It was unsettling and comforting at once.

"Maybe," he said. "Or maybe I'm just a liar like you think everyone is. Eh? You think everyone strings everyone else a line? Crap. Who has the time for that shit?"

Perhaps they were drinking beer now. Or was it vodka? She found it hard to tell after a while.

"You know what I mean," she said. "You should know. The sweet young thing who has AIDS and doesn't tell you. Or me. I'm lucky so far. Are you? Or who sucks you for your money. Or josses you 'cause he's into denim and Nordic looks."

"Okay, okay. I give up. Everybody's a creep but you and me."

"And I'm not so sure about you."

"Likewise, I'm sure. Have another. So, if you're so pure, what about the ethics of it?"

"What *about* the ethics of it?" she asked. "Do you think I went through all that sex without paying attention? I had nothing else to do but watch other people come. I saw that old cult movie, where the aliens feed on heroin addiction and orgasm, and the woman's not allowed orgasm so she has to O.D. on smack. Orgasm's more decadent than shooting heroin? I can't buy that, but there's something about a world that sells it over and over again. Sells the thought of pleasure as a commodity, sells the getting of it as if it were the getting of wisdom. And all these times I told you about, I saw other people get it through me. Even when someone finally made me come, it was just a feather in his cap, an accomplishment, nothing personal. Like you said. All I was was a program, they plugged into me and went through the motions and got their result. Nobody cares if the AI finds fulfilment running their damned data analyses. Nobody thinks about depressed and angry Mannboard ROMs. They just think about getting theirs.

"So why not get mine?" She was pacing now, angry, leaning that thin body as if the wind were against her. "Let me be the one who runs the program."

"But you won't be there. You told me how you were going to hide out, all that spy stuff."

She leaned against the wall, smiling a new smile she thought of as predatory. And maybe it was. "Oh, yes," she said. "I'll be there the first time. When Max and Kozyk run this thing and it turns them on. I'll be there. That's all I care to see."

He put his big hands on the wall on either side of her and leaned in. He smelled of sweat and liquor and his face was earnest with intoxication.

"I'll tell you something," he said. "As long as there's the real thing, it won't sell. They'll never buy it."

Angel thought so too. Secretly, because she wouldn't give him the satisfaction of agreement, she too thought they would not go that low. *That's right,* she told herself, *trying to sell it is all right—because they will never buy it.*

But they did.

A woman and a computer. Which attracts you most? Now you don't have to choose. Angel has made the choice irrelevant.

In Kozyk's office, he and Max go over the ad campaign. They've already tested the program themselves quite a lot; Angel knows this because it's company gossip, heard over the cubicle walls in the washrooms. The two men are so absorbed that they don't notice her arrival.

"Why is a woman better than a sheep? Because sheep can't cook. Why is a woman better than a Mannboard? Because you haven't bought your sensory add-on." Max laughs.

"And what's better than a man?" Angel says; they jump slightly. "Why, your MannComp touchpads, with two-way input. I bet you'll be able to have them personally fitted."

"Good idea," says Kozyk, and Whitman makes a note on his lapboard. Angel, still stunned though she's had weeks to get used to this, looks at them, then reaches across the desk and picks up her prototype board. "This one's mine," she says. "You play with yourselves and your touchpads all you want."

"Well, you wrote it, baby," said Max. "If you can't come with your own program. . . ."

Kozyk hiccoughs a short laugh before he shakes his head. "Shut up, Whitman," he says. "You're talking to a very rich and famous woman."

Whitman looks up from the simulations of his advertising storyboards, smiling a little, anticipating his joke. "Yeah. It's just too bad she finally burned herself out with this one. They always did say it gives you brain damage."

But Angel hadn't waited for the punch line. She was gone.

(1988)

BRUCE STERLING

We See Things Differently

This was the *jahiliyah*—the land of ignorance. This was America. The Great Satan, the Arsenal of Imperialism, the Bankroller of Zionism, the Bastion of Neo-Colonialism. The home of Hollywood and blonde sluts in black nylon. The land of rocket-equipped F-15s that slashed across God's sky, in godless pride. The land of nuclear-powered global navies, with cannon that fired shells as large as cars.

They have forgotten that they used to shoot us, shell us, insult us, and equip our enemies. They have no memory, the Americans, and no history. Wind sweeps through them, and the past vanishes. They are like dead leaves.

I flew into Miami, on a winter afternoon. The jet banked over a tangle of empty highways, then a large dead section of the city—a ghetto perhaps. In our final approach we passed a coal-burning power plant, reflected in the canal. For a moment I mistook it for a mosque, its tall smokestacks slender as minarets. A Mosque for the American Dynamo.

I had trouble with my cameras at customs. The customs officer was a grimy-looking American white with hair the color of clay. He squinted at my passport. "That's an awful lot of film, Mr. Cuttab," he said.

"Qutb," I said, smiling. "Sayyid Qutb. Call me Charlie."

"Journalist, huh?" He looked unhappy. It seemed that I owed substantial import duties on my Japanese cameras, as well as my numerous rolls of Pakistani color film. He invited me into a small back office to discuss it. Money changed hands. I departed with my papers in order.

The airport was half-full: mostly prosperous Venezuelans and Cubans, with the haunted look of men pursuing sin. I caught a taxi outside, a tiny vehicle like a motorcycle wrapped in glass. The cabbie, an ancient black man, stowed my luggage in the cab's trailer.

Within the cab's cramped confines, we were soon unwilling intimates. The cabbie's breath smelled of sweetened alcohol. "You Iranian?" the cabbie asked.

"Arab."

"We respect Iranians around here, we really do," the cabbie insisted.

"So do we," I said. "We fought them on the Iraqi front for years."

"Yeah?" said the cabbie uncertainly. "Seems to me I heard about that. How'd that end up?"

"The Shi'ite holy cities were ceded to Iran. The Ba'athist regime is dead, and Iraq is now part of the Arab Caliphate." My words made no impression on him, and I had known it before I spoke. This is the land of ignorance. They know nothing about us, the Americans. After all this, and they still know nothing whatsoever.

"Well, who's got more money these days?" the cabbie asked. "Y'all, or the Iranians?"

"The Iranians have heavy industry," I said. "But we Arabs tip better."

The cabbie smiled. It is very easy to buy Americans. The mention of money brightens them like a shot of drugs. It is not just the poverty; they were always like this, even when they were rich. It is the effect of spiritual emptiness. A terrible grinding emptiness in the very guts of the West, which no amount of Coca-Cola seems able to fill.

We rolled down gloomy streets toward the hotel. Miami's streetlights were subsidized by commercial enterprises. It was another way of, as they say, shrugging the burden of essential services from the exhausted backs of the taxpayers. And onto the far sturdier shoulders of peddlers of aspirin, sticky sweetened drinks, and cosmetics. Their billboards gleamed bluely under harsh lights encased in bulletproof glass. It reminded me so strongly of Soviet agitprop that I had a sudden jarring sense of displacement, as if I were being sold Lenin and Engels and Marx in the handy jumbo size.

The cabbie, wondering perhaps about his tip, offered to exchange dollars for riyals at black-market rates. I declined politely, having already done this in Cairo. The lining of my coat was stuffed with crisp Reagan $1,000 bills. I also had several hundred in pocket change, and an extensive credit line at the Islamic Bank of Jerusalem. I foresaw no difficulties.

Outside the hotel, I gave the ancient driver a pair of fifties. Another very old man, of Hispanic descent, took my bags on a trolley. I registered under the gaze of a very old woman. Like all American women, she was dressed in a way intended to provoke lust. In the young, this technique works admirably, as proved by America's unhappy history of sexually transmitted plague. In the very old, it provokes only sad disgust.

I smiled on the horrible old woman and paid in advance.

I was rewarded by a double-handful of glossy brochures promoting local casinos, strip-joints, and bars.

The room was adequate. This had once been a fine hotel. The air conditioning was quiet and both hot and cold water worked well. A wide flat screen covering most of one wall offered dozens of channels of television.

My wristwatch buzzed quietly, its programmed dial indicating the direction of Mecca. I took the rug from my luggage and spread it before the window. I cleansed my face, my hands, my feet. Then I knelt before the darkening chaos of Miami, many stories below. I assumed the eight positions, bowing carefully, sinking with gratitude into deep meditation. I forced away the stress of jet-lag, the innate tension and fear of a Believer among enemies.

Prayer completed, I changed my clothing, putting aside my dark Western business suit. I assumed denim jeans, a long-sleeved shirt, and photographer's vest. I slipped my press card, my passport, my health cards into the vest's zippered pockets, and draped the cameras around myself. I then returned to the lobby downstairs, to await the arrival of the American rock star.

He came on schedule, even slightly early. There was only a small crowd, as the rock star's organization had sought confidentiality. A train of seven monstrous buses pulled into the hotel's lot, their whale-like sides gleaming with brushed aluminum. They bore Massachusetts license plates. I walked out on to the tarmac and began photographing.

All seven buses carried the rock star's favored insignia, the thirteen-starred blue field of the early American flag. The buses pulled up with military precision, forming a wagon-train fortress across a large section of the weedy, broken tarmac. Folding doors hissed open and a swarm of road crew piled out into the circle of buses.

Men and women alike wore baggy fatigues, covered with buttoned pockets and block-shaped streaks of urban camouflage: brick red, asphalt black, and concrete gray. Dark-blue shoulder-patches showed the thirteen-starred circle. Working efficiently, without haste, they erected large satellite dishes on the roofs of two buses. The buses were soon linked together in formation, shaped barriers of woven wire securing the gaps between each nose and tail. The machines seemed to sit breathing, with the stoked-up, leviathan air of steam locomotives.

A dozen identically dressed crewmen broke from the buses and departed in a group for the hotel. Within their midst, shielded by their bodies, was the rock star, Tom Boston. The broken outlines of their camouflaged fatigues made them seem to blur into a single mass, like a herd of moving zebras. I followed them; they vanished quickly within the hotel. One crew woman tarried outside.

I approached her. She had been hauling a bulky piece of metal luggage on trolley wheels. It was a newspaper vending machine. She set it beside three other machines at the hotel's entrance. It was the Boston organization's propaganda paper, *Poor Richard's*.

I drew near. "Ah, the latest issue," I said. "May I have one?"

"It will cost five dollars," she said in painstaking English. To my surprise, I recognized her as Boston's wife. "Valya Plisetskaya," I said with pleasure, and handed her a five-dollar nickel. "My name is Sayyid; my American friends call me Charlie."

She looked about her. A small crowd already gathered at the buses, kept at a distance by the Boston crew. Others clustered under the hotel's green-and-white awning.

"Who are you with?" she said.

"*Al-Ahram,* of Cairo. An Arabic newspaper."

"You're not a political?" she said.

I shook my head in amusement at this typical show of Soviet paranoia. "Here's my press card." I showed her the tangle of Arabic. "I am here to cover Tom Boston. The Boston phenomenon."

She squinted. "Tom is big in Cairo these days? Muslims, yes? Down on rock and roll."

"We're not all ayatollahs," I said, smiling up at her. She was very tall. "Many still listen to Western pop music; they ignore the advice of their betters. They used to rock all night in Leningrad. Despite the Party. Isn't that so?"

"You know about us Russians, do you, Charlie?" She handed me my paper, watching me with cool suspicion.

"No, I can't keep up," I said. "Like Lebanon in the old days. Too many factions." I followed her through the swinging glass doors of the hotel. Valentina Plisetskaya was a broad-cheeked Slav with glacial blue eyes and hair the color of corn tassels. She was a childless woman in her thirties, starved as thin as a girl. She played saxophone in Boston's band. She was a native of Moscow, but had survived its destruction. She had been on tour with her jazz band when the Afghan Martyrs' Front detonated their nuclear bomb.

I tagged after her. I was interested in the view of another foreigner. "What do you think of the Americans these days?" I asked her.

We waited beside the elevator.

"Are you recording?" she said.

"No! I'm a print journalist. I know you don't like tapes," I said.

"We like tapes fine," she said, staring down at me. "As long as they are ours." The elevator was sluggish. "You want to know what I think, Charlie? I think Americans are fucked. Not as bad as Soviets, but fucked anyway. What do you think?"

"Oh," I said. "American gloom-and-doom is an old story. At *Al-*

Ahram, we are more interested in the signs of American resurgence. That's the big angle, now. That's why I'm here." She looked at me with remote sarcasm. "Aren't you a little afraid they will beat the shit out of you? They're not happy, the Americans. Not sweet and easy-going like before."

I wanted to ask her how sweet the CIA had been when their bomb killed half the Iranian government in 1981. Instead, I shrugged. "There's no substitute for a man on the ground. That's what my editors say." The elevator shunted open. "May I come up with you?"

"I won't stop you." We stepped in. "But they won't let you in to see Tom."

"They will if you ask them to, Mrs. Boston."

"I'm Plisetskaya," she said, fluffing her yellow hair. "See? No veil." It was the old story of the so-called "liberated" Western woman. They call the simple, modest clothing of Islam "bondage"—while they spend countless hours, and millions of dollars, painting themselves. They grow their nails like talons, cram their feet into high heels, strap their breasts and hips into spandex. All for the sake of male lust.

It baffles the imagination. Naturally I told her nothing of this, but only smiled. "I'm afraid I will be a pest," I said. "I have a room in this hotel. Some time I will see your husband. I must, my editors demand it."

The doors opened. We stepped into the hall of the fourteenth floor. Boston's entourage had taken over the entire floor. Men in fatigues and sunglasses guarded the hallway; one of them had a trained dog.

"Your paper is big, is it?" the woman said.

"Biggest in Cairo, millions of readers," I said. "We still read, in the Caliphate."

"State-controlled television," she muttered.

"Worse than corporations?" I asked. "I saw what CBS said about Tom Boston." She hesitated, and I continued to prod. "A 'Luddite fanatic,' am I right? A 'rock demagogue.' "

"Give me your room number." I did this. "I'll call," she said, striding away down the corridor. I almost expected the guards to salute her as she passed so regally, but they made no move, their eyes invisible behind the glasses. They looked old and rather tired, but with the alert relaxation of professionals. They had the look of former Secret Service bodyguards. The putty-colored fatigues were baggy enough to hide almost any amount of weaponry.

I returned to my room. I ordered Japanese food from room service, and ate it. Wine had been used in its cooking, but I am not a prude in these matters. It was now time for the day's last prayer, though my body, still attuned to Cairo, did not believe it.

My devotions were broken by a knocking at the door. I opened it. It was another of Boston's staff, a small black woman whose hair had been treated. It had a nylon sheen, it looked like the plastic hair on a child's doll. "You Charlie?"

"Yes."

"Valya says, you want to see the gig. See us set up. Got you a backstage pass."

"Thank you very much." I let her clip the plastic-coated pass to my vest. She looked past me into the room, and saw my prayer rug at the window. "What you doin' in there? Prayin'?"

"Yes."

"Weird," she said. "You coming or what?"

I followed my nameless benefactor to the elevator.

Down at ground level, the crowd had swollen. Two hired security guards stood outside the glass doors, refusing admittance to anyone without a room key. The girl ducked, and plowed through the crowd with sudden headlong force, like an American football player. I struggled in her wake, the gawkers, pickpockets, and autograph hounds closing at my heels. The crowd was liberally sprinkled with the repulsive derelicts one sees so often in America: those without homes, without family, without charity.

I was surprised at the age of the people. For a rock-star's crowd, one expects dizzy teenage girls and the libidinous young street-toughs that pursue them. There were many of those, but more of another type: tired, footsore people with crow's-feet and graying hair. Men and women in their thirties and forties, with a shabby, crushed look. Unemployed, obviously, and with time on their hands to cluster around anything that resembled hope.

We walked without hurry to the fortress circle of buses. A rearguard of Boston's kept the onlookers at bay. Two of the buses were already unlinked from the others and under full steam. I followed the black woman up perforated steps and into the bowels of one of the shining machines.

She called brief greetings to the others already inside.

The air held the sharp reek of cleaning fluid. Neat elastic cords strapped down stacks of amplifiers, stencilled instrument cases, wheeled dollies of black rubber and crisp yellow pine. The thirteen-starred circle marked everything, stamped or spray-painted. A methane-burning steam generator sat at the back of the bus, next to a tall crashproof rack of high-pressure fuel tanks. We skirted the equipment and joined the others in a narrow row of second-hand airplane seats. We buckled ourselves in. I sat next to the Doll-Haired Girl.

The bus surged into motion. "It's very clean," I said to her. "I expected something a bit wilder on a rock and roll bus."

"Maybe in Egypt," she said, with the instinctive decision that Egypt was in the Dark Ages. "We don't have the luxury to screw around. Not now."

I decided not to tell her that Egypt, as a nation-state, no longer existed. "American pop culture is a very big industry."

"Biggest we have left," she said. "And if you Muslims weren't so pimpy about it, maybe we could pull down a few riyals and get out of debt."

"We buy a great deal from America," I told her. "Grain and timber and minerals."

"That's Third-World stuff. We're not your farm." She looked at the spotless floor. "Look, our industries suck, everyone knows it. So we sell entertainment. Except where there's media barriers. And even then the fucking video pirates rip us off."

"We see things differently," I said. "America ruled the global media for decades. To us, it's cultural imperialism. We have many talented musicians in the Arab world. Have you ever heard them?"

"Can't afford it," she said crisply. "We spent all our money saving the Persian Gulf from commies."

"The Global Threat of Red Totalitarianism," said the heavyset man in the seat next to Doll-Hair. The others laughed grimly.

"Oh," I said. "Actually, it was Zionism that concerned us. When there was a Zionism."

"I can't believe the hate shit I see about America," said the heavy man. "You know how much money we gave away to people, just gave away, for nothing? Billions and billions. Peace Corps, development aid . . . for decades. Any disaster anywhere, and we fell all over ourselves to give food, medicine. . . . Then the Russians go down and the whole world turns against us like we were monsters."

"Moscow," said another crewman, shaking his shaggy head.

"You know, there are still motherfuckers who think we Americans killed Moscow. They think we gave a Bomb to those Afghani terrorists."

"It had to come from somewhere," I said.

"No, man. We wouldn't do that to them. No, man, things were going great between us. Rock for Detente—I was at that gig."

We drove to Miami's Memorial Colosseum. It was an ambitious structure, left half-completed when the American banking system collapsed.

We entered double-doors at the back, wheeling the equipment along dusty corridors. The Colosseum's interior was skeletal; inside it was clammy and cavernous. A stage, a concrete floor. Bare steel arched high overhead, with crudely bracket-mounted stage-lights. Large sections of that bizarre American parody of grass, "Astroturf," had been dragged before the stage. The itchy green fur, still lined with yard-marks from some forgotten stadium, was almost indestructible. At second-hand rates, it was much cheaper than carpeting.

The crew worked with smooth precision, setting up amplifiers, spindly mike-stands, a huge high-tech drum kit with the clustered, shiny look of an oil refinery. Others checked lighting, flicking blue and yellow spots across the stage. At the public entrances, two crewmen from a second bus erected metal detectors for illicit cameras, recorders, or handguns. Especially handguns. Two attempts had already been made on Boston's life, one at the Chicago Freedom Festival, when Chicago's Mayor was wounded at Boston's side.

For a moment, to understand it, I mounted the empty stage and stood before Boston's microphone. I imagined the crowd before me, ten thousand souls, twenty thousand eyes. Under that attention, I realized, every motion was amplified. To move my arm would be like moving ten thousand arms, my every word like the voice of thousands. I felt like a Nasser, a Qadaffi, a Saddam Hussein.

This was the nature of secular power. Industrial power. It was the West that invented it, that invented Hitler, the gutter orator turned trampler of nations, that invented Stalin, the man they called "Genghis Khan with a telephone." The media pop star, the politician. Was there any difference any more? Not in America; it was all a question of seizing eyes, of seizing attention. Attention is wealth, in an age of mass media. Center stage is more important than armies.

The last unearthly moans and squeals of sound-check faded. The Miami crowd began to filter into the Colosseum. They looked livelier than the desperate searchers that had pursued Boston to his hotel. America was still a wealthy country, by most standards; the professional classes had kept much of their prosperity. There were those legions of lawyers, for instance, that secular priesthood that had done so much to drain America's once-vaunted enterprise. And their associated legions of state bureaucrats. They were instantly recognizable; the cut of their suits, the telltale pocket telephones proclaiming their status.

What were they looking for here? Had they never read Boston's propaganda paper, with its bitter condemnation of everything they stood for? With its fierce attacks on the "legislative-litigative complex," its demands for sweeping reforms?

Was it possible that they failed to take him seriously?

I joined the crowd, mingling, listening to conversations. At the doors, Boston cadres were cutting ticket prices for those who showed voter registrations. Those who showed unemployment cards got in for even less.

The prosperous Americans stood in little knots of besieged gentility, frightened of the others, yet curious, smiling. There was a liveliness in the destitute: brighter clothing, knotted kerchiefs at the elbows, cheap Korean boots of iridescent cloth. Many wore tricornered hats, some with a cockade of red, white, and blue, or the circle of thirteen stars.

This was rock and roll, I realized; that was the secret. They had all grown up on it, these Americans, even the richer ones. To them, the sixty-year tradition of rock music seemed as ancient as the Pyramids. It had become a Jerusalem, a Mecca of American tribes.

The crowd milled, waiting, and Boston let them wait. At the back of the crowd, Boston crewmen did a brisk business in starred souvenir shirts, programs, and tapes. Heat and tension mounted, and people began to sweat. The stage remained dark.

I bought the souvenir items and studied them. They talked about cheap computers, a phone company owned by its workers, a free database, neighborhood co-ops that could buy unmilled grain by the ton. ATTENTION MIAMI, read one brochure in letters of dripping red. It named the ten largest global corporations and meticulously listed every subsidiary doing business in Miami, with its address, its phone number, the percentage of income shipped to banks in Europe and Japan. Each list went on for pages. Nothing else. To Boston's audience, nothing else was necessary.

The house lights darkened. A frightening animal roar rose from the crowd. A single spot lit Tom Boston, stencilling him against darkness.

"My fellow Americans," he said. A funereal hush followed. The crowd strained for each word. Boston smirked. "My f-f-f-fellow Americans." It was a clever microphone, digitized, a small synthesizer in itself. "My fellow Am-am-am-am-AMM!" The words vanished in a sudden soaring wail of feedback. "My Am/ my fellows/ My Am/ my fellows/ Miami, Miami, Miami, MIAMI!" The sound of Boston's voice, suddenly leaping out of all human context, becoming something shattering, superhuman—the effect was bone-chilling. It passed all barriers, it seeped directly into the skin, the blood.

"Tom Jefferson Died Broke!" he shouted. It was the title of his first song. Stage lights flashed up and hell broke its gates. Was it a "song" at all, this strange, volcanic creation? There was a melody loose in it somewhere, pursued by Plisetskaya's saxophone, but the sheer volume and impact hurled it through the audience like a sheet of flame. I had never before heard anything so loud. What Cairo's renegade set called rock and roll paled to nothing beside this invisible hurricane.

At first it seemed raw noise. But that was only a kind of flooring, a merciless grinding foundation below the rising architectures of sound. Technology did it: a piercing, soaring, digitized, utter clarity, of perfect cybernetic acoustics adjusting for each echo, a hundred times a second.

Boston played a glass harmonica: an instrument invented by the early American genius Benjamin Franklin. The harmonica was made of carefully tuned glass disks, rotating on a spindle, and played by streaking a wet fingertip across each moving edge.

It was the sound of pure crystal, seemingly sourceless, of tooth-aching purity.

The famous Western musician, Wolfgang Mozart, had composed for the Franklin harmonica in the days of its novelty. But legend said that its players went mad, their nerves shredded by its clarity of sound. It was a legend Boston was careful to exploit. He played the machine sparingly, with the air of a magician, of a Solomon unbottling demons. I was glad of his spare use, for its sound was so beautiful that it stung the brain.

Boston threw aside his hat. Long coiled hair spilled free. Boston was what Americans called "black"; at least he was often referred to as black, though no one seemed certain. He was no darker than myself. The beat rose up, a strong animal heaving. Boston stalked across the stage as if on springs, clutching his microphone. He began to sing.

The song concerned Thomas Jefferson, a famous American president of the 18th century. Jefferson was a political theorist who wrote revolutionary manifestos and favored a decentralist mode of government. The song, however, dealt with the relations of Jefferson and a black concubine in his household. He had several children by this woman, who were a source of great shame, due to the odd legal code of the period. Legally, they were his slaves, and it was only at the end of his life, when he was in great poverty, that Jefferson set them free.

It was a story whose pathos makes little sense to a Muslim. But Boston's audience, knowing themselves Jefferson's children, took it to heart.

The heat became stifling, as massed bodies swayed in rhythm. The next song began in a torrent of punishing noise. Frantic hysteria seized the crowd; their bodies spasmed with each beat, the shaman Boston seeming to scourge them. It was a fearsome song, called "The Whites of Their Eyes," after an American war-cry. He sang of a tactic of battle: to wait until the enemy comes close enough so that you can meet his eyes, frighten him with your conviction, and then shoot him point blank. The chorus harked again and again to the "Cowards of the long kill," a Boston slogan condemning those whose abstract power structures let them murder without ever seeing pain.

Three more songs followed, one of them slower, the others battering the audience like iron rods. Boston stalked like a madman, his clothing dark with sweat. My heart spasmed as heavy bass notes, filled with dark murderous power, surged through my ribs. I moved away from the heat to the fringe of the crowd, feeling light-headed and sick.

I had not expected this. I had expected a political spokesman, but instead it seemed I was assaulted by the very Voice of the West. The Voice of a society drunk with raw power, maddened by the grinding roar of machines. It filled me with terrified awe.

To think that once, the West had held us in its armored hands. It had treated Islam like a natural resource, its invincible armies plowing through the lands of the Faithful like bulldozers. The West had chopped our world up into colonies, and smiled upon us with its awful schizophrenic perfidy. It told us to separate God and State, to separate Mind and Body, to separate Reason and Faith. It had torn us apart.

I stood shaking as the first set ended. The band vanished backstage, and a single figure approached the microphone. I recognized him as a famous American television comedian, who had abandoned his own career to join Boston.

The man began to joke and clown, his antics seeming to soothe the crowd, which hooted with laughter. This intermission was a wise move on Boston's part, I thought. The level of pain, of intensity, had become unbearable.

It struck me then how much Boston was like the great Khomeini. Boston too had the persona of the Man of Sorrows, the sufferer after justice, the ascetic among corruption, the battler against odds. And the air of the mystic, the adept, at least as far as such a thing was possible in America. I thought of this, and deep fear struck me once again.

I walked through the gates to the Colosseum's outer hall, seeking air and room to think. Others had come out too. They leaned against the wall, men and women, with the look of wrung-out mops. Some smoked cigarettes, others argued over brochures, others simply sat with palsied grins.

Still others wept. These disturbed me most, for these were the ones whose souls seemed stung and opened. Khomeini made men weep like that, tearing aside despair like a bandage from a burn. I walked down the hall, watching them, making mental notes.

I stopped by a woman in dark glasses and a trim business suit. She leaned against the wall, shaking, her face beneath the glasses slick with silent tears. Something about the precision of her styled hair, her cheekbones, struck a memory. I stood beside her, waiting, and recognition came.

"Hello," I said. "We have something in common, I think. You've been covering the Boston tour. For CBS."

She glanced at me once, and away. "I don't know you."

"You're Marjory Cale, the correspondent."

She drew in a breath. "You're mistaken."

" 'Luddite fanatic,' " I said lightly. " 'Rock demagogue.' "

"Go away," she said.

"Why not talk about it? I'd like to know your point of view."

"Go away, you nasty little man."

I returned to the crowd inside. The comedian was now reading at length from the American Bill of Rights, his voice thick with sarcasm. "Freedom of advertising," he said. "Freedom of global network television conglomerates. Right to a speedy and public trial, to be repeated until our lawyers win. A well-regulated militia being necessary, citizens will be issued orbital lasers and aircraft carriers. . . ." No one was laughing.

The crowd was in an ugly mood when Boston reappeared. Even the well-dressed ones now seemed surly and militant, not recognizing themselves as the enemy. Like the Shah's soldiers who at last refused to fire, who threw themselves sobbing at Khomeini's feet.

"You all know this one," Boston said. With his wife, he raised a banner, one of the first flags of the American Revolution. It bore a coiled snake, a native American viper, with the legend: DON'T TREAD ON ME. A sinister, scaly rattling poured from the depths of a synthesizer, merging with the crowd's roar of recognition, and a sprung, loping rhythm broke loose. Boston edged back and forth at the stage's rim, his eyes fixed, his long neck swaying. He shook himself like a man saved from drowning and leaned into the microphone.

"We know you own us/ You step upon us We feel the onus/ But here's a bonus/ Today I see/ So enemy/ Don't tread on me/ Don't tread on me. . . ." Simple words, fitting each beat with all the harsh precision of the English language. A chant of raw hostility. The crowd took it up. This was the hatred, the humiliation of a society brought low. Americans. Somewhere within them conviction still burned. The conviction they had always had: that they were the only real people on our planet. The chosen ones, the Light of the World, the Last Best Hope of Mankind, the Free and the Brave, the crown of creation. They would have killed for him. I knew, someday, they would.

I was called to Boston's suite at two o'clock that morning. I had shaved and showered, dashed on the hotel's complimentary cologne. I wanted to smell like an American.

Boston's guards frisked me, carefully and thoroughly, outside the elevator. I submitted with good grace.

Boston's suite was crowded. It had the air of an election victory. There were many politicians, sipping glasses of bubbling alcohol, laughing, shaking hands. Miami's Mayor was there, with half his City Council. I recognized a young woman Senator, speaking urgently into her pocket phone, her large freckled breasts on display in an evening gown.

I mingled, listening. Men spoke of Boston's ability to raise funds, of the growing importance of his endorsement. More of Boston's guards stood in corners, arms folded, eyes hidden, their faces stony. A black man distributed lapel buttons with the face of Martin Luther King on a background of red and white stripes. The wall-sized television played a tape of the first Moon Landing. The sound had been turned off, and people all over the world, in the garb of the 1960's, mouthed silently at the camera, their eyes shining.

It was not until four o'clock that I finally met the star himself. The party had broken up by then, the politicians politely ushered out, their vows of undying loyalty met with discreet smiles. Boston was in a back bedroom with his wife, and a pair of aides.

"Sayyid," he said, and shook my hand. In person he seemed smaller, older, his hybrid face, with stage makeup, beginning to peel.

"Dr. Boston," I said.

He laughed freely. "Sayyid, my friend. You'll ruin my street fucking credibility."

"I want to tell the story as I see it," I said.

"Then you'll have to tell it to me," he said, and turned briefly to an aide. He dictated in a low, staccato voice, not losing his place in our conversation, simply loosing a burst of thought. " 'Let us be frank. Before I showed an interest you were ready to sell the ship for scrap iron. This is not an era for supertankers. They are dead tech, smokestack-era garbage. Reconsider my offer.' " The secretary pounded keys. Boston looked at me again, returning the searchlight of his attention.

"You plan to buy a supertanker?" I said.

"I wanted an aircraft carrier," he said, smiling.

"They're all in mothballs, but the Feds frown on selling nuke power plants to private citizens."

"We will make the tanker into a floating stadium," Plisetskaya put in. She sat slumped in a padded chair, wearing satin lounge pajamas. A half-filled ashtray on the chair's arm reeked of strong tobacco.

"Ever been inside a tanker?" Boston said. "Huge. Great acoustics." He sat suddenly on the sprawling bed and pulled off his snakeskin boots. "So, Sayyid. Tell me this story of yours."

"You graduated magna cum laude from Rutgers with a doctorate in political science," I said. "In five years."

"That doesn't count," Boston said, yawning behind his hand. "That was before rock and roll beat my brains out."

"You ran for state office in Massachusetts," I said. "You lost a close race. Two years later you were touring with your first band—Swamp Fox. You were an immediate success. You became involved in political fund-raising, recruiting your friends in the music industry. You started your own record label. You helped organize Rock for Detente, where you met your wife-to-be. Your romance was front-page news on both continents. Record sales soared."

"You left out the first time I got shot at," Boston said. "That's more interesting; Val and I are old hat by now."

He paused, then burst out at the second secretary. " 'I urge you once again not to go public. You will find yourselves vulnerable to a leveraged buyout. I've told you that Evans is an agent of Marubeni. If he brings your precious plant down around your ears, don't come crying to me.' "

"February 1998," I said. "An anti-communist zealot fired on your bus."

"You're a big fan, Sayyid."

"Why are you afraid of multinationals?" I said. "That was the American preference, wasn't it? Global trade, global economics?"

"We screwed up," Boston said. "Things got out of hand."

"Out of American hands, you mean?"

"We used our companies as tools for development," Boston said, with the patience of a man instructing a child. "But then our lovely friends in South America refused to pay their debts. And our staunch allies in Europe and Japan signed the Geneva Economic Agreement and decided to crash the dollar. And our friends in the Arab countries decided not to be countries any more, but one almighty Caliphate, and, just for good measure, they pulled all their oil money out of our banks and into Islamic ones. How could we compete? They were holy banks, and our banks pay interest, which is a sin, I understand." He paused, his eyes glittering, and fluffed curls from his neck. "And all that time, we were already in hock to our fucking ears to pay for being the world's policeman."

"So the world betrayed your country," I said. "Why?"

He shook his head. "Isn't it obvious? Who needs St. George when the dragon is dead? Some Afghani fanatics scraped together enough plutonium for a Big One, and they blew the dragon's fucking head off. And the rest of the body is still convulsing, ten years later. We bled ourselves white competing against Russia, which was stupid, but we'd won. With two giants, the world trembles. One giant, and the midgets can drag it down. So that's what happened. They took us out, that's all. They own us."

"It sounds very simple," I said.

He showed annoyance for the first time. "Valya says you've read our newspapers. I'm not telling you anything new. Should I lie about it? Look at the figures, for Christ's sake. The EEC and Japanese use their companies for money pumps, they're sucking us dry, deliberately. You don't look stupid, Sayyid. You know very well what's happening to us, anyone in the Third World does."

"You mentioned Christ," I said. "You believe in Him?"

Boston rocked back onto his elbows and grinned. "Do you?"

"Of course. He is one of our Prophets. We call Him Isa."

Boston looked cautious. "I never stand between a man and his God." He paused. "We have a lot of respect for the Arabs, truly. What they've accomplished. Breaking free from the world economic system, returning to authentic local tradition. . . . You see the parallels."

"Yes," I said. I smiled sleepily, and covered my mouth as I yawned. "Jet lag. Your pardon, please. These are only questions my editors would want me to ask. If I were not an admirer, a fan as you say, I would not have this assignment."

He smiled and looked at his wife. Plisetskaya lit another cigarette and leaned back, looking skeptical. Boston grinned. "So the sparring's over, Charlie?"

"I have every record you've made," I said. "This is not a job for hatchets." I paused, weighing my words. "I still believe that our Caliph is a great man. I support the Islamic Resurgence. I am Muslim. But I think, like many others, that we have gone a bit too far in closing every window to the West. Rock and roll is a Third World music at heart. Don't you agree?"

"Sure," Boston said, closing his eyes. "Do you know the first words spoken in independent Zimbabwe? Right after they ran up the flag."

"No."

He spoke out blindly, savoring the words. "Ladies and gentlemen. Bob Marley. And the Wailers."

"You admire him."

"Comes with the territory," said Boston, flipping a coil of hair.

"He had a black mother, a white father. And you?"

"Oh, both my parents were shameless mongrels like myself," Boston said. "I'm a second-generation nothing-in-particular. An American." He sat up, knotting his hands, looking tired. "You going to stay with the tour a while, Charlie?" He spoke to a secretary. "Get me a Kleenex." The woman rose.

"Till Philadelphia," I said. "Like Marjory Cale."

Plisetskaya blew smoke, frowning. "You spoke to that woman?"

"Of course. About the concert."

"What did the bitch say?" Boston asked lazily. His aide handed him tissues and cold cream. Boston dabbed the Kleenex and smeared make-up from his face.

"She asked me what I thought. I said it was too loud," I said.

Plisetskaya laughed once, sharply. I smiled. "It was quite amusing. She said that you were in good form. She said that I should not be so tight-arsed."

" 'Tight-arsed'?" Boston said, raising his brows. Fine wrinkles had appeared beneath the greasepaint. "She said that?"

"She said we Muslims were afraid of modern life. Of new experience. Of course I told her that this wasn't true. Then she gave me this." I reached into one of the pockets of my vest and pulled out a flat packet of aluminum foil.

"Marjory Cale gave you cocaine?" Boston asked.

"Wyoming Flake," I said. "She said she has friends who grow it in the Rocky Mountains." I opened the packet, exposing a little mound of white powder. "I saw her use some. I think it will help my jet lag." I pulled my chair closer to the bedside phone-table. I shook the packet out, with much care, upon the shining mahogany surface. The tiny crystals glittered. It was finely chopped.

I opened my wallet and removed a crisp thousand-dollar bill. The actor-president smiled benignly. "Would this be appropriate?"

"Tom does not do drugs," said Plisetskaya, too quickly.

"Ever do coke before?" Boston asked. He threw a wadded tissue to the floor.

"I hope I'm not offending you," I said. "This is Miami, isn't it? This is America." I began rolling the bill, clumsily.

"We are not impressed," said Plisetskaya sternly. She ground out her cigarette. "You are being a rube, Charlie. A hick from the NIC's."

"There is a lot of it," I said, allowing doubt to creep into my voice. I reached in my pocket, then divided the pile in half with the sharp edge of a developed slide. I arranged the lines neatly. They were several centimeters long.

I sat back in the chair. "You think it's a bad idea? I admit, this is new to me." I paused. "I have drunk wine several times, though the *Koran* forbids it."

One of the secretaries laughed. "Sorry," she said. "He drinks wine. That's cute."

I sat and watched temptation dig into Boston. Plisetskaya shook her head.

"Cale's cocaine," Boston mused. "Man."

We watched the lines together for several seconds, he and I. "I did not mean to be trouble," I said. "I can throw it away."

"Never mind Val," Boston said. "Russians chain-smoke." He slid across the bed.

I bent quickly and sniffed. I leaned back, touching my nose. The cocaine quickly numbed it. I handed the paper tube to Boston. It was done in a moment. We sat back, our eyes watering.

"Oh," I said, drug seeping through tissue. "Oh, this is excellent."

"It's good toot," Boston agreed. "Looks like you get an extended interview."

We talked through the rest of the night, he and I.

My story is almost over. From where I sit to write this, I can hear the sound of Boston's music, pouring from the crude speakers of a tape pirate in the bazaar. There is no doubt in my mind that Boston is a great man.

I accompanied the tour to Philadelphia. I spoke to Boston several times during the tour, though never again with the first fine rapport of the drug. We parted as friends, and I spoke well of him in my article for *Al-Ahram.* I did not hide what he was, I did not hide his threat. But I did not malign him. We see things differently. But he is a man, a child of God like all of us.

His music even saw a brief flurry of popularity in Cairo, after the article. Children listen to it, and then turn to other things, as children will. They like the sound, they dance, but the words mean nothing to them. The thoughts, the feelings, are alien.

This is the *dar-al-harb,* the land of peace. We have peeled the hands of the West from our throat, we draw breath again, under God's sky. Our Caliph is a good man, and I am proud to serve him. He reigns, he does not rule. Learned men debate in the *Majlis,* not squabbling like politicians, but seeking truth in dignity. We have the world's respect.

We have earned it, for we paid the martyr's price. We Muslims are one in five in all the world, and as long as ignorance of God persists, there will always be the struggle, the *jihad.* It is a proud thing to be one of the Caliph's *Mujihadeen.* It is not that we value our lives lightly. But that we value God more.

Some call us backward, reactionary. I laughed at that when I carried the powder. It had the subtlest of poisons: a living virus. It is a tiny thing, bred in secret labs, and in itself does no harm. But it spreads throughout the body, and it bleeds out a chemical, a faint but potent trace that carries the rot of cancer.

The West can do much with cancer these days, and a wealthy man like Boston can buy much treatment. They may cure the first attack, or the second. But within five years he will surely be dead. People will mourn his loss. Perhaps they will put his image on a stamp, as they did for Bob Marley. Marley, who also died of systemic cancer; whether by the hand of God or man, only Allah knows.

I have taken the life of a great man; in trapping him I took my own life as well, but that means nothing. I am no one. I am not even Sayyid Qutb, the Martyr and theorist of Resurgence, though I took that great man's name as cover. I meant only respect, and believe I have not shamed his memory.

I do not plan to wait for the disease. The struggle continues in the Muslim lands of what was once the Soviet Union. There the Believers ride in Holy Jihad, freeing their ancient lands from the talons of Marxist atheism. Secretly, we send them carbines, rockets, mortars, and nameless men. I shall be one of them; when I meet death, my grave will be nameless also. But nothing is nameless to God.

God is Great; men are mortal, and err. If I have done wrong, let the Judge of Men decide. Before His Will, as always, I submit.

(1989)

PAUL PREUSS

HALF-LIFE

The open window is a bright rectangle of sunshine, filled with scintillating disks of green—at this distance my worn-out eyes will no longer resolve the leaves of the poplars, stirring in the summer air.

Beyond the trees, the Alps are a smudge of blue streaked with white; flecks of white, trembling randomly upward through the cobalt sky, detach themselves from the greater white that is the crown of Mont Blanc. Could I focus on these specks I would surely see them for what they are, small live things, cabbage butterflies. But cataracts and crude operations have almost destroyed my sight, and I imagine the fluttering specks not as butterflies but as bits of my soul, leaving me, fragment by fragment.

"Madame . . ."

I feel the doctor's fingers against my cheek and turn to let him remove the thermometer from my dry mouth. He takes it off somewhere into the shadows and studies it in silence. When I stretch numb fingers to him, he surrenders the instrument without protest.

I raise my head and fumble for my thick-lensed glasses, fishing them up by the cord around my neck. With the glass tube of the thermometer at just the right distance, I manage to focus on its scale.

"Thirty-nine degrees." Is that pitiful whisper my own voice? "It's lower." My head falls back against the pillow, my hand drops to the stiff sheets, and I suppose the thermometer rolls away. The doctor retrieves it before it falls to the floor. I am too tired to be ashamed.

"A good sign, Mé." Eve is sitting close to the bed, almost leaning on it, as she has taken to doing these last few days; her need to reassure me is urgent. "The fever has broken. You're going to be better now."

"It was not the medicines," I say, for I want no more of these ignorant and painful attempts to cure me. My eyes seek the radiant window. "It was the pure air, the altitude. . . ."

"Yes. It was a good idea for us to get out of Paris, wasn't it?" My daughter reaches to take my hand; I picture what I cannot see clearly, her dark, solemn features, her glossy brown hair pulled back. Her face is an echo of mine when I was her age, her darkness a sort of negative of my paleness, and I think—not only because her darkness is Pierre's—she is more beautiful than I was.

My once-bright hair is now sparse and white and so fine I cannot control it; my face is wrinkled, my mouth still set in the straight line that formed there, without my realizing it, when I left childhood behind—but now deeply bracketed by creases. How stern I must seem! I fix my daughter with that frightening, that demanding stare; a question plagues me. "Was it done with radium or mesothorium?"

"I . . . I don't . . ."

It comes back. "The decay product of the emanation. My mind must be wandering." The more important question recurs. "When are they returning from Stockholm? They promised to see me."

"Who promised, sweet?"

"Irène and Fred. Fred made a very provocative speech." I try to mimic my son-in-law, but my thin voice does no justice to his baritone: " 'We are entitled to think that scientists, building up or shattering elements at will, will be able to bring about transmutations of an explosive type.' Where is the evidence to support such a statement?"

Eve has no answer and clearly thinks I am raving. She reaches for my hand, but I irritably withdraw it. "It was printed in all the newspapers," I grumble.

The point, of course, is not that Fred *has* no evidence for these speculations, but that he and Irène have not presented the evidence to *me.*

"I'm afraid I have not seen the reports," Eve whispers.

"Well, well, then, Eve . . ." I have never exhibited the slightest favoritism between my daughters, but I suspect that in the midst of her love, Eve—the musician, the writer—resents me for not telling her how to conduct her life so as to please me better. Irène never needed to be told.

Why am I suddenly so weary, so cold? I sense Eve gently lifting the thick glasses from my closed eyes. She does not realize that they weigh nothing.

The door opens and I hear Dr. Lowys's brisk tread leaving the room, followed a moment later by Eve's light footsteps. Relieved of their presence, I allow my eyes to reopen. The massed leaves outside my window cast their shadows against the white enameled wall, gathering and organizing themselves like dark figures on a cinema screen, tentative and jerky. . . .

Horseshoes clatter on the cobbles. Iron tires screech. A gruff voice mumbles: "This Curie's place? We got a consignment from the station."

"Pierre," I call out joyously. "It has arrived—come see!" I sweep the flyaway hair from my eyes; the laboratory smock flaps behind my long black skirts as I dash into the paved courtyard, slick with dew in the weak Parisian sunlight. Workmen are already pulling the heavy sacks from the back of the coal wagon, piling them on the cobblestones.

Dear rough-bearded, close-cropped Pierre emerges from the shed that serves us both as laboratory and stands with hands clasped behind him, observing the unloading of the sacks with a proprietary air—or thinking of something else altogether, as he so often is.

Pierre and I have been married for three years. He is older than me, certainly wiser; he and his brother were making discoveries of fundamental importance while I was still self-exiled to Poland's sugar-beet plains, working as a governess and hoarding my rubles to send my sister to medical school. But my constitution is hardier than his, this rugged-looking Frenchman of mine, and it is my choice to do the heavy work.

And my ideas have managed to capture his imagination; he has married his researches as well as his person to mine, and science consumes our lives. Our newborn Irène is necessarily in the care of her nurse and her loving grandfather, Pierre's father, for most hours of the day. The sad set of her mouth is already fixed, earlier than was my own.

The heap of sacks in the courtyard rapidly grows into a miniature mountain of pitchblende, the ore already processed to remove the uranium metal, which is useful in ceramic glazes. But in these sacks of worthless residues, miniscule amounts of other elements remain, or so we are determined to prove: we have named them polonium and radium, and they surpass uranium in their power to charge the air and make shadows on sealed photographic plates—the property to which I have applied the term *radioactivity.* The challenge is to isolate our new elements chemically, in order to establish their actual existence.

Unable to restrain my enthusiasm for this stuff which has cost us so much of our meager earnings in freight charges, I take a knife from one of the workmen and slash into the sackcloth. Soft brown earth spills onto the paving stones. I plunge my hands into the rich dirt and scoop it up in my fingers; the loamy soil is mixed with pine needles from Bohemia, from the mines of St. Joachimsthal.

It is the first day of a labor that will consume my strength for four years. . . .

Eve follows the doctor down the hall of the sanatorium. In her mother's room she has seen what she has seen, and she knows what she has to do; ahead she hears familiar voices: the doctor's polite murmur, and the smooth, assured baritone that could only be that of her brother-in-law.

"We arrived last night," Frédéric is saying. "Would it be convenient to see her now?"

"I'm Dr. Lowys," says the doctor. "And you are the Professors Joliot-Curie . . . ?"

As Eve comes into the waiting room Frédéric turns to her, mildly surprised. He is a tall, thin-faced, clean-shaven man; Eve thinks his looks worthy of a cinema star; he is as handsome as Chevalier. She hesitates. The sight of him with Irène stirs vague excitement, edged with coppery resentment. She avoids his glance, looking past him instead to the wall calendar behind him. July 1934. It occurs to her—rather inanely, she reflects—that the weather could not be more glorious.

Clutching her notebook, she pushes herself forward again, moving toward her older sister—Irène is as dark and beautiful as she, with an even more solemn expression—and they embrace, quickly and efficiently.

"Pardon us, please," says Frédéric, turning back to the doctor with some embarrassment; he is not the sort to forget the social amenities. "Under the circumstances . . ."

"Of course. Madame Curie was just speaking of the two of you. You have been in Stockholm?"

"Stockholm?" Frédéric looks at Eve with a quizzical expression. "What's this about Stockholm?"

"Mé is confused," Eve tells him. "She was quoting a speech you supposedly made—something about the destructive power of the elements. As if you were accepting the Nobel Prize."

"She was remembering Pé's Nobel speech," Irène says.

"No," says Eve, "I think she dreamed that her hopes for the two of you had come true."

"Well, certainly we share those hopes," says Frédéric. "What do you say, doctor? Is she . . . ?"

"If you would like, you may just step in and look at her—but please don't disturb her rest."

Irène turns implacable eyes upon the doctor; one who did not know her as well as Eve would assume that the grief that shone from them was for her mother's sake, but Irène has worn this expression of loss since early childhood. "She is dying, then."

The doctor nods. "It cannot be long. Her temperature is falling rapidly."

"But she does not know, and she must not be allowed to suspect," Eve says vehemently. "If we were all to gather suddenly at her bedside, she would realize . . ."

"Eve, we will not waken her," Frédéric says firmly.

They enter the sickroom. Eve promptly resumes her chair at her mother's bedside, watching them.

Frédéric stands in the sunny room watching Marie's labored sleep. Tears pool in his eyes. His natural warmth—Eve can feel it—makes him want to go to her, to this woman who has been his beloved teacher, the founder and chief of the institute where he has worked all his professional life. He wants to take her frail body in his arms.

Fred tenses to move, but Irène's hand on his arm restrains him. "Remember our promise." Her expression is inscrutable. They stay a moment longer, watching Marie in silence, then Irène tugs at Frédéric's sleeve and they creep silently out of the room.

Eve, watching them go, releases a tiny sigh and returns her burning attention to the motionless shape of her mother on the bed.

The shadows on my wall shift and coalesce. It is night. I take Pierre's hand as we stand alone in the empty shed. On all sides, on every shelf and tabletop, bottles and test tubes glow with blue luminescence.

Those four years, those tons of residue—when the weather was good, we processed it outside, in the cramped courtyard of our makeshift laboratory. When the weather was bad, we breathed the fumes indoors, under the leaking glass roof. In all seasons, in all weathers, I shoveled and carried and poured, stirring the boiling caldrons with an iron rod as tall as I.

When the crude ore separations were complete, we patiently coaxed the metallic salts to precipitate, working on the rude pine benches, using the glassware and electrical apparatus we had made for ourselves. Eventually we obtained enough of the pure chloride—a few tenths of a gram laboriously separated from each ton of brown dirt—for the chemical proof that radium is indeed the new element we have claimed.

I squeeze his hand.

"Pierre, do you remember saying you hoped that when we found radium, it would have a lovely color?"

"I got more than I hoped for, certainly." His dark eyes sparkle in the glowworm darkness. "These are like fairy lights."

"Also useful lights! With a little of the salt, I have been able to read in darkness with perfect ease."

Pierre never condescends to me, but he laughs now. "It will not replace gas or electricity, I think—in all this time we have made less than a gram of it."

We know that the concentrated salts of radium glow with more than visible light. The glass vessels in which the chloride is stored turn a lovely purple. The cotton wadding in which these vessels rest eventually crumbles to powder. Radium burns the flesh without heat, as our colleague Becquerel and I discovered accidentally—an effect Pierre established somewhat more methodically, giving himself a festering wound on the arm which did not heal for weeks.

The physicians tell us that this intense radiation penetrates deep into the body, and that dense tumors absorb more of the radiation than ordinary healthy tissue. These discoveries, we are delighted to learn, suggest new treatments for disease.

Our friends urge us to patent our methods for radium extraction. We agree that we could not do such a thing; the benefits of science are not to be diluted by the quest for profit. . . .

Frédéric and Irène stand in the sanatorium's sunny anteroom, where Eve has introduced them—at their insistence—to the distinguished specialist from Geneva. The man stands nervously by, his coat already over his arm and his bag already in hand.

"The first thing I did was to review the blood assays," he is explaining, "and I found that the count of white corpuscles and of red alike were falling rapidly."

"What could that mean?" Frédéric asks.

"I reassured madame that it was not the previously diagnosed gallstones, as she seemed to fear, and that we would perform no unnecessary surgery."

"Very well, then," Irène says impatiently. "And your diagnosis?"

He pauses to hum a little, deep in his throat, before he announces, "Pernicious anemia in its extreme form. I instituted what means of treatment were available, but as you see I was called too late. Much too late. I'm afraid I must now excuse myself. Sir. Madame." The doctor moves jerkily toward the door. "My taxi . . ."

Eve does not fail to note Irène's skeptical eyebrow, raised as she watches the doctor depart.

Nor does Frédéric. He shakes his head at Irène. "A physician of his stature, a patient of hers . . . one can hardly blame him for his discomfort."

Irène stares at the potted palm in the corner of the room, then studies the geometric pattern of the faded Shiraz carpet on the floor. She turns her dark stare upon her younger sister. "So. We are barred from her room."

Eve flushes. "Mé clings to the belief that she has a passing fever. If she sees us all lined up like mourners . . ."

"Eve has reason, I think," Frédéric says, insinuating himself solemnly into the sisters' broken argument.

Irène nods once, sharply. "Well, Fred . . . do you have the proofs of the paper with you?"

"Yes. They are in my case."

"Shall we look at them?" she suggests. "While we are waiting?"

"If we can take a walk outside first. I must have a cigarette if you expect me to get any thinking done."

They leave Eve standing in the anteroom, her cheeks rosy with apprehension. She turns slowly and walks toward the sickroom, where time and her mother dream entwined dreams.

Pierre's voice reaches me, muffled and far away. "Will I see you at the laboratory?"

"Too much to do today." I am upstairs, feeding Eve, planning how I will do all today's necessary errands. "Don't get wet."

Pierre slams the door behind him and hurries out into the blustery weather. April is wet this year, 1906. . . .

He walks beside the rain-swept Seine, toward the university.

Lunch with the science faculty in the rue Danton—the subject is laboratory safety—then a futile trip to his publisher, closed down by a strike . . . now he is heading toward the river again, toward the laboratory, unexpectedly early, with the prospect of a good afternoon's work ahead of him. The rue Dauphine is crowded with traffic, its sidewalks too narrow for umbrella-carrying pedestrians to pass without jostling, and there is danger of receiving an umbrella's rib-end in the eye. Pierre steps off the curb, following a horse-drawn cab. The rain comes down harder; the surface of the street, freshly paved with asphalt, is black and slick. The blind black enclosure of the high cab prevents him from seeing ahead. Why is the driver dawdling?

I am with Pierre, hovering a little above his shoulder, and I can see what he cannot, the iron-tired freight wagon loaded to the top with bundles of clothing, which has just entered the crowded street, crossing the quai from the Pont Neuf, drawn by two young and windy horses.

Lost in thought, daydreaming again, Pierre forgets where he is—I try to scream, to warn him, but no sound emerges from the airy O of my mouth—as impatiently he steps out from behind the slow cab and collides with the oncoming team of horses. His umbrella flies from his grip. He clutches at the harness of the nearest horse to prevent himself from falling, but the steaming beast rears up, startled, and Pierre's feet slip on the wet pavement. As he falls the onlookers shout with horror, giving voice to my voiceless agony. The wagon driver hauls back on the reins with all his strength, but the horses are wild with fear, for the street has erupted in panicked cries.

The horses clatter over Pierre, past him. He lies in the middle of their path, untouched by their iron-shod hooves. The front wheels of the wagon grind into the pavement on either side of him. He lies still, safe. Seconds more . . .

There is to be no miracle. The left rear wheel rolls over his head, crushes his skull into sixteen fragments, spatters his brain in the gutter. Already my despairing consciousness has wheeled away into the low-lying clouds—

—back to our home, to await the arrival of his body at my door. . . .

This body now on the bench is muddy like his; its head is a mass of blood-soaked bandages like his, but ten years have passed since I held Pierre's crushed head in my arms, and this is a boy in uniform, still barely alive.

I arrange the X-ray source and check the current from the van's generator. Irène, eighteen years old—intransigent, darkly beautiful—holds the plates. A surgeon stands by, his long apron painted with blood like a corner butcher's, red on brown from ankle to chest. In a few minutes the images of the shell fragments will appear on the developed photographic negatives, sharp and black; knowing where to cut, the surgeon will cut with somewhat more precision than he is accustomed to.

The young men are dying in the indescribable muck of Verdun and the Somme, dying by the tens of thousands, by the hundreds of thousands, eventually by the millions. Of the French alone, nearly two million men will be counted dead or will have vanished into the liquefied earth by this war's end.

I have established two hundred radiological stations. My radiological corps numbers twenty mobile X-ray vans, including the Renault I drive myself. In Paris I supervise the preparation of ampules of radium emanation and train others in their use as a radiation source. X rays were not my speciality, but in the interests of the wounded I have learned what I need to know.

This form of radiation too will save lives. I will see to it.

"I irradiate the target with alpha rays from the source." It is Fred's voice, speaking to Irène as he leans over the table—

—but he is not here, he could not be here, we have not met him yet. "The Geiger counter is crackling like crazy," he says, and indeed there is a sound like frying sausage—"but when I take the source away from the target . . ."

The frying continues. "The counter ought to stop," says Irène. "The target is still emitting."

I am somewhere halfway between myself and darkness, with no sense of where I am in space, but I have a sudden conviction of where I am in time. It is less than a year ago from now, the fall of 1933. I watch as my daughter and son-in-law bend to their experimental equipment: a polonium source, an aluminum foil target, an ionization chamber. . . .

"I'll do it again," he says. "Mark the time."

Irène looks at her watch and listens endless minutes until the Geiger counter's clicks drop off, becoming indistinguishable from the normal background level. "Perhaps a few seconds over ten minutes."

"It's been just that every time," he says. "It falls off as a succession of half-lives."

"Then so it must be."

"But by what sequence? None of the known isotopes . . ."

"If the aluminum is capturing the alpha particle, then immediately emitting a neutron . . ."

"Then decaying to . . . ?"

The answer would be a new isotope of phosphorus, but she does not say it. "What if something's wrong with the counters?" she says instead, abruptly ending the speculation.

He does not argue with her. "Gentner's a specialist, let's have him verify that the instruments are in working order." Fred straightens his shoulders, backing away from the equipment with reluctance. He smiles his dark-eyed smile. "For now, let's be off—to deal with that damned dinner. For the sake of the institute, of course."

"Don't pretend to be so glum, Fred." My daughter grants him as much of a smile as she can manage. "You are as much a socializer as a scientist."

"I prefer to think of myself as a social*ist*," he says happily, shrugging off his laboratory coat.

They are soon gone, leaving me, and the place is dark, except for the glowing bottles and tubes. . . .

This is not the shed, long since torn down. This is the Radium Institute of the University of Paris, at number 1 rue Pierre Curie; the Curie name is carved in stone over the entrance. There are trees in the courtyard; the rooms have high ceilings and smooth white plastered walls, and the basic equipment of a good chemistry laboratory is to be found here. This is the place I have built in Pierre's name.

Fred and Irène know what they have found, but they will not permit themselves to believe it. Not yet. They have been too often humiliated—that *annus mirabilis* of physics, 1932, held no wonders for them. They had discovered the positron but failed to realize it; an American had claimed the prize. They had discovered the neutron but failed to realize it; an Englishman had claimed the prize. But this time . . .

When they return from their dinner party, there is a note on the bench from Gentner: "The Geiger-Müller counters are in good working order."

To see the look on Fred's face is as good as reading his firm English prose in *Nature* for the first time, when he announces their triumph to the British, to the Americans, to the world: "Our latest experiments have shown a very striking fact: when an aluminum foil is irradiated on a polonium preparation, the emission of positrons does not cease immediately when the active preparation is removed. The foil remains radioactive and the emission of radiation decays exponentially as for an ordinary radio-element. . . .

"The transmutation . . . has given birth to new radio-elements. . . ."

This time they will not fail to claim the prize. . . .

Satisfied, I allow myself to open my eyes. Eve looks up from her ink-smudged notebook and leans forward, willing herself not to intrude, but listening for any word that I might have for her.

From the lawn the voices of Fred and Irène float through the open window, distant and indistinct, and I catch the pungent odor of Turkish tobacco. Eve suppresses a spasm of ill temper. What if Frédéric and Irène disturb me with their distant conversation, she is thinking. What if I smell his cigarette? What will she do about that? Eve can hardly slam the window shut or shout at them to be quiet. What will she do about her sister and brother-in-law? What will she do about her love and jealousy?

No matter; my eyes are closing again. Eve goes back to her writing. She believes that I am asleep, but I am not. Instead, my consciousness has worked some slack in its mooring; I seem to be able to take up a stance quite apart from my own body. The thought neither thrills me nor disturbs me; it is a thing to be observed.

I am looking down upon my wasted self lying on the high white bed in the sunny white room. Beside the bed, my weary younger daughter, hunched over her notebook, is at work on the biography of Madame Professor Marie Sklodowska Curie. She cannot become an extension of her mother, as Irène did, yet with her skill with words she hopes to fix my life on the page. I see the repetitious phrases she has copied into her notebook, as distant from me but as sharp as images seen through a reversed telescope; they are inscriptions from the letters she and Irène wrote to me as children: "Darling Mé," "My Sweet darling," "Sweet Mé. . . ."

On the floor nearby rests a pair of soft, ankle-high Navaho moccasins—my most comfortable footgear, given to me when I visited the Grand Canyon. Outside the window, Fred is still talking—he is so much better at it than the rest of us—and I can hear him quite distinctly:

". . . I will never forget the expression of intense joy which came over her when Irène and I showed her the first artificially radioactive element in a little glass tube. I can still see her taking in her fingers (which were already burnt with radium) this little tube containing the radioactive compound—as yet one in which the activity was very weak. To verify what we had told her she held it near a Geiger-Müller counter, and she could hear the rate meter giving off a great many clicks. . . ."

I swiftly rejoin myself, reminded of an important matter. "Eve! The paragraphing of the chapters ought to be done all alike."

Eve looks up, startled. "What, Mé?"

I have frightened her, but never mind. "The paragraphs about artificial elements were added so late. I worry that . . ."

"Please don't worry," Eve says, soothing me. "It will be a fine edition."

"Yes, yes." My voice hardly troubles the air. "See to it." I know she will see to it; it is the sort of thing she cares for. So I dart off, clear out the window, to hear what Fred is going on about—

". . . As Madame Curie put it, it was like a return to the glorious days of the old laboratory. This was doubtless the last great satisfaction of her life. . . ."

Fred too! Well, I did say that about the glorious old days, but Fred is too bold! As if there were to be no more great satisfactions in this life. As if I am to be spoken of only in the past tense.

Is it in irritation, then, that I fly on toward the snows of Mont Blanc, as fitfully as one of the little white butterflies that tumble through the summer air, leaving Fred to stroll and smoke his cigarette and pontificate?

I am caught on an updraft and mount swiftly higher. Soon the air grows cold and thin, and still I soar. Down there, the cold is creeping up the shriveled limbs that no longer contain me; even my numb fingers, normally insensitive to temperature, feel the cold.

I have the unsettling sensation that the Earth is rearranging itself, down below.

I can see nothing distinct, but my senses are far from numb. There is a tang in the air, tantalizing, familiar—the scent of sagebrush. I know it from that interminable train ride through the American west, across the furred plains and through the skeletal mountains.

A voice comes to me in the darkness, booming and harsh, stripped of its resonant frequencies by crude electronics. At first I am reminded of the excruciating speeches I sat through on my American tours; are any people more lavish than the Americans in their public displays of affection? Even their president, who was among the worst . . .

But this voice, rolling in echoing waves as if across vast open spaces, has nothing to say. It only counts.

Three. Two. One. . . .

A thing boils out of the fragrant dark, an obscene bubble devouring the endless sage flats with its savage glare, flaring across the distant dry mountains. I hear the strangest sound I could have imagined coming out of the darkness: the cheers and hearty laughter of men, a mob of them, watching this excrescence of light.

I feel a great wind and a flush of heat across my cheeks. My butterfly consciousness goes tumbling on the bosom of the wind.

Afterimages are playing inside my eyelids in negative rainbows; meanwhile the joyous shouts become louder, a triumphant chorus mounting like the final movement of Beethoven's Ninth Symphony—

—becoming strident now, sour now, until the voices are no longer joyous, until they have become infused with a quality of questioning, and then of horrid certainty, of agony and terror.

All around, splotches of black liquid are falling. The slick wet pavement of the rue Dauphine which tilted from under Pierre's desperate feet has turned to a bubbling mass of asphalt. People are fleeing along the melting boulevards, toward the boiling river. I have been in this landscape before, this tumble of rubble lit by the candelabra of burning trees; I have looked out upon the no-man's-land of the western front. But this population—these outstretched arms, these uplifted faces—these people are orientals.

Images flicker in front of me like a grainy silent film. I linger on a shadow-picture etched on a granite porch—the image of a whole body, sitting there when it must have been taken by the very thing that took its picture. Then the hot wind takes me.

Through the rolling clouds I hear the denatured metallic voice again: *Three. Two. One. . . .*

A horror of light, bursting upward through layers of cloud, streaking outward along thin cloud layers, discoloring the surface of the ocean.

Three. Two. One. . . .

An ocean heaving itself toward heaven but failing to escape the earth, falling back in a million Niagaras upon the hole in itself that was a coral island.

Tri. Dva. Adin. . . .

A frozen steppe vaporizing in a concussion as of a ravening comet, falling upon the Earth.

Surely these are terrible natural disasters. . . .

Three. Two. One.

"I don't want it! I want to be let alone," cries the feeble old woman on the bed.

Dr. Lowys, the narcotic needle poised in his manicured fingers, looks at Eve.

Her fingers are ink smudged from her scribbling. "Do as she wishes," she whispers.

The doctor lowers the needle. "You should know . . . ," he begins softly.

"I know." Eve abandons her book and gathers her mother's hand into both her own.

The doctor moves to the far side of the bed, reaches out, and takes the stiff and calloused fingers of the old woman who lies there, the old woman who refuses to see the inevitable.

Outside, barred from the room by the fierce solicitude of her younger sister, Irène waits with Frédéric, talking physics.

The death watch goes on for sixteen hours. Only when the sun strikes the high peaks of the Alps does Marie's heart stop beating.

"Madame Pierre Curie died at Sancellemoz on July 4, 1934. The disease was an aplastic pernicious anemia of rapid, feverish development. The bone marrow did not react, probably because it had been injured by a long accumulation of radiations."

She was sixty-six. The true name of her disease was leukemia.

Not until the following year, 1935, were Irène and Frédéric Joliot-Curie awarded the Nobel Prize in chemistry, "for synthesizing new radioactive elements."

In 1956, at the age of fifty-nine, Irène died of leukemia.

In 1958, at the age of fifty-eight, Frédéric died following internal hemorrhaging of uncertain etiology.

In 1906, at the age of forty-six, Pierre Curie died in a street accident. In 1988, as these words are written, Eve Curie is alive and active in various good causes.

In the nature of things, as specified by quantum mechanics, one cannot predict the lifetime of an individual atom. For the radioactive elements, however, one can specify a half-life: the time required, on the average, for half a given population of atoms to decay to another element, or elements—its daughters—by the emission of some collection of alpha particles, electrons, gamma rays, neutrons, positrons, neutrinos, antineutrinos, and so on. Half-lives, mere averages, have been measured with great precision.

The half-life of the most stable isotope of uranium, a naturally occurring element, is four and a half billion years.

The half-life of the most stable isotope of thorium, a naturally occurring element, is fourteen billion years.

The half-life of the most stable isotope of polonium, a naturally occurring element, is 138 days.

The half-life of the most stable isotope of radium, a naturally occurring element, is 1,620 years.

The half-life of the most stable isotope of radon, or "emanation," a naturally occurring element, is three days, nineteen hours, and forty-eight minutes.

The half-life of phosphorus 30, the first known artificially radioactive isotope, is three minutes and fifteen seconds.

The half-life of plutonium 239, the first artificially prepared fissile isotope, is 24,360 years.

The half-life of the human species varies by era and culture; consult appropriate actuarial tables.

The half-life of planets is undetermined; the experimental sample is too small.

(1989)

MARGARET ATWOOD

Homelanding

1. Where should I begin? After all, you have never been there; or if you have, you may not have understood the significance of what you saw, or thought you saw. A window is a window, but there is looking out and looking in. The native you glimpsed, disappearing behind the curtain, or into the bushes, or down the manhole in the mainstreet—my people are shy—may have been only your reflection in the glass. My country specializes in such illusions.

2. Let me propose myself as typical. I walk upright on two legs, and have in addition two arms, with ten appendages, that is to say, five at the end of each. On the top of my head, but not on the front, there is an odd growth, like a species of seaweed. Some think this is a kind of fur, others consider it modified feathers, evolved perhaps from scales like those of lizards. It serves no functional purpose and is probably decorative.

My eyes are situated in my head, which also possess two small holes for the entrance and exit of air, the invisible fluid we swim in, and one larger hole, equipped with bony protuberances called teeth, by means of which I destroy and assimilate certain parts of my surroundings and change them into my self. This is called eating. The things I eat include roots, berries, nuts, fruits, leaves, and the muscle tissues of various animals and fish. Sometimes I eat their brains and glands as well. I do not as a rule eat insects, grubs, eyeballs or the snouts of pigs, though these are eaten with relish in other countries.

3. Some of my people have a pointed but boneless external appendage, in the front, below the navel or midpoint. Others do not. Debate about whether the possession of such a thing is an advantage or disadvantage is still going on. If this item is lacking, and in its place there is a pocket or inner cavern in which fresh members of our community are grown, it is considered impolite to mention it openly to strangers. I tell you this because it is the breach of etiquette most commonly made by tourists.

In some of our more private gatherings, the absence of cavern or prong is politely overlooked, like club feet or blindness. But sometimes a prong and a cavern will collaborate in a dance, or illusion, using mirrors and water, which is always absorbing for the performers but frequently grotesque for the observers. I notice that you have similar customs.

Whole conventions and a great deal of time have recently been devoted to discussions of this state of affairs. The prong people tell the cavern people that the latter are not people at all and are in reality more akin to dogs or potatoes, and the cavern people abuse the prong people for their obsession with images of poking, thrusting, probing and stabbing. Any long object with a hole at the end, out of which various projectiles can be shot, delights them.

I myself—I am a cavern person—find it a relief not to have to worry about climbing over barbed wire fences or getting caught in zippers.

But that is enough about our bodily form.

4. As for the country itself, let me begin with the sunsets, which are long and red, resonant, splendid and melancholy, symphonic you might almost say; as opposed to the short boring sunsets of other countries, no more interesting than a lightswitch. We pride ourselves on our sunsets. "Come and see the sunset," we say to one another. This causes everyone to rush outdoors or over to the window.

Our country is large in extent, small in population, which accounts for our fear of large empty spaces, and also our need for them. Much of it is covered in water, which accounts for our interest in reflections, sudden vanishings, the dissolution of one thing into another. Much of it however is rock, which accounts for our belief in Fate.

In summer we lie about in the blazing sun, almost naked, covering our skins with fat and attempting to turn red. But when the sun is low in the sky and faint, even at noon, the water we are so fond of changes to something hard and white and cold and covers up the ground. Then we cocoon ourselves, become lethargic, and spend much of our time hiding in crevices. Our mouths shrink and we say little.

Before this happens, the leaves on many of our trees turn blood red or lurid yellow, much brighter and more exotic than the interminable green of jungles. We find this change beautiful. "Come and see the leaves," we say, and jump into our moving vehicles and drive up and down past the forests of sanguinary trees, pressing our eyes to the glass.

We are a nation of metamorphs.

Anything red compels us.

5. Sometimes we lie still and do not move. If air is still going in and out of our breathing holes, this is called sleep. If not, it is called death. When a person has achieved death a kind of picnic is held, with music, flowers and food. The person so honoured, if in one piece, and not, for instance,

in shreds or falling apart, as they do if exploded or a long time drowned, is dressed in becoming clothes and lowered into a hole in the ground, or else burnt up.

These customs are among the most difficult to explain to strangers. Some of our visitors, especially the young ones, have never heard of death and are bewildered. They think that death is simply one more of our illusions, our mirror tricks; they cannot understand why, with so much food and music, the people are sad.

But you will understand. You too must have death among you. I can see it in your eyes.

6. I can see it in your eyes. If it weren't for this I would have stopped trying long ago, to communicate with you in this halfway language which is so difficult for both of us, which exhausts the throat and fills the mouth with sand; if it weren't for this I would have gone away, gone back. It's this knowledge of death, which we share, where we overlap. Death is our common ground. Together, on it, we can walk forward.

By now you must have guessed: I come from another planet. But I will never say to you, *Take me to your leaders.* Even I—unused to your ways though I am—would never make that mistake. We ourselves have such beings among us, made of cogs, pieces of paper, small disks of shiny metal, scraps of coloured cloth. I do not need to encounter more of them.

Instead I will say, take me to your trees. Take me to your breakfasts, your sunsets, your bad dreams, your shoes, your nouns. Take me to your fingers; take me to your deaths.

These are worth it. These are what I have come for.

(1990)

KATE WILHELM

And the Angels Sing

Eddie never left the office until one or even two in the morning on Sundays, Tuesdays, and Thursdays. The *North Coast News* came out three times a week, and it seemed to him that no one could publish a paper unless someone in charge was on hand until the press run. He knew that the publisher, Stuart Winkle, didn't particularly care, as long as the advertising was in place, but it wasn't right, Eddie thought. What if something came up, something went wrong? Even out here at the end of the world there could be a late-breaking story that required someone to write it, to see that it got placed. Actually, Eddie's hopes for that event, high six years ago, had diminished to the point of needing conscious effort to recall. In fact, he liked to see his editorials before he packed it in.

This night, Thursday, he read his own words and then bellowed, "Where is she?" She was Ruthie Jenson, and *she* had spelled *frequency* with one *e* and an *a.* Eddie stormed through the deserted outer office, looking for her, and caught her at the door just as she was wrapping her vampire cloak about her thin shoulders. She was thin, her hair was cut too short, too close to her head, and she was too frightened of him. And, he thought with bitterness, she was crazy, or she would not wait around three nights a week for him to catch her at the door and give her hell.

"Why don't you use the goddamn dictionary? Why do you correct my copy? I told you I'd wring your neck if you touched my copy again!"

She made a whimpering noise and looked past him in terror, down the hallway, into the office.

"I . . . I'm sorry. I didn't mean . . ." Fast as quicksilver then, she fled out into the storm that was still howling. He hoped the goddamn wind would carry her to Australia or beyond.

The wind screamed as it poured through the outer office, scattering a few papers, setting a light adance on a chain. Eddie slammed the door against it and surveyed the space around him, detesting every inch of it at the moment. Three desks, the fluttering papers that Mrs. Rondale would heave out because anything on the floor got heaved out. Except dirt; she seemed never to see quite all of it. Next door the presses were running; people were doing things, but the staff that put the paper together had left now. Ruthie was always next to last to go, and then Eddie. He kicked a chair on his way back to his own cubicle, clutching the ink-wet paper in his hand, well aware that the ink was smearing onto skin.

He knew that the door to the pressroom had opened and softly closed again. In there they would be saying Fat Eddie was in a rage. He knew they called him Fat Eddie, or even worse, behind his back, and he knew that no one on Earth cared if the *North Coast News* was a mess except him. He sat at his desk, scowling at the editorial—one of his better ones, he thought—and the word *frequancy* leaped off the page at him; nothing else registered. What he had written was "At this time of year the storms bear down onshore with such regularity, such frequency, that it's as if the sea and air are engaged in the final battle." It got better, but he put it aside and listened to the wind. All evening he had listened to reports from up and down the coast, expecting storm damage, light outages, wrecks, something. At midnight he had decided it was just another Pacific storm and had wrapped up the paper. Just the usual: Highway 101 under water here and there, a tree down here and there, a head-on, no deaths. . . .

The wind screamed and let up, caught its breath and screamed again. Like a kid having a tantrum. And up and down the coast the people were like parents who had seen too many kids having too many tantrums. Ignore it until it goes away and then get on about your business, that was their attitude. Eddie was from Indianapolis, where a storm with eighty-mile-per-hour winds made news. Six years on the coast had not changed that. A storm like this, by God, should make news!

Still scowling, he pulled on his own raincoat, a great black waterproof garment that covered him to the floor. He added his black, wide-brimmed hat and was ready for the weather. He knew that behind his back they called him Mountain Man, when they weren't calling him Fat Eddie. He secretly thought that he looked more like The Shadow than not.

He drove to Connally's Tavern and had a couple of drinks, sitting alone in glum silence, and then offered to drive Truman Cox home when the bar closed at two.

The town of Lewisburg was south of Astoria, north of Cannon Beach, population nine hundred eighty-four. And at two in the morning they were all sleeping, the town blacked out by rain. There were the flickering nightlights at the drugstore, and the lights from the newspaper building, and two traffic lights, although no other traffic moved. Rain pelted the windshield and made a river through Main Street, cascaded down the side streets on the left, came pouring off the mountain on the right. Eddie made the turn onto Third and hit the brakes hard when a figure darted across the street.

"Jesus!" he grunted as the car skidded, then caught and righted itself. "Who was that?"

Truman was peering out into the darkness, nodding. The figure had vanished down the alley behind Sal's Restaurant. "Bet it was the Boland girl, the young one. Not Norma. Following her sister's footsteps."

His tone was not condemnatory, even though everyone knew exactly where those footsteps would lead the kid.

"She sure earned whatever she got tonight," Eddie said with a grunt and pulled up into the driveway of Truman's house. "See you around."

"Yep. Probably will. Thanks for the lift." He gathered himself together and made a dash for his porch.

But he would be soaked anyway, Eddie knew. All it took was a second out in this driving rain. That poor, stupid kid, he thought again as he backed out of the drive, retraced his trail for a block or two, and headed toward his own little house. On impulse he turned back and went down Second Street to see if the kid was still scurrying around; at least he could offer her a lift home. He knew where the Bolands lived, the two sisters, their mother, all in the trade now, apparently. But God, he thought, the little one couldn't be more than twelve.

The numbered streets were parallel to the coastline; the cross streets had become wind tunnels that rocked his car every time he came to one. Second Street was empty, black. He breathed a sigh of relief. He hadn't wanted to get involved anyway, in any manner, and now he could go on home, listen to music for an hour or two, have a drink or two, a sandwich, and get some sleep. If the wind ever let up. He slept very poorly when the wind blew this hard. What he most likely would do was finish the book he was reading, possibly start another one. The wind was good for another four or five hours. Thinking this way, he made another turn or two and then saw the kid again, this time sprawled on the side of the road.

If he had not already seen her once, if he had not been thinking about her, about her sister and mother, if he had been driving faster than five miles an hour, probably he would have missed her. She lay just off the road, facedown. As soon as he stopped and got out of the car, the rain hit his face, streamed from his glasses, blinding him almost. He got his hands on the child and hauled her to the car, yanked open the back door and deposited her inside. Only then he got a glimpse of her face. Not the Boland girl. No one he had ever seen before. And as light as a shadow. He hurried around to the driver's side and got in, but he could no longer see her now from the front seat. Just the lumpish black raincoat that gleamed with water and covered her entirely. He wiped his face, cleaned his glasses, and twisted in the seat; he couldn't reach her, and she did not respond to his voice.

He cursed bitterly and considered his next move. She could be dead, or dying. Through the rain-streaked windshield the town appeared uninhabited. It didn't even have a police station, a clinic, or a hospital. The nearest doctor was ten or twelve miles away, and in this weather. . . . Finally he started the engine and headed for home. He would call the state police from there, he decided. Let them come and collect her. He drove up Hammer Hill to his house and parked in the driveway at the walk that led to the front door. He would open the door first, he had decided, then come back and get the kid; either way he would get soaked, but there was little he could do about that. He moved fairly fast for a large man, but his fastest was not good enough to keep the rain off his face again. If it would come straight down, the way God meant rain to fall, he thought, fumbling with the key in the lock, he would be able to see something. He got the door open, flicked on the light switch, and went back to the car to collect the girl. She was as limp as before and seemed to weigh nothing at all. The slicker she wore was hard to grasp, and he did not want her head to loll about for her to brain herself on the porch rail or the door frame, but she was not easy to carry, and he grunted although her weight was insignificant. Finally he got her inside, and kicked the door shut, and made his way to the bedroom, where he dumped her on the bed.

Then he took off his hat that had been useless, and his glasses that had blinded him with running water, and the raincoat that was leaving a trail of water with every step. He backed off the Navaho rug and out to the kitchen to put the wet coat on a chair, let it drip on the linoleum. He grabbed a handful of paper toweling and wiped his glasses, then returned to the bedroom.

He reached down to remove the kid's raincoat and jerked his hand away again. "Jesus Christ!" he whispered and backed away from her. He heard himself saying it again, and then again, and stopped. He had backed up to the wall, was pressed hard against it. Even from there he could see her clearly. Her face was smooth, without eyebrows, without eyelashes, her nose too small, her lips too narrow, hardly lips at all. What he had thought was a coat was part of her. It started on her head, where hair should have been, went down the sides of her head where ears should have been, down her narrow shoulders, the backs of her arms that seemed too long and thin, almost boneless.

She was on her side, one long leg stretched out, the other doubled up under her. Where there should have been genitalia, there was too much skin, folds of skin.

Eddie felt her stomach spasm; a shudder passed over him. Before, he had wanted to shake her, wake her up, ask questions; now he thought that if she opened her eyes, he might pass out. And he was shivering with cold. Moving very cautiously, making no noise, he edged his way around the room to the door, then out, back to the kitchen where he pulled a bottle of bourbon from a cabinet and poured half a glass that he drank as fast as he could. He stared at his hand. It was shaking.

Very quietly he took off his sodden shoes and placed them at the back door, next to his waterproof boots that he invariably forgot to wear. As soundlessly as possible he crept to the bedroom door and looked at her again. She had moved, was now drawn up in a huddle as if she was as cold as he was. He took a deep breath and began to inch around the wall of the room toward the closet, where he pulled out his slippers with one foot and eased them on, and then tugged on a blanket on a shelf. He had to let his breath out; it sounded explosive to his ears. The girl shuddered and made herself into a tighter ball. He moved toward her slowly, ready to turn and run, and finally was close enough to lay the blanket over her. She was shivering hard. He backed away from her again and this time went to the living room, leaving the door open so that he could see her, just in case. He turned up the thermostat, retrieved his glass from the kitchen, and went to the door again and again to peer inside. He should call the state police, he knew, and made no motion toward the phone. A doctor? He nearly laughed. He wished he had a camera. If they took her away, and they would, there would be nothing to show, nothing to prove she had existed. He thought of her picture on the front page of the *North Coast News* and snorted. *The National Enquirer?* This time he muttered a curse. But she was news. She certainly was news.

Mary Beth, he decided. He had to call someone with a camera, someone who could write a decent story. He dialed Mary Beth, got her answering machine, and hung up, dialed it again. At the fifth call her voice came on. "Who the hell is this, and do you know that it's three in the fucking morning?"

"Eddie Delacort. Mary Beth, get up, get over here, my place, and bring your camera."

"Fat Eddie? What the hell—"

"Right now, and bring plenty of film." He hung up.

A few seconds later his phone rang; he took it off the hook and laid it down on the table. While he waited for Mary Beth, he surveyed the room. The house was small, with two bedrooms, one that he used for an office, on the far side of the living room. In the living room there were two easy chairs covered with fine, dark green leather, no couch, a couple of tables, and many bookshelves, all filled. A long cabinet held his sound equipment, a stereo, hundreds of albums. Everything was neat, arranged for a large man to move about easily, nothing extraneous anywhere. Underfoot was another Navaho rug. He knew the back door was securely locked; the bedroom windows were closed, screens in place. Through the living room was the only way the kid on his bed could get out, and he knew she would not get past him if she woke up and tried to make a run. He nodded, then moved his two easy chairs so that they faced the bedroom; he pulled an end table between them, got another glass, and brought the bottle of bourbon. He sat down to wait for Mary Beth, brooding over the girl in his bed. From time to time the blanket shook hard; a slight movement that was nearly constant suggested that she had not yet warmed up. His other blanket was under her, and he had no intention of touching her again in order to get to it.

Mary Beth arrived as furious as he had expected. She was his age, about forty, graying, with suspicious blue eyes and no makeup. He had never seen her with lipstick on, or jewelry of any kind except for a watch, or in a skirt or dress. That night she was in jeans and a sweatshirt and a bright red hooded raincoat that brought the rainstorm inside as she entered, cursing him. He noted with satisfaction that she had her camera gear. She cursed him expertly as she yanked off her raincoat and was still calling him names when he finally put his hand over her mouth and took her by the shoulder, propelled her toward the bedroom door.

"Shut up and look," he muttered. She was stronger than he had realized and now twisted out of his grasp and swung a fist at him. Then she faced the bedroom. She looked, then turned back to him red-faced and sputtering. "You . . . you got me out . . . a floozy in your bed. . . . So you really do know what that thing you've got is used for! And you want pictures! Jesus God!"

"Shut up!"

This time she did. She peered at his face for a second, turned and looked again, took a step forward, then another. He knew her reaction was to his expression, not the lump on the bed. Nothing of that girl was visible, just the unquiet blanket and a bit of darkness that was not hair but should have been. He stayed at Mary Beth's side, and his caution was communicated to her; she was as quiet now as he was.

At the bed he reached out and gently pulled back the blanket. One of her hands clutched it spasmodically. The hand had four apparently boneless fingers, long and tapered, very pale. Mary Beth exhaled too long, and neither of them moved for what seemed minutes. Finally she reached out and touched the darkness at the girl's shoulder, touched her arm, then her face. Abruptly she pulled back her hand. The girl on the bed was shivering harder than ever, in a tighter ball that hid the many folds of skin at her groin.

"It's cold," Mary Beth whispered.

"Yeah." He put the blanket back over the girl.

Mary Beth went to the other side of the bed, squeezed between it and the wall and carefully pulled the bedspread and blanket free, and put them over the girl also. Eddie took Mary Beth's arm, and they backed out of the bedroom. She sank into one of the chairs he had arranged and automatically held out her hand for the drink he was pouring.

"My God," Mary Beth said softly after taking a large swallow, "what is it? Where did it come from?"

He told her as much as he knew, and they regarded the sleeping figure. He thought the shivering had subsided, but maybe she was just too weak to move so many covers.

"You keep saying it's a she," Mary Beth said. "You know that thing isn't human, don't you?"

Reluctantly he described the rest of the girl, and this time Mary Beth finished her drink. She glanced at her camera bag but made no motion toward it yet. "It's our story," she said. "We can't let them have it until we're ready. Okay?"

"Yeah. There's a lot to consider before we do anything."

Silently they considered. He refilled their glasses, and they sat watching the sleeping creature on his bed. When the lump flattened out a bit, Mary Beth went in and lifted the covers and examined her, but she did not touch her again. She returned to her chair very pale and sipped bourbon. Outside the wind moaned, but the howling had subsided, and the rain was no longer a driving presence against the front of the house, the side that faced the sea.

From time to time one or the other made a brief suggestion.

"Not radio," Eddie said.

"Right," Mary Beth said. She was a stringer for NPR.

"Not newsprint," she said later.

Eddie was a stringer for AP. He nodded.

"It could be dangerous when it wakes up," she said.

"I know. Six rows of alligator teeth, or poison fangs, or mind rays."

She giggled. "Maybe right now there's a hidden camera taking in all this. Remember that old TV show?"

"Maybe they sent her to test us, our reaction to *them.*"

Mary Beth sat up straight. "My God, more of them?"

"No species can have only one member," he said very seriously. "A counterproductive trait." He realized that he was quite drunk. "Coffee," he said and pulled himself out of the chair, made his way unsteadily to the kitchen.

When he had the coffee ready, and tuna sandwiches, and sliced onions and tomatoes, he found Mary Beth leaning against the bedroom door, contemplating the girl.

"Maybe it's dying," she said in a low voice. "We can't just let it die, Eddie."

"We won't," he said. "Let's eat something. It's almost daylight."

She followed him to the kitchen and looked around it. "I've never been in your house before. You realize that? All the years I've known you, I've never been invited here before."

"Five years," he said.

"That's what I mean. All those years. It's a nice house. It looks like your house should look, you know?"

He glanced around the kitchen. Just a kitchen—stove, refrigerator, table, counters. There were books on the counter and piled on the table. He pushed the pile to one side and put down plates. Mary Beth lifted one and turned it over. Russet-colored, gracefully shaped pottery from North Carolina, signed by Sara. She nodded, as if in confirmation. "You picked out every single item individually, didn't you?"

"Sure. I have to live with the stuff."

"What are you doing here, Eddie? Why here?"

"The end of the world, you mean? I like it."

"Well, I want the hell out. You've been out and chose to be here. I choose to be out. That thing on your bed will get me out."

From the University of Indiana to a small paper in Evanston, on to Philadelphia, New York. He felt he had been out plenty, and now he simply wanted a place where people lived in individual houses and chose the pottery they drank their coffee from. Six years ago he had left New York, on vacation, he had said, and he had come to the end of the world and stayed.

"Why haven't you gone already?" he asked Mary Beth.

She smiled her crooked smile. "I was married, you know that? To a fisherman. That's what girls on the coast do, marry fishermen or lumbermen or policemen. Me, Miss Original No-Talent herself. Married, playing house forever. He's out there somewhere. Went out one day and never came home again. So I got a job with the paper, this and that. Only one thing could be worse than staying here at the end of the world, and that's being in the world broke. Not my style."

She finished her sandwich and coffee and now seemed too restless to sit still. She went to the window over the sink and gazed out. The light was gray. "You don't belong here any more than I do. What happened? Some woman tell you to get lost? Couldn't get the job you wanted? Some young slim punk worm in in front of you? You're dodging just like me."

All the above, he thought silently, and said, "Look, I've been thinking. I can't go to the office without raising suspicion, in case anyone's looking for her, I mean. I haven't been in the office before one or two in the afternoon for more than five years. But you can. See if anything's come over the wires, if there's a search on, if there was a wreck of any sort. You know. If the FBI's nosing around, or the military. Anything at all." Mary Beth rejoined him at the table and poured more coffee, her restlessness gone, an intent look on her face. Her business face, he thought.

"Okay. First some pictures, though. And we'll have to have a story about my car. It's been out front all night," she added crisply. "So, if anyone brings it up, I'll have to say I keep you company now and then. Okay?"

He nodded and thought without bitterness that that would give them a laugh at Connally's Tavern. That reminded him of Truman Cox. "They'll get around to him eventually, and he might remember seeing her. Of course, he assumed it was the Boland girl. But they'll know we saw someone."

Mary Beth shrugged. "So you saw the Boland girl and got to thinking about her and her trade and gave me a call. No problem."

He looked at her curiously. "You really don't care if they start that scuttlebutt around town about you and me?"

"Eddie," she said almost too sweetly, "I'd admit to fucking a pig if it would get me the hell out of here. I'll go on home for a shower, and by then maybe it'll be time to get on my horse and go to the office. But first some pictures."

At the bedroom door he asked in a hushed voice, "Can you get them without using the flash? That might send her into shock or something."

She gave him a dark look. "Will you for Christ's sake stop calling it a her!" She scowled at the figure on the bed. "Let's bring in a lamp, at least. You know I have to uncover it."

He knew. He brought in a floor lamp, turned on the bedside light, and watched Mary Beth go to work. She was a good photographer, and in this instance she had an immobile subject; she could use time exposures. She took a roll of film and started a second one, then drew back. The girl on the bed was shivering hard again, drawing up her legs, curling into a tight ball.

"Okay. I'll finish in daylight, maybe when she's awake."

Mary Beth was right, Eddie had to admit; the creature was not a girl, not even a female probably. She was elongated, without any angles anywhere, no elbows or sharp knees or jutting hipbones. Just a smooth long body without breasts, without a navel, without genitalia. And with that dark growth that started high on her head and went down the backs of her arms, covered her back entirely. Like a mantle, he thought, and was repelled by the idea. Her skin was not human, either. It was pale with yellow rather than pink undertones. She obviously was very cold; the yellow was fading to a grayish hue. Tentatively he touched her arm. It felt wrong, not yielding the way human flesh covered with skin should yield. It felt like cool silk over something firmer than human flesh.

Mary Beth replaced the covers, and they backed from the room as the creature shivered. "Jesus," Mary Beth whispered. "You'd think it would have warmed up by now. This place is like an oven, and all those covers." A shudder passed through her.

In the living room again, Mary Beth began to fiddle with her camera. She took out the second roll of film and held both rolls in indecision. "If anyone's nosing around, and if they learn that you might have seen it, and that we've been together, they might snitch my film. Where's a good place to stash it?"

He took the film rolls and she shook her head. "Don't tell me. Just keep it safe." She looked at her watch. "I won't be back until ten or later. I'll find out what I can, make a couple of calls. Keep an eye on it. See you later."

He watched her pull on her red raincoat and went to the porch with her, where he stood until she was in her car and out of sight. Daylight had come; the rain had ended, although the sky was still overcast and low. The fir trees in his front yard glistened and shook off water with the slightest breeze. The wind had turned into no more than that, a slight breeze. The air was not very cold, and it felt good after the heat inside. It smelled good, of leaf mold and sea and earth and fish and fir trees. . . . He took several deep breaths and then went back in. The house really was like an oven, he thought, momentarily refreshed by the cool morning and now once again feeling logy. Why didn't she warm up? He stood in the doorway to the bedroom and looked at the huddled figure. Why didn't she warm up?

He thought of victims of hypothermia; the first step, he had read, was to get their temperature back up to normal, any way possible. Hot water bottle? He didn't own one. Hot bath? He stood over the girl and shook his head slightly. Water might be toxic to her. And that was the problem; she was an alien with unknown needs, unknown dangers. And she was freezing.

With reluctance he touched her arm, still cool in spite of all the covering over her. Like a hothouse plant, he thought then, brought into a frigid climate, destined to die of cold. Moving slowly, with even greater reluctance than before, he began to pull off his trousers, his shirt, and when he was down to undershirt and shorts, he gently shifted the sleeping girl and lay down beside her, drew her to the warmth of his body.

The house temperature by then was close to eighty-five, much too warm for a man with all the fat that Eddie had on his body; she felt good next to him, cooling, even soothing. For a time she made no response to his presence, but gradually her shivering lessened, and she seemed to change subtly, lose her rigidity; her legs curved to make contact with his legs; her torso shifted, relaxed, flowed into the shape of his body; one of her arms moved over his chest, her hand at his shoulder, her other arm bent and fitted itself against him. Her cool cheek pressed against the pillows of flesh over his ribs. Carefully he wrapped his arms about her and drew her closer. He dozed, came awake with a start, dozed again. At nine he woke up completely and began to disengage himself. She made a soft sound, like a child in protest, and he stroked her arm and whispered nonsense. At last he was untangled from her arms and legs and stood up and pulled on his clothes again. The next time he looked at the girl, her eyes were open, and he felt entranced momentarily. Large, round, golden eyes, like pools of molten gold, unblinking, inhuman. He took a step away from her.

"Can you talk?"

There was no response. Her eyes closed again and she drew the covers high up onto her face, buried her head in them.

Wearily Eddie went to the kitchen and poured coffee. It was hot and tasted like tar. He emptied the coffee maker and started a fresh brew. Soon Mary Beth would return and they would make the plans that had gone nowhere during the night. He felt more tired than he could remember and thought ruefully of what it was really like to be forty-two and a hundred pounds overweight and miss a night's sleep.

"You look like hell," Mary Beth said in greeting at ten. She looked fine, excited, a flush on her cheeks, her eyes sparkling. "Is it okay? Has it moved? Come awake yet?" She charged past him and stood in the doorway to the bedroom. "Good. I got hold of Homer Carpenter, over in Portland. He's coming over with a video camera around two or three. I didn't tell him what we have, but I had to tell him something to get him over. I said we have a coelacanth."

Eddie stared at her. "He's coming over for that? I don't believe it."

She left the doorway and swept past him on her way to the kitchen. "Okay, he doesn't believe me, but he knows it's something big, something hot, or I wouldn't have called him. He knows me that well, anyway."

Eddie thought about it for a second or two, then shrugged. "What else did you find out?"

Mary Beth got coffee and held the cup in both hands, surveying him over the top of it. "Boy oh boy, Eddie! I don't know who knows what, or what it is they know, but there's a hunt on. They're saying some guys escaped from the pen over at Salem, but that's bull. Roadblocks and everything. I don't think they're telling anyone anything yet. The poor cops out there don't know what the hell they're supposed to be looking for, just anything suspicious, until the proper authorities get here."

"Here? They know she's here?"

"Not here here. But somewhere on the coast. They're closing in from north and south. And that's why Homer decided to get his ass over here, too."

Eddie remembered the stories that had appeared on the wire services over the past few weeks about an erratic comet that was being tracked. Stuart Winkle, the publisher and editor in chief, had not chosen to print them, but Eddie had seen them. And more recently the story about a possible burnout in space of a Soviet capsule. Nothing to worry about, no radiation, but there might be bright lights in the skies, the stories had said. Right, he thought.

Mary Beth was at the bedroom door again, sipping her coffee. "I'll owe you for this, Eddie. No way can I pay for what you're giving me." He made a growly noise, and she turned to regard him, suddenly very serious.

"Maybe there is something," she said softly. "A little piece of the truth. You know you're not the most popular man in town, Eddie. You're always doing little things for people, and yet, do they like you for it, Eddie? Do they?"

"Let's not do any psychoanalysis right now," he said coldly. "Later."

She shook her head. "Later I won't be around. Remember?" Her voice took on a mocking tone. "Why do you suppose you don't get treated better? Why no one comes to visit? Or invites you to the clambakes, except for office parties, anyway? It's all those little things you keep doing, Eddie. Overdoing maybe. And you won't let anyone pay you back for anything. You turn everyone into a poor relation, Eddie, and they begin to resent it."

Abruptly he laughed. For a minute he had been afraid of her, what she might reveal about him. "Right," he said. "Tell that to Ruthie Jenson."

Mary Beth shrugged. "You give poor little Ruthie exactly what she craves—mistreatment. She takes it home and nurtures it. And then she feels guilty. The Boland kid you intended to rescue. You would have had her, her sister, and their mother all feeling guilty. Truman Cox. How many free drinks you let him give you, Eddie? Not even one, I bet. Stuart Winkle? You run his paper for him. You ever use that key to his cabin? He really wants you to use it, Eddie. A token repayment. George Allmann, Harriet Davies . . . it's a long list, Eddie, the people you've done little things for. The people who go through life owing you, feeling guilty about not liking you, not sure why they don't. I was on that list, too, Eddie, but not now. I just paid you in full."

"Okay," he said heavily. "Now that we've cleared up the mystery about me, what about her?" He pointed past Mary Beth at the girl on his bed.

"It, Eddie. It. First the video, and make some copies, get them into a safe place, and then announce. How does that sound?"

He shrugged. "Whatever you want."

She grinned her crooked smile and shook her head at him. "Forget it, Eddie. I'm paid up for years to come. Look, I've got to get back to the office. I'll keep my eyes on the wires, anything coming in, and as soon as Homer shows, we'll be back. Are you okay? Can you hold out for the next few hours?"

"Yeah, I'm okay." He watched her pull on her coat and walked to the porch with her. Before she left, he said, "One thing, Mary Beth. Did it even occur to you that some people like to help out? No ulterior motive or anything, but a little human regard for others?"

She laughed. "I'll give it some thought, Eddie. And you give some thought to having perfected a method to make sure people leave you alone, keep their distance. Okay? See you later." He stood on the porch, taking deep breaths. The air was mild; maybe the sun would come out later on. Right now the world smelled good, scoured clean, fresh. No other house was visible. He had let the trees and shrubbery grow wild, screening everything from view. It was like being the last man on Earth, he thought suddenly. The heavy growth even screened out the noise from the little town. If he listened intently, he could make out engine sounds, but no voices, no one else's music that he usually detested, no one else's cries or laughter.

Mary Beth never had been ugly, he thought then. She was good-looking in her own way even now, going on middle age. She must have been a real looker as a younger woman. Besides, he thought, if anyone ever mocked her, called her names, she would slug the guy. That would be her way. And he had found his way, he added, then turned brusquely and went inside and locked the door after him.

He took a kitchen chair to the bedroom and sat down by her. She was shivering again. He reached over to pull the covers more tightly about her, then stopped his motion and stared. The black mantle thing did not cover her head as completely as it had before. He was sure it now started farther back. And more of her cheeks were exposed. Slowly he drew away the cover and then turned her over. The mantle was looser, with folds where it had been taut before. She reacted violently to being uncovered, shuddering long spasmlike movements.

He replaced the cover.

"What the hell are you?" he whispered. "What's happening to you?"

He rubbed his eyes hard and sat down, regarding her with a frown. "You know what's going to happen, don't you? They'll take you somewhere and study you, try to make you talk, if you can, find out where you're from, what you want, where there are others. . . . They might hurt you. Even kill you."

He thought again of the great golden pools that were her eyes, of how her skin felt like silk over a firm substance, of the insubstantiality of her body, the lightness when he carried her.

"What do you want here?" he whispered. "Why did you come?"

After a few minutes of silent watching, he got up and found his dry shoes in the closet and pulled them on. He put on a plaid shirt that was very warm, and then he wrapped the sleeping girl in the blanket and carried her to his car and placed her on the backseat. He went back inside for another blanket and put that over her, too.

He drove up his street, avoiding the town, using a back road that wound higher and higher up the mountain. Stuart Winkle's cabin, he thought. An open invitation to use it any time he wanted. He drove carefully, taking the curves slowly, not wanting to jar her, to roll her off the backseat. The woods pressed in closer when he left the road for a log road. From time to time he could see the ocean, then he turned and lost it again. The road clung to the steep mountainside, climbing, always climbing; there was no other traffic on it. The loggers had finished with this area; this was state land, untouchable, for now anyway. He stopped at one of the places where the ocean spread out below him and watched the waves rolling in forever and ever, unchanging, unknowable. Then he drove on. The cabin was high on the mountain. Up here the trees were mature growth, mammoth and silent, with deep shadows beneath them, little understory growth in the dense shade. The cabin was redwood, rough, heated with a wood stove, no running water, no electricity. There was oil for a lamp, and plenty of dry wood stacked under a shed, and a store of food that Stuart had said he should consider his own. There were twin beds in the single bedroom and a couch that opened to a double bed in the living room. Those two rooms and the kitchen made up the cabin.

He carried the girl inside and put her on one of the beds; she was entirely enclosed in blankets like a cocoon. Hurriedly he made a fire in the stove and brought in a good supply of logs. Like a hothouse orchid, he thought; she needed plenty of heat. After the cabin started to heat up, he took off his outer clothing and lay down beside her, the way he had done before, and as before, she conformed to his body, melted into him, absorbed his warmth. Sometimes he dozed, then he lay quietly thinking of his childhood, of the heat that descended on Indiana like a physical substance, of the tornadoes that sometimes came, murderous funnels that sucked life away, shredded everything. He dozed and dreamed and awakened and dreamed in that state also.

He got up to feed the fire and tossed in the film Mary Beth had given him to guard. He got a drink of water at the pump in the kitchen and lay down by her again. His fatigue increased, but pleasurably. His weariness was without pain, a floating sensation that was between sleep and wakefulness. Sometimes he talked quietly to her, but not much, and what he said he forgot as soon as the words formed. It was better to lie without sound, without motion. Now and then she shook convulsively and then subsided again. Twilight came, darkness, then twilight again. Several times he aroused enough to build up the fire.

When it was daylight once more, he got up, reeling as if drunken; he pulled on his clothes and went to the kitchen to make instant coffee. He sensed her presence behind him. She was standing up, nearly as tall as he was, but incredibly insubstantial, not thin, but as slender as a straw. Her golden eyes were wide open. He could not read the expression on her face.

"Can you eat anything?" he asked. "Drink water?"

She looked at him. The black mantle was gone from her head; he could not see it anywhere on her as she faced him. The strange folds of skin at her groin, the boneless appearance of her body, the lack of hair, breasts, the very color of her skin looked right now, not alien, not repellent. The skin was like cool silk, he knew. He also knew this was not a woman, not a she, but something that should not be here, a creature, an it.

"Can you speak? Can you understand me at all?"

Her expression was as unreadable as that of a wild creature, a forest animal, aware, intelligent, unknowable.

Helplessly he said, "Please, if you can understand me, nod. Like this." He showed her, and in a moment she nodded. "And like this for no," he said. She mimicked him again.

"Do you understand that people are looking for you?"

She nodded slowly. Then very deliberately she turned around, and instead of the black mantle that had grown on her head, down her back, there was an iridescence, a rainbow of pastel colors that shimmered and gleamed. Eddie sucked in his breath as the new growth moved, opened slightly more.

There wasn't enough room in the cabin for her to open the wings all the way. She stretched them from wall to wall. They looked like gauze, filmy, filled with light that was alive. Not realizing he was moving, Eddie was drawn to one of the wings, reached out to touch it. It was as hard as steel and cool. She turned her golden liquid eyes to him and drew her wings in again.

"We'll go someplace where it's warm," Eddie said hoarsely. "I'll hide you. I'll smuggle you somehow. They can't have you!" She walked through the living room to the door and studied the handle for a moment. As she reached for it, he lumbered after her, lunged toward her, but already she was opening the door, slipping out.

"Stop! You'll freeze. You'll die!"

In the clearing of the forest, with sunlight slanting through the giant trees, she spun around, lifted her face upward, and then opened her wings all the way. As effortlessly as a butterfly, or a bird, she drew herself up into the air, her wings flashing light, now gleaming, now appearing to vanish as the light reflected one way and another.

"Stop!" Eddie cried again. "Please! Oh, God, stop! Come back!"

She rose higher and looked down at him with her golden eyes. Suddenly the air seemed to tremble with sound, trills and arpeggios and flutings. Her mouth did not open as the sounds increased until Eddie fell to his knees and clapped his hands over his ears, moaning. When he looked again, she was still rising, shining, invisible, shining again. Then she was gone. Eddie pitched forward into the thick layer of fir needles and forest humus and lay still. He felt a tugging on his arm and heard Mary Beth's furious curses but as if from a great distance. He moaned and tried to go to sleep again. She would not let him.

"You goddamn bastard! You filthy son of a bitch! You let it go! Didn't you? You turned it loose!"

He tried to push her hands away.

"You scum! Get up! You hear me? Don't think for a minute, Buster, that I'll let you die out here! That's too good for you, you lousy tub of lard. Get up!"

Against his will he was crawling, then stumbling, leaning on her, being steadied by her. She kept cursing all the way back inside the cabin, until he was on the couch, and she stood over him, arms akimbo, glaring at him.

"Why? Just tell me why. For God's sake, tell me Eddie, why?" Then she screamed at him, "Don't you dare pass out on me again. Open those damn eyes and keep them open!"

She savaged him and nagged him, made him drink whiskey that she had brought along, then made him drink coffee. She got him to his feet and made him walk around the cabin a little, let him sit down again, drink again. She did not let him go to sleep, or even lie down, and the night passed.

A fine rain had started to fall by dawn. Eddie felt as if he had been away a long time, to a very distant place that had left few memories. He listened to the soft rain and at first thought he was in his own small house, but then he realized he was in a strange cabin and that Mary Beth was there, asleep in a chair. He regarded her curiously and shook his head, trying to clear it. His movement brought her sharply awake.

"Eddie, are you awake?"

"I think so. Where is this place?"

"Don't you remember?"

He started to say no, checked himself, and suddenly he was remembering. He stood up and looked about almost wildly.

"It's gone, Eddie. It went away and left you to die. You would have died out there if I hadn't come, Eddie. Do you understand what I'm saying?"

He sat down again and lowered his head into his hands. He knew she was telling the truth.

"It's going to be light soon," she said. "I'll make us something to eat, and then we'll go back to town. I'll drive you. We'll come back in a day or so to pick up your car." She stood up and groaned. "My God, I feel like I've been wrestling bears all night. I hurt all over."

She passed close enough to put her hand on his shoulder briefly. "What the hell, Eddie. Just what the hell."

In a minute he got up also and went to the bedroom, looked at the bed where he had lain with her all through the night. He approached it slowly and saw the remains of the mantle. When he tried to pick it up, it crumbled to dust in his hand.

(1990)

DIANE GLANCY

Aunt Parnetta's Electric Blisters

Some stories can be told only in winter
This is not one of them
because the fridge is for Parnetta
where it's always winter.

Hey chekta! All this and now the refrigerator broke. Uncle Filo scratched the long gray hairs that hung in a tattered braid on his back. All that foot stomping and fancy dancing. Old warriors still at it.

"But when did it help?" Aunt Parnetta asked. The fridge ran all through the cold winter when she could have set the milk and eggs in the snow. The fish and meat from the last hunt. The fridge had walked through the spring when she had her quilt and beading money. Now her penny jar was empty, and it was hot, and the glossy white box broke. The coffin! If Grandpa died, they could put him in it with his war ax and tomahawk. His old dog even. But how would she get a new fridge?

The repairman said he couldn't repair it. Whu chutah! Filo loaded his rifle and sent a bullet right through it. Well, he said, a man had to take revenge. Had to stand against civilization. He watched the summer sky for change as though the stars were white leaves across the hill. Would the stars fall? Would Filo have to rake them when cool weather came again? Filo coughed and scratched his shirt pocket as though something crawled deep within his breastbone. His heart maybe, if he ever found it.

Aunt Parnetta stood at the sink, soaking the sheets before she washed them.

"Dern't nothin' we dude ever work?" Parnetta asked, poking the sheets with her stick.

"We bought that ferge back twenty yars." Filo told her. "And it nerked since then."

"Weld, dernd," she answered. "Could have goned longer til the frost cobered us. Culb ha' set the milk ertside. But nowd. It weren't werk that far."

"Nope," Filo commented. "It weren't."

Parnetta looked at her beadwork. Her hands flopped at her sides. She couldn't have it done for a long time. She looked at the white patent-leathery box. Big enough for the both of them. For the cow if it died.

"Set it out in the backyard with the last one we had."

They drove to Tahlequah that afternoon, Filo's truck squirting dust and pinging rocks. They parked in front of the hardware store on Muskogee Street. The regiments of stoves, fridges, washers, dryers, stood like white soldiers. The Yellow Hair Custer was there to command them. Little Big Horn. Whu chutah! The prices! Three hundred crackers.

"Some mord than thad," Filo surmised. His flannel shirt-collar tucked under itself. His braid sideways like a rattler on his back.

"Filo, I dern't think we shulb decide terday."

"No," the immediate answer stummed from his mouth like a roach from under the baseboard in the kitchen.

"We're just lookin'."

"Of course," said Custer.

They walked to the door leaving the stoves, washers, dryers, the televisions all blaring together, and the fridges lined up for battle.

Filo lifted his hand from the rattled truck.

"Surrender," Parnetta said. "Izend thad the way id always iz?"

The truck spurted and spattered and shook Filo and Aunt Parnetta before Filo got it backed into the street. The forward gear didn't buck as much as the backward.

When they got home, Filo took the back off the fridge and looked at the motor. It could move a load of hay up the road if it had wheels. Could freeze half the fish in the pond. The minute coils, the twisting intestines of the fridge like the hog he butchered last winter, also with a bullet hole in its head.

"Nothin we dude nerks." Parnetta watched him from the kitchen window. "Everythin' against uz," she grumbled to herself.

Filo got his war feather from the shed, put it in his crooked braid. He stomped his feet, hooted. Filo, the medicine man, transcended to the spirit world for the refrigerator. He shook each kink and bolt. The spirit of cold itself. He whooped and warred in the yard for nearly half an hour.

"Not with a bullet hole in it." Parnetta shook her head and wiped the sweat from her face.

He got his wrench and hack saw, the ax and hammer. It was dead now for sure. Parnetta knew it at the sink. It was the thing that would be buried in the backyard. "Like most of us libed," Aunt Parnetta talked to herself. "Filled with our own workings, not doint what we shulb."

Parnetta hung the sheets in the yard, white and square as the fridge itself.

• • •

The new refrigerator came in a delivery truck. It stood in the kitchen. Bought on time at a bargain. Cheapest in the store. Filo made sure of it. The interest over five years would be as much as the fridge. Aunt Parnetta tried to explain it to him. The men set the fridge where Parnetta instructed them. They adjusted and leveled the little hog feet. They gave Parnetta the packet of information, the guarantee. Then drove off in victory. The new smell of the gleaming white inside as though cleansed by cedar from the Keetowah fire.

Aunt Parnetta had Filo take her to the grocery store on the old road to Tahlequah. She loaded the cart with milk and butter. Frozen waffles. Orange juice. Anything that had to be kept cool. The fridge made noise, she thought, she would get used to it. But in the night, she heard the fridge. It seemed to fill her dreams. She had trouble going to sleep, even on the clean white sheets, and she had trouble staying asleep. The fridge was like a giant hog in the kitchen, rutting and snorting all night. She got up once and unplugged it, waking early the next morn to plug it in again before the milk and eggs got warm.

"That ferge bother yeu, Filo?" she asked.

"Nord."

Aunt Parnetta peeled her potatoes outside. She mended Filos's shirts under the shade tree. She didn't soak anything in the kitchen sink anymore, not even the sheets or Filo's socks. There were things she just had to endure, she grumped. That's the way it was.

When the grandchildren visited, she had them run in the kitchen for whatever she needed. They picnicked on the old watermelon table in the backyard. She put up the old teepee for them to sleep in.

"Late in the summer fer that?" Filo quizzed her.

"Nert. It waz nert to get homesick for the summer that's leabing us like the childurn." She gratified him with her keen sense. Parnetta could think up anything for what she wanted to do.

Several nights Filo returned to their bed, with its geese-in-flight-over-the-swamp pattern quilt, but Aunt Parnetta stayed in the teepee under the stars.

"We bined muried thurdy yars. Git in the house," Filo said one night under the white leaves of the stars.

"I can't sleep 'cause of that wild hog in the kitchen," Aunt Parnetta said. "I tald yeu that."

"Hey chekta!" Filo answered her. "Why didn't yeu teld me so I knowd whad yeu said." Filo covered the white box of the fridge with the geese quilt and an old Indian blanket he got from the shed. "Werd yeu stayed out thar all winder?"

"Til the beast we got in thar dies."

"Hawly gizard," Filo spurted. "Thard be anuther twendy yars!"

Aunt Parnetta was comforted by the bedroom that night. Old Filo's snore after he made his snorting love to her. The gray-and-blue-striped wallpaper with its watermarks. The stovepipe curling up to the wall like a hog tail. The bureau dresser with a little doily and her hairbrush. Pictures by their grandchildren. A turquoise coyote and a ghostly figure the boy told her was Running Wind.

She fell into a light sleep where the white stars blew down from the sky, flapping like the white sheets on the line. She nudged Filo to get his rake. He turned sharply against her. Parnetta woke and sat on the edge of the bed.

"Yeu wand me to cuber the furge wid something else?" Filo asked from his sleep.

"No," Aunt Parnetta answered him. "Nod unless id be the polar ice cap."

Now it was an old trip to Minnesota when she was a girl. Parnetta saw herself in a plaid shirt and braids. Had her hair been that dark? Now it was streaked with gray. Everything was like a child's drawing. Exaggerated. The way dreams were sometimes. A sun in the left corner of the picture. The trail of chimney smoke from the narrow house. It was cold. So cold that everything creaked. She heard cars running late into the night. Early mornings. Steam growled out of the exhaust. The pane of window glass in the front door had been somewhere else. Old lettering showed up in the frost. Bones remembered their aches in the cold. Teeth, their hurt. The way Parnetta remembered every bad thing that happened. She dwelled on it.

That cold place was shriveled to the small upright rectangle in her chest, holding the fish her grandson caught in the river. That's where the cold place was. Right inside her heart. No longer pumping like the blinker lights she saw in town. She was the Minnesota winter she remembered as a child. The electricity it took to keep her cold! The energy. The moon over her like a ceiling light. Stars were holes where the rain came in. The dripping buckets. All of them like Parnetta. The *hurrrrrrrrr* of the fridge. Off. On. All night. That white box. Wild boar! Think of it. She didn't always know why she was disgruntled. She just was. She saw herself as the fridge. A frozen fish stiff as a brick. The Great Spirit had her pegged. Could she find her heart, maybe, if she looked somewhere in her chest?

Hurrrrrrr. Rat-tat-at-rat. *Hurrr.* The fridge came on again, and startled, she woke and teetered slightly on the edge of the bed while it growled.

But she was a stranger in this world. An Indian in a white man's land. "Even the ferge's whate," Parnetta told the Great Spirit.

"Wasn't everybody a stranger and pilgrim?" The Great Spirit seemed to speak to her, or it was her own thoughts wandering in her head from her dreams.

"No," Parnetta insisted. Some people were at home on this earth, moving with ease. She would ask the Great Spirit more about it later. When he finally yanked the life out of her like the pin in a grenade.

Suddenly Aunt Parnetta realized that she was always moaning like the fridge. Maybe she irritated the Great Spirit like the white box irritated her. Did she sound that way to anyone else? Was that the Spirit's revenge? She was stuck with the cheapest box in the store. In fact, in her fears, wasn't it a white boar which would tear into the room and eat her soon as she got good and asleep?

Hadn't she seen the worst in things? Didn't she weigh herself in the winter with her coat on? Sometimes wrapped in the blanket also?

"Filo?" She turned to him. But he was out cold. Farther away than Minnesota.

"No. Just think about it, Parnetta," her thoughts seemed to say. The Spirit had blessed her life. But inside the white refrigerator of herself— Inside the coils, an ice river surged. A glacier mowed its way across a continent. Everything frozen for eons. In need of a Keetowah fire. The warmth of the Great Spirit. Filo was only a spark. He could not warm her. Even though he tried.

Maybe the Great Spirit had done her a favor. Hope like white sparks of stars glistened in her head. The electric blisters. *Temporary!* She could shut up. She belonged to the Spirit. He had just unplugged her a minute. Took his rifle right through her head.

The leaves growled and spewed white sparks in the sky. It was a volcano from the moon. Erupting in the heavens. Sending down its white sparks like the pinwheels Filo used to nail on trees. It was the bright sparks of the Keetowah fire, the holy bonfire from which smaller fires burned, spreading the purification of the Great Spirit into each house. Into each hard, old pine-cone heart.

(1990)

LISA GOLDSTEIN

Midnight News

Stevens and Gorce sat at the hotel bar, watching television. Helena Johnson's face nearly filled the entire screen. Snow drifted across her face and then covered the screen, and five or six people in the bar raised their voices. The bartender quickly switched the channel, and Helena Johnson's face came on again, shot from the same angle.

She had told the reporters she was eighty-four, but Stevens thought she looked older. Her face was covered with a soft down and her right cheek discolored with liver-colored age spots, and the white of one eye had turned as yellow as an egg yolk. The hairdressers had dyed her hair a full, rich white, but Stevens remembered from earlier interviews that it had been dull gray, and that a lot of it had fallen out.

"I lived at home for a long long time," Helena Johnson was saying in her slow scratchy voice. The reporters sat at the bar or at round tables scattered throughout the room and watched her raptly. The bar, which the hotel called a "lobby lounge," had once been elegant, but two months of continuous occupancy by the reporters had changed it into something quite different. Cigarette butts had been ground into the lush carpet, drinks had been spilled, glasses broken. "Well, it was the Depression, you know, and I couldn't move out," the old woman said. "And girls weren't supposed to live on their own back then—only loose girls lived by themselves. My father had been laid off, and I got a job as a stenographer. I was lucky to get it. I supported my family for two years, all by myself."

She stopped for a moment, unwilling or unable to go on. The camera pulled back to show her seated on the bed, then cut to the small knot of reporters standing in her hotel room. Stevens saw himself and Gorce and all the rest of them. He remembered how tense he'd been, how worried that she wouldn't call on him. One of the reporters raised his hand.

"Yes, Mr.—Mr.—" Helena Johnson said.

"Look at that," Stevens said in the bar. "She's senile, on top of everything else. How can she forget his name after two months?"

"Shhh," Gorce said.

"Capelli, ma'am," the reporter said. "I wondered how you felt while you were supporting your family. Didn't it make you feel proud?"

"Objection," Gorce said in the bar. "He's leading the witness."

"Shhh," Stevens said.

"Well, of course I was proud," Helena Johnson said. "I was putting my younger brother through college, too. He had to stop after two years, though, because I lost my job."

Her manner was poised, regal. She reminded Stevens of nothing so much as Queen Victoria. And yet she hadn't even finished grade school. "Look at her," he said in disgust. He raised his glass in a toast. "This is the woman who's going to save the world."

No one knew how the aliens had chosen Helena Johnson. A month after they had appeared, their round ships like gold coins above the seven largest cities in the world, they had jammed radio frequencies and announced their terms for a meeting. One ship would land outside of Los Angeles, and only twenty reporters would be allowed to board.

Steven's first surprise was that they looked human, or at least humanoid. (After the meeting scientists would speculate endlessly about androids and holograms and parallel biology.) Stevens sat on an ordinary folding chair and watched closely as the alien stepped up to the front of the room. Near him he saw reporters looking around for clues to the aliens' technology, but the room was bare except for the chairs and made of something that might have been steel.

"Good afternoon," the alien said. Its voice sounded amplified, but Stevens could see no microphone anywhere. "Hello. We are your judges. We have judged you and found you wanting. Some of us were of the opinion that you should be destroyed immediately. We have decided not to do this. We have found a representative of your species. She will make the decision. At midnight on your New Year's Eve she will tell you if you are to live or die."

No one spoke. Then a bony young woman, her thin black hair brushed back and away from her face, jumped up from her seat. It was the first time Stevens saw Gorce in person, though he had heard of her from his colleagues. He held his breath without knowing it. "Why do you feel you have the right to sit in judgment over us?" she asked. Her voice was level.

"No questions," the alien said. "We will give you the name of the woman who is to represent you. Her name is Helena Johnson. She lives in Phoenix, Arizona. And there is one more thing. Brian Capelli, will you stand please?"

Capelli stood. His face was as white as his shirt. The alien made no motion that Stevens could see, but suddenly there was a sharp noise like a backfire and Capelli's chair burst into flames. Capelli moaned a little and then seemed to realize where he was and stopped.

"We have power and we will use it," the alien said.

Not surprisingly, with every state and federal organization mobilized to look for her, Helena Johnson was found within two hours. She lived in a state-sponsored nursing home. She was asleep when the FBI agent found her and when she woke she seemed unable to answer the simplest question. "What is your name?" the agent asked. Helena Johnson gave no sign that she had heard him.

But within a month she seemed to have accepted the situation as her due. The government put her up in the best hotel in Washington and hired nurses, hairdressers, manicurists, companions. She had an ulcer on her leg that had never been seen to at the home, and the government sent out a highly paid specialist to treat it. Another specialist discovered that she wasn't so much disoriented as hard of hearing, and she was fitted with a hearing aid.

She granted interviews with the twenty reporters daily, then screened the tapes and deleted anything she didn't like. The world discovered to its dismay that Helena Johnson's life hadn't been an easy one, and everything possible was done to make it easier. Television programs now played for an audience of one: stations showed *The Nutcracker Suite* over and over again because she had talked about being taken to see it as a child. Newspapers stopped reporting crime and wars—crime and wars had, in fact, nearly disappeared—and ran headlines about the number of kittens adopted. She got an average of ten thousand letters a day; most of them came with a gift and about a third were marriage proposals.

"So my co-worker, Doris, she said the boss would let you stay on if you would, well, do favors for him," Helena Johnson was saying. "You know what I mean. And I decided that I'd rather starve. But then the next day I thought, well, it's not just me that's depending on the money I earn. It's my parents, and my brother who I was putting through college—did I tell you about that?—and I decided that if he asked me I'd do it. I'm not ashamed to tell you that that's what I thought." The camera cut to the reporters again. Most of them were nodding sympathetically. "So the next day I was called into his office. I was called alone, so I thought, here it comes. Usually when he fired you he called you in in a group. He was standing behind his desk—I can see it now, as clear as day—and he opened his mouth to say something. And then he shook his head, like this, and he said, 'Forget it, girl, go home. You're too ugly.' "

"I wonder if that guy's still alive," Stevens said in the bar.

"I hope for his sake he's dead."

"Gone to the grave never knowing he doomed the world with one sentence."

"She doesn't seem too bitter."

"Who knows what she seems? Who knows what she's thinking? Look at her—she looks like the cat that ate the canary. She's going to play this for all it's worth."

"I got married at the beginning of the war," Helena Johnson said. "World War Two, that was. I was thirty, a bit old for those days. My husband met one of those female soldiers over there in Europe, one of those WACs, and left me for her. Left me and our baby son."

"Is that when you went back to your maiden name?" Gorce asked.

"Yes, and that's a very sharp question, young lady," Helena Johnson said.

"I don't see why," Stevens said, in the bar.

"Because she wants to talk about herself, that's why," Gorce said.

"My husband's name was Furnival," Helena Johnson said. "Isn't that a dreadful name? It sounds just like a funeral, that's what I always thought. I went back to my maiden name as soon as I heard about him and that WAC. They tell me he's dead now. Died in 1979. I lost track of him a long time ago."

"And then you had to raise your baby all by yourself," Gorce said.

"That's right, I did," Helena Johnson said, smiling at her. "And he left me too, soon as he could get a job. He was about seventeen. Seventeen, that's right."

"Have they found him yet?" Stevens asked in the bar.

"They traced him to that trailer camp in Florida," Gorce said. "He left last April, and they haven't been able to pick him up from there. Probably on the run."

"You'd be too."

"I don't know. This could be just what she needs, an emotional reunion with the prodigal son. Make great television."

"The prodigal son has a record as long as your arm—assault, armed robbery, breaking and entering . . ."

"Do you think the Feds will grant him that pardon?"

"Probably."

On the screen the interview was coming to an end. "Anything else you want to say, Miss Johnson?" the hired companion asked.

"No, I'm feeling a little tired," she said. "Oh, I did want to thank—what was his name? Oh, dear, I can't remember it. A young man in Texas who sent me this ring." She held the back of her hand to the camera. The diamond caught the light and sparkled. "Thank you so much."

Her face faded. "The Dance of the Sugar-Plum Fairies" came on over the credits and several people in the bar groaned loudly. The bartender turned the sound down and then turned it back up for the nightly news.

"Good evening," the anchorman said. "Our top story today concerns the daily interview with Helena Johnson. During the course of the interview Miss Johnson spoke once again about her childhood and growing up during the Depression, about her marriage and son. She had this to say about her husband."

"Good God, she's the most boring woman in the world!" Stevens said. "Why do we have to sit through this drivel again?"

"You know why," Gorce said. "In case she's watching."

"In other news, the government reported that the number of survivors of the Denver fire-bombing stands at two," the anchorman said. "Both the survivors are listed in stable condition. Both have burns over fifty percent of their bodies. Skin grafts are scheduled to begin tomorrow."

"God, that was stupid," Gorce said. "I wonder whose idea it was to attack that ship."

"Well, how the hell could we know? All we'd seen them do was burn a chair, and any special-effects man could have done that. What if they were just bluffing?"

"And now we know," Gorce said.

"Now we know."

"Government sources say the bombs were not nuclear weapons," the anchorman said. "There is no radioactive fall-out at all from the bombing. Miss Johnson has sent both the survivors a telegram expressing her wishes for their speedy recovery."

"Bully for her," Stevens said.

"Come off it," Gorce said. "She's not that bad."

"She's a horror. She hasn't called on me once the last three days, and you know why? It's because I accidentally called her Ms."

"I feel sorry for her. What a hard life she's had."

"Sure you do—she loves you. Look at the way she beamed at you all through the interview today. But I guess you're right. I guess she's been lonely. She was only married a year before her husband was called up."

"I didn't mean just her marriage—"

"Now don't go giving me that feminist look," Stevens said, though in fact Gorce's steady gaze hadn't changed. "You know what I meant. If they're not married they usually have a career, something they're interested in. Like you. But this woman had nothing."

"Were you ever married, Stevens?"

"No." He looked at her, surprised by the question. "Relationships don't work out for me. Too much traveling, I guess. How about you?"

"No," she said.

On the screen a scientist was summarizing the latest attempt to communicate with the ships, and then the news ended. "Stay tuned for *Cinderella* following tonight's news," the announcer said over the credits.

"*Cinderella!*" Stevens said, disgusted. "Come on, guys. She can't be awake this late."

"Shhh."

"What—you think she'll hear me? She's on the top floor."

The bartender turned the television off. Stevens and Gorce ordered another round. "You know what I was thinking?" Gorce said. "Have you thought about these aliens? I mean really thought about them?"

"Sure," Stevens said. "Like everyone else in America. I've got a new theory, too. I bet it's a test."

"A what?"

"A test. It doesn't matter what the old bitch chooses, whether she wants us destroyed or not. It's like a laboratory experiment. They're watching us to see how we act under pressure. It we do okay, if we don't all go nuts, we'll be asked to join some kind of galactic federation."

She said nothing for a while. The dim light in the bar made her face look sallow, darkened the hollows under her eyes. "You ever read comic books when you were a kid, Stevens?"

"Huh? No."

"That's what it always turned out to be in the comic books. Some kind of test. All these weird things would happen—the super-hero might even die—but in the end everything returned to normal. Because the kids reading the comics never liked it when things changed too much. The only explanation the writers could come up with was that it had all been a test. But I don't think these tests happen outside of comic books."

"Okay, so what's your theory?"

"Well, think about what's happening here. These guys have set themselves up as the final law, judge, jury, and executioner all rolled into one. Sure, they picked the old woman, but that's just the point—*they* picked her. They probably know how she's going to vote, or they have a good idea. What kind of people would do something like that?"

"I don't know."

"Pretty sadistic people, I'd say. If there was some kind of galactic federation, wouldn't they just observe us and contact us when we were ready? I mean, we were on our way to blowing ourselves up without any outside help at all. Maybe these people travel around the galaxy getting their jollies from watching helpless races cower for months before someone makes the final decision. These aliens are probably outlaws, some kind of renegades. They're so immoral no galactic federation would have them."

"That's a cheerful thought."

Gorce looked around. "Hey, where's Nichols?"

"I don't know. He said something this morning—"

"What?"

"He was going to try to talk to her alone."

"He can't do that."

"You're damn right he can't. Look at all the security they've got posted around her."

"No, I mean he can't get a story the rest of us don't have. We've got to go up there."

"Forget it."

"Come on. We can stop by for a visit or something. Play a game of cards. She'll be happy to see us."

"You're crazy."

"All right, you stay here. I'm going up and talk to her. She won't mind—she likes me."

"Gorce—"

Gorce stood up. "Gorce, don't do that! For God's sake—*Melissa!*"

He wouldn't have remembered her first name if they hadn't done interviews with each other for their respective news stations. "This is Melissa Gorce, reporting from Washington," she'd said, and he'd thought that he couldn't have come up with a name less like her. Using it seemed to work. She stopped, and the mad light in her eyes went out. "Okay," she said. "Maybe you're right."

The next day, at the daily interview, Stevens found out how right he'd been. The number of FBI guards at the door had been doubled, and when his ID had been checked and he'd finally been let in he saw that Nichols was gone.

"He tried to get inside her room last night," Capelli said. "The guards said they were reaching for their guns when they saw this bright flash of light go off. He was practically unrecognizable—they had to check his dental records to make sure it was him."

"He'd been Denverized," another reporter said, trying to laugh.

"He wanted to commit suicide, you ask me," Capelli said. His hands were shaking.

"You see?" Stevens couldn't resist saying to Gorce. "You see what I mean?"

The two cameramen finished setting up, and Helena Johnson's companion opened the floor to questions. No one brought up the dead reporter and Helena Johnson didn't mention him; maybe, Stevens thought, she didn't know. To Stevens's relief she called on him for the first time in four days.

"I was wondering," he said, "how you spend your time. What are your hobbies?"

She smiled at him almost flirtatiously. He was surprised at how much hatred he felt for her at that moment. "Oh, I keep busy," she said. "I look through my mail, though of course I don't have time to answer all my correspondence. And I watch some television, I watch videotapes people send me, I have my hair done . . . I enjoy mealtimes especially, though there's a lot of food my stomach can't take. Do you know, I'd never eaten lobster in my life until last week."

Gorce was right, he thought. She does like talking about herself. If they survived New Year's Eve he'd have to keep in contact with Gorce—she was one smart woman.

Someone asked Helena Johnson a question about her father, and the old woman droned on. She's already told us this story, Stevens thought. There were a few more questions, and then Gorce raised her hand. Helena Johnson smiled at her. "Yes, dear?"

"What do you think of the aliens, Miss Johnson?"

"Gorce!" Capelli whispered behind her. The other reporters thought he'd lost his nerve at the first press conference, when his chair had burst into flames behind him.

"I suppose I'm grateful to them," Helena Johnson said. "If it wasn't for them I'd still be in that dreadful old age home."

"But what do you think of the way they've interfered with us? Of the way they want to make our decisions for us?"

Capelli wasn't the only reporter who became visibly nervous at this question. Stevens felt he could have cheerfully strangled her.

"I don't know, dear. You mean they want to tell us what to do?"

"They want to tell you what to do. They want to force you to make a choice."

"Oh, I don't mind making the choice. In fact—"

Oh, Lord, Stevens thought. She's going to tell us right now.

The companion stepped forward. "Our hour with Miss Johnson is almost up," she said smoothly. "Do you have anything else you want to say, Miss Johnson?"

"Yes, I do," the old woman said. "I wanted to say—Oh, dear, I've forgotten."

The companion moved to the desk and brought her a slip of paper. "Oh yes, that's right," Helena Johnson said, looking at it. "I wanted to tell everyone not to get me a Christmas present. I know a lot of people have been worrying about what to get me, and I just want to tell them I have everything I need."

So give a contribution to charity instead, Stevens thought, but Helena Johnson seemed to have finished. Did she neglect to mention charity because she knew there would be no charities, or anything else, in a few weeks? It was amazing how paranoid they had all become, how they analyzed her slightest gesture.

The companion ushered everyone out of the room. The reporters went downstairs to stand in front of the hotel and tape a short summary of the interview for their stations. Upstairs, Stevens knew, Helena Johnson and the cameramen were going over the footage, editing out parts where she thought she looked too old, too vulnerable or too uncertain.

He felt depressed by the interview, by Nichols's death. The old lady hadn't given them any hope at all this time. What would he be doing a few weeks from now? If she said no, he could probably have his pick of assignments. But if she said yes he'd be charred bones and ashes, like poor Nichols, like all the people in Denver. God, what a horrible way to die. She had to say no, she had to.

On New Year's Eve everyone was either watching television, getting drunk or doing both at once. The last show would be broadcast live. Stevens had taken a sedative for the final interview, and he knew he wasn't the only one. There had been no commercials on any network for the last five hours; if the old lady said no, Stevens had heard, there would be commercials every three minutes.

They were let into the room for the last time at exactly midnight. "Hello," Helena Johnson said, smiling at all of them. The smell of fear was very strong.

"I have been chosen by the aliens to decide Earth's future," she said. "I don't understand why I was chosen, and neither does anyone else. But I have taken the responsibility very seriously, and I feel I have been conscientious in doing my duty."

Get on with it, Stevens thought. Yes or no.

"I have to say I have enjoyed my stay here at the hotel," she said. "But it is impossible not to think that all of you must consider me very stupid indeed." Oh, God, Stevens thought. Here it comes. The old lady's revenge. "I know very well that none of you were interested in me, in Helena Hope Johnson. If the aliens hadn't chosen me I would probably be at the nursing home right now, if not dead of neglect. My leg would be in constant pain, and the nurses would think I was senile because I couldn't hear the questions they asked me.

"So, at first, I thought I would say yes. I would say that Earth deserves to be destroyed, that its people are cruel and selfish and will only show kindness if there's something in it for them. And sometimes not even then. Why do you think my son hasn't come to visit me?" The yellow eye had filled with tears.

Oh, shit, Stevens thought. I knew it would come to this. He had heard her son was dead, killed in a bar fight.

"But then I remembered what this young lady had said," Helena Johnson said. "Miss Gorce. She asked me what I thought about the aliens interfering with our lives, with my life. Well, I thought about it, and I didn't like what I came up with. They have no right to decide whether we will live or die, whoever they are. All my life, people have decided for me, my parents, my teachers, my bosses. But that's all over with now. My answer is—no answer. I will not give them an answer."

No one moved for a long moment. Then one of the agents stationed outside the door ran into the room. "The ships are leaving!" he said. "They're taking off!"

Suddenly everyone was cheering. Stevens hugged Gorce, hugged Capelli, hugged the FBI agent. The reporters lifted Gorce and threw her into the air until she yelled at them to stop. I hope the camera's getting all this, Stevens thought. It's great television.

The reporters, quieter now, came over to Helena Johnson to thank her. Stevens saw Gorce kiss the old woman carefully on the cheek. "You'd better leave now," the companion said. "She gets tired so easily."

One by one the reporters went downstairs to the bar. Helena Johnson and Gorce were left alone together. Stevens went outside and waited for Gorce near the door. He wanted to tell her she'd been right to ask that question.

Gorce seemed pleased to see him when she came out. "What'd she want to talk to you about?" he asked.

"She wanted me to ghostwrite her autobiography."

Stevens laughed. "No one would read it," he said. "We know far too much about her as it is."

"It don't matter—they've already given her a million dollar contract."

"So what'd you say?"

"Well, she offered me ten percent. What do you think I said? I said yes."

"Congratulations," he said, happy for her. Outside he heard police sirens and what sounded like firecrackers.

"Thanks," she said. "Do you want t-t-to go out somewhere and celebrate?"

He looked at her with surprise. He had never known her to stutter before. She wasn't bad-looking, he thought, but too bony, and her chin and forehead were too long. She had to have gotten her job through her mad bravery and sharp common sense, because she sure didn't look like a blow-dried TV reporter. "Sorry," he said. "I told my girlfriend I'd call her when this whole thing was over."

"You never told me you had a girlfriend."

"Yeah, well, it never came up," he said. "See you, Gorce."

She looked at him a long time. "You know, Stevens, you better start being nicer to me," she said. "What if the aliens pick me to save the world next time?"

(1990)

JOHN KESSEL

INVADERS

15 November 1532: that night no one slept. On the hills outside Cajamarca, the campfires of the Inca's army shone like so many stars in the sky. De Soto had reported that Atahualpa had perhaps forty thousand troops under arms, but looking at the myriad lights spread across those hills, de Candia realized that estimate was, if anything, low.

Against them, Pizarro could throw one hundred foot soldiers, sixty horses, eight muskets, and four harquebuses. Pizarro, his brother Hernando, de Soto, and Benalcázar laid out plans for an ambush. They would invite the Inca to a parley. De Candia and his artillery would be hidden in the building along one side of the square, the cavalry and infantry along the others. De Candia watched Pizarro prowl through the camp that night, checking the men's armor, joking with them, reminding them of the treasure they would have, and the women. The men laughed nervously and whetted their swords.

They might sharpen them until their hands fell off; when morning dawned, they would be slaughtered. De Candia breathed deeply of the thin air and turned from the wall.

Ruiz de Arce, an infantryman with a face like a clenched fist, hailed him as he passed. "Are those guns of yours ready for some work tomorrow?"

"We need prayers more than guns."

"I'm not afraid of these brownies," de Arce said.

"Then you're a half-wit."

"Soto says they have no swords."

The man was probably just trying to reassure himself, but de Candia couldn't abide it. "Will you shut your stinking fool's trap! They don't need swords! If they only spit all at once, we'll be drowned."

Pizarro overheard him. He stormed over, grabbed de Candia's arm, and shook him. "Have they ever seen a horse, Candia? Have they ever felt steel? When you fired the harquebus on the seashore, didn't the town chief pour beer down its barrel as if it were a thirsty god? Pull up your balls and show me you're a man!"

His face was inches away. "Mark me! Tomorrow, Saint James sits on your shoulder, and we win a victory that will cover us in glory for five hundred years."

2 December 2001

"DEE-fense! DEE-fense!" the crowd screamed. During the two-minute warning, Norwood Delacroix limped over to the Redskins' special conditioning coach.

"My knee's about gone," said Delacroix, an outside linebacker with eyebrows that ran together and all the musculature that modern pharmacology could load onto his six-foot-five frame. "I need something."

"You need the power of prayer, my friend. Stoner's eating your lunch."

"Just do it."

The coach selected a popgun from his rack, pressed the muzzle against Delacroix's knee, and pulled the trigger. A flood of well-being rushed up Delacroix's leg. He flexed it tentatively. It felt better than the other one now. Delacroix jogged back onto the field. "DEE-fense!" the fans roared. The overcast sky began to spit frozen rain. The ref blew the whistle, and the Bills broke huddle.

Delacroix looked across at Stoner, the Bills' tight end. The air throbbed with electricity. The quarterback called the signals; the ball was snapped; Stoner surged forward. As Delacroix backpedaled furiously, sudden sunlight flooded the field. His ears buzzed. Stoner jerked left and went right, twisting Delacroix around like a cork in a bottle. His knee popped. Stoner had two steps on him. TD for sure. Delacroix pulled his head down and charged after him.

But instead of continuing downfield, Stoner slowed. He looked straight up into the air. Delacroix hit him at the knees, and they both went down. He'd caught him! The crowd screamed louder, a scream edged with hysteria.

Then Delacroix realized the buzzing wasn't just in his ears. Elation fading, he lifted his head and looked toward the sidelines. The coaches and players were running for the tunnels. The crowd boiled toward the exits, shedding thermoses and beer cups and radios. The sunlight was harshly bright. Delacroix looked up. A huge disk hovered no more than fifty feet above, pinning them in its spotlight. Stoner untangled himself from Delacroix, stumbled to his feet, and ran off the field.

Holy Jesus and the Virgin Mary on toast, Delacroix thought.

He scrambled toward the end zone. The stadium was emptying fast, except for the ones who were getting trampled. The throbbing in the air increased in volume, lowered in pitch, and the flying saucer settled onto the NFL logo on the forty-yard line. The sound stopped as abruptly as if it had been sucked into a sponge.

Out of the corner of his eye, Delacroix saw an NBC cameraman come up next to him, focusing on the ship. Its side divided, and a ramp extended itself to the ground. The cameraman fell back a few steps, but Delacroix held his ground. The inside glowed with the bluish light of a UV lamp.

A shape moved there. It lurched forward to the top of the ramp. A large manlike thing, it advanced with a rolling stagger, like a college freshman at a beer blast. It wore a body-tight red stretchsuit, a white circle on its chest with a lightning bolt through it, some sort of flexible mask over its face. Blond hair covered its head in a kind of brush cut, and two cup-shaped ears poked comically out of the sides of its head. The creature stepped off onto the field, nudging aside the football that lay there.

Delacroix, who had majored in public relations at Michigan State, went forward to greet it. This could be the beginning of an entirely new career. His knee felt great.

He extended his hand. "Welcome," he said. "I greet you in the name of humanity and the United States of America."

"Cocaine," the alien said. "We need cocaine."

Today

I sit at my desk writing a science-fiction story, a tall, thin man wearing jeans, a white T-shirt with the abstract face of a man printed on it, white high-top basketball shoes, and gold-plated wire-rimmed glasses.

In the morning I drink coffee to get me up for the day, and at night I have a gin and tonic to help me relax.

16 November 1532

"What are they waiting for, the shitting dogs!" the man next to de Arce said. "Are they trying to make us suffer?"

"Shut up, will you?" De Arce shifted his armor. Wedged into the stone building on the side of the square, sweating, they had been waiting since dawn, in silence for the most part except for the creak of leather, the uneasy jingle of cascabels on the horses' trappings. The men stank worse than the restless horses. Some had pissed themselves. A common foot soldier like de Arce was lucky to get a space near enough to the door to see out.

As noon came and went with still no sign of Atahualpa and his retinue, the mood of the men went from impatience to near panic. Then, late in the day, word came that the Indians again were moving toward the town.

An hour later, six thousand brilliantly costumed attendants entered the plaza. They were unarmed. Atahualpa, borne on a golden litter by eight men in cloaks of green feathers that glistened like emeralds in the sunset, rose above them. De Arce heard a slight rattling, looked down, and found that his hand, gripping the sword so tightly the knuckles stood out white, was shaking uncontrollably. He unknotted his fist from the hilt, rubbed the cramped fingers, and crossed himself.

"Quiet now, my brave ones," Pizarro said.

Father Valverde and Felipillo strode out to the center of the plaza, right through the sea of attendants. The priest had guts. He stopped before the litter of the Inca, short and steady as a fence post. "Greetings, my lord, in the name of Pope Clement VII, His Majesty the Emperor Charles V, and Our Lord and Savior Jesus Christ."

Atahualpa spoke and Felipillo translated: "Where is this new god?"

Valverde held up the crucifix. "Our God died on the cross many years ago and rose again to Heaven. He appointed the Pope as His viceroy on earth, and the Pope has commanded King Charles to subdue the peoples of the world and convert them to the true faith. The king sent us here to command your obedience and to teach you and your people in this faith."

"By what authority does this pope give away lands that aren't his?"

Valverde held up his Bible. "By the authority of the word of God."

The Inca took the Bible. When Valverde reached out to help him get the cover unclasped, Atahualpa cuffed his arm away. He opened the book and leafed through the pages. After a moment he threw it to the ground. "I hear no words," he said.

Valverde snatched up the book and stalked back toward Pizarro's hiding place. "What are you waiting for?" he shouted. "The saints and the Blessed Virgin, the bleeding wounds of Christ himself, cry vengeance! Attack, and I'll absolve you!"

Pizarro had already stridden into the plaza. He waved his kerchief. "Santiago, and at them!"

On the far side, the harquebuses exploded in an enfilade. The lines of Indians jerked like startled cats. Bells jingling, de Soto's and Hernando's cavalry burst from the lines of doorways on the adjoining side. De Arce clutched his sword and rushed out with the others from the third side.

He felt the power of God in his arm. "Santiago!" he roared at the top of his lungs, and hacked halfway through the neck of his first Indian. Bright blood spurted. He put his boot to the brown man's shoulder and yanked free, lunged for the belly of another wearing a kilt of bright red-and-white checks. The man turned, and the sword caught between his ribs. The hilt was almost twisted from de Arce's grasp as the Indian went down. He pulled free, shrugged another man off his back, and daggered him in the side.

After the first flush of glory, it turned to filthy, hard work, an hour's wade through an ocean of butchery in the twilight, bodies heaped waist-high, boots skidding on the bloody stones. De Arce alone must have killed forty. Only after they'd slaughtered them all and captured the Sapa Inca did it end. A silence settled, broken only by the moans of dying Indians and distant shouts of the cavalry chasing the ones who had managed to break through the plaza wall to escape.

Saint James had indeed sat on their shoulders. Six thousand dead Indians, and not one Spaniard nicked. It was a pure demonstration of the power of prayer.

31 January 2002

It was Colonel Zipp's third session interrogating the alien. So far the thing had kept a consistent story, but not a credible one. The only consideration that kept Zipp from panic at the thought of how his career would suffer if this continued was the rumor that his fellow case officers weren't doing any better with any of the others. That, and the fact that the Krel possessed technology that would reestablish American superiority for another two hundred years. He took a drag on his cigarette, the first of his third pack of the day.

"Your name?" Zipp asked.

"You may call me Flash."

Zipp studied the red union suit, the lightning bolt. With the flat chest, the rounded shoulders, pointed upper lip, and pronounced underbite, the alien looked like a cross between Wally Cleaver and the Mock Turtle. "Is this some kind of joke?"

"What is a joke?"

"Never mind." Zipp consulted his notes. "Where are you from?"

"God has ceded us an empire extending over sixteen solar systems in the Orion arm of the galaxy, including the systems around the stars you know as Tau Ceti, Epsilon Eridani, Alpha Centauri, and the red dwarf Barnard's star."

"God gave you an empire?"

"Yes. We were hoping He'd give us your world, but all He kept talking about was your cocaine."

The alien's translating device had to be malfunctioning. "You're telling me that God sent you for cocaine?"

"No. He just told us about it. We collect chemical compounds for their aesthetic interest. These alkaloids do not exist on our world. Like the music you humans value so highly, they combine familiar elements—carbon, hydrogen, nitrogen, oxygen—in pleasing new ways."

The colonel leaned back, exhaled a cloud of smoke. "You consider cocaine like—like a symphony?"

"Yes. Understand, Colonel, no material commodity alone could justify the difficulties of interstellar travel. We come here for aesthetic reasons."

"You seem to know what cocaine is already. Why don't you just synthesize it yourself?"

"If you valued a unique work of aboriginal art, would you be satisfied with a mass-produced duplicate manufactured in your hometown? Of course not. And we are prepared to pay you well, in a coin you can use."

"We don't need any coins. If you want cocaine, tell us how your ships work."

"That is one of the coins we had in mind. Our ships operate according to a principle of basic physics. Certain fundamental physical reactions are subject to the belief system of the beings promoting them. If I believe that X is true, then X is more probably true than if I did not believe so."

The colonel leaned forward again. "We know that already. We call it the 'observer effect.' Our great physicist Werner Heisenberg—"

"Yes. I'm afraid we carry this principle a little further than that."

"What do you mean?"

Flash smirked. "I mean that our ships move through interstellar space by the power of prayer."

13 May 1533

Atahualpa offered to fill a room twenty-two feet long and seventeen feet wide with gold up to a line as high as a man could reach, if the Spaniards would let him go. They were skeptical. How long would this take? Pizarro asked. Two months, Atahualpa said.

Pizarro allowed the word to be sent out, and over the next several months, bearers, chewing the coca leaf in order to negotiate the mountain roads under such burdens, brought in tons of gold artifacts. They brought plates and vessels, life-sized statues of women and men, gold lobsters and spiders and alpacas, intricately fashioned ears of maize, every kernel reproduced, with leaves of gold and tassels of spun silver.

Martin Bueno was one of the advance scouts sent with the Indians to Cuzco, the capital of the empire. They found it to be the legendary city of gold. The Incas, having no money, valued precious metals only as ornament. In Cuzco the very walls of the Sun Temple, Coricancha, were plated with gold. Adjoining the temple was a ritual garden where gold maize plants supported gold butterflies, gold bees pollinated gold flowers.

"Enough loot that you'll shit in a different gold pot every day for the rest of your life," Bueno told his friend Diego Leguizano upon his return to Cajamarca.

They ripped the plating off the temple walls and had it carried to Cajamarca. There they melted it down into ingots.

The huge influx of gold into Europe was to cause an economic catastrophe. In Peru, at the height of the conquest, a pair of shoes cost $850, and a bottle of wine $1,700. When their old horseshoes wore out, iron being unavailable, the cavalry shod their horses with silver.

21 April 2003

In the executive washroom of Bellingham, Winston, and McNeese, Jason Prescott snorted a couple of lines and was ready for the afternoon. He returned to the brokerage to find the place in a whispering uproar. In his office sat one of the Krel. Prescott's secretary was about to piss himself. "It asked specifically for you," he said.

What would Attila the Hun do in this situation? Prescott thought. He went into the office. "Jason Prescott," he said. "What can I do for you, Mr. . . . ?"

The alien's bloodshot eyes surveyed him. "Flash. I wish to make an investment."

"Investments are our business." Rumors had flown around the New York Merc for a month that the Krel were interested in investing. They had earned vast sums selling information to various computer, environmental, and biotech firms. Several of the aliens had come to observe trading in the currencies pit last week, and only yesterday Jason had heard from a reliable source that they were considering opening an account with Merrill Lynch. "What brings you to our brokerage?"

"Not the brokerage. You. We heard that you are the most ruthless currencies trader in this city. We worship efficiency. You are efficient."

Right. Maybe there was a hallucinogen in the toot. "I'll call in some of our foreign-exchange experts. We can work up an investment plan for your consideration in a week."

"We already have an investment plan. We are, as you say in the markets, 'long' in dollars. We want you to sell dollars and buy francs for us."

"The franc is pretty strong right now. It's likely to hold for the next six months. We'd suggest—"

"We wish to buy $50 billion worth of francs."

Prescott stared. "That's not a very good investment." Flash said nothing. The silence grew uncomfortable. "I suppose if we stretch it out over a few months, and hit the exchanges in Hong Kong and London at the same time—"

"We want these francs bought in the next week. For the week after that, a second $50 billion. Fifty billion a week until we tell you to stop."

Hallucinogens for sure. "That doesn't make any sense."

"We can take our business elsewhere."

Prescott thought about it. It would take every trick he knew—and he'd have to invent some new ones—to carry this off. The dollar was going to drop through the floor, while the franc would punch through the sell-stops of every trader on ten world markets. The exchanges would scream bloody murder. The repercussions would auger holes in every economy north of Antarctica. Governments would intervene. It would make the historic Hunt silver squeeze look like a game of Monopoly.

Besides, it made no sense. Not only was it criminally irresponsible, it was stupid. The Krel would squander every dime they'd earned.

Then he thought about the commission on $50 billion a week.

Prescott looked across at the alien. From the right point of view, Flash resembled a barrel-chested college undergraduate from Special Effects U. He felt an urge to giggle, a euphoric feeling of power. "When do we start?"

19 May 1533

In the fields the *purics,* singing praise to Atahualpa, son of the sun, harvested the maize. At night they celebrated by getting drunk on *chicha.* It was, they said, the most festive month of the year.

Pedro Sancho did his drinking in the dark of the treasure room, in the smoke of the smelters' fire. For months he had been troubled by nightmares of the heaped bodies lying in the plaza. He tried to ignore the abuse of the Indian women, the brutality toward the men. He worked hard. As Pizarro's squire, it was his job to record daily the tally of Atahualpa's ransom. When he ran low on ink, he taught the *purics* to make it for him from soot and the juice of berries. They learned readily.

Atahualpa heard about the ink and one day came to him. "What are you doing with those marks?" he said, pointing to the scribe's tally book.

"I'm writing the list of gold objects to be melted down."

"What is this 'writing'?"

Sancho was nonplussed. Over the months of Atahualpa's captivity, Sancho had become impressed by the sophistication of the Incas. Yet they were also queerly backward. They had no money. It was not beyond belief that they should not know how to read and write.

"By means of these marks, I can record the words that people speak. That's writing. Later other men can look at these marks and see what was said. That's reading."

"Then this is a kind of quipu?" Atahualpa's servants had demonstrated for Sancho the quipu, a system of knotted strings by which the Incas kept talleys. "Show me how it works," Atahualpa said.

Sancho wrote on the page: *God have mercy on us.* He pointed. "This, my lord, is a representation of the word 'God.' "

Atahualpa looked skeptical. "Mark it here." He held out his hand, thumbnail extended.

Sancho wrote "God" on the Inca's thumbnail.

"Say nothing now." Atahualpa advanced to one of the guards, held out his thumbnail. "What does this mean?" he asked.

"God," the man replied.

Sancho could tell the Inca was impressed, but he barely showed it. That the Sapa Inca had maintained such dignity throughout his captivity tore at Sancho's heart.

"This writing is truly a magical accomplishment," Atahualpa told him. "You must teach my *amautas* this art."

Later, when the viceroy Estete, Father Valverde, and Pizarro came to chide him for the slow pace of the gold shipments, Atahualpa tested each of them separately. Estete and Valverde each said the word "God." Atahualpa held his thumbnail out to the conquistador.

Estete chuckled. For the first time in his experience, Sancho saw Pizarro flush. He turned away. "I don't waste my time on the games of children," Pizarro said.

Atahualpa stared at him. "But your common soldiers have this art."

"Well, I don't."

"Why not?"

"I was a swineherd. Swineherds don't need to read."

"You are not a swineherd now."

Pizarro glared at the Inca. "I don't need to read to order you put to death." He marched out of the room.

After the others had left, Sancho told Atahualpa, "You ought not to humiliate the governor in front of his men."

"He humiliates himself," Atahualpa said. "There is no skill in which a leader ought to let himself stand behind his followers."

Today

The part of this story about the Incas is as historically accurate as I could make it, but this Krel business is science fiction. I even stole the name "Krel" from a 1950s SF flick. I've been addicted to SF for years. In the evening my wife and I wash the bad taste of the news out of our mouths by watching old movies on videotape.

A scientist, asked why he read SF, replied, "Because in science fiction the experiments always work." Things in SF stories work out more neatly than in reality. Nothing is impossible. Spaceships move faster than light. Atomic weapons are neutralized. Disease is abolished. People travel in time. Why, Isaac Asimov even wrote a story once that ended with the reversal of entropy!

The descendants of the Incas, living in grinding poverty, find their most lucrative crop in coca, which they refine into cocaine and sell in vast quantities to North Americans.

23 August 2008

"Catalog number 208," said John Bostock. "Georges Seurat, *Bathers.*"

FRENCH GOVERNMENT FALLS, the morning *Times* had announced. JAPAN BANS U.S. IMPORTS. FOOD RIOTS IN MADRID. But Bostock had barely glanced at the newspaper over his coffee; he was buzzed on caffeine and adrenaline, and it was too late to stop the auction, the biggest day of his career. The lot list would make an art historian faint. *Guernica. The Potato Eaters. The Scream.* Miró, Rembrandt, Vermeer, Gauguin, Matisse, Constable, Magritte, Pollock, Mondrian. Six desperate governments had contributed to the sale. And rumor had it the Krel would be among the bidders.

The rumor proved true. In the front row, beside the solicitor Patrick McClannahan, sat one of the unlikely aliens, wearing red tights and a lightning-bolt insignia. The famous Flash. The creature leaned back lazily while McClannahan did the bidding with a discreetly raised forefinger.

Bidding on the Seurat started at ten million and went orbital. It soon became clear that the main bidders were Flash and the U.S. government. The American campaign against cultural imperialism was getting a lot of press, ironic since the Yanks could afford to challenge the Krel only because of the technology the Krel had lavished on them. The probability suppressor that prevented the detonation of atomic weapons. The autodidactic antivirus that cured most diseases. There was talk of an immortality drug. Of a time machine. So what if the European Community was in the sixth month of an economic crisis that threatened to dissolve the unifying efforts of the past twenty years? So what if Krel meddling destroyed humans' capacity to run the world? The Americans were making money, and the Krel were richer than Croesus.

The bidding reached $1.2 billion, at which point the American ambassador gave up. Bostock tapped his gavel. "Sold," he said in his most cultured voice, nodding toward the alien.

The crowd murmured. The American stood. "If you can't see what they're doing to us, then you don't deserve our help!"

For a minute Bostock thought the auction was going to turn into a riot. Then the new owner of the pointillist masterpiece stood, smiled. Ingenuous, clumsy. "We know that there has been considerable disquiet over our purchase of these historic works of art," Flash said. "Let me promise you, they will be displayed where all humans—not just those who can afford to visit the great museums—can see them."

The crowd's murmur turned into applause. Bostock put down his gavel and joined in. The American ambassador and his aides stalked out. Thank God, Bostock thought. The attendants brought out the next item.

"Catalog number 209," Bostock said. "Leonardo da Vinci, *Mona Lisa.*"

26 July 1533

The soldiers, seeing the heaps of gold grow, became anxious. They consumed stores of coca meant for the Inca messengers. They fought over women. They grumbled over the airs of Atahualpa. "Who does he think he is? The governor treats him like a hidalgo."

Father Valverde cursed Pizarro's inaction. That morning, after matins, he spoke with Estete. "The governor has agreed to meet and decide what to do," Estete said.

"It's about time. What about Soto?" De Soto was against harming Atahualpa. He maintained that, since the Inca had paid the ransom, he should be set free, no matter what danger this would present. Pizarro had stalled. Last week he had sent de Soto away to check out rumors that the Tahuantinsuyans were massing for an attack to free the Sapa Inca.

Estete smiled. "Soto's not back yet."

They went to the building Pizarro had claimed as his, and found the others already gathered. The Incas had no tables or proper chairs, so the Spaniards were forced to sit in a circle on mats as the Indians did. Pizarro, only a few years short of threescore, sat on a low stool of the sort that Atahualpa used when he held court. His left leg, whose old battle wound still pained him at times, was stretched out before him. His loose white shirt had been cleaned by some *puric*'s wife. Valverde sat beside him. Gathered were Estete, Benalcázar, Almagro, de Candia, Riquelme, Pizarro's young cousin Pedro, the scribe Pedro Sancho, Valverde, and the governor himself.

As Valverde and Estete had agreed, the viceroy went first. "The men are jumpy, Governor," Estete said. "The longer we stay cooped up here, the longer we give these savages the chance to plot against us."

"We should wait until Soto returns," de Candia said, already looking guilty as a dog. "We've got nothing but rumors so far. I won't kill a man on a rumor."

Silence. Trust de Candia to speak aloud what they were all thinking but were not ready to say. The man had no political judgment—but maybe it was just as well to face it directly. Valverde seized the opportunity. "Atahualpa plots against us even as we speak," he told Pizarro. "As governor, you are responsible for our safety. Any court would convict him of treason, and execute him."

"He's a king," de Candia said. Face flushed, he spat out a cud of leaves. "We don't have authority to try him. We should ship him back to Spain and let the emperor decide what to do."

"This is not a king," Valverde said. "It isn't even a man. It is a creature that worships demons, that weaves spells about half-wits like Candia. You saw him discard the Bible. Even after my months of teaching, after the extraordinary mercies we've shown him, he doesn't acknowledge the primacy of Christ! He cares only for his wives and his pagan gods. Yet he's satanically clever. Don't think we can let him go. If we do, the day will come when he'll have our hearts for dinner."

"We can take him with us to Cuzco," Benalcázar said. "We don't know the country. His presence would guarantee our safe conduct."

"We'll be traveling over rough terrain, carrying tons of gold, with not enough horses," Almagro said. "If we take him with us, we'll be ripe for ambush at every pass."

"They won't attack if we have him."

"He could escape. We can't trust the rebel Indians to stay loyal to us. If they turned to our side, they can just as easily turn back to his."

"And remember, he escaped before, during the civil war," Valverde said. "Huascar, his brother, lived to regret that. If Atahualpa didn't hesitate to murder his own brother, do you think he'll stop for us?"

"He's given us his word," Candia said.

"What good is the word of a pagan?"

Pizarro, silent until now, spoke. "He has no reason to think the word of a Christian much better."

Valverde felt his blood rise. Pizarro knew as well as any of them what was necessary. What was he waiting for? "He keeps a hundred wives! He betrayed his brother! He worships the sun!" The priest grabbed Pizarro's hand, held it up between them so they could both see the scar there, where Pizarro had gotten cut preventing one of his own men from killing Atahualpa. "He isn't worth an ounce of the blood you spilled to save him."

"He's proved worth twenty-four tons of gold." Pizarro's eyes were hard and calm.

"There is no alternative!" Valverde insisted. "He serves the Antichrist! God demands his death."

At last Pizarro seemed to have gotten what he wanted. He smiled. "Far be it from me to ignore the command of God," he said. "Since God forces us to it, let's discuss how He wants it done."

5 October 2009

"What a lovely country Chile is from the air. You should be proud of it."

"I'm from Los Angeles," Leon Sepulveda said. "And as soon as we close this deal, I'm going back."

"The mountains are impressive."

"Nothing but earthquakes and slag. You can have Chile."

"Is it for sale?"

Sepulveda stared at the Krel. "I was just kidding."

They sat at midnight in the arbor, away from the main buildings of Iguassu Microelectronics of Santiago. The night was cold and the arbor was overgrown and the bench needed a paint job—but then, a lot of things had been getting neglected in the past couple of years. All the more reason to put yourself in a financial situation where you didn't have to worry. Though Sepulveda had to admit that, since the advent of the Krel, such positions were harder to come by, and less secure once you had them.

Flash's earnestness aroused a kind of horror in him. It had something to do with Sepulveda's suspicion that this thing next to him was as superior to him as he was to a guinea pig, plus the alien's aura of drunken adolescence, plus his own willingness, despite the feeling that the situation was out of control, to make a deal with it. He took another Valium and tried to calm down.

"What assurance do I have that this time-travel method will work?"

"It will work. If you don't like it in Chile, or back in Los Angeles, you can use it to go into the past."

Sepulveda swallowed. "Okay. You need to read and sign these papers."

"We don't read."

"You don't read Spanish? How about English?"

"We don't read at all. We used to, but we gave it up. Once you start reading, it gets out of control. You tell yourself you're just going to stick to nonfiction—but pretty soon you graduate to fiction. After that, you can't kick the habit. And then there's the oppression."

"Oppression?"

"Sure. I mean, I like a story as much as the next Krel, but any pharmacologist can show that arbitrary cultural, sexual, and economic assumptions determine every significant aspect of a story. Literature is a political tool used by ruling elites to ensure their hegemony. Anyone who denies that is a fish who can't see the water it swims in. Or the fascist who tells you, as he beats you, that those blows you feel are your own delusion."

"Right. Look, can we settle this? I've got things to do."

"This is, of course, the key to temporal translation. The past is another arbitrary construct. Language creates reality. Reality is smoke."

"Well, this time machine better not be smoke. We're going to find out the truth about the past. Then we'll change it."

"By all means. Find the truth." Flash turned to the last page of the contract, pricked his thumb, and marked a thumbprint on the signature line.

After they sealed the agreement, Sepulveda walked the alien back to the courtyard. A Krel flying pod with Vermeer's *The Letter* varnished onto its door sat at the focus of three spotlights. The painting was scorched almost into unrecognizability by atmospheric friction. The door peeled downward from the top, became a canvas-surfaced ramp.

"I saw some interesting lines inscribed on the coastal desert on the way here," Flash said. "A bird, a tree, a big spider. In the sunset, it looked beautiful. I didn't think you humans were capable of such art. Is it for sale?"

"I don't think so. That was done by some old Indians a long time ago. If you're really interested, though, I can look into it."

"Not necessary." Flash waggled his ears, wiped his feet on Mark Rothko's *Earth and Green,* and staggered into the pod.

26 July 1533

Atahualpa looked out of the window of the stone room in which he was kept, across the plaza where the priest Valverde stood outside his chapel after his morning prayers. Valverde's chapel had been the house of the virgins; the women of the house had long since been raped by the Spanish soldiers, as the house had been by the Spanish god. Valverde spoke with Estete. They were getting ready to kill him, Atahualpa knew. He had known ever since the ransom had been paid.

He looked beyond the thatched roofs of the town to the crest of the mountains, where the sun was about to break in his tireless circuit of Tahuantinsuyu. The cold morning air raised dew on the metal of the chains that bound him hand and foot. The metal was queer, different from the bronze the *purics* worked or the gold and silver Atahualpa was used to wearing. If gold was the sweat of the sun, and silver the tears of the moon, what was this metal, dull and hard like the men who held him captive, yet strong, too—stronger, he had come to realize, than the Inca. It, like the men who brought it, was beyond his experience. It gave evidence that Tahuantinsuyu, the Four Quarters of the World, was not all the world after all. Atahualpa had thought none but savages lived beyond their lands. He'd imagined no man readier to face ruthless necessity than himself. He had ordered the death of Huascar, his own brother. But he was learning that these men were capable of enormities against which the Inca civil war would seem a minor discomfort.

That evening they took him out of the building to the plaza. In the plaza's center, the soldiers had piled a great heap of wood on flagstones, some of which were still stained with the blood of the six thousand slaughtered attendants. They bound him to a stake amid the heaped fagots, and Valverde appealed one last time for the Inca to renounce Satan and be baptized. He promised that if Atahualpa would do so, he would earn God's mercy: they would strangle him rather than burn him to death.

The rough wood pressed against his spine. Atahualpa looked at the priest, and the men gathered around, and the women weeping beyond the circle of soldiers. The moon, his mother, rode high above. Firelight flickered on the breastplates of the Spaniards, and from the waiting torches drifted the smell of pitch. The men shifted nervously. Creak of leather, clink of metal. Men on horses shod with silver. Sweat shining on Valverde's forehead. Valverde stared at Atahualpa as if he desired something, but was prepared to destroy him without getting it if need be. The priest thought he was showing Atahualpa resolve, but Atahualpa saw that beneath Valverde's face he was a dead man. Pizarro stood aside, with the Spanish viceroy Estete and the scribe. Pizarro was an old man. He ought to be sitting quietly in some village, outside the violence of life, giving advice and teaching the children. What kind of world did he come from, that sent men into old age still charged with the lusts and bitterness of the young?

Pizarro, too, looked as if he wanted this to end.

Atahualpa knew that it would not end. This was only the beginning. These men would suffer for this moment as they had already suffered for it all their lives, seeking the pain blindly over oceans, jungles, deserts, probing it like a sore tooth until they'd found and grasped it in this plaza of Cajamarca, thinking they sought gold. They'd come all this way to create a moment that would reveal to them their own incurable disease. Now they had it. In a few minutes, they thought, it would at last be over, that once he was gone, they would be free—but Atahualpa knew it would be with them ever after, and with their children and grandchildren and the million others of their race in times to come, whether they knew of this hour in the plaza or not, because they were sick and would pass the sickness on with their breath and semen. They could not burn out the sickness so easily as they could burn the Son of God to ash. This was a great tragedy, but it contained a huge jest. They were caught in a wheel of the sky and could not get out. They must destroy themselves.

"Have your way, priest," Atahualpa said. "Then strangle me, and bear my body to Cuzco, to be laid with my ancestors." He knew they would not do it, and so would add an additional curse to their faithlessness.

He had one final curse. He turned to Pizarro. "You will have responsibility for my children."

Pizarro looked at the pavement. They put up the torch and took Atahualpa from the pyre. Valverde poured water on his head and spoke words in the tongue of his god. Then they sat him upon a stool, bound him to another stake, set the loop of cord around his neck, slid the rod through the cord, and turned it. His women knelt at his side and wept. Valverde spoke more words. Atahualpa felt the cord, woven by the hands of some faithful *puric* of Cajamarca, tighten. The cord was well made. It cut his access to the night air; Atahualpa's lungs fought, he felt his body spasm, and then the plaza became cloudy and he heard the voice of the moon.

12 January 2011

Israel Lamont was holding big-time when a Krel monitor zipped over the alley. A minute later one of the aliens lurched around the corner and approached him. Lamont was ready.

"I need to achieve an altered state of consciousness," the alien said. It wore a red suit, a lightning bolt on its chest.

"I'm your man," Lamont said. "You just try this. Best stuff on the street." He held the vial out in the palm of his hand. "Go ahead, try it." The Krel took it.

"How much?"

"One million."

The Krel gave him a couple hundred thousand. "Down payment," it said. "How does one administer this?"

"What, you don't know? I thought you guys were hip."

"I have been working hard, and am unacquainted."

This was ripe. "You burn it," Lamont said.

The Krel started toward the trash-barrel fire. Before he could empty the vial into it, Lamont stopped him. "Wait up, homes! You use a pipe. Here, I'll show you."

Lamont pulled a pipe from his pocket, torched up, and inhaled. The Krel watched him. Brown eyes like a dog's. Goofy honkie face. The rush took him, and Lamont saw in the alien's face a peculiar need. The thing was hungry. Desperate.

"I may try?" The alien reached out. Its hand trembled.

Lamont handed over the pipe. Clumsily, the creature shook a block of crack into the bowl. Its beaklike upper lip, however, prevented it from getting its mouth tight against the stem. It fumbled with the pipe, from somewhere producing a book of matches. "Shit, I'll light it," Lamont said.

The Krel waited while Lamont held his Bic over the bowl. Nothing happened. "Inhale, man."

The creature inhaled. The blue flame played over the crack; smoke boiled through the bowl. The creature drew in steadily for what seemed to be minutes. Serious capacity. The crack burned totally through. Finally the Krel exhaled.

It looked at Lamont. Its eyes were bright.

"Good shit?" Lamont said.

"A remarkable stimulant effect."

"Right." Lamont looked over his shoulder toward the alley's entrance. It was getting dark. Yet he hesitated to ask for the rest of the money.

"Will you talk with me?" the Krel asked, swaying slightly.

Surprised, Lamont said, "Okay. Come with me."

Lamont led the Krel back to a deserted store that abutted the alley. They went inside and sat down on some crates against the wall.

"Something I been wondering about you," Lamont said. "You guys are coming to own the world. You fly across the planets, Mars and that shit. What you want with crack?"

"We seek to broaden our minds."

Lamont snorted. "Right. You might as well hit yourself in the head with a hammer."

"We seek escape," the alien said.

"I don't buy that, neither. What you got to escape from?"

The Krel looked at him. "Nothing."

They smoked another pipe. The Krel leaned back against the wall, arms at its sides like a limp doll. It started a queer coughing sound, chest spasming. Lamont thought it was choking and tried to slap it on the back. "Don't do that," it said. "I'm laughing."

"Laughing? What's so funny?"

"I lied to Colonel Zipp," it said. "We want cocaine for kicks."

Lamont relaxed a little. "I hear you now."

"We do everything for kicks."

"Makes for hard living."

"Better than maintaining consciousness continuously without interruption."

"You said it."

"Human beings cannot stand too much reality," the Krel said. "We don't blame you. Human beings! Disgust, horror, shame. Nothing personal."

"You bet."

"Nonbeing penetrates that in which there is no space."

"Uh-huh."

The alien laughed again. "I lied to Sepulveda, too. Our time machines take people to the past they believe in. There is no other past. You can't change it."

"Who the fuck's Sepulveda?"

"Let's do some more," it said.

They smoked one more. "Good shit," it said. "Just what I wanted."

The Krel slid off the crate. Its head lolled. "Here is the rest of your payment," it whispered, and died.

Lamont's heart raced. He looked at the Krel's hand, lying open on the floor. In it was a full-sized ear of corn, fashioned of gold, with tassels of finely spun silver wire.

Today

It's not just physical laws that science-fiction readers want to escape. Just as commonly, they want to escape human nature. In pursuit of this, SF offers comforting alternatives to the real world. For instance, if you start reading an SF story about some abused wimp, you can be pretty sure that by chapter two he's going to discover he has secret powers unavailable to those tormenting him, and by the end of the book, he's going to save the universe. SF is full of this sort of thing, from the power fantasy of the alienated child to the alternate history where Hitler is strangled in his cradle and the Library of Alexandria is saved from the torch.

Science fiction may in this way be considered as much an evasion of reality as any mind-distorting drug. I know that sounds a little harsh, but think about it. An alkaloid like cocaine or morphine invades the central nervous system. It reduces pain, produces euphoria, enhances our perceptions. Under its influence we imagine we have supernormal abilities. Limits dissolve. Soon, hardly aware of what's happened to us, we're addicted.

Science fiction has many of the same qualities. The typical reader comes to SF at a time of suffering. He seizes on it as a way to deal with his pain. It's bigger than his life. It's astounding. Amazing. Fantastic. Some grow out of it; many don't. Anyone who's been around SF for a while can cite examples of longtime readers as hooked and deluded as crack addicts.

Like any drug addict, the SF reader finds desperate justifications for his habit. SF teaches him science. SF helps him avoid "future shock." SF changes the world for the better. Right. So does cocaine.

Having been an SF user myself, however, I have to say that, living in a world of cruelty, immersed in a culture that grinds people into fish meal like some brutal machine, with histories of destruction stretching behind us back to the Pleistocene, I find it hard to sneer at the desire to escape. Even if escape is delusion.

18 October 1527

Timu drove the foot plow into the ground, leaned back to break the crust, drew out the pointed pole, and backed up a step to let his wife, Collyur, turn the earth with her hoe. To his left was his brother, Okya;

and to his right, his cousin, Tupa; before them, their wives planting the seed. Most of the *purics* of Cajamarca were there, strung out in a line across the terrace, the men wielding the foot plows, and the women or children carrying the sacks of seed potatoes.

As he looked up past Collyur's shoulders to the edge of the terrace, he saw a strange man approach from the post road. The man stumbled into the next terrace up from them, climbed down steps to their level. He was plainly excited.

Collyur was waiting for Timu to break the next row; she looked up at him questioningly.

"Who is that?" Timu said, pointing past her at the man.

She stood up straight and looked over her shoulder. The other men had noticed, too, and stopped their work.

"A *chasqui* come from the next town," said Okya.

"A *chasqui* would go to the *curaca,*" said Tupa.

"He's not dressed like a *chasqui,*" Timu said.

The man came up to them. Instead of a cape, loincloth, and flowing *onka,* the man wore uncouth clothing: cylinders of fabric that bound his legs tightly, a white short-sleeved shirt that bore on its front the face of a man, and flexible white sandals that covered all his foot to the ankle. He shivered in the spring cold.

He was extraordinarily tall. His face, paler than a normal man's, was long, his nose too straight, mouth too small, and lips too thin. Upon his face he wore a device of gold wire that, hooking over his ears, held disks of crystal before his eyes. The man's hands were large, his limbs long and spiderlike. He moved suddenly, awkwardly.

Gasping for air, the stranger spoke rapidly the most abominable Quechua Timu had ever heard.

"Slow down," Timu said. "I don't understand."

"What year is this?" the man asked.

"What do you mean?"

"I mean, what is the year?"

"It is the thirty-fourth year of the reign of the Sapa Inca Huayna Capac."

The man spoke some foreign word. "Goddamn," he said in a language foreign to Timu, but which you or I would recognize as English. "I made it."

Timu went to the *curaca,* and the *curaca* told Timu to take the stranger in. The stranger told them that his name was "Chuan." But Timu's three-year-old daughter, Curi, reacting to the man's sudden gestures, unearthly thinness, and piping speech, laughed and called him "the Bird." So he was ever after to be known in that town.

There he lived a long and happy life, earned trust and respect, and brought great good fortune. He repaid them well for their kindness, alerting the people of Tahuantinsuyu to the coming of the invaders. When the first Spaniards landed on their shores a few years later, they were slaughtered to the last man, and everyone lived happily ever after.

(1990)

NOTES ON THE AUTHORS

Poul Anderson, born in 1926, began his long and full professional career in John Campbell's *Astounding* in 1947. He writes both science fiction and fantasy; among his many novels are *Brain Wave* (1954) and *Three Hearts and Three Lions* (1961), and his stories have won several Hugo and Nebula Awards. He lives in Orinda, California.

Eleanor Arnason lives in Minneapolis. Her stories have appeared in *Orbit* and *New Worlds*, and she has published three novels: *To the Resurrection Station* (1986), *Daughter of the Bear King* (1987), and in 1992 *A Woman of the Iron People*, which co-won the first James Tiptree, Jr., Award.

Margaret Atwood, who lives in Toronto, was born in 1939. She has published over thirty books of poetry, fiction, and literary criticism. *Survival* (1972) helped define the study of Canadian literature, and her work has been highly influential in Canada and abroad. *The Handmaid's Tale* (1986), a cautionary novel of the near future, won the Arthur C. Clarke Award and the Governor General's Award for Literature. Her newest collection of stories, *Good Bones* (1993), contains several science-fiction pieces.

Greg Bear, born in 1951, came to prominence in the late seventies. He is a multiple winner of Nebula and Hugo Awards; some of his stories are collected in *Tangents* (1989); his novels include *The Forge of God* (1987), *Eon* (1985), and *Blood Music* (1985). He lives in Seattle.

Gregory A. Benford, born in 1941, lives in Laguna Beach and is professor of physics at U.C. Irvine. His major novels include *Timescape* (1980), which won the John W. Campbell and Nebula Awards, and *Beyond the Fall of Night* (1990), a collaboration with Arthur C. Clarke. He has written science articles, and scripted and hosted a TV series, *A Galactic Odyssey* (1989).

Michael Bishop lives in Pine Mountain, Georgia; since 1974 he has been a full-time writer, published in all major science-fiction magazines. He has won two Nebula Awards, had a story in *Best American Short Stories 1985,* and has published several story collections and nine novels, among them *No Enemy But Time* (1982). His latest work is *Count Geiger's Blues* (1992).

James Blish (1921–1975) left an indelible mark on the field of science fiction as a critic (under the name William Atheling) and fiction writer. Among his major works are *A Case of Conscience* (1958), the linked collection *The Seedling Stars* (collected 1957), and the *Cities in Flight* tetralogy (collected 1970).

Michael Blumlein, who lives in San Francisco, has written for stage and film and is a practicing physician. "The Brains of Rats" was a World Fantasy Award finalist, and gives its title to his collected stories. He has published two novels, *The Movement of Mountains* (1987) and *X, Y* (1993).

Marion Zimmer Bradley, born in 1930, began writing as a young fan, and publishing as a professional in the sixties. She is best known for the Darkover series of stories and novels, including *Darkover Landfall* (1972) and *The Shattered Chain* (1976). *The Mists of Avalon* (1983) retells the Arthurian legend from the point of view of Morgan le Fay. She lives in Berkeley.

Edward Bryant, born in 1945, began publishing in 1970. He received the Nebula Award for "Stone" in 1978 and for "giANTS" in 1979. His novel *Phoenix Without Ashes* (1975) is a collaboration with Harlan Ellison. Bryant lives in Denver.

David R. Bunch, poet and fiction writer, has kept well out of the limelight in St. Louis while contributing a unique voice to science fiction. His first story appeared in *If* in 1957. Many of the stories he wrote in the sixties were gathered in the novel *Moderan* (1971). More recent work appears in *Bunch* (1993).

Octavia Butler, born in 1947, published her first science-fiction story in 1971. She won the Hugo Award in 1984 for "Speech Sounds," and the Nebula and Hugo Awards for the novella *Blood Child* in 1985. Her novels include *Wild Seed* (1980) and the *Xenogenesis* trilogy. She lives in Los Angeles.

Pat Cadigan's short fiction appears frequently in the Best of the Year anthologies and is included in the three-author collection *Letters from Home.* She holds the World Fantasy Award. Her novels include *Mind-*

players (1987); *Synners* (1991), which won the 1991 Arthur C. Clarke Award; and *Fools* (1992). She lives in Overland Park, Kansas.

Orson Scott Card, who began publishing in 1977, won both the Nebula and the Hugo Awards for *Ender's Game* in 1986, and in the following year for the follow-up novel *Speaker for the Dead.* He has also won the World Fantasy Award. A prolific writer, one of his recent novels is *Lost Boys.* He lives in Greensboro, North Carolina.

Michael G. Coney came from England to Canada in 1972, and lives on Vancouver Island, British Columbia. He is proprietor of Porthole Press. Among his science-fiction novels are *Syzygy* (1973) and *Winter's Children* (1974). He has a story collection, *Monitor Found in Orbit* (1974).

John Crowley, born in 1942, has been a documentary screenwriter as well as fiction writer. Beginning with his first novel *The Deep,* he has often combined elements of science fiction and fantasy in his work. *Engine Summer* appeared in 1979 and the World Fantasy Award-winning *Little, Big* in 1981. The novella *The Great Work of Time* won the same award in 1990. His most recent novel is *AEgypt* (1987).

Avram Davidson, born in 1923, has been writing for fifty years and publishing for forty-eight. He has won the Hugo, Edgar, and World Fantasy Awards. His seventeen novels include *The Phoenix and the Mirror* (1969) and its sequel *Vergil in Averno* (1987). Collections include *The Enquiries of Doctor Esterhazy* (1975) and *Or All the Seas with Oysters* (1962). He lives in Bremerton, Washington.

Samuel R. Delany, born in 1942, published his first novel at the age of twenty. He has several Nebula Awards for stories (including "High Weir") and for his novel *The Einstein Intersection* (1967). His critical writings, such as *The Jewel-Hinged Jaw* (1977) and *The American Shore* (1978), earned him the Science Fiction Research Association's Pilgrim Award. His most recent book is *They Fly at Ciron* (1993).

Philip K. Dick (1928–1982) was one of science fiction's most original and distinctive voices. Early stories such as "The Father Thing" (1954) introduced themes that are developed more fully in his novels: alternative realities, simulacra, and ambiguous contacts with the divine. Dick won a Hugo Award for *The Man in the High Castle* in 1963 and the John W. Campbell Award for *Flow My Tears, the Policeman Said* in 1975. The 1982 film *Blade Runner* was loosely adapted from Dick's novel *Do Androids Dream of Electric Sheep?* (1968). Other major novels include *Martian Time-Slip* (1964), *Ubik* (1969), and *Valis* (1981). All his stories have recently been reissued in a series of volumes.

Candas Jane Dorsey, born in Edmonton in 1952, is a professional poet, editor, and fiction writer. She edited *Tesseracts 3* with Gerry Truscott, and her collection *Machine Sex and Other Stories* was published in Canada by Porcepic Books and in England by The Women's Press. She is editor of River Books, Edmonton. Her autobiographical note ends: "Has cats, of course."

Suzette Haden Elgin, born in 1936, drew on her Ozark upbringing and linguistic training for her *Ozark Trilogy* (1981). *Native Tongue* (1984) and its sequel *The Judas Rose* (1987) explore the relation between language and gender politics. Retired from San Diego State University, Elgin returned to Arkansas to found the Ozark Center for Language Studies.

Harlan Ellison, born in 1934, is an editor, screenwriter, media critic, and award-winning story writer. His honors include a Writers Guild of America Award for "Demon with the Glass Hand" (1965), the Nebula and Hugo Awards for "Repent, Harlequin, Said the Ticktockman" (1966), several other Nebulas and Hugos, the Edgar Allan Poe Award for "The Whimper of Whipped Dogs" (1973), and a Special Hugo Award for editing the groundbreaking anthology *Dangerous Visions* (1968). No cats.

Carol Emshwiller, born in 1921, began publishing her innovative short stories in 1955. Recent publications include the novel *Carmen Dog* (1990), a novella, *Venus Rising,* and two collections of stories, *Verging on the Pertinent* (1989) and *The Start of the End of the World* (1990). She lives in New York City.

Karen Joy Fowler, born in 1950, began publishing short fiction in 1985. In 1987 she won the John W. Campbell Award. She has a story collection, *Artificial Things* (1986), and her most recent book is the novel *Sarah Canary* (1991). She lives in Davis, California.

William Gibson, born in 1948 in South Carolina, has lived since 1969 in Vancouver, British Columbia. His first novel, *Neuromancer,* won the Hugo, Nebula, Ditmar, and Philip K. Dick Awards in 1984, and set the style for what became known as cyberpunk. His other novels are *Count Zero* (1986), *Mona Lisa Overdrive* (1987), and *The Difference Engine* (with Bruce Sterling, 1990). His stories were collected in *Burning Chrome* (1986).

Diane Glancy is a poet, essayist, and fiction writer, winner of the 1990 Native American Prose Award for *Claiming Breath,* a book of essays. She has also published *Lone Dog's Winter Count* (poems, 1992), and *Trigger Dance* (short stories, 1990), which was awarded the Charles

Nilon Fiction Award. A professor at Macalester College, she lives in St. Paul, Minnesota.

Molly Gloss, who lives in Portland, Oregon, has been publishing short fiction in magazines and anthologies since 1981. *Outside the Gates,* a novel, was published in 1986. Her Western historical novel *The Jump-Off Creek* was a P.E.N.-Faulkner Award finalist in 1989. A science-fiction novel, *The Dazzle of Day,* is forthcoming.

Lisa Goldstein lives in Oakland, California. Her novel *The Red Magician* won the 1983 American Book Award for best paperback fiction. She is a notable short-story writer, and her novels include *Tourists* (1989) and most recently *Strange Devices of the Sun and Moon* (1993).

Phyllis Gotlieb, born in 1926, lives in Toronto. Her active and distinguished writing career includes four books of poetry; seven novels (six of them science fiction), the most recent being *Heart of Red Iron* (1989); and two collections of stories. She co-edited *Tesseracts 2*.

Eileen Gunn, born in 1945, lives in Seattle, and has been publishing in science-fiction magazines and anthologies since 1978. "Stable Strategies" was written when she returned to fiction from the world of commerce; she says she thinks of it as a slice-of-life story.

Joe Haldeman was born in 1943 and divides his time between Gainesville, Florida, and Cambridge, Massachusetts, where he teaches at MIT. After service in Viet Nam he became a full-time writer and since 1977 has published stories, poems, *Star Trek* novels, adventure novels, and the story collections *Infinite Dreams* (1978) and *Dealing in Futures* (1985); his science-fiction novels include *Mindbridge* (1976), *Worlds Enough and Time* (1992), and the Hugo and Nebula-winning *Forever War* (1974).

Zenna Henderson (1917–1983) wrote principally about two milieus she knew well: the classroom and the American Southwest. Both are found in the stories of interstellar refugees she called The People. Her collections include *Pilgrimage* (1961) and *Holding Wonder* (1971).

Sonya Dorman Hess, born in 1924, lives in Taos, and is a poet and fiction writer. Her collection *Poems* (1970) won the Rhysling Award from the Science Fiction Poetry Association. "When I Was Miss Dow" (which, like most of her fiction, was published under the name Sonya Dorman) received a Nebula Award.

James Patrick Kelly, born in 1951, lives in Portsmouth, New Hampshire, and has been writing professionally since 1975. His stories have appeared in many anthologies and he has twice won the Theodore Sturgeon Award for short stories. His novels include *Planet of Whispers* (1984) and *Look Into the Sun* (1989). He reports that he has too many hobbies. His cat status is unknown.

John Kessel lives in Raleigh, North Carolina, where he is a professor at North Carolina State University. He has published fiction since 1975, and won a Nebula Award for his novella *Another Orphan* and the Theodore Sturgeon Award for a short story, "Buffalo." His novels are *Freedom Beach* (with James Patrick Kelly, 1985) and *Good News from Outer Space* (1989). A story collection, *Meeting in Infinity,* was published in 1992.

Damon Knight, born in Oregon in 1922, early became a member of the New York writer/fan group The Futurians. He began publishing fiction in 1941, and has been writing for fifty years. Among his novels are *A for Anything* (1961) and *Why Do Birds* (1992). He edited the admirable and influential series of original-story anthologies, *Orbit,* for many years, and his equally influential critical writing, collected in *In Search of Wonder* (1956), was honored with the Hugo Award.

Nancy Kress began selling her short fiction in the mid-seventies. In 1985 she won the Nebula Award for "Out of All Them Bright Stars." "Beggars in Spain" won both the Nebula and Hugo Awards for 1991. Her novels include a fantasy, *The Prince of Morning Bells* (1981), *An Alien Light* (1988), and *Brain Rose* (1990). A story collection is entitled *Trinity and Other Stories.* She lives in Brockport, New York.

Raphael Aloysius Lafferty was born in 1914 and has been publishing fiction since 1960. His twenty novels include *Past Master* (1968) and his major story collections are *Nine Hundred Grandmothers* (1970), *Strange Doings* (1972), and *Does Anyone Else Have Something Further to Add?* (1974). Many of his deeply imaginative stories, such as "Continued on Next Rock," are set in Oklahoma, where he lives.

Ursula K. Le Guin, born in Berkeley in 1929, lives in Portland, Oregon, and has published four books of poetry, two of essays and criticism, and many novels and short stories in a variety of genres including realism, fantasy, science fiction, and children's books. *The Left Hand of Darkness* (1969), the four *Earthsea* books (1968–90), and *Always Coming Home* (1985) are among the best known. She has many awards, the most recent the Oregon Institute of Literary Arts' H. L. Davis Prize for *Searoad* (1991). Has cat.

Fritz Leiber (1910–1992) began publishing in the thirties as a fantasist; his "Fafhrd" stories founded, and excelled in, the subgenre known as Sword and Sorcery. He also wrote inventive fantasies in modern settings, such as *Conjure Wife* (1953; filmed as *Burn, Witch, Burn*), and science-fiction novels such as *Wanderer* (1964). He crossed genres freely in his short stories, collected in *The Best of Fritz Leiber* (1974) and *Worlds of Fritz Leiber* (1976), but by no means all his best work has yet been reprinted. He had six Hugo Awards, three Nebulas, and the Grand Master of Fantasy Award.

Katherine MacLean, born in 1925, published her first story in *Astounding* in 1949. "The Missing Man" won a Nebula Award in 1971. Her stories, published in many magazines, are collected in *The Diploids and Other Flights of Fancy* (1962), *Trouble with Treaties* (1975), and *The Trouble with You Earth People* (1980).

Vonda N. McIntyre, born in 1948, began publishing in the early seventies and in 1973 won the Nebula Award for "Of Mist, and Grass, and Sand." The expanded version of this classic story, *Dreamsnake* (1978), won both the Nebula and Hugo for best novel. Recently she has been writing *Starfarers,* a four-book series, the last of which will come out in 1993. Her short fiction was collected in *Fireflood and Other Stories* (1979). She lives in Seattle. Has foster-cat.

Barry N. Malzberg, born in 1939, began publishing in 1968 under the pen name K. M. O'Donnell. He has written more than twenty science-fiction novels, including *Beyond Apollo* (1972), which won the John W. Campbell Award, and is a prolific short-story writer. *The Engines of the Night* (1982) is his collection of critical writings on science fiction. He lives in Teaneck, New Jersey.

Pat Murphy, who lives in San Francisco, began publishing in the early eighties. Her second novel, *The Falling Woman,* won the Nebula Award for novel in the same year (1987) that her *Rachel in Love* won it for novella. *Points of Departure* (1990), a collection of short fiction, won the Philip K. Dick Award. Her most recent novel is *The City, Not Long After* (1989).

Frederik Pohl, born in 1919, has led a long and full life in science fiction. A Nebula and Hugo winner, his often brilliantly ironic works include *The Space Merchants* (with C. M. Kornbluth, 1952) and *Gateway* (1977), and many short stories. Editor of the magazines *If* and *Galaxy* in the sixties, he has also edited many notable anthologies.

Paul Preuss lives in San Francisco and has published eleven novels since 1980, including *Starfire* (1988) and *Human Error* (1985), and collaborated with Arthur C. Clarke on the *Venus Prime* series. He is a writer, editor, and producer of films. His latest novel is *Core* (1993).

Michael Resnick, born in 1942, lives in Cincinnati. He received a Hugo Award in 1989 for "Kirinyaga" and another in 1991 for a story in the same series, "The Manamouki." His novels include *Santiago* (1986) and *Ivory* (1988).

Kim Stanley Robinson sold his first story in 1976; in 1984, his novella *Black Air* won the World Fantasy and John W. Campbell Awards, and he has a Nebula Award for the novella *The Blind Geometer.* His novels include *The Wild Shore* (1984), *Pacific Edge* (1990), and most recently *Red Mars* (1993). He lives in Davis, California.

Joanna Russ, born in 1937, lives in Seattle and is a professor at the University of Washington. Her first science-fiction story was published in 1957. She has won Nebula and Hugo Awards and the O. Henry Prize for short fiction. Among her novels are *The Female Man* (1975) and *And Chaos Died* (1970); story collections include *The Adventures of Alyx* (1983) and *Extra Ordinary People* (1984). She received the Pilgrim Award for her literary criticism. Her nonfiction includes the splendid manual, *How to Suppress Women's Writing* (1983).

Pamela Sargent has been publishing since the mid-seventies; her thirteen novels include *The Shore of Women* (1987). She has two collections of stories, and has edited five anthologies, including the three influential *Women of Wonder* anthologies. She lives in Johnson City, New York.

James H. Schmitz (1911–1981) specialized in humorous science fiction, often with resourceful young female heroes, such as Telzey Amberdon in the series of that name. His best-known novel is *The Witches of Karres* (1966).

Robert Sheckley, born in 1928, lives in Portland, Oregon; he published his first story in 1952. Best known as a short-story writer and humorist, he won the Jupiter Award with "Suppliant in Space." His collections include *Can You Feel Anything When I Do This?* (1971), and among his novels are *The Status Civilization* (1960) and *Options* (1975).

Lewis Shiner lives in Houston, and came to prominence in science fiction in the eighties; he is the author of several dozen short stories, several comics, and four novels, including *Deserted Cities of the Heart* (1988), *Slam* (1990), and most recently *Glimpses* (1993).

Robert Silverberg has written many kinds of fiction and nonfiction, and used to fill entire magazines with stories under various pen names. He began doing his finest work in the sixties, and has received many Nebula and Hugo Awards for both novels and stories. His short fiction is now being reprinted in a multi-volume collection. Among his best-known novels are *Dying Inside* (1972), *The Book of Skulls* (1972), and *Lord Valentine's Castle* (1980). He lives in Oakland, California. Has cats.

Clifford D. Simak was born in rural Wisconsin in 1904. A journalist and fiction writer, he wrote twenty-eight novels and over a hundred short stories—*Way Station* (1963) and "The Big Front Yard" won Hugo Awards. He was given the International Fantasy Award for *City* (1952) and was a Grand Master of the Science Fiction Writers Association. His was a warm, well-loved voice in science fiction for over fifty years. He died in 1988.

Cordwainer Smith was the pen name of Paul Myron Anthony Linebarger (1913–1966), a professor of political science at Johns Hopkins University. Linebarger, who spent much of his youth in China, worked for U.S. Intelligence in the Far East during the Second World War and later wrote scholarly studies of Chinese politics and psychological warfare. He used the name Felix Forrest for two non-science-fiction novels before entering science fiction as Cordwainer Smith with "Scanners Live in Vain" (1950). His only novel in the field is *Norstrilia* (1975). His extraordinary stories, most of which are related by their future-history setting, were reprinted in various collections, among them *You Will Never Be the Same* (1963) and *Stardreamer* (1971).

Bruce Sterling has been publishing since 1976, and his stories appear frequently in the Best of the Year collections. He edited the anthology *Mirrorshades* (1986), which showcased cyberpunk as a category of science fiction. His novels include *Schismatrix* (1985) and *Islands in the Net* (1988), and his story collections are *Crystal Express* and *Globalhead* (1992). His most recent publication is a nonfiction work, *Hacker Crackdown.* He lives in Austin.

Theodore Sturgeon (1918–1985) was writing stories of considerable stylistic elegance and psychological subtlety long before most readers of science fiction could hope for more than good plotting and invention, which he also supplied. Among his best stories are "Thunder and Roses" (1947), "A Saucer of Loneliness" (1953), and "Slow Sculpture" (1970). Some of the best known of his novels are *The Dreaming Jewels* (1950), *More Than Human* (1953), and *Venus Plus X* (1960). His innovative fiction was rewarded with many prizes, including the Nebula, Hugo, and International Fantasy Awards.

Michael Swanwick began publishing in 1980; he has been a frequent Nebula Award finalist, and won the Theodore Sturgeon Award for short fiction; in 1992 he won the Nebula for his novel *Stations of the Tide.* He lives in Philadelphia.

James Tiptree, Jr., was the pen name of Alice Sheldon, born in 1916 in Chicago, daughter of a distinguished family of explorers. She served in Air Force Intelligence during the Second World War and after it in photo intelligence in the CIA. In the fifties she earned a Ph.D. in clinical psychology and began writing fiction. Her brilliant, disturbing stories are to be found in five collections, including *Star Songs of an Old Primate* (1978), *Warm Worlds and Otherwise* (1975), and *10,000 Light-years from Home* (1973). Her two novels are *Up the Walls of the World* (1978) and *Brightness Falls from the Air* (1985). She won two Hugo and three Nebula Awards (one as Raccoona Sheldon, a second pen name), and was awarded, but refused, the Nebula Award for "The Women Men Don't See."

John Varley, born in 1947, currently lives in Portland, Oregon. He began publishing science fiction in the mid-seventies and promptly won the Nebula and Hugo Awards. As well as screenwriting, he has written a trilogy, *Gaea,* and his stories are collected in *The Persistence of Vision* (1980).

Howard Waldrop was born in 1946 and has lived in Texas since 1950. First published in 1970, he has been a full-time writer since 1980. His story collections are *Howard Who?* (1986), *All About Strange Monsters of the Recent Past* (1987), and *Night of the Cooters* (1991). His first novel was *The Texas-Israeli War: 1999* (with Jake Saunders, 1974), and recently he published the novella *A Dozen Tough Jobs* (1989).

Andrew Weiner, born in London in 1949, has lived in Canada since 1974. His first story was published in *Again, Dangerous Visions.* Since then he has published nonfiction and many stories in the magazines; a story collection, *Distant Signals and Other Stories* (1989); and a novel, *Station Gehenna* (1988).

Kate Wilhelm was born in 1928 and lives in Eugene, Oregon. Among her many prizes are the Hugo Award for her novel *Where Late the Sweet Birds Sang* (1976), a 1986 Nebula for "The Girl Who Fell into the Sky," and a 1989 Nebula for "Forever Yours, Anna." Her novels, many of which cross or blend genres, include *Juniper Time* (1979) and the recent *Death Qualified* (1991). Her latest story collection is *And the Angels Sing* (1992).

Connie Willis, born in 1945, lives in Greeley, Colorado. She is a multiple award winner for her short stories; "Fire Watch" won both the Hugo and Nebula Awards in 1982. Her collection is named *Fire Watch* (1985). She has published two novels, *Lincoln's Dreams* (1987) and *The Doomsday Book* (1992), and a forthcoming collection is titled *The Last of the Winnebagoes.*

Gene Wolfe first dazzled science-fiction readers with *The Fifth Head of Cerberus,* and since that debut has written prolifically. He holds the World Fantasy Award and two Nebula Awards, one for "The Death of Doctor Island" and one for *The Claw of the Conciliator* (1981), third volume of the tetralogy *The Book of the New Sun.* His short fiction has been collected in *The Island of Doctor Death and Other Stories and Other Stories* (1980) and *Endangered Species* (1989). Among recent works are *Soldier of the Mist* (1986), *Castleview* (1990), and *Nightside the Long Sun,* the first volume in a new series. Born in 1931, he lives in Barrington, Illinois.

Roger Zelazny has been publishing since 1962. Among his many awards are three Nebula and six Hugo Awards. His story collections include *The Doors of His Face, the Lamps of His Mouth* (1971) and *Frost and Fire* (1989), and among his novels some of the best known are the *Amber* series, *The Dream Master* (1966), *This Immortal* (1966), and *Lord of Light* (1967). Born in 1937, Zelazny now lives in New Mexico.

ACKNOWLEDGMENTS

"Kyrie" copyright © 1968 by Joseph Elder; first published in *The Farthest Reaches,* New York, Trident, 1968; reprinted by permission of the author.

"The Warlord of Saturn's Moons" copyright © 1974 by Eleanor Arnason; first appeared in *New Worlds 7* (U.K.) and *New Worlds 6* (U.S.), reprinted in *New Women of Wonder;* appears here by permission of the author and the author's agent, Virginia Kidd.

"Homelanding" copyright © 1990 by Press Porcepic, Ltd.; first published in *Tesseracts 3;* reprinted by permission of the author.

"Schrödinger's Plague" copyright © 1982 by Greg Bear; first published in *Analog,* 1982; reprinted by permission of the author.

"Exposures" copyright © 1981 by Abbenford Associates; first published in *Isaac Asimov's Science Fiction Magazine,* 1981; reprinted by permission of the author.

"The Bob Dylan Tambourine Software & Satori Support Services Consortium, Ltd." copyright © 1985 by Interzone; first published in *Interzone,* No. 12, 1985; reprinted by permission of the author.

"How Beautiful with Banners" copyright © 1966 by James Blish; first appeared in *Orbit 1;* reprinted by permission of the Author's Estate.

"The Brains of Rats" copyright © 1986 by Michael Blumlein; first published in *Interzone,* No 16; reprinted by permission of the author.

"Elbow Room" copyright © 1980 by Random House; first published in *Stellar #5 Science Fiction Stories;* reprinted by permission of the author.

"Precession" copyright © 1980 by Edward Bryant; first published in *Interfaces,* Ace Books, 1980; reprinted by permission of the author.

"Speech Sounds" copyright © 1983 by Davis Publications, Inc.; first published in *Isaac Asimov's Science Fiction Magazine,* 1983; reprinted by permission of the author.

"2064, or Thereabouts" copyright © 1992 by David R. Bunch; first published in *Fantastic,* 1964; reprinted by permission of the author.

"After the Days of Dead-Eye 'Dee" copyright © 1985 by Pat Cadigan; first published in *Isaac Asimov's Science Fiction Magazine,* 1985; reprinted by permission of the author.

"America" copyright © 1987 by Davis Publications, Inc.; first published in *Isaac Asimov's Science Fiction Magazine,* 1987; reprinted by permission of the author.

"The Byrds" copyright © 1983 by Michael G. Coney; first appeared in *Changes;* reprinted by permission of the author and the author's agent, Virginia Kidd.

"Snow" copyright © 1985 by Omni Publications International, Ltd.; first published in *Omni,* November, 1985; reprinted by permission of the author's agent, Ralph M. Vicinanza.

"The House the Blakeneys Built" copyright © 1965 by Avram Davidson; first appeared in *The Magazine of Fantasy and Science Fiction,* 1965; reprinted by permission of the author.

"High Weir" copyright © 1968 by Galaxy Publications; first published in *If,* October, 1968; reprinted by permission of the author.

"Frozen Journey" copyright © 1980 by Playboy Magazine; first published in *Playboy,* 1980; reprinted by permission of the Author's Estate and the agents for the Estate, Scott Meredith Literary Agency, Inc.

"When I Was Miss Dow" copyright © 1966 by Sonya Dorman; first appeared in *Galaxy;* reprinted by permission of the author and the author's agent, Virginia Kidd.

"(Learning About) Machine Sex" copyright © 1988 by Candas Jane Dorsey; first published in *Machine Sex and Other Stories,* Tesseract (Porcepic) Books, 1988; reprinted by permission of the author.

"For the Sake of Grace" copyright © 1969 by Mercury Press; first published in *The Magazine of Fantasy and Science Fiction,* 1969; reprinted by permission of the author.

"Strange Wine" copyright © 1976 by Harlan Ellison; first published in *Amazing Stories,* 1976; reprinted in *The Essential Ellison,* Morpheus International, 1991; appears here by arrangement with, and permission of, the Author and the Author's agent, Richard Curtis Associates, Inc., New York. All rights reserved.

"The Start of the End of the World" copyright © 1981 by Terry Carr; first published in *Universe 11,* Doubleday, 1981; reprinted by permission of the author.

"The Lake Was Full of Artificial Things" copyright © 1985 by Davis Publications, Inc.; first published in *Isaac Asimov's Science Fiction Magazine,* 1985; reprinted by permission of the author.

"The Gernsback Continuum" copyright © 1981 by Terry Carr; first published in *Universe 11,* Doubleday, 1981; reprinted by permission of the author and the author's agent, Martha Millard.

"Aunt Parnetta's Electric Blisters" copyright © 1990 by Diane Glancy; first published in *Trigger Dance,* University of Colorado Press, 1990; reprinted by permission of the author.

"Interlocking Pieces" copyright © 1984 by Molly Gloss; first appeared in *Universe 14;* reprinted by permission of the author and the author's agent, Virginia Kidd.

"Tauf Aleph" copyright © 1981 by Phyllis Gotlieb; first published in *More Wandering Stars,* Doubleday, 1981; reprinted by permission of the author.

"Stable Strategies for Middle Management" copyright © 1988 by Davis Publications, Inc.; first published in *Isaac Asimov's Science Fiction Magazine,* 1988; reprinted by permission of the author.

"The Private War of Private Jacob" copyright © 1974 by Universal Publishing and Distributing Corp.; first published in *Galaxy,* 1974; reprinted by permission of the author.

"As Simple as That" copyright © 1971 by Zenna Henderson; first appeared in *Holding Wonder;* reprinted by permission of the Author's Estate and the Estate's agent, Virginia Kidd.

"Rat" copyright © 1986 by Mercury Press, Inc.; first published in *The Magazine of Fantasy and Science Fiction,* 1986; reprinted by permission of the author.

"Invaders" copyright © 1990 by Mercury Press, Inc.; first published in *The Magazine of Fantasy and Science Fiction,* 1990; reprinted by permission of the author.

"The Handler" copyright © 1960 by Greenleaf Publishing Company; reprinted by permission of the author.

"Out of All Them Bright Stars" copyright © 1985 by Mercury Press, Inc.; first published in *The Magazine of Fantasy and Science Fiction*, 1985; reprinted by permission of the author.

"Nine Hundred Grandmothers" copyright © 1966 by R. A. Lafferty; first appeared in *If;* reprinted by permission of the author and the author's agent, Virginia Kidd.

"The New Atlantis" copyright © 1975 by Ursula K. Le Guin; first appeared in *The New Atlantis*, Hawthorn Books, Inc., 1975; reprinted by permission of the author and the author's agent, Virginia Kidd.

"The Winter Flies" copyright © 1967 by Mercury Press, Inc.; first published (under the title "The Inner Circles") in *The Magazine of Fantasy and Science Fiction*, 1967; reprinted by permission of the author.

"Night-Rise" copyright © 1978 by Katherine MacLean; first appeared in *Cassandra Rising*, ed. Alice Laurance (New York: Doubleday, 1978); reprinted by permission of the author and the author's agent, Virginia Kidd.

"Making It All the Way into the Future on Gaxton Falls of the Red Planet" copyright © 1974 by Barry N. Malzberg; first published in *Nova 4*, Walker, 1974; reprinted by permission of the author.

"The Mountains of Sunset, the Mountains of Dawn" copyright © 1974 by Vonda N. McIntyre; first published in *The Magazine of Fantasy and Science Fiction*, 1974; reprinted by permission of the author and the author's agent, Frances Collin.

"His Vegetable Wife" copyright © 1986 by Interzone; first published in *Interzone*, 1986; reprinted by permission of the author.

"Day Million" copyright © 1966 by Rogue Magazine; first published in *Rogue Magazine*, 1966; reprinted by permission of the author.

"Half-Life" copyright © 1989 by Paul Preuss; first published in *The Microverse*, Bantam: Spectra, 1989; reprinted by permission of the author and the author's agent, Jean V. Naggar Literary Agency, Inc.

"Kirinyaga" copyright © 1988 by Mercury Press, Inc.; first published in *The Magazine of Fantasy and Science Fiction*, 1988; reprinted by permission of the author.

"The Lucky Strike" copyright © 1984 by Terry Carr; first published in *Universe 14;* reprinted by permission of the author.

"A Few Things I Know About Whileaway" copyright © 1975 by Joanna Russ; first appeared in *The Female Man;* reprinted by permission of Beacon Press.

"Gather Blue Roses" copyright © 1971 by Mercury Press, Inc.; first published in *The Magazine of Fantasy and Science Fiction*, 1972. Copyright reassigned to Pamela Sargent in 1977. Reprinted by permission of the author and her agent, the Joseph Elder Agency.

"Balanced Ecology" copyright © 1965 by Condé Nast; first published in *Analog*, 1965; by permission of the agents for the Author's Estate, the Scott Meredith Literary Agency, Inc.

"The Life of Anybody" copyright © 1984 by Robert Sheckley; first published in *Is That What People Do?*, Holt, Rinehart, Winston, 1984; reprinted by permission of the author.

"The War at Home" copyright © 1985 by Davis Publications, Inc.; first published in *Isaac Asimov's Science Fiction Magazine*, 1985; reprinted by permission of the author.

"Good News from the Vatican" copyright © 1971 by Asberg, Ltd.; first published in *Universe 1;* reprinted by permission of the author.

INDEX